The Herries Chronicles Volume 1

Hugh Walpole was born in New Zealand in 1884, the
son of a clergyman. Sent to England, he was
educated at Canterbury and Cambridge, becoming a
schoolmaster and later a book-reviewer. His first
novel, *The Wooden Horse*, was published in 1909.
During the First World War he served in Russia
with the Red Cross, receiving the Order of St George
and being made a CBE. *The Secret City*, published in
1919, about the Russian Revolution, won the Tate
Black Memorial Prize. The *Herries Chronicles*, his
most ambitious work, was written in the early 1930s.
He was knighted in 1937. Hugh Walpole never
married. He died in 1941.

Also by Hugh Walpole
The Herries Chronicles Volume 2

Hugh Walpole

The
Herries Chronicles

Volume I

Pan Books
in association with
Macmillan London

Rogue Herries first published in Great Britain 1930 by Macmillan & Co. Ltd
Published 1971 by Pan Books Ltd
Judith Paris first published in Great Britain 1931 by Macmillan & Co. Ltd
Published 1971 by Pan Books Ltd
Both books are copyright in all countries which are signatories to the
Berne Convention
This omnibus edition first published 1985 by Pan Books Ltd
Cavaye Place, London SW10 9PG,
in association with Macmillan London Ltd
9 8 7 6 5 4 3
All rights reserved
ISBN 0 330 28852 0
Printed and bound in Great Britain by
Cox & Wyman Ltd, Reading

Rogue Herries

Why are we so alive if not to change the body into soul?

Oh, how good it was to live! I thank Thee, God,
Thou Who gavest me life!

King David, RENE MORAX

Contents

Part One

THE CUCKOO IS NOT ENCLOSED

Part Two

'FORTY-FIVE

Part Three

THE WILD MARRIAGE

Part Four

THE BRIGHT TURRETS OF ILION

Over this country, when the giant Eagle flings the shadow of his wing, the land is darkened. So compact is it that the wing covers all its extent in one pause of the flight. The sea breaks on the pale line of the shore; to the Eagle's proud glance waves run in to the foot of the hills that are like rocks planted in green water.

From Whinlatter to Black Combe the clouds are never still. The Tarns like black unwinking eyes watch their chase, and the colours are laid out in patterns on the rocks and are continually changed. The Eagle can see the shadows rise from their knees at the base of Scafell and Gable, he can see the black precipitous flanks of the Screes washed with rain and the dark purple hummocks of Borrowdale crags flash suddenly with gold.

So small is the extent of this country that the sweep of the Eagle's wing caresses all of it, but there is no ground in the world more mysterious, no land at once so bare in its nakedness and so rich in its luxury, so warm with sun and so cold in pitiless rain, so gentle and pastoral, so wild and lonely; with sea and lake and river there is always the sound of running water, and its strong people have their feet in the soil and are independent of all men.

During the flight of the Eagle two hundred years are but as a day – and the life of man, as against all odds he pushes towards immortality, is eternal . . .

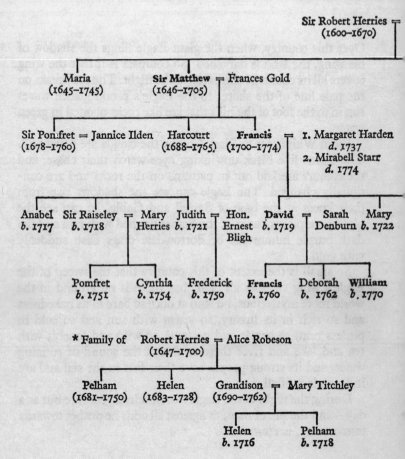

Sir Robert Herries ⊤
(1600–1670)

Maria   Sir Matthew = Frances Gold
(1645–1745)   (1646–1705)

Sir Pomfret = Jannice Ilden   Harcourt   Francis   = 1. Margaret Harden
(1678–1760)   (1688–1765)   (1700–1774)   d. 1737
                                                          2. Mirabell Starr
                                                             d. 1774

Anabel   Sir Raiseley = Mary   Judith = Hon.   David = Sarah   Mary
b. 1717 b. 1718   Herries b. 1721 Ernest   b. 1719 Denburn b. 1722
                                         Bligh

Pomfret   Cynthia   Frederick   Francis   Deborah   William
b. 1751   b. 1754   b. 1750   b. 1760   b. 1762   b. 1770

* Family of   Robert Herries = Alice Robeson
              (1647–1700)

Pelham   Helen   Grandison = Mary Titchley
(1681–1750)   (1683–1728) (1690–1762)

                              Helen   Pelham
                              b. 1716   b. 1718

FAMILY

Margaret Blaikie

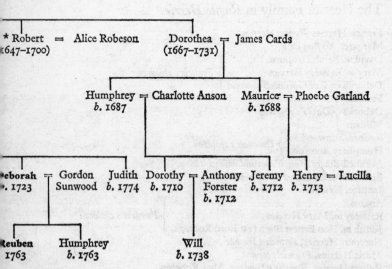

* Robert = Alice Robeson   Dorothea ⊤ James Cards
(1647-1700)   (1667-1731)

          Humphrey ⊤ Charlotte Anson   Maurice ⊤ Phoebe Garland
          b. 1687   b. 1688

Deborah ⊤ Gordon   Judith   Dorothy   Anthony   Jeremy   Henry = Lucilla
b. 1723   Sunwood   b. 1774   b. 1710   Forster   b. 1712   b. 1713
                                         b. 1712

Reuben   Humphrey   Will
1763   b. 1763   b. 1738

The Herries Family in *Rogue Herries*

Francis Herries (Rogue Herries)
Margaret, *his first wife*
David *m.* Sarah Denburn
Mary *m.* Raiseley Herries   } *Francis's children*
Deborah *m.* Rev Gordon Sunwood
Francis
Deborah   } *David's children*
William
Reuben Sunwood
Humphrey Sunwood   } *Deborah's children*
Mirabell Starr, *Francis's second wife*
Sir Pomfret Herries, *Francis's brother*
Jannice, *his wife*
Anabel
Raiseley *m.* Mary Herries   } *Pomfret's children*
Judith *m.* Hon Ernest Bligh (1st Lord Rockage)
Harcourt Herries, *Francis's brother*
Maria Herries, *Francis's aunt*
Robert Herries, *Francis's Uncle m.* Alice Robeson
Grandison, *his son, m.* Mary Titchley
Pelham
Helen   } *Grandison's children*
Humphrey Cards, *Francis's cousin, m.* Charlotte Anson
Jeremy
Dorothy *m.* Anthony Forster   } *Humphrey's children*
Will Forster, *Dorothy's son*
Maurice Cards, *Humphrey's brother, m.* Phoebe Garland
Henry, *his son, m.* Lucilla Vane

Part One

THE CUCKOO IS NOT ENCLOSED

THE INN–THE HOUSE

A LITTLE BOY, David Scott Herries, lay in a huge canopied bed, half awake and half asleep.

He must be half awake because he knew where he was – he was in the bedroom of the inn with his sisters, Mary and Deborah; they were in the bed with him, half clothed like himself, fast sleeping. Mary's plump naked arm lay against his cheek, and Deborah's body was curled into the hollow of his back and her legs were all confused with his own. He liked that because he loved, nay, worshipped, his sister Deborah.

He knew also that he was awake because, lying looking up, he could see the canopy that ran round the top of the bed. It was a dull faded green with a gold thread in it. He could see the room too, very large, with rough mottled white walls and a big open stone fireplace; there was a roaring, leaping fire – the only light in the room – and he could see very clearly the big, shining brass fire-dogs with grinning mouths like dragons and stout curly tails.

He knew, too, that he was awake, because he could see Alice Press sitting there, her clothes gathered up to her knees, warming her legs. He did not like Alice Press, but she always fascinated him, and he wondered now of what she was thinking, so motionless, her head with its red hair pushed forward, her naked neck above her silver brocade.

He knew that he was awake, because he could hear the sounds of the inn, voices calling, doors banging in the wind, steps on the stair, and even the snap-snap of horses' hoofs on the cobbles of the yard. He could hear the wind too, rushing up to the windows and shaking the panes and tearing away again, and then he shivered, pleasantly, luxuriously, because it was so warm and safe where he was and so cold and dangerous outside.

Then he shivered again because he remembered that he, with the others, must soon plunge out again into that same wind and mud and danger.

He would like to stay thus, in this warm bed, for ever and ever.

But, although he was awake enough to know all these things, he must be asleep also – asleep because, for one thing, the room would not stay still, but leapt and rollicked with the fire. All the things in it moved; the fire-dogs grinned and yawned; over a large armchair of faded red silk, oddly enough, some harness had been slung, and it lay there in coils of silver and dark brown leather, and these coils turned and stretched and slipped like snakes. Then against the wall there was a long, thin mirror in tarnished silver and, in this, Alice Press was most oddly reflected, the side of her face that was shown there being very thin and red, her hair tawny-peaked like a witch's hat; her eyebrow jumped up and down in a terrifying manner.

Only David was not afraid. He was a very fearless boy. But he thought, as he lay there and watched, how ugly she was in the mirror, and that if his father saw her thus he would not chuck her beneath the chin and so make his mother unhappy. And, although he was not afraid, he was glad nevertheless that Mary's warm arm was against his cheek and the round shape of Deborah's body against his back.

Because it might be that after all Alice Press was a witch. (He had always had his secret suspicions.) The way that she sat there now, so motionless, bending forward, was just as though she were making spells – and the silver harness blinked and the glass of the mirror trembled as the flame of the fire rose and fell again.

Then, again, it must be that he was still asleep because, although he knew that he was lying in his bed, he knew also that he was yet bumping and tossing in the coach. In that coach they had surely been for weeks and weeks, or so at least it had seemed to his tired and weary body.

At first when they had set out from Doncaster – how long ago? – he had been all pride and pleasure. It had been a fair and lovely morning – one of the last of the late summer days. The sun was shining, the birds singing, such gay bustle about the cobbled courtyard of the inn, the maids looking down from the windows, the hostlers busy about the horses, the postilions polite and eager to his father, all of them, Mother and Father Roche and Alice Press and Mary and Deborah fitting so comfortably into the soft warm inside of the coach, that had even pictures of hunting painted on the walls and little windows with gold round the edges.

Yes, it had been all gay enough then, but how miserable it had soon become! He could not now divide the days and nights from one another: moreover, he was still there in the coach, bumped up and down, thrown here and there, sleeping, waking with cramp and pins and needles, and Deborah crying and needing

comforting, and Mary cross, and his mother frightened, and
Alice Press sulky. Only Father Roche, reading in his purple book,
or looking steadily in front of him, never perturbed nor upset
nor unhappy, always grave and kind, and miles and miles away
from them all!

Then the Great North Road, which had sounded so fine and
grand when he had first heard of it, how different it was in reality!
Not fine and grand at all, but full of deep ruts and mud so fearful
that again and again the coach was hopelessly stuck in it, and
everyone had to pull and push, cursing and swearing. Once they
were almost upset. The coach went right over on its side and the
horses went down, and they were all on the top of one another.
He, David, had a bruise on his right leg, and his mother's cheek
was cut.

The farther they went the colder it became. They seemed,
almost at once, to leave summer right behind them.

Nor were the inns where they stopped fine and clean like the
Doncaster one, but cold, draughty, and the floors and walls often
crawling with spiders and other more evil things.

He seemed, lying there in the bed watching the leaping fire, to
be transferred suddenly back into one of the worst of them –
where, tired and bruised with the rough travelling, he had
stumbled into the low-ceilinged, ill-lighted, ill-smelling room,
huddled with his mother and sisters at a dirty table in a dim
corner, and there stared out into the rude, confused babble –
men, women, children, dogs, drinking, shouting and singing, the
dogs waiting, mouths agape, while the food was tossed to them,
four men playing at some game in a corner, a man with a fiddle
and a monkey dressed in a crimson jacket dancing in the middle
of the sandy floor, the heated damp of the room rising to the
ceiling and trickling in wet smeary streaks down the walls, a
smell of straw and human breath and dung and animals and
tallow – and in the middle of this his father standing, in his dark
purple riding-coat, his high hat cocked, his waistcoat of silver
thread showing between the thick lapels of his coat, his whip with
the silver head in his hand – like a god, like a king, demanding a
private room, aweing at last the fat landlord, round like a tub,
causing all that coarse roomful to feel that a great man had come
among them. There was little, tired though he was, that David
had not that night noticed, from the painting of the King over
the fireplace to a swinging gilt cage with a blue bird, and a man
who said he was from the wars and crept to their table on his
wooden stumps showing that his right hand had no fingers . . .

Yes, he remembered everything of that night (was not the man with no legs and no fingers over there now by the fire watching Alice Press, her back of stiff brocade?), because on that night a great happiness had come to him. He had slept with his father. His father and Father Roche and himself had slept in the one small, dirty room, all three on the low, dirty bed. At first it had been almost terrible because his father had been in one of his rages, cursing the place and the dirt and the cold, cursing his family, too, for persuading him to the expense and danger of a private coach, when they would all of them have been so much better on horseback.

Then, seeing his little son straight and sturdy there in his smallclothes, looking up and waiting for orders as to whether he should go naked to bed or no, with one of his sudden gestures he had caught him up and hugged him, then thrown off only his outer clothing, then taken David and wrapped him, close up against himself, in his great riding-coat – and the two of them stretched out on the bed, Father Roche bodily beside them but spiritually a world away.

How wonderful that night had been! David had slept but little of it. He had lain close against his father's heart, his hands across his father's breast, feeling the great beat of the heart and the iron ribs beneath the thin shirt, his cheek against the smooth softness of his father's neck.

That had been a great happiness, but after that night there had been only trouble. On the high ground towards Kendal they had suffered a fearful storm of wind and rain. It had seemed to them that the end of the world had come; the coach had sunk into the mud so that for hours they could not move it. They had been warned, at the last town, that they must beware of footpads, and at every sound they had started. Quite a crowd of travellers had been accompanying them for safety – farmers, pedlars and other pedestrians. The weather perhaps had saved them. All the footpads were within doors, warm and cosy beside their fires.

In Kendal they had left the coach and had ridden the remainder of their journey on horseback. David, tired though he was, had found that glorious, riding in front of his father, mounting the hills, then dropping under the faint misted morning sun down beside the miraculous waters and mountains, a land of faery such as David had never dreamt of, sheets of white and silver, the mountains of rose and amber and the trees thick with leaves of gold.

They had ridden into Keswick in the afternoon, quite a

cavalcade of them, with their possessions on pack-horses, the
women and children so desperately fatigued that they could
scarcely keep their seats. So, in a dream, to the inn, and the
children stripped of their outer clothing and flung into the great
bed, the two little girls at once dropping off into heavy slumber.

So should David have done, but instead he had lain there in
this strange state of waking sleep. It was, possibly, that he was
too greatly excited. For months past, in their home outside Doncaster, he had been anticipating this journey. He had not been
happy in the Doncaster home. His father had been so much
away, his mother so unhappy, there had been no one save his
sisters with whom he could play. He had hated the stuffy little
house, the rooms so small and dark, the country surrounding it
so dull and uninteresting. And always there had been this unhappiness, his father angry and rebellious, his mother often in
tears, Alice Press, whom he hated, supposedly looking after the
children but doing nothing for them, gentlemen arriving from
Doncaster, drinking, playing cards, singing and shouting all
night long. His only interest had been his lesson with Father
Roche, who, while teaching him Latin and Greek, would talk to
him about many wonderful things, about London with its
palaces and theatres and gardens that ran down to the river, and
Rome where England's rightful King lived, and then of God and
Heaven, and how one must live to please God – to obey Father
Roche in all things and to keep secret in his heart everything that
Father Roche told him.

The only other entertainment had been the times when he was
with Nathaniel and Benjamin, the men-servants. Nathaniel
taught him the small-sword and cudgel, and Benjamin taught
him to box and to wrestle, and he had been twice with Nathaniel
to a cock-fight and once to the village to see a bear baited.

Nevertheless, had it not been for his father and Deborah the
days would have been heavy indeed. He was a boy of passionate
affections and his whole heart was given to his father and his
sister. His love for his father was worship and his love for
Deborah was protection.

His father was entirely a being from another world like St
Michael or St George who came in the Christmas plays. His
father who was so handsome and splendid could do no wrong,
although when he was drunk he was hard to understand; when
he beat Benjamin until the blood ran down Benjamin's back
David was sorry for the man, but yet was certain that his father
was in the right.

But Deborah was of his own flesh and blood. So, too, was Mary, but he did not care for Mary. She, although she was so young, had already her own independent fashion of living and, because she was so pretty, could have her way when she pleased, which she very well knew. But Deborah was not pretty and was often afraid. Deborah believed that David could do anything, and she always came to him when she was in trouble and trusted him to help her. He could do no wrong in Deborah's eyes, and so he loved her and guarded her as well as he could from every harm.

At the thought of Deborah he turned a little and put his arm about her, which she feeling, although deep in sleep, recognized by a little dreamy murmur of pleasure.

Just then he heard the door (which was behind the canopied bed so that he could not see it) open, and an instant later it was all that he could do to withhold a cry of pleasure. For it was his father who had entered, who was now standing quite close to them, looking down upon them. David closed his eyes – not because he wanted to be deceitful, but because he knew that his father wished that he should be asleep.

Nevertheless, one look had been enough. His father was resplendent! For days and nights now he had seen him soiled and disarrayed with the storms and struggles of that awful journey, muddied and blown and uncaring whether he were neatly kept or no. There were times when his father seemed to prefer dirt and disorder, and they were bad times too. An unkempt wig, tarnished buckles and buttons, a soiled cravat, and David had learnt to know that the disarray and rebellion were more than physical.

Only an hour ago David had seen him striding about the courtyard of the inn, mud-splashed to the thighs, raging and swearing. That had been his last thought before he had fallen into this half-slumber, that his father was still out there in the wind and rain ordering Benjamin and the rest, seeing to the horses that were to carry them the final stage of their weary journey. But now, how resplendent in the white-walled fire-leaping room! David in that one glance had seen it all.

The fine curled chestnut wig, the beautiful claret-coloured, gold-embroidered coat with the long spreading skirts, the claret-coloured breeches and grey silk stockings, the fluted grey-silk waistcoat stamped with red roses, the little sword at his side – ah! glory upon glory, was anything in the world anywhere so glorious as his father thus! No, nothing in London or Rome of which

Father Roche had told him – nothing that China or India itself could show!

His heart swelling with pride and happiness he lay there, pretending to be asleep, watching through half-closed eyes. He saw then an odd thing. He saw his father, on tip-toe, approach the fire, steal upon Alice Press, she motionless gazing into the flame, lean forward, put then his hands, deep in their splendid white ruffles, lightly about her face, closely across her eyes. She gave a little scream, but David knew that at once she was aware who this was.

Laughing, Francis Herries withdrew his hands. She looked up, smiling that strange smile of hers, half pleasure, half rebellious anger.

'Why, sir' (she was, like David, greatly surprised at his grandeur), 'what fine feathers we're wearing!'

'Hush,' he put his fingers to his lips, 'the children are sleeping.'

'I fancy so. They sound still enough. Poor babies – after such a devilish journey!' She turned again from him and stared back into the fire. 'You are dressed to meet your brother?'

'Why not to meet yourself, beautiful lady?'

He was laughing, that careless, jolly, kindly, good-to-all-the-world laugh that, as David knew, came only when he was happy. So he was happy now! David was glad.

'Myself?' She turned to him fully, showing the deep swell of her bosom beneath the brocaded vest. 'No, I think not. God! that I had not consented to come on this madcap journey.'

For answer he bent down and, still laughing, caught her head in his hands, brought his mouth to hers, kissed her on the lips, the cheeks, the eyes, then, almost violently, flung her away from him, straightening his body as he did so.

'Do you like that better? Does that make you more content with your journey?'

'No, why should it?' She shrugged her shoulders, turning back to the fire. 'Do you love me? No. Then what is a kiss?'

'Love – and love.' He laughed. 'I am no captive to it, if that's your meaning. I visit it, wish it good day, spend a pretty hour in its company – so I am never weary of it nor it of me. Love? And what do you mean by love?'

'I mean,' she answered fiercely, 'those foul, filthy, beggarly days and nights of mud and dung and stinking beds; the pains and bruises that I have known on this journey and the idiocies of your wife and the wailings of your children and the evil dirty tempers of yourself . . . And what do I receive in return for these things?'

She rose up suddenly and turned to him – a tall broad woman, with scarlet hair and a white face, who would soon be stout.

David, watching her, had never seen her like this, so alive, her big eyes with the fair, faint eyebrows staring, the big bosom under the silver brocade heaving, the big mouth in the pale face half open.

Francis Herries looked at her gently, kindly and with amusement. 'What do you get?' speaking low so that the children should not be waked. He put a hand on her shoulder, and she stood strong and sturdy without moving. David could see her full face now in the mirror and he watched absorbed because it was so awake. Always it had been yawning, the lazy eyes half closed, the cheeks heavy with indolence as she sleepily ate sugar-plums and cakes and sugar-figs.

'What do you get? . . . Something. Nothing. And what is there to get? A little hugging and fumbling, sweating and panting, and then satiety.' He looked at her even with more earnest study, as though in truth he had never seen her before, and her eyes did not fall before his. 'You elected to come – to the end of the world. No roads. Savages. A chill house with the rain always falling – and the ghosts of all your sins, my dear.'

She, with a sudden movement that surprised him, caught him round the cheek and with her white face against his ruddy brown one whispered eagerly, furiously in his ear. The fire leapt as though in sympathy with her urgency, and the figures swayed and swelled in the silver mirror.

Francis Herries withdrew from her slowly, carefully, as though he would not hurt her, no, neither her body nor her soul. But he was many, many miles away from her as he answered:

'So that's the way of it . . . To leave them in the mud and rain and find sunshine, the two of us, alone – alone.' He smiled – a beautiful smile, David, who did not understand the most of this strange conversation, thought. 'Alone with me, Alice, you'd be in despair in a half-hour. No one has been alone with me ever and not suffered the intensest weariness. I have suffered it with myself, recurring agonies of it. And you are not made to be wearied.

'Nevertheless, you will be infinitely dull. Days of rain and mud in a half-tumbled house cut off from everything but the savages. It's your own choice, my dear. And only my body to comfort you. My body without my soul, I fear. My soul has flown. I lost it a week back. I shall find it doubtless on a tree in Borrowdale.'

David saw that she did not understand him, that she gazed at him with a look that he himself did not understand, a look of rage, of love, of uncertainty, of disappointment. She was not very clever, Alice Press. Young though he was, David already had an instinct of that.

His father came softly to the bed and looked down on them. David, his eyes tightly closed, could nevertheless see him, the gold of his coat, the white silk of the lapels, the curling splendour of the chestnut wig. It was as though his father were weaving a spell over him – his eyes so fixedly closed that they burnt. A spell, a spell! The crystal in the silver mirror turning, Alice Press mounting her broomstick and riding through the dark heavy-hung sky, and his father riding on a silver horse into the moon and stars . . . A spell! A spell!

'Wake up! wake up!'

It was Alice Press's soft white hand shaking his shoulder. He opened his eyes. His father was gone as though he had never been. They were to be up and have their clothes on and see their good uncle and aunt – Uncle Pomfret and Aunt Jannice.

The two little girls, like little round fluffy owls bewildered by their sleep, dazed with the strange light of the leaping fire, fastened their own clothes. Mary was eight years of age, and Deborah seven, and they had been taught from a long time to do for themselves. They had been wearing their winter dresses these last days, and Mary's had dark fur edging the green velvet and Deborah's grey fur upon crimson. David was dressed in a short yellow jacket and long tight breeches, buff-colour, reaching down to his ankles. He tied Deborah's ribbons and points and fastened her shoes. She was very frightened. She was scarcely as yet awake. She did not know what this great room was nor where they were now going. She was terrified of her Uncle Pomfret and Aunt Jannice. She was weary, utterly weary after the days of the journey. She wanted her mother. She, like David, hated Alice Press. She was like a little downy bird, her head covered with soft flaxen curls. She stood there biting her lips so that she would not cry. Had David not been there she *must* have cried. But she stood near him looking up into his face. Where David was no harm could come.

It was now time for them to go down, but they had to delay because Mary must have her horn-book to carry with her. It was a fine one, and its back was of gilded and embossed leather, crimson with silver wire. David knew at once why Mary must have it. It was to show off before Aunt Jannice that she might notice how exceptional a child Mary was.

They searched here and there. Mary had had it with her before she fell asleep. Alice Press swore and threatened. It was of no use. Mary had a marvellous obstinacy when the purpose was concerned with herself. The horn-book was found beneath one of the fire-dogs, and Mary walked out, holding it virtuously by the handle, her head up as though she were leading a procession.

They went down the wooden staircase, which was from Elizabeth's time, very beautiful and broad, the newels thick and strong, the handrails framed into the newels, the balustrade beautifully arcaded, a lovely symmetry of delicacy and strength. In the hall below it was very dark, save in the doorway that looked out into the street where the light of the afternoon still gleamed in pale shadow against black cloud. Great gusts of the gale blew into the hall, at the end of which was a huge stone fire-place with a roaring fire. On broad tables candelabra held many candles that also blew in the wind.

Across the shining floor servants, drawers, maids, men from the kitchen were constantly passing into the wild light and out of it again. Uncertain though the light was, it was enough for David to see his father, standing very stiff and upright, his mother also, and a lady and gentleman who must, David knew, be his uncle and aunt.

The children were brought up to their parents. Mary at once went to her mother, caught her mother's hand, and so stayed, looking very pretty. David kissed his aunt's hand, bowed to his uncle, then stood straight and stiff beside his father. His uncle Pomfret was a big, broad, stout man with a very red face, large wide-open eyes and a little snub nose. He was dressed in rough country clothes, his long boots were splashed with mud. He smelt strongly of wind, rain, liquor and the stables. He seemed good-natured and friendly, laughed much and struck his leg often with a riding-whip. Aunt Jannice was thin and tall, with a peaked face and a big brown wart in the middle of her cheek. She wore a broad hat and had a curly brown wig which sat oddly about her yellow leathern face. She was very composed, dignified and superior. She contrasted strangely with David's mother, who was always so stout and red and flustered and was given to breaking into odd little hummings of tunes from simple nervousness.

David knew that there was nothing that irritated his father so much as this habit of hers. But David's attention was fixed upon his father. He wished desperately – although he did not know why he wished – that his father had not dressed so grandly. Only half an hour before he had been so proud of his father's grandeur, now he was ashamed of it.

He was sure that Uncle Pomfret and Aunt Jannice were laughing at his father for being in such grand clothes. Not that his father would care, but he, David, cared for him. Uncle Pomfret was much older than his father (he was indeed twenty-two years older; he was the eldest, as Francis Herries was the youngest, he fifty-two years of age and Francis only thirty). He looked as though he might be David's grandfather.

There was indeed no physical resemblance between the two brothers. David discovered also another thing – that they were all striving to persuade his father of something, and his father was very obstinate. He knew how his father looked when he was obstinate, he smiled and was haughty and said little. So it was now.

They were trying to persuade him to stay in his brother's house at least tonight and not to go on in the wind and wet and darkness into Borrowdale. But his father only smiled. He had planned to be in the house tonight and be in the house he would, and the others should be there too.

David saw that his mother was very near to tears, her round mottled face all puckered, and she bit continually at her lace handkerchief. She was desperately weary, poor woman, and afraid and very unhappy.

'Why, blast you and damn you, brother,' said Uncle Pomfret very heartily. 'You must stay with us tonight or prove yourself most unbrotherly. We had always expected it so— Had we not, Janny? There's no road over to Herries. You are going among the savages there, brother. I can swear you were dismayed enough at seeing this griddling little inn after your great Doncaster houses, but this is Paradise to what you're going to. Don't say I didn't warn you now. Damn me for a curmudgeon, brother, if I bottomed you into doing it – but tonight you shall stay with us. There's your lady sunk with weariness, and the babes too, damn me if they're not.'

He shouted all this as though across a windy common, and all that Francis Herries said to it was:

'Herries sees us all tonight, and we'll take our luck with the road.'

'You'll be the rest of this day on horseback,' his brother

assured him. 'There's not a cart in Borrowdale, brother, nor a
road to carry one. It's all horseback round here. Damn it, you're
in Chiney in Borrowdale, but never say I didn't warn you. You
wanted cheap living and you've got it. Naked bottom and bare
soil! that's life in Borrowdale.'

David had never heard so rough and coarse and hearty a voice,
and it seemed to him strange that this big red man should be his
father's brother. He jumped, too, from the sharp contrast when a
moment later his aunt spoke:

'Come now, Francis. Have some softness for the family. The
children can scarce stand with their weariness. Margaret, persuade him. There is room enough with us for so long as you
please to remain.'

Her voice was cold and thin like the steady trickle of a determined pump. When she spoke, she stared in front of her, looking
neither to right nor left, as though she were reciting a set piece.

David's mother, thus appealed to, very nervously and not
looking at her husband, answered:

'Indeed, it's very kindly of you, Jannice. We are weary and
'tis late. Tomorrow would be time enough.'

'There, brother!' Sir Pomfret broke in with a roar, 'have you
no tender parts? Your wife and the children at least shall stay
with us. You shall ride alone if you are resolved – you and the
priest,' he added, suddenly dropping his voice.

'There – that's sufficient,' Francis Herries answered sharply.
'My wife will be thankful enough when she's there and settled.
In an hour's time the horses will be moving and ourselves on
them. Thank you for your goodwill, brother. And now for a
meal. It is ready and waiting.'

It was now late for dining. To the children, indeed, it would,
before this tremendous journey of theirs, have seemed an incredible hour, for their dinner had been at three of the afternoon
ever since they could remember, but now all their customs and
habits were in ruin, and they accepted, poor things, blindly and
without a murmur, what came to them.

They were, however, all three, too tired to have an appetite. In
the little private room they were crowded about the small table.
David to his distress was next to his uncle, who roared and
rattled and laughed as he helped the food, so that it was like
being seated next an earthquake.

There was a good baked pie of a leg of mutton, and roasted
chickens with pease and bacon, and a fine fruit tart that would,
at another time, have made David's mouth water. There was

much wine, too, and of this Uncle Pomfret began to drink very
heartily indeed, and shouted to the others to do the same. The
noisier he became the more upright and magnificent was Aunt
Jannice.

Very fine, especially, was she when she rose to wash her spoon
in a bowl of water behind the table, so that, having just used it
for pease and bacon, it should not now be soiled for the fruit
tart. David's mother, who had never seen anyone do this before,
could not hide her staring wonder.

David, in spite of his weariness which made everything
around him like a dream, fancied that his aunt was storing all
things up in her mind, so that for many weeks she would be able
to retail to her genteel friends all the strange things that this
wild family had done. He did not love her the better for fancying
this.

But he was in so dreamy a state that he could be sure of
nothing. He, in his half-dream, saw – and he knew that his
mother saw this too – that his father was drinking in a defiance of
his stout red-faced brother. He knew what his father was like
when he was drunken, and he hated his uncle that he should
tempt him. Throughout this journey his father had been very
fine, drinking nothing, aware perhaps of the charge there was
upon him. And in any case he drank little when Father Roche
was there.

But in everything that he did, while his brother was present,
there was defiance. There had been defiance in his grand clothes,
defiance in his refusing to stay in Keswick, defiance now in every
gesture. David, because he adored his father, knew all this with a
wisdom beyond his years. Meanwhile, in this dreamy state, it
was all that he could do with his wits to defend himself against
his uncle, who was pushing pieces of meat and of pie on to his
plate and even holding his head back and poking food into his
mouth. But once when he was about to force some wine down
his throat Francis Herries called out quietly:

'Nay, brother, leave the boy alone. He shall have wine when
he wishes for it. It shan't be thrust on him.' Pomfret broke out
into a flurry of magnificent and filthy oaths. He then thrust
David in the ribs and cried at him: 'Why, damn thee, boy, dost
thou not follow thy father? He's a lecherous foul-dealing knave
enough, I'll be bound – no Herries, an he ain't. Drink thy uncle's
health, boy, and be damned to thy father!'

'Pomfret!' said Aunt Jannice. It was enough. The uncle was
cowed like a dog under a whip and took some sugar-plums from

a plate and swallowed them, three at a time, like a confused child. David looked across to his father. It seemed to him then, as it was to seem to him increasingly in the coming days, that they were younger and elder brother, not father and son. And, indeed, there was only the difference of nineteen years between them.

In his dreamy state it seemed to him that he and his father were circled round with light together, they two, and that his father's crimson and gold shone, and the room burnt against its panelling with a strange and sombre glow.

But his next thought was for Deborah. With every attention that his uncle had permitted him he had watched her and had seen that she was very unhappy. Poor child, with weariness and fear of her relations and her seated distance from David, she was nearly distraught. She did not understand what had happened to her, but it was something terrible. She understood that more terrible things were shortly to occur. David, watching her, could at last endure it no longer; her frightened eyes, the way that her head bobbed and nodded and then bobbed again, her fashion of pretending to eat and not eating, hurt him as though it were himself.

While his uncle was busy with a long and excited account of his country sports and pastimes, with vociferous curses on the French and praise of the Hanoverian succession, he stepped from his chair and went to her side, bending forward and whispering to her.

But, alas, this kind attention was too much for her; she broke into sobs, not loudly but with a soft titter-witter like a wounded bird.

Uncle Pomfret broke off his account of what he would do to a French Papist an he caught him, to tumble into a bellow of laughter.

'Why, pox on it, here's a little master . . . comforting your sister . . . Why, damn it, boy, but I like your heart. There's a good one for the ladies. He knows a thing or two, I warrant. But come hither, little Deb. Come to thy old uncle. He'll buy thee a baby, one of your china sorts with pink cheeks, none of your stuffed rags. Come to thy uncle, Deb, and he'll comfort thee.'

'David.' It was his father's voice. 'Leave Deborah. Come to me.' He went up to his father, fearless, but not knowing whether a caress or a blow was to be his fate. Then he looked into his father's eyes and saw that they were soft and humorous and knew that all was well.

'Go, find Benjamin. We must shortly be starting.' Then, turning to his brother, 'She has babies enough, Pomfret; she is weary, and there's a bed at Herries waiting for her.'

He did not hear his uncle's retort, which was something fine and free about beds and ladies and general courtship. He was glad to be away, he didn't care if he never saw his uncle or aunt again; he hated them and Keswick and the inn. But coming into the bustle of the kitchen where serving-men and maids were shouting and pushing, where dogs were waiting for chance pieces of food, and a man with a feather in his broad hat was seated on the corner of a table playing a fiddle, the stir and adventure of it all heartened him and he was glad that he was alive and pushing, shoving forward into this grand new world. The kitchen smelt of everything in the world – meat and drink and the heat of the great fire. He looked around him and found Benjamin seated in a corner near the fire, his arm round a girl. She was feeding him with pieces of meat off his plate.

'Benjamin,' he said, ordering him as though he were a hundred years his master, 'my father says that it's time for the horses.'

Many of them heard him and turned laughing, and a big woman with an enormous bosom would have made him come to her, and a brawler wanted him to drink, but he fixed his eyes on the stout Benjamin, who put his plate down, gave the girl a kiss, and came without a word. So much power had Francis Herries over his servants.

Benjamin was plump and rosy; he should have been a fine figure of a man, but he could eat all day without ceasing. This was one of the reasons that he was beaten by his master, but he bore his master no grudge. Everything that came his way he took, and over the bad he shrugged his shoulders and over the good he laughed and grunted.

First of all he loved himself, then food, then women (all kinds, young, old, ugly and fair – there was not the ugliest woman in the country who was too ugly for him, and with his round, rosy cheeks, merry eyes, broad shoulders and stout legs he could do what he would), then cock-fighting, dog-fighting, football, bear-baiting, rat-hunting, witch-hunting, all kinds of sport (he was himself not a bad sportsman with the staff and cudgel, and boxing and running and swimming), then every kind of a horse, then young David, for whom he cared, perhaps, more than for any other single human being, but not for him very deeply, only lazily and with easy good-nature. He was from the South, and had, as yet, no good word for this northern country.

He grumbled as they made their way into the dusky yard. 'Pox on it,' he said, 'I'll pepper my own legs with shot, but I thought his honour would give us another hour's quiet and plenty. What's he want riding on tonight for? There's but few like the master for a restless spirit . . . I'd match that white dog in the kitchen there,' he went on irrelevantly, 'for a hundred guineas against the grey bitch the master had in Doncaster. There's a dog. You could see he never blinked a bird in his life. And you needn't tell master I was kissing Jenny neither! They all say their name's Jenny—'

'I shall not tell him,' said David proudly.

'How many miles is it from this Borrowdale to Keswick?' asked Benjamin.

'Around seven, I fancy,' said David.

Benjamin nodded his head but said nothing. 'It's a little inn as you might say, this,' he remarked. 'Small beside the south-country inns. Not much business in this little town. Kendal's the way the business runs. Not but there won't be some sport in Borrowdale. I may be a poor man and not bred for writing and accounts, but I know a dog when I see one.'

David missed many more of his remarks. For one thing Benjamin was always talking, not like the other man Nathaniel, who was a little spare fellow, very silent and grim, and anyone who was often with Nathaniel must accustom himself to think his own thoughts while Benjamin chattered. Besides this, David again was in his dream state. As he stood in the yard listening to the horses striking the cobbles, hearing the curses of the hostlers, smelling the hay and straw, catching the sharp cold of the breeze about his face, he seemed to move, not on his own feet, but through the air, alighting here and there and then up again, softly, breezily like the wind.

Thus dreaming he found himself standing with the others at the inn door. Father Roche was there, and Alice Press, his father, mother, uncle, aunt, and his sisters – all dreamy and wavering together. A crowd had collected to watch their departure. A great wind was hurrying through the sky above the black gables and chimneys, carrying soft grey clouds with it, and between the clouds once and again a burning star stared and vanished. The horses were stamping and pulling at the heads. Everything was ready for this last ride.

In the doorway stood the stout host of the inn, bowing as Francis Herries very grandly thanked him for his courtesy. Uncle Pomfret laughed and shouted. Then, as it seemed, a

moment later one of life's great happinesses had occurred, for
David was sitting a horse in front of his father. He had expected
that he would be in front of Nathaniel, because all the way from
Kendal he had been with his father, and surely such luck would
not come to him twice. But here he was pressed against his
father's body, and he could feel the movement of his thighs and
above his head the throb of his heart, and in his face the wind
was beating like a whip.

They were off, trotting over the cobbles, the horse slipping
now and then in the mud or refuse, his father stiffening as he
pulled at the reins, and at their side seen dimly his mother,
pillion behind Father Roche with Mary in her lap, Alice Press
with Deborah pillion behind Benjamin, the rest duskily in the
rear.

The little town was very still; a light glimmered here and
there through a shutter, a watchman going from his warm room,
perhaps, to his night-duty passed them swinging his lamp, a
chair in which a lady highly muffled could just be seen went
swiftly with its bearers round the corner. They turned out of the
square to the left, and the clatter that they made as they swept
round the corner drew some heads to the window and an
aproned man with a candle in his hand to the doorway. Then as
they began to clear the town another thing occurred. David was
aware that certain figures were running at their side and a man
on a little nag was keeping pace with them. The same thing had
happened to them on their way to Kendal, when a number
of farmers and others had gone with their coach. That had
been because of footpads, and now this must be for the same
reason.

That made his heart beat faster. They were passing out of the
guarded town and were running into dangerous country,
dangerous country that, although he did not know it, was to be
his country for many a year. He had perhaps some sense of it
there under the biting wind, for he shivered a little and drew
closer to his father.

They pulled up a little hill and were aware now at once of the
open country, for the road beneath them was treacherous. The
horses began to walk, and even so they slipped and stumbled in
the mud. In the centre the path (it was little more than a path)
was hard and well-trodden but on either side a quagmire. There
was a faint silver misty light in the sky, but this shifted and
trembled with the driving clouds. On the left of them there were
thick trees, but on the right the landscape sloped to the mere, and

in front of them were black shadows that waited like watchers for their coming, and these, David knew, were the mountains. He was aware then of a further thing, that his father was drunk. Not bestially drunk. Not ferociously drunk. Happily drunk. His body closed a little about his son as he sang softly the children's game:

> 'Lady Queen Anne who sits in her stand,
> And a pair of green gloves upon her hand,
> As white as a lily, as fair as a swan,
> The fairest lady in a' the land.
> Come smell my lily, come smell my rose,
> Which of my maidens do you choose?
> I choose you one, and I choose you all,
> And I pray, Miss Jenny, yield up the ball.
> The ball is mine and none of yours.
> Go to the woods and gather flowers;
> Cats and kittens hide within;
> But all young ladies walk out and in.'

David knew the words very well, because, although this was a girls' game, he had played it to please his sisters. His father repeated again:

'And I pray, Miss Jenny, yield up the ball – And I pray, Miss Jenny, yield up the ball.'

Why had he chosen the name Jenny? Was not that the name by which Benjamin had called the kitchenmaid? Did they, as Benjamin had said, always cry Jenny for a name? His father swayed slightly as he sang, but the horse seemed to understand. In any case they were going slow enough. No harm could come. A little man trotting at their side called up to them:

'I have a fiddle with me, your honour, and will play to you by your fire.'

And Francis Herries answered him happily: 'I'll swear you have a fiddle and know how to play on it too.' Then he began to talk very pleasantly to his young son. The path now was bending down until it almost touched the mere, and David could hear the little waves, driven by the wind, slapping the shore and rippling away again into space.

All his life he was to remember that moment; the clap of the horses' hoofs on the path, the slap and ripple of the water, the little panting breaths of the man running beside them, the warmth and intimacy of his father's body, the dark woods above them, the black hills in front of them, the fiercely moving sky, and the gentle good-humoured voice in his ear.

'And so, David, we are passing into the perilous country where the savages live, where there is only hay to eat and dirty water to drink, where it rains for a hundred days. Dost thou think there will be bears there, David, my son?'

'I don't know, Father. I hope so,' said David.

'Bears of one family or another there will be, and snakes in the grass and peacocks on the garden wall. Is it not as though we were escaping? Escaping from what, think you?'

'We are not escaping,' answered David proudly. His voice came in little jolts. They were now on harder ground and were moving more swiftly. 'You would never run away.'

'No, would I not? Art thou so sure, little son? I have run from the lions in my time and then again I have braved them. But this is the most perilous adventure of all. We will not come from this save with our naked skins; and if I am hard pressed will you always stay by me, David?'

'Always,' said David, nodding his head. 'I could never be frightened an you were there.'

'Couldst thou not, couldst thou not, my son? Although the she-devil with the silver hams and the glassy tongue came to down us both?'

'I'm afeared of no woman,' David answered, but the trees now were gathering about him very darkly, and it was cold. In spite of himself he shivered a little.

His father laughed, bent forward and touched ever so lightly with his lips the boy's neck.

'So we are together, side by side, whatever the peril – for ever?'

David straightened his back. 'Yes, sir,' he answered proudly.

'’Twas a maid in the inn said her name was Jenny when I kissed her,' his father said, 'though she's no maid any more. Not by my doing, I had no time to test her virtue. Eh, little son?'

David understood this only vaguely. 'I don't like women,' he said.

'Not your sister Deborah?' His father laughed softly, deeply, as though he were thinking of other things.

'I love Deborah,' David answered.

'And your Aunt Jannice?'

But David did not reply. He could not. He was fast asleep, leaning back against his father's breast.

He woke again with a start to see that all the horses were at a standstill and were gathered about a small stone bridge. At that same moment, as though it had been arranged, a round moon, cherry-coloured, broke out from shadowy banks of cloud.

She stared down at them, and at once, as it seemed in his sleepy half-wakened state to David, the clouds fled away; she sailed gloriously in the sky of shining light scattered with stars. The world around them was like a world seen through glass, pale and unreal, with the trees and hills of ebony sharpness. A hamlet was clustered beyond the bridge and the river, which was running full and throwing up, under the moon, little white waves alive and dancing.

After a consultation they moved on upwards over a little hill with hills on their left side and the flooded gleaming river on their right. It was all very quiet and still. The storm had altogether died away. No one spoke, and the only sound was the hoofs of the horses, now soft, now sharp. The scene was now to David, who had only all his life seen flat and shallow country, incredibly wonderful.

They were passing through a gateway of high rock into a little valley, still as a man's hand and bleached under the moon, but guarded by a ring of mountains that seemed to David gigantic. The moonlight made them larger and marked the shadows and lines of rock like bands of jagged iron. In colour they were black against the soft lighted sky and the myriads of silver stars. A little wind, not sharp and cold as it had been before, but gentle and mild, whispered across the valley.

As they advanced, the only live things in all the world, it seemed that in a moment someone must break the strange moonlit silence with a cry: 'Ahoy! ahoy! who comes to meet us?'

But not even an owl hooted from the listening trees. After a while one mountain detached himself from the skies, coming towards them – large, sprawling, very dark and solid, with a ragged edge. To the left of this mountain there was a straight thin ledge like a tight-rope, and on the right a very beautiful cluster of hills, in shape like the grouped petals of an opening flower.

Then quite suddenly they stopped. 'That is the house on the left of us,' someone said. It was the first voice for half an hour, and the hills seemed to repeat: 'Yes, that is the house.' The horses trotted over soft, rather boggy, grass, up a little hill, through a thick group of trees, and at once they were all outside a rough stone wall that guarded a ragged, grass-grown courtyard. David looked at the house and was sadly disappointed. Under the black hills it seemed so very small, and in the white moonlight so cold and desolate. It appeared to be two houses: on the right it was high, with a gabled roof and thin latticed windows; then it dropped suddenly to a low rough-seeming building with shaggy farm byres at its hinder end. He noticed, especially, the windows of the higher house, because there were two little attic windows like eyebrows, and he could see, because the moonlight made everything so clear, that the door of this house had handsome carving. But the other building was low and shabby and forsaken.

While they waited at the gate three dogs came out furiously barking, and directly they were followed by a broad thick-set man, walking clumsily, who hurried down to meet them.

Then a light was in the doorway, but still the house watched, cold, desolate, under the moon, with no greeting for them.

'So – we are home,' he heard his father murmur.

Then he felt himself picked up in his father's strong arms, lifted, then carried across the courtyard.

His father set him down, and he ran over the threshold of the doorway. The hall where he stood was flooded with moonlight, and opposite him were two shining suits of armour. People were moving and talking behind him, but he did not hear them.

He was first in the house. As he stood there in the moonlight he, who had been asleep so long, was suddenly awake.

And he made his compact with the house.

THE MOUNTAIN

CHARLES FRANCIS HERRIES woke when the light of the fine new day was throwing silver shadows across the misty fields. Pushing back the creaking diamond-paned window, standing there in his purple bed-gown he looked down on the courtyard, the thick clustered yews that guarded, as though with fingers on their lips, the house, the ragged stone wall, then, beyond, the river, the thatched roofs of the nearest yeoman's farm, the fields and the dark sombre hills.

He drew a deep breath, flung off the bed-gown and stood there naked. He did not feel the cold, nor the sharp crisped air; he was at that time impervious to all physical pain and discomfort, a magnificent creature in all bodily force and feeling. He stared out, then looked back into the little, thin, low-ceilinged room. It was furnished scarcely at all – only a narrow truckle-bed on which he and his son had been sleeping – David, his flushed cheek against his arm, still lay there soaked in sleep – a big carved chest with the date 1652 roughly cut upon it, a mirror on the chest, and against the farther wall some old green tapestry (very faded) that flapped and rustled now in the breeze from the open window. There was one high-backed and clumsy chair, and into this his clothes had been carelessly flung. David's little things, carefully folded, were on the top of the chest.

He felt his body, punching it here and there, pinching it, kicking out a leg, stretching an arm. He might have been proud that he was so handsome and in such splendid health – such marvellous health indeed, considering the life that for ten years now he had led. But he was scornful of that as he was of everything else. What good had his beauty, health, strength brought him? Not so much good as that silver moon setting now in a pale rosy sky beyond the latticed window.

He stood there, the breeze blowing on his bare back and thighs, looking down on his little son. Here, too, he was scornful. His young son loved him, but would he love him as the years passed and he grew to realize his father? Would there not develop in him that same withdrawal that seemed to come to every human creature after a short contact with him – yes, even to so poor a thing as Alice Press, who was already beginning to look at him with that strange, surmising glance? David at present trusted and adored him, and in the centre of Herries's universal scorn, scorn of himself, of all human beings, of the round world and all that moved in it, there stayed this pleasure and pride that his young son so thought of him. That he could neither deny nor reject. But for how long was it to remain? Would he take any steps to retain it? He knew himself too well to fancy that he would.

He turned again to look out of the window on to the scene that was to be his now, he was determined, for evermore. Whatever came of this step that he had taken, whatever misery, ruin, disgrace, he would hold by it. It was final. Only thirty years of age, he yet seemed to see far, far into the future, and something told him that at the very last these dark hills would encircle him.

The hill that chiefly his window faced seemed especially to tell him this. The houses of this time in this country were not built that their tenants might look out on beautiful views, but rather for safety and shelter, tucked tight in under the hill, guarded by heavy yews.

Beyond the fields, in far distance, this humped, lumpish hill, Glaramara, sprawled in the early morning light. Herries knew well its name. For so long as he could remember he had known precisely how this house must stand, and all its history. In 1565, the year following the founding of the Company of Mines Royal, Sir Francis Herries, his great-great-grandfather, had come from his house Seddon, north of Carlisle, in part charge of the 'Almaynes', the foreign miners, and built him a little house here, called it Herries, and, at last, liking it and the country, had lived in it altogether, giving up Seddon to his younger brother.

In all his young days at Seddon, Francis had heard of Herries, the strange house in the strange country, shut in under the mountains behind rocky barriers, cut off from all the world. His grandfather, Robert Herries, had tried for a while to live in it, but it had been too isolated for him. That, too, his father Matthew had found, and had moved back to Seddon, and after this the old house had been held by a yeoman, Satterthwaite, farm-buildings had been added to it, and much of the older house had been allowed to fall into ruin.

When Francis's elder brother, Pomfret, had made a fortune in speculation (this largely by chance, because Pomfret was no brilliant financier) he had built him his house in Keswick, caring nothing for Herries, which, although so near to him, seemed yet at the very world's end.

Satterthwaite, a clever yeoman above the abilities of his fellows, had done well for himself, and built a farm-house over towards Threlkeld. It was then, after some years of desolate neglect, that Herries had been suggested to Francis by his brother, and, driven both by his romantic love for the notion of it and by his own desperate circumstances, he had accepted with an eagerness that had amazed the unimaginative Pomfret. Yes, an eagerness that was amazing even to himself. What was it that had driven him? That part of him that loved to be alone, that loved to brood and dream and enfold about him, ever closer and closer, his melancholy and dark superstition and defiant hatred of the world. That part of him, too, that felt, as neither Pomfret nor Harcourt, his brothers, felt, his passionate pride in his family. Why that pride? God only knew. There was no reason for it. The Herries men had never done great deeds nor supplied to the world famous figures. For hundreds of years they had been drunken, robbing Border freebooters; only, in Elizabeth's time, his great-great-grandfather, Francis, having some good fortune at the Court, had pushed up a little the family fortunes.

That Francis had been a hard-headed fellow, a flatterer, a time-server, a sycophant, but not ungenerous if he got his way, and no fool at any time. Elizabeth had a fancy for him, would have kept him with her, and was none so well pleased when, quite eagerly, he accepted the opportunity of surveying the foreign miners who were sent to Keswick.

Something hurried him thither, that odd strain that was for ever cropping up in every Herries generation, the strain of the dreamer, the romanticist, the sigher for what was not, the rebel against facts; and in that old Elizabethan Herries this romantic dreaming went ill enough with hardness, his pushing ambitions, his desire for wealth.

Between the two stools of temperament he fell to the ground, as many another Herries had done before him. This land in Borrowdale caught his fancy; he stayed on and on there, losing at length his interest in the mines, mooning, a dirty unlaced old man, behind the rocks that bounded that valley, keeping company with the yeomen, pursuing their daughters, drinking, riding, dicing – dying at last in his old tumble-down house, a little soiled rat of a man with ale dribbling at his ragged beard.

That was great-great-grandfather Herries. The place had done something to him, and Francis Herries, gazing now out of his window, thought it an odd fancy that this same sprawling hill, Glaramara, had looked across into that old man's eyes, seeing them grow ever more bleary, more dim, more obstinately sodden.

And so it might be with him! He had come even as that old man had come, in the vigour of his prime and strength, and he had in him those same things – that longing for what was not, dream of Paradise round the corner, belief in a life that could never be. And in him also, riding him full strength, were lechery and drunkenness, lasciviousness and cruelty.

As he stood there, idly gazing, he had a passionate family feeling. Not for individuals. He hated Pomfret, despised Harcourt, cared nothing for his cousins, the children of his uncle Robert, who lived London way, nor for his other two cousins, Humphrey and Maurice Cards and their children, Dorothy, Jeremy, and Henry. Humphrey Cards, a man a good deal the elder of Francis, lived now at Seddon and was said to be a tight-lipped Quaker. Francis had never seen the Cards brothers; they inhabited London when he, as a boy, lived at Seddon, but Pomfret knew them and despised them both.

No, there was not one of the family for whom Francis cared a rap, neither agricultural Pomfret and his yellow-faced wife, nor

bachelor Harcourt, there on the edge of that dirty sea-coast at
Ravenglass, nor the purse-proud Kensington children of Uncle
Robert with their family coach and fine Queen Anne house and
garden, nor Humphrey at Seddon, nor ship-owning Maurice
(his eyes, they said, so deeply stuck into his business that he
could see nothing else) down at Portsmouth – not for a single one
of them had he a warm feeling or a kindly thought – they were
all rogues and fools together – and yet here he was, new-come to
this tumbled old ruin, gazing out on a couple of shabby hills and
some grass-greasy fields, and his heart was swelling, at
the thought of Herries and of the Herries men and women
before them, the Scotch and English blood that had gone to the
making of them, the English soil that had seen the breeding of
them.

He felt suddenly the cold, and with a shiver pulled to the
window and took on his bed-gown again.

There was a pump in the yard behind the house – he could
hear the handle going; he would go and soak his head under it.
He pulled on a pair of breeches, thrust his feet into some slippers,
and then softly, lest he should wake his son, stole out.

The morning was deepening now, but the small heavily
paned windows let in little light.

The part of the old house that remained had not been ill
designed, the rooms lofty and the staircase wide enough for two
to go abreast, still something of a wonder in Queen Anne's day
and exceedingly unaccustomed in Elizabeth's.

This old house was of two floors, a most unusual thing in that
country, the court-room, the dining-hall, the withdrawing-room
leading one from the other. Out of the court-room a stair led to a
loft that held the three bedrooms, two very small (in one of them
he had slept last night with David, in the other Alice Press with
the two little girls), and the other larger, containing a grand bed,
and in this his wife was still sleeping; Father Roche had a small
room below.

On the ground floor there was the entrance-hall and the
kitchen, and on to the kitchen abutted the farm-buildings rented
by Satterthwaite. These were a diminutive example of the yeoman's dwelling. This building was slated, the ridge made of what
were known as 'wrestlers', slates notched so as to interlock. The
rest was primitive enough, the upper floor open to the oaken beams,
an oak partition portioning off the sleeping-place for master and
mistress.

Below was the house-place, the parlour and the kitchen. A

man and his wife called Wilson had been caring for the house ever since the Herries family had forsaken it.

Coming down the rickety stair from the loft in the dim light, Francis Herries could see at once that their care had been neither vigilant nor arduous.

He stood in the dining-hall and looked about him. In that dim air without a sound in the world it seemed forlorn and desolate enough.

At the withdrawing-room end there was a raised dais, and at the court-room end, opposite the dais, some high oak screens, intricately carved.

Along one wall hung a fine spread of tapestry, fresh and living still, worked in colours of red, brown, amber, dark purple, its subject a hunting-scene, so handsomely wrought that all the wall seemed alive with straining hounds and noble horses, hunts-men winding their horns, and for their background dark hills and clustering trees.

This was a fine piece, and Herries, looking at it, wondered that it should be so well preserved. For the rest the hall was furnished barely – one long oak table, some stiff-backed chairs, a carved chest, and a portrait hanging above the dais.

It was this portrait that drew now Herries's attention. In the dim light it seemed marvellously alive. He did not question but that it was the portrait of old great-great-grandfather Herries himself. It had been undoubtedly painted after his coming to Herries, possibly by some wandering artist who had strayed into these wilds or by some London friend passing through Kendal on his way to Scotland – whoever had executed it, he was, in that wavering light, alive and dominating. An old man, his face wrinkled and seamed, his head poked forward out of some dark furs, his eyes dimmed, half closed, and one thin hand stretching forward out of the picture, as though to seize some prize or arrest some attention.

What Francis Herries felt, looking at it, was that there was here an odd resemblance to himself. Was it in the eyes? How could that be when his own were so bright and eager? Or the mouth? But this mouth was puffed and seemed as you looked at it to tremble. Or the skinny neck between the furs? Or the grasping hand? He looked at it, nodded his head as though the sight of it had decided some problem for him, and passed on down the stairs, through the shabby little entrance-hall into the open.

Behind the house he found an old-fashioned pump, and

leaning against the wall, scratching his head and yawning, was Benjamin.

By the side of the pump was a wooden bucket. He signed to Benjamin to come and help him, stripped (this was the blind side of the house, and in any case he did not care who might see him). Benjamin splashed him. The water was ice-cold. He pulled on his breeches again, bid Benjamin rub his chest and back. He was in a splendid glow.

Over the low wall he could see the lights of the sky clustering about Glaramara's shoulders. Long swaths of yellow lay across the pale ivory, and the edge of the hills rippled with fire. A bird sang, a little uncertainly, from the yews, and in the fresh stillness other birds could be heard beating their way through the shining air.

Benjamin, his mouth open, stared at his master, waiting for orders.

'Strip, you devil,' Francis Herries said, laughing. 'You are sodden with sleep.' Benjamin stripped at once, and his plump, stout body began to shiver and quake as the cold air caught his flesh. Francis laughed, then filled the bucket and splashed the water over the man, who did not, however, flinch, but stood there, shaking, but at attention.

'I will repay your courtesy,' Francis said, and seizing him, rubbed his naked body with a ferocious vigour. Then, giving him a kick with his soft slippers, cuffed him on the cheek and bid him put on his clothes.

'How does this place seem to you, Benjamin?'

Benjamin, pulling up his breeches, answered:

'We shall come to a handsome knowledge of one another's customs, hidden here from the world – but 'tis a good place for horses.'

Francis Herries looked about him. 'I haven't seen so clear a water nor smelt so fresh an air for years. But you can leave me when you will. I'll have no man stay who's a grumbler.'

'If I would leave you, master,' Benjamin answered with that odd, half-sulky, half-humorous speech that was so especially his, 'I'd have left you long ago. There's been often reason enough.'

'Why do you stay then?' asked Herries.

Benjamin, rubbing his wet head, answered: 'I can't tell. There's no reason for why I do things.' He paused, then added: 'Where you are, master, there's food and dogs and horses. Day come, day go, life is the same anywhere in the world, I fancy.'

'And when I beat you?'

'All men are beaten,' answered Benjamin, shuffling inside his clothes. 'I'd sooner be beaten by you than another.' He added, looking about him at the hills as though he were seeing them for the first time – 'The fellow in the house tells me there's fine bull-baiting, wrestling and other games round these parts. Life's not over for us yet, master,' and, as he shuffled off with his fat walloping walk he grinned at Herries, showing himself half servant, half friend; half hireling, to be kicked, beaten, abused; half equal, knowing secrets and sharing confidences that must breed equal contact.

As he turned to go back into the house Herries saw, looking at him from the corner of the housewall, an old, bent, infinitely aged woman. She had long, white, ragged hair, and a thin, yellow face. She stood without moving, looking at him.

'Who's that?' he asked Benjamin.

'The house-man's mother.'

The old woman raised her hand as though to feel the wind, then disappeared.

He went into the house to see his wife. The bedroom was dark. He pulled back the curtains and then stood by the window looking across at her. That was a fine bed in which she was lying, the curtains of faded crimson velvet, the woodwork splendidly carved. Crimson velvet, torn and shabby, was tacked also on to some of the panelling of the walls. There was a portrait of a young lady in a green dress and a white ruff over the fireplace.

His wife was yet sleeping. He came to the bed and stood there watching. There was something pathetic in poor Margaret Herries as she lay there, happy for a while at least in dreamless slumber. All the anxieties, woes and bewildered distresses that attacked, so increasingly, her waking life were for the moment stilled.

She looked a fool as she slept. She was a fool, she would always be one, but there was something gentle, kindly, appealing in her stout characterless features. And it might be that there was more character there than anyone, herself most certainly, at this time knew.

Maybe Herries, as he looked at her, felt something of this. Drawing his purple gown closely around him, he gazed at her, lost in his own disappointed ironical thoughts.

Why in folly's name had he ever married her? They had been young enough, he eighteen, she seventeen. They had been idiots enough, he vain beyond all vanity, she adoring beyond all conceivable adoration; she had been pretty, innocent and wealthy.

Her father, Ephraim Harden, a very successful City merchant, had died a year before their meeting, her mother being already long-time dead. She was an only child and sent to an aunt in Carlisle on a holiday. They had met at a Carlisle ball, he handsome, without a penny, loathing the dull life at Seddon, where he hung on because he had no means wherewith to live in any other more lively place.

Seddon was still his brother Pomfret's at that time, and Francis and his brother Harcourt were permitted to remain there on a kind of tolerating sufferance. How he had hated that place with its dull grey walls, its poverty and greasy indolence. You might say that this place, Herries, to which he had now come was dull and grey enough, but, from the first moment seen on that moonlit night, he had thrilled to it. It had touched, and he knew this absolutely, some deep fundamental chord in him.

But Seddon and brother Harcourt! Harcourt with his thin, shanky frame, peering eyes and most exasperating cough, his passionate absorption in his books, so that he was only happy when they were piled high around him, sending up their dusty thick smell on every side of him. Harcourt who, in his twenties, had been a gay spark in London, an acquaintance of Swift and Addison and Steele, who had helped in the exposure of the great Psalmanazar, been present at the trial of John Tutchin, and even spent an evening with the infamous Mrs Manley of the *New Atalantis*!

But as Harcourt had grown, his zeal for letters had grown with him; he had abandoned the town, buried himself in Seddon with his books, and then, at Francis's marriage, taken himself to the sea-coast, near Ravenglass, where he lived, a contented hermit.

It had not been altogether Francis's desire for money that had driven him into marriage with Margaret Harden. His motives were never unmixed in anything that he did, always there was nobility with his greed, tenderness with his cruelty, humour with his pessimism. He cared for her prettiness and innocence. He might have had her without the marriage ceremony, her body and her money too, she adoring him so that from the first moment she could deny him nothing, and he did not.

Nor was it only his weariness with Seddon. From the first he had realized that it was likely that Margaret Harden would weary him more than ever Seddon had done. He had felt a tenderness (which he might now allow was principally a weak sentiment) for this lonely orphaned girl, tied, until some man should carry her away, to the strings of a dumpy, frowzy aunt whose only interest was in cards and the scandals of the country town.

He had been stung to the venture also by the sharp pleasures of rivalry. The neighbouring squires, the sparks of the little town, even some of the graver, more aged officers of the garrison, had seen in Miss Harden's pretty face and splendid fortune an exciting prize. But from the first moment of Francis Herries's appearance there had been no chance for any other. He had been for her, poor silly fool, the god of all her dreams and maiden longings.

Yes, she had been cheated as vilely as he – nay, in the issue of it, much more vilely. She was no judge of men, poor thing, and had thought him as noble in character as he was handsome in person. The aunt, tired swiftly of the burden of this innocent girl for whom cards were too intricate a pleasure, and scandal too distressing a pastime, was delighted to have her off her hands.

Herries had, indeed, considered the thing at some surprising length for a boy so young, but even at that age he had no illusions about himself, knew himself very well for what he was. But he wanted the money, her face pleased him, he had a certain kindness for her, and so the thing had been.

Looking down at her now he could not believe that, so short a while back, she had been that pretty, slender girl. Marriage had at least agreed so far with her that, in the very first year, she had begun to thicken. The three children that had come to her (the only happiness the poor lady had known) had not assisted her beauty; you could not believe that now she was but twenty-nine years of age.

And he would swear that all their quarrels and distress had not been his fault alone. She had never tried at all to grow to his taste and wishes; she had developed in nothing during the twelve years of their life together. She had no curiosity, no inquisitiveness, no sensitiveness, no humour – only sentiment, a liking for good food, a weak indulgence of the children and an infinite capacity for tears. Unfortunately all his ill-temper, his infidelities, his squandering of her fortune had not caused her to love him less; rather she adored him more today than when she had married him. Even this last insult, of carrying Alice Press to this place with them, had not stirred her resentment.

It was that above all that irked him. Although he had tried again and again to kill it, he had deep shame at his treatment of her – a shame that never drove him to better behaviour, but that for ever irritated and vexed him. Had she abused him, sworn at him, there would have been some reason for him to despise himself less, but this submission to his unkindness made him, when he was conscious of it, hate her for his reproach of himself.

Not one of his mistresses had ever been anything to him, and Alice Press the least of all. He had taken them in a kind of impatient scorn of their eagerness. What did it matter, one thing more or less, since all had gone so ill?

She was stirring. She raised her arm, let it fall again, sighed in her half-sleep, sighed again and woke. Seeing him, she gave a little cry. He must have looked wild enough standing there in the half-light, his shaven head with its short, bristling hairs, his chest showing bare through the lapels of the bed-gown.

'Francis!' she said, and smiled that trusting, half-deprecating, appealing smile that he so thoroughly detested.

'It is a fair morning,' he answered, 'and time you were about.'

'I know.' She raised herself, putting her hand modestly over her breasts. 'I was dreaming. I dreamt that my Aunt Hattie was here again and her dog Pompey, and that she was giving it chocolate.'

'Thank God,' he answered grimly, 'that the reality is more gracious. You are at Herries, and the cesspool below this window is in full odour, and there is a witch in the house.'

'A witch?' she cried, alarmed. She was crammed with superstitions, old wives' tales of warlocks and broomsticks, prophecies and magic spells.

'A witch. I saw her but now alight on her broomstick, scratch a flea from her ear and whisper with her familiar hedgehog.'

Margaret Herries smiled that nervous smile with which she always greeted his pleasantries, not knowing whether he were in jest or earnest; whichever way her conclusion went she was always wrong.

Now she thought that he was jesting and tittered. Also she was but half awake and could not see his face clearly in the half-light. He came nearer to the bed and bent over her. He was moved by one of those sudden and to himself most exasperating impulses of compassion.

'You had best stay where you are,' he said. 'The last week has been exhausting enough for a hide-bound alligator.' He smiled, sat down on the high bed's edge and touched her hand.

'Lie here, and the woman shall bring you some food.'

Margaret was awake enough now. Any kindness from this

adored husband set her heart wildly beating, her cheeks flushing, her tongue dry in her mouth.

'If you think it wise—' she stammered. She had a desperate impulse to press his hand, even to put her arm up, pull his head towards her and embrace him, but she knew by bitter experience how dangerous those actions would be. Her hand lay pulsing in his.

'Margaret,' he said, 'if you find that I have done you wrong to bring you here, if you cannot endure the remoteness of the place and the savagery of the inhabitants, you must go for intervals of every year to some town. York is not so far – even Scotland. There is Carlisle . . .' He broke off, remembering certain old scenes in Carlisle.

'And you shall take the children with you. Only you shall not keep David too long. I have done wrong to bring you to this forsaken country.'

The flush yet on her cheeks, she answered:

'Whilst you care to have me here, Francis, I care to stay.'

It was the most aggravating thing that she could have said. It called up in its train a thousand stupidities, placidities, nervousnesses, follies that had, in their time, driven him crazy with irritation. Never a mind of her own, always this maddening acquiescence and sentimental fear of him.

He drew his hand away.

'The rocks that hem us in are not more implacable than your amiability, my dear. I remember that your aunt, prophesying (how truly!) our wedded bliss, said that you had a nature, mild, trustful and clinging. With what knowledge of human character she spoke! Cards and the frailties of her neighbours yielded her human wisdom. Then you shall not go – you shall stay and love and cherish your husband, caring nothing for the odour of the cesspool, the machinations of the household witch, the rustic brutalities of the neighbouring yeomen! I will see that some food comes to you.'

He got up from the bed with that abrupt, impatient movement that she knew so well. She recognized, poor lady, that she had already lost her momentary advantage, how she could not tell.

She looked at him, loving his every feature, then said:

'Yes, Francis, I thank you.'

She was an exasperating woman. As he went from her room he felt that he did not care how unhappy she might be in this desolation to which she had come. She might make friends with the pigs for all that he cared, and good luck to her. And she was

but twenty-nine and growing fatter with every hour! Was ever
man so cursed?

And yet once again, as, later in the day, he rode out on his black
horse, Mameluke, he was affected by his compassion. He had
escaped them all; he had not stayed for the meal which now that
it was past three o'clock would soon be on the table. He must be
alone and facing his own strange thoughts.

At first, as Mameluke trotted quietly along the rough path, he
did not notice the country round him. He saw for a while
nothing but himself and he saw himself in a mirror, his features
caricatured by the distorting glass, his body lengthened to a
hideous leanness, his forehead peaked to a white cone-shaped
dome. Well, thus he was – and thus. This sudden quiet, this
hush of the fields and sharp, refreshing coldness of the air
seemed to bring the issue of the situation before him in sharper
form than it had taken for many months.

The issue was this – that unlike all the men and women that he
knew, the squires and boon-companions of Doncaster, the
women, loose and otherwise – alone of them all he longed for
something that he could not touch. He had a vision, a vision that
took, when he was with Father Roche, a religious shape, when he
was with Alice Press a fleshly, with little David a pride in family,
with the beauty of landscape and fine stuffs and rare pieces a
poetic, but all these only forms and vestures of a vision that was
none of them, but of which thing all were. And with this vision
there was the actuality of his life – his life wasteful, idle, cruel,
sensual, selfish, vain. He did not, as he rode now on Mameluke,
turn his head away from a single aspect of it.

He had once dreamed a dream. It was some five years back at
the end of a race-meeting in Doncaster. He had stayed in an inn
in the town for the night. Drinking heavily, he was yet not drunk
as were his companions. He had shared a room with one of them,
pulled his boots off him, flung him down on his bed, where he
lay loathsomely snoring. Himself he had gone to the window,
pushed it open and stared out on a splendid night flaming with
stars.

And there, it had seemed, propped forward on a little chair, his
head almost through the window (so that he might easily have
tumbled on to the cobbles below), he had fallen asleep. Had he
slept or no? How many times since then he had asked himself
that question! In any case, through his dream he had seemed
to hear the sounds of the night. The slow, lazy call of the

watchman, the love duet of cats, the rumbling of a country cart on distant cobbles, the snores of his neighbour, these had been behind and through his dream.

His eyes open, he would have sworn, staring into the stars he had beheld a vision. He was in a region of vast, peaked, icy mountains. Their fierce and lonely purity, as silver-pointed they broke the dark sky, caused him to cry out with wonder. The sky was dark; the mountains glittering white, they ringed round a small mere or tarn, black as steel in shadow.

There was absolute silence in this world. Then as he looked he saw a great white horse, glorious beyond any ever beheld by man, come, tossing his great white mane, to the edge of the mere. He hesitated, lifting his noble head as though listening, then plunged in. He swam superbly, tossing his mane, and Francis could see silver drops glistening in the icy air. He swam to the farther edge; and then Francis was seized with an agonizing terror lest he should not be able to climb, out of the mere, up the icy sides of the cliff that ran sheer into the water. That moment of suspense was fearful and compounded of a great love for the splendid horse, a great tenderness, a great reverence and an anguish of apprehension.

Then, tossing his mane once more, the beautiful horse mounted out of the mere, strode superbly across the ice and vanished. Then, again, there was great loneliness.

Waking from this dream and staring back at the little room, stuffy and smelling of drink, the floor tumbled with clothes, his thick, open-mouthed, red-faced companion, he knew an instant of acute, terrible disappointment. For a moment he thought that he would throw himself out, end everything, so as to kill the disappointment; and perhaps it would have been as well had he done so, because, since then, that disappointment had been always with him.

The more that he had hated the noise and filth and confusion of his life in Doncaster, the more he had plunged into it. Now, as he slowly passed along the darkening path that was leading him gradually into the shadow of the hills, he saw one incident after another of the Doncaster life, stretching out their hands to him as though they were figures that kept pace with him. The foolish duel with young Soltery, a quarrel about nothing when they were both drunk, Soltery who was terrified, and then more terrified yet that he should seem terrified. He saw young Soltery's eyes now, as they faced one another in the early morning light on the fields outside Doncaster, eyes of a frightened, bewildered child – and he had shot away one of young Soltery's ears, so that he would be disfigured for life.

Or fat Maitchison the surgeon with his brilliance, his obscenity, his odd beliefs in magic and other humbug – that foolish night in Maitchison's rooms when they had defied the Devil, smashed the mirror, stripped Maitchison's mistress naked and painted her yellow. He could see now the room, furniture overturned, the glass of the big mirror scattered over the floor, and fat Maitchison with gusts of drunken laughter painting the naked back of the swearing girl . . . And the sudden opening of the door, the breeze blowing in from the street, the candles going out, and someone crying that bats were hanging on the ceiling . . .

Yes, the races, the cock-fights, the bull- and bear-baiting, the debauchery and smells and noise – a roaring in his ears, a stink at his nostrils, and always in his heart this longing for the icy peaks of his dream, the black tarn, the splendid horse with the snow-white mane.

He was young, and should do something with his talents. That he was talented he knew. They all told him so. He had infinite courage, splendid physique, an interest and curiosity in many things. What should it be? Which way should he go? And meanwhile the years slipped by, and now, obeying some mad, mysterious impulse, he had cut himself right off, hidden himself among the savages.

Was he to laze here, slouching about, making familiars of the yeomen, riding with them, chaffing their wives, perhaps seducing their daughters?

For what had he come here? He only knew that already the place was working into his veins – the silence, the air with an off-scent of ice in it, the hills that were perhaps only little hills and yet had so strong a power – witchcraft hills, hiding in their corners and wrinkles magic and spells. As he rode on, the outside world was beginning to slip ever farther and farther away from him. His was the only figure in the landscape; the whole country, as the afternoon shadows lengthened, seemed naked. Above the clustered group of mountains at the end of the valley a little minaret of pale grey clouds was forming, one cloud stealing upon another as though with some quiet purpose; a purple shadow fell over these hills as though a cloak had been suddenly dropped over them.

He saw on his right then a group of buildings. His empty world was in a moment peopled with life. Near him at the fork of the road was a small crowd gathered about a pedlar who had slung his box off his neck and rested it on a flat stone. Herries drew nearer and, sitting his horse, watched quietly.

The scene that had been a moment before wild and haunted was now absolutely domestic. Three healthy, red-faced girls stood there, their arms about one another's necks, laughing and giggling, one stout yeoman, some farm boys, and a little man, tow-coloured like a wisp of hay, who, by his drab dress, should be one of those itinerant parsons and schoolmen who went from house to house in country districts, taking odd services of a Sunday and teaching the children.

The pedlar was a tall, thin scarecrow of a man, having on his head a peaked faded purple hat, and round his neck some of the coloured ribbons that he was for selling. By his speech, which was cultivated, he was no native, and, indeed, with his sharp nose and bright eyes he seemed a rascal of unusual intelligence.

The little scene was charming in its peace and security. Some cattle were being brought across the long field, two dogs at their heels; a voice calling in rising and falling cadence sounded, as it seemed, from the hills, and in the foreground there was the sharp humorous note of the pedlar, the laughter of the girls and young men and, once and again, the deep Cumbrian accents of the yeoman.

At first they had not noticed Herries, but when one of the girls, looking up, gave a cry of surprise, they were not disturbed, and after a glance went on with their private affairs, governed by a certain dignity and independence of their own.

The pedlar, however, was aware of him although he continued his patter. He had 'Fine thread satins both striped and plain, Persia nets, anterines, silks for scarves and hoods, shalloons, druggets, and some Scotch plaids.' On his tray there were some pieces of fine bone lace, Chinese boxes, necklaces, gold rings set with vermilions, several gold buttons, and red watch bottles ribbed with gold – or he said it was gold. And some books. Chapbooks and calendars, *Poor Robin, The Ladies' Diary*, some old sheets of the *London Gazette*, and some bound volumes of Plays. These things of fashion looked strange in the open fields before the little country group, who fingered and laughed and fingered again. The jewellery, indeed, had a false air, but the ribbons and lace were pretty, and above, Herries must fancy, the purses of the locals. Herries noticed, too, that the pedlar did not seem too intent upon his sales or purchases, and that his sharp eyes went everywhere, and especially to Herries and his horse.

He thought to himself that this would not be the last time that he would see that pedlar.

The shadows of the hills now covered the valley; the light flashed palely above Glaramara and then fell. Herries turned his horse towards home. As he moved away the little tow-haired parson detached himself from the others and approached him.

His long parson's coat was green with age, shabby and stained, and his breeches were tied about the knees with string, his bony fingers purple with cold, his nose red; but he had about him a very evident dignity. He bowed, but not subserviently.

'It has been a fine afternoon,' he said, keeping pace with Mameluke's gentle step.

Herries, impressionable ever to the moment's atmosphere, his spirit touched now by some quiet and happiness, answered, as he could when he so pleased, with charm and courtesy.

'The day falls quickly in these valleys.'

'And the light is for ever changing,' the little clergyman answered with pleased eagerness. 'You are newly arrived here, sir?'

'But yesterday.'

'I know everyone in this neighbourhood – man, woman and child. You are the gentleman who has come to Herries by Rosthwaite?'

'I am,' answered Herries.

'There has been much interest in your coming, sir. It will be the wish of everyone that you will find it pleasant here, and stay with us.'

'Do you also belong here?' asked Herries.

'I do the Lord's will and go whither He sends me. For some years now I have taught the children of these villages, assisted at services, done what the Lord has bidden me.'

'You are not a native of Cumberland then?'

'No, sir, I am from the South. I was born in Bideford in Devon. For many years I was chaplain to the Earl of Petersham.'

'Why, then, have you come here? It must seem a severe exile to you.'

'The Lord spoke to me in a dream and ordered me to go North. I was to walk forward until I saw a naked man tied to a tree, and in that place to abide and do His will.'

'Where saw you your naked man?'

'After many months, begging and preaching my way through the country, I came at last to the village of Grange on a summer evening. And above the river where the bridge is, I saw a man naked and bound with ropes to a tree. The men of the village were throwing stones at him: he was near death. He had been caught robbing a yeoman of the place of two hens. I urged them to release him, the Lord prevailed, and afterwards I lodged in his house. I lodge there yet.'

'And what, then, do you teach the children?' asked Herries, entertained by this simplicity.

'The Lord's Word, the Catechism, and, when they wish it, Greek and Latin.'

'You have no family?'

'My wife is with God.'

The dark was falling more swiftly now, and it was difficult to see the path. Herries jumped off his horse and walked beside the clergyman.

'What is your name?' he asked him.

'Robert Finch.'

'How shall I like this place? It is cut off from the world.'

There was a sudden odd note of scorn in the little man's voice as he answered:

'It *is* the world, sir. Here within these hills, in this space of ground is all the world. I thought while I was with my lord Petersham that the world was there, but in every village through which I have passed since then I have found the complete world – all anger and vanity and covetousness and lust, yes, and all charity and goodness and sweetness of soul. But most of all, here in this valley, I have found the whole world. Lives are lived here completely without any thought of the countries more distant. The mountains close us in. You will find everything here, sir. God and the Devil both walk on these fields.'

'And if I believe neither in God nor the Devil?'

'You are a young man for such confident disbelief. God was speaking to me now, and has told me that you will find everything that you need for the growth of your soul here in this valley. You have come to your own place, sir. You are young and strong, but the day will come when you will remember my words.'

Herries looked back down the path. In the dusk he could see it point like a pale, crooked finger straight at the heavy black hump of Glaramara that was dark against lighter dark. Again he felt ice in the air and shivered.

'They are little hills by your foreign sort,' he said, 'and yet they impress.'

The small voice beside him answered:

'They are the loveliest hills in all God's world.' Then it continued, taking another tone, very mild and a little anxious: 'You have children, sir?'

'Three,' answered Herries.

'If you were in need—' he hesitated. 'My Greek and Latin are good, and I have authority with children. If I could serve you—'

Herries laughed.

'I must warn you,' he said, 'there is a priest in the house.'

There was a pause while the wind, rising, began to blow fiercely, swaying the branches and turning the dead leaves about their feet.

The voice began again: 'He instructs your children?'

'A little.'

'Your own religion?—'

'Nay, I am no Catholic. I have told you I have no religion. How think you, Mr Finch? In this drunken, debauched world what is your God engaged upon? He is busy elsewhere improving some other planet.'

'Christ died upon the Cross suffering a worse bewilderment.'

Herries laughed again.

'Well, you shall try your luck upon them. But we are a wild house, Mr Finch, and may, in this desolate country, become yet wilder.'

They had come to the gate that led to Herries. They paused. To Francis's surprise the little man laid his hand on his arm.

'You are young, sir. I have ten years' advantage of you. I fancy your wildness does not frighten me.'

'On thy head be it then,' Herries cried, as he led Mameluke up the path. The way here was very rough, and he began to curse as he hit the loose stones, plunged into mud, fearing that his horse might stumble and damage his knees. His mood was changing with the swiftness that belonged to his moods. Oddly enough his mind had turned to Father Roche. The little clergyman had reminded him. Why was he burdened with this priest and the risks and penalties connected with his presence? It was true that just now there was a lull in the Catholic agitation, but it might burst out again at any instant. Herries did not doubt but that Roche was busied in a thousand intrigues both political and religious, and they were intrigues with which he had no sort of sympathy. Jacobitism made no appeal to him – he hated the French influence behind it. He wanted no king for England who would be ruled by French money and ambition. Moreover, he took in any

case but little interest in politics, and had no romantic feeling for
that world. Nor had the Catholic religion attraction for him; he
despised what seemed to him its mummery, the child's play, as
he saw it, of its tinkling bells and scented air. But Roche's influence over him was strong and subtle. Ever since his first meeting with the man some five years before, it had persisted. And
for what reason? Roche was stern, unsympathetic to all Herries's
pleasures, showed no warmth of feeling to Herries (no warmth of
feeling to anyone, indeed, save little David), used Herries's house
quite openly for his own private purposes, had carried on in
Doncaster, as Herries well knew, a network of plans and plots
with an odd audacity and defiance. When he spoke intimately
with Herries it was to rebuke him. And yet Herries would endure
from him things that from another he would most furiously
resent. Where lay Roche's power? In the continued suggestion
that he held somewhere a solution for Herries's sickness of soul?
Not in any dogma lay that solution, but in something deeper,
something far more profound . . .

But (and here the house with its lighted windows loomed
suddenly up before him as though it had been pushed up
through the rough ground) was the priest to remain? Why? He
and Alice Press should both be sent packing. One must start
fair in this new place – and for a moment before he pushed back
the heavy door he had a picture before his eyes of the country
group in the fading afternoon light, the coloured scene, the quiet
and the animals and the purple-shaded hills. Here in this good
land there should be no place for the priest and the woman . . .
Here in this good land – and a moment later he was caught into
one of his dark, bestial, frantic rages.

He had left his horse outside the door and, calling Benjamin,
pressed up the staircase to the little tapestried dining-hall. A
high, thick-clustered candelabrum was burning on the table, all
the candles blowing in the winds that came from the floor-cracks,
the slits in wall, roof and window.

At the table his wife was seated crying. Alice Press, very gay
in a crimson gown, was turning scornfully away from her, even
as he entered. The three children were playing together by the
oak chest. Over all the room there was a frantic disorder. Some
of the boxes, brought by the pack-horses the night before, were
there, and scattered about were suits, gowns, china, stuffs, linen,
children's toys.

A strange thick scent of burning wax, damp straw and odours
from the neighbouring cesspool lay heavy about the candle-shine.

He had ordered that the boxes were not to be touched until the morrow, when he could supervise the opening of them.

By whom had he been disobeyed? Both women began to chatter, his wife wailing, Alice Press loud and shrill and defiant. The little girls began to cry. At that moment Benjamin, a foolish smile on his chubby face, appeared at the stairhead.

Francis Herries caught him by the neck, then, raising the riding-whip that was still in his hand, cried:

'What said I to these boxes? Hast thou no wit, thou lubber-pated bastard?'

Benjamin shouted something; everyone began to call aloud at once. The room, the house, the world was filled with shouting and stink and a raging anger.

To come thus, from an afternoon so quiet and promising, to this vileness! Anger boiled in his heart, choking him. He had Benjamin's coat off his back, struck the bare flesh again and again, lashed him about the head, the legs, the thighs, and when suddenly the man hung his head and began to droop in his arms he let fall his whip and began to beat him with his hands, letting him at last drop, a huddled, half-naked heap.

The man had fainted. Raising Benjamin's head, Herries was suddenly remembering how that morning in the fresh air by the pump he had rubbed in friendliness the man's body while the birds wheeled through the sky.

A sickness caught him at the heart. He told David to run for some water, but before the boy had returned the man was reviving. He was lying back, his head on his master's knee. He looked up, then, flicking his eyelids, said:

'It was not by my word, master, that the boxes were opened.'

Clumsily he rose to his feet; he caught his coat to his bare chest—

'I'll be rubbing the horse down,' he said, and stumbled down the staircase.

FAMILY

POMFRET HERRIES lived at this time in one of the most beautiful houses in Keswick. It was beautiful, not by his own taste or fancy, but because he wished to have a better house than any one of his neighbours.

This has always been a habit with certain of the Herries. Desiring this, he chose for architect that strange, saturnine hermit, old John Westaway, known in Keswick for a madman and the best architect in the North, a desperate traveller who knew Italy as you might know Skiddaw, who had been invited again and again to London, but preferred to live in his little house above the river, seeing no one, liking no one, buried in his books and art treasures. All over the North Westaway's fame ran. He was an old man now, had been, it was said, in his youth the friend and intimate of Chesterman and Van der Vaart and Vanbrugh, a curmudgeon, a surly bachelor, in league, some whispered, with the Devil himself, pottering about that house, with its pictures and statuary, and his dark Italian servant – a devil, but the finest architect, it might be, in England.

He had made Pomfret pay for his fancy, and when it was done Pomfret had grumbled so that you might hear him from John o' Groat's to Land's End – but it was a beautiful house. People came from Kendal and Carlisle and Penrith to look at it, so that at the last Pomfret and his wife had grown proud of it and spoke of it as entirely their doing.

In fine proportion, its roof covered with red tiles, the wrought ironwork across its front showing like lace against the stone, the house was oblong without gables. The windows were for their period most modern. They were sash windows, a great rarity, and they were beautifully spaced. The doorway had fluted columns and over it there was a charming and delicate fanlight.

The house was outside the town near to Crosthwaite Church, and the gardens ran down to the weeds and rushes of the lake-end. The garden held lime trees and the lawn was bordered with tubs of orange and bay trees. There was a little terrace and a rosy wall of red brick, and beyond the formal garden a meadow, the lake and the rising hills. To the right some greenhouses, a flower garden and a kitchen garden.

Inside, the house was wide, spacious and full of light. First a pillared hall, on the right the parlour, on the left a fine, wide staircase opening into a splendid saloon. Beyond the parlour a large bedroom leading to a greenhouse. On the upper floor other bedrooms.

Pomfret's chief pride was the saloon, the decoration of which Westaway had designed and executed – the subject was Paris awarding the apple. Lady Herries had been disturbed by the naked goddesses until it was seen that no one else minded.

In this fine house Pomfret inhabited only one room, a dusky

apartment crowded with guns, stuffed animals and fishing-rods.
Here he drank merrily with his friends.

Lady Herries's home was the parlour, where she read her
medicine books, scolded the maids, suffered in a bitter silence
that ancient lady, Pomfret's aunt, fed a screaming macaw, and
gave her neighbours tea and chocolate. The three children had
their own room far away at the top of the house.

There was a great array of domestics, from Mrs Bellamy the
housekeeper to little Peter the black boy, who had been purchased in London, shivered in the cold, and stole everything that
he, with safety, might.

Mrs Bellamy was of the family of Mrs Slipslop, and made all
the mischief both in the house and in the neighbourhood that
time and talents permitted her.

They could scarcely be called a united family, for they were
never together. Pomfret diced, drank, rode, hunted with his
masculine friends, who liked his company because he was stupid
enough for them to rob him at will. Jannice, his wife, bullied him
when she was with him, forgot him when she was not. She loved
him only when he was ill, and this was often enough, for his intemperate habits and his swinish feeding caused him constant
attacks of biliousness and vertigo. There was nothing that
Jannice Herries loved like a medical treatise; her familiar and,
after Mrs Bellamy, most constant companion was old Dr Ellis,
who would discuss with her by the hour the whole works of that
excellent practical physician, Dr Thomas Sydenham!

She experimented on her staff, her family and any neighbours
who would permit her. Little Peter, who was sick every other day
from stealing confitures from the store-room, was her most
unhappy patient. And yet, of course, this is not all that can be
said about Pomfret and his lady. At heart they were kindly and
well-dispositioned. Only they had no imagination, and had been
covered with a thin skin of wealth that, like a rash upon their
souls, discomforted them, made them uneasy, suspicious, unhappily proud.

Pomfret loved his children, but did not know how to approach
them. He cuffed them and spoiled them and cuffed them again.
He was generous-natured and desired that his friends should be
happy, but he suspected that they laughed at him, and so was
pompous and grand when he wished to be easy and familiar.

His money he had made, as he well knew, from his obedience
to the advice of a London friend, Hartwell, who, at a certain
moment, had directed his affairs.

Although his companions robbed him he had wisdom sufficient to leave his affairs in Hartwell's hands. He pretended to a knowledge of commerce and exchange; it was, as he knew in his heart, a bare pretence. He did nothing well, rode badly, shot badly, fished badly. He knew moments of great unhappiness.

Jannice Herries was also without imagination. She was acrimonious and bitter, but she knew that this was not her real life. Somewhere real feeling was hidden, but day succeeded day and nothing was done. She knew that she was unpopular among the ladies of Keswick, but she swallowed every compliment that Mrs Bellamy gave her, and at the end was more lonely than before.

After her interest in medicine her most active passion was her hatred for Pomfret's Aunt Maria, that very ancient lady, who, born in 1645 and for a time in the fashionable world, was now a hideous remnant of a dead and musty past. She longed for this old lady to die, and would have poisoned her ere this, but alone of the household Aunt Maria refused all of her niece's drugs. She was now eighty-five years of age.

Finally with both Pomfret and his lady there remained a constant uneasiness about their wealth. It had come so oddly, without any true justification. It might go as oddly again. They had witnessed in the last twenty years a series of financial panics. Now with the abominable French ready for any villainy, all this new-fangled independence of servants and labourers, who knew what the next event might be? The Catholics were listening at every window. Why, here was Francis Herries coming to live in the neighbourhood and bringing with him quite openly a rascally priest. Although Walpole and the Whigs were in, who knew how strong was their power?

Jannice Herries's favourite remark to Mrs Bellamy was: 'Things are not as they were.'

To which Mrs Bellamy with a shudder would reply: 'No, my lady. If I know my own mind there was never a truer word spoken.'

'And what will you do, Bellamy, if your master is ruined?'

'Heaven strike me dead if I ever desert you, my lady! Marry come up, don't I know a virtuous place when I see one?'

But Bellamy had been lining her pocket for many a year, and being Mrs Bellamy only by courtesy had her eye on a handsome victualler in Kendal, whose hearth and home she proposed to encompass and govern on the first signs of distress in the Herries country.

The three children, Anabel, Raiseley and Judith, lived in their own world. They, like their father, were Herries of the unimaginative, matter-of-fact breed. They took things as they came, and each, in his or her own fashion, worked quietly and obstinately for personal profit. Anabel was good-natured, plump and easy. Raiseley was clever. It would not be true of him to say that he was without imagination, but it was imagination of an educational kind.

He was studious, priggish, aloof and cold, rarely roused to anger but unforgetful of the slightest injury. He had the wise, calculating side of the Herries blood; he was studious, honest to chilliness, and despised both his father and his mother. Judith would be beautiful; she was dark and slender and already cherished her beauty as her most important asset.

These three were all typical Herries on the stony side of the family character. They saw everything in front of their noses and nothing beyond. They did not mind in the least their social isolation. They might condemn one another, but united at once in condemnation of all other children.

They were waiting now in their high, chilly room for the visit that their cousin in Borrowdale was to pay them. Only the little boy, they understood, was coming with his father and mother. They had already gathered from the conversation of their elders that Uncle Francis was a disgrace.

Of the three of them at this time it may be said that Raiseley and Judith held out no hope of later humanity; for Anabel, because of her good-nature and a certain carelessness that went with it, there were possibilities.

On this afternoon the three children were in their chill room quietly busy. Judith was seated motionless in a high chair, a collar round her neck, a board tied to her back. This was for her figure. She was watching the grandfather clock in the corner. Five minutes of her daily half-hour remained. This half-hour was valued greatly by her, because she knew that this discipline was for the benefit of her beauty. She was only nine years of age, but had already a grave and considered air. Anabel, who was thirteen, was curled up in the window-seat looking at the pictures of some chap-books, *Babes in the Wood, Bluebeard, Little Tom Thumb*. But she was not reading. She knew the old stories by heart. She was wondering what her little cousin would be like.

She, unlike her brother and sister, was sometimes lonely. She confessed it to no one, but she loved parties and fun. Maybe this little boy would be agreeable.

Raiseley was yawning over his Virgil. Mr Montgomery, who

came every day to teach him Latin and Greek, had but just now gone.

'Jam pater Aeneas . . .' murmured Raiseley, and fingered a little box in which he had a cocoon concealed. He hid this from his parents and Mr Montgomery, because they would disapprove if they knew. But soon the cocoon would be liberated. No one told him any of the things that he wanted to know about animals, about the stars. Now, when he thought of these things, a new expression came into his eyes. He was suddenly alive with a questioning, investigating alertness. His cold, pale, pointed features gained an interesting sharpness. The book fell from his hand. There were many things that he would know one day; they should not stop him pursuing his knowledge. Mr Montgomery with his sing-song voice, his perpetual cold at the nose, his eagerness to please, how Raiseley despised him!

He would like to see Mr Montgomery whipped as little Peter was whipped, or standing as the man they had seen one day in the pillory in the market, his face smeared with the mud and the yellow of the eggs that people had thrown at him. And, as he thought of these things, his face achieved an added sharpness, coldly, intellectually speculative— 'Jam pater Aeneas . . .'

He looked at the little pile of books beside him – A Guide to the English Tongue, by Thomas Dyche, schoolmaster in London; Paul's Scholars' Copy-Book, by John Raynor; The Use of the Globes.

He did not look at them resentfully. He would extract from them everything that they had to give him.

'Judith,' he said, 'I should know more than Mr Montgomery knows in a year or two. I would think it fine to see him in the pillory as a week back we saw that man.'

Judith, motionless, her eyes on the clock, answered: 'We are to go downstairs when our uncle and aunt come. I am to wear the grey-blue.'

Anabel, from the window, said: 'I like David for a boy's name.'

'I heard them say,' went on Raiseley, 'that Uncle Francis is always drunken and beats Aunt Margaret.'

'But he is very handsome,' said Judith. 'He was wearing such fine clothes the other day that Father was shabby beside him.'

'Fine clothes,' said Raiseley scornfully, 'and they living in mud and dirt up to their elbows! They say that Borrowdale is full of witches and giants – wolves too. I would like mightily to see a wolf. I shall ask Uncle Francis to take me.'

The clock struck the half-hour. Judith very carefully separated herself from her board and collar. At that same moment the door opened. They were told that it was time for them to dress.

David and his mother had indeed already arrived.

Poor Margaret Herries had been for weeks dreading this visit. It was now a month since they had come to Herries, and the weather had been so terrible that the ride to Keswick had been impossible. It had rained and rained; not as it rained in Doncaster, with gusts and flurries and pauses and whispering, but in a drenching flood, falling from the grey, lowering sky like sheets of steel.

And the mountains had crept closer and closer, and the cold stolen into the very webbing of the sheets, the torn tapestries beating against the wall, and the mice boldly running for comfort to the peat fire. A horrible month it had been, but with all the courage at her command she had faced the rain, the isolation, her loathing for Alice Press, gathered her children round her as she might and made what she could out of the situation.

Oddly enough she had not been unhappy. Francis had been ever close at hand. He did not go off for nights at a time as he had done at Doncaster. That might come later – but at present it was as though the place cast a spell upon him. He pottered about the house, rode out to Stye Head, walked up Glaramara and the neighbouring hills, wandered along the lake by Manesty and Cat Bells, made himself known to some of the neighbouring yeomen, was silent often enough, drunken at times, angry once and again, but on the whole more her companion than he had been since their first marriage year.

And so there had increased in her heart her ever-constant loyalty to him. What she had suffered watching the degradation of his reputation during these past years no one would ever know. She would never tell. Here it was as though he had begun a new life. Stories long commonplace round Doncaster would here not be known. He would start again, and she would do everything in her power to assist him. Only his brother's family could spoil this fair beginning; she had seen and heard enough already to feel that Pomfret and his wife were Francis's detractors and would from the first take care to be dissociated from any scandal.

She was as fiercely prepared to fight her brother- and sister-in-law as any lioness in defence of her cubs, but her trouble was that she was not a lioness. She was a coward; while she was riding pillion behind her husband and her son, she was aware that at the first sight of Jannice in her own domain she would lose courage, she would tremble, she would show faint-heartedness. Francis had things that he must do in Keswick. He would come later to his brother's house to fetch her. She must face Pomfret and Jannice alone.

So she stood, David at her side, in the little hall with its rounded pillars, its stone floor in black and white squares, its fine picture of an Italian scene, with dim greys and purple for colour, hanging on the right of the staircase.

They were ushered into the parlour. It was lit with candles, and David had never seen such a room. But before he could examine the room he must be startled by the persons in it, by his Aunt Jannice, who was dressed superbly in a high wig mounted over a cushion and decorated with roses and daisies, her hoop spread about her, the outer skirt of crimson velvet and the front of her dress white and silver. On one brown cheek she wore a black patch. She was grander than any lady that he had ever seen; no one who came to their house in Doncaster had dressed like that. Young though he was, he realized that her thin, meagre figure and brown complexion ill suited such finery.

But his childish attention was soon drawn from his aunt to the terrific figure who sat in a high chair under the window. This was his Great-Aunt Maria.

He would never have believed, had he not seen it with his own eyes, that any person could be so old and yet live. Her wig of a bright brown colour was arranged in a fashion of fifty years ago, falling about her strange mask of a powdered, painted face in long curled ringlets. Over one eye was a black patch. Her green bodice was peaked, and her full, open sleeves were caught together with jewelled clasps. Her wide skirt was of purple satin. Her fingers, so thin that they were like the ivory sticks of a fan, were loaded with jewels.

On her lap was a small King Charles spaniel.

She appeared a painted image. Except for her one visible eye nothing in her face moved. David was a polite little boy, but again and again he had to stare. Here was a portent, a revelation in his young life.

The little black boy was standing behind Lady Herries's chair, and as soon as greetings had been exchanged they all sat down. The little black boy handed chocolate; a bright purple macaw in a gilt cage by the window screamed.

For a little while there was a terrible silence. The room was very hot; there was a large log fire. The sky beyond the window was bright with a silver glow.

When the talk had started David could look more easily about him.

He was indeed enchanted with the softness and beauty of everything. Beyond the wide window he could see the trim hedges, the paved path, the fountain with a strange stone bird, long-necked and violent-beaked, rising out of it, and beyond the fountain the line of trees guarding the waters of the lake.

Within the room there were countless objects that he longed to examine more closely, a screen worked in gold thread, a silver casket, a clock with the sun, moon and stars on its face. But more than these, the terrible old woman with her strange ringlets, her painted face, the cascades of her bright purple dress, the sharp-pointed fingers weighted with flashing jewellery . . .

'Indeed,' his aunt was saying, 'I wonder at Mr Flammery. 'Tis a poor child that doesn't know its own father, and there's a multitude of his own poor children must be in a fine confusion.'

This puzzled David, who, looking first at his aunt and then at his flustered mother sweating in the face with the heat of the room and the agitation of this her first so important visit, wondered how it could be that any child should not know its own father. He of a certainty knew his well enough.

'Yes, indeed,' his aunt continued, looking, as he was even now old enough to discern, with an odd mixture of curiosity and contempt at his mother. 'You must be well aware, Margaret, of the world into which you have come. In winter I doubt that you'll be able to move a step. You live in the heart of savages, and when the lake is too wild for passage and the roads all of a muck to your armpits the civilized world will be as distant from you as the Indies.'

'I don't doubt,' said Margaret, flushing and perspiring the more, for she knew that it was at her own abandoned Francis that these remarks were made, 'but that the days will pass. There's sufficient to do about the house to take a month of winters . . .'

David then was aware that his great-aunt's eye had turned in his direction. He was fixed by it as a rabbit by the eye of a snake . . . It was as though he, sitting on the edge of his chair, and this very ancient lady, both of them motionless, were holding some strange secret communication. Then he was aware of something further – that his great-aunt was about to speak.

In an odd, cracked but exceedingly piercing tone she said: 'God save His Gracious Majesty.'

The worst had happened. The old woman was silent often enough for days together, and this was well, because she was a

burning fanatical Jacobite. The terrors into which her dangerous
political opinions had again and again plunged Pomfret and his
wife were both ludicrous and tragic. Sometimes for weeks she
kept to her room, and on every occasion that saw her enter that
sanctuary everyone about her breathed the hope that it would be
for the last time, but her powers of revival were incredible, and
down once more she would come to sit and watch and await her
awful moment.

She had been born on the 14th of June, 1645, the day of the
battle of Naseby, but her great days had been during the last
years of Queen Anne, when she had known Godolphin and
Marlborough and been received by Lady Masham, having her
feet planted in both camps.

But she had been nevertheless, heart and soul, Jacobite, and,
it was said, played some part in the intrigues of those last
dramatic months. The Elector of Hanover had been for her the
Devil himself, and when his cause had been definitely won she
had retired from London, professed openly her Jacobite sentiments and chattered and prayed for the coming of the Day.

No one had much regarded her; she had lived in a small house
in Winchester, until, her brain softening, Pomfret, driven by one
of the kindest and gentlest impulses of his life, had given her
shelter and protection.

How many thousands of times since then he had longed for her
decease was a secret between himself and his Maker.

Now with terror and dismay Jannice Herries heard her speak.
Here was their skeleton clattering straight out from the cupboard
and before that fool Margaret Herries. But Margaret was too
deeply buried in the warmth of her confusion to pay much
regard. Only the little boy felt the power of those few cracked
words; something spoke in his heart, some strange sympathy
that he suddenly felt, to which he quite blindly and unknowingly
responded. He was to remember at a later time this queer
muffled moment.

The situation was immediately saved for Jannice Herries by
the entrance of her children. The children had beautiful manners.
Mrs Bellamy in black silk, her hands folded across her stomach,
stood behind them – the boy bowed, the little girls curtsied.
Anabel's eyes smiled at David. He was quick enough at once to
perceive that the other girl was thinking of her own looks. She
was like his own sister Mary in that.

And then the eyes of the two boys met, and they knew one
another at once for foes. David had as friendly a heart as any

boy in the kingdom, but he realized an enemy when he saw one. One straight look at Raiseley's cold reserve and proud consequence and something within him said: 'I hate my cousin.' Just as the cracked voice of the old woman speaking to him five minutes before out of an ancient past was to return to him with significance in years to come, so that first glance exchanged with Raiseley was to influence the Herries family fortunes for many future generations.

Looking at Anabel, David thought to himself: 'That's a friendly girl.' He was uncomfortable among these grown-up persons, and hoped that it would be suggested that he should go with his cousins to see the garden or their toys. He would like finely to inspect more closely that fountain of the beaked bird or to hunt among the reeds at the water's edge.

But no suggestion was made. He too was standing now, his hands stiffly at his side as his father had taught him. The room grew ever hotter and hotter, and with every moment he felt more indignantly Raiseley's scornful eyes upon him.

Margaret Herries must talk to her nephew and nieces. She was never at her ease with children.

'Fine children,' she said nervously to her sister-in-law, 'and seemingly in grand health.'

The word 'health' was the trumpet to sound the charge to Jannice Herries, who answered proudly: 'Fine and sound they are, sister. Six months last sennight Judith here was sorely threatened with the Falling Sickness – hast thou heard of the Antepileptic Crow, sister?'

'I fear not,' said Margaret timidly.

''Tis a perfect cure for the Falling Sickness. Judith was cured by the crow. Deplume and eviscerate a large crow, casting away its Feet and Bill; put into its Belly the Heart, Liver, Lungs, Bladder of the Gall, with Galangal and Aniseeds; bake it in a new Earthen Vessel well shut or closed in an Oven with Household Bread; after it is cooled, separate the Flesh from the Sides or Bones, and repeat this Operation of baking the second or third time, but taking great care that it may not be burnt, then reduce it into a fine powder.' She recited this in a high sing-song as though it were poetry, her eyes almost closed. Opening them she saw that Margaret was gazing at her with great humility and reverence. Maybe the woman was not such a fool after all. She would make, it might happen, something of a companion. A kindliness stole about Jannice Herries's heart. It would be something to have a friendly creature near her whom she could

patronize and gratify and instruct. The days in truth were lonely
enough . . .

'You must come and see us at Herries,' Margaret went on to
the children.

'Yes, ma'am,' Raiseley answered, gravely bowing. 'It is said
that there are wolves in Borrowdale. I would gladly see a wolf.'

Margaret smiled timidly. 'David shall show you the wolves.
He has been already in the mountains. Have you not, David?'

Judith, who, since the Falling Sickness had passed as a topic,
felt perhaps that she was not receiving sufficient attention,
smiled her prettiest smile, so that her aunt, thinking how beautiful a child she was, said, speaking directly to her:

'My little girls, Mary and Deborah, will wish to show you
their toys and babies.'

'Yes, ma'am,' said Judith in her softest, gentlest voice, so that
her aunt looking at her loved her.

Once more they were interrupted, and this time it was the two
men of the family. David waited for his father's entrance. First
there was Uncle Pomfret, red-faced, noisy, with his: 'Well,
then – here's all the family! Haste away! Haste away!' and then a
sudden look of almost childish discomfort and unease. Quietly
behind him David's father, kindly today and, for David, so handsome in his dark suit and lace ruffles that all the colour in the
room went out before him, dimmed to abasement.

Yes, his father was in good humour today, coming forward and
kissing the old lady's hand, saluting his sister-in-law's brown
cheek, turning then to the children, pinching the cheeks of the
girls, tapping Raiseley on his shoulder . . . How proud of him
David was and how ardently longing for the moment to come
when he would catch that glance and, perhaps, that smile. But
for a while he did not. His father paid him no attention. The
parlour was overcrowded with figures and the sound of Uncle
Pomfret's demonstrations. Now he was being jolly with his
children: 'You will be the death of your poor father . . . I
promised your mother to give up half the afternoon to your
entertainment, and wasn't I to show you the best pack of dogs in
England? But no, Mr Montgomery don't allow. Pox on Mr
Montgomery – and here's your uncle and little cousin come to
visit us – yes, and your aunt too . . . Pleased to see you, sister . . .
and there's no Mr Montgomery to stop a family welcome,
odrabbit it! I am determined upon your being good children now
and welcoming your little cousin . . . a fine boy, brother Francis.
He shall come a-hunting. Canst ride, boy?'

'Yes, Uncle,' said David, 'a little.'

'That's more than thy cousin Raiseley can do then. Put him on a horse and he's like the Witch of Endor on a broomstick . . . Wilt thou learn to ride then, Raiseley, to please thy father?'

This public mockery was anguish to Raiseley, nor did he fail to ledger it in the account against his young cousin. But his pale face did not alter; no shadow of a change was upon it. Looking his father in the face, he answered steadily:

'I will learn, sir, an you wish it.'

'An I wish it!' His father broke into a roar of laughter – 'Hark to that now! An I wish it! Have I wished, then, to have a milksop for a son? 'Tis all your Montgomerys and their Latin grammars that have spoilt thee, boy – Here,' catching David suddenly by his breeches and raising him in the air, 'here's the spit of a tree! Here's a lad knows a dog when he sees 'un, that I'll wager! Wilt come with thy uncle hunting, David?'

But he waited not for an answer. He was aware that his wife thought him foolish and noisy. He turned confusedly to chatter to his sister-in-law.

It was then that David had a word with his father. They were standing a little back from the others. 'David, you are to go now. Your mother will ride home with me. You will find Father Roche to the left along the road. He is waiting now at the turn to Crosthwaite Church. You will ride back with him.'

At once David obeyed. He turned, bowed to his great-aunt, kissed his aunt's hand, heard above his head the excuses for his departure, smiled at his girl cousins, exchanged one look with Raiseley and was gone.

How proud he was to be treated thus – as though he were already a man!

He pushed open the heavy house-door, stepped through the courtyard, between the high gates and into the dusky road. It was almost dark; shadows lay about the broad path and little winds ran whispering about his feet.

A great sense of adventure possessed him. Behind him was the lighted town, near him the warm house with its fires and talking company, and outside the house the garden with the bird fountain and all its ordered discipline running to the wild edge of the lake with the clustered reeds. Young though he was, he yet felt the humanity and safety of this world crowded with all its persons so diverse as the ancient lady and little Peter and Cousin Raiseley, his enemy. All this within firelit walls, but, outside, the long road running, as though on a secret purpose, below the

mountain that seemed to him huge in the night air, Skiddaw; by
now he knew its name. But here, also, there was a church, and
men might ride with ease, and at short distance all the traffic of
the town. But away from it the road ran on, curving at the lake's
end, running up the hill, then above the lake's side until at last it
reached that little bridge and the high rocks behind it that were
the barrier of his own dark country. There was danger, there,
romance and adventure. Cousin Raiseley had said that there were
wolves there. He did not know how that might be, but a month's
living there had shown him how strange and removed a world it
was, and already it was beginning to pull at his boy's heart, so
that he was ready to defend it and feel that he was citizen of it.
Yes, he would know every tree, every rock, every corner of it
before long; he would push his way into every one of the
mysteries . . .

He had been walking swiftly down the road, a little afraid,
although he would not have owned it to anyone, of the sound of
his own footsteps, when he saw at the parting of the two ways a
horse and a figure standing beside it.

The figure came to meet him, and at first he did not recognize
it, because Father Roche was dressed as an ordinary gentleman
in plain riding-clothes.

'Father Roche,' he whispered. He had not intended to
whisper, but the silence and loneliness of the road commanded
him.

He was taken up and in another moment was seated in the
front of the saddle. They started off.

'Not Father Roche any more,' the figure behind him murmured. 'Mr Roche . . . the times move, and we must move with
them.'

His voice had tonight more than ever before the power to
move David. He was himself already excited and stirred, and, as
they moved over Derwent Hill, through the village of Portinscale
and then up over Swinside Hill, with every step they seemed to
be moving into some mysterious country, and it was Father
Roche's power and spirit that was leading them. Was he then no
longer a priest? Could you at one moment be a priest and then,
at the next moment, not? Was it at his father's orders that he had
ceased to be a priest? But for the moment he was too deeply
excited by his own experiences. 'Uncle Pomfret's house is very
grand. It is grander than ours at Doncaster. There is a garden
with a fountain that is a bird's head, and a clock with the sun and
moon on its face. My great-aunt Maria is a very old lady – she

looks a hundred years. She has long hair falling about her face. My cousins were present, and my cousin Raiseley is very grave as though he thought well of himself . . .' He paused, then added: 'We will fight one day. And I shall win.' His little back straightened and his short legs tightened about the horse's neck. 'Uncle Pomfret always speaks at the top of his voice. He lifted me by my breeches and said that I should go hunting with him. Will my father permit me, think you?'

'Yes, David, when you are older.'

David sighed. 'It is always when I am older. My cousin Raiseley asked whether there were wolves in Borrowdale. He said that he wished to see one, but I doubt it. I think he does not care for dogs and horses and wild animals.'

They were going more slowly now, climbing the hill. It was bitterly cold, even a little snow was falling, and a few stars were like points of ice in the sky. They were climbing to high ground. There were three paths on this farther side of the lake, but as Father Roche had been warned in Keswick only one was passable for a horse and that the highest.

'My Great-Aunt Maria,' David went on, drawing a little back on Father Roche for greater warmth, 'said once "God save His Gracious Majesty". Aunt Jannice was vexed, so that I knew that it could not be the King in London. It is forbidden, is it not, to speak of the other King in Rome?'

Father Roche drew the boy closer to him. The time had come, then, to speak. The boy was now of a sufficient age. For years now he had been waiting for this moment, and he was well pleased that it should be at this instant, cold and sharp under the winter night sky, with the world so silent on every side of them. It had been the lesson of his life that he should have no human passions, and he had learnt it well, but in spite of all his lessons human feeling had grown in his heart for this boy and this boy's father. There were many other plans and schemes in his life that went far beyond his momentary relations with the Herries family. He stayed with them only because it suited his larger purposes to do so, but growing up in his heart in these last years had been the longing to turn this boy on to his own paths. During these weeks since coming to Borrowdale David seemed to have grown in mind and perception. He was already wise in some things beyond his years.

'David, will you listen a little as we ride? I have wished for some time past to speak to you. You are of an age enough now to understand.'

David nodded his head proudly. The only sound in all the world was the clap-clap of the horse's hoofs on the frozen ground.

Father Roche went on: 'There was a King in England once who was a martyr. Wicked men in the malice of their hearts slew him, and so interfered with one of God's most holy laws — the Divine Right that He hath given to those whom He has appointed as His rulers on this earth. This martyr, King Charles of blessed memory, was, perhaps more than any other man on this earth, near in his sufferings to our Saviour Himself. When Christ suffered there was darkness over all the land, and so when King Charles was under trial there were mighty wonders in the sky. You have read of the centurion who was assured that He was the Son of God, and his servant was healed; so with the Blessed Martyr, one of his guards was driven by conviction of sin to repentance. Did they not part our Sovereign's garments among them? Even so have they taken his houses, his possessions, his very garments from our master . . . And in his life, in his gentleness, his courtesy, his love of his fellowmen, did King Charles approach most closely that blessed prototype.'

Father Roche paused. The road ran now over Cat Bells and Brandelhow; from its bend the land dropped straight to the lake, which could be seen now like a dark mirror of jet below hills that were faintly silver. The horse's breath rose in front of them in clouds of steam; facing them was the hump, black as ebony, of the Castle Crag, and, more gently grey, the hills behind it. For young David, to whom this view was to become one of life's eternal symbols, he was to hear always, when he beheld it, the beautiful, melodious voice of the priest and to see again the scattered steely points of the stars in the velvet sky.

'His was an unrenounced right of sovereignty. None could take it from him. He had been placed there by God, and man had no voice in that choice and circumstance. He was murdered and betrayed by the sons of the Devil . . .'

A thrill of sympathy touched David's heart. Oh, had he been there, he would have died for that King!

'Even as Christ did, so could he work miracles. Have you ever heard how, being taken by his captors through the town of Winchester, an innkeeper of that city, who was grievously ill and suffocating, flung himself on his knees before His Majesty, crying "God save the King!", and the King said: "Friend, God grant thee thy desire," and the tumours and sores disappeared, and the man was made whole? And the kerchiefs dipped in the King's blood after his death had also this miraculous property.

'His son had also this virtue, and, it is said, touched one hundred thousand persons to cure them . . . Since this family appointed by God to rule over England have been in exile God's face has been turned away from us. Nothing is so sure and certain in this world as that our beloved country shall not again prosper until our rightful King returns to us. Do you understand what I have been saying to you, David?'

'Yes, sir,' answered David in an awed voice.

They clattered through the little village of Grange. Some woman came to a lighted door to watch them pass. Under the stone bridge the river, flooded with the recent rains, rushed to the lake. They turned into their valley under the dark rocks. 'The time may come, David, when every true man will be challenged. Under which King, God's or man's? What will thy answer be, boy?'

'Under God's King, sir,' answered David.

'Keep silence about what I have said even to your father, but talk to me when you have a mind. Wonder at nothing that you may see me do. I shall come and be gone again, but wherever I may be I shall know that I can trust thee . . .'

'Yes, sir.'

'You will not be afraid if a day should come . . .'

'No, sir. Only my father . . .' It was not for him then to know how little in later harsh fact this picture of God's King would affect him.

'Your father is my friend. He knows me.'

'Yes, sir . . . Will he, too, be ready when the day comes?'

Roche hesitated—

'Every true man who loves his God and his country will be ready.'

'Yes, sir,' answered David again, suddenly sleepy and very cold. Loyalties? He now had many. To his father, to Deborah, to this King in Rome. Life was beginning to be filled with great adventure. There was his father in his dark suit with the silver cuffs, there was the old lady a thousand years old, Cousin Raiseley, whom he would one day fight, his uncle who would take him out hunting, the King in Rome who made people well by touching them, Father Roche who was now no more a priest, his mother whom he loved and Mrs Press whom he hated, and the old woman in Herries who was a witch, and the hill with the caves, and the more distant hills, where one day he would make great discoveries.

They turned to the house, black and cold under the scattered stars. But it was home, and there would be fire and something to eat, and then falling asleep in the room where his father would afterwards come . . . and then the King in Rome . . .

He was shivering with cold when Father Roche lifted him down from the horse and carried him in.

THE DEVIL

DAVID LOOKED up at the woman whom he so thoroughly detested, with fearless eyes.

'I went out because I wanted.'

'Yes, and the muck and all you've got into,' she answered crossly. 'But it isn't for me to say, I've no authority. And the horses not returned yet from Keswick, and the hills darkening the whole place. I hate this house – from the first instant I set foot in it I've hated it. A nice, pretty kind of life for one who's young enough and handsome enough for a frolic or two.'

She swung the silver chain that lay about her neck and touched the crimson velvet of her sleeves.

'And you fast with the priest all the morning,' she continued, her sharp eyes darting about the shadowy room. 'What is it he must speak so long about with a child like you?'

'He teaches me Latin,' David answered quietly.

'Yes, and many another lesson, I'll swear,' she answered.

He could see that her ears were ever straining for a sound.

'Ugh!' she shivered, 'the rain's coming down again, and all the old tapestries flapping against the wall. It wasn't so in Doncaster, I can promise you, before your father engaged me.'

'No,' said David, hating her.

'No, indeed. There was music there and dancing and the Fair at midsummer and the Plays at Yule. But here . . .'

She broke off. She thought that she had caught the clap of the horses' hoofs on the ragged stones of the little court. She sprang to the darkening window, then turned impatiently back, caught the flickering taper and held it to the leaded pane. Once again she was disappointed. There were no horses there – only the tap of some branches against the wall and the seeping drip of the rain.

'Why did you come here?' asked David.

She struck her hand violently on the table – 'Why? why? why?' she answered passionately. 'You are a child. How should you know? And yet—' She came over to him, caught him by the shoulders and stared into his eyes. 'You hate me, do you not? Young though you are, you know enough for that. You all hate me here and wish me gone. And most of all that priest – who has persuaded him against me.'

'He is not a priest now,' answered David. 'He is only Mr Roche now.'

'No priest? Yes, that is fine talk. Once a priest always a priest. And where has he gone this afternoon, riding away to Keswick? Where is it that he goes for nights together?'

'I don't know,' answered David.

'I'll tell you more,' she continued. 'He can be in prison any day. There are the laws against the Catholics, and he serving Mass in that upper room. Have I no ears nor eyes? So he shall be in prison if he returns and I have my way.'

She stopped again to listen. The house was intensely silent. The two little girls were with their mother in her room. There could be heard even through the rain and the wind the noise of falling water, the swollen stream tumbling down the side of the hill at the house's back. She stood thinking, then came closer again to David. He moved as though he would shrink from her, then firmly stood his ground.

'David, do you not think you could speak to him, to your father? When nobody else is by – he listens to you. I have noticed that when no other can speak to him he can be patient with you. Ask him if he will not ride out with me for an hour – I would tell him certain things. For weeks now I have not been alone with him, and I shall go mad . . . this desire . . . this longing . . .'

She broke off as though the words choked her, putting one hand to her throat and with the other gripping the boy's arm. David saw that she was in great suffering, and could have been sorry for her had he not hated her so. He remembered that night at the Keswick inn when his father had come in and kissed her. He hated that she should touch him, but he did not move.

'You must speak to him yourself,' he answered. 'My father, these past weeks, has had business in Keswick and in the country here.'

'Business in Keswick!' she answered scornfully, pushing him from her so that he almost fell. 'Fine business! Such as he had in Doncaster. Riding into Keswick to play at cards and look at the women, stumbling about in these mucky country paths to find a girl with bright eyes . . .'

David cried: 'You shall not speak against my father. When he wishes to talk with you he will tell you. Yes, it is true that we all hate you here and wish you gone. My mother cries because of you. You struck Deborah when she had done no wrong. You should return to Doncaster, where there are games and music . . .'

He was trembling with rage and with a desire that in some way he might persuade her to go. Oh, if only she would go away. . .

But already she had forgotten him. Her ears again had caught a sound, and this time she was not deceived.

The clatter of hoofs was on the stones of the court, and at the same instant Margaret Herries, the two little girls beside her, appeared, holding a light, at the stair's head.

'Is he come? Is he come?' she cried eagerly, and then started down the rickety stairway, moving heavily and awkwardly, the children close behind her.

The hall, that had been only a moment before so dark and drear with the faint light and old Herries sneering from the wall, was now all alive.

Francis Herries in his deep riding-coat, Wilson following him with candles, entered, and his wife and the children ran to him. Alice Press stayed in the dusk. They could see at once that he was in a good mood. He laughed as he saw them, caught Deborah and David to him, bent forward and kissed his wife.

'Yes, something to eat and drink. I'm parched and famished. The rain blew against us like the plague. I thought Mameluke would have fallen twice, and it was such thick darkness along Cat Bells that it was God's miracle we were not in the lake.' He pulled Deborah's hair. 'Thou knowest there's something here for thee and for Mary too – the other pocket for David . . .' Laughing and shouting with excitement, they felt in the pockets and pulled out the bundles. For Deborah there was a 'baby' with bright flaxen hair and a dress of green silk, for Mary a toy tea-set, cups and saucers decorated with pink roses, and for David battledore and shuttlecock.

With every moment the room grew more lively. A big log fire was leaping in the open fireplace. Wilson and his daughter were setting the table; Benjamin had come in (Nathaniel had left them at Martinmas), a bottle of wine in either hand, his round face smiling with the pleasantry of the familiar servant who knows that tonight he has nothing to fear from his master's temper. Only Alice Press stood back against the wall, without moving, her hand against her heart.

Francis Herries, his riding-coat flung into a chair, stood before the fire, his legs spread, warming his back.

'Dear brother Pomfret is to visit us tomorrow,' he said. 'He will condescend to take the journey. Keswick was a pool of muck; you couldn't stir for the mud. And so, Deb, you love your baby?'

Deborah was sitting on a stool at her mother's feet, hugging her doll. She was in an ecstasy of happiness, rocking the doll in her arms, then straightening it to smooth its stiff hair, her eyes shining, looking at her brother every once and again to see that he was sharing in her pleasure.

Francis Herries, looking out at them all, hummed in a half-whisper the children's song:

> 'Lady Queen Anne who sits in her stand,
> And a pair of green gloves upon her hand,
> As white as a lily, as fair as a swan,
> The fairest lady in a' the land.'

Tonight he was well content. The mood was upon him when everything seemed fair. It was good thus to come home to his own, to find the candles shining and his own things about him, and his children, whom he loved, longing for him. The devil of restlessness was not with him. That afternoon in Keswick he had won three fine bets at the cock-fighting. He had drunk just enough to make the world glow. Even Margaret, his wife, could seem, close to him, neither so stout nor so foolish . . . Ah, if they would let him alone, his little pack of demons, he could make a fine thing of this life yet.

His eyes, roaming, found Alice Press, motionless against the wall. His voice changed.

'Have the babies been good?' he asked her.

She came forward into the candlelight.

'Well enough,' she answered, and turning sharply, left the room.

The food came in. The others had dined long ago, but they crowded about him as he ate, and Benjamin stood behind them, smiling beneficently, as though they were all his handiwork.

While he ate and drank he told them little things about his

Keswick day – how they had been baiting a bull in the market-place and two dogs had been killed; how there had been a medicine man pulling out teeth, and he had pulled two wrong ones from an old woman, and she had demanded her money back, but he had not given it: the old woman's son had fought him and knocked his tub over; how he had had a talk with old Westaway, the architect of Uncle Pomfret's house, and what a strange old man he was and had been the world over and seen the Pope in Rome and the Czar of all the Russias, and spoke in a shrill piping voice, and trembled with anger, so they said, at the sight of a woman; how there was a little black boy for sale like the one Aunt Jannice had, and some splendid dogs, big and fierce, who would do finely for defending the house in the winter; how there had been in the market-square the day before a gathering of those strange people, the Quakers, and they had been set upon and two of them stripped naked and splashed with tar; how they told him that there was a band of robbers now in Wasdale that came down from Scafell and had murdered two shepherds in the last week; and there was a fine gathering of gentlemen for the cock-fight and he had not done so ill there . . .

Here he broke off; he knew what Margaret thought of his cock-fighting – another evening he might have teased her and been pleased to see the fear come into her eyes, but not to-night . . . He was young as David tonight. He had David on his knee, his hand fingering his hair. His wife, Margaret, was praying: 'Oh, Lord, let this last a while. Let this last a while.'

After his supper they played Blind-man's Buff. Francis Herries's eyes were bound with the handkerchief. The children ran, screaming and laughing; Margaret herself played and ran into his arms, and once again – after how many years – her husband had his arms about her, held her, kissed her cheek. It was David's turn to be blinded, and, as he stood in darkness, he could hear all the sounds – the crack and tumble of the fire and the hiss of the falling ash, the rain against the window, the breathing of the people about him; and it seemed to him that all the room was lit with red light and old great-great-grandfather Herries came down from his picture-frame and ordered him to come to him. He ran forward; an instant of awful terror came to him. But all was well; it was into Benjamin's arms that he had run, and as he felt the stout, soft body with his hands he screamed with excited relief: 'It's Benjamin! It's Benjamin!' – then Benjamin was blind man.

*   *   *

After breakfast the whole world is filled with light. Everything
moves together. Round Herries the entire universe centres itself,
spreading out to endless distances that are mysteries – China,
Pera, the kingdom of Samarkand – but pouring all its waters into
this one deep purple pool – purple of Glaramara, purple of the
shadows and eaves and door-post, purple of the feathers in the
peacock fan carried by the Princess in Deb's chap-book, purple
of the darker river shadows that lie beneath the spume and froth
tumbling through Grange to the lake. Through the shadows of
this purple February morning, David, standing at the road-bend,
Deborah beside him, saw the moving of all the people around
him – Alice Press yawning at the window, his father drinking his
breakfast ale; Benjamin in the little court, his hand on Mameluke; his mother hearing Mary her morning prayer; the old
witch grandmother Wilson silent against the wall, her white
kerchief about her chin, leaning on her stick; Wilson himself
moving to the cows; then, a little more distantly, Moorcross, the
home of the statesman Peel – Peel, the tallest, stoutest man
David had ever seen – famous for his wrestling, with a boy of
David's own age, whom David would like to know; and beyond
the Peels again, all Borrowdale, with the names that were becoming part of him, Rosthwaite and Stonethwaite, Seathwaite
and Seatoller, and the hills, glittering on this lovely morning,
Glaramara, Scafell, the Gavel; wolves, maybe, above Stye Head,
and robbers, his father had said, in Wasdale, and fairies, gnomes,
devils, witches . . .

Deb's hot hand held his more tightly.

'What are you looking for, David?'

What was he looking for? He did not know. But this was to be
a day of days. His happiness last evening, the games, sleeping on
the small pallet beside his father's bed and then waking to so
wonderful a day! After all the rain and wind, this stillness and
shining glitter, small fleecy clouds like puddings or puppies
plump against the shadowed softness of the blue, the branch of
no tree stirring, so clear that the crowing of a cock far away towards Seatoller could plainly be heard, but, as always here, the
sound of running waters, now one, now two, now fast as though
an urgent message had come to hasten, now slow with a lazy
drawling sound . . .

He knew that today he could have the small shaggy pony,
Caesar, that his father had bought from Peel. It was a whole
holiday. Mr Finch would not appear. No one would care what
he did nor where he went. He would like to ask the Peel boy to

go with him, but he was shy, and the Peel boy spoke so odd a language and then, of course, had his work to do . . .

At that instant, so miraculous is life, the Peel boy passed them. The Peel boy was bigger and stronger than David, very broad of the chest and thick of the leg; his eyes were blue and his hair very fair; his cheeks were rosy, and he whistled out of tune. He was whistling now, but when he saw Deborah and David he stopped. He paused and smiled.

'Good day,' said David, also smiling.

''Day,' said the boy, shuffling his feet. They grinned and said nothing.

'Have you a knife, please?' David asked.

'Aye.'

David did not need one, but when the large rough cutlass was put in his hand he chipped off the small branch of a tree.

'Thank you.' He tried again. ''Tis a fine day.'

'Aye.'

'We have holiday.'

'Aye.'

'I shall ride Caesar to the valley end.'

'Aye.'

Then the Peel boy bobbed his head and went on down the path. He turned back.

'You may have t'knife,' he said.

'Oh, no, I thank you,' said David, very greatly touched. Then seeing disappointment – 'Well – if you wish —'

He took the knife, and the Peel boy, delighted, started down the path again, whistling once more out of tune.

The day was well begun.

He walked slowly back to the house, his hand tight in Deb's. She asked: 'David, may I come with you on Caesar?'

'No,' he answered, 'I go alone.' He felt her hand give a little quiver – 'Why, you are not afeared? I shall be back by dusk.'

She nodded her head bravely. 'I shall wash my new baby.' But she had something in her mind. She noticed so much more than Mary. She was exceedingly sensitive and would always be. She would always live alone, however many people were near her, and would give herself in passionate devotion to one or two, realizing that it was the law of her life that she should give rather than receive.

Already, although she was only seven years of age, she knew of many little things in and around Herries that no one else had seen – the face of a woman, thin and sharp, carved on the oak chest in the dining-hall; a ruby ring that old great-great-grand-father Herries wore on his finger in the picture; the way that Alice Press had of looking scornfully at her fingernails; the fashion that old Mrs Wilson had of walking like a blind woman, her eyes tightly shut; the coarse crowing laugh of her grand-daughter – and she knew everything about David: the straight-ness of his back when he was standing waiting for something, how one leg would rub against the other when he began to be eager in talking about something; his smile, when one end of his mouth seemed to curl more than another; the roughness that a wind would make of his hair when he wore no cap, the beautiful coolness of his forehead when he let her put her hand on it. She did not know that she knew these things – she had as yet no self-consciousness.

The most common sensation for her would always be fear, and the constant duty of her life would be building up sufficient courage with which to meet it. Apprehension would attack her at every turn. It was as though she had three skins less than other folk. Even as a baby she had seen shadows in the room that no one else had seen, heard footsteps that no one else had heard. Things assumed significance for her beyond all fact and reason. There had been a tree in the Doncaster garden, stout in the trunk, thinly carved in its branches. How she had hated that tree, what terrors undefined it had brought to her, how, in all the other excitements of leaving Doncaster, this had been predomi-nant – that she need never see that tree again!

And here at Herries already there were terrors. Alice Press and old Mrs Wilson of course – these were natural alarms – but also the pump in the yard, the two suits of armour within the house-door that seemed to her to have faces, one white and one yellow, and the steps of someone walking on the floor of the parlour-loft when they were in the dining-hall.

All around her, everyone was insensitive. It was not a time when people noticed such things. There were witches and war-locks, fairies and gnomes, but they were real and active with persons as positive as the serving-man or the night-watchman. She kept – as she was always to keep – everything to herself. David alone understood something of her sensitiveness, and this not because he shared it with her, but because he loved her so deeply that she was like part of himself. Only when she was with him she knew no fear. Her confidence in him was as though he were someone divine. Where he was no fear could come, no evil live.

This morning as they neared the house he wanted to go into the yard behind to see whether Benjamin were there. She shrank back.

'Come, Deb. Benjamin hath a new puppy Peel's man gave to him.'

She shook her head and, breaking from him, ran in by the front door. He remembered then that he must see his mother. Every morning he was with her for half an hour, and read out of the *Life of King Arthur* or the Bible for her. He read very well; he liked books when there were not horses and dogs and games like football and battledore. But today he did not want to read. It was not a day for books, and as he moved slowly into the house, he felt impatient with his mother. He shared a little with his father the intolerance of her clumsiness, her habit of tears, her absent-mindedness, and, as with all of us when we are impatient with those who love us, he wished that she did not love him quite so much.

She was so easily hurt. She was always asking him what he was doing, where he was going, with whom he had been; and although there was no reason at all why he should not tell her everything, he inclined to be secret with her because of her curiosity. Then he had seen, so many times, his sister Mary flatter and cheat her mother because of something that she had wanted, and that made him honest to the point of discourtesy. He loved her better when he was not with her; he hated Alice Press because she made his mother unhappy, but he did not mind also making her unhappy. Now, when he went in, he would be forced to tell her about what he was going to do, how he would ride Caesar to the valley's end, and fish in the stream below Stye Head and watch to see if a wolf should be prowling under Glaramara. And he did not want to tell her these things. It would spoil them a little, make them more ordinary and less adventurous.

He found her in her room, alone, the room darkened by the big canopied bed; it was a little chill.

He saw at once that today there would be no reading. His mother, dismayed and distraught, was standing in the middle of the room, her hand at her cheek, her eyes crowded with alarm.

So soon as she saw him she began: 'No, David . . . Leave me . . . This is too vile . . .' She was not near to tears: no, for once anger had mastered her. She had even a certain grandeur, pulled to her full height, massive, her gaze upon the door. Before he could wonder, someone had come in, and at once a spate of words broke about the place; the room crackled with fury.

He knew, without turning, that it was Alice Press; no need to question that shrill voice that rose in a kind of sweeping tide of temper to a scream.

'And so you mean to banter me, madam – a fine figure before your own children. Was I put here to direct them or no? It is no disparagement to a woman, I suppose, that before all your household I should be told my place and then left to find it by their easy insulting courtesy. Oh, no, indeed – I am not to be averse to every slavish duty that a gentlewoman can be put to, having been dragged from Doncaster by the heels, and then flung into this muck-heap and cesspool to keep proper company with old witches, who by rights should be stripped of every cloth on their backs and then thrown to the river to let them sink or swim! Oh, no, you say, I honour you ever more and more, but I insult you as I may, and as convenience suits me. I do not remember to have ever had the pleasure of witnessing your own rules of law and order in this house or any other. You are quiet enough until the fit moment comes to abuse me properly, and then you have words enough . . . I can't express the satisfaction, truly, that it gives me to know the meaning of your feeling towards me, and if I should go naked and be on my knees before you, that would give you satisfaction, perhaps – you who have not your own children to order, nor your husband to bed with you – yet you would teach *me* my lesson and my proper order in this house . . .'

She paused for breath. David saw her now, her pale face crimson, her hands clenched, her breast heaving.

'I will not have you,' Margaret Herries answered, 'abuse my privileges. It was not by my wish nor order that you were here. God knows I have surrendered in these years many of my proper rights, and God He also knows that I have suffered my own bitterness, and such it may be must come to every woman, but yet I am mistress in this house.'

'Mistress!' Alice Press broke in, 'and in a fine house! Mistress when there is such a master here and a house where the mice and rats are the true familiars. Mistress you may be in your own privacy, but mistress, as the veriest hireling on this place knows, in no public fashion. Mistress! Then who is master here? Know you your master and his company? Ask your master his pleasure in Keswick and the drabs that he fumbles, so that after barely a six-months' stay in this place his name is a byword! Mistress—'

'I will not,' Margaret Herries broke in. 'This is enough. I have suffered your company long enough, but now it is you or I who go – and I care not how soon!'

'Go!' Alice Press moved a step forward. 'Yes, though we had been at the same charity school and I had gone the round of neighbours asking for bread, I would not go at your bidding. No, nor do aught else at your bidding. Neither I nor anyone else in this place. You for a weak trembling fool who have neither the courage nor the discipline to bid a mouse go when you would wish it. Oh, I could tell you things, madam, that would make your eyes sore. I have waited in patience, borne your insults and laughed at your silly little pieces of pride, but now at last my silence has lasted long enough . . .'

Silence fell on the room. Francis Herries stood in the doorway, and David moved towards his mother. He came close to her, scarcely knowing that he did so, and suddenly he felt her trembling hand on his shoulder and steadied himself that he might support it.

'Well,' Herries said quietly, looking about the room, 'here is a scramble . . . the whole house shares in it.'

For once Margaret Herries was not cowed. Her hand tightening on David's shoulder, her voice trembling ever so lightly, she replied to him:

'Mrs Press has some complaint that I have ordered her unjustly before the servants. She has been impertinent . . .'

David saw, and triumphantly, that it was the other woman who was afraid. In a voice that was strangely stilled after its earlier shrillness, looking straight at Herries, forgetting, it would seem, that there was any other in the room, she answered:

'I have my place here, a place that you have appointed me. Your wife has forgotten . . .'

Herries smiled.

'Your place? No place unless you yourself fulfil it.'

It was possible that in that one quiet word she saw her sentence; she had known, it might be, that for months it had been coming to her. It might be that, beyond that again, she realized now her folly in provoking this scene, in forgetting a patience that it had been, this last year, no easy task to tutor her natural hot temper towards.

'I have fulfilled it,' she answered proudly. 'It is you who have neglected to keep me in it.'

'That may well be,' he answered lightly; 'there is so much to be done and little time to see to it all. And now I advise that you

leave us . . . Wherever your place may be, it is certain that it is
not in this room.'

She would, it seemed, speak; then with another glance at him,
her colour now very white, she passed through the door.

He looked at his wife with a strange mixture of scorn and
kindliness.

'You should know better, Meg, than to suffer her impertinence . . . but at least you shall not suffer it long.'

He went out. David felt still the pressure of his mother's hand.
She did not move; then, at last, turned from him, went to the
window and stood there looking out. There was nothing that
he could do – only he would never speak to Alice Press again.
Never! Not though his father whipped him till the blood ran.
With this high resolve he left the room, and then, after a pause,
the house. He hated it and everyone in it.

He found Benjamin and Benjamin found Caesar. No one prevented him; from the outside court the house within seemed
dead. No sound came from it. It was strange that by merely
closing a door you shut everything off – anger, fears, greed, joys.
Already, at his early years, it seemed to him that one of the ways
to secure happiness was to escape from people, to be by yourself
in the open.

He wasn't happy as he found his way, past Moorcross, on to
the main path, but he was too young and too healthy to be unhappy for long. And there was the consciousness that he was
sharing now more in real grown-up life than he had done in
Doncaster. But why had his father brought Alice Press with him
from Doncaster? That was what he *could* not understand. It was
from her that all the trouble came, she who made his mother
unhappy, his father angry, Deb frightened, himself in a rage.
Were she gone, they would all be tranquil again. But *why* had
his father brought her? Why had he kissed her in the inn? There
was something strange here that caused his heart to beat and his
cheeks to redden. Children then lived from the earliest years in
contact with great grossness of word and action. David almost
from babyhood had been aware of the physical traffic between
men and women, had at the age of seven seen a woman give
birth to a child in the streets of Doncaster, but he had as yet
translated none of these physical acts to mental or spiritual
significance.

Life from the very first was for him far coarser and more
brutal than it would be for his great-grandchildren, but for that
reason, perhaps, his consciousness of it was purer and less

muddled than theirs would be. In any case he drove these things very swiftly from his mind as he drew out from the Rosthwaite hamlet into the open country.

Open country, indeed, it was. At this time it was scarcely cultivated save in a few fields round Seathwaite or Rosthwaite. It lay in purple shadows with splashes of glittering sunlight, a lost land, untenanted by man, no animal anywhere visible, dominated entirely by the mountains that hemmed it in. To David's right ran the path up to Honister, where the mines were; this country was forbidden ground, for here all the rascals and outcasts of the neighbourhood would congregate to scrape among the mine refuse and then sell the scraps of plumbago to the Jews in Keswick, who would meet them at The George or The Half-Moon and then bargain with them. The stories were that titanic battles were fought above Stye Head and on Honister between rival bands of robbers, disputing their plunder, and it was true enough that many a time, walking up Honister, you would find a dead man there, by the roadside, his throat cut or a knife in his belly and often enough stripped naked.

For David, that road up to Honister was the most magical passage of all, and one day he would investigate it, robbers or no robbers, to its very heart; but today he was out to catch fish, and it was by the bridge under Stye Head that he would catch them – were he lucky! It was not a great day for fishing with this glittering sun and shining sky.

The farther he got from Herries the happier he became. Of late he had been cluttered about with people. All of them – his father, his mother, Deb, Mary, his cousins, Father Roche, the Press woman, old Mrs Wilson and her son, Peel and his boy – some of them he loved and some of them he hated, but all of them hindered his perfect freedom.

He, he was wise enough even now to realize, would always be hampered by people – you couldn't be *free* of people, nor did he want to be – but there would be moments and days when you would be free, absolutely, nakedly free, and, oh! how glorious they were!

It was such a moment now.

Caesar was no very magnificent steed, but he was a good enough pony, and quite able to grasp his own moments of freedom. As they came deeper under the hills the path was so rough and uncertain that David let him pick his own way. The group of mountains that closed the valley in were lovely in their wine-grape colour under a sky that had been a stainless blue, but that

now, in the fashion of these parts, was suddenly the battlefield
for two angry clouds, one shaped like a ragged wheel, the other
like a battering ram. The wheel was a thin grey edged with silver
and the ram was ebony. The empty valley – the little boy on the
pony was the only moving thing in the whole landscape – seemed
to wait apprehensively as the wheel and the ram approached one
another. The sun appeared to retreat in alarm, but the wheel
stretched out a wicked hand with swollen fingers and seized it –
then the ram crashed down upon it.

The end of the valley was darkened although behind him, by
Castle Crag, the sun was in full glory, and the world blazed like a
sheet of dazzling metal. Within the shadow it was cold, and
David, shouting to give himself company, kicked Caesar forward.

He came now to three houses, brooding like witches at the side
of the rough path, quite deserted, it seemed, open, like many of
the other cottages, to the sky.

Before the third cottage stood three men and a girl. David felt
his heart beat at the sight of them. They were the wildest-looking
men he had ever seen. They were copies the one of another,
seemingly of the same height and the same age, the age maybe of
his father, broad and strong, and all with dark rough beards. The
girl was only a baby, younger than David, slight and dark like
the men, but rosy-cheeked, and, as David passed them, she was
laughing. One of the men stepped forward and stood in David's
way.

'A fine day,' he said.

David nodded. He was frightened, but he wouldn't let anyone,
not even Caesar, know it. He wished, though, that the sun would
come out again.

'Where'st going?'

The man had a deep, rumbling, husky tone with a rasp in it.

'To fish at the bridge.'

'To fish at the bridge?' All the men laughed.

'Pass, little master.' The man stepped back and ironically
doffed a very filthy and greasy hat. Then David, seeing the
laughing eyes of the small girl fixed upon him, smiled.

She had in her hand a small switch. She ran into the path,
struck Caesar's buttocks and then, as he started forward,
laughed with a shrill crying tone like a bird. He looked back and
saw her standing in the middle of the path against the sun.

He cared nothing for girls – Deb wasn't a girl, she was his
sister – but it did seem to him exciting and adventurous that this
small girl should be quite alone with these three wild men, and,

apparently, happy with them. She was perhaps the daughter of one of them. It might be that they were some of the robbers who came down from Stye Head and murdered defenceless people and returned. Well, there was nothing about him for them to murder. He had a tin with worms in it, and a home-made fishing-rod and a few pence. He was safe enough.

The country now grew ever wilder and wilder. A rough, ragged stream, swollen with the rains and the snow from the tops, rushed along over a deep bed of slabs and boulders. Fragments of rock lay everywhere about him here, so that he had to dismount and lead Caesar. Above his head the two clouds had made truce and after a meeting had separated, one now in the form of a ship that, lined with silver, sailed off into the blue, the other dispersed into a flock of little ivory clouds that stayed lazily, as though playing a game, in lines and broken groups. The sun had burst out again and flooded all the land. David had already learnt that, in this country, the sky was more changeable than in any other in the world, that if you lived here your days were bound up with the sky, so that after a while it seemed to have a more active and personal history than your own. It became almost impossible to believe that its history was not connected with yours, keeping pace with you, influencing you, determining your fate. He had never considered the sky very greatly at Doncaster, but in this world, it drove itself into your very heart. The brilliant sun now struck sparks from every stone, while every splutter of the stream against a boulder flung into the air a shower of light. The whole valley glittered, while above it the mountains, streaked like a wild beast's skin with snow, were black.

He came to the bridge, let Caesar loose, clambered over the smooth wet stones to the deep, green pool under the waterfall, chose his worm and began to fish below the pool. There was shadow here from an overhanging tree and the curve of the bridge. He was exceedingly happy. He had the great gift of complete absorption in the task or play of the moment. He was never to know the divided moods, divided loyalties of his father. His character was not subtle, but steadfast, fearless, unfaltering. He did not realize for how long he fished. He moved below the bridge and then back again. He caught nothing. He never had a bite. The sun was too bright. He sat, his legs apart, his eyes intently fixed on the water. A shadow was flung. He looked up.

Leaning on the bridge, looking down at him very gravely was a pedlar with a coloured hat and a sharp bright face. He had rested his pack on the bridge's wall.

'A fine sun today,' said the pedlar.

David nodded.

'Too strong a sun for good fishing,' said the pedlar.

David sighed. 'That's true.' He scrambled up to the sward above the stones. He looked at the pack.

'Have you something for me to buy?' he asked, smiling. He had some money in his purse – money his father had given him – and it would be pleasant to buy something for Deborah.

The pedlar shook his head.

'Nothing for you.' Then he felt in a pouch at his waist. 'Do you fancy boxes? I have a little box here . . .' He fumbled, then brought out a small silver box and gave it to David. His hand was nut-brown, with long, thin, tapering fingers. It was a beautiful little box. On one side was carved a picture of girls dancing round a maypole, on the other a picture of gentlemen hunting.

David looked at it, then shook his head. ''Tis a beautiful box, but I have not money enough.'

The pedlar smiled. 'It is yours. Keep it until your marriage day.'

'Thank you,' said David, dropping it into his pocket. 'But I shall never be married.'

'You will be married,' said the pedlar, 'and have fine sons.'

'How do you know?' asked David, looking into his tin and seeing that the worms that remained were few and poor. He would not fish any more. He found bread and meat in his pocket and offered some to the pedlar, who took more than his share and ate voraciously.

'I know everything,' said the pedlar. 'I am the Devil.'

David believed him. He looked both wicked and gay as he stood there in the sunlight, and Francis Herries had always told him that the Devil was both these things.

'I am not afraid of you,' said David, laughing. 'My father has always told me not to be afraid.'

'I know your father,' said the pedlar, licking his fingers after the bread and meat and looking as though he would like also the piece that David had in his hand. 'Your father is an old friend.'

'He is the finest man in the world,' said David proudly. 'Why will you not show me the things that you have in your pack?'

'I am weary of showing them,' said the pedlar, yawning and displaying a splendid row of sharp white teeth. 'Time enough. You shall see them one fine day.'

'If you are the Devil,' said David, who was always interested in everything, 'you can tell me where there is good fishing.'

'There is good fishing everywhere,' said the pedlar, 'if you
have patience. You have patience. It will carry you through
the world – patience and courage, two stupid qualities but valuable.'

'Do you live round here?' David asked.

'Here or anywhere. When you have lived for ever as I have,
one place or another is the same.'

'Do you never grow any older?' David asked.

'Never,' said the pedlar. 'A wearisome business. Good day.
We shall often encounter one another. Keep the little box. I am
not, in my intentions, always unamiable as people say.'

He shouldered his pack, started up the Stye Head and was
quite suddenly lost in the sunlight.

David jogged back happily through the sunny afternoon. He
took his time; he saw no human being. The sun falls behind the
hills like a stone over this valley, leaving in the sky a long, wide
strath of white and blue. When David reached Herries the
shadows were straddling giants across the little stone court.

He found his father alone in the shadowed hall; he leant across
the long table, on which a map was spread. 'He's looking grand,'
David, who relished him in his plum-coloured coat, thought,
'and he has a temper.' So, like a knowing puppy, he slipped
quietly past the fading fire. In the room above he heard Deborah's funny little piping voice, singing to herself or her baby.
Beyond the leaded window the sky was a lovely pale green like
early spring leaves and the low spread of the land was purple
again as it had been in the morning. Against this gentle, pure
light the room was very dark, although two candles were lit.

His father saw him.

Without looking up from the map: 'Where have you been,
David?'

David told him. It might be that there would be a whipping
or it might be that there would be a game – you never could tell
with his father.

'Thou hast missed thine uncle, boy.'

David had nothing to say to that – as there was a pause he
filled it.

'I saw the Devil by the bridge.'

His father did not answer but suddenly raised himself.

'David, come here.' David came to him.

He put his arm round his neck. 'David, I love no one but
you – no one – no one in all the world. And I hate your uncle.
Remember this day, for on it I surrender all wishes for a good

union between your uncle and me. Silly, patronizing fool!' He
looked furiously about him at the table which was clustered with
a mess of things – tankards, a platter with bread on it, a riding-
whip, a velvet glove with a jewelled clasp. 'I'll twist his neck for
him, brother or no brother, an he comes this way again. Aye, you
should have seen your uncle riding his fine horse and stepping
over the muck and cobbles, he fat as an otter and red as an
infant's bum. 'Tis his lady wife sent him to spy the land out –
a fine stretch she'll be the wiser for his coming – a dark house, a
dull woman and his debauched good-for-nothing brother . . . I'll
warrant he's sad that he had me here – a fine tear on his famous
reputation. And now that I'm here I'll stay. The place charms
me, naked though it is. There's some ale for you, David. Drink
to your good-for-nothing rump of a father, naked-bottomed in a
cesspool and pleasantly forgot by the gay world.'

But David didn't drink. He felt in his pocket and brought out
the little silver box.

'The Devil gave me this,' he said.

His father, his eyes angry yet good-humoured, wandered
round the room then came to it.

'A pretty thing. And how did the Devil look?'

'He was a pedlar. He said he knew you.'

'Yes – there is a pedlar here I have spoken with . . .'

His mind was away, then he caught his son to him and held
him close.

'My good brother's son is a damned smug; and gives him no
joy – I can beat him there.'

He crooked his son's chin upwards and looked at him. David
gazed back at him fearlessly.

'Remember this day,' his father said. 'We shall be alone
against the world, you and I.'

CHINESE FAIR

HERRIES RETURNED, one September morning, after his walk
abroad, without his coat. It had been one of his finest, the plum-
coloured coat laced with silver. He walked into the house in his
white sleeves, and the old witch, Mrs Wilson, leaned over the
top of the stairs and smiled. She never laughed. 'You're grand
without your coat,' she said. They seemed to have a kind of

understanding, the two of them. He, as did all the valley, believed her to be a witch. He thought none the worse of her for it. He was happy this morning like a boy. It was a bright fresh morning, with clean white clouds leaning negligently on the hills. With the beauty and the youth and the kindly look that he had when he was happy, he was a good sight for an old witch. And she was no misanthrope. Life was too busily interesting for her to despise mankind.

'I'm going to the Fair,' he said like a boy.

She nodded her head, put out her long brown hand, and touched the white linen of his sleeve.

'You're not to give t' coat,' she said. 'It'll be remembered.'

He didn't care whether it were remembered or no. Out on the Watendlath path, looking up at a bright silver waterfall poised like a broken ladder against the green cliff, he had seen by the stones of the beck a dead man with his throat cut and a woman shivering beside him. A dead man was no extraordinary sight; this man was naked save for his shirt, and his white legs stretched stiffly as though they had been carved. The woman did not cry nor ask for alms, but she shivered in the keen September air. He did not speak to her, but obeying the impulse of the instant, took off his plum-coloured coat and threw it over her trembling shoulders. He strode back to the house. Seeing Benjamin in the yard, he leaned from the window and bade him go and fetch the woman to the house. Ten minutes later Benjamin returned to say there was no sign of woman or man.

He did not care. He was too cheerful in spirit to be bothered by a dead man or a shivering woman.

He sat in his sleeves at the window looking out on to the beautifully coloured world, Glaramara plum-coloured like his coat, and the long stretch of green valley.

He was like a schoolboy about this Fair. It was an accidental chance-by-night Fair for Keswick. It had been intended for Kendal and then for Carlisle, a motley company of entertainers and rogues and rascals travelling slowly to Scotland.

But the smallpox was savage this summer in Kendal, and so they had changed to the smaller town. In the past Keswick had had few Fairs but its own. It was too small a place. The chartered Fair on the 2nd of August for the sale of leather, and the Cattle Fairs on the first Thursday in May and on each Thursday fortnight for six weeks after; on the Saturday nearest Whitsuntide and Martinmas for hiring servants, and on the first Saturday after the 29th of October for the sale of cheese and rams.

Saturday the year through was market-day for provisions and
corn.

But these Fairs were local, and business was their purpose.
This present Fair was the maddest, wildest thing in Keswick's
memory. It would be generations before the week of it would be
forgotten. They said, too, that there was a company of Chinese
people travelling with the Fair, and they wore strange clothes,
such as had never been seen in that neighbourhood, and they
juggled with gold balls and swallowed silver swords, and had an
old man with them three hundred years of age. It was always
afterwards called the Chinese Fair.

But it was not of the Fair that Herries was now thinking as he
sat at the window. He was thinking of how well satisfied he was
with this place. He had been here full two years, and his strange
instinct that had driven him here had been right. He already
loved the valley, and had even now caught some of the sense of
its intimacy that led its inhabitants to cling to it with an obstinacy
and stubbornness that made them a byword for the rest of the
world. It was said that the men of Borrowdale were so stupid as
to be scarcely human, and that they did such idiotic things, like
building a wall to keep the cuckoo in their valley, that they must
be half-witted – that they never stirred from their valley, that
some of them had never even seen Keswick, that they spoke a
strange language of their own and were like men in a dream.

Herries had heard how the people in Keswick and from Newlands and St John's and the rest mocked and gibed, but he knew
now what it was that held the men of Borrowdale: although he
was not yet one of them (they were greatly suspicious of new-
comers), one day he would be. Something was in his blood that
was in their blood: it was a doom, a judgement, the fulfilment of
a prophecy.

He thought of other things too, as he sat there. He was well
pleased that he had cut himself off from his brother and his
brother's family. Since that day when Pomfret had ridden over
to Herries he had never set foot in his brother's house. Margaret
and the children had visited – he did not care whether they did or
no – and when he met Pomfret in Keswick he talked with him,
but he had never been within his brother's door.

He loved his pride, his fierce intolerance. He cherished it, fed
it, adored it. It had been one of his fears, on coming to live in
Herries, that perhaps he would find his brother a better fellow
than he had thought he was, and so would be forced to see him
and keep company with him because his heart drove him.

That was why, on the first evening at the inn, he had worn his finest clothes – because that might annoy his brother, and then Pomfret would appear less pleasant than he was. And so in the event it had been. Now he cherished his scorn of his brother – it was a fine silver flower in his coat.

The thing, however, of which he was mainly thinking now was what he should do to be rid of Alice Press, for rid of her he would be. Although so reckless a man, he knew, as every imaginative Herries has always known, that you can't rid yourself of past deeds. Kill a fox, give your coat to a trembling woman, drink of the water of Sprinkling Tarn, and you are a doomed man. He was doomed because he had kissed Alice Press, doomed because he had shot off that young fool's ear in Doncaster, doomed because on entering Herries he had put the right foot before the left, doomed anyway and a thousand times a day; but to be bored, because he was young and full of life, was a worse thing than to be doomed. And he was bored by Alice Press, bored to the very hilt of his sword. He thought now that he had always been bored with her, although there had been, at the very first, a flashing moment of startling splendour. Now he was bored with everything about her, from her heavy sallow face, her long sad brooding gaze at him, her stealthy eagerness to be alone with him, down to the paste buckles on her scarlet shoes, the scarlet shoes that he had once bought for her on a Fair day in Doncaster, and that she wore now in persistent petulant reminder. Moreover, she had been insulting to Margaret, and he would have no one rude to Margaret but himself. Yes, he must be rid of her, but how?

He looked out at the great shoulder of the hill. 'How, old Glaramara? You are old enough to know. Come and tell me your plan.'

As though in answer to his question, hearing a deep breath he turned round to find Alice Press at his side.

She was very grand in black velvet, with a heavy silver chain and her scarlet shoes.

She came close to him, and the scent that she used, a scent of roses, stifled his nostrils.

'Francis,' she said, her large sombre eyes staring into his. 'You will take me to the Fair, will you not?'

'No,' he answered, smiling at her and patting her white hand. She drew her hand away from the arm of his chair.

'You promised me.'

'I break my promise.'

'You must not. I am bent to go. You have been unkind to me all these months, and I have borne you no grudge. I knew that I could wait. Today it shall be like one of our old times.'

'Old times never return,' he answered her, looking at her with an intentness that matched her own. How strange it was, this passing of love! A never-ending marvel! At one moment the merest touch of the hand is Paradise, at the next, dead flesh.

'Have you not been selfish in this,' she went on quietly, 'and blind too, perhaps? Because you are tired of loving me you think our intercourse is at an end. But no intercourse is at an end when two have loved one another as we have.'

'Loved!' he interrupted her. 'Love and love! Do you call that love? I have never known what love is. 'Tis a wonder that waits always round the corner. If ever I do know, then I will be faithful. But *our* love! My dear, you use words too lightly.'

He hit her hard there, but she gave no sign. Her eyes did not quiver.

'Of course you are faithless,' she said. 'I have always known that, but I am not quite like the other women you have kissed. I always told you I was not. You cannot rid yourself of me so easily.'

'Can I not?' He looked at her speculatively. 'I have never been false to you. I warned you not to come here. I told you what it would be. Go back to Doncaster, my dear, and find a better man.'

That 'better man' hit her the hardest of all, because, although she thought him rotten, he was yet better for her than any other man in the world. A woman's bitter fidelity is always the honestest thing she has.

'Take me with you to the Fair today,' she repeated, 'and we will see. I've made no request for months but have faithfully stayed in this house, suffered every scorn at the hands of your wife, been hated by your children, been faithful to your interests – now, today, you will take me to the Fair.'

'I will not,' he answered, smiling up at her. 'David is the only one who goes with me.'

She turned past him and stood facing him, with her back to the window, blotting out the scene as though she thought that the mountain, at which he gazed so persistently, was her enemy.

'Listen, Francis. You are a bad man but a fair one. Here is a bargain. You have spoiled my life, shamed me before everyone, wrecked all my prospects, but I will feel nothing for all this if you will give me this day, one day as we used to have it, as we had it in Doncaster that Fair day when you bought me these shoes.' He knew that she was saying to herself: 'If I can but get him from this house and away with me as he used to be, I can charm him again.'

He answered her unspoken thought. 'You cannot charm me any more, not by one day nor by twenty. It is over. All done. I never promised fidelity. I never loved you. I have never loved anyone save my son. These things are not for our asking, my dear. Nature is rough when she tosses us our moods. "This one for you," she says, "and this for you," and no tears or scarlet slippers will change her indifference. Blame no one. Life is not understood by scolding.' Then he went on very kindly. 'Alice, go back to Doncaster and forget me. There was that fellow – how was he named? Matthew Priestly – he always loved you. He loves you, I doubt not, still. Blow no more on these dead coals. Forgive my indifference. It is the fault of neither of us.'

She saw something in his face that she understood. She gave him one long look and then slowly went. An hour later he was riding with David to Keswick. He could not quite rid his mind of her. Oddly enough it was now in connexion with David that he thought of her. David, ever since that quarrel between the two women, had kept his vow. He had refused to speak to Alice Press. The woman had taken it for the most part with a cold, haughty indifference, as though she could not be disturbed by the impertinence of a child, but yesterday there had been a scene. She had demanded of Herries that he should make his son answer her. Herries had ordered him. David, with set face and an odd little frown between his brows that was his father's own, had refused. Herries would whip him for disobedience. David, his body drawn tight together, kept to his refusal. He was stripped and whipped. Herries drew blood from his young son's white back, because he loved him so dearly and was so deeply bored with Alice Press. David put on his shirt and jacket without a word.

'And now will you speak to her?' his father asked him.

'No,' said David.

Then his father kissed him and gave him some fine ointment for his back. Today it was as though this had never been. David was in perfect happiness as he rode Caesar, laughing and chattering as he did sometimes when he was excited, making Caesar gallop on the free turf of Cat Bells, coming down into Portinscale as though he were heading a charge. The boy was growing. There would soon come a time when he would judge with a man's thoughts. He was a fine boy, of a stiff, brave, honest character, full of courage and obstinate. What would he think of his father?

The Fair was on the farther lake side of Keswick, on the broad meadows that ran to the lake's edge, not far from Pomfret's grand house, and it pleased Francis to think how greatly Pomfret must dislike to have all this rapscallion world at his very door. Keswick, at this time, was a town of one fair street and a huddle of filthy hovels. In the minor streets and 'closes' the cottages, little houses and pigsties were thronged very largely with a foreign and wandering population – riff-raff of every sort who came to steal plumbago from the mines or were wandering their way northward, off the main route; these houses were crowded with foul middens and encroached on by large open cesspools, pigsties and cowsheds. The refuse stagnated and stained the air and tainted the soil. Here were women of ill-fame, hucksters, thieves, many Jews who paid high prices for the stolen lead. At once on entering the town you were in another world from the honest and independent country of the statesmen and yeomen of the valleys – these statesmen who for centuries had lived on their own land, their own masters, and owed no man anything.

In the former year, 1731, in Keswick, out of a population of some twelve hundred, nearly five hundred persons had died of smallpox, cholera and black fevers. During the summer months the channels of ordure, the cesspools, became intolerable, and in the lower parts of the town respectable citizens could scarcely breathe.

The natural inhabitants of those parts, however, showed no discomfort and made no protest.

On this fine morning the principal street was shining with its white cobble-stones and a throng of people who pressed hither and thither, giving themselves up with complete child-like abandon to the fun of the occasion. The Fair had spread from its proper surroundings out into the street, and David and his father had to push through the groups surrounding booths and cheap-jacks and fancy quacks.

But the Fair itself, when they reached it, was a glory.

So many were the booths and stalls that the waters of the lake were invisible. On every side were announcements of wonders.

'Here is the Dancing on the Ropes, after the French and Italian fashion, by a Company of the finest Performers that ever yet have been seen by the whole World. For in the same Booth will be seen the two Famous French Maidens, so much admired in all Places and Countries where they come, for their wonderful Performance on the Rope, both with and without a Pole; so far outdoing all others that have been seen of their sex, as gives a general satisfaction to all that ever yet beheld them, to which is added Vaulting on the High Rope and Tumbling on the Stage.'

And here again: 'Here is to be seen a little Fairy Woman lately come from Italy, being but Two Foot Two Inches high, the shortest that ever was seen in England, and no ways Deformed, as the other two Women are, that are carried about the streets in Boxes from House to House for some years past, this being Thirteen Inches shorter than either of them ... Likewise a little Marmozet from Bengal that dances the Cheshire Rounds and Exercises at the word of Command. Also a strange Cock, from Hamborough, having three proper legs, and makes use of them all at one time.'

Here was a play announced in front of a booth all gay with crimson cloth and gold tinsel –

'An Excellent new Droll called *The Tempest* or *The Distressed Lovers*. With the English Hero and the Highland Princess, with the Comical Humours of the Enchanted Scotchman, or Jockey and the three Witches. Showing how a Nobleman of England was cast away upon the Indian Shore, and in his Travels found the Princess of the Country, with whom he fell in love, and after many Dangers and Perils was married to her; and his faithful Scotchman, who was saved with him, travelling through Woods, fell in among Witches, where between them is abundance of Comical Diversion. There in the Tempest is Neptune with his Tritons in his Chariot drawn with Sea-Horses, and Mairmaids singing . . .'

And then the marvellous animals: 'The true Lincolnshire Ox Nineteen Hands high and Four Yards long, from his Face to his Rump, and never was Calved nor never sucked, and two years ago was no bigger than another Ox, but since is grown to this prodigious Bigness. This noble Beast was lately shown at the University of Cambridge with great satisfaction to all that saw him . . .

'The large Buckinghamshire Hog above Ten Foot long ... the wonderful Worcestershire Mare, Nineteen Hands high, curiously shaped, every way proportionable; and A little Black Hairy Pygmy, bred in the Deserts of Arabia, a Natural Ruff of Hair about his Face, Two Foot high, walks upright, drinks a glass of Ale or Wine, and does several other things to admiration; and the

Remark from the East Indies; and the little Whifler, admired for
his extraordinary Scent.'

Although David did not know it, some of these same animals
must have been of an amazing age, because the celebrated Mr
Pinkeman had himself shown them in the days of Queen Anne.

For David, however, hours must pass before he could take in
any detail. He did not know that already behind the colour and
show there was disgust and discontent on the part of the show-
men, because the takings were so small, and there was no one
there but gaping country-fellows, the discontent leading in the
last day of the Fair to a free fight and riot that spread, before all
was over, into the heart of the town.

It all seemed to him so grand and magnificent that there had
been nothing in the world like it before. Walking close at his
father's side he was caught up into a world of colour and scent –
the faint September blue held the flare of the fires that blazed
upon roasting meat and fish, popping corn and scented sweetmeats, the thick swaying tendrils of smoke that crawled about the
booths, the waving of coloured pennants, the flaunting of flags,
and, under this shifting roof of colour, everything broke and
mingled again, dogs nosing for food, naked children sprawling in
the mud, mummers in gold and blue, women, bare-breasted,
shrieking after their men, tumblers somersaulting, a monkey
loosed, dragging after him a silver chain, his face weary with age
and loneliness, three dwarfs in crimson hose, with huge heads,
counting money, a black woman, a yellow kerchief round her
head, selling silver rings, clowns, soldiers, girls dressed like
angels with white wings, the booths with the drum beating and
shrill trumpets blowing, men stripped to the waist, their skin
pouring sweat, fighting before a shouting crowd, everywhere
eating and everywhere drinking, men tumbling women and
women fingering men – and through these crowds the countrymen, the farmer, the dignified statesman, the gaping yokel moving like strangers, suspicious, aloof, and gradually tempted by
ale and women and silver, by noise and food and curiosity,
tumbling into the reeking tub and so kicking and shouting and
screaming like the rest as the sun went up the sky.

Yes, hours passed. Somewhere, at some time, David had a
sudden curious vision of all the colour, reek and noise of the
Fair parting like a drawn curtain, and there in the clear space was
the lake, misted yellow under a misted sun, cool and still, the
line of Cat Bells rising softly above the woods on the farther side,
the water still without a ripple, very cool and sweet. Then it

closed again, and the stench of roasting meat and uncleanly bodies and painted boards melting in the heat of fires and frying corn and burning wood swept over him again, bringing with it into the very heart of his nostrils the whole pageant of bright colour, purple and gold and saffron, and the odd wildness of a thousand faces, eyes staring, mouths agape, and a roar of bells and whistles, shouts and curses and cries, the neighing of horses and barking of dogs and the shrill human scream of a crimson-pated cockatoo.

He was aware then that he had lost his father. He stood for a moment dismayed. On every side figures were pushing against and around him; now someone would run past him shouting; now two singing, falling from side to side, would lurch drunkenly his way; now with a cry, as though it had come from the ground itself, there would be a rush from a whole group; and all of this dreamlike – a flash of a sword, a trembling coloured flag, a creaking board of a booth, a ringing silver bell, the scream of the crimson-pated cockatoo, the wail of the lost monkey dragging his silver chain, a man bending a woman backwards against a boarded trestle, a naked muddied baby crying for its mother, all in a dream; where the clear, tranquil, golden-misted lake was, there was reality.

But he had no fear; he would see his father again; it was fine to be independent in a noisy world and to hold your own against the Devil. So, looking around him, he saw that he was before the very booth where he had most set his heart, the booth where the Chinamen were. On the outside of the booth a Chinese curtain hung in brilliant splashes of gold and red, a temple, a grove of golden bells, soldiers in armour, a bridge of blue, and in front of the curtain a Chinaman with a yellow face and an ebony pigtail was inviting everyone to enter. A bell clanged, the Chinaman called out in a shrill voice and at the same moment the thick pushing crowd shoved forward. David was caught in it, carried off his feet; he was pressed against smelling clothes and warm, sweating flesh; he clutched, that he might not fall, at a man's waist and held to it; his fingers stuck to the damp waist-belt and his arm was driven into a soft belly. For a moment he was almost under a dozen feet, then lifted up again on the sheet of a thousand smells and so almost hurled into the inside of the booth. He did not know whether he should pay money or no, he had lost his breath and found himself enclosed within the thick arm of a huge country-fellow, black-bearded, bare at the neck; their sense of one another was instantaneous, and the black-bearded man

laughed, standing him in front of him, pressing him back against
his chest, his hot naked arm against David's cheek.

He could see where he was. He was high on some raised
boards. Everything around him was quiet. The noise of the Fair
had been shut out. On every side of him the people with staring
eyes, speechless, stood waiting. A little empty stage was in front
of him and above it some curtains idly flapped.

All his senses were centred on this empty stage. It became to
him full of omen and suspense. What was about to happen?
Who would come there? A very ancient man came with a long
face of yellow parchment. He wore a long stiff garment of purple
brocaded silk. He sat, quite silently and quite alone, on a little
round stool. He was motionless, carved in colours against the
dark shadows of the flapping tent. He looked neither to right nor
left, was unaware of the sweating crowd. Perhaps he was the
Chinaman who was three hundred years old. If you were three
hundred years of age you would not pay attention to any crowd;
you would have seen so many.

Then the curtains parted, two young men in gold trousers,
stripped to the waist, their bodies glistening, came and threw
into the air coloured balls. They threw up a dozen balls at once,
and the balls, green, yellow, red, made whirls of colour above
the head of the old man who never moved.

Then there came two short fat men with very yellow bodies;
they were clad only in loincloths. Standing in a corner of the stage
they began silently to wrestle.

Then six young men came in trousers of gold and jackets of
silver; they had poles up which they climbed; they threw ropes
to one another and with pointed red slippers on their feet walked
on the ropes. Lastly a number of little yellow-faced children,
also dressed in bright, shrill colours, ran silently forward,
spread their legs and their arms and stood in a pyramid: the
child who climbed to the top and stood balancing there with his
little feet seemed only a baby with tiny black eyes and a doll's
pigtail.

Now all of them – the young men with the balls, the naked
wrestlers, the men balancing on the ropes, the pyramid children
who suddenly melted to the floor and were turning like bright
bales a hundred somersaults and cartwheels – were moving
ceaselessly round the old man who sat motionless on his little
stool, never flickering, you could be sure, an eyelid. Faster and
faster they turned, but always without a sound, and as they
moved the tightly-packed crowd moved with them: the crowd

began to sway and to murmur: everyone was smiling: the black-bearded countryman who smelt of good fresh dung put his arm tight round David's neck, pressing his body to him. They were all smiling as though they were in a dream, and it must have seemed to many of them that they too were tossing balls into the air, turning somersaults, climbing poles, balancing on ropes. Their bodies must have appeared free to them and clean and strong: the ordure and the filth, the daily toil, the cruelty and sickness and pain, the darkness and rain and cold freezing nights, the life with animals and the wrestle with the hard ungrateful soil, the penury and ignorance and darkness, the loneliness of rejected lovers, the injustice of tyrannous masters, the narrow, constrained horizons, the proud brutalities of a swollen-headed upper class against whom they struggled dumbly, whom one day – and that day was not far distant – they would conquer – all these hard things fell away, the sky was bright and clear, the air fresh like crystal, all for a moment was joy and happiness in a free world where it was always day.

As for David he could see nothing but the silent old man sitting on his stool. The old man seemed to be staring directly into David's eyes. However David moved his head he could not escape that old man. He began to be frightened. He wanted to run away. The old man appeared to have a message especially for him. In another moment something terrible would happen. His father was in danger. And it spread beyond the moment – all his life he would remember that old Chinaman, and whenever he remembered him he would shiver with apprehension. Life was dangerous, and you could only know how dangerous it was when you sat quite still and listened, waiting for a sound to break.

Anyway, he must go. He must find his father.

He wriggled away from his black-bearded friend, then, dropping down from the raised boards, pushing through legs and arms, shoving with his head now this way, now that, at one instant stifled by the human stench, at another brought up against a solid body that would never move again, at last he was by the flap of the tent and tumbled into the free air, leaving behind him, it seemed, a crowd hypnotized, in a trance, a dream . . .

He was in the open air again and frantically hungry. It must be afternoon. The sun was high in the sky.

So, looking rather desolate and half lost, his father, Francis Herries, saw him. Herries was a little drunk and soon would be more so. Somewhere in the heart of the Fair where they were bargaining about cattle he had discovered an old woman with a store of wine. She sat under an awning, on either side of her a cask of wine. A strange woman, very fat, with a purple face. She did not seem to want to sell her wine, but sat there idly. Once and again she broke into a strange raucous song in a deep, rumbling voice. She ladled the wine out of the casks into long, thin glasses: the wine was a shilling a glass, Portuguese on one side of her, Florence the other. Herries drank the Portuguese. What was it? He neither knew nor cared. Was it White Vianna or Passada or Barabar? Carcavellos or Ribadavia? He drank many glasses. The old woman did not speak to him nor he to the old woman. After that everything entertained him. He had always been very easily amused by little things, and there was something in him that liked the stench and the common crowd and the press of animals human and other—

He watched for a long while two men who, drunk with gin, tumbled about in the mud together. Close beside him was a fellow selling medicines. The two drunkards, suddenly weary, kissed one another and lay there in the mud head by head, looking up at the sunny sky.

The quack, long, thin and brown, like a gnarled tree-branch, with a high black hat – 'Here's a plaister will cure old Ulcers and Fistulas, Contusions, Tumours and any Dislocations or Hurts, and when it has performed Fifty Cures 'twill be ne'er the worse but still keep its Integrity.'

He moved leisurely, looking for a pretty face. Where were all the pretty women? Here at least not one. The country girls hanging on the arms of their lovers were each more blowzy than the other. There seemed to be none of his own class here. What was it that gave him a sudden sense of freedom so that he was happy as though he had thrown off bonds?

All these strange faces interested him, wizened and twisted and swollen; he could throw off his fine clothes, put on these tinsel rags and go wandering with them, drinking, wenching . . . Then looking about him he saw his small son. With a pang of reproach, oddly sharp as he saw his air, half defiant, half frightened, he cursed himself for the rottenest parent. To leave that child in such a place, at such a time! And yet he did not move at once towards him, but watched him, loving him, proud of him, sturdy and self-reliant among all the oddities, the shouting, the flaming fires. Whatever occurred that boy would not cry out, but would stand on his courage to the last, letting endurance father

him were no other father there. And was not that because he had
no spirit of imagination? Imagination was the devil. Let your
fancy move and there, by that booth where the boxing was, you
could see the sun roll down from the sky and sweep them all –
pimp and trollop, bully and jade, monkey and dwarf, Indian and
Chinaman – with its fiery heat, screaming into perdition. As he
one day would go. But David would not stir, not till he felt his
duty was done.

Then he moved forward and was happy to see the boy's
pleasure spring into his eyes at sight of him.

'Did you think me lost?'

'No, Father. I've been in the Chinaman's tent.'

'And what did you see there?'

'There was an old man, they say he is three hundred years old,
and young men throwing balls.'

Then he added rather wistfully:

'Father, I'm hungry.'

'Come, we'll eat then.'

They moved through the packing crowd and came to a kind of
temporary hostelry. It had a grander, larger front than the
booths, and, inside, there were long trestle tables with benches
stretched on the grass and at the far end a defended fire with a
grid. The place was very full with people eating and drinking,
and many were already drunk, singing and shouting. David and
his father found places at the end of the tent near the fire. A
stout jolly man with an apron and a white cap asked them what
they would have. There was Pudding and Roast Beef, Boiled
Beef and Ox Tripe, Pigeons, well moistened with butter, without
larding.

'Pudding and Boiled Beef,' said David. It was then that he
saw that his father had been nobly drinking. He was too
thoroughly a boy of his time to be disturbed by drunkenness, but,
during these last weeks, he had grown greatly and taken a more
manly place in the world, and in nothing more than in his
attitude to his father. His father was weak where he himself
would never be. He did not know this with any priggish sense of
virtue: it came to him simply that there were times when he
must look after his father just as there were times when he must
look after Deborah.

He was a sort of guard to them, not because he was better than
they – all his life and through everything that happened he
would always look up to them, but only because he loved them.

He was uneasy now, as looking about the tent he felt that in

some way or another this was not a place for his father to be
riotous in. The men and women around them were of mixed
kinds: there were some sober and solid yeomen and townsmen,
eating their meat with grave seriousness, with the Cumbrian air
of guarding their own; there were some rascals of the Fair's own
company, one of them in a shabby gay jacket of gold thread,
another like a pedlar in a crimson cap (he reminded David of the
Stye Head Devil who gave him the little box) with a small
gibbering monkey sitting on his shoulder. With them were two
loose women very gaudily attired, laughing and shouting. One of
the women fondled the pedlar, thrusting food into his mouth.
Near his father was a group of better-class people. They might
be townsmen from Kendal or Penrith. One was very stout with a
double chin and little mouse-eyes. He was rather drunken already
and spilt his meat on his green velvet waistcoat. Another was a
little man, thin as a spider, with a shrill feminine voice. He was
over-handsomely dressed with an elaborately curled wig, a full-
bottomed coat of bright blue, and many rings on his fingers. He
was also drunken, and said many times over that he wanted a
full-bosomed woman to go to bed with, that he might wake in
the morning and find her near to him.

Herries, as was his way when he was drunk, had become very
grand and proud. The wine that now was brought to him, added
to the wine that he had already had, increased his grand dignity.
David, who very soon had eaten all that he wanted, began to be
unhappy and to plan some way of escape out into the air again.

Glancing here and there he knew that there were a number in
the tent who had recognized his father. He had long known that
there was much curiosity about his father and his father's family,
as to why he had chosen to exile himself in Borrowdale, as to his
dangerous liking for women, as to his mingling with anyone he
met and caring nothing for the quality of his company, as to his
having a fine mistress hidden away there in Herries and his
flaunting her full in his wife's face – David knew that all these
things were said and that already a queer chancy air had grown
about the building of Herries, and that they had all become the
more suspicious to the outside world because on their first
coming they had sheltered a Roman Catholic priest (and who
knew on what errand he had vanished less than a year ago?), and
had under their roof the most famous witch in Borrowdale.

All this was in David's mind and consciousness. His determination was set on getting his father away before some open
scandal occurred, and through all the murk and smell of the

crowded tent, stinking of meat, spilt drink and unclean bodies of men, he saw the old Chinaman's eyes, that Chinaman who was three hundred years old and sat like an image.

His father was very haughty, ate and drank without speaking to anyone. He seemed like a god to his son, sitting there so grand and handsome with his thin, brown face, his clear eyes and the silver waistcoat with the ruby buttons.

The spidery man in the full wig buried his nose in his glass, and then, in his shrill high voice, bowing to Herries, said:

'A drink with you, sir.'

Herries drank.

'I am from Kendal,' the little man went on, while the very stout fellow laughed immoderately. 'I have come hither to see the pretty women, but by Jesus there are none!'

'There are several,' Herries replied, eyeing him severely.

'There are several.' The little man tittered: 'You are fortunate, sir. My name is Rosen – may I be honoured by knowing yours, sir?'

'My name,' said Herries very proudly, holding up his glass and looking at the beads of colour in the yellow wine, 'is Charles Henry Nathaniel Winchester, Duke of the Pyrenees and the district of the Amazon.'

Mr Rosen became very serious. His little brow was puckered.

'I understand you, sir – a secret, between gentlemen.'

'There are women here,' said Herries, 'but no gentlemen – all the gentlemen are at the lake's bottom feasting with the mermaids.'

'I have heard,' said Mr Rosen, who realized only the last word of Herries's sentence, 'that a mermaid was indeed seen off the northern coast of Scotland a month back. I was told by one who had read of it. I could go to bed with a mermaid,' he hiccuped, and looked gravely distressed, 'were her tail not too long. Could one choose one's mermaid?'

It was then that a terrible thing occurred. David, more and more restless, seeing that the tent was now fully crowded, that several had moved near to them and were listening, had his eye on the tent's door. Through it he could see a patch of bright sunlight, a woman dancing on a tub and many figures passing in shadow. It was clear by the door. Someone entered, a woman, Alice Press.

He stared, first thinking that he was blinded by the sunlight, then that he had mistaken some other woman of a like figure for her – there was no mistake. She was wearing the black velvet dress of the morning. He could see the silver chain lying against it. And she wore the scarlet shoes. She stood quite by herself staring about her. She looked up and down the tent. Then she saw Herries. She saw him, looked full at him, then very slowly began to move up the tent.

David's eyes were fixed. He had become an image of apprehension and fear. He could see only the green waistcoat of the fat man and that down it there was trickling a little stream of wine, while his big belly rose and fell in spasms of laughter. He did not look at his father, but he knew, quite suddenly, that his father had seen her. He felt for a moment his father's hand touch his shoulder, then he heard Alice Press's voice.

'I have come, you see. Will you give me something to eat?'

There was a place at Herries's other side. She took it with great ease and composure, but David, who, because of his detestation of her, had her in his very bones, knew as though it had been himself that she was suffering from throbbing nervousness and a devilish fear.

Herries, his face very stern, answered her quietly.

'Yes, since you are come . . . What will you have?'

She ordered something from the smiling man with the apron, and, attempting a perfect ease, looked about her. She must have seen at once that no women of any quality were there, but only drabs and Fair ladies. All stared at her. At the door-end of the tent a thick rabble was quarrelling and laughing at its own affairs, but at the fire-end all eyes were upon her.

She smiled swiftly at Herries, and then began to talk.

'A kind fellow from Seathwaite brought me. I watched him passing. 'Twas dull at the house and the day bright, so I thought that I would venture for an hour. But I am hungry and 'tis three o'clock. 'Tis a gay Fair and of a size for a little town, as large as the Doncaster Fair. There are things to buy, I can be sure – will you buy me something, Francis?' She put her hand for a moment on his arm, laughing in his face. 'Yes,' he answered slowly, 'I will buy you something.' He did not look at her, but stared in front of him as though he were lost in thought.

Her food was brought, and she began nervously to eat. The heat of the tent, her fear and excitement had brought colour to her sallow cheeks. The black dress suited her and her full half-revealed bosom. The little spidery man in the blue coat regarded her with all his eyes, his mouth open, the stout man also.

She continued talking:

'And will you take me to see the sights? There is a Chinaman three hundred years old and a play . . .' She broke off. She was gathering courage. ''Tis time you showed me the world again.'

Herries, for the first time since she had come, looked at her.

'I will show you the world. It would be ungracious did I not when you have come so far. First you shall eat . . .'

It was then that the little Mr Rosen of Kendal caught up his courage and spoke to her. He raised his glass.

'May I drink to you, madam? You honour us by your company.'

She smiled at him, raising her glass, but her nervous thoughts were fast on Herries.

'We are all friendly together here,' she said. 'Pleasant company. Can you tell me, sir, whether the Chinaman has truly three hundred years?'

'They say so.'

'A very Methuselah. Are you an inhabitant of Keswick?'

'My town is Kendal.' The little man's eyes were now bursting from his head at the sight of the lady's opulence and beauty. ''Tis a finer town than Keswick.'

'Larger. 'Tis not for me to say that 'tis finer. We who are citizens of it have our private conceit.' He sighed, swelled out his chest, felt for the hilt of his sword.

After a little she looked at Herries. 'I have done eating,' she said. 'Will you take me to the sights?'

Herries drank his glass, looked at it after, with a firm hand, he had placed it on the table, then turned to her gently.

'Alice,' he said, 'as you have taken this on yourself so you take the consequences. When we leave this tent we part . . . You do not return to Herries.'

His voice was quiet, but he had not wished especially to lower it. Mr Rosen and his stout friend, and indeed all at that end of the table, heard the words.

The colour in her face deepened. She put her hand to her bosom, an action of hers that David knew well.

'Come, then,' she said, half rising, 'this is too public a place . . .'

'Nay.' He put his hand on her arm, holding her down. 'You have chosen it. Before we move hence you must tell me that you understand – at the tent door we part. You go no more to Herries.'

Her rage at the public insult – her temper was always beyond her command – flushed her cheeks. She, too, had in these ten minutes been drinking to give herself control. David saw her white hand pressed with desperate force on the table until the blue veins stood out.

'Be ashamed,' she murmured. 'In this place . . .'

'Yes,' he replied. 'In this place. I want your assurance.'

'No, then,' she cried, her voice suddenly rising. 'You bought me. You shall keep me.' It was odd how, with her anger and the freedom from the drink, the commonness that was in her blood suffused, like a rising colour, all her body and spirit.

'I bought you. Yes,' he answered quietly. 'Then I can sell you again.'

Everyone around them was silent. The stout man, very drunk, rolling his head, suddenly exclaimed:

'Aye, and who would not have her, this beautiful lady – though she cost him – his – his house and – and – horses?'

But David saw that she was very afraid.

'Francis, you have been drinking. I did wrong to come – I confess it – I will do all that you wish. But not here – not in this place . . .'

But he went on steadily.

'You have said it. I have bought you, and now, our bargain being ended, I will sell you again.' He fixed Rosen with his eye: 'You, sir, how much will you give me for this lady?'

Several men murmured shame, but everyone here was very drunken: there was some laughter, and a man began to sing a song. A woman very gaudily dressed and painted had come over and, leaning her bosom on the stout man's back, eagerly watched the scene.

'You insult the lady,' little Rosen began, half rising from his seat and feeling for his sword: then something in Herries's face constrained him, and he sat down again.

'I am indeed serious,' said Herries sternly. 'This lady and I are weary of one another and would part, but she is mine and I would have compensation. You, sir,' staring into Rosen's face, 'how much will you give for her?'

Alice Press rose – 'I will pay you for this . . . in good coin . . .' She made as though to go, but he rose also, laid his hand again on her arm, then, his voice clear so that all heard, said: 'This lady is for sale – for the one who will bid the highest.'

Cries broke out – some were laughing, some swearing, most too drunken to understand the affair; the garish woman laughed loudest of all.

A man said: 'Five silver shillings.'

Rosen, fuddled but struggling, in his funny feminine voice

screamed: 'You are a filthy dog – you shall be caned for this—'
Nevertheless he could not take his eyes from Alice Press. His
whole body hung towards her.

Herries answered him quietly.

'Come, sir, will you give me forty shillings?'

'He'll give forty shillings . . .' some drunken voice murmured
like a refrain. The garish woman cried shrilly: 'More than she's
worth, the bitch.'

Something happened then to Rosen. With a frenzied gesture
he plunged his hand in his pocket, flung down on the table a heap
of silver coin, then leaned forward, his face almost in Herries's.

'I'll take her. I'll take her. She shall come if she's willing – I'll
care for her – zounds and the devil, I will – an she's willing.'

The money struck the table, and some of the coins, like live
things, danced in the air, springing to the ground. A heap,
shining there, lay before Herries.

'Have her then,' he said. 'I drink to you both.'

As he did so Alice Press turned to him and struck the glass
from his hand. The wine splashed in his face.

She said something to him that no one could hear. Then
clearly:

'You shall never be free from this.'

She looked about her once, proudly, and David, who still
hated her, nevertheless at that moment mightily admired her.

Then she turned, brushed through the men and was gone.

Mr Rosen rose and hurried after her.

Herries picked up one of the pieces of silver, looked at it
intently, then placed it in the deep pocket of his coat.

Quietly, without any haste, he went out. David, his head up,
his eyes shining, followed him.

THE SEA – FATHER AND SON

IT WAS on a windy April night in the year 1737 that David and
his father arrived at a new understanding together. The manner
of it was on this wise.

The years that had passed since the very public exit of Mrs
Alice Press had suffered this and that figure to rise for a moment
before their indifferent background, and then to be whirled like a
tumbled leaf into windy space.

There had been the cheerful, friendly Gay, who, dying of an inflammation of the bowels in three days, had drawn this unusual sincerity from Mr Pope: 'He was the most amiable by far, his qualities were the gentlest ... Surely if innocence and integrity can deserve happiness ...'

It was Mr Pope's profound opinion that they could not.

On the 13th of March, 1734, one Mr William Bromley had proposed that 'leave be given to bring in a Bill for repealing the Septennial Act, and for the more frequent meeting and calling of Parliaments' – and the echoes of that appeal were one day to affect even the remotest hearthstones of Borrowdale.

Other figures, oddly contrasted, beckon for a moment on the mirror. Bolingbroke, cursing everyone save himself, takes boat for France on a windy June morning; then Louis of France, making rude gestures, fingers at nose, that he may irritate, polished sophisticate that he is, the barbarian Stanislaus; and a heavy-jowled, good-tempered cynic is fingering women in a gilded London bedroom and refusing most resolutely to be irritated by either Louis or Stanislaus. He has seen, with a smile, the packing of Bolingbroke's boxes, has sighed and smiled cynically again because Nature that leaves so many dullards lagging on the stage has taken the great Arbuthnot after only sixty-eight years of noble brilliance, has snorted with his closest friend and intimate, snuff-taking Queen Caroline, over the rude, personally insulting dispatches posted indignantly by His Gracious Majesty, the Emperor Charles the Sixth, and has turned with a grunt back to his women and bottles again, strong in this policy of masterly inactivity, this heavy-jowled, good-tempered, massive-bellied cynic Walpole.

One more, before the mirror darkens and the months hurry to a more desperate destiny – a bright-cheeked, rosy boy receiving his baptism of fire at the siege of Gaeta, aged only fourteen, Don Carlos touching the boy's arm with his long hand, and thus angering Caroline and George in their London palace so that they must send to Walpole to soothe them – that boy Charles Edward, whose happiest moment, maybe, is just this when, from that little close-walled flowered garden, he looks across, a fire of ambition at his heart, to a thin line of smoky plum-coloured hills.

In Borrowdale, at Herries, David and his father, on the morning of the 10th of April, 1737, were preparing to ride over to Ravenglass to spend several nights with brother Harcourt.

David, who was almost eighteen now, and had broadened, strengthened, darkened, so that you would not know him for the same little boy who had pretended to sleep in the four-poster at the Keswick inn, knew nothing of Gay or Arbuthnot, of *The Beggar's Opera* or the malicious devilries of Mr Pope; but he knew by now a great deal about Borrowdale.

He knew the name of every Statesman in the valley and the faces and bodies of most of the humans there. He knew the innermost, intimate history of every possible fishing locality, the name of every bird, the lair of every fox. He had seen a wolf round the Glaramara caves, he had seen a golden eagle fly in the sun above Castle Crag, he had shared (without shame or shrinking – that sensitiveness did not belong to his time) in nearly every bull-baiting, dog-fighting, cock-fighting that the valley had to offer. He had learnt something of the spinning and weaving, and there had not been a Christmas Feast, a stanging at Twelfth Night, a pace-egging at Easter, a late summer rushbearing, a Hallowe'en or a local wedding at which he had not played his part. He was as popular (although he did not know it and would not have thought of it had he known it) as his father was not.

His whole young life had become absorbed by this valley world and by the close history of his own immediate family. They had been the seven happiest years of his life. He was a boy no longer. He was on the threshold of his manhood.

This journey to Ravenglass was to show him this. He had been anticipating eagerly a visit to his uncle Harcourt ever since he had first come to Herries. Uncle Harcourt was to be different, different from anyone he had seen or known. Harcourt had lived in the great world, he cared for the Arts, he was brilliantly read, a scholar, he could answer many of the questions that, for years now, David had been longing to ask.

For, although he loved everything that had to do with the outside world, he had, too, an intellectual eagerness that was perhaps the growth from seeds that Father Roche had sown. This had not been satisfied.

Simple, gentle little Robert Finch had come and taught the three of them what he could. That had not been a great deal. From the outside world the family at Herries had been more and more shut off.

Here, in spite of his externally happy life, lay the reason for the apprehension and misgiving that were in David's heart. For himself all might be well, for his family and for those whom he loved, all, as he very thoroughly knew, was not well at all.

The clouds had begun to gather after the scandal of the Chinese Fair. That scandal had been in its effects infinitely more public than seemed at the time possible. It had, indeed, been shameful enough for himself, and its effect on him had altered the whole balance of his character. Although five years now intervened he could yet see and feel every detail of it, the close and ill-smelling tent, the leaping fire, the genial host, the garish woman with the painted face, the bright blue coat of the little shrill-voiced man, the silver coins lying on the table, the broad stout hand of Alice Press stark on the table-board – but it had been, it had seemed, a private drama for himself and his father. For months he had caught no outside word of it. All that they had known at home had been that Alice Press was gone, and for ever: that had been relief enough.

Then, even to his boy's ears, bit by bit and piece by piece the story had come to him: the Peel boy knew it, Benjamin knew it, at last, as he found, his mother and his sisters knew it. It was a story incredibly distorted. It seemed to him, when at last he met it face to face, to have no relationship to the truth. Of course he hotly defended his father – but the mischief was done. Here was the man who had sold his woman in public for 'thirty pieces of silver'. Even to that country tradition in that uncouth time the event was memorable.

It clothed his father with a kind of 'apartness' – yes, even for himself. His father had always been for him like no other man, but that had been, in his youngest years, a difference of glory. Now it was a difference of peculiarity.

His was a character that must face everything truly and honestly as it came to him, and now he must face this – that his father could do shameful things and yet feel no shame. This, oddly enough, made him love his father more than he had done before, but it was a love very different from the earlier one. Now he must guard and protect this man who moved under some kind of influence that was straight from the Devil. David, of course, believed in the Devil – did he not know him as he was in human form?

His father must be loved and guarded because he was different from other men, but no longer could he be worshipped – and this brought him nearer to David. There had been from the beginning something fraternal in their relationship. That was now strengthened.

Other changes had come upon Francis Herries in these five years. He was not the beautiful, young, elegant person that he had been on his first coming to Herries. His body had stoutened, his dress was more slovenly, his air more careless. He bore at times – although he was worlds apart from him – an odd re-semblance to his brother Pomfret. At least you could tell now that they were brothers.

In mood he was very much as he had been, gay, charming, sullen, angry, kindly, cruel. He did not appear to feel his apart-ness. He had his acquaintances in Keswick, men with whom he rode, betted and attended the country events, also women. But David now knew he carried his secret life within him and was never, for an instant, unaware of its presence.

They would have been, as a family, more thoroughly isolated than in winter they were, had it not been for David's country popularity on the one side that made him friends with everyone in the valley and, on the Keswick side, strangely enough, because of David's sister Mary.

Mary was now fifteen years of age and Deborah fourteen. Mary was handsome – she would be a true Herries woman, big-boned, broad-breasted, carrying herself with that mixture of arrogance and confidence and grace – that blending of hardness and courtesy, of indifference and kindly attention, that brought in every country, society, and age such Herries women to the front. She was indeed hard, determined, and ambitious. Of her true feelings for her father she had given as yet no sign, but she must from her very earliest age have felt that he was her enemy, her thwarting opponent in every desire and longing that was hers. In truth, every element in him must have always been dis-tasteful to her, his recklessness, his irony, his grossness, and, above all, his unconsciousness of and disregard for public opinion. For she was cautious, unaware of subtlety, grimly virtuous and alive to every public wind that blew.

Very early, indeed, she must have surveyed the scene and decided that not for her were the isolation of Herries, the mire of Borrowdale, the rusticity of the country company, the coarseness and crudity of living. She had never any eye for any beauty save her own, her only tenderness was to herself, and she had a power of cautious waiting on the event, an ability to spin over months and even years the web of her own secret plans, that was both in its strength and secrecy extraordinary.

Very soon she had begun to turn her eye to Keswick and her cousins there. That was her future world, or rather the stepping-stone to a larger, grander one, and, at once, she began to use it. Very early she won the admiration of her uncle and aunt. She was in truth the very type that they could understand and admire.

She found, as she grew older, ways and means of reaching Keswick that only ruthless determination could have taught her. At first her father had angrily forbidden her his brother's house, but soon he had grown indifferent and lazy. He had never cared for this daughter of his. He did not mind where she went. When she was fourteen she persuaded her mother that she must have dancing-lessons and, riding her own horse, would vanish into Keswick and no one question her.

It may have been that Pomfret and his wife found a certain triumph and pleasure in thus alienating one of the children of Francis, but it is more probable that they had not enough subtlety of mind for this. They gained a certain definite pleasure in hearing the child rail against her father, as she did in quiet, measured, determined tones, but soon it was reason enough that she was there simply because she dominated all the family and had already a kind of social power and authority that neither they nor their children would ever acquire.

Of Deborah, as she grew older, no one save David ever thought. She was not a pretty child. Pale of face, very thin of body, silent. Only her brother knew her and the rare, sweet spirit that she had.

It was from her that he obtained his deeper and more subtle consciousness of the beauty of the country around him. Child though she was, she was sensitive to the minutest beauties – a brown dry tree on a moonlight night, a glittering stream, the softness that snow on the hill-tops gives to the reflective valley, the yellow bunches of leaves on the oak tree, the purple depth of the lake seen beyond a bank of primroses, the low singing of the swallows, the whiteness of frost-bleached stones, the sudden flashing out of lights after a sullen storm, a brown stream running turbulently below a white cottage – above all, the sky of whose pageantry this country seemed more than any other to offer extravagant splendours. She would watch it constantly with a deep enwrapped contemplation, and yet she did not seem a dreamer, helped with a steady unobtrusiveness in all the business of the house; but she was, like her father, although in a very different way, a spirit alone, the only citizen of her mysterious world.

She had a passion for no other human being save David. More than anyone else in the family, she was attentive to Margaret Herries, never irritated by her stupidities or exasperated by her tears; but she had no close contact with her. That was, it might be, her mother's fault. It was her husband whom Margaret

Herries loved, ceaselessly, deprecatingly, monotonously, and her daughter Mary whom she admired. She would ask Mary wistfully about Keswick and Pomfret and Jannice. She did not go to see them because she was afraid of them and because her husband would be angry if she did, but theirs was the life that she would have preferred had she had the good fortune – to be in a fine house in a lighted town with company and cards and an occasional ball – but these only if Francis shared them with her.

As he did not choose that life she preferred this isolated one so that he shared it with her. Shared was perhaps too strong a word for anything that he did with her. He told her nothing, approached her always with that same mixture of sarcastic humour and rough careless kindness: she would never understand him at all; perhaps if the moment of comprehension had ever come to her she would not have loved him any longer, so that it was well as it was.

This, however, can at least be said, that, after Alice Press's departure, she was happier than she had been before. If he had other mistresses she did not know of them, and like many another wife, after her and before, so long as she did not know she did not question.

So these years had passed, a strange, slow mist of isolation creeping up around Herries, a mist not of fact but of suggestion, an atmosphere that slowly marked off this family as different from other families, a family of another colour, as though they had been, these Herries, of foreign blood, and had come from some very distant land where odd beasts dwelt and dangerous rivers ran.

It was just about now that, for the first time, someone said in Keswick: 'He's a rogue, Herries – a fantastic rogue.'

Meanwhile, in this April month, Francis and his son David rode together to Ravenglass to stay, for several nights, with brother Harcourt. They rode over the Stye Head Pass and down into Wasdale. David rode on Caesar, and Francis on a little shaggy horse that he called Walpole because he had a belly and was cynically indifferent to any morality. The little horses picked their way very carefully up the hill with deliberate slowness.

No one hurried them. The day was grey and still with little pools of sunlight in a dark sky. The hills had snow on their tops, but in the valleys the larches were beginning to break into intense green flame. As they wound up the Pass, the hills gathered about them, not grandly and with arrogant indifference as larger hills do in other countries, but with intimacy and friendliness as though they liked human beings and were interested in their fates.

By the Stye Head Tarn it was grim and desolate. This Tarn lies, an ebony unreflecting mirror, at the foot of the Gavel – beyond it, to the left, soft green ridges run to Esk Hause and the Langdales and lonely Eskdale.

Above the green stretches there are the harsh serrated lines of Scafell Pike and the thin edge of Mickledore. It was here, however, and on this day that David had his first sharp consciousness of the Gavel, the grand and noble hill that was one day to watch him struggling for his life.

It was not to be seen at its finest here from the Tarn, for it sprawled away to the right almost without shape and form: nevertheless the spirit of it, dauntless, generous and wise, seized and held him. The sunlight, hidden elsewhere, broke above its head and caressed it; long strathes of water, blue like the cold spring streams that ran below the snowdrops, spread about its shoulders.

The whole expanse of land here is wide and strong, so that although no plan or form is visible it makes of itself a form, the Tarn, the green stretches, the grouping hills having their own visible life without any human thought or agency to assist them.

They stayed for a little while beside the black Tarn. Herries, climbing the Pass, had been very genial, speaking of anything that came into his head, of a bull-baiting in Keswick, of funny days in Doncaster and of his old long-ago life near Carlisle. When he was thus he and David were like brothers. But suddenly now beside the Tarn he became morose and gloomy. He withdrew into himself. In silence they rode down into Wasdale, along the road, past the little church to the long lake's edge. Here there was great beauty, the grey lake without a ripple and descending into it the black precipitous Screes, savage and relentless, while on the bank where they rode everything was soft with golden sand, green shelving meadow on which sheep were grazing, and the larches bursting into leaf. All the afternoon they rode in silence turning inland over rough, dull country.

It was not until they came to Santon Bridge that Francis Herries broke the silence.

'Thy Uncle Harcourt is Jacobite. He is a romantic jackanapes. Let him not talk thee over.' Then he laughed, twisting himself round on his horse to look at his stolid, thickset, square-shouldered son. 'Not much romantic notion in thy head, David.'

David to his own surprise did not answer. Perhaps it was that the scene had now of itself become romantic. They were riding through thick woods, and between the spaces of the trees the evening sky was faintly rose. A bird, singing, seemed to accompany them. But it was not only the place and the hour. David found that his father had unexpectedly touched something in him that was deep and fervid. Was this the consequence of that ride, seven years ago, with Father Roche? He could hear the melody and worship of the priest's voice now – 'Even as our Blessed Saviour, so the King . . .'

And, realizing this, he was aware that there was something in him here that his father could neither govern nor command – nay, something that his father could not touch. And yet the folly of it! What did he know about Jacobitism, its rights or wrongs? And yet he seemed in those few moments between the dark trees to have started some conflict with his father.

'Where has Father Roche been these years?' he asked.

Herries tossed his head. 'How do I know? He is a fool, a fanatic. He had fine parts but must needs waste them on a mare's nest . . .' Then he added abruptly: 'He hath been in Rome, tying the Pretender's shoe-strings.'

He went on as the evening gathered under the rosy sky. 'He had a power over me. He has had a power over many. But, believe me, if ever he returns it will be for no good. An ill-omened bird. Yes, a fanatic – better that, though, than a half-nothing like your father. David, have you ever dreamt a recurring dream?'

David shook his head, laughing.

'I am too heavy of nights to dream.'

'I believe that.' Walpole stumbled. Herries pulled at him with a curse.

'I have a dream . . .' He stopped abruptly. 'There are the lights of Ravenglass. We are almost in.' They came clattering over the cobbles of the little place and smelt the salt sea and heard the sharp questioning cry of the gulls. A fellow standing in a doorway directed them to Harcourt's house.

Although it was now dark David could see the little square white-fronted house thrust back from the street in a small, walled garden. He smelt, as they waited by the door, the sting of the sea and an aromatic scent of herbs and could see here and there the faint yellow of blowing daffodils.

A little old man, very ancient, in a white wig, knee-breeches, and with large silver buckles to his shoes, holding a candle above

his head, opened the door cautiously to them, after much un-
bolting and unbarring and rattling of chains. A moment later
Harcourt Herries was there to greet them.

They all went together round with the horses to the stables
which were at the back of the garden. The stars were coming out
and a strong wind blowing. They returned to the house, and
Harcourt, a silver candlestick held high in either hand, led them
up to their room.

In the candlelight as he stood and talked to his brother, David
could see him clearly. He was a little thin spindle-shanked man
very elegantly dressed in an old fashion. He had the high, white
forehead and the air of breeding that belonged to the Herries,
the breeding that even Pomfret could not quite lose. You could
see that he was brother to Francis, but although he was only
twelve years older, forty-nine to Francis's thirty-seven, he might
have been his brother's father.

His face was thin and drawn and covered with a network of
wrinkles; his body was so slight and delicate that as with rare
china you might expect to see through it.

Everything about him was refined, from the thin gold ring
with a green stone on his finger, to the rich rose-colour of his
skirted coat. His voice, when he spoke, was very gentle and kind,
and there was in it a note, full and harmonious, that resembled
something in Francis's voice.

He looked exceedingly fragile as he stood in the candlelight
beside his brother, whose body was beginning to thicken, and his
nephew, whose strength and health shone through his young
limbs. He had things about him that were like Francis and Father
Roche and Deborah, the three people for whom David had, in
his life, cared the most.

Harcourt left them to wash off the dirt and weariness of the
ride. The jugs and basins in the room were of old beaten silver,
and round the top of the four-poster ran a fine tapestry with
friezes in rose and old saffron.

Before they went down, Francis said to his son: 'You will find
no woman in the house. Harcourt was once in his youth crossed
in love. He cannot abide women, and will have none about him.'

Downstairs in a charming panelled parlour they had a meal
that was to David a delight. The candlelight trembled before the
dark panels.

It was late indeed for dinner, but there was fine fare – a grand
salmon, a patty of calf's brains, a piece of roast beef, a dish of
fruit with preserved flowers, spinage tarts, sweet with candied

orange and citron peel mixed with the spinage, marrow and
eggs, and fresh fruit, pears and China oranges and muscadine
grapes. There were French wines, Pontack and Hermitage, and
later when the table was cleared and showed a pool of splendour
under the candles, a bowl of Brunswick Mum, the most intoxicat-
ing liquor known to man. Neither Harcourt nor his nephew was
drunk. The boy felt perhaps that for the first time, outside his
own house, he was treated as a man. Harcourt was a most charming host, telling them in his gentle voice the romantic things
about Ravenglass – how its name meant grey-blue river, how
three rivers – the Esk, the Irt, and the Mite – joined here to make
the almost landlocked harbour, how once the Romans had been
here and made a camp. How in those days it was a place of importance, had its charter in the beginning of the thirteenth
century, and at Muncaster Castle near by, the Penningtons
would take refuge from the sea raiders, how Henry VI, fleeing
there after a lost battle gave his host an enamelled bowl of green
glass, 'the Luck of Muncaster', how still there was traffic in the
harbour and much smuggling to and from the Isle of Man, which
was but forty miles away. He said that, as he sat there in his
room, he could see the Romans and the men of the Middle Ages
and all the busy citizens of the place, when it was a prosperous
town, come crowding about him with their long, thin faces
and strange distant voices – and at that Francis, who was now
drunk with the Mum, laughed at him and called him a romantic
fool.

It was then that David felt again an odd wave of antagonism
to his father sweep over him.

There was something moving between them, something new
that had never been between them before: soon it would appear
and would be defined.

He became in that first evening attached to his uncle, and it
was plain enough that his uncle delighted in him; on the next
morning, which was cold and windy, Francis was oddly morose
and, saying very little to either of them, went off by himself.
Uncle and nephew sat by the coal fire in the parlour.

Harcourt talked of the days when he was a boy in the London
of Queen Anne. He had been fourteen years of age when he first
went there. He had been present at the sacking of the New Court
in the Sacheverell riots and had seen the huge bonfire of its
furniture in Lincoln's Inn Fields; he had had nights on the *Folly*,
the Thames barge opposite Whitehall, although it had already
then fallen out of fashion; he described the coffee-houses as

though he were still frequenting them – Anderton's, the Bay Tree, Button's, Child's, where you might, an you were lucky, see learned celebrities like Dr Mead and Sir Hans Sloane; or Don Saltero's, set up by Sir Hans Sloane's servant, where there was a collection of curiosities such as the Queen of Sheba's cordial bottle, Gustavus Adolphus's gloves and King Charles II's beard which he wore in disguise in the Royal Oak.

He had been a great lover of the drama, he told David, a faint flush of enthusiastic memory staining his wrinkled cheek.

In the Dorset Gardens Theatre, he had witnessed a performance by the lovely Mrs Tofts. This theatre was pulled down in 1709, and the world of pleasure knew it no more. In the Theatre Royal, in Drury Lane, he had been thrilled by the performance of the second part of *The Destruction of Jerusalem*. He would never forget the splendour of Mrs Rogers as Berenice.

But his chief love had been the Italian Opera. He had himself been present at the great event of its opening on the 9th of April, 1705, when Vanbrugh and Congreve had been there and Mrs Bracegirdle had spoken the Prologue. The opera on this occasion had been *The Triumph of Love*.

As he talked he seemed to recreate about him all the distant and vibrating life of that old time, already so quaint and unmodern, with the busy scenes on the river, the perils of the night Mohawks, the chatter of the shops and coffee-houses, and great figures like the Queen and Harley and Marlborough moving in splendid ghostly grandeur.

But what held young David and made this talk memorable to him for ever was the note of wistful and yet acquiescent regret in his uncle's voice. That had been the time when life had been so full of energy and eagerness: everything had been promised then – love and fame and great company – now in this little house, with the sea-coal's thin glow between the fire-dogs, the whisper and rustle of the sea beyond the dark windows, the sense of the little dead and abandoned town once of so busy a prosperity, the remoteness, the half-death-in-life, the eternal melancholy of the indifferent passing of time ...

Nevertheless, Uncle Harcourt was cheerful enough. He opened with delicate, reverent fingers his bookcases and produced his Spensers and Miltons and Ben Jonsons. His favourite poet was Mr Pope. He had Lintot's *Miscellany* with the first publication of 'The Rape of the Lock', and the earliest editions of the *Iliad* as the volumes appeared from 1715 to 1720.

But most of all did he love the 'Elegy to the Memory of an

Unfortunate Lady', and, with tears in his eyes, recited, his voice quivering a little as he spoke:

'By foreign hands thy dying eyes were closed,
By foreign hands thy decent limbs composed,
By foreign hands thy humble grave adorned,
By strangers honoured, and by strangers mourned!
What tho' no friends in sable weeds appear,
Grieve for an hour, perhaps, then mourn a year,
And bear about the mockery of woe
To midnight dances and the public show!
What tho' no weeping Loves thy ashes grace,
Nor polished marble emulate thy face!
What tho' no sacred earth allow thee room,
Nor hallowed dirge be muttered o'er thy tomb!
Yet shall thy grave with rising flowers be drest,
And the green turf lie lightly on thy breast:
There shall the morn her earliest tears bestow;
There the first roses of the year shall blow;
While Angels with their silver wings o'ershade
The ground, now sacred by thy reliques made.'

So long as he lived David was never to forget that scene – the little man, his wig a trifle awry, the volume in one hand, the other hand behind the heavy skirt of his coat, the gentle, melodious voice, the rain, that had now begun to fall, beating on the pane, the distant surge of the sea, the steady friendly murmur of the grandfather's clock. He was not imaginative as his father was; he was never to care very passionately for art and letters, but he made, in this morning, a new friend and acquired for ever some sense of the tragedy of the passing of time and the deep intangible beauty of old loyalties.

His uncle afterwards began to speak of his father. David at once perceived two things, one that his uncle had in his youth deeply loved his father. His older years had given him a protective maternal love of him. There was something very feminine in Uncle Harcourt's nature, and more and more as the morning passed he reminded David of Deborah. And, secondly, Harcourt was greatly distressed at his brother's appearance. He had not seen him for six years and although he said but little and asked but few questions David could see that some unexpressed alarm worked in him.

He spoke of Francis's youth, of how he had been always

different from the others, capable of the greatest things, but that some instability had always checked him. 'He hath always imagined more than he grasped, dreamed more than he could realize. There is a wild loneliness in his spirit that no one can reach.'

Then coming and putting his hand most affectionately on David's shoulder he added: 'But he hath bred his greater self in his son, who will fulfil his dearest hopes. I can see that, and it gives me great happiness.'

They were thus affectionately together when Francis Herries came in. He stayed in the doorway then came forward. 'A very pretty picture,' he said. They were both immediately conscious of anger in his voice. David drew away from his uncle, getting up and moving to the window.

'Welcome, brother,' said Harcourt 'Be warm by the fire and tell us where you have been.'

'Nay,' Francis continued, his voice dry with sarcasm, 'I am one too many. I have a book to read – in my room.' But Harcourt came across to him, laughing, put his hand on his shoulder and drew him to the fire.

Francis was like a child. He sat by the fire, his feet stretched out, and sulked. Their evening meal was not very gay. David felt in every vein antagonism to his father. To repay his brother's courtesy with such childishness! At the age that he had, to sulk and pout like an infant! And yet behind the childishness there was something real. Jealousy? Loneliness? Discontent? Through the evening the antagonism between them grew. By the close of the meal David was miserable. This was none of the old childish quarrels that ended in a beating. And yet what was it about? Where was its growth? A ride through darkening woods, drunkenness over Mum, a flurry of rain ...

Sitting there Harcourt raised his glass. 'The King!' He crossed the glass in the air.

Francis sprang to his feet. 'None of that humbug, brother! The boy has enough nonsense in his head.'

Harcourt flung his glass behind him. It smashed on the wall.

'I have drunk my toast in my own house,' he answered evenly.

An idiotic moonlight fluttered at the window, very feeble and wavering.

Francis walked to the door, stayed, then came back and put his hand on his brother's shoulder. 'I am become too serious. I have had a day with only ill thoughts for company.' Then, surprisingly, he turned to his son. 'Will you come out with me, David? There is a moon.'

The boy nodded, then turned, smiling, to his uncle:

'You will not be lonely for an hour?'

The little man smiled back at him.

'Mr Pope will drink a glass with me.' They all smiled at one another. Friendliness had suddenly returned.

Francis and David walked out into the little street, which was quite deserted. There were two sounds, the even whisper of the sea and some drunken fellow at a distance shouting a chorus. The moonlight was a faint, grey, glassy shadow dimming the sharp outline of the houses, but at the sea-edge it was stronger, flooding the water and giving an unreal size and shape to the distant sand-dunes that lay like lazy, grey whales on either side of the harbour.

A little boat stayed very faintly rocking at the shore's edge.

'Shall we take the boat out to the sand?' Francis asked. 'There's no one to prevent us.' They climbed in, Francis took the oars and in silence rowed over the water.

It was not excessively cold, and as they went forward the clouds shredded away, the moon came out riding in a misty, starless heaven. Round her was a ring dark red in colour.

David wondered what his father was going to do. He had some purpose. David on his side felt his own independence resolutely strengthen. Some subservience that there had always been to his father was no longer there. The boat shelved gently on to the sand and they stepped out. The sand was hard and crisp under the feet: the dune was naked save for a thick black post that stood up, like a finger in the moonlight. They walked over the dune and stood on the farther side. The sea was stronger here, coming in fiercely and drawing back with a powerful grating reluctance. They stood together looking out.

'I will not have you play with this Jacobite folly,' Francis said suddenly. 'Understand me in this. You are a child – your uncle is an old dreamer and babbles of Queen Anne.'

David straightened his shoulders. 'I have played with no Jacobite folly,' he said. 'I have only spoken of it once and that for a brief while.'

Francis felt the new tone in the boy's voice. 'You had some fine intimate confidences with your uncle,' he said scornfully. 'I should have remembered that he has a way with young men. Had I remembered I would not have brought you.'

In each of them anger was rising; their isolation, thus standing quite alone in a bare world that was all moonlight and water, increased their sense of opposition.

David said coldly: 'I am no child, Father, any longer. I must have my own judgement. My uncle is a generous host. Today you have left him all afternoon and he has not seen you for six years.'

His father turned to him passionately. 'And so the babe has grown . . . By Christ, I'll sit meekly by and have my son read me a lesson. Has the hair grown above your belly yet, and how many women are with child by you?'

David stood his ground, but strange old fears, born of whippings and terrors and childish nightmares, crowded over the sand-dune and caught at his feet. 'I am on the edge of manhood and you should know it. I have been child to you long enough. If I find my uncle careworthy I have a right to care for him. It is time when I must think for myself. I love you, Father, as I love no one else alive. There is a bond between us, and, I suppose, will always be, that we can have with none other. You have often recognized it. But I am my own man. I have my own life to carry, and yield my liberty to no one—'

Francis laughed. 'Your liberty – who constrains it? You speak bravely of love, but there is also a word duty. When I say bend you shall bend. When I command you shall go. No doubt but your uncle's flattering enlarges you – but not with me . . . come here.'

David came close to him. Francis caught his cheek and pinched it. 'You are mine, my fine son – strip now. Here, under this moon. I will run you naked into the sea – cold bathing for a rebellious son. That shall cool thy Jacobite notions. Strip then.'

'I will not,' David said. He was trembling from head to foot, but neither with chill nor with fear.

'You will not? . . . Better for thee far to obey. Strip – naked as you were born.'

'I will not,' David said again.

Francis had in his hand a small cane with gold-stamped head. He raised it and struck David across the cheek with it. David caught it, flinging it far into the sea.

They stood staring the one at the other.

'That – never again,' David said quietly. The moonlight showed the red weal from his eye to his mouth – 'The last time . . .'

Francis stayed without a word. Then he turned and walked away across the sand.

David stood there looking at the red ring around the moon, knowing that something fundamental that would affect all his life had occurred. He had the quality of common sense in melo-drama; the unreality of any scene did not lead himself to unreality. This was unreal, the desolate sand, the crazy moon red-ringed, the mildewed sea, his father's assault, his own action – all unreal and yet at their heart a real and true fact, that he was child no longer.

He waited: he was sure that his father would return and that then, perhaps, they would be companions as they had never been before. His father did return, slowly coming across the sand, his figure thin and hard in the soft moonlight.

When he was near David went up to him, holding out his hand and smiling. 'You must know for yourself,' he said, 'that the water is too cold. And for your cane you shall have another.'

Francis caught him, gripped his shoulder, then stood close, his hand against his wounded cheek.

'You are a boy no longer. You are right in that. But I have been jealous today, suffering torture for you.

'Always I have been judged to lose anything where I put value, and to catch to me closer than a flea anything that was worth-less.

'For years I have been prepared for you to go like the rest. When you were a baby I would watch and say, "Now, in a moment his eyes will change. He will know me for a rogue." And then, as one accident after another passed and still you were the same, I would say, "He is only a child. He hasn't heard. He hasn't years enough to understand." When my temper or my lust has driven me I have thought, "This will take him away the sooner," and I have almost wished for that, because my dread of losing you would be the earlier satiated. And now, today, watch-ing your happiness with your uncle, I went out so that he should tell you everything – how as a child I did this and as a youth that, this way a rogue, that way a villain.

'I thought, "When I return he will know me for what I am, and our time together will be over. Then everything and every-one will have gone from me and I need fear no more."

'And I came in and saw his arm about your neck and hated you, loving you never so dearly as then. Never so dearly – save now.'

He broke off, then drawing David closer to him, waved his hand at the moon. 'The red ring – so it was when I ruffled my first girl, twelve years of age as I was, in a hay-loft.' Then he

turned David towards him and looked at him: 'One day you will
go from me – but not yet.'

David, smiling, said:

'Why should I ever leave you? I have no light sentiment about
persons. You and Deborah I could never leave. You have told
me,' he went on, hesitating a little, 'that I have no imagination
nor fancy. I think that is true. I see what is before me and only
that. But I am the easier faithful. I have noticed that those who
have much fancy are but rarely steadfast. But this I know. Were
I made more cleverly I would be of less enduring service to
you.'

He said this with a very grave air, as though he had long been
elderly.

His father answered him: 'There are only nineteen years
between us, and as time goes they will lessen. Soon we shall be of
an age: then you will pass me and be old before I am weaned.
But remember this,' he touched the boy's arm lightly, almost
withdrawing from him, 'whatever others say, I have it in me to
be faithful – only as yet I have found neither cause nor person
nor quality fit for that fidelity. I say this with no arrogance. I
know what I am, and that is no fine thing. Nor do I say that with
modesty. God may answer, if He is, for it is He that has made a
man in a mouldy broken image of a divine ambition . . . But
always with us Herries there have been one or two who see
farther than they can reach and hope for more than they shall
ever get.

'Their place is to break up that pattern formed so beautifully
by such as your dear Uncle Pomfret. So the strife goes on, and
will always go between the marred angels and the belly-filling
citizens who have their fine houses and thank God they are not
as others.

'The Herries have always been thus, and will always be, so
making a fine study for your social observer.

'But I can dream of beauty, and if one day it is put in my
hand . . .'

He broke off. 'What I would say,' he added, kicking the sand
with his shoe, 'is that crab-apples are deceiving when they shine
in moonlight, and the taste is stale.'

Then, almost passionately, he cried:

'Ah, but stay by me, David. I am going the wrong way, and
what matters it? It is only another man lost. But one day I may
be faithful to something, and then I would have you witness of
it.'

David, who only saw the principal fact, that his father needed him, answered, as Ruth once answered:

'I will never leave you.'

His father, looking at him ironically, said:

'Your imagination saves you, Davy. That you have none, I mean. But you have made a vow here. I must have something for the loss of my gold cane.'

And then, the wind once more rising, whipping up the waves, they turned back across the sand.

CHRISTMAS FEAST

THE DECEMBER weeks that winter of 1737 were wonderful. Frost held the valley: Derwentwater Lake was frozen from end to end for thirteen days; the hills were powdered with thin patterns of snow hardening to crystal under a blue sky.

The valley was now truly enclosed. The outer world did not exist for it. The autumnal rains had been very violent, and, after them, Borrowdale barred its door.

The Herries family itself took the fashion. Even Mary deserted her Keswick cousins. As Christmas approached they were all caught into the general eagerness. In every house in the valley such a baking and brewing was going on as the Herries children had never seen in their Doncaster days. And the materials for this were all self-provided. No going into Keswick for town provisions. The valley was sufficient for itself. Down the path below Herries the Statesman Peel would be striding, his hands in huge home-made mittens, his jacket buttoned up to his chin, passing his dairymaid who, with her piggin in her hand, was hurrying to the cow-house, relishing the warmth and smell of the cows after the bitter cold that descends from the snowy hills; the boys sliding on the little pond beyond Herries in their wooden clogs, the blue sky, the snowy hills over all, the Wise Man with the pink ribbons to his moleskin hat moving up the road to Seathwaite, witches hiding, no doubt, in the Glaramara caves, the Devil warm at a farmhouse fire with his pedlar's pack, and all the wives and daughters washing, baking, churning; the puddings and pies will be enough for all Cumberland.

As Christmas approached more nearly David became uneasy and restless. It may have been that there was something ominous

for him in the strange isolation of this valley. It was not that he
was dull; every moment of the day seemed to be filled. He was
now friend to all the valley. Whatever they might feel about his
father there was no differing opinion about himself. His handsome looks and splendid body (he promised to be a giant both in
breadth and height; he was already as tall as his father), his
courage, openness and sincerity, the absence of all conceit and
social arrogance, his simplicity, a certain animal lack of subtlety,
his kindliness of heart and warmth of feeling – here promised to
be a man of no ordinary colour, and everyone realized it. He had
that greatest of all powers – he loved his fellows without being
conscious that he loved them. Had he been a little less simple he
might have seen them more justly, but in the end have judged
them more untruly.

With all its simplicity, his character, as it was developing, was
not uninteresting. His fearlessness, honesty and warmth of heart
gave even his smallest adventures a richness of colour. He was of
the race around whom legends grow: already people told stories
of his strength, of how he had bent an iron bar in Peel's kitchen,
beaten a shepherd from Watendlath, and whacked a Seathwaite
farmer at singlestick and he champion of the valley – small
stories, but he was already talked of beyond Bassenthwaite and
over Buttermere and Loweswater. Borrowdale was the proudest
of all the valleys and the stickiest to foreigners, but its natives
already showed signs of adopting young Herries. Young Herries,
but no other of the Herries family. It was possibly of this that
David was subtly aware, partly this that roused his uneasiness.

It seemed to him that this valley had entrapped them. He was
not sorry to be entrapped – he was happier here than he had ever
been anywhere – but the sense that they were caught and held
roused his fear. It was the only fear that life perhaps could give
him – the fear of confinement – and now not so much for himself
as for his father. He was growing now to be a man and ever since
that night at Ravenglass he had been on shoulder-level with his
father. His father seemed to him more alone than anyone in the
world. No one in the valley was his friend. He was someone of a
different nation from all of them – from his own son as well.

And the valley, because it was at this time almost savage in its
isolation, hated and feared, like all savage things, what was
different from itself. David loved his father now more than he
had ever done, but he understood him less the older he grew, and
feared for him more with every day.

He saw with his own eyes once a small child run from his

father screaming. He did not yet know that the mothers of the valley told their babies that Rogue Herries would eat them if he caught them.

Nearer to David's father than any other man in the valley was Statesman Peel. He was himself a rather isolated man, gigantic in build but silent, keeping to himself. Rendal Peel, his son, David's dearest friend, was frightened of his father and could manage no contact with him. He too was a silent boy, adoring David, following him like a dog.

So there they were this Christmas that was fated to add another legend to the Herries story. Rogue Herries who sold his woman for thirty silver pieces and Rogue Herries who was slashed in the cheek by young Osbaldistone . . . Nothing stands still. The course that the lives of Francis Herries and his son David were to take was largely fashioned that winter.

All England was at this time wrapped in superstition: the Age of Reason was only now stirring in that romantic womb – and no valley in England was more superstitious than this little one of Borrowdale. Perhaps you could not call it superstition, so active a part in daily life did they play, pixies and warlocks, gnomes and little green Johnnies, the Devil and his myriad witches. It was not far back that men of Borrowdale, seeing a red deer on the hills, had thought it a horse with horns and pursued it for a magical twist of the Devil; and the wall to keep in the cuckoo would yet have succeeded had it been but a story higher.

It was unlikely that David, a child of his time, would escape this magic. As he sat now, a week before Christmas, with Deborah before the open fire in the Herries hall and saw the snow swirl like twisting worsted beyond the leaded panes, he felt that they were both held there by a spell – the spell, it might be, of his wicked old ancestor hanging on the panelled wall.

His great shoulders and long legs sprawled beyond his chair; his fair head was thrown back; his eyes, warm in spite of their bright blueness, stared into the black beams above him. Deborah, seated at his feet, looking up at him, thought that she had never seen anyone so splendid.

'Deb, why is it that they hate Father so?'

For how long now had this question been hovering between them!

'There is a separateness about Father.' She stared into the golden cavern that hung, lit with sparks of fire, between the black logs. 'They cannot understand him nor he them.'

'Deb, do you understand him?'

'Yes, I fancy so. He dreams of what life should be and because it falls so far behind his dream he abuses it.'

David let his hand fall on her hair.

'I am no dreamer, but I can see how a man in this life may have ambitions to alter it. I am a poor oaf, Deb. I love every moment of the day. Just to feel the blood in my veins is enough for me. Such a day as yesterday with Rendal on the Gavel when, from the summit, you could look out to the sea like a green shawl and all the tops hushed with snow . . . That's enough for me, Deb. And always will be. I shall never go from here. I shall never do anything in the world . . . I cannot be unhappy like my father.' Then he added, dropping his voice: 'I am afraid for our father.'

And she whispered: 'I also.'

They had never, although their lives had been so intimate, confessed so much to one another, and in their young hearts, courageous and generous, there beat a tremendous impulse of loyalty and protection to him.

They offered their young bodies and their strong souls as shields and bucklers for his protection, whatever he might do or be. No matter how valueless his worth they were his guard and would always be.

Deborah looked up to David and clasped his hand; as they looked at one another that was what they meant. Then they both saw, leaning a little heavily against the windowledge, their mother. Her face was pallid: her hands gripped the wood. She was like a heavy ghost: she had made no sound and her eyes did not move.

'I am unwell,' she suddenly gasped. 'I have a sharp pain at my breast.'

David jumped up and ran to her. He put his arm about her and with his great strength almost carried her up the little stairs to her room. She smiled very faintly as he laid her on the bed.

'The pain is nothing,' then, closing her eyes, she murmured, 'Christ is kind . . . He moves gently . . .' She caught her son's hand. 'Don't tell your father . . . How cold it is in this valley.'

She was better again by Christmas Eve, and was up seated in the hall, watching them dance to the fiddle of old Johnny Shoe-string, whose bow squeaked like a dying hen. That was the happiest evening they had yet had in Borrowdale. The hall was bright, the fire leaping, the candles burning, the floor shining. Wilson had hung three old flags that had been buried in the oak chest, one of crimson with a white cross, one of faded purple and

one of green. Whose flags? From what wars? No one knew. The
holly was thick with red berries that year and hung from the
rafters. They could hear the bells ringing from the Chapel above
the splash and crackle of the fire. Francis was a child, younger
than any. They danced till they sank on the floor with weariness.
Margaret Herries never moved her eyes from her husband.

Next night, Christmas night, they were invited to Statesman
Peel's. It was not as it was in most parts of England where, at
Christmas time, the Squire was the King of the Castle and his
subjects were graciously bidden to enjoy his hospitality with a
proper sense of his grand benignancy and their inferior peasantry.
In Borrowdale every Statesman was master of his own house and
owed allegiance to no one. Every Statesman's house was open on
Christmas night to all the world, rich and poor. There were the
guests, indeed, who had their special places there, but the doors
were wide open to the stars and the line of friendly hills and the
hard-frosted road.

Peel's kitchen this night was a place of splendour. Its warmth
and colour, its happiness and hospitality, stretched to the
farthest heavens. Glaramara and the Gavel looked in at the
windows, the Derwent rolled its waters past the door, and every
star scattered its light over the roof-tree.

There is no house like Peel's house anywhere in England any
more, but, as it stood then, in its life and strength and happiness, it was thus. It was a strong place, secured with strong
doors and gates, its small windows crossed with bars of iron. It
held three rooms on the ground floor and two on the second
storey.

The front door was covered with a low porch, the entrance
from which was called the 'thresh-wood' or threshold, and on this
thresh-wood crossed straws, horseshoes and so on, were laid to
hinder the entrance of witches. From this there was a broad
passage through the house called the 'hallan'; sacks of corn were
deposited here before market-day, pigs were hung after killing,
and there was a shelf over the door where sickles hung and car-
pentry tools were laid.

In Peel's house the hallan opened straight into the 'down-
house'. This was in his case the great common room of the
family, the place of tonight's Christmas Feast. Here, in the
course of the year, everything occurred, baking, brewing,
washing, meals, quarrelling, courting, tale-telling. This down-
house had no second storey but was open to the rafters. In later
days a second storey was often built over the downhouse. The

sides of this room were smeared with clay and cow-dung. Joints
of meat hung dry for winter use. From the smoky dome of the
huge fireplace dropped a black sooty lee called the 'hallan drop'.
Under this the women knitted or spun wool or flax, the men
sometimes carding the wool, the children learning their lessons,
the old men telling their tales. At the opposite end of the passage
was the mill-door and beyond this another passage known as the
'heck', and this heck was terminated by a huge octagonal post.
Into this post sometimes a hole was bored and in it a piece of
cow-hair secured by a wooden peg for the purpose of cleaning
combs, and behind the heck was a bench.

The windows were separated by stone munnions, and here
were the Bible and Prayer Book, *Tom Hickathrift* and Sir
William Stanley's *Garland*.

The chimney wing was spacious. Indeed, this was a really vast
chamber, for it was the 'house' or dwelling-room and 'down-
house' or kitchen thrown into one. Part of it therefore stood for
kitchen with the great chimney and hearth; here, on the heap of
wood ashes, was the 'handreth', an iron tripod on which was
placed the 'girdle' for baking oat-bread. Before the fire stood a
spit. The two standards, which were three feet high with seven
hooks, were hinged, so that they could be folded and put away
when not in use. The spit, a slender rod, was six feet in length,
and on the rod were two pairs of prongs to hold the meat, and
beneath it a dripping-pan. There was a handmill or 'quern', a
malt mill, a spindle and a 'whorl', a spinning wheel. In the
chimney wing were hung hams and sides of bacon and beef, and
near the fire-window was an ingle-seat, comfortable most of the
year save when the rain or snow poured down on to the hearth,
as the chimney was quite unprotected and you could look up it
and see the sky above you. Such was the kitchen end of the
room. The floor tonight was cleared for the dancing, but at the
opposite end trestle tables were ranged for the feasting. Here was
also a large oak cupboard with handsomely carved doors. This
held the bread, bread made of oatmeal and water. On the mantel
and cupboard there were rushlight holders and brass candlesticks. In other parts of the room were big standard holders for
rushlights.

All these tonight were brilliantly lit and blew in great gusts in
the wind.

Francis Herries, arriving with his children, David, Mary and
Deborah, found that already everything was in a whirl. Peel himself greeted them magnificently, standing his six foot four,

splendid in his dark coat of native fleece and buckskin breeches, and Mrs Peel, stout, very red of face, in russet, all the little Peels (and there were very many) gathered together behind her.

Many were already dancing. It was a scene of brilliant colour with the blazing fire, the red berries of the holly glowing in every corner, old Johnny Shoestring in bright blue breeches and with silver buckles to his shoes perched on a high stool fiddling for his life, the brass gleaming, faces shining, the stamp of the shoon, the screaming of the fiddle, the clap-clap of the hands as the turns were made in the dance – and beyond the heat and the light the dark form of the valley lying in breathless stillness, its face stroked by the fall of lingering reluctant snow.

After the first greeting the Herries family stood quietly by the wall. Fragments of talk, slow cautious words like the repetition of some magic recipe, circled the light.

'Hoo ayre ye today? Hey ye hard ony news? . . .'

'Ye say reet, nowt se sartain. Gud day. Ayre ye all weel at heam? . . .'

'Aye, they said she was worth brass . . .'

'Whya, he's nobbut read about it; what can he knaw? I sud think if he minds his awn job it'll be as weel.'

Peel came and asked Francis Herries to sit by him. His elder girl took Mary and Deborah. David found Rendal.

Francis had come with some of the gaiety and happiness of the preceding night and, as always when he was happy, it seemed to shine in him. He was dressed simply tonight in a suit of grey and silver; although in these last years he had stoutened and broadened he was still handsome beyond all ordinary men. His charm, when he was charming, was so gracious and natural that it won everyone near him.

From the moment of his entering every eye had been upon him. To these people of the valley, although they had talked for months of his wickedness, cruelty, and the strange mystery that led him to isolate himself in this loneliness, he was yet at sight something miraculous and magnificent beyond belief. He was the Dark Angel of their secret dreams.

Romantic – but to himself he was not romantic. As he sat there beside Peel, he could feel the old devilish struggle beginning in him. Partly this was an evening after his heart. He cared nothing for class – all the world was his fellow. He liked to see this common happiness; he could feel in this little, hot, sweating, smelly world all the animal satisfaction that had no ill in it.

He would set them all, had he his way, eating, drinking,

fornicating, singing – the whole world singing over its surfeited belly – and mingled with this a tenderness, a kind of familiar protection so that he could love these owl faces, these humped bodies, these spindle legs for their little homely tragedies and satisfactions.

> So go we all
> Down the dark path,
> Alien, to the friendly tomb.

This sense of common luck with the veriest hind was something that had always separated him from Pomfret, Harcourt and the rest – yes, and from his own children.

Tonight he could feel it to the full as the rushlights scattered streams of light in the wind and the smell of unwashen bodies, perspiring chaps, dogs' offal, burning wood and cooking meat gathered in the air, and all the faces turning in the middle of the room, dilated with the music and the movement – dog faces, horse faces, pig faces, bird faces – but gathering an extra humanity as they felt happiness encouraging them and leading them on to confidence.

He would jump down and share this with them, the drink and the food and the tousling the girls. But he was alone. He could share nothing with anyone. His touch was enough; at the feel of it everything withdrew. Within the heart of the burning candle he was isolated; at its core it was ice. He was ringed with flame and could not get out.

He looked at Peel whom he liked, his big body set back, his broad face spread in laughter: he looked at David whom he loved, moving into the middle of the room crowded now with faces. No one was alone save himself, and he by his own mysterious fault. He was well aware by now of how suspicious they were of him.

This suspicion had blown like a subtle poison through the valley. What had he done to create it? Been drunk once or twice, kissed a girl or two, lost his temper on an occasion – nothing definite save that foolish affair with Alice Press . . . She had spoken truly. Since that day he had never been rid of her.

But he knew well that it was no positive deed on his part that had separated him. It was something in his spirit. They suspected that battle that was never still in himself, disgust fighting with longing, lechery with an icy purity, a driving dream with sodden reality, the devil in him that would never leave him alone, try as he would to throttle it with self-contempt, irony and the discipline of his impulses.

Sitting now beside Peel he envied that great healthy body, that steady mind, that serene soul, and even as he envied knew that this very thought was separating him, driving him into loneliness and this bitter isolation.

The door would open and the snow blow through in little impatient gusts and all the valley would pour in with it. The room was crowded now against the wall and in the corners. The ale was passing round, and voices were loud and laughter ferocious. But everyone behaved in seemly fashion: a dignity, that seemed to radiate from the grand figure and quiet hospitality of the host himself, pervaded the place. Only – as Francis Herries could feel – he could sniff it in the air – there was a kind of madness behind the dignity, something that belonged to the witches and old crippled warlocks, to the naked shapes playing under the stars above Seatoller, to the broomsticks flying dimly like thin clouds towards the moon.

Suddenly there was a cry: 'They coom. They're here.' It was the 'Play-Jigg'. This was the drama in verse played by the actors who, tonight, were passing from Statesman's house to Statesman's house.

Johnny Shoestring ceased his playing, the dancers vanished, the centre of the room was clear. Packed against the walls now were bodies and faces, legs and backs. There was whispering and tittering, but quite clearly in the immediate silence could be heard the hiss of the snow hovering down through the open chimney on to the fire.

They came forward. Francis was amused as he saw that the Master of these Ceremonies was his old friend the pedlar, David's Devil. Very roguish he was tonight in a cocked purple hat and purple tights showing his thin, spidery limbs, his face with its crooked ironic smile, and his black shining eyes.

He introduced his little company, Old Giles, a bent old man with a long chin, Pinch, a clown, a stout and jolly fellow, a husband and a wife, and young Go-to-Bed who at once in a high, shrill treble introduced himself:

> 'My father is old and decrepit,
> My mother deceased of late,
> And I am a youth that's respected,
> Possessed of a good estate.'

The old couple did a little dance of joy at this, and then Pinch the clown came forward and asked young Go-to-Bed if he wanted to increase his fortune. Of course young Go-to-Bed was eager, so Pinch introduced him to Old Giles, who said he would show him how to make money out of nothing. This young Go-to-Bed was delighted to know, so Old Giles told him that he must have his arse kicked a dozen times by friend Pinch, and then he must put his head in a bucket of water and then must sit up a night alone in a churchyard: all these things young Go-to-Bed performed to the infinite delight of the audience, especially in the churchyard when Pinch, dressed as a painful ghost, emptied a sack of flour over young Go-to-Bed and set the dogs on to him.

The 'Jigg' ended in a grand dance and in this the audience soon joined. Go-to-Bed, his face white with flour, led off with Mrs Peel, and Peel took the Old Lady, and soon all the room was turning to Johnny Shoestring's music.

Still Francis Herries did not move. He was alone on the raised seat near the fire-window. All his children were dancing; even Mary now had forgotten her superior airs and breeding and was smiling at young Curtis, son of a Newlands Statesman. The pedlar came across to Francis.

'Good day.'

'Good day,' said Francis.

'You are not dancing, sir.'

'In my own time,' said Francis.

The pedlar stood there smoothing his hands down the sides of his legs with a look of infinite satisfaction.

'It is very cold up at the valley end,' the pedlar said, 'but the moonlight warms the air. Leave this and take a walk with me.'

Herries felt an impulse to go. The thought of the cold, the black ridge of the hills, and the sky silver-thickened, the freshness, the icy air, was fiercely attractive. His dream – the splendid horse breasting the dark lake under the icy spears – seemed to penetrate the very heart of the thickly smelling, heated room. Close to him the hams and the dried beef swung ever so slightly in the great chimney. A country girl mopped her sweating brow. Beyond the fire-window he fancied that he could hear a cow, desolate in the dark field, lowing for its calf, but of course there would be no cow outside at Christmas. He was about to say that he would go when the pedlar touched his arm.

'Here are strangers,' he said, pointing with his long white finger.

Francis Herries followed his direction and saw pressed near

the door at the hallan end a man and a woman and a child. The
man was rough, bony, with long black hair that tumbled on to
his shoulders, the woman white-faced, crouching a little as
though she feared a blow, and pressed against her dress was a
very young child. It was the child that held Herries's notice. She
could not have been above seven or eight years of age, her face so
white that it might have been blanched by moonlight. But it was
her hair that was astonishing. She was wearing a little peaked
man's cap of grey with a russet feather in it and under this her
hair fell almost to her tiny waist. Its colour was flame. Flame.
Francis, incredulously smiling at his interest, repeated the word.
Flame. As though her head were on fire. Flame smouldering,
with a sudden movement of her little shoulders glancing in
coloured shadow as though it were alive. It sank into darkness as
fire does, then lifted into amber and rolled about her head in
smoky sombre red. She pressed farther back against her mother,
and the flame seemed to creep across the dress, to move, to stir,
then to lie there, idly licking the dull stuff.

Between this fire the little face looked out, the face of a tired
baby, weary, scornful, ironically interested and alone.

'I have never seen such hair,' Herries said, as though to himself.

'Come and burn your hand in it,' said the pedlar.

Herries got up and looked about him. The brightness of that
baby's hair seemed to have dimmed and hushed the room. The
candlelight was smoked, the voices, the laughter, the trampling
of feet shut away behind glass. Herries followed the pedlar
across the floor. As they approached the man frowned and
drew his body together animal fashion. He was all animal,
he smelt animal, looking out with sharp suspicious eyes from
his shaggy black hair. The woman did not move, but looked
up at Herries. The pedlar smiled at her: 'Hey, Jane Starr,' he
said.

Then the woman spoke to Herries: he was astonished at her
voice, which was soft and musical and without any real accent.

'You have forgot me, sir.'

He smiled down at the child. 'I fear that I have.'

'Once you gave me your coat,' she said softly, staring into his
eyes. So that was it! The morning of the day that was to prove so
eventful to him, the morning of the Chinese Fair. The tang of
that walk came back to him, his happiness, the freshness, the
waterfall clinging like a ladder to the rock, the dead man, the
patient woman.

'You were welcome to it,' he said, looking at her for the first time. Her face was not comely. White and weary, but there was strength and courage in it.

'And this is your child?' he asked.

'My child,' the woman answered. But the man made no movement, only stared moodily into the whirling room. It was strange that her voice was so soft yet came clearly through all the racket and din of voices, music and stamping feet.

'Of what age is she?'

'Eight,' the woman answered.

Eight! – and so independent and alone in this jostling cruel world. He thirty-seven, and yet already there was some kinship between them . . .

'What is her name?'

'Mirabell,' and then after a little pause with a quick glance at the man beside her – 'Mirabell Starr.'

Mirabell Starr – so he heard for the first time the name that would never leave his consciousness again. He could be very sweet with children. He squatted on his hams, his silver sword trailing on the floor. He put out his strong hand and took her tiny one.

'Mirabell. That is a man's name, you know . . . Shall we be friends?'

Her strange grey eyes, shining with deep lights, regarded him very gravely. She sighed, then very indifferently answered:

'If my mother wishes.'

Her voice was low, sweet and distant, a little as though it were caught in the echo of a shell. He was charmed with it. Squatting a little lower he put out his arm and drew her in to him, pressing her gently between his knees. The silver thread on his sleeve rubbed her neck, but she did not draw back. Nor did she come to him of her own will.

'Where do you live, my pretty?'

'I live with my mother.'

'And where is that?'

The woman spoke.

'We are from Ennerdale, sir.'

'Ah, from Ennerdale.'

At last, drawing a little breath as though he foretold the emotion that it would give him, he put up his hand and stroked her hair: it seemed that a wave of pleasure passed through his body. Its texture was infinitely soft and lay against the back of his hand like music.

'How come you here? You should be at home on Christmas night.'

The man spoke for the first time. 'We have no settled place. I am a horse-dealer.' His voice was rough and very ungracious, but it had no tang of the North.

Herries caught the child closer. Her head was almost against his breast, and it was as though his heart leapt towards it to greet it. He felt in his pocket and found a charm, a Negro's head in gold with ruby eyes – it was a charm against the ague.

'Will you take this from me – a Christmas gift?' he asked.

For a moment, to steady herself, she laid one tiny hand on his thigh while with the other she took the little Negro. A thrill of happiness ran through him. She looked at the charm very gravely.

''Tis against the ague,' he told her. 'You will not catch it an you keep this with you.'

She looked up at her mother, then at the man.

'It is very pretty,' she said. 'I thank you.' But although her expression was that of a grown woman her fingers tightened round it as a baby's would.

He kissed her forehead, then straightened himself to his full height.

'I wish you good day,' he said, bowing to the woman very slightly, then turned and walked into the room. He turned confusedly like a man in a dream. For a while he could not see the room clearly. Strange coincidence! That this should be the woman whom carelessly that morning he had for a moment protected! What had been her history? Who was the dead man, who now this present animal, this horse-dealer, horse-thief he did not doubt? She did not look a woman who would pass lightly from man to man – but what did she at all in that company? Mirabell . . . Mirabell . . . So the child was called. Poor little misery, already bearing in her eyes the knowledge of hardship, cruelty, aloneness. What a life must she have with such a man and his company! Almost he was tempted to turn aside, go back and make some mad demand for the child's protection. A nice affair – to be mixed in such a throng! As though there were not already scandal enough. But he looked back nevertheless. There was no sign of them. They were hidden by the dancers. The Christmas Feast was at its height.

This was a scene from Breughel. The trestle tables were piled with food, pies and puddings, hams and sides of beef. The drink was for the most part ale, but there was creeping into the valley now that new destroying devil of the English countryside, the demon gin. There were signs of it here tonight – men were pressing the girls now, their faces flushed, their hands fumbling for breast and side. The women were giggling, the dogs snapping at food and legs and one another. An old man with long white hair, thin as a scarecrow, was dancing very solemnly alone in the middle of the floor, twisting his body into corkscrew shapes. At a table near the chimney a group of old people were playing at cards. But wildness was coming in, coming in from the caverns of the hill, and the high, cold spaces round Sprinkling Tarn and the lonely passes above the listening valleys. It was Christ's Day no longer. He had been turned out when the wind had changed, and all the doors and shutters of the house had rattled their shoulders at His going.

Peel himself felt perhaps that his hand was losing its hold on the scene. And perhaps he did not care. He was a man of his time, and that was a rough time, a cruel and a coarse. They had a small, wild, starving dog, strayed in from the valley, and they had tied him to the leg of a table, and were holding meat just beyond his nose, while he yelped in his agony of hunger, and his little fierce protesting eyes darted wildly about the room.

Up in the half-darkness of the hallan one of the shepherds was stripping to a whispering group of men and girls to show his tattooed body, made when he was in the Indies as a boy, marvellous, they say, a whole love-story on his legs and back. Although the night was bitter, couples twined closely together wandered out of the house up the road, kissing to the eternal murmur of the running water.

Then the house-door burst wide and a strange crew broke into the room. They came shouting, singing and very drunk. Their shoulders were powdered with snow, and their frosty breath blew in clouds about them. This was a party that had ridden over from Keswick and Portinscale and Grange, had found their way under the moon to Rosthwaite, and now, drinking at every stage, were turning back again (an they were sober enough to ride) to Keswick. Here was the Lord of Misrule and his followers, a young fellow with very flushed face, a crown awry on his crooked wig, his clothes of purple satin and gold, carried on the shoulders of four half-naked men blacked like Indians and followed by a motley baggage-heap dressed fantastically as jesters, Chinamen and clowns. There was a Hobby-horse and old Father Neptune with his trident. They burst the doors, then paused to arrange their procession. The naked

Indians threw off their cloaks in which they had been wrapped against the cold, caught up their young Lord of Misrule and shouldered him, and so marched up the room, followed by the Jester with his bauble, a lady with a flaxen wig and very naked bosom, Neptune and a posturing, shouting throng.

The natives of the valley drew back against the wall. Here were foreigners from the town, and though their intrusion was no new thing at a Christmas time, yet it boded no good. It had ended before in a bloody riot and so might do again. Francis had been looking for his children, and finding them had bidden David take his sisters home, then, if he would, return. So he was once again alone, a great stillness in his heart in the midst of the riot, once or twice looking to see whether he could catch sight of the child and her mother: it seemed that they were gone.

Watching this new invasion he found that he recognized three at least of the company, two from Keswick. The Lord of Misrule himself was young Cuthbertson, son of a wealthy merchant; one of the black men young Fawcett, a Squire's eldest boy; and the Jester himself with his cap and bells Osbaldistone from Threapthwaite, near Whitehaven. Young Osbaldistone was often at Keswick, and Herries had been with him at cards and cock-fighting. There was no love between them. Herries had won his money, which the young fool could ill afford to lose, and Herries had kissed a girl that Osbaldistone had also been pursuing.

At the sight of him a spasm of revolt and disgust caught his heart. He had drunk nothing: he had been moved tonight by the courteous friendliness of Peel, by the happy simplicity of the earlier part of the evening, and, at this last, by his meeting with the child. Apart and reserved as he seemed standing there alone, yet his heart had been filled with kindliness and an almost child-like desire to be friends with the world.

At the sight of this rabble he was tempted to slip away and find his bed. Had he gone, the whole course of his life would have been other. Nevertheless our lives are dictated by character, not by chance. Some foolish pride kept him. He fancied that from the corner by the fire-window the pedlar sardonically watched him. It was true that many eyes were on him, as they had been all the evening; so, because he had some conceit and felt a challenge in the air, he stayed.

Events followed then with dreamlike swiftness. Afterwards if he ever looked back to this night it seemed to him that he had from the very first been trapped. He could not have escaped; he did not pity himself for this (in all his life-history from the first page to the last there was no self-pity), but he did ask himself whether he could have avoided the event: he could not.

The procession settled itself about its Lord: drink was brought: there was much sham ceremony: subjects knelt and sentences were passed; the lady in cloth of gold with the naked bosom was proclaimed Queen. The peasants stood around, mouths agape, the little wild dog, who had been forgotten, yelped dismally, then broke his rope, crawled to a corner where he feasted ravenously. Everyone was at ease again. Dancing took the floor. Figures, fantastic, painted in orange and scarlet and purple, laughing, singing, kissing, whirled and turned; some fell upon the floor and lay there. Still in the farther corner the old people, like characters painted on the wall, played gravely their cards.

Young Osbaldistone, his cap awry, the laced waistcoat unbuttoned, pursued a girl and encountered Herries. He stopped short.

Herries gravely bowed. Osbaldistone looked. The drink cleared from his eyes. He straightened himself. He was a cold-tempered, severe lad in his natural life, debauched enough but ready at any moment to clear debauchery from his system. He stood back fumbling the hilt of his sword.

'Mr Francis Herries.'

'Mr Richard Osbaldistone.'

He yet stuttered a little. The drink was not all cleared. 'Dick to my friends,' then added softly, 'but not to you, Mr Herries.'

No one heard him. Herries frowned. He did not want a quarrel with the boy here, not tonight, Christmas night, and in Peel's house. He bowed.

'I wish you good evening,' he said and turned.

Osbaldistone touched his shoulder. Herries, turning back, was amazed at the hatred that formed and edged the other's face like a mask. To hate him like that! And for what? For nothing – a loss at cards, a girl's kiss. No – for what he himself in his very spirit was. And at the consciousness of that his heart sank and his anger grew.

'You will not wish me good evening,' Osbaldistone said. 'I will have no good evening from you. Since our meeting of last week I have been determined on a word with you. You are a cheat, Mr Herries, a liar and – it may be – a coward. For the last we will see.'

Then he raised his hand and struck Herries's cheek. Miraculously, this, too, no one saw. It gave the dreaminess of this strange hour an added colour – the shrill, discordant music of the violin, the thick steaming air, the great chimney with its smoky fire, the figures confused in colour, unreal in chin and eye and limb, the movement striving, it seemed, to make significant pattern – and yet Herries quite alone in a frozen place with this boy who hated him.

But no man had ever struck him and had no answer. He frowned sternly on young Osbaldistone, who was breathing now fiercely as though driven by some terrific emotion.

'Not here,' he said quietly. 'There is a green behind the house. The moon is bright. I will join you there in an instant. But take care; we must go separately. My host tonight is my friend.'

At once, again as in a dream, young Osbaldistone had disappeared. Herries looked about him. Oh! how desperately he did not wish this to happen! It was from no fear for himself. But he seemed to be haunted tonight by the past; something was pulling him back into that other life that he had abandoned; something would not let him escape.

But he must find a second. It must be, if possible, someone not from Keswick. The less that this was known . . . He turned towards the door and saw the pedlar standing against the wall, smiling ironically and stroking his thighs with his hands.

'You can do me a service,' Herries said. The pedlar followed him out. The moon was full. No snow was falling.

Against the green behind the house everything was marked as though it had been cut from black paper, the ridge of hill, the roof-line, the thick wall of jagged stones.

Osbaldistone was waiting there and Fawcett, a stout, plump youth, absurd with his blackened face and thick cloak heavily furred. He came to Herries.

'For God's sake, Mr Herries, this must be avoided . . .' His teeth were chattering.

'Too damned cold for talk,' said Osbaldistone.

They spoke in whispers.

'If Mr Osbaldistone will apologize for his insult,' said Herries.

'I will not,' said Osbaldistone.

They faced one another: every detail in the scene was clear under the moon. It was indeed bitterly cold. The frost seemed to creep upon the flat stones that lay about the field. Herries was aware of the tiniest details and would remember them all his days. A snail-track glittered in crystal on the farm wall behind him; a little wind ran over the grass, fluttering the light snow that lay loosely on the ground, and on the path beyond the field he could see the moonlight shine on the ice that the cold was forming on the little pools.

They advanced. At once he knew that Osbaldistone was no swordsman – and a moment later Osbaldistone knew it too. Again the thought tapped Herries's heart: 'How he must hate me to run this crazy risk!' and again 'Why?' In another moment or two he was aware of the sword's instinct, something much more deadly and determined than his own. He could never strike another's weapon with his and not feel that separate aliveness in his blade, as though it said: 'You have called me out. You have liberated me. Now I am my own master.' And now he was very curiously aware that he must restrain this creature, use all his force and power, otherwise the boy would be hurt. But as they parried and struck and parried again a warmth of companionship with his sword swelled in his throat as though it had said to him: 'Come. We are comrades now. We march together. You wouldn't desert me when you have brought me so far.'

His pride in his accomplishment grew in him. His body grew warm, taut, eager. He forgot his opponent, felt only the moon shining above that cold field, the splendid panoply of stars exulting in his skill.

He had the boy utterly at his mercy, and, at the same moment, the boy's face swung down to him as though it had been lowered from a height. He gazed into it and saw terror there, the certain expectation of instant death.

Death. Yes, one more link in the ridiculous binding chain. This time at least he would be master of his fortune.

He lowered his blade and stepped back. An instant later Osbaldistone's sword had carved his right cheek in two, a deep riven cut from temple to chin.

His face was flooded with blood. Dropping his sword, the field whirring about his ears like a top, he sank to his knee.

He heard young Fawcett cry 'Enough . . .' and a word about honour, then the frosted stones leapt up and hit him into darkness. But before he sank he felt the pedlar's hand on his arm.

DEATH OF MARGARET HERRIES

DEBORAH FOUND her way one March afternoon through Stonethwaite Valley home.

She had been as far as the Stake Pass, turned back, stayed where the waterfall tumbles over the rocks before the Grasmere turning, looked up at the quiet hills lying against the quiet sky, then down again to the tumbling stream that spread fanwise over the white stones shining in the sun under the water.

Spring was so late here that hardly yet were there signs of it, but Deborah saw every bud and smiled at every pushing green. The spirit of spring was in the faint rain-washed blue of the sky, the purple shadow that hung intangibly about the branches and the pale primrose sunlight that fell in white patterns on rock and stone. The air was cold and snow streaked even the lowest hills.

She was a very slight and lonely child as she walked over the green turf that here in this valley was like the ancient lawns of noble families, so smooth it was and deep. She would soon be fifteen, but children in those years were almost women at fifteen. And she had had much to make her mature. Since her mother had fallen so ill this Christmas, since Mary had grown so proud and was so often with her cousins in Keswick, all the duties of the house had fallen on to Deborah. She was hurrying now for fear of what might have happened while she was away. All last night she had sat with her mother, fighting a thousand terrors, her mother's strange ceaseless talk, the house that was never still, the calling of the owls, but worst of all the anticipated presence of old Mrs Wilson the witch. Since her mother was ill Mrs Wilson had been for ever appearing, now here, now there. She spoke little, but at first had offered again and again her remedies. Deborah could hear her now in her odd, croaking voice pressing her herbs, her spells, her incantations. Deb had from the very first been terrified by the old woman, but against her will she had been forced to realize that there was something pathetic and something kind in the old wrinkled face, the little eyes almost hidden by the brown lids, but now anxious and be-seeching like an animal's. The old snuff-nosed, wrinkled-faced Doctor Absom, their only resource, once a fine doctor in Carlisle but reduced by liquor to a peddling house-to-house livelihood, had soon stopped her solicitings. He had threatened her in so many words with the gaol for a witch. She had not spoken again after that, but she was always, night and day, hovering there. It seemed, so her son said, that she had formed some affection for Margaret Herries. He said, almost apologetically, that he had never known her take to anyone before as she took to Mistress Herries; and Deborah, walking now in her cold green valley, seemed still to be haunted by her presence, and, against her fear, something forced her to wonder whether after all Mrs Wilson's magic might not be of more value than the old doctor's dirty ministrations, he never sober, stinking of snuff, and with bleeding ever his principal remedy.

Poor Margaret! She had been bled enough. There was no more blood left in her. She was dying. Nothing could save her.

The stroke that had slashed her husband's face had struck her down. He had made nothing of it. His face was bound. He had called it a scratch, but from the first instant she had seen deeper than this, had known that here was something predestined.

Child though she was, Deborah had marvellously understood her mother's longing. She was perhaps the only living soul in the world to understand what her mother's love for her father was, how for years she had been praying the God in whom she believed to give her opportunity to show that love without foolishness. Now it might be that the moment had come, and she was too weak to offer it. Not that Herries gave her opportunity: he would have no pity, no tenderness, no allusion to the event. No one spoke to him of it. Everyone pretended that nothing had occurred.

But Deborah knew how her mother ached over him as though he were a child bullied at school and the agony that it was to her, far surpassing her bodily pain, that she could say nothing. She rose to great heights of character in these last days.

But for Deborah life had never yet been so threatening. How would it be when her mother was gone and she alone with her father? Again and again she tried to beat down her fear of him, but it seemed to be something in her very veins. There was David. Had there not been David she might have turned and run back, over the Stake Pass to Langdale and Grasmere, wandered the world and never returned. So long as David was there she could endure any test, but would he always be there? Anyone as wonderful as he must be caught into the outside world. They would call for, shout for him! And then . . . as the light fell and she thought of the darkening house, her father with the fresh purple scar that ran from temple to mouth, catching up one corner of his lip, of her mother's room, of Mrs Wilson, her white cap, the black stick on which she leaned, she stayed for a moment by the wall of the field and the little chapel looking back to Glaramara, her hand at her throat, her knees trembling.

The thought of David reassured her and she smiled. Where he was no harm could come.

At the turning in of the grassy court two figures made her pause

–two men on horseback. In the fading afternoon light she could not at first tell who they were, then, realizing, amazement stayed her: they were her uncle Pomfret and her cousin Raiseley.

They had but now arrived, for they got from their horses as she came to them (she was pleased indeed to see how clumsy Cousin Raiseley was as he climbed down). Uncle Pomfret greeted her with a confusion of heartiness and embarrassment, which showed that he was in no way at ease over his visit. She curtsied and he kissed her, swimming her in an odour of ale and snuff. He was becoming a mountain of flesh. His belly swung before him. Cousin Raiseley, who was pallid and thin as his father was purple and corpulent, bowed to her gravely. She hated her cousin Raiseley because David did. 'Hey, little lass . . .' (her uncle addressed her as though she were a favourite hound) 'here's your old uncle come all the way through the muck to cheer your poor mother up.' He threw a cautious look around him. 'And your father . . . is he about?' She replied quietly. She did not dislike her uncle. There was something kindly and simple about him. She thought: 'He hates coming . . . It's his good nature.'

David came out to them, and Deborah flushed with pride as she saw his splendid strength beside his pale shambly-kneed cousin. Benjamin was called to care for the horses, and they all went into the house. What deep shame Deborah felt as they climbed the stairs! She knew Raiseley would be seeing everything, sniffing the farm-smells, the dung and the cesspool, hearing the trickling of water, catching the gleam of the damp on the walls, and, as they came into the upper hall, marking down the holes in the furniture, the bareness of the rafters, the tapestry that was never still against the panelling. She hated Raiseley the more because her home was shabby.

In the hall now there were David and Mary. It was Mary, of course, who at once commanded the scene. She flung her arms around her uncle's short, thick neck and kissed his ill-shaven chin, then with a smiling demureness that was beautiful to witness offered her cheek for Raiseley to kiss, which he did with a very pleasant eagerness.

Uncle Pomfret explained with a great many oaths and confused sentences that he and their Aunt Jannice had been distressed indeed to hear of the grave illness of poor Margaret and that Aunt Jannice had sent with him some cures and recipes.

For himself, would it be possible for him to see her?

The room was dark. The evening glow penetrated the little

windows very thinly. Suddenly a figure bearing high two lighted candlesticks appeared on the staircase. It was Francis, his face quivering in the blown flame of the candles. He seemed very tall in that semi-light, in a long, purple dressing-gown, and the scar was leaping on his face.

It might be that Pomfret had not expected that: he stared, his thick legs wide planted, his chin raised. He said afterwards to his wife: "'Twas no man standing there. Someone raised from the dead. The cut lined on his cheek.'

Francis said no word, but came slowly down. Then he placed the candlesticks on the table and holding out his hand said quietly: 'How are you, brother?'

Pomfret began a tumbled and confused explanation, but in a whisper as though he were in church there; finding the whisper arduous, broke into a kind of congested roar, then sank to a whisper again.

Francis nodded his head.

'That was kindly thought . . . Margaret would wish to see you. She is awake – but she is sadly weak.'

He picked up the candles and led the way upstairs again. Pomfret, stepping with his big feet as though on eggs, followed him.

The children, left alone together, were embarrassed. Even Mary, conscious perhaps that the eyes of her brother and sister were upon her, had very little to say. At last Raiseley muttered something about going to see after the horses. He started down the stairs, and David stoutly marched after him. In the dusk, wrapped in the cold air, the two stood stiffly side by side. At last Raiseley, patronage in every word that he uttered, said:

"'Tis isolated here . . . and muck at every step.'

David, anger throbbing in his throat, answered:

'It is no place for soft bodies.'

'Nor for active minds,' Raiseley answered.

'Keswick,' David said with a scornful laugh, 'is scarcely the Athens of the world.' (He thought this a fine phrase and told Deb of it afterwards.)

Raiseley sniffed. He had a maddening habit in this as though he suffered from a perpetual cold.

'I wonder, cousin,' he said, 'that you can endure the mud and rain and nothing but yokels for company. But maybe it suits you.'

'It does,' David answered. 'Better than by your looks Keswick might.'

Raiseley laughed. 'Keswick is no abiding-place. I shall be in London in a six-months.'

'Well,' said David, 'for me you can keep your London. There is air here and space, horses to ride and hills to climb. There is no finer spot in England.'

'I can understand that you would find it so,' Raiseley answered.

The poor white worm – David thought – one crack with the singlestick and he'd go over. One push with the thumb and down he'd be! He hated him with every pulse in his body, but at the heart of the hate there was a sort of wistfulness. He would be clever, Raiseley, and getting a fine education. Already he would know so many things that David would never know.

The darkness fell. Benjamin held a flare. The horses clamped with their hoofs on the grassy stones. The two boys stood without speaking, hating one another. Then the two men came out. They were very quiet. Margaret on her death-bed had brought them closer together than they had ever been or would be. Pomfret's simple heart was deeply touched.

'Poor soul,' he said. 'Poor soul . . .'

'She is a woman of great courage,' Francis said.

'Poor Margaret,' their voices echoed on the night air. Pomfret and his son climbed on to their horses.

'That was kindly of you, brother,' Francis said, and held for a moment Pomfret's hand.

'Come and visit us. There is a bed for thee,' Pomfret answered, bent down and kissed his brother's cheek. Then they rode away, their horses stumbling over the dark track.

Francis went back into the house. From these few whispered words both children had realized that their mother was indeed dying. They stood there close together in the dark courtyard, the wind that had suddenly risen whistling about their heads. Deborah began to cry. She clung to David, who put his arm around her, holding her very close. She was a little hysterical with lack of sleep, too incessant labour, fear of the future.

'Oh, David, I'm frightened. Mother will die and you will go into the world and I shall be left here with Father . . . I don't want to be left . . . I don't want to be left. 'Tis cruel, this valley, when you are alone in it, and there are spirits in the house. The house hates us. There has been no luck for us since we came to it, and I'm weary of the mice and the holes and the shabbiness that will not be cleaned . . . Oh, David, don't leave me here alone . . . Don't leave me!'

She sobbed on his breast and he comforted her. 'Deb, little Deb. There's no fear. I'll not leave you. Mother will be happier gone. She was never rightly settled here and the rain and wind destroyed her. Poor Mother. She will be warm again and comforted if there's a heaven as they say, and if there's none she'll not be aware of it. But, Deborah, you must not fear Father. He's worst with anyone who fears him.

'He will love you an you go to him bravely. He has himself a shyness of spirit. See how happy the three of us will be together – and you are the bravest of us all. The house is well enough. I'd have it a thousand times before that popinjay place of Uncle Pomfret's in Keswick.

'And I'll not leave you. I'll never leave you. You are the only woman in all the world I love, Deb, save our mother.'

Deborah smiled through her tears.

'There'll be a woman for you one day: every woman who sees you must love you.'

'Ah, but it takes two for that,' David answered laughing. 'There was a girl once up by Seathwaite hit my horse with her stick. Do you know, Deb, it was but a moment and I've never seen her since, but she had a face like a laughing rose . . . For the rest they are all alike. I warrant marriage is a false tale. I would be free, and who is free with a wife?'

Deborah sighed.

'I shall be left one day . . . 'Tis so silly, but although I'm fourteen years I'm frightened of the dark . . . The true dark when there are only owls and mice. And Mistress Wilson. David, is she truly a witch?' She dropped her voice to a low whisper.

David tightened his arm round her. 'I think she's a witch,' he whispered back. 'She never sleeps. She has a fire with blue flame. She makes dolls of wax. I've seen one with a needle through. But she cannot touch thee, Deb . . . Christ is at the back of thee, and all the holy angels.'

'Maybe,' Deborah answered, shivering against his breast, 'she is a good witch. I'm sure she means no ill to our mother. Maybe she would have cured her.'

But David shook his head. 'Better our mother die 'than be cured of the Devil,' he answered. Then he folded his little sister yet more closely in his arms and kissed her.

'I will swear an oath, here in this place, never to leave you, Deborah. An I marry, you come also. And if I do not marry, you shall ever keep house for me and Father. Now listen, little sister, I will swear. By Christ and His holy angels I, David Scott

Herries, will never, while breath is in my body, leave thee, Deborah Herries – unless,' he hurriedly added, 'there is hunting on the hills or travelling to see new countries – an adventure, you understand. You would not hold me from that.'

'I would not hold you from anything,' Deborah answered, standing on tip-toe to kiss him. 'I am not that sort of selfish woman. I know that you will have a grand life, David, of adventure and enterprise, and do you think I would hold you back? I love you too well.'

She was quite happy now, and, their arms around one another, they went into the house.

Francis Herries had gone to his wife's room. He sat there beside the big bed, very patient, staring into the round light of the two candles. Margaret lay, her eyes closed, breathing stertorously. There were beads of sweat on her brow, and her two hands, tightly clenched, lay on the coverlet. Little Absom had gone for a meal but would return. It might well be that Margaret would die before he came back, but it did not matter; he could do nothing.

Herries sat there without moving, looking at his wife. He had never loved Margaret: he did not love her now nor did he let sentiment chafe him, but, as he watched her, he was sorry that her life had been spent with a man whom she could not understand.

It was this lack of comprehension that affected him most deeply as he sat there. She had loved him, but had not understood him at all. He had not loved her, but had understood her only too well.

All human relationships seemed to him miserable things as he sat there – all false, all betraying. Well, for himself, it did not matter. On the Christmas night at the moment when young Osbaldistone had slashed his cheek, he had finished with human beings. As he felt the blood gush over his face he had, at that instant, stepped aside from all his fellows. He had been coming to that point through many months. Now the division was made.

In the weeks that had followed, he had nursed his cut with a quiet sense of completion. He knew that he would be marked for life and terribly, that this would be the first thought that all men would have, the first thing that they would see.

He could look back now and understand that for years he had been slowly separating himself from his fellowmen. His fault or theirs, what mattered it? Their fault because he had a dream that could not be fulfilled, or his because he was ever putting himself wrong with them by loss of temper or arrogance or other passion? So he was done with them. Even poor Margaret was leaving him. Only David remained. David he could not separate himself from, but he was sure that the hour would come when David too would go. But that would be for David to recognize.

And instead of human beings, he would embrace this valley, this soil, this house itself. He had plans that he would get some land from Peel, that he would sow corn, grow trees perhaps, have cattle. He would work with his own hands here. All day and every day during those last weeks he had, when he had not been at Margaret's side, been digging and cutting wood, mending holes, carrying water, Ben, Wilson, David, assisting, but going and coming, whereas he stayed, sweat pouring from him, his nails grimed with dirt, his face raised to Glaramara, then bent again to the ground. And it seemed to him that the soil came and built itself about his heart. He was earthed in: the smell and the tang and the grit of it were in his eyes and his nostrils. He was growing his own hair. Soon it would be long about his brows. His heavy boots were caked with mud, and when he straightened himself this fresh, sharp ache in his back called out to him with a friendly voice.

Margaret stirred. Her hands rose and fell with a little flutter as he had so often seen them do, and a rush of memory swept over him. How badly he had treated her, and how she had asked to be badly treated! What absurd ironic fate had driven them together? Why was life thus, so that you were caught of your own good intentions and held in a trap to which there was no purpose? He had meant to do her kindness and had done her nothing but ill: but was not that indeed the whole motto of his life?

He could think of so many occasions when he had returned from some ride or visit meaning so many courtesies to her, and she, in the very first word, had roused his ironic irritation. And how poor was he that, knowing her love for him and that she was stupid and could not help herself, he had not been kinder to her, more indulgent! His sins had been frightful, thrusting his mistresses under her very nose, coming back drunk to her and forcing her against her will, until in the last matter of Alice Press he had been most evil of all. For all this he must pay, and when the day came for payment he was not to squeal about injustice.

He thought then of her many, many kindnesses and of her great patience, but the thought of her patience only again exasperated him. Why had she been so patient? It would have been better had she been rash with him sometimes and called him what he was. And so, as most men do who have ill-treated their wives, he came to an odd mixture of feelings, of shame and irritation, of self-blame and wonder that women could be so persistently provoking. At least he was glad that now she suffered no pain.

She stirred and woke. She looked about her without raising her head from the pillow. Then she saw him and smiled, and then, as she had done on a thousand other occasions, checked her smile lest he should think it foolish.

'What hour is it, Francis?' she asked him in a thin, very distant voice.

'Six of the clock,' he said, bending forward and taking her hand. That pleased her and she smiled again.

'My head is very clear . . . I have had strange dreams. I would speak to David. May I?'

He nodded. That 'May I?' touched him deeply. In the first year of their marriage when she had been a young girl and first afraid of him, she had said about this or that little pleasure and excitement, 'May I?' and often enough he had answered: 'No, you may not.'

Now he nodded and went from the room to fetch his son.

He sent David in. The boy came and stood by the bed, his breadth blocking the window. Then a terrible pity and tenderness for his mother, self-reproach for himself, and a consciousness of the imminence of death wrung his heart. He dropped on his knees, put out his great brown hands and took her thin white ones. He seemed for the first time in his life now to realize her. There had always been somebody or something else standing in his view of her. He had caught from early babyhood something of his father's idea of her. Now, when it was too late, she seemed to stand before him as she really was, going on this journey all alone with no one to help her. The room was so dark that it was only by the candlelight that he saw her face, and in that flickering gleam she was not foolish any more – she had courage and dignity, and these things all her life she had never seemed to him to have before.

She put up her hand and stroked his hair. Her voice was faint and he had to lean nearer to her to catch her words. Her arm fell about his neck.

'Davy, I've not been a wise mother to you . . . I've not been a wise woman, but I have loved you with all my heart.'

'I know you have, Mother,' he answered.

'I want you to promise me . . . never to leave your father.'

'1 will never leave my father.'

'It is strange,' she looked at him rather timidly, 'that love does not bring understanding. I have loved Francis so much but have never known the way to be easy with him.' She paused between the sentences, and David heard the wind tugging at the leaded panes, and in some way the little sound, as of a friendly companion, was comforting and understanding.

'It is too late now for me not to fear your father. Oh, Davy, how have I said again and again, "Now you must not mind him," but I have always minded him and the sight of him has made my heart beat and driven every word from my head. I know so well why he should be irritated with me. How should I not know, being so irritated with myself? But that is all over . . . past . . . away . . .' She stopped, lay back, closed her eyes. David placed his arm around her and held her close to him. He could feel the sweat of her body beneath the nightdress. 'I meant to make him proud of me and I have not. I meant that he should continue in love with me and he was not. I meant many things and have not wrought them, but—' and here her voice grew stronger and she seemed to wake to new life, 'I have given birth to a fine son who will be heard of in the world. Oh, I am proud of you, Davy, my darling, my darling.'

He held her closer, moved to his very soul, because in all these years she had never told him how she loved him.

'And you are strong and grand and fearless. You will be a man among men so that they look up to you and come to you. So, Davy, my darling, you must never leave your father, who is alone and will be more alone as the years go.' She raised herself a little on David's arm.

'Breed sons, my David. Great, strong-limbed men like yourself. Davy, Davy . . .' Her hand clutched his sleeve. 'I am no Herries, but I have borne a son to the Herries. Though they have mocked me, in my womb was carried the finest of them all, and from your seed, David, all the grand Herries shall come.' She sank back and the strangest elfin smile came to her lips. 'Your aunt and your uncle have bred niddering children, but two hundred years hence there shall be Herries who shall know that it was I, Margaret Herries, who gave suck to the man of them all . . . Your children, Davy . . . You must have men children to carry the Herries name further . . . further . . . further . . .' She seemed exhausted. She lay back on the pillow and he bent and stroked her forehead. 'Wrong thoughts, Davy,' she whispered, 'for a dying woman, but they have struck your father in the face and your sons must revenge . . . I have loved him so . . . even now to have his cheek against mine, his poor wounded cheek.'

'Shall I call him, Mother?' David whispered.

'Nay.' She smiled again. 'He would not know what to do or say. He was ever awkward in a scene. Like a child . . . I would have been mother to him rather than wife, but he would not allow me. Dear Francis . . . Francis, dear . . .'

Then she motioned him to raise her up. Her face was against his. She kissed him. Her lips were damp with sweat.

'Is it not odd that I who have been afraid all my life should not now be afraid? Our good Lord understandeth my awkwardness. His arms are around me . . . To die is simpler than to live . . .'

He laid her down again. Her hand closed with exceeding tightness about his.

'Dear Francis . . . Call him, Davy . . . I am dying.'

Gently he unloosed his hand, went to the door and called softly: 'Father, Father.'

Francis came in, and kneeling by the bed put his arms round her and held her as her spirit passed.

Her last words uttered against his cheek: 'Francis, dear.'

Part Two

'FORTY-FIVE

LAUGHTER OF A SPANIEL

MARIA HERRIES died on the morning of February 14th, 1745, thus missing by exactly four months the attainment of her hundredth year.

This lamentable failure afforded great grief and a sense of affronted egotism to the whole of the Herries family. Bad news flies apace, and in a surprisingly short time the event was known to, and greatly bewailed by, the children and grand-children of Robert Herries in Kensington, the family of Maurice in Portsmouth, of Humphrey at Seddon, and the Golds (only far relations-in-law, but nevertheless of a very definite Herries con-sciousness) in Edinburgh.

They all united in blaming Pomfret and Jannice for this disaster, and indeed very rightly, for who was to blame if they were not? Having kept the old lady alive so long, the least for them to do was to keep her alive that little bit longer. Moreover, it was pleasant to blame Pomfret and Jannice, who had made money in a very sudden and vulgar manner, in a fashion that was not the Herries manner: Herries always inherited, or if they worked, did so slowly and cautiously and with an air of indifference.

Wealth meant little in the Herries blood: they had not at all like certain other famous English families the sense of property. They were indeed quite above and outside this sense, because to be Herries was enough and, rich or poor, you were of an equal and exceptional importance. No, the Herries pride (of which there was always God's plenty) was based on two magnificent foundations: England and Common Sense. When you said English you said Herries, and when you said Herries you said No Nonsense. In this lies any interest that there may be in a study of Herries' family history – that there was something in the Herries blood demanding that their castle of common sense should be persistently attacked, and almost always from within. Again and again these attacks occur, and with every fresh battle new history is made. 'I am a sensible man,' chanted the first Herries, striding across the naked body of his enemy, Romance or Illusion – and so ever since have his stalwart descendants chanted.

'The man's a fool.' 'The woman's an ass.' 'I can't think what he's after.' 'A madman.' 'A lunatic.' 'A dirty dog.' 'Traitor to his

country.' 'An artist.' 'A ne'er-do-well.' 'Fantasy.' 'Imagination.'
'An atheist' – such and so have ever been the words and phrases
of contempt in the mouths of following generations of Herries.

And rightly so. For just as Common Sense has always served
them soundly and well in all their history, so have Imagination,
Originality, the hopeless pursuit of the shining star, led them to
ruin and disaster, public scandal and disgrace. They have learnt
to dread and with justice the dreamer; he has ever haunted the
sleep of right-minded Herries men and women.

This Common Sense, on the other hand, has been with them
no unstudied art. They have penetrated every nook and cranny
of this temple, have studied with hundreds of years of patient
learning the shifting features of the God.

At the moment of birth young Herries know precisely the
sensible thing to do, how to watch and wait, to avoid all eccentricity, to embrace only those things and persons that are of good
report and general repute, to believe only in what they see, to
handle only what they can in reality touch, to give their blessing
to all that is normal, firmly traditional, safely found. Within the
world of common sense they are kindly, generous and open-
hearted: let them for a moment stray into that howling wilderness
of stars and mandrakes and they are ferocious and bloodthirsty:
alarm partly makes them so, the knowledge given to them by
history that they are a family especially susceptible to attacks of
the dreamer's incongruity, the rebel's immorality. They go,
therefore, armed to the teeth: divided as they sometimes are
(being yet human) among themselves, they unite instantly at the
call of one of their members: ''Ware Wolf!' They have made
England what it is: they are rightly proud of their magnificent
achievement.

But, it must be repeated, their principal interest to the
observer of them is that they have, at their heart, the poison of
their qualities and intentions. Every generation, it seems, is condemned to this warfare against its own home-born traitors, and
from this warfare comes always a stouter, more determined
resolve.

The death of Maria Herries, so lamentably previous, offered a
fine example of their common sense in action. One thing that had
never been understood by them was that Herries men must die
so soon. It was natural for the majority, who waste their days in
dreams, in pursuit of the thing that is not, in longing for what
does not exist, to wear themselves untimely away, their proper
punishment and condemnation. But for Herries, who never ran

after a vain thing nor stared at the moon, life should be inde-
finitely extended, and because they believed in a just God (the
God of the contemporary majority) it was hard to see why His
justness did not perceive exactly this.

There had been already examples in history of what a Herries
could do when he tried. Old Polyphemus Herries, barnacled and
lichened with tradition, who eight hundred years ago in Fife (the
Herries were all Scottish then) had lived to a hundred and sixty
one; old Mary Herries of the Wars of the Roses, who, defending
Lancaster Castle, upset pots of boiling pitch on to the heads of
invaders, she had lived to a hundred and thirty-nine, and had had
fifty-eight grandchildren. Ronald Herries, friend of James I,
had lived in sin and iniquity into his hundred and twentieth
year – a black sheep, but honoured by the Herries because of his
arrogant resolve to beat Death back to Hell, which for a hundred
and twenty years at least he succeeded in doing, then drink had
him and he died, his head in a butt of Canary!

Since old Ronald no one had passed the century, although
Elizabeth Herries of Charles I's time had been ninety-three, and
little Johnny Herries the hunchback, uncle of Maria and
Matthew, had seen ninety-four.

Old Maria as she approached the century had become an
object of reverence to all of them, and Pomfret and Jannice,
hitherto contemned, had been more honourably considered for
preserving her. Here again was something that the Herries did
better than anything else – show Death that they would stand no
nonsense.

There was nothing that the Herries prided themselves upon
more justly than the health and excellence of their bodily vigour.
They were not eccentric in this; they did not produce strong
men for exhibition at a fair, or wrestlers at a pageant, but just
vigorous, sound Englishmen with no nonsense about them,
destined to die calmly in their beds at a ripe old age. And how
often these last years had the words been murmured in Kensington, in Portsmouth, in Carlisle, in Edinburgh, at Seddon, at
Hatton, at Brighthelmstone. 'The Herries live long . . . Maria
Herries in Keswick neareth her hundredth year . . . Nothing
ails her . . . She is bled once and again . . . She has all her
teeth.'

And now she was gone and had missed her goal. A hundred
in four months' time! The irony of it!

By an odd coincidence it happened that for Maria's funeral there
was a remarkable Herries gathering. Movement over considerable

distances was not easy, although easier than it had been, but it was not difficult, of course, for Humphrey Cards, his wife Charlotte, his daughter Dorothy, her husband Anthony Forster, and their little son Will to come over from Seddon, and Grandison, son of Robert, cousin of Pomfret and Francis, had been paying a visit in Edinburgh with Mary his wife, and Helen and Pelham his children, so they came down: and last but not, of course, least there was Henry, son of Maurice Cards, and Lucilla his wife. In this company three quite separate impulses of the Herries blood could be traced.

Humphrey Cards, hidden away at Seddon, had been suspected of turning Quaker. He had at any rate been oddly religious enough to frighten all decent-minded Herries. His daughter Dorothy, who had married one of the Northumberland Forsters, was grimly religious enough, but not, thank Providence, in any eccentrically dangerous fashion.

Dorothy Forster then (cousin to a more famous Dorothy Forster of this same time) represented the spiritual vein of the Herries body.

Her thin, pale, ramrod-straight body, her dark clothes and quiet misgivings about her other fellow-humans, made this manifest.

Robert's son, Grandison, and his children Pelham and Helen represented fashion. They lived in Kensington, and everything outside London was too odd and peculiar to be true. Grandison had never understood how a Herries could bring himself to live out of London – it was a sort of *lèse-majesté* against the blood. His eyes, protruding out of his round pale face, expressed perpetual surprise and wonder. He was tall, stout and most elegantly dressed. Clothes were of great concern to him, and food, and the order of entrance and exit. Not greatly distinguished in the village of Kensington, he was an exquisite in Keswick. Aunt Jannice thought him the most marvellous creature in all the world, and had he but allowed himself to be bled more frequently he would have been perfect.

His girl Helen was in no way remarkable, but his son Pelham promised well as the Herries rake of his generation. There must always be a Herries rake, and he must go so far and no further. He must gamble, drink, womanize to a certain degree, fight duels enough for glory and not enough for scandal, be handsome and dashing and outrageous, but always within the limits of common sense. Other Herries must be able to shake their heads over him, but admire him too, and at last when a new younger rake is maturing he, the elder, must marry a virtuous girl with wealth, settle down and breed a family.

Young Pelham, aged at this time twenty-seven, understood all this perfectly, and had in fact a certain private store of ironic amusement which bewildered at times his fat father and irritated his august mother.

This mother, a magnificent figure, both snobbish and stupid on a large scale, had been a Titchley and, as everyone knows, it is difficult for a Titchley to yield place even to a Herries. She had in fact never quite yielded. She was still just enough rebel against the Herries tradition to need watching; not that she was interesting in her rebellion – she neither thought nor spoke enough to be interesting. Only once and again she would look at a stray Herries with a dumb air of wonder as much as to say: 'In a Titchley world this creature would not be permitted.'

In her quite young days she had known Sarah Marlborough and although now she was in a Kensington set she always got Court news before anyone else.

Henry, son of Maurice, and Lucilla his wife, represented the third strain in the Herries blood. Henry, who was thirty-two years of age, was thin and spare, with eyes gravely fixed. They were fixed upon the markets and he never permitted them to rest anywhere else. For one brief moment of sensual delight he had allowed them to rest upon his wife Lucilla. Ten years ago she had been a beautiful girl. Three years following their marriage she had been attacked by the smallpox, and, quite naturally, after that business had claimed him again. They had no children; the multiplying of coins of the realm was their only increase.

Henry was able and kept his eyes open for all the mechanical improvements and developments that were now beginning to alter the country, how permanently and irretrievably even he did not suspect. He was one of the first men in England to be aware of the deep importance of John Kay's invention of the fly-shuttle in 1733, of John Lombe's discovery in Italy of those improvements in machinery that gave such an impetus to the silk trade, and, in later years, he was to recognize at once the value of Crompton's mule, of Highs's water-frame and the spinning jenny of Hargreaves.

Oddly, with all his cleverness, his attention to business and parsimonious industry, he was never to make a fortune. This too was characteristic of the Herries; they were never in their money-making destined to be middle-men because if, in their tribe,

genius showed its head it was instantly suspect and exiled. Henry
was no genius, but he was industrious, honest, cross-grained,
conceited and quite without poetic fancy. That was well, for had
this last been his he would have been unfaithful to Lucilla, who
was no woman to endure patiently infidelity.

Gathered there together on some general ground, had they for
an outside observer any physical characteristic in common?

Only this: that in them all there was some attribute of the
horse – Pomfret the cart-horse, Dorothy Forster the funeral
hack, young Pelham the dashing pony, his father the well-fed
favourite of the Countess's barouche, Henry the little dark horse
of the race-meeting, and so-and-so . . . these traits of chin, high
cheek-bones, long forehead, brooding, patient and unimaginative
eyes marking the Herries tribe, giving them their place in
English life and history.

And with all this they had great qualities.

They had a great force of fidelity, so that under pain of urgent
torture they would not desert their loyalties, their loyalties of
creed, of family, of ethics, of social conduct. These loyalties
were English, and therefore the easier because no light of imagination was ever let in upon them. Two hundred years ago they
had been, to a letter, the same: two hundred years later they
would not have changed to a hair's-breadth. They were loyal to
their country, to their family, to their loves, to their friends, with
a stolid wonder that anybody could be anything else. When those
ill-smelling traitors were discovered within their own households
(as with every generation they were discovered) that taunt of
disloyalty was the first stone that was flung.

As to their country so also to them disloyalty meant everything
that was base; abnormality, cowardice, the vilest selfishness,
dirty living, obscene thinking. And the certainty of their judgements was only equalled by the swiftness.

It was tragedy for the Herries that they must live in a constantly changing world. When, as now with Maurice's son
Henry, these changes were sharply perceived, the Herries strain
of orthodox tradition modified the use that was made of them.
Loyalty came in there.

The changes were always unfortunate, even when they were
most inevitable. The old days were always the good old days for
the Herries; that was why, for example, Harcourt, who on this
occasion had come over from Ravenglass, was accepted by all of
them as a perfect member.

For him only all that was old was worthy. It had been Mr

Pope's only fault that he was not old enough. The thought that old Maria had been born on the day of the Battle of Naseby embalmed her, even though she had so impertinently missed her hundredth birthday, with an especial fragrance.

And behind this reverence there was something very kindly and genial. The Herries men especially were warm of heart. Pomfret and Harcourt, Robert's sons, and in the younger line, Francis's David, young Pelham – there was strong generous humanity here. Only, faced with what they thought to be heresy, vain worship of false gods, treachery to Church or State, to Country and the Marriage Vows and sound fact, only then they were as fierce, as prejudiced, as bloodthirsty as any Spanish Inquisitor. And for confidence in their own eternal rightness there was no family in Britain to rival them.

Here, then, they were, two days after Maria's funeral, on an afternoon of driving rain, gathered together in Jannice's withdrawing-room: lean Henry and his pale-faced Lucilla, little dainty Harcourt, Mrs Dorothy black and austere, Pelham's mother stout and frosted, Pelham gay in a coat of orange and silver, Raiseley bitterly envious, Grandison fat and flabby, amiable Anabel and beautiful Judith – the Herries stable – one of these Herries family gatherings that any Herries chronicler is compelled in their history to confront.

Jannice, Lucilla, Grandison, his wife Mary and Helen their daughter, were busy at Ombre. The men, bored with the wet, had come in to take tea with the women. Henry was giving Pomfret a rather patronizing lecture on profit and loss (he thought Pomfret the veriest fool), Pelham was tantalizing Raiseley with London splendours and besieging the lovely Judith with all his polished arts, and on the crimson sofa the dead Maria's spaniel lay, staring with sad angry eyes at the hated company.

The room was lit with candles, but the curtains were not drawn, and beyond the windows a furious sky tore in sweeping battalions of smoky clouds from horizon to horizon. Today as so often in this country of clouds the sky imposed itself upon the farthest interior seclusion. The glittering furniture of the room, the gilt of the chairs, the jewellery of the little clocks and boxes, the crimson silk, the shining silver candlesticks, the amber of the fluttering flames of lights and fire surrendered without question to the black shapes of the sky that seemed so vast and threatening, dragging at the distant tops of the hills as though to fling them across the lake on to the houses of the town.

Everyone in the room was irritated by the storm, but no one asked for the curtains to be drawn. There had been also during these last days other irritations.

The friendly scorn felt in different degrees by them all for their host and hostess reacted upon themselves. It was exasperating to feel that a Herries, whose hospitality they had accepted, was below the proper Herries mark, and Pomfret, who was only at his ease when he was out of doors killing something, who was always too uncomfortable in his wife's presence, had flustered through these days, now roaring in a noisy and false good humour, now putting on an air of deep seriousness that his words, alas, only betrayed, now sinking into a schoolboy silence of discomfort.

Jannice too was unhappy. For many years now she had been comfortable here in her own little circle, testing neither her wit nor her beauty against broader standards. But she detested the large pompous body of Grandison's wife after the first half-hour of her arrival. For Mary Herries, Jannice had the double aggra-vation that she was neither a Titchley nor a worthy Herries. She had indeed, with her provincial airs, her silly cures and recipes, her little conceits and ugly appearance, everything against her. Pomfret had never cared for his wife so protectively as during these last days when 'the Titchley woman', as he called her, had mocked with every word. He longed to humiliate fat Grandison, to put him on a horse that would throw him at the first ditch, to fire a gun in his ears, to win his money at a cock-fight, even to strip the clothes off his flabby body and soak him in the lake. He would show these Kensington puppies what real life was like up here in the North Country. Even as he listened to Henry Cards's dry words, hoping that he might gather a business wheeze or two, his other ear was on the Ombre table listening to the thick voice of Mary Herries as she instructed the others in the Ken-sington fine shades of Ombre play.

Mary Herries indeed was indignant with every pulse in her large body at the company that she was forced to keep. The very cards that Jannice had provided seemed to her contemptible with their old-fashioned pictures of 'the Bishops in the Tower, Popish Midwife, Captain Tom, Army going over to the Prince of Orange', etc. They were Jannice's best cards, 'the best superfine Principal Ombre cards at 2s 9d a Dozen'. She had been playing with them these twenty years. If good enough for anyone in Keswick, why not for anyone in Kensington?

Mary Herries had other causes for dissatisfaction. She knew

that her son Pelham was attracted by Jannice's girl Judith. She
adored her son; this was the strongest, fiercest motive of life for
her. His handsomeness, cleverness, gaiety, made her the proudest
woman in all England, and her pride was the more defended
because it was mingled with a worshipping fear of an irony in
him that she would never understand.

That by any horrible chance he should throw himself away
on the girl of these country bumpkins was terrifying to her. Fool
though she was she could see that Judith was a dark beauty:
dressed properly and educated in Kensington she might make
others than her son stare. She knew too that Pelham meant as a
rule but little by his gallantries – there was already a fine list of
momentary conquests behind him – but the dullness of these
last days (was it for ever raining in this pernicious country?), his
idleness and something arrogant and distant in Judith might
lead to some desperate impetuosity. She could scarcely hold her
cards as she thought of some dreadful crisis suddenly exploded
before them: her husband, poor fool, would perceive nothing,
and would never dream of acting until all was over.

And she had a further irritation. This was the King Charles
spaniel on the crimson sofa. This, the last of dead Maria's many
spaniels, was the only true mourner of that poor lady. She was
missing her now with every wheezy breath that she drew. She
was old, fat, the victim of many pains and tortures; life had long
ago been misery to her had it not been for the touch of those
strange dry fingers, the scratch of those multitudinous rings, the
warmth of that thin shrivelled body, a bag of bones under the
coloured shining silks. Alone she had shared her mistress's
recent life, her longings, her prides, her greeds, her ignorances,
her loneliness. Alone she had called out of that aged woman, so
nearly deceased long before the actual moment of death, tenderness and unselfishness, the only cause in her of anxiety for another. During those long nights when Maria had lain looking up
at a remorseless ceiling, seeing pageants of vanished scenes and
figures, her pride her only refuge, the spaniel had breathed
against her withered hand, rested its head against her dried
bosom.

Together they had faced a world that seemed to them both
worthless and ugly; all the old glories were over, but so long as
they were together pride would sustain them both.

Now they were no longer together, and the spaniel, only
aware that her mistress called her no more, ached her old heart
away in angry wasted rebellion. But there was more than despair

and loneliness there. There was also a spirit of impotent and sarcastic rage. She was of blood royal, descendant of a line of kings.
It had always seemed to her that Jannice and Pomfret, their offspring also, were low and degenerate creatures. She hated that
they should touch her, and when Raiseley or Judith teased her,
her whole soul rose in affronted disgust. While Maria lived she
had been protected, and in sublime confidence of her dear
mistress had been able to scorn those others, but now she knew
that she was open to the world . . . Pains racked her, dim fears
besieged her, and with these the scorn that she knew her mistress
had felt ever increased within her.

She was no Herries: her alliance had been to a single soul, not
to the herd. So now as they passed around her with their strange
scents and movements and sounds she hated them even as she
despised them, and most bitterly of all she hated and despised
the stout, crackling, silk-swishing, fan-waving, scent-distilling
Mary Herries.

It may have been that in this woman beyond the others she
detected false arrogances and knew that of them all it was she
who would have most fiercely affronted her mistress. In any case
it was upon Mary Herries that she fixed her filmed and fading
eyes, concentrated her aching body, curled her upper lip, showing two sharp and yellow teeth.

Mary Herries was telling some tale of a friend: 'But a miserly
temper. She is as expressive to her husband as a casket of jewels.
Many's the night I've seen her lug out her old green net purse
full of old jacobuses while her waiting woman in the room behind
is diving into the bottom of her trunk hoping for a stray piece or
two . . .' when she was aware of the spaniel's eyes.

She moved her chair ever so slightly and was aware of them
the more. The spaniel was laughing at her, or maybe it was the
spirit of old Maria that mocked her through the dog.

She felt suddenly an accumulation of miseries: she saw
Grandison her husband as he stood in his night-shirt, his ugly
naked toes spread, his bristling head bare of its wig, and in that
figure, so deeply accustomed that it seemed to be part of her
own, she groaned at the weariness of her life. What was all this
pretence of Kensington finery, this elaborate mention of old
Duchess Sarah, Sir John and the rest, when a yard away Pelham
was making eyes at that hoydenish country girl, and her stomach
ached beneath her tightened stays and her feet were pinched in
their silver shoes, and Grandison, scratching at his wig for the
thousandth time, cleared his throat over his cards preparatory to

playing the wrong one? What were these Herries but second-rate country bumpkins? Henry with his spare money-calculating eyes, who yet could make no fortune, Dorothy in her thin black with her psalm-singing pieties, Pomfret stinking of drink and the miry road, his miserable Raiseley with his splay feet and mean little nose. Oh! she was sick of the lot, she had messed her life through her own silly folly, storms of rain beat the windows and the spaniel mocked her!

A point had come in the game and she flung her cards on the table. 'I play no more,' she said in her thick soft voice that was like the stirring of suet in the pan. She had been winning (a fact that until now she had quite honestly not noticed) and at once she was aware that Jannice Herries found in this the reason of her withdrawal.

Jannice had not at sixty improved in appearance. She was thinner, more sallow, more drawn and by her odd unsuited clothes more painfully quartered than ever.

'An old witch,' thought Mary Herries.

'A fat mean cook of a woman,' thought Jannice.

'Why, cousin, you are winning,' said Jannice sharply. 'You must give us our revenge.'

But Mary Herries, raising her stout body painfully, pushing back the chair, feeling freshly the agony of her pinching shoes, answered:

'That dog should be poisoned.'

Everyone felt the unseemliness. A Herries, the oldest of all the Herries, had been but two days buried. This was her dog, all that remained of her, almost you could say a Herries dog. But worse followed.

Mary, her voice quivering to an unexpected plaintiveness: 'I am sick to death of this: it rains and rains again. Maria is happily buried if it was here that she must look out of window.' Then with a toss of her head, the painted flowers in her white wig nodding their petals, she waddled from the room, her little feet protesting with sad little creaks against the weight that they must carry.

Grandison knew what this meant. She was feeling Titchley, and when she felt Titchley he was in for a terrible hour. He hastened after her. The dog still laughed, motionless like a dead dog.

But the men, Henry and Pomfret, young Pelham and Harcourt, like all Herries men when a woman made a scene, came together. Young Pelham, leaning back against the purple brocaded chair near the door, smiling, said: 'My mother has vapours often enough at this hour. She will be happy only in a land where the sun always shines. I appeal to you, sir' (smiling at Pomfret), 'this is a handsome country, but it rains unduly.'

'It would not be so handsome a country,' said Harcourt, 'did it not rain so frequently.' And he turned from them, looking out of window across the lake to the hills where a sudden flash of pale sunlight had pierced the storm, striking an arrow of gold that cleft Cat Bells in two. He loved it, every stick and stone of it! How he loved it! And as he looked, a deep homesickness for his own home at Ravenglass, his little garden, his gleaming book rows, the faint flash of the sea beyond his windows, took him.

All of them in that room caught from him some sense of English soil. The men moved together to the window and stood there side by side looking out. They were Herries in this: that however far they might be drawn from the English soil, they yet belonged to it. Even in Kensington they felt the stirrings of ancient waterways and the tuggings of prehistoric roots. Which partially explains perhaps that they were never good travellers abroad, queasy, irritable, of an arrogant critical mind; and if they must settle in a foreign land they must turn it speedily to a Scottish or English likeness.

They felt now that urgent need to break out into the open air that every Herries feels when his women are badgering him.

Pomfret's indignation at the insult to his wife was mingled with a twofold satisfaction: it was not he who for once was the clown of the occasion and, although he would never confess to this, his own dear Jannice had been found to be less than perfection. There came to him indeed at that moment, gazing out at the steel wall of rain that fell now like a vengeance from the muddy sky, a thought of what life would have been had Jannice never existed. He cast an uneasy backward glance at the spaniel, who was now wheezily sleeping. How many things dogs knew, and how greatly the more at ease he was with them than with humans! Now with a dog! . . .

And he thought again of Jannice, of how to this day, although they had been married so long, he was afraid of her, afraid of that sudden sharp tap in her voice like a knock on the window, that chilly glaze of contempt in her eye when he had been an especial fool. Yes, and his own children . . . Only Anabel was friendly and easy, and she was easy with all the world.

He was sixty-seven years of age now, a tun of a man with a floating hulk of a belly, and he was lonely as perhaps were all men of sixty-seven. Only with horses and dogs and a drinking parson and a swearing friend or two, killing, hunting those animals that he yet so dearly loved, only thus might he for a driving hour cheat himself of his loneliness. Staring out of window, not hearing anything of the voices in the room behind him, he thought suddenly of his brother Francis. Why, he could not say. He did not think of him more often than he must, partly because he was a scandal, partly because he loved him. At heart it might be that Francis was more to him than anyone else in the world: Francis, digging away in that miry patch of stinking mud in that nook-shotten valley, Francis shouted at by the peasant children, Francis, adulterer and vagabond, known to have sold his woman at a public fair, to have killed his wife with unkindness, to have driven one of his own daughters away from her home, to be sheltering under his roof the most notorious old witch in the country, Francis – 'Rogue Herries' to all the world, so that he brought with every hour disgrace on the Herries name – yet Pomfret loved him. His mind flung back to that first windy evening when Francis and his family arrived in the town, Francis so young and handsome then in all his gay clothes, and to that other time, the day that poor Margaret died, when he had ridden over to Herries and Francis had been so grave and kindly, so noble in spirit, and he, Pomfret, had kissed his brother, loving him and wishing in his own clumsy speechless way to protect him.

Oh! Francis was bad and not to be mentioned, but through the sheets of rain Pomfret had a mad, monstrous wonder of a moment whether, if he had been with him out there in rugged tumbled Herries, life might not have been richer, more valorous, better worth . . .

And so wondering, turning because he heard the door open, saw to his stricken, open-mouthed amazement his brother, Francis Herries, standing in the room.

He had not seen his brother for three years; the last time had been in a Keswick street when Francis, riding past on a huge kind of cart-horse, had patronized Pomfret and sent him home in a fuming fury.

But now how strange he looked standing there, wearing his own black shaggy hair, muddily booted to the thighs, his long brown coat faded and stained, his face brown and spare, the shape and form of it altered by the deep white scar that ran from brow to lip. His face was yet shining with raindrops, water dripped from his boots, the back of his brown hand shone with rain. Years back he had promised to be stout; now he was lean and spare, and seemed of an immense height. He had aged strangely. Pomfret had a quick vision of him that other first time at the inn when glittering in gold and crimson he had been so young and handsome. Now the soil was in the furrows of his cheeks.

To Jannice, staring from above the card-table, it was as though the Devil had sprung out of the floor. Francis was to her as the Devil. Sharing no blood with him, disliking him from the very first, her dislike was now hatred – hatred mingled with deep fear. For years he had threatened everything in which she believed, her morality, her family, her social position. Especially her social position. Every little success in Keswick was threatened with the consciousness that only a mile or two away there was this sinister figure, outlaw, adulterer, vagabond, and, because she never saw him, her sense of his evil power grew and grew with imagination. She was a woman compact of superstition. Witches and warlocks, mandrakes and goblins were as real to her as her own children. The two worlds were, with her, one. Had Francis been arrested for dealings with the Devil and been burnt at the stake she would not have thought it an injustice.

She had sworn that never again should he pass her door. He was here, and it seemed to her as she looked across the room at him that fire and brimstone smoked at his nostrils.

Harcourt was the first to speak. He was enchanted with pleasure. He came forward, holding out both hands: 'Francis, my dear brother!' That explained to the others who this was. Young Pelham, greatly interested, thought: 'So this is my dangerous and exiled relation. This is a man. Worth the lot of us here.' He was drawn naturally to the rebel in life. He had a complete intellectual appreciation of rebellion, although his love of comfort would always keep himself on the side of safety.

Francis looked about him, bowed to Jannice and Dorothy Forster, then, smiling (his smile was odd now because the scar caught his upper lip and twisted it), said:

'Forgive me. I would not have intruded, but, passing, thought that I would greet the family . . . very briefly. It can be so seldom that we are all together. Not, you know,' he continued, smiling more broadly, 'that I enjoy family gatherings, and I fear that I have not impertinence enough to invite you to Herries, unless anyone has an affection for potato-gathering. But I would not wish to be remiss in paying some reverence to my great-aunt.'

He looked at the handsome boy by the chair. 'You must be Grandison's boy?'

Francis rested for a moment his hand on his shoulder. 'You should know my son David,' he said. 'If you care for the country, a day or two at Herries . . . But I suspect that you have better things to do.'

Pomfret here blustered forward. 'Well, brother, damn it, now that thou art here . . . a drink in this damp weather . . . Why, damn it, man . . .' Then, conscious of his wife behind him, stopped abruptly.

'Nay, nay,' said Francis, smiling. 'My horse is outside and I have business. I heard you were all here. Doubtless you thought of me and wished my presence but were shy of asking me.'

He saw the spaniel, crossed to the sofa, bent down and stroked it. 'Poor bitch. You have as little place here as myself. I'll be coming to see thee one of these days, Harcourt.' Then was gone abruptly as he came.

INTO THE CAVE

FRANCIS HERRIES rode off into the rain, his mind a strange torment. To enter that house over whose threshold he had not stepped for so many years had been an impulse of the moment. He had been inside before he had known that he was going, and, brushing past the startled man-servant, he had entered that room and almost blinked, like an owl, at the unaccustomed light. It had been more than the candlelight; to himself who had been having for so long no intimate contacts save with the wind, the air, the hard grit of unyielding soil and the soft friendliness of the land after rain, these figures were like fish swimming in a strange sea. Like fish, and yet they had tugged at his heart.

He had entered the house in a childish play-acting spirit of dare-devil as though he would say 'Bo!' to a goose, but the very sight of silly Pomfret with his hanging belly and little Harcourt whose eyes had shone with pleasure at sight of him, and that handsome lad Grandison's boy, and all his Herries blood had pressed about his heart. It was to conceal this – which had been as violent as an unexpected blow in the face – that he had moved to the dog, stroked it, said those false sentimental words – the

play-actor in him again. But behind the false sentiment there
had been that swift ache of loneliness.

He knew it: he could confess it to himself: for all his intolerance and truculence he would have loved to stay with the
men, with Pomfret, Harcourt, young Pelham, even with stiff
Henry and flabby-faced Grandison, spent the night with them,
laughed and drunk and changed bawdy stories with them, felt
HERRIES again, felt the family blood in him and all England
behind his tread and that ancient old tree-man whispering in his
ears the ancient Herries password . . . and then perhaps to have
taken the boy Pelham off to Herries and to have shown him
David, who was a giant now and the hero of the countryside and
the simplest, grandest Herries of them all. Then to have put on
his decent clothes again and found a good horse once more
(Mameluke buried beneath the yews behind the house) and
ridden off to Seddon for a week or two, and then perhaps to stay
with Grandison in Kensington . . . He! He grinned, the rain
blinding him as he climbed the steep hill to Cat Bells. That was
never again for him nor would he care for it did he have it. In a
day he would be quarrelling with Harcourt, mocking Pomfret,
laughing at Grandison, corrupting Pelham. But the Herries
blood was there. He had been a fool to enter that place.

There was something further for him to consider. In Keswick
that afternoon he had talked with Father Roche. He had been
crossing the market-place, his head up, looking neither to
right nor left, in enemy's country and knowing it, when a
country fellow dressed like a carter had touched his arm. He had
turned about with his accustomed haughty stare, and that voice,
once so powerful over him, came back to him across all the years.
He knew him immediately, the voice with its seeming musical
resonance, the eyes with their strange commanding glow belonging to one man only in the world. Roche had smiled, his broad
hat pulled over his brows. Francis had asked him to Herries.
Roche had refused, saying that he was on his way to Carlisle.
The business was urgent. Very shortly the world would hear
startling things. The hour for which they had all been waiting so
long had struck at last. The voice was not raised, but behind it
was that old fanatical undoubting spirit, and it had for Francis
its ancient power. Standing there in the market-place, the rain
soaking down upon them, the old times swung back, days in
Doncaster when it had seemed to him that he would follow
Roche anywhere, evenings when it had appeared no odd fancy
that, threading the stars, God and all His cohort of angels, the

chariots of fire and the horsemen thereof, could plainly be dis-
cerned. Roche had given him an address – Walter Frith, in charge
of John Stope, English Street, Carlisle. He would be found there.
They had parted.

So all the old life was swinging back. You could not escape it,
throw it off as you fancied, dig yourself into the very stomach of
the soil – one tap on the shoulder, one glance through the dark
branches of the yew and you were caught again. As Francis rode
down to Grange Bridge the rain cleared. The clouds were rolling
away above the Castle Crag, and a faint fair wash of crocus
spread in a sea of light over the black pointed hill. On either side
above Watendlath and the slow slopes beyond Grange white
fleecy mists still lay low like bales of wool, but you could feel the
light that burnt behind them, and the soft fields beyond the
stream towards the lake were richly green.

He crossed the little bridge, turned to the right, rode between
the trees beside the swift river along the track to Rosthwaite. In
the village he had not seen a soul. It had been like a dead place.
And well it might be. All the valley from Seathwaite to Grange
had been cursed that winter. Misfortune had followed misfortune. Cattle had died, agues and fevers and plagues of pests had
seemed to choose the valley for their camping-ground, and at the
last smallpox had come, had raged right down the valley and
only here. None over in Grasmere nor the other way in Newlands nor more than ordinary in the Keswick slums. The valley
had been marked out. He knew well enough what the people
were saying, that there was a curse, a spell, and he knew further
that the old Wilson woman under his own roof was marked as
the agent. And he knew that behind her he was himself marked
out.

Yes, and he knew more than that; that, had it not been for
David, weeks ago the roof would have been burned down over
his head, Herries a heap of ashes and himself, perhaps, stoned to
death. He did not care for their hatred, but he did not wish to die.
There was something in life that was, like the beat of a drum,
insistently enthralling. He had always felt it: he would never
escape it: and it was as though, did he live long enough,
he would discover the answer to this incredible mixture of
beauty and filth, wizardry and commonplace, stagnation and
unceasing activity. He did not want to die, but he did not want,
either, that it should be by permission of his son that he should
live.

But this was not for long. David was going: he knew it as

though David had told him. And he did not want David to go. No, he did not ...

David was now twenty-five years of age, six feet five inches tall, as broad as a wall, the strongest man in the county beyond question, and many thought, with his fair blanched hair, blue eyes and splendid carriage, the handsomest. Let that be as it might. It did not matter. He was simple, modest, a man without words, quite direct in thought and act and with few subtleties. He had, for his years, scarcely stepped farther than Seascale on one side, Penrith on the other, very rarely left his valley, made few friends in Keswick, though all the world was friendly. His own valley loved him and said, as Francis well knew, that Rogue Herries had never fathered him. And yet he was clear Herries enough, the line of his jutting chin, the high strong cheek-bones made him plainly of the 'horse' family. He moved, tossed his head, swung his body like some high-bred animal, held, confined.

For eight years now he had helped his father in the land around Herries, ploughing, planting, digging, all as he very well knew, but never said, to little effect. His constant companions were his father and Deborah; he was friend to all the valley, but had no other close intimacy save that old childhood one with Peel's boy, Rendal, who was now a man almost as big and strong as David himself. Of love affair there had been as yet, it seemed, no sign.

He was a man of few words save possibly with Deborah. When he went to sport or meeting, to hunt or local games, and performed some miracle of strength, he came home afterwards without a word of it. His thoughts were certainly slow in labour: you could almost see them move behind his smooth clear forehead. He had a long, slow laugh that began as a murmur, spread into a long rumble, ended in a roar. He had a slow temper. He had two faults: that he was suspicious of men and, although courteous in manner, desperately hard to make a friend of. And he never forgot nor forgave an injury. When, that is, he had proved it to be one. He paid no attention to gossip, drank as men drink, but kept the effects of it to himself. He showed no resentment at the cruelties, foulnesses, obscenities of his time. He was a man of his time. He did not trade with women because he did not as yet apparently care very greatly for women's company save Deborah's. He was tongue-tied with women and impatient of their ways. He did not care very much for any company and preferred best to be away on the hills

alone. He was very Herries in some things: in his passion for
England – he had all the Herries's ignorant contempt for and
dislike of foreigners; in his interest in the family – he would ask
his father many questions about Herries history and relationship; in his inability to see anything that was not in front of his
nose.

It was his father who was the rebel, not he. Unless he were
passionately roused – a very rare thing – there was something
lazy and comfort-loving in his great size and strength. He seemed
to be never physically tired, but he liked to lie back staring into
fire or sky, seeing nothing, perhaps thinking nothing, letting
light and warmth soak into him.

But what were his thoughts of his father? How many times, in
the instant of digging or planting, hoeing or carrying, walking or
riding, Francis had looked up at the sky, at the long hump of
Glaramara, or, from Grange, at the opening flower of Skiddaw,
and asked himself that question. David was infinitely kind, ceaselessly patient. Since that night so long ago at Ravenglass no word
of impatience had passed his lips, he had shown no angry movement towards his father. But they had moved, these last years,
with a sort of mist between, loving one another and yet distrust-
ful: or Francis on his side at least had held distrust. What must
David feel about his father's isolation, self-adopted, ironically
self-proclaimed, and about the ever thicker wall of hatred built
by the world against him?

We love most, perhaps, those of whom we are a little afraid.
David was the only creature in the world of whom Francis was
afraid, and this was a fear only of a sudden blazing word, a glance
of contempt. Then, the word spoken, the glance flung, Francis
would pass into the final ostracism.

When Mary, two years earlier, had left him, Francis thought
that the word would be spoken. Mary, who had grown increasingly beautiful and contemptuous, had gone without a sign one
morning to her aunt in Keswick. She had sent a letter from there
saying that she would not return. No other word came from her.
They heard that she went afterwards to stay in Carlisle, then that
she was back in Keswick, then in London. Then it was said that
Francis had beaten and abused her. He smiled at that. In earlier
days he had beaten David often and Deborah on occasion: on
Mary he had never laid a finger.

Would David blame him for Mary? He did not. David blamed
him for nothing. Was his silence criticism? Maybe not. He
was always so very silent. Once, when they were together in

Langdale, Francis looking down the long green sward and then up to the Pikes, rosy in sunset, said:

'You must hate me, David.' And David, after a long silence while the birds swept above their heads home, answered:

'I have three friends. You are one – and the first.'

But what comfort, his irony urged on him, was he to find in that? David had not answered his question, only asserted his loyalty; and David's loyalty was so unsubtle that it offered no reward to one's pride.

Not that Francis's pride was in question. He was so proud that his son's approval or disapproval altered nothing. He was so proud that he would tell his son to go to the devil did he patronize him. But he did not patronize him. He stood at his side and worked with him. That was all.

So he rode into the little stone court of Herries, shouted to fat Benjamin to come for his horse, and longed, as he stumbled up the dark staircase, to see David waiting for him.

David was there. He was standing in the dark brown room upon whose surface the firelight was very faintly flickering, listening, and so intent was his attitude that Francis also stayed motionless by the door: the only sound in the room was the soft settling of the ash from the piled logs.

'What is it?' Francis asked at last. Then he heard, but so faint that it was like the scratching of mice on the wainscot, a trickling, crooning sound; someone, at a distance, behind walls, was singing, singing in a high-pitched murmur of a voice a little tune like an incantation or a prayer monotonously reiterated.

'Mrs Wilson,' David said, then coming close to his father and laying his hand on his arm: 'She sings to keep herself company. She's afraid.'

'Of whom?' asked Francis, although he knew the answer.

'They are very impatient . . . I've been telling her she should go from here.'

'Turn her from this roof . . . after these years?'

'No, no . . . Help her to the Low Countries. At the Hague there is some family she was nurse to once. They would take her. We could secure her a passage.'

'She is old,' Francis answered. He liked the warmth of his son's body close to his. He hoped that David would not move. That visit to the family had made him lonelier . . .

He put his arm across David's vast shoulders. His long brown fingers pressed a little into the smooth warmth of his son's neck.

'I think she is going mad with terror,' David said. The room too seemed a little mad: the dusk wrote letters on the wall with the firelight and then erased them again. The wind that was getting up and rattling the leaded panes drowned the little song and then by contrast raised it again. It was more dangerous in the dusky room because both men believed in witches and thought that Mrs Wilson was one.

Then Benjamin came clumping up the staircase, holding the lighted candles in their tall silver candlesticks in either hand, and Deborah came in to lay the table for some supper; there was life and movement and the little song could be heard no more.

Deborah, who was now twenty-two years of age, was little and insignificant until you noticed her eyes, which were large, soft, grey, very beautiful. Her shyness was her trouble. She could not be courageous about people. She was afraid of every person in the world save David, and especially of her father. She had had the same fear for seven years, ever since the death of her mother, that David would go and leave her with her father alone. That fear was now a torture, and no reassurance on David's part could comfort her.

Francis knew, of course, that she was afraid of him, and that exasperated him. Every time that she shrank from him his old ironic dislike of himself increased in him and she was included in that. When the supper had been cleared away and she had gone up to her room, the two men were left alone in front of the fire. The rain had returned and in violence; it slashed the panes, roared with the wind away, then fell again upon the house as though it would batter it to the ground; the fury passed and the rain softly stroked the windows, whispering indecent and chuckling secrets, then ran in a hurry as though it were pattering after someone, burst after that once more into a frenzy of rage and exasperation . . . an evil frustrated old woman, the rain that night.

Secure from it the two Herries drew close together. Suddenly they were intimate as they had not been for months. Francis put his hand on David's broad thigh, drawing his great body a little nearer to him. When he told him about his visit to the family that afternoon David was excited.

'Oh, why did you not stay?' he said. 'The awkwardness would have worn away. How did Cousin Pelham look? And Henry Cards . . . and Cousin Dorothy . . .' He sighed. 'I would that I'd been with you.'

Francis sharply withdrew his hand. 'You could go . . . Why don't you?'

David shook his head, laughing. 'What would they want with me? I've no head for their company. No, no. It was your opportunity, Father. But you frightened them.'

Francis said: 'David, I've been wishing to ask you. We've been working side by side these years. It's come to but little. Everything here must seem to you cursed, the house, the soil, the life, the loneliness. I fancy that it's in that very cursedness of the place that I find some salvation. I would have it hard and ungrateful. Here for the first time in all my days I've found response to my own temper and some aggravating comfort. But for you! Already you are doing good business in Keswick and with your friend in Liverpool. Why should you stay? There's no place in the world where you wouldn't make your way, and you should see the world, find a woman of your own breed, not bury yourself, in this windy hole for hinds and pigs . . . I'm other than you. The dirt of the soil is more to me than any man, aye, or woman either. I am stuck here, my feet in the clay, and am accustomed. But it is not your abiding-place and will never be.'

He was amazed then at how roughly, after he had ended, his heart was beating as he waited for the boy's answer. What would it be here without David? How could he endure it? But better that David should go rather than he should indulge his father by staying. Francis would take no patronage. Yes, but his heart hammered as he waited.

David was slow as always. At last he answered: 'I'm glad you've spoken at last, Father. All these months I've wondered what was in your mind. But I can't leave you. We're bound together, I fancy, different though we are. And yet . . . there *is* something I should say. Father, why should we stay by Herries? The place has never cared for us. As a boy I ran first into the house and shivered at its greeting. Everything has been wrong for you here. The people have been wrong for you, the soil stubborn; nothing that you have planted has grown: you have been with every year more alone here. Why should we stay? We owe nothing to the house. In the South together, the three of us, where it is warmer and the sun shines and people's hearts are more friendly . . . Father, let us leave here. Everything has been wrong for you here.'

'No,' his father answered in a strange, low voice, as though he were speaking to something within him. 'Everything is not wrong for me here. Here is my home, the only one I've ever known or shall know. I feel the touch of the peat, the scratch of the dried bracken, and it is my place.'

His voice had its accustomed ironic tone. 'So they've been persuading you, David, my son? "Take your father away, David
Herries. He stinks in our noses, he is warlock and dirty liver and
murderer maybe. Remove his carcass or we will remove it for
you." They've persuaded you, David . . . but there must be
more than a word before they can move me. I am stuck fast, and
there's my ghost to come after me when they've knocked my
head in and scattered my entrails for dung over their fields:
there's still my ghost, David.'

David got up. His voice was cold with anger when at last after
a long while he spoke.

'That is unjust. No man could persuade me against you save
yourself. I am no traitor. But guard yourself against irony with
me. I am a fool, you know, and may understand it wrongly.'

He went out.

So that was that. Herries was alone. He got up very early next
morning, washed himself at the pump and went off, walking, his
head in the air, not caring a damn if he never saw his bullock of a
son again. Or he said not. His heart within his heart ached, as it
always did, for his son. That heart would have gone, waked the
boy, embraced him. The only heart to which David responded,
the only one that he understood. For David had all the simple
sentimentality of his period; for him there were these actual
contrasted powers, God and the horny Satan, Michael and all
the angels, dragons and rescuing princes, shepherds, shepherdesses, and the ravening wolf, the good old man by the fireside
reading out of the Book to his family clustered at his knees,
wedding bells and Innocence wed under roses to Purity and
Strength. Yes, David believed in all these things. He saw life
like that.

Francis, as he strode off into the early morning rain that sung
about his ears in a feathering mist, said aloud: 'I'm done with the
boy. What's the use? . . . No ground between us,' and the rain
whispered in his ear: 'It's a lie! It's a lie!' Once he almost turned
back. It would be very easy to run up those stairs, climb to
David's room, see him sunk in sleep there, his chest bare, his
knees curled up. Francis knew how he lay, his cheek on his hand,
dreaming of his princesses and his shepherdesses. He had no
more subtlety than that. The Herries sentimentalist. No, not
conscious enough to be called anything. A sweet-breathed, mild-
eyed animal, with the obstinacy of a mule, the strength of a
horse, the fidelity of a dog. He should be breeding. He should be
let out, like a stallion, to the women of the country to get fine

sons. All this true enough did you forget his heart, which in its strength, sweetness, sympathy, durability was of another order from the animal. There was his immortality, and, likely enough, the immortality of all of us.

For there was immortality in us! The great white horse of Herries's dream striking up from the ebony lake to the icy peaks. Sentimentality, that again, thought Herries, and arrogance, planning for your little peapod of a marionette so handsome a destiny. But the very fact of the planning . . . Why this burning, eager, rebellious, longing fury between his miserable bag of bones, the thick coiled entrails, the stringy nerves, the flat-faced pancreas, that silly mechanism that one blow from a fool could tumble as a child tumbles a toy. Burning there between the bones and fat, the blood and gristle, this fierce arrogant ambition, this persistent dream, this lovely vision . . . 'All we like sheep . . .' Nay, like gods rather, lost in a strange land.

Herries often, as he dug and sweated, cursed the reluctant soil and his aching back and blistered hands, turned back and back to those same common platitudes, fresh to him because they were his own and mingled with so many strange things for which he could find no words. His brain, heart, generative organs: how to reconcile these three in a common harmony and drive them to a fine destiny, his brain that was clogged with lack of education, his heart that led him only to self-contempt, his generative powers that had known their best days, and they nothing to boast over. All keys to some event, but all out of control and discipline, all leading to silly ends.

Not intelligent enough, not kind enough, not even lecher enough. A botched machine set in a country veiled with mist . . .

He had crossed the fields, passed the little cottages of Seatoller and the yews, and started up the hill to Honister. On the left of him Hause Gill tumbling in miniature cataracts with the recent rain, on the right of him the ever-opening fells. He drew great gulps of air into his lungs. That was for him, that unenclosed fell. As soon as he reached a point where the moss ran unbroken to the sky all his troubles dropped away from him and he was a man. There was no place in the world for open country like this stretch of ground in Northern England and Scotland, for it was man's country: it was neither desert nor icy waste; it had been on terms with man for centuries and was friendly to man. The hills were not so high that they despised you; their rains and clouds and becks and heather and bracken, gold at a season, green at a

season, dun at a season, were yours; the air was fresh with kindliness, the running water sharp with friendship, and when the
mist came down it was as though the hill put an arm around you
and held you even though it killed you. For kill you it might.
There was no sentimentality here. It had its own life to lead and,
as in true friendship, kept its personality. It had its own
tempers with the universe and, when in a rolling rage, was not
like to stop and inquire whether you chanced to be about or no.
Its friendship was strong, free, unsentimental, breathing courage
and humour. And the fell ran from hill to hill, springing to the
foot, open to the sky, cold to the cheek, warm to the heart, unchanging in its fidelity. As he breasted the hill and turned back to
look across Borrowdale the sky began to break.

He stared, as though the scene were new to him, to Glaramara
and then over Armboth to the Helvellyn range. It was new to
him: never before had it held those shapes and colours nor
would it again: with every snap of the shuttle it changed.

Now across the Helvellyn line the scene was black and against
the black hung the soft white clouds. Borrowdale glittered in sun
like a painted card, flat, emerald and shining. Above his head all
the sky was in motion: beyond him over Honister tenebrous
shadows thrust upward to one long line of saffron light that lay
like a path between smoking clouds. All the fell smelt of rain and
young bracken, and two streams ran in tumult across the grass,
finding their way to the beck. The sunlight was shut off from
Borrowdale, which turned instantly dead grey like a mouse's
back; then the sun burst out as though with a shout over the low
fells that lay before the Gavel. A bird on a rock above the beck
began to sing.

He was filled with a delicious weariness. He lay down there
where he was, his full length on a thin stone above the beck, and
on that hard surface fell happily, dreamlessly, asleep.

He woke to a strange sense of constriction. He moved and
found amazingly that his arms and legs were tied with rough
rope. He raised his head and stared into the eyes of a man who
sat motionless on a rock near him. A horse grazed in the grass
close by.

Francis stared at the man: the man stared back again.

'You sleep fast,' the man said. 'I bound you and you didn't
waken.' He was a man with a thin dry face, long shaggy black
hair, a coat and breeches of some colour that had faded into a
dirty green. He looked like part of the fell. His legs were thin and
long and sharp. He was not young, fifty years of age maybe.

'Why have you bound me?' Herries asked quietly.

'You are my prisoner,' the man replied.

'My body is – for the moment,' Herries answered.

The man was, from his voice, not of the North. His tone was firm, quiet, reflective.

'You are Herries of Herries in Rosthwaite.'

'Yes. How do you know me?'

'I've seen you many times.'

'What have you against me?'

'Nothing.'

'Then why have you bound me?'

'You are my prisoner,' the man answered again.

'Yes; but why?'

'I have a curiosity to ask you some questions. Would you come peacefully with me?'

'Whither?'

'By Honister.'

'Yes,' said Herries.

'You swear it?'

'Yes.'

'Then I will untie you.'

He came forward and, quite gently, with some care, undid the bonds.

Herries sat up and felt his arms and legs where the rope had been, but he had been bound only a moment or so: it was the binding that had waked him. Then he rose and stretched himself. The man also got up. He was of great height and very thin with a long nose. His face was pitted with smallpox marks.

They started to walk together forward to Honister, the man leading the horse. The air was deliciously fresh and the sky filled now with little dancing white clouds.

'What is your interest in me?' Francis asked at last. They were on the higher ground, about to turn the corner, and before he turned he looked back and saw, picked up by the sun, on the low ground before Armboth a little wood of silver birch. The sun hung over the little wood in a brooding lighted mist and the thin silver trunks stood up proudly, burnished. Herries, because of what happened afterwards, was never to forget them.

This fellow was a man of not many words, but at last he said, long after Francis's question:

'Can you recall, once, many years gone, you gave your coat to a woman by the road?'

'Yes,' said Herries, his heart beating.

'And once later on a Christmas night you talked with her?'

'I remember,' said Herries.

'I was there, that second time,' the man said.

'There was with her,' Herries said, 'a young child.'

The man nodded. 'The woman was my sister. The child was her child and is with me yet.' He waited a while and then went on. 'I bound you because you would not have come with me else. Or I thought so. They say in the valley that you are the Devil and eat human flesh.'

Herries looked at the man smiling. 'Do you think so?'

The man looked back at Herries.

'No,' he said. 'When my sister died she said I was to give you the only thing she had. I have kept it for you.'

'But why,' asked Herries, 'must you bind me to give it me?'

The man answered: 'Our place is rough in Honister. We are in bad repute here, my brother and I, though not so bad as yourself. I thought you would fight before you came, and because of my sister I would not strike you. Are you as bad as men say?'

'I am as bad,' answered Herries, 'as other men. And as good. We are as the fancy hits us.'

The man nodded his head gravely. 'That's true. One man's life is this way, another's that. We have little choice.'

They struck up the fell to the left and climbed. The man led the horse patiently and with kindness. When they were high on the moor they could see the guards of the mines pacing on the path below.

All the fell rolled beneath them now like the sea, and the clouds rolled above them, driven by a sunny dancing wind. On the brow of the hill the man took Herries's arm, led him over boulders, dipped down the shelving turf, then pushed up again on the hinder shoulder of Honister.

Then, loosening his grip, he vanished. Herries stood alone, hearing no sound but the wind and running water. He could see, icily blue, the thin end of Buttermere Lake far below. He heard a whistle and saw the black head of the man just below him. He went down.

He saw then the grey opening of a cave in the hill, fenced with dead bracken and furze. He followed the man in. At first he could see nothing, but could smell cooking food, an odd sweet scent of flowers and a musty animal tang. The man had his hand on his arm and very gently, as though he were speaking to a child, said: 'Sit you there. You can sleep if you will. The straw's dry.' Francis turned back, shifting the bracken a little; and the sun flickered on to him, dancing before his eyes.

But he did not wish to look about him. He was oddly uncurious and infinitely weary. Why this weariness? It was as though the kind black-haired man had laid a spell upon him. So he slept, long and almost dreamlessly. The nearest to a dream was that he was led again through the incidents of the morning, following the lean man over ever-darkening fell, then was pushed from a height and heard, as he raised himself from a hard cold ground, a voice say to him: 'Into the cave! Into the cave! You have been outside too long.'

With that he woke, wide-eyed, oddly happy, extremely hungry. He sat up and looked about him. The sun streamed in from the fell. He could see all the cave, which was not indeed quite a cave, but rather the opening of some deserted entrance to a long-neglected mine. In the black cavern beyond him there was a fire and on the fire a round black pot. A girl sat on the ground watching the pot.

At once he knew her. Her hair, which fell all about her face and almost to her waist, told him – there was no colour like that anywhere else in the world; but something thin, poised, intent, alert, independent, in her attitude also told him: his eyes saw once again that figure never in all these years lost sight of, the tiny child, crowned with its flaming hair, pressed back against its mother's skirts. Instinctively, he put his hand up to his cheek and felt his scar.

He had found her again. He had the oddest sense of having reached the end of some quest, a sense of rest, of fulfilment, of motionless certainty.

'Well?' he said quietly.

'Well?' she answered, without turning or taking her eyes from the fire. 'So you've waked?'

'I've waked.'

'I never saw a man sleep so sound.' Then after bending forward and stirring the fire she added, but still not looking at him: 'So you've come at last.'

'At last?'

'Yes. I knew that you would come one day.' Her voice, he noticed, had the very same sweet, remote tone that all those years ago it had had. Seven years, and they were as though they were yesterday.

He got up and stretched himself. His clothes were stuck with bracken. He came across to the fire, looking at her hair that was dark in the cave like the sombre shadows in flame when the smoke is thick. Even now she did not look up.

'Well, I have waited for you too,' he said.

At that she turned and looked up at him, and as his eyes met hers he knew two things: that he loved her and that he had never before, in all his ventures, known at all what love was. He knew, instantly afterwards, a third thing: that he meant nothing at all to her and that she would be glad when he went. He knew that by the way that she looked beyond him to the mouth of the cave, a little impatiently, her mind on the fire and also on some possible escape for her.

She was a child, under eighteen. He was over forty. This folly . . .

But he could not take his eyes from her. They were locked there, and all his body moved in its inner spirit towards her so that already, although his hand had not touched hers, his arms were round her, his head, so heavy with fruitless work and anger and impatience, resting on her child's breasts.

'How did you know,' he said at last, his voice husky, 'that I would come one day?'

'Oh,' she answered, 'Mother would speak of you, and my uncle, and I would see you in the woods, Borrowdale-way. I begged once of your son by Stonethwaite. He gave me a silver shilling. He is the finest man I have ever seen. He has the grandest body. But I could never love him. He is too thick. But I have seen too much love.'

'You are only a child,' Herries said, 'and cannot know.' The force within him was too strong. Had it meant death in the next moment he could not have prevented himself. He put out his hand and touched her hair. But it did not mean for her anything at all. She did not move her head but allowed him to stroke it as he would.

He felt that, and his hand came back to him. Then she got up from the fire, straightening herself. Her body was very thin and still a child's body, but lovely to him in its slender line, the long legs and high carriage of the head and the lovely bosom, breathing on the very edge of maturity.

'My uncle is out watching,' she said. 'The guards are active today. They killed two men last night. Some day soon they will find this place and then we must move on again.'

'What does your uncle do?'

'My two uncles. Oh, they do what they can. Steal from the

mines and sell to the Jews in Keswick, or they poach, or my uncle George fights in the Fairs . . . whatever comes. But they are hoping for news soon from France. Then we will go to Carlisle or Scotland maybe.'

'From France?'

She smiled. 'They never tell me anything. Why should I care? It is all the same to me. One day they will be killed, and I shall sell myself to some wealthy man.'

'You would do that?'

'And why not? I must have food. To feed my body, I give my body. What is my body? It is not myself. That I keep for my own.'

'If your uncles are killed, you must come to me. I will take care of you.'

She looked at him, smiling. 'You are very ugly, and they say in Borrowdale that you are very wicked. I don't care if you are wicked – but how rich are you?'

'I am very poor.'

'Then why should I come to you if I don't love you?'

'Because I would care for you and work for you and protect you.'

'Maybe I should lie with your son. Would you still protect me?'

He turned his eyes away from her.

'Yes; even then.'

She put her hand lightly on his shoulder.

'No; if I ever came to you I would be honest. My mother always said a woman must be honest or she is nothing. Men can be as dishonest as they please. That is the difference between men and women.' She smiled at him like a small child, enchantingly. 'I would be honest if I came – but I will never come.'

Her two uncles crossed the light. They were in excellent spirits, amused by some joke they had had with one of the guards. One of them, Anthony, had rabbits and a hare.

They all sat round and ate. The food was excellent: savoury meat cooked in the pot, tasting of herbs and sun and all the rich juices in the world. There was good wine too. The two men – Anthony was round and fat, with a broad chest and short thick neck: he was coloured dark brown and had sharp suspicious eyes like a ferret's – curled up and went to sleep.

All through the sunny afternoon, while the clouds raced past the cave's entrance driven by the wind, Herries sat where he was, silent, watching the girl. She sat quite near to him, sewing at some garment and then afterwards lying back on the hay, the sun on her cheek, and falling easily, comfortably asleep.

He sat there thinking of nothing, nothing at all. He did not want to move. The air was cold although the sun shone, but he was hot with a kind of fever; once and again he trembled. Once he leaned forward and touched her cheek with his hand. He withdrew abruptly as though he had, by so doing, pledged himself to some awful danger. But he did not think at all, neither of his past nor of his future, nor of himself in any way. He simply knew that his fate had come and that whatever way he turned now he could not escape it.

He did not want to escape it. He, forty-five years, she sixteen. This child who cared nothing for him and perhaps never would care. A child of vagabonds. That did not matter. He was himself a vagabond. They were both outcasts. He sat staring there like a drunken man or an idiot. There was utter silence in the cave; only the wind, rushing by outside, sometimes cried out like a struck harp not quite in tune.

When the shadows began to lengthen and the sky beyond the cave was a pale washed blue with no clouds in it, the men stirred and woke together. George looked gravely at Herries as though he were going to lecture him. Then he got up, found an old green box behind the fire, fumbled in it and brought to Herries a simple rough silver chain with a little crucifix of black wood on its end.

'This was what she left for you,' he said.

Herries expected that he would say more. He had spoken in the morning of questions that he would ask. But he said no more, only stood there as though dismissing him.

Herries took the chain. He did not want to go. He wanted with a desire stronger than any that he had ever known to stay, but the two men stood there waiting for him to go.

The girl had waked, stretched her arms, then walked to the cave opening: the evening wind blew her hair so that it seemed to be fire blowing about her head and against the grey stuff of her dress.

'Hadn't you questions that you would ask me?' he said.

'No,' said the lean man.

'I don't understand why you brought me here.'

'To give you that.'

'Well, then, tell me your names.'

'I am George Endicott. He is Anthony Endicott.'

'And the girl?'

'The girl's name is Mirabell Starr.'

'Maybe we shall meet in another place.'

'Maybe.'

'In Carlisle, perhaps?'

'Maybe.'

Anthony, the fat one, turned back into the cave as though the matter were closed. George held his hand out.

'I bound you because I was afraid you wouldn't come.'

Herries exchanged a handgrasp.

'That's no harm. I shall keep the chain. My thanks for the meal. At Herries there's a meal for you.'

Then he went out of the cave. He held out his hand to the girl.

Lowering his voice, staring into her eyes, he said: 'You have promised to come to me if you are all alone.'

She answered like her uncle.

'Maybe,' she said. She let him hold her hand, and for a moment, in the wind that was now very strong blowing from the sea, his body pressed against hers.

'I will be good to you,' he said.

'So they all say,' she answered, 'until they've got what they wanted.'

'I shall never get what I want,' he answered. He longed to kiss her pale thin cheek, but the indifference in her eyes humiliated him. So he turned, bending his head a little, and went up the fell, not looking back.

WITCH

MRS WILSON stood, as was her habit, at the foot of the stairs, listening and looking up. No one was moving in the house. It was after midday. She knew that Herries was digging at the back of the house, that his son was away for that day in Keswick, that his daughter was in Rosthwaite and Benjamin the servant at the stable: she was therefore quite alone in the house.

She stood there endeavouring to make up her mind to what was for her a great venture. She was planning to go to Grange. She had not been out of that house for six months: she had not been in the village of Rosthwaite for a year. This enterprise of hers needed immense resolution and courage. Although, since early morning, she had been summoning her will to this expedition, she was not yet completely resolved on it.

Old Tom Mounsey, deaf and dumb, had contrived to send her word that his wife Old Hannah Mounsey was dying and wished to see her before she went. Hannah Mounsey, once Hannah Armstrong, a gay and beautiful young thing, was Katherine Wilson's oldest friend. She was now, like Katherine, so old that she didn't know how old she was. And she was dying. She was the first human who had asked to see Katherine Wilson for more than twenty years.

The old woman had been strangely stirred by the summons. She was so old that the days of her youth were as yesterday. They were very vivid and alive to her. She saw Hannah still with red cheeks, bright flaxen hair, and a blue gown. She heard Hannah laugh as she hid with Katherine in Statesman Armstrong's barn, while young Johnny Turnbull had searched for her to fumble and kiss her. Young Johnny Turnbull had been hanged in Carlisle for stealing a sheep. As everyone knew, it was not he who stole the sheep but Daniel Waugh.

She was very old, but she could make the journey. Her legs could still carry her. It would take her two hours or more to walk to Grange, but she could do it. It was not her legs that frightened her. Something else.

She was frightened of the outside world, and with reason. The outside world hated her. They hated her as much as they were afraid of her.

They said she was a witch. Was she a witch? She did not know. They said that the troubles of the last year were her doing. Were they? She did not know. Sometimes she thought that they were and felt an odd impulse of power. Was it true that by crooking her finger or nodding her head she could kill sheep, scatter the palsy, burn hay-ricks, poison food? It might be so. She did not know.

It was not of course true that she could fly on a broomstick or that she had danced naked with the Devil in Glaramara caves.

But she *had* danced naked in the woods one moonlit night. That was a great many years ago. Many, many years. She had had a child by Joe Butterfield because of that dancing. The child had been happily still-born, and Joe Butterfield had been gored to death by his own bull many years back . . . He had been a fine big young fellow, with a tattoo of a mermaid on his chest.

She could not remember many things, and many things she

remembered in every detail. But all that she wished now was to be let alone: all the passions save fear had died right down in her. Her love of fun and gaiety, her recklessness, her vicious tempers, her courage, her loyalty to those whom she loved, her passion for her son who, after living in this house with her so long, had left her, all these fires had sunk to grey ashes. The only thing remaining to her was fear.

The first time that she had been really afraid was one day shortly before the coming of these Herries, when, walking out on the path to Seathwaite, some boys had thrown stones and shouted 'Witch!' after her. Long before this she had been suspected of witchcraft, she and Mary Roberts and Ellen Wade and Alice Leyland. Alice Leyland had been much older than the others. It may be that Alice had been a witch. She had made an image of Gabriel Caine and burnt it at a slow fire, and he had died within three days.

She had, too, her famous love-philtre, and Katherine herself had mixed this in her own man's drink, a year after their marriage, when he was going with the Hoggarty girl in Keswick. It had not, however, caused him to leave the Hoggarty girl, not until she had had the smallpox and grown ugly.

The old woman sat down at the foot of the stairs. Did she dare to venture into Grange? She sniffed danger in the very air, but that might be her fancy. Much of it might be her fancy. She had stayed alone in this house until she scarcely knew what she believed. But, from the very beginning, there had been something about her that set her apart from the others. She had been a pretty girl: they had all said so. She had cared for men no more and no less than the others, but the difference had been that men were not enough: no, love was not enough, nor courting, nor childbirth, nor any of the dreary, dull, day-by-day life in that dreary, dull valley.

She must have excitement, but then, after that, it was not excitement that she wanted, not excitement only. She was curious, inquisitive. She wanted to see *into* things, and when she had seen Alice Leyland and the others dance naked across the grass under the moon and then vanish into the black wood she had been curious to see what they did there. So she, too, had danced naked into the wood, and all that had happened had been Joe Butterfield's baby.

Had it not been for that odd sense of power that sometimes came to her she would have left it alone.

But there had been hours when she felt that she held all the

valley in her hand to do with as she would. She felt that sometimes even now. What was that accompanying her, lifting her up,
taking her to the very verge of some discovery? Was it only her
fancy? In later years she had yielded to the temptation to see in
the eyes of others that look of fear, of terror . . .

When they came to her, as they used to do, to ask her to heal
their cattle, to help them with a lover, to injure an enemy, she
had always told them to go away again, that she knew no spells,
no charms, had no powers.

But they did not believe her, and she did not believe herself.
Had she no power? Why was it then that she would rise in the
night and walk to the window and see the shadows under the
moon come flocking to her call, and had she not killed Janet
Forsse by looking at her after Janet had called her a witch outside Rosthwaite Chapel? Had not Janet gone home, lain down on
her bed and died? That had done her much harm, that death of
Janet. They had feared and hated her from that moment. She
had felt the power rise in her breast, fill her breast, well into her
eyes. But was that truth or falsehood? Janet had eaten meat from
a poisoned pot and so died . . .

All her life she had wished others well. Only when they insulted her she must turn and defend herself. And in these last
years, from loneliness, desolation, unhappiness, she had scarcely
known what she did. She had made wax figures, watched from
the window, spoken sometimes with shadows. Why not with
shadows when no one else would speak with her?

Everything had been worse with her since the coming of
Herries. From the first day she had hated the father and loved
the son. The father had something in common with her. Although she was an untaught woman, and he was a grand gentleman, yet they shared something. He had looked at her and she at
him. It might be that he was the Devil. Some thought so in the
village. It might be. He looked like the Devil once and again.
Perhaps he could answer the questions that she never dared to
ask. She was afraid of him, and she hated him. She had always
loved his son David since, as a little boy, he had run first into the
house. All that was simple and good and maternal in her responded to him. He had always been kind to her, talked to her,
asked her how she did, and now that he was the finest, grandest
man in the valley she was proud of him, as though he had been
her work. When his mother had died she had wanted to protect
and care for him. He had not needed her – he needed no one –
but she prayed for him night and morning.

That had been until the last year, but in the last year fear had grown in her breast, swallowing up everything else in her.

The thing that she feared most now was to dream, because in her dreams she was quite unprotected. So soon as she slept she was outside the house in the naked road, or the house was without walls, or she was on the mountainside. Then while she waited alone in this awful space she could hear them coming, hundreds of them; the present and past came together – Alice Leyland, Joe Butterfield, Turnbull, Hannah Armstrong, and with them many strangers. But they all looked alike. They had terrible faces, and that look in the eyes of lust and hatred, curiosity and pleasure. Years ago, when a young woman, she had seen a boy stoned to death in Keswick market. They said that he had burnt a rick. That look then had been in their faces. It had been perhaps also in her own.

In her dream they came always nearer and nearer, quite silent, and she had no strength to escape them. Then one had called 'Witch!'

She would awake trembling and the sweat would run down into her eyes; then she would sigh with relief at the respite, and would get up and touch the familiar things, the clock, the settle, the pots and pans, to reassure herself.

When her son had left her he had said nothing, but had looked at her once before he went, and the look in his eyes had held fear, just as her own eyes held fear. She had not tried to keep him. Only after he had gone she sat and remembered all the things he had done as a child and especially when he had sucked at her breast and she had crooned songs to him.

And now should she go in to Grange? It might be that it would break the spell, it might be that she would meet folk who would be kind to her, and, seeing Hannah again, she would recover her courage.

She moved slowly back into the empty kitchen. She was still strong. Her bodily health had been always amazing; she had never known a day's sickness, and that, too, had made her some-times wonder whether she were not under the Devil's especial protection.

She stirred about the kitchen, raising her head, sniffing the air, her brown face was a network of wrinkles, her hair was snow-white, her eyes dimmed in vision. She moved on her legs easily and with freedom.

Suddenly she knew that she was going into Grange: it was as

though someone had bent over and whispered in her ear. The
great grey cat, with one eye green and one brown, her only friend
in the world, had come and rubbed itself against her legs. It was
he, perhaps, who persuaded her.

Every witch must have a cat. She had seen Alice Leyland
once take a glove that she had soaked in blood and water and rub
it on her cat's belly, murmuring some spell . . . What were the
words? She had known them all once. Words, words, words . . .
words from where? They had come to her once, without her own
desire: there had been the day when she had seen Statesman
Peel's man rubbing between the horns of his oxen the grease
from the Paschal Candle, eyeing her as he did so. Yes, then,
against her own will, not at all by her agency, the words had
come to her lips. He had seen her lips move and had told them in
the village.

But her cat. She bent down and stroked it, letting her old
dried fingers press into the fur, liking to feel the cat's response as
it bent its back a little, stiffening, stretching its legs, its eyes
closing with pleasure. She had thought often that her cat knew
more than she did. Watching sometimes at night from the
high window she had seen it slip off across the fields, moving
with quiet secret purpose, just as Alice Leyland had once
moved. The cat and Alice Leyland knew things that she would
never know.

She went to the cupboard and found her cloak and high-
crowned, old-fashioned hat. She found her crooked, gnarled
stick. She started out.

When she came into the path beyond the courtyard her heart
beat so furiously that she must stop: it leapt with wild angry
stabs as though it were telling her not to go. For a whole year
she had not been beyond the courtyard. She was encouraged by
the stillness of the world about her, not a sound save the running
water that was never silent, and the scrape, from behind the
house, of Herries's spade as it struck the hard soil. She was always
scornful of Herries's labour; the soil here was like stone or mire,
harsh, ungrateful, contemptuous: it hated Herries as she did. A
little pleasure stirred her heart as she thought of Herries's labour
and the small reward he had for it.

She walked down the path, moving with marvellous strength
for an old woman. She thought that she heard the cat following,
and she turned to forbid it, but there was nothing there.

It was a grey, overhanging, autumn day with no wind: the
light on walls and trees trembled once and again as though

thunder was coming, but the leaves that still lingered, brown and
shrivelled, on the trees, never shivered.

She walked as she had lived, in a half-dream. Sometimes it
seemed to her that figures were walking with her, sometimes that
she was alone. When she reached the river she muttered a little
with pleasure, as though she were blessing it. Perhaps she was.
This river, the Derwent, had been part of her from birth. Her
parents' cottage had bordered it: her first instinct as an infant
had been to find it, and now, because for so long she had not
seen it, she greeted it again as an old friend. There had been a
time in her life when, if she did not see it every day, she was
miserable. From Seathwaite to the lake she had known every
inch of it, its deeps and shallows, its moods of anger, rebellion,
calm, blue content, shrill chatter, acquiescence, curiosity; its
colours, brown like ale, blue like glass, grey like smoke, white
like cloud; she had bathed in it, fished in it, sat beside it. Often,
shut up in that house, she had listened to it, especially when it
was in flood; then it was happiest, most violent. It was the only
thing in the world now that she could trust: it would never harm
her. It did not care whether she were witch or no.

As she passed beside it now, happy in a dim confused way at
recovering it again, she seemed to speak to it, telling it how sorry
she was that it was shrunken, that its stones and boulders must
be exposed, and its voice have fallen to a murmur. Never mind.
The rains were coming again. Patience, patience . . . And as she
looked her husband rose out of it, his brown tangled beard wet,
his eyelashes dripping water, his breast, thick with soaking hair,
exposed, his flanks too shining with damp fine yellow hair, his
toes crooked about the stones of the river-bed; his bare arm rose
up as he brushed his hair from his eyes as he used to do. He
called out something to her, and his voice had just the old
husky growling note, but she could not hear what he said.

She walked on, resolutely, her stick striking the path, her head
in its high black hat, and very far away, beyond Grasmere maybe, the thunder dimly rumbled. She gathered confidence as she
went: a silly old woman she had been to stay in that dark house
letting fear gather upon her. She would not wonder now but it
was that devil Herries that had put those thoughts into her head.
It was himself that the people hated, and she had taken his contempt for her own. Just because, forsooth, some boys had
thrown stones after her and a labourer cast a word at her, she had
hidden away and missed her proper company. It would be good
to see Hannah once more. Hannah was dying, they said, but she

would be able enough to remind her of the old days when they had both been young and happy together. One kindly look from Hannah's eyes would be a fine thing, and she would walk all the way back to Herries again and show the village that she was no witch, but an old woman who liked company and chatter and friendly faces in candlelight.

As she walked, strength seemed to increase in her. She had no ache nor pain in all her body. She was still good for life. Death had not got her yet. She breathed the air, even though it were close and packed with thunder, and as the hill grew steeper by the Bowder Stone, she set her knees to it and braced her back and climbed bravely to the turning of the road. Then, at the sight of the Grange cottages across the river, again her courage failed her. She was passing Cumma Catta Wood, a place that she had always feared because, when she was a girl, young Broadley had drowned himself in the pool there below the wood. It was a pretty place, a little hill thick with trees hanging over a broad pool, where the river gathered itself together for a while and stayed tranquilly reflecting the sky. But they said that young Broadley haunted it, and that, in ancient days, there had been pagan sacrifices there. You could see the two projecting stones where the sacrifices had been.

The old woman moved on. She paused before she crossed the bridge that raised itself up like a cat's back over the divided strands of the river. The Grange cottages, huddled on the other side, seemed to be waiting, watching for her.

Their faces were white, shining in the grey shadows of the thundery air.

She crossed the bridge, wondering that she saw no human being: she must herself, to those who, behind dark window-panes, watched her, have seemed a curious figure alone in that still grey landscape, in her high hat and black cloak, tapping with her stick.

She knew Hannah's cottage, a little grey dwelling twisted like a crumpled ear over the river. She knocked with her stick on the door. There was no answer, and she had never felt the world so breathlessly still. The rattle of her stick on the door had been so sharp that she would not knock again. She pushed the door back and went in. The interior was very dark and smelt of damp hay. Some hens ran squawking from under her feet into the open. Her eyes were dim and the light was dusk, but she soon saw that the very old man, Hannah's husband, was sitting in a chair by a black, empty grate and that a large stout woman was bending over him, making signs with her hands. But he did not look: he stared, without any movement, in front of him.

The woman looked up and saw Mrs Wilson. She stared then with a start of recognition, turned as though she would motion to the old man, then turned again, and, with a muttered explanation, almost hurled her stout body out of the cottage. Mrs Wilson could hear her feet hastening over the cobbled path; once more there was breathless waiting silence . . .

The old man could not hear her, could not speak to her. She was as old as he, but he looked infinitely older. He was a little man like a grey nut, and on his head he was wearing a bright-red nightcap. It was of no use to waste time with him, so she fumbled her way up the twisted wooden staircase. Halfway up she paused: she was suddenly very tired. Her legs were aching and she was a hundred years old. The door of the room at the stair-head was open and she went in. A large four-poster bed with faded red hangings occupied most of the room, placed a little unevenly on the crooked wooden floor. Hannah Mounsey was stretched out on the bed in her grave-clothes, her long, thin face, with the closed eyes, looking spiteful, because the mouth had fallen in and the sharp brown chin stuck forward aggressively.

So Hannah was dead, an old grey bag of bones under the long white clothes. This was young Hannah with the flaxen hair and blue gown. There was a faint odour in the room, and a mouse scuttered across the floor. Beyond the dim, diamond-paned window you could hear the Derwent carelessly running.

Death was nothing odd to Mrs Wilson, yet peering half blindly over the bed she shivered. She would not be greeted by Hannah, then; her journey had been fruitless. Suddenly she felt a deep sorrow for herself. Hannah was gone, the only one who in all these years had sent for her. Nobody now wanted her at all. To pass from this dead house to the dead house Herries was all the same. And yet she had the capacity still to love someone, to take trouble for someone or something. She was not dead, as Hannah Mounsey was, and she had a sudden vision of herself coming out· on a sunshiny morning, sitting outside her cottage, other neighbours gathering round, all of them chatting, laughing together.

Then something made her prick up her ears: she did not know what it was, but it was something that caused her altogether to forget the dead woman on the bed. Fear leapt into her body. Her legs were trembling, so that she caught the post of the bed. She had a sense of being trapped, and yet when she listened again there was no sound, only the careless running of the river. Nevertheless, she knew that there was reason for her fear. She looked about the room, at the looking-glass, the wooden box painted with red hearts, a chair with a thin curved back. She listened, her head bent forward, her hat a little crooked. There was a sound behind the soundlessness; the still air was full of it, and the odour of musty decay in the room grew with every second stronger. She must get out, get away, get to Herries.

Although her legs that had been so strong were now trembling like slackening cord, she found her way down the wooden staircase. Nothing was changed in the room below. The old man in the red nightcap still sat there without moving, staring in front of him.

She pulled back the door, peered out on to the ragged garden, and beyond it the grey smooth running water, and beyond that the field rising to Cumma Catta Wood. Then, although no sound reached her, she turned and stared, across the cobbled path, into a group of faces.

Men and women, close together as though for protection, were gathered at the end of the cobbled path. They stood, huddled together, not speaking, staring at her. Although she could not see well and was so deeply frightened that it was as though her heart were beating in her eyes, yet certain faces were very distinct to her. One belonged to a large stout man in a brown wig and green coat and breeches. His face was red as a tomato and his eyes wide and staring. There was the smooth white face of a young woman; a face with a black beard; there was a young girl's face, very fresh and rosy, with a mole on one cheek.

She looked back behind her; there was no way out there, only a thick rough-stone wall. They could easily stop her if she ran in front of the river.

She walked forward towards them, leaning on her stick because her knees trembled so badly, and at her movement a hoarse whisper broke the thick air: 'T'witch . . . t'witch . . . t'witch.' She stopped, rubbing at her eyes with her hand. The people stood and she stood; then, not knowing what she was doing now, she turned back towards the cottage door.

Her movement released them. A second later two had her, one, the big red-faced man, dragging at her arm, the other a little man with a hump who caught her with twisting hands round the waist.

She heard someone cry: 'A trial! A trial!' She tumbled on to her knees, not for supplication but because, her legs shaking as they did and the man dragging her, she had no strength. She looked now a ridiculous old woman, her hat knocked sideways, her head bent, one thin arm up as though she were shielding herself. But having gone so far with her they paused. The two men stood away from her. The rabble – for it was now a great crowd, some having run and told the others what was toward – broke into every kind of babel, some shouting one thing, others another.

Meanwhile she stayed there murmuring: 'Oh, Christ save me! Oh, Lord Christ save me! Oh, Christ save me!' but her thoughts were like wild terrified birds flying from one place to another, so that she was thinking of her knee that was cut by the sharp stone, of Hannah lying dead, and of a great weariness that had seized her, turning all her body to water. But mostly she was afraid of the large red-faced man. Then, in the pause, life coming a little back to her, she looked up and searched some of the faces to see whether there was kindness in any of them. With a horror that was the most terrible confirmation of all her earlier fears, she realized that all these faces had that look that so often, alone in Herries, she had anticipated: the look of lust and hatred, curiosity and pleasure. And they all seemed strangers to her.

As was perhaps to be expected, it was a woman who took the next step. A long, thin, elderly woman whose head wagged on her neck as though it were loosely tied there.

Crying out something in a shrill, high voice like a bird's, she rushed forward and, bending down, struck the old woman on the cheek. It was as though that had been a signal. The crowd tumbled across the path, loosed, it seemed, by a word of command. A funny babble of sound came from them, not human, not animal: 'Swim her!' 'Swim her!' 'Sink or swim!' A little girl danced delightedly round and round, like a leaf spinning, crying: 'T'witch! . . . T'witch! . . . T'witch!'

Inside the cottage, the widower of Hannah Mounsey sat staring in front of him, hearing nothing, seeing Hannah as a young, laughing, fresh-faced girl. He moved his hand a little, enclosing with his arm her waist.

They dragged Mrs Wilson along the path, bumping her head on the stones, pulling her by her feet and her hands. They tumbled her out on to the green sward between the bridge and the river.

Then again they stood back from her. She crouched there, her head hanging forward. Her hat was gone, her white hair was loose about her face, her gown was torn, exposing her withered

brown breasts; she clasped her arms together over these. Tears
trickled down her cheeks.

There was a desperate impulse in her now to say something,
but she could not speak. Her terror urged her that if she could
only make them listen she would persuade them that she was no
witch, but only a harmless old woman who had never done any
harm.

But she could not speak: fear constricted her throat, and her
tongue moistened her dry, dead lips. Her other thought was that
soon they would hit her again. She bent her head over her arms
to shelter herself from the blows.

The crowd now had no individual consciousness. Some cried
that they must take her to the little house at the back of the
village and that she must be tried there all in proper order and
decently. But these were the minority. The others must see her
swim; then they'd know whether she were witch or no. Then
there was a moment's strange silence. Every voice fell. For an
instant the only sounds were the very distant rumbling thunder,
the running river and the old woman's crying, a whimper like a
child's.

Three women ran forward. They bent down over her; shouting they tore her clothes from her. They threw her clothes over
their heads into the crowd. They tore her flesh as they dragged
her things away. One stood up, tugging at her white hair, and so
she pulled the thin, bony body up, raising it to its knees.

Someone threw a stone. It struck the body between the breasts.

Then the stout, red-faced man, shouting as though he were
proclaiming some great news, called for order. Everything must
be done properly. No one should say that they were out of
justice. He strode forward, laughing. He caught the body in his
arms, then dropped it again as he felt in his breeches pocket,
from there brought faded green cord. He took the body again
and roughly, as though he would tear one limb from the other,
took the right foot and fastened it to the left hand, the left foot
and fastened it to the right hand. So trussed, she lay motionless.
Then suddenly raising her face, which now streamed with blood,
she sent forth two screeches, wild, piercing, sounding far over
the crowd out into the village, down the road. Then her head
fell again.

Triumphantly he raised her in his arms, holding her, her head
against her knees, as a woman might an infant. He danced her
for a moment in his arms. Then he ran forward, the crowd shouting, yelling, laughing, and up the bridge some children ran that

they might see better, singing and dancing: 'T'witch . . . t'witch . . . t'witch.'

He lifted his stout arms and flung her out, high into air. The little white body gleamed for a moment, then fell, like a stone, into the water.

Herries straightened his aching body and leaned on his spade. He had been clearing a patch of hard, stiff ground. Later there should be an orchard here: he saw it in his eye, the strong, gnarled trunks, the blossom, the apples hanging in shining clusters, the sun blinking through the leaves.

He spat on his hands and bent again to the spade. Around him nothing had grown well save a strange ruffian-like grass that had sharp-pointed blades like jagged knives. Some stunted blooms, some ragged naked vegetables. It was the wrong place, the wind caught it too fiercely, there was not sun enough, the soil was too resolutely stubborn. Meanwhile, to the house many things should be done. Windows were broken, pipes had fallen; one corner towards the hill had tumbled right in, and stones lay in a careless heap.

Nevertheless, the house looked stout and obstinate, its colour was of a pale gentle ivory, stained here and there with orange and pink, stains of rain and wind. Its feet were dug resolutely in the ground. It was alone but not lonely, defiant but not complaining.

Herries, raising himself again, turning to look at it, loved it.

He saw fat Benjamin, sweat pouring from him, hurry towards him.

'They are drowning Mrs Wilson, by Grange Bridge, for a witch.'

He turned and listened as though he expected to hear something. Only a faint rumble of thunder over Grasmere way. He said nothing to Benjamin, but dragging on his old faded long-skirted coat, strode into the yard. Benjamin, silent as himself, brought out his horse.

At once, without a word to one another, they rode off along the rough track to Grange. Then, after a little, Benjamin, in the husky voice which ale, weather and stoutness of body had produced in him, explained that he had been riding back through Portinscale. Passing Grange he had heard that the old witch Wilson was in Mounsey's cottage, saying spells over his dead woman, and that they were going to have her out and 'swim' her. He had hastened on to his master.

Herries had long been expecting this. He did not doubt but that Mrs Wilson was a witch. He had a horror of her for that. He was glad that now she would be out of his house. He felt no pity, no sense of a hunted thing, of a crowd lust-baiting. Such feelings were not of his time, class or education.

Had he been a magistrate and she been brought before him with evidence of her dirty dealings, he would have condemned her without hesitation and watched her sentence without a shudder. But here he also was involved. His pride drove him to protect his house. They would touch one of his servants? He would see to it. He hated them as he rode, the whole dirty foul rabble of them.

Then as he went something else moved in him. Since his day in the Honister cave a new element had stirred, a kind of softness, a glow of unanalysed, almost unrealized kindliness. He had not wanted it. He would scorn it if he dragged it into daylight.

But he did not drag it. It stayed within him like a secret fire that burnt stealthily without his feeding it. Every little thing was happier to him now than it had been.

His gaze softened, even now as he stared through the trees at the river, pounded up the hill, saw the humped bridge and the crowd at the water's edge.

He leapt off his horse and came down to them. He spoke to no one. As he came to the stream he saw an old white bundle of flesh with hair that streamed behind it rise, eddy in a little pool, sink again.

He plunged in, waded up to his thighs. The crowd said no word. The body rose again right at his hand. He plunged his arms in and caught it, dragging it to his breast. The head wagged against his coat.

He turned, standing and looking at them all for a moment, then breasted his way back to the bank. On dry ground he felt his hands chill against the bare flesh, so he laid the sodden body delicately on the ground, took off his faded coat, wrapped it round, then, holding the little corpse like a child against his shirt, strode up the hill, all the people silently withdrawing from him.

He mounted his horse and rode away.

THE ROCKING WOOD

As THEY rode through the rocking wood, the wind tearing at their heels, Herries talked to David.

It was the wild stormy afternoon of Friday, November 8th, 1745. It had been Herries's suggestion that they should be riding to Carlisle. For months now he had been longing for this.

In the *Scots Magazine* for July, at the barber's in Keswick, David had read:

'There have lately been several rumours of some designs upon Scotland or Ireland by the Pretender's eldest son.' Then, a month later, at that same barber's, it was said that there had been a landing in Scotland.

Now this very morning Keswick was frantically buzzing. The rebels were in Jedburgh. At any moment they would be South . . .

Francis Herries had shown no interest. His mind was elsewhere. David even was surprised at his own indifference. His principal thought was of Father Roche. After all these years his chance had come! After all these years! David was a child again riding under Cat Bells, his body tight between Roche's thighs, and that beautiful, persuasive voice in his ears: 'Even as our Lord suffered . . .' But he was practical now, was David, a grave and serious man with a liking for the steady security of the reigning dynasty. He had been prospering lately. He had bought land near Cockermouth. He had an interest in two vessels trading from Liverpool. There was a farm at the back-end of Skiddaw that he might buy if things went well. He had no hunger for rebellions . . .

But the romantic soul still breathed close to his heart. The memory of Roche could stir it, some woman one day, but most of all, now and ever, his love for his father, this strange man, removed in temperament, thought, passion so far from him, so mysterious and alone. Of late so silent, but united to him as no other human being was united.

Therefore when, quite suddenly, in the dark hall at Herries last evening, his father had said: 'Shall we ride tomorrow to Carlisle?' David had at once agreed. No more than that. No reason given. In all these years at Herries David had been only once to Carlisle, his father twice. But it seemed that now, riding alone together, they might come to some fresh intimacy. It must come from Herries. David was a man of few words and deep shyness in close relations. There was something, too, in the isolation of Herries that drove speech deep down. They talked less and less in Herries.

They were silent out of Keswick until they rode into the woods below Skiddaw. A terrific wind was surging among the trees; all the wood was rocking, and light mists spun and shifted over the two humps of the mountain-top that were powdered with snow thin like smoke. Beyond the wood Bassenthwaite Water was whipped into curls of white and angry spray.

Herries began to speak, his thought that had followed its own secret course ever since they left Herries breaking into spoken word: '. . . When I came to the river's edge she was bobbing, a white bundle, in the water. I strode in and picked her out, and they stood there while I carried her off. At that moment, David, when I held her wet and sodden against my body I felt something new in me. I had been coming to that as I had been coming to many things through these years . . . She cried against my heart although she was dead. She cried something, telling me a road to go. She was a witch and foul-living. In all those years that she was with us, David, I don't doubt but that she was evil.

'But she had been alone as I also had been alone. They hated her as they hated me. Not that I care at all for their hatred, but there was a bond in our loneliness. I had always known it.' (He thought, as he went on: Why am I telling him this? He can never understand that loneliness. He will never feel this thing that I feel.) '. . . I have had to bear my difference all my life, David, as she had to bear it. By no choice and no wish. I have no faith in God. I have never had; but for those of us who are different there is a compulsion to listen that is almost a faith. Nature, I suppose, chooses once and again to separate a few from the rest. She understands them and speaks to them. But why should we who are thus separated expect human nature to understand? Human nature must protect itself. I perceive that it must be so. Human nature is narrower than Nature, less wise and less secure.

'We who are different cannot come into that general company, however we may desire it. It is our lot. Myself, I do not grumble at it. What have I ever done worse than these others, than Pomfret or Harcourt? But every dice has been loaded against me, every act removed me further . . . Nothing strange there, since it is understood. Think you that she was a witch, David?'

Through the groaning of the boughs and the rocking wind David's voice came out sturdily:

'Most certainly she was a witch, Father.'

'Yes . . . most certainly. They were cruel because they were afraid, and I was compassionate because I, too, have suffered. Do you think it has meant nothing to me that I could not be like other men? I, too, have my pride, my sense of honour, my friendliness, although it does not do to speak of these things. But with them all, my brothers, my wife, my mistresses, my children, that final intimacy has been forbidden. Only with my own kind could I be intimate, and I could not find my kind. Often I have wished to put my case' (Herries thought: I am putting my case to him now and he does not understand it at all, not a word of it), 'but my case has not been their case. I am, in some sense, it must seem to them, against Nature, but it is not against Nature but rather against human nature.

'Nevertheless, there is compensation in loneliness. I am grow- ing to find that. There is strength in it, and a compelled wisdom. I learnt that from the witch. The evil that she knew was not so weighty as the strength that she caught from her isolation. They might stone her, but their stones would not bring her into their company nor would they stay her. Nothing can stay us, no physi- cal death.' (He smiled to himself thinking: All these words go to the wind. He has not caught any of them.)

And David, stolid on his horse, his back broad as a wall, his head finely set, was thinking: 'He is talking to me now as man to man. He has never before done that. But this talk of feelings: I can't be with him there. What's the use of it? I love him what- ever he is, different or no, but it's uncomfortable to speak openly about love . . . Easier here, though, with this wind blowing and the trees creaking. If the *Calliope* does well this voyage I could pay a price for that farm. It will mean leaving Herries. It must come to that one day. But not yet. I must take Deb with me and that would leave him alone. I can't leave him alone; and he wouldn't go from Herries. But one day if I marry, which I shall . . .'

He felt the cold rain on his face and the wind swooping down and then up again. He threw back his head, stretched his great chest, turned to his father, smiling:

'Maybe, Father,' he said, 'you force yourself to be different by thinking that you are. Folks take one for what one says one is. You have always refused them, thought poorly of them, fright- ened them maybe. Will you never leave Herries, Father?'

'Leave Herries?'

'Aye. Maybe I'll buy that farm at the back of Skiddaw –

Penhays . . . John Tennant and I have done well lately with the *Calliope* and the *Peggy Anne*. If this Pretender doesn't upset the world . . . Herries is a hard place, Father. No soil, no sun, rock and mire. They have this thought of you in the valley and will never be rid of it.

'But at Penhays you could have your own land and work it, and it would be brighter for Deb . . .' He waited, then continued more shyly. 'Uncle Pomfret loves you, Father, at heart. I know he does. Aunt Jannice is sick now and has little say. My dear cousin Raiseley is in London. If we were at Penhays we would be more in the world. At Herries . . .' He broke off, afraid suddenly, as he had so often before been afraid, of his father's anger. Some word would be spoken and all the good of their talk be gone, and they would ride on in offended silence. David had his own temper in his own way and it showed most easily with his father, simply because he loved him most.

But today he need not have been afraid. His father turned to him with a strangely childlike, ingenuous gaze as though he were David's junior and had been asking advice from him.

'Herries is a bitter place for you and Deborah. I've always known it. But for me there is none other nor ever can be. I'm held there and it's for ever. But you will go, of course, when the right time comes. And, for that, I may not be alone. It may be that, one day, I shall marry again.'

The rocking wind, as though driven by that word to a frenzy of derision, cracked in his ear: 'Marry again! He'll marry again! Crack! Crack! Crack! He'll marry again!' David brushed the rain from his eyes. Marry again! He thought that his father had done with women. For a long time now there had been no sign of any traffic with them.

'Well,' he said, 'have you seen a woman?'

'Yes . . . there is someone. She is a child. She could only need me through weariness and fear of loneliness. But I am in love again. Again! I have never loved before. I am very happy in the mere thought of it.'

David had an instant of deep comprehension and of an aching affection for his father. With a swift vision of imagination, born only through love and exceedingly rare with him, he saw his father as he had been, so handsome and grand. As he was now, his face disfigured, his body gaunt and bent with digging and grubbing . . . Could a woman care for him now? A sense of his father's isolation came over him as it had never done before.

Now, however, they had come out of the woods and were in

open country across which the icy rain was blowing in furious
sweeps. On a good day a great stretch of land spread grandly to
the Firth and the hills behind it, but now everything was blotted
out.

For Herries, although today he could not see, this coming into
the open was like walking out of a house and closing the door
behind him. That was why he chose this route, because he loved
it. The regular riding path was by Threlkeld. That little world of
hills and lakes was gone in an instant, folded away. On a clear
day you could look back and see Skiddaw, the Helvellyn
range, the group above Stye Head, Grasmoor and the rest lying
gently like lions above the land, their heads resting on their
paws. One step and you were in a new world, a world as romantic perhaps in spirit as that other, but not this, as beautiful but
not with this beauty. That odd sense of magic, so that with one
foot forward you lost it. He would always, on reaching this spot,
know a little shiver of fear that when he came back again that
lovely country would be gone, a mirage dreamed of by him and
by him perhaps alone. But today in his head he carried with him
the rocking wood. The trees creaked around him long after he
had left them.

The wind fell: the rain drew off: the air was colder. The thick
sky watched them maliciously and once and again sent down a
flake of snow to spatter their eyes.

They had come into new country in another sense. The
cottages and farms that they passed gave them a consciousness of
agitation. Women stood at the doors. A man called after them
some question. A horseman rode past them furiously towards
Carlisle. Unconsciously themselves they drove their horses
faster, the mud scattering up about them as they went.

'The Pretender may be in Carlisle ere this,' said David
suddenly. 'What then?'

'We'll ride back again,' said Herries.

'What do you think, Father? Has he a hope? In Keswick they
wished him back in France, to a man they did. Disturbing their
affairs. It's odd to remember it, but I thought it a fine thing as a
boy when Father Roche spoke of it. Now, because I may buy a
farm, I see other things. Is Roche in Carlisle, do you think?'

'Yes, so I fancy. When I was a boy at Seddon, in '15, thirty
years ago, there was a peacock screamed under the hedge by the
pantries. I thought him the finest, most defiant bird in the kingdom, and when they were out in '15 he was like the Old Pretender, that bird. I had a fancy about him that if their foray

failed he'd die; and, sure enough, he died. Died of spoilt pride.
I've always thought rebellion a grand thing, but now I don't
know . . . I love this ground and the men on it, although they'd
thank me little if they knew it. If Charles Edward has his way,
every field will be blood-stained. Either way my peacock dies . . .
No, he can't win. He's too late. And if he wins it can be only for a
moment. Hanover's a hog by my peacock, but he's made his sty
of our home, and it's quieter for him to lie there. I told Roche
once that the notion of beauty to a plain people like the English
is too upsetting. They stand by their stomachs. They are poets
only by protest.'

The scene cleared: the sky lifted and the snow fell faster. A
man on a horse passed them, then drew up and waited for them.

He was a short fat man on a short fat horse, hunched forward
rather absurdly, not a good rider. He had a dark-crimson coat
with silver buttons: his face was round, red and anxious, rather
a baby face with open wondering eyes and startled eyebrows.

'I beg your pardon, gentlemen—'

They drew up their horses.

'Are you for Carlisle?'

David said that they were.

'What news have you?'

'None.'

'Ah, things are bad.' The little man looked at them beseechingly, as much as to say: 'Be kind to me. Tell me some good
news, even though it's lies. Tell me anything, only that I may
calm down and regain my dignity.' It was plain enough that he
was frightened of Francis Herries, who, straight on his horse, his
scarred face showing pale and impervious under his broad black
hat, was silent and grim enough. David, with his health and rud-
diness and open smile, reassured him. He confided in him.

'You see, gentlemen, I'm riding out of my way, but I had the
news at Sockbridge last night that the rebels were in Jedburgh,
and that they were already moving South. My God, they may be
in Carlisle at this instant, and my poor wife and Hetty . . . I said
to Mr Wordsworth – Mr Richard Wordsworth, Superintendent
of the Lowther Estates, I was today staying under his roof, my
worthy friend; maybe you know him, gentlemen? – 'Sdeath, Mr
Wordsworth, I said, it can't be that they are in Carlisle already,
and our house in English Street, the very centre of the town, my
wife sick of a nervous complaint these last five years, ever since
William Gray, the best surgeon in the whole of Carlisle, gentlemen, cut her for the bladder. And it isn't as though Hetty had a

head on her shoulders neither. The sight of a soldier makes a fool of the child, and these breechless Highlanders are beyond law, as we all know well enough. Eh, gentlemen, forgive this uneasiness, but I fancied that you'd have some good news, maybe of a defeat or a rout and the Pretender taken, or driven back to France again, where, Heaven is witness, it were better for him to have stayed.'

The words came with panting eagerness, but there was a childish simplicity and good nature behind them that won David, who was as childish, simple and good-natured as himself.

'I fear, sir,' he replied, 'we can give you little comfort. We are riding from Keswick where we had only the news that you yourself have had. We know nothing of what is happening in Carlisle.'

The little stout gentleman looked anxiously about him. 'It's cold,' he said, 'and the snow is in our faces. Would you give me the courtesy of your company? With every step we may be meeting danger. I am no coward, but I will confess that this news has quite unnerved me. It is only what I have been expecting these thirty years, but that it should drop on to us when I was away from home and my wife none too well . . .'

'Certainly we will keep company,' said David cheerfully. 'I think you are unduly apprehensive, sir. We should have heard, I am sure, were the Pretender already in Carlisle. I scarcely think that the Royal troops will allow him so much advantage. If one may go by the common feeling in Keswick the sense of the country is against him, and a company of raw Highlanders is hardly a match for an English army. Moreover, the farther they come from their own Highlands the less stomach they'll have for the job.'

This was the kind of comfort that the little man was needing, and in return for it, as they went forward, he gave them all his history. His name was Cumberlege, John Cumberlege of the Moor House, English Street, Carlisle, and he was a corn-dealer like his father before him. He had had three children, and two had died in infancy, one of the staggers and one of the croup. He had been twice married, and Hetty, his only child, was of the second marriage. He was of good standing in Carlisle, and numbered among his friends there the worthy Dr Waugh; young Mr Aglionby, Mayor of the City; Thomas Pattinson, Deputy-Mayor; and Colonel Durand, Commander of the City. They might see from this how safely they might trust themselves to his company. He had also much to say of his late host, Mr

Richard Wordsworth, who had but recently been appointed
Receiver-General of the County of Westmorland.

Altogether, as they jogged along, he recovered in this general
recital of his famous friends a good deal of his natural confidence
and genial humour.

David was glad of the little man's companionship. Francis
Herries had fallen into one of his grim and arrogant moods again
and would vouchsafe not a word. The afternoon was early dark,
and there was a spectral air over the scene.

Indeed, the uncertainty of the situation influenced David in
spite of himself. Moving thus through the cold dusk over a flat
and silent land one could not be sure that at any moment one
might not stumble upon the whole of the Prince's army. Where
were they? How had they fared? It might be that this adventurer
was truly destined for some glorious success and England would
fall into his hands like a fine plum? Then back the Catholics
would come again and with them the French dominance, and
who knows after that the sequel? At this all the Herries English
rose rebellious in David's soul. He wanted no French power here
nor Catholic either. It was at this moment, perhaps, little Cumberlege pressing near to him, the few chill snowflakes striking
his cheek and a great silence on every side of him, that he knew
once and for all what he was. Scottish ancestry or no, he was
English Herries. Men and women for two hundred years afterwards were to have some consequence in their lives from this
moment of conviction.

Little Cumberlege asked them where they were lodging in
Carlisle.

David told him that they had no settled place.

'Then, sirs, you must come to us. To be frank with you, I shall
relish your company. There's no man in the house but the boy
Jeremiah, and he's a witling with a wall-eye. I only took him to
pleasure his father, who did me a service in '32, the year they
hanged Humpy Dillon for sheep-stealing. You're a man of your
inches, sir,' he added, looking appreciatively up at David, 'and
might render us a service at a dangerous pinch.'

David looked at his father, who said no word. He smiled at the
eager excited little man, the skirts of whose crimson coat stuck
out from his fat buttocks as though with an indignant life of their
own.

'For tonight at least,' David said, 'we'll take you at your word
and thank you.'

A strange world had now come up about them, for the wind

had dropped, the snow ceased to fall, and instead a fog rolled in thick grey folds across the fields. This fog was to take a great part in the alarms and fears of the coming days: many, looking back afterwards and telling their story, gave it a personal form and body as though it were a creeping devil of an especial malignancy created by the Pretender himself.

David, who was never given to vague imagination, himself felt it an oddly alive thing. It came creeping towards them, now slipping along the road on its belly, licking the horses' hoofs, then raising a white swollen arm, wreathing their necks with it, then slipping away again, mounting into a wall in front of them, closing about them, stifling them, blinding them, dropping again to a thin shallow vapour that swathed the hedges with spider-web.

For Herries, it filled his dreams. For half an hour now he had not realized where they were nor cared. He rode forward, possessed by his vision. Since the word 'Carlisle' had, carelessly perhaps, passed Mirabell's lips it had been his one thought to go there. But with that burning impulse came also the resolve not to be defeated by it, because he felt that, let him surrender to it, and he would be beaten. Some prevision of the future told him that this journey taken through the fog, into the Lord knew what, was the beginning of a pursuit for him that was far more than physical, and, being spiritual, must fail in its aim.

He stared through the fog, her body, her soul, dancing in front of him. A child who had given him no single thought, a vagabond, ruthless and heartless perhaps, intolerant certainly of any of the bonds that he would put upon her. But all his history had led him to this, his rebellions, scorns, arrogances, dreams, self-contempts, Alice Press and the like, his wife Margaret, every woman whose tongue he had ever twisted beneath his own led him to this. He wanted nothing for himself, only to be good to her, to know that she was happy, that she had what she wanted. That she had what she wanted! Ironic, ironic desire, for it would not be himself that she longed for . . . And so he rode on.

They came upon Carlisle quite suddenly and were challenged at the gate.

Carlisle had at this time a population of some four thousand persons, the majority of these living within its walls.

The Castle Walls and Citadel had still their original force: the Castle was held by a non-resident governor and a company of invalided veterans: the city gates were shut at the firing of the evening gun. Nevertheless, its life as a centre of warfare was now

still and dead. The union of the kingdoms of Scotland and
England had silenced the Border warfare, turned guns into
knitting needles and cannon-balls into peppermint rock. Here,
perhaps, lay the root of the Prince's advantage, that any Scottish
invasion of England was by now undreamt of in Carlisle and the
town was in no way prepared for it.

On this evening the bustle at the gate was tremendous. The
Herries would most certainly not have been admitted had they
been alone, but their little friend, Mr Cumberlege, had not said
too much about his popularity in Carlisle. Especially did a large,
pompous and terribly flustered military officer appear delighted
to see him, even to the extent of embracing him. He was not, Mr
Cumberlege explained, *sotto voce*, a real and proper military
gentleman, but rather a volunteer, in his time and natural state a
wealthy bachelor with a taste for wine and a talent for the game
of bowls, moreover a relation of good Doctor Bolton, the Dean of
Carlisle. He had in his private garden a fountain with a naked
mermaid who blew water out of her tail, considered by many a
marvel.

At the moment he was thinking of neither bowls nor mermaid,
but was in a dreadful flutter of indecision.

Scouting parties had been sent out to discover, if they might,
the Rash Adventurer's (such was the title decided on by those
who wanted to land safely in the ultimate result) whereabouts.
That afternoon, so Mr Bolton told Cumberlege, Lieutenant Kil-
patrick had advanced beyond Ecclefechan and sighted a body of
rebels. A Scottish quartermaster, seeking quarters for his troops
in Ecclefechan, had been seized and was now in Carlisle Castle.
That was as much as was known for the present.

A strange contrast was to be found in Mr Bolton's manner, he
suddenly rapping out most authoritatively a military order, then
sinking his voice to a nervous, confidential murmur with John
Cumberlege, who was as apprehensive as himself. They made a
funny enough pair, their contrast in size, their bodies starting at
every sound, and once when a horseman clattered over the
cobbles suddenly clutching one another as though for protection.

They rode up English Street to Cumberlege's house, which
was a neat little Georgian building with a brass knocker on the
door showing a sea-fish swallowing a trident, and a sundial on
the lawn by the street, and a fine little gate with small dragons
on either side of it. A good light burning in a cresset over the
door blew in the wind. The street was deserted. The fog had
cleared, and the sky was full of cold and glittering stars.

'Come in. Come in, gentlemen,' said Cumberlege, looking about him before he opened his front door as though he scented a Highlander round every corner. 'It's a poor hospitality I shall offer you, taking me unexpected and my wife an invalid, but—' and here he dropped his voice still further, 'there's wine in the house. Wine too good for the Highland rabble that's coming upon us.' And then to himself, as he unfastened his door: 'Poor Bolton! Poor Bolton! I'll wager he wishes himself back safe with his mermaid.'

Half an hour later they were seated in Cumberlege's gay little dining-room, a beef pie, an apple tart and some of the finest Madeira in front of them. It was a handsome little room with dark-red wallpaper hung with scenes from Mr Gay's master-piece, 'The Beggar's Opera', and a handsome oil painting of Mr Cumberlege's grandfather in a green coat and ruffles, over the mantelpiece. A noble old gentleman with a face like a codfish and a neck so thick that it was no wonder to hear, later in the evening, that he had died of an apoplexy. Silver candlesticks, a glass bowl of oranges and figs, a fire in the hearth, the curtains warmly drawn, and best of all Cumberlege's daughter Hetty, who was as pretty a dark child as David had ever seen.

Two things were very plainly visible: one that to John Cumberlege this daughter was the life and light of his being. He sat with one stout arm round her and fed her with figs as though she had been a child in arms, his eyes moving ever and again about her pretty face with its nose a little snub, its eyelashes beautifully dark and long, its rounded chin and soft cheeks, as though all his happiness were there.

The other evident fact was that the child had fallen in love with David at sight. She sat there shyly smiling at him, her cheeks flushed, her eyes burning with pleasure and adventure. She was in a dress of white calico sprayed with pink roses, as David was long after to remember. A pretty face was a pretty face to David. Many times of late he had thought that he must fall in love, but Keswick did not offer so many varieties. Now he wondered whether his fate were not here. It was not, but it was near enough to make his heart beat, his tongue stammer and his big body move clumsily as though, in spite of itself, it must be impelled towards her.

John Cumberlege too, perhaps, as he looked across the table at David, had his dreams. It was true that he knew nothing about these visitors of his, and the elder was alarming in his taciturnity and grim seclusion, but you could not look at the younger Herries and doubt him. Honesty was in every glance, every breath, simplicity, a courageous rectitude.

For Hetty Cumberlege this threat of the Scottish invasion was a grand and enchanting game. Was it true that the Prince was the most beautiful young man? When he came to the city would there be routs and balls as she had heard there had been in Edinburgh? For herself she didn't care what her father thought; she was all for seeing him, and it would be a wicked shame were he stopped before he got to Carlisle. But he would not be. He was already there. He had been at Ecclefechan that day. Perhaps tomorrow he would be in the city, and if there was a ball she had no dress fit to wear. But oh, she was glad her dear father was safe (this with an especial hug of her father, a blushing glance at David). Mother had been in a great way all day and hadn't had her afternoon sleep and had been bled again this evening, and she had run to the window and the door a thousand times to see whether he were not coming, and would there be firing and the windows broken and people wounded?

Why shouldn't the Prince come into the town if he wanted to? That was the feeling of most of the militia anyway, and it was only that old jackanapes Colonel Durand who was for everybody fighting. She was sure that no one wanted to kill anyone else, the idea was perfectly horrid. And as the Madeira mounted into David's head and the weariness bred of his long forty-mile ride dazzled his eyes, it seemed to him that he was already kissing those blushing cheeks and stroking ever so gently that bare and gleaming shoulder.

Francis Herries said no word beyond mere politeness. He could not. He saw the figures of little Cumberlege and his daughter, the silver candlesticks, the glittering glass about the fruit, the portrait of old Cumberlege senior, in a thin and gauzy dream. He was here in Carlisle, and every beat of blood in him urged him, weary though he was, to go out and search for her. It seemed to him that there was more than mere vague urgency in this. Opposite him where he sat was a small round mirror with a dark oak frame. Its glass was blistered and cracked with age, so that the candle-flame flickered and redoubled in it, and the colours of the room, dark crimson, white and green, were a blurred and mellowed fog. Staring in it, half-asleep maybe, the voices coming to him with a faint chirping hum, he seemed to see that child Mirabell step into the mirror, break the misted colours, turn to him that strange, cold, indifferent face, gravely surveying him, oddly and harshly inviting him.

He pushed his napkin and wine-glass from him and asked his host to excuse him while he found a little air in the street. His head was hot and he must cool it before he went to his bed. He was aware that they felt, all three of them, a certain freedom from restraint at his departure.

In the street the wind had now quite fallen and only, as though dropped by the multitudinous shining stars, thin flakes of snow fell lazily as though they were too indifferent to reach the ground. No one was about. There were few lights in the windows. The sense of suspense might have been his own imagining, but it seemed to him that behind the doors and the windows folk were listening. He could hear the hearts throbbing, could see the eyes straining, and over his head and about his body the stems and branches of the rocking wood seemed still to be beating and groaning. He had been in that wood all day. He was not clear of it yet.

As though led by a guide at his elbow he turned up a dark and narrow street that was as silent as an empty pocket. On his right there was a light blowing above the name, 'The Silver Horn'. Here as well as another place. He pushed back the heavy wooden door and stumbled on to the uneven stone floor of an inn-room filled with a rough glare of men, women, smoke, thickly smelling of dried fish, tobacco and stale drink.

He sat down at a long deal table, men, countrymen, farmers, making easy way for him, too deeply intent on their talk to consider him. A thin wasp of a serving-man brought him some ale; a heavy thumping clock, hiccuping once and again as though it had taken in the drink as steadily as its customers, tick-tocked just above his head; a parrot, whose bright-green colour he could just see swaying on a perch through the smoke, called out in a thick husky caw; and still through it all the wind and creaking of the morning's wood kept him company.

He discovered soon enough that there was only one topic and that the natural one. Where was the Pretender and where his Highlanders? Even now they might be at the walls. What would Durand do? What Pattinson the Deputy-Mayor, young Aglionby being safely away in the country somewhere? What would the Dean and Chapter do? What would the Cumberland and West-morland Militia do? What was everyone going to do? Were they all to be blown to bits? What was Wade going to do? What was the King in London doing that he hadn't sent any reinforce-ments? Didn't he care what happened to old Carlisle, and if he didn't why should old Carlisle care what happened to the King?

Ah! but those Highlanders! Here fear crept through the smoke, skins went shivering, the tick-tock of the old clock took on a deeper tone. Those Highlanders . . . Hadn't you heard, then, of what they'd been doing in Edinburgh and Glasgow, of the women they'd been raping and the destruction they'd been causing? The story went tonight that back at Kelso Spital they had shot all the sheep, hanged all the farmers, drunk the warm blood of the sheep like so many cannibals. There was the tale, too, of the farm-wife at Langholm who refused to tell the rebels where her husband had hid the horses and cattle, she lying in bed with a new-born child. She refused, even though the rebel officer threatened her with cutting down the beam that supported the roof of the farmhouse. He cut away at the beam, but it stoutly withstood, and the house was spared.

And what of Carlisle? What is the good of holding out, the Castle as rotten as it is, the Gate not covered by any outworks, the Wall over the Lady's Walk very low with neither parapet nor flank to defend it, the old gateway not defended by any flank, and we having nothing to oppose seven thousand rebels save a few invalids? . . . Surely better, then, to let the Pretender come in under guarantee of decent behaviour on both sides. Hick, hick, hick, stammered the clock. It was then that, staring through the smoke into the light of the roaring fire, Herries saw Mirabell.

This gave him no sense of surprise nor question of undue coincidence. It seemed to him the most natural thing in the world that she should be sitting there, and his only sensation was one of great happiness, a happiness oddly tranquil and secure. He had at first no ambition to speak to her, only to sit there and know that she was alive and in the same room with him.

He could not, from where he was, see her very clearly. She was wearing an amber-coloured hat with a feather in it and a deep dark-red cloak with a high collar; he could see, from where he was, that the cloak was faded and old. He could not deny but that she seemed bedraggled and shabby. He could not distinguish her features, only sufficient to know that it was surely she, but indeed where else in the world was there hair of such a colour? It was piled up, burning between the tawny colour of her hat and her white neck, a fire in smoke and under creaking windy trees.

He was half-asleep, perhaps, with weariness, or the heat of the room bemused him, but after a little while it appeared that he and she were quite alone in the wood and that they rode forward silently to some unknown destination.

After a while he wished to see her more clearly, rose from where he was, pushed through the farmers and countrymen and came to another place across the room. He was sitting in a corner now, near the fire, quite close to the bright-green parrot; it was fiercely hot, but he did not feel the heat.

He was beside her now, and at once his heart was shot through by a sharp and intolerable agony. That was no exaggerated figure of speech. It was like that. He felt the pain before he realized the cause. This cause was that, beside her, his arm around her red cloak, was a young man, a fellow of little more than twenty perhaps, yet a boy with a boy's fresh colour, a boy's laugh, a boy's bright eyes. Those eyes were fixed on her and her eyes on his. That they loved one another, and to a pitch that excluded the scene and everything in it, was clear to any casual onlooker. How sharply, deeply clear to Herries, in whose ears might be echoing yet the crash of the derisive boughs. 'Crack-crack! Crack-crack! He means to be married! He means to be married!'

As he watched he saw her hand come out and take the broad brown hand of the young man. Then she smiled at him, a shy, delicate, happy child's smile that drew her, although they did not move, deep into the young man's heart.

Her note for Herries had always been her remoteness; he had never seen her intimate with nor close to anything. He had never dared to imagine how she would look when she was in love. His only hope had been that she had never known what that was, and so he had wondered whether he might not be the first to teach her. For he had taught in his day many lessons in love. Now he knew that that would never be.

When some control came back to him he studied the boy carefully. He was dressed roughly in a dark coarse coat and homespun breeches, and gaitered to the thigh for riding. His body was slim and well-formed, he carried his head high: everything about him was honest and upright, strong and smiling. He was a proper man. It was after concluding this (and his pride allowed him to flinch from no challenging comparisons) that Herries noticed a third figure. This was a thick, short, black-bearded fellow who sat behind the pair, swinging his legs from the table-end. His face was covered with a shaggy black beard and his hair lay in a black tangle over his forehead. There was black hair on the back of his hands. He was dressed soberly and cleanly, and his large, steadily open, black eyes never left the face of the girl.

Once and again he said a word to her, but when he spoke it did not rouse the girl, who smiled at the boy as though it were he who had spoken. But they were all three of them very quiet, not joining at all in the conversation around them, making a little world and history apart by themselves.

For Herries it was as though a new fresh chapter of his life had opened. When we fall in love the desire in us is so strong that we argue a like desire in the other, and stay cheated so long as we may. Well, his cheat was over, but he was in no kind of way released from her. He realized at once that he was only the more strongly bound because he would never forget now how she looked when she was in love, and would never again be able to defend himself against her with a sense of her remoteness.

Often since the day in the cave, lying on his bed, working in the field, riding solitary up Stonethwaite, standing on Esk Hause and seeing the valleys glitter and smile beneath him, he had wondered how she would look at him the first time that she knew she could trust him. For that was what he had meant to do; by great kindliness and patience to make her trust him as she had never trusted anyone before. Now he knew that that would never happen.

He saw, too, how all his actions since the day in the cave had been for her. He had never once been free of her. When he had taken the witch from the river and held her to his heart it had been this child that he had held. All the new compassion and softness that had lately been growing in him so that the sterner, more ironical part of him had been frightened at the change and tried to drive it away, all this had been from her. It had been as though he had been educating himself out of the nastiness and pride of his earlier life, so that he might be ready for her when she came to him: and now she would never come.

She would never come. The trees of the wood gathered about his head very thickly and now with silence because the wind had died. The green parrot swung from bough to bough watching him with beady eyes. Then he heard her speak, and her voice was as deeply familiar to him as though he had been in company with it all his life.

She spoke to the parrot.

'For a penny,' she said, 'I'd wring your neck, you evil bird.'

The young man, looking at her as though he would drown her in his love, answered in a voice that was roughly boyish and eager:

'I shall buy the bird for you.'

And she answered, holding his hand very tightly: 'Two is company.'

The black-bearded man behind them swung off the table and stood, thick and stocky, looking up at the parrot. He went up to it and stroked its neck. The parrot bent its head, eyeing him obliquely with a beady eye.

Herries had seen enough. He went out, into the street.

SIEGE IN FOG

HERRIES WOKE early the next morning, and under a sharp agitation of disturbance and fear. The room in which he was lying was foreign and strange to him. His eyes slowly picked up one thing after another; the faded green hangings of his bed, the uneven boarding of the floor, a print hanging against the dark panel of the wall, showing apprentices playing football in the Strand, and another with a crudely coloured presentation of Bear-Baiting. On an old chest under the window was a bowl of thick green glass, rough in texture so that the colours of the green glass seemed to shift and change.

The light from the window was dim. There was no sound anywhere.

Where then was he? With a rush as of charging horses, events, pictures, words came back to him. He sprang from his bed as though, at once, he would hasten out into the street and start about his affairs. He went to the little window and pushed it back. A thin, wet, wispy fog met him. He was in the house of Mr Cumberlege of Carlisle. He was also in the 'Silver Horn', and close to him Mirabell Starr was looking into the young man's eyes, while the green parrot rocked on its perch. And he was in the ground behind Herries, digging while Glaramara humped its back over him and the light came down in misty ladders over Stye Head, and he was rowing slowly from Lord's Island, while the water slipped in ripples of steel from hill to hill.

He passed the back of his hand across his eyes, pulling himself together. He was here in Carlisle. The Prince and his High-landers . . . Mirabell . . . this green bowl above whose colours the thin fog shifted . . . His hand touched his bare chest and felt for the chain and the wooden cross that Mirabell's mother had left for him. He had not been without it since that day, and now, as his hand touched it, a new determination came to him: that he would find the child and talk to her and see how he might serve her. She was not for him and now would never be, but he might help her.

He stretched his legs and his arms, smiled; his face just then was kindly, not sardonic, but a little old and rough, battered and torn above his body, for his skin was fair and delicate like a woman's.

The door creaked open, and David came in. He was in an excitement unusual for his calm temper. He was fully dressed.

'Father, what are we going to do? They say this morning the town's under siege. There's a fine to-do, and half the city's downstairs swearing the militia are going to give in before they are fairly started, and the other half's in the street screaming about the Highlanders, and there's a fog so thick you can't see the back of your hand. Are we going to stay here? I doubt if we can get out now if we want to.'

'Of course we stay,' said Herries, sitting on the bed's end and swinging his bare legs.

'What did you hear last night when you were in the town?'

'Oh, naught, but that a parrot has green eyes.'

'Old Cumberlege loves me like a son this morning. He's plucky enough for himself, but his lady and his lady's woman are raped already by bony Highlanders in their imagination. They can't tell whether to be sorry or glad. The girl's brave, though. She calls me her brother.'

David grinned and put his arm around his father's bare neck.

'So we're to stay here?'

'Of course we're to stay, seeing we can't get out.'

'But who are we for? The Prince and his Highlanders?'

'For ourselves.' Herries stood up, stretching his arms. 'We're in a green city with warlocks and witches. Take care of the witch downstairs, David. Or love her if you wish to. A fog's the place for true love. My stomach's empty. Is there any food in this siege, or do we live from now on upon snails and puppies' tails? And water. There's a tin basin here, but no water.'

'I'll fetch you some.'

David returned with a bucket of water. He watched his father bathe. 'You're strong. Stronger than you used to be.'

'Aye, I'm strong – and damned ugly. The fog's to my advantage. Hast kissed the girl downstairs, Davy?'

'Yes, I kissed her.' David was crimson. 'She liked it.'

Herries, drawing on his hose, laughed.

'Good enough now. There'll be tears later.' They went down the crooked stairs, arm-in-arm.

But that day went for nothing. For the most part father and son were together, walking the town, watching the country people (for it was Martinmas Hiring Day), listening to a thousand silly rumours and stories.

At three in the afternoon there was a real sensation. A party of fifty or sixty horsemen appeared on Stanwix Bank, overlooking the city. The road was crowded with country people going home. When these were cleared away the ten-gun battery of the Castle fired, but the troopers were in safety by then.

Francis was in his little room washing his face in the tin basin when the guns fired. The floor seemed to quiver; the little panes of the windows rattled; a scatter of birds flew past, and there was a woman's scream, shrill and sharp, through the house. Then silence.

He went to the window. The fog was clear and the sky silver with threads of blue above the crooked roofs. He leaned out. On a cobbled corner of the side-street (he could see only a fragment of it) a man stood, looking up. Herries had the oddest fancy, seeing dimly in that faint afternoon light, that it was the pedlar standing there, the pedlar whom he had not seen since that Christmas night of the duel . . . Oddly like him, with a peaked cap, the thin straining body. He fancied that he could certify the sharp, piercing eyes. He stepped back into the room in whose dusk the green glass bowl was the only light. Of course it was not the pedlar, but the fancy held him.

He yet seemed to have the echo of the guns in his ears, and the woman's scream. What was to happen to him here? An odd burning shiver ran through him like the first warning of a fever: he knew in that second, staring into the green glass of the bowl, that one of the crises of his life was approaching. He knew it quite certainly. He did not care for his life – it was not of so precious a quality to him – but this crisis that was coming was of deep import and would change, whichever way it went, all his fortune, physical and spiritual.

He knew it, as though the guns had blown away a veil from his eyes.

He went out to see what was toward. The country people were all hastening home. There was a stir in the Square like a scare among sheep when a wolf is by. Little groups collected like flies round sugar, and yet over all the bustle and movement there was a strange hush as though no one dared to raise a voice. He heard the names pass back and forth: 'Wade', 'Durand', 'Aglionby', 'Waugh', 'Pattinson'. The pigeons came strutting at his very feet, and above the roofs the sky suddenly tossed up arms and wreaths of red and gold, proclaiming the setting sun.

He turned his steps towards the Cathedral. In the Close everything was very still. Someone stood in a side door of the Cathedral looking up at the flaming sky. It was as though everyone he saw were straining an ear for the sound of the guns again.

Someone was speaking to him. 'A fine evening, Mr Herries.'

He turned, as one turns in a dream, because he knew the voice. He passed his hand before his eyes, and in his ears the cannon dimly sounded, for it was Mirabell Starr very quietly standing there.

'I have followed you, Mr Herries – most indecently. I saw you ten minutes ago.'

She looked at him with that clear-eyed indifference so known to him. But she was pleased, perhaps. The sky sank to smoky grey, and he could scarcely see her face. The bells chimed five o'clock. But she was glad to see him, less indifferent than she had been. He caught that and cherished it. She looked a baby, wearing the same shabby red cloak. His heart throbbed. He held himself sternly at attention, his arms stiff at his sides, lest he should touch her.

'I'm bold to address you.'

She saw in his eyes that he was worshipping her, this odd, ugly, elderly, scarred man.

She was frightened, perhaps, and for the honest child that she was wanted to put everything in a clear, defined light.

'I followed you—' she caught her breath a little. 'I wanted to tell you . . . There at Honister, when we talked, I told you that I didn't believe in love. Well, now, you were kind and asked me to come to you if I needed anything, and my mother trusted you, so you must know I am very happy and I love someone, and he loves me.'

'That is good,' he said sternly. 'And it is a good man you love?'

'Yes, it is a good man.'

'He will care for you?'

'Oh, always.'

'I am happy. But you should not be here. This town will be dangerous now.'

'I have been in danger all my life,' she answered. 'Danger is nothing – for myself,' she added hastily.

Then, smiling at him so sweetly that his heart ached, she said quickly:

'I wished you to know. Goodnight,' and was gone.

He stood without moving, for how long he did not know.

There was a bitter, almost despairing, pain at his heart, such as he had never known before. He had always been too proud to despair of himself, but now, under the black shadow of the Cathedral, he really despaired. He was isolated, ostracized, hateful to all men. At once, at first sight of him, these Cumberleges had drawn back . . . That he could face, but now, all pride flung aside, all fear of weakness discarded, he felt the bitterest anguish. Because, for a moment, he had been in touch with a kind of joy, a sort of happiness that he had not known before existed. He had seen it in the distance, stretched his hand, touched its wings; it had flown. Sternly, his back against the Cathedral wall as though he were hammered on to it, he stared in front of him, his palms gripped. He had not known before that his love for her was so deep that the hooks of it were in his very entrails. He knew now, and that he would always love her so.

On the following morning, the Sunday, Francis and David were summoned to the defence of the city. The fog was this morning thicker than ever and added to the general confusion and increasing alarm. Every kind of rumour was about. No one knew where the Prince and his army might be. Some said that he was already inside the city. Some said that Wade and his forces were marching to relieve them, others that they were to be left to their fate, their children would be eaten alive, their women raped and the houses burned to the ground.

Among the most gloomy of Carlisle's citizens was Mrs Cumberlege, who continued to scream from her bed of sickness. At one moment she succeeded in staggering as far as her doorway (rumour had it that she could have staggered a great deal farther had she so wished) and crying: 'The Highlanders are here! The Highlanders are here! Help! Help! We are all to be murdered!'

This was, of course, desperately upsetting for Mr Cumberlege, who was forbidden by her to leave her defenceless in the house. At the same time he wished to do his duty as a loyal citizen and surrender himself to Colonel Durand's orders. It ended in his slipping, with Herries and David, off into the fog, and leaving her in the care of her beautiful daughter.

They went to the Castle and were enrolled for defence. Prospects were not cheerful. From the room in which they stood, crowded about with an extraordinary tumbled and disorderly mixture of old men, young men and boys, they could hear the echo of trowel and hammer on the city walls. The original garrison was but eighty old 'invalid' soldiers. The guns were so ancient that they were reputed to have been, in the jest of the drinking-bouts and tea-parties, Boadicea's. Durand had augmented them with ten small ship's guns brought from Whitehaven, and the old ruined walls were now in course of being altered that they might fit these.

Forty townsmen were in charge of the Whitehaven guns, and another eighty served the Castle artillery.

Confusion was the more confounded by the bringing from neighbouring towns and villages of small companies of militia, but their arms were of different bores, and every man made his own ball fitting the size of the piece.

All the worst trouble, Herries soon perceived, came from these same militia. Colonel Durand had proposed that the militia officers should do duty by detachment from their several companies, but this they emphatically and turbulently opposed, and drew lots, among themselves, for their posts. The result of this was that there was no order nor discipline, and men wandered where they would and were already demoralized and fatigued.

As the morning drew on, the confusion in the room where Herries was grew ever more active. Men ran about like children, crying out, fingering arms in so uncertain a manner that it was likely at any instant that one would blow another to pieces, starting up and running to the windows, chattering, crying, shouting, now boasting, now bewailing. An old countryman stood near Herries, an ancient man with a long grizzled beard who, again and again, called out: 'Who is for the Lord? Who is for the Lord?' Little Cumberlege walked to the window and back, stopping every other minute by David, whose strength and imperturbability seemed to give him an immense satisfaction. It seemed to be impossible for the present to come near Durand, who was in an inner room.

Then, about midday, the fog rolled off, and a young man with a long yellow face like a turnip came in shouting:

'They are upon us. The whole army. At the very walls.'

He had scarcely spoken when the guns were heard to fire. 'That's from Shaddon Gate,' someone cried. There was a moment of transfixion when everyone stood, not seeing what to do, where to go, waiting for they knew not what. Then two men ran in, shouting hysterically:

‘We have beat them. They are retreating.’ And almost at once the fog came down again, blotting everything out.

Some said now that they had retreated all together, others that it was but a blind, others that they had marched round to the other side of the city and were already creeping about the streets.

Some swore that they could hear the skirl of the Highland pipes. Even for Herries who, in such an affair, had no unsteady nerves, there was an odd thrill from the knowledge that in the brief interval of clarity the whole of the Prince's army had been seen at the very walls. It was true, then. They were in the real heart of this situation, not imagining it. Shortly there might be – nay, surely would be – massacre and bloodshed. And where would she be in this? A chance bullet? A drunken Highlander? His whole body trembled . . . The old countryman clutched his arm and peered into his face.

‘Who is for the Lord? Who is for the Lord?’

It was late in the afternoon before he and David were marched off to the part of the wall that was their post. As they marched through a portion of the town it had a weird effect, because the order had gone out that there were to be lights in all the lower windows, darkness in the upper. The fog, too, hung high, so that they seemed to be stepping along a stream of uncertain watery glow, while above them was a bank of blackness. All was silent; behind the lighted windows there was no sound. Against his will every man was listening for the guns.

No one spoke. They might have been moving to some secret rendezvous. Herries had at his side a short, round, very stout, little man who groaned, panted and seemed to be bursting with some tremendous secret.

They paused at a lighted corner while their destination was settled. At once the little fat man, whose face was beetroot colour (his head trembled with a queer jerky movement), burst into the middle of excited, despairing sentences as though he were continuing a long, already uttered speech. He caught Herries's arm and held it, and this oddly pleased him. There was someone in this foggy world who did not shrink from him.

‘. . . The eldest but five and a half . . . One every year, and the five of them alone in the house with their grandmother, deaf as a post, to mind them . . . I said to them that I would not be gone a half-hour, and what service can I be with a musket, serving out butter and sugar for the last twenty years? . . . But what do you think, sir? Shall we beat them off, do you think? My sister would have been in to mind them, but only two days back she was on a visit to Allonby to her brother-in-law, as indeed I told her at the time that he was but inviting her to take advantage of her. He was never a man, from his boyhood up, to do a thing and not expect anything back for it, as Margaret my sister has herself said many a time . . . and the children crying their hearts out in the dark . . .'

The light from a flare that someone carried swung in the breeze, as though a tongue were licking the cheek of the fog. In that sudden illumination Herries saw two things: that David was not with him and that quite close to him, almost in touch of him, was Mirabell's young lover.

At that knowledge he caught his breath as though he expected a blow. The boy (for he was little more) stood stiffly, his head up-staring straight into Herries's face.

He did not, of course, recognize him, but he looked at him as though he would know him. And yet he was looking beyond him. Herries saw now that he was not seeing anyone. He was swimming deep in his own thoughts, and his mouth was smiling.

The order came again to move forward. The young man was very near to him. It was as though he had been placed there in David's stead.

The little fat man stayed close at Herries's side. Whistling ejaculations came from between his lips. 'Eh, sirs! . . . Eh, sirs!' 'The pity of it! The pity!' 'The waste in this town!'

Mirabell's boy, the second coincidence. First the 'Silver Horn' and now this. He felt a dead weight upon him, as though he were caught in some trap. The conviction that had been with him in his room when he heard the first gun, came back to him, that he was moving to some deep crisis in his affairs and that all his future would depend on the way that he now acted.

Oddly, at the very first sight of him under the flare, he knew that he hated him.

Inside the wall they took their places. Someone came round and told them where they were to go, and that at a certain time they would be relieved. At once it was evident that there was no discipline. The fog had lifted again and a few faint, very small stars could be seen.

Men were moving about, talking to one another. The fat man, his hand once more on Herries's arm, was about it again. '. . . Only yesterday, being Martinmas Hiring, I engaged the girl, but when she saw the trouble in the city nothing would stay her. I offered her a double wage if she'd bide with the children. She'd be safer, too, here than out in the country, but when they fired that cannon it frightened her. Not a word would she hear . . .'

The young man stayed at Herries' side as though he knew that was the place for him. Yes, he had a fine, clear, noble countenance. No fear there, no meanness. His slim body was strung to the full height of discipline and obedience. Still on his lips was that little, happy smile.

Herries, as though under command, spoke:

'The fog clears,' he said.

The young man turned as though he had been recalled from a great distance.

'They must be at our very feet,' he said. 'It will be cold before dawn.' He smiled, then he added: 'I have a friend who was with me until ten minutes back. We wished to be together.'

Three men came past, peering. One of them stopped.

'I have found you,' he said. That thick growling voice was guide enough for Herries. He knew that the company was now completed. The face, with its black hair, peered close at Herries. Herries could see him again as he stepped to the parrot, tickling its neck with his finger.

'I had lost you,' the young man said.

'I am never lost,' he laughed deep as though in the coils of his stomach. 'Well, sir,' he said to Herries, 'this is a play.'

Herries nodded, turned away, looked out to the grey web of the night, its texture dotted with lights that seemed to sway and stagger because the mist came in drives, advancing and retreating.

They took their places, quietly, the three of them together, and stood there without moving. An immense time seemed to pass. The cold grew very intense.

Herries thought: 'Here I am, these two with me, not by my own choice or intention.' He felt growing up in him the old man that he had by now, he thought, discarded. Something seemed to him to come through the night and the fog and the cold and place in him one evil thing after another, as you pile stuff in a cupboard. 'And now this I'll add. And now this. Yes, and this we must have.'

Evil things, lecheries, lusts, cruelties, meannesses, desires to hurt, to maim, purposeless maliciousness. And he himself seemed to look on, coldly and with external deliberation. All his love for the child, Mirabell, was tarnished and coarsened. He now lusted for her in exactly the way that, in his younger days, he had lusted for many women. His hands touched her hair, her small child's face, her little breasts, her waist, her knees, coldly, with desire but no fine passion.

His evil thoughts spread over the walls into the dark plain beyond. He saw the Prince's army encamped, and it seemed to him that he could stare into every tent. Each place was peopled with evil men, men cruel and mean and lascivious as he was. They were crawling over the country, carrying naked women on their backs, naked women whose hair was loose about their bodies and down whose faces tears were pouring. He saw a farm, the house, its windows shuttered for the night, the farm buildings stacked with provender, the animals sleeping in their places, the master in the upper room asleep, his head resting on his wife's breast.

Through the gate, a little bent man, a flare in his hand, crept. He stooped lower, setting the flare now here, now there. The flames sprang up. The byres were caught. The animals screamed. The fire ate the walls of the house with greedy avaricious gestures. White faces were at the windows. There were screams, cries, odour of burning flesh. The woman, held in her man's arms, watched the flames crawl nearer . . .

The little bent man moved about the country, doing here one evil thing, another there. Herries moved with him, his body cold, like marble, his heart burning.

All the men in the Prince's camp seemed to stir before him. They moved closer to the walls, and in all that army of eyes there was anticipatory lust and longing for suffering in others and destruction and ruin. Herries himself seemed to lead them on, saying: 'Here is a good place . . . And here are women . . . Here are houses to burn.'

A shiver of bad desire ran through him. It was as though he had been sleeping there on his feet and wakened. It might be so. Everything was very clear about him, the dark ramparts, the white faces of men.

He could have said: 'I see men crawling like lice, and that is all that they are. Poor, lowest and meanest of all created things.' He tried not to think of anything. He knew that if he went much further he would face thoughts that were lower and viler than any that he had ever known. But someone went on piling the cupboard high with these. 'Here is a new one. Here is one that I have found. And here another . . .'

He turned a little and talked to the black, short man at his side, who, like the boy, had neither moved nor spoken all this time.

'What do you think,' he asked, 'of this adventurer's chances? Will he reach London?'

With that odd growl as of an animal roused by some sense of danger, the man answered: 'I neither know nor care. He can take this place when he wishes – and all England for me.'

'Doesn't it matter to you then?'

'Why should it? There is food and drink under any king. One ruler is like another, unless oneself has the chance of ruling.'

'Are you in Carlisle by hazard?' To Herries it was as though, beneath this conversation, other words were being said and other meanings of deep import were being intended.

'I am anywhere by hazard. One place is as another to me.'

'I have seen you before,' Herries said. 'The other evening at the "Silver Horn".'

'It may be,' the man replied. 'I have been there.' He spat against the wall. 'Some of us may be dead men before morning.'

'Why do you stay here,' asked Herries, 'if you are indifferent? You lose your life, maybe, for nothing.'

'My life!' The man growled a chuckle. 'I have no life. I have only moments. I am hungry, I eat. I am thirsty, I drink. I want a woman, if I can I take her. Life stops. Well, why not – when it has never begun?'

'Then you have no fear of death?'

'No. If there's no life, there's no death. There is only the body. One fills it. One empties it. One seizes with it what one can.'

Herries said: 'Then you regret nothing that you have ever done?'

'Only what I have wanted and have not had.'

'You are fortunate, then,' Herries answered. 'You have no scruples, no regrets.'

'Regrets! No! Why? Where I am strong enough I conquer. Where I am weak I take to my heels.'

'Why, then, I ask again, are you here? In this bleak place, in danger, where nothing is to be gained.'

'Ah, perhaps something is to be gained.'

The thin, faint light was enough for them to see one another's faces, and suddenly, at the same moment, they stared, the one at the other. It was indeed a strange look. Herries, gazing into that shaggy face with the bristling, black hair, the light, fiery little eyes, the low chill brow, felt that he had seen this face before, and often. He felt, too, that the man was coldly, deliberately, and without interest in anything but his own purpose, asking him to do something. What he could not tell.

'That's a deep scar you've got,' said the man.

'Yes.'

'Did you kill the man who gave it you?'

'No,' said Herries.

'I would have done: drawn and quartered him. You see my hands?' He held them out, hideous hands, the backs thick with black hair, the fingers stumped and gnarled.

'They are strong. I could strangle an ox with them.'

Herries, moved by some curiosity, touched one. It was ice-cold and damp.

'Yes. You have strong hands.'

For the first time the young man spoke:

'He is so strong that he can lift a cart with them. Can you not, Tony?'

The man did not answer. The boy went on: 'Is it not strange, sir, standing here in this cold mist, waiting for we know not what and for no real reason?' His face was charming, as he turned it to Herries. 'I am all for a fight in the open, and when you know the cause, but this chill waiting . . . and I would be loth to die, just now.'

'The boy's in love,' said the man. 'He's thinking always of his beautiful girl. Isn't it so, Harry?'

The boy laughed.

'That is no business for this gentleman,' he said. 'Another man's love affair is dull news.'

And so they would move, these men, stirring so quietly under the wall, their eyes burning, their hearts thick at the thought that with a knock or two this town would surrender. And then what fun there would be for them! No house closed to them, the women cowering in the bed-curtains; their 'Hallo! you there . . I have you!' Dragging her out, pulling back her head, loosening her hair, tearing her clothes from her – her neck, her breasts, her eyes staring in terror, the crackle of flames, the tramping of men, the warm trembling body slack in their arms . . .

'And out on the Fell I have seen the shepherd whistling to his dog and the sheep come in a cloud, while the sun strikes the stream like mirror-glass. That's what I want and will have, when this is over.' It was the boy speaking.

The man growled at his side. 'The lad's a poet. He writes reams of it. There's books already enough in the world.'

'But this, sir, too, is wonderful. Can you not feel it to be so?

The town so dark behind us and the land so dark before. We standing on so narrow a parapet that one cannon-ball would tumble it to dust. If 'twere only myself I were thinking of . . .' He sighed and turned impulsively to Herries. 'Oh, sir, we standing as we do in this dark, strangers, need not be afraid of rashness. Have you not felt often how unsafe it is to love? The agony of another's safety . . . The pain of parting . . .' He broke off. They were all very close together, and their voices low.

Herries felt that he was alone there and that these two were but voices of his own different warring selves.

The mist was thick again and the cold very sharp. They stood instinctively the closer.

It was then, with a sudden pang as though an enemy had struck a blade into him, that he realized the intensity of his hatred for this boy. This had been approaching him for a long while, keeping pace with all his other evil thoughts, but now it had outpaced the others and crept all over his body like a fever. His hands shook. He did not trust himself to speak because his voice would shake.

This was the boy loved by Mirabell. Had he not come she would have learnt to love himself. Aye, she would. With what woman had he ever failed? No matter if he were older now and face-scarred, when he chose to put forth his charm what woman resisted him? And most certainly she, a child who, in spite of her boasts, could know so little about men, would have surrendered to him. But now her heart had been taken by a chit of a boy, beardless, simple, a baby poet. She would love him and then rue it, live with him a week and tire of it. A few years and she would be a woman, complex, tyrannous, passionate. And was this boy companion for such a woman?

But, more than conscious thought, his body was moving him towards some action. His hands about the boy's throat in that thick darkness, his hands strong as iron, one throttle, a little murmured cry. There would be no witness save the other fellow, and, with that, Herries, although no word had been spoken, was aware that it was the black-faced fellow's desire that he should do this. He was aware that the man hated the boy as he did. The fellow was very close to him, thigh pressed to thigh, and even as this knowledge came to him he felt the cold, damp, hairy back of that other hand on his.

One squeeze of the fingers about the throat . . . In the hurry and panic of this especial crisis no one would hear and no one know.

His body shook now so that, touching the thick, hard body close to him, he knew that the man felt this trembling and was aware.

The fellow said to him: 'At what hour did they say they would relieve us?'

But behind the spoken words were these others: ('We understand one ·another, we two. Do this and there will be no sound . . .')

He replied: 'At midnight.'

(And his answer: 'I wish for no understanding with you. What I do I do for myself.')

The man growled: 'The cold is more biting with every second.'

(And behind the words: 'Press your fingers into his windpipe. I will keep guard.')

Herries answered: 'The cold will be worse for the second watch.'

('Keep guard for yourself. I am my own guard.')

The man's cold hairy hand touched Herries's fingers.

'This town can stand no siege unless Wade relieves it.'

(And behind the words: 'It will be quickly done. Catch him by the neck. Press his head back.')

Herries said: 'Well, Wade should have been here today were he coming.'

('But it is my affair. Leave me alone to my own deed.')

The boy's voice came from what seemed an infinite distance: 'I wonder what the hour should be. I have missed the Cathedral clock.'

And from a greater distance yet some other voice: 'Eh, but it's cold . . . awful cold. There'll be snow before morning.'

Every evil act of Herries's life seemed to come to him there, all that had been unrestrained, uncontrolled, self-willed and cruel. The days in Doncaster, Margaret weeping on her bed, Alice Press at the Fair, and it was he who with his own hands had bound the naked witch . . .

He seemed to encircle Mirabell, his adored, with one arm and with the other he touched the boy's neck.

The boy turned, but Herries allowed his hand to stay against the warm skin.

('One twist of the head and you have done it. I will keep silence as though it had been myself.')

Then desperately, out of the mist, from some place that was not his own heart, some sort of a prayer issued: 'Oh, God, who dost not exist, help me now for I am in perilous trouble. Oh, God, who art not, save me from this sin.'

He touched barely the boy's neck, but he felt as though he held him in his arms, and all the hatred, all the aching lonely desire for the girl so indifferent to him, all the insistent urge to kill, was in the power behind his hands, his arms, his beating heart, his straining body.

It seemed to him that he threw him over the parapet and that nothing had been done.

The boy laughed.

'Your hand is cold,' he said.

Herries dropped his arms.

'I could wrestle with you to be warm,' he said.

'Well, let us wrestle then,' said the boy laughing.

Herries answered shuddering: 'I must go to find my son.'

He stumbled off into the dark. Figures were moving, voices murmuring. And then there was a great silence as though all the world had been stricken dumb.

He pressed up against the rampart of the wall, his forehead clamped to the cold stone. And so he stayed.

THE PRINCE

CHARLES EDWARD, with his army, entered Carlisle city on Monday, November 18th.

This was the climax of days of panic and despair. There is no need here to recover the episodes of that unhappy week, to recall once again how, after unfortunate Deputy-Mayor Pattinson had gaily sent word to London that the Prince had retreated, and been officially thanked for the news, he discovered only too quickly the error of his judgement; or how, to a growing accompaniment of terror and dismay, the citizens of that gallant town learnt that they were deserted and betrayed; or how on the 15th the Highlanders were within eighty yards of the city wall and answered the disheartened fire of the garrison with scornful jeers, 'their bonnets', one commentator remarks, 'held high aloft at the end of their trenching spades'.

After this, do what Durand might, there was pandemonium in the city. That brave man did his utmost, 'assuring them', to quote again the chronicler, 'that they need fear nothing from the rebels, that they were in a very good condition to defend themselves, and that if they would continue to behave with the same spirit and resolution they had hitherto shown, the rebels would never capture the city'.

It was the militia who brought the panic to submission. To the mess-room at the 'King's Arms' they retired, and this was their Declaration:

'The militia of the counties of Cumberland and Westmorland having come voluntarily into the city of Carlisle for the defence of the said city, and having for six days and six nights successively been upon duty in expectation of relief from His Majesty's forces, but it appearing that no such relief is to be had, and ourselves not able to do duty or hold out any longer, are determined to capitulate, and do certify that Colonel Durand, Captain Gilpin and the rest of the officers have well and faithfully done their duty.'

Durand, after reading this, made one more attempt to reason with them, but they would listen to no reason and no argument.

'The majority of the officers insisted that they were resolved to treat with the enemy for themselves.'

One last attempt was made; the townsmen, having better guts than the poor militia, refused to capitulate, determined to hold the Castle, collected provisions and munition in the Castle, but, alas, the militia 'melted away through the night, and on the morning of the 15th Durand was left with his eighty "invalids" and a capful of brave townsmen'.

On this a messenger who had been sent to the Prince returned with these words: 'That he would grant no terms to the town, nor treat about it at all unless the Castle was surrendered; likewise, if that was done, all should have honourable terms, the inhabitants should be protected in their persons and estates, and everyone be at liberty to go where they pleased.'

These terms, better than the citizens had expected, decided the matter. The Duke of Perth entered and took possession of the Castle and city. The capitulation of Carlisle was effected with the loss of one man only, and he a rebel.

On the 16th of November the Duke of Perth, on the steps of the Cross in the centre of the Market-Place, proclaimed King James III, and the Town Clerk and members of the Corporation went out to Brampton, where the Prince was, and, on bended knee, yielded him the keys of the city.

So, on the 18th of November, the Prince entered the city, and

David Herries and Hetty Cumberlege were among those who saw him enter.

That was a happy day for David. It was for him, and for many thousands of others who were there, like passing out of a nightmare. Strong of purpose, courageous and unflinching as he was, these last days had begun to test his nerves. 'If only,' he had thought (as he was to think many times again in the course of his life), 'folk would keep their mouths shut.' The thick foggy weather, the uncertainty of the future, the possibility of massacre and fire, the sense of futility from beating against all these nerves and ill-controlled passions, were beginning to frighten him.

For himself he did not care, and in his father he had absolute faith, but these trembling and crying women were another matter. Little Hetty Cumberlege was among the bravest of them, but on her, too, the wild stories and frenzied anticipations were having their effect. Had he been in love with her it would have been simpler. A sort of glory would have come from that. But although he wished to be, he could not. He could not understand that. She was pretty and charming, and herself as far in love with him as her childishness and inexperience allowed her to be. A word, a kiss, one passionate movement and she would have been his. But he could not make that movement.

Yet she woke him to a consciousness of women as no one before had ever done. He was twenty-six years of age and had never yet kissed a woman, save in friendliness. Now, even in these few dark troubled days, he looked at the women about and around him with new eyes. Hetty Cumberlege had done that for him. But he did not love her. He was sorry, but he did not.

The consciousness that she was ready to love him at a moment's turn embarrassed him terribly. He wished that he had Deborah there to advise him. Every look from Hetty's eyes (and she gave him a great many) made him feel ashamed. He would have liked to love her. He felt now that it would be delightful to love someone, but that someone would not be Hetty.

He would have spoken to his father about his troubles, but his father had been removed from him in some strange absorption of his own. His father had shown a surprising gentleness and kindliness these last days, but he had been alone. And by his own wish.

So here David and Hetty were watching the Prince enter Carlisle. The crowd by the city gates was so thick that they caught only a glimpse of him. David was far taller than the

majority around him. He saw, as a flash of sun struck from the
heavy winter clouds, the fine white horse and on the horse a
youth with a gallant air, his head up, a smile of pride and
courtesy and triumph on his lips. He looked like a king. He was
happy that morning as, had they all but known it, he was never
to be happy again. The horse tossed its head, a hundred pipers
played, and the sun went in again behind the clouds.

So then they went home. There was a very lively company in
the parlour. Mrs Cumberlege had found the general excitement
too much for her retirement, and there she was laid out on the
sofa. To David she was truly an amazing sight, for her stoutness
and shortness of figure gave her, lying there with a handsome
China shawl over her knees, the appearance of a bolster. Her
face was very red and she had on top of it her best wig, powdered, curled and greased, dressed high over a large cushion and
decorated with imitation fruit and a little ship with silken sails.
Mr Cumberlege was there, two ladies, and a jolly old fellow with
a wooden leg, who announced himself as Captain Bentley. He
was apparently a stranger in the house, and could not be sufficiently polite to Mrs Cumberlege, whose stout cheeks were all
smiles and whose head nodded with pleasure so frequently that
the little ship travelled on stormy seas indeed.

The talk was, of course, all of the Prince. An amazing calm,
and even gaiety, had for the moment come upon the town. It
would not last, but, just now, no one was alarmed any longer.
The Prince was here. He was charming, handsome, and who
knew but that in a week or two he might be master of the
country? Moreover, his Highlanders were here too and were be-
having with the greatest propriety. Not a single act of riot or mischief had been reported. It was whispered indeed that a number
of ladies were sadly disappointed . . .

The white favour was becoming for women with every
moment more popular.

As to Captain Bentley, you might think that there was no
Prince and no Highland invasion. He sat on the edge of his chair,
which creaked beneath his weight and the glory of his plum-
coloured breeches and silver buckles, and forced upon Mrs Cumberlege incidents of his personal experience. He was very
honest about his drink, and proud of it too. He declared that he
could swallow a bowl of punch and two mugs of bumbo without
any difficulty whatever, and told a long tale of how, being in
Wapping, he had a fierce toothache and could find no one but a
woman to pull the rogue, which she did with so muscular an

arm that he thought she must be a man in disguise, until inquiring further he found that she was a woman indeed.

'Fie! Captain,' said Mrs Cumberlege, laughing most friendlily at him, upon which he would have bent forward to whisper in her ear had not the stink from her wig been too strong for two by no means sensitive nostrils. He had also a grand tale of how in London a month or two back he had seen a show of moving pictures. Truly marvellous. You could see a coach roll out of the town, and a gentleman in the coach saluted the company, and you could watch ships sailing upon the sea and a man come to light a lamp in the Tower. In return Mrs Cumberlege had a sister-in-law who had seen a live griffin at a Fair and he had shot fire from his mouth, which had so sadly frightened her sister-in-law that she had given birth to triplets before her due time.

There was a bowl of punch, and both Mr Cumberlege and Captain Bentley became very merry indeed, and even the three ladies found their sentences coming none so clearly.

During all the gaiety Hetty and David sat close together in the bow-window. The streets were now dark outside, but many people were about. The cobbles echoed their steps. There was laughter and singing, and everywhere you felt the sudden relief, the freedom from panic.

Romance, too, was in the air. For good or ill this young and beautiful Prince was now in their city. Everything, it seemed, was giving way before him. After all, was he not one of our own people, no foreigner? Had not that sound of 'James III' cried on the steps of the Market Cross a pleasant echo in the air?

And for Hetty Cumberlege, too, this was the most romantic hour of her life. This huge young man, who sat so close to her, so brave, so strong, so proper a man, she thought that he loved her and presently would say so. It was true that she feared his father, but he would not live always with his father. It seemed to her impossible that they could be related, so different were they. The candles burning in the room, the flickering firelight, her mother for once in a good mood: now surely it was designed that he would speak.

How marvellous a chest he had, how beautiful a neck, what glorious eyes, how direct and honest he was: she could trust herself to him for ever. A little shiver ran through her body. She hung her head. She did not dare to look at him.

And David said never a word. His was not a quick nature, but yet quick enough for him to realize, with an awful sense of horror, that she was waiting for him to speak. He could see it in her hanging head, her trembling hands. This was for him the most terrible moment of his life. He longed to move, but was frozen to his chair. He heard the merry Captain and Mr Cumberlege trolling a song from an infinite distance. What must he do? By whose fault had he tumbled into this dreadful dilemma? She was so sweet, so young, so pretty. She would be wonderful for any man to hold in his arms, to press his cheek to hers; and yet he did not want to hold her. He wanted only to escape from the room. His great clumsy body seemed to him to fill the room and to swell ever larger and larger as he stayed there.

'There are many people yet abroad,' he said.

She raised her eyes, looked at him, and dropped them again.

'Yes . . . But it is cold. I think there will be snow.'

'At Herries, where we live . . .' he began desperately.

'Yes?' she said, looking into his eyes again.

'Wintertime the snow lies on the Fell to a great depth. Many sheep are lost in it.'

'Poor things,' she said.

'Sometimes in winter they must carry a corpse over the hills from valley to valley. When the snow is deep 'tis no light matter.'

'I like the summer best,' she answered.

How he longed to say: 'Hetty, dear, I like you so, but I don't love you. I wish I did.' Instead he told her about his sister Deborah. She was not interested. Her hand stole out and nearly touched his breeches. Had she touched him he might have yielded, and all his life, and the lives of many future Herries, been other, but her hand stole back again.

'Father is greatly pleased that you are here,' she ventured.

'I am glad,' he answered.

'And Mother too.'

'I am very glad.' She meant that someone else was greatly pleased too, but she did not say so.

'We must be returning home in a day or so,' he said, his face burning. 'I have business, an interest in two vessels in Liverpool. And maybe I shall purchase a farm.'

'You are very young for so much business,' she said, and again she looked at him.

The thought came to him that this proclamation of his prosperity might be considered a foreword to a proposal, so he said hurriedly:

'It is not much. A small venture.'

If something did not happen soon he was lost. Something did

happen. His father saved him. The door opened and Francis Herries came in.

David, his heart thumping his deliverance, went to meet him. Hetty, a minute after, left the room and running up the stairs, closing her door, threw herself on her bed in a passion of tears.

Herries meanwhile had had his own strange hour. He felt, because of it, soft and gentle to all the world. That night struggle on the wall had left him first as a wounded, then as a convalescent man and, in this convalescence, he was oddly gentle.

He felt a great and persistent weariness throughout his body, and everything about him – the town, the people, the crisis – was removed behind a sort of dream-curtain. Just now this Mirabell Starr was the only real thing to him in life. She was more real by far than he was to himself.

That same afternoon he had seen and talked to her. He had been wandering through the streets, lost in his own thoughts, but getting behind them an impression of this day's events very different from the one in Cumberlege's warm parlour. There was relief, it was true, but beyond the relief a sulky stiffening, a sense of humiliation and apprehension. It was as though, with a kind of second-sight that he had, he could feel the doom that was coming to this place, could touch Cumberland's swollen cheeks and smell the hot stench of that black hole where nearly four hundred poor wretches, huddled and trampled like cattle, were, in so short a time, to pant their strangled lives away. He could see, it might be (and yet not see), brave Coppock drawn on the smart new sledge through the English Gate to execution, and gaze upon that sad procession now only two months distant, the officers with their legs tied under the bellies of their horses, the privates on foot marching like felons, two abreast, fastened by rope. If he did not see these things he felt them in the air, which was growing with every moment colder and was made bitter by a driving wind that held in its lap a steely sleet.

He had reached the farther end of English Street and was about to turn when Mirabell all but ran against him. Three times now within the week chance had brought him to her, or perhaps it was not chance. There was to be one more . . .

She was cloaked up against the wind and seemed to him infinitely young and fragile. They encountered under a lamp-flare, and she knew him at once. She smiled. He could see that she was in some fear, and that stirred him at once to a sharp passion of protection.

'Mr Herries,' she said.

'You should not be out alone,' he answered her quickly. 'Not now, towards evening, the streets as they are.'

She did not repulse him. She seemed glad of his company.

'I am going to my lodging,' she said rather breathlessly. 'In Abbey Street. Behind the Cathedral. I have a room there.'

They started along English Street. She looked back.

'You see no one following us?'

'No,' he said. 'Who should be following you?'

'No one . . . but now, the town as it is . . .'

'Take my arm. No one shall touch you while I am here.' The pride he felt as he said that! And the rush of blood to his heart as he knew the touch of her hand on his arm!

'I know who it is,' he went on. 'A short, thick, black-bearded man with a chill hand.'

'You know? Yes. Anthony Thawn. But how do you know?'

'I saw you, a week back, in the "Silver Horn". I was quite near to you. There was a green parrot and this fellow stroked its neck.'

'Yes. He is a friend of Harry's. Harry is my lover. I am greatly afraid of him, Mr Herries. I have never been afraid of anyone before, and it is not for myself now but for Harry. He pretends to be his friend, but I know that he is not. He was first a friend of my uncles. He was with us here when we first came to Carlisle. Then when my uncles went to Scotland he stayed. He would make love to me if he dared. Harry is so simple that he thinks Thawn is his friend. I have told him no, but he will not believe me. Always when I leave them alone I am afraid of some evil . . .'

She poured all this out as a little child might, confident in her hearer's interest. And indeed Herries was interested, so deeply that it seemed to be his own history to which he was listening.

'I have seen your lover. He also was at the "Silver Horn". He has a noble face.'

'Harry! Yes, he is noble! When we go from here he will marry me and we will live in London, where he has a brother. Harry is a poet. He is writing a grand poem on "Dido and Aeneas". I can't tell whether I have·the names rightly. I have never had any education.'

'But could you live in London, when you have been always in the open? Seeing you on Honister I had thought you could never endure a town.'

'I could live anywhere with Harry. He also loves the country as I do, and when he has made a little money we will come back to the mountains. He will find patrons for his poem. He says that is often done.'

How different, Herries thought, love has made her. She is still a child, but all the wildness and rebellion are gone. His heart ached, but the touch of her hand on his arm consoled him. Perhaps he could help them, these two, and in being a friend to them find his salvation. They were both so very young.

'This fellow Thawn,' he said, 'if he troubles you I will rid you of him.'

But she shook her head. 'That is not so easy. He is very strong.'

'I, too, am strong,' said Herries.

'I have no fear,' she answered confidently, 'when I am with Harry. It is when I am away from him. He trusts everyone. He can see no harm in anyone. If he had had my life he would not be so trusting, as I am always telling him.'

They were skirting the Cathedral. They would not have many more minutes together.

'I told you,' Herries said, 'on Honister that I am always by you if you need me. Will you promise me, if you are afraid, to come to this place? It is in the very middle of the town, only five minutes from here. If I am away I will let them know, so that they can always find me.' He gave her the name of Cumberlege's house. 'Do you promise?'

She looked at him, then nodded her head. 'Yes, I promise.' She sighed, he thought, with some relief. 'Here is my lodging,' she said.

Abbey Street was a quiet, staid place behind Tullie House. It was a thin house with neat stone steps and a light in the upper window.

'Thank you. I am sure that Harry is here. The light is in my room.' Her voice had changed to a radiant happiness. She had already, he thought, almost forgotten him. She ran up the steps and into the house. He watched her until she was gone.

All that night he dreamt of her.

Events moved swiftly with him then. That next day, November 19th, was to be a marked day for him his life long, and for more than one reason. He left Cumberlege's house after three of the afternoon; by six of the evening that had occurred which gave his life a new strain never again to be lost.

By the Market Cross he was confronted with Roche. He had been expecting this meeting. Roche had in Keswick told him where he would be found in Carlisle, but Herries had not sought him out. Roche belonged to his old life, not to this one. But here Roche was and recognizing him instantly; indeed Francis Herries, with his proud arrogant carriage, his scar, his high sturdy figure, was not a man easily passed.

Roche's pleasure at the meeting was moving. He was dressed in civil clothes, but as a very grand gentleman. The grandeur suited him well. His black coat was of silk, elaborately laced, and at his side there was a slender gold-hilted sword. He wore a tie-wig and a three-cornered hat of dark felt and laced. His pale, long, aristocratic face was grave and dignified, and not jubilant as Herries would have expected it to be.

He caught Herries's arm and walked with him as though he would never let him go again.

'Well,' said Francis, 'your prophecies have been found true. You must be a happy man.'

But Roche was not altogether a happy man. As they walked, their cloaks close about them because of the bitter wind, Roche, dropping his voice, spoke his doubts. All was not as well as it ought to be. True enough that, with Edinburgh and Carlisle in their hands, the Government forces apparently dismayed, they had prospered to a marvel. But there were dissensions in the camp.

'His Royal Highness is but a boy, and has had little experience as yet of governing men. How could it be otherwise at his age? But there are the Irish. They have great importance, perhaps too great, in his councils. There is Lord George Murray. He is stiff-necked and obstinate and hates the Catholics. He has but now sent in his resignation because His Royal Highness had left the Duke of Perth and Murray of Broughton to arrange the terms of surrender without consulting Lord George. His Royal Highness had written Lord George a very sharp letter in which he had said that he was glad to hear of his particular attachment to the King, but was sure he would never take anything as a proof of it but his deference to himself. This to Lord George, who considered himself the God Almighty, was a bitter word. But they could (Roche was forced to confess) ill afford to lose Lord George, who had a great sense of strategy and the discipline of armies. The Lord knew they needed discipline (here Roche sighed), and it was hard to come by in such an ill-composed army as theirs.

'There was, too, great division of opinion as to the next steps to be taken. It was said that the Government was sending an army of ten thousand under Sir John Ligonier to Staffordshire.

Some were for a return to Scotland, others for remaining here to wait the rising of the North Country Jacobites. The Prince himself was for marching forward.'

Herries could see that Roche was in great perturbation of mind and longing for a confidant. He seemed to have no doubt at all as to the direction in which Herries's sympathies would lie, and was, it appeared, ready to confide to him any secret. He had aged very greatly since Herries had had any long talk with him, but that was natural enough, for a number of years had passed and he had been engaged in much perilous enterprise. But he had changed, too, in spirit. He seemed to have no longer anything of the religious zealot about him, but was completely the man of affairs, and with the discovery Herries also realized that all Roche's old influence over him had gone, his power and his charm.

He was eager to know what Herries felt to be the mood of Carlisle. Were they for the Prince? Had Herries not seen in the reception of the Prince's entry a disposition to enthusiasm? One more success and might it not be that the whole of the North would turn?

Herries said what he could and, snatching at any encouragement, Roche insisted that he should come now to see His Royal Highness and assure him of this. Even though it were only for five minutes. He was himself on his way there.

Herries had no wish to be dragged into any definite partisanship, but against this his curiosity to see the Prince was very great. So he went with him.

The Prince was lodging at the house of Mr Charles Highmore, Attorney-at-law. This was a white-fronted house on the west side of English Street, standing back some yards from the main thoroughfare.

Roche and Herries passed under an archway, sufficiently wide for a carriage drive. Above the archway was a big bay-window, and the whole house seemed spacious. There were glimpses of a fine garden at the back of it.

At the doorway and in the entrance hall there was a great bustle. A big fire burnt in the hall, officers were standing in groups, messengers coming and going. Leaning over the banisters of the wide staircase Herries saw two small children watching wide-eyed all that was going forward. Roche, begging Herries to seat himself for a moment in the hall, vanished behind a green-baize door.

Herries waited there. He realized that his presence caused

very considerable interest. One stout, thick-thighed officer, grandly dressed, warming his back at the fire, stared at him persistently. He was always afterwards, for no reason that he could define, to remember this officer with his swollen cheeks, pug nose, legs tight within their sky-blue silk breeches.

It seemed to him, although this impression may have been unwarranted, that there was some carelessness and disorder over the hall bustle, too much shouting and calling out and casual argument. Only a giant Highlander, who must have been some seven feet in height and was broad in proportion, stood motionless near the entrance. It was at him that the two children, breathless on the stairs, principally gazed.

It was cold and exceedingly draughty. The fire blew out of the open fireplace in flurries of smoke and flame. Some faded green tapestries of gods and goddesses feasting flapped on the wall. Near the baize door a group of young officers stood in whispered consultation.

He had taken this all in (and for the rest of his life it would remain with him), when he saw Roche come through the door and approach him.

'His Royal Highness,' he said, 'is most anxious to see you.'

He followed Roche through the door (pursued, as he knew, by the curious eyes of everyone in the hall) into a small, darkly wainscoted room. There was a table with a bowl of fruit, a finely carved fireplace and some high-backed chairs. On the mantelpiece was a big gold clock, very handsomely mounted, with the moon and stars portrayed and a Cupid with a small gold hammer to strike the hours.

Only two persons were in the room. One was a plump gentleman with a good-natured kindly face, who stood turned to the window that he might see better some papers held in his hand.

The other was warming himself at the fire. This was a lad in a grave handsome dress of dark purple, wearing his own hair, a diamond star at his breast. This boy's face was of a most delicate oval shape, the chin weak, the mouth rather too full. His splendour (for he did that day seem splendid) lay in his eyes of a deep eloquent brown, bold and haughty, brave and inquiring, and in the magnificent carriage of his beautifully shaped head, the carriage by natural right divine of a king and a ruler of men. His hair was of a fair brown, catching the light so that it seemed gold-tipped.

This was Prince Charles Edward.

But he was a boy, a child, an infant! Herries, in that first glance and then as, bending a knee and kissing the hand, he looked up into those eyes, was transfigured by surprise.

He had known that the Prince was but twenty-five, about the age of his own David; he had himself again and again wondered what it must be for such a boy to be in charge of so wild and tumultuous and kenspeckle an army, but in some imaginative fashion the events of these last weeks had altered his vision. The Prince, seen only through event, had grown and aged in the consequence of his successes. But now, face to face, why, beside David himself who could have taken him across his knee and with one gesture broken him, he was unbelievably a child.

And then, rising from his knee and exchanging with him look for look, Herries had a curious moment of vision.

It is an old tale that a drowning man sees in one instant the whole course of his past experience laid out as on a map. So now Herries, looking into that young man's eyes, had, in one moment of time, a vision of a world.

In Paris carts rumbled over the cobbles under a snowy sky, the French King lolled on his bed, scratching his stomach, yawning, then stretching a fat naked leg to see whether last night's drinking had dulled the use of it. A courier, waiting in the cold hall with dispatches, shivered and thought tenderly of his new mistress. At Calais the snow was beginning to fall, and along the deserted beach an old man in rags that blew in the wind wandered, searching for sea-trove. On the Dover Road a coach plunged up the hill, while within it, rolling in sleep one against another, two men and a woman dreamed of money, lechery and food.

The clouds gathered ever more thickly over Europe. In Vienna it was a blizzard, by the Hague the sea was rising and tumbling in huge swollen billows along the deserted shore. In London the Hanoverian King stumbled as he climbed the stairs, swore a German oath, wondered for the hundredth time which among his treasures he must take with him to Hanover if a sudden flight caught him. He had a violent cold and that old pain in the left side that hurt him when his nerves were out of order.

All through London that afternoon panic was spreading. No one had any thought but for himself and his. A man swung from ledge to ledge above a back court of the Strand, his pocket stuffed with rings and necklaces. He dropped eight feet, stumbled and was up, running through the falling snow, like a shadow, down to the river. In a room lit only by the firelight a lover was

buttoning his smallclothes, a lady arranging her hair before a
mirror. The clouds descended ever lower and lower over
London. Out of a window and above the river a lady was leaning,
looking out to hear whether even now she could catch the Highlanders coming. On the Great North Road the coaches were
running, and two miles before Doncaster three footpads were
waiting, their horses shivering in the cold. Such a snowy night
was good for the trade.

Up on the fells above Brough and Appleby it was desolate
indeed. A shepherd, trying to shield himself from the fierce
wind, searched for some lost sheep, calling to his dog, glancing
up at the sky as though it had some personal and especial message for him.

In Kendal and Penrith and Keswick, men sheltering by fires,
busy over their money-making, had only one topic. The Pretender was in Carlisle. Carlisle had fallen. First Edinburgh and
now Carlisle. An old man, dying in a farmhouse by Caldbeck,
wandered in his delirium and called for the girl of his heart, now
forty years dead. Two women, in a rich house by Grange,
quarrelling over cards in their high gilded drawing-room,
paused suddenly to listen, because above the fall of the stream
under the bridge they seemed to hear the tramp of soldiers . . .

What did Herries see? What did Herries hear? He only knew
that before him was a child, ignorant, impetuous, brave and
tragic, and that as he breathed, as his hand went to finger the
lace at his throat, as he felt for the skirt of his purple coat stiff
with whalebone, Europe, carrying on its wheeling surface, as on
an indifferent turntable, the hearts, the souls of these little men,
wheeled another turn in her history, this boy for a single bitter
instant the moving force.

Tragedy! Herries could see it in every stir and flicker of the
flame behind him. This boy to rule England, this boy to meet
those heavy, cumbrous, cruel forces now advancing to encounter
him! He could, in that second of understanding, have taken that
boy in his arms, hastened with him to deep obscurity, protected
him until the crisis was past.

Then the Prince spoke, and it was a king who was speaking.

'Mr Herries,' he said, smiling most charmingly, 'you are
welcome. Mr Roche here says you are an old friend of his.'

'Yes, sir. It was pleasant to meet again.'

'And what do you think of the feeling in this city? Is it
favourable to us?'

'I am a stranger here, sir. From the little I have seen I would say that feeling is divided. Many are waiting to feel the current of the wind.'

The Prince looked at him. Here was a man. Young though he was, he was no poor judge when his prejudices were not already stirred and his liberty not threatened. Years later, in 1771, when he was sheltering shabbily under the roof of the tailor Didelot, hunting round for a wife, the Irishman Ryan introduced him one drunken evening to a tall lean fellow, with a scarred face, a famous ragamuffin duellist. Lolling, paunchy and red-faced, on the shabby sofa, looking up at the fellow, Charles Edward remembered that other man with a scar. Where had it been? And when? In the close, hot, smelly room, thick with smoke and stinking with drink, his bemused mind went back to that other scene: Carlisle, high burning hopes, courage, pure ambitions, England open before him, and that strange, stern, ugly fellow who carried himself and spoke like a leader. The grease dropping from the slobbering candle was mixed with his own maudlin tears. That day . . . and this . . .

'Sheridan, this is Mr Herries of Keswick.'

The stout man turned from the window, smiling. They bowed and shook hands.

'What do you advise, Mr Herries; that we should go forward or stay where we are?'

The unexpected and casual directness of this startled Herries: he fancied that some lack of caution in it had startled Sir Thomas Sheridan, too, and not for the first time.

His natural honesty, as always, drove him.

'I cannot tell what information Your Highness has obtained. I am sure that time is a most important element in your favour. I am sure, too, that many who are secretly on your side are waiting for your success before they join you. If by pressing forward very rapidly you are likely to reach London within a very brief period of time, I should push forward. If your progress is likely to be slower, then I should remain in the North until more of your friends come out to you.'

'Yes, yes . . .' answered the Prince impatiently. Then it seemed that he caught Sheridan's eye, for he turned abruptly back to the fire, stared into it a moment, then wheeled round to Herries again.

'Of what sort of a place is Keswick, Mr Herries?' he asked.

'It is a small town, sir, very remote from the world.'

'Your place is in the country?'

'Seven miles from Keswick, in a valley beyond the lake.'

' You have much rain there, I have heard.'

Herries smiled. 'It is a changeable climate, sir. We have every sort of weather.'

The Prince shrugged his shoulders. '*Peste!* Every sort of *bad* weather. I know the changes; hail one fine day, sleet another, snow a third. You should try the south of France, Mr Herries. There it is all sunshine and beautiful ladies.'

Herries smiled. 'I have no doubt, sir. But I love this cold North Country. It has something magical for those who feel it.'

The Prince laughed.

'Eh, Sherry? Shall we leave this business we're on and settle down in the mountains to shoot bears and frighten the wolves? Poor Sherry! Mountains and bears are not for your stomach. For myself, I don't know. But, Mr Herries, you had better come with us. We will lead you into the sunshine.'

Herries paused, then looking the Prince between the eyes he answered: 'I am afraid the public world is no longer for me, sir. I am forty-five years of age and no very good company.'

The Prince looked back at him, honestly and quietly. They liked one another.

'*Eh bien!* Yours is no doubt the better part. We have little choice in our destinies, I believe. Fate is with us, and then, a change in the wind . . .' He shivered, made as though he would kick the fire with his foot, half turned his face.

'At least you wish me well.'

Herries said: 'I will always wish you well, sir.' He hesitated, then went on: 'I would only say that I love England with a passion. I believe that you have the same love. And, were I younger—' He broke off. 'I hope you will believe, sir, in my sympathy.'

The boy looked at him with some touching appeal in his eyes. There was fear there, some hint of dismay and confusion as though, only now, he were beginning to realize the impossibility of the task that he had at first so gaily shouldered. Herries's heart went out to him, just as it might have gone to David in trouble.

He bent the knee and kissed the hand again, bowed and left the room.

In the street again he said goodbye to Roche, promised to meet him shortly, saw him vanish into the dusk. He did not know that he was never to set eyes on him again.

A little bemused, he stood hesitating. Then, as though he could step no other way, he turned down English Street towards the Cathedral. It was not dark yet: there was a queer, green, owl-ish light through which snowflakes were falling, fragments of ghostly wool. Very few persons were now about. He crossed into Abbey Street, which was quite deserted. He stood in the shadow by the long wall of Tullie House. It was cold, but he did not feel it. There was no wind.

How absurd! He was watching, like any young moon-calf, outside his mistress's window. There was no light in the demure, thin-lipped house, where she was lodging. He could see the number – Thirty – in clear Roman numerals above the door. There was no stir of life anywhere.

But he knew the strangest satisfaction in standing there. It was as though he were protecting her, although, for all he could tell, she might be in the other end of the town. And there was also a sense that he was expiating a little the frantic temptation that he had known on the wall. That gave him, oddly enough, the only conviction of sin that he had ever known. He had done many evil things in his life and had dealt ironically with them all. But this . . . He had stepped farther then into monstrous countries than ever before. Was it only because this had touched her? Or because he was, in his old age, developing a new sense of sin? Time perhaps that he did. Or was it that sentimentalism, a senti-mentalism of the very kind that he had always most despised, was creeping over him? Or was it a sort of frustrated lust? Because he would not yet possess Mirabell he imagined a noble aim in himself? Ah, that last, God forbid! He did not want to possess her – or at least not that mainly – he wanted to care for her, be good to her, make her happy . . . And then, having used her, would he not tire of her and forget all his nobility, as he had with so many women before her? For the instant the picture of Alice Press came back to him; Alice Press when he had first seen her, when he had first had her, when he had tired of her, hated her, sold her . . .

He nodded his head to himself. Yes, this was most truly some-thing other, something quite new in him, something growing, like a plant, in his soul. If there were indeed a soul . . . If there were not, there was at least something in him that was not only animal; his great white horse plunging through the black lake, climbing the splintered hills – she was, for him, of the world of that dream.

The door of the house opened. He was almost opposite it, but the shadow, thickening as the early winter darkness crept upon the city, covered him.

Two came out. They were Mirabell and her lover. He caught her face for a moment under the light by the door, and she seemed in an ecstasy of happiness. She was pressed close to the boy, who had his arm around her. He watched them go, quietly, down the street. He was never afterwards to know what still kept him there. His business was over. She was well protected, and, as his constant irony drove him to perceive, by the only protection that she coveted. She had, he could not doubt, lost all awareness of him. Perhaps, after seeing him, she had told her lover, and together they had laughed at the thought of that ugly, elderly courtier, laughed kindly but with the selfish, indifferent confidence of blissful lovers.

He felt the cold now and drew his cloak close about him. Yes, it was cold and he was alone, and the street was very silent. He was conscious again, as he looked at the light above her door, of a sense of doom that lay over the city and over the Prince whom he had just left and, it might be, over himself. For himself he did not very much care.

But for Mirabell . . . Mirabell . . . Mirabell . . . An absurd name . . . a man's name. He looked back to that Christmas feast so long ago, the woman standing by the door, the child huddled against her skirt. It had been that woman's romantic notion to call the child Mirabell after some play perhaps. Congreve's *Way of the World*, was it? or perhaps she had heard the name spoken or seen it on a news-sheet. Mirabell . . . Mirabell . . . Yes, the mother to whom he had once given his coat must have been a romantic creature, filled, he had no doubt, with unsatisfied longings.

The door opened again. A man came out. It was Thawn.

Herries caught his black face in the light, but there was no mistaking the fellow's walk, that lurch, that slouch, that roll from heavy foot to heavy foot. He walked, too, with his head sunk between his thick shoulders as though he had no neck.

An animal, by God, a wild hairy animal, possessed by the Devil. He paused by the door. He was considering something, and his face was as evil as a face may be and yet be in some sort human. Then he lurched away, moving, in spite of his awkwardness, with great speed.

There began then a strange pursuit. Herries followed as though he had been ordered to do so. But it was like a pursuit in a dream. They seemed to move in a dead city. Herries could never remember afterwards that he passed a living being. As he moved anxiety grew in him. He had no reason, but with every step his fear increased. Thawn never looked back, nor hesitated. He seemed to know exactly his direction and purpose.

They kept to the dark side-streets, came to the Castle, skirted it and, turning a corner near the city wall, saw the girl and boy but a little in front of them.

Then it was they whom Thawn had been following.

The girl was standing folded by her lover's arms. His back was towards them.

There was a sudden alteration in Thawn's movement. He walked more swiftly, but very silently. His feet made no noise at all.

At that same instant Herries understood.

He ran, crying 'Look out! Look out! . . . Take guard!' But he was too late. The boy turned, but with that same movement Thawn struck, his black arm, the pale chill of the back of his hand, the knife shining. Herries caught these and his thick, pulsing, stertorous breath like a bear's grunt.

The boy fell without a cry, and Thawn was gone, moving like a shadow into the shadows of the dusk.

The girl flung herself down, then stared up at Herries, not seeing who he was.

Herries knelt, pulled the shirt down, felt the heart. The boy was dead. His own hands were a mess of blood.

'He's dead,' he said, touching her hair, which fell, loosened, about his hands.

'You lie,' she answered.

Then he bent his will and purpose to do all that should be done.

Part Three

THE WILD MARRIAGE

CANDLELIGHT RESPECTABILITY

ON A beautiful summer afternoon, in the year 1756, David and Deborah rode into Keswick. Deborah was proud because, for the first time, she was riding her new horse, Appleseed, that David had given her. Old fat Benjamin had named him. It seemed to Deborah a very pretty name. She was excited, too, because they were riding in to a Ball and were to sleep three nights at Keswick. Although Deborah was now thirty-three years of age, a very great age indeed, she was still wildly excited by a Ball. She could not think how David could remain so calm.

But David was always calm. As she looked at him now, gigantic (he was six foot six inches in height, and broad with it) but placid, smiling to himself at some notion that was, she was quite sure (she thought to herself), to do with ships or tallow or grain, she loved him more than ever, but was a little indignant with him too. She would have liked to stick a large and sharp pin into the rough broadcloth that covered his immense, immovable back.

It was a Ball at the Assembly Rooms (the first of the season), and they were to stay for three nights with, technically, Uncle Pomfret, in reality, Cousin Raiseley and sister Mary.

In the year 1750 Cousin Raiseley had married sister Mary. Deborah who, in spite of her placidity, had some good strong feelings within her, hated her cousin Raiseley and had always disliked her sister Mary. It was, she had thought at the time, a very suitable match, only she had supposed that Mary would have made a smarter one. Heir to a baronetcy though he was, Raiseley was, after all, with his poor health and country background, no very great catch for anyone. It was true that his social value had risen a little after his sister Judith married the Honourable Ernest Bligh, who might, with good fortune, be one day Lord Monyngham, but Judith, after her marriage, disregarded her family entirely, and never again came near Keswick – no, not even when her mother died.

It was well known, too, that neither Raiseley nor Mary had been a grand success in London. That was why, perhaps, they had married one another, a fellow-feeling making them wondrous kind. So back to Keswick they had come, Raiseley to cheer the remaining years of his poor old father, who could not move for

the gout, Mary to rule the household, and so much of Keswick
as she could ensnare, most tyrannously.

They did not often invite Deborah to come and see them, and
Deborah had determined to refuse when they did, because Mary
would not see her father, would not come out to Herries, would
not speak to him if she saw him in Keswick.

'If Father is not good enough for Mary I am not,' said Deborah,
and then sighed because there were so many who would not
speak to her father.

But now, on this occasion, her father had insisted that she
should go. He had kissed her, looking at her with that queer,
ironical smile that still, even after all these years, frightened her
so strangely.

'Thou'dst best go, Deb. And maybe there'll be some spoiling
of the Egyptians. Anyway, it will help Davy.'

So they had left him, standing in the little grass-grown courtyard with fat Benjamin and Benjamin's thin wife Marjorie
(whom he had married out of Newlands some ten years ago),
standing there gaunt and shabby, grand and lonely, shading his
eyes against the sun, then turning back to the old house with that
odd, absorbed, dreaming look as though he had already forgotten them, almost, with that one turn of the heel, putting them
out of existence.

They were climbing up out of Grange, and soon the lake came
into view. It was an early autumn afternoon of crystal clarity;
the lake, Skiddaw, and Saddleback behind it, were as though
they were enclosed in a series of mirrors. The lake was a bowl of
pale-blue glass, cracked here and there with silver splinters.
Over a portion of it shadows of rose amber tumbled with a faint,
rippling stillness, as though one were breathing on it to stir it.
Lord's Island lay on this silver-blue like a ball of ebony ruffled
at its edge by the silhouette of its trees. On the farther side the
fields, bright green in the sun, rose to the slopes of Saddleback
that was beginning gently to change from amber to purple, and
behind the dark line of the hill the sky was almost whitewashed,
with a little colour.

So, as the eye travelled upwards, it moved from dark to light,
from light to dark, but always with the tranquillity of perfect
harmony. The air about them, as they rode, shared this crystal
purity with the scene. One pale cloud, blown open into the shape
of a great white rose, travelled over their heads.

For Deborah this Lake had grown to have almost a magical
splendour. Although Rosthwaite was some miles away, she

walked continually to Grange, to Manesty, even to Portinscale, to sit beside it, listen to the trees whispering and the broken ripple of the tiny waves against the stones. Even physically she had some kinship with the Lake. In no way beautiful, rather broad and shapeless of figure, her pale gentle face, her hair faintly gold, her steady honest gaze, her spiritual *quietness* belonged to the coves and shallows and wooded shelters of the Lake-side. There was strength and force, too, behind her gentleness, just as the Lake had strength and force. She lived securely and proudly within her borders as the Lake lived.

As they rode she noticed all the trees, mountain-ash, holly, ivy, hawthorn, yew; and they were all transformed for her into a sort of glory. Rocks here and there by the side of the lake glittered in the sun. She thought to herself how passionately moving this world would be were she seeing it for the first time on such a day. She would surely say to herself: 'This must be a very holy place.' But now that she knew it so very well it was not less holy, and in every different mood it seemed to have a different holiness.

David broke the beautiful silence.

'We're coming to a new time, Deb, a modern world; with these new toll-roads our valley will be enclosed no longer.'

'It will be better for riding to Keswick.'

'Aye, there'll be good things doubtless, but it will be sad to see the old world go. I doubt that you will find anything grander in the world than our Statesmen – Peel and Elliot, and Curtis and Ramsay, more self-dependent, more self-sufficing, owing nothing to any man . . .'

'They have been cruel to Father,' she answered fiercely, an odd fierceness to come from her placid countenance.

'Nay, not cruel,' he answered with his customary slowness, as though he thought every word out before he uttered it. 'He's strange to them, and I don't wonder. These last eleven years – we've talked of it many a time – he's been like a man lost. Since the Rebellion, when we were in Carlisle, he's been a "fey" man. As though he were searching for something he could never mind. He loves me, I know, but he'll tell me nothing. He's as strong and hearty as he was twenty years gone – more hearty for all the walking he does – but it's of no avail to try to keep him to business. He is happier walking the Fell than any other way, he's happier silent than speaking, happier alone than with company. There was something in Carlisle, all those years ago . . .' He broke off, then turned on his horse towards her, speaking more rapidly: 'I've never told you, Deb. I've never told any man. There was a night in Carlisle – after the Prince made his entry – I was climbing into my bed: I had gone an instant to the window to see whether the snow was falling. I heard the door open and turned. Our father was in the doorway, white as a cleaned stone. He stumbled and held by the bed post. I thought he would fall and ran to catch him. He held by my shoulder. His nails dug into the flesh. I asked him what it was, whether he were sick. He nodded his head and looked as though he did not see me. He put his hand flat on my naked heart.

'"Aye, sick," he answered me, "and unhappy, Davy." Then he went out. I did not dare to follow him. I waited, listening for a sound. There was none. In the morning he was as he has been since – closed, lost and alone. They are right to fear him, Peel, Curtis, and the rest. He's a man lost.'

Deborah answered at last:

'He was never as we were, never like any other. But I love him now as I never did. I always feared him. Now I would be proud to comfort him, would he let me.'

'Aye, but he will not let you – nor anyone.'

They rode on silently for a time. Then David spoke again.

'I have a hard evening, Deb,' he said. 'I've to tell Christina that I'll not be marrying her.'

'Oh!' cried Deborah. 'I'm glad!'

'Yes.' He nodded his head. 'You never liked it, Deb. I fancy you will never care for me to marry. But it must be one day. I must have children. But it'll not be Christina who'll be their mother.'

'What's decided you?' she asked him.

'I do not love her. I have never loved her. I thought she'd be grand for a wife, in all the outward things, you understand. Mellways would be a fine house and there's broad land with it. She's kind, but wearisome. Her voice has a fearful monotony. And she doesn't love me herself. It's her dogs and her horses that have her real fancy. She's been thinking I'd be good for looking after the horses.' He chuckled in his slow, drawling way. 'And her eyes are not even,' he added.

'I'm glad, I'm glad.' Deborah almost sang it. 'I knew that you were not lovers and that she would contemn Herries and would take you away and would think me a dolt. Aye, she does that already.'

David sighed. 'But it will be uneasy telling her. I'm not grand at speeches. Love's a strange thing, Deb. You go to your bed thinking that you love a girl and you wake in the morning to know her eyes are crooked . . .' He hesitated, then went on: 'I should be marrying. I was six-and-thirty last Martinmas, and I've money enough now. But it's the children rather than the woman I dream of.'

Deborah answered: 'You're in luck, Davy, because you're a man. I'm younger, and yet I'm now an old maid. I could have loved a man, but no man has ever fancied me.'

'Tonight, maybe,' said David. 'Don't lose heart, Deb.' But he didn't say it with great conviction. It was true. Deborah had always been an old maid and would always be one. Not like her sister Mary, who had made eyes at men since she was a baby.

As they rode through Portinscale village over the stream by old Crosthwaite Church into Keswick (the shadow of Skiddaw, russet and silver-grey, sprawling above them), he fell into thought.

He had very much to think of. He was a boy no longer, a man of thirty-six. Things were approaching a crisis, and he must come to some man's decision. He could see, looking back over the last ten years, that he had been almost incredibly influenced in his actions by his father's: incredibly because his father had neither by word nor action tried to influence him, had told him indeed, again and again, that he must break away, make his own life now, leave him and even forget him.

His affairs had developed beyond all reasonable expectation during those years. The little enterprise in Liverpool that had started with a share in two small trading vessels had grown until he had his finger now in half a dozen Liverpool ventures. He had bought land in Borrowdale, beyond Keswick towards Troutbeck and at the farther end of Bassenthwaite towards Cockermouth. It was not that he had a brilliant head for commerce, but he was notably honest and upright, very sure if also slow, kindly and agreeable to deal with. He had, too, a wider and deeper sense of the social changes that were moving under his feet than had most of the men around him. He perceived that these years that followed the '45 Rebellion were opening up the North. He could not perceive that he was now living at the commencement of England's great new industrial life, but he understood something of the new inventions and sniffed more in the air. It would be fifty years yet before the world that he foresaw was in true being, but, in his own small individual way, he was part of it.

But, with this new and exciting world of affairs, his father would have no touch; nay, would not, could not. He had been willing, almost eager at first, to help in the little Keswick office that David had now for his own behind the Assembly Rooms towards the Kendal road. He had a brain far abler and more brilliant than David's, but it would not stick into these items of lading and shipping and transport. He did not care: he could not bother with it.

So, after a while, he slipped back to Herries, and David was glad that he went, for not only did he confuse any issue that he touched, but his own unpopularity with the outside world hampered the business at every step. It was not only the old evil reputation that he already had, but the new evil reputation that he was for ever creating. He no longer kissed the women and gambled and drank with the men. It had been better maybe if he had. He held aloof from all social contact; when he met a man he looked at him with his cold ironic eyes and as often as not turned on his heel without a word, and this, as David knew, not from scorn, arrogance or pride – these fires had remarkably died in him – but rather that his mind was altogether elsewhere, searching for something, dreaming of something, regretting, hoping – at least in no mood for Liverpool trade.

So back to Herries he went. Here, too, he was odd, almost to madness. He would have no stranger in to improve the house. He or Benjamin or David might support a tottering wall, mend a gaping stair, fill in a window – no strangers. Nor would he permit David to buy more land to go with the house. There was at one time a fair lot available that would have made Herries a fine property, but Francis would have none of it. He dug still in his one or two barren fields as he had always done, planted what would not grow, dug to sterility, and was quiescent. This and his rovings gave him a kind of restless contentment. With every year he roved farther – looking for what? for whom? On horse or on foot he had covered all the country from Shap to Gosforth, from Uldale to Stanley Gill. Every stream and every hill he knew. Here, in this soil and rocky fell, lay his passionate devotion. One of two; the other unsatisfied.

To David and Deborah his manner remained always the same, jestingly ironic, scornfully loquacious, lovingly friendly of a sudden, then for a day, two days, a week utterly silent, while his eyes roved, his ears were a-cock listening for a step. It was keeping company with a haunted man.

But where in this lay his influence? David could not say, except that quite simply he loved him. He loved him, it seemed, more with every year and understood him less. As Deborah had once said, where she and David left off, their father began. He was in country that they had never so much as seen a map of.

But things were reaching a crisis. David hated Herries. He had perhaps always at heart hated it since, the first of that family, he had crossed its threshold and seen those chill suits of armour receive him. He hated the house for its darkness, gloom, damp, moth-eaten, grudging spirit. He hated it because of the things that had happened there – the long-ago evil of Alice Press, his mother's death, old Mrs Wilson the witch, and all the superstition and avoidance that had grown up around his father there. He wanted to leave it to die its own death. He was convinced that if he could take his father away from there his father would become another man. This odd wearisome passion his father had for finding something that would put everything right and fair would die in another, healthier atmosphere. David loathed everything that was dark and damp, morbid and introspective, superstitious and nightmare-ish. These things, he thought, did not properly belong to his father, but had been bred in him by the place.

At his engagement to Christina Paull he had expected a settlement. They would live near by Penrith, and his father would live with them. But Christina had plainly denied that, and so had his father. His father had loathed Christina, calling her a 'tight-nostrilled bitch', but had in no way persuaded David against the marriage.

'A mare like that,' he had said, 'cannot step in between our lives together, not though you live in China.'

And David had found that true. Without saying a word, his father had in some way shown him how truly impossible Christina would be.

David had been greatly relieved to see the impossibility; but yet, did it mean that he was never to escape his father, never have his own life, nor children, nor freedom? Why did he love his father so fiercely, when he did not at all understand him and often was infuriated by him? There was some bone in him that was his father's bone. That was the only answer.

As they rode into Keswick he shook his head with a kind of despair, and Deborah, who had been riding quietly on Appleseed beside him, looked up as though she expected him to speak. But he said nothing, only sighed very deeply.

And so they came to old Uncle Pomfret's house.

Externally it had not changed very much in the last twenty-five years. When David, as a small boy, had first seen it on that memorable occasion of his visit with his mother, it had seemed a palace of a shining and a glittering splendour. Now it was a small place. The trees had grown in the garden, the fountain, once of so incredible a beauty, was now diminished and stained with rain: *sic transit gloria!*

But within Mary had made everything as fine and modern as Raiseley's stingy habits would allow her. She had two footmen, and in the saloon (which appeared now to David amazingly small) a beautiful Bury four-backed settee and some exceedingly handsome Chippendale chairs with cabriole legs.

Although, as David very well knew, she cared nothing at all for literature, she had *Sir Charles Grandison*, Thomson's epic poem, *Liberty*, and Glover's tragedy, *Boadicea*, prominently displayed on her table.

He regarded his sister critically: never having liked her, he had not denied her opulent beauty. She was yet beautiful, but was too thin and haggard, and her eyes and mouth wore a discontented and peevish expression. The Herries, because of their prominent horse-like bones, were not advantaged by thinness. Her cheeks were strongly painted, and her wig very high and decorated with pompoms.

She greeted her brother and sister with the condescension she always used, but, David thought, with a certain anxiety, as though she would, if she knew how, win them to her side. At their entrance the two infants, the boy Pomfret, aged five, and Cynthia, aged two, were in course of display to their reluctant relatives. They were plain children, the girl clear Herries, thin, pale and bony, the boy plump, with the features of his grandfather. They howled lustily, and had to be removed by their fat kindly Aunt Anabel, whose complacency seemed armoured against any vexation.

The little parlour was hot and over-filled with Herries. Grandison, his wife Mary, and Cousin Pelham were there; Uncle Harcourt, now sixty-eight years of age, frail and delicate like a piece of china; and Dorothy Forster, stiff in creaking black, as gloomy and funereal as ever.

Pelham was the grand one of the party. He was now thirty-eight years of age, still a bachelor, very elegant indeed, and kindly with it. He seemed to Deborah's country eyes the handsomest man she had ever seen, with his slim body, suit of black and silver; he was Herries at its most elegant. All the Herries breeding seemed to have concentrated in his repose of bearing, humorous knowledge of the world, languor, superior indifference. Deborah could not but wonder what it was that had brought him to so rustic a ball in so small a country place.

It was his mother who had brought him, he having gone to her, as on many another occasion, to see whether she had a plan that would relieve him of some of the more tiresome of his debts. These were the only occasions when he did go to her, her maternal solicitude and anxious care of him boring him exceedingly. But he was always courteous to her when he *was* with her, making up in manner what he omitted by his constant absence.

This time she had the excellent notion that Uncle Harcourt might be of use. Here was a source untapped, and, if Herries gossip were to be trusted, a rich source too. It stood to reason that a bachelor, living alone in a world-away seclusion like Ravenglass, with no one but himself to consider, must have a fair sum of money put by. Moreover, little Uncle Harcourt was sixty-eight, and, as things were, could not be expected to live for ever . . . So Pelham had already suggested to his little uncle that he should come and stay for a while at Ravenglass, and the charm of his manner had been no whit abated by the obvious reluctance of his uncle (who was not born yesterday) to have him.

Mary Herries, stout, overbearing and ill-mannered, had tried to subdue her personality to the desperate needs of her son, and had wooed Harcourt like any sucking-dove. This had been no easy task for her, and the entry of the large handsome David, who was, she knew, Harcourt's favourite nephew, did not please her at all. She gave David the barest of greetings, and poor Deborah no greeting whatever.

Deborah indeed found her ultimate comfort with poor old Uncle Pomfret alone in his room, trophies of the chase mouldering about him, and his leg (already huge enough) swollen to twice its natural size and laid out on a chair in front of him.

Poor Uncle Pomfret, rotten now with gout, and deserted in his own house, seventy-eight years of age, and no one caring whether he lived or died! Gone were all his blustering, hunting years; gone his oaths, his country pastimes, his childish prides, his simple pleasures!

When his wife Jannice had died, he had thought, poor fool, that it was not a bad thing. She had worn him to an irritable thread with her medicines, tempers and dominance. Now, on how many a lonely afternoon he would wish her back again! His gout would have been for her the very thing that she wanted! Would she not have loved to posset him and bleed him and cosset him! Might they not have found in their mutually sick old age a mutual love and comfort?

It was true that his daughter Anabel did for him what she could, but it was Anabel's mania these days to be, of all things incongruous with her stout form and rosy cheeks, a blue-stocking.

She had corresponded with Mrs Delany and sent a long screed to Lady Mary Montagu on the smallpox, and, on a visit to London, she had attended a meeting in Mrs Elizabeth Montagu's famous Chinese drawing-room in Hill Street. Nothing would hold her after her return, and although she was kind to her old father when she thought of him, she forgot him for most of the time.

So there poor Uncle Pomfret was, and tears poured down his cheeks as Deborah sat beside him, stroked his puffed and swollen hands and settled his pillows. Huskily he asked her how her father did, and could not hear enough of what she had to tell him.

'Brother Francis! Brother Francis! He was closer to me than any of them. But I was afraid of your aunt, my dear . . . And Francis didn't want me, didn't want any of us . . . I mind when I went to see your poor mother afore she died – poor soul! Sitting up in bed for manners' sake when she was almost gone. Francis felt her going, although he was always too clever for her . . . Here, bend thy head a moment, little darling, and I'll whisper thee something.'

Deborah bent her head and felt his hot liquorish breath and the odd touch of his burning hand against her fresh cheek.

'When thou hast a man, don't take one too clever like thy father, for he'll dream without thee; nor stupid like thy old uncle, for he'll not dream at all. Do thou the dreaming, and he'll never leave thee.' He thought this mighty clever and lay there chuckling until the chuckle brought on the gout, and his pain was a torment to see.

On the third night was the Ball.

They did not go until nearly eleven o'clock, because they were the gentry and it was not genteel to go too early.

The Assembly Room was a small room, even by Carlisle or Kendal standards, but to Deborah it seemed like Paradise indeed.

She would have clapped her hands, had she dared, at the shining candles, the little gallery (with its gilded scroll where the musicians were, the alcoves where the food was – jellies, syllabubs, cakes, orgeat, lemonade, fruits and the rest – the gleaming floor, the hangings of red and blue, the rows of benches down the side all covered with persons in the most beautiful dresses.

It was the second ball only of her life, although she was thirty-three, and by contemporary standards an old maid. But she did not look thirty-three that night in the new dress that David had bought for her in Liverpool. This dress was not grand, with its modest hoop and gentle frills and fichus, but its rose colour went prettily with the freshness of her cheeks and bosom. Her figure was too large and full, but this tonight gave her strength and honesty, and she had always masked gracefully, like the well-born lady that she was.

At first she could see little, because of her terror of the enormous Mary Herries at whose side she seemed remorselessly attached. Mary Herries and Grandison were almost the largest persons in the room, and looked double their natural size because of their magnificent clothes. Mary Herries's hoop was as wide as the globe, and her wig, in which nestled birds, flowers and fruit of the gayest colours, towered to heaven.

Grandison in crimson and silver, as stout as he was tall, as superb in his own estimation as he was stout, was thought by some of the yokels peering in through the door to be the King of England. Well, they were Herries from London, and so must show these country bumpkins!

In a brief while, happily, they forgot Deborah, and she was able to sit on a bench and look at the world.

The townspeople were dancing country dances; the minuets would come later.

Deborah, who had a sharp Herries eye, saw many things: how the townspeople grew demure with the appearance of the gentry and plainly less happy; how little Mr Gibbon of the china shop (whom she knew well and liked greatly) was already drunken, and his wife in an agony of alarm; how charming Pelham was, moving about so gracefully, speaking to everyone with such kindness; how greedy and sulky Raiseley was, going to one of the alcoves by himself and helping himself to syllabub; how grand Mary thought herself, moving about among the townspeople as though she owned all of them, but always with that unhappy, discontented look in her eyes; how speedily David had caught a glimpse of Christina Paull and moved hurriedly in another direction (and what a darling, and how handsome and how superior to everyone else in the room!); and what fun the country dances were (her feet were moving to the gay tinkling little tune!), and how she did hope that someone presently would invite her to dance; and what fun balls were, and why had she not been to more of them; and how the girls clustered together and giggled and made eyes at the men (and how odd it was that she had not a girl friend in the world, nor had ever had one), and—

At this moment she was aware that someone was sitting very close to her, and this someone a man. She turned round and saw, next to her on the bench, a short, sturdy little clergyman with a chubby face.

He must, she thought, be someone's private chaplain, perhaps from the Castle at Cockermouth or one of the grand country houses. He looked a gentleman (she stole several very careful glances). Many of the clergymen known to her had been little better than the peasantry, living a life of the utmost poverty and treated accordingly. Most of the grander clergymen she had heard of never went near their parishes, and visited Bath or Harrogate.

This clergyman – his hair was tinged with grey – looked healthy, strong and a gentleman. She thought him very pleasant. And apparently he thought her so, for presently he shifted his broad shoulders and turned to her, smiling most charmingly. He apologized for not allowing her room and stood up that she might have more. She, blushing, begged that he should sit down again. But he looked very well standing there on sturdy legs, his face a fresh colour, his eyes (as she was ashamed to notice) very large and fine.

'Pray, sir, be seated,' she said, smiling in her turn.

'I fear I incommode you.'

'Why, no, sir, there is room.'

He sat down again.

'The music is excellent,' he remarked.

'For a little place, I agree,' Deborah replied, feeling a proper woman of the world.

Very soon they were talking. He told her that he was but newly come to the neighbourhood, being in charge of a Cockermouth parish. He told her that he had been chaplain to Lord and Lady Padmont in Rutlandshire, and very kind patrons they had been. She discovered, too, that he was greatly interested in Nature and especially in birds, and this was a great link between them, because she was interested in Nature too.

Then he asked her whether she would not care for a little refreshment, and they walked together to the alcove. She did not know whether she were not exceeding proper modesty in this, but after all she was thirty-three and he was a clergyman.

Then, over a syllabub, he introduced himself. His name was Gordon Sunwood, the Sunwoods of Gloucestershire. He was, he told her, thirty-eight years of age and (blushing at the confession) a bachelor.

He then added, touching (quite accidentally) the back of her hand with his, that he was a bachelor because he had not until now seen anyone who combined the qualities of a saintly spirit, a beautiful person and a merry heart. He wasn't sure, he added, whether the last were not the most important of the three. He did enjoy a joke, and had found nothing in Holy Scripture to condemn such a taste. But there: of course, were he ever so fortunate as to discover the Fair Divinity with the triple merit, it was unlikely that she, on her side, would be ready to share his modest Parsonage and slender stipend. But to *that* he must add (this he almost whispered, sinking his voice to an incredible roguishness) a certain little fortune of his own, left him by a friendly aunt, so that things were not so bad, and in case of offspring . . .

But, at this point, Deborah could only decide that he had been drinking a little. And yet, even though he had, she could not but think him charming. It was true that clergymen were little higher in the social scale than hostlers or dairymen, but Deborah was no snob and, considering that she lived in a tumbledown manor with a father ostracized by all the countryside, she had no reason to be. In any case she did not care. She liked this little man with the round bullet head and cheeks like a russet apple and thick sturdy back and warm voice and clear twinkling eyes. Nay, although she had spoken with him but ten minutes, she more than liked him already. And this was her first adventure with a man in all her thirty-three years!

David meanwhile was having an experience less agreeable than that of his sister. He noticed neither the shimmering candles nor the fiddle, fife and drum, nor the orgeat and syllabub. He had eyes only for Miss Christina Paull, and they were not, alas, eyes of love.

He wondered as, fixed into a little corner with this lady, he glanced at her, how he could ever have contemplated matrimony with her. And as with many a man before and after him, behind the immediate misery of his horrid task was a glimpse of the glories of later freedom.

Miss Paull made things more easy for him by, most rashly, laying down some laws for their future comfort. She was a very determined young woman, Amazonian in build and colour, smelling freshly and quite pleasantly of the stables and spreading her legs apart as though she were always, in her imagination, astride a horse.

What she wanted to say was that she was very sorry indeed, but that after their marriage David must leave his father behind him. She had heard rumours that he intended to move his father along with him.

David saw his advantage. Like many another who contemplates diplomatically a quarrel, he snatched at any trivial excuse for one.

'My father is not to be moved thus lightly,' he said. 'If he cares to come with me, he will come.'

Christina, with that kindly good-humoured patronage that she applied to all human beings (regretting that for their own advantage they were not horses or dogs), explained patiently that she meant no criticism of his father; she had no doubt but that he was an excellent man. Nevertheless he was not a comfortable man, not an easy man, not an ordinary man. Married persons were better without relatives in their house.

That was undeniable. David did not contradict it, but, shifting his huge body on the little gilded chair until it creaked again, he remarked that perhaps, maybe, after all it were possible ... The words choked in his throat.

But Christina Paull knew well enough what it was that he intended to say. She was not at all sure but that he was right. She was as independent as any of her feminine descendants two hundred years later were likely to be. Her only relation was her old father, who was drinking with the stable-boys most of the day and drunk with the neighbouring Squire all the night. Nevertheless she had, since her plighting with David, heard so much of his own scandalous father that she was already half shrinking from her bargain.

She was no very sensual female; men would never mean very much to her, but David had caught her with his strength, health, amazing bodily vigour. But when she had bedded with him a month or two and the novelty of it was worn a little, what then? – there would be the father, the strange family history, witches and adulteries and general vagabondage ... She was not so sure.

But David was quite sure. His mind was suddenly clear, his courage certain and undaunted.

He smiled at her charmingly, as though he were offering her a kingdom, and said:

'We'll not be marrying, Christina.'

She took his statement as clearly as he gave it.

'It is, perhaps, wiser.' She looked at him, and liked him better than she had ever done before.

'I think,' she said, 'I'm not a marrying female.'

In his relief David would have offered her the gold of the Indies had his hands contained the treasure.

He nodded his head. 'I also. Marriage is a hampering state.'

She laughed, then bent towards him, tapping his shoulder with her fan, like a horse in skittish mood. It was a frank age. 'There is nothing against going to bed with you, David, on a dark night,' she said.

David crimsoned to his fair hair.

'I doubt that you'd like it,' he said. 'I'm a heavy sleeper.'

So they parted most excellent friends; and, a year later, Christina married Sir Roger Bollinger, who knew more about horses, cock-fighting and the breeding of spaniels than anyone in the north of England. She had nine children, and behaved to them as a bitch does to her puppies, caring for them when they were young and tender, but, when they grew, forgetting them entirely in the odours of the stable and the ardours of the chase.

And David – but that is another story.

The minuet was over. David, watching its last delicate graces, was amazed to see that his Deborah had for her partner a little stout parson, who, strutting, preening, flaunting, bowing, was like a cock before its mate.

The dance concluded, the little parson bowed and retired after showing Deborah to a seat. There David found her. She was flushed, her bosom heaved, her eyes shone; she was prettier than he had ever seen her. He seated himself beside her.

'Why, Deb,' he said, 'what's this? A clergyman?'

She seemed scarcely to hear him, then turned to him and answered: 'He is the Reverend Gordon Sunwood. He is of a Gloucestershire family. He has now a living in Cockermouth. He has been very attentive, David.'

David took her hand between his. 'Dear Deb . . . And is he already a suitor?'

She took her hand away. 'That is unkind. He has only talked with me a little. He is interested in Nature, and has a remarkable knowledge of birds.'

David chuckled. 'Beware, then, of his bird-nesting.' Then,

boyishly happy over his freedom, he went on: 'It is done, Deb. The task is over. She is of the same mind. As I am no horse nor a rare-bred dog, she is to be yet a maid. And we are good friends over it.'

Deborah almost danced on her bench.

'Oh, Davy, I'm so glad. 'Twould never have done. She'd have made you sleep in a kennel and given you a fine bridle. Oh, Davy, I am so happy! I was never so happy before nor saw anything so beautiful as this is! Are not the lights fine? – and although I had not danced since Christmas, Mr Sunwood found me "exquisite". That is what he said! I – exquisite! But to watch the world and its follies; I swear I could sit here the night through!'

'Yes,' said David, smiling at her, 'with the bird-fancier at your side.' As he looked at her, a tender compassion over her happiness pervaded him. She who had for so many years, without grumble or complaint, borne the closed-in, stifling, melancholy life of Herries, making no friends, having no gaiety, fighting her fears and loneliness and depression without a word to anyone, there was courage and character there! And to be so deeply pleased with this little country scene and amateur gaiety! Shame on himself and his father that they could have suffered it so long!

He could have kissed her there where she sat before them all, but they were interrupted by the portentous figure of Aunt Mary Herries, who hung over them like a battleship and finally demanded his company.

But Deborah was not to be alone for long. Of all amazing things, the elegant and wonderful Pelham had sought her out and was sitting at her side.

She would have been afraid of him had she been less happy. As it was, he caught her happiness and her freshness, and to his stale thoughts, plain though in truth he thought his country cousin, there was charm and pleasure here. His heart was good, though his morality was worn.

He was at his most delightful. Timidly she asked about London and the grand world. Gaily he told her tales and anecdotes and adventures, all of a decorous kind. He told her how a friend of his, Mr Spencer, had married Miss Pointy, and come up to town in three coaches-and-six with a company of two hundred horsemen.

He gave her dreadful details of the Lisbon Earthquake. He described to her the London fashions: how gowns were pinned rather closer than before, hoops as flat as though made of paste-board and as stiff, the shape sloping from the hips and spreading at the bottom, enormous but not so ugly as the square hoops. Heads now very variously adorned, pompoms with some accompaniment of feathers, ribbons or flowers; lappets in all sorts of sizes; long hoods worn close under the chin, the strings go round the neck and tie with bows and ends behind. Night-gowns worn without hoops. He was as gay and attentive as though she were the only lady in the world. It was true that he did not ask her to dance, but perhaps he was wearied of dancing.

Before he left her, very earnestly looking her in the eyes, he said: 'Dear Cousin Deborah, pray for me on occasion. I wish all the world well, save myself. I have the taste to be a monk, but, alas, not the character. I am going to the devil as fast as may be, but have dreams of another world.'

As he said this, he had, she thought, a strange look of her father, something ironical, regretting and doomed. She felt very, very tender towards him. But when he was gone, the most charming and distinguished person in the room, her eyes were looking, her heart was beating for her little clergyman. She could not help herself. She did not know whether it were right or wrong. She did not care.

And he returned to her. He bent towards her, sinking his voice to the most delicious of confidential whispers. He told her that he had been thinking only of the moment when he might come to her. He offered her his arm. They walked the length of the room together. He complained of the heat. She acquiesced. They passed behind the hanging curtains, pushed a door, and they were in a little yard at the back of the Assembly Rooms, under a sky sheeted with stars, a faint breeze whispering at their ear.

'You will take cold.'

He put his arm about her. She leaned against him, and could feel his heart beat against her arm.

He asked whether he might write; she murmured 'Yes'. And he bent his head and kissed her, the first kiss from a lover that she had ever received.

So the evening had gone well for Deborah.

THE WILD MARRIAGE

THEY RODE off next morning in the pouring rain. This rain was the especial and peculiar property of the district, rain that must often fall behind any chronicle of human lives here.

It was rain of a relentless, determined, soaking, penetrating kind. No other rain anywhere, at least in the British Isles (which have a prerogative of many sorts of rain), falls with so determined a fanatical obstinacy as does this rain. It is not that the sky in any deliberate mood decides to empty itself. It is rain that has but little connexion either with earth or with sky, but rather has a life of its own, stern, remorseless and kindly. It falls in sheets of steely straightness, and through it is the rhythm of the beating hammer. It is made up of opposites, impersonal and yet greatly personal, strong and gentle, ironical and understanding. The one thing that it is not is sentimental.

The newcomer is greatly alarmed by it, and says: 'Oh, Lord! Lord! how can I live under this!'; the citizen of five years' habitation is deprecating to strangers but proud in his heart; the true native swears there is no rain like it in the world and will change it for none other.

Any true chronicler of the Herries family will be forced, frequently, to speak of this rain.

David and Deborah, their horses, Absalom and Appleseed, passed through it as though it were their only wear. The whole country was blotted out by it, the lake quite invisible, the hills smothered in quilted cloud. The path, that could not yet be dignified by the name of road, was in a condition of indescribable mire and ruin. It needed a very little to make it difficult; tomorrow it would be impassable. But the horses plunged and waded their way through, while the trees bent to the deluge and the hammer beat, beat, beat in the clouded barriers of the mist.

David and Deborah were very happy, riding home. They said very little to one another, because it was difficult to talk through the rain and because each had important thoughts to investigate and arrange.

David was happy because he liked (as all true Herries like) his meeting with the other Herries. He had felt a warm companionship with his poor old Uncle Pomfret, with Uncle Grandison, with dear little Uncle Harcourt and especially with Cousin

Pelham. With all of them, different as they were, there had been a blood tie which he had recognized and they also.

Pelham had shown especial friendship and had invited him to London. David thought that he would go. It would be good for his business; he felt, too, a sympathy with this world of brocade, silver candlesticks, soft voices, delicately nurtured women. He had been a savage too long. He knew now that he was not much longer for Herries. He was happy, too, because he had escaped from Christina Paull, and escaped so politely, with neither harsh words nor hurt feelings.

And Deborah? Deborah swam through the rain in a streaming and glorious splendour. Her happiness was so great that she was truly and magnificently born again. The kiss of last evening had transformed her. She rode, her head up, her eyes alight, her mouth curved in a retrospective smile. She did not doubt but that she would marry him. He had not asked her, but he would. He was honest and good. A clergyman? Well, but she was very suited to be a clergyman's wife and the mother of a clergyman's children. At the thought of the children her heart hammered with joy to answer the hammer of the rain. How good, how generous, how well-wishing life was!

So they rode, and it was not until they were feeling their way cautiously through the mud below the Bowder Stone that Deborah was suddenly uneasy. What distressed her? She could not say. She was very sensitive to these mysterious, unreasoning impressions, and especially in this valley, which had always seemed to her to have a peculiar, magical quality of its own. She told herself at first that it was her thought of Mrs Wilson and her horrible death that still, after all these years, lingered with her. She always hated Cumma Catta Wood, with its pagan sacrifices and scent of murder. But soon, as they turned down the lane that led to Rosthwaite, she knew that it was not that.

She was increasingly apprehensive. It might be her dislike of Herries; especially it seemed to her dreary and forbidding after the social brightness of last evening. But it was not Herries alone. On the little mound that rose above the shaggy path that led to the house her father was standing. They could see him, waiting there in the rain, his cape over his head, leaning on his stick.

David said: 'Father is waiting for us. Something has occurred.'

And Deborah, as so often she had felt before at the thought of her father, knew a sickening apprehension of dismay. Some evil thing had come.

Then when she was face to face with him she knew that he was radiantly, wildly happy. She had never seen this light in his face before. It transformed him, even as she herself had been transformed last evening. At the sight of his happiness she, too, was happy again. Her apprehension left her, and when he held her and kissed her wet cheek she stayed with him, letting his arm encircle her.

He was happy and he was shy too. They had dismounted from their horses, but he kept them there. 'Wait!' he said. 'Before you go to the house . . .' He seemed like a boy, in spite of his grey hair, long about his neck, and his figure, bent a little from his persistent labours.

'There is someone . . . I must tell you . . .' He stammered a little. He put his arms about both of them, drawing them to him, and the rain fell all round them in walls of silver steel.

'There is a lady here in the house; this very day I am to marry her. Davy, Deb, be kind to her. She is strange here . . . Please me in this.' His voice was triumphant, as though he wanted all the world to hear his news.

They were bewildered; intent upon their own affairs, this sudden transition was amazing, paralysing. Marriage? Their father? Now? At once? At Herries? But whom? Was this some sudden freak, mad gesture, crazy eccentricity?

'Marriage, Father? Today? Here?' David was stammering in his turn.

'Yes – today. Here.' His father mocked him, pressing him closer to his side. 'I was in to Keswick yesterday. I have been bustling; have been with the surrogate, and have the licence. And this afternoon there will be the clergyman. Don't be angry with me, Davy, for not telling you. For eleven years now I have served my 'prenticeship, and she has come to me of her own free will. These last months it has gone hard with her. Be gentle with her.'

David was silent. What was he to say? Who was this woman? Another Alice Press? But behind his almost breathless astonishment was the thought that this new move would, whatever else it involved, help him to his own freedom. But then, as they neared the house-door, his love for his father overwhelmed every other emotion. It might be that this would be some woman who would be good to him, care for him, devote herself to his comfort.

He turned at the house-door and put his hand on his father's arm. 'If this is for your happiness, Father,' he said, 'Heaven bless her, whoever she may be.'

He had in his mind (thinking still, possibly, of Alice Press) the image of some large opulent woman who had caught his father's fancy. He mounted the stairs and turned into the dining-hall, which was, even now in this morning hour, brilliantly lit by a high cluster of candles on the broad table and a great fire in the open fireplace. Under all this splendour the tapestries, the portrait of old Herries leapt in the air, and the room was alive with the drumming of the rain on the panes.

A girl in some dress of flaming orange and crimson, seated on a low stool, was crouching towards the fire, her head in her hands.

As they all came in she turned round facing them, and then, seeing them, jumped to her feet as though to defend herself.

The three stood for a moment motionless by the stair-head while the girl confronted them. She made indeed an astonishing picture. For David she would always be the figure of that first moment. But it was not for him the first moment. He recognized her at once as the 'robber-girl' (so he used to call her) whom, in the old long-ago days, he had met up and down the roads, begging of him, mocking him once and again, always – to his Herries sense of order and decency – the outlaw and vagabond.

But indeed she had changed since then. That had been a child: this was a woman. She was of a bitter thinness, tall, and her small white face like a mask set with fierce hostile eyes. Her wonder, then as now, was her hair, which fell in ringlets about her shoulders and in the firelight was, with that glow, its own lambent flame. Her dress was fantastically over-coloured: a bodice of bright orange with silver buttons, a hooped skirt of the old-fashioned shape a burning crimson, and faded yellow shoes. She was, in her small peaked face, like an angry child, but her body was mature and her hands, long, thin and very white against her dress, those of a grown woman.

Francis Herries went across to her. 'Mirabell,' he said (and David wondered at the gentleness of his voice), 'this is my son, David, and this my daughter, Deborah. They will be loyal to you and devoted as they have been always to their father.'

David went over to her and took her chill, lifeless hand.

'We are old friends,' he said smiling, 'so it is not hard to be new friends too. I hope you will be happy with us.'

She did not answer, but looked at him with her fierce, protesting eyes.

Deborah went and kissed her on the forehead. 'Indeed I hope so,' she said.

The girl, at the touch of Deborah's lips on her forehead, trembled, but still said nothing.

Herries said to his son: 'Come away, Davy. I have business with you.' He smiled back at the two girls. 'We will return, but you will be better friends without us.'

He clattered down the stairs, David following him.

Deborah, left alone with this strange hostile creature, had an impulse to turn and flee. A sort of terror seized her, as was often the way with her; but her own deep happiness, which nothing here could touch, reassured her, and there was something in that white, small face and the wide, staring eyes that moved her heart. That her father was to marry this wild girl seemed to her an incredible thing; but everything about her father was incredible to her, and had always been.

She came close to her.

'I did not hear your name,' she said. 'Mine is Deborah.'

'Mirabell.'

'Mirabell! What a pretty name!'

'No, it is a crazy name. My mother had it from a play. It is a man's name.'

Deborah did not know what to say, what question to ask, but the girl broke in fiercely:

'You may hate me as much as you will. It matters nothing.'

'But why should I hate you?' Deborah asked.

'To be here, in your house, a stranger. It is not my will. I have no will any more. I came to your father yesterday because I was hungry. Once, many years ago, he told me to come. If I had had food I would not have come. They put me in prison in Kendal for a wanton. I was three months in their filthy gaol. And then for two weeks I have been hungry. Your father has been good to me; therefore because he wishes to marry me I will marry him, and then, when he is weary of me, I will go away again.'

She spoke in a kind of fierce defence of herself, her eyes never still, roaming about the room like those of a captured animal.

Deborah was touched to pity. She put her arm round the girl and drew her down to the settle by the fire.

'Oh . . . in prison! How cruel! And hungry for two weeks!' She caught her cold hand and held it to her.

'Cruel? No. Why? I may have robbed or lain with men, asking them in the streets.'

'Well . . . If you did . . . Still it is cruel. Kendal gaol . . . I have heard of it.'

'I did not steal nor lie with men. But only because I was proud. Now I am proud no longer. Anyone can do anything with me.' Her thin body under her gay dress shivered.

'But now you must be happy,' Deborah said. 'We will make you happy, all of us.'

'No, you cannot make me happy. I can never be happy again, but I will work for your father and give him what he needs – if I can.'

'And Father has known you a long while?' Deborah said.

'Since I was eight years old. And now I am twenty-seven.'

'You must not be unhappy . . .'

But the girl drew away from her, rose up, stood looking down on her.

'Happy? Unhappy?' she said scornfully. 'That is nothing . . . It is only that when you have been hungry long enough you must have food.' She turned her back on Deborah and stood looking into the fire.

They were silent then, until Herries came back. After this he dominated the scene. In their own separate fashions they all surrendered to him. The strange girl seemed to have a driving desire to make herself of use, and, speaking to no one, moved down and up to the kitchen, taking plates from Benjamin's wife, helping with the potatoes, rubbing the silver – all with a kind of hostile fierceness.

Herries showed his wisdom by not attempting to prevent her, nor did he speak to her, but his eyes were never away from her when she was near to him. It was as though he could not believe in his luck. He had thrown off his years. He was almost a boy again. His body was straightened, the thin, pointed face with the high bones had lost its grey pallor and was flushed with colour. His head was up and his voice rang with joy.

He had been shopping in Keswick, raided the neighbouring farms, stirred Mrs Benjamin (who could cook when she liked) to make pies and puddings. Soon a great feast was laid out on the broad table under the portrait of scornful old Herries. There was a fine paste of almonds with candied cherries, plums and currants. There were two fowls, a splendid pie (for which he must have paid dear, thought David, remembering also that it was his mother's money that bought it), wheaten loaves, China oranges, walnuts and plums, candied Madeiras, citrons and muscadine grapes.

To drink, there was to be a grand bowl of punch made after Major Bird's famous recipe, Batavian arrack and good honest ale.

For whom was all this? Were there to be guests, and if so, who? No questions were asked. Everything went forward.

The little chapel was only a step away. The rain, too, had now ceased to fall, and the sky was filled with little round fleecy clouds stained with blue shadows.

Herries appeared in his grandest dress, a suit that had lain in the big oak chest for many a year, something almost of Queen Anne's reign, strangely out of fashion, its colours faded, fitting oddly with his ugly scarred face and long grey hair. He had a dove-coloured waistcoat woven with gold. His cloth coat was of cinnamon colour, his sword was silver and gold-hilted, with figures on the handle, and he carried a cane with an amber head.

A strange pair the bride and bridegroom made as they started out together down the lane, he walking very proudly, she, her arm through his, hanging her head and looking like a gipsy from a fair. Deborah and David walked behind.

At first no one saw them. Some men and women were working in one of Peel's fields, and looking over the hedge caught a sight of all this glitter and colour. Then an old woman at a cottage door had a glimpse and called out after them. Then some children playing by the great oak tree near the inn had a sight of them, and all came trooping after.

At the door of the inn there was a little wizened, hunch-backed pedlar selling his wares. He, too, came hobbling behind.

Little Rosthwaite Chapel by the village was one of the smallest in England, and passing under the porch Herries and David had to bow their heads.

The clergyman was waiting for them, and almost at once the little place was filled with the children, the pedlar, some old women. For Herries the scene was some dream long dreamt by him, now accomplished in reality. Since the moment when she had come knocking at the door of Herries and he had opened it to her (would that be for ever the most miraculous moment of his life?), his happiness had been so strong, so universal, so overwhelming that he could neither realize nor see objects outside it. There *were* no objects outside it. This joy had covered all the world like a great cloak of surpassing brilliance. The others, David and Deborah, had but just ridden off to Keswick. He had gone back into the house and set about polishing the silver on some harness. The knock had sounded through the still, withdrawn place, mingling with the eternal murmur of running water. He had seemed to know that the knock announced great news, for he had hastened down the old stairs, flung open the door. And there she had been in the little grass-grown court, at fainting-point with hunger, in her bright shabby clothes. He had caught her in his arms and carried her in. From that moment his happiness, unquestioning, undoubting, had risen like a wave all about him and drowned him. He scarcely saw the girl herself in his triumph.

She was here; she needed him, and she would stay. Would she marry him? Yes, she would marry him. At once? Yes, at once if he wished it. Would she stay with him? Yes, she would stay with him. She acquiesced in everything, while he fed her and gave her drink. He placed her in Mrs Benjamin's care, then went out for the licence, the parson, the grand food, the liquor and a chain of fine gold that he bought off a Jew in Keswick. All that night he lay alone on his naked bed, seeing only her, thinking only of her, staring into radiant bliss. How David and Deborah would take it scarcely stirred his imagination. He loved them. He hoped that they would be glad; but if they were not, the brilliance of his happiness would not waver.

So now, when he stood in the tiny chapel and took Mirabell Starr for his wedded wife, the shabby little place was ablaze with glory. He bent and kissed her cold unresisting mouth, then passed down the aisle again between the children, the hunch-backed pedlar and the old women. Outside a crowd of people had gathered. He waved his hand to them and, in a voice ringing with joy, told them that they would one and all be welcome at his house. They all followed after, whispering among themselves.

Deborah's memory may be the truest mirror to catch the scene that followed. Into the heart of her old age that scene remained as something framed off by itself, apart in colour and shape and fashion, something wild and fantastic beyond conception.

First, the quiet of the Borrowdale road and the little grey village, the peaceful sky in which all the little clouds were turning rose as the sun went down, the barking of dogs, the fields softly lit by the gentle sun, Rosthwaite Fell a kindly guardian hovering above them, ducks waddling in silly procession, an old woman sweeping her doorway – and through this placid quietness Herries and his bride in their silver and cinnamon, their orange and crimson, he marching as though he were conqueror of the world, she beside him, looking in front of her, neither to left nor right, her face a mask; then David, striding towering over the rest but shy of this pageantry; herself, Deborah, feeling the rosy sky, the pale green of the sunlit fields, the dark shadows of the hills and, as she was always to remember, the conscious-ness of her new life that the kiss of the night before, pervading everything, had given her. And, after them, the whole rabble of the village, gathering force with every step, children running to keep up, farm boys, women from the fields, old dames from the cottages, dalesmen and labourers, headed by the little round fat clergyman and the hump-backed pedlar, all of them crowding along, but, so strangely, not speaking above a whisper, wondering in excited awe what it was now that Rogue Herries would be at.

Deborah knew this well enough, and one question she was soon asking was: Would they step into the house? For many, many years Herries had been forbidden, warlock ground to them. Had not the witch, Mrs Wilson, lived there, and was it not back there that Rogue Herries had taken her after her drowning? Had he not lived there with his painted woman of the town, had not his poor wife died there? – poor soul, poor soul! Aye, it was a wicked house, evil enough, a place of spells.

But now it was as though they themselves were under a spell. They followed as though the pedlar were piping some magical tune that they could not resist. Deborah knew, too, that they had recognized, well enough, the bride. Already she was aware of the scandal that that would be, only adding to the other scandals.

It seemed that every step that her father took must only be the more fatal to his name. They had seen the girl in the roads, on the Fell, begging, dancing, stealing, one of the robbing gipsies, and now Rogue Herries had married her. And he fifty-six, who should surely now be repenting of his sins (that were so many) and making ready for the next world, where, whatever he did, his place could be no easy one.

She knew so well what they were thinking, and, when they came to the bend of the road where the lane to Herries, turning up to the right over the stream, met it, she felt the pause, the hesitation.

Herries and his bride went on, the pedlar and the clergyman went on, a second's wavering and the crowd followed too. Coming to the gate before the courtyard they waited. Herries turned, his grey head bare in the evening light; he waved, with a sort of joyful gesture, his stick with the amber head in the air. He cried:

'Here is food and drink and no grudging. Welcome, my friends, this day at least. We will drink to the bride.'

He marched on, carrying his hat in one hand, waving his stick in the other. They all followed. An odd and wild scene it was after that. The two old suits of armour had never seen the like. The dark stair was narrow. They crowded up it, pressing upon one another, still whispering, no word above a whisper.

The clergyman, sweating with the pace at which they had gone, and the pedlar were the first to follow into the dining-hall. The pedlar, as though he owned Herries and all in it (he had a crooked body and a pock-marked face and thin strands of carroty hair on his bald poll), laid his pack on the table and scattered the contents. 'A bride's gift!' he called in a funny cracked voice. 'A bride's gift! What will you have, lady? A grain gold watch-chain, cambrics, gold buttons, watch bottles . . . What will you have? A gift for the beautiful bride!'

Soon they were, most of them, in the room, peering about them, staring at the old chest, the tapestries, the portrait, the wide stone fireplace. They crowded together like animals, but many of them, although they were in the witch's house, re-membered their Cumbrian manners, than which there are no finer in dignity and self-respect and courtesy the wide world over. Many of them might have fled, it could be, had it not been for David, but they knew Mr David Herries, they trusted him to see that they would come to no harm; not his fault that he was the son of the Devil, who had danced with witches and now married a gipsy. And another reason why they did not go was that they could not, for there were so many crowded on the stairs that they could move neither up nor down.

They might have been forgiven that day for thinking that Herries was of another world. He stood at the end of the table, lit by the jumping fire, the scar standing out on his face, even his clothes – in spite of their grandeur – of another age, and his voice was strange, glorified, filled with a triumphant power as though he had won a great victory, or, as an old woman said that night, 'made new contract with t'Divil'.

He filled the glasses and the cups with the brandy and the arrack and passed them round. This was fiery stuff, stronger than their accustomed ale, so it was no wonder if soon their voices were loosed.

The feasting began, only the bride, sitting at the table-end with the bridegroom, did not eat and did not speak. Herries seemed not to see her. He pressed those close to him, his children, the clergyman, the pedlar, a stout broad-shouldered dalesman with a vast black beard, a farming woman with crimson face and swelling breasts, already a little drunk, all of them near to him he pressed to eat the fowls and the pie, the fruit and the mound of beef. Soon they were eating right enough, and as the drink went round they began to pull at the food, the more drunken of them reaching across the table, cracking the nuts and catching the shells in the air, and throwing pieces of flesh to two or three hungry dogs who had crept in with them.

Then Herries rose to make a speech. He had drunk very little, but he seemed a drunken man, his hand trembling, and his eyes, always brilliant, now glittering with an eager fire.

'Friends and neighbours,' he said (and the pedlar, looking round him, echoed in his shrill cracked tones, 'Friends and neighbours'), 'I welcome you all here on this the happiest day of my life. The moon is silver in the sky' (now once again the rain was pouring down torrentially and clattering at the panes), 'and all the good dogs are baying at it. This is the valley of our hearts: in every stream there are fish of gold, and on the hills through the heather the blessed angels are picking the blackberries and singing under their wings as the rabbits run from their holes to listen to them.

'In no other valley in the world can these things be, and to-night, when the stars are blinded by the light of our happiness, the Old Man will be tramping the road, his pack under his elbow, and the stones hard to his stubborn toes. That is what happens in our wonderful valley, so drink to the Bridegroom and the Bride, whose nakedness your loving thoughts will cover and whose roof is your roof, and the snail on the wall has left his silver track for your guidance. Drink, friends and neighbours, and tumble downstairs as you may.'

No one understood a word of it, and for years after there were some who said that Rogue Herries, on his marriage night, had invoked the Devil. They had heard him with their own ears, had they not?

Then an old man, very grave and reverend, with a white beard and a nobly shaped head, stepped forward to make a speech.

'We mun thank Mr Herries,' he said. 'When I was young, we did varra weel off labscourse en stirabout fur dinner and we'll do varra weel yet. But Mr Herries has grudged neet.' He wandered off into disconnected reminiscence. 'Folks was harder lang sen . . . When I was a lad wi' a bit of bluemilk cheese en breed I never ailt nowt . . . In my opinion ther's nowt bangs good muck . . . good muck wi' plenty o' suction in't 'll bring a crop any time. Anyways it's nobbut dry work talking without summat to sup on, and ther's plenty to sup on here . . . But cuntra's turned upside-down. It'll be lang afore they see any mair times like t'oad uns . . . any mair times like t'oad uns . . . afore t'Rebellion . . . afore t'Rebellion . . .'

His voice sank into his beard; moreover, the noise now was too general for him to be heard. The arrack was having its way. There was stamping and singing, some child was crying. They were crowding more and more about the table. A glass fell and crashed. The rain slashed the windows until they rang again.

Deborah had watched the riot growing. In spite of the festivity there was a false element in it. Her father's happiness had something protesting in it, and was made the stranger by the girl's silence. David was doing what he could for friendliness, moving among them all in his quiet natural fashion, but with the heat of the great fire, the strength of the drink, the ferocity of the storm outside, a crisis seemed to be mounting over them.

It came, and with a wild suddenness. The pedlar, whose little skimmy eyes had scarcely left the face of the new Mrs Herries, had been coming ever closer to her. He seemed himself to be mad with some sort of sensual desire or arrogant conceit. At first he fingered the orange sleeve of her coat, then bent forward, put his hand under her chin, lifted her face. 'A kiss,' he said, 'from the happy bride.'

A moment later Herries's fist had crashed into his misshapen ugly face, and he tumbled backwards into the noisy crowd. Herries, pressing after him, seemed to be seized with an exultant rage. He struck right and left.

Everyone scattered to the door, and, as he pursued them, they turned pell-mell, one upon another; men, women, children were heaped to the door, were stumbling, leaping, flying down the stairs, rushing into the court, away, away through the gate, and down the lane, as though the Devil were after them.

In a leap of the fire the room had been cleared, the table, the floor messy with food, glasses overturned, only the pedlar, unconscious, flat on his back.

'You with the rest!' cried Herries, and, picking him up, threw him down the stairs, ran down the stairs after him, picked him up again, dragged him through the court, threw him over the wall into the lane, returning then, found his pack still on the table, picked it up, stuffing ribbons and chains and gold buttons back into it, ran down with it, and threw that too over the wall. The rain came soaking down upon it.

Back in the hall again he saw that Deborah and Mirabell were gone. Only David stood, tall and considering, above the ruined feast.

Herries broke out, roaring with laughter.

'Well, Davy . . . Our first hospitality.'

And David answered, picking up an orange from the table

and biting into it with his teeth: 'Well, Father, you made the punch too mighty for them.'

By evening a quiet contentment seemed to have come to them. No sign of the feast, no sign of the feasters. An hour before, Herries had gone out to look for the pedlar to see whether he were killed or no. There was no glimpse of the pedlar, nor of his pack; only the cold muddied path, the trees sighing under the rain.

Now they were all about the fire, Deborah sewing, David doing his accounts at the table, Herries in the oak chair with the big arms to it, and Mirabell quietly near to him, silent as before but a little flush now in her face, and looking up once and again, first at one of them, then another. The riot had, it seemed, in no way disturbed her. She had known many like it before.

Herries's joy was quiet now and tranquil. He would look at her, an odd smile playing about his lips, then glance away again.

He nursed his knee, bending forward towards the fire. The old house seemed to fit into their mood. Somewhere Benjamin could be heard, beyond the rain, raucously singing a tune. He was drunk a little. The room was dry and warm for once; the firelight played about the brown figures in the tapestry and threw a strange shadowing on the beams. Sometimes a mouse scratched behind the panelling. Deborah was thinking of love, David of business. It was plain of what Herries was thinking. No one knew Mirabell's thoughts.

The evening wore on, the storm died down, and with the cessation of the rain all the rivers and streams of the fields and rocks seemed to rush into the house. The whole valley was vocal with running water, and some little wet stars came out and blinked between the black driving clouds.

Deborah and David went to their beds. Deborah, before going, bent down and kissed Mirabell's forehead.

When they were gone, their doors closed, and all silent again, Herries rose and said to her softly:

'Mirabell . . . speak to me. Say that you have trust in me.'

'Yes,' she said. 'I have trust in you.'

He stooped and picked her up. He carried her, her hair strayed across his breast, up the stairs, along the tumbling passage to the little room where he had slept with small David on their first night in the house.

He laid her on the bed, knelt down beside it, stroked her hair, kissed her eyes and mouth; then, very tenderly, with a gentleness of a woman, he undressed her. When she was naked he took her in his arms again, and, with one hand free, turned down the bed, and laid her in it, smoothing the pillows for her head.

Then he knelt down beside her again.

'My darling,' he said, 'when I saw you in the cave on Honister I loved you so that I knew then and for ever where my haven was. After that day I have had no other desire than that, to worship you and serve you. Many of my days have been evil, but I have had no shame of that. I let things pass me by because my eyes were set on a dream. I knew always that in some place or person or act there lay the fulfilment, so that when I came to it I would find myself. I was always searching. No man has been more lonely than I, and by my own fault. I would receive no pity, that most contemptible of the vices, and I would give none, but I could be honourable could I find a place for my honour, and I could serve if I could see an altar. And now I have found it. I have years left. I am strong. There is no task too hard for me now I have got you, and if you stay with me no unhappiness can touch me.'

She looked at him then, full in the face. Then she put her hand up and, very gently, stroked his cheek where the scar was.

'You know,' she said, almost in a whisper, 'that I loved once and when he was killed I was slain too. I am a dead woman, Francis. I was a child when I talked to you in the cave. I was a woman at that moment in Carlisle. I care for you. I feel sorry for you. But I have no love for you. I told you yesterday. I can never love anyone again, I think. And so I wish that you did not love me so much. But you have shown me more kindness than anyone has ever shown me. I will do my very best to please you. Indeed I will.'

They remained for a while, he kneeling by the bed, she stroking his cheek. Then he took off his clothes and went in with her.

He put his arms round her and held her icily cold body close to his heart. Her head was on his breast and suddenly she began to cry, without sound, but he could feel her tears wet against his arms. She cried for a long time, he consoling her and stroking her long hair.

THE VOICE

IT WAS not strange, when you think of it, that the valley should now determine that it was a witch Herries had married.

It was, after all, only what they had expected him to do. It was, after·all, only what they had always expected her to be. After the wild marriage party, so grotesque in its conclusion, every sort of fantastic story was abroad. Some said that Rogue Herries had, all in a moment, shown a fiery tail between his coat-ends and that two brown crooked horns had sprung out from behind his ears. Others that the girl had flown of a sudden above the table and was carrying in her right hand a broomstick. All agreed that they had been beaten with mysterious blows from a hundred invisible arms. The pedlar, who seemed, with his hump and carroty hair, to have settled down in the valley, went about everywhere whispering, in his cracked voice, stories about Herries.

No, this was not odd, but what was strange was that, as the months passed, Mirabell won the name among them of a good witch, almost of a kind of well-wishing fairy. No one could quite say how this idea began to grow. It was not that she did anything for them; she did not, indeed, take any part in the lives of the farmers and dalesmen. It was said (and most of the stories came from Mrs Benjamin, who was a very talkative woman and had friends in Rosthwaite, Seatoller, Seathwaite, Grange, everywhere in the valley, in fact) that she was busy all day in the house, quietly going about her duties. That she was kindly to everyone, never out of temper, never proud nor haughty, never gay, but never sad either. She was not a bad witch in any case; only a poor gentle woman who had let her spells lie forgotten in their pack. Nevertheless the village children were warned not to speak to her when she went about, walking or riding, with her flaming hair and the brilliant-coloured clothes that she loved to wear.

After a time the village women began to pity her. They could not charge Herries with unkindness to her, although that they would have loved to do. It was plain enough that he worshipped her and would do anything in the world for her. He was a changed man, Mrs Benjamin declared, when she was about, although he would curse and swear and strike Benjamin with his whip or cane, as he had always done, when she was away.

The story was gradually told that Mirabell Herries had been in love with the Devil himself, who had been disguised as a beautiful young man, and then, when she saw her sin, she had fled from him and been broken-hearted ever since. This, the farm-women said, might happen to any woman. She was not to be blamed for it.

Within the house David and Deborah became greatly attached to her. This did not say that they had any intimacy with her. She remained apart, reserved, secret, but she was in all her ways so gentle, so ungrudging in her service to all with whom she came in contact, that even the old wind-blown house itself seemed to gather a warmth and kindliness from her presence in it.

They must feel, too, their father's worship of her. Oddly they did not resent that nor charge her with taking his love from them. It was her purpose plainly that she should take nothing, but only give, and that shyly, as though she had no right to think that her gifts would be received.

There came a day, a warm dim February day, when Deborah was taken a little closer into this girl's privacy, and that perhaps because of Deborah's own confidence to her.

It was, as often happens in this country, a sudden flash of sun and warmth and promise between storms of wind and rain.

When they saw how it would be the two of them rode out under Cat Bells through little Braithwaite village, up Whinlatter, and then, finding a sheltered corner and letting their horses feed in the grass by the road, seated themselves where they could look down upon Bassenthwaite, smooth under the sun like a gold shield, and across to Skiddaw that opened like a flower of steel and silver against the windy sky.

Deborah, moved by some quick impulse, told Mirabell that she had a lover; Mirabell turned towards her with a gesture of more eager friendliness than she had ever shown to her.

'Oh, tell me about him,' she said. So Deborah, with the sedate deliberation that, even when she was in love, could never leave her, told Mirabell about the Keswick Ball, and the little clergy-man and the kiss under the stars.

'And I had a letter yesterday delivered by horse from Cocker-mouth,' she added, blushing and looking very happy in spite of her sedateness. 'Is it not foolish to be so in love at my years? . . . But then he is not a boy,' she added, smiling with love at the picture of him in her heart. 'I fancy that we are greatly suited,' she said, feeling for the letter in her bosom.

She read the letter, while the breeze rustled over the Fell and

the shadows passed like wings of gigantic birds across the slopes
of the hills.

'MY DEAREST FRIEND – When I had read your letter I
grumbled, for I would have had it so lengthy that it would
stretch the reading of it until I might see you again. I have
now read it twelve times and could, were I put to it, read it
blindfolded and make no mistake in it. It was a sweet letter
nevertheless, and I love you at my heart with so great a devotion that I cannot subscribe to your absence, you resting in
my heart and so being never away from me.

And so you being here in my parlour, what do you think of
it? Everything is smart and everything elegant. There are the
short candles and the long ones, the tea-urn and the two
screens with the Chinese figures upon them, of which I have
told you already. And even now I have been busy on my sermon, whose text is: "Suffer the little children", and I have also
a Latin inscription to compose for the tomb of Mr Harvey, the
principal solicitor of Cockermouth, who passed away a sennight back, as I fancy my last letter informed you. There is
also my good dog Rufus at my feet, who already loves you
who are now his only mistress, and has looked at your letter
with an obeisance marvellous in so dumb a beast.

Two chairs also are newly come to the parlour, purchased
by me a fortnight back at the sale of poor Mrs Newbiggin's
effects (of this also, I think, I have told you). They have a
certain lameness at the moment, but I know how to steady
them against your coming. When am I next to *expect* a letter?
They are as careless at the Crown as at every other inn in the
country, and the thought that a letter from you may be even
now in the wrong hands is a constant anxiety for me.

You know how I love you, my dearest, and that with every
hour my love increases . . .

'The rest is nothing,' said Deborah, folding it up and looking
at Mirabell with a sudden anxiety. After all, how slightly she
knew this woman, how different their natures and origins. Such
a letter might seem to her the last foolish pettiness, and if she
laughed . . .
But Mirabell did not laugh. She turned and, drawing Deborah
to her, kissed her. This she had never before done of her own
accord.
'You are happy,' she said. 'That is a very kind letter. No one

has ever written me a letter. He would have—' She broke off, stared down with her strange elfin eyes to Bassenthwaite, that is always from a height like a lake ebbing its life away between marshy strands; then crept closer to Deborah as though she sought protection from something.

'You are all so kind to me. As no one has ever been. And I wish to return your goodness, but I am outside it. I want to be drawn into your friendliness, but my spirit is dead. My mother, after my father had been killed (he was slain by my uncle, who had always hated him), told me that when he was stabbed every other was stabbed also. She lived with dead people after that. I was so young that it meant nothing to me then, but now . . . Oh, how well I understand!'

'Had you some tragedy then?' Deborah asked. She knew, of course, that there had been tragedy here, but she had never asked any question. Her father had told her nothing.

'It has always been tragedy all my life, but never tragedy that touched me – until this last. My father was murdered, struck in the back in the dark by my uncle. My mother died on the Fell in the rain, her feet deep in mire, no one near us but the kites and the sheep. Then I was with my other uncle, wandering, thieving, hiding, escaping, in caves, on the Fell, begging in the street, beaten, always moving from one hill to another, from one road to another. I was ravished when I was twelve. I had seen four men foully murdered before I was sixteen years of age; one was all night dying, his head in my lap, his blood soaking my clothes. But nothing could touch me. I was apart, by myself!' She sprang up, as though inspired, and cried: 'Ohè! Ohè! Ohè!' and her call echoed from hill to hill, perhaps from Grasmoor down Crummock to Red Pike, from Red Pike to Langdale, from Langdale to Coniston Old Man.

'I would call and so thrust them from me. With my call I expelled them. Touch me? I was not there to be touched!' She called again and heard the echo come back. Then she crouched down once more close to Deborah, her hand on her arm.

'Your father came and found me in a cave on Honister Crag. I told him that day that I was myself, free, by myself, and it was true. But I had remembered him. He gave me that when I was a child with my mother.' (She felt in her dress and brought out the golden head with ruby eyes that he had given her at that Christmas feast.) 'He went away, but I still remembered him. He is not easy to forget. He is a Man, not half a man or a piece of one, but a whole one made in one block like a carved stone. I remembered him, but I did not care for him. I cared for no one; only the memory of my mother made me lonely sometimes, and when men wanted me then I was lonely too, because I hated men.

'Then—' (she broke off, caught her thin breasts with a sudden pathetic, driven gesture as though she must control some beating impulse) 'we came to Carlisle. My uncles were much on the Border, thieving, wrestling, carrying messages. They had been for a long time working with the Scottish rebels, you see, and were paid by them as secret agents. After the Prince landed they went to Edinburgh. I was left in Carlisle. There was a man whom they knew there, a devil, he was evil as Satan, and more evil than that; they knew what he was and what he intended to me, but they were still his friends, and for that I will never forgive them, nor speak to them, nor drink with them, neither here nor in eternity.' Her face was suddenly cold and mask-like with hatred.

Deborah had never seen that figure, the white mask-like face, so small, so carven, so cold under the red smoke-gleaming hair. But she was full of pity, and she put her arm out and drew Mirabell closer to her.

'This man said he loved me; he was hideous in his body as in his soul: squat, black, always cold to the touch. He came to my bed and I fought him. I dug my nails into his eyes, and naked as I was I forced him to creep away, under the smoky candle, his tail between his legs, dog as he was. He did not attempt me again, but he watched me; he was always there watching me, waiting until my uncles should return. He thought they would give me to him. Then Harry found me. We loved at the very first sight, as I came to the door of my house on a fine morning, he riding by. It was always a surety. He was beautiful, he was brave and noble-hearted, he was young and a grand poet, he was mine and I was his . . . And oh! Deborah, Deborah' (she began to weep, tears pouring down her cheeks, beating her hands, clenched, against her breast), 'Thawn killed him, he stabbed him in the back, he fell dead at my feet, and I dead with him! Deborah, Deborah!' (she turned, clinging, holding to Deborah's body) 'what shall I do? I am not alive. I died with him. When he fell, I fell! Oh, how shall I live again if Harry cannot come back to me? He comes. He beats at the window. When I lie beside your father I hear him crying. When I am moving about that dark house he is a light ahead of me, but I can never come to him, and he can never come to me. I want him so, but he is dead on one side of the wall, and I am on the other. What shall I do when you are so kindly to me, and your father loves me so, and I only a ghost in the middle of you? Oh, what shall I do? Oh, what shall I do?'

In all these months Deborah had never seen her display feeling. She had been kind, and had served them all, and been quiet. Now she clung to Deborah, sobbing on her breast, holding Deborah's arms, weeping as though her heart were all tears.

'Hush! Hush!' Deborah kissed her hair, her forehead, keeping her very close. 'It will pass. It will pass. We will all love you and have a home for you. You are not alone any more. We love you. We love you.'

But Mirabell raised her head, staring into the faint pale sky as though she would find some answer there. 'It will never pass,' she said. 'It is eleven years now, and it was yesterday that he died at my feet.'

She quieted as suddenly as she had cried out. The clouds came over, gathering together in fleecy, windy companies, cloud forming with cloud in ribs and ripples of gauzy vapour. Soon all the sky was a ribbed shore of pale ghostly sand. The fells grew black, and little streams that laced their forms were rents in their strong flanks. Bassenthwaite paled, as the sun withdrew, into the curve and colour of a grey shell. The wind raced over the moor and up the Fell, suddenly liberated, delighting in its freedom. It was cold and sharp with the tang in it of sheep's dung and new young bracken and coming rain.

'Let us go home,' said Mirabell. 'It is cold.'

They mounted their horses and turned down the hill. For Deborah, Mirabell's story had flung the whole life at Herries into a new, dramatic and, for her timidity and quiet mind, sinister shape. Mirabell was something now apart from all of them; she was to be pitied, cared for, comforted, but she could give none of them anything. She could not give her husband anything. She did not love him at all. Through all these months Deborah had supposed that in her own strange way Mirabell loved her father, and now it appeared that she had no love for him, but thought only of some ghostly young man who had been dead for eleven years. Well, but if she did not love her father who himself adored her so! Why, that must mean torture for her father, despair, misery. What end could it have but disaster?

This was the first moment in Deborah's life, now as their horses were picking their way through the stream that runs through Braithwaite village and starting up the winding hill to Cat Bells, that she truly loved her father without any sense of fear or dismay. She was overwhelmed with pity for him, caught after all his rough and lonely life into this great passion for someone who did not love him, and could not. 'Oh, poor Father, poor Father!' she thought. 'How he must be suffering, and under what restraint!' She remembered all his goodness and gentleness these last months, and how, when Mirabell was there, so quietly and with such courtesy he waited on her and cared for her. Deborah's heart, that was all softness and tenderness, ached for him. She cared, too, for Mirabell. It was not her fault that she had come, and she was doing all in her power. But so little was in her power! Nothing was in her that he needed, and yet she was his only need!

That evening in the house Deborah watched with a new understanding and sensibility. And Herries seemed to detect that there was some change in her. She went with him to the door of the house before going up to her bed. The wind that had risen while they looked down on Bassenthwaite was now raging through the valley. It carried in its arms a new young slender moon, and seemed to be tossing it from leafless tree to leafless tree. The trees bent with their bare arms to catch it and then tossed it in and out of the rushing clouds. There was a great noise, a noise of streams, of branches cracking, of the wind itself, and the beams and rafters of the old house.

Herries listened, loving it.

'One wind more and everything will tumble,' he said. 'You'd best go, Deborah, before the fall.'

She timidly put her hand through his arm and stood close to him.

'Father, I love Mirabell,' she said.

'I am old for a husband,' he said, seeming not to hear her. 'When I was young I ranged from door to door, and now that I have found her I am old, bent, twisted . . . Deborah, will you not marry before it is too late?'

She wondered whether he had heard something. She herself had said nothing. It had not yet seemed the right time. She nearly spoke then, but she did not. While he wanted her, she must stay.

'One day, Father . . .' she said, 'but not now.' And then the wind, with a great scream of happiness and freedom, drove them indoors.

The following day Herries took his wife, riding pillion, into Keswick. He was terribly proud of her. He wanted to show her to everyone; he knew what they said of her, that she had been gipsy, tramp, thief. That was nothing. It was the truth for him that she was glorious, extraordinarily, magnificently glorious. She was as glorious to him now as she had been before he married her. And she was also as mysterious. Intimacy had not made her less mysterious. But perhaps, although he did not know it, there had been no intimacy. Did he know that? He was a deep man who knew many things, but often did not realize them.

She rode behind him into Keswick in a crimson dress with gold buttons. He was in his old shabby country clothes, wearing his own hair. When he touched her he was happy so that he could sing, but behind his happiness he was unhappy: he had questions that he wanted to ask her and he did not dare.

As they drew near to the town, along the path and across the watery meadows, people were walking and riding. In the Town Square there was a thick pressing multitude. He asked a fellow what the matter was, and someone told him it was the Methodists, and then another fellow volunteered that it was George Whitefield, the most remarkable preacher of them all.

Herries was interested in all that he had heard of the Methodists, who had now for a number of years been strengthening their position in the country, and especially of this Whitefield, concerning whom and his extraordinary preaching he had had, like everyone else at this time, many reports.

He knew that this was a courageous man who was ready, for his religion, to meet any form of contempt, abuse and danger. He knew that he was sincere, of deep piety, of constant energy, of selfless industry. Against these things he weighed what he had heard of his emotionalism, theatricality and fanaticism, all qualities to which Herries, by his own reserved and private mind, was deeply hostile.

He had heard that Whitefield had but one desire, to save souls for God, that often he preached fifty or sixty hours in the one week, and that his journeys, involving as they did at that time so much physical discomfort, were ceaseless.

He knew, too, that he was a man free of all meanness; his bitterest adversary did not attribute to him small ambitions, petty jealousies, sly revenges. He appeared to Herries, from what he had heard of him, to be feminine in his hysteria, weak-nerved, histrionic, ill-balanced, but he was, even because of these defects, exactly suited to move great masses of people by impassioned appeals, passing from place to place like a torch of fire.

When he heard that it was Whitefield who was here he decided that he must listen to him. He backed his horse out of the crowd, and, dismounting, took the horse by the bridle and Mirabell by the hand, finding some higher ground where he could watch what was going forward.

He told Mirabell of the reason for the crowd. She did not seem to be greatly concerned, but, as he had noticed before when she was in any crowd of people, to be looking about her searchingly, as though she would find someone.

He stood, his arm around her, holding her close to him. He felt as though some crisis were arriving between her and himself; this was no new feeling, but had been present with him for the last two months or more, and he knew that was because something was urging him with every day more pressingly to ask her certain questions with regard to himself. He was aware, too, that it was better that he should not ask these questions, that her answers might precipitate a crisis that would make him much unhappier than he had ever been before. But he could not help himself. With every hour he was urged further. He must know, he must know – whether now, after these months, she did not love him a little, a little, a very little . . . the first stirring of some new emotion in her . . . and at the thought of asking her and of her answer he trembled as though with cold.

Very soon he was aware of a voice coming to him very clearly over the heads of the people. He could see, only indistinctly, any figure. The crowd, of every type and order of person, was packed tightly across the Square; they seemed to press against the houses behind them, as though they would bend them back. It was an intent and silent crowd, so intent that the urgency seemed to spread to the distant line of hills, Causey and Cat Bells and Maiden Moor, beyond the roofs, so that they, too, were listening.

The figure was indistinct, someone lit with the pale February sun, a body of grace and good proportion, but it was the voice that came straight to Herries, as though it were to him alone that it was appealing. He realized then that every man and woman in that crowd felt as he did, that it was to him or her alone that the voice was speaking. At once, hostile though he was to public emotion and theatrical display, he yielded to the beauty of the voice. It was, beyond any sort of argument, by far and far the most moving and lovely voice that he had ever heard. Every word was distinct and clear, running to him with a separate and special urgency, and the words were bound into a general rhythm most melodious and musical; yes, it was like music, the perfect and rounded notes following one after another, to make, at the fitting moment, a completed harmony. So lovely was the voice that for a little while he did not listen to the words, then they were forced upon his attention with a pressing gentleness, as though someone, very gracious and kindly, were at his elbow, saying, 'You must hear this; this is for you and for you alone. It has great importance for you.'

He listened then with the utmost attention.

'It is simply as an occasional preacher that I am come to preach the Gospel to all that wish to hear me, of whatever denomination. I have nothing to do with denominations, for it is the righteousness of Jesus Christ that I am preaching, and that righteousness has no denominations. You have heard many times of the righteousness of Jesus Christ, and at every time you have been wearied or indifferent to Him or busied with affairs. It may be that this is the last time you will hear of Him and the last time that I shall preach of Him. Here into this town He has come, knowing that it is for the last time, but you do not know. The clouds have circled over your heads, the sun is about to set and, setting tonight, it will not come again. You are returning to your homes, your candles are lit, your children are at your knee, and distantly from over the hills there is the faint sound of a trumpet. The sound is distant, for the hills cover it, and your many daily businesses, the food for gossip, the food for the belly, the food for pride and vanity, these make a babel in your ears and blot out the distant call. But soon,' and here the voice rose to a high bright summoning call, 'the trumpeters have crossed the hills. The trumpeters have crossed the hills! The trumpeters have crossed the hills!'

He paused as though he were listening. It seemed that everyone else was listening too. The crowd was tense and concrete, as though its eager attention had moulded it into one man. Across the silence there struck stray sounds, the crowing of a cock, the sharp bark of a dog, the stamping of some horse's hoofs against cobbles. These emphasized the stillness. They could see the hills where the trumpeters were. They could name them – Skiddaw and Saddleback, Helvellyn and Fairfield, Langdale Pike and the Gavel, Seatallan and Haycock, and through that circle of grey listening hills they could see the trumpeters moving.

The voice took a personal colour. 'The Trumpeters come first, moving down the valleys, and after them the cohorts of the Saints in their shining armour, and after them the Priests and Prophets with judgements in their hands, and after them' – the voice sank to a whisper and through the crowd there ran a little rustle of apprehension – 'after them the Great Judge Himself.'

There was silence again. A stout country-woman near Herries began to sob.

'Who in this valley shall be ready for that awful army? Now, outside your door, there is one summoning blast. No time for preparation, for hiding the things that should not be seen. THY JUDGE IS THERE... THY JUDGE IS THERE... And He is just and He is merciful. Yes, but He is just. Think not only of the mercy; think also of the Justice...' And then, with a sudden agonizing, beseeching cry: 'Oh, my hearers, the Wrath to come, the Wrath to come!'

There was a terror and imminent fearful apprehension in that last cry that even a man like Herries, steeled against every sentimental appeal, could not resist. He started as though someone at that instant came running to him, crying out that the end of the world was upon him. He looked hastily around him, as though a wild animal or flaming fire were at his back. And on the crowd the effect of that cry was immediate and tremendous. Superstitious, ignorant, simply and often savagely moved, cut off as they had been for many centuries from all contact with a larger world, they were ready to be seized by any swift emotion, ready and eager. Here Whitefield, however, had won his hardest victory, for these North Country people were not Celts as the Cornish and Welsh were. They were neither dreamers nor fanatics. As Herries knew, five years before they had stoned the Methodist preacher almost to death, and the whole district from Kendal to Carlisle had a name of great danger for the sect.

But they would not stone Whitefield now. He himself began to be moved with the crowd; his body swayed, his arms rose and fell, his voice was torn with distress and urgency. Tears, they said afterwards, were pouring down his cheeks. He picked out men and women from the crowd. 'Oh, sir, are you indeed ready? Have you your garments packed for the journey, your horse harnessed, and your conscience clear? For Heaven and Hell, Death and Judgement are not names only for you. They are real, they are present. Eternity is a true word and Everlasting Punishment is no lie. Can you be led to the Judgement Seat before that awful crowd of Witnesses and not tremble? Your deeds are behind you. There is no hope now that they may be altered, for they are written in the book. There is the pause. You have made your plea. You are waiting for the sentence, and even as you stand here now, so it is certain that you will stand before your God.

Eternal Damnation! Damnation for ever and ever more, suffering
and torment and the agony of a repentance that is out of time!'

His voice sank again to a pleading whisper, while now his
utterance could be heard to be broken with sobs. 'O God, where
is Thy mercy? O God, whither shall I turn?' Then, with a great
cry that ran, glittering, resonant through the air: 'In Christ
Jesus! In Christ Jesus only is there any hope! But even He is
Just.' His voice was now of an awful solemnity: 'Sinner, I must
do it. I must pronounce sentence upon you.' Again there was a
terrible silence, and then, in a voice of thunder as though the
very cobbles of the town must rock:

'Depart from me, ye cursed, into everlasting fire!'

The crowd began to cry out: 'O Christ, save me!' 'Christ be
kind to me!' 'God have mercy upon me!' Men were pushing
against one another to reach nearer to the preacher, tears fell
from many eyes, and suddenly, with a great burst of sound that
had in it something gloriously strong and victorious, the hymn
'Our God, our help in ages past' broke out and was carried, it
must seem, far beyond the confines of the town.

The voice had ended and Herries was freed. He turned to find
that Mirabell was clinging to him, her face very white, her eyes
closed.

'Come. It is growing dark. We will go home.'

She nodded. He led his horse out of the crowd and then, in a
little dusky side-street where there was a deep silence, he lifted
her on to the horse and climbed on behind her. With his arms
about her he started away. The horse went gently.

Herries thought: 'There is this Damnation then. I, too, shall
be damned with the rest.' He had stirred to a consciousness,
through this scene, of a general movement behind his own
personal history, of some new world coming to England. Ten,
five years ago those men and women would have driven Whitefield with stones and abuse out of the town. Now he held them,
although it might be only by a kind of superstition and sentiment. He felt that all around him there was a new consciousness,
a fresh curiosity, a novel enterprise. For himself, he belonged to
the old world that was passing. He had still a link with the boy who,
sniffing his way through Queen Anne's London, had not been so
far removed from the Rebellion, the tumbling of King Charles's
head, the Plague and the Great Fire. But David and Deborah
had no touch with that world at all; it was a dream, a fairy-tale to
them. David's enterprises were consciously engaged, through his
vessels and the things that they carried, with other worlds that

were not dream-worlds of adventure and romance, as China and
India and Russia had been to Francis's childhood, but definite
practical places in which men walked on their legs, ate mutton
for their dinner and read the news-sheets. Everything was
opening up before him, and at the same time closing in about
him. This very rough path on which tonight his horse was
picking his way would soon be a toll-road that would carry carts
and carriages. This modern world so novel, strident, ill-fitting.
In the hearts of those people listening to Whitefield he had detected a new curiosity. And (here his Herries blood drove him)
he disliked and distrusted this modernity. Queen Anne's age
appeared to him as something infinitely quiet, cosy, picturesque
and easy.

They were talking now of inventing things to make the lot of
the common people easier. The common people! No one had
thought of the common people when he was a boy. Why invent
things only to make them restless? He thought of the old London
scenes, so dim now in memory; the crowds on holiday all upon
pads and hackneys, Mob's Hole where the ox, roasted whole,
was eaten, the dancing to a bagpipe, the fiddlers scraping, an old
trooper from the Royalist wars tootling upon a trumpet. The
shopping in the New Exchange, that he had so adored as a boy,
the beautiful ladies in coach or sedan chair, the ladies with their
pets, marmosets and Barbary doves, scarlet nightingales and
milk-white peacocks. And the Coffee Houses which to him,
taken there as a boy on a London visit by Harcourt, twelve years
his senior, had seemed the great paradise of glory; the Coffee
Houses with the fine glass lanterns hanging without, the pretty
Phyllis smiling at the bar, the young swells of a morning,
whether at Searle's or Squire's or the Grecian, dressed, as Steele
had it, 'in gay cap and slippers with a scarf and party-coloured
gown'. The drinking, the smoking, the gaming, the singing – oh,
the Life, the Life that it was! . . .

And now, now, how drab and busy this new world, with no
respect from youngsters to elders, no romance, only money-
making, business, and the whole world in your pocket!

It was his age. How old he was, and only now his true life
beginning!

At that his arms tightened about her body, he bent forward
and touched her neck with his lips. He fancied that she yielded
to him a little. Did she or no? How often, in these last months,
he had wondered that!

And then the temptation that had been behind him so fearfully all day rushed to his lips. He could not stay it now. He had run in upon his fate.

'Mirabell,' he said, 'I must ask you a question.' He felt his heart hammering in his breast. His hands trembled.

'Yes,' she said, and then, most unexpectedly, asked him one: 'Do you think there can be a God, Francis?'

A God? A God? What did it matter whether there were a God or no now when the only urgency in this world was, had she come to love him a little.

'That Methodist thinks so,' he answered her lightly.

'Those poor people whom he threatened with damnation, what right has God to judge them, having made them so? And yet—' she looked round at him into his eyes. 'He had a great eloquence. I saw the trumpeters coming through the valley.'

'Mirabell,' he began again, 'I must ask you a question.'

'Yes,' she said patiently.

'Am I,' his hands tightened about the reins, 'am I so very old to you?'

'Old! Why, no!'

'I am old. All my life is behind me and yet, loving you, it is but beginning.'

She said nothing.

He went desperately on: 'You told me on your wedding night that you did not love me, that you could not. I have never questioned you again. But now it is too much for me. I can wait no longer. Have you not, in these months, learnt a little, a very, very little, to have love for me? Or is it, can it never—' He broke off, so terribly agitated that he could not speak.

At last she answered, turning round again, and looking up at him like a little child.

'I do not feel you old. I feel you so very good, better far than I had ever thought. But love . . . are we not friends, good friends, trusting friends? I am not made for love. Only once, and that was a dream. But your friend . . .'

Then he broke out (although he knew very well the fool he was, and that maybe in these words he was breaking up all the foundation of their happiness together): 'Friend, friend, friendship! What is that for a man? I have never had a friend. I do not want a friend. But my love for you is eating me up, tearing at my heart. As that man today desired his God so I desire you. It must be. I cannot live if I haven't it. Your cruelty . . . I lie with you in my arms and you are not there. I touch you and you are gone. I must have a little of you, a touch, a breath, a word that is yours meant for me. I am in torment, dying of thirst, of hunger . . .'

He could not make the words, he held her, letting the reins fall, as though he would drag her into his very breast. He felt her body stiffen against his.

'No,' she said, almost beneath her breath, 'I will not lie to you. I cannot. Even though you kill me I will not be dishonest. It is not my fault that I am apart. I am apart from all the world, yes, and from myself.

'Francis, I would give you everything. I have never but once wanted so to give myself, but I cannot. I cannot! Oh, I should never have come! I am wicked, I am a cheat . . . I care for you so much, I would give everything to make you happy. But love – it escaped me that night. I cannot find a way to get it back.'

He answered nothing. He rode the horse more swiftly. After a long time, fear in her heart, longing to comfort him, she spoke again:

'I would do everything. Teach me. I will learn.'

He said, between his teeth:

'I have my answer. You have so generous a heart. I will be patient.'

As they rode on (and now it was very dark) her unhappiness seemed to her more than she could bear.

SAGA OF DAVID

I

THE YOUNG SARAH

THE place has now come for David's story. These events occurred in early May 1758. David was in his thirty-ninth year in the course of them.

David did not appear a man of thirty-eight at this time. His face was very young, unlined, fresh in colour, strong in profile, with the prominent bones of all the Herries, but his forehead was as clear and smooth as a young boy's. Just at this time, because he was working considerably at the little Keswick office, he was beginning to stouten. His huge frame would gather fat very easily. But this did not diminish his strength, which was now, and would be for another fifteen years, prodigious. It was at this time that he picked up Statesman Peel in one hand and Benjamin with the other and held them, without any effort, suspended for a considerable time.

Men would come from Ennerdale and Eskdale to see him wrestle, and they said that he was, if he pleased, a terrible man with his fists. The twisted carroty-haired pedlar, Peter Dolfin, who was now for ever hanging around Rosthwaite and Grange, hated him and said that he would be hanged for murder any day that he lost his temper. But he never did lose his temper these days. There was a certain sluggishness in him at this time (except when he was occupied on his business; then he was wide awake enough). This is the story of how he lost his sluggishness.

The most remarkable thing about him, as he grew, was the sweetness of his nature. This sweetness of temperament has been a continuous strain in the Herries blood. There has been no generation lacking certain examples of it.

This is no merit to its possessor, entails no virtue, deserves no reward. It is a quality of personality extremely vexing to many who think it sentimental and untrue to life. It is not sentimental because it is a quite natural element in the character of the possessor, and the possessor is unaware that he has it. David did not find life gentle, kindly or considerate. He knew that it was fierce, callous and dangerous. It was companionship with a tiger who, with one careless scratch of the paw, produces tragedy, ruin, catastrophe, and then yawns his indifference. But although he knew life to be dangerous and quite heedless of his personal good luck, his nature drove him to choose the better parts of the men and women about him, to enjoy the happy and bright moments, to perceive beauty without having any imagination about it, to wish everyone well and to rejoice at others' good fortune. It was easy for him just now because of his superb health, but afterwards, in bouts of pain, distresses and anxieties, the loss of someone who was dearer to him than all else, this sweetness of nature did not leave him. It came, as it always comes, from something remote and deep, beyond the business of the body, a central radiance of spirit.

He was, of course, no saint. He was exasperated, sulky, unjust, as everyone is, but only for the moment. These moods never dwelt in him. They tried him and found him uncomfortable as a living-place.

During this year 1758 his sluggishness did not prevent him from restlessness. After he had freed himself from Christina the restlessness increased. He began to wish, as he had never wished before, to make love to someone. He had matured very late. In Liverpool on an occasion he had gone with a woman and, after a brief moment of physical excitement, had known that such encounters were for ever barren for him. But his restlessness was not springing only from need of the love of woman. He seemed to have, at this time, no exercise for his warm, affectionate heart. He was, and had always been, quite undemonstrative, but he must have someone to love. He had loved his father and Deborah, and, in lesser degree, Peel's son. But Rendal was dead (killed in a brawl in Penrith), Deborah's mind elsewhere, his father married again.

It was his father's marriage that mainly caused his restlessness. He had never, in his own simple and unexperimenting mind, suspected the possibility of such utter absorption in another as he perceived now was his father's case. He himself realized the attraction of Mirabell, he thought her beautiful and gentle, and strangely different from other women, but he soon saw that she did not love his father, but was doing what she did from a sense of gratitude and duty. He saw, too, that his father was hungry and thirsty for what he could not have, and that his soul was set on this eluding quest. His father had, for the time, forgotten him. And so, because he loved his father with an unanalysed persisting love, having its roots in his very earliest years, he missed increasingly his contact with him. He did not know how to recover it again; he never knew, in his relations with people, how to change anything. He could not analyse nor examine himself. He had never done such a thing in his life, but he felt, as a loving animal feels, isolated and pushed aside. He blamed no one, felt no jealousy, but was increasingly, with every week that passed, lonely. His business, although it interested and occupied him, was nothing to him compared with his relations to one or two people.

So, although he did not know it at this time, he was very lonely and would soon be very unhappy.

More and more it became clear to him that he must marry. Well, what then? Could they all live together at Herries? There was room enough, but the sense of drama, of events that happened always just out of sight, began to bewilder him as though he were beginning to be asked to look in many different directions at once. This was no place for his wife, whoever she might be. There was some money (his mother's, as he often ironically reflected), but everything was shabby, out-at-elbows. It was not that they did not wish to have everything in fine colour, but there was some movement inside the house itself; as soon as a window was mended a door was off its hinges. Everything blew against the wall and along the floor. There was a draught in every corner, and rats behind the panelling.

In the old kitchen, where Mrs Benjamin officiated, everything accumulated. Mrs Benjamin was slatternly and careless. Nobody minded.

His father's wife helped about the house as though she were a servant. Those seemed to be the times when she was happiest, when she was carrying plates, sweeping floors, polishing the brass and silver. She was oddly most at her ease with old Benjamin. It was as though they had some secret friendly understanding. As though they had come from the same place . . .

Herries would enter and find her scouring the plates. He could not endure that; he would ask her to go and dress in her finest, and then he would sit her in the high-backed chair in the dining-hall, and he would change his clothes (he had been, as usual, digging, trying to turn rock into pasture, plucking up weeds, or simply standing staring at Glaramara, watching as it turned from amber to purple, purple to jet, jet to silver), and then there they would sit, the two of them, she in gold and crimson, he in cinnamon and silver, on either side of the fire, saying nothing at all.

No, all this was too eerie for David. He didn't know what would happen soon; something, he thought, that would make them all unhappy.

And no one wanted him. When he rode in from Keswick, evening time, he would see them sitting like that in the firelight. They were two ghosts to him. Everyone now was just out of his reach. He had never been so alone in his life before.

So one day he rode over to Wasdale. He went to see about some sheep that, he had heard, were for sale, and cheap. They belonged to a man called Denburn. This man Denburn was a gentleman, they said, from London, fallen on evil days. He had a tumbledown farm at Wasdale Head called Scarf Hall, a place half gentleman's house half farm. They told him in Keswick that Denburn was a ruffian, but clever, had a library of books that he set great store by. He had a daughter too.

He had some sheep, and David wanted some for his fields by Herries, so he rode over.

It was dark when his horse (he was riding Deb's Appleseed) had picked its way to the bottom of Stye Head, and it was difficult to find his way. He found his path across Lingmell Beck, and then plunged into a black thicket of trees. Here he stumbled for

a long while, hearing water tumbling all about him, and the wind
roaring down the pass.

He was not a man to mind wind and tumbling water, but he
was uncomfortable nevertheless. This lake-end valley, cut off
from the world, was an excellent rendezvous for smugglers from
the sea-coast, only a few miles away. The inn at that time, the
Wasdale Inn, was a wretched place, as he well knew, both in
accommodation and reputation, but it was there that he must pass
the night.

As he blundered among the trees, scarcely able to see his
thumb before his mouth, he felt for his knife and his pistol. He
might need them before the night was through.

He came through the wood and almost stepped on to the inn.
There was a light in the window; he banged on the door, which
was opened by an old woman with a shawl over her head and a
shabby patch over one eye. He called for someone to look after
his horse, and a lad went with him to a tumbled stables at the
rear.

After seeing to his horse's comfort (poor comfort, but all that
he could have) he stood for a moment swallowing the mountain
air, looking up at the great shoulders of the Gavel behind him
and the black sprawl of Lingmell, the sharp edge of the Pike in
front of him. The night was clear. Stars, as the dusk faded into
night, were breaking, in their thousands, into the stuff of the sky.

Reluctantly he shouldered his way across the floor of the close-
smelling inn-room. All eyes were upon him as they well might
be. He was so tall that he could, standing on his toes, touch the
ceiling; so broad that he seemed to be at elbows with every man
there. It was a small place, dim with the smoke from the fire,
smelling of food, ale, dung, human unwashed bodies. The bodies
were there, a dozen men, the old woman and another. His eyes
were on her instantly. She was turning to go as he came in. She
was dressed for riding, and wore a large hat with a feather and a
great gold buckle that glittered and flashed in the firelight.

She was a young girl of strong, sturdy build, an open laughing
face, broad shoulders, big-breasted, brown-haired. She might be,
David thought, of any age from seventeen to twenty. She was
tall, carrying her head grandly on her shoulders. As David came
in her head was half turned, she laughing at someone, striking
her whip against her thigh.

She was the most natural, open creature David had ever seen.
Beside her was a man of some fifty years, very tall and skeleton
thin. This man was dressed quietly in grey coat and breeches

with a white stock; he wore a brown tie-wig. His face was as
sharp and pointed as his body was thin and long. He had very
thick, dark, beetling eyebrows and his complexion was sallow,
his face deeply furrowed. A very ugly man. As he talked he bent
his body about as though he would snap it.

For the rest there was the host of the inn, Sol Beddowes, who
was as thick, black, and dirty as a tar-barrel, some rough fellows
who might be smugglers, and one or two honest dalesmen. But
David's eyes were all for the girl.

He spoke to Beddowes; was, with a brusque word, told that he
could have a bed, came to the fire and so was companion to the
man and girl. He heard someone say 'Mr Denburn', so he spoke:
'Am I speaking to Mr Denburn?' he asked. The long sallow
hatchet of a face wheeled slowly in his direction and the little
eyes receded into the eyebrows.

'I am Mr Denburn.'

'My name is Herries,' said David. 'I have a piece of business
with you. May I come and call on you some time tomorrow?'

The body rose, as though on its heels, and leaned towards him
like a whip, then the voice, cold, chill, and filled with self-import-
ance, answered:

'Business of moment?'

'To the advantage of both of us, I fancy,' he answered.

'I am at home tomorrow evening.' Then he added, a little
more graciously (he had been examining David with great care,
and appeared to find him interesting), 'but possibly you prefer to
be away before evening. . . I could arrange a meeting in the
morning.'

David, with a thought of the girl, answered that the evening
would be a perfect appointment. He knew that the girl had been
intently aware of him, and, suddenly, he looked at her, catching
her gaze. She did not flinch, but looked at him squarely, then
smiled.

'A dark night to come over the Pass,' she said. Her voice delighted him, rich, warm, deep. It was as though he had heard it
before, many times, and recognized it, coming home to it. He
was excited by the sound of it, as he had never been by a woman's
greeting.

Mr Denburn went to the door. She followed him. Before she
went out she looked back, smiling again, and David smiled too.

Until he slept he thought of her. Was he in love at last? He sat
by the fire, looking into the flames, his legs stretched out, as he
loved to sit, talking to nobody, thinking slowly and steadily.

He remembered the women he had ever made any court to. The woman in Liverpool, a woman in Seatoller, Christina, one or two more. Little approaches that had been amusing, casual, leaving his heart alone. This was different: already it was different.

It seemed to him, poor David, the newest, most unusual experience in the world. It *was* unusual possibly. Strong healthy men in that age were seldom as virgin as he at thirty-eight.

He felt about twenty, and as he thought of her with every thought he was younger. He recalled the tones of her voice again and again with a happy luxury. She was only a child in years, but the voice seemed to him to have in it wisdom, fun, and good health, three splendid things as he saw the world.

When he went to his bed in a little room over the stables he found that he must share it with a stout dalesman. At any other time there would have been trouble. Tonight he did not care. The dalesman was asleep and snoring like a pig, his hairy chest heaving under the candle. David shoved him to the wall. He only grunted and turned on his side. Then David lay down, pulling up his knees, as he had to do in most beds, and, instantly, with a happy smile on his face, he was asleep.

He did not, unfortunately, dream of the brown-haired young woman, but he found himself in the little dark wood, lost, bewildered, stung by sharp thorns, his feet in plosh and mire. Beyond and above him on Stye Head someone was waiting for him, someone in peril, and it seemed, oddly enough, that this someone was himself. Did he not reach this figure to rescue him there would be disaster, but with every effort that he made his feet stuck the faster and the thorny trees tore his face more savagely. The voice from Stye Head called to him: 'Help. Help! I can do no more!' He made a last gigantic effort for freedom, and woke to find himself clutching the hairy throat of the stout farmer, his knee planted on his chest. Even this did not wake the slumberer, who, lost in his own pleasures, murmured: 'Coom, lass, pour oot for t' lot.'

David could not sleep after that. He lay there, listening to a first lonely bird, smelling the stuffy odour of straw, blanket, dried cow-dung that the room enclosed. He lay, his arm behind his head, gazing at the grey square of the little window, wondering how now, in clear day-time, he would find her. Was it perhaps only his longing to be in love that had cheated him? Would he discover her now like the rest, ordinary pleasant womanhood, with no magic about her? He didn't know. He wished urgently that he could summon her there, immediately, that he might satisfy that question.

At last he got up and went out. The fresh morning air caressed his eyes, his mouth, as though it loved him. He found the beck and washed his face and hands in it. It was icy cold. The light crept out above the black edge of the Pike, the trees came forth as though rising from their sleep, the hills moved grandly into their places. The few birds and the whispering beck greeted him with a happy, aloof indifference.

He didn't see her again until the evening.

Scarf Hall was hidden in the woods under Green How.

When David came to it the moon sailed out from above the Screes and an owl hooted. The house swam in a pale light that flowed about it like green water. An odd building surely; one old tower and on either side of it bow-windowed circular rooms like ears. The grass and bushes of an entangled nettled garden spread almost to the old door, whose front was lined with thick iron bars, studded with large flat-faced nails. Out of one of the upper windows a garment was hanging to dry, and it flapped humorously in the moonlight. A big white cat came out of the shadows and rubbed itself against David's legs, mewing.

He banged the old knocker, that was an old man's face with nose and chin meeting, against the thick wood. His knock resounded as though it would wake the heart of the Screes, but it didn't disturb the cat that continued to mew and rub against his boots.

After a while an old man, holding a lamp high, unbarred the door and opened it an inch. David must have looked giant-tall in that moonlight, for the old man nearly dropped the lamp in his astonishment. But he had been told maybe that there would be a visitor, so he opened the door wider, and the cat slipped into the hall.

He was a funny old man, bent and hairy, wearing a green apron. He had quite a little company of hairs on the end of his nose. Without a word he led the way, David striding after.

They were seated about a table in a dining-room eating and drinking. Because of the odd uneven shape of the tower this room was like a box with its corners pushed in. It seemed that the corners of the ceiling (which was an ornate one, painted with faded pink-bottomed cherubs festooned with chains of roses) would fall in also, for they bulged as though under a heavy weight. The room was badly lit with two candles in silver candlesticks.

There was a spinet in one corner and a large yellow globe like a huge dried melon in another. The white cat was curled up on the broad window-seat.

About the table were Mr. Denburn, Miss Denburn, an ancient lady in rusty black and a high white wig, and a broad thickset coarse-looking fellow with a round red face like a sun. In the poor light Mr Denburn was more sallow and hatchet-faced than ever. With his long protruding chin his face had the shape of a yellow-pointed shoe, and his eyebrows looked as though they were made of horsehair and fastened on with glue.

He tried to be genial this evening, but geniality was difficult for him. He bade David welcome, pushed a cold pie towards him, and filled his glass with wine. The thickset man was introduced as Captain Bann. He was drunk quietly, and, it appeared, in no good temper.

'I must offer my apologies,' David said. 'My business is with some of your sheep, Mr Denburn. I should have told you so last evening. You will be forced to have two visits from me.'

But Mr Denburn was delighted to speak of his sheep. His self-sufficiency was amazing. To hear him speak you would think that there were no sheep like his in the whole of northern England – and yet David knew that he was a poor farmer – almost no far-mer at all. While he spoke he wriggled his body up and down, as though there were a perpetual itch between his shoulder-blades.

In a very patronizing tone he cursed the neighbourhood, the climate, the Hanoverian government, the war with France, and humanity quite in general. He gave David to understand that he had for long led a life in London very different from this present one; that had it not been for certain rogues and vagabonds he would now have his place at court, and that he had rendered this same cursed Hanoverian family much personal service in the '45, but that he could wish now that the Pretender had pushed on to London when he might have done, and thrown the whole London lot into the Thames.

'Aye, aye,' gurgled Captain Bann, his nose in his glass. 'Pox on the lot and into the Thames with the bastards!'

At this point Miss Denburn and the ancient lady rose to retire, and David hurried to open the door. The cat stretched itself and followed them out. At the door he bowed and Miss Denburn curtsied, smiling with the greatest friendship as she did so, and he, as she smiled, felt his body tingle all over.

Returning to the table David found that the two gentlemen were regarding his physique with great interest. Indeed Captain

Bann, who was now far gone in liquor, proposed that the two of them should strip there and then and try a fall. There should be stakes which Mr Denburn should hold. He was beginning immediately, swaying on his stout legs, having taken off his coat, to undo his stock. David, however, firmly declined the honour.

It was shortly plain enough to him that these were two very considerable scoundrels. They had an understanding which hinted at many mutual past knaveries, and Mr Denburn was the master of the other. Denburn did not drink; his eyes under the absurd eyebrows were never still. He cracked walnuts in his sharp bony fingers as though he were cracking beads.

Captain Bann was made quarrelsome with drink, and wished to provoke David to some argument. He spilled wine on the table-cloth and paddled his fingers in it, even flicking a drop or two into David's face. But David was not to be provoked. It occurred to him, however, that had Denburn been of that mind the two of them would have set upon him without any uneasiness of conscience; it was an unpleasant notion to have Denburn's long fingers at his windpipe and the Captain's brawny shoulders pressed on his stomach. That he could manage them both he did not doubt, but it was a lonely spot, lonely and most ominously silent. There was no sound at all but the tapping of a branch against the pane behind the green curtains.

So, very shortly, he made his excuses to depart. Denburn did not attempt to stop him, and they arranged for a morning visit to the sheep.

He had no further word with Miss Denburn.

Quite early, however, next morning he encountered her, and had with her what was for him a very eventful conversation. Waking again very early (this last night he had had his bed to himself) he went down to the lake and stood watching the silver ripples break from the mirror, running out of the glassy stillness as though with childlike delight into the young stiff reeds at the water's edge.

He stood there, looking down, as the light broadened over the Screes, heard steps, looked up and saw Miss Denburn. She had not seen him in the half-light, but was walking along the lake path, her head up, her body beautifully free, taking in the morning air.

He straightened himself and bowed, smiling very shyly. He had read few romances and little poetry, books gave him poor pleasure, but if he had he would have known that this was a fitting time and place for a lovers' meeting. As it was, he did not think of himself as a lover but only as David Herries, delighted at the presence of a most beautiful lady. In actual truth he did not think consciously of anything at all.

She was as little self-conscious as he. To reveal a secret, she had fallen in love with him instantly at first sight in the inn yesterday. It had seemed to her as natural as mounting a horse. She had fallen in love a number of times in her young life already. She thought falling in love exceedingly pleasant. She was by nature impetuous and fond of all natural things – eating, sleeping, hunting, fishing, chattering, loving, hating.

When she saw a handsome thing she went directly towards it. David was by far the handsomest man she had ever seen. She had thought about him incessantly since first meeting him and how she might meet him again without anyone else being by. She had come out this morning on the chance. He was the kind of man she fancied would be up early.

Had he said at once this morning: 'I love you. Marry me,' she would have answered at once: 'Yes, I will,' without a moment's proper hesitation.

All her life she had been with bad, ugly-thinking, vilely-acting men, and she would have followed a tramp to get away from them. It was the mercy of a sometimes benevolent Providence that young Sarah was not by now wedded to a tin kettle and a baked hedgehog with a rabble of ragged children at her skirts. She had no caution whatever. But, as David was shortly to learn, escaping from Mr Denburn was not so easy as it might be.

As a matter of history David did, within a surprisingly short time, tell her that he loved her. As has been already explained, he was in a state very imminent on declaring his passion to someone or other, and this was a girl most exactly after his physical desire. Whether they were, either of them, after the spiritual needs of one another was something neither gave a thought towards. By good chance for the blood-history of many later Herries they were, both of them, fine creatures. Every once and again these chancy things happen fortunately.

In any case, Sarah looking at him with the smiling eagerness with which a young puppy looks at some human who promises a walk, David naturally advanced in boldness very swiftly.

They walked beside the lake together while the sun came over the hill and worked patterns of gold into the black reflections of the precipitous Screes. Over their shoulders Middle Fell looked down upon them benevolently.

David began with becoming modesty. He explained some facts about himself and that he lived at Rosthwaite in Borrowdale.

'I know Rosthwaite,' she remarked reflectively. Then she added: 'My name is Sarah.'

He told her that he had a business with Liverpool trade, that he was buying land thereabouts, and, in fine, that things were going well with him.

'You are married, Mr Herries?' she asked him, giving him a very quick look and thinking him so handsome that she longed to pull his ears.

No, he was not. He looked at her as he said it, and blushed. Gathering boldness, he asked her whether she lived alone here with her father, and said that it must be bleak enough in the wintertime.

She startled him by the answer:

'Mr Denburn,' she said, 'is not my father.'

He was astonished indeed.

'No. He is my uncle. My parents are both dead. My father died in the year previous. My uncle is my guardian.'

David was encouraged then to hint that it had not seemed to him natural that Mr Denburn should be her father. He hinted that he did not like Mr Denburn.

'Like him indeed!' her voice rang out. 'He is detestable! I have always hated him. He was my father's brother and held a strange influence over my father. In his last years my father was, I fear, quite in my uncle's hands. I inherit some wealth – no great sum – from my dear mother. I was their only child. My uncle removed to this lonely spot that he might influence my determination. It is his desire that I should marry that pig of a Captain whom you saw besotted at the table last night.

'My resolve for my own independence irritates them vastly. I am only seeking some opportunity to return to London. But this guardianship is strict. Even now the Captain is, I wager, if he is not sleeping off his drunkenness, somewhere on the watch. If not the Captain, then my uncle. You see, Mr Herries, I am a captive.'

She said it laughing, and he greatly admired her spirit, but he fancied that behind her laughter there was an apprehension. She was not, he imagined, as happy as she seemed.

She told him that she must return. Even now it was dangerous for her to be away.

He offered then his assistance, in any sort, in any kind. And a moment later, without realizing the extravagant speed of his progress, he was telling her that he loved her, that he had loved her

at the first sight in the inn, that he had never truly loved anyone
before, and that he would love her, he fancied, for ever and ever.

'What!' she cried. 'You the age you are and the handsome
man you are and never loved anyone before!'

'Never!' he declared, and with more truth than she could
dream of. She did perhaps, young as she was, realize that there
was something different in the freshness and sincerity of his declaration from the ordinary fashion of men.

Her eyes softened and her face shone with pleasure as she
looked at him. She could not help herself. He was so very delightful. She gave him her hand and told him that she would meet
him again that afternoon. She would walk across the fields to a
farm at the foot of Lingmell with the old woman who was her
duenna. She would see that the old woman did not disturb them.

They parted like two children enchanted with one another's
company. He was very young for his years.

He saw Mr Denburn that morning and Mr Denburn's sheep.
He bought the sheep and hated Denburn. He would in any case
have hated him, but now, because he knew that Sarah was oppressed by him, it was difficult for him to keep his hands away
from him.

Denburn of course noticed nothing. As with all self-appreciat-
ory persons he was lost in his own glories. Because David said
little he discovered him to be good company. His condemnations
covered the whole world: no one and nothing escaped them.
With his scorn there was mingled a mean anger and an avaricious
greed. He would have haggled over the sheep's price for an hour
but David gave him at once what he asked. He scarcely saw the
sheep, he did not see Denburn at all; he saw only young Sarah
with all the glories of heaven about her head and himself in bliss
at her feet. He also saw himself as the inevitable father of her
children. When he had left him and was back at the inn he went
up to the stuffy little chamber, into which the May sun was now
pouring, sat on the miserable truckle-bed and endeavoured to
control his fire. But he could not. It lapped him around with a
burning, shining flame. Never, in his thirty-eight years, had he
approached this sensation of worship, happiness and almost
agonizing wonder. He had not known that love would be like this
nor that it could descend with such precipitate suddenness. He
had no doubts about its issue. He would shortly marry Sarah and
that was enough.

How he would marry her, snatch her from her captivity, did
not yet occur to him; nor did he at present think of his father nor

Deborah nor Herries. He had never been able to think of more than one thing at a time.

And so when he met her on a sunny meadow under Lingmell he could not at first speak at all.

The ancient lady who accompanied her had been left in the farmhouse asleep. It was her virtue that, placed in a comfortable chair, her handkerchief over her face, she fell instantly asleep, like any bird with a cloth over its cage. Sarah had discovered this pleasant trait in her and profited by it.

So in that meadow, the shadows from the hill gathered about it as they walked, they confessed their love. It was not, it could not be, a very lengthy business, when two are instantly of the same mind, afraid of nothing and regardless either of the present or future.

David, when at last he found words, said: 'I told you this morning. I must repeat it. I cannot help it if you are angry. I have been thinking of you incessantly since the morning and I must tell you again that I love you.'

Sarah replied: 'I am not angry at all. I loved you the first instant in the inn.'

David said (but not meaning it): 'You should consider it. I am very old.'

And Sarah answered: 'Young men never pleased me.'

Then he kissed her, very gently, not as he intended to kiss her later on.

They were both so exquisitely happy that for a long time they could not speak at all but looked at one another, walked a little and looked at one another again.

After a while it occurred to them (the gathering shadows warned them) that the old lady would soon wake and that something must be done.

'Of course,' David said, 'you must come away with me.' He stood drinking in her loveliness. She was none of these thin willowy women that you could crack over your knee, but strong, broad-breasted, of noble carriage, health, vigour, energy, simple directness in every look and gesture. A third, watching them, might have thought them of the same family.

'Of course I must,' said Sarah and then moved, with more practical directness than he, on to the difficulties.

It seemed, at first sight, an easy matter. All, David said, that she had to do was to walk out of the house. He would have a horse at hand, and so, over the Pass and home. Indeed his first suggestion was that she should come with him immediately.

That, so eager and impetuous were they, might have been (and much trouble spared them) were it not for the old woman. Sarah would not leave her to the fury of her uncle. She must go when the old lady was not on duty. From this she would not stir.

David began now to be once more his true, slow, cautious self. This needed thinking of; there was Herries, there was his father. There were his own affairs. He hesitated less than ever as to his purpose, but everything must be soundly based at home, ready for her when she came.

He discovered then that she was being guarded as a prisoner. Although she might laugh with her young indomitable courage, he began to realize that these last months had been torture for her, and that, had he come or no, she would not in any case have endured much more of it. A more suspicious soul than David might at this point have asked himself whether she were not using him only as a means of escape. But with all his simplicity he was astute. He knew that she was in his own state of blissful bewildering love.

They could not, in fact, make any very serious decisions that afternoon. After a sentence they would stop and walk in a world together so magical and removed from argument that all plans were monstrously unreal. The most that it came to was that, early tomorrow morning, he would take his sheep home, and then shortly return to take her after the sheep.

Only it must be soon. For every reason, but chiefly because waiting seemed an incredible folly – it must be soon.

Once again he kissed her, behind the thick body of a chestnut tree (lest they should be observed), and this time it was a long embrace, with all heaven in it. That was the first true kiss of David's life.

Once, as they neared the farm, she turned to him, and there was a new seriousness in her voice. 'Do not think,' she said, 'because I have told you so quickly that I love you that it is a light word. I have been moving to this my whole life long.' She spoke as though she had already lived an eternity. And he very gravely answered: 'I will love you, dear Sarah, for ever.'

They came into the farm and found the old lady fast sleeping under a red handkerchief, and snoring lustily.

SAGA OF DAVID

II

THE FIGHT ABOVE WASDALE

ABDUCTIONS were common enough at that moment in the world's history; they roused no sort of comment unless the persons concerned were of social or financial splendour. David and Sarah were of neither. It was in fact a completely minor affair to everyone save the few persons concerned.

It was unimportant to David's father. David hinted to him that he had discovered the lady and might, if fortune favoured, bring her home. Herries was digging. He looked up, his face muddy, his eyes angry at withdrawing from their proper business.

He told David to go to hell, find anyone there he fancied, and do with her what he pleased. He was in one of his old moods, cursing the mud that splashed into his face, cursing his aching bones, but happy and tranquil in his occupation.

And David in his turn was angry in the old way. He abused his father handsomely, and going into the house felt a proper relief. He could do as he pleased: whatever way he went his father would be behind him.

In the doorway he met Mirabell. She was standing there watching a flight of birds cutting their way through the fresh spring air.

She was holding in both hands a tub filled with dirty water, her thin spare arms straining to the weight. Her face, beautifully pale like ivory under the tawny hair, was raised to the sky with a childlike pleased curiosity.

She smiled shyly at David. 'You see them best on the Fell,' she said, 'where you may follow them for a fine distance . . . The hills have taken them.'

He tried to relieve her of the tub but she wouldn't allow him. She was always shy with him, eager to please him without giving him any of herself.

But what he felt now was the amazing contrast that she made with young Sarah. On every occasion that he saw a woman now, Sarah was the more wonderful to him. This fancy of his father's – he liked her, felt kind to her, would be glad to please her, but she was a fade-away unhappy wisp, holding herself in against everybody, while Sarah!—

At the thought of her he was in such a glow of happiness that he could have picked Mirabell up in his arms and tossed her like a feather.

She, with her funny, almost witch-like perception of the moods of others, said:

'You're happy today.'

'I am,' he answered, throwing his arms up to the sky. 'I am! I am! I am!'

He was in a mood to tell her of it.

'I have found a maid – over the hill. I'm going to fetch her back, and marry her.'

To his surprise Mirabell was happy, as though good news had come to herself.

'I'm glad. Where will you live?'

'Here.'

'Yes, don't leave your father.' She put down the tub and caught his great hand in her thin bony fingers. She looked up at him, smiling. 'Is she young? And beautiful? And a fine mother for your children?'

'She is young and beautiful, and a fine mother for my children,' he repeated after her, smiling back at her. They had never come so close together before.

'Bring her here, Davy. There is room enough.'

'Oh yes,' he answered, looking up at the old house where in one corner the roof was slipping, and where a chimney cocked sarcastically with a drunken leer. 'There is room. But, Mirabell, why should we not all go from here? There is money enough for a fine place where they can take Father newly. Here they have always hated him. Persuade him, Mirabell.'

But she shook her head. 'In that I can't move him. He is stuck in the place.'

'For you he'd do anything.'

'No. That – never.'

Then she picked up the tub again, moved into the court, and over her shoulder repeated: 'Bring her here, Davy. Good luck to your hunting.'

Next morning he went back to Wasdale. He walked over. After much thinking he had decided that a horse would be a danger, that he must be as little visible as possible before the event. He was inclined at this moment to consider but lightly of the whole business.

For Sarah to escape from two such elderly ruffians as Denburn and the Captain would be surely no problem. It seemed to him as he walked under a clear blue sky, singing, the very simplest thing in the world . . .

In the little valley by the beck under the Pass at the foot of Lingmell there was a deserted shepherd's hut that he had marked on the last occasion. This, he thought, would do very well to pass a night in without observation.

He reached it in the late afternoon when the light was failing. The silence was profound, broken only by the gentle running of the beck. There was a sweet air scented with water and fresh grass. He sat in the little hut on a pile of dry bracken while the colours faded and the sky whitened, thinking, happily, triumphantly, of all the joy that was coming to him. He hadn't known that love could so change the world in a second of time.

He stretched his body out, his arms behind his head, and looked up at a little hole in the turfed roof through which the sky was like a crystal cup.

His imagination had Sarah in his arms, and he whispered to her: 'My darling, my little love,' and enjoyed himself hugely.

When it was dark he went out. He met nobody until before he reached the wood of Scarf Hall. The world seemed to be entirely deserted.

When he came to the grass-grown drive he stole carefully to the rear of the tower to see whether a window were open. On the left side he found a window brilliantly lighted. The shine streamed out, illuminating a strange little garden that had once been carefully tended. There was a thick box hedge with animals cut upon it – a cock, a swan, a dog – and in the centre of the little lawn a square sundial. This was all lit with the pale shadowed light from the candles in the room.

Standing in the dark by the box hedge he could see into the room. The table, whose surface shone like a mirror, had on it a large bowl of fruit, a bottle of wine, and a board of red and yellow chessmen set out as though for play. The white cat was curled up near the yellow globe. A large silver candelabrum with many branches threw a fine dazzling radiance over the broad figure of the Captain, who was seated, alone in the room, at the table, his large red face between his hands, staring in front of him, a grand picture of drunken stupor. The room was so still that it might have been a painted scene.

After a while a breeze descended among the trees and, as though he had been roused by that (although he could not have heard it), the Captain took the bottle of wine with a shaking hand, filled a long thin glass, raised it to his mouth, drank it, and then, amazingly, climbed to his feet and shook his fist threateningly and savagely in the air, at nothing in particular.

He was the picture then of a man very angry and very foolish. His rage seemed to possess him for he suddenly, with a curve of his stout arm, swept all the chessmen off the board, raised the board itself and flung it to the ground. Then he stared about him as though he had just awakened from a dream. It was odd enough to see all this in dumb show and hear no sound.

A thin cold rain began to fall, pattering among the leaves.

The door opened, the Captain turned, and, miracle of miracles, Sarah entered. She was dressed exquisitely in a silver dress, and she carried a candle. When she saw the Captain she would retire again, but he stumbled to the door and stood with his back to it.

She blew out the candle, placed it quietly on the table and turned to him, her head raised. She said something to him; he replied, very ludicrously falling on one knee. She came to the window and at that same moment David stepped forward into the light. He stood there in an agony of apprehension lest the Captain should see him, but the Captain, drunken as he was, could not balance himself on his knee and sprawled to the floor.

Sarah laughed (and a fine splendid sight it was to see), stepped over his body and, at the moment that her hand was on the door, looked back into the garden.

She saw him. Heaven be thanked, she saw him! Her face was rosy, she put her hand for an instant to her breast, then left the room. The Captain lay there where he had fallen, his face in the chessboard.

Some window must have been slightly open, for the candles began all hurriedly to blow as though they were laughing at the Captain, and in that same new flurry of wind Sarah had joined David by the hedge.

They exchanged no word. He drew her face to his, his hands were about her neck, the rain blessing both of them.

At last, withdrawing from one another, they began to laugh in sheer joy of seeing each other again. He drew her away into the back of the little garden out of the light, then hurriedly told her his plan: 'It must be tomorrow night. I will be here in this same place. At what hour?'

She whispered back: 'At this same time. But I may not escape at once. I will come from that window . . .' Then in sheer happiness she caressed his face with her hand, tracing his mouth, his eyes, his nose.

'I hadn't dreamt it would be so soon. I have watched two evenings. I must pull your ears. It was the first thing in the inn I desired.'

'You will be damp. The rain—'

'Kiss me again. Hold me tightly. If I had other clothes I would come now . . .'

'Do you love me? Have you thought of me?'

'I love you so . . . I haven't ate a thing these two days. My uncle . . .'

She broke off, listening. The Captain had come through the window, lurched on to the bright square of lawn, took off his wig and lifted his naked scalp to the rain. He stumbled towards them, holding his wig in his hand.

'Water,' they heard him say. 'Damned refreshing . . . cool to the head.' He rocked into the sundial which he clasped with both arms.

They waited, scarcely breathing, while he hugged the dial. Then they kissed again, a long embrace, suddenly not caring for the Captain. She came out into the light, walked right past him, through the window into the house.

He stood, scratching his head, not knowing whether he had seen anything or no. David slipped away.

He slept the sleep of the innocent, the just and the healthy that night in the hut and dreamt of nothing and nobody. He woke to a cold day with a great wind that drove bellying grey clouds in riotous hurry over the hills as though preparing for some grand show when the clouds should be packed away. All day they rolled, leaving the tops clear, sharp and cold beneath their smoky procession. All day David stayed in the little valley, eating the bread and meat that he had brought with him and drinking out of the stream. He climbed the Pass as far as Stye Head then, to warm himself. It was but a little way down into Borrowdale. There could be but little trouble in the affair. They would be at Herries by early morning.

He had but one encounter; a thin wiry choleric Squire with some hounds who, attended by two men, was going up the Pass as he came down. The Squire wanted company and held David by the coat while he enlarged on his affairs. Like another Squire of his time he was all for 'lending' anyone who disagreed with him 'a flick'. He had a long matter in his head about an estate that joined his own, somewhere, David gathered, Eskdale way.

'Join the two and there's no larger estate in the kingdom. I had rather bate something than have the pox of a fellow advising me on my own ground.' He had an especial cursing fury at the towns and London in particular. 'I'd be a Hanoverian 'fore I'd show my arse among their smoking chimneys. Pox on all Hanoverians and Presbyterians either. Thou must come drink a bottle at my table. I'll show thee some trees and some horses also. You show your fancy very plainly. I'm ne'er mistaken in a man. Thou'rt no Hanoverian.'

He would then back with David and drink with him in the Wasdale Inn. Then, to David's consternation, suggested they should impose themselves on Scarf Hall. He knew, it seemed, Denburn. 'He's a mean varlet,' and he'd doff his clothes to give him a lick as soon as spit in his face; nevertheless there'd be wine there and they'd make a rousing night of it.

It took a quarter of an hour's good work to dissuade him from this and to push him on up the hill again, but at last, swearing at his men and his hounds, he vanished round the bend, his little wiry legs the last visible part of him.

The only merit of this adventure was that it was pleasant to realize the general unpopularity of Denburn. All humankind doubtless loathed him. David had through the afternoon some apprehension lest the testy Squire, in search of good liquor, should turn and descend again, and he watched the Pass with some anxiety. But there was no figure on the Pass. Doubtless he had gone, cursing, down into his own place in Eskdale.

The rain threatened all day but never fell. When at last darkness came, the hills were clear and later there would be a moon.

In the little garden again he performed the silliest act of his life. Looking back afterwards he never could see what drove him to it. It may have been the cold, which was bitter, or impatience to bring things to an issue, or sheer childish playfulness.

In any case the garden was chill, half an hour's waiting made him stamp his feet with restlessness, the house was dark without a visible light. He stepped over the lawn, brushing against the sundial, felt for the window of the dining-parlour, found it un-latched and was inside.

There he paused, his hand on the table-edge. He listened; there was not a sound but a hysterical clock that giggled some-where like a schoolgirl. He opened the door, crept into the hall, a wavering candle turned the corner, and in a moment he had the old lady in his arms.

He clasped her to him as though he loved her, his broad hand over her mouth, and pulled her, lighted candle and all, back into the parlour, and closed the door very quietly behind him. The old lady was in a strange garment of faded green, her grey hair about her shoulders and on her lined wrinkled face an expression of such convulsive terror that it touched his compassion. But she did not speak, only gaped at him, her mouth open like a young bird's. He took the candle from her trembling hand and set it down on the table.

'You love Miss Denburn,' he said hurriedly. 'I know you do. Miss Denburn is in great peril and must be away with me tonight. I would not put you to any sort of inconvenience, madam, but every moment has its danger. Assist us and you shall be rewarded magnificently.'

Her mouth opened and shut. She kept plucking at her green gown that it might cover her négligé. The leaping candle made the queerest figure behind her on the wall. She said at last in the oddest voice, between a squeak and a whisper:

'There's the Captain coming down and we're all undone.'

He saw from that that she was on the right side and had probably been already warned by Sarah, but she trembled like a flower and, he feared, might at any moment drop to the ground in a faint.

So he pushed her into a chair, poured some wine from a decanter on the table into a glass and made her drink it. She gasped and gurgled, but, it was plain, enjoyed it.

'Now, madam, you must return to Miss Denburn and tell her that I am waiting for her here. Then go to your chamber and remain there.'

He spoke sternly, but he smiled. And she, to his astonishment, smiled back at him, put her finger to her lip with an evident enjoyment of the conspiracy and, clutching her gown about her, stole softly out of the room again.

A moment later, listening in the darkness, he heard the Captain's voice. The Captain was not drunk tonight. He sounded another man, rallying the old lady with quite a deep dignity and precision.

She, David gathered, was endeavouring to escape up the stairs and he detaining her.

'No shame on your attire, Sister,' he was saying (that plainly his jocular name for her). 'You shall drink a glass with me – a handsome night-cap. The moon will be up and we will salute it through the open window.'

She replied something and then David could hear her hastening upstairs. A second later the Captain was through the door, so near to David that he could feel the hot breath on his cheek.

He was himself pressed back against the wall as flat as his great body would allow, his hand ready on his sword-hilt.

The Captain went past him and began to curse for a light. He had a fashion, it seemed, of talking to himself. 'Curses on the dark! 'Tis a house of no discipline. But I'll not drink this evening. I'll match Ned with his sobriety, blast his superior elegance. And I'll not be longer here neither; it's a job or it's no bargain, nasty skinflint.'

He moved to the window. David could see his broad bulk, in the thin light that preceded the moon, his hands in his breeches pocket, his legs straddling. He continued to talk as an angry boy might: 'I'm no such fool as he'd think me, as he'll find in his own time. The girl's well enough, but she hates me sober and loathes me drunk.

'And there's Jane at Newmarket. . . A shrew's a shrew however much gold she carries. . . And this plaguy country where it rains like Egypt's plague, and no company to make a night of it . . .' He yawned prodigiously, then, with an exclamation, found in his pocket what he wanted. He fingered the tinder-box, struck a light, turned and saw David.

In another second he would have shouted but with a leap David was across the room, had knocked the light from him and hurled him with a crash to the ground, his hand over his mouth. The noise of the crash must surely rouse the house and as, after that, they struggled, David's ears were alert for Denburn's footsteps. But there was nothing save the chattering clock that seemed suddenly to redouble its pace in a violent excitement.

That was no mean struggle. The Captain must in earlier days have been a man of his hands, and even now, weakened by lazy living and drink, his big body had energy. Had David been free it would have been a matter of a few moments, but as it was he must keep his hand over the man's mouth, which hampered him sadly. The Captain wriggled like a worm, now bottom up, then with his legs twisting like a centipede's, then with a sudden force in his belly that turned it into iron, pressing against David's arm. He had his hand in David's eye and was knuckling him lustily until, throwing his body on to the man's stomach, David had a free arm and could press the other's hand back to the floor.

Their panting breath and the roll of their bodies on the floor was the only sound.

Then the door was open and there was a light. David could not turn to see and had an awful fear it was Denburn. But it was Sarah's voice:

'Quick,' she said. 'My uncle is on the stairs.'

'The bands from the curtains,' he gasped. 'Fasten his legs.'

With admirable energy and dexterity she had them there and (as she told him later) tied them about those stout ankles with the greatest satisfaction. She was as brisk as though her life had been spent in such tasks.

'The garden-house . . . Over the lawn . . .'

They pushed the window and dragged him out. David's wide and deep kerchief was over his nose and mouth, the curtain-bands over his arms and legs. These were temporary enough and would stand little resistance, but for the moment they must do.

David's huge arms dragged him across the lawn (his head bumped the sundial), through the path by the box hedge, and, hidden in thicket, there was the garden-house. It was a small enough place, piled with straw and gardening-tools, but they bundled him in, closed the door and bolted it. Then they ran.

By the path that skirted the lake-end they stopped. She caught his hand and leaned against him, recovering her breath. They listened intently. It was strange after those moments of hot panting struggle to stand still in a world, cold, motionless, at their feet the grey rounding of the lake and about them everywhere the dim shapes of the hills. The house, the room, the heaving body of the Captain, all in China . . .

A dog barked somewhere. The reeds rustled. He held her to him as though she were part of himself.

'Now . . . how long may that garden-house bolt last?'

'Not long; the wood is rotten.'

David laughed. 'He had an immoderate taste of my fingers . . . Come. We'll do the kissing later. There's no time . . .'

They were off again, through the little gathering of houses, then the foot of the Pass.

'Soon there'll be the moon.'

Before they started to climb, in that strange milky glow, they turned towards one another and kissed. Her immediate ready courage of the last half-hour pleased him most divinely. That was the companion that he would have, a man in swiftness, eagerness of perception, a woman when the softer time demanded it.

He was proud of her mettle beyond any personal pride that he had ever known.

'You did that bravely. Oh, I love you a thousand times for it!'

She took his head in her hands, fondling it, bending it to her breast. 'I did not know that love would be thus,' she murmured. Silly stuff to both of them had they heard others whisper it, but they might be allowed it, the night before them being sterner than they knew.

Indeed so little concerned were they that they started up the Pass hand-in-hand, like two children.

She told him her adventure. The old lady had warned her, she had started down the stairs when she heard the crash of the tumble. Then there was panic for her! What to do? To go forward and risk what she might find below or to turn back and wait? The door of Denburn's room opened. It was dark on the stair and she waited, listening for his movement. He asked her from his door had she heard anything.

'Only an owl,' she had called back to him, her heart thumping. He went in again, closing his door, and once more she listened. Now everything was still save the clock. Only the white cat (that had doubtless slipped through the door when the Captain opened it) slithered up to her, rubbing against her legs. She had taken that as an omen, and so went forward. Then, most foolishly, when she saw the pair of them struggling on the floor she had wanted to laugh. The Captain's broad beam and his knuckle in David's eyes . . .

But at the thought of that she caught David's hand the tighter.

So they walked on, unconscious of anything save the splendour of being in love, of the health of their bodies. One hundred and fifty years later a descendant of theirs would be walking up this same Pass with the lady of his choice to whom he had just declared his passion. She had accepted him, but, as he kicked the rough shale from under his feet, he would be wondering, in the manner of his time, whether he had done wisely. She was pretty enough, but might she not sicken after children? Of course with birth-control methods as safe as they were . . . Her nose certainly went blue with the cold (although tomorrow was the first of May it was damned cold) and her taste in Chinese art was uncertain . . . 'Darling,' he was, a hundred and fifty years later, remarking, 'that book of Breasted's shows quite plainly . . .'

And now at this same moment David, looking back down the milky path and feeling at his sword, said most happily: ''Twould be no bad place for a fight . . . if your uncle has the stomach for it.' Only the wind, whistling by, answered them. There was no suspicion of a pursuer.

He kissed her again. He really couldn't kiss her enough; this kissing was so different from any that he had ever known.

Then the moon peered over the edge of Lingmell. She scarcely showed herself, a fingernail of pale colour, but she was rising; very soon the Pass would be flooded with light, the moon that ushered in May.

But it was not to be just yet. There drifted, in the odd fashion of inconstancy that these hills have, sudden filmy wisps of mist, the edges of the thinnest gauze, having no especial purpose, rising from nowhere, born of nothing, so thin as to be transparent with the dim preface of the moon behind them. And at the same moment a new wind began to shrill up the valley between Lingmell and the Pass.

David after many years knew this country well and something in the wind told him that these vapours would not remain transparent for long. An odd unanalysed anxiety caught him. Mist was the one thing of which he had not thought.

'Oh, look!' Sarah caught his arm and pointed to the valley. ''Tis as though a great kettle were boiling.' The vapour was coming up towards them in spirals of smoke and, you might suppose, little clouds of steam. David was not imaginative, but, in his anxiety to have this adventure safely over, he was ready to fancy some active agency down there in the valley, some enemy raising a huge fire of damp logs to send up a torrent of twisting smoke.

'We must press on,' he said. 'The Pass can be cursedly confusing in the mist.' The thin gauze skirted the Pass like a live thing and as it thickened above them, obscuring the rising moon, the world darkened again and chilled, the wind whispering at their ears.

An odd thing happened then to David. He fancied that his father was walking beside them. He could almost see the man, tall and powerful, with his long hair, his shoulders a little shrunken, his whole body moving forward with that obstinate energy that was so peculiarly his, his eyes staring into some imagined dream of space.

It was as though he said: 'There is trouble for you now, and so I am here. You have taken this girl in a single second, forgetting our bond together. But you will not be permitted to forget it. We are Herries always, and we Herries are always together against the world whether we wish it or no, and so it will always be. Our bond is for no time or termination. It endures infinitely. A weariness, perhaps, but nevertheless a law.'

Indeed David may at this moment have been thinking these things, for he was suddenly conscious of his father, and not very long ago, at Herries, his father had said something of this kind to him when he asked him why he did not marry, and added that marriage would be no escape for him because he was indubitably a Herries, and must always belong to those of his own blood rather than to anyone from outside.

It was only for a second in time that David saw his father striding there beside them, but it was a second that contained many centuries in its form.

The incident thirteen years back, in Carlisle, came to him when he had watched in the fog on the walls. He had lost his father and then, in the early morning, his father had found him. There had been an extraordinary relief in that reunion, something far beyond the immediate circumstance of the incident.

Now again, for nearly two days, he had lost his father, absorbed by his sudden love for this girl. His father had held him once more and, for that moment, it had been as though Sarah did not exist.

He had her again, catching her hand. The Pass was really steep here with a sharp edge, and the mist was now boiling up from the valley in thick rolling masses of cloud.

He stayed her to caution her, and at that same instant the tops cleared, the moon sailed out, full and faintly red-cherry coloured. Everything was illuminated, the Gavel on their left, Lingmell, Scafell, the Pike, the rough track of the Pass winding down into the valley.

They turned to look back, and there, sharply clear in the moonlight, pressing up the Pass were two figures, Denburn and the Captain.

Each saw the other and stood transfixed. David was happy.

'If only the mist holds off I can deal with them. They won't use their pistols so long as you are here. Oh, but I'm longing for a cut at your uncle—'

The distance between them was short. The two men were standing on a green promontory that stretched out of the Pass over the valley, looking to Wasdale and the sea. They were exceedingly clear in the moonlight, first like statues, then beginning with feverish energy to scramble forward up the Pass. Denburn shouted something and David, laughing, shouted back:

'Ohè! Ohè! Ohè! Cut-throat and Captain! I'll buy you both for a farthing.' He was like a boy again at the thought of a fight.

'I could meet them here,' he said reluctantly. 'At this bend.
I'd have the command of the path.'

But Sarah urged him on. Her courage, although she would
never let him know, had failed her. She didn't want him to fight,
she was sick in the stomach, she was suddenly a child of her own
really tender years. She had been brave enough in the house
because that had been a matter of escape, and her uncle had not
shared in it. But now he was almost upon them, and all the terror
and sense of malignant power with which he had always possessed
her returned to her.

Since she had been an infant in the little house, with her father
and mother, in Kensington village, she had known this. She had
caught it first, perhaps, from the terror that her father and
mother had of him.

When he had reached to her and tried to take her on his knee,
she had shivered and gone pale with apprehension. The comfits
that he had given to her had always seemed to her poisoned, the
touch of his hand the touch of a frog.

The natural buoyancy and health of her disposition had prevented this from breeding in her any permanent unhappiness.
Her terror of him was intermittent, only really present when his
physical body forced her to realize it. It was his physical
body that she realized now. Although he was only a manikin of a
figure against those moonlit hills, he was as real and powerful as
though he were there beside them. She was sure that he
would kill David! He had the evil power. There was something
in him that must be stronger than the goodness and courage in
David.

So she urged David forward, running ahead of him, and he
followed, joy in his heart that now he might at last settle with
that dirty fellow who had ill-treated his beloved Sarah, stroking
his sword-hilt as though it were the best friend he had.

They had reached the turn, climbed the boulders, came to the
point where the signpost now assists the aspiring tourist, saw the
tarn lying before them black under the moonlight.

'I will meet them here,' David said, his pistol in one hand, his
sword drawn in the other.

Sarah implored him to go on. He saw then her terror and was,
privately, disappointed in it.

'I will but make a statement or two,' he said quietly, but with
the obstinacy of a small boy. 'Your uncle must understand my
feeling for him before I take you from him. That is justice.'

Then he saw the rising ground that leads past Sprinkling Tarn

and Allen Crags to Esk Hause. 'That would be better,' and, with
her following him, he took the higher fell.

Then, without an instant's warning, the moon was blotted out
again. The mist swept up in an array of thin cloud that veiled the
hills, the fell, the tarn. Before it thickened into a wall of white
muffling vapour they saw the two figures round the corner and
start up the fell towards them.

'Now we are caught indeed,' David whispered. He stood
listening. He felt for her hand, clutching it. 'Don't move from
me,' he cautioned her. ''Tis easy to miss in this cloud. I must
listen for their step.'

But, as always in that mountain-mist, listening he heard every
imagined sound. Rocks seemed to fall from a great height, water
rose in a whirlwind from the lower ground, voices were everywhere, animals rustled at their feet, there was secret laughing, an
army of curses, the ringing of bells, and behind and around all
this a dead cold stillness like the grave.

Forgetting his own caution and thinking he heard his enemy,
he moved away from her.

Again he listened, and suddenly, quite near to him, so that it
was almost at his ear, he heard the Captain's voice: 'I'll not
move till this mist thins. It's the Devil's work . . .'

David turned and there, looming right up at him, and seemingly twice its natural size, was the Captain's body. The Captain
saw him at the same instant and immediately a shot struck the
wind. The echo of the pistol fire was volcanic, as though the
whole system of rock and fell had split with one heave.

Then they were breast to breast and, a moment after, sword to
sword. It was the strangest duel, their bodies visible one moment,
invisible the next, the swords flashing as though with life of their
own, lunging into emptiness, coming up sharply in defence
against no opponent, and for David always the agony that he did
not know where Denburn was; he might have Sarah in his arms
by this; and there was also the part that the mist itself seemed to
take in the affair, eddying around him, sweeping by with a swing
of the wind's arm, beating against him, as though with a personal
meaning.

He realized very quickly that the Captain was in a rage, and
that the anger was personal because they had trussed him and
piled him in the garden-house.

At first he muttered the dirtiest oaths: his personal vanity had
been meanly affronted: but soon his strength began to fail him.
The tussle with David earlier that night, the pressure up the Pass,

the force of his age and his evil living all swiftly told on him. He made a lunge into cold fog, staggered with the impetus, and David's sword was through his arm. With a gurgle as though he had tumbled into a tub of water, he dropped.

David turned to find that the mist had slipped off the lower slope and was hastening, like a live thing, up the hill, torn away like a theatre curtain and flinging into the moonlight all the higher ground as far as Sprinkling Tarn. He could see the edge of that water a curdled grey against banks of vapour. The clouds were everywhere thinning, and the moon shone behind them with a thin glow, giving the shadows of watery ghosts to every rock and stone. As the mist pulled away Sarah ran to him: at his feet curled unconscious was the Captain; quite near to them Denburn, his sword in his hand, watching them. Phantasmal all these figures were, in a world so shadowy and faint that with every moment and shift of the clouds it was a new world.

So David put his arm about Sarah and thought he would say a word to her uncle.

'Go home, Uncle,' he cried. ''Tis cold, and you must be abed. Sarah has said her farewells. She leaves thee the white cat. She is weary of thy company. Go home, go home. Thou art old for the fells at nightfall.'

He saw from where he was that Denburn had no pistols. He was flicking his sword back and forth. The moon was now in full splendour again, and the clouds had rolled back to veil the Gavel and crowd the Pike. The stretch of moor, the edge of the tarn, the Stye Head Tarn below them were brilliantly lit, and all the hills were ebony.

Denburn answered: 'You have killed my friend, ravished my house where you were hospitably entertained, and shall most immediately repent of it.'

The charge of broken hospitality vexed David, for it was, in a manner, true.

'I have not killed your friend,' he answered. 'You had best gather him together and go home with him or he will catch an ague. As to your hospitality I ask you now, with proper deference, have I your leave to wed your niece Sarah Denburn, whom I love and shall cherish always? I have money enough, and prospect of more. I am thirty-eight, and in admirable health. Give us your blessing and I will carry the Captain down myself.'

To this Denburn answered with some foul oaths. His voice had an odd note of surprise in it, as though he could not credit his senses that anyone should treat him with so arrant a disrespect.

'Well then,' said David, 'I will beat thee home for a dirty rascal and bragging bully. Run now, or I'll drive thee down.'

He moved forward. Denburn said nothing, but circled round
towards the hills, then ran forward up towards Sprinkling Tarn.

There was something oddly comical in this long man with his
waggling moonlit shadow running, but there was method in it.
He found his higher ground with the Tarn behind him to the left.

'I'm afraid of no long-legged country bastard,' he cried.
'Leave the girl and go to your own place or I'll slit your ears.'
Even here there was yet this odd note of astonished disappoint-
ment that he should be so inelegantly treated.

David moved up to him; he saw then that Denburn had been
skilful in choosing his place. The moon, richly full, stared down
at him; the shadows were baffling and at every step upwards he
was under a disadvantage.

Their swords touched and it seemed to Sarah that the hills
crowded nearer to watch the better. For her it was indeed the
issue of her whole life.

Were David even wounded to unconsciousness she knew that
she had no hope of Denburn's mercy after this affront to his
pride. She crouched, watching, her hands clasped, her eyes hot
and burning. She might possibly have aided him. Already she
understood David well enough to realize that if she did he would
never forgive her.

But Denburn was no very able swordsman. On higher ground
though he was, David, whose reach was tremendous and eye certain, drove him step by step towards the Tarn. Denburn lunged,
parried, lunged again with fury, overbalanced, and David had
struck his sword from his hand. David himself was no very grand
swordsman although he inherited an instinct of it from his father.
He had wished all his days to do precisely this, in the manner of
all the approved tales and poems.

With joy at his heart he followed the pattern of the romancer.
His foot on Denburn's sword, he threw his own on to the turf.

'Now, Mr Denburn,' he said, 'we'll wrestle for it.'

Very certainly he meant to kill him. The man was a dirty misshapen dog who had done nothing but evil and had no right to
be in this beautiful world at all. Especially had he no right to be
in a world that contained young Sarah.

So he ran forward and they were locked excellently in one
another's arms. Denburn was wiry and his fingers were quickly
about David's neck. David too was embarrassed by his height
and, whether it were his anxiety for Sarah, his climbing to higher

ground, or some extra energy that he had put into his swordplay, certainly he could not find his usual easy strength.

Denburn was strong in two particulars. His fingers would not be dislodged from David's throat, his feet would not be dislodged from the ground.

Sway as they might it seemed that his feet had some magic contact with the soil. The fingers tightened and there was a firm thought in David's brain. What if after all he were to lose this? His breath began to come pantingly. The fingers dug inwards like live things with their own live purpose. It was as though his eyes were being pushed from their sockets. The moon rose like a flaming disc, hurled itself through the sky and swept back to its place again, while the black shoulders of the hills rocked and bent. His knees began to sag and the turf to run up to him like the swaying deck of a vessel. He released one arm to catch at those hands, tore at them, but they neither bent nor shook. Only pressed deeper. Denburn's head came curiously towards him, the eyes small, detached, the mouth curved and, as always, coldly self-pleased.

'O Christ!' The voice came from far away, from the very heart of the red and fiery moon.

'I am a strangled man . . .'

He reeled, and with that reel lay the fortune of his destiny. Denburn's hand was shaken. David's body rose; like a dog he shook his throat free. His giant arms crushed the other's in a great grip. He lifted him from his feet, raised him in air, turned staggering with him, and flung him into the Tarn.

The man splashed, sank, did not rise. Heaving with gusts of strangled breath David waited. The ripples died under the moon, but Denburn did not come again. The scene was as still as a glass mirror and the quiet wonderful.

Yet he waited. Then, when he saw that for a certainty Denburn would never return any more, he ran to Sarah.

HERRIES IN 1760

BEAUTY is aroused by Beauty and change answers to change. But in this valley at this time Beauty was spread in vain for natives. They had not yet learnt to find it in the eyes of the outsider. Poet Gray nine years later, peering to find Castle Crag and

Glaramara 'indescribably fearful', was to open a gate that has grown since then most uncomfortably wide.

As to change; perhaps in no corner of England had the escapades and accidents of history made less stir than here. Looking over the flat green surface sheltered so tenderly by its protecting hills, you may see the monks of Furness Abbey riding their nags on survey of their property, or Sir Wilfred Lawson of Isell protecting his German miners, or Radcliffe of Derwentwater in the Civil War turmoil dredging peasants from the Borrowdale fields to support the King and to meet in that conflict their own near neighbours who, under Lawson of Isell, fought for Parliament, stored munitions on St Herbert's Island, burnt the Radcliffe house on Lord's Island, and, riding up Borrowdale over the Stake Pass to Rydal, pleasantly sacked Rydal Hall.

And so to present memories, the old men and women of 1760 who could remember well enough the events of '15 when the Radcliffe house was still standing on Lord's Island and the last Lord Derwentwater lost his poor young head, dying by the axe as a last distinction – and so the Rebel Hunts on the hills after the '45, the terrified fugitives hiding behind the kitchen door, and Butcher Cumberland waiting in Carlisle. And now there was the new road, and more new roads after it, and soon Gray's postchaise and, later, the little boy struggling over his sums at Hawkshead School, and the eyes of the world turning in wondering patronage towards this small square of ground . . .

On this very afternoon of early November 1760, David Herries was looking out from his fields behind Herries on to a scene that no events could alter, that would for two hundred years to come wear the same quiet face. This November weather is cold and sharp, but the sun is out lying flat upon the fields; some of the sheep are away on the fells, on the lower slopes of Thornythwaite and High Knott and Watendlath, some are cropping the short turf in Stonethwaite, some hiding from the wind in the crannies and coverts of the rocks.

The valley has just learnt that on October 25th old George II fell down dead in Kensington Palace. No one has been greatly stirred by this. Only some of the women gave a thought to a young Prince, only twenty-two years of age, a Prince who is really English at last, who says in his opening speech that 'he glories in the name of Briton'.

But, for David, this news meant something. He could not see young Charles James Fox, a boy of eleven, standing in front of his father and reciting in a shrill treble and with proud gestures

lines from *Samson Agonistes,* nor John Wesley, in spite of his
fifty-five years, preaching at five in the morning and finding it a
'healthy exercise', nor Joseph Priestley, twenty-seven years of
age, nosing his nonconformist way to his principles of oxygen,
nor Samuel Johnson, an odd fifty or so, pushing his cumbrous
path through the Strand, cracking his fingers as he went – he
could not tell what the larger world might be at, nor indeed why
it should be at anything at all (he was never a philosopher), but
he did know that a crisis was arriving in his own affairs that must
be met and met with courage and wisdom, and that, behind his
own personal crisis, the solitude and isolation both of this valley
and of his own history were passing and could never return again.

What must he do? What was the right thing not only for himself but for all?

He had married Sarah Denburn in May 1758. It was now the
fourth of November 1760. From then until now, he and his wife
had resided at Herries. Last evening (and here he leant his arms
on the little rough stone wall, staring out in front of him, not feeling the cold, so lost was he in his grave anxiety and distress for
what had occurred) there had been a terrible scene. It had been,
of course, the fault of his father; it had been only the worst of a
number like it that, through this past year, had increasingly
occurred.

It came in the first place from this cursed obstinate determination of his father to remain at Herries. When on that early May
morning he had brought Sarah down to Herries it had seemed
natural enough, even inevitable that they must stay. In the first
place they had remained to face any trouble that might arise. The
Captain, who on that eventful night had found his own way back
to Wasdale, had at once, nursing his wounded arm, ridden off to
his own place, wherever that might be, without word to anyone.
David, remembering the chessmen scattered on the floor and the
futile gestures of vexation, fancied that he had not regretted
Denburn.

No one else, it seemed, had regretted him either. His body had
been found a week later by some of the smugglers who used the
Borrowdale–Ravenglass secret paths for their expeditions and
were none too anxious for much investigation. They had left the
body at the Wasdale Inn, and ridden away. That Sarah Denburn
had married David Herries was proof enough that the Herries
family knew something of the matter, but Denburn, it now
appeared, was so deeply loathed and David himself was so widely
popular, that no more questions were asked. In any case, a

murdered man or so found in the hills was no matter for much curiosity.

The only local consequence of it was that once again 'old Rogue Herries' was connected with darkness. His son had killed the father, and married the daughter (as Sarah was in the outer world supposed to be). They skipped David in their superstitions, allowing him to do as he pleased, but the Rogue had another deed to his reckoning – and, as the wives whispered over the kitchen fires, ''twould most surely not be the last'.

But for David, worried just now as perhaps he had never been in his life before, there was no superstition or rumoured chatter involved; there were facts, definite and hard.

The main fact was that the stress and odd circumstance of his father's marriage had been increased and aggravated by the arrival of his own beloved Sarah in this dark, damp and tumbledown place. If David had loved her at sight in Wasdale that love was nothing at all compared with what he felt for her now after a year and half of matrimony.

She was ideally his desire. In her freshness, common sense, cheerfulness, kindness, tenderness she combined for him all the possible virtues. She had with these one fault only, and that would be no fault in any place of her own – it was that she must be putting anything to rights that she saw wrong.

It was not that she was meddlesome, but she was young – even now, after all this matrimony, but twenty-two – and where she saw dirt, incompetence, neglect, she must alter it. Not then with any officiousness or judgement of others, but she must alter it.

What she needed, as David only too clearly saw, was a place of her own. She had done what she could to Herries. She had in a way transformed it. Swept the corners, cleaned the floors, stopped the doors from creaking, ridden pillion with David to Penrith and Kendal to buy a chair, a table, and even, miraculously, a harpsichord. She aired the beds with warming-pans, mended her father-in-law's small-clothes, taught Mrs Benjamin new dishes (and Mrs Benjamin didn't thank her for it) and, through it all, was cheerful, merry, never out of temper, always busy and, it seemed, happy. Only David knew that she was not happy.

Deborah adored her (she pining, poor dear, to be married, and crying on Sarah's shoulder over it). Herries himself liked her. He found her merry and pleasant company. He didn't care how often she whisked about the house with a broom, or told Mrs

Benjamin how to keep the kitchen clean, or scrubbed the old worm-eaten floors. He liked to hear her play on the harpsichord, and often, with her, his old humorous ironic nature would return; he would have fits of his old playfulness again, and race her about the house; and hide behind doors to jump out on her. At these times he seemed to have half his sixty years, and they, the girl of twenty-two and the man of sixty, had a wonderful comradeship. Indeed, David was bitterly reflecting, were it not for Mirabell, they might be now a happy family.

Mirabell! Mirabell! Mirabell! He repeated the name, that had always seemed to him a fantastic and stupid one, aloud. He was beginning to hate her.

He hated her (he had always definite and solemn reasons for everything) because she made (wantonly, as it seemed to him) his father so unhappy, and because she, Mirabell, hated Sarah.

Sarah did not hate Mirabell; on the contrary she liked her, was sorry for her, would have made a friend of her had it been possible. It was true that she did not understand her, but who could understand this melancholy, dreamy, unnatural woman who, although she was now thirty-one years of age, was yet a child in so many things?

His exasperation with her began before he had realized her attitude to Sarah. Why could she not give his father more of what he desired? Even though she did not love him could she not pretend it? Women were good at pretending. Even though she had once had a lover must she mourn him for ever? To watch his father's unceasing tender care of her, to feel his unresting devotion, and to discover at the end of it his unhappiness – this was exasperating enough.

But when she began to avoid Sarah, not to speak to her could she help it, to leave a room when Sarah entered it, his exasperation grew to something deeper. It seemed (David was not good at these states of mind) that Mirabell's dislike had its origin in a resentment that Sarah took to herself the management of the house. She fancied, poor silly child, that it had been her affair. On a day she burst out before them all; this was the only thing she could do, the only service she could render, and now this service had been taken from her. Why, she was mad in this! What had she ever done before Sarah came but carry plates hither and thither, rub the furniture, make the beds? She had had no talent for managing the house at all. How could she, she who had been a gipsy, a liver in caves, a companion of rogues, smugglers?

It was marvellous enough that she had the decency, the

decorous manners that she had; how could she hope to be a house-woman in the fashion of Sarah who was gentle-born?

And there was more than this. She must always fancy that Sarah was mocking her, noting her country habits, laughing at words that she used, and the rest. Sarah never mocked her; she could not do anything so unkind. It was true that Sarah felt her difference from the rest of them, but she did not show Mirabell that she felt it.

Still the hostility grew, and with that hostility the girl's unhappiness, and with that unhappiness his father's strange outbursts of rage. They were roused always in the same way, and directed always against Mirabell. He seemed to rush from serving her and loving her directly into a tempest of passion when, before them all, he would abuse her, order her out of the room, surrender to a fit of dreadful violence. Then, after a while, a sort of horror would come into his eyes, as though he had done an awful thing, he would sit silent among them, then leave them and go to her.

When he abused her like this she answered nothing, only her pale face grew paler, and she would hang her head and go. She never disobeyed him, never answered back to him, was indeed submissive to everyone. It was perhaps this very submissiveness that exasperated David, not being himself a submissive man.

Well, it could not continue. Sarah could endure little more of it. If his father would not leave Herries then he and Sarah must leave it. On the other side there was the promise made to his dead mother and made to himself that he would never leave his father.

But against this there was now the strongest reason of all: Sarah was with child. Such a scene as last night's was impossible for her in her condition. The crisis had arrived. There was a fine house, half manor, half farm, to be bought in Uldale, behind Skiddaw. Just the place for him in which to start his family. But to leave his father . . . What must he do? What must he do?

He turned at a sound and saw Sarah coming across the field to him. He was exceedingly pleased to see her. She would understand precisely the point that he had reached.

She came to him, and put her hand on his broad shoulder. She didn't speak. Clasping her with his arm he drew her closer.

'Dearest, it is cold for thee. We will go in.'

She laid her head on his shoulder.

'I am weary, Davy. Mirabell has tears in every word that she speaks, and your father does not speak at all, and there is a pool of water under the stair.'

He stayed thinking; then, looking down into her face, he said, as though he had at last reached the conclusion of long doubt: 'Yes, we must go.'

She waited, then said: 'It has been wrong here for me from the beginning. Why? I have no immoderate vanity, but I had not intended officiousness. Davy, *am* I so officious? How can I know? Deborah says not. . . In all those ill years after my mother's death what I did for my father was necessary. Anything to protect him against . . .' (She stopped. Inured to any sort of beastliness though she was, that death on the fell still haunted her.) 'But I was a child. I grew to be a woman that night you took me away. And being of a sudden a woman I must justify myself – for myself, you see, and for you whom I loved. Have I interfered too greatly in this last year? But what could I do? The discomfort, the disorder, the uncomeliness—' She caught him closer to her with her arm about his neck. 'And why should Mirabell grudge it? I would not take her place. I have not, I could not – but to stay still and watch the dirt grow. 'Tis ill enough in a morning when your father, black and half naked in his old robe stained with drink, takes his ale . . . I would not have you like that, not though you reach a hundred, but I have said nothing, all these months, not a word. But last night – that rage and Mirabell lying speechless at his feet! Oh no, Davy, it's not to be endured. 'Tis not wholesome nor natural . . .'

'It shall not be endured, dear one,' he said, kissing her. 'I have been in the wrong to persist in this. It is settled. We will go to Uldale for a time at least. I must tell my father.'

But Sarah was an understanding and tender-hearted woman. She realized something of the long history that lay, far back, between those two.

'But you cannot leave him. We must think out a plan. To be at Uldale part, and here part, or for him to come—' She broke off, wrinkling her brow. In her heart at that moment she felt that she could not endure Herries another instant! How she loathed it, with its old musty furniture, its draughts and dripping water and constant disorder and rats and owls! The thought of a good, clean house at Uldale, a house of her own and David's that their children should be born in! Away from these strange underground disturbances that she could not understand any more truly than David. That brought her to her next word:

'Davy, your father and Mirabell are in another world from you and me, from Deborah too. We see things plainly as they are, and always will. A road is a road to us, and a house a house. But

Mirabell and your father see nothing as it is. I cannot sit still like a puss in the corner to wonder which way the wind is blowing. For me, give me a fireside and you, a square screen to keep off the draught, a work-basket, and I can do well enough; but for them they see neither screen nor work-basket. But always something beyond the window that they have not, or once had or would have, or will have if they wait long enough.

'We must be doing something, they must only be thinking. Your father is sixty, and has been here these thirty years doing exactly nothing.'

'Yes,' said David, 'because facts are not sufficient for him. He could have done well with them if he would; you may call it an epidemical distemper, a madness, but he bears his condition with grand fortitude. He could not change it. He must have more than facts, and find something that will be a key for him to all existence.'

''Tis well,' said Sarah dryly, 'that he has money sufficient to keep him, even though it is your mother's, and a roof over his head, even though it is full of holes.' Then her heart reproaching her, she went on: 'Nay, I care for him greatly and would for Mirabell too if she would let me. 'Tis their unhappiness that distresses me. If I could bring them together I would never say a word for our going. But our being here separates them the more. They are of another world than ours. They are poets, maybe, and see everything fantastically. We' – she laughed, and pressing her cheek against his, very lightly bit his ear – 'we, Davy, are the farmers of this world, and are for ever taking our eggs to market.'

'And poor Deb,' he added. 'She cries her eyes out to be with *her* farmer *and* to have a child by him. 'Twill be too late an she does not hasten.'

Sarah looked back at the house, her strong broad body pulsing with health, her cheeks glowing with the cold. 'That he can remain here and love it so! What he sees here or feels! If she would but love him as he loves her, then his dream would be fulfilled, I suppose, and he understand the universe . . . As he loves her! But no two love alike. Do we love alike, Davy?'

'I love thee the more.'

'Nay, no man loves a woman the more. You love me but you love also your Liverpool trade, and the fields here, and the sheep, and a cock-fight in Keswick and chatter with the Keswick men . . . Heigh-ho! We women – a poor circumstance to be a woman and a poor end, were it not for the children,' she added more softly. 'What's a man beside a child?'

They turned to go back and saw Herries coming towards them.

When he was near he had the face of a naughty child conscious of guilt. He wore a plum-coloured coat with silver buttons, and at his side a little sword with a chased silver hilt. He had dressed up and shaven properly. Thus, his head high and with that look of a child caught out in his odd angular face, high-boned, crooked with its scar, lined, stern and gentle, scornful and friendly, thus David, knowing that the moment had come at last when he must leave him, loved him. Sarah too wanted, as she saw him come so proudly and yet so submissively, to comfort him, the thing in all the world, as she knew, that he would most resent.

'Well,' he said angrily to David. 'You will kill her of ague in this wind. Bring her in.'

He looked out over the landscape, over the scrubby, stony ground, thick with bush and tree, here cleared for cultivation, there wild again. That was what he loved, that wildness! He looked on to Rosthwaite Fell and Glaramara behind it, greeting them.

'Softly,' said David, laughing. 'Sarah has tolerable strength. She does not faint at sight like the town ladies.'

He turned to them and looked at her with his old ironic smile. He bowed to her gravely. 'Madam, my daughter-in-law, I am an old gentleman reaching dotage and beg to be excused for most unhandsome meddling.' He took her hand in his and went on most gently. 'My dear, forgive me. I forget sometimes my place. But soon you will be gone, and free; then you will look back and pardon me because you have a loving heart.'

'Be gone!' she cried. 'Why, in what condition? . . .'

He shook his head, smiling, at both of them.

'Why, you know, I'm no such fool. I lost my temper painfully last night, my dears, and now you have been saying: "Poor old man, it is too terrible," and David has said "You cannot endure it, my love," and Sarah has said "Nay, my dear, you must stay with your father," but meanwhile there is a fine property at Uldale, and there is a child coming who must have a clean place to be born in, and – there are other things.' His face was suddenly stern. He looked out to Rosthwaite Fell as though to find comfort there. 'Davy has spoken of his promise to stay by his father, and Sarah has told him that he must not break it, and both of them are thinking how a way can be found.' He put a hand on David's shoulder. 'Is it not thus?' he asked.

It had been so exactly thus that they could neither of them answer him. He nodded.

'Yes, and so the property must be bought at Uldale, and I will trot over on my nag for a glass of ale and then – most contentedly trot back again.'

It was done. There was nothing to be said. In the hearts of all three of them they knew that it was the inevitable necessity. No one had spoken of Mirabell, but she was there, the final cause.

So David rode over to Uldale and in a short while was the owner of the manor farm and the land about it.

This was a modern house that had been standing only some ten years or so, charming in spirit and colour, built for comfort rather than display. Above it ran the moor free and unfettered to the skyline, and from that moor you could see behind you the Solway Firth and the Scottish hills, before you across the valley to Skiddaw and Saddleback, and then, curving to the right, the whole range from Helvellyn through the Pike and the Gavel to Robinson and Grasmoor.

Under this glory the house nestled, catching the sun, sheltered from wind and rain.

As David looked upon it, its walls faced with red brick that was already mellowing, the sash windows of happy proportions, the roof with its strong cornice, the dormer windows, the trim garden, the farm-buildings, the little orchard, a great pride and happiness filled his heart.

He seemed to know, as though someone had whispered to him, that this was to be the home of his children and his children's children, and that he was beginning here a history that must have eventful consequences far beyond his own small consciousness.

All the world here seemed open and free. Near to Cockermouth, Keswick, Carlisle and Penrith, he was in the main world and was a man of that world. As he rode back to Herries he felt as though he were plunging into the dark bowels of the earth.

Weeks of restraint and discomfort followed. Sarah felt a desperate guilt. Mirabell seemed to show by attempting a shy, awkward friendliness that she was herself to blame, and poor Deborah, when she knew that she was to be forsaken, could not disguise her terror.

Nevertheless, in her heart, when she heard that David was going, she felt certain of her own coming freedom . . .

On the last night that they were together David and Herries sat up late by the fire. They did not speak much. David tried at last to say something.

'Father, it isn't a real parting. There'll be always a room for you and for Mirabell too. 'Tis no distance. It will be a pleasant change for you. And I will come here whenever you need me.'

Herries grinned. 'We are fastened together for life, Davy, but I don't care for having you by. That's the truth. I'm set on another plan from yours. Thou art a fine healthy lump of flesh and wilt breed children like a rabbit, fine children, I don't doubt, with no maggots in their heads. I've always had a maggot and it's made me lonely. By desire, mind you. I prefer it. I love you against my will, Davy, for you are everything that I would not be. To make money, build a house, have land, breed children, honour the King, pay your taxes, leave your mark on the country though it may be but the impression of your bottom on your counting-house chair, I can see 'tis an ambition as good as another. Myself I've stuck in the mud here for thirty years, been given a contemptible name, done nothing whatever save see the house drop over my head, married a wench from the road who doesn't love me, although she'd wish to, poor lass, out of a churchy kind of gratitude. . . 'Tis as useless a life as a man can find and as pitiful, but I've had moments, Davy, that you will never know, and 'tis by the height of your divining moments that life must be judged. I love this woman that I have got here as you and Sarah will never love, in the entrails, Davy, down among the guts, my boy. And I'll have her yet, struggle as she may, and when I have her I'll know what the stars are for and why the moon's a silver treachery and what God has in His anointed beard . . . And they'll not drag me from this house till the rats are gnawing at my toes and there's lice in my ears. For this is my home, this spot, this ground, this miry waste, and here I'll die – and the third day I'll rise again. I love thee, Davy, but thou art the damnedest fool of a good fellow that was ever made between sheets. So goodnight to thee, my little son.'

After which he yawned loudly, stretched his arms, scratched his thigh and stamped up to his bed.

After this it was Deborah's tragedy. Poor Deb, a woman now of thirty-seven, an age at this time when, still unmarried, you were an old maid and as good as buried. She looked her age too, for she was broad and massive-bosomed, with sturdy arms and haunches, and a wide good-natured double-chinned face. She looked well in a mob cap, aproned and in pattens.

Nevertheless her little clergyman loved with a devoted unfaltering patience. He did not mind how broad she grew – he was no slim beauty himself. He would wait for ever if need be. He told her so again and again in his letters which were filled with love and little snatches of news and pieces about his health and his food.

'Little Love –' (he always addressed her thus, nor saw any humour in it) 'I had a fine visit yesterday to Sir Whickham Partridge's seat at Highloft. The gardens are very fine, of uneven ground diversified with valleys and hills. There is also a monstrous fine dairy with churns of butter, prints and skimming dishes all of the handsomest kind. We had fine weather and a most pleasant journey... I have had three Baptisms in the last four days, but one infant hath died of the croup since and is now safe in the arms of Christ Jesus, which is all the better for the family in that there are nine of them already and the man, a good honest fellow, making little at his business – he is a cordwainer... Little Love, you say nothing in your last letter about our marriage, for which I pray night and morning. I wait on your circumstances, which are, I know, uneasy of settlement. But my sister is ready to receive you here whenever the proper time comes.'

Or again:

'I rejoice at the good account you give of your health, Little Love. You have so cheerful and happy a disposition that you are able to endure the discomforts of your watery valley... The bed in the guest-chamber has gone weak in one leg, and my sister Mary slept there the last two nights and found it unevenly balanced in the morning... Thou knowest how dearly I love thee, Little Love, and wait only thy signal for all to be in readiness here...'

Yes, he could wait for ever, but she could not. Four years gone and nothing done. Four years gone and not a word said to her father. Whether he guessed or no she could not say. He was a strangely perceptive man and, when he wished, a strangely silent one.

After Mirabell came, for a while Deborah conquered her fear of him. He was softer, gentler, and seemed himself to care for her more openly. Then she might have spoken to him about her little clergyman. She had no reason to suppose that he would be angry. Why should he be? He had never shown any dislike of her marrying, or that he wanted to keep her with him for ever. But he would laugh. He would look at her in that terrible ironical way and, with a word or two, drive her into the very centre of the shyest reserve.

But what of that? He cared for her in his own fashion. He would not be unkind to her, he would even give her his own sort of ironic blessing. But here the accumulated effect of her years with him, of her old frights and old loneliness, her sense of his strangeness, above all, her terror of some sudden outburst of rage, held her back. Again and again she would tell him; again and again she postponed the occasion.

Then after David brought home Sarah it seemed certain that she would go. There was no need for her now that Sarah was here, but then, as the new situation developed so uncomfortably for them all, as Mirabell retired unhappily more and more into herself, Deborah stayed because she seemed to be the only link between Mirabell and Sarah. They liked her, both of them, although Mirabell said very little. But she, out of her own reserves and deep shynesses and perception of tiny things, understood Mirabell's wild, unhappy heart better than any of them, and Mirabell knew it.

But, when Sarah and David departed, her mind was made up. She would wait no longer. Stay in this house alone with the two of them she could not. They did not need her. She could do nothing for them; it was between Mirabell and Sarah that she had been able to help, never between Mirabell and her father.

Another thing also drove her to her decision – the knowledge that Sarah was going to have a child. That was the one ever-present, ever-dominant idea, the children that she would have.

She thought of it, dreamt of it, whispered the names that she would give them (to herself). But she was thirty-seven; soon it might be too late.

So a week after David and Sarah had gone she wrote a little letter:

MY DEAR LOVE – I can wait no longer nor suffer you to wait neither. On Tuesday next I shall be in Keswick at four of the clock standing at the corner by the Assembly Rooms. – Shortly to be your True and Loving Wife,
DEBORAH HERRIES.

I have not told my Father and shall bring only a small Basket fearing to upset him with my News.

When the letter was dispatched by the carrier, her happiness flooded over her in a radiant shower. Why had she not done this before? She could not tell. A spell seemed to be broken. Surely then it would be easy to tell her father. 'Father, dear, next Tuesday I am going to Cockermouth to be wed with a clergyman.' But she could not say it even now. She knew how he would take it.

'Wed with a clergyman? Bedded with a parson?' and then his eyes, loving her but despising her too, then his shrug of the shoulder as he went out to his digging, or his tramp over the fells, or his riding to some distant valley. She also said nothing to Mirabell lest she should afterwards be charged with deceitfully keeping a secret. But on the last evening she went over to her and kissed her.

'Dear Mirabell, remember I am for ever your friend.'

The girl (for she seemed still a child with her slender body, little breasts, small rounded head) looked at her from under her pile of fiery hair and said, smiling:

'Why, Deborah, are you going on a journey?'

'Maybe,' whispered Deborah, nodding her head. Mirabell suddenly clung to her, resting her little head between Deborah's big breasts.

'Come back again one day. And if you travel think of me who would like to travel too.'

'Aye,' Deborah said, 'I will come back.' They kissed then, very lovingly.

When she kissed her father goodnight that evening he was abstracted, reading a play of Shakespeare's, *Antony and Cleopatra,* and calling it nonsense one minute and miraculous marvel the next, so he nodded goodnight, scarcely seeing her.

Next morning she rode into Keswick on Appleseed. Herries was out in the fields, cutting scrub away, and did not see her go. She left on the dining-table a letter:

DEAR FATHER – I have gone to Cockermouth to be wed to a clergyman, Mr Gordon Sunwood. I have known him these four years but did not tell you, not to weary you with it. He is a Good Man, I am sure. I shall write to you at Cockermouth and then we will come to visit you if you wish us. – Your loving Daughter,

DEBORAH.

Herries did not return until evening. He saw the note on the table and read it. He read it again and then again. He smiled, then he laughed, then he threw back his head, roaring.

Then he called loudly for Mirabell. When she came he shouted:

'We are alone. We are alone. We are alone!'

He strode to her, caught her up, held her high, then kissed her over and over. His old wild joy of his wedding day seemed to have returned.

'Poor Deb! She is wed to a parson, to a stummicky, bottomy, garlic-smelling parson. I love my daughters, I cherish them, I give them all I have, but now they are gone and I have done my duty, my duty, my full and fitting duty. They are gone and we are alone, my Sweet, my beloved, my darling wife . . . You and I, and there is no one to care for you but I, and no one to watch when we kiss nor when we quarrel . . . I love my Deborah, but I like her better away sitting on the fat knees of her rummidgy parson, breeding young parsons to fill the pulpits with their precious tidings . . .' He set her down on a chair, knelt before her, his head bent into her lap. 'Mirabell, there is no one in the whole green world but ourselves.'

When at last he was quiet she said anxiously: 'Is Deborah gone then?'

'Aye, Deborah is gone to wed with a parson.'

'Ah, that was what she meant when she kissed me last evening.' She shivered a little, but he could not see her; then, straightening her thin body against the chair, she said:

'And now if there is no one else you must be served by me.'

'Nay, nay,' he said. 'I shall be server, and you shall be the queen, for you are my love whom I adore. And shall ever adore through this death and the next after it and after that, to eternity again.'

But she, as though she had not heard him, and were following her own thought said: 'The Trumpeters coming through the valley . . . I know that they must come.'

That evening he would not allow her to do anything, made her sit in the high chair at the end of the table, served her with food and drink, and at last when he had his own, sat on a stool at her feet. 'Deborah is a good woman,' he said once, 'and will make her parson happy,' and that was the only allusion he gave her.

Mirabell seemed to feel his happiness and respond to it. They sat together by the fire and she told him of her adventures with her uncles, and times that she could remember in London, and she let him hold her hand and stroke it, and when he kissed her she returned his kiss.

He rose and went upstairs and came again with a small cedar-wood box. He poured the contents on to her lap. They lay glittering there. There was a gold Moco stone chain set in gold, a necklace with pearls and vermilions, a gold watch, a rumphlet of diamonds set in silver and gilt, a large rose diamond set in silver and fastened to a bodkin, a gold ring with seven diamonds in the form of a rose, and a diamond cross.

She cried out at sight of them, a child now in her pleasure. He told her that they had been his mother's and that he had kept them for a fitting time to give them to her. He did not tell her that he had been storing them for the day when at last she would, freely, of herself, tell him that she loved him. She had not yet told him, but now that they were alone again, with everyone out of the way, soon, soon she would tell him.

He knelt before her and hung them all on her until she glittered and glistened in the firelight, all the stones winking and shining under the flame of her hair. Her fingers were loaded with them, and her neck and bosom, and she wore the diamond cross in her hair.

Then, very friendly together, they sat at the table while he gave her her writing lesson. At this, and at reading, she was very slow and stupid. It seemed that she *could* not learn. But tonight she was docile, and did her utmost to please him, sitting there in her old gown and covered with jewels.

She went to sleep quietly that night in his arms. He slept also. Later he woke to find that in her sleep she had got out from him, and was standing at the window in her nightdress, beating at the panes and crying:

'Harry, Harry! Take me out! I can't get out! Harry, Harry, I can't get out!'

He could hear her sobbing. He lay very still. Later she came into bed again, and he stayed very quietly, longing to touch her and to comfort her, but doing nothing. So he lay for many hours beside her in great trouble.

THE LOVER

HERRIES and Mirabell were alone in the house.

Except for Benjamin and his slatternly greedy wife there was no human being near them. Herries watched Mirabell as a cat watches a bird, and he watched out of love and terror lest at any moment she should escape.

Now most truly he was paying for all the infidelities of his long life. He knew in the depths of the bitterest truth what the anguish of unrequited love was. He was sixty-two years of age and had never yet known such burning desire of the flesh, burning because it was eternally unsatisfied. Night after night he might lie with Mirabell and do with her what he would, and night after night, when she slept, he would get up from bed and walk the house like a frantic ghost because she did not love him.

But this agony bit far deeper than any unsatisfied desire of the flesh could do. He was ready to surrender any physical connexion for ever and ever if only she would love him a very little, and she was ready to give him everything she had out of kindness.

And so they came terribly to fear one another. She was afraid of his rages, his silences, his miseries and his absences. She was so fond of him that when he was away she longed for him to return so that she might be kind to him, and then, when he was there, she longed for him to be away again because she found that she could not give him the love that he desired.

Although she was now thirty-three years of age she was still very much of a child, and she was hoping that suddenly one morning she would find that she loved him. She was so fond of him that she could not understand why that fondness was not love. But it was not. Her heart never beat the harder when he was coming. Her face never flushed when he looked at her with passionate desire; at such times there was terror in her heart and she would wonder whether this night perhaps she would find that she could not surrender her body to him any more, and must tell him so.

That would be fearful, that night when it came. They both trembled at the idea of it. She thought that perhaps after she had shuddered apart from him, he would get up and go out and kill himself. She knew that he was aware of her reluctance, and that he loathed himself for pressing her. Sometimes when he had not, but had only kissed her and turned over to sleep, she almost loved him, put her hand up to caress his cheek and then put it down again lest he should take it as a sign that at last she really loved him.

But, although she guessed so much, she did not guess the half of his real torture; how before every step that he took towards her he hesitated lest she should make some movement, exclamation, sign that showed how she shrank from him.

She was troubled, too, by an increasing stifling sense of imprisonment. It was not only that now he watched her every step. It was also the personality of the house that she had always hated from the first. It watched her even as its master did. There were things in it that were spies, she was sure: the portrait of the old Herries in the dining-hall, the two suits of armour, the drunken tumbling chimneys. She could hear the suits of armour clanking after her at night, and she would stay in her room, the door ajar, listening to them as they whispered about her.

She hated it that always there was the same view from the windows and the yard. All her life long she had wandered, and now, wherever she looked, she must always see those two horrid hills, Rosthwaite Fell and Chapel Fell. The very hills that were Herries's passion were her loathing, and she hated most of all the way that he would talk about them as though they were persons and his very dear friends. They *were* persons and her very dear enemies.

But worst of all for her – and this thing, as the months passed, became an obsession – was her consciousness of all the little stone walls running up the sides of the hills. All her life long these stone walls had been the dearest things in the world to her. When she was an infant and could not walk, they would put her, wrapped in a shawl, under one of these walls out of the wind. As she stayed there, she could see the wall running, like a live thing, first across the turf straight like a taut string, then suddenly turning and leaping upwards until it was lost at the high bend of the hill. Over all this landscape she saw these little walls running, gay, free, vigorous, and when she walked – the wind blowing her hair – pressing up the side of the hill, the wall went with her, keeping her company. Now she was tied to this house. From the back of the yard she fancied that she could see a thin black line on Rosthwaite Fell; this was the wall and it would run to the ridge, then straight with only the sky over it, then it would dip again, catching its breath in the little valley before it mounted up again. Tears would fill her eyes as she gazed, and an impatience that made her heart beat angrily.

'He is kind to me, he loves me, but what would it hurt him if I were gone a week? I would return.' But would she? She could not honestly answer that. She was honest above all else. With all her faults of childishness, temper, rebellion, ignorant boasting, she was immaculately honest. It was because she knew that if she once went away she might never return that she never begged him that he might let her go.

Another thing her honesty showed her to her great distress and pain. She was beginning to forget Harry. This was the cruellest thing of all, because she had nothing with which to replace him. In all her bitterest distress at the agony of having lost him, there was a kind of bitter happiness because her love for him, although he was gone, was so wonderful. A thousand times a day she would recall everything that he had said and done, how he had looked here, how he had smiled there, what his eyes had done when he told her that he loved her. They had not had so very long a time together, so that the collection of her memories must be conned over and over. But the years had passed, and the conning had become almost mechanical; her honesty drove her to discover this and then drove her further, to realize that days and even weeks went by and she did not think of him at all.

She was indeed a strange mixture of childishness and maturity, of anger and submission, of knowledge and ignorance. Her best parts were her kindliness and honesty and a kind of instinctive poetry she had, and her industry. She always wanted to be at work on something, but unfortunately she had no gift for housework or keeping a place clean, or remembering what she must do. Untidiness seemed to follow her; things were broken, forgotten, disordered wherever she was. Nor would she learn. Her stubbornness was terrible. In these two years, Herries had taught her neither to read nor write. She would begin a lesson with him in all docility. He, for so restless and scornful a man, was marvellously patient with her. The lessons would start, both of them in great amiability, then her stupidity would irritate him, she see that he was checking it, and so she would burst into tears and run to her room.

What she liked best was when they sat in front of the fire, she on a cushion at his feet resting her head on his knees and he telling her stories. Then there was a great peace between them; he would forget his passion for her and be only her friend, and she would feel so kindly to him that she thought that in another moment she would love him.

They mingled strangely little with the outside world. Deborah lived, serenely happy, with her little clergyman in Cockermouth. She had only one grief – that as yet she had no children and soon she would be too old. But a Wise Woman had told her that she would have two sons, and Wise Women knew. David rode over often from Uldale although he was so busy a man. He was always urging his father and Mirabell to go and visit them, and Deborah too sent pressing invitations. But Mirabell would not go any more. She was frightened of Sarah, so efficient, businesslike, normal and happy. She thought that Sarah despised her, and so in her heart perhaps Sarah did.

But no. Sarah was of too generous a nature to despise her. She could not understand her. Mirabell with her odd looks, baby face, bright-coloured untidy clothes, sudden silence, odd sayings, was incredible to her. She did not understand her at all, and remembered that she was only a gipsy. Sarah was not a snob, but it was a time when the middle classes thought of the peasants as of another world from themselves, like dogs or cats or horses. Then Mirabell could not bear to see the neatness and grandeur of Uldale. It was not really very grand, but it seemed so to Mirabell with its solid walls and fine fires and trim garden, clocks and pictures and comfortable beds. There the rain did not drip through the roof, nor were the meals thrown anyhow on to the table, nor did the beds stay unmade all the day long. After a day's visit to Uldale she came back to Herries resolved to set everything into marvellous order. The next morning she was up in the dark busy and eager. But nothing would go her way; after she had swept, the dust was still there, the mud seemed to walk of itself into the house and lie about the stairs, the mice would come on to the table and nibble at the bread. And Herries did not care; he did not mind in what disorder he was living. He would curse Benjamin and his wife in a splendid rage, and then forget it all again. He was always dreaming, of the weather, the country, the clouds, the running water, and of herself.

So, this winter of 1762, things went from bad to worse.

A week before Christmas there was a great frost. A frost that holds is, in this district, rare; but round Christmas there is much cold spicy weather, the air nutmeg-scented, the waters running down all the hills with a tinkle of ice in their chuckles, the trees are red, amber to rose, and the sky grey, dove-winged, often very clear and shot with stars.

Mirabell was having a reading lesson in a house as still as the dead. A great fire leapt in the stone fireplace and the light of it clambered about her jewels and her orange-coloured dress. She

had a silver shawl over her hair to see what it looked like, and
when she should have attended to her lesson she was moving her
head against the old round cracked mirror that hung by the window to see how it shone. It was not vanity that moved her, but
childishness and restlessness; this last because out in that grey
frost-held world she knew that the little walls were running up
the iron-clad hills to the grey snow-gathering sky. On such a late
winter's afternoon she would be running ahead of her uncles over
the turf, through the keen icy wind, to reach the edge of the Tarn.
Here the water would lie black under a thin crinkle of silver ice,
and the first cold stars would come out, and perhaps the slip of a
frozen moon . . .

Herries, his patience constrained with difficulty, was reading
out of Swift's *Polite Conversation*. He chose this work because the
English was good and the words were mostly of one syllable. Also
it entertained Mirabell because of the pictures of, as it seemed to
her, ridiculous polite society.

It was Herries's plan to read a piece very slowly and with great
patience. Then Mirabell was to read it after him. This did not
please her. She liked him to read straight on. What did it matter
whether she herself should learn to read or no? He was always
there to read to her.

Herries read:

'MISS. Lord, Mr Neverout, you are as pert as a Pear monger this morning.

NEVEROUT. Indeed, Miss, you are very handsome.

MISS. Poh, I know that already; tell me news.

(*Somebody knocks at the Door. Footman comes in.*)

FOOTMAN (*to Col.*). An please your Honour, there's a Man
below wants to speak to you.

COL. Ladies, your pardon for a Minute.

(*Col goes out.*)

LADY SMART. Miss, I sent yesterday to know how you
did, but you were gone abroad early.

MISS. Why, indeed, Madam, I was hunched up in a Hackney Coach with Three County Acquaintance, who called upon
me to take the Air as far as Highgate.

LADY SMART. And had you a pleasant Airing?

MISS. No, Madam; it rained all the Time; I was jolted to
Death, and the Road was so bad, that I screamed every Moment and called to the Coachman, "Pray, Friend, don't spill
us."'

Herries paused. Mirabell was seated beside him, her head screwed round to the mirror.

'You don't attend,' he said sharply.

She looked back quickly to the book like a frightened child. 'I do indeed,' she said hurriedly. 'What a childish Miss, to scream every moment because the coach jolted her! I could make her scream if I had her here.'

'Come,' said Herries sternly. 'Now you shall read.' He did not wish to be stern. His hand was very near her flaming hair that was now ungathered and fell about her shoulders under the silver shawl and over the orange satin gown. It needed all his strength not to stroke it. His hand would move up and then down again while his heart thumped beneath his waistcoat. He must not touch her. All hope in an ordered lesson would be over if he did. She would sit on the floor in front of the fire and demand a story – a woman, thirty-three years of age. At least she did not look a day more than twenty. So, to check himself, he was stern.

'Cease glancing at that mirror,' he said, 'and read this for me.'

She began, very slowly:

'MISS. Lord! Mr Nev-er-out, you are as p e r t as a Pea—'

She stopped.

'What is this long word?'

'Pear,' he answered.

'Pear.'

'Monger.'

She looked at it and shook her head. 'I have never seen such a word before.'

'No, doubtless. But how will you ever learn to read if you see only the same words every time?'

'Why should I learn to read?' she asked. 'Why do you force me? There are many ladies can't read. Besides I am not a lady, and will never be one. There are other things I can do, but not this.'

'You are thirty-three years of age.'

She jumped up.

'And older, older, older! I'm just as young as I was when I was five. I knew everything then and nothing. It is the same now.'

It was true. As he looked at her he saw her both as woman and child and loved her as both.

'Yes, that is true,' he said sadly. 'I am neither old enough nor young enough for you.'

'Oh, don't let us talk of ourselves!' She turned away to the mirror again. Then she softened, coming back with a smile. 'Oh, Francis, take me as I am! I cannot change with your wishing it nor you with mine. We must make what we can with what we've got.' Then she threw the silver shawl on to the table.

'I will go and do some sweeping,' she said. She was interrupted by a noise at the door. It was Benjamin, who said that there were some children there to sing carols. Then there was a strange light in Herries's eye, a curious smile at his scarred mouth. It was many years that the children had not come near his house to sing carols. Proudly he had always said that he did not care whether they came or no. But he did care. It seemed like a good omen that they should come to his old house at last.

So he ordered Benjamin to have them up, and soon in they trooped, some seven or eight boys and a short stout man in a red coat and with a double chin and a big belly.

They stood all together over by the fire, close, as though they were a little frightened. They had doubtless heard things about the house and its owner. But the sight of Mirabell reassured them. She was enchanted with them. She loved children, being a child herself, and now she clapped her hands, and went and stroked their cheeks and asked them their names, speaking in broad Cumberland just as they did.

Then she stood near Herries: his arm was about her, and so they listened to the music. All their years afterwards they remembered this scene and especially one carol. The stout fellow had a little viola on which he played very sweetly. The boys, at a sign from him, all lifted up their heads together like young birds and began to sing.

They sang 'The Three Kings' and 'The Cherry Tree' and others, but it was this one, 'The Angel Gabriel', that Mirabell never afterwards forgot. The simple sweet tune greatly touched her, and later she learnt the words and remembered them, she who could never get anything that Francis taught her by heart. It was, she would afterwards think, the last scene of her childhood – yes, her childhood, although now she was thirty-three, and the background had always exquisite beauty in her memory – the grey frosted world outside hard like iron, and inside the room everything melting in the coloured firelight, the flickering ceiling, the crimson logs, the faces of the children, and Herries himself, grave and kind and generous-hearted, as she liked best to see him.

So the children sang 'The Angel Gabriel':

> The Angel Gabriel from God
> Was sent to Galilee,
> Unto a Virgin fair and free
> Whose name was called Mary:
> And when the Angel thither came,
> He fell down on his knee,
> And looking up in the Virgin's face,
> He said 'All Hail, Mary!'
>
> Then sing we all both great and small,
>   Noël, Noël, Noël;
> We may rejoice to hear the voice
>   Of the Angel Gabriel.
>
> Mary anon looked him upon,
> And said, 'Sir, what are ye?
> I marvel much at these tidings
> Which thou hast brought to me.
> Married I am unto an old man
> As the lot fell unto me;
> Therefore, I pray, depart away,
> For I stand in doubt of thee.'
>
> Then sing we all, both great and small,
>   Noël, Noël, Noël;
> We may rejoice to hear the voice
>   Of the Angel Gabriel.
>
> 'Mary,' he said, 'be not afraid,
> But do believe in me.
> The power of the Holy Ghost
> Shall overshadow thee;
> Thou shalt conceive without any grief,
> As the Lord told unto me;
> God's own dear Son from Heaven shall come,
> And shall be born of thee.'
>
> Then sing we all, both great and small,
>   Noël, Noël, Noël;
> We may rejoice to hear the voice
>   Of the Angel Gabriel.

This came to pass as God's will was,
Even as the Angel told.
About midnight an Angel bright
Came to the Shepherds' fold,
And told them then both where and when
Born was the child, our Lord,
And all along this was their song,
'All glory be given to God.'

Then sing we all, both great and small,
    Noël, Noël, Noël;
We may rejoice to hear the voice
    Of the Angel Gabriel.

Good people all, both great and small,
The which do hear my voice,
With one accord let's praise the Lord,
And in our hearts rejoice;
Like sister and brother, let's love one another,
Whilst we our lives do spend,
Whilst we have space let's pray for grace,
And so let my Carol end.

Then sing we all, both great and small,
    Noël, Noël, Noël;
We may rejoice to hear the voice
    Of the Angel Gabriel.

When they had ended Herries could not do enough for them.
That strange mood of excited gaiety that sometimes swept over
him was on him now. He sent old Benjamin to the kitchen for
cakes and sweetmeats; he would stuff the children till they were
sick. He took the smallest, who would not be older than six or
seven, on to his knee, and a great softness of feeling pervaded
him when he saw that the child did not shrink but played with
his heavy gold chain and told him his name, Richard Watson.
Was the legend finished then? Was he no longer Ogre or Rogue?
Oh, this was surely a good omen for him, and now everything
would be right with Mirabell too. Before they were in bed she
would tell him that at last she loved him . . .

The boys had lost all their shyness, and were moving about the
room, filling their mouths with cake, and examining everything.
He gave the fat man richly from his purse, and clapped him on

the shoulder. He carried little Richard on his shoulder down the stairs when they were all going. He saw them from the door with their lighted lanterns go across the frosty court. He saluted the myriads of stars so bright above the black line of the hills with a wave of his arm before he came back into the house.

He stood in the doorway of the room smiling at her, and she smiled back at him. She was sitting at the fire humming to herself the 'Angel Gabriel' tune.

> 'Like sister and brother, let's love one another,
> Whilst we our lives do spend.'

He went to her at once, made her sit on a cushion at his feet, and, following on the triumphant current of his mood, drawing her head back against his knee, burst into a wild flow of talk:

'It is the first time all these winters that the children have been here. They've gone to every house but this one. Why should I care whether they have come or no? But I have cared, and now that you are here I have wanted everyone to be friendly. Yes, for the first time in my life I've wanted friendship . . .'

He drew her closer to him, and she felt his hands hot and trembling against her cheek.

'Don't be angry with me. Don't turn me away. You must shrink because my hands are old, old and dry, but there's no age in my heart. I *was* old when I came here first, proud and young. I thought I could do just what I liked then – with anyone or anything. But I've learnt wisdom. Time has taught me. I haven't done what I liked with anything. Even the soil – I haven't even a fine potato out of it. And the trees have all gone crookedly against me, and the wind has blown the hills sideways. But I toiled on, because I knew that there was an answer somewhere to my question if I refused to be beat.

'What's my question been? I don't know myself. That's the odd thing. I don't know either the question or the answer. I puzzle my head sometimes till it breaks. Yes, breaks. Splits like a fig. Then I think the answer will be in there. It must be. That's the thing that spins round and round and asks all the questions. But if it has the questions then it must have the answers too. These questions. Why is the sky grey today, my dear, and being grey, with a touch of rose to it, why does my heart thump? Why cannot I leave this place, this tumbled heap of stones, but must hang on always staring at a humped hill and a pocketful of rank grass? Yes, split your brain and dig in the mess with your fingers for the answer.

'Nay, it's not in the brain but in the wind behind the brain and the soft sly voice behind the wind. Ah, that voice! I tell you, Mirabell, there are times when I've almost heard it. I've stood on Honister, where I found you, my darling; I've stood there listening, and He's been almost in my hand. A sly dog, conceited of His power, with all the beauty that He's got and all the strength to frighten us. And at the last, maybe lazily, out of idleness, He drops a present into our lap, a golden rose, a string of glass beads.

'I say damnation to His power. I care not a rabbit for it, but 'tis the mystery plagues me, Mirabell, the oddity, grotesque like a map of China, bits here and there, offal and star-dust together. That's why I stare and stare, looking at a hill or a tree or a lump of this rotten soil, for the secret may be in any place, and by a hair's-breadth of laziness we may have missed it.

'The Herries have always been like that, one mystery-monger and the rest good sober citizens. David's the sober sort. There have to be both in the world. But David finds nothing odd. It is all as it should be. But for me, until I found you, there's been no answer.

'Now, if you loved me, there'd be an answer to every question. I am your lover, Mirabell. I'm not an old man past sixty, but young and strong, always your lover. Can you love me a little, Mirabell? I have been patient all this time with you here. Is it coming to you a little? I am so hungry for it. I think I must not be without it much longer. Mirabell, Mirabell. Love me a little, a very little . . . I want you so.'

His voice ended in an almost breathless whisper and she held herself taut so that he should not feel the shiver that was running through her body.

At first while he talked she had been hypnotized by his voice, but had not listened to his words. It was comfortable here by the fire; she liked him when he was kind and friendly. She always loved his voice when he was telling her a story or talking about his ideas. She found his ideas incomprehensible. She did not understand one of them. The things that he said were completely unreal to her. This mystery that there was in life, she could not see any of it. Her own life was clear enough. She had been beaten and ill-treated and must fight for herself, then she had loved a man, as many a poor girl had done before her, and he had been murdered most foully, and after that this man had been kind to her and given her a home. She could not love him; that was not

her fault; she was generous, she would give him anything, but
that was something that you could not give unless it happened so.
There was no mystery here.

He was always talking of staring at stones and trees. When he
came to this her mind slipped away and she would think of other
things - of the little walls running away under the frosty air, of
old Mrs Benjamin who was a slattern, of Sarah's fine household
gifts (odd how often she thought of Sarah!), and tonight of those
children singing their carols. How fresh their voices had been,
how fresh and how sweet!

But when he came to his love-making, fear snatched her back
to attention. Oh, how she hated it, that now so familiar change
from friendliness to love! She was like an animal caught, all her
senses alert for any chance of escape.

Everything was changed. The tone of his voice, the touch of
his hand; she could feel all his body trembling behind his fingers.
Not a simple lustful desire to possess her - that she could have
understood and to that she would have submitted - but this
thing, far more deadly, this praying, pleading passion that she
should love him. How could she when she did not? Oh, how
could she? ... There was danger here, dreadful danger both to
herself and to him. Yes, she held herself taut lest that inner revulsion should escape her and rouse his fury. It was, she understood,
fury and rage and disgust with himself rather than with her, but
that did not make it less awful.

'I love you, Mirabell, dear, dear Mirabell . . . Give me a little
in return . . . Love me ever so little.'

Stiff against him, her head up, staring into the fire, she
answered:

'We are so happy thus, Francis. Let us stay tranquilly . . .'

'Tranquil!' He caught her closer. 'A fine word to use, but I
have never been tranquil. I have not been worthy of any tranquillity.'

She understood that. This man was in reality the shyest and
most modest she had ever known. She did not comprehend men
who were fighters with themselves. Every man in her life had
taken himself for what he was and thought no more about it. But
this man was different. She did dimly perceive that everything
in his history - rebellion, outrage, ostracism, irony, sense of
beauty - had come from his own restless dissatisfaction, and that
if she saw his soul naked it would be a soul on its knees. But she
did not want to see his soul bare. Any close terms with him meant
violence and the demand for something that she hadn't to give.

Moreover on an occasion like this her fear was so great that such
wits as she had were away.

'Let us read again,' she said, trying to smile at him. 'I will be
cleverer this time.'

He put his hand to her neck and held her head up to him.

'Understand this. I am out of breath now. I can endure no
more. You must love me. You can if you will. You have love in
you. You could give it to that other man. And have I not done
more for you than he could ever do, more in every way? Has a
man ever loved you as I love you? I want nothing . . . Love me
and I will never ask you a favour. Love me and I will sleep in
another bed. Love me and I will work for you like a dog. We shall
leave this place that has always fretted you. We shall go where
you will and I will never even kiss your hand. I will not touch
you, Mirabell, if you can love me a little. My heart is starved . . .
after these years . . . I have no more power to resist.'

He was at her feet, kneeling. All his pride was gone, all his
power over himself. His scarred face lifted to hers, if she had
been able to see it, was beautiful.

But she could not see it; she was so frightened that she could
see nothing. This was the worst that he had ever been. With a
little cry she tried to rise. He caught at her dress. He held her
round her knees.

'Say that you love me even though you do not. I will cheat
myself.'

But she could not. Her lips moved but no words came. He
caught her, pressing his face to her bosom. Then he felt her
tremble. That flung him into madness. He had been always
afraid of this and had been on his guard. Now he guarded himself no longer.

'I will beat you into it. Can you stand outside me and I not
compel you to come in? Have I waited so long for naught? Have
I no strength?' He caught her and strained her to him. He covered her face, half averted, with kisses. He dragged her head back
by the hair and kissed her neck, tore her gown open, burying his
face in her breasts, murmuring: 'An you will not come to me, I'll
make you . . . I shall conquer your stubbornness, do you see? You
are inside me, at my heart . . . shall never escape . . . I carry you
with me.'

Her fear was so frantic that she managed to break away from
him and crying out: 'Oh, never, never any more!' ran, half
naked, across the floor and up the wooden stairs. She heard him
stumbling after her, crossed the dark passage, found her room,

bolted the door with its wooden bolt and then crouched against the wall, listening. She thought that he meant to kill her, but it was not the fear of death that frightened her, but something far deeper, a mingled terror and sorrow for him was part of it.

He came to the door and battered on it, shouting: 'Come out, then ... I will end it for us both ... Come out that I may finish it.'

He paused, and the silence in the house was terrible; not only in the house but in all the frost-bound, star-shadowed world outside. There was moonlight in her room, splashed against the wall. Her eyes devoured the door.

He battered again, then flung all his weight. The whole house rang to his blows, the door that was very old cracked. He kicked and it fell.

From the doorway he saw her crouched against the wall. He waited, his breast heaving.

She did not speak, she could not. So they stared at one another.

His madness left him. The moonlight seemed to lap it up. He knew that he had done something for which he would never forgive himself.

He turned and with hanging head went away.

MIRABELL IN FLIGHT

THERE is a work of particular interest to members of the Herries family – *Letters in England, 1757–1805* – edited by Dorothea Leyland (Satters and Bonnin, 1876).

This is a book worthy of more general reading. Miss Leyland tells us how, after the purchase by her father of Rockington Hall in Shropshire (the home of the Durward Herries from 1830 to 1854), she discovered in an old oak chest a red leather box stuffed with old letters. They were hard to decipher, yellow and torn, but after some difficulty and the exercise of much patience they were all transcribed.

They included letters preserved and formed into little packets neatly tied with red ribbon by that solemn and serious Mary Titchley, wife of Grandison Herries and mother of the gay Pelham; of all of whom we have already caught glimpses.

They were not of necessity letters written entirely to or by members of the Titchley and Herries families, although these formed the larger portion of them. This, one may suppose, was why Miss Leyland decided against giving the collection a family name. The volume excited very much less attention than it deserved. There was not at the time of its publication the interest in eighteenth-century minutiae that there is today. It has been long out of print. In any detailed chronicle of the Herries family during the years included by it, it must be of great value.

There is one letter – dated April 4th, 1763 – which is pertinent here. It is written to Pelham Herries (at this time a bachelor of forty-five years of age living in King Street, St James's) by his cousin Frances Titchley, a single lady of middle years who was at the time making a tour of Scotland and the North of England with her brother Reginald and his wife.

After certain details that do not here concern us (the full letter can be found on page 331, in the volume above referred to) it proceeds as follows:

. . . I was about to close my letter without communicating to you my most interesting Adventure, most interesting at least to Yourself who, if you will remember, begged me to ascertain any News of your Cousin whether in Keswick or the Barbarous Wilds of Borrowdale.

In my own solitary Person I had not the courage to invade the Fortress of dear Raiseley and dearer Mary. You know how they are thought of by the Family as a Pair of Unconscionable Ogres from whose Hospitality no Cakes and Ale are to be hoped for, but only the Chilly Fingers of Uneasy and Insincere Politeness. In short, dear Pelham, neither Reginald nor Coelia would accompany me on a Call and I would not go alone, so although we were three whole days in Keswick and expecting momentarily the most Inconvenient of Meetings we escaped without a sight of them.

Blame me if you will, dearest Pelham, but remember that you have not yourself been over Punctilious in your Obedience to Inexorable Duty.

You know that I can always see more faults in my own Performances than I love to think on, but at least You shall not be entirely Disappointed in me; I have something yet to offer you.

You know that Reginald has, from his Cradle, a love of the Horrible and that no Terror is so Great but that he must tickle his Palate with it. We have seen, as I have told you in my other letters, Sights of Superb Splendour and the Grandest Magnificence in Scotland. For my part I felt that I had seen enough

and even my Love for You was not Spur sufficient to drive me
into the (so rightly named) Jaws of Borrowdale to catch maybe a
glance of the ferocious Herries who inhabits there. But you
know how 'tis the nature of the Common People to hate all
Novelties and the nature of Reginald to be drawn by them, so
when the Boots at the Keswick Hotel assured us that there was
Nothing in Borrowdale to be seen but Horrid Crags and Violent Waterfalls this decided Reginald immediately. He was
ready indeed to go alone, and Coelia, when she heard that the
only Transport was on Horseback, decided violently against
going but, a little thro' Charity to myself and a great deal thro'
Charity to You because I was aware of your Eager Curiosity to
hear something of your strange Francis for whom you bear,
you always tell me, so odd an Affection, I agreed to accompany
Reginald and to share with him whatever Perils and Dangers
there might be.

Strong Temptations rise within my heart to make of this a
story as fearfully absurd as any thing in the History of Miss
Betsy Thoughtless, but I will spare your Sensitive Feelings
and I am sure you will consider my Behaviour has been very
handsome. In short we set out on the fairest of Young Spring
Days and discovered the most lovely of England's uninhabited
though Cultivated Vallies. I say Uninhabited but am not quite
Literal. Houses and Farms there are scattered here and there
in a wilderness of Scrub under the Frowning Eyebrows of
horrid Crags and Precipices. Whatever you wish to offer up to
your Idol, Taste (and you know that I have ever applauded
your taste in the Arts, extravagant tho' some of your Relations
have found it) as We saw it under a brilliant Sun with fresh
Green glittering from a recent Shower I was not altogether resolved against coming to live in these Regions for the remainder of my Days and indeed might seriously so consider it were
it not for the too close Juxtaposition of dear Raiseley and Mary.
But now to my Story. Our Guide, who both in his Corpulency
and abruptness of Speech reminded me strongly of Uncle Roger
(whose Partiality for green corn partridges and ill success at the
Oxfordshire Poll you will certainly remember) showed us the
Beauties and Curiosities of the district as we passed them, the
Ingenuity of the Bowder Stone, the Beauties of the River Derwent, a wood above the river where not so long back they
drowned a Witch, but I will not detain you with these, knowing, dearest Pelham, your Unmitigated Impatience with anything that has not to do with a graceful Ankle or a Pack of

Cards, and so proceeding over the Wildest Country, all Horrid Boulders and Little Trees growing in grotesque profusion, we approached at length the village of Rosthwaite. You have heard me say that I am a Philosopher only in the fields, and never in the Fields but when the sun shines, so should I have been most surely a Philosopher now, but I confess to a most unphilosophical Tremor when the Guide says, as quietly as you please, 'And that is the House of Herries,' pointing with his stick to a strange Building on a rising Hillock so near to us that only a rivulet and a rustic Bridge divided us.

The Afternoon was gathering in and the Shadows fast falling across the Valley. There was a Purple Light over all the scene and the Mountains had assembled in front of Us as though to close us in with their Black and Jagged Sides. It was a fearful Scene, dear Pelham, and I am thankful indeed that I had Reginald with me Who being destitute of all Imagination suffers no Distress from Nature at her darkest nor the forebodings of Man's untimely End. How Strange, how Abandoned, how Desolate this House of Francis Herries! I have seen you draw a Gothick Hog-sty for a customary Freeholder in Northamptonshire but this would be entirely beyond your Pencil.

From where our horses stayed We could see the deserted grass-grown courtyard, Walls from which the bricks were already falling, windows so Dark that they must be always foreign to the Sun, and the Garden behind a tangle of Weed and Stone. The House must be in part Elizabethan or of an earlier date and it had, in this Shadow that crept about the silent Valley, so unhappy an Air that I have never seen a House speak so eloquently. And now see what follows! We had been watching in silence for some five minutes when of a sudden a Woman comes into the Doorway.

She stands for a moment in Hesitation then crosses the Courtyard and turns down the Path towards us. We had, as You might imagine, a Perfect View of her and I ask you to imagine how Romantick a Picture with this tumbling dark House behind her and the Black Hills on every side and no Sound in the World. As she came towards Us I saw that she was beautiful or so Unusual as to be named a Beauty. She passed us by silently as a Ghost might. She wore nothing over her Head, and her Hair was the Reddest in Hue I ever saw. Over her shoulders she had a Orange Shawl.

Her Face was small and white like a Child's but by her Person I should say she was near thirty Years. Lost in her

Thoughts she gave us no Notice. Then, when She was scarcely past us a man came from the same door, walks to the Lane, sees her in front of him and also draws near to us. This was of course your admired Francis.

He also passed Us without the merest Glance, slowly as though He would not accompany the Figure in front of him but yet would keep Her in His Eye.

You have seen Him, Pelham, and so I need not waste Paper in describing Him to you, but how Striking and how Strange is his appearance. His Clothes are Shabby and stained with mire. He had a Black Hat and a Coat with wide old-fashioned skirts of rusty Brown, he was gaitered to the Knee.

But his Face – scarred on one Cheek from brow to lip – his Eyes of a most tender and Romantick Cast, grave and yet kindly, his Body so straight (save for the slightest stoop of the Shoulder) that although You tell me He is over Sixty it is yet difficult of Belief. There seemed a sort of Desperation in his eye although You, knowing my Romantick Disposition, will attribute this Embroidery to my excess of Sentiment.

He passed Us and followed the Lady but, as I have told You, not to be up with her but rather to keep Her in his Watch. We saw her turn into the shadow of the darkening Road. He slowly behind her and so the two of them out of our Sight.

Forgive, dearest Pelham, the Length of this Epistle but I had resolved that I must give you the fullest details of this Occurrence although Reginald pshaws me and assures me that We have seen nothing at all but a husband and wife on their Daily Walk. For myself there is something more Romantickal and I will confess to you that I have altogether fallen in Love with your Francis and would perhaps try my Fate with Him were he not so obviously already Captured.

My Health is much after the old fashion; yours, I hope however, is quite recovered . . .

There is nothing further in this letter that calls for attention. The other view of Francis and Mirabell during this month is Deborah's. For a long time past Deborah and her husband had been demanding a visit. Francis had never come near to them since Deb's marriage.

One afternoon towards the end of April, Francis and his wife (riding pillion) appeared outside the little, squat, rosy-faced rectory. The Reverend Gordon Sunwood was cleaning out the pigsty. Deborah was baking a cake. She arrived at the doorway, her face rosy from the heat of the fire, her hands thick in dough.

She was pleased and frightened at the same time. They looked so strange sitting silently on a large black horse as though they had been conjured out of the ground.

It was altogether the strangest visit. There seemed no actual reason for it. Neither seemed glad to be there. But, by the second day, Deborah seeing that something was terribly amiss between the two of them, her warm heart was deeply touched and she tried to draw close to them. No easy matter. They were like foreigners who are uncertain of the language spoken around them. They looked foreign, too, sitting in Deborah's amazingly neat and bright parlour with its shining brass, its handsome pictures of King George and his Queen, its Chippendale chairs.

But altogether it was the prettiest of little rooms, hung round with India paper, with Chelsea china, and a pagoda, and a looking-glass in a frame of Chinese paling.

This room was Deborah's pride, and how happy she was, sewing by the fire, listening to the steps on the cobbles, and interrupted once and again by the fat, cheerful countenance and round plump person of Mr Sunwood, who would look in to tell her about the new litter of pigs or how the hens were laying or the text he had chosen for his next sermon or how Mrs Jameson, the lawyer's wife, was faring in her childbirth.

Deborah had all she wanted in the world, for now she knew that she was to have a child. (She was delivered of boy twins on the morning of October 3rd, 1763.)

Socially, too, the Sunwoods were very popular. It must be remembered that Deborah had never all her life long known what social popularity was. There had been always over them the atmosphere of her father's sin and social impossibility. She had also been in Doncaster too young to know what society was, and at Herries there was no society.

She yielded herself, therefore, now to all the friendliness and neighbourliness with a full will, and happy were her days. But all her life came back to her full flood in the presence of her father; yes, right back to her infancy when they arrived at Keswick on that stormy afternoon and Alice Press sat beside the fire.

Old shadows, old terrors. She was not afraid of him now quite as she had been; married life had given her independence. Besides, he was strangely kind and gentle. He seemed to have lost all his authority, acquiesced in anything that was suggested; he charmed Deborah the most by his exceeding courtesy to his wife, rising to offer her any attention, always with his eye on her.

But they talked scarcely at all together, only smiled occasionally, and then as though they were strangers.

Deborah did her best to come to close terms with Mirabell and, until the final evening, altogether failed. She took her over the little house, showing proudly all her treasures. Especially the bedstead in which Mr Sunwood and his lady enjoyed their marital comforts. This was a mahogany bedstead with fluted posts and dark crimson hangings. Other glories of the house were a walnut-tree writing-table, three India-back walnut-tree chairs with stuff silk damask seats, a pier-glass in a black and gold frame, blue and white china, and a Turkey carpet.

It may be wondered what contrasts Mirabell made in her heart between this and Herries. Poor woman! A house like this, cosy, warm, clean, bright with frilly things, and an air everywhere of love and safety, had never been, all her life, in her way. Would she have cared for it or would it have driven her wild? If it had been this that she wanted, and she had urged Francis Herries sufficiently towards it, there is little doubt but that he would have tried to get it for her. She did not belong to this comfort.

With every hour Deborah felt the distance between them growing. Physically they were of separate worlds, Deborah plump, with cap and apron, keys at her girdle, with her bright happy face, placid too and yet sensitive with that perception, kept by her from childhood, of small unexpressed things.

It was this perception that made her bond with Mirabell, that separated her from Sarah and David and gave her kinship with her father, although she feared him. She was in that way nearer to her father than to her own husband. She watched Mirabell. She saw her stand near the mirror in the parlour, half reflected in it. Her face was elfish, both tragic and impatient. Under its great burden of hair it was poignant in its loneliness. And at last Deborah, unable to endure the woman's silent suffering any longer, caught her in her arms and held her there.

'Tell me, my dear, what is it? What is wrong? Why are you unhappy?'

Mirabell did not try to escape as Deborah had thought that she would. She stayed there looking down.

'We are both unhappy,' she said at last, 'because I cannot give him what he would have, and he has done something for which he will never forgive himself.'

Deborah drew her to a chair. She felt close, close to her. She suddenly seemed to understand her as she never had before, understand the good honest heart, her wild nature uneasy at captivity, her gratitude for his kindness to her, her misery because she could not love him. These things were all told to her as though Mirabell had spoken.

She did speak; she looked up into Deborah's face, seemed to find comfort in those quiet eyes.

'It is all my own sin, all because I came to him for shelter that first time when I was hungry.' She began to speak passionately as Deborah had seen her do once before above Bassenthwaite Water.

'I could not know then; I was a child in so many ways. I knew that he loved me, but not that for so long, with so much refusal, he would still love me. His love is terrible; it is like a pain in his heart and in mine. If I cared nothing for him it would be easy. I would have told him and left him. But how can I not care for him when for so long he has been so good to me, and for so long asked nothing in return? Now at last he does ask something. He cannot help himself . . . And then there is more. I am imprisoned in that house. I am a woman now, not a child, and it seems that I am a woman accursed because I cannot rest anywhere. I think that when Harry was killed I was struck a blow here at my heart. I can feel it, a pain that nothing can heal. After all, I am of no family and of no place. I am not in my own world with him. If I loved him, then nothing would matter, but because I cannot . . .'

She broke off, threw up her head. 'I have a great scorn of women who go about bewailing everything. We had a woman once who was like that; she was mistress of one of my uncles. "Oh," she was always saying, "he has struck me," or "He neglects me," and therefore he did strike her, no blame to him. I would wail about nothing of myself, but to see him so wretched when I care for him . . .' She broke off again, then turned eagerly to Deborah. 'Oh, you don't know, Deborah, how good he can be! He is quite changed now. Of course he is older, but it is not only age. There is a new gentleness – can you not see it?'

'Yes,' said Deborah, 'but it is because he is unhappy.'

'I know, I know!' Mirabell caught Deborah's arm. 'I cannot endure that quietness, not for much longer. If we could speak together – but, after Christmas last, he will say nothing concerning the two of us. There was an angry scene. He beat down the door of my room. I thought he would kill me. I would not have cared had he, but the fit passed and since then he has had a shame that has no cause. What is that – beating the door down? He himself has done many things worse – and to me what have they not done? Beaten me and kicked me, and many worse things. I would not have minded if he had beaten me, but it was of a sudden to withdraw, as though he had done some shameful thing.'

'That is because he loves you,' said Deborah.

Then Mirabell said, dropping her voice very low:

'It cannot go on like this. It must have a turn. It were better for him that I were not there.' And then, with the oddest smile, looking close at Deborah again: 'And perhaps I am not there. No woman at all. The real woman is somewhere else and loves him. I feel that I have no soul, that I must go out to find one.'

At that Mr Sunwood came in and they had supper.

Deborah had one word with her father. After supper he went to the door with her to see the rich red spring moon. He stood there, feeling through all his body the peace of the little town. The cobbled path, the white houses shining in the moonlight, the rooms behind them with their warmth, no sound, and the moon riding through the serene sky. But he turned to her:

'I will not accept this world of ghosts,' he said. 'He has laid it thus, so and so. "And now you take it," says He. "This is good enough for you." But it is not good enough. It is a botch, a mess, a frustration, and man is frustrated in the middle of it. But for every man, one twist and it would be right enough. "Jog this for me a turn to the left," says Man, "and I shall have comfort." "Not I," says God. "Jog it yourself if you can."' He laughed and tweaked Deborah's ear very gently. 'Thou art happy, Deb?'

'Very, Father,' she answered.

'Aye, so I see. And I like your parson, even though he likes not me.'

'Oh, but he does,' said Deborah indignantly.

'Nay,' said Herries laughing. 'I am an old serpent in his nest. I can see him wondering, as we sit at table, "Now, how doth my adored Deborah come from that thief's loins?" But 'tis my seed, Deb, that you are, never shame thy mother else.' He sighed, shrugging his long shoulders. 'Poor sainted Margaret! Old days. Think you that she is behind that moon now, Deb, watching us?'

'Where Heaven may be,' said Deborah.

'Aye, where Heaven may be – a plaguy caterwauling place.'

Taking all her courage she said: 'How sweet Mirabell is, Father; and she cares for you most deeply.'

He looked at her as though he had not heard, then, very low, staring at the moon and speaking into the air:

'She has no right to care. I have treated her very evilly;

everything in me turns to evil.' Then, shrugging his shoulders again: 'Come in. Do you know that I am sixty years old and more? Every part of me from nose to belly, from belly to knee-joint, is aware of it. Only I, I myself, will not recognize it.'

They went inside, and next morning the two rode back to Herries.

As they rode Mirabell knew that he had some fresh plan in his head. She heard him laugh softly to himself, saw him turn to look back at her, then toss his head as though he were proud of making his mind up. And she was intensely miserable. She had never before known such misery. When Harry had been killed, that had been unhappiness of another sort – deep, biting agony with grandeur in it; this was unhappiness that came from failure. Somehow in these years, with all the chances that she had had, she should have made a better job of it. Had Deborah's parson felt passion for her but she no passion in return, would she not have made the best of it, have satisfied him in some way, have 'taken him in' for his own good as so many women must do with their men?

Ah, but Deborah's parson and her Herries, what different men they were! There was no one like her Herries (here she felt a queer sort of pride) for oddity, suddenly stepping inside himself where you could not get him. And herself and Deborah! Here, too, there was a bed-rock difference. Deborah was a lady and she, Mirabell, was not. She did not know what she was – something for nothing, an absurd misfit belonging to no place, no person. And here such a bitter sense of desolation came to her that it was all she could do to hold back her tears.

It would never do that he should see her weeping, so she turned away blinking at the thin sunshine radiant with promise. Derwentwater lay below them. The air seemed to be filled with the sound of waterfalls, and in contrast to this delicious murmur the lake was softly still. One boat floated upon it, the hills were most delicately reflected in purple shapes, a looking-glass world. Lord's Island was a cloud of green. Everything was freshly green – the copses, the hawthorns. Birds were singing everywhere – bullfinches, robins, thrushes – and on all sides the gentle fields sloped lazily up to the rocks and spurs of the hills that would soon have a shadow of green smoke on them from a hint of the new bracken.

Such peace must seem unreal when life is at impossible odds, but for Mirabell this free and open nature had always been the only true certain thing that she knew. She did not analyse it, she could not have described it, because it was part of her, and, just as she was at a loss about her own moods and nature if she were asked for any definition, so she was at a loss here. But the lake, that had slipped so beautifully down between the hills and now lay in perfect peace, rose up to her and for a moment drew her into its own tranquil reassurance.

For some days after their return Francis Herries kept his plan, whatever it was, to himself; then at last one evening he told her.

Herries was at its best in the spring and the early summer. Daffodils blew about its walls, birds were everywhere nesting, the old rooms seemed to take the sunlight more readily, the windows could be flung open; the place lost its musty smell of ancient cobweb and leaking wainscot. Herries himself worked all day on the ground, and now at last, after all these years, it seemed to be responding and yielding to his long care of it. People, too, seemed to be losing some of their long avoidance. Women would greet him at their doors as he passed, men exchange 'Good day' with him, and sometimes children would hang about the court-yard, stroke the dog and watch Benjamin groom the two horses.

They were standing by the wall at the house's back looking at the light fading over Rosthwaite Fell, when he turned abruptly to her and said:

'Soon we shall be leaving this.'

For a moment she did not understand what he said. He repeated it, looking at her shyly, but watching her to see the surprise of pleasure flash into her eyes.

'Leave Herries?'

'Yes . . . Since our visit to Deborah I have been thinking. This is no place for you. You have always hated it. We will find a bright trim house like hers, with modern walls and India paper on them, no dripping water, no disorder . . . a proper parlour for you to sit in.'

'Leave Herries? . . . But you love every stone of it.'

'Yes. But you do not. I can do you that service.'

She was terrified. A mature, profound understanding came to her at this moment. There was some crisis at this time when she became a woman. It may have been this. She saw in a flash of intuitive comprehension that this was his last throw. If she had learnt anything about him during these years with him, it was that Herries was everything to him, that it had a power over him, as some places have over some men, deeper than thought, deeper than reason.

She saw in his eyes, in their light dancing attack on her, that he was saying: 'Now – now – you must love me. I have found a way at last. I am giving up everything, the only thing I've ever really cared for. *This* must win you.' And she knew, as she looked about her, at the darkening fells, the stony fields, the house that seemed to grin malignantly at her, with what loathing she regarded it, with what poignancy she felt the pathos of his abnegation, with what wretched certainty she knew the hopelessness of his desire.

A panic seized her. She felt as though she could run to the house and beat on it with her hands until they bled.

'You must not. You shall not. Do you not realize that I have no power to change this, that no giving up of anything can alter it? Oh, I am wretched indeed to have come, wretcheder to stay, cheating you, cheating myself, when I care for you so. If I did not care it would be easy. But I do not love you. I shall never love you. Nothing can change it.'

'This can change it,' he said. 'We will go from here where you will. It is this house and its discomfort that has chilled you. I was a fool not to have seen it before. I know my way.'

She bowed her head. There was only one thing for her to do.

In the four days that followed, she must have gone, again and again, over every aspect of it. By leaving him might she not liberate him? What was her presence to him save a goad, a torture? She was by now obsessed with this sense that she had, from the beginning, only harried him, and that now the harm that she did was touching insanity. Leaving Herries, what could there be for him but continual remorse and regret with no compensation?

Possibly she had never cared for him so tenderly and so regretfully as now. Those last days of April when the sun shone and the water glittered on the rocks, and green burnt like fire, they moved apart, he, it seemed, resolved that he had won her by this last surrender to her, but suffering, it may be fancied, a brutal hurt with every glance that the house gave him. She saw that he dug no longer, nor planted, nor went out to the hills.

During those last nights he never touched her, and she, lying awake at his side, hated with shivers of revulsion this passion that seemed so necessary to men that they must die if they could not have it.

Oddly, the more deeply she cared for him, the more now she detested the thought of his physically possessing her. She wanted no man ever to touch her again.

On the last night of April, a starless, moonless night, about two of the morning, she rose from his side, crept to the other room where some clothes were, wrote on a piece of paper, left it where he should see it, and fled. By seven o'clock she was on the coach for Kendal.

That night by an odd chance he slept heavily, having been much awake other nights. When he woke and saw that she was not with him in bed, he went to the passage and called her.

It was May Day; the light over the house was dim. All the way down the stairs he called her. On the table where he had so often tried to give her lessons was a piece of paper, and very childishly written:

It is beste to goe. You will have Piece better without me.
                                           MIRABELL.

He stood, holding the paper towards the window, reading it over and over, rocking on his feet.

The sun, surmounting the hill, pierced the window, but he saw nothing.

ULDALE

I

FOUNDING OF A FAMILY

MEANWHILE David and Sarah had made a fine start of family life at Uldale. They had two children – Francis, born in 1760; and Deborah, born in 1762. They were both grand healthy children.

David, indeed, was at last in his full and proper element. You could see this in the happy confident gaze that he threw over his wife, his children, his square house with its rosy brick set so comfortably in its little walled-in garden, his little farm, his servants, his farm hands, and even over the high and swelling downs stretching towards Scotland and the sea – all, in a sort of fashion, his, because he loved them with a personal love and was proud of them with a personal pride.

This was what he had always been intended to be – patriarchal founder of an English family with his great stature, huge limbs, splendid carriage.

As he strode about the soil, his flaxen head up, his chest spread, his eyes shining with health and vigour and happiness, he was already the patriarch gathering these men and women, these beasts of the field and birds of the air under his protecting shelter.

He was now forty-three years of age, and had much worldly wisdom hidden in his round solid-looking head. He was beginning to make very real profits through his Liverpool trade, and, had he wished, could have become a wealthy man. He had the talents, the persistence, the courage. But here the real Herries strain came out in him, also the touch of softness of sentiment that belonged to the little boy who had adored to ride in front of his father, who had hated Alice Press and been thrilled by the dreams of Father Roche. The Herries strain in him made him weary of money-getting, just as it began to be important.

Herries did not care for property; they were too proud to think it worthwhile to amass it. They cared so much for family, for their own standing, their own importance in England, that no vulgar amassing of wealth could do anything but damage their self-approval. But then again their family pride was so unself-conscious, so completely taken for granted, that they never thought of it, talked of it or defended it. The English have always had this quality of confident security, and this makes them remote from the rest of the world and will always isolate them whether their island continues to be an island or no. It accounts for their universal unpopularity, for their insular stubbornness, their hypocrisy and their profound calm in a crisis. It accounts also for a generous warmth of heart hidden under an absurd armour of frigid suspicion of strangers. It accounts for their poetry, their lack of imagination, their peculiar humour, their irritating conceit and ignorance in foreign countries, and a certain naïve youthfulness which is both absurd and attractive.

Any history of any English family must be concerned with this confident security and the shocks that it receives from time to time. These shocks never ultimately affect it; the history of any English family therefore is, basically, comedy rather than tragedy; comedy decorated with incongruous things like spring flowers, teapots, the Battle of Trafalgar, London fogs, beer and country vicarages. This confident security is the true reason of our magnificent sequence of great poets. Poetry is roused by sheer rebellious indignation, so vilely exasperating is it to anyone with imagination.

David, however, thought in these days little of poetry. He was so busied from early morning (he was up at five-thirty every day) until evening, that life flashed like a meteor before his eyes and was gone.

In actual fact the times were propitious for him. There was possibly no period in the history of the village labourer so black, degraded and hopeless as that between the years 1760 and 1832. Let there follow some items important in the Herries family chronicle. The agricultural labourer at this time earned fourteen pence a day or eight shillings a week, and his wife, were she lucky, might earn sixpence a day. Here are some of the things that the labourer must provide for his family: candles, 3d; bread or flour, 1s 8d; yeast and salt, 4d; soap, starch, 2½d; tea, sugar, butter, 1s; thread, worsted, 3d. The weekly total would be some 8s 4½d or £21 15s 6d per annum, his earnings being £20 16s:

In addition to the weekly expenses, there were clothing, rent, fuel, amounting to some £8, and leaving the happy villager with a yearly deficiency of nearly £9. He could buy neither milk nor cheese. He could not brew small beer save for some especial occasion. So difficult was it to obtain soap for washing that they burned green fern and kneaded it into balls. A quarter of wheat cost in 1787 forty-eight shillings, and that amount was trebled later.

Everywhere and in every way the labourer was oppressed by the farmer. Landlords and farmers were, at this time, advocating enclosures everywhere. The common field system was utterly wasteful; far better to throw all the fields into large farms.

David found that here in all the country that stretched between Uldale and Carlisle matters were very different from the independence and security of the Statesmen in Borrowdale and Newlands. There a labourer could rise by thrift and diligence until he should be in some sort his own master. In all the country districts about Uldale, by enclosure the labourer was losing his right of cutting fuel on the common, his piece of land, his pig and cow. Privilege of gleaning after harvest, whereby poor families often obtained enough corn to last them through the winter, was also now withdrawn.

Signs of the new world were also to be found in the arrival of the middleman; the farmer sold his corn to the miller, the miller to the mealman, the mealman to the shopkeeper, the shopkeeper to the poor.

In short, the halcyon time for the poor man at work on English fields was over, never, alas, to return.

David was fortunate in that his farm was small and his means were large. His heart was warm and kindly, his character patient, his intelligence shrewd. It was not long before his name began to be known for wise charity and true understanding; it would not be long before 'Squire Herries' was his designation.

His whole heart and soul rose to his new position. He was founding a family, not a new family, but a new branch of the finest family in the world, the Herries of England. Here, from every possible motive, both his spiritual and physical energies were engaged. At the heart of it were his wife and children. Here both his love and his pride knew no bounds. Beyond them were all the Herries (with one very important exception).

After he had been at Uldale a year or so, he wrote to various relations informing them that here he was, and that they were welcome to a bed and a sup any time they passed that way.

In dueness of time he heard from Cousin Pelham, a very gay and frivolous epistle, saying that Uldale was the very place for flight when the bailiffs should become too pressing; a stiff angular letter from Dorothy Forster, complaining of the weather and her rheumatism; a grand document from London from his cousin Judith (now the Hon Mrs Ernest Bligh), informing him that her social duties were so onerous that she was sadly afraid that she could spare no time for the bleak North (where, she knew well from her unhappy youth, it always rained); a delightful letter from dear Uncle Harcourt (now seventy-five years of age), wishing his nephew every prosperity, but intimating that gout had him by the leg and David must come to Ravenglass to see him rather than he to Uldale. There were others: Will Forster, now twenty-five years of age, who wrote from Alnwick to inquire about the hunting; an aunt of Pelham's, an ancient Titchley, who, drinking the waters at Bath, begged him to subscribe to her Home for Indigent Sedan Chairmen; and young Morgan Gold of Edinburgh, who wrote to ask David to be a subscriber and patron to his forthcoming epic, *The Tower of Babel*.

In one way and another David felt his bag had not been a bad one. This was his first step towards bringing the family together, making it a real force and power in the progress and happiness of England.

It was England that he always ultimately saw; England expressed in the downs, streams and hills of his own surrounding country; England in the names so immediately close to him – Skiddaw Forest, Bassenthwaite Common, Great Calva, Bowscale Fell, Blackhazel Beck, Mungrisdale, Scarness, Jenkin Hill; England in the little streets of Keswick; England spreading and dipping and rising again, through town and country, from county to county, until on every side it claims the sea.

His patriotism was like the patriotism of most men, founded on a stone, a flower, the sound of a stream, a clod of earth, the rustle of a tree, but it spread from these things until it embraced the earth, the moon and stars at one reach, and dug pits in his soul at the other.

All fine enough, but there was one festering strand in his ambition which was not so fine. That was his hatred of and scorn for his dear cousin and brother-in-law, Raiseley Herries.

Raiseley, who was forty-five years of age now, had never been a very fine physical specimen, and now, from idleness, a bad constitution and much early coddling, had developed into as complete a valetudinarian as his mother had ever been. In his youth he had had brains of a rather scientific sort, but for lack of encouragement and because of a bad education they had run to seed. He had not had all the best chances. His health had always been bad: *that* was not entirely imagination. His marriage had been unfortunate. Mary, David's sister, had never cared for him, had indeed never cared for anyone but herself, nor did her two children, Pomfret, aged twelve, and Cynthia, aged nine, care for him either. His appearance was distressing, his long thin face yellow like a turnip, frequently coloured with the ravages of dyspepsia, his lanky body gaudily and untidily clothed, always on his features the malcontentedness of a thoroughly disappointed man. He added to these unamiable qualities an overweening pride in his position and a hasty but cowardly temper.

His quarrel with David had begun at a very early age, from that day, in fact, when David had paid his first Keswick call with his mother so many years ago. For long Raiseley had had the best of it. David, living in disgraceful obscurity with a father who was the scandal of all the world, was no very possible rival. It was true that Raiseley had married David's sister, but this was because Mary had turned her back on her family and disowned them all. Afterwards matters had not been improved by the fact that whenever Mary wished to scorn or abuse her sickly husband (and these occasions were not rare as the intimacies of marriage strengthened) she found an easy weapon in the size and ability of her brother (whom, nevertheless, herself she termed for many years 'clodhopper'). It was not, however, until David came to Uldale that the feud was really proclaimed.

At first when they had heard of David's purchase of the place, both Raiseley and Mary had laughed scornfully. Their position

in Keswick was nothing very fine (they were not even contemptuously popular as old Pomfret had been before them), but they
nevertheless represented the only kind of Herries of which Keswick socially had any cognizance. It was not so much that English
society in the middle of the eighteenth century was snobbish, as
that the members of it simply felt that those who were not members of it were not human. It was easy enough. A man who was
not a gentleman was hanged for stealing a sheep or whipped at
the public stocks until the blood ran, or a child would be imprisoned in a gaol too filthy for rats for stealing a loaf of bread, or a
woman who was not a lady would suffer the grossest of public
indignities for no reason other than that she answered her mistress impertinently.

There was no question but that any Herries was a gentleman;
unfortunately Francis Herries had declassed himself completely,
and must be therefore doubly disowned. How ridiculous then of
his son to expect, because he bought a small property in the
neighbourhood, that he would be received or accepted! It was
true that Rogue Herries's daughter had been accepted, but that was
because she had disowned her monstrous father at the earliest
possible moment, and then had been washed, as it were, pure in
London's chastening waters before returning to Keswick. David
not only approved of his monster of a father, but openly declared
his devotion to him, and was seen with him as often as possible,
yes, even though the man, after selling his mistress in public and
murdering his first wife, had married a common gipsy off the
fells.

Oddly enough, none of these things seemed to stand in
David's path. After all, he was not new to Keswick; he had done
business there since he was a boy; everyone knew his rectitude,
his courage, his humour. He was a proper man; he could carry an
ox on one shoulder; stripped, he could fight any man in the North
Country. Had he not carried off his wife single-handed from the
villain of a father and a posse of attendant villains? True, he had
killed the man, there under Esk Hause. The thing was already an
epic, and ballads had been written about it.

This was the Keswick view, and soon neighbouring squires
were calling at Uldale, and David was hunting, fishing, shooting
with them, and it began to be noised abroad that some of the jolli-
est evenings to be enjoyed in Cumberland were to be found at the
Fell House, Uldale.

It was then that the bitterness of his hatred for his brother-in-
law was felt to the full by Raiseley Herries. His view of life was

in any case a bitter one. Ill-health made him bitter, a conviction of wasted brains and opportunities, disappointment both in his wife and his children, hurt vanity, wounded conceit – these all made him bitter.

David's scorn and contempt for Raiseley was a bad, unworthy element in his warm, generous, noble nature, as Sarah well knew and deplored.

'It isn't worthy of you,' she would say after he had boasted to her of some small triumph, 'and one day it will come back badly to you. Our children will suffer for it, if not ourselves.'

'Not they!' said David laughing, throwing his babies up into the air and catching them. ''Tis an old feud, Sarah, my love, and it began with his laughing at my father when we were infants together. With his wheezly, flammering body, I could break him over my head.'

And so in pride and scorn and derision he rode himself over to invite the two of them to his first grand festivity, this May Day, 1763. Sitting his horse outside their door, a magnificent sight for all to see, he gave his messages to young Pomfret, a stout, sturdy boy, who carried his head proudly so that David took to him at sight.

It was plain that young Pomfret had been trained to disapproval of his uncle, but he could not drag his eyes from the horse.

'Wilt have a ride?' asked David, laughing.

But young Pomfret shook his head and ran into the house.

Sarah also shook her head when David returned and laughingly told her of it.

'Why should we breed our children to this? What affair is it of theirs that you and Raiseley Herries have a spite?'

She was nursing her own baby, Deborah, not yet a year old, as she spoke. She looked down, smiling, her eyes bright with love. 'We have had feuds enough in our lives – my uncle and your father; now there must be peace. This is not like you, Davy; it is not your generosity.'

'I feel no generosity,' he answered sharply. 'My sister left us and stayed in Keswick to mock us. Raiseley has been our enemy since he was weaned.'

But Sarah shook her head. 'Then it is the more reason the thing ceased. It has lasted long enough. See that you are not proud, Davy, in your new place. Of all things pride is the worst.'

He bent over the mother and child, himself a child at that instant. 'I have reasons for my pride. Two good reasons.' Then, kissing her, his great hand cupping her chin: 'And how can I not be proud when I love you so? Having such a wife, what is a man worth an he is not stiff with pride?'

So Mary and Raiseley Herries did not come to the May Day Feast at the Fell House. But all the rest of the world came.

It was a grand May Day, soft and warm. David had the downs above his house for his games – for the Archery, the Football, the Wrestling and the Dancing. Upright on the downs, its head proudly lifted to heaven, was the Maypole, its hanging streamers lazily lifting like live things in the breeze. He stood with Sarah on the lawn in the brick-walled garden to receive his guests. He wore a plain suit of mulberry trimmed with silver. His fair hair (he was beginning, as were many others, to wear – save on very state occasions – his own hair) shone in the sun. His rosy face – strong, clear-eyed, broad-browed – beamed happiness. Sarah stood beside him in a pretty grey dress, the hoop sprayed with roses, a fine white wig with cherry ribbons, and she wore silver shoes. She looked as healthy, confident, happy as he.

Around them, too, everything was happy: the pigeons cooed, cows softly lowed, birds sang in the elm tree, young Francis was sturdy enough in his three years to stand beside his mother holding tightly to her with one hand and with the other cracking his whip.

David and Sarah insisted on receiving all alike; today there were to be no class distinctions. David had sent invitations to all his old friends in Borrowdale, and many of them had ridden over – Peels and Satterthwaites and Mounseys and Bells. Sarah, although truly she was no snob, could not but be gratified to see how the gentry and their wives were appearing – Mr Bonstead from Keswick, Squire Osmaston and his lady from near Trout-beck, Squire Worcester and his lady from the other side of Threl-keld, the Peaches and Sandons and Ullathorpes from Keswick, the Brownriggs all the way from Patterdale, the Newsomes of Newlands, the Robertsons of St John's in the Vale, the Kendals from the other side of Bassenthwaite.

Soon Sarah found that she was compelled to observe social distinctions, so she led Mrs Osmaston and Mrs Worcester and old Miss Mary Peach and the Misses Gwendolyn and Frances Brownrigg out to the seats that had been arranged on the down with an awning to protect them from the wind. The farmers and their wives and children gathered in their own groups, and splen-did Statesmen like Richard Bell, towering with his white head and six foot five above all the others, and George Satterthwaite, like a bull for thickness and strength, walked on the springing

turf as though they owned the world and were rightly proud of
it.

Yes, this was perhaps the happiest day of his life for David. It
had come to this: that he had now his true independent place in
the world, his place, his wife and children, this turf on which
he was treading, this English turf under English hills, watered
with English streams – these things were his and he owed them
to no man alive. Men of all kinds, from old Osmaston, who was
a sort of king of Cumberland at this time, from Richard Bell, as
noble-hearted as he was ironically cautious and loyally steadfast,
to old Ducken the ploughman, who was now moving towards the
Maypole, a string of children at his heels, these men and their
womenfolk had greeted him, welcomed him, received him into
their world.

And he thought as he stood there, his legs spread, his head up,
his face flushed with happiness, of himself as a small boy at Herries listening to Alice Press as she screamed at his mother; of the
Chinese Fair and the ancient Chinaman with the old, old face; of
that awful scene in the tent when his father sold Alice Press; of
how he stood in the courtyard sparring with Raiseley while his
mother was dying upstairs; of old Mrs Wilson the witch; of the
ride to Carlisle; of that awful moment when his father, looking
a dead man, had come into his room in Carlisle; of the day when
Mirabell had met them in Herries – a thousand other scenes were
called up by his memory. He knew now that, in spite of his devotion and loyalty to his father, that strange mist of disgrace and
isolation had always been hanging over him, although he was too
proud to acknowledge it.

Now at last, at last he was clear of it!

All this while his eye was on the road beneath him to see
whether his father and Mirabell would appear. He had, of course,
sent word to them – a special letter on horseback – that they must
most certainly come. He wanted them to come; it would not be
a real complete day for him if his father were not there, but with
that, if he were honest with himself, there was a feeling too that
they would be strange, his father and Mirabell, in this company.
They were always strange, his father with his arrogant look that
went so oddly with his scarred face, his silence, his sudden ironical statements, his wandering eye so that his mind seemed to be
always elsewhere, and Mirabell like a play-actress with her gaudy
clothes and ill-easiness in proper and normal company. He wanted them to come, but he dreaded a little what the result of their
coming might be.

Now everything is in movement. The coloured ribbons of the Maypole flash in constant change against the blue of the sky and the green of the turf. The girls pass like notes of music sounding in regular rhythm against the air.

On a grassy mound above the road an old man with two chins and a frizzy white wig stands fiddling, and he has an attendant piper. Birds fly across the sun, bells sound, clouds lighter than smoke, with the soft colour of swan's down, collect and hover and disperse.

Beyond the Maypole there are benches, a barrel of ale, apples soaked in sugar and thick flat cakes crammed with raisins, damp in the middle. Men and women cluster here; there is wrestling, kissing and hugging and drinking, and, beyond them, as the sun slides down the sky, the sloping black side of Skiddaw catches the light: it is as though it rolled its coat off and spread there, basking, while the clouds are shadowed across the shining surface. And David stands, his head up, breathing the air, catching the light, feeling that the whole world is his, joy in his heart.

A farmer passes. He turns, laughing, rolling his thick back towards the Maypole.

'T'dancing is grand,' he says. Osmaston's huge body draws near, seeming to darken the sun with its bulk. He happens very gravely to talk politics with young Herries. 'Now Grenville . . . And these American Colonies? . . .' They are just beginning, in other places beside Uldale, to seem impertinent.

Sarah's task was harder today than her husband's. About her were seated, their hoops spreading wide around them, the Misses Gwendolyn and Frances Brownrigg and the great Mrs Osmaston. Mrs Osmaston was a tremendous lady, with her high white wig, her enormous white bosom half naked to the sun, her round white arms. With all this massive flesh her features were small and tightly pinched together. But out of her little mouth a tremendous voice proceeded, deep and bass like a man's, and with this voice she had been accustomed for forty years to give commands to all around her, save only her husband whom she resolutely obeyed. She was like a great white whale lying there in the sun. She had never been out of Cumberland in her life, and had all the knowledge of and confident scorn for the rest of the world that such determined staying-at-home produces. She had been, both in the '15 and the '45, an ardent Jacobite, and could never say enough about the Hanoverian dynasty. Many of her oaths and similes were of an excellent coarseness, and she alluded to all the natural processes of man with much freedom and gusto.

When in good humour, as she was today, she would slap her
friends on the back or pinch their arms or yield them even more
familiar gestures. She often made the oddest noises, and was, in
honest fact, none too cleanly in her person, so, as her own devoted
husband said, ''twas best to sit to windward of her'. Better than
all else, she loved to discuss the love affairs of her neighbours and
friends, and had, as she said, 'a nose for copulation like the nose
of a dog for a hare'. She liked Sarah and told her so. Seated there,
her great knees wide-planted inside her hoop, her fat arms akim-
bo, she told one bawdy story after another and was ably abetted
by the Misses Brownrigg, who, being supposedly virgins, had
their eyes eternally at the keyholes of all their neighbours' bedrooms.

Sarah, a woman of her time, was amused by the bawdy stories
when she could keep her ear to them, but she must watch first
one side, then another, to see that all went well, that nobody was
offended, that everyone, even to the smallest child of the least
important labourer, was happy. But everyone was happy. Happiness was everywhere.

Now it was time for the great Football game. Everyone
streamed towards the upper down where the game was to be.
The goals were distant nearly half a mile the one from the other.
There were few rules, if any; all cunning and trickery were at
advantage, but brute force was the greatest power of all. There
were fifty players a side to start with, although before the game
ended there were nearly a hundred a side. It was a match between
the Uldale men and the Keswick men, wide latitude allowed for
district partisanship.

It was a superb sight to see the hundred men – farmers, labourers, townsmen, woodsmen, sailors from the coast, dalesmen,
shepherds – stripped to their smallclothes, rush together with
great shouts of joy and triumph. The ball rose into the air and at
once the battle began, clumps of men binding together, arms
locked, rushing head down to meet other bands with a great
crash of neck and shoulder.

Soon the giants on either side were to be seen. Willie Peel of
Mungrisdale with his two sons, a mountain of a man, his sons as
big as he, the three rushing forward, the ball at their feet, lesser
men clinging to their sides and buttocks, leaping at their necks,
trying to trip them at the feet, while to meet them came John
Ringstraw and his brother George from Threlkeld, men like bullocks, crimson of face, thick of neck, with backs like walls. Willie
Peel meeting John Ringstraw, for a while all lesser men drew

back and watched them hurl themselves the one at the other, arms interlocked, backs straining, legs planted for a throw, while the air was beaten with the shouting and all the dogs barked and the shadows lovingly stroked the sides of Skiddaw. Then Willie's belt was burst and his smallclothes were flapping about his ankles; nothing mattered that to him, and he played for the rest of the game half naked, but the ball now had passed to a wily little devil, Jock Mounsey from Grange in Borrowdale, who was away across the downs with the thing at his feet, half a hundred men after him.

All the downs now rolled like a sea towards the sun and the hills. Little waves of dark shadows broke the pale primrose glow. Skiddaw and Blencathra grew dark, and seemed to billow with gestures of lazy self-indulgent satisfaction out towards the tender colours of the May Day sky.

And against this fair scene the battle rose and fell. Little Mounsey was for a while detached, a small figure springing along like a deer, controlling the ball as though it were tied to his shoe-strings, but then the two Grimshaws, stocky shepherds from Troutbeck, had caught him up. One of them tripped him and he fell, but before the ball had turned back to the goal at Skiddaw end half a hundred men had arrived and thrown themselves upon it.

Here now was a *mêlée* in the grand old style, no quarter asked and no quarter given. Over the ball in a wriggling, writhing heap twenty men were lying, and over these another thirty were striving, while behind them were the outguards, arriving from every part of the field, and, if they could not reach the central scrimmage, wrestling and boxing on their own. So that now there was a grand and noble sight, this central mass of heaving men, detached groups of fighters, and the spectators shouting, roaring, the dogs barking as though they were mad. The fine ladies themselves cursed and swore in their interest, and it was all that her husband could do to prevent Mrs Osmaston from rushing on to the field of play and lending assistance.

All is fair in love and war, and no chronicler would dare to catalogue some of the things that were done in that scrimmage; shirts were torn from many a back, once and again a head would rise, as though seeking for the stars, and stare vacantly skywards, blood pouring, eyes blackened, and once and again, a figure for an instant stood completely stark and so faced the world in utter nakedness, like some primeval hero before clothes were.

Then, alive with its own devilry, the ball suddenly emerged

and sped forward, pursued by Willie Peel and one of his sons.
Willie, his long hair flying, naked to the waist, his shaggy chest
broad as a wall, his eyes on fire, crying his war-cry 'Peel! Peel!
Hey Peel!' was well away, the ball at his feet. Staggering that so
huge a man should run so swiftly and keep the ball at his toe with
so astounding an accuracy, but now he was away from them all,
the field streaming at his feet, and in his size, strength and beauty
he joined partnership with the strength and beauty of the scene,
the grand type of all Cumbrian strength, sureness of purpose,
largeness of grasp, as good as anything the world has seen, and
as lasting.

The only man in his way was Jock Elliot of Crosthwaite, and
he was a kind of ogre of a man, almost deformed, so short of
stature, so thick, so shaggy, with such long swinging arms.

With a great grin, his little eyes burning under his black bristling eyebrows, he advanced to meet Willie Peel. Peel tried to 'slip'
him, but, heavy though Elliot was, he was agile too, and was in
front of him. Their bodies met with a shock that would have slain
two ordinary men and could have been heard, you would swear,
away in the streets of Keswick itself.

The two men drew a breath and closed. A moment later Peel
had Elliot in his arms, held him as though he loved him dearer
than any woman, and actually raised him from the ground.
Elliot's head was up. He seemed to be staring at the heavens as
though imploring the gods to do him this last great service, then,
his short legs about Peel's thighs, he brought him crashing to the
ground, himself on top. That seemed to end their struggle. They
lay, full length, one on the other, softly heaving, while the world
roared its approval and, gently, quietly, rosy clouds drifted like
miniature galleons towards the west.

But the ball was out again. Three men had it and were racing
towards the Uldale goal. All Uldale drew its breath; soon most of
the remaining audience, save the very aged, were rushing into
the field to join the game.

David too. He had been all this time like a dog straining at the
leash. Now stripping off his mulberry coat and flowered vest, he
rushed into the fray. Peel's two sons were with him. Together
they raced the field, and David as he ran, felt that this was truly
the grandest moment of his life, with the wind brushing his
cheeks, the mountains crowding to meet him, the turf strong and
resilient beneath his feet.

He touched the ball; it passed to young Isaac Peel, then over
to Rumney Peel, back to himself again. He could feel the field

streaming behind him. Two men were in their way. David feinted; the ball obeyed him like a living thing, and now the three of them, sharing for an instant a comradeship that was as true and strong as though long companionship had made it, were away, away with only the hills to meet them.

Skiddaw smiled; Blencathra clapped his hands; all the rosy clouds sang together; and to the roar of the approving world, the ball slipped between the posts.

Glorious never-to-be-forgotten moment – and David, turning, throwing his arms high for victory, saw, quite near to him, above the road, waiting beside his horse, the figure of his father.

He moved towards him, joyfully greeting him. Then he paused. Something very terrible had occurred. He felt it come, through the lovely evening air, darkening the sky, dimming the sounds of the games, removing him to a circle of silence wherein he stood alone with his father. Afterwards he remembered that he had thought: 'Why, he's old . . . and a terrible thing has come to him.'

In Herries's voice when he greeted him, however, there was no tremor, and his hand, in its long black glove, was hard and firm. His clothes were dark, his face was pale, drawn, as it often was, a little crookedly. Whence did David have his sense of some disaster?

Herries said, very quietly, but holding his son's hand:

'Davy, has she been here?'

'She? . . . But who?'

'My wife.'

'Mirabell? No. Is she not with you?'

'She left me early this morning, and I must find her.' The hand in David's gave a slight quiver.

'Why did she leave you?'

'I cannot say. But I must find her.'

David put his hand on the other's shoulder and felt an odd pride that it should be so hard and strong. All this while he had been looking into his father's face, and now, beneath the customary ironical gaze and twisted mouth, he felt such a force of controlled agony that he dropped his eyes. He had never yet loved his father so deeply as now, when he realized that he was unable to help him.

'She cannot have gone far,' he said urgently, longing to do or say something to assuage that unhappiness. ''Twas a momentary pique or resentment. She had secret moods unlike other women—'

But Herries stopped him, raising his hand and gripping his son's shoulder so fiercely that David winced. He wore only his shirt.

'No, it was no pique,' Herries said quietly. 'I had told her that we would leave Herries because I fancied that she would be happier so. She thought it would kill me to leave Herries, so, for my comfort, she went away. I must find her that she may understand.'

He turned, stroking his horse's neck.

'Father, I will come with you. I will sleep with you tonight, and tomorrow—'

Herries shook his head, smiling.

'Nay, this is my affair. You are a good son, Davy. I shall find her. Nothing in heaven or hell shall stay me.'

He mounted his horse.

'Return to your guests. Farewell.'

He started down the white road and, before he turned the corner, looked back once and waved his hand.

HERRIES STARTS HIS SEARCH

VERY early the next morning, Herries, after bidding farewell to Benjamin, his servant and friend, started out on his search.

Part Four

THE BRIGHT TURRETS OF ILION

RETURN OF A WANDERER

ON a sharp clear autumn afternoon of the year 1768, Mr Simeon Harness; pastor, schoolmaster, and general man-of-all-work in the districts of Rosthwaite, Watendlath and Seatoller, climbed to the top of the Brund Fell and looked appreciatively about him. With so little a climb he had reached an elevation of great splendour. He was a short, pursy man, normally scant of breath, but for the last five years he had walked these tops on his daily occupations, and so friendly and kindly had they come to seem to him that he did not realize any arduousness in surmounting them.

His own home – two rooms of a farmhouse – was in the hamlet of Watendlath, the smoke from whose chimneys he could see now lazily curling beneath him.

He had indeed a fine view. On these tops you could walk for miles and scarcely be compelled to descend. Beloved names came to meet him as he looked. Towards Derwentwater, Brown Dodd and Ashness Fell and High Seat; towards Thirlmere, Armboth and Watendlath Fell; towards the Langdales, Coldbarrow and Ullscarf and High White Stones. The ranges lay all about him in shapes more human than those of his friends, moulded and formed, now sharply with rocks and steeples and slanting cliffs of shining colour, then gently in sheets of flaming bracken lifting to smooth arms and shoulders embossed like shields of metal. Wild profusion, and yet perfect symmetry and order. One colour faded to another, purple cliff above orange sea, deeps of violet under shadow of rose, and a great and perfect stillness everywhere.

When he turned and looked across the valley to Stye Head he saw, falling over the Gavel and Scafell, ladders of sunlit mist that were indeed to his devout soul like steps to heaven. It did not seem strange to him that, on a sudden call, one should climb these ladders and so, to the sound of trumpets, pass into that other glorious company.

He sighed. He did not wish to pass over. He supposed that there was still much work to do, but there were times when his scattered flock seemed to be past all stirring, when, if he looked back, he had achieved exactly nothing at all, when the pain in his side, which had been his constant companion ever since, three years before, some drunken revellers had in the friendliest of spirits thrown him off a hayrick, was sharper than he could silently endure, when his own sins, his ingratitude to God, his liking for ale, the greed of his stomach, and the sudden sharp temptation of a handsome woman, mounted crimson-high – on such occasions, in spite of all fortitude, he sighed for the ladders of God.

He had a round bare face like a baby's, wore a small tie-wig and a coat and breeches of rusty black, and carried in his hand a worn copy of Mr Chapman's translation of the *Iliad*, which appeared to him to be, after the Bible, the finest book in the world.

It was his intention, although the afternoon was chill, to sit on the ground, with his beloved hills all around him, and read. He knew that in a short time the peace of the scene would steal about him and quieten his distresses. This magical charm had never failed him. He sat down, facing the silver ladders, and opened his book, gathering the skirts of his coat about him for greater warmth and smiling amiably at the three or four sheep who were tranquilly grazing near him.

He began to read:

<blockquote>

Fires round about them shined,
As when about the silver moon, when air is free from wind,
And stars shine clear, to whose sweet beams, high prospects, and the brows
Of all steep hills and pinnacles, thrust up themselves for shows,
And even the lowly valleys joy to glitter in their sight,
When the unmeasured firmament bursts to disclose her light,
And all the signs in heaven are seen that glad the shepherd's heart;
So many fires disclosed their beams, made by the Trojan part,
Before the face of Ilion, and her bright turrets showed.
A thousand courts of guard kept fires, and every guard allowed
Fifty stout men, by whom their horse ate oats and hard white corn,
And all did wishfully expect the silver-thronéd morn.

</blockquote>

He repeated the phrases aloud that the hills might also enjoy them.

'The lowly valleys joy to glitter in their sight.' The 'bright turrets' of Ilion. The 'hard white corn'. 'The silver-thronéd morn.'

He was himself something of a poet and had once written an

'Elegy to Sophia Countess of Balebury', his one-time patroness.
It had, of course, never been published, but he showed it once
and again to an intimate.

All very well to be a poet, but when you had but thirty pounds
a year, a pain in your side and a sadly lascivious nature, where
was the time for poetry? He was concerned too for the country.
The fate of the American Colonies was dwelling just now heavily
on his conscience, although no others of his friends seemed to be
concerned with it. Grenville's Stamp Act of three years before
had appeared to him an injustice unworthy of his country's great-
ness; but on the other hand he had only now, in a belated news-
sheet, been reading of the episode of the sloop *Liberty* in Boston
and the abominable riots that followed the seizure of the cargo.
Hard, hard the ways of this world; so easy would men only love
one another, but that very thing how difficult, as he could see in
his own case, because try as he might he could not love Willie
Richards, the farmer in whose house he lodged, as he truly
should.

So he sighed and envied the sheep, then smartly abused himself for an ungrateful wretch whom God had placed in this marvellous world, hemming him in with ladders of silver and gold,
extending to him with every new day the signs of His grace and
favour, while even the pain in his side was troublesome but a little
and nothing at all compared with what many poor folk had to
suffer. He could not, however, return tranquilly to his Homer.
He was sitting on a natural platform of turf, and now he rose and
walked back and forth, two hands clasped behind his back, his
eyes drinking in the constant change of scene as the light and
shadow ran beneath the sun, his mind biting on its troubles, its
successes (as when last Sunday forenoon he had preached in
Keswick market-place to some hundred souls), its fears and
surrenders.

He had just thought that his stomach was queasy and it was
time he made his way down to Watendlath for a meal, when, looking in the direction of the Pikes, he perceived someone approaching. This was a man moving with a remarkably easy and resolute
stride, and, as he came nearer, Mr Harness saw that he carried
on his back a bundle and in his hand a very stout staff.

The stranger (for Mr Harness could see at once that it was
no one familiar to him) appeared to hesitate as to his choice of
descent; then, seeing the little clergyman, he came to meet
him.

Now, close at hand, he was clearly remarkable for his height, his strong leanness, his white hair (he wore his own hair, which was cropped to his neck), and for the unusual character of his features. His eyes were large and brilliant, his countenance haughty and reserved but marked by a deep scar which ran from the forehead to the upper lip.

So soon as he saw the scar Mr Harness knew who it must be. This was Herries of Herries in Rosthwaite, the extraordinary man who had gone mad after his wife, a common gipsy woman, left him. That at least was the gossip of the valley. Although Mr Harness had been for five years at Watendlath and Herries had been on several occasions during that period at his home, Mr Harness had not yet seen him.

Opinion locally differed as to whether the man were mad or no. Some said that he had been always crazy since he first came there; others that he was not mad at all but cursed by God; others that he was not wicked even, but only a poor soul with whom everything had gone wrong. And a few said that he was a good man and generous and very wise. It was true at least that after his wife left him opinion became gentler towards him, and the old term 'Rogue Herries' had a note of kindliness in it; but it was still said everywhere that once he had had league with the Devil, had lived with a witch in his house and, when they drowned her, carried her home and buried her in his garden.

So, for all these opinions, Mr Harness was greatly interested to meet with him.

'Good day,' he said smiling.

Herries took off his broad black hat and wiped his forehead.

'It is warm walking,' he said, looking at Mr Harness with a very kindly expression in his dark eyes. His hat off, there was something indeed very remarkable in his appearance, for his hair was of a most beautiful snowy whiteness that seemed to catch the afternoon light. His face too was brown and spare with health.

'Have you come far, sir?' asked Mr Harness.

'From Furness.'

'That is a long distance. By Langdale is shorter.'

The other laughed. 'I am sixty-eight years of age, but have no sense of it.'

'Sixty-eight!' said Mr Harness in admiration. 'You are accustomed to walking, sir?'

'I never knew what true health was before I adopted it.' Then he added very simply, 'My name is Herries and I am going to my house in Rosthwaite. Perhaps you are yourself going that way?'

'My name is Harness,' answered the other. ''Tis odd that we have not met before.'

'I have heard of you, sir,' said Herries. 'We will go together, then.'

As they turned he went on: 'I have been all day alone and shall be glad of a little company. 'Tis odd how you may walk these hills for a week and meet no human soul. There was a time when I preferred my own company to any man's, but now it may be that I know my own self too well.' Then, after a moment's pause, he added very quietly, 'I have been for a long time in search of my wife who left me in a misunderstanding five years ago.'

'I have heard something of it,' said Mr Harness, gravely.

Herries nodded his head. 'I speak of it to everyone I meet, for it may by chance happen that they have heard of her.'

Mr Harness was very sympathetic. He liked this man.

'It is scarcely likely,' he said, 'that she will have remained all these years in the district.'

Herries nodded. 'Nay, it is not likely. But the North Country was her only home. Though she has gone south for a while she will return. Of that I am certain.' Then, very cheerfully: 'But these are personal matters; I know did you have news of her from anyone you would inform me. I am hoping that she may be at my house, waiting for me. I have considerable hope. It is three months since I was here, and as this is the only spot of the whole earth for me it is a great happiness to return.'

'Have you been far, sir?' asked Harness.

'I have been for the first time for many years in London.'

'And pray tell me, sir,' said Mr Harness, eagerly, 'how did you find the Town? I have, alas, never been there, and must trust to the descriptions of others.'

'I found it grievously altered,' said Herries. 'There is scarce any of the old Town left. They are pulling down here and destroying there until it is pitiful to realize that in a year or two the character of the Town will be gone. 'Tis this craze for modernity. I assure you, sir, there is such a rush and tumble in these days that one must hesitate to cross the street for the fierceness of the traffic.

'But what appears to me the most lamentable is that the Town is losing its character, and might be as modern as the town of New York for its new buildings, the vulgarity of the people, the craze for wealth, and the rest. But indeed, sir, I am an old country cousin, and 'tis a shock to my system to comprehend that Queen Anne is truly dead.'

'You spoke of the town of New York,' said Mr Harness. 'Pray tell me, did you hear much talk of our American Colonies?'

'Scarce a word. America is too remote for men to worry over.'

Mr Harness sighed. 'I fear there is a great injustice there. We shall worry before all is done.' He went on more tentatively: 'And you heard no news of your wife in London?'

'No, sir, I did not. I had one evening, however, an odd adventure.'

'Pray let me hear it, sir,' said Mr Harness.

'I was minded one evening to go to the theatre. They were playing the *Othello* of William Shakespeare. Before the first act was over I was conscious that there was a fellow near to me who was aware of my nearness to him. I looked again and again, but could see only his back. After a while he turned, and I perceived that he bore an odd resemblance to a fellow many years ago in these parts, a pedlar, a vagrant who, by accident rather than any design, had played some part in incidents of my former life here.

'I am a man of no superstitious feeling. This world is interpenetrated, we cannot but doubt, with many others, but it is our business to deal with this one and leave the rest to a future time. But it has ever been my misfortune to be dreaming when I should be most practical, and to see my way cloudily when I should be most exact.

'The lights were blowing, there was a wind stirring in the theatre, and I had a strange conviction that in another moment or so I was to die. I don't know, sir, how it may be with you, but life has so tormented me with its riddle that to die without any answer to it has always seemed to me an exasperating indignity.

'The theatre grew dark to me, the wind blew about my ears, the candles leaping before my eyes, and the fellow of whom I have spoken appeared to come close to me and whisper with malicious amusement in my ear. The theatre was crowded to my eyes with dancing figures grotesquely attired, and in the centre of them I seemed to see my wife begging me to come to her.

'In the increasing uproar of wind and light and many men shouting, I fought my way towards her, this fellow at my side striving to prevent me. With the utmost difficulty, and after much roughness, I reached her, and, at the touch of her hand and the consciousness of the great joy that we both were feeling, everything seemed to be made clear to me. I wondered that for so long it should have been so perplexing. The intensity of that joy made my past life of no account ... We fell together, our hands clasped, between a crowd of whirling figures, the candles dancing before our eyes. Such a mutual death was greater than anything that life had been. It was in all the experience of a moment, but so vivid that it was impossible to deny its positive occurrence. Nevertheless I had not vacated my seat, nor missed, I fancy, any detail of the play. When, in my clear mind, I looked for this fellow again he was not there.'

'It was a dream,' said Mr Harness gravely. 'God has many fashions of making Himself clear to us.'

'Well, well,' Herries answered briskly, with a smile. 'It may be so. But I doubt the benevolence of your God. He is plaguily roundabout in His plans for serving us, nor have I found life so sweet that I am minded to thank Him so heartily for what He has done for me.

'It may be,' said Mr Harness, 'that sweetness is not its purpose, but rather a very varied experience for the growth of our poor wisdom. The beauties of Nature and the unexpected nobility of man under severe trial are sufficient justification for living, to my mind.'

Herries answered quietly: 'An God will give me my wife again, I will ask Him for no further justification.'

They were reaching now the foot of the Fell and approaching the road. It was plain that with every step Herries's pleasure at returning to his home was increasing. They turned left towards Rosthwaite, and walked very happily together along the path that ran down above the river bed. It was a beautiful evening of great quietness; the air smelt sweetly, and the sky was rosy above the hills.

Mr Harness, thoroughly at ease with his companion, talked freely on his affairs, how the pain in his side troubled him, and how his appetite was shamefully strong, and he had been drunk ten days back, and sung, he was afraid, a number of lascivious songs. But the Devil was always round the corner with a remarkable knowledge of each individual's weakness. They parted in great friendliness, and Herries went on up to his house.

At the entrance to the little court he hesitated. Dusk was coming rapidly now, and he could see only dimly the stone wall, and beyond it the huddled dark mass of the house, its line ragged against the sky. A little wind had come with the evening, and was whistling and whining over the ground, a tune so familiar to him in its thin desolation, mingled as it was with the rhythm of running water and the chill of oncoming night, that it was like the hand-grip of a friend. But it was not the wind to which he was now listening. How often, during these last years, he had waited thus on his return!

Sometimes he had been absent only a week, sometimes months, and once, directly after her flight, nearly a year had passed. Always the same. Listening, his hand on the gate that was swinging now on its hinges, because he must postpone a little longer the moment when he would put it to the test whether she were waiting for him or no. One day it would be – of that he had no doubt – but how soon? How soon? Could he endure this time the blow of the disappointment? He set back his shoulders, looked up to the last yellow strands that struck like whips across the darkening sky, then went forward with a firm tread.

The door was open. He could see the familiar things, the old armour, the yellow-faced clock like a moon against the shadow, and he could hear the sounds, the clock's voice, a banging door monotonously complaining, and the stir that there was always about the old house, rats in the wainscot, maybe, and the dust of the years sifting from ceiling to floor.

She was not here. He knew it instantly. Never mind; she would come – if not now, another time. Tomorrow, soon, it could not be long delayed. So he went slowly up the old creaking stairs, stood in the dark hall, and then shouted for Benjamin. He was suddenly very weary, dropped his bundle and stick on the floor, and sank into the armchair by the fireplace.

Soon he heard Benjamin come clambering up the stairs. A moment after, Benjamin was in the doorway, holding two lighted candles, his face wreathed in smiles.

'Master! Master! You're back!'

He set the candles on the table, and came over with his old familiar rolling gait like a shapeless porpoise. His face was round like the moon, he had three chins now, and a belly that hung over his stout legs like a pillow, but he was not soft. His hair was short and erect on his head, his eyes wore their old expression of sound surprise, and on his nose there was the same old brown wart. The same! Of course he was the same! It was as though Herries had taken him with him on his travels. He came to his master, and his master greeted him with his old gesture, pulling him towards him, pinching his cheek, then driving him away again with a smack and a gentle kick.

'Well, old ass, old noddle, with us again . . . with us again . . . The world over, and thy round face always behind the candles – Satan be thanked for it!'

Benjamin went on his knees and pulled off his boots, looking

up once and again into Herries's face with a pleasure that was
none the less precious for being simple. Herries rested his hand
on the broad back. So she had not come, she was not here. One
more delay – how many yet would he endure?

He drove it from him.

'Food, fire, drink, Benjamin. There has been no one here?'

'Master David, master. Miss Deborah once. Statesman
Peel . . .'

'Aye; more of that in a moment. Has Mrs Benjamin a fowl or
can slaughter one? Has she a pie? I could eat thy own chaps, thou
monstrous swine.'

The man sat back on his haunches.

'My wife is gone, master.'

'Gone!' Herries sat back astonished. 'What! A-whoring!'

'No, poor woman. She's dead.'

'Dead! Dead! Why? how? when?'

'''Twas Midsummer Night. She'd had a pain in her belly. I'd
cursed her for a whining woman, and told her I'd take a whip to
her, always moaning about her belly as though she'd a child there
and was eight months gone. But it was real enough. She wasted
day after day to the thinness of a hickory stick. She wouldn't eat,
she who could swallow a leg of mutton and a beef pie quicker
than any woman. And she was gentle – terribly gentle and for-
giving. I cursed her for that too, but she could do nothing with
it. "My temper's gone down with my belly," poor soul, she'd say.
Mother Dawlish of Stonethwaite physicked her. There's no one
finer. She has herbs from Solomon's time, they say. But 'twas no
use. Comes Midsummer Night, as fine and warm an evening as
you could search for, but she was mortal cold and would lie in
my arms, a thing she'd not wished for these many years. She had
never been a loving-tempered woman, and would always be in a
tantrum if I wanted to press her a bit. But now she was there,
with my arms round her and a mighty pain in her belly, poor
thing, and as fine and warm a night of stars and moonshine as
you'd wish for. She was wandering at the last, wanting a green
nettle to tickle Tom Prommice that she'd had a mind to be married to before I plagued her. Aye, all she wanted was a green
nettle and I had none for her, and so she passed, with the moon
coming in at the window, there in my arms.'

'Why, poor old Benjamin!' Herries drew him closer, enclosing
his neck with his hand. 'You are alone – and I also. And since
then, there has been no one with you in the house?'

'No one, master, and many's the night I've thought I've heard her tread – lop-lop-lop, heavy-heavy-heavy, and then a kind of skitter-skatter with the flop of her slipper. I've risen from my bed to look for her, but it's been the wind or the rain coming in through the roof at the left end there.'

'So we're alone here.'

'None the worse for that.' Benjamin straightened himself and rose. 'I'll light the fire and have a grand meal for you.'

Herries nodded. 'And you need no woman to help you?'

Benjamin turned near the door. 'We shall do without women. I'm wise now, so that I'd rather have my sleep than a woman. That's what life teaches you.'

Well, thought Herries, life hadn't taught him that yet. Quietly, as he often did, in an attitude of cool dispassion, he considered this longing for Mirabell. What was it that drove him? Certainly not lust. That it had never been. Certainly not self-pity or fear of loneliness. In one sense he had never been lonely, in another he had never been anything else. What was it, this hunger? He supposed that in human beings there was always through life this search for fulfilment, and through life to death most men never found it. They managed well enough without it, had no time to speculate, snatched at whatever substitutes they could find and made the most of them.

But with some men this search was ceaseless. It would for ever be the theme of all their days. The poets made poetry of it, the conquerors hacked kingdoms out of it, the madmen plaited straw in their hair. He had been one of these. It had never let him rest, and when he saw Mirabell the question was answered for him. He had loved her in the only true sense of love, that of finding completion in another soul and remaining settled there like a kernel in the heart of a nut. Everything moved by law whether there were a God or no, and this was a law, as certain and ordered as the movement of the stars, that he should love Mirabell. Did she love him, then the order was completed, and one more fragment of perfect movement was added to the multiplicity of the rest. But she did not. She had never loved him for a single moment. So here was another jangled piece of disorder added to all the others.

He had had a strange life, not, he thought, an unhappy one. It had been too interesting for that, but it was a fierce business, ferocious in its wildness, surprising in its beauty, ironical in its foolishness, mysterious in its purpose, but always invigorating, powerful, infinitely worth while.

He watched old Benjamin light the fire, smiling to himself to think that after all this life, this struggle, these passions, rebellions, and desires, this should be all that was left to him, this old fat man who was like a dog in appetite, lack of vision, and fidelity. Oh, and David also.

'So my son has been here?' yawning in sleepiness.

'Mr David has been here, master, and once he brought his babies with him.'

'How do they grow?'

'Grand children, fat and greedy.'

'And how is my son?'

'Not a more content man in the county, master. "Well, Benjamin," says he, "how scrub does this place look! It wants a pail of water," says he, "and the doors are all loose on their hinges!" "Well, Mr David," says I, "it is a tolerable place for Master and me because we're at ease in it," says I, "and 'tis better to be where you're at ease, however scrub it may be, than in a palace where there's no small-beer nor a bull-baiting." "Why, Benjamin," says Mr David, "you're a philosopher." "I leave that to the master," says I, "and suit my bottom to my own stool." But he's always friendly. He's a smiling gentleman, and they say he has a fine house. I've not been there myself, though he's asked me.'

'Aye, he has a sound imagination,' said Herries, 'and a sound belly. Phantoms and apparitions are not in his company, and he's the happier for it. I'm glad he's well.'

'So am I too,' said Benjamin, happy to see his master so cheerful, 'for he is a grand strong man, and can wrestle any other in the county, and he's breeding a grand family that will last to Judgement Day, I should think.'

When the food came Herries made Benjamin sit down beside him, and told him of some of his adventures. The old man had a great ear for marvels. Nothing was too miraculous for him to believe. Herries told him how he had seen in London a man with a furry tail that stuck out of his breeches, and a woman with a beard to her waist. Also a mermaid in a tank of water.

Benjamin sighed, watching to see whether Herries was relishing his food.

'A mermaid! That's a woman with a fish tail. I've heard of such. And what would be her issue, master, after lying with a man? Fish, think you?'

'More mermaids,' said Herries. 'They sing so sweetly that no man can resist embracing them.'

'Did the one you saw sing, master?'

'She was melancholy, poor creature, being a captive, and did nothing but sigh, and the tears poured down her cheeks.'

''Tis a shame,' said Benjamin, banging the table, 'to keep them for a show. Why did you not break the tank, master, and plunge her into the sea again?'

'I'm no knight-errant any more, Benjamin. I have lost my fire.'

'Not a bit of it, master,' said Benjamin cheerfully. 'You shall see how merry the two of us shall be here. I can cook to your fancy, and the trees are growing and I've got bricks round the chimney, and the horses are in fine trim. You shall see how grand everything will be!'

Left alone, Herries lay back and looked at the fire, strange thoughts crowding on to him; the scenes of the last months, lonely hillsides, crowded inns, the noise and smells of streeted towns, lights and flares, clouds and wind, odd voices and shouting strangers, all the bustle of a world. He had not been unhappy in it. There had been something as spectator that had pleased his ironic fancy, and there had been always the driving passion of his unresting search. But that other earlier life, now so remote – pictures now crowded about him – the mad restless life at Doncaster, the arrival at Keswick, and poor old Pomfret with his oaths and nervous violence, the night ride out to his house, poor Margaret, Alice Press . . .

His visions stopped there. He drove them back. Of what use? All, all had been a preparation for Mirabell. He saw her, a tiny child clinging to her mother in the noise of the Christmas games, standing beside him on Honister, speaking to him shyly in Carlisle: 'I wanted to tell you . . . I love someone. . .', that fearful moment when, above the dead body of her lover, she turned, not seeing him, staring into the face of her tragedy, the marriage day, in the little Chapel, afterwards the huddle of the villagers tumbling down the stairs, and again when he had carried her to their bed . . . these too he must drive back. But his longing he could not control. His longing for nothing more than her presence. Were she here now, sitting opposite him at the fire, he would not pester her for love. Were she returned, he would never speak to her of love again – only that she should be there!

He smiled at his old age, his white hair: he as a lover! But this love had nothing to do with age nor with physical strength nor with beauty. He did not love Mirabell for her beauty. She was not beautiful. She was not clever, nor had she the arts of the woman. But she was his wife, his child, his mistress, his friend, and he felt a kind of triumph because nothing could rob him of this, his only feeling for her that death itself would not destroy.

If only for five minutes he might speak to her he was sure that he could persuade her to stay with him. There was nothing now to frighten her. He did not want her now to love him, that is, if she truly could not.

But at the thought of the bliss that it would be if she loved him, his heart beat so thickly that he could sit still no longer. He tried to rise, to find that one of his legs would not stir. The pain was so sharp and so sudden that he cried out. A wave of pain covered his body. He thought that he would faint. Then, while he gritted his teeth, it passed again. Benjamin returning at that moment, he called out to him to help him.

'Why, master, are you lame?' The old man helped him up.

'Aye; take me to bed. I'm old. This leg failed me a sennight back.' But he grinned at the top of the stairs. His leg was better again.

'That won't beat me. But see me to my bed, and talk your non-sense, old fool. I'll not have ghosts in my room tonight.'

And Benjamin, whose mind was literal, told him how the old woman Carpenter of Grange had been chased in Cumma Catta Wood by the ghost of the old witch Wilson, who had barked like a dog, and flame had come from her mouth.

'She will not plague me,' said Herries. 'I carried her in my breast once for all her witchcraft.'

He kept Benjamin at his side far into the night.

ULDALE

II

FAMILY LIFE

SARAH HERRIES one fine summer day had a tea-party. Not by her own intent. She had but recently risen from the delivery of her third child, William Benedict Herries, who was born on a damp day in June, 1770. Why Benedict, said everyone? No one knew. Sarah thought it a nice name, and David was so happy at having another son that he didn't care what they called him. Why was David so happy? He had two children already, and children are, they say, very expensive. They were not so expensive then. There were more servants, much more space, much

more indifference to infant complaints. Children wailed, were
not attended to, ceased wailing. But David cared nothing for
expense. Here was another Herries. He saw himself in the rôle of
Abraham with Herries scattered about him like the sands of the
sea.

Sarah did not mind. This was to be the last of her children and
she would have been sad had she known. She was strong, resolute, happy, maternal. This was the grand time of her life.

Squire Osmaston and his wife rode over on this fine summer
day, and the O'Briens happened to be out in their new carriage.
This was a year or two before the Carlisle Post Coach, which
went from Carlisle to London in three days. The world was opening up. You could travel so fast now that there was no escaping
a neighbour, did he wish to see you. So fast, but not so securely.
The O'Briens had a house between Carlisle and Bassenthwaite.
They had come ten miles in their carriage and were shaken to
pieces although this was summer weather and the roads were dry.
They were shaken but proud. The Squire and his lady had ridden
over on two enormous horses who looked, as young Maurice
O'Brien whispered to their friend, Colonel Assheton-Bolitho-
Carmichael, who had ridden over with them, like 'animals out
of the Mythology'. The gentlemen were drinking in the parlour
while the ladies sat in the garden sheltered from the winds by a
charming little Gothic temple which Sarah, who was sharing the
universal taste for Gothic, had had constructed.

So there they were. David was unfortunately in Borrowdale,
where he had been staying the night with his father. Sarah,
warned by her maid Nellie, who had spied the chaise, had quickly
changed her housework clothes for a large orange hoop and an
upper dress of silver which suited her very handsomely. Mrs
O'Brien and her two daughters, Katherine and Olivia, were very
finely dressed, so finely that they took up most of the space in the
temple, but Mrs Osmaston had on a muddy riding-suit, her wig
awry, and her hat on anyhow. She sat as usual with her legs
spread, her hands on her hips, looking like the Wife of Bath,
temp 1770.

Sarah enjoyed it all hugely. She loved to have friends about
her, to play hostess, to sit in her own grounds with her house at
her back, to know that her children were well, the cows in the
paddock not ailing and her own bodily vigour returning to her at
last after some very languid weeks. Talk, talk! What were they
talking about?

About a boil on the Osmaston back, about clothes in Carlisle, about the incredible impertinence of servants and the high vails that they everywhere demanded, about Miss Nancy Souper of Hardcross and her illegitimate baby that she'd had of a local doctor, about a shepherd who had been hanged last week for stealing two halters and a hammer, about colds and chills, about everything in the world and nothing at all.

The new baby was brought out for inspection and was considered strong, healthy and the spit of his father. The baby, who was withdrawn howling, led to a very animated discussion of the comparative virtues of Doctor James's Powder and Bishop Berkeley's Tar-Water. Dr James's Fever Powder, nothing could rival it. It had saved the lives of Royalty, was good for everything from smallpox to distemper.

The powder rose in a happy cloud before the ladies' eyes. Of a sudden, life was secure and confident. Incredible that anyone should ever die! Mrs O'Brien (whose voice was small, very precious, as though every utterance were worth its weight in gold) gave it as definite fact that between the year 1750 (when the powder first began to be in reputation) and the close of the year 1763 fewer had died, upon an average, than in any preceding thirteen years, upon which Mrs Osmaston, kicking out her leg, scratching her dirty wig and barking like a dog, remarked that this was no virtue in a powder. For her part this business of keeping Inconsiderable People alive when they were greatly better dead was vastly overdone. The world was largely too filled with unnecessary persons. In the good old times, which were better in every way than the present, when someone ailed, if he or she were of a sickly constitution the illness finished them, and a good thing too, for who wished the countryside to be peopled with ailing imbeciles who were for ever about to be ill or recovering from illness and a nuisance to everyone about them? Had she had her way she would have strangled Dr James at birth and saved this world a monument of trouble and expense.

Mrs Osmaston always grew vigorous in the open air. Houses stifled her. She was only really happy with dogs and horses, men who told her bawdy stories and ladies with whom she might exchange scandal. Her heart, however, was kindly and generous, her life a constant protest against the conventions of a ridiculous society. It was told of her that when the Squire in her own village had put a girl in the family way, and the girl was turned out by her drunken but virtuous father, she had taken the girl into her own house and nursed her until she was well again.

What was life to her? a succession of following the hounds,

tramping the fells after the fox from dawn to dark, eating and drinking vast quantities of everything, bullying and loving her thick-hided husband, scolding her friends, crying over *Clarissa*, chatting with every huntsman and stable-boy in the district, driving all her household to church of a Sunday and encouraging the parson to be drunk after dinner.

Mrs O'Brien was a sententious and sentimental woman with all the belief of her time in capital letters. Mrs Osmaston shocked her very deeply and she could not forbear to say:

'Why, Alicia, to speak so destructively you condemn both our Maker and His Divine Purposes. Why should we practise the virtues of Compassion and Indulgence on behalf of our Fellows if this world is not an Education and an Improver of our frailties? Olivia, my love, turn your cheek. The sun is catching it.'

'I cannot for my part,' said Mrs Osmaston, 'do with your Sensibilities and Virtues. We are not put here to be Virtuous, but to cause as little trouble to our fellow-mortals as may be. And the proof is that if you have a flea down your back you think nothing of your Sensibility but off with your smock and snap him between finger and thumb.'

Both the O'Brien girls tittered at this. Mrs Osmaston was so very droll! Olivia was all Sensibility, but Katherine inclined towards dogs and horses and a drink with the gentlemen. They both despised their mother, but feared her. Underneath her sensibilities she had an iron hand.

'We have had,' said Mrs Osmaston, who enjoyed teasing Mrs O'Brien, 'the oddest cousin from London. He would have pleased you mightily, Julia. He was all sensibility. He was in raptures over every country sight. He was ever talking of the Elysian fields and 'gentle showers' and 'rivers of dew'. A sheep sent him into ecstasies. He was all for discovering hillocks and haycocks and dusky trees. At the last he was discovered lying under a haycock with a milkmaid, where his processes were, I don't doubt, as ordinary as though he'd been fiddling with a chambermaid in Piccadilly. But his hair was all straw and he was whipped through the fields by a jealous shepherd, so his experiences were at the last sufficiently Arcadian.' Mrs Osmaston roared with laughter, slapping her thighs. 'The shepherd had his breeches down and whipped his bare skin, so that he could not sit to cards that evening. He returned to town next day and is the less Arcadian for his visit.'

All the ladies laughed and had anecdotes of a similar kind to furnish, and then there must arise the accustomed arguing as to the relative virtues of Mr Fielding and Mr Richardson. Those two gentlemen entered the Gothic temple, their spirits comfortably enjoying the salubrious air and the female society. Mr Fielding liked the pretty Olivia best, with her pink and white, her air of a rakish prude and her fine legs (which, being a spirit, he could plainly discern under the lemon-coloured hoop), and little Mr Richardson preferred Mrs O'Brien who was after his own heart.

'But Grandison!' cried Mrs O'Brien, 'how tenderly imagined, how proudly conceived! What Ideal Behaviour and Constant Fidelity!' and Mr Richardson planted a kiss on her broad brow which seemed to her like the tickling of a fly so that she brushed the place with her hand.

'A —— for your Grandison!' said Mrs Osmaston very coarsely. 'Now Jones is the man for my money and for Katherine's too, I don't doubt. What, Katherine! Would you let Jones touzle you were he here? Would you beat Sophia out of the field, girl? I'll wager if your mother's back were turned you'd not hesitate.'

It was well perhaps that the gentlemen were coming across the lawn. Squire Osmaston was drunk and Mr O'Brien nearly so. They were singing a hunting catch which rang prettily through the summer air, but they hushed as they drew close to the temple.

Mrs Osmaston rose to control her lord and master.

'You're drunk, Peter, and will never reach home in safety.'

He staggered a little, then slapped her fat neck with a hearty friendliness.

'I'm a little drunk and a little sober. My good horse Robin knows how to carry me. I have not been drunk for a week past and, for that, my fair hostess will forgive me.'

Everyone was readily forgiven on so lovely a summer evening. They all moved to the road where the fine new chaise was vastly admired and the two enormous horses solemnly held by Ralph, David's farm man. The scene was thick with gold dust like a bee's wing and the trees smelt of honey.

The chaise was away first with a great waving of arms and shouting of goodbyes. Before she mounted her charger Mrs Osmaston put her stout arm round Sarah's neck and embraced her.

'I am fond of you, my dear. I am a foolish old woman who chatters a world of nonsense, but there's a bed for you and a horse to ride with us any time you desire it. Now then – huppety-hup—' With a leap she was in the saddle and settled there as though she were part of the horse's anatomy. The Squire too, drunk though he might be, had no trouble in mounting, and a fine pair they made, facing the country as though they were king and queen of it.

The Squire had some last confidential word. 'There's a tale,' he said to Sarah, looking at her solemnly from the back of his horse, 'a damnably good tale that I must tell your husband. 'Tis a tale of an orange and Mrs O'Brien's pet monkey. 'Tis the wittiest, handsomest . . .'

'Whoop!' cried Mrs Osmaston, giving his horse a whack with her whip, and off they went down the road, a cloud of dust behind them and the sky golden over their heads.

The horses' hoofs rang on the road, then peace resumed its power.

Sarah walked a little while in her garden before going into the house. Although the sun, a smiling gold penny, had almost perched its chin now on the ledge of the hills, the air was yet richly warm and the cool of the evening mingled with it most freshly.

All the sounds were of the summer evening, bees were yet humming, the men were calling to the cows, and a thrush was singing from the thick luxury of an oak tree as though it had but just come into the noblest of fortunes. Sarah's heart beat with the conscious appreciation of the goodness of life. She could not believe that she was thirty-two! Thirty-two! Thirty-two! And she knew old ladies in Keswick with Brussels caps on their heads not a day over thirty. But she was younger now than she had ever been. In those hard years with her uncle she had been old. She saw herself as a child of fifteen, standing before one of his infernal rages and calculating with the wizened wisdom of an old witch how she would drive him into a certain position and make a bargain with him there. Her youth had begun with that almost miraculous appearance of David there in the Wasdale Inn. She had loved him at sight, and thrown herself at his head and won her liberty.

But afterwards, over that last scene on the Pass, a cloud hovered. There had been something evil then. She had hated her uncle, she had owed him nothing, he had not cared what misery he had planned for her, but still in his death there had been a cloud of evil. She would never be quite free of it.

For a moment the garden had been darkened and the humming of the bees dimmed, but she was of too healthy a nature to prolong any morbidity, and so, singing to herself, her strong freshly-coloured body moving freely in its orange and silver, she walked her garden.

She loved this place because it was so open. Although in the manner of the time the garden was a little arranged with its temple, box hedges and ornamental paths, yet it ran boldly into open country, the down rising above it on the one side, the road running under the hills on the other. But she loved it in reality because it was the home of her husband and her babies. She was all maternal.

David was her child more than her lover. She understood him now, she thought, with completeness. She had all the woman's tender irony at the ridiculous things that seemed to him important, at his absorption in minutiae; she had, too, the woman's almost jealous envy at his ability to throw off his moods, to forget his passions, to take everything with a light mind.

Was there anything for which men finally cared? David loved her, of course, but a little as a child loves its mother. If another child calls him to play a game, off he goes, forgetting his mother until he needs her again. But Sarah had a great understanding and a splendid gift for taking things as they were. She did not wish David to be different in anything, but were he different she would suit herself to his condition. Standing under the oak tree, looking over to Skiddaw's sprawling shoulders, she speculated a little as to how it would have been if David had had his father's temperament. She did not understand Francis, and yet felt that perhaps at the last she could have understood him better than did any other.

He was old now, but finer, more striking than he had ever been, with his white hair and long nervous figure, of which every part seemed to be imaginatively alive. She could not understand that he should love someone desperately, without end, for ever. David would not. Did she die he would never forget her, would care for her always, but he would marry again and be happy, and the second wife would listen to his plans and share his activities, and be mother of his children just as she was. The knowledge did not make her sad. All she wanted was that he should be happy, happy always and vigorous always and noble-hearted always.

Smiling at the thought of him, she went into the house to her children. They were brought down to the parlour.

Francis was ten and Deborah eight. Deborah was as sweet-natured and unselfish and happy as Francis was reserved and driven in upon himself. Both were pretty children, Francis very dark, slim, aristocratic, never familiar with anyone, fearless, but oddly tempered. He would be distressed for no reason, happy for no reason. He liked best to be by himself. Whether he was fond of his father Sarah could never be sure. He allowed his father to play with him, responded to his father's demands on him, was for the most part obedient. He did not appear, though, to miss him when he was absent, nor showed excitement on his return.

He adored his mother. With her he was not demonstrative, but you could tell that everything she said or did worked in his own bosom responsively, and he would watch her, when he thought that she was not looking, with loving meditative eyes.

Deborah, on the other hand, loved everyone, and gave herself to everyone. She had no self-consciousness, no pose for effect, no selfish motive in anything. She was like any other child in small things – temper, disappointments, aggravations – but everything was quickly over. The serenity of her temperament carried her always on a calm sea. She was as fair as her brother was dark, like her father in that, although slender and delicately made. David worshipped her.

In the parlour they were endlessly happy. There was the China wallpaper, with the white and blue pagodas, temples, bridges and flowers. There was the spinet at which their mother sang. There was the cabinet with the silver boxes and gold chairs and little Chinese figures. There was the music-box with the King and Queen on its lid, who marched to the tinkling tune. There was the animated carpet with the battle worked on it – cannon firing, horses rearing, Captains waving on their men; and there was the comfit-box with the sugared cherries and the cakes of marzipan.

This evening young Francis stood at the window watching the sunset fall over Skiddaw. He was like his grandfather in this at least, that he could not have enough of this country. He had not as yet seen much of it; but now, as he looked out, he was swearing to himself that he would not rest until every stone and tree of it was revealed to him. What did he see there if he looked hard enough? The mountains opened, and, carried by the wind, you struck with your golden shoes the centre of a group of hills like men watching you. Here was a pool, icy and black, and suddenly into the middle of it there plunges a beautiful white horse . . .

''Tis the white horse,' he cried excitedly, turning from the window to Deborah.

'A white horse?' asked Sarah, thinking of a new shawl, the gold buttons of David's coat, whether Mrs Osmaston ever wore a clean wig, and if not why not, and why David was not returned.

'Why, yes, Mama . . . We told you. The ice breaks and it swims to the shore.'

Some story, she supposed, that Mrs Monnasett, nurse, housekeeper and general confidante, had been telling them. Mrs Monnasett needs many pages to herself, but cannot have them – with her passion for plums, her belief in witches and centaurs, and her play-acting, so that, give her a handkerchief and a deal board, and she can be Cleopatra, Jane Shore and Mrs Elizabeth Montagu without shifting her wig. But did anyone suppose that David or Sarah made Uldale, made the children, made the sun turn grey before an east wind, and the milk sour before thunder? No, no. It was all Mrs Monnasett.

And now it was time for the children to hear the music-box and to have one sugared cherry apiece. Francis listened to the tune and saw five small Negroes in gold-laced jackets dance across the carpet. One carried an ivory cane with a blood-red knob to it, and he had only one eye. Where the other eye should have been . . . So he suddenly began to shudder, to shudder and shiver and tremble. He knew now that he would see that empty place where the eye should be all night, so quite without warning and quite foolishly he was sick on the carpet.

Sarah could not understand it. She had never been sick in her life. Perhaps Mrs Monnasett would understand. She was better with Francis than was anyone else.

'After one tune he was sick . . .'

Francis lay, very small and very white, in his four-poster that had green curtains with roses.

Mrs Monnasett, so large that she filled the room, her black hoop billowing about her, a silver chain rising and falling on her breast, took his hand, and continued her fairy-story about Queen Anne. 'But the Princess was resolved to see the Queen, although she had only a rag upon her, so she said to the Lord-in-Waiting, who was fingering his snuff-box made of one green emerald, "Sir, there is a spider in the Queen's closet." Now if there was anything that Her Majesty had a distaste for 'twas a spider, as everyone in the Court knew, and only a week back five hundred and thirty-one spiders had been thrown into the kitchen fire, and made such a smoke that the Royal Cook had turned a dish of Peacock into a Canterbury Pudding by the misfortune of the smoke blinding her eye. Therefore the Lord-in-Waiting hastened as swiftly as his stout legs would carry him, and the Princess, following . . .'

Sarah, sitting awhile to watch that the boy was comfortable,

wondered what Mrs Monnasett's history might be. No one knew.
She had been living for several years in a little green cottage outside Keswick when Sarah met her, and had herself suggested
that she should come to Uldale, for 'I love children,' said she,
'and am never happier than in their company.' And so indeed it
seemed, for she had no interest at all in Society, but cared only
for being with the children, and talking to her little white dog,
Mr Pope, and eating as many sweet cakes as she could find.
'Which is the reason of her great stoutness,' thought Sarah, but
she was truly a Blessing for the house, and long might she remain.

David was home. She could hear him calling 'Sarah! Sarah!',
so she hurried downstairs, and he was there in the parlour, larger
than ever before perhaps. He was delighted to see her, but gave
her that kiss which husbands give their wives when they have
been a long while married and are thinking of someone else.

'You would not consider him fifty years old,' thought Sarah
proudly. His brown tie-wig was pushed back a little from his
forehead, and he slapped his great thigh.

'Here is Paradise. Here, come.' He sat down in the big chair
and she sat close to him, her hand on his knee. 'I'll tell you, I
hope you were frightened out of your senses for me because I did
not return.'

Sarah smiled. 'I am never frightened when you are away, but
I had a party, and you were sadly missed.'

'Aye, that for certain,' he grinned. 'But I have the ague and
the fever and the toothache as well. That house is of paper, and
will be blown away with the first wind, and there my father sits
with old Benjamin on his hams beside him, listening to every
mouse in the passages.'

'How is he, Davy?'

'Oh, well enough. He was but just returned from another of
his journeys. He is crazed, and yet he is not crazed. He is as content, I believe, as ever he was in his life, but he will never rest
until he has found her, although what he will do with her when
he has found her no one can tell. But he will never find her. She
is dead or gone abroad or changed into an apple tree. But he is
resolved that she will return.'

'He and Benjamin are quite alone?'

'They sit like a pair of quarrelling lovers. "You shall have veal
today, master," says Benjamin. "I shall not," says my father. "But
you shall," says Benjamin, and he gives him veal and my father
beats him. And all the while the house rocks and mumbles, and
the mice sit on the tables and the rain beats through the ceiling.

And next week he will be off again and walk a hundred miles, asking of every sheep has he seen his wife. But he is sane enough. He began with me, examined me on all the family, and confounded me with his knowledge. He has been, too, to see Deb's two boys, and can tell you where they are in Arithmetic, and that Deb has a new China piece in her cabinet and a black cat with no tail.'

'Will he not come here for a week and have good food and a warm bed?'

'He does not want good food nor a warm bed neither.'

Sarah sighed, then, looking up at David, laughed.

'How is it that he is your father and you so different?'

'I am not so different. We have a great bond of common feeling. 'Tis odd, Sarah, but I am more comfortable with him than with any other human on the globe, save yourself. I have a feeling, Sarah, that if Mirabell were to return and give him satisfaction by loving him, and they to settle down together, he would become very like myself.'

That was clever of him, thought Sarah, who, like all loving wives, wanted always to prove him strong in the direction where he was undoubtedly weak.

They began then, sitting very close together, to gather all the tiny important things – Davy's toothache, how Molly the mare had cast a shoe, whether Forrest the head farm man was lazier than was natural, the eternal mystery of Mrs Monnasett, and so to Francis who had been sick on the carpet for no reason, and thence to the baby Will who had chewed his coral – and through it all their happiness, their security, their mutual trust, their luck that they had one another.

And David the Patriarch – this is the last view of him just now – staring into the Chinese pagodas, the bridges and the Immortal Temple, sees a Great Tree stretching to heaven, and hanging from its million branches Herries, and Herries, and Herries.

Beneath the tree lies England – her valleys, her rivers, her great cities, and the rocks of her invincible coast – and over England the Tree beneficently stretches its green shade.

There are enough Herries here for a thousand years, and who is that so fatherly protective on the topmost branch?

Who but David himself? He draws Sarah close to him and, with his broad arm around her, kisses her.

But it is England that he is embracing.

THEY MEET IN PENRITH

FEB. 4TH, 1772

THE Peel Towers have faded, the refugees from Culloden are bones beneath the turf, the poet Gray has more than three years back 'dined with Mrs Buchanan on trout and partridges', and Herries has stayed, rested his bundle on the slope of the hedge, and stood with his back to a friendly oak to settle in his mind whether there be three roads or one stretching before him in the dim February light.

His fever, which had become by this quite a friendly companion to him, often brought him to such an uncertainty. He called it his Fever because he did not know what other name to give to it. It came and went as it pleased, having quite a cheerful and independent life of its own. You could never tell what it would be about.

It gripped him in its strong arms at any time, and supplied for him the queerest fancies. You could scarcely call it a sickness because, although it weakened his limbs, dimmed his eyes and beat him about the head, it provided him also with an odd exhilaration and gave him many fantasies. Sometimes it drove him to bed because his back and legs refused to carry him any longer, and, had his will been less strong, he might have yielded to it then more completely, for nothing pleased him more than to lie, the Fever with him, on his bed in Herries and see the strange sights that the Fever brought him, and hear, always a little removed, the sounds, the running of water, the beating of drums, the rumbling of thunder, that echoed in his ears.

But he was not defeated by it. He would boast to it: 'Nay, Fever, I like your company once and again, but you shall not weaken me. This picture that you are showing me of a chariot filled with monkeys and a bark with gold apples is entertaining enough, but tomorrow I go about my business again.'

And the Fever, being a good-natured fellow, would recognize his stubbornness and let him have his way.

On this dark afternoon it was as stubborn as he. He shivered with the chill, his body was as though bruised by a tumble, his head was on fire. So he stood against the oak tree and wondered whether there were three roads into Penrith or only one.

'Ah, well,' said the Fever, rattling inside his head like a loose button, 'you are seventy-two years of age, you know. You haven't the power over me you once had.'

Yes, but *were* there not three roads? He had walked only from Appleby that day, and he must press on to Herries. But how could he press on when there were so many roads to choose from? They mingled and divided and mingled again. They ran to his nose, leapt skywards, rolled like strips of white boarding down an implacable hill.

He wiped his brow, which was damp with sweat, and that seemed to quieten him, for now there was but one road stretching in a subdued and orderly manner to the foot of the town.

He picked up his bundle and went on. In the main street there was no one about. Near to him was a lighted window (for early though it was, the town was already dark) and over the doorway hung a sign, 'The Green Parrot', with a painting of a fine green bird with an ironical eye. A parrot? A parrot? Once before there had been a green parrot in a room filled with talk, and a man. . . But he could not settle the matter. After the Fever had left him he would investigate his memory.

There was a small bare panelled room with a table and a bench, so he sat him down and soon a stout old man in a green baize apron came to attend to him. This old man had a broken nose and a hand without a thumb, but he was pleased to see company. There was something about Herries that always won him attention wherever he might be. He brought him ale and bread and meat, and then sat beside him for fellowship's sake. The old man was called Andrew Greenship, and at once, as though he had spoken with no one for a hundred years, told Herries all his history. He had been a soldier in the old days and fought in the Low Countries. His thumb had been severed by a Hanoverian hatchet, and his nose broken in a fight about a gold piece. He had gout when the weather was bad, and for the most part trade was poor. But mostly he wanted to talk about his son who had gone to make his fortune in London, had returned without making it, and was now a curse to his father. He was in Carlisle at the present, but would soon be back again wanting money from his father, and with a pack of women and dogs at his heels and no place to put them. The old man could not understand it. Why were things as they were? Why were there not cakes and ale for everyone? For his part his only comfort was a dog called Mulberry, who was the cleverest dog in all Cumberland and Westmorland, and once let him set his teeth in another dog . . .

The Fever waved its hand and departed. The room was warm,

the fire burnt brightly, and the red curtains were cosy about the windows.

On the wall was a play-bill. At the Theatre Royal, Penrith, they were presenting *Othello,* by Mr William Shakespeare, to be followed by a farce, *There is No Wife like a New One.*

'The Players are here?'

But are they not here? Andrew had not himself seen them, but he had heard them grandly spoken of. Tonight was their last performance. But Andrew was inquisitive. Who was this old man, so fierce and so courteous, travelling only with a bundle? He asked many questions. Herries answered them all. He had been far, he was a great traveller, he knew London, he had seen the King, he, too, had a wife and children. But after all he was a mystery. He gave nothing of himself away, and his eyes moved as though he could see a penny through a wall of houses. When he rose from his hard bench Andrew was amazed at his height and strength.

'How old would he be?'

Seventy-two years! and Andrew was but sixty-three come Michaelmas. Andrew had not for many a day seen a man he liked better the look of, but he was one of your gentlemen, a nobleman maybe, taking his exercise for the fun of the thing, as noblemen were apt to do.

There came in a little, stout, self-important apothecary-chirurgeon. He had been his rounds in the country and had his saddle-bags filled with boluses and electuaries. In his skirt pocket he had his sand-glass and wanted to take Herries's pulse with it.

He had had a busy and, it is to be hoped, profitable day; one lady had been treated for the vapours, and one lady, alas! for the itch. He was in a temper, too, for in Appleby he had not heard the 'Gardey Loo', and some of the contents from an upper window had missed his head indeed, but struck his long-skirted coat, and it would never be clean again.

He recovered over his ale and the warm, close, smelly comfort of the low-ceilinged room. He described with gusto a recent visit to Edinburgh, the ladies in their gigantic hoops, their heads and shoulders covered with green and scarlet plaids, the green paper fans with which they warded off the sun, their red-heeled shoes, the dirt and filth and narrowness of the stairways, the streets crowded with the rude and impertinent 'caddies' carrying messages and parcels, the theatre where he had seen *The Mourning Bride* and *The Country Wife,* the cock-fights, the taverns where the advocates drank their morning sherry, and the bacchanalian nights in the meanest of 'oyster cellars', where you would enjoy raw oysters and porter, and dance with both the lowest and the highest ladies of the town.

Aye, that was a life in Edinburgh, but after a week of it you longed for your work again, and here he was, who had dined a fortnight back with the Bishop in Carlisle, and had to pay a whole guinea in vails to the servants, and was tomorrow night to have a grand feast in Keswick with some fellow apothecaries, and where he would be the following morning no one could tell.

It was this fellow's talk that kept Herries where he was and so led to the events that followed. The apothecary, whose name was Summers, lighted his eye on the play-bill on the wall; and although he asserted that it would be a poor enough affair, and laughed at the 'Theatre Royal' which would be a makeshift of boards in a tent, he licked his lips all the same, for he loved a play and would see one in any place. Very politely he invited Herries to accompany him. Herries meanwhile had been hit by an odd coincidence. He was always catching now at coincidences and omens (having little else to go by) and, while little Summers was talking, had remembered fully what the 'Green Parrot' signified to him. No need now to recall that scene in Carlisle; did he let himself, his fancy would pull him back into the very centre of it. He held himself off from it, but it kept knocking just outside his heart. He would stay the night here. He turned and asked Andrew whether he had a bed. Aye, if he did not mind sharing a room with a post-boy. No, Herries minded no company. His brain was on fire now with the thought that somehow, somewhere, something would come of this coincidence. How many many times before he had trusted to similar coincidences he did not now regard! Every occasion was a new one, filled with hope and happy prospects. His cheeks glowed, his hands trembled.

'The old gentleman,' said the apothecary aside to Andrew, 'has a fever. It would be wise if he permitted me to bleed him.'

But they both of them had a certain fear of this strange old gentleman who sat quietly there by the window, a smile on his lip and the light of eagerness in his eye. When the time came for them to be going, he marched off with Summers as though he were going to his wedding.

The weather now was fine, the air sharp, the evening very dark.

It was a strange theatre that they were introduced to, the arena a stable and the tiring-room a hay-loft, as they could very easily see. Everything was open and exposed. On some wooden steps, leading up to the loft, Othello sat, his face fittingly blackened,

wearing a long and very soiled white robe, drinking out of a pot
of ale. He would drink, and then start up in a state of very honest
fury to instruct with many curses two or three yokels who were
learning, even at this late hour, to trail a pike in a soldierly fashion. In spite of his spasmodic rages he did not look to be a bully,
having one of the roundest and mildest of faces, with a small snub
nose and eyes that, although they rolled whitely in their black
disguise, could not deny their essential amiability.

The arena was but poorly filled, dimly lit with candles that
guttered in all the breezes of heaven, and very powerfully to the
nose came the odours of cows and horses and the pungency of
dung.

Little Summers had plenty to say, and fortunately needed no
answer, for Herries, sitting very upright, his hands clasped over
his staff, his eyes staring straight before him, surrendered to the
strange fever of expectation that now, as in times altogether past
recording, swept him into breathless excitement. How well he
knew, had he dared to reckon, this repetition of circumstance!
The omen, a tree, the name of a street, a woman's hair, a printed
word, the fire of confident assurance, the bitter unavailing disappointment. Every time he would be cheated, every time make
ready for the next occasion.

Presently there was a sharp altercation. A large stout red-faced
farmer, two ladies in attendance, came and sat next to the apothecary, and soon, the ladies wishing for more room than was rightly
theirs on the bench, the large farmer began to sit all over the little
apothecary, who had, it seemed, a temper as fiery as a bantam's.

'You have paid, sir, for *two* seats?'

The farmer slowly shook his head, and his thick sides quivered
with laughter. This excited the apothecary to a frenzy, and he
most inappropriately called the farmer a puppy.

The two ladies then began to take part in the affair, saying that
they supposed the gentleman must be from Keswick or Kendal
or some other rough part, and for themselves they did not see
why they should lower themselves to speak with common persons; they'd never done so yet, and had no intention of now beginning. Both sides of the dispute appeared to amuse the farmer
greatly, for he could do nothing but shake with silent laughter,
say 'Aye, Aye,' turning his head from one side to the other, and
murmur something about 'Coom back a bit,' moving, however,
himself not all. So the apothecary leant over his broad chest, and
was about to make some very rude remarks to the ladies, when
what seemed to him the very great beauty of the younger lady

struck him so forcibly that his face was suddenly wreathed in
smiles, he was apologizing for his abruptness, and was seated at
the other end of the bench in no time at all. This, instead of
angering the farmer, but appeared to amuse him the more, and,
as the young lady was apparently not displeased, all was well.
But the little altercation had confused Herries, and he had not
realized that the play was begun.

There was a door at the back corner of the stage, and when
this was opened a cow could be seen feeding in its stall. The
scenery was a piece of tattered cloth hung crookedly from a rafter,
an old gilt chair and a green-painted table. Against the front of
the stage a number of children and boys had gathered, and were
clustered, open-mouthed, in an attentive group watching the
antics of the actors. A stout woman in a soiled crimson hoop,
with a shawl over her head and a small black dog in her lap, sat
on a chair near a candle, holding a prompt-book.

Herries soon lost himself in a mixture of falsehood and reality.
The rustic scene, the smell of the cows, and the evening air lifted
him back into his own world at home, and he could see the trees
blowing in dark fan-like clusters above the familiar gable-end.
Shakespeare had always been a glory to him, at a time, too, when
he had no great popularity, and soon he was caught up anew into
the familiar story and once more felt the ringing beauty of the
words.

Othello came down to the candles, and, forgetting the Duke
and the attendant senators, addressed his rustic audience, pausing at times for a word and turning impatiently to the lady with
the red hoop, who must hesitate before she discovered the place.
Nevertheless the atmosphere was caught. Venice and her waters
did their business yet once again of tricking a mortal soul or two
into a foolish trust in the fidelity of beauty.

The little black dog barked.

'She loved me' – said Othello, wiping his nose with the back
of his hand,

> —for the dangers I had pass'd,
> And I loved her that she did pity them.
> This only is the witchcraft I have used;
> Here comes the lady; let her witness it.

and then, from among the cows, holding her long train that it
might not be soiled by the dirt, Mirabell came in.

He did not see her. She had spoken her words:

My noble father,
I do perceive here a divided duty,

before he realized her.

Then it came to him, quietly, inevitably, as though it had been from the beginning arranged that it should be like that.

That was Mirabell, her hair, her small child's face, her body looking stout and thick beneath the shabby tawdry dress of white satin. On each cheek was a splash of red paint, and behind this her little face was oddly white and her eyes staring.

Yes, this was Mirabell. It was as he had always expected it, if not here, why, then at another place. Soon he would go, when this mummery was over, behind and fetch her away. They would stay the night in Penrith, and tomorrow would be home. At the thought of home and Mirabell there again he began to tremble. It was as though someone were slowly shaking him from head to foot. Someone also was shouting in his ear, and everything in front of him was swimming in a mist of shapeless colour.

It began at once to be incredible to him that she should be there and not recognize him. Why did she not cease all this foolishness and suddenly cry out: 'Francis! Francis! Francis, I am coming home!'? At that he began to wonder why he himself was not crying out. He clasped his staff with a fearful intensity. His arm shook above it, and unknown to himself a tear was trickling down his cheek.

Very soon he would have risen from his seat, pushed his way through the country people, but fortunately she turned, and, as Othello, his eyes on the boys who were teasing the little dog from the front of the stage, said: 'Come, Desdemona,' she gathered up her dress, glancing to see that she did not trip over a hole in the boards, and at his words, 'We must obey the time,' she vanished through the door.

Herries rose instantly and pushed through the crowd, mounting with steady steps the wooden ladder that led to the hay-loft.

Here there was a torn curtain. Shaking it aside he stood just within, leaning a little on his stick. On the floor two children were playing with some stones and string. They had tied the string to one of the stones and were dragging it, bumping, over the cracks in the floor. There was a wooden table piled with theatrical properties, and on the table a long thin man was sitting, powdering his hair, while a woman bent over him mending a hole in his faded sky-blue tights. A little fat man in a full bottomed wig and red satin breeches was looking at himself in a cracked glass and adjusting on his head a tin helmet. From below came the lowing of a cow for its calf and the voice of Iago, very high-pitched and trembling with dramatic irony.

The woman mending the sky-blue tights was Mirabell.

One of the children cried out. She looked up.

So they looked at one another after these many years. She was old, worn, ill. That was his only thought – that he must take her at once, without an instant's delay, and have her cared for. Her beautiful hair had lost its lustre, the blobs of red paint on her cheeks seemed to sharpen the lines, the shadows, the thinness of that child's face that yet was a child's face no longer, but a woman's, weary, ill-fed and drawn.

And what did she see? An old white-haired man leaning on a stick. But what happiness was in her heart when she saw him! Yes, the shock of it surprised herself. The only friend that she had in the world. Was that ungrateful, perhaps, when the simple, kindly player, Othello, Julius Caesar, Jaffier, Prospero and Falstaff, cared for her, was good to her? Yes; say, then, the only friend that she herself wanted. How much greater the ties of those years that she had lived with him had been than she knew! Had she done right to leave him? Had he been happier without her? Was it by chance that he saw her now? Had he ever seen her, wished for her? Would he want her to return with him, or had he come only to give her a good day for the sake of old times?

All these thoughts pressed upon her in that first moment as she looked at him.

She dropped the needle and went over to him. Then she was moved to the very depths of her being when she saw that he was so profoundly shaken at the sight of her that he could not speak, but, his hand trembling on his stick, tears falling, turned his head away that she should not see.

She put her hand on his arm and led him to the corner of the room by a little broken window that was stuffed with paper. The two men said nothing, paid no attention. It was nothing to them that an old man should speak to her, or, for that, a young one either.

'Don't cry,' she said. 'How happy I am to see you!'

When he could command himself he put up his hand and touched her hair. Then he said:

'You must come with me. As soon as this is over. We will stay tonight in Penrith, and tomorrow go home.' Then, before she could answer, he went on: 'I have been searching for you ever

since you went away. I was in London looking for you.' He was
so fiercely excited that his words came breathlessly, as though he
had been running. 'But it is no matter – now that I have found
you.'

'Yes.' She had to give herself time to settle her own problem
of honour and duty. 'I have wondered so many times – whether
you thought of me, what you did. But you have been ill. Your
hair is white.' She smiled. 'We are both old now.'

His eyes never left her face, never moved. They were as beautiful, as strong and piercing as ever they had been.

'I will come to fetch you as soon as the piece is played.'

But she must postpone telling him how she was placed. Things
were not so simple as that. But, for a moment, she wished that
they had been. How she wished it! She was so weary, she was so
bad an actress, this life was so mean and dirty. To go back with
him, to be cared for and loved . . . She would let him love her now
in any way that he wished. One thought of the rest that it would
be! To sit in that chair in Herries and hear the running water;
Herries that once she had hated! But she drove all the pictures
back.

'You have wanted me then? You have missed me? I have so
wondered . . . But listen.' She began to speak quickly, holding
his arm with her hand. 'A man here – he is playing Othello – has
treated me with great kindliness. I was very sick – it is five years
back – dying, I think. He was acting in the town. He is good,
most generous-hearted, and I am a shabby actress, but, when he
might have had a position in London had he left me, he would
not. He is drunk sometimes, but even at that he is kind.

'I have never loved him, but if I leave him now he will lose
all – his interest, his work. He has no one else. Those are his two
children by another woman. She is dead of the smallpox. They
too, they think I am their mother, poor babies. Francis—'

He broke in fiercely. 'You left me. You can leave him then.'

'I left you because I thought it right for you. You were only
unhappy.'

'And what have I been without you?'

'You are strong. Adam is weak. If I left him he would not do
anything but die in a ditch, and the children would die. We have
so little time. I will see you again, most truly I will. Did you
know what it is now to hear your voice . . .' She broke off. That
was not the way. She began to be tormented. She could go with
him now, without one word to anyone. When she saw him holding her with his eyes, her own longing to be loved by him again,

to be warmed by him, to be protected by him, began to pervade her like a happy faintness. Instinctively she drew nearer to him, and he, suddenly raising his head proudly, put his arm around her.

Othello came in.

At the sight of him Mirabell's torment grew. In his foolishly blackened face, his dirty dishevelled turban, his fat good-natured cheeks, she felt all his commonness and by contrast Francis's aristocracy. This was a spiritual thing, not a social. This heavy fat man who when he was hungry crammed his food into his mouth like an animal, who was so simple and foolish that he knew nothing of the world but the little scandals of the hedge-rows and the dirty anecdotes of the roadside inns, who was kindly because he·had not the wits to be aught else, who, when he was fuddled, would kneel at her feet, crying and kissing her worn soiled hands until she was ashamed, who was feckless and lazy and vain, boastful and ignorant, weak and little – and Francis who looked now, standing in that dingy attic, a king among men, Francis so mysterious in his breeding, Francis who loved her so that he had searched all England for her! – she did not draw back from his arm as her shabby Othello approached them.

She made them known. She realized that her man, Adam Betty, at once perceived that this newcomer was a patron, some-one who might possibly raise them all up in the world. He spoke to him with a mixture of humility and boasting.

'Small quarters, sir, bu.t the Muse must be served. Shake-speare! I kneel to him! So wise a connoisseur as yourself must have some points from which a humble player . . . But my Othello – the Heart is there, the Heart! The Noble Moor is trans-lated into this rough barn, and Miss Starr's Desdemona – ah, there, sir! you will have a performance of a Natural Sublimity—'

But Mirabell could not endure it. She saw Herries's courtesy, his head a little bowed as he listened, but also his almost mad impatience, so that she feared that at any instant he would break into some desperate declamation.

Othello was a little drunken. He swayed a trifle on his legs, and was now sending a small boy in a shirt and ragged breeches for further liquor. The scene was becoming intolerable to her. The wretched place, the figures pressing about them, the conscious-ness that soon she must return to the stage, the shock of Herries's presence there, her longing for him (which was by far stronger than she would have supposed), the consciousness of a new dig-nity and fineness in him as an older man that there had not been

THE BRIGHT TURRETS OF ILION

before, above all, the ache for the rest and care that he would give
her, all these tore at her heart.

Then there was a little incident. One of the children, the smaller, thin and spare, in a shawl and a tattered red kilt, with bow legs and the expression of an aged woman, running to its father, tumbled over a crack in the floor and fell howling to the ground.

At once its father, who had been grandiloquently orating, rather to the general world than to Herries, of his rendering of other rôles in Mr Shakespeare's plays, lost all quality as actor, and became only a simple and affectionate parent.

As he bent over the child and raised it, speaking to it gently, drying its tears with the corner of his dirty gown, catching it in his arms and kissing it, he was a man of dignity and feeling. He was the man who had been good to her when everyone else had abandoned her, who needed her, who trusted in her. He turned and, smiling through his sooty blackness, gave her the child.

'You see,' she said, turning to Francis, 'that we cannot speak together here. I must tell you of everything more fully. It is not, oh, believe me, it is not so easy a thing. You shall meet me afterwards – yes, yes, I promise you.'

He looked at her as though he would never let her go. He did not care that she was worn and shabby. This was a love that had no dictation from outside things. But he saw that it was true that they could not talk there.

'I have your promise?' he asked, touching again with a shy secret movement her hair.

'Yes, yes . . . Later. At ten o'clock I can be free. There is a place beyond the Castle on the left of the road towards Keswick. There is a gate there with a deserted cottage. Wait for me there.'

She had spoken in a hurried whisper, rocking the child in her arms. He saw that there was nothing more to be done here. He knew that she would keep her promise, so, with one last look at her, he went.

After that he walked he knew not where. A soft rain began to fall, but he did not realize it. He realized nothing but the hunger to have her with him again. He heard the three-quarters strike on the church clock, and, hurrying as though by chance she might be before her time, went to the place. He found it without difficulty, although the night was very dark.

He stood there by the gate in the rain. He was ill again, although he did not heed it. His legs were trembling and his head was on fire. Many lights were dancing in his eyes. But he thought only of the clock. His heart leaping, he heard it strike the hour, counting aloud the strokes.

Now she would come, in another moment she would be with him. The quarter struck, then the half-hour. The silence grew with every minute more menacing. It was as though the town, the dark night, everything in the world were holding her back to taunt him. He ran into the road, then a little way towards the town. He began to call then, louder and louder. No one came. The clock struck eleven. The silence was not broken.

The quarter struck again, and once more the half-hour.

He began to run. It might be that she had said some other place. He was in the town, which was now utterly black under the rain. He ran, calling her name. Two hours later, a blind, fiery, unconscious impulse leading him back to the 'Green Parrot', when old Andrew with candle and nightdress opened the door to the knocking, Herries fainting, fell into his arms.

PHANTASMAGORIA IN THE HILLS

HERRIES lay for six months moving into Death's arms and then slipping out of them again. It seemed to him like that, but Death was no grisly skeleton with grinning bones, but a place of light and space where there was a great singing emptiness and a hooded brooding sun. He moved and was bathed in a curious lethargic contentment; 'So this is where one goes,' his complacency told him, but he was allowed only to sniff the air and shade his eyes from the light, when pulleys dragged him back to a hot fire, aching limbs and a will to live.

He was a very old man in those times to live at all with such an illness. The town took a sort of obstinate pride in his recovery. Wagers were laid. Sir Humphrey Paddock, an ancient knight whose house was at Cross Trees, a mile outside the town, bet the little black boy that his wife had brought up from London against Squire Bantock's famous mare, Marjorie, that Herries would not die. It was as well that he won, for he did not tell his lady, who was attached to little Pompey, and there would have been the domestic devil to pay had he lost.

Old Andrew obtained quite a notoriety and an added custom from his guest's struggle with death. Old Andrew was prouder of Francis than he had ever been of anyone in his life. Heaven

knows where he got his affection for him from. The snob in him
perhaps. He had always worshipped Quality quite frankly, and
when, twenty years later, in his very old age (he lived to be almost a hundred), men praised the Revolution in France as the
beginning of a grand new world, his indignation was a sight to
witness.

But his affection for Herries went deeper than that. He tended
him like a woman, would scarcely have left his room had it not
been for the necessities of his trade and for Benjamin.

In the first delirious weeks Herries was always calling for
Benjamin, so Benjamin was sent for. He came and set up a jealous
imperious rule that no one could defeat. He had all the unreasoning suspicion that anyone who is accustomed to Keswick has for
anything that happens in Penrith. He wore an air of exceeding
knowledge. No one understood his master but he. He would talk
oracularly, in the inn-parlour, to anyone who cared to listen,
about the great man that his master was, and the wise man and
the mysterious.

It became after a while bruited abroad that Herries had shut
himself up for many years in his lonely house because he was discovering the Philosopher's Stone or some such thing. Benjamin,
and indeed many of the citizens of Penrith, had still a medieval
mind, and any marvel was welcome.

But when Benjamin was in his master's room, caring for him,
his tenderness and devotion were wonderful.

'Come now, come now,' he would say, wiping the sweat from
the brow, smiling into the staring eyes, smoothing the sheets
about the body. 'There's no fear to trouble you. Softly, master,
softly. Hold to my hand now and you'll know that there is no one
can come after you. Nay, nay. There's no one here but Benjamin.
Yes, yes. She'll be with you presently. She has but gone out for
a breath of air and so that you may sleep a little. Softly, master,
softly. All is very well. Lie still and rest then.'

Being by nature a man of fancy to whom any fable was welcome, he indulged himself by uttering any kind of marvel that
might be expected to comfort his master. His fancy was closely
allied to his literalness, so that if he stated that Mirabell had been
but just now in the room, he must describe her dress that was
sweet with sprigs of roses and say that her hair had a silver comb.
He would tell Herries that all the town, aye, and the County too,
was at the door inquiring how he did, and that coaches packed
with Countesses waited in the street, and Marquises and Dukes
sent messages of condolence. But nothing mattered to Herries,

who lay, for many a day and night, his long thin fingers twitching the sheets, his eyes pitifully staring, his haggard cheeks as white as his hair.

Nothing finer can ever be recorded of old Andrew than that he endured, without too much argument, Benjamin's patronage and superiority. The two old men even achieved finally a kind of alliance together against the rest of the world.

Little Summers always afterwards asserted that it was he who saved Herries. Certainly he bled him often enough, and could be seen many times a day tramping up and down the wooden stairs, his sand-glass, almost as big as himself, in his hand.

But whether it was Benjamin or Summers or Fate or Herries's own constitution, he did, in spite of medical treatment and enough dirt and ignorance to slaughter a cityful of old men, recover. The day came when he was carried downstairs to the back-parlour by Benjamin, where he lay on a sofa in the sun, with canaries in a cage twittering above his head and a distant view of the dim hills through the window.

After that he gained strength amazingly, and it was in mid-July that he stepped with Benjamin into a hired chaise, bade old Andrew farewell, and departed for Herries.

He had become very silent. No one knew now what was in his mind. David, Sarah, Deborah had all been to visit him in Penrith, and they had felt that they were with a stranger. He asked them no questions, heard their news with courteous indifference, seemed to feel no connexion with them. His only request was that he should return as speedily as possible to Herries, and there was a glow in his cheek and a smile on his lips when the chaise stumbled up the rough lane (there was path enough now for a carriage), and he was once more inside the little grass-grown courtyard.

He went quietly about the house from the top loft to the dark cellar beneath the kitchen, touching everything and making sure that it was there.

He talked often with great and excited incoherence, then for many days he would be quite sensible and coherent, then for days silent. But he asked no questions about anything, nor mentioned Mirabell's name.

There was an old white horse that he had had for some years, called once ironically by him the Paladin. It was a horse of a rather comic appearance, short in the leg and very bare of feature, with a large black patch over one eye that gave it an extraordinarily innocent and amiably foolish expression. Herries took now a fancy to this horse, and every day rode out on it. But he went no longer for any journeys. Every evening he returned.

No one knew of what he was thinking. You could not say that he was mad, because if you did he would in another moment show so much sense and consciousness of the true life about him that you were (if you were Benjamin) dumbfounded.

But he thought himself that he was growing mad, that he was less certain with every day as to the reality of anything. He had been all his life scornful of other men's acceptance of reality; that had been one of the principal reasons for his division from them. On the other side, he knew that now, for the first time in his life, he was not honest with himself. There was something within him that he would not examine. He had always despised humbug, and now he was himself a humbug, because there was a great hurt and unhappiness in his breast that he would not examine.

He would not glance down at anything that was past. Something was not here, something that he had passionately desired. No matter. Let it lie. He could not procure it. It was gone. To call it up, long for it, stretch out his hands to it, meant madness. And he also would not think of the future. He did not know what was coming. Maybe that lighted chamber of Death with the hooded sun, maybe a man in armour riding him down, maybe old age and food in your belly. He would look only at the present, this rustling tapestry on the wall, this old hill beyond the window-pane, this chair with the crusted gold sunk into its wood, this green slipper with the silver buckle, this halter that gaped from its hook on the wall. But here is your trouble, old man. Who knows what these things are? – the tapestry, the hill, the chair, the slipper, the halter – maybe they are cheating you. They are not what they seem. The tapestry is an old woman whispering, the slipper a fallen leaf, the house and the hills around it a well in which you are sunk up to your very neck. You think you are alive and are not. You were dead months ago and lay stretched out with the sheets to your chin and the candles blowing at your feet, and now that you are dead you have the power to see double, two of everything, and the trees like men walking.

He would catch Benjamin's arm at a time, and would say, chuckling: 'We are both dead, old friend, and no one knows it.' Benjamin did not mind. It was only his master's way.

So Herries would ride out on the Paladin to think of these questions, and would return in the evening, his head none the clearer.

He was always at his most sensible when David or Deborah

came to visit him. He would sit in his chair by the fire or walk with them gravely over his territory, showing them an apple tree or a cabbage or the new marigold. But he never asked them questions. He listened with great pleasure to Deborah's stories of her twin boys, of their cleverness, courage and remarkable natures, of Mr Sunwood's sermons, of how they had been to visit the Bishop, of their friends the Wordsworths and the grand house they had, of the new road to the North, of the many visitors to Cockermouth, and of Lady Freshwater's garden that had three cascades, a Gothick Temple and a statue of Minerva.

He listened, too, when David told him of his farm, of his business, of his hunting, of his children and his horses. He enjoyed it all. He was glad that they should come, but so soon as they were gone he forgot all about them. He walked about the house at night talking to himself. Benjamin would get up and follow him lest he should do himself a mischief. Once he pulled Benjamin out of bed to show him the moon over Rosthwaite Fell. Another night he crept into Benjamin's bed and lay there shuddering, his arms about the other's neck. Once, talking very sensibly and in perfect command of his faculties, he spoke about his wife Margaret, but as though she were there in the house.

'You are not to speak to her of this. She is sensitive to all that I say, poor soul, but if she would not fear me we would do better. You have seen yourself how she trembles if she thinks that I am angry. I cannot bear a trembling woman, and never could. You could say to her not to be afraid, for there is nothing to fear in me. I have not been in a rage since the children were little.'

Nevertheless he would sometimes be in a rage for no reason whatever, and then he would shout and storm just as he did in older days. His best friend and visitor, who seemed altogether to understand him, was little Mr Harness the clergyman, who came often to see him, and thought nothing that he did or said odd at all.

Mr Harness, in fact, had a theory that Herries was as sane as any man, but elaborated and fantasied things, in order to hold himself from thinking. He had a hope that religion would assist him. He brought with him certain beloved books from his little library – Henry Dodwell's *Christianity not Founded on Argument*, Butler's *Analogy*, Warburton's *Divine Legation*, Law's *Serious Call* and *The Way to Divine Knowledge*.

It may be that Herries read these works, maybe not. No one will ever know. He did not discuss anything with Mr Harness so much as throw out casually to him stray observations, as:

'The Planets, I fancy, must have a hearty detestation of their God. To be held by an iron hand in one order, always to obey a Law made without any consultation of them. A Planet having a trifle of Independence would prefer to fall to fiery ruin . . . So Satan snapped his fingers.'

Mr Harness had no liking for Chaos.

'No, you would not. You are too good a man. Nor do I fancy that if God walked in this garden, I would myself be doing anything fine or bold. He has had the experience to make Him ready for any occasion. But I would ask Him one thing – whether He is not at some time wearied of His power, and wishing that He could Himself be a rebel once and again against it.'

And he said once to Harness:

'What men call madness is only to have a picture of your own. I make my own vision of things more independently as I grow.'

Had you asked him at this time what his condition was, he would have told you, perhaps, that he saw three things to other men's one – or perhaps Mr Harness was right, and he busied his brain with pictures because he did not wish to look into reality.

In any case the great day of his life arrived, coming to him blindly as all our great days come. It was May 16th, 1773. He rode out after his early dinner on the Paladin. He sat up very straight and stiff, wearing his old broad-brimmed black hat, his legs reaching far down because the Paladin's legs were short, his eyes staring straight in front of him as though he were setting out on some urgent quest.

Benjamin stood at the top of the path watching him anxiously. He was never certain when he saw his master thus depart whether he would ever welcome him back again.

It is possible that Herries had some notion that this was a great day, or it may have been only that the sun was shining strongly on field and hill, powdering the valley with gold-dust; it is true that his heart beat strongly with expectation. He would not ask himself any longer what it was that he expected, but he smiled sometimes grimly to himself as he went, and, as was his habit, he talked to the Paladin.

'What is your will today? Where do we go? Make use of your imagination. You shan't flick your ears at the sun. Unmannerly behaviour . . . There's no graciousness in you.'

He came to a field off the road near Stonethwaite hamlet where some men and boys were baiting a little bull with two dogs. He got off the Paladin, leaving him to crop the hedge, and went into the field. There was no reason. He had nothing against the baiting of bulls, which was the habit of the time. Or, rather, he had had nothing. It may be that now, seeing three things instead of one, he was in advance of his period. The little animal was mad with terror and pain. One of its legs was torn and bleeding, the skin above one eye was ravaged and the blood poured down its face. But like Wesley's bull it could not be roused to much vengeance against its tormentors, but only pawed the ground, lowered its head, and raised it again.

Herries went up to it, put his hand on it, stroked it, and it did not stir, only stood there trembling. The men knew him well enough, and, thinking him a crazy old man, let him have his way. A stout red-faced farmer promised him that the bull should be let alone, and to his own later surprise kept his promise. He didn't know, he said afterwards, but the bull and the old man seemed to have an understanding. Witchcraft . . .

So then Herries got on to the Paladin again, and they ambled forward until they reached Seathwaite, and then past the hamlet wandered on along the well-known path into the pool of the hills. It was that time of the afternoon when on a fine day in early summer this end of the valley holds all the sun in a blaze of gold, while the hills above it are black. Herries came to Stockley Bridge, where once long ago his son had talked with the Devil, let the Paladin wander, and sat down on a flat stone above the clear green pools that Grain Gill makes for its own sweet pleasure.

From above him and around him Glaramara, his old friend, and Allen Crags and Great End and the Gavel looked down and saw him, far below them though he was, a black figure in that blaze of gold.

Whatever he was at other times, he was not clear in his head just then, for he saw, out of the tumbling stream, from behind the casual rocks, from the green bracken of the Fell, figures rise on every side of him. He did not know whether they were men or women, nor did he care. They rose like flopping scarecrows, and came trooping, ambling, appearing and disappearing, making signs at him, passing him without heeding him, flying in the air like jackdaws, until at last an odd old creature with a wrinkled face marked with lines like a map, its texture also of parchment, came and crouched on its thin shanks beside him.

The air was exceedingly peaceful, the green pool between the grey stones pure and still, the sunlight over all, so that Herries did not mind a talk.

'Where are you from?' he asked idly, watching two flies circle above the pool.

'From nowhere at all. But it is a fine evening.'

'It is indeed,' said Herries. 'And your companions. Where do they hail from?' For he could see behind the black cloak of his neighbour the dark cloaks of many others beating like birds' wings in the air.

'Also from nowhere.'

'If I give you something,' said Herries (for the shadow with the parchment face had a begging eye), 'will you go away?'

'What have you of any value?'

'I have only one thing,' said Herries, 'upon which I lay any value, save my house, my son and my servant. That is a silver chain that I wear around my neck. It was left to me once by a lady who was dead. That I will not give you. But I have a spade, some trees, a horse, a picture of an ancestor and two suits of armour. Also a witch's bones in my garden. To any of these you are welcome.'

The black-cloaked beggar moved his bony hams derisively.

'Poor property,' he said, 'at the end of a long life.'

'Am I then at the end?' asked Herries with interest.

'Not absolutely. Why have you retained so little?'

'I cannot tell,' said Herries. 'I have never had a saving nature. When I was young I scattered my seed like grass – if I may be for a moment poetical. Now I am old and I have only one desire and one dream.'

'What is your dream?' asked the shadow, but more from politeness than interest. He yawned indeed, raised a bony hand, but did not hide a cavernous mouth.

'I have dreamed of a noble white horse who swims a black pool and mounts hills of ice. But I pray your pardon. My dream can interest no one save myself.'

'Not at all,' said the shadow politely. 'And what is your desire?'

'That is no man's business,' said Herries abruptly.

'As with the rest of us,' said the shadow, crouching a little nearer, 'you have found life a silly thing with no meaning.'

Herries nodded at the pool.

'Inconsequent. Without an answer. But I have seen hints that there may be an answer elsewhere. Were men themselves less foolish there is beauty and adventure enough to balance the rest. Not, you understand, that I am of any wider intelligence than my fellows. I have been always beyond ordinary foolish. Nor do I regret it.'

The shadow plainly found his acquaintance uninteresting. He rose like a black beanstalk.

'One thing I will tell you,' he said. 'You are but at the beginning of your journey. My felicitations on your companion. Keep your spade, your scar, your fine white horse. You will need them.'

The company now darkened the air, which was very chill. The sky was grey. The hills shone with ice, and at Herries's very feet was the black still pool that he had so often seen before. It was no surprise to him, therefore, to behold a moment later the beautiful white horse go plunging in.

Once again he saw him, but now he was closer to him than he had ever been before. His great head, with its flowing mane of snow, clove the water, breaking its blackness, and Herries could feel the superb strength of the body as it drove its path. Then came the moment of struggle when the horse must plant his hoof on the slippery slant of the icy rocks. He could see more clearly than before how he raised his head in a superb agony of effort, how the hoofs slipped and slipped again, how it seemed as though he must fall back into the icy water, how every muscle was straining, how the glittering hills looked on with stern indifference.

All Herries's own vitality, everything that he had put into life, any past gallantry or courage or discipline, he seemed to give to aid his friend. Then with a great controlled burst of energy, that last effort was made and the ascent was won.

The white mane was shaken in triumph, the water dripped from the white body like rain, and he was off piercing the hills until he was like a silver arrow flying skyward.

Herries smiled and rubbed his hands. And there was no pool, there were no icy hills. Only the fellside, the bubbling stream, and all the valley grey now because the sun had sunk behind the rim of the purple tops. He had slept then. The Paladin was cropping the grass close at hand, and the stars were creeping out into soft green sky. Between sleeping and waking, now that you were old, it was no great matter. Life melted from one to another, and the dividing wall became with every breath the less opaque.

He supposed that he had slept. Then sleep was more real than waking.

He climbed on to the Paladin and rode dreamily home. But this time, as he came up the path to the house, he could see, dusky though it was, Benjamin waiting at the gate. He ran forward, caught the Paladin's bridle.

He was shaking with the excitement of some news.

'Master! Master!' He pulled, in his quivering eagerness, at

Herries's arm. 'She has returned. The mistress is here. She is waiting for you by the fire!'

THEY ARE ALONE AND ARE HAPPY

SHE was standing against the wall beside the window, straight against it as though she must have something behind her in case of attack. She had a grey shawl over her head, a faded green upper dress and a shabby red hoop. She looked old and monstrously weary. That had been Benjamin's first thought when he saw her come slowly across the courtyard, that she was fearfully weary.

Herries did a very touching thing. He went straight across the room to her, put his hand up, and stroked her pale cheek. Then he bent his head and kissed her hand.

'Forgive me,' he said, 'but I have been dreaming much of late. I supposed this also was a dream.'

They stood very close to one another, looking into one another's faces for what seemed to Benjamin, who stood without moving at the door, a long time.

Then she spoke quickly, and never taking her eyes from his face.

'Before everything I must tell you that I have come here to explain to you. That is why I have come. I can go again as easily. You must know why I broke my promise to you of meeting you on that night.

'After you were gone, my protector – the man you saw, the player – made a scene of great jealousy. He had seen that we were known to one another; he overheard our appointment. He was mad with a strange new anger and fear that I had never before seen in him.'

She caught her breath, putting her hand to her breast. 'It was as though he knew that you were the only friend I had in the world. Often he had seen me with other men and been unmoved. Now he told me that if I went that night to see you he would kill himself. I believe he would have done it. I considered my duty. I thought . . . that if I saw you again . . . I might stay with you. There were the children. So we left Penrith that evening after the play. I sent a messenger to you with a letter, but he never found you or said he did not.

'And a month back Adam left me for a young woman who had lately joined our company, taking the children with him. I had been ill. He left me without money – this was in Salisbury – and I have slowly come back. Let me stay with you tonight, and then if you wish it tomorrow—'

She swayed, reeled, would have fallen had he not caught her.

She was ill from nothing but exhaustion. When she was in bed Herries fed her with strong soup and hot wine. She thanked him with a smile, put her arms around his neck and kissed him, then, sighing with a sense of safety, turned and slept. She slept all that night, all the next day and all the night after. She slept like a young child, her head in her hand.

Herries sat for most of that while at her side. He slept a little, but was always starting out of his sleep to see whether she were there. Very gently he would put his hand out and touch her heart, to be sure that she was breathing.

Benjamin said to Mr Harness: 'He's in such joy at her return that it's like to turn him crazy altogether.' But that was just what it did not do. He walked directly away from his dreams and fancies, leaving them behind him like discarded clothes. He came down to the door to speak with Mr Harness.

'It is my wife who has returned, sir,' he said. 'We are friends, I am happy to think, and therefore I would wish you to give me joy, for this is the most cheerful thing that has happened to me in all my life.

'I have been, since my illness, a trifle dazed in my head, the rather I fancy because it was not healthy for me to see things exactly as they were, but now I am very well, and you may wish us a long life together.'

'Indeed I do,' said Mr Harness, but thinking that seventy-three was an advanced age to begin life at. 'I am most heartily pleased, sir, and will offer my duty to your lady when she is well rested.'

On the morning of the second day, while Herries was sitting beside her bed and the sun was pouring in at the window, she awoke entirely refreshed. For a moment she did not remember where she was; then, when she saw his white hair and eager look, such a shadow of happiness and relief swept her face as was moving to see, for, poor thing, everything was very different from when she had gone away: she had suffered so many hardships and known so little rest that it was not only the added years had aged her.

They talked a little quietly and she had her hand in his.

Then he said, after kissing her cheek: 'There is but one thing that I must say. I pray you not to leave me again, for this time it would be my death.'

'Nay, I will never leave you any more, Francis.'

'For I am not as young as I was. Be angry. Have things as you will. I shall not pester you now to love me. Only you must not go away.'

She repeated again: 'I will never leave you any more.'

He said then in his old way: 'We are a couple of fools to make promises. Was ever a vow kept in this world? But I cannot endure the thought . . .' He turned his head aside. 'I will not ask you to make a vow. Only do not go – unless you must.'

'And you will not leave Herries?'

'No. I will never leave Herries now.'

It was natural that in the first weeks there should be a certain awkwardness between them. There were the old things to remember and the new things to expect.

Each found the other at first changed. It was only after a while that these superficial alterations dropped away and they discovered that the old spirit shone there.

But there *were* changes, real and true ones. Each was altered by trial. The shock of her going and then his long illness in Penrith had softened Herries to a more patient acquiescence. It was as though he had peeped through a door into another room and seen certain things there that excited his curiosity and so made him less stirred by his present surroundings. It was also that her absence had been so terrible to him that, now he had got her again, he was contented in her mere presence, not wishing her to be this or that, but only near him.

Also it was as though he had found an answer to the question that he had been asking all his life. He had found justification. Finally he was so happy that he asked no more questions. It was enough that she was there and wished to remain there.

The principal difference in Mirabell was that she was a child no longer. It was not only that she was now forty-four years of age, for there are some who carry their childlikeness with them to the grave, but also trouble, loneliness, sickness had given her that kind of sanctification that comes through sorrow.

Not that she was miserable or went about the place with a sad mouth. It was only that at first she could not realize her security.

What occurred was that presently happiness began to seep into the house. It is dangerous to speak of happiness, and cowards knock on wood for protection. But there are times in a man's life when it comes, at first slowly in a trickle, then rising ankle-deep, then flooding the window, at last brimming the chimneys. There is also no source of happiness quite so sure and true as the real love of one human being for another; this too seems at first incredible and very often when it has climbed waist-high sinks again, but real love is a true thing although it needs two fine-natured persons to make it true. One is not sufficient.

Nevertheless, as a matter of history, happiness flooded this old house at last and must therefore be mentioned although many would speak of ague, toothache, blights among the cattle or a hanging in the barn.

The old house soaked it in. A muddled old house it was by this, a jumble of chimneys, gables and crooked corners. What shapeless buildings! Sties like an alderman's coffin, stables like byres and byres like the ruins of Rome. Peat-stacks, dung-hills everywhere, poultry scratching in the grass-grown court, ducks everywhere garrulous, weeds hip-high, and, rather by their own volition than from any care taken of them, in their proper seasons, daisies, marigolds, jonquils, pansies, orange-lilies, gardener's garters and honeysuckle.

The old house with its cocked impertinent chimneys, its wainscots and irregular windows and ghost-haunted stairways sinking, slowly sinking into this growing height of vegetation that, encouraged by the overlooking hills, climbed patiently to heaven.

Into all of this their happiness crept. After a month or two you could feel it everywhere. Deborah and her clergyman, David and Sarah, who came in due time to pay their respects to the returned bride, all felt it. They felt also that they were not really wanted.

Mirabell was most happy to see them and was very much more at her ease with them than she had been, but no one else was wanted. Happiness is like that – a cheerfully selfish thing.

Mirabell sat there and in her heart wondered what it was that had, on that other occasion, made her run away. It was as though she looked back upon another woman, a strange, uneasy, restless creature who had not wanted this and had been discontented with that. She did not ask herself yet whether now she loved Herries. Like himself she bothered herself with no questions. She wanted to be sure that she was there.

There were times when they would suddenly look at one another, both needing the same assurance.

It could be said that all that Mirabell felt for a long while was that this was a safe haven and that any other haven would have done as well. No one could tell. She did not examine the question. The haven was Herries and Herries was the haven, both man and house. She could not imagine that there could be any other. This was, after all, the only one that she had known her whole life long.

Slowly, piece by piece, some of the things that she had suffered came out. The poverty, discomfort, dirt, weariness, insult that were the inevitable companions of touring players. To the man himself she was always loyal. He had meant very well by her always. He had loved her in his own way, and the two poor children, sickly, ugly, thrown from one hardship to another, had had only herself to look to. He had on the whole, save for a momentary impulse or two, been faithful to her. After his first passion for her had worn away she had wondered that he had kept her, for, most certainly, she was not beautiful, she was often ill with hunger and cold, and she was an astonishingly bad actress.

She could remember her lines and that was all. She could never imagine herself anything but what she was. The plays seemed to her mostly foolishness, Mr Shakespeare no better than another. She had not managed well for him. She could not cook anything fit to be eaten nor keep a place in order. Her only merit was her fidelity.

So, when at last the other girl joined them – a black-haired, fierce-tempered woman, a remarkable actress in the more fiery parts – she did not wonder that he went away with her. She would have been happy at her freedom had it not been for the two poor children, who hated the black woman and cried whenever they saw her. Poor Adam! To what miserable end must he come. Poor, stupid, good-hearted Adam to be eaten by a tigress!

Then, as months went, she forgot all the past. This new happiness burnt all the old things as a fire burns straw. They, both of them, she and Francis, went forward into a new world and lived one grand day after another. Oddest of all, he became young again. His brain was unclouded, his limbs vigorous. This was his Indian Summer.

But nothing stands still. Everything now was an inevitable sequel to all that had gone before, but a new sequence was being created.

In the autumn, that was very wet, full of howling winds, and thick at the foot with sodden leaves, Mirabell found that she was watching Francis with an odd anxiety and restlessness. Whenever he left her she was uneasy, and she would stand at the thin window that looked over the court waiting to see him turn the bend, pause at the gate, and then look up to the window, thinking, as she knew, of her. It was not that there was any true reason for uneasiness. All through that year he was strong and well, and although Benjamin, who liked gloomy tales and prophecies, told her fearsome stories about his fever, there was no sign of its return. When he lay at night with her, putting his arms round her, she falling to sleep in the hollow of those arms, his body was like iron, marvellous for so old a man.

Nor was there any reason, as once there might have been, to fear any outside hostility, for that had died. The 'Rogue' was used in friendly fashion when it was used at all.

Nevertheless she never saw him leave the house without fearing that he would not return. All this time, with Benjamin, she managed the house. The only other was a wild girl called Bethany, of whom a wandering woman, who had died five minutes later, had been delivered in a ditch near Seathwaite.

If she was not quite right in the head, at least she did what she was told, and developed after a time a passionate devotion to Mirabell. So the house went none so badly.

But this anxiety of Mirabell's grew. She did not know what was the matter until on an evening after Christmas it was made clear to her.

That same afternoon Herries had ridden on the Paladin into Keswick to see the lawyer about money matters. She could never but smile when she saw him go, so erect on the fat horse, with his legs so long, his head stiffly set under his broad black hat. So soon as he had turned the corner and was out of sight, with a sigh she left the window and went to the oak chest where there was some linen to be marked. Looking into the chest, under the linen she saw a cedar box, and, opening it, found piled pell-mell together the jewels with which formerly he used to dress her. Gathering them together, she went to the table and sat down with them, and was filled with memories.

She could see herself now seated at the table, the jewels in her ears and hair and round her neck, while he patiently tried to teach her to read. Tears filled her eyes. How good he had been to her! She had never been able to learn anything from him, and that was strange, because she had learnt her lines in the plays easily from Adam. There had been something then between her and Francis that had prevented this contact. Now there was nothing. They stood bare breast to breast.

With that she sprang up in a great terror. She lit candles, piled logs on the fire, and, although it was far too soon, began to listen for his return. It was one of those quiet winter afternoons, so still that you could almost hear a robin's step. She looked out of the window, and a round red sun was sinking over fields and paths that glimmered faintly with a white shadowed frost. There was no sound in the house save the logs on the fire that chattered crisply one moment and then broke into a sort of music like bubbling water, and Bethany who was singing below stairs.

She went to the head of the stairs and listened. Then she tried to work and could not, went down to the kitchen and talked with Benjamin, came back again, going to the window, although beyond it now all was black, then watched the stars come out like very distant fires, then listened to the wind getting up and roaming, whistling about the house. All this time her panic grew. Oh, if he did not come! But he would not. She knew that he would not. Something had happened: he had been suddenly ill. This was a premonition. The house was alive with it. Every board, every rafter creaked with it. There were steps on the stair, and he came in.

She ran to him, flung her arms round him, drew him to the fire. He could feel how she was trembling.

'But what? . . .' He stood smiling down at her. 'You are trembling.'

'I thought you would not come.'

'But why?'

'The house was so still. You were away so long.'

He sat down, drew her to him, laid his hand on her hair.

'It was not so long. There was no one in the town. Not a leaf stirring. I read a tale somewhere once of a Dragon who, very hungry, came to the town for a meal. There was only the King's Prime Minister there – the others were away hunting – an old dry man. The Dragon licked him all over, but found that he was so lacking in juices that he dropped him from his jaws and returned sulkily to his cave. I was such an old man today. An old man on an aged horse in a frosty town . . .'

'I was afraid . . . I am always afraid when you go out.'

'Then you care for me to return?'

'Care!' He felt her body draw closer to his. 'I love you, Francis. I didn't know surely until today. I had not thought. But I love you so dearly that I live only when you are near me. I was looking at the old jewels in which you used to dress me. How could I then have been so ungrateful? But we cannot force love. And I was busy with selfish grief for Harry. Then in those years away from you I learned that in the whole world there is no one who is like you. It is a pity that I have learnt it only now when I am old . . .'

'We are both old,' he said, smiling. 'I have learnt some things too.'

So it had come at last. At last! At last! His happiness prevented any words. Nevertheless, when a moment later Benjamin came in carrying some logs and dropped one, he jumped up and cursed him with all his old fervour, then threw his riding-gloves at him.

But that evening they sat for a long time by the fire hand in hand, saying nothing.

Then, in the spring, Benjamin died.

One evening he had a rheum. Next day a cough tore his chest in two. On the day following, every breath he took cut like a knife. But he would not go to bed. He had a superstition that once you went to bed in the daytime you never got up again.

Illness, too, was new to him. He had had blows and kicks and bruises and cuts, but never an illness like this. This sharp pain in his chest drove him to remember his father, who had had a cake-shop in Taunton. His father had been one of the fattest men in the South of England and one of the best-natured. It was from him that Benjamin had his own good nature. His cake-shop, which had been a famous one (and Benjamin might have suc-ceeded to it and been a wealthy man today had he not thrown a plate at his stepmother and run away to seek his fortune), was very small, and his father filled all of it with his handsome brown peruke, his three chins, and his white apron. It was his father's belief that he was grandson to a nobleman by a country-girl's mistaking her road home on a dark night. In any case he had an 'air', a tone, a something, and everyone noticed it, and bought his cakes the more readily.

Little Benjamin, sitting in the room behind the shop and smel-ling the rich plummy smell of good bakery, would wonder whether his grand jolly father wouldn't burst the wall of his shop with his huge shoulders, swinging stomach, roaring laugh.

And then, one evil day, his father caught this pain in the chest. Benjamin, who was then about fourteen years of age, had never seen anyone change as his father did. He suffered so terribly (he said that a hundred knives were slicing him into pieces) that they put him to bed, and there in the big four-poster that had the canary-coloured curtains (Benjamin remembered every aspect of that room – the two chairs, of which his mother was so proud, of dim gilt, covered with silk embroidery, and on the table in the window a bowl of dried rue and sweet-briar – he could smell its sleepy perfume yet) he lay, his chins grimy with the unchecked beard, and in his eyes a look of terrified surprise.

He lay there and said nothing, save one day that he could no longer smell the thick hot scent from the bakery. They knew then that the end was near, and a day later, staring with that same surprise as though it had been impossible to conceive that it was this had been waiting for him, he died. So, a month later, Benjamin threw a plate at his stepmother and ran off to seek his fortune.

It was going to bed that did it. In spite of the pain from the knives his father should have stood on his two feet and defied them all.

But now when, after all these years, Benjamin had this same pain of the knives in his chest, he felt terror and he felt defiance. So they meant to play him the same trick, did they? He had learnt a thing or two from his old father. He'd defy them by standing on his legs – yes, let them do their worst. So they did. They knocked him down there on the kitchen floor, where he lay with two broken plates beside him, and Bethany ran crying to her master.

Benjamin was put to bed then whether he wished or no. A doctor was found, a young fellow this time, Parling by name, a tall bony lad with great ambitions and a speculative mind, lodging in Grange because he was reading for a thesis.

When Parling looked at Benjamin, stripped his chest, listened to his lung, two opposite worlds met. Parling was all for the future, Benjamin saw only the past. Benjamin regarded the young doctor with horror. Two hours after his departure (he leaving a very serious report of the old man's condition with Herries) Mirabell, sewing by the fire, hearing a sound, turned to see Benjamin, dressed in his working clothes, swaying on his feet, at the end of the room. She ran to him. He tried to push her off. 'Stand on your feet! Stand on your feet!' he cried, clutching her arm and staring wildly beyond her. 'They can't catch you if you stand on your feet.' A fearful bout of coughing racked him and he fell forward. With great trouble she held him, he so heavy and she so slight, until Herries came and, bearing him in his arms like a baby, laid him back in bed again.

After that he was partly away in Taunton and his childhood, and partly clinging to Herries. His love for Herries came out in him like a child's dependence on its mother. He had stood by his master so long, through so many evil reports and mischances, that to go anywhere now without him seemed an incredible thing. And a great part of the while he confused Herries with his father.

He smelt the bakery. He saw the boy come into the room with the long tray and the dark brown cakes lying on it, all in rows like a game, and he felt the saliva gather in his mouth as though he were a little dog; then he heard his father's thick deep voice (as though he were himself an enormous Cake speaking), 'Chut! Chut! Be careful, boy! . . . I'll flog thee for a stumble,' and then the beneficent smile as he looked at the tray so approvingly and rubbed his fat hands that seemed to have always in their interstices fragments of flour.

But across this vision drove Herries. Herries in his proud youth, Herries stripped in the open waiting to have the water dashed over him, Herries riding his fine horse, Herries having his boots pulled off, Herries shouting for his dinner.

In his rambling talk many of his private anxieties that had never risen into expression when he had command of himself came out.

'Master, master, I'm coming . . . Aye, hurry, hurry! It is past the hour and no one come . . . If I break it he'll mind, but there's always a stumble or a trick for a man's feet. Coming! Coming! What more can I do? He would have me every place the same time, and then nothing but kicks after all's said . . . Aye, they can name him names, but what do they know? So it is, Master Davy, so it is. But you go by the field to the left there. They say there's a fine trout or two. I'll not tell your father.

'Coming, coming, master! That's his joke. Every gentleman has his own fun – and every man too for that. There they go! Tumble them down the stairs! Tumble them down them!

'I'll set a dog to them an they come shouting their bawdy nonsense . . . Nay, but, Father, I said naught. But she's not my mother. I'll do her bidding. She shall let me alone though. If she strikes me I'll not stay . . . 'Twas a woman with a green petticoat had the paper. She's gone in a coach and had a monkey with her . . . He's gone a long while. It's lonely, this house . . . If I did tumble her there's no sin. And if there's a child the old man won't know it. I'll be rubbing Unicorn down. There's an hour before sundown. Steady now! Steady! 'Tis dark in this house before you've time for a lantern . . .'

The day before he died he recovered his senses altogether. He lay very placidly, looking at the ceiling and smiling to himself. On the next evening, which was warm so that the window was open, he heard them calling the cows in.

'The country's a fine place,' he said in a weak, quavering voice.

'Doncaster was not much, master. But here there's always a bustle. Are you happy now, master?'

'Yes,' said Herries, 'I'm happy.'

'I'm glad of it. There has been another look in your face since the mistress came home. And where would I have been without you? Dandering around, coming to no good, for I had always a leching for women. But I wouldn't have bided in one place for any woman. No, I would not. Nor worked for any woman neither. 'Tisn't right for a man to work for a woman. It is against nature. That's what my father always said, and he'd had a multitude of women in his time . . . You've been a good master to me and I've been a good man to you. There's satisfaction in that certainly.'

Then he began to count slowly to thirty or forty, and then begin again. It may have been cakes that he was counting, or cows or horses. So, counting, he died.

After the funeral they were alone in the house, for Bethany, feeling that a funeral was a festival, had gone merrymaking.

'We are alone in the house, my dear,' said Herries.

She kissed him, then, a happy triumph showing in her face, answered:

'No, we're not alone, Francis. Nor will be again. Old woman though I am, I am to have a child. How am I for a clever woman?'

She danced around the room, and he, looking at her, saw all her youth come back to her. Her hair flamed; she was as she used to be when he implored her to love him. Now he did not need to implore. She was his completely.

DEPARTURE FROM HERRIES

MRS HENNY came now on the scene.

Mrs Henny was a southern woman who for ten years had been living a widow in Grange. She was a lady of all trades – nurse, midwife, cook, friend of all the world and, in the modern manner, a witch. One may see how different the modern manner (temp 1774) is from the old, because whereas, years ago, Mrs Wilson had been persecuted and drowned, Mrs Henny was the most popular woman from Seathwaite to Portinscale.

Young women indeed came to ask her advice from districts as distant as Shap and Kendal. There was no one, they said, so successful in promoting a hesitating love-affair, no one with so sound a knowledge of herbs and simples. She sold charms, verses, and prophecies in packets, and kept in cages birds that told your fortune. She was in fact a 'good' witch, and was never known to do anybody any harm.

In appearance she was a little thin-boned woman with bright sharp eyes, a jutting chin, and she liked to wear wide black hoops and long black gloves on her hands.

It was she herself who suggested to Herries that she should come and 'do' for him. She could cook, she told him, she could nurse; there was a child coming and no midwife in Cumberland her equal. It was not strange that he, already most anxiously nervous about his wife's condition, should agree to her proposal; it was only strange that Mrs Henny, who had a nice little cottage of her own in Grange, just on the farther side of the bridge, where she had a most thriving trade, should wish to come. And there was only one possible explanation. She was the most inquisitive old woman in England.

Her curiosity was her devouring passion. She had been a girl of uncertain morality in her youth, not from any sensual laxity but only because she found that promiscuous affection provided her with more excellent secrets than any other mode of living. She had an amiable nature and did not wish to use these secrets to anyone's hurt, but know them she must.

It was for the same reason that she began, later in life, to dabble in love philtres, prophecies and potions – only that she might be confided in. That it was lucrative was for her an entirely secondary consideration.

It is probable that for years now her bright little eyes had been fixed upon the Herries house and her ears strained to catch the slightest sound from it. The tales about Herries were so many, he and his house were now so legendary that she was not the only one who would look up from the path and see a light burning in a window there and long to know the truth. Mrs Herries's return must have excited her yet further; when she heard of Benjamin's death, and that there was to be a child, she saw her opportunity.

On a warm spring evening of 1774 she arrived with a black box and a cage of canaries. To do her justice, although she may have come there from curiosity, she very speedily fell in love with both of them.

She was a warm-hearted old woman in any case, but the two things that she loved were power and a satisfied curiosity. Here she very quickly had both. They told her anything that she asked and they let her do what she wished. They were in truth so deeply absorbed the one in the other that they had no energy for asserting their rights.

'She couldn't enough confess,' she confided to her friends in Rosthwaite and Grange, 'the fashion with which they loved. In the heart of male and female,' she declared, 'you will ever find a principle of self-love and vanity, and this makes us very unwilling to give way to one another in anything. It is the desire of most females to have lovers, but for the most part it is because they wish for admiration. It is indeed the only way we females have of raising ourselves in Society.' But in this instance Mrs Herries appeared to have no appetite for flattery but desired only to serve Mr Herries, which was the stranger in that, after being married to him, she had left him for many years. His worship for her was odder yet, for she was not an educated woman, was most unskilful about the house, and although her hair was of a fine colour, no one could call her beautiful, nor was she, in strict parlance, a lady. Mrs Henny had always let it be known in Grange that she was herself a lady, her father a clergyman and she herself early married to a clergyman who, as in the case of Mrs Laetitia Pilkington, had treated her shamefully and abandoned her. However, she followed the parallel no closer. She was therefore a judge of the Upper Classes and Nobility, and she must observe that never, in all her wide experience, had she known a gentleman of the very finest birth, as Mr Herries undoubtedly was, accustom himself so admirably to a wife who was not gently born. They suited one another in everything and could not endure to be out of one another's sight.

His, Mrs Henny considered, can have been no easy nature to subdue, for, old though he was, he had yet a fiery temper and a very ironical tongue, but to his wife he was always the gentlest and most amiable of mortals. Mrs Herries, poor thing, had the look of one worn out with life. She had ever an air of apprehension if he was not near her. She had been tossed about, Mrs Henny – who was something of a poet – continued, so fiercely by life's cruel waves that she could not believe that she had reached a haven at last.

As for her child, this was her first, she was very old at forty-four for childbirth and had no strong constitution. It would be an uncertain situation. Meanwhile, they stayed hand in hand by the fire, or went out walking together, saying but little, wishing only for one another's company.

Such was Mrs Henny's account, listened to with the greatest interest by the ladies of the neighbouring villages, who had not for a long while had such a first-hand account of doings in Herries. And they on their part revived all the old stories – of the fine rake that he had been when he had come so long ago to Herries, of his selling his mistress at the Fair, killing his wife by unkindness, burying the witch in the garden and the rest. He was a changed man, they reckoned, and it only showed what God's adversities could do.

Nevertheless Mrs Henny, with all her curiosity, perceived one thing only dimly: the gathering anxiety with which they watched one another as the year advanced.

He had good reason for his care of her. As the child strengthened in her womb, he was more and more reminded of her age and her weakness. She seemed, as he lovingly watched her, to regain the slender childlike features that once had stirred so deeply his tenderness. She was a mature woman now in her control, knowledge of life and patience, but it was a child's face that looked across the table at him. So, lover although he was, he was also increasingly maternal; he could not watch and care for her enough.

This was also the emotion that was growing in her, for she now with every week saw increasingly that he was old. The fever returned to him at nights and he would shiver in her arms. His memory sometimes played him tricks, and his body that had served him so marvellously for so long sometimes betrayed him. The leg that had given him trouble once failed him again. He would pretend that it did not and she would pretend that he was stronger than he had ever been, and each hid the trouble from the other.

In July, Bethany ran away with a soldier she found in Keswick.

The summer was cold and wet; with October there came glorious fiery days, burning with colour, and then, in the first weeks of November, a first powdering of snow on the hills.

He began now to feel a fierce and biting anxiety that never left him. The nine months were past and the child was not born. She appeared to suffer very little discomfort. Possibly at no other time in her difficult life had she shown such courage and hardihood as she did now. She was always cheerful, and when he was there seemed the happiest woman in the country.

Mrs Henny, who had so vast an experience, said that it was no matter that the child should be delayed; it was often so, and for the best nine times in ten.

On a day in November, Herries took her in a hired chaise to the

Lake. The carriage stumbled over the rough path, which was bad for her; but she insisted. They stood for a little while in the wood below Cat Bells, pleased at the scene. The water was as still as glass, and the snow that brokenly covered the hills was reflected in it like a multitude of white fleecy feathers. The bare trees were brown and sunny; the light travelled like a silver arm resting upon hill after hill. Never before had they felt their love so strongly as then. It was love too mature and settled for many words and, most truly, too deep for tears. It had come out of great sorrow and anxiety, many mistakes, much selfishness, some anger and petulance, and it was now purified of everything save itself.

'I have never known whether there is a God,' said Herries. 'I am no more sure now than I was forty years ago. But I always said that if I had you, and you loved me, I would thank Him.'

'I love you with all my heart.'

'I know it. And so take off my hat to the old monster.'

And he took it off and bowed to the fleecy feathers in the Lake.

'Life has a meaning,' he said. 'At last, at last it has a meaning. One fine hour is enough.'

Then he took her back to the chaise, wrapping her warmly.

'When I am sententious, my dear, you must punish me. To talk about life so is in the worst manner of Mr Richardson, whom I detest. But even he shall not hinder my telling you that I love you.' And he kissed her cheek.

A few days later, David rode over to see him. He was greatly distressed to see how very ill the old man looked. But he said nothing of it to either of them.

As he stood by his horse before his departure, with his arm around his father's neck, a powerful sense of his love for his father overwhelmed him. It seemed to him that in spite of his affection for his wife and children, his absorption in his affairs, his pride in his position, none of these things truly touched him as deeply as this emotion.

He spoke of Mrs Henny.

'She cares for you properly, Father?'

'Yes, yes.' He looked up laughingly. 'She is distressed today because this morning she found her birds dead. She sees an omen in everything.'

'Why will you not bring Mirabell to us? She shall have every comfort and the child shall be born under Sarah's care.'

'No, no,' Herries answered impatiently. 'Of course the child must be born here in Herries.'

'How you love this place!' David looked about him. 'In all these years you have never failed it.'

'Nor has it ever failed me,' answered Herries stoutly.

'And you have never failed me either, Father,' said David. 'After all this there is no one in the world I love as I do you.'

But Herries was not feeling sentimental.

'Aye, we've been bound together, different as we are . . . There, get along. The snow is coming.' He gave his son a friendly push, then turned into the house, not looking back.

That night he was very ill. There was no doubt but that the worry of these last weeks brought it on. They put him to bed and summoned the young doctor. For a fortnight he was delirious and knew nobody. Then he was in his senses again, but was too weak to move. He lay there and Mirabell lay by his bed. He never took his eyes from her face.

The snow was falling heavily. The first day a wind blew and the snow piled up against the house and began softly to climb the windows. There was a still white light all about the house.

Sharply, about midday, Mirabell was taken with her first pains. Mrs Henny put her to bed. They lay in two rooms adjoining and the doors were open that they might speak to one another.

He called to her: 'The snow is climbing the windows. Is it light in your room?'

And she answered very cheerfully, that he should not know what she was suffering:

'Yes. I can see its shadow. Are you better? I would come to you. I shall be stronger tomorrow.'

'Are you warm? Is Mrs Henny with you?'

Her pain was terrible. She could not answer. Mrs Henny came to his room and told him that she was sleeping.

But when the spasm had passed, she called out:

'Is your head well now? Soon I will come myself and see.'

His head ached strangely. The snow was coming into the room, mounting higher and higher. Some of it touched his lips and it was bitter like blood, but behind the confusion, the flashing lights, the roar of water, his mind held on to her, and, in a voice very feeble but clear, he answered: 'Yes . . . Yes . . . I am better . . . but it is dark.'

Her pain rose and swallowed her. She thrust down a shriek of agony lest he should hear her. She had one last thought. She seemed to cry it triumphantly, although it was truly so faint that the old woman who was delivering her did not hear it.

'Francis . . . dear, dear Francis!'

Her child was delivered, and some moments later she died.

Herries, who was ever a fighter, rose in his bed to come to her. He saw her standing in the doorway, the snow whirling softly about her head.

Gladly he called to her.

'Mirabell! Mirabell!'

Then sank back, as it seemed to him, in her arms.

There was silence in the house for a brief moment. Then there was a thin wailing cry. The old woman and the new-born child were the only living things in the house.

Judith Paris

for
J. B. Priestley

I have kept my faith, though faith was tried,
To that rock-born, rock-wandering foot,
And the world's altered since you died,
And I am in no good repute
With the loud host before the sea,
That think sword strokes were better meant
Than lover's music – let that be,
So that the wandering foot's content.

W. B. YEATS

A PREFATORY LETTER

MY DEAR JACK,

There is in general no reasonable excuse for burdening a novel with a Preface or any sort of statement; a novel should show in itself its purport without outside emphasis. But, after the publication of *Rogue Herries*, I saw that with the next 'Herries' volume there must be a note of explanation. And for these reasons:

First: when a reader sees another instalment of Herries history he may think it necessary that he should read the first in order to understand the second.

Secondly: after *Rogue Herries* had made some friends it was in some places assumed that '*now*, of course, I would write a sequel'.

And thirdly: the principal criticism of *Rogue Herries* was on the ground of its diffuseness.

I must explain then that, firstly, the story of *Judith Paris* may be followed without any knowledge of her father or curiosity as to her descendants. Then, far from considering a sequel to *Rogue Herries* for the first time *after* its publication, I must here confess that I had, more than twenty years ago, the plan of writing the history of an English family that should cover two hundred years and that should have, throughout, the same English scene for its centre. This was, I think (although Mr Galsworthy may correct me), before the later Forsytes were thought of, or any suspicion of Sagas hung in the literary air.

Thirdly, I hope that when any who are interested realize (possibly with dismay and indignation) that there are to be, in all, four volumes of Herries history, certain details and characters will not seem so unnecessary, nor certain scenes so diffuse.

I would like, very modestly, to defend the fact that I write, and must write, from my own point of view. I can see that the Herries family offers, in its history, subject-matter for every kind of historian. But my view of the Herries in these volumes is frankly a romantic one.

Every historian, whether of a country or a family, is compelled by his temperament to his own individual vision. I can see that there is a Herries history that is realistic, one that is comic, one that is scientific. Any of these might be more broadly convincing than my own, but I must mix my own colours and stand by the result.

As to diffuseness, compression in such a scheme as this is not easy. I might have written a novel, a long one too, only about Jennifer. Even with Judith I have been compelled to squeeze ten years of her life into one chapter. Those ten years could well be the subject of another novel. The Rockages at Grosset fascinate me, but my theme compels me to keep them minor. And how much more I know about Georges Paris in London or Charlie Watson in Watendlath than I have space to tell!

Every scene and character has been deliberately chosen by me because of the book's continuous theme. At the awful word 'Theme', however, I feel that I am growing altogether too serious and solemn.

My intention is simply to record scenes from the life of an English family during two hundred years of English change and fortune, and beyond that to pay a tribute to a part of England that I dearly love.

Judith Paris may be read as a quite independent novel, but the four books are seen together in my mind as a piece of gaily-tinted tapestry worked in English colours.

Affectionately yours,
HUGH WALPOLE

Contents

Part One
ROGUE'S DAUGHTER

Part Two
WATENDLATH

Part Three
THE BIRD OF BRIGHT PLUMAGE

Part Four
MOTHER AND SON

The Herries Family in *Judith Paris*

Judith Herries, *afterwards Judith Paris,*
daughter of Rogue Herries and Mirabell
Georges Paris, *her husband*
Adam Paris, *her son*
David Herries, *son of Rogue Herries*
Sarah, *his wife*
Francis *m.* Jennifer Cards
Deborah *m.* Squire Withering } *their children*
William *m.* Christabel Carmichael
John
Dorothy } *Francis' chidlren*
Walter, *William's son, m.* Agnes Bailey
Uhland
Elizabeth } *Walter's children*
Deborah Sunwood, *daughter of Rogue Herries*
Rev Gordon Sunwood, *her husband*
Reuben
Humphrey } *their children*
Sir Pomfret Herries, *son of Sir Raiseley Herries, m.* Rose Dymock
James
Rodney } *their children*
Cynthia, *Pomfret's sister*
Carey Bligh, 2nd Lord Rockage
Maria, *his wife*
Carey *m.* Cecily Fowler
Phyllis *m.* Stephen Newmark } *their children*
Madeline, *Rockage's sister*
Jeremy Cards, *son of Humphrey Cards*
Prosper Cards, *son of Henry Cards, m.* Amelia Trent
Jennifer *m.* Francis Herries
Robert } *Prosper's children*
Morgan Cards, *Prosper's brother, m.* Ruth Ormerod
Montague, *his son*
Warren Forester, *great-grandson of Humphrey Cards*

Part I

Rogue's Daughter

FORECHAPTER

THE OLD WOMAN and the newborn child were the only living things in the house.

The old woman, Mrs Henny, had finished her washing and laying-out of the bodies of the child's father and of the child's mother. She had done it alone because she had been afraid to leave the house with no one alive in it save the newborn child. Now she was exhausted and, in spite of her labour, fearfully chilled, for the snow, although it fell now more lightly, was piled high about the doors and windows as if, with its soft thick fingers, it wished to strangle the house.

She was very cold, so she drank some gin, although it was not as a rule her weakness. The bodies of Mr and Mrs Herries lay, the eyes decently closed, the pale hands folded, each in its proper bed.

A fine heat burnt through Mrs Henny's old body. The gin was good. Then her head fell forward and she slept.

The old house rattled and squealed in the wind that was rising up now that the snow had almost ceased to fall. Feet seemed to creep up and down the stairs, fingers were at the windows, but the dead and Mrs Henny slept on.

Then, in the room where the old woman, the child, and its mother were, from the window a piece of glass, very old and dark green like weeded water, was loosened with the wind and fell tinkling to the boards. The snow blew in like a live thing and the room was icily chilled.

The child that had been sleeping felt the cold and began to cry, a shrill cry on one note. But Mrs Henny heard nothing, the gin holding her fast.

Squire Gauntry – little Tom Gauntry – riding along the Borrowdale path just below the house on the farther side of the little bridge, heard the cry. It was strange that from so weak a creature the cry should be so clear. He heard it, and he pulled up his horse; the six hounds who were with him stopped also. The snow had but just ceased to fall and for the first time that day. It was so unusual in that country for there to be so heavy a fall that he halted and looked about him in wonderment. The roofs of Rosthwaite, all the hills, the fields, were buried in the white smooth covering, and now, for the first time, light began to break through. The grey stuff of the snowy sky was torn and a faint green field spread over the dim hills, and the snow began shyly to sparkle. The wind blew the top of the snow into little smoking spirals. Some rooks flew, like black leaves, cawing, breaking the sacred silence. The green field spread.

Herries, the house, raised on its little hill, to Gauntry's right, seemed to be overwhelmed by the snow, huddled, shapeless, helpless, and out of that white shapelessness this thin, desolate, tiny cry continued.

Gauntry was eager to be home; his high black riding coat was heavy with snow, he was weary and chilled, but there was something in that cry that moved him. A hard-bitten little man, leading always his own life and telling everyone else to go to the devil, nevertheless he was sentimental too: so he turned his horse, crossed the bridge over the stream, and, followed by the six hounds, guided the animal through the snow, and, striking with his whip on the gate of the courtyard, holloaed three times.

There was no answer at all. The silence settled down again. There was no sound but the thin persisting cry. He hesitated as to his next step. He had met Herries once and again, but had no intimacy with him. Indeed, no one had. He was said to be a queer customer, one not easy to deal with, one who would not thank you for uninvited interference.

Gauntry was just like that himself, and, for that very reason, had always felt a sympathy with Herries. He liked a man who told the world to go to the devil: it was what the world was meant for. Nevertheless, he was tired, cold, thirsty. Why should he put himself about for a man who would only curse him?

Then something about the stillness of the house hit his attention. The place was but a ruin in any case; under the snow he could fancy how the boards creaked and the chimneys rocked.

He dismounted from his horse, pushed wide the old, grumbling gate, the snow falling thickly from it, then, followed in silence by the hounds, crossed the courtyard.

The house door was unbarred. The iron handle turned easily. He entered, to be met by two rusted suits of armour stationed at the foot of the stairs. Still there was silence everywhere, save for the lament of the child.

How cold the house was! He shivered, drawing his cloak tighter about him. Then again he holloaed. No answer. Where the devil were they hiding? Not a sound, not even a clock-tick. Up the creaking stairs he went, the dogs padding after him.

He came to a room hung with faded brown tapestries; there was a portrait of a wicked-looking old man in the dress of Elizabethan times, dead ashes in the stone fireplace, remains of a meal, bread, a mutton bone, on the table.

He called again: 'Herries! Herries!' but this time softly. Something in the place constrained him. Lord! how cold the house was!

A narrow wooden stair led higher, so on he went, the hounds following, crowding one another on the stair but making no sound.

At the stairhead there was a room. He pushed the door, entered, then stood there looking.

First he was aware that the snow was blowing in through a broken window, and then that a child lay in a wooden cradle. It was the child's cry he had heard. Then he saw that in a chair near the bed an old woman was asleep, and at her side was a bottle, tumbled over, spilling its contents on the floor. Then, stepping forward, he saw farther. On the bed a woman was lying. He saw at once that she was dead. Her red hair was spread about the pillow, her eyes were closed, and in her face there was a look of great peace and contentment.

Mrs Herries! He had heard of her many a time, but had never seen her. She had been a gipsy girl when Herries married her. She had run away from him, and then returned. Herries' second wife, the only woman, they said, whom he had ever loved. Gauntry bent forward and touched reverently the cold, thin hands. Yes, she was dead. Where, then, was Herries? Roughly he shook the old woman by the shoulder, but she would not stir. Only her old head rolled. He called softly 'Herries!', then went to the cradle, and the infant, who must be but newly born, at once ceased to cry.

He went to the door and listened, then seeing a room close by pushed softly into it. Herries himself was lying in bed there. Going closer Gauntry saw that he, too, was dead – an old man, his face scarred, but he, too, seemed to smile in great contentment and happiness.

Both, then? Both dead? He turned back to the other room, again shook the old woman, but saw that the drink held her fast. He stood there wondering what he should do, while the hounds sat on their haunches by the door and watched him.

Through the dusk the snow sparkled like diamonds, and

somewhere a solitary bird began its chirping. The infant did not cry, but seemed to watch him.

'Old woman!' he cried. 'Wake up! Wake up!'

But she would not wake. What must he do? The child must not be left here in this bitter cold: he could see that it was very warmly wrapped. Every preparation had been made for its coming. Poor woman! Poor Mrs Herries! Died in childbirth maybe, and Herries himself dying in the next room. Strange end to a strange life!

A tenderness seized him as he looked at that thin childish face, those thin delicate hands! What lovely hair she had! Herries had loved her, they said, almost to madness.

Well, someone must be told. Herries' son, David Herries, at Uldale must be told. Someone in Rosthwaite village must be fetched. But he could not leave that child there to start its melancholy cry so soon as he was gone. No, he could not. Very delicately for so dried and rough a little man he picked up the child, wrapping round it its warm bedding. Were it warm enough it would not suffer. They were hardy children in Gauntry's world. He was pleased that the child did not cry, but lay there in his arms contentedly.

Then he went out, down the stairs, across the courtyard, led the horse with one hand, and so, followed by the hounds, crossed the little bridge.

He knocked on the first cottage door in Rosthwaite. An old, wrinkled woman opened it. He told her of what he had found. She exclaimed something incoherently of witches and warlocks; another woman came, they chattered together. Two men joined them.

After many wonderings, forebodings and murmurs they started off up the hill to the house, in a group together as though they were afraid.

He stood there, considering. He did not wish to leave the child. It would be late when he was home. He would take it to his own place, Stone Ends, that night, and the family at Uldale should have it in the morning.

Yes, he did not want to leave it. Poor baby; it trusted him and seemed to watch him lest he should go away. Both dead in the one hour! He was helped to his horse, the child lifted to him by a village girl, then he called to the hounds and rode away. The infant, warm under the thick wrapping, uttered no sound.

LIFE AT ULDALE

IN THE AUTUMN of the year 1785 David Herries was sixty-six years of age, his wife Sarah forty-seven, his children, Francis twenty-five, Deb twenty-three and Will fifteen; his little half-sister, Judith Herries, was eleven.

They all lived at Fell House, Uldale. Uldale is on the farther side of Skiddaw and looks over the moor to the Solway Firth. The sprawling flanks of Skiddaw spread between Uldale and the town of Keswick.

In 1785 Marie Antoinette was playing hide-and-seek with her ladies in the gardens of Versailles, William Pitt was Prime Minister of England, Jane Austen was ten years old, and a Keswick boy of sixteen had just been hanged for stealing a leg of mutton. Nevertheless, this is a poor way of reckoning history, especially at Uldale, where the crops mattered and cock-fighting mattered and old Mrs Monnasett had only this very moment died.

History, of course, begins anywhere and everywhere. For Judith Herries it began, perhaps, when little Tom Gauntry found her squealing under the closed and lifeless eyes of both her parents. She never reckoned it so; she reckoned that it began on this autumn day when, after looking at Mrs Monnasett's corpse, she was whipped by her half-brother David.

This at once shows the ludicrousness of her position. She was eleven years old, and yet was sister to David Herries, who was sixty-six, and, yet more absurd, aunt, or at any rate half-aunt, to Francis, who was twenty-five, and Deb, who was twenty-three.

To make the matter more complicated yet and surely most improper, she was in love with her nephew Francis. For excuse you may say that she loved and hated alternately everyone around her a hundred times a day.

One of the disgraceful colours to this first notable event in Judith Herries' life was that Mrs Monnasett was but just dead and lying in state in the Blue Room. It was, indeed, because Mrs Monnasett lay there that the trouble began.

Fell House was a pleasant building, square-shaped, its brick rose-coloured, a walled-in garden, many fruit trees, the farm buildings with all the animals and the odours, a Gothic temple beyond the lawn, pigeons in the loft, swelling downs stretching almost to the sea, Skiddaw against the windows, and the road where the coaches ran not so far away that you could not hear the horses.

Life for Judith should have been agreeable there. They all wished to love her, and there was nothing in the world that she liked better than to be loved, but it had all been spoilt for her from the very beginning because she preferred so infinitely the life at Stone Ends, where Uncle Gauntry drank, hunted, beat her, loved her, taught her to ride, to hunt, to prepare the birds for cock-fighting and to learn everything there was to learn about men and women.

She was only eleven, but she knew more, far more, about everything than her half-niece Deb, who was twenty-three, or that other Deborah, her half-sister, who was married to a clergyman at Cockermouth and had two grown sons.

Uldale was by far too tame for her, and yet she loved them all and yearned for them all to love her. She knew, though, even at this age (she had known it long ago), that they could not really love her, for her mother had been a gipsy woman taken by her father off the fells and married by him when he was already an old man. She knew that David and Deborah, his children, had been ashamed of this marriage and had despised him for it. (They had not despised him for it. She would learn that one day.) Oh yes, they could not love her at Uldale, because she was the daughter of a gipsy who had been found one day dancing naked on the roof and could swear most horribly. But at Stone Ends they did not mind whose daughter she was and allowed her to do whatever she pleased.

Now on this afternoon in October they had but just finished dinner, Mrs Herries, Deb, Will, and Judith. Mr Herries and Francis had ridden to Newlands to see about a piece of land. Mrs Monnasett was to be buried the following day. The house was quite still. Mrs Herries went to the China Room to write a letter to her sister-in-law, Mrs Sunwood of Cockermouth. Deb was for the dairy, Will away on some secret purpose of his own. No one needed Judith. She stood, listening to the stillness of the house, halfway up the staircase, her fingers in her lip, considering. She was an odd little creature, even as odd little creatures go. She was very small, although made in excellent proportion, save that her red hair, which hung in ringlets, seemed weighty for her head. Her complexion was pale and would always be so: she had the horse-features of all the Herries, prominent nose and cheek-bones. She was, in fact, no beauty, but there was very much character in her bright and challenging eyes, the resoluteness of her mouth. When she smiled she could be very winning. She could also look exceedingly impertinent, and, when angry, with her red hair, her pale face, and perfectly balanced, lightly swinging body, she could seem a flying fury. She had tiny hands and feet; of these already she was boastfully proud.

She was dressed in a red bodice with silver buttons and a small orange hoop. She wore red shoes. This was her best dress, bought for her in Carlisle on a birthday by David Herries, who alternately loved and hated her. She was supposed to wear this grand dress only on very special occasions; she put it on most days of the week, but although she wore it so often it was as fresh as when it was new. She had, from the first, that gift of being clean and spotless in all her circumstances as a piece of china. That was a dirty age, but Judith had always a passion for washing; no water was too cold for her; she was so hardy that nothing ever ailed her. One out of every three children at this time died before it was four years of age. Judith had never known an ache or pain. They said that it was because Tom Gauntry had carried her on the very day that she was born through all the snow and ice from Borrowdale to Stone Ends. If that hadn't killed her, nothing would.

She stood, swinging a red shoe, sucking her thumb, and considering. She had intended to go to the corner of the road and watch for the return of Mr Herries and Francis. She loved Francis madly, passionately, although he was her nephew. She loved his thin delicate body, his pale austere face with the dreaming eyes, the soft gentle voice. He should have been a woman, people said, and that was why so few understood him, but Judith understood him and she would willingly (she thought) die for him. She would not, of course, in reality die for anyone, having now and always a fierce and tenacious hold on life. But she fancied that if he said (in his soft dreaming voice) 'Judith, pray jump from yonder window and break all your bones', she would jump. The fact that he considered her very little, scarcely ever thought of her, made no difference. She loved him only the more fiercely. He and Uncle Gauntry were the gods of her fiery, agitated, dramatic world.

As she stood there the stillness of the house forced itself ever more upon her attention. She had intended to go to the road, but what an opportunity this was to creep in and look at Mrs

Monnasett! She had seen dead people before. There was the boy in Bassenthwaite village who had been beaten by his master and had suddenly (most ungratefully) died; she had been walking with Will and they had come on him lying against the Cross on the Common. There had been the beggar who came to their door one summer night to ask for food, and he had fallen dead while walking away up the hill. She was no stranger to death, and thought, in a general way, little of it. But Mrs Monnasett was different. Judith had known her all her life. She had been nurse and tyrant and friend to all the children. She had been there for years, ever since Francis and Deborah were born, and what a strange woman she had been, with the hairy mole on her cheek, the strange stories that she used to tell, the songs that she used to sing, the ghosts she had seen and the witches she had known, and, more than all, the little gold box that she carried with the charm of a snake's skin and the queer-smelling foreign root; would she have that little box with her yet, even though she were dead?

Judith had thought that the charm would prevent her from ever dying. She would live for ever. But no, she had not. She was dead now and the worms would eat her. Had she the little box yet with her? Judith considered. She and Will had been forbidden to go near the room, but that forbidding only made the matter more charming. She would have a whipping, but she had had many, and when David Herries whipped her she had only to sob in a certain strangling way and he was always sorry for her and would kiss her and let her have a pinch of snuff out of his box. Yes, the risk was nothing. Softly she stole up the stairs.

As it happened, Mrs Sarah Herries was at that same moment writing of Judith to her sister-in-law, Mrs Deborah Sunwood. She sat in the China Room, pleasant and sunny, the low windows looking across to Skiddaw. The room was handsomely furnished with some pagodas and vessels of Chelsea china, in which were set coloured sprigs of artificial flowers. The walls were hung with a Chinese wallpaper and, to quote an old Herries journal, 'A looking-glass, enclosed in a whimsical frame of Chinese paling, stood upon a Japan table over which was spread a coverlet of the finest chintz.' Yes, a pretty room, burnished now with the last orange glow of the setting sun, for it was after five, and Sarah Herries must light the candles.

She stood there a moment watching the trembling flame, a handsome woman in a rose-coloured hoop, wearing her own hair, a fine bosom, and the face stout a trifle but kindly, good-humoured and patient.

She was thinking, perhaps, as she held the snuffer in her hand and glanced at her broad figure in the looking-glass, that her life had been cast in pleasant places since that day so many years ago when David had snatched her out of Wasdale and fought her uncle on the Stye Head Pass.

She was thinking of that and of her Will, whom she adored, and her Francis, whom she adored not quite so much, and of her fat good-natured Deborah, whom, because she took a trifle after herself, she loved a little less . . . yes, ever so little less. And then her thoughts turned, as they always did were they given any freedom at all, to her beloved, worshipped David, the fire, the heat, the passion of her happy life, still the most handsome of all human creatures although he might be stout now, still the best of all humans although he might on occasion drink himself under the table or lose at faro with Squire Osmaston and the others the money that he had put aside for the purchase of Brandon's field. Her eyes were wet a trifle, the candle flame danced mistily as she sat herself down in the dark Irish Chippendale chair to write to her sister Deborah.

There was nothing in the world that she liked better than to write to Deborah, for she understood so precisely the importance of everything that Sarah thought important, was interested in all the cures that Sarah practised on the children, thrilled to the heart when she heard that wicked Cousin Pelham, now nearly seventy and old enough to reform (but he never would), had sent Sarah all the way from London by coach and carrier a Chippendale bookcase with a Gothic design in the cornice and rosettes on the lower panels.

Yes, Deborah understood everything, and most especially did she understand about Judith.

This, then, was the letter's first part, the candle flame trembling, the China paper dancing, the outer world fading to a silver star and the white tone of the climbing road.

MY DEAREST SISTER – I hope that you were not disappointed of your lodgings in Kendal and that the boys took care for you. I can give but little account of these last days for, as you know, we have had Kate Morris' children with us while the house in Keswick was set to order. Their visit had like to have been fatal to me for they not being acquainted with the Semblance of Manners nor trained indeed to anything but having their own Way perfectly in all things that were bad enough without our Judith's added wickedness to excite them.

There is also now Mrs Monnasett dead in the House and last Tuesday the new Coachman that we had from Mr Newsom of Newlands was drunk returning Home from Penrith and the postillions also and like to have overturned us on a gallop against a Post coming through Threlkeld.

However, dearest Deborah, you are aware that my Nature is both Tranquil and Harmonious and that if I might but be sure that the Beneficient Creator is not on occasion busied with His Attention in other more interesting Directions I would not trouble for drunken Coachmen or anything else.

Mrs Monnasett is to be buried tomorrow forenoon.

I am happy that I consider nothing more disagreeable than Learning in a Female for Mr Huxtable the Tutor of Kate's children has been here a week and found us all Savages save Francis.

With him he must talk Greek and all the Indian Languages and has Mr Young's *Night Thoughts* at his Finger End and Mr Pope's *Essay on Man* sprouting from his Eyeballs – a Man heavy of figure and such a Comedy on a Horse that it would do you good to see. But Judith who must always carry everything too far put a Cracker under his Chair and a Mouse in his Wig for which David whipped her, but not I fear so severely as she merited. But Mr Huxtable showed no Impatience, reminding us that Alexander the Great and Diogenes were Characters alike for their indifference to Trifles, the one holding the World as his Tub, the other his Tub as the World or some such Nonsense.

And now in Seriousness, my dearest Sister, I have been so gravely disturbed over Judith that last Tuesday I was blooded and on two occasions my throat has been excoriated.

For the Child has a Devil that there's no exorcizing. She is now high and now low and not altogether bad; David indeed swears that she is not bad at all and has as good a Heart as anyone in this house, which may be in Truth enough save that if she has a Heart she has also a Temper and a Disposition to Evil that I swear poor child is as great a Trouble to Herself as it is to Us.

I have no doubt as I have often said to you before but that it had its commencement in Mr Gauntry's love for her as a Baby. We have forbidden her his Place for the Present. I have

no Need to tell you, Sister, of the scandalous Conduct now
current in Stone Ends. It is the Talk of the Countryside. The
last Time Judith was there they had been wanting to make
her drink with him and I must not be ingreateful to the Squire
when I acknowledge that he will not have her contaminated
and in any Case she can, with a marvellous Discretion for a
child of her years, manage the whole Establishment at Stone
Ends that she has under her little finger. It is Managing that
she is always after and has been from a Baby. All the satisfaction that I have is that she has not yet learnt the Fashion
of managing me nor ever will, but to see that Chit of a Child
with her red hair and Herries Nose giving orders to my Will
and Deb is so Unnatural as to be only partly Decent. Monnasett could deal with her and would have it that her Temper
was from her Consciousness of and Uneasiness at her unlikely
Parentage, but I have not seen her so Sensitive but have found
again and again a brutal insensibility to the wants and opinions
of others.

For the present she is in a Pretty Tantrum because she is
forbidden Mr Gauntry's and if we do not watch her she will
be over there in a trivet. She has found out, I fancy, that I am
not to be feared although I am not yet assured that she has
found out that I am to be loved. But am I indeed? She is too
odd a changeling for either David or myself to be certain of
our Hearts towards her. It was the same with her mother, poor
Mirabell, who as you will well remember, dearest Sister,
never loved me because I was too Settled a Wife and Domestic
a Woman for her. And this Child also could be in her turn
Domestic when she wished. She is in fact of a Mixture so odd
that it needs a more perceiving Woman than myself to fathom
her, only it is Plain enough that she must have her Way in
everything and Dominate all those around her. Then,
granted her Desires, she will let her Heart speak and has a
Generosity that is not to be checked. Nevertheless I am filled
with Fears for the future. As she grows her Nature becomes
more clear with every hour and this house is in a Turmoil
over her . . .

As to your Complaint, gentle purging is to be advised;
no vomits but if your stomach flags four to eight drops of
Elixir of Vitriol is excellent and if feverish three spoonfuls of
a decoction of the bark by boyling one ounce and a half in a
quart of water to a pint. I must tell you, dearest Deborah,
that since the days that Cupid set Hercules to the distaff he

has not had a nobler conquest than mine over the straightening
of the cupboard room in the new . . .

The remainder of this letter has nothing for our purpose.

It is Herries history, however, that at the moment when Mrs
Sarah Herries was doing her best to place Judith upon paper,
the same Judith was with the utmost gentleness and caution
opening the door of the Blue Room where Mrs Monnasett
was lying.

Entering, she was both pleased and sensually alarmed by the
dim candle-fluttering light that hung about the room, making the
blue pagodas on the wallpaper, the high tallboy, seem of infinite
mystery, and the blue tester hangings and overlay of the bed
sway in some dimly felt stirring of the breeze. Not that she was
frightened. Judith did not know now, did not, for many years,
know what it was to be afraid. The day would come, and in a
room not unlike this present one, when, hearing her beloved
Francis enter the hall below, she would know, but that was not
yet.

She approached the bed; it was one that had always most
especially attracted her with its reeded and fluted columns,
delicately carved with acanthus leaves. There were very few
things, even at this early age, that she did not notice. The candles
were standing at the bed-head, and Mrs Monnasett, very yellow
against the white of the pillow, her black hair spread, her large
strong hands neatly folded, lay there, her lips curved in a
sardonic smile. So, Judith reflected, often in real life she had
smiled as though she knew more, far, far more than anyone
around her. And so, indeed, Judith was very sure that she did.
If she had not been an actual witch she had been as near to it
as not to matter. Judith had known that all the domestics and
hands about the farm had thought her one. Yes, she had known
everything, and now what did she know? Did Death tell you
anything more? She looked as though, behind those closed
eyelids, she was seeing a thousand things. A fire burned in the
room. It was hot, and there was a faint cloying smell of cor-
ruption. Judith came very close, stood on her toes because
the bed was high, and touched with her warm fingers the dead
hand. It was not only cold like iron but hard like iron. Where
was Mrs Monnasett now? With God? Asking God questions?
Telling Him, perhaps, things that He did not know. But, above
all, had she the little gold box with her? Judith did not intend
to steal it, only to see whether they would bury it with her.

She looked about the dim dark room, sniffing the faint decaying odour like a little dog. The heavy curtains at the windows fluttered, the blue pagodas on the wall seemed to run a race, the fire crackled and sputtered, mice would be behind the wainscot, but none of these disturbed Mrs Monnasett, who lay there, growing surely with every moment more yellow, and the mole black upon her cheek, smiling her secret smile because of the things she knew that others didn't. But had she the little gold box with her? Had she? Had she? Judith must know.

She stood at her tallest, leaned over and, with a shiver of excitement at her daring, felt with her hand, under the clothes, in the hollow of Mrs Monnasett's breasts.

She had scarcely touched that chill flesh when there was a voice at the doorway, a voice of horror and disgust.

She nearly lost her balance and, half tumbling, started away from the bed to see Mrs Herries, holding high a lighted candle, in the doorway. The child assumed at once the attitude that she always had when she was set for trouble. She flung her head back, held her hands behind her and waited.

'Judith! Come out of here.'

She followed Mrs Herries from the room. In the passage she stood by the door like some small wild animal ringed about with enemies.

'What were you doing there?'

'Nothing.'

'Nothing! That is a lie!'

'I wasn't doing anything.'

'You wicked child! You had been forbidden to enter the room.'

'Yes, ma'am.'

'You confess your disobedience?'

'Yes, ma'am.'

'And at the bed you were touching—' Sarah Herries' voice broke in her disgust and revulsion.

'I wished to look at Mrs Monnasett – and bid her farewell.'

Sarah Herries sighed. This strange child! But there was feeling there, tenderness. The child had heart. And all would have been well had not that odd impulse to absolute honesty that would, throughout Judith's life, force from her such inconvenient avowals burst from her now:

'I wished to see whether Mrs Monnasett had yet with her the gold box with the charms.'

'You wished to see – what?'

'Whether she had yet the little gold box with the charms.'

'You would see . . .' Mrs Herries broke off. Her nature was kindly, wise, tolerant, but she did not understand this child any better than in the earlier days she had understood the mother. And just as then elements would arise that sickened some sound English normality in her, so now with Judith there would be often moments when she hated this child, in reality hated her so that she wished her out of her house and her family, a thousand miles away, never to return.

She felt this revulsion now, a sort of sickness. To search the corpse for a gold box – a child of eleven. She was afraid of what she might do, so she said: 'Go to your room and wait there until I come to you.'

Judith, without a word, turned and went.

Her room was a small one under the roof. From her window she could see the road, the hills, the woods that stretched towards Bassenthwaite. Here she had her treasures – a candle-stand that Francis had given her, a china jar, old and cracked, but with lovely orange flowers on it, that she had begged from Mrs Monnasett, two 'babies' – rag dolls from her own babyhood – a fox's brush that Tom Gauntry had sent her, a piece of China silk, a faded and stained battle-piece in a black frame that she had found in a cellar, a treatise on cock-fighting, and a Bible that Reuben Sunwood had presented to her last Christmas-time. Here she would sit on a small oak-panelled armchair and watch from the window the outside world that she so desperately loved.

Now she banged the door behind her, kicked off her red shoes and stood scowling. She hated Fell House and everyone in it save Francis. She knew that she had been wrong to go and look at Mrs Monnasett, and more wrong still to touch her. Her immaculate honesty forbade her to blame Mrs Herries for any injustice. She had been right to be angry, the punishment that would follow would be just. She was so much wickeder than all the others, as she very well knew. Here was no portrait of a poor, ill-treated little girl. They tried to love her; it was her own fault that they could not. But with every breath that she drew she was longing for Tom Gauntry – the odd, rambling, ill-shaped house with the smell of dogs and horses and drink and dung and cooking food and musty curtains, with the noise and laughter and songs, with the freedom and airy indulgence as though all the doors and windows were for ever open – that was her life, that the place into which she had been taken on the very first day of her existence, and Uncle Tom with his twisted brown face and twisted brown body, his funny bow legs and his hoarse whisper and his cry to the hounds and his oaths and angers – *he* understood her as no one else in the world did . . . And then, cutting across that picture, as so often it did, was another one, quite opposite, that made her understand the Herries decency of Uldale, made her, in certain moods, finely handy about the place, in the store cupboards, the dairies, so that she could sew and bake and clean with the best of them, and understand too when Will (for whom she did not really care) would tell her, with all the gravity of a grown man, of how he would advance the Herries family and have money in all the banks and buy land everywhere – all this she could understand and believe in.

Yes, but at this precise moment she was a little girl of eleven in one of her hellish tempers, one of her incoherent rages, so that she could swear in proper Cumberland just like any of the girls or men about the place, so that she was mad to be out of the house and over the fells, sniffing the peat, hearing the water of the mountain streams run and the tug of the sheep at the grass and the sharp bark of the sheepdogs . . .

She turned, her eyes furious and her little feet stamping, at the sound of the open door. Francis Herries had come in.

At the sight of him she forgot for a moment all her trouble. He was still in his riding clothes. He must have come straight to her after his arrival. His face was so beautifully peaked and serious under his brown wig, his legs in their riding boots so handsomely shaped and his eyes so far away, so mysterious . . .

She drew her breath sharply as she always did when she saw anything that seemed to her beautiful. How she loved him! And he, from his great height, looked down gravely to the odd little figure with the defiant mouth and the red hair and rebellion in every inch of her.

He slapped his whip against his thigh.

'Father is coming shortly to beat you. I thought I'd best prepare you.' Then he smiled, a lovely winning smile which, in anyone more self-conscious, must have been artificial. But Francis Herries, as he never thought of himself, never thought of his smile either.

'I know.' Her eyes devoured him. 'I don't care as long as you've come.'

'What have you done, you little devil? Why can't you be good?'

'I can't be good,' she answered defiantly, 'because my father married a gipsy. And I'm happy he did,' she added.

This was an old familiar statement of hers. She was always dragging in the gipsy. It seemed to Francis to be in bad taste, so he said again:

'What have you done this time?'

'I went in to see Mrs Monnasett.'

The thought and image of death, so familiar as to be less than nothing at all to the men and women of his time, always affected Francis Herries with a queer tremor of mystery and horror. It seemed to him revolting that this child should have been in Mrs Monnasett's room.

'Why must you do that?' he asked.

'To see if she had her little gold box.'

'What box?'

'A box of spells that she had.'

He said nothing and turned to the door.

With a little tremor in her voice she said: 'Please punish me.'

He turned back. 'Punish you?'

She broke out passionately, an unusual passion for so young a child.

'I didn't know that it was wrong, but if you had told me not I would never have gone. Punish me and you will see. I will do anything you tell me, stand in icy water or let the rats in the cellar gnaw me or sleep in the stable.'

He looked at her, met the intense absorbed devotion of her eyes, and was greatly touched. When he could come out of his dreams and notice human beings he loved them, loved all humanity. He was humble also, and found it strange that any-one should care for him. This small child, standing there in her stockinged feet and coloured hoop, adoring him, moved him. They were friends from that moment, although neither realized that it was just then that their long alliance was formed. He spoke lamely enough:

'Punish you? No. Why should *I* punish you?'

They could say no more because at that moment David Herries came in. He carried a riding whip, was in his riding clothes, looked exceedingly sheepish. He had been always of great size and immense strength. Now, at sixty-six, he was beginning to be corpulent, had a red face and something of a belly, but looked very much the same kindly, obstinate, un-imaginative boy who had, nearly thirty years before, carried his Sarah away from the dark house in Wasdale.

He looked sheepish because he hated this business. Francis went out. Judith bent over the chair and he whipped her. Neither said a word until it was over. She replaced her little clothes, then stood, her lip trembling, because she was very near to tears but would not cry, near the window.

Her stockings were crooked, which seemed to David very pathetic, and without knowing it she had her hand on her back where it was sore.

He filled the room with his great bulk, and his red face was creased with kindliness. He scratched his bare head, pushing his wig a little awry. He talked because he saw that she was near to tears.

'Now, Judith, why must you do such a thing? 'Tisn't decent to be in the death-chamber, and it was against all orders, as you very well knew. Now, then, it is over, isn't it? Never to be spoken of again . . .'

He went and picked her up and kissed her. Had he known it (and it had been always one of David's weaknesses that he was not clever at perceiving things), this was, of everything that he could do, the thing that she detested most.

To be picked up, like a tiny baby, to be dangled in the air, to be held close to this huge man and feel his bristly cheek and smell the odour of liquor and horses, to have her neck pricked by the sharp buttons of his coat, and, worst of all, to have his great heart hammering in her ear, this was the final ignominy!

She stayed passive, only when he would kiss her mouth she turned her head aside. He put her down with a grunting sigh. She was a problem, this child, just as her mother Mirabell had been before her. He did not understand her at all.

He looked at her, smiled an awkward, clumsy smile, muttered, 'We shall say no more about the thing,' and stumped away.

She stood there, considering. She did not want to see any of them ever again, save Francis. Somewhere a clock sounded six. A cart rattled down the Fell road. She went to the window and looked out. It was almost dark; the hills were shadows against shadow.

Then she smiled.

She knew what she would do.

STONE ENDS

SHE WAS SO made that once a plan came to her nothing in the world was going to stop her, and every pulse of her body beat to that one purpose.

She flung back the narrow diamond-paned window, found a cloak and a shawl, left the red shoes for thick country ones. No time was wasted, and as she worked for her purpose her small mouth was set, her chin was out. Nothing was to stop her in such a mood. She didn't think of consequences (she was never to think of them as she should do), recked little that this second disobedience in one evening meant trouble for her more serious, perhaps, than any that she had yet encountered.

She had been out of that window before. There was still light enough for her to see the old crooked water pipe that jerked an arm round the farther end of her casement, then there was the water butt, then the stone passage leading to the stable. But she had a long descent on that pipe. She clung to it with hands and feet, her chin and nose rasped by its casing. Her small legs trembled, the shawl blew against her face, she felt (or imagined that she felt) spiders' thread in her hair, then her feet found the water butt, she held her body together and jumped.

She fell on her hands and knees, and the black cat, Solomon, ran from under her very feet, scrambling up the monkey-tree. Her knees were bleeding, her hoop under her cloak was torn. But she stood, holding her breath like a proper conspirator, to hear whether the noise had made any stir. There was no sound but the owl hooting. It seemed that a breath of light had blown back again into the sky. Over the garden wall, the Caldbeck fells were outlined as though a row of candles were lit behind them.

It was the moon; later that moon would strengthen, and the freshening wind would blow the stars up. All the garden scents were crowding the night air. She was very cheerful indeed, and, pulling the cambric tight about her face again, stepped across the irregular paving of the yard, called very softly, 'Barnabas! Barnabas!' At once the little black horse with the white star on his forehead put his head over the paling. In another moment she had unbarred the door and was leading him out, stroking his nose.

Barnabas understood perfectly what she wanted. She mounted

the black outside the gate and, her legs spread very wide, her hair flying, was away up the road. A mile later, the first delirium of freedom passed, she began to consider ghosts, witches, and warlocks. She was not afraid, but there was the man with the face like a rat, the woman with two heads, the lost soul of Judas that whimpered like an infant, the old woman with a rat on her shoulder, the lovely lady on the skeleton horse, the old woman with three beards, the soldier who had lost his head in the wars and carried it in his handless arms, the coach with the eight devils and the fiery horses, the lady of Caldbeck who walked searching for the child that she had murdered.

And worse, perhaps, in actual fact, than any of these, the highway robber who had been hung in chains on the path between Thistlebottom and Whelpo, although there were now only his bones remaining.

She was not afraid of any of them, but she repeated aloud to herself the Lord's Prayer and so much of the Creed as she could remember, and then the names of the places near her home – Ireby, Snittlegarth, Binsey, Aughertree, Nevin Tarn, Orthwaite, Over Water, Braefell, Branthwaite. It comforted her that Barnabas trotted comfortably along as though he knew precisely his destination, but it comforted her yet more when she met a cheerful gang of pack horses, the bell-horse first with his pleasant noise. They were carrying peat from the moors in halts, old-fashioned wicker baskets that were very soon now to give way to carts.

Judith called out to the men as she passed them, waving her hand, and they talked that night about the witch that had greeted them (on a black horse) and had waved in the air hands shining with flame.

Stone Ends, Tom Gauntry's place, was a mile beyond Caldbeck. She made no further encounter. The clock of Caldbeck Church struck seven as she trotted through the deserted little street.

On the dark road beyond Caldbeck she met two drunken soldiers who stood in the road and waved at her. They had a lantern; one had a wooden leg. She leaned forward on to Barnabas' mane and cursed them in good Cumbrian. She called them 'Hulkers' and 'Lubbers' and 'Dummle-heads'. She told them that they gave her 'a nasty dwallow taste in her mouth' and that they'd better 'jump up and knep a daisy'. She must have astonished them, perched on the horse, her red hair flying about in the uncertain circumference of the lantern that waved in their

drunken hands. At any rate, they did nothing, and stood aside
to let Barnabas by.

So she arrived at Stone Ends. This was a rough-cast building
of no height, with an outside gallery and stair. There were
mullioned windows, great trees overhanging the mossy slates and
round thick chimneys. There was a garden with a clipped hedge,
the fells everywhere beyond, a rough plot of flowers, some out-
buildings, a sundial, a little stream.

Lights burnt in the windows, but Judith did not need a light.
This little place had been familiar to her since her babyhood,
her only true home. She tied Barnabas to the gate and went
cautiously to the porch. She was not certain how she would be
received. Old Gauntry was not always the perfect host, especially
when taken unawares. Riding Barnabas so soon after the beating
had not improved the soreness of her seat. She did not want
another whipping, nor to be sent directly back to Uldale again.
So, with her ear to the heavy door, she listened. Little listening
was needed. The chorus of revelry was clear enough. They
would have been hunting, she decided, and were now in process
of becoming drunk as soon as possible. *That* did not frighten
her. She had heard often enough: 'Now this is a fine fox we've
killed and it munna be a dry one.' The important thing was to
ascertain the *stage* of drunkenness at which they had arrived.
She knew that between the first and second hour they would
all be in a state of exceeding friendliness.

She was, however, given no time to consider. The door opened
and Wull shoved his hairy head out. Wull (or William Flint as
was his proper name) stood to Tom Gauntry as the Fool stands
to his King. Judith would never forget the agitation with which
she had first beheld him. In her babyhood she had been told
that he was the Hobthross, the Brownie who lurks in old houses –
works all night for the family to whom he has attached himself,
stretches himself before the fire, churns the milk for the girls,
and can be heard singing at his tasks. A kindly spirit, but wild to
look at, with his shock of hair, his broad ugly face, his misshapen limbs. Just so was 'Wull', and when she was an infant
he would love to pull faces at her until she howled with rage.
She was never frightened of him, but only angry. Later he became her friend, then her warm ally. He poked his ugly head out
at her now.

'Wull! Wull!' she whispered.

Sometimes he was a complete fool, sometimes most intelligent. He would tell her about himself with a broad grin: 'Ah'm

nobbut a bit goffish.' It was probable that he was not 'goffish' at all, but knew exactly what he was doing. When he saw who it was he let her in. The house-place was filled with dogs and smelt like a midden. Judith did not mind the smell in the least. The dogs were everywhere; every kind of dog. They ran at her when they saw her, barking and tumbling all over her. Some of the hounds were bigger than she. They all knew her. One, a spaniel bitch, Clara, adored her, had followed her once almost all the way back to Uldale.

When Clara saw her she was in an ecstasy of happiness, springing up and down, yapping on a shrill high note, her beautiful large eyes beaming with joy. Judith asked Wull how many gentlemen there were in there. He didn't know; about twenty maybe. They had had a grand day's hunting and had killed over by High Hesket. He cuffed the dogs and quieted them, but the noise had been heard. The room door opened and Tom Gauntry came out. He stood with his funny crooked legs straddling. He was fairly drunken. When he saw Judith he gave a loud 'Yoicks! Yoicks! Tally-ho! Tally-ho!' and they came crowding to the door. Judith recognized a number she knew – young Osmaston, Squire Watson, old Birkmyre, Statesman Peel – also two ladies.

Gauntry came over to her and picked her up and carried her shoulder-high into the room where they were dining. Oddly enough, what she hated in David Herries she liked in Uncle Tom.

'And why the hell have you come?' he asked her.

'Because I wanted,' she answered.

From her height she looked over the scene, which was for her no new one. The room was not large. They were crowded about the round table upon whose shining surface the candles guttered grease. Food was piled everywhere – mutton, beef, puddings; wine was spilt on the table, and almost the first thing that Judith noticed was the naked head of old Dunstable, robbed of its wig, lying forward in a puddle of wine. He had succumbed already.

Most of them had not. Sitting now, sharp-eyed, on a chair beside Uncle Gauntry, she saw very quickly that there were two boys there, boys of about her own age. It was not unusual that boys should be there, and one of them she knew, little Johnny Peel, two years younger than herself. It would later be said of him that he was 'lang in the leg an' lish as a lizard', and someone in the *Gentleman's Magazine* was to record that 'he

seems to have come into this world only to send foxes out of it'.
He was of Caldbeck village, but there was no hunt already that
he wasn't attending within any radius from Penrith to Cockermouth, Cockermouth to Carlisle. It was said of him already that
he could do thirty miles in the day and not be tired of it; later
on it was to be fifty. But Judith knew that boy before; he didn't
interest her. The other was another matter. She had not hitherto
allowed her young life to be much encumbered with boys. On
the whole she despised them; of late, especially, her real worship
of Francis Herries had veiled her sight.

But this boy struck through to her deep consciousness. How
often afterwards she was to look back to this moment when, as
she sat perched up on the chair beside Tom Gauntry, her little
sharp eyes flashed across to the table to the equally sharp eyes
of that small, black-haired, bullet-headed urchin, who was
grabbing any food that he could see. Very characteristic that
Judith's first vision of him should be of greedy rapacity! But
(also how characteristic of him!) it was not merely greed. While
he snatched at meat and bread and the thick pastry of the beef
pie his little black eyes were flashing about him, humorous,
contemptuous, but as alive as fire-balls!

'Who's that?' Judith asked of Gauntry. He was, as she had
hoped, at the cheerful side of his drinking, singing a catch,
shoving food into his mouth, exchanging bawdy stories with all
and sundry.

'That!' he laughed, following her eyes. 'That's the Frenchy!
There's his mama!' pointing a chicken bone at a lady farther
along the table. There were only two women here, one of them
the wife of young Squire Osmaston, a flaxen-haired, broad-
bosomed, opulent lady at the moment chucking Sam Newton
under the chin. This other was different. She sat upright like a
maypole and was black as a raven. Marvellous black eyes, she
had, a lovely shapely bosom, and silver ornaments in her dark
hair, which was her own and unpowdered. You could see,
Judith decided, that she was the little boy's mother. They would
be French then. Judith had heard of Paris, where silks and
brandy came from. She had seen a print of the French Queen
dancing in a great hall lit with flambeaux. This lady looked as
though she could be a queen were she given the opportunity.

The noise and confusion now were very great. Old Dunstable had slipped beneath the table.

Wilson of Ireby was standing on his chair proposing healths;
fat Dick Conyngham of Penrith and a thin young man with a

crooked nose were embracing. Voices rose and fell, then suddenly the chorus, everyone joining together:

> *Then chink and clink your glasses round*
> *And drink to the Devil below the ground.*
> *The more you drink the better you be*
> *And kiss the lasses upon your knee.*
>> *Chink, clink!*
>> *Chink, clink!*
> *The Devil himself can't drink like me.*

Then young Drayton of Keswick, whose sweet tenor was famous for miles around, stood up and sang the song of 'Beauty Bathing':

> *Beauty sat bathing by a spring*
>> *Where fairest shades did hide her;*
> *The winds blew calm, the birds did sing,*
>> *The cool streams ran beside her.*
> *My wanton thoughts enticed mine eye*
>> *To see what was forbidden:*

> *But better memory said, fie!*
>> *So vain desire was chidden:*
>> *Hey nonny nonny O!*
>> *Hey nonny nonny!*

> *Into a slumber then I fell,*
>> *When fond imagination*
> *Seemèd to see, but could not tell*
>> *Her feature or her fashion.*
> *But ev'n as babes in dreams do smile,*
>> *And sometimes fall a-weeping,*
> *So I awaked as wise this while*
>> *As when I fell a-sleeping:*
>> *Hey nonny nonny O!*
>> *Hey nonny nonny!*

The beauty of the words, of the voice, seemed for a moment to sober them.

>> *Hey nonny nonny O!*
>> *Hey nonny nonny!*

they sang, and down the fat cheeks of Dick Conyngham drunken tears were coursing.

No one appeared to think it strange that the child should be there. Most of them knew her; she seemed to belong to the place, and for many of them that happy time was now approaching when nothing anywhere seemed strange, when the candles on their silver stalks swam like gold roses in a shimmering haze, and the moon, now delicately rising beyond the uncurtained windows, was quadrupled in its pure serenity; now, through the open door, the dogs were coming in to pick up what trifles they might from the scattered floor, and a thousand clocks were ticking their friendly chatter on a thousand walls. No one thought of the child, not even Gauntry himself; only Clara, the spaniel bitch, coming in with the rest, had found her and was sitting behind her chair.

Judith ate very little and drank nothing. It was no unusual thing at that time for a child to be drunk. The children of the poor lay in the gutter drowned with gin. In the back parts of Keswick town Judith herself had seen them. But something in her, connected possibly with her immaculate personal cleanliness, had made her, so long as she could remember, detest liquor. When she was only a baby some friend of Gauntry's had tried to make her drink Madeira, and she had screamed, beaten his face with her hands, torn his nose with her nails. She didn't like the smell of it very much, but in a scene like this the stench of wine and heat and unwashed human bodies, dogs and horses, candle grease and cooked meats, was so familiar to her that she never thought of it.

What she did think of, though, was that when the drinking and rioting had reached a certain pitch she would leave them, for they were then no longer of any use to anybody.

It neither shocked nor distressed her that they should lie about the floor with their heads in puddles of wine. She preferred in fact the rough-and-tumble riot here to the orderly drunkenness at Fell House, and she had on several occasions watched while Wull and Andy and Matthew had stripped Uncle Gauntry and laid him in his naked bed. What she did mind was that they were all so stupid when they were 'gone'. She was quickly developing that passion, afterwards to be so strong in her and so irritating to her acquaintances, of hating to waste a single moment! Her restless energy was, later, never to leave her for an instant alone. They were a waste of time, these stupid hours when they all lay about, dribbling and drabbling, with the moon high, the wind fresh, blowing the stars about the sky. She might as well be in her bed, which was where, indeed, she *would* be had she remained at Uldale.

Her bright eyes searched the room. She saw one thing, that the French lady was absorbed by Mr Drayton, who had sung 'Beauty Bathing'. He was a good-looking man, Mr Drayton, slender and straight, with yellow hair like a blazing candle, and he wore a beautiful flowered waistcoat. There were gold buckles on his shoes. The French lady liked him, that was plain. They stood, the handsome pair of them, gravely by the window, away from the litter, noise and mess; quite suddenly Mr Drayton took the French lady's hand. Now was the time, then, for Judith to speak to the little French boy.

She stepped off her chair and, followed by the spaniel, came round to where the French boy was sitting. She touched his shoulder. He turned round and smiled at her.

'Come out,' she said.

He came at once, making a last grab at a handful of raisins before he went. They ran hand in hand, as though they had known one another for ages, into the dark hall, where the fire was blazing, and the dogs, as though they owned the house and everyone in it, were moving about, snapping at one another, yawning, lying down to sleep, climbing the stairs, gnawing bones, scratching for fleas.

The two children sat close together beside the fire.

'I know. You're French,' Judith said.

He spoke without an accent, as though he were English. He gave her, rather reluctantly, some raisins. The truth is, she took them.

'I was born in London,' he told her.

'Oh, I want to see London!'

'Is your hair in truth that fine colour?' he asked, pulling it.

She slapped his face, not lightly but with genuine feeling. He got up, his eyes blazing. He stood there, his sturdy little body trembling with anger. It seemed that he would kill her. But he thought better of it. His hand to his cheek he sat down again.

'Because you are a girl I won't hurt you,' he said.

'Hurt me!' She was indignantly scornful. 'No one can hurt me!' Then she went on: 'I was whipped this noon.'

They were friends again. She, taking more of his raisins, asked him how it was if he were French he had never been in France.

'My papa and my mama are French born,' he told her.

She asked him his name.

'Georges.'

And his other name.

'Georges Paris.'

'But Paris is a town.'

He told her there were people called Paris too. He told her then (he always from the very earliest time loved to talk about himself) that his father was dead, that his mother liked England to live in, that they lived for the most part in the village of Hampstead, near London. Hampstead was on a hill, and at night you could see all London lit up from their window. Judith wanted to tell him something about herself. Her name was Judith Herries, her mother had been a gipsy, she lived with her half-brother at Fell House in Uldale. She could ride and swim, had a horse called Barnabas (it wasn't in fact her horse at all, but it made it grander to say so), could stand on her head, train a bird for fighting, and so on, and so on. Mrs Monnasett was dead and would be buried tomorrow. She had run away and would be whipped on her return.

But he wasn't interested. He could do nothing but look at her hair. He had never seen anything like it in his life before.

Then her mind ran away from him. The place where they were was lovely to her, with the leaping fire, the moonlight, the dogs. She thought of Statesmen and farmers and boys and horses – all friends of hers. She liked to hear the men singing in the distance. All her troubles were far away; tomorrow, the whipping, Fell House. In an impulse of general happiness that had little to do with the boy she put her arm round his neck, drew his head towards her and kissed him. He did not mind that at all and pulled her hair – but gently. And she did not, this time, smack his cheek.

Dreamily she went on: 'Maybe when I'm grown I shall marry you. But I must have dogs and horses, and we must have our house near to this. But you must not be drunken.' Then, pushing his head away from her, she asked sharply: 'But what shall our children be – French or English ?'

'French,' he answered her quickly.

'No, they shall not. English.'

'French.'

'No, English.'

'Then I'll not marry you.'

She pinched him in the place where it hurt the most. In

another moment they were fighting, rolling on the floor, all the dogs yelping. But they were interrupted by a greater agitation, for the door suddenly swung open, there was a shout and clatter, and into the hall came fat Dick Conyngham riding Judith's Barnabas. Poor Barnabas was in any case overweighted by the huge body that rode him; he was frightened also. He came kicking into the hall, the dogs setting up an infernal din.

'The stairs! The stairs! I'll ride him to the attic!' and Conyngham drove the little horse towards the staircase, waving his fat arms like a madman.

They all came pouring in out of the other room, those of them who could stand, to see Barnabas kicking with his hind legs and Judith raging like a mad thing.

She rushed to little Gauntry, catching him by the arm: ' 'Tis my Barnabas ... He has no right ... He'll break his knees!' and Gauntry, who had been singing the tail-end of some chorus, was suddenly, in the manner of drunken men, in a terrible rage and rushed at Conyngham. The fat man drove the horse at the stairs, but in a moment they had him on the floor and were kneeling on his stomach.

Barnabas, wild now with the lights, the dogs, the fire, began to prance madly hither and thither; and Judith, fearing nothing, had caught him, was carried off her feet as she hung to his mane, crying 'Barnabas! Barnabas! Dear Barnabas! They shall not touch you!' The little horse knew her hand and voice. He snorted, pawing the wood floor with his hoofs; he looked wildly around, then he suffered her to lead him away.

She took him this time to one of the outhouses. She stood there in the soft moonlight wondering whether after all she would not ride home again. Not far from her was the lower end of the garden that held a little pond with a statue of an armless lady. The little pond was like a curved shell of ivory, and the lady was green in the moonlight.

A moment later they all rushed past her, a shouting and singing rabble. Fat Conyngham was to be ducked in the pond for that he had taken a lady's horse without her permission. They were not like men at all, but shadows that the moon had made. They were stripping him; a moment he escaped and ran, a ridiculous pink figure, bald-headed, across the grass. They chased him around the sundial, caught him; there was a splash, and she could see a spray of water dazzle the air.

She rubbed her nose in Barnabas' mane. Should she go home? She was lonely, a little frightened. They had never been so wild

before in this place. The house did not seem to be her friend
any longer, only the quiet fells that stretched beyond it, with
the boggy peat, the sheep cropping, the eternal sound of running
water.

It seemed of a sudden comforting to have Sarah Herries'
arm around her. She was a child again. She was not *truly*
frightened. She had never been frightened. She would not be
frightened now. But in absolute truth it would be pleasant to
be in her bed with the cherry curtains, to hear the owl hooting
and Deborah Herries snoring not too far away.

Then, because she would never grant to either God or Man
that she could be afraid of anyone or anything, she threw up
her head defiantly at the moon, stroked Barnabas on the nose,
whispered to him that she would not be long away and went
back to the house.

They were still dancing and singing round the pond. The
garden had a fantastic air like a witches' sabbath. The house
was now deserted and empty. The dogs were for the most part
away, the moonlight stained the floor, the fire was low. No sign
of the French boy, no sign of anyone. She peeped through the
door, and there were two men, asleep, with their heads on the
table. The candles guttered.

She herself felt a fearful weariness. She was aching for sleep.
She staggered on her little féet. Her shoes hurt her, her beautiful
dress was torn, the place where she had been whipped was
smarting. She would find the room upstairs that was generally
hers. The thought of sleep was so delicious as to be incredible.

She sat down halfway up the stairs, and with her head in her
hand dreamily considered herself. She had learnt to do this
early in life, because, observing things and people, she had
realized that if you do not consider yourself no one else is going
to. But when she began to think of herself it was always to her
mother and father that she was led.

Years ago she had persuaded Tom Gauntry to take her,
pillion-fashion, to see the house where she was born. They had
ridden into the heart of the valley of Borrowdale, and there, on
a little hill above the village of Rosthwaite, was standing this
strange tumbledown house. She could not credit her own sharp
eyesight when she saw it. They had tied the horse to the gate
and walked in the grass-grown courtyard. It was late April,
and the smaller daffodils were blowing under the wind. A storm
was coming up over Glaramara, and flashes of sun glittered in
cold sharp gleams and were gone again. Under the wind and the

hurrying cloud the house looked desolate enough. Judith, used to the noise and vitality of Stone Ends, the luxury and comfort of Uldale, could not believe that this was where her father had lived for so many years. Some peasant lived there now. Two very dirty children, sucking their thumbs, lurked in the doorway. Behind the house a waterfall glistened against rock. There was the sound of running water everywhere. It looked as though one 'fuff' of wind would blow the place down.

That day 'Uncle Tom' told her to the smallest detail of how he had found her, the snowstorm, her wailing cry, her father and mother dead. But he would never tell her enough about her father. He had not known him, he said. Neither would David and Sarah tell her much, although he had been David's father, and so David must know everything. David would tell her only the grand things, how passionately through many years he had loved her mother, how tall he was and strong, how noble he was, and went his own way whatever people might say. 'Whatever people might say—' Judith nodded her head over that. People had said a good deal, no doubt. She only wished that she could have been there, standing at her father's side, to tell those people what she thought of them. To tell those people what she thought of them— Her head was nodding, and had not the moon been shining straight into her eye she would have fallen into deep slumber. As it was she was suddenly awake. She would find the room and the bed . . .

She climbed the stairs, looked out of the window on to the outside gallery and the fell beyond, pushed back a door. She stood there. Her heart seemed to stop its beating. The almost bare room, with only the yellow-curtained bed, two chairs, a chest, was sunk in moonshine. In the middle of the moonlit pool the French lady was standing quite naked. Behind her, her clothes were piled on the boards. She stood, her legs together, her arms raised above her head, her black hair loosened about her shoulders. Her breasts were full and firm. She was smiling.

At her feet, clad only in his shirt, young Drayton was kneeling, his hands about her naked waist, his eyes raised in an ecstasy to her face.

They never spoke nor moved. Judith saw that something glittered sharply in the light – the diamond buckle of her shoe, lying on top of her clothes.

Then the child heard him speak:

'Oh, how beautiful you are! Oh, how beautiful you are!'

But the French lady only smiled.

Judith turned away. Her shoes made clop-clop on the boards. She sat down on the top of the stairs.

What had she seen?

Something that she would never forget, something that hurt her.

She began to cry very softly, lest anyone should hear her. She cried and cried. She wanted to go home. She wanted someone to care for her.

Huddled up, now only a baby lost and bewildered, crying and sobbing, there with her head against the banister she fell fast, fast asleep.

SUNWOODS IN COCKERMOUTH

DEBORAH HERRIES, the daughter of Francis Herries, sister of David Herries and half-sister of Judith, married, early in 1761, the Reverend Gordon Sunwood, a clergyman who lived in the town of Cockermouth. Mr Sunwood had no particular cure, but after his marriage published two admirable works – one *A Treatise on the Magnificat*, the other *The Hope of Grace to Come*, or *Sinners at the Feet of Jesus*. This second work had a very real sale throughout the North of England. He was in considerable request as a preacher. In 1765 his aunt, Miss Mercia Sunwood, died in the town of Exeter, bequeathing him a very reasonable fortune.

They had two boys, twins, born in the year 1763, Reuben and Humphrey.

Deborah Herries had been always, unlike her sister Mary and brother David, of a quite unambitious disposition. For the first half of her life she had lived quietly with her father at Herries in Borrowdale, perfectly content to care for him and offer him as much love and affection as he was willing to accept.

After his second marriage, however, which occurred when he was well on in years, she considered that she was no longer needed by him (which was perfectly true), left him and married her clergyman in Cockermouth. She had loved Mr Sunwood from the first moment of seeing him at a ball in Keswick, and he was indeed exactly suited to her, being as kindly, well-disposed, unenterprising and equable as she. She differed from him greatly in her perceptions; she had a good deal in her of her father's poetry, very much more than had her brother David, who had, however, been always much closer to their father. She had been kept from her father by a sort of terror of him. being never very comfortable with persons who were scornful or sarcastic, or liable to sudden temper or indignation.

Mr Gordon Sunwood had been a rest and refreshment to her after her life with her father, for, as his rotund body, snow-white hair and kindly rosy face portended, he could with the greatest difficulty be angry with anyone or anything, and then only for a moment at a time. Methodists, Wesleyans, Quakers, Dissenters of any kind – these were almost the only animals who could rouse him to any sort of genuine indignation.

Marriage with Deborah excited him to a kind of mild am-bition, and it is quite certain that he would never have written or, having written, would never have published his two books had she not stirred his faculties.

Having published them he exhibited a natural pride very evident in most authors, who have, from time immemorial, found it difficult to conceive that theirs are not the only shining fish in the literary ocean.

When Deborah's twins were born the cup of her joy was full. And, as is not the case with all optimistic parents, her joy continued, for as the boys grew in physical stature so also they grew in kindliness of nature and obedience to their parents.

They were, one is happy to record, by no means angels, but their vices were mild ones, and their faults just sufficient to keep them properly human. Humphrey had by far the easier dis-position of the two. Tall, slender and flaxen-haired, life was for him one long adventure. He was as restless as he was merry, so popular at the Cockermouth school that it was entirely to his credit that he should wish to be constantly with his parents.

Everyone spoke well of him, and it is not, perhaps, altogether to be wondered at that his charm became his principal asset and an easy substitute for hard work and diligence. His parents succeeded in affording him his residence at St John's College, Cambridge, and, if he did nothing there but secure the pleasant good wishes of his fellow-men, that was more than many others succeeded in securing.

After Cambridge the question was what should be done with him. He would hear of nothing but London, and to a lawyer's office there he went. On this bright afternoon in early November of the year 1785 his proud mother was excitedly occupied in reading his first letter from the Metropolis.

Humphrey's twin brother Reuben had quite another history. They had only small resemblance to one another whether in character or in physical appearance. And yet the bond between them was almost fantastic. From their first conscious moments they had been all in all the one to the other; theirs, indeed, was a love that nothing in life would be able to influence. Humphrey, volatile, restless, and woman-lover as he was, yet knew no emotion so unyielding and passionate as this for his brother. For Reuben, Humphrey was always and ever in a world apart. Reuben was unlike Humphrey in that he was stout, clumsy and plain. He was not uncleanly in his person, but his clothes never fitted him, nor could he be brought to consider the practical details of daily life. His eyes were good and faithful, his mouth, although too large, kindly and tolerant, but his nose was ludicrously ill-shaped, his hair wild and of a dingy colour, his limbs uncouth and ill-disciplined. From his very early years he had been of an intensely religious mind. It had been always understood that he would be a clergyman. At the age of sixteen he joined the religious society of St Bees, but was there for a year only, finding that he could not come to the same mind with the authorities.

He returned to his parents' house in Cockermouth, and to their considerable grief had in the last five years shown little progress in anything; his favourite occupation was to walk the hills for days on end by himself, and he could be seen striding along the roads, talking aloud and snapping his fingers in the air.

He was devoted to his parents, amiable and docile. There had, however, been strange rumours of late concerning him, not of any immorality or cock-fighting, or gambling, but of something that was, in his father's eyes, very much worse: a suspicion that he was concerting with the Methodists. A well-known Wesleyan itinerant, Mr Jeremy Walker, had been seen in his company. There was a rumour that he had taken part in some sort of outdoor meeting. His father had not yet dared to ask him whether there was any sort of truth in this. He knew well his son's honesty, but Mr Sunwood was grievously disturbed in his mind.

Their home on the outskirts of Cockermouth was a pretty place, looking out to the fields and woods, having a garden filled with sweet-williams and pinks and hollyhocks in their due season, and an arbour and a trellis for roses. In the parlour there was a rosy chintz and some fine pieces of mahogany, in Mr and Mrs Sunwood's bedroom a grand four-poster and a dressing-

chest with a lattice of Chinese decoration. At the corner of
the stair there was a round-faced clock of Irish Chippendale.
There were spindle-backed chairs, a Bury settee and a fine
Turkey carpet in the dining-room. These things were the very
pride of Mr and Mrs Sunwood's hearts. There was a maid-
servant called Rebecca, a cat, Timothy, and a boy, who worked
(when he felt inclined) in the garden, named Jacob. Deborah
herself cared for the preserving, pickling and daily cooking.
She and Rebecca kept the little house as clean and shining as a
new saucepan. They were, both of them, so proud of it that
they dreamt of it at night.

Deborah had but seldom any time for rest and reflection; she
did not, indeed, desire it. On this particular afternoon, however,
she was expecting her sister-in-law, Sarah Herries, and some
members of her family to dinner at four o'clock; they would
remain for the night and return to Fell House on the following
day. Everything was ready for them, the Guest Room prepared,
the dinner preparing. All day she had had with her Humphrey's
letter. Only now was she free to settle herself and read some of
it. Her excitement was as intense as though Humphrey himself
had made a sudden unexpected appearance.

Mr Sunwood came in from tending a pig, who led (unwitting
his destiny) a greedy and contented life in a sty at the back of
the house; close together on the settee, his hand resting often
on her plump shoulder, they read the letter. Humphrey began
with loving messages to everyone. Then he had many things
to tell of London: the eating-house where he had paid a shilling
for his dinner of meat and pudding, the Thames with its fine
bridges and noble arches, the hackney coaches, the dangers
of the streets where the coaches and carts crowded so closely
that there was scarcely room to move, and the noise so fierce
that you must step into the quiet of a shop if you wanted to
converse with a friend, a ship on land near the Tower that was a
trap for pressing simple people into being sailors, the signs
outside the shops with 'Children educated here', 'Shoes mended
here', 'Foreign spirituous liquors here', the general drunkenness,
so that the common people were always far gone in gin and
brandy. He had visited Vauxhall with the son of his master,
Mr Hodges, and had much to say about the paintings and statues,
the rotunda and the orchestra therein.

The most exciting news to his parents, however, was that
he had taken dinner with his mother's cousin, Sir Pomfret
Herries, who had a fine house in Kensington: Pomfret was the

son of Deborah's first cousin Raiseley, who had once owned a
fine house in Keswick but was now with God. Deborah's memory
flew back to her cousin Raiseley, a sickly and arrogant youth
who had been for ever at war with her brother David. It had
seemed that there would be a family feud there, but when
Raiseley had in later years moved to London, and the Keswick
house was sold, communication had altogether dropped.

It seemed, however, that this child Pomfret, whom Deborah
remembered as a little stout boy beating David's big black
horse with a toy whip, now a man of thirty-four or so, had done
well for himself in the City, married a clergyman's daughter,
and begotten of her body two healthy children.

Well, feud or no feud, Pomfret Herries had been kind to her
boy, and for that she would forgive him all old scores. Young
Humphrey described the splendour of the Kensington house,
the garden with its fountain and statues, the many servants,
the rich food and wine. Cousin Pomfret was large and stout
('like his poor grandfather before him,' sighed Deborah, with a
sudden desire to go somewhere and be kind to that poor old
man with his red face and pimples, suffering so sadly from gout,
sitting alone and deserted in the Keswick house by the Lake).
And now there was this new Pomfret with his children and handsome wife sitting in his grand Kensington house, forgetting
no doubt that he had ever had a grandfather. Time flies, thought
Deborah, and this is a modern world that we are in. Those old
days are gone for ever! There was indeed a certain moment's
melancholy in this excited acceptance by her son of this new life.
She had lost him! – he who only a moment ago had been rolling
naked on this Turkey carpet while she turned the tunes in the
music box – and, her eyes a little tearful, she placed her chubby
hand on her husband's chubby arm that she might feel securely
that he, at any rate, was still with her.

Mr Sunwood loved his son, but so confusing is this modern
life that there were four things in his head all obscuring and
dimming the things that Humphrey had to tell him. That was
the worst of these days: you never had a moment's peace. There
was his friend Mr Forster, who wanted a midshipman's place
for his boy, and hadn't Mr Sunwood some interest; there was
his own wickedness in sitting up almost all night at cards two
days back at Mr and Mrs Donne's, and although he had lost
but a shilling in all it was a habit that must not grow on him;
and there was the funeral of Mrs Hardacre tomorrow and he
must see that his black silk hatband had its proper white love-

ribband; there was their own dinner, too, this very day. Sarah and David Herries were accustomed to good fare. Deborah had told him that there would be a couple of rabbits smothered in onions, a couple of ducks roasted and an apricot pudding. He himself had seen to the wine, punch and beer. And what was that that Deborah was reading to him? 'A girl staying in the house, Nancy Bone, has a lovely figure, and we laughed and joked much together. I sat beside her when we played Forfeits, and I have bought her today a purse made of Morocco leather. For dinner we had a turkey roasted, a boiled chicken, blancmange, tarts, a damson cheese . . .'

Deborah, her eyes shining, said: 'If it should be a match between our Humphrey and this Nancy . . .' upon which, throwing to the wind all the other concerns that had been plaguing him, and realizing only her, the best wife God had ever given to man, he put his arm around her broad shoulders, kissed her on the lips and pinched her ear for an audacious matchmaker.

He was about to ask 'And where is Reuben?' when they heard the clatter of the horses on the cobbles. A moment later and there in the doorway were Sarah, David and their youngest boy.

Everyone was very happy; they were sitting in the parlour, and little Rebecca, looking her best in her fresh cap and ribbons, was offering wine and cake, and Jacob was caring for the horses.

Mr Sunwood, although he would acknowledge it to no man, was always a little shy of his brother-in-law, David Herries. He was always hoping that this hesitation would shortly be conquered and had even prayed to God about it, but on every fresh occasion the shyness was there. For one thing David Herries was now a great man in the county, his influence everywhere felt, and men said that one of these days he would be knighted. Mr Sunwood could never feel perfectly assured that David had not a little despised his sister for marrying a simple clergyman. Then David was a great man physically too, enormous he looked now as he spread about the settee with his snow-white wig, which he still occasionally wore, his round red face, his full-skirted blue coat and silver waistcoat, his immense thighs and legs in their riding boots, his silver spurs.

But no one could have been kinder than David was to his brother-in-law. There was no condescension in his heart to anyone, he had no pride anywhere in his heart save that he was a Herries and had done something to raise his branch of the

Herries family in the world. It was strange indeed to see how
the moment that David and Deborah his sister were together
again, the Herries family feeling was suddenly everywhere.

The house, the furniture, the cake, the wine, Rebecca and
the cat, little Mr Sunwood himself, all became adjuncts of the
Herries Family, whether they would or no. That was a way that
the Herries people had.

Nevertheless David and his brother-in-law discussed the
affairs of the nation in quite a broad general spirit. David had a
great deal to say about the recent rejection of Pitt's Reform Bill.
He was glad indeed that it had been rejected. If ever there was a
true Tory in the world it was David Herries, and Mr Sunwood
agreed with him, being as Tory in Church as David was in
State. David's voice had a way of rising to a regular boom when
his feelings were roused, and they were roused now. He could
not himself see that there was anything wrong with Parlia-
mentary Representation. He would have things left as they were.
For all that he could see, this was nothing but a plot on the part
of the Yorkshire freeholders to put a check on the authority
of their good and wise King. He shook his great head over
these new times. Why couldn't we leave things as they were?
This discontent of the lower orders boded no good. What was
this chatter about their Rights? When he had been a boy they
had had no Rights and were contented enough. He recalled
the admirable behaviour of a servant his father had had, Benjamin he had been called. The more you whipped him the better
he was pleased, and he had died in his father's arms. David never
perceived the incongruity of his remarks in that he himself
could never beat anyone and was notorious for over-indulging
his servants. Mr Sunwood, however, agreed cordially and sighed
over these new times, and was afraid that there were many
fresh changes coming.

Sarah and Deborah meanwhile were talking together as
eagerly as any two women will who are very old friends, and
have not seen one another for a while. Sarah, although she did
not at present declare it, was paying this visit because, above
everything, she wished to discuss with Deborah the urgent
matter of Judith. Deborah, on her side, was longing for the
moment when she might begin about Humphrey's letter and
his visit to the Pomfret Herries.

Sarah had the greatest opinion of Deborah's sound common
sense. Judith's escape to Tom Gauntry's on the evening of her
whipping had had most momentous consequences. David had

ridden over to Stone Ends and brought her home. From then until now her nature had changed. She was obedient, docile, with flashes of fiery temper, strange impetuous affections; Sarah, whose nature was equable and always under control, could not understand her at all: she felt, too, that she was alone in this, for David had not the art of understanding temperaments. Francis could do what he liked with the child, but would not, so there you were ...

Meanwhile one member of the household was in his attic room drumming with his fingers on the window. This was Reuben. He could not decide to go down. He had seen them arrive. The one of them that interested and touched him most was not there – Judith. She came in his heart after his brother and his mother, and so warm, so almost passionate, were his affections that she would have been surprised indeed had she known of them. As yet she never thought of him; she had seen him but seldom, and he was no figure to appeal to a child, with his lanky hair, his stout ill-shapen body and his untidiness.

But if she had been there he would have come down. He would have endured his awkward distrust of himself before his grand uncle and his discomfort before the sharp critical eyes of young Will his cousin. Had Judith been with them he could have sat and looked at her lovely hair, and perhaps done her some little service.

But he knew what they thought of him. He could hear his uncle ask why he was not at some work, saving his parents their charges. He had seen his uncle stand by the horse, giving his riding coat to Jacob, revealing the splendid clothes. Why was he never to be like that? Why was everything in him just so turbulent and disordered, as though he heard from a great distance some Call to the obeying of some Order, and yet could not distinguish what that Call might be – and why, oh, why, was something driving him now towards a step that must enrage his father and make his brother grieve?

It had been only a year ago that Mr Walker had given him an ill-written, exceedingly ill-printed *Life of John Wesley*, and this book had been for him, since then, almost his Gospel. Everything related in it had seemed to grow into his own nature. When he read that Wesley wore his hair flowing loose upon his shoulders to give the money that would be spent in caring for it to the poor, that seemed to him a divine action. When he read Wesley's words: 'I would as soon expect to dig happiness out of the earth, as to find it in riches, honour, pleasure (so called) or indeed in the enjoyment of any creature. I know there can be no happiness on earth, but in the enjoyment of God, and in the foretaste of those rivers of pleasure which flow at His right hand for evermore. Thus by the Grace of God in Christ I judge of happiness. Therefore I am in this respect a new creature': his soul thrilled within him; it was almost as though he saw God Himself standing before him and the light of His Countenance shining upon him.

When he read of how Whitfield on the afternoon of Saturday, February 17th, 1739, stood upon a mound, in a place called Rose Green, his 'first field pulpit', and preached to the Kingswood colliers, he felt that he would have given all that he had might he but have stood at his side on that great occasion.

He read how Wesley preached at Gwenap, in Cornwall: 'I stood on the wall, in the calm still evening, with the setting sun behind me; and almost an innumerable multitude before, behind and on either hand. Many likewise sat on the little hills, at some distance from the bulk of the congregation. But they could all hear distinctly while I read "The disciple is not above his Master", and the rest of those comfortable words which are day by day fulfilled in our ears.'

Oh, those comfortable words! Why had he not too been there on that beautiful evening, following that great man's counsel?

Above and beyond all, there was the necessity for the New Birth. 'One will ask with all assurance, "What! Shall I not do as well as my neighbour?" Yes; as well as your unholy neighbour, as well as your neighbours that die in their sins; for you will all drop into the pit together, in the nethermost hell. You will all lie together in the lake of fire, "the lake of fire burning with brimstone". Then at length you will see (but God grant you may see it before!) the necessity of holiness in order to glory, and, consequently, of the new birth; since none can be holy, except he be born again.'

None can be holy except he be born again! So he was not holy. No, indeed, he was not. He was filled with a loathing and hatred of himself, of his body, but far more of himself, his character and true person. He knew himself for a glutton, a coward, an idler, filled with vanity, sensual thought, ingratitude.

But it was worst of all that he should not know which way he should go. He had seen during the last year something of Mr Walker and his friends; he had been to some of their meetings and was not happy there. There was something of his father in him, more than he knew; something perhaps of the Herries blood of his mother. The violence and hysteria in the meetings repelled and silenced him. And they, too, felt that he was not with them. What he wanted he could not tell, save that he must serve God, and must in himself bring about some entire change. Poor Reuben! He was just now the loneliest young man in the world.

He leaned from his window and listened to the sounds of the little world about him. Some horse was impatiently pawing the cobbles, a pedlar sharply cried his wares, a flock of sheep came hurrying under the window, pressing together with their wide, startled, stupid eyes; the shepherd, an old man, with a white shaggy beard, wearing a wide black hat, called shrilly and with an absent mind to his sheepdog. Beyond these movements the wood lay in dark shadow, motionless as though painted on the silver sky. Every fibre in him responded to this lovely world. He must get out into it. He would not go down to his aunt and uncle. He would see them later in the evening. Had little Judith been there—! And at the thought of her, although he had no sensual feeling for her (was she not, ludicrous thought, his aunt ?) he became quite suddenly disturbed by consideration of women. They flocked, like a covey of bright shining birds, about him, settling on his head, his shoulders, his hands, ruffling their feathers, crimson and silver and gold, with their sharp beaks pecking at his cheeks, smiling at him out of their hard, bright eyes. His body was burning, his heart roughly beating. The Devil himself was with him in the room, which had become hot and airless. The sun was sinking, and the wood, as though stricken by the hand of God, was ebony. The silver sky was a camping-ground for tents of crimson; shadows of approaching evening stole across the brightness of the field. His room was evil and filled with temptation. Not realizing that he was hurrying to the turning-point of his life, he hastened softly down the stairs, along the passage, into the path before the house.

The little town was embraced by the rosy light of approaching evening. Fresh breezes from the sea ruffled the hair and wigs of the citizens; not far away the kindly hills caught the light. The streets were narrow, ill-paved, and of a certain odour, but it was the time when the labours of the day are drawing to a close, many were at their dinner, children ran playing from door to door.

At the door of Jacob Hilton's Library young Mr Clementson, flour-dealer, was having a pleasant word with Mr Fletcher of the

'King's Arms', and here was the Carrier coming in from Workington.

They all knew young Reuben Sunwood well enough and greeted him kindly, but he had the sense (perhaps with some truth) that they regarded him oddly and avoided too plain a recognition of him for the Methodist company he was keeping.

So he turned off the main street up a dark and narrow way, thinking of his own troubles, his evil temptations, his loneliness, his perplexed opinions, and found himself, almost without knowing it, in the coachyard at the back of the 'Black Bull'.

He had been attracted here, it might be subconsciously, by the shouts and laughter of a pushing, pressing crowd. He was among them before he knew. He stood there watching. In the middle of the yard there was a cleared space, and in the cleared space a post. Chained to the post was an old, ragged and exceedingly weary bear. Near to the bear, held in the arms of two stout young men, was a small brown-faced man, his forehead streaked with blood. It seemed that he was a foreign pedlar of some kind from his long black hair, his brown complexion, a torn jacket of crimson with a silver chain. It was soon clear that he was a foreigner, for he jabbered ceaselessly in a strange tongue, words pouring from him in a tangled, agitated flow. Once and again he would raise his little body as though he would break away, and then his voice jumped into a shrill scream of protest that roused bursts of laughter from the onlookers.

Kneeling on the ground were two men who held in leash a bulldog and a small terrier, and these two dogs were madly straining to be free that they might get at the bear.

Everyone was hurling bets into the air, and close to Reuben a short thick-set man sucking a straw was taking bets down in his book. The excitement was intense; it was months, a tall farmer near Reuben told him, since there had been a bear to be baited.

Above the hubbub and bustle, clouds of saffron sailed tranquilly over the sky that was now white as moonlit water. Two children hung between the balusters of the inn balcony, laughing at the little pedlar.

At first it seemed to Reuben that he was not concerned in the matter. The bustle and noise, the friendly stomach of the large farmer against which he was pressed, the general air of goodwill and happiness was a relief to him after his own silly and selfish perplexities. There was very much of the child in him, and he liked above all to have happy people around him. To see animals baited was no fresh thing to him; he had been accustomed to such sights since he was a baby. The cruelty of his time was natural to his time and so was no cruelty. He pushed himself forward that he might see the better.

Then he encountered the face of the bear. An encounter it was, as though the pale sky, the crowd, the inn buildings had been swept into lumber and only he and the bear remained. The bear raised its old sad wrinkled face and looked at him. Age was there, bewilderment was there, but what was there, beyond all else, was Reuben himself. Reuben looked at Reuben.

The bear was fastened to the post by a rusty chain that went round his middle and his foot. His body was chafed in a number of places, where life had been hard on him. The long brown shaggy hair of his body was tangled with mud and dirt, and above his left eye there was a deep cut from which blood dripped.

It was this that Reuben first saw, how he raised his paw clumsily, slowly, as though he were resolved to be cautious, and wiped the blood that trickled down his nose. From under his thick tangled brows his eyes looked out, melancholy, slow and brooding. It was these eyes that seemed at first to be exactly Reuben's own. He knew how often his gaze had been fixed upon himself and the world in which he moved with exactly that same perplexity and sadness. The bear's loneliness was his own loneliness.

Then the bear began quietly to realize that he was in the middle of his enemies. Carefully, with that same caution, he moved his head to look for his master, and when he saw him held with his coat torn and his brown breast bare he began to be angry. (Just, Reuben thought, as he would himself slowly, in the middle of his enemies, begin to be angry.) But with his anger there rose also slowly his sadness and his bewilderment. He shuffled with his feet; his paw rose and fell again. He began to roll his head. Then he tried to break from his chain, and when he found that he could not, he jerked his head towards his master. Then again rubbed the drops of blood from his nose.

Something very grand entered into him, the grandeur of all captured and ill-treated things. He lifted his head and stared from under his jutting brows at the crowd, and was at once, with that single movement, finer than all of them. He was no longer Reuben. Reuben had been left behind and was now one of the crowd.

Then a large fat man without a hat, his hair tied with a brown ribbon, in red faded breeches, strode forward and undid the chain. Everyone shouted. The bear, bewildered, hesitating, rubbed his nose again, then, like a man in bedroom slippers, shuffled towards his master.

At the same moment the two dogs were loosed. Everyone began to shout together. It seemed to Reuben that it was towards himself that the dogs were running.

The bulldog instantly attacked the bear, caught his leg and hung on there. The smaller dog stayed back, whining.

The world was pandemonium. Men were laughing, yelling, moving, so that the crowd rocked like a wave. But the bear stood doing nothing; he only raised his paw and stroked his nose. He was a very old bear, who had been travelling for an infinity of years; he was very weary and did not understand why things were as they were.

The bulldog loosed his hold, sprang at the bear's throat, missed and rolled over. The bear sank on all fours, and, rolling his head with a blind gesture, seemed to be asking of them all what they were about.

It was then that Reuben, pushing violently his way, broke into the centre and ran to the bear. Then everything happened swiftly and, for the crowd, comically. A bear or a man, it was the same to the crowd. The bulldog bit Reuben's leg. Something struck his face. There were shouts and cries. Lightning broke from heaven, and the multitude of men, faces, heads of hair, hands, rose in a swirl like a shifting canopy of black flies and carried him sky-high. Then he fell, fell into a pit that was black, that had the mouth of a fish, opening, shutting, opening again. But as he fell somewhere, triumph, joy, freedom – things that he had never known – broke like silent fireworks in his heart . . .

Many generations after, he was sitting in a chair in the parlour of Mr Candlish the bellman. He knew him well, a short pursy fellow with a wart on his nose. Mrs Candlish had bound his head. One eye was closed. A little crowd in the doorway surveyed him. Someone held a candle. He smiled feebly on them all, climbed to his feet, found that he could walk, although his body ached and blood trickled from under the bandage.

He said that he would go home now, thank you. No one stayed him. They were silent when he limped past them, and stared after him in silence as he hobbled down the street. He did not know at all why he was happy, but he was.

He had not far to go. Every step was an agony. He opened his house-door and pushed into the parlour, where they were at

dinner. With his one eye from under his bandage he saw his
Uncle David, shining in splendour, his father pouring wine, his
mother – her face suddenly springing into terror at the sight of
him – his aunt, and his little cousin Will, who watched everything and missed nothing that anyone said.

He saw the table piled with food, the candles that danced in
their silver holders and the harpsichord in the corner. Someone cried out; he swayed in the doorway, tried to ask for some
wine, could not, fell fainting at his mother's feet. As he tried
to catch her hand he smiled.

He was the bear, and none of them knew it.

FIREWORKS OVER THE LAKE

FOR THE EVENING of June 23rd, 1787, Mr Joseph Pocklington of Vicar's Island announced that there would be fireworks discharged from his own ground *if* the weather were
fine.

If the weather were fine! How that phrase beat its anxiety
in a thousand hearts, for not only was it a question of the fireworks, but the band, organized by Mr Peter Crosthwaite, of
Crosthwaite Museum, would play airs from Haydn and Mozart,
and there would be dancing in Crow Park, to say nothing at all
of the boats that there would be on the Lake itself, the Chinese
lanterns, and the dark recesses of the water hidden from the
inquisitive glances of the moon.

Would there be a moon? Yes, there would be a moon. Mr
Crosthwaite himself, who, after serving his country for twenty
years in the Navy, had but recently returned to his native place
with a most interesting collection of curiosities, promised that
there should be a full and lustrous moon.

It mattered little where you went on that early morning of
June 23rd. Every riser had the same idea; nightcap after nightcap might be seen hanging from the window, sniffing at the
weather. From the windows of the 'Royal Oak' and the 'Queen's
Head', from John Powe's where the Old Club for so many years
held its meetings, from the attics of the 'Shoulder of Mutton',
from the Excise Officer at the 'George and the Dragon', from
Abel Graves the hairdresser's and Mr Lancaster the patten-
maker's, from the toll-gate at Brown Top – yes, and much

farther afield than these ... right around the Lake, from Stable
Hill and Burrow and Low Low Door, High Low Door and
Grange, Borrowdale Common and Manesty Nook, Mutton Pye
Bay and Branley, House End and Water End, Finkle Street and
Portinskill. Yes, and beyond these again, from Newlands
and Rosthwaite, Stonethwaite and Watendlath Braithwaite and
Bassenthwaite, even to Buttermere and Uldale and Caldbeck
and Threlkeld – even to Penrith and Grasmere, to Patterdale
and Ambleside, the news had run and the nightcaps were at all
the windows, whether of mansion or Statesman's farm, of shop,
of meeting-house or humble cottage.

For these nights on the Lake, *if* only the weather were fair,
were nights to stir the poets to song, and they *did* stir the Keswick poets to song. Are not those poems to be found in Keswick
archives to this very day?

Mr Pocklington himself loved to give pleasure to the people
of Keswick, and the people of Keswick loved to have pleasure
given them. And was not Mr Pocklington a fine man, seeing
that he owned so much land around the Lake and had his
place on Vicar's Island and at Ashness and at Fall Park, and
had set up a wonderful Druid's Circle in the pleasantest imitation
of the real one above Keswick?

If only the sun would shine, everyone and everything was in
favour. And the sun *did* shine. It rose above a curtain of mist
that cut the Lake into half, turned the islands into clouds of
emerald, touched Skiddaw with rose and the sharp edges of
Blencathra with ebony.

All the gardens of Keswick – and at that time Keswick was
filled with gardens – glittered in the sun. Then, as now, no
gardens in England could grow sweet peas and pinks and stock
better than the Keswick gardens. On a summer day, such as
this one, Keswick smelt of flowers, save only in the slums, behind
Main Street, where the odour was quite another one. But here
dwelt only gipsies and whores and smugglers from St Bees and
Ravenglass, and they didn't matter to anyone.

So the day lengthened; the air was balmy, Mr Crosthwaite
took out his flute and tuned it; Miss Evins the schoolmistress
practised her dancing steps privately in her bedroom; the
'Royal Oak', the 'Queen's Head', the 'Shoulder of Mutton'
prepared for an infinity of custom; all the children were beyond
human discipline; Mr Pocklington's gardeners guarded the
fireworks, and from distant silent valleys the horses had set
out, the ladies riding pillion as happy as though there were not

a heartache in the world. All the Herries would be there. It was a proud day for the Sunwoods, for their Reuben was but just returned from France, where he had been these last two years; and all the Herries from Uldale – David and Sarah, Francis, Deborah, Will and Judith – rode out in the forenoon and had dinner in state at the 'Royal Oak'.

William Herries, now seventeen years of age, small, short, spindly-legged, an arrogant nose in the proper equine Herries style, a thin rather tight mouth that could, and often did, break into a very charming smile, and clothes neat, correct and most unobtrusive, this William Herries was, as he always had been, exceedingly old for his age.

He himself knew that this was so; he had realized for the last ten years at least that he was quite the oldest of them all. Without any sense of condemnation, without any outward show of superiority, he had long felt a very real contempt for all the other members of his family – for his mother because she was jog-trot, his father because he was conservative, his brother Francis because he was a dreamer (here was his severest contempt), and Judith (could she be reckoned as one of the family) because she was mad and had no control of her emotions. (Strangely, though, here he recognized in Judith some spirit of mastery closely akin to his own.)

He recognized that he was superior to every member of his family but chiefly in this: that he knew so exactly what he wanted to do with his life and how he would do it.

His father, poor man, had a kind of notion that Will would follow himself in his trading business, would work in Liverpool for a while, travel in the East for a while, and finally, having doubled the value of everything, settle down as Squire of Fell House.

Some of this prophecy was, indeed, correct. Will *would* follow his father in the business, would in truth double it and more than double it, but *not* from Liverpool. It was in London that Will Herries intended to make his career. It was not at all that Will objected to business; that was not the kind of snob that he was. Now, with all England's glorious foreign conquests, with the India Trade, the China Trade and the rest, now was the very time to make a fortune. But it was to be a fortune made in the grand manner, made in the very heart of the universe, made against the very strongest opposition, and made – here was the fount and crown of the whole ambition – made for the HERRIES' glory.

Will was nothing if he was not Herries, and Herries practical, material, of the earth earthy. He was sentimental about nothing; he was most certainly not sentimental about this. He did not know in what distant childish dreams this ambition had not had its birth, to make a fortune and with that to take his place at the head of the Herries family. So that men everywhere might say: 'That is a Family, that is. It has houses and barns, gardens and fields, ships and horses and sheep and cattle. *That* is what a Herries can do.'

He saw neither poetry nor romance in this ambition. It seemed to him a perfectly practical logical plan. He would not mind if, at the end of it, one day he returned to Uldale as its master. He cared for this North Country if he cared for any country at all. There was something in its bleak spaces, its coldly blowing winds, its little stone walls running like live things about the fells, its glancing, shining waters, its cleanliness and strength and honesty, that was akin to his own strong unfaltering purpose.

He had, of course, the defects of his qualities like all of us, and it was one of his defects that he made no allowance for the poetic, incalculable quality in human nature. He thought, even now at the young age of seventeen, that he could always calculate with perfect safety. He knew exactly what his father and mother would do and say. His father with his large hearty good-nature, his simple laughter; his ability for seeing what was under his nose, and his stupidity in thinking that that was all that there was; his common sense that stopped just short of real knowledge; his sentimentality (Will, like many another practical man and woman, mistook for sentimentality quite deep and genuine feeling); his boisterous physical life, love of food, of drink, of hunting, of horses, of cock-fighting and card-playing and wrestling and football; his kindliness and satisfaction with small material things. Will knew that most of the business was now left to Mr Metcalfe and his son, his father's partners in Liverpool, and he despised his father for so leaving it. He had a good-natured regard for his father and he despised him thoroughly.

He really loved his mother; it was perhaps the strongest human feeling that he had, and this was chiefly because he thought that she managed the house very well, ruled the servants and had everything in order, but she was always doing what seemed to him silly sentimental things.

For his elder brother Francis he felt a contempt that was almost savage. Francis stood for everything that he despised; he did nothing, but hung in idleness about the house, reading, dreaming, saying absurd, ridiculous things, seeing poetry in everything, liking to be alone, simply cumbering the ground. He had not even the natural passions of drinking, wenching, gaming. He was nothing, nothing at all.

From them all, with a self-control that argued well for his future success in the world, he completely hid his scorn. To them all, he appeared a quiet, obedient, studious boy, who did what he was told and gave no trouble.

Francis possibly had some suspicion of the iron will and determined purpose that was developing there, but no one knew what Francis thought about anything. The only other person who had any accurate knowledge of Will was Judith. His own attitude to Judith was a peculiar one. He had to confess that Judith perplexed him. He had to confess regretfully enough that to sum her up as wild and foolish was not sufficient. She was, it was true, all of these things, but she appeared to be something else besides.

The relation between them was exceptional. Judith was now approaching thirteen years of age. She, like himself, was older than she looked, except that, at times, she looked old enough to be eighty. She had all the colour, all the oddness, all the uncertainty, irresponsibility, that he distrusted and condemned. It was natural enough, he considered, when you thought of her mother. But besides this was her desire to dominate everyone with whom she came in contact, and this was like his own desire except that she wanted it for other reasons. She wanted power because of *people*, he wanted it because of *things*. He had sensual feeling like anyone else, and had had already two experiences. She had sensual feeling too, but it was quite different from his, because whenever she cared for anybody (and she cared for fifty different people a week) she threw herself into it as though this were the only affection of her life, while he always knew that people were nothing, that no one ever cared for anyone else very long.

And he told himself this, although right before his eyes were his own father and mother who had loved one another for so many years and would do so to the end. But his father and mother had so much ridiculous Sensibility – and very little Sense at all.

Nevertheless it remained to him puzzling, this relation of his with Judith. Defensive or offensive? She wished to dominate

him as well as the rest of her world. It amused him sometimes
to allow her to think that she did.

So he remained, this young man of seventeen, watching,
waiting, calculating all his chances.

The night was enchantingly warm. They went down to the
Lake in a body – David in his fine rose-coloured coat, wearing
his own hair clubbed and powdered (an increasing fashion);
Sarah in a fine hoop of silver with little roses; Deborah, red in
the face with pleasure and happiness ('blowzy', Will thought
her); Judith, a fascinating little hat on the side of her red hair
and a little hoop with silver ships painted on it; Will, very
soberly dressed in brown, demurely in the rear; Francis, slim,
aloof.

Mr and Mrs Satterthwaite of Bassenthwaite village walked
down with them. Mrs Satterthwaite's talk was all of servants;
a new one, Mary Benson, recommended by Mrs Blane, five
pound a year, tea twice a day, good at cookery and understanding
her needle. Well, we hope, don't we, that it will turn out for the
best ? But they begin so well, don't they, up so early, ready to
milk the cow, and then, where are you ? A month later, already
in child from the cowman or drunk on the parlour floor. Yes,
where are you ? All the sky, milky now with golden fleece
before the sun's setting, is crowded with maids flying like witches,
mocking their mistresses, and men, bare as they were born, down
the wind after them. Do what you will, it is all Nature, and what
do you say to Mr Bradby, the new schoolmaster in Keswick ?
A sensible and good-natured man, unmarried – and at once
Mrs Satterthwaite's two daughters, single and plain, poor things,
always left to their own thoughts at every dance in the neighbourhood, staying in Carlisle at this very instant with an aunt
to see whether *she* couldn't do something about it, filled the
scene and checked the conversation.

Not for Judith. She was so happy that she must dance along
the path as she went, chattering to Francis, although she knew
that he was listening to nothing that she had to say.

Everywhere, on every side of her, people were moving forward
to the Lake, and all of them as happy as she. She loved that
people around her should be happy; she was to love that as long
as she was alive. If only they were happy and *also* did what she
told them, she asked nothing more of life.

And tonight, everything was perfection. She had had her
own way in everything, was wearing the clothes that she wanted,

there would be dancing under the trees and they would be in a boat on the Lake, the moon would rise, and then, best of all, there would be Fireworks – Fireworks, of all things in life that she loved best! Could she have seen Mr Joseph Pocklington, she would have flung her arms around him and kissed him. She did not mind what she did when she was happy. Her soul and body surrendered then completely to the emotion of the moment. Nothing existed for her except that moment.

Even Will, who thought it foolish, indeed, when you were a little short thing with a pale face and so many people around you, to dance along so that all must notice you, was forced to acknowledge to himself that her happiness was infectious. He himself hoped to have his arm around some feminine waist before the evening was over.

When they gained the lakeside it was beautiful indeed. The Lake, whose waters scarcely moved, only a trembling shudder of pleasure once and again mysteriously stirring, had caught flakes and scatterings of gold from the last rays of the sun as it fell behind Cat Bells. Vicar's Island lay like a dark hand upon the water. Under the trees there were booths with many things to buy. Someone was playing a fiddle. Everywhere boats floated, and the oars plashed like music through the air.

Happiness? Happiness? Where is it? Where is it? Here, now, this very moment, with the movement of the people under the trees, the fiddle and the soft distance of the orchestra on the Meadow, before one's eyes the silver stretch of water spreading to the hills that lay like friendly elephants (thought Judith, who had never seen an elephant) humped against the sky. Yes, here is Happiness, because here is Mystery and promise of Adventure. One cannot quite see who is moving beneath the trees. One step and whom may one not encounter?

Two boats were waiting for the Herries family in the charge of old John Blacklock, who was so broad in the waist and thick of the leg that he was like one of the sights at the Fair, two bodies with one head. This head and face, too, were so thickly covered with hair that his eyes shone out like a friendly animal's from a bush. Judith always talked Cumberland to him.

She greeted him now with: 'Noo than what, John?' which pleased him greatly. In his opinion she was a 'gay fewsome lass'. When the weather was bad, he would come out to Uldale and work in the garden for a week or more.

But there was at once a real excitement for her, because Reuben was there. They were waiting for them – little Mr

Sunwood, very neat in his best parson's clothes; Deborah, always so kind and comfortable; and Reuben, a trifle neater for his two years' sojourn in France, but otherwise very little changed. She liked Reuben, in part because of the power she had over him, in part because of his modesty and warm-heartedness. She even understood his shyness, although it was so far from anything in herself. It was, indeed, part of her character that she should care more for Francis and Reuben, so unlike her in temperament, than any other of her relatives.

And at once her power for having things as she wanted them was apparent. A child of less than thirteen, she was in five minutes seated under an oak tree, the Lake spread in front of her, and settled around her were Reuben, Francis, and Will. It was true that they were there to take a breath and look about them before the activities of the evening began for them, and were scarcely conscious, perhaps, that Judith was there, or it was Reuben only who was conscious. Will, as usual, had his sharp eyes fixed on everything at once and was absorbed in considering how he should turn things to his own advantage, and of what Francis was thinking no one could tell, but very quickly Judith had fastened her personality upon all of them and was taking the lead.

So they talked, the background of the fading evening, the faintly rustling trees, the moving people, voices, music forcing from all of them a gentle comfort and well-being that drew them all together in general friendliness. In after days these voices of the lost and ghostly past of this moment would visit them again.

For Judith, as she sat perched on the bole of the tree, a cloak over her shoulders, her shoes shining in the dusk, it seemed to her, as it had seemed to her a thousand times already, that life was at this very moment beginning. She was so happy that she should have been afraid, but she was never afraid when she was happy.

'Reuben, tell us about France. Did you see the King and Queen?'

But Reuben had very little to tell about France. Something about Lourdes, where there was a castle on a rock; State prisoners were sent there by *lettres de cachet*. Here they died of despair and misery. At Pau he had been shown the cradle of Henry IV, which was the shell of a tortoise. At Bordeaux he had seen Dauberval the famous dancer. He had visited Versailles and had seen men walking in rags of the direst destitution. There

was a wonderful botanical garden there. In the Castle at Cham-
bord he had been shown the room where Marshal Saxe had
died. It was said that he had been run through the heart by the
Prince of Conti in a duel. And so on. And so on. Little things,
unalive, related by him in his shy, hesitating voice so that, Will
thought impatiently, he turned everything to dullness. But how
could it be other ? How could he, in this quiet homely comfortable scene, tell them of the things that had been burning in his
heart – the filth, oppression, cruelty, suffering ? Tell them of the
man whom he had seen in Tours beaten to death before his
eyes, because he had taken a log from the Seigneur's wood,
or the two girls ravished by the son of the Lord of the Manor,
one of them within a week of her wedding, or of the horde of
starved creatures that he came upon on the road outside Paris,
scarecrows, their bodies shivering in the bitter wind ? The bear
again, lodged now close in his heart, he the protector of it; how
could he speak of that to Will or Francis Herries ? So his voice
died away, and he felt the scornfulness of Will's eyes.

'When I am grown,' Judith cried, 'I shall go to France. I shall
see the French Queen and dance in Versailles. I shall see India
and China and the savages of the West Indies. What will you
do, Will ?'

He smiled. It was always his way to be courteous and friendly
to everyone. Besides, nothing in the world interested him so
greatly as to think of what he would do when he grew up, a time
that was very near to him already.

'I shall build the Herries fortunes,' he said in that voice, a
little mocking, a little ironical, so that if anyone objected to what
he said he could declare that he had never meant it. 'I shall have
a larger fortune than any other Herries, and then, when I have
accumulated it, I will tour the globe and return to make another
fortune.'

'And will you not marry ?' asked Judith greatly interested.

'I shall marry,' said Will gravely, 'and so increase the Herries
stock. I shall have six children,' he added mockingly.

To their surprise an angry voice broke on the scene – surprise
because it was the voice of Francis, who seemed never to be
disturbed nor to wish to join in their childish conversations. But
he was disturbed now, and at the sight of his disturbance two
fish-shaped clouds above Vicar's Island joined hurriedly together
the better for self-protection.

'There, Will; that's your fancy. It's you, yourself. Money-
bags, children, more money-bags. God, what ambition !'

It was a sharp interruption and rather frightened all of them. Francis was twenty-seven years of age and so in another world from their own. He had never mingled with them; he was like a ghost to them with his thin, handsome face, his cold blue eyes that could on a sudden so strangely burn, the severe suit of grey and silver that he so generally wore. Will might despise him, but there was fear mingled with that scorn.

And now suddenly he was standing, all shadows around him, his voice that had been always so chill and reserved beating with emotion.

'You shall have your money-bags if you want them. What is easier? And getting them you will have nothing. And is that all life is to you? Are you so blind that you can see no ghosts behind the money-bags and ghosts behind them again? Have you only your physical parts to cram food into your swelling belly?'

('I have no swelling belly,' Will thought complacently. 'I have an admirable figure.')

Francis went on, coming close to them, standing over them. His anger was gone as soon as it had come. He spoke now gently.

'When I was small I had a dream of a grand white horse breaking from an icy pool and breasting the rocks, tossing its mane. I have not dreamt that for a long while, but I know that that dream is more real to me than all the chairs and sofas, the mutton pies and shoe buckles. How can you not tell that that only is real in this world, that vision of ice and strength breaking it, and if we have not seen that we have seen nothing? Who can tell what is Reality? But this at least I know, that I shall never know happiness until I have seen more than you will ever see, Will, my young brother.'

'Thank you for nothing, Francis,' Will answered, looking up at him and smiling. 'I prefer my money-bags to your white horses.'

'Aye, I know what you think,' Francis broke out passionately. 'What you all think. That I loaf at home and take what my father gives me ... Wasting ... wasting.' His voice broke. 'Our grandfather was so. He was searching all his days and never found anything ... Forgive me, I have been absurd. This world itself is absurd to me, but behind it ... behind it ... there are Wonders. Forgive me ... forgive me,' and to their utter surprise he turned and vanished into the trees.

For a moment they were all in a great discomfort. It was so

agreeable an evening. They had not the slightest notion of Francis' meaning and they did not wish to spoil his pleasure. Judith, who loved him, would have wished to have run after him, to have taken his arm and comforted him. But to have comforted him for what ? She could not tell.

And at that moment, fortunately, the first fireworks broke like a sigh in the darkening heaven. Everyone said 'Ah!' and then 'Ah!' again, just as a hundred years after, and a hundred years after that again, they would sigh with pleasure and strain their eyes upwards. So now they gazed. Everywhere they were gazing, in the little flower-scented streets of Keswick, lovers waiting among the Druid stones, shepherds on Blencathra, watchers by the Watendlath Tarn, children gathered by the cottages in Newlands and under Castle Crag and by the waving reeds of Bassenthwaite.

A star broke into a silver cluster, another into points of blue, another showered drops of gold. In the hills the echo called and answered. For a flash all the faces were lit with a white radiance, the dancers paused in the Meadow, the trees on the Island were fiery and then the darker for their flame.

For Judith it was a moment of sheer ecstasy. She sat, her head back, her hat behind her neck, her legs uptilted, and at every rush as of wings, at every gentle crackle of sound, at every fresh miracle of blue and gold she murmured, her hands tightly clasped. She forgot everything and everyone in that beauty. A star burst, and showers of silver flecked the sky.

She sprang up and ran to the Lake edge. Others were crowding there, and she stood with them, her head bare, gazing upwards. Three rockets burst together, and the sky was scattered with stars. 'Bravo!' 'Bravo!' 'Bravo!' everyone shouted. She clapped her hands; everyone was clapping with her. Again the hills called and answered. Then the pause came, a sudden deep and mysterious silence. The Lake was now infinite. Far, far away, where the hills were packed together, a faint radiance was gathering, the coming moon. Real stars began to twinkle.

Out of this dark lovely world a voice spoke to her: 'It is better in a boat.'

She knew the voice well; in the last two years she had thought of it very often. It was the French boy of Tom Gauntry's.

The lanterns had been lighted and were swaying from the trees. She could see him quite plainly. He was just the same, only taller, in a very grand coat and breeches with gold braid. Under his hat his hair was as black as ever, and his eyes as black. His mouth was just as impudent. She grinned at him, a childish grin.

'Fetch me a boat then.'

What would Sarah think? It would mean perhaps another beating. She had been ordered not to go near the boats until they told her. The thought of being alone with the French boy was most exhilarating. She watched him while, without another word, he was in a boat, had pushed it towards her and, like a grown man, with fine ceremony, handed her in. As she stepped in she glanced about her to see whether any of the family were near. No sign of any of them. She fancied that she heard Sarah's voice, and in a sudden panic pushed from the shore. Many other boats were now moving, and, in the distance, they were singing.

'Quickly,' she cried, with delight, 'or they will see us.'

They floated away: the oars touched very gently the water as though they were whispering to it their pleasure in the evening. As they moved, the shore behind them came out, with all the dark figures, the lights like jolly smiling faces among the trees, and shadows dancing on the Meadow to a thin faint tune that was reedy like wind through wallpaper.

'Where have you been?'

'In London with an uncle.'

'And your mother?' She saw the room, the beautiful naked woman, her arms raised, the diamond buckle shining.

'My mother is dead.'

'Dead?' And at the moment a firework broke in the sky again, this time a circle of fierce rasping flame that whistled with the hiss of an angry cat.

Dead? Judith shivered. Then for these two years the picture that had transformed her, that had changed her from a thought-less baby into something, something very different ... that picture had been for nothing, of a dead woman.

'Why did she die?'

'What is it? I cannot hear.' He had leaned forward on the oars.

'Why did she die?'

'She died of the smallpox.'

'When was it?'

'A year back.' He spoke quite indifferently.

'Did you not care?'

'No. She was unkind to me.'

'She must have been very gracious; a beautiful lady. Her hair was so dark.' Judith shivered again. She wanted to return to the shore, to be with her own people. And, surprisingly, something else dominated almost every other feeling, that she wanted to kiss the French boy. Hateful, when his mother, his beautiful mother, had for her, at any rate, only this moment died.

'How old are you now?' he asked her.

'Twelve – nearly thirteen.'

'I am sixteen.'

'What are you doing here? Why are you not with your uncle?'

'My uncle is in Carlisle. I am with Gauntry until he fetches me. I like this country. Soon I shall come to live here.' Then he added, laughing: 'Is your hair yet the same colour? I have thought of your hair often.'

Because she wanted to kiss him and because she mustn't, because she was only twelve and he sixteen, she flipped water in his face. He laid down his oars in the boat, moved near to her and roughly kissed her, cheeks, eyes, mouth. She pulled her head free and smacked his face just as she had done two years before. But he did not move. He sat quietly beside her, his hand at her waist. She did not move either. Fires were burning now on Vicar's Island, the set-pieces of the fireworks. A trellis-work of flame ran like live things from tree to tree. All the Lake near the Island glowed, but in the distance it was very dark, with a smoky sheen on it, the first fore-shadowing of the moon.

She sat there in perfect happiness. She hoped that he would kiss her again. He did so. Then she returned his kiss.

'I shall be whipped if they know about it.'

'My mother whipped me, but my uncle dare not. When my mother was angry she could kill a man.'

'Was she long ill of the smallpox?'

'No. A month. I was glad when she died. Do you love me?'

'No.'

'Later you will. You are only a baby. In two years I will write you a letter, and perhaps you will come to London.'

'Will you want to marry me?'

'Perhaps. You have such beautiful hair.'

Judith considered. In two years she would be nearly fifteen. She could marry soon then and leave Fell House and live in France.

'If I married you should we live in France?'

'Maybe.'

'Will you have money and a house and horses.'

'Yes. Of course.'

'And we will have children?'

'Yes. Of course.'

'We will have six children, and I want to see the French Queen dance in Versailles.'

'I want to live in this country and have dogs and horses.'

'But will you not take me to France for a visit?'

'Maybe.'

They kissed again. She kissed him like a child, just as she kissed Francis. Then quite suddenly she knew that she must return to the shore. At once, at once! She was afraid of him and of the Lake that seemed dark now because the fireworks had died away.

She told him to take her to the shore.

'No. We will stay here.'

Then he saw another Judith. She stepped from him, and, the boat rocking under them, went to the oars and began to row. She could do anything with a boat or a horse.

'If you leave me now I will never see you again,' he said to her fiercely. She made no answer, and a moment later had scrambled over the boat's edge and had landed.

That was the last she saw of him, standing up very dimly against the dark water.

She ran in to the trees and, quite breathless, tumbled straight into Reuben and his mother.

'I was lost,' she said. 'Where are they?'

She put her hand under Reuben's arm and smiled at him so sweetly that he was enraptured. She looked such a baby with her pretty hat crooked, a little breathless.

'We will go and find them,' he said.

THE FUGITIVE

HOW DOES A house first know that changes are coming to it? or does a house know? Are we not attributing to it emotions, fears, agitations that are not its real property? The answer depends on yourself. What you see, hear and feel is for yourself alone.

It is certain in any case that in that winter of 1788–9 Sarah Herries, just arrived at her fiftieth birthday, knew that some change was at hand. It was the first unhappy winter for her since

- since when? Since she had lived with David at Herries.

Had she cared for wider issues she might have realized that the change was not only here, but in all the civilized world. She did not, however, care for wider issues, had never done so. It had never meant anything to her that the American rebels had thrown tea into Boston Harbor, that old Chatham had the gout, that Fox made an unholy alliance with North, that young Pitt pored over *The Wealth of Nations* at Cambridge, that men were trampled to death by the horses of noble carriages on the roads outside Paris, that Necker sat up all night biting his thumbs over the impossible business of turning twice-two into five. If she had known of these things she would not have cared.

But she did perceive that nothing now went right in the house, that doors swung on their hinges and refused to close, that the Chinese figures in the Blue Room tumbled, through nobody's fault, and were broken to pieces, that the cows gave no milk and the horses went lame.

Twenty years earlier she would have hunted for witches. Now she could only discover that David was becoming an old man, that she herself was fifty and that everyone in her family was at odds. She was a sensible woman, who refused to surrender to superstition, but things were going wrong, and as she lay at night awake in the big four-poster beside David she could hear the wind come whispering down from Skiddaw and must listen, do what she would, to a hundred steps creeping about the stairs and mysterious voices behind the curtain.

But there were unhappy evidences more material than steps and voices.

The first trouble was on the day after the firework evening on the Lake. At dinner Will had suddenly said to Judith:

'Well, miss, you enjoyed, I trust, your pleasant trip in the boat last night.'

No one knew why he said it. He did not care for Judith, but he bore her no especial malice. He did not himself, perhaps, know why he said it. It came no doubt from his deep restless love of power. He was only a boy, but he could turn them any way he wished.

All might even then have been saved had it not been for Judith's implacable honesty.

'You were in a boat?'

'Yes, ma'am.'

'With whom?'

That she would not say: with a gentleman, yes. For a brief period, to see the fireworks better. David beat her. The child said nothing, only afterwards alone with Will she told him that she would not forget his kindness.

'I wanted to see how it would go,' he told her quite honestly. He admired her then, such a little thing, standing on her toes to make herself seem taller. She bore him apparently no grudge.

'It shall not be for long,' she said, nodding her head like a woman of forty. She turned on her toes, pirouetting. 'I'll be a woman very shortly.'

But for the moment, as the consequence of this indiscretion following many others, she was in great danger of the one and only thing that she dreaded – of being sent to Miss Macdonald's Academy at Carlisle.

She had heard something of this school from Margaret and Hetty Worcester of Threlkeld, who attended this place for a time, and she did not like what she had heard. They rose at six winter and summer, ate a piece of bread and then had an hour's schooling. Then there was 'Punishment Hour', wherein, it seemed, the Misses Macdonald indulged in an orgy of whipping, six stripes of the rod for a small offence, and a 'proper whipping' meant that you fetched the rod, kissed it, and then, before the school, were stripped, 'mounted' on another girl's back and beaten till the blood came. Hetty Worcester gave an admirably detailed description of it. Judith knew well that before she suffered that ignominy there would be a murder done. Not that Hetty thought much of it, for in her home everyone was whipped, the maids and the grooms, the dairy girls and even the tutor. Nevertheless, Judith knew that a week in Miss Macdonald's Academy and she would be a vagrant loose upon the world, and for that she was not yet ready.

While her fate hung thus in the balance the relations between Sarah and Judith developed uncomfortably. Judith bore her sister-in-law no grudge, she knew herself to be a difficult ill-disciplined child, but the difference between their ages was so great and their characters were so ill-suited that, as Judith grew, trouble was bound to come.

Sarah in her heart cared for nothing at the last resort but David. She loved her children, but David was her adoration. She could not endure to see him vexed, even for a moment, and now she realized that Judith was constantly vexing him. He understood her as little as did Sarah. He was too kindly-natured to exercise his authority sufficiently. Judith was for ever

escaping him. After all she was not his child, but his half-sister.
There were many times when she seemed to him her mother
come alive again.

He was a great deal at home now; went to Liverpool very
seldom. He trusted the Metcalfes for everything, and soon Will
would be in Liverpool. Therefore he was much at Uldale. He
loved every stick and stone of it, and he could be seen, his body
casting a vast shadow, pottering over the sunny lawn, looking
up as a great hurrying cloud flung its shadow over the Fell,
examining the horses, watching the maids working in the dairy,
going over accounts with Mr Matcham the agent, or simply
leaning on the stone wall and gazing across the white road at the
low sprawling shape of Skiddaw.

So, being at home thus, he was always tumbling upon Judith
and Francis; Judith, her ringlets flying, riding Barnabas or
sliding down the banister of the great staircase, or, in another
mood altogether, standing motionless, watching, waiting – what
was the child about and why did she look so damnably like her
mother?

Or Francis, twenty-eight years of age now, always so slim,
elegant, apart, silent – and doing nothing. Twenty-eight and
doing nothing! For you could not call reading Cowley or Milton
or Shakespeare anything, or roaming aimlessly the countryside
(and greeting no one as he went) anything. His father would
catch him writing in a book and when he would ask him of it he
would close the book and, secretly, deep in himself, would
answer the question by saying:

'Nothing, sir.'

Once David lost his temper, and only once.

'I'll not keep you here idling.'

An hour later Francis came down the stairs in his riding coat,
Andrew the boy carrying his valise. He was going away, and
David knew that it was for ever. David found then how deeply
he loved him. Afterwards he pleaded with him: why were
they drifting so far apart? Could they not open their hearts
to one another? And Francis answered: 'Oh, sir, would to God
I could! Something silences me. I will work, father, anywhere
you place me . . . in your Keswick office . . . I will do all I can.'

What an echo of ghosts was here! For had not David's father
once, in the dead years, said the same? For a moment Francis
Herries the Elder stood there, that same ironical twist to his
lip that his grandson had.

So Francis went to work in the Keswick office, and he was

useless. All he cared for was to read poetry and philosophy.
Poetry and philosophy! So, loving one another deeply, they
drifted further and further apart.

But Judith was a greater mystery for poor David, who would
sit back in his armchair before the fire, his legs spread, his great
bulk at ease, but his honest friendly face twisted with perplexity.

He wanted to do what was right by the child. She was his
own father's daughter; but the truth was that neither he nor
Sarah felt that she had anything to do with him at all. At one
moment she was a child of her proper age, at another almost
a woman, ordering the men and maids in the place as though
she commanded it. She had a good heart, he could tell that, but
when she couldn't get her own way she was a devil, not raging
nor crying but her sharp, pale, little face cold and savage under
her red hair. And he sometimes thought that she hated Sarah.
They didn't forbid Gauntry's to her any more. What was the
use? She would simply go there, and one day, if they were not
careful, she would never come back, and what a scandal that
would be! Besides, there was no harm in little Gauntry, and
he loved the child like his own daughter.

So David went over all his perplexities, feeling perhaps, as
Sarah did, that changes were coming. When things were too
difficult for him he would ride over to Worcester's or Osmaston's
and play cards all night or get drunk and be carried up to bed.

Meanwhile he clung to Sarah, his wife, ever more deeply.
She was his real friend, had always been. He loved Deborah,
his daughter, but in his heart found her a little dull; he was a
little afraid of Will, who always knew better than he himself
did; Francis, whom he loved best of his children, was a mystery.
So he stayed with Sarah and was only truly happy when she was
by.

In March of the new year they decided that Judith should pay
a visit to the Sunwoods in Cockermouth. Maybe they would
manage her. Judith was very happy to go. She was very happy
to go, but never dreamt before going that when she was there
she would be so happy to stay.

She had visited a number of times at the little house, but had
had no notion that it would suit her so perfectly to live in it.
It was the very size that she liked, small, compact, comfortable.
Everything in it went on under her very nose; she could have
her fingers in every pie, in Deborah's cooking and preserving,
sewing and cleaning, in the dealings with the pig, in all the little
affairs of the town, the gossip, the tea parties, the expeditions

on fine days, the cosy conferences round the fire on wet ones. In
five minutes she had Mr Sunwood entirely under her control,
he would read his sermons to her, she would listen to his
accounts of his Quadrille parties, enjoy by proxy the first piece
of roasted swan that he had tasted at a grand party at the Castle,
and even advise him as to the right time to take a good dose of
rhubarb.

But the element that made this visit so enchanting was her
quite unexpected friendship with Deborah. Deborah was nearly
sixty-six years of age and Judith only fourteen, yet the difference
in their ages seemed to make no division between them at all.
Judith was hungering for affection with all the ardour and excitement of her temperament. She was separated from Francis and
also (although of this she tried to prevent herself thinking) from
Georges, the French boy. So she was ready, in any case, to
throw herself upon Deborah and Reuben. But she soon discovered that she had never been brought into contact before with
anyone at all like this stout, soft-eyed, soft-voiced, gentle-
hearted woman. The people whom she had hitherto known had
not (save for Reuben, and he had been two years away) been
gentle-hearted – not Gauntry, nor Sarah, nor Will, nor even
Francis.

The first thing that drew her to Deborah was that Deborah
let her do anything that she wished, and the second thing was
that Deborah told her so much that was new and exciting about
her father.

They sat together beside the fire, Deborah sewing and Judith
leaning forward, her chin cupped in her hands, and Deborah
recovered for the child her own childhood. This gave Deborah
herself a surprising happiness and pleasure. No one in her own
family had asked her questions about those days. It was her
husband's belief that he had rescued her from some wild sort of
savagery and the less said about it the better, and her sons had
never shown any curiosity. But this strange child, with her
ardent, eager, impetuous spirit, brought her father back to her
as though he were with them in the room. *Her* father! *Their*
father! And at the thought that they had, both of them, she
nearing the end of her life, the child only beginning hers, the
same father, a bond of affection was formed and remained. She
soon discovered that she herself loved to recall that long-ago
time, the wild Borrowdale valley, so cut off and remote, the
old house rocking to every wind, the death of her mother and
her own fear at being left alone with her father, although she

loved him. Her devotion to her brother David, such a wonderful
boy, the strongest boy and man in the valley (different, she was
forced to confess, from the stout, rather lazy monarch of Uldale),
the old witch, Mrs Wilson, who lived with them and was drowned
in the Derwent by the villagers, her own lonely thoughts, love
of natural things, shyness – then the ball in Keswick and the
little clergyman coming to sit beside her and make love to her,
her father's strange marriage to Judith's mother, and then the
unhappiness of that odd woman, her flight, her father's loneliness and madness and search, and always the tumbledown house
and the isolated valley behind and through it all.

She let Judith ask as many questions as she wished and answered all that she asked. Judith recovered the personalities
of her father and mother as she never had done before. They
became alive to her. She saw Francis, her father, the scar
marring his face, tumbling the villagers down the stairs after
the wedding. She saw Mirabell, her mother (it was part of her
oddness that she should have a man's name), breaking her heart
because the man she had loved had been murdered under her
eyes in Carlisle. She saw Francis, her father, setting out in
search of her, wandering over England looking for her, at last
capturing her again, and then the two of them dying together in
that lonely house.

Something grew in her as these two ghosts were drawn to her
side. *Her* ghosts and only hers. No one alive in the world had
the right to both of them as she had. She was never, after this,
to lose the fancy that all her life long there were three of them
moving about together through the world.

'Oh, if but I had been there,' she cried. 'I could have made
them so happy!'

And Deborah, in her turn, recovering thus her young days,
felt her heart warm in her for her dear, lost father. Only she
and David in all the world thought of him any more – and now
this child. How could she not but love her?

Judith was easy enough to love in such a case. She asked nothing better than to love and be loved in return: it was only when
someone was an enemy, or she thought was an enemy, that her
fierce hostility flamed out. Even then she could be generous and
large-hearted. She wished Will no evil because he had betrayed
her about the evening on the Lake. She could not be mean nor
spiteful about little things.

They were both large-hearted, she and Deborah.

Then something more drew them together. Judith discovered

that Deborah was very unhappy. For eight months she had had no word from her son Humphrey. Mr Sunwood pooh-poohed the whole business. The boy would write when he had leisure; the Post was a very uncertain affair; he, himself, would soon make a journey to London and see the boy.

But none of this could comfort Deborah. They had heard nothing, either, from his master. The last news had been a year ago. At first the boy had written frequently. He had been last home a year and a half ago and had been well and merry, but, even at that, she had fancied that he had said too little about his work. It was all his pleasure, his visits to Vauxhall, how he had seen the good King and Queen, been to a picnic in Twickenham, travelled down the river with the Pomfret Herries, and so on, and so on. But of his work very little. And that was a year and a half ago.

As Judith listened to all this her impatience leapt into flame. But why didn't someone go to London? Why didn't Mr Sunwood or Reuben? She would go herself. Why should not she and Deborah go? It was a shame to leave it in this uncertainty ... She jumped up and ran about the room, tossing her red ringlets in the air.

But Deborah, smiling, shook her head. It wasn't so easy to go to London, a very long journey. Mr Sunwood felt no alarm, why should she? Reuben had his work at Mr Stele's the solicitor's. Oh, it was all right. She was sure that all was well. Humphrey was such a good boy. Any day there would be a letter. And she would look across the room at the little bottle-green window and shake her head, and her eyes would swim in tears.

So Judith went to Reuben. Reuben was changed by his two years in France, more remote. He was tidier, but alas! little cleaner. It was not at that time important that you should be clean, and Judith was peculiar in wishing for cleanliness. When Mr Sunwood came in from attending to the pig he was not very clean and would sit down to his dinner without thinking of it. But Reuben's linen, his small-clothes, oh, they wanted a deal of attention! His hair was not brushed and fell untidily about his shoulders. His shoes were often caked with mud. In his attic there was always a close stuffy smell, terrible untidiness, his bed where he used to lie, his hands behind his head, looking up at the attic roof, staring and thinking, sadly tumbled. Judith never came into the room but she longed to set about it with a scrubbing brush and a pail of water. But she loved him none the less, his fat loose body, his kindly, large,

wondering eyes. He was generous and soft-hearted like his
mother, but so often like something that had lost its way. He
moved at times as though he were blind. He was a dreamer
like Francis, but what an incongruous comparison he made with
that slim, elegant, severe figure! And he had told her once that
if he were afraid of anyone in the world it was of Francis.

Then one evening she came up to his attic and found him
lying on his bed, his coat off, his shoes off, his stockings halfway down his legs, and he was talking to himself, while a long
drunken candle guttered on a chair beside the bed.

She herself held a candle. She stood for a moment listening to
him:

'Oh, Lord! Oh, Lord!' he was saying, 'I am a sinner. I have
no courage in my heart. I am a poor wretch. Oh, damnation!
Damnation! I long in my heart after women and go the way I
should not! Oh, Lord, Lord! . . .'

She stopped this peroration by crying in a very solemn voice:
'I am the Devil and have come for your soul, O Reuben!' and
he, hearing her, jumped from the bed and stood blinking at her
like an owl.

'Do you truly long after women?' she asked him a little later,
when they were both sitting on the bed close together, the candles
throwing great shadowy shapes on the wall.

'Yes, I do.'

'Well, then, you should marry.' She nodded her head, swinging her little legs and wishing for the thousand-thousandth time
that they were longer.

'No woman would have me.'

'No, not while you are so untidy in your clothes. Why don't
you brush your hair and have a new ribbon for it? And there is
a hole in your stocking.'

'I hate Mr Stele and his office,' he said suddenly. 'I was so
happy the day I saw the bear. That was a sign, and I did not
follow it.'

'They sent you away to France,' she said, 'because of the
bear.'

'Yes.' He nodded his head. 'And one day in the road beyond
Tours – a hot glaring day – I saw Jesus Christ standing there.
He stood right in my path; the sun was shining in His hair.
He looked at me so kindly and said: "Reuben, feed my Lambs."
And I have done nothing, nothing.'

'For how long did He stay there?' she asked. She had a very
practical mind and no sense of religion at all. She could not

help that. She wished to have it, but she found it very difficult to believe in anything that she did not see.

Reuben pulled up his stockings. He was always aware that she disliked his untidiness. She herself looked so neat now in her little orange hoop and brown shoes.

'He did not stay long,' Reuben sighed. 'It was the second time. He came to me once at St Bees.' He put his hand timidly and took one of hers.

'Judith,' he said. 'You are so brave. Show me what to do.'

'Yes, I will show you,' she answered, coming close to him. 'Go to London and see Humphrey.' She felt him tremble.

'I dream about Humphrey,' he answered her, 'every night. I know that he is in great trouble. One of us always knows when the other is in trouble. I know that Mother also is grieving, but I am afraid to go to London. I am afraid of everything. I would not know how to behave in London nor what to do. They would all laugh at me, and I cannot bear to be mocked. London is so vast, and there is so much noise there . . .' He broke off, plucking with his fingers at his clothes.

'No, but you must go,' she answered. 'I will never speak to you again if you do not. It is your duty to your mother. Do you love me, Reuben?'

'Of course.'

'Then go to London or I will never see you again.'

She began then eagerly to speak of what he would do and just where he should go. She seemed to know everything about London, although she had never been there. His cheeks kindled, there was light in his eyes. Yes, he would go. He would ride into Kendal and take the coach there. He would speak to his father . . . And then he shrank back. But all the people, so many strangers, the lighted streets, he would be lost.

'Well, if you do not go, I am finished with you.'

She stood in the middle of the floor, her head up, scorning him. And at that moment some of her strength entered into him, entered into him never to leave him again. He went to the window and looked out across the darkness. Then he looked back into the lighted room and saw her standing there. He cried out in a kind of frenzy:

'I'll go! I'll go! I'll go!'

How often in other places, in later times, he remembered that scene! And then she danced about the room like a mad thing, caught his hands and made him dance too. She ended by tying his hair with a new ribbon and finding another pair of stockings for him. She hoped that he would find a woman in London to make him happy, and she also hoped that he would not, because she wanted to have him all to herself.

Howbeit, events moved faster than Reuben. Before he could speak to either his mother or his father something very terrible occurred.

Years and years afterwards Judith would remember that March afternoon and its sudden storm sweeping her off her feet into an adventure that would have its consequences for all her life.

She and Deborah had been shopping in the town. It was market day and proper March, with a sky that was here pale green, there pale blue, while little busy clouds like torn sheets of grey paper flew and scattered under cross tugs of wind. The sky was swept with streams of light that flooded out into glory, throwing sheets of pale silver colour on to field and wood.

It was one of those days when everyone in the little town was conscious of the near neighbourhood both of the mountains and the sea. The wind had begun with little anticipatory gusts, as though it were trying its forces to see whether they were strong and sound, then, as everything went well, it increased its power, began to find pride in its strength, and soon, doubtless, would be bellowing with vainglory. You could see in your mind's eye Ennerdale, that was not far away, ruffling into little flakes of foam, its waters chocolate-coloured, while the sky above the hills was all busy with its traffic, sending clouds hither and thither, flashing light now on, now off, under order of the March gale. All the hills, black and grim, gathered like conspirators close about the waters. On the other side of the town there was the sea, the wind tugging at St Bees Head, and all the shipping tossing maliciously in Whitehaven Bay.

The booths of the market were creaking and cracking, cloths blowing about, the pedlar forced to cover his wares, ropes straining, doors rattling, everyone clinging to their hats and wigs.

Then with a shriek of whistling fun the wind and the rain came, driving straight up the street, sweeping the trestles and boards away, carrying the whole town with it as though it would toss it into Ennerdale.

Judith and Deborah went scurrying home, hats, wigs, pieces of cloth, fragments of wood, dogs, cats, shrill voices, laughter, all hurrying through the air, it seemed, with them.

Safe in the little house again, panting for breath, wet, blown, laughing, they looked about them, while the rain rattled on the windows crossly because they had escaped it. They stared under wet eyelashes about them, and the first thing that Judith saw was a letter, lying innocently on the table: it was addressed 'Miss Judith Herries'.

She snapped it up.

'A letter?' asked Deborah.

'Yes.'

'From Uldale, I warrant.'

'Yes,' said Judith. It was not a lie because she had not yet looked at it. It lay warm in her wet hand. She thought it would be from Sarah, summoning her home. Who had left it there? Had David perhaps ridden over, or Francis? It might be that they would spend the night. But she wouldn't go back to Uldale. She was too happy where she was. She wouldn't go back until she had seen Reuben safely away to London ... She had got thus far. She was climbing the stair to her room. She saw what it was. It was from Georges Paris. He was in Cockermouth. He asked her to meet him in the parlour of the 'Greyhound', five o'clock that evening. He would wait until six.

Her first thought was of his impertinence, then that he should have the spunk to leave the letter at her very door where anyone might read it, then that she wouldn't go, nothing should induce her, then that she would greatly like to see him again just to tell him what she thought of him, then that she would take Reuben with her (it would be so amusing to see Georges' face of disappointment), then that this would be the first time of seeing him since the evening on the Lake, then that she would not go but would send a letter by Reuben, then that perhaps she *would* go just to see what he was like now ...

By this time she was in her room and laughing at the thought of an adventure. For it *was* an adventure. Georges was always an adventure. She would wear her orange hoop ... But in this weather with the streets swimming in water! She heard the maid calling her to dinner. Three o'clock. There would be plenty of time before five ...

By the end of the meal she was uneasy. She was always uneasy when she thought of Georges. She determined that she would take Reuben with her.

Behind the parlour there was a little room with nothing much in it but a large yellow globe, a powder-stand and a shaving-table. It could be turned into a guest room at a crisis. She pulled Reuben in there after her. The little windows looked out on to a narrow crooked path that ran through fields to a shaggy wood,

on fine days a pleasant prospect, but this afternoon you could
see nothing but the storm that swung in sheets of rain across the
scene, the drops on the panes in the windows rattling like little
pellets from a shotgun. From a side door of this room there was a
short passage and another door opening on to the field.

When she had Reuben in the room with her, she suddenly
thought – no, after all, she would not tell him. Why should she
not go alone ? Georges could not harm her. They would be in a
public place. She was not afraid to smack his face again if need
be. She was not afraid of Georges nor of anyone. So when she
saw Reuben, still wiping his last draught of ale from his mouth
and smiling in that uncertain way that he had when he was not
sure how she was going to use him next, she burst out laughing.

'Reuben—' she said, and then she paused.

'Yes,' he said obediently.

'It's raining.'

'Yes,' he said again, wondering.

'But I am going out into it.'

He said nothing.

'And no one is to know. I shall go by this door.'

He looked at her in perplexity. She could always do as she
liked with him, but after all she was but a child. Her small
stature and something innocent in her wide-open eager eyes
always made her younger than her age, just as the resolved
dominating lines about her mouth made her older. Nevertheless,
she was young to be going out into the town alone, and in this
weather, and what could she be going for but to see a man ?

At the thought his heart beat thickly, his stout cheeks coloured,
he plucked at his coat.

'You shall not go alone,' he said. 'I shall accompany you.'

'Oh no, you will not !' she answered laughing. 'You shall stay
here and keep them quiet. If they ask where I am you shall say
I am busy working – and so I shall be.'

'Busied at what ?'

She stood on her toes, pulled his head down, and kissed him.

'Never you mind. I am your aunt.'

'I shall accompany you,' he said firmly.

She looked at him. Would it be better perhaps, after all, that
he should ? She was *not* safe with Master Georges. She remembered a moment in the boat, when, in an instant, at a touch of his
hand, she had been warned.

Many visits to Stone Ends had acquainted her with life.
Children were not children for long in those days. *Should* she

take Reuben with her? And it would tease Georges so that he should be there. And Reuben was so strong, so safe, so devoted. A sudden impulse of great affection for him, one of those impulses that were often all through her life to rise in her, straight, unalloyed, from her heart, influenced her now. She put her hand on his arm.

As she did so they both heard, quite clearly through the slashing and angry rain, a rap on the window. Her hand tightened on his arm and they turned. The rap came again, urgent, imperative. They stared and at first could see nothing. In any case there would have been only a pale, fading light, but now with the storm all was darkness. Reuben hurried to the window and pressing his face against the pane stared out. He could see a shadowy form.

'There is someone there,' he whispered to Judith, then, hurrying through the little passage, opened the outer door. The wind almost blew the door to, but holding it firmly he looked out.

'Who's there?' he called softly.

A moment later his fingers were grasped by a cold hand, he had been drawn back into the passage, a figure soaking with wet was pressed close to him, and his brother Humphrey's voice was in his ear, nay, at his very heart.

'Reuben . . . for God's sake – no sound . . .'

'Humphrey!'

'Yes. Is there anyone there?'

'Only Judith.'

But Judith, hearing the whispering voices, had come into the passage. Humphrey, pushing past them, had peered into the little room, seen that there was no one there, hastened to the door and bolted it, then turned to them both:

'No one must know. Not Father nor Mother. No one. Get me something to eat. Oh, God, I am so weary!'

He sank into the only chair in the room, murmuring again, 'Food. Food, and secretly.'

Reuben didn't question. It was, as it always was with his brother, as though this were part of himself, soaked with rain, fugitive, in some frantic plight, hiding from the world. He moved as though hurrying to save himself, undid the bolt and was gone.

Judith bolted the door again. Her heart was moved at once to eager pity and a desire to help. When she had last seen Humphrey he had been so young, so handsome, so self-confident, so sure of himself and his ability to manage any situation in life; now another man was there, utterly weary, exhausted, his head

back, the water dripping from the capes of his coat, his hair long
and matted, his face pale, haggard, and his eyes that had been
so gay and happy now restless, hunted, brimming with despair.

He seemed to her to be years older, older than himself, older
than Reuben, and he seemed, beyond that, to be mysterious, a
man from some world that she had never before realized, a man
who should, by right, speak to her in a strange language.

He wasted no time, did not ask her why she was there, did
not consider her except as an agent of assistance for him.

'I have been an age outside. I could not see clearly who was in
the room. I had to risk something. Thank God, it was Reuben!'

His words came in gasps. His hands moved ceaselessly.

'I've had no food for two days. I have tramped from
Kendal . . .'

She was intensely practical, as she always was in a crisis.
'You must take off your coat. It is dripping. You must have dry
things.'

He got up from the chair and she helped him to take off the
shabby soiled riding coat. His body was trembling; he was wet
through to the skin. The thing that moved her most was that his
eyes were never still, searching the globe, the powder-stand,
the dull green portrait of some old Sunwood ancestor, the dark
bulging window against whose panes the rain, falling now gently,
pressed.

She did not stop to ask him why he was there, nor what
catastrophe had plunged him into this disaster, but his fear
infected her. She was not in the least afraid, but she listened,
as he did, to any outside sound. She realized that whatever
else happened his mother must not now see him. She did not
know the reason, but she understood that he was bitterly
ashamed to see his mother, that, beyond any other possible
disaster, that was the one he dreaded.

Her sense of this made him still more mysterious to her and
touched her heart yet more deeply. Towards anyone pursued
she was always to be sympathetic, although there was some true
Herries in her that placed her also on the side of justice. In
herself she was to be always both pursued and pursuer.

Reuben scratched on the door and came in, not clumsy nor
shy any more, but swift, silent, efficient. He was acting for the
stronger part of himself. He closed the door very gently behind
him, bolted it softly. He had half a cold mutton pie, bread,
cheese, ale.

Humphrey drew to the little table, devoured the food frantically. He seemed just then like an animal, his ears pricked, his eyes everywhere, his hand curved close about the meat.

'Mother is with Father,' Reuben whispered, 'listening to his sermon.'

'He is wet to the skin,' Judith answered. 'He must change everything.'

Reuben went out again. She stood by the door, letting him finish his food. Life was like this. She had seen it already countless times. Mrs Osmaston's maid had stolen stockings, had fled and been caught in Keswick, jailed there; a pedlar had murdered a woman in Keswick for a shilling, he had been chased by a crowd of men and boys to Threlkeld and stoned there to death...

'Yes,' said Humphrey, speaking quite clearly out of the half-light illumined only by one blowing candle. 'And now I must get to the coast. I am so weary. God, if I could sleep for twelve hours.'

'What is it?' she asked. 'What has happened?'

His face, pale, drawn, the hair shaggy on his forehead, looked up at her. She felt as though he were her child.

'I killed a man in London. Over cards.'

'Have you any money?' she asked him.

'Nothing – now. It is all gone.'

She came over to him and stroked his hair back from his forehead. With a gesture of infinite weariness he leaned his head, wet with rain as it was, back against her childish breast.

'I shall sleep,' he murmured. 'How soft your hand is!'

Reuben knocked; she unbolted the door. He came in with clothes on his arm. At once, as though a desperate hurry were now his accustomed state, Humphrey jumped up and stripped. Judith helped him. This was no time for maidenly modesty, and she had seen many a man naked before.

When he was finished he sat there holding Reuben's hand in his. The three of them began a quick whispered conversation. On the one thing he was determined, that his father and mother shouldn't know. Nothing would shake him in that. He told them very little of what had happened. Things had been going badly for a long while. Some fierce love-affair he had had with Nancy Bone: Pomfret had forbidden him the house. After that Judith had a picture of some dark underground London, gutters running with water, sudden flares of light, gambling, little rooms in crooked inns, life by the river, curious interludes of some great man like Mr Fox or Mr Burke, a struggle up again to larger rooms, then down again, fights in that same gutter, swinging shop-signs, a narrow street crowded with carriages, a woman looking from a window, a fight, some fat man with a wound in his breast, and all the while it seemed to be rain and fog . . . She was to have this queer picture of London for years until the reality gave her another one.

But the one thing that stood out clearly was that he must escape from England. Some port . . . Whitehaven . . . It was then that she had her idea. With a flash of inspiration she thought of Georges Paris. She had long known that young Georges with other friends of Gauntry's had dealings with some sort of traffic on the Cumberland coast. Some kind of smuggling perhaps. She had been too much of a child for them to take her into any kind of confidence, but her last time at Stone Ends there had been a Captain Barnett, a thin green-faced man like a nettle, who had praised young Georges for his enterprise in some Whitehaven or St Bees expedition.

She did not doubt but that that was what brought Georges into Cockermouth this afternoon. He would do anything for her; he should help to get Humphrey out of the country. Once again in a moment she took the situation into her hands. She acknowledged without a tremor to Reuben that it had been this Georges Paris whom she had been going to meet. Was he to be trusted? Of course he was to be trusted. He was her friend. She had known him for years. He would do anything that she told him. They followed her. What else? Something had to be done at once. They must not stay in this house. There was no other plan.

Only Reuben said one thing that often afterwards she was to remember: 'If he does this for you, are you under some obligation to him?'

Feverishly eager to be off, as she always was when she had a plan, she tossed her head. She did not even answer, but almost pushed them both in front of her, through the little passage and out of the door.

That brief journey from the house to the 'Greyhound' was the most exciting thing that had yet happened in her life. She was in charge of the expedition; the men followed meekly. That sense of power, the strongest sense in her, drove her like a charm. Without her, Humphrey, all of them, would have been lost. Now she would direct the affair like God Himself. The rain had ceased; the little cobbled streets were gloomy and deserted. They left Humphrey in the shadow of the yard of the inn and went quickly up the wooden staircase to the parlour. No one was

about. In the parlour, a small panelled room, a little sea-coal
fire was smoking and two candles guttering. Someone came
forward. It was Georges, almost hidden in the capes of his
riding-coat. She saw at once that he was angry because she was
not alone. She felt herself forty years of age at least as she took
his hand, introduced Reuben. He had never seen her so beautiful.
Indeed he had never thought her beautiful, only strange, unusual, in some antagonistic way appealing to his senses. Now,
in the half-lit smoky room, in all her colour, her small hat with a
feather, her hair, her little face ivory-coloured and in expression
mischievous, kindly, proud, all together, she seemed to him for
the first time a woman. He put his riding whip on the table,
clasped his hands behind him. He longed to kiss her. Who was
this big clumsy oaf of a fellow with her ?

Very quickly Judith explained, keeping him greatly at a
distance, very lofty, commanding rather than requesting.

And she saw, a moment later, that he found an opportunity
in all this. It was the first real request that she had ever made of
him. He asked no questions about Humphrey. A relation of
hers in distress . . . He must get to sea swiftly and quietly . . .
Had he a friend ? . . . Was there a boat ? . . .

By chance he had a friend. He paused and looked at her
oddly.

'If I do this for you—?' he broke off. They had both, concerned in their own personal drama, quite forgotten Reuben.

He forced her eyes. She would not be brow-beaten by him,
so stared proudly back at him, at his dark eyes, black hair, thin,
proud, restless face.

She said nothing. He, as though satisfied, nodded his head.

'Where is the gentleman ?'

They passed to the staircase. As they went down she whispered to Reuben: 'Have you any money ?' He nodded his head:
'I had thought of that.'

They had found Humphrey in a panic of nervous anxiety.
How strange it was to Judith to see what circumstances could
do to a man! He had been so easy, gay-hearted, confident. Her
whole being ached for him. She would have liked to go with him,
share his adventure wherever it might be, see that he was not
cold, hungry, lonely. As they hurried down a dark side street,
stumbling over gutters, holes in the road, refuse, she put out a
hand and caught his. For a moment she held it, hot, dry,
quivering . . .

They stopped before a door below the pavement; a little flight of steps went down to it. Georges went ahead of them and knocked. While they waited, a man, swinging a lantern, passed them. He did not look at them, but Judith felt as though it were the whole town staring. Then the door opened a little way, a head peered out, some words were exchanged. They all went in. The place was a large cellar, a lantern hanging from a hook, some farming implements in corners, a pile of hay, and, seated on an overturned barrel, a man of an enormous corpulency. His coat was open at the neck to allow room for his three chins. His cheeks were purple above a yellow beard and his nose had been slightly flattened on one side in some fight, but his eyes were large, clear and merry. His hand was a roll of beef and his thighs so huge that it was a wonder any breeches could ever contain them. He rose to receive them, and standing, his legs wide, he was like a vast amiable monster at home in its cavern. He smelt of oil, fish and whisky, but it was plain that he admired Judith immediately, hanging over her with a merry possessive look as though at any moment he would pick her up and slip her into his deep coat pocket.

It was clear also that he knew young Georges Paris very well and understood immediately what was wanted. He never looked at Humphrey, who had slipped into the shadow, nor addressed a word to him. His name, it seemed, was Captain Wix. His voice was deep, rolling, and had the same kindliness as his eyes. Those eyes scarcely left Judith. Straddling on his legs he kept looking at her while Georges quickly whispered. He nodded his head several times, took a great chequered handkerchief from his pocket and blew a blast on his nose.

'It will be good enough for charges,' he rumbled to Georges.

Judith who was adoring this adventure, the dark close cellar, the straw, the swinging lantern, and the sense of having arranged the whole affair, spoke then and said that they had money with them.

'Keep it, lady,' growled Captain Wix. 'Tis no matter.' He became gallant and was inexpressibly comical. 'I have a ship,' he informed her, 'like a daisy. An' you come for a trip in her you shall be as safe and trim as in your mama's parlour. I'll have the cabin done up special for you.' He bent towards her, beamed at her with the greatest kindliness: 'Now what do you say to a piece of fine lace? A present from a friend who knows the coast of France like his own hand. What do you say now to a little trip?'

But here Georges intervened. He drew the gigantic creature

aside, speaking to him very seriously rather as a king speaks to his subject. The matter, it seemed, was concluded. They were to leave Humphrey in Captain Wix's charge.

Reuben went to his brother. When he rejoined them there were tears on his cheeks. Judith then kissed Humphrey.

He spoke with sudden desperation. 'My mother mustn't know . . . I will beat them yet . . .' Then fiercely, catching her hand: 'There's no God . . . Naught but injustice, no mercy . . . I shall find my way yet.'

Captain Wix kissed her hand.

When she went up the little steps again with Georges she felt suddenly helpless, very tired, six years old, and so cross with him that she did not thank him, only said 'Good night' quickly and walked up the street.

Georges, before he went downstairs again, looked after her, smiling. He felt very important, very wise, a ruler of men.

DEATH OF DAVID

THE JULY HEAT bathed the little town in its ardour, but breezes, stealing from the Lake, from the higher woods, from Skiddaw forest and Blencathra shallows, carried the scent of flowers everywhere. The town slept. Some sheep wandered dreamily down Main Street, the dust blew in little spirals between the hedges toward Crosthwaite Church, the post-chaise waited outside the 'Royal Oak', two young men, with nothing whatever to do, lounged up against the wall of Mr Crosthwaite's Museum. A little way up the street a small group waited for the arrival of the Good Intent post-coach from Kendal. It was five minutes past four of the afternoon, and nine out of every ten of Keswick's citizens were still discussing their good liquor and digesting the day's dinner.

Francis Herries came down the sunny street, riding from Penrith. He was, in this July of 1789, twenty-nine years of age and as handsome a bachelor as the counties of Cumberland and Westmorland contained. He was, however, as awe-inspiring as handsome. No young lady anywhere, not even the pretty daughters of Mrs Herring of Bassenthwaite, reputed the most daring young women in the whole of the North of England, had ever attempted a flirtation. He was immensely clever, they said,

was for ever reading. It was true in any case that he had no
close friend – now, riding down Main Street, he seemed alone
with his own shadow.

He may have been half asleep, may have been deeply lost
in some speculation, when he felt a hand laid on his bridle.
He looked down and saw little Mr Summerson the Surgeon,
short, stout, very gay in a purple coat, looking up at him.

'Have you heard the news, Mr Herries?' he asked.

'No,' answered Francis. 'What news?'

'The Bastille in Paris has fallen.'

Francis straightened himself. 'The Bastille?—'

'Yes, sir. Fallen to the Revolutionaries. I know no more. I
had it from Mr Jobling, who has just ridden in from Kendal.
The news is quite certain.'

Francis smiled. 'Thank God, sir. Thank God. This means a
new world.'

Little Mr Summerson looked as though he were not so sure,
but Francis did not wait to hear what he had to say. His heart
triumphant, as though it were by his own agency that this great
deed had been brought about, he passed along the road to
Bassenthwaite now like a conqueror.

The Bastille fallen! The Bastille fallen! It must be true.
Summerson had been certain of it, and if it were indeed so,
then all the secret wishes of his heart were gratified. Secret indeed, for there had been no one in whom he could confide.
The secret history of his mind had been born with him perhaps;
he had always, to his own thinking, been different from all the
others, but its first real mature food had been the treatise of
Helvétius on 'Mind' and 'The System of Nature' of Holbach.
Holbach's work especially had seemed to explain the whole of
life to him; its system of metaphysics had exactly suited his
speculative untrusting nature, his instinctive cynicism, and its
eloquent ardour for physical science had become his ardour also.

Voltaire's scepticism and good sense, the absence of all
fanaticism and mysticism had carried him yet further. He delighted in his clear ideas, his ironical banter, and his determination to make the world a wiser place so that ultimately it
might become a better one.

His education had then been completed by the influence of
Rousseau. The *Contrat Social* seemed to him the Bible of the
new world. This sentence of Rousseau's, 'The moment the
Government usurps the sovereignty, the social compact is
broken, and all the simple citizens regaining by right their natural

liberty are forced, but not morally obliged, to obey' became his gospel.

Had his youth been spent in a larger and more varied society much of the effects of these doctrines might have been worn away in contact with older and more experienced minds. But there had been few with whom he could discuss anything. His nature was in any case reserved; some inherent shyness forbade confidences; his father had views utterly divorced from these; his father was conservative absolutely in religion, politics, agriculture, everything. Will's mind was quite selfish and practical, his mother was not interested in ideas. Judith was only a child.

He made no friends among the gentlemen of the neighbourhood; there were very few gentlemen to make friends with. He knew that had any of them seen into his mind they would have regarded him as traitor to everything in which they believed.

At Penrith there was a certain Mr Frederick Moore, an elderly man, a retired Army officer, who thought as he did, but went much further. Mr Moore was, indeed, a fanatic, and in that displeased the reasonableness of Francis' mind, a strange man, solitary, embittered, intensely dogmatic. But he lent Francis books and pamphlets, and they had many talks together.

Rousseau was Mr Moore's god, and he very quickly became Francis' also. They would neither of them see that Rousseau himself recoiled from many of his own opinions and conclusions. Passionately they out-Rousseaued Rousseau. They disregarded such sentences as: 'If there were a people of gods, they would govern themselves as a democracy. So perfect a form of government is not suited for men' and 'The best and most natural order is, that the wise should govern the multitude, provided that one is sure that they govern it for the profit of the multitude and not for their own'.

But Francis, although he thought continually about Government, had only the simplest notions of the matter. Had he been a fanatic like Mr Moore he would have gone further, but just as his nature held him back from extravagance so also it prevented inspiration. He felt that he was fortunate that he was born to be a citizen of a new world, but in cruel fact he was neither the child of the old world of reason nor of the new world of feeling. He had the misfortune to sympathize deeply with the unhappiness of a vast multitude of human beings, who were only now growing conscious of their rights, but he was an aristocrat by instinct although a democrat by reason – and was too reserved, too lonely, too self-suspicious to venture into any kind of demonstrative action.

He had followed, as well as news-sheets, pamphlets, books, and Mr Moore permitted him, every movement in France – the doctrines of the Economists, who contended for the inviolability of private property, the shameful consequences of the stupid despotism of Louis XV, the iniquitous taxes, the brutalities of the upper class, the exemption of the nobles from taxation, Necker's poor attempts at reform in 1780, the monstrous sale of offices, the increase of tyrannies that followed Turgot's fall, Necker's failure in 1781, and after that the growing incompetence of everybody and everything: the luxury and ostentation of the Court of Versailles, the unpopularity of the Queen, the amiable weakness of the King, the Assembly of Notables by Calonne, their dissolution – until at last he had felt that he was almost a personal witness of the most dramatic of the recent events, the *coup d'état* of May of last year, the convoking of the States-General by Brienne, the strength of the Third Estate, the gradually rising tide of disorder, the flood of revolutionary pamphlets, the bad harvest of '88, and the fearful winter that succeeded it, the freezing of the Seine, the prominence of Mirabeau and Sieyès, of Barnave and Dupont and Bailly, the Oath of the Tennis Court on June 20th.

The Oath of the Tennis Court was the last absolute news that he had had until today; for the last month he had been living in a ferment of expectation and feverish excitement. He could not understand that the men and women around him took so slight an interest in these events. If they spoke of outside affairs at all it was, at the most, in a late day, of the King's sickness, the possibility of a Regency, some new gambling scandal of Charles Fox or the eccentricities of Mr Pitt. The small business of the countryside contented them all.

So he had moved, poor Francis, as though he carried a bomb in his breast. There were times when he thought that he would cross to France and take part in the great crisis that was developing there, but his self-distrust, his natural love of England and his home (cherished passionately in his heart, unguessed at by anyone save possibly Judith) held him where he was.

This great news today released him! The world was free! The strongholds of all the tyrants had fallen! This was to be a symbol that would stand to all the world for the new freedom!

These may seem empty phrases enough set down upon paper, but in Francis' heart they were flames and torches. In very truth, as he rode now under the July sun beside Bassenthwaite, he felt as though every constriction, every doubt of himself, every shyness and stupid caution were now released.

France would lead the way for all the world. He saw Louis with his fat good-natured face, Marie Antoinette with her gay beauty, seated grandly on their thrones by the will of their people. He could almost hear, beside these quiet sparkling waters, the wild cheers, the frantic shouts of joy that must fill the Paris streets. And now all men would hear them, and would be ashamed of their lethargy, their shameful lazy injustice and indifference.

He was indeed ashamed of himself. As he rode along he felt born again; his life had been most selfish. It should be so no longer. At any cost to himself he would take part now in forwarding the new justice and uprightness that was come into the world. As he rode he could have sung his happiness aloud.

He did not doubt but that his father, with all other men, would see the grandeur of this event. His father was a just man, although an obstinate. He loved his father dearly (who could help but love him?), although he was shy of him. How this new era in France would bring them together, would bring all men together and would lead to a new era in England also! As he turned up the lane to Fell House his eyes were dim with tears of joy.

And at once, so characteristically, he was checked by contact with his fellow human beings. A maid, coming from the dairy carrying buckets, Will's tutor seated reading on the lawn, his mother stepping down the staircase as he entered the house, all these drove him at once to silence.

His stout good-humoured sister met him at the turn of the stairs. He had nothing at all in common with Deborah. She had all the good-natured domesticity of a thoroughly contented Herries. So absolutely satisfied was she with herself, her family, all the little circumstances of her surroundings, that in all her twenty-six years she might be said never to have suffered an ache of a pain, whether of body or of soul. She was handsome in a large-boned Herries fashion, was never irritable, never excited, never curious about the nature of other people, always ready to do anything for anyone.

How ridiculous to say to her: 'Deb, the Bastille has fallen!' It would be to her exactly as though you had said: 'Deb, the cat has kittened!'

Having washed, brushed, changed his linen, he came downstairs again, walked into the garden and discovered Judith mocking the tutor. Mr Langbridge was shortly leaving them. Will was now nineteen and did not need a tutor. Mr Langbridge was long, gaunt, perpetually hungry, brilliantly founded in the classics (which was of no use at all to Will), hoping to be a clergyman, of a fanatically serious mind. He understood no sort of humour, and it delighted Judith to hold long conversations with him, asking him gravely about his health, his studies, and his home in Dorset. For he detested the North, with its dark clouds, its rain, the savagery of its people, its bare strong hills. He was a perpetual exile. She stood in front of him now, her hands behind her back, her eyes twinkling, but her expression very serious.

Francis, coming upon her, realized quite suddenly that she was a woman. She was old for her fifteen years in her self-possession, young in her childish impulses. He knew that she adored him, just as she had always done; it had been a long faithful service on her part for which he had made little return. There was something about her small stature, pale face, and almost savage unlikeness to the average Herries order that frightened him, and yet he had long ago realized that she was the only one in this family who ever remotely understood him.

He realized it again now, for as she turned to him he saw that she immediately recognized him to be under the power of some very strong excitement. Mr Langbridge pulled his long lanky body together, rose, very solemnly bowed to Francis and stalked away.

She looked at him, half roguishly, half with that affection that she could never keep from her eyes when she was with anyone of whom she was fond.

'Dear Francis,' she said, dancing about the lawn on her very small feet, 'you have got a secret. I can see that you have. And none of the family is worthy of it.'

She turned towards the house and they both saw David, followed by Will, coming towards them. The whole scene, the rosy brick house with its chimneys and gables and pigeon-loft, the dairy and stables behind it, the moor that was like a heaving green curtain moved with the intensity of the sun, the blue sky without cloud, the lawn so brilliant in colour that it hurt the eye, the trimmed hedge, the Gothic temple, the sprawling shadow of Skiddaw, the figures in their gay clothes, David in purple, Judith in green, Francis in silver, this moment of heat and colour would be remembered by all of them for ever.

David, carrying a riding whip, moved heavily.

'Well, Francis,' he said, 'what news in Penrith?'

'Great news, sir,' Francis answered.

'What! has Pitt a fresh plan for the franchise?' David asked with good-humoured scorn. All Francis' notions seemed to him those of a child. But it was a half-sneer on Will's superior face that drove Francis on.

'No, sir,' he answered. 'The Bastille has fallen to the People of Paris.'

They all stayed, rigid, transfixed. David said at last:

'Where did you have the news?'

'Mr Summerson told me in Keswick. He had it quite surely from Kendal.'

David raised his head and looked at everything, the buildings, the walls, the garden, as though assuring himself that they were all still there, safe and secure. Then he said slowly: 'If this is true it is terrible news.'

'I think,' Francis broke out, 'that it is the grandest news the world has ever had.'

Judith, who cared nothing for the fall of the Bastille in comparison with the immediate dangers of the scene, saw David's broad hand tremble about his riding whip.

'Then you advocate rebellion,' he said slowly, 'murder, revolution . . .'

'Yes,' Francis answered hotly, 'if these things are to bring justice back into the world.'

'Justice!' David's whole body trembled. 'Justice for the dirtiest mob of cut-throats that ever fouled a country. Justice for ingratitude, for disloyalty to a worthy King . . .' He half turned towards the house, then, his face swollen, it seemed, with anger, he came nearer to Francis. 'You are not my son if you find this foul rebellion glorious.'

'Then I am not your son,' Francis cried. 'I have long suspected it. For years I have watched your blindness to the way the world was going. For how much longer do you think a million men will suffer at the orders of one, and of one weaker, more selfish, more tyrannous than they could ever be? Thank God, men are to be free at last, free from tyrants, free . . .'

'From tyrants like myself?' David cried, his anger now quite uncontrollable. 'A fine thing for a son . . .'

'Take it as you will,' Francis answered, his words biting on the air. 'There is tyranny everywhere, here as well . . .'

Some long accumulation of small persistent differences,

always unsettled, mingling with the heat of the July day and
their deep love, always checked, always running into perverse
courses, combined to produce in them both a furious anger.

'By God, for less than that . . .' David cried.

'If your pride is hit,' Francis answered, 'it is by your own will.
It is time that your eyes were opened.'

'I'll have no rebellion here,' David shouted. 'No rebellion
here. Your gutter-friends may for the moment have their way
in Paris. I am yet master in this house.'

'No more!' Francis cried. 'Many masters are falling.'

David raised his riding whip and struck Francis on the cheek.
They were silent then, and the cooing of the pigeons ran like
water through the air, the only sound. Francis bent his head.
David dropped the whip.

'Francis,' he began in a thick low guttural, turned a step
and fell, like a log, to the grass. He was carried in. It was a
stroke. Mr Summerson the Surgeon was fetched from Keswick.
David was bled. Consciousness returned to him, but he could
not speak, and his left side was paralysed.

Francis went about the place with his head up, his features
cold and severe, and agony in his heart. No one, except Judith,
knew that he felt anything. His mother would not speak to him.
That moment, running out on to the sunlit lawn at the sound
of a cry, had changed Sarah Herries from a cheerful normal
woman of her world into a creature of one impulse and one
impulse only. Nothing now was alive for her in the world save
David, her house meant nothing to her, her children meant
nothing to her, she meant nothing at all to herself. She would
not speak to Francis. She looked through him as though he
were not there. She regarded none of them very intently. They
were shadows to her. She seemed in one half-hour to become
of a thinner, straighter figure; the colour left her cheeks, her
eyes held a steely radiance, her voice a hard metallic ring.
Something masculine that had been perhaps always in her personality came out now very queerly, save when she was in
David's room; there she was soft, gentle, maternal. David had
always been her child; now her love for him burnt with twice
the earlier intensity because he was altogether dependent on her.
He lay there, a huge bulk, beneath the clothes, only his eyes
moving.

Judith watched all this with an acute perception, but in the
first weeks her thoughts were all for Francis. She longed to tell
him what she felt; at last she had her opportunity.

One evening, a cold wet August night drawing on, at the turn of the stairs on the upper passage beyond her room, she ran into him in the half dusk. His hands held her in the first shock of contact. She could feel how they trembled. And at once, deeply moved by that trembling, she began, not weighing her words nor thinking of anything but that she must comfort him:

'Don't go. Don't go. I have been wanting to speak to you for these weeks past. I know that you have always a little mocked at my affection for you – indeed I have mocked at it a little myself – but it gives me a right, after all these years, to tell you that I am the only one in all this house who understands you. Don't grieve about him, Francis dear. It was not your fault, indeed, indeed it was not. You had to say what you believed that day, and I know that he admired you for that behind his anger. The stroke must have come in any case – Mr Summerson says so. And his heart, too, has been weak these years past. So soon as he is better he will send for you and tell you that he loves you—'

'My mother will not allow me to see him,' Francis interrupted her.

'She cannot prevent you if he wishes it. As soon as he can speak he will ask for you. I know that now he is sorry and is grieving for you.'

His voice shook. 'No, I must go and never return. I have been a curse to this place. Only I can't go without a word from him. I am waiting only for that—'

'Yes. He is better today. Mr Summerson thinks that in a week or so he will be able to speak a little. The paralysis is only on one side.'

They were in the dark together; neither could clearly see the face of the other, but Judith knew that Francis was crying. Half a child, she was greatly inclined to cry, but she only stood close to him, her hand on his arm.

'You have always been the best friend I have had here,' he said at last.

'And I will be,' she answered.

Afterwards she could not but reflect that she was always better with anyone who was in distress or desired her help. She liked above everything to feel that she was needed, and yet she had a strong contempt for any weak-willed person who was for ever relying on others. What she liked was to assist or direct those who normally were quite able to assist themselves. What she would have done now to have helped Sarah had Sarah

but invited her! But Sarah needed no one's help, and least
of all Judith's. She allowed Deborah to do things for her, and
very remarkably Deborah began to develop under this crisis,
but Judith she completely disregarded.

This, again, was why Judith had no sort of contact with Will.
Will relied on no one but himself and took no one into his
confidences. He gave the impression that he was watching every
move, every phase of the situation, weighing it all that he might
turn it in the best way to his advantage.

The house very quickly suited itself to the new circumstances.
Everything turned now around the room where David was lying.
He had been always greatly popular with his servants; unlike
many men of his time he had always seen them as separate
individuals, was constantly inquiring about their families and
circumstances, had a jolly, natural, healthy interest in all of
them. He had been the one of the family for whom they cared,
who stabilized their loyalty. His simple animal health and boyish
pleasure in little things had always pleased them. He had been
an indulgent but not a foolish master; they were very sorry now
for his misfortune.

David rose with infinite slowness and caution from a sea of
darkness. Wearily he pushed aside fold after fold of heavy clinging cloth that hindered his sight. Then, tired out, he lay back
to resist no longer, and saw swaying above his head a gold
rose set in a green cloud. He heard, a little after, from an infinite distance a voice speaking to him. Someone touched him,
and he sank instantly back into the dark sea whose waters,
smooth like oil, lapped him round and lay upon his eyes and
mouth. Aeons later he saw again the gold rose on the green
ground, and once again heard the voice, and knew that it was
Sarah his wife who was speaking to him.

He raised very slowly his right hand and touched the chill
flesh of his breast beneath his shirt. Then he would raise his
other hand, but he had no other hand. His perceptions moved
with infinite slowness. After, as it seemed to him, a lifetime of
patient watching he realized that the gold rose was fixed in
its place above his head, and that there were other gold roses.
Then, after another infinity of time, he knew that these
gold roses belonged to the tester of the bed in which he was
lying.

His wife's voice was often in his ear. She made a noise like a
bird, like a mouse; the noise came and went and came again.
He was immensely susceptible to light. A wave of light would

slowly sway in front of him, would be withdrawn and then return with greater intensity.

There came a time when he wished to speak about this light but he could not. He could speak no more than a dead man. But he was not dead at all. An urgent pulsing life began to beat within him. This life was connected with nothing that he saw or heard. It had a wild riotous time of its own within him: it laughed, it sang, it wept, it sighed, but it was imprisoned, and it longed to get out. His eyes began to take everything in – the room with the purple curtains, the piece of green tapestry, the crooked legs of the chairs, Sarah, Deborah, the maid, once and again Will. He saw and recognized them all, but he could not speak, nor had they anything to do with the wild life inside him. When he knew this he pitied himself and them; tears, help-less tears, rolled down his cheeks, and his wife wiped them away.

He knew now all the things that they did to him – the things the surgeon did, how it was when they turned him in bed (he was a very heavy man and it was not easy), and when they put a new shirt on him, washed his face. Sarah kissed him, and he touched her cheek with his right hand.

He was never by himself. At night candles were burning, and Sarah sat there, sometimes sewing, sometimes reading a book, her eyes continually going to meet his eyes. He was ashamed at some of the things she must do for him, but she was his wife, he had lain with her in his arms; he would lie there staring at the gold roses and think of how often he had buried his hands in her hair.

He was glad that she was always there, because he was lost in that wild turbulent life within himself, and she was all that there was to call him back. Then one night he was far away. He was standing on a deserted beach beside a lonely sea. Some-one was beside him, a man, and quite suddenly this man raised a stick to strike him. He seized this stick, broke it in half and flung it into the sea. After that this man never left him. He was very tall, thin of face, and he had a scar that ran from eye to lip. The man stood beside him on a green lawn, and this time it was he who had the whip; he raised his hand and struck; as he did so the man changed. He was young, and after he was struck he bent his head.

David lay there for a long while striving to reconcile these two figures. They were the same and were not the same. At one time they seemed to be himself; then they were separate, then together again.

One grey ghostly morning he awoke and knew everything. The man who had wished to strike him was his father; the man whom he had struck was his son. He knew everything. He had been ill, and was lying now in his bed, while beyond the window a bird sang, and near him the candles were almost burnt out, and Sarah sat in a high chair, her head forward, asleep. He passed then, struggling all alone, hours of terrible agony. His left side was dead; there was no feeling nor motion in it. His heart bled for his son. He could think of nothing but that. He must see his son. He must see his son. He raised his right arm: he tried to shout and to shout again. No sound would come. His father and his son. He must ask them both to forgive him; until he had done that there was no peace for him.

At last the door opened; someone came in, carrying something. Sarah woke and came to the bedside. His eyes besought her. He raised his hand. His agony of mind was terrible, for he could not reach her. How strange that he could not reach her! After all these years together, their love, their intercourse, their friendship. She was the mother of his children, and he could not reach her. Strange low mutterings came from his mouth. His eyes implored her, begged of her.

The light, grey, webbed, hung like a film about the room, and in this film she moved. At length she bent down to kiss him, and as she did so, his eyes were so near to hers that she must have seen the agony in them. He made sounds that seemed to him explicit prayers, but she could understand nothing.

It was three hours later that the surgeon understood sufficiently to send for a paper. Then David wrote in a large sprawling hand the word 'Francis'. Francis came. They were alone in the room together, and David spoke the first word since his illness. 'Forgive.' His voice was strange, cracked, with a slur in it, but Francis understood and knelt beside the bed. David, with his trembling right hand, stroked his hair.

After that he could not bear to have Francis out of the room, so that the two of them, Francis and Sarah, were there together. But Sarah would not speak to her son nor look at him if she could help it. David began then the slow business of seeing that two and two make four. There were some things that he could not understand at all. He did not know why he had struck his son with a whip, nor why he was sometimes there quite clearly in the room with his wife beside him and at other times he was in the little dark house in Borrowdale, following his father, hearing his father's voice, and behind the voice the wind rustling the tapestry, and the noise of water falling down the rock.

He slept a great deal, and in his dreams he climbed the rocks, ran across the springing turf of the Fell, stood on the Pass with Sarah in his arms, watching his enemy climb the road towards him.

At times again he would be dreadfully unhappy. Tears would roll down his cheeks; he would wipe them feebly with his hand. But why he was so unhappy he could not tell.

But at these times an infinite pity for himself overwhelmed him. 'Poor David. Poor, poor David. Poor, poor David.' Was there ever anything so sad as poor David – and, from a great distance away, he watched this poor David and sympathized so deeply with his loneliness, his helplessness, the injustice of his state.

After a time words came back to him. He could say 'Francis. Sarah. I don't want. Goodnight.' He mumbled them; his mouth was twisted.

His brain conceived a new map of the world for him. There was the room where he lay. Pieces of furniture became alive and personal to him. A china table, a tea-kettle stand, chairs with faces. He liked especially a ribband-back chair covered with red morocco, a real friend of his, that would smile and wave his leg at him. The tapestry on the wall, its subject Susanna and the Elders, was also his friend. He liked Susanna's kindly breasts and her shining thighs. He was glad that he had not allowed Sarah to make the house in the Gothic style, as she had once planned to do, after Horace Walpole or some other London absurdity. He had an honest scorn for artists and writers. She had wanted a wallpaper printed in perspective, windows with saints in painted glass, and even arrows, long-bows and spears.

Poor Sarah! What a good woman, how wonderful a wife she was to him! He liked her to sit beside the bed and be near to him. He would smile a crooked twisted smile and murmur her name. Yes, all this was real enough. Summerson with his hour-glass, the basins and glasses, old Ballard the manservant with his handsome white wig, Will, Judith, and, above all, Francis. Deborah too, good girl. She had a genius for moving quietly, big woman though she was: no hand so soft as hers, and – best of all – she breathed good-humour. He wanted no sad faces about him; in Sarah's eye he detected sometimes a look of terror and that he would not have because it made himself afraid . . .

Yes, all this was real enough. But beyond the room he could not be sure where he was. The landscape was the landscape of

his young life, and although in this room he was tied to the
heavy four-poster, once he was outside the room he could move
where he wished. Every part of Borrowdale was open to him.
All the old places: beloved Stonethwaite, with its tumbling
stream, the springing turf of Stake Pass, the swinging birds above
Honister, hundreds more; the wrestling bouts, the high room
of old Peel's with its blazing fire and broad rafters, the taste
of the dried salted beef and mutton, the oatmeal puddings, the
bull-ring in Keswick, when on a grand day in the market place
you must sit on an adjoining roof to get a view, the shearing days
with the chairing and the bell-ringing, Twelfth Night when the
lighted holly tree was carried from inn to inn – all had departed
from him so long, long ago, killed by the later modern times, but
now he was back in them again, all his health and vigour were
returned, he was the strongest man in all the valley, and every
hill knew him, Glaramara smiled on him, Eagle Crag was his
brother, Sprinkling Tarn his sister, Sea Fell his lover . . .

He lay there, motionless, smiling, his blue eyes fixed on the
gold rose. They thought that he was imprisoned there, a helpless
hulk. Little they knew! He was free again, as he had not been
for many a year.

His father now accompanied him everywhere. His father
digging that intractable ground, riding with him to Ravenglass,
sitting beside him at the old stone fireplace in Herries, his hand
on his thigh, his father and Mirabell, his father and Deborah,
his father who had been always closer to him than any other
human being.

They wished to pull him back from this happiness, this freedom, this strength of body, and cold running air of the fells,
smell of the bracken, sound never stilled of running water. The
sheep moved, the sun glistening on their fleecy sides, the shepherd whistled to his dog, the clouds rushed out and covered the
sun that yet escaped them, mocking them and flashing a shield
of light upon the distant brow . . .

'Hold on to me, Father. They are dragging me back. I will
catch your arm. They shall not separate us . . .'

It was time for him to be washed, to be turned in his bed.
The smell of the sick-room was there, the chair with the red
morocco, Susanna with her breasts, Sarah's grave face and that
look of terror in the eyes. Only Francis and Judith knew his
father. That child with her pale face and red hair, hair like
Mirabell's. Poor Mirabell . . . but no, she was not to be pitied,
for she loved his father at the last . . .

His mouth crookedly formed the word 'Judith'. She came to the bedside, not frightened like Sarah, smiling, standing on her toes to be level with the bed. He took her hand in his. It lay there warm and soft.

'Judith.' That was the last word that he spoke.

For he was swung away in a great torrent of light. He flew on the air, kicking his limbs free, his head up, his hair tugged at by the wind. Away and away, over Borrowdale and Stonethwaite, over Sea Fell and the Langdales, over Waswater, black like ebony . . . What freedom, what happiness!

He shouted; 'Oh, hoi! Oh, hoi! Oh, hoi!' He came swinging down until the turf sprang beneath his feet. He was leader in an immortal chase. 'Oh, hoi! Oh, hoi! Away! Away!' The scent of the bracken and the falling leaf, the touch of the stone of the little running walls! He had caught a cloud and swung into the dazzling sun. Old Herries was at his side, the moulded shoulders of the Tops were beneath his hand, the ruffled water of the Lakes spun to the swirl of his great strength.

'Follow! Follow! Away, away!'

His father and he, masters of the air, friends of every hill, laughing with every twist of tarn and river, raced towards the sun . . .

Watching the bed, they saw his body lie motionless: the eyes stared.

Sarah's scream brought Deborah running into the room.

QUARREL AND FLIGHT

JUDITH AWOKE TO a sudden consciousness of distress. She had been very happily asleep curled up in the corner of the settee with the green Chinese dragons. These dragons had pursued her very pleasantly in her dream, large amiable creatures with green scales; from their bodies flakes detached themselves (as they ambled along) and lay like green pennies on the hot dry sand.

It was so hot, this sandy country, that she woke with a start to find the warm spring sun shining in through the window on to her face. She looked about her, bewildered, on to the Sheffield-plated candlesticks and the blue and white china in the corner cupboard. With the final release from her dream she pushed a large, fat, beery, and most affectionate dragon away from her and sat up, listening. What she heard was Sarah, in the room across the hall, talking to herself.

Sarah was not talking to herself, she was talking to David. Judith knew exactly how it was; Sarah was walking quietly up and down the room and was begging David to return, was telling David that she could not endure life without him, was asking David how he could have left her.

These outbursts were becoming rarer with Sarah, but they were still constant enough to fill the house with uneasiness. She had been for years the happiest, most normal of women. One man's death had changed her from that into this suffering remote figure, who was battling, who had been battling for months, to recover her security. Soon she would be armoured again safely against life, but the old Sarah was dead, vanished for ever, and happiness was, for the time, gone from that house.

It was part of Judith's character that she had no patience at all with nerves or hysteria. It was a period when women enjoyed and fostered all the artificialities that might give them an important place in a world designed entirely for men. 'Vapours' were the order of the day for the majority of God's females. If they could not rouse attention by one manoeuvre they would rouse it by another.

Judith had never had the 'vapours' nor would she ever have them. Nevertheless, she was near sixteen, and had the understanding, in many things, of a grown woman. Her education in life had been, thanks to Tom Gauntry and his friends, early and thorough. She realized that this was no nonsense nor affectation on Sarah's part. David's death had simply taken away from her all the ground on which for years she had been standing. She was fighting to regain her sure footing; she would regain it. Meanwhile she would allow no one to help her.

Now, as Judith listened to that murmuring voice, she longed to go and help her. She knew, if she did go, the kind of treatment that she would receive. The only person in the world who could assist her now crossed the hall and went in to her. Deborah's soft comforting voice could be heard. A little later the two women passed out into the garden together.

It was one of Judith's deepest chagrins that in all this crisis she had been of no use at all. It was Deborah, of all people, who had saved the situation, stout dull Deborah who was suddenly the principal figure in the house, was kind and tactful with everyone, managed the servants, entertained the local gentry, kept the accounts, prevented Will (when at home) and Francis from open quarrel and understood Judith, it seemed, better than anyone had ever done. This had been that quiet woman's chance and she had seized it.

In the year that followed David's death the situation had demanded exactly such a woman as Deborah. She had always seemed slow, unobservant, uninterested; now it was apparent that she observed much and was never uninterested. She was greatly assisted by limiting her horizon to her own affairs. That France was in revolution, that her mother was in hysteria, these were not her business. She had loved her father as well, possibly, as any of them, but her father was dead, life must go on, the cows must be milked, intercourse with neighbours resumed. She quietly assumed direction of the house.

Had Will been there her domination might not have so quickly succeeded, but Will was in Liverpool, forming new contracts with Mr Metcalfe. Francis also was away for days at a time. The house became the abode of the three women, and had it not been for Deborah, catastrophe would have rent it from attic to cellar. For Sarah, in the strange unnatural world that she now inhabited, had a fierce and unresting grudge against Judith. Judith's name had been the last word on David's lips, it was into Judith's eyes that David had looked before he turned his head on the pillow and passed. Judith was to Sarah still the strange unaccountable child that she had been ten years ago. At that time a girl of sixteen was often a mature woman, but Judith was for Sarah still a rebellious intriguing child, born of a gipsy. These things are mysteries, but beyond question there mingled now in Sarah's feelings about Judith something of her old uneasiness with Mirabell. Mirabell, Judith's mother, had never liked her, had indeed refused her kindliness and friendliness. Here was Mirabell born again.

But Judith was not Mirabell; she was fiercer, more readily hostile and resentful, far more dominating. She would not let Sarah hate her without making some return for it. It was not her fault that David had said her name before he died. If anyone wished to make a friend of her she was ready, but she was ready – oh, exceedingly ready – for anyone who wanted her as enemy.

Deborah disregarded all this. She was loving to Sarah, loving to Judith, loving to Francis, to whom even now, after these many months, his mother would not speak. Deborah took the situation and kept it, for the moment, safe. She could not keep it safe for long – it was charged with violence and danger – but what she could do she did. She indulged also her own fancy. Her fancy was, and had always been, for social amenities. She loved tea-drinkings, card parties, evenings, when some neighbour 'put up' four or six couples for a dance, expeditions of a moderate kind to some interesting site or historic building, and, above all, the chatter that circled around love-affairs and interesting engagements.

She had now entirely her own way in this, for Sarah was living altogether in her own world. When a decent interval had passed since David's death, neighbours came and went at Uldale with an easy frequency unknown for some time past. There were the Redlands of Thornthwaite, the Darlingtons from Whelpo, the Berrys of Roseley, the Carringtons of Forest Hall. It was suddenly a woman's world, and a world that seemed to Judith ridiculous in its obsession with trifles and incredible in its indifference to all outside events.

Deborah's principal friends were the Redlands of Thornthwaite – Squire Redland, his stout pleasant wife, and the two handsome Miss Redlands – and the two Miss Berrys of Roseley. The elder Miss Berry was the great gossip of the district. She found everything amusing and left everything scandalous. The Miss Redlands, dark, big-boned, handsome women, were the flirts of the district. Their thought was only of men. Mrs Redland had a genius for the arrangement, in other people's houses, of teas and suppers, parties at cards and little musical occasions.

Hours – and for Deborah most enchanting hours – would be spent in the discussion of social combinations and permutations. Mrs Redland had the talent of making any house in which she happened to be visiting appear instantly as her own. She was massive, enjoyed bright colours and had a laugh like a trooper. She would arrange herself on the settee with the green dragons and instantly begin:

'But, my dear Miss Berry, we must not be too nice. Invite them all. Why not ? They are a standing example of good humour and amiable intention, and I am sure Mr Frank Fuller, although he may be the oddest creature in the world, is a gentleman, which cannot be said for Mr Beaton, who has a store of underbred finery quite amazing.'

And little Miss Berry, with her sniff that suggested an eternal cold, would observe:

'Mr Beaton is a coxcomb as everyone knows. But there is nothing to be ashamed of in being a coxcomb. What he enjoys the most is an evening of noisy entertainment, and for my part there are times when noisy entertainment is the thing. Ask Mr Beaton by all means. That will make six couples exactly.'

'And this time,' Mrs Redland would say, looking about her, 'we will make the dining-room of use by shifting the pianoforte. Last time there was not room for anyone to have real enjoyment.'

And Judith, listening, would wonder that Deborah had the patience to submit to these ladies who ordered the house as their own. But, indeed, she herself was not at all popular with them. They wondered why this sulky sarcastic girl was there. Was she 'out' or was she not 'out'? Was it true that she was the love-child of some peasant courted in the ditch by that old ruffian of a Herries, who had died in a hut in Borrowdale?

David was only a year dead, and they were dancing in his house. But if Sarah made no objection to it had anyone else a right? Sarah's face was now a mask. She sat in her upstairs room, looking from her window. There were some days when no one came to the house at all, and then, so eerie was the silence, so threatening the atmosphere, that Judith understood why Deborah encouraged her sociabilities.

But with every week the inevitable crisis drew nearer. Francis was absent during all that summer. Will came and went, but in November, two days after Judith's sixteenth birthday, Francis returned – and life was permanently changed for them all for ever after.

His return was innocent and quiet enough. There was a storm of rain. Skiddaw was hid in purple shadow and over its head an ebony lake of cloud hung like a reflection. Beyond it, towards the sea, faint strips of blue sky showed that it was but a shower. The rain fell like thunder. Mrs Redland and one of her daughters, the two Miss Berrys, Deborah and Judith sat in the parlour and waited for the rain to pass. A dance – arranged entirely by Mrs Redland – was to take place in the following week at the Darlingtons'. The Darlingtons were lazy, but good-natured. They did not mind at all that Mrs Redland should consider their house as hers so long as she did all the work for them. She was now in high feather. All the invitations had been successful. There were to be eight couples.

Mrs Redland was pretending to be angry with Miss Berry's imitation of old Miss Clynes, whose teeth clicked in her head like castanets. 'For shame, Miss Berry, you shall not mimic her! And as to young Mr Clynes, he is perfectly satisfied with his sheep and his farm.'

'Yes,' cried Miss Berry in an ecstasy of enjoyment at her own

sense of fun and humour, 'and they say that coming in the dark
into the house one day he took his aunt for one of his sheep that
had been straying all the afternoon. "Shoo! Shoo! Shoo!" he
cried. And you know how the good lady, when she is but half
awake, baas for anyone who is close to her ... Well, well, I've
no doubt but the young man will make a match of it with Jane
Bastable. Poor thing. She missed the dancing master last year,
although she trudged into Keswick twice a week and oftener ...
"Baa, baa!", and it wasn't until the young man lit a candle that
he saw how things really were.'

Miss Berry's imitation was most lively, and they were all in a
roar of laughter over it when the door burst open and Francis
Herries, the capes of his riding coat dripping with water, stood
there, glared fiercely for a moment, and was gone.

Judith, who had been sitting by herself in the window
watching the black cloud above Skiddaw shred into a dozen fish-
tails, hating Mrs Redland and Miss Berry, wondering what end
all this unhappiness in the house could have, seeing him, sprang
up and went out.

She saw him standing in the hall, that was dark with a kind
of smoky reflection of the rain, as though bewildered. He looked
at her, and without a word turned into the little room that had
been always David's sanctum, a cold and cheerless little room
now; here were cases with old books that David had never read,
but his chair was there, a table with some of his papers and the
prints of Derwentwater, Keswick, Borrowdale that he had dearly
loved.

Judith followed Francis there. He had flung off his cloak and
turned to her, his face working with anger and impatience.

'The house is changed,' he said bitterly. 'It is no home for
either of us any more ... Where is my mother?'

'In her room. Oh, Francis, I am so glad that you have returned!'

'I have come back with a purpose. This cannot continue.
My mother must speak to me for there are things that must be
settled. This silence has lasted a year, and I will have no more
of it.'

He looked so unhappy, so desolate, as he stood there that her
heart ached for him, and the anger that had been piling up all
these months at the treatment of both himself and her reached at
that moment its crisis. She felt that the time had come for a
settlement, and she was glad of it.

'Oh, Francis, isn't it the strangest thing! She loved you so.

She was always so kind and so good. I have thought that it was a sickness that would pass, but you are right; it must be brought to an issue . . .'

She recollected in that instant the scene in the cellar at Cockermouth, when Humphrey Sunwood, outcast and fugitive, had said farewell to her. Now she and Francis were outcast and fugitive: for no fault of theirs. She thought, standing in that room, of David's kindliness and benignity. Were his ghost with them now he must grieve at these circumstances. Oh, if he were only here, if he were only here!

'You do not know,' Francis went on rapidly, his voice trembling with emotion, 'that two weeks ago from Penrith I wrote to my mother. I said everything in that letter, of my love for my father, of my great unhappiness, that I was the cause of his sickness, that I would never, never, so long as I lived, forgive myself for that, but that I loved her too, that I loved her the more for my own fault, that I had borne patiently all these months her silence and that I had well deserved it, but that this must have some limit because I loved her, because I loved our home . . .' His voice broke. He turned, leaned his head on his arms against the fireplace. For a little the only sound in the room was the driving rain. When he looked up and spoke again his voice was stern and resolved.

'She did not answer my letter. I have waited these two weeks. So now it must end. I must know one way or another.'

'Yes, it must end,' Judith answered. 'For all our sakes . . .'

'I am going to her now.'

He left the room. She stood there, heard him mount the stairs. In a little while the rain had stopped. She heard the ladies come out, chatter, laugh, depart. Deborah came past the open door, but did not look in, and moved slowly into the servants' part of the house. Still there was no sound from upstairs. Then, quite sharply, Francis' voice rang out, one word cutting the air like a snapped stick. Judith, driven by an impulse that was entirely beyond her governance, ran up the stairs, stayed for a moment, then, her face hardening into resolve, walked down the passage.

She pushed Sarah's door open and went in. The room that Sarah had chosen for herself after David's death was a small bare one. Over the fireplace was a highly coloured, badly painted picture of David. It had been done by some travelling artist some ten years before, and showed David complacent in full wig, a crimson coat and flowered vest, red-cheeked, exceedingly amiable.

He grinned down at Sarah, his wife, who sat in a chair of crimson morocco; her hair, her face, grey, her dress black, a ghost of desperate anger and unhappiness. It was the unhappiness that Judith, standing in the doorway, first saw, then, a second later, she was engulfed in the anger as though she had to push up her head to avoid drowning in it. She closed the door.

'I will not speak either to him or to you!' Sarah cried, her hand trembling on her chair.

Francis, in entire command of himself, was by the window. He came forward.

'I am glad you have come, Judith,' he said. 'I would have a witness to this. After twelve months my mother has at length addressed me . . .' He went close to her. His voice was tender and full of affection. 'I cried out at what you said, Mother, but you have a right to say what you wish. You have told me to go and never to come back. I will go, but not before you have heard me.'

She did not look at him, but, half rising in her chair, spoke to Judith.

'I know that you are on his side,' she said, 'but that is no new thing. Ever since they brought you to this house as a baby you have made nothing but evil here. You have never belonged here, and it is quite fitting that you should take the part of the son who killed his father, leaving us all desolate.'

Even as her face was a mask hiding some real woman under it, so her voice was not her own. Judith had a queer perception of the old, rather tired, very quiet woman that Sarah would be after this sickness was over, as unlike the woman that she had once been as this present woman was unlike. She had a strange conviction, as though someone spoke to her, that throughout this scene she must keep that old tired woman in her mind, so she would be kinder and more just.

No one could be more just or more decent than Francis.

'Listen, Mother,' he said. 'You *shall* attend to me, for later when you look back you will be glad that you heard me. You loved Father. God knows I did also. My love is something; you cannot take it from me. But I could not deny my nature, neither for you nor Father nor anyone. That nature has always put me by myself, alone. I tell you now so that you may remember it after, that I would change it, God knows how I would change it, if I could. And is it not enough that I must carry with me all my life the knowledge that it was my insane obstinacy that killed Father; is not that some punishment for a man? Did he not himself forgive me? Was he not the most generous-hearted of men, and can we not now, who both loved him, find some ground in his generosity and make a peace? Mother—'

He approached her. She drew back violently, almost pushing the chair over. Then she rose, swept by him as though he were not there, and went to the window.

'Very well,' she said, 'if you wish it you shall hear me. I was a happy woman; you have made me an unhappy woman. I had a home, a husband whom I loved; I have nothing any more. You say it was only your nature. Very well, I am an enemy of that nature. I was your mother. I am so no more. I do not know you. You may remain in this house if you will. You have the right. I believe the house is now yours. I will leave it if you wish. But understand, if you stay and I stay I do not know you. We remain as strangers.'

She beat her hand against her black dress, her fingers scraping the silk as though her control was almost exhausted. Yet her eyes, looking beyond them both into some mysterious distance, seemed to say: 'I am imprisoned here. These words are not mine. I do not know who is the speaker.'

Francis turned to Judith with a gesture as though of despair.

'No,' he said, 'I will not go like that. I am no stranger to you whatever I have done. You have borne me, suckled me. I have lain on your breast. Things cannot be ended . . .'

'Listen then,' she interrupted quickly. 'I was once a girl, very unhappy. Your father came and rescued me, fought for me, married me. From the first moment that I saw him I worshipped him. I bore him three children. Now I have but two. Can you understand *that* then? That . . . That . . .'

But Judith, furious with what seemed to her the theatrical falseness of a woman hugging with a sort of selfish joy the self-inflicted tragedy, broke in:

'I have something to say in this. I am a woman, Sarah, as you are a woman. I am a child no longer. What right have you to fancy your grief is yours alone? For a year and more you have walked by yourself, hugging your wrongs, and you have hugged them so long that you are a comic figure, not real at all. We have all endured your nonsense long enough. Oh yes, you can order me to go. I know that I have no place here any more. I am going. But Francis is another matter. For a whole year, with absolute patience, he has endured your tantrums and bewailings. He is offering you now your last opportunity. Lose it, and when you come to your senses again you will whistle for him back and whistle to empty air. If I were your daughter I could show you something. You adore David, yes, but you allow the house to be filled with chattering women, and Mr Finch comes with his fiddle from Keswick, and the pianoforte is moved to have room for another two couple, and—'

She paused for breath. She was in one of her rages, almost dancing on the Turkey carpet.

Sarah broke into her pause.

'No, you are right, Judith. You are no child of mine. Thank God for it. We, at least, have been strangers always. I see no kind of reason for you to intervene in this. Francis is the master here now. If he wishes you here I have no say. If you think me a comic figure, that also is of no importance. I did not ask you to come and wrangle here. I may be allowed, perhaps, another room where I may be by myself. When you have finished, if you wish to stay here, I will go.'

Then Francis turned to her, his face lit with a most noble generosity and kindness.

'Mother, listen. Why should you cut yourself off? You have been angry with me long enough. Were Father here he would laugh at all of us. There are never so many in the world who are our own stock, our own flesh and blood, that we should separate ourselves from those we have. I have told you that all my life long I shall carry with me the burden of my father's death. But life is not over for that. Would my father wish us, because he is gone, to spoil our lives for him? He would be the last, the very last in the world, to tolerate it. He loved life, every piece of it, and he loved friendship and fellowship and the forgetting of injuries. He never grudged an injury his whole life long. You know that he did not. He has forgiven me, although I cannot forgive myself. Dear Mother, in his name, forgive me too. Let me be your son again; come out and make this house real. I will be as true a son to you—'

She broke in: 'No. No. Never! You, both of you together, do you think I cannot see into your hearts? Do you think this treachery is a new thing to me? Make no mistake. I know you – and now, perhaps, you will allow me to find another room.'

Judith cried: 'You shall not go like that. Listen. You say that I have been false to you all my life long. I know that I haven't been good. I have always found discipline hard; not *your* discipline, Sarah. Any discipline. But I think, looking back, that you were always very kind to me. You never saw that I was always older than I should be, that I was disgraced by my own impulse to be for ever making new resolutions that I couldn't fulfil. There was no more evil in it than that. The greatest kindness you could ever show me was to let me have my own way that I might quickly discover how foolish my own way was. But there was no more wilfulness than that. I have always cared for you, Sarah, and now when I leave you, as I shall do this very night, I want you only to remember afterwards that I would tell you truths while I can and wish you well.

'And it is for that, because I wish you so well, that I beg you not to lose Francis. He is right. David's death is no reason for any separation. Keep him with you. His situation should secure your compassion, not your anger—'

Francis broke in: 'Judith, you are not to go.'

But Sarah was already at the door: 'Our worlds are separate, Francis,' she said, more quietly than she had hitherto spoken. 'You have thought me comic, Judith, in my selfishness. There you are doubtless right. Only I pray God that you may never know the unhappiness that I know. I did not think there could be such an unhappiness in the world and anyone live with it.'

She opened the door and went out.

Judith stared at the picture of the rubicund and complacent David.

'When he was alive,' she said, 'Sarah was quiet enough in her affections. She loved him, but not to any desperation. Francis, I hate women with their exaggeration and sentiment. There is something rotten here like a poison.'

He sighed wearily, stroking his forehead with his hand.

'No. There is a reality in it somewhere. I always knew that we were nothing to her compared with my father. He filled her whole vision, and now she is lost.'

'I will never be that for a man,' Judith answered sharply. 'Mark you that, Francis. Never, never, never!'

She went up to him, stood on tiptoe, kissed his forehead.

'Dear Francis, goodnight.'

He did not attempt to stop her, but stood there, lost in his own problem.

'Even he,' she thought, 'does not want me here.'

Indeed, when she reached her room, she felt more desolate than ever before in her life. She belonged now to exactly no one at all.

She must go at once, this very night, but she had no doubt at all as to what this going meant. She was going now once and

for ever. This place was never again to be her home, or so at least
she thought, being no witch to see in a glass her future.

She looked about her little room that had been the same ever
since her babyhood. There was the oak-panelled armchair, the
tallboy, the bed with the faded cherry-coloured hangings.

She got out of the drawer her childhood treasures: the fox's
brush from Tom Gauntry, the book on cock-fighting, the china
jar with the orange flowers, the two rag 'babies' and, best loved
of all, the Bible with the wood-cuts that Reuben had given her.

She smiled when she looked at them, but smiled quite without
sentiment. Her childhood was over, quite finally, for ever. And
she was not sorry. It had been a mischancy ill-fitting time. Yes,
that was one thing, but this sudden exile into a vast uncanny
world was quite another. Suppose Tom Gauntry didn't want
her? He was growing old now and was uneasily under the
domination of his cook, Emma Furze ... Oh, well, if he didn't
want her, there were other places. She could work; she wasn't
afraid of anyone.

Then, quite unaccountably, she wanted to cry. Indeed,
indignantly, she brushed some tears from her eyes. How she
wished that Reuben was here! He loved her, and only he in all
the world. Poor clumsy, fat-faced, kindly Reuben. She hadn't
seen him for six months. Deborah Sunwood, too, was altered
since Humphrey's troubles, not the same bright tranquil woman
as before, and Reuben was so restless that he might be away
from Cockermouth any time.

Something had happened to them all, just as it was happening
to the larger, outside world, breaking up all the old moulds,
busily forming new ones that would be, no doubt, very like the
old ones when they were settled.

But the thought of the change and of some movement in the
world very much larger than her own little trivial affairs stirred
her to action. There were no tears any more. She would go to
Stone Ends tonight, and if they did not want her there she would
move on. What of London? There were Herries there, who would
help her. After all she *was* a Herries, whatever they might say.
And at that she thought suddenly of Georges Paris. She had
seen him once and heard from him twice since the adventure
with Humphrey in Cockermouth. The time she had seen him
had been at Stone Ends; they had not been alone, had had few
words, but there had been something in a kind of mocking
proprietary air that he had had that had not altogether pleased
her. Nevertheless, he had grown extraordinarily handsome,

slender, dark, with a sort of sword-like sharpness and brilliance. He shone among all those befuddled squires and hunting men at Gauntry's like a prince in disguise. Oh no, she was not romantic about him. She knew his selfishness and conceit and laziness well enough, but when he was near to her, looked at her, touched her, he stirred her blood, and she liked her blood to be stirred. She liked anything, any risk, any danger, rather than stagnation. That Georges Paris *was* a danger she never disguised from herself for a single moment.

Well, she must be moving. She wanted to get away from the house, away from Sarah's sickness, from Francis' unhappiness, from Deborah's chattering women, as quickly as might be.

She began to turn everything out, her possessions, clothes, hats and shoes, until they lay all over the room. Then she decided to take nothing with her. She would ride over on the cob to Stone Ends and send for her things.

She smiled as she remembered the time when, years ago, after David's whipping her, she had climbed out of the window and ridden away.

It should not be so dramatic an exit this time.

But, in honest fact, when at last she walked out of the house she heard no sound, she met no one. It was as though she were going out of a dead house.

Out of a dead house into life.

MADAME PARIS

SHE WENT ALONG on her horse – clop-clop, clop-clop – and with every ring of the road she was more surely leaving everything behind.

She saw nothing, thought of nothing outside herself. The separate strains fighting for order in her mind slowly, by a kind of reluctant agreement, as though they were obeying commands against their will, sulkily settled themselves.

'I have left everything behind me, and I am going out into nothing – or perhaps everything. Everyone with whom I have had to do has been showing Sensibility about something, even Will. But I wish to show Sensibility about nothing. I have only myself to consider. Even Francis does not need me. I am nearer to my dead father and mother than I am to anyone else. But

there also I will not show Sensibility. They are dead and dead
for always. I shall never see them or speak to them. I may have
feeling in me that comes from them, but they cannot help me.
They will not weep if I come to disaster. They will not answer
if I call. Who is in my life ? David is dead. Sarah has just thrown
me out, Will and Francis think of themselves, Deborah is
nothing, Deborah Sunwood has her husband and is grieving
for Humphrey, Reuben thinks about God, Tom Gauntry to
whom I am going is old and loves his cook, Georges – Georges
wishes to kiss me when he sees me. Otherwise I am nothing to
him. There is nobody at all who needs me. So far as I can tell,
I have not a penny in the world, although Francis would, I
suppose, give me some money if I asked him. I shall not ask
him. I have no friends, no money, no work.

'I am sixteen years of age, with fine hair, a poor complexion,
a nose too large, and ridiculously small stature. I have no
especial intelligence, but I know when persons are speaking to
me and I remember something of what they say. I have never
been afraid of anybody or anything, but I have not as yet met
anybody or anything to be afraid of.

'I have never had a lover, but am very ready to have one. I
am curious about love. I expect that love itself is nothing very
fine, but I could care for somebody very deeply. I would wish to
have children that I might care for them. Is this Sensibility ?
I do not mind whether it be so or not.

'I know nothing as yet about the outside world, but I am
extremely inquisitive concerning it, nor do I believe, like Mrs
Redland or Miss Berry or Deborah, that it spreads no farther
than Kendal. I would be interested to see many countries, and
the Revolution in France is a very exciting event. I would like
to see Mr Pitt and Mr Fox and the King and Queen (although
they do not appear to be interesting).

'I fancy that I have no very good Disposition. I have a violent
temper and dislike to be opposed in anything, but when my
affections are roused there is nothing I will not do. Is this
Sensibility ? I fancy that it is.

'I am not a child any more but a woman. When did this
change come to me ? I think that day in Cockermouth with
Humphrey. I had no concern that day as to what happened. I
knew that whatever happened I could master it.

'I love this part of England. This is undoubtedly Sensibility,
but I do not mind if it is. I do not wish ever to live anywhere
else, although I wish to see other places. I would like to marry

a man here, and have children here close to where I was born . . .

'Because of my father I am very proud to be a Herries. I would like to meet all the different Herries, although I am sure that I should not wish to be with most of them very long. I find that it is in my nature to hate people very much and to love people very much, and also to laugh at everybody and also myself when I am very angry.

'I do not think that there is a God or that Reuben saw Him on the road outside Tours. If there is one He is stupid because He has so much power and makes very little of it. Neither Francis nor Georges thinks there is a God.

'When I have some money I shall be very good at managing it. I am very good at managing anything if no one is in my way. I am not sorry for Sarah as I should be. She likes to be miserable, because she has never been miserable before. It is a new feeling for her. I am sorry for Francis, because he will remember all his life about David, which is a sad waste of time. I am resolved to make my life very amusing.'

With this she discovered that she was outside the gate of Stone Ends. The house was dead. A thin quarter moon hung like a wisp of pale rag over the end of a dirty silver-edged cloud, and, washed by ghostly mist, the house showed nothing human. She tied the horse to the gate and walked up the irregular stone path to the old worm-eaten door. At the sound of the banging knocker all the dogs in the house set up a fearful yelling and barking.

There was a pause, and Judith felt desperately cold and frightened. Suppose the old man didn't want her? He had been always good to her, but now he was aged and ailing, and under the thumb of his cook, people said. Suppose he didn't want her? And the wind, blowing sharply from Skiddaw, rustled all the plants in the weedy neglected garden in melancholy echo. One thing she noticed. The fountain was no longer playing. That had been Tom Gauntry's great pride, and his boast was that, however badly things went, he would always have enough water for the fountain. An owl hooted.

'You see,' said the owl, 'we haven't water enough any longer.'

There was a great unrasping of bolts from within, and then the door slowly opened. Old Tom Gauntry, holding a blowing candle, stood there, and a comical figure he looked. He was in a nightdress, black stockings and dingy slippers, and he wore a very long nightcap with a red worsted tip to it. Over his nightdress he had flung an old riding coat. He peered out, shivering,

his old wrinkled face like an anxious monkey's. When he saw
who it was he gave a cry.

'Judy. By God, 'tis Judy!'

He looked so comical, with his nightcap, his nose dripping,
his unshaven chin, that she couldn't help herself. She began to
laugh, and then the cold and her own most uncertain situation
in some strange way forcing her, once she had begun to laugh
she couldn't stop. She pushed past him, to get in out of the cold,
and then laughed and laughed and laughed.

'Judy! For Almighty sake shut the damned door. I've a cursed
cold on me.'

'I must go and look after the horse first,' she said. 'Where's
Wull?'

He began calling 'Wull! Wull! You devil, where are you?
Wull! Wull!,' and all the dogs began to bark.

While she was standing there she could take in the scene,
which was certainly funny enough. The old hall stank of dogs,
drink, damp. Dogs as usual were all about the place, scratching, sleeping, suddenly lifting up their heads and howling. In the
stone fireplace a great fire was roaring up the chimney. In the
ingle two old men, one in an untidy wig, one bald-headed, were
sitting. On a table near them was a large bowl with a ladle in
it, and, her head resting on the table, slept Emma Furze, a tall
woman, snoring lustily.

'Hush!' said Judith. 'You'll wake her.'

'The last trump won't wake her,' cried Gauntry. He was
rather drunken, but not badly so. 'Wull! Wull! Where the hell
are you?'

Wull appeared, yawning, scratching his untidy head, his
shirt hanging out over his breeches.

'Take Miss Judith's horse to the stable.' He put his old horny
hand on her arm. 'Come to the fire and get warm, my pretty.'

She came to the fire and was introduced to the old men.

'This is my ancient friend, Mr Jeremy Cards. He's a relation
of yours. And this is Joe Twisset, he's a relation of none but the
devil.' He kicked and cuffed the dogs, who, however, knew Judith
and jumped about her, licking her hand. She went to the fire
and stood in front of it roasting herself. She smiled on the two
old men.

She was suddenly happy. She was at home here. The dogs,
the smells, the old men, they were all right. She could manage
it all very comfortably.

Gauntry was delighted to see her. She was, as he explained to

the two old men, his especial pet, his pride, his joy. And although
he was rather drunk he meant it all. The two old men were
rather drunk too, but blinked their eyes in the firelight, rubbed
their hands and looked happy.

'But why, my pretty, have you come so late? You should be
abed, a child like you.' Sniff, sniff, sneeze, sneeze. 'I've a hell
of a cold, a damnable hellish cold, and I'm not as young as I
was.'

Judith explained that she had left Fell House for ever. She
said very little about it. She had taken off her hat, and her hair
burnt in the firelight. The old men looked at it admiringly.

'Yoicks! Yoicks! Hurray for ever!' Gauntry was delighted.
'Didn't I know it was coming? "Wait a bit, you old devil," I
said to myself. "She'll be coming to you. Just be patient a
trifle." This is your cousin,' he added, pointing to the old man
in the wig, 'and it's certain he's delighted to see you. Aren't you,
Jeremy?' he shouted in the old man's ear. 'This is Judy Herries,
daughter to Francis. She's your cousin, you old bastard!'

Old Jeremy Cards rose on his trembling legs and made a low
bow.

'I knew your father, my dear, and a fine grand man he was.
I was born in 1712, I was, and I'm seventy-eight years of age
and got my full sight and everything, but my hearing's failing
a trifle. My right ear's the one for you to speak into if you'll be
so good. It was in 1763 I saw your father last in the town of
Kendal, and I remember like yesterday . . .'

'Well enough, well enough,' Gauntry broke in. 'You must
drink something, my pretty, and then we'll find a bed for you.
Before she wakes,' he added, suddenly dropping his voice.
'Better get settled before she wakes. Although I can manage
her, mind you. She's afraid of me, she is, but she's a good soul
when she's sober, and an old man like me can't be expecting
young beauties at his time o' life. Down, Roger, get out of it,
Trixie . . . The dogs know you well enough. So they should. This
is your proper home, my dear. Didn't I find you when you were
not a day born? By God and I did! Have something to warm you,
my pretty.'

She was glad enough of the hot strong drink. Wull came in to
say that the horse was stabled. The old kitchen clock rivalled
Mrs Furze's snores. All was cosy and comfortable.

Judith told the three old men about the scene at Uldale,
and they nodded their sympathy, but old Jeremy Cards was
galvanized to an extraordinary life by the very mention of the

Herries family. So David was dead! Aye, aye – a pity, a pity! He'd
known him as a fine young man who could cross-buttock anyone
in the country. When would that be now ? Aye, 1742, just before
the Jacobite troubles, he'd seen David wrestle a man in Newlands, a great bullock of a man he was too, but David was the
prettiest lad stripped – and there came before Judith's eyes a
David whom she had never known, young, fresh, strong-
limbed. Behind him were other Herries, old Maria who had
lived to be almost a hundred, Pomfret and Jannice in Keswick,
little Harcourt at Ravenglass, and Jeremy's own people, his
father Humphrey, who had been born in 1687, and his mother
Charlotte, who loved dancing and was a Beauty in the days of
Queen Anne. The old man went rambling on, putting his skinny
finger to his bare poll and wiping his eyes, that the smoke
made to run, with a large yellow handkerchief. The logs fell to
crimson ruin in the fire, and all the dogs slept.

Old Jeremy sighed: 'All dead, buried, and the worms have
eaten them. But the family goes on. I daresay there'll be Herries
sitting in this same spot a hundred years from now.'

He seemed, Judith thought, a brave old man, because he was
quite alone in the world and hadn't a penny. He stayed about in
the district, in any house that would keep him. He didn't want
much, a drink, a bite, and the fire to sit beside. As he told them,
most of his days were now swallowed by dreaming. 'It's hard to
tell what's a dream.' Yes, that was true. It was hard to tell.

It occurred to Gauntry that the girl might be hungry. She
acknowledged that she was, and the old men all said that they
were hungry as well, so the host scuttered off in his clop-clop
slippers to find them some food. He returned with a mutton
ham and a piece of a pie. Some of the dogs woke up and came
sniffing round; then Emma Furze woke also. She raised her
head slowly from the table, stretched her arms and yawned.
Then she saw Judith and stared as though her eyes would burst
from her.

'This is little Judy Herries, Emma,' said Tom Gauntry
nervously.

She stood up. She was a big woman. She had large black eyes,
a fine bosom, and she stood with her legs spread like a trooper.

The old man looked at her apprehensively.

'Oh, is it ?' she said.

Judith rose and held out her hand. But Mrs Furze was uncertain as to whether she saw two Judiths or three, so, to avoid
any silly mistake, she walked off a little unsteadily.

'She will be most agreeable,' said Gauntry, 'in the morning. She has a totally different nature in the morning.'

The mutton ham was extremely good.

In the morning, indeed, Mrs Furze shed tears upon Judith's shoulder. She arrived in Judith's room before Judith was awake and sat for a long while moodily observing her. Judith, before many weeks were out, was to know all Emma Furze's history, was to know, too, that there was much merit in her if also some melodrama. Emma was to play an important part in Judith's story. But for the moment, Judith, after a most healthy sleep, awoke to see this big woman balanced on a small chair and tears rolling down her nose. Tears, whether male or female, had always an instant effect upon Judith's heart, so now in a moment she was out of bed and, in her thin shift, was kneeling on the bare boards by Emma's side, imploring her to tell her trouble.

What, now as ever, was not Emma's trouble! At present it was difficult enough to disentangle. Emma, as Judith soon heard, had been an actress, and fine words were her pleasure. Words poured from her like the water from Lodore after heavy rains, and out of all the confusion nothing was immediately to be gathered. There had been a villain somewhere, 'a villain of uncultivated manners and corrupt heart'; there had been 'a smiling innocent babe'. She had been 'tossed on the waves of a sea of sorrows' and so, 'washed up' on Tom Gauntry's 'shores', had consented to be both his cook and his mistress.

Her tale was so lengthy, so incoherently mingled with tears, the boards of the floor were so hard, that Judith was compelled to rise, whereupon Emma also rose and, folding Judith to her bosom, embraced her very warmly, told her that she would 'worship her for ever' and, becoming instantly practical, asked her what she would have cooked, with what clothes she might supply her; stated that, in fact, she was her servant for life. She was very quickly of the utmost cheerfulness, laughing and plunging about the bare room. It was thus, in this ridiculous manner, that Judith made one of the principal friendships of her life.

The next occurrence was, of all amazing things, the appearance of Will Herries. Two days after Judith's flight he appeared on a grand calm morning when the grass was still silver with frost and the scent of the Fell was stung with the breath of icy running water. The grass of the little tangled garden was crisp and crackling under Judith's heels. She looked up and saw Will, sitting there very stiff and reserved on a fine coal-black horse. She had not seen him for a long while. She thought he was in Liverpool. He looked older, thinner, better pleased with himself than ever, and he had all the pursed-up solemn air of a man who finds himself immensely important.

Their conversation was short. He did not come down from his horse, but was quite friendly. She stood near him, her hand on the bridle, looking up at him and often smiling. He seemed to her so very pompous.

'Where are my things, Will?'

'Your things?'

'My handsome possessions, my marriage portion, my livelihood. There is a dress and a cap, two pairs of shoes, a cracked china jar, the brush of a fox, a Holy Bible . . .'

He looked severe. 'You must ride back with me, Judith.'

She laughed. He couldn't but feel that she was a lively attractive little thing, standing there in the crisp morning air with the Fell and the old house for her background. He saw, too, with surprise that she had become in the course of a night or so a woman.

'Ride back? Is that your mother's wish?'

He leant over towards her confidentially. He always prided himself on his diplomatic gifts.

'Now, Judith. These are women's quarrels. You know well enough that my mother has been a sick woman since my father's death.' (He said *My* Mother and *My* Father as though they had been his own most especial private property.) 'A sick woman . . . But it will pass. It is already passing.'

'Has she spoken of me?'

'No. She has kept to her room.'

'Has she spoken to Francis?'

Will's upper lip, that was thin and tight like whipcord, was sharp.

'Francis is greatly to blame. He is my brother, but I cannot acquit him of fault.' (He said *My* Brother as though, rather reluctantly this time, he owned him.)

Judith broke our fiercely:

'He is *not* to blame . . . David's attack would have followed whether Francis were aggravating or no. You know well what the surgeon said. And after David's death Francis did everything that was possible. Sarah hugs her misfortune. She is not alone in losing a husband.'

Will said severely: 'You forget that she is my mother.'

'I forget nothing at all. Least of all do I forget that I never belonged at Uldale, Will. This is an old shabby place, and there are only old men in it, but it has always been my home more than the other. A poor taste, but my own. And so long as Sarah is living we can never be under the same roof. No, here is my place and here I stay.'

Will looked sternly about him as though he were making a quick businesslike survey of the house, grounds, view, and found them of exactly no value at all.

'You know of Gauntry's bad repute?' he asked.

'Oh, Will,' she answered lightly, smiling at him. 'Who shall cast stones? There is not one of us without his detractor—'

This made Will uncomfortable. He looked for a moment as though he were going to ask Judith whether she had heard anything about himself. He had all the sensitiveness to personal reputation that belongs to very selfish men. However, all he said was:

'You yourself are a Herries, Judith, and in this part of the country the Herries have a reputation.'

She interrupted him laughing. 'There's another Herries in the house here already – Jeremy Cards. He knew my father.'

Will's expression was as though he had smelt some strong odour, which, indeed, as they were not far from the midden, he might have done.

'I have heard of him. A disreputable old man . . .' He saw apparently that there was nothing to be done. He was relieved, perhaps, that it was so. 'So you will not come?'

'No, Will. I am happier here.' She asked him: 'Are things going well with you?'

He looked at her kindlily. He liked anyone who took an interest in his affairs.

'Well enough . . . I am to go to London very shortly.' (He said London as though it were *His* London, just purchased by him.) 'I'm glad. They say there's a deal of money there.' He nodded very seriously. 'Liverpool is too small a place,' he told her.

He shook her hand, was minded to pat her head, but refrained. Then he rode off, she calling after him:

'Remember that my things must be sent.'

He turned in the saddle, nodded gravely and disappeared.

She went in to find Tom Gauntry huddled in an old bed-gown over a grumbling fire, dogs spread all around him. He looked up at her smiling, but his old face was wrinkled with pain. Her heart ached for him.

'That was Will Herries,' she said cheerfully. 'He asked me to return to Uldale. I say nay, like the girl in the ballad, and that is the end of that.'

'That is the end of that,' whispered the coal in the fire. 'Are you sure that you are wise?'

He put out his dry bony hand and took hers: 'Here has always been your home, and so long as I'm alive it shall be. But maybe that's not so long. My back aches and my head's like a turnip. There's a hunt today, Threlkeld way. Hunting's over for me. And I'll never be on a horse again neither ... Strange, strange! I've lived my life on horses ... But it's been a long life. Emma likes ye, my pretty. She's got a heart, Emma has, poor silly soul. She'd skin herself for anyone she's fond of – *has* skinned herself a hundred times, poor girl. It's mortal cold this morning. And yet I'm hot in the head, as though there were coals of fire blazing away. It's the devil to be an old man – better go while you're active.'

She nodded her head. 'I think,' she said, 'I could deal with whatever came. I feel that way on a fine crisp morning. Uncle Tom, what am I to do today? There are a thousand things – I'll ride over to Bassenthwaite village. There's a woman there a marvel with herbs. David had her once for his leg . . .'

The old man rolled his head. 'Nay, nay, I'm past everything but dreaming, damn my bones. Don't you worry, my pretty. When you've had a pain in your leg a long while it's a kind of friend.' Then he added quite casually as though he were saying nothing at all: 'Georges may be riding over from Whitehaven today.'

Her heart began to hammer. 'Georges Paris?'

'Aye. He's grown a fine young man, but he'll burn his fingers one of these days. He's in with a lot o' rogues. I've told him, but he don't listen. Thinks he can manage them. Very confident young man is Georges.'

Before she could say anything or even reason with herself about her foolish excitement Emma Furze joined them. Judith saw that she had smartened herself. She had a black hoop and a silver band in her dark hair. She looked really handsome as she stood there. There was something both foolish and good in her face; her black eyes were large and always brimming with emotion; at the slightest excuse her breast would heave and swell. She looked at Judith with a childlike smile of pleasure.

'I saw a fine man on a horse and said to myself, "He's come to take her away." I was tortured by the anxiety, my dear.'

'You need be tortured no longer. No fine gentleman shall take me away.'

With a sigh of relief Emma sat down beside them. How pleasant it was for Judith in the fresh quietness of the morning, no sound in the house but the old clock ticking and a mouse scratching behind the wainscot!

Judith asked Emma some questions, and out her history tumbled in an overwhelming flood – some of it at least. As Judith was to discover, there were endless, endless chapters to it; she had led, it seemed, a thousand lives, and was yet, according to her own account, but two and thirty.

Her first part had been that of the Duke of York in *Richard the Third* at the Birmingham Theatre, then Cupid in *The Trip to Scotland*, then Prince Arthur in *King John*, then Bath, where Mr Palmer gave her five shillings a night. Her first girl's part was Sukey Chitterling in *Harlequin's Invasion*. She drew from her bosom a packet of papers, yellow with age and greatly torn; she read to them with every possible dramatic gesture some of her notices.

'On Tuesday night Miss Pomeroy ("My name at that time, my dear") made her appearance in *Isabella*; and, although the audience went with such strong prejudices in favour of the fashionable Melpomene, yet never did Mrs Siddons draw more genuine tears from an audience. It is impossible to conceive what a high-fashioned picture this lady gave of Isabella's woes, and how nearly she arrived to nature in almost every scene. There were no studied pauses, to purchase, by vacancy of time, the approving hands of the audience, and yet the house echoed with repeated marks of approbation. Her shriek at the discovery of Biron had a good effect, but was rather that of terror without amazement, than of terror and amazement mixed. When the public consider that this Miss Pomeroy is that Miss Pomeroy who performed Cowslip . . .'

Old Jeremy came stealing down the stairs to join them. He was blinking his eyes and yawning, for he was only now awake, but Emma's dramatic voice, the great rise in it as she came to the word 'terror', her sudden declamation of Isabella's most moving lines, soon stirred him. It was as good, he declared, as being at the Theatre and with nothing to pay. The dogs barked, Wull came to the door and listened, and Judith, who had never seen a play, was entranced.

Very early in the afternoon the light vanished behind the hills, and the house was a place of shadows. Judith riding in from Caldbeck, and, chilled to the bone, hurrying to the fire, saw Georges Paris standing in the firelight. No one else was there. It was the same as when they had run, that first time, from the supper-room, and she had smacked his cheek.

She would not smack his cheek now. He had grown a man, slim and tall in his riding coat and riding boots, his black hair tied in a queue, his handsome self-confident face bright with life, fun, energy, adventure.

He saw, too, a changed Judith. From the child whom he had left there had grown a child-woman, charming in her small buoyant independence, throwing her hat beside her and shaking her red curls just as she used to do, holding out her hand to him at once in their old friendship.

'How d'ye do, Georges? I'm happy to see you again.'

'By heaven,' he thought, 'she's somebody . . . I'm glad I came.'

For he had been in two minds about it. Stone Ends was in no sort of way the place it had been. Gauntry was ill, only old men there, flea-bitten dogs, and the strange woman, half cook, half play-actress, in command. Georges was profoundly convinced that he could live but once and must waste no time. Had he been present when Gauntry needed he would have helped him to his last shilling, for he was impetuously generous, but he was happy in living for the moment and in finding the moment always exciting.

And now this Moment was Judith. He had not expected to find her here and certainly not supposed that she would, at his very first glimpse of her, affect him so strongly. He had thought of her, forgotten her, thought of her again. He lived for excitement, and only accepted the things and people that could contribute to that. Since he had seen her he had had adventures enough – on the Cumberland coast, on the Solway, in Holland, in London – to satisfy, he thought, any man. What he did not recognize – as we never recognize the truest things about ourselves – was that all these adventures had been scattered with a thin second-rate dust, as though, with everything that he touched, he robbed it of a degree of fineness. He had first-rate moments and a great quality of happy fearless adventure when things went well, but he had second-rate ambitions, second-rate vision, second-rate reactions. He was a fine young man with a soul, through no fault of his own, inevitably shabby. Was it perhaps in Judith's power to raise him into a finer world? He did not think so, because he was convinced that no world could be finer than the one he was in; and she did not think so, because she never, all her life through, saw herself as a moral agent in anything. She never thought at all about moral qualities in the abstract.

At any rate, simply as a factor in the intricate course of Herries history, it must be recorded that on that afternoon, November 24th of the year 1790, Judith Herries and Georges Paris, standing beside the fire in the hall of Stone Ends, fell in love with one another.

Judith knew at once what had happened to her. She was always extremely clear-sighted about herself. Now if he attempted to kiss her she would not smack his cheek. But she did not intend that he should kiss her. She was in fact very cool to him indeed.

He had intended to stay the one night at Stone Ends and then ride on to Penrith, where he had business of an especially interesting nature. He was by present occupation a smuggler and just now a prosperous one. But his intention was to find a little place somewhere in the district, a rather remote place if possible, and make it his centre. This was not only a business ambition. He had a true love of the country, possibly the truest thing in him; he liked nothing better than the old life of hunting, fishing and the rest that he had had in the earlier days at Stone Ends. Sensuous enough, he nevertheless vastly preferred men to women as companions. He had long pictured to himself a small farm somewhere that could be the centre both of his business and his pleasure. Now that he was in funds was the time to purchase such a place. He certainly would not be in funds for ever.

So, at the very first instant of seeing Judith walk across the floor towards him, in a flash it had come to him: 'Here is the woman you want.' He had always considered her, even as a child, a most sensible capable person. There was some hard common sense in Judith that had always roused his keenest admiration. She knew this country and liked it. She would run a house well, would manage men with authority. She had no ties. She had pluck and courage and, he surmised, would not trouble herself too deeply about transgressions of the law. Now that he beheld her again he remembered how greatly he had been impressed in Cockermouth by her decision and resolution. She was not strictly a beauty, but there was something very attractive to the senses.

When he wanted anything he always, in five minutes,

concluded that it was his. He wasted no time at all; before they had been half an hour together he was making ardent love to her.

Emma Furze was in her room that night imploring her to be careful.

'He is not for you – no, never, never!' She held Judith's hand and spoke as though the fate of nations were in danger.

'What have you against him, Emma?'

'He has no character, no fine feelings. I have known men and been betrayed by them too. They are all false, and this young man is French as well.'

'They are not all false,' said Judith, thinking of Francis and Reuben. 'But you must recollect, Emma, that I am acquainted with Georges Paris since I was a baby.'

'Yes, but now you are in love with him. You were not and now you are. Love blinds poor women. Men are never to be trusted for a single instant. They are filled with cruelty and caprice. On the most vain and frivolous pretexts, whenever their temper is in the least ruffled, they cast you aside. They behave with propriety only when it is to their advantage.'

'Well, my dear, you need not fear. I know myself.'

But did she? She lay in bed looking at the moonlight washing the door. She was in love – and for the first time. Did she know that? Her cheek was hot as she fell asleep. And her dreams were of a fiery splendour and a happiness that she had never touched before.

It was plain enough to everybody next day that Georges remained at Stone Ends only because of Judith. He carried on his courtship with an impatient ardour that had a great deal of very real passion in it. He was ruthlessly selfish about everyone else. Gauntry he patronized, the two old men he disregarded, Emma Furze he detested. Like many sensual men nothing exasperated him more than having to be in the company of a woman who was most unattractive to him. Emma exasperated him by her apparent vagueness. She seemed to him to live entirely in a world of make-believe. He declared that she did not know where France was nor that Paris was the capital of that country: neither politics nor money meant anything to her at all. She lived entirely in a world of the passions, except when she was cooking. (She was a very excellent cook.) She was vague and ignorant and absent-minded except when someone for whom she cared was in question; then she was as sharp as a needle. He knew at once that she was his enemy so far as Judith went, and he loved her none the better for that knowledge.

So things moved swiftly. Judith was in a strange state. He caught her when she was isolated from all her claims and associations. Everything played into his hands. When her things arrived from Uldale, with them came a letter from Reuben. It was very short.

DEAREST JUDITH – I am going with Humphrey to France. There is the centre of all the movement for the Betterment of Mankind. I shall learn there in that New World how to help Mankind. I shall think of you so often, dearest Judith. I love you with my whole Heart.

REUBEN SUNWOOD

France! It had taken Reuben as it had taken Francis. And now it seemed that it must take her too. But what a different France hers! For Georges seemed to care nothing for his parents' country, save that he got lace and brandy from it, nor did it concern him at all that there was a Revolution there. What was Georges in reality? Did she know him? Did she see him as he was? Was Emma in the right about him? But, as the days went on, she could not think any more. She had never been in love before. She had not known that it would be this strange fiery heat, mist before the eyes, all the outside world sounding dim to the ear.

The house, the old men, Emma, all grew faint and unreal to her, and Georges was ever more clear. He seemed to her most beautiful, and now, because he also was in love, he was most tender.

In these chill frosty December days he was at his very best. There were in him somewhere noble instincts; he wanted her so fiercely (as he wanted anything withheld from him) that his very desire brought him close to her and he caught some of her fineness. He had been in love again and again since he could remember, but now three things were united that had perhaps never been before – desire, perception of character, and practical advantage. There was wisdom in his choice of her, although the very thing that now attracted him, the strong domination of her will and purpose, would be, when passion had died, the last thing that he would want in her.

She held out against him so long as she could, but he was too strong for her. It seemed to her that this had been foreshadowed since her sharp farewell to him in Cockermouth. He had looked at her then as though he knew that one day she would come to him.

But she was never less assured about him than at the moment before she submitted. Coming down the stairs she saw him standing in the hall that was lit by a blazing fire. He was dark black, standing motionless there, as though he were waiting for her. She paused on the stair, and the thought struck her heart: 'This man is my enemy.' Then she came down, and a moment later she was in his arms.

Afterwards he was speaking in all sincerity when he said:

'My dearest, I will care for you with my whole heart. You can make me noble and fine. This is a new beginning. There is nothing you cannot make of me.'

Lying in his arms she was wildly happy with that fierceness of intensity that was always hers in everything that she did. But she had never surrendered herself before to anyone save the ghost of her father. No one had held her and loved her and stroked her hair and kissed her with passion. She did not know that it could be so sweet. What vows she made of service and devotion! How she would work now that she had someone to work for!

She did not ask him where he would take her, whether he had money to keep her! She could work for them both; at what she did not inquire.

Her cheek against his, she stayed in a trance. Perfect happiness had come. How could she ever have thought that she did not know him? She knew him utterly. She had always known him as she knew herself.

She was so very young.

Part II

Watendlath

FRANCIS RIDES OVER

THIS BOOK IS the history of a country, England (not of course, the whole history); of a family, Herries (nor the whole history of that); and of certain members of that family especially – Judith Paris first, then, after her, of Reuben, Will and Francis (and not, of course, their whole history either).

But the Herries are English, and Judith, Reuben, Will and Francis are Herries. At the heart of this family there is a struggle and in each of these individuals a struggle. The history of that struggle is the history of this book, is the history, perhaps, of every book that has ever been written.

The history of any country and the history of any family is continually presenting strange underground movements of ebb and flow, and to these movements members of the country and of the family are for ever responding, although they may themselves be quite unconscious of it. Moreover, the actions of one individual will often permeate the whole body of which he or she is a part; even slender characteristics may affect it as the shape of Cleopatra's nose swung Egypt, Napoleon's passion for hot baths France, and Mrs Fitzherbert's virtuous tenacity England.

So the determination of Will Herries' prominent chin affected just now the fortunes of the whole family of Herries. They may be said to have swung upwards upon it.

In 1791 Will Herries moved to London and married there a Miss Christabel Carmichael, a young woman with a fine waist, something of a fortune, a doting father; against these benefits must be set a slight cast in one eye and a rather hysterical temper. Will cared nothing for the first and soon dominated the second. He was determined to get on, and, as in this life everyone gets what he wants if only he wants it hard enough, he did get on, and speedily.

He was soon known in the City as a man of prudence and enterprise nicely commingled. His business was especially in Indian trade, tea, silks and spices. He had a pretty house in the village of Chelsea, and in February 1792 Mrs Will Herries gave birth to a son, Walter, who, with his opening shout to the world, proclaimed that he also meant to get on and to waste no time in doing so.

It would, however, be an exaggeration to say that at this time any other members of the Herries family were at all aware that they were about to swing upwards on the point of Will's chin. As was always the Herries characteristic, there was perfect self-confidence everywhere until disintegrating imagination broke in and threatened it. The Family was at this moment divided, unlike Gaul, into four parts. There were the Herries of Uldale, Sarah and her children, Francis and Deborah; the Pomfret Herries of Kensington, with whom poor Humphrey Sunwood once on a time visited; the Cards of Bournemouth, Prosper Cards who married Amelia Trent and had offspring, Jennifer, born in 1770, and Robert, born in 1771; and, fourthly (but in their own opinion absolutely firstly), Lord and Lady Rockage of Grosset Place in Wiltshire. Judith Herries, sister to Raiseley and first cousin to David, had, many years before, bewildered into matrimony the Honourable Ernest Bligh, who in his gout-ridden and exceedingly ill-tempered old age had become Lord Monyngham, then Viscount Rockage. Of them had been born three children, Frederick, who died, Carey in 1755 and Madeline in 1756. Carey, now Lord Rockage, had two offspring – Carey the younger, born in 1780, and Phyllis, born in 1782.

Lord and Lady Rockage, his sister Madeline, his children Carey and Phyllis, lived all in penniless grandeur at Grosset in Wiltshire, where the rain trickled through the roof, the trees creaked and wailed, and the cold of the stone passages carried rheumatism into the bones of all who suffered it.

Lest these family branches should seem confusing it may be said that the Uldale family stood for Country Life, Pomfret's family for London, the Cards in Bournemouth for Social Intercourse, and the Rockages for the Ruling Classes; yes, and more than that, for two strong elements of the Ruling Classes at the end of the eighteenth century in England, namely the arrogance of a dominating Aristocracy and the narrowness but courage of Methodism.

This book is not, however, in the main the history of the Rockage fortunes. There is a story there, in that odd proud group of the family, that should command a book of its own.

To have suggested to either the Rockages or the Cards of Bournemouth at this time that Will Herries was an important relation would have been to invite derision. But Will's time was approaching.

Possibly Francis, up in Uldale, had more foreknowledge of

it than any other. He knew his brother. Indeed, very often, Francis, who was without any personal conceit, felt that he knew everything about his own immediate relations, that he knew too much for anyone's happiness. He had in fact a very special quality of psychological penetration. He was now grown very handsome for those who did not find his figure too slender. His features were sharp but delicate, his colour fresh and gentle; he carried himself with a strongly reserved dignity, was always clothed with perfect simplicity but in absolute taste.

He wore an air of melancholy, no pose of the period, but very real indeed. These years were, in fact, very unhappy.

They might well be so. Uldale was, at this time, no cheerful place. He held himself there because he thought it his duty. A bailiff managed the farm, but Francis managed the bailiff – and everyone else as well. He had far more authority than cheerful stout David had ever had; he was the friend of no one, and would have been unpopular in his remoteness had there not been a very proper pride in him. He was the Aristocrat of the district, and everyone was pleased that there should be an Aristocrat. His melancholy reserve lent not only the house but all the district an air. Unlike his sister Deborah, who was in and out of all the houses of the neighbourhood with her giggle, her two little dogs and her passion for gossip, he went nowhere and entertained only with reluctance.

But it was on his relations with his mother that the whole house hung.

Sarah Herries was now an aged and shrunken woman. In the spring of 1792 she was fifty-four years of age, but she looked another ten. Her hair was white; she dressed always in the deepest black, her shoulders a little bent as she walked slowly, leaning on an ebony cane. Her eyes were scornful, as though she said always to the world: 'You took from me the only thing for which I ever cared. What do you expect of me now?'

Now that her features were more slender there was a resemblance between herself and her son. The stout and chattering Deborah seemed to have no relationship with either of them.

Sarah had not, of course, forgiven Francis; she would never forgive him. She would never forgive him, but she surrendered to his influence. She allowed him to do what he would with the house and everyone in it. She found indeed no interest in either contemporary life or persons. She sat, either in her own upstairs room or in the temple in the garden on a fine day, staring in front of her, at the bad blowzy painting of David or the china

figures or across the sunlit lawns to the sweep of Skiddaw or
the Scottish hills. Her lips moved; her thin pale hands beat
together a little on her lap. She was in no way deranged. Any
question asked of her she answered sharply and with a certain
shivering impatience.

She allowed Deborah to chatter to her for so long as she
would, and Deborah flattered herself that but for her jolly
brightness and good-nature the house would fall into ruins.
But Deborah also abandoned everything to Francis. She paid
visits with increasing avidity among the neighbours. She was a
great player of cards, a passionate gossip, surely a destined old
maid. But Destiny does not always work to pattern.

Francis behaved to his mother with unfaltering courtesy and
an unflinching patience. But it seemed to him that life could
not continue for very much longer like this. His real life was
imprisoned within him like a fire within an ivory bowl. The
bowl would crack, and the fire burn the hand that held it.

He was thirty-two. His life was passing. And a day came when
his endurance broke.

In the evening he sat opposite his mother in the China Room,
while a thin coal fire whispered grumpily between them. The
curtains, with their stamped pagodas and blue tilted bridges,
were drawn. A small King Charles spaniel bitch lay at Francis'
feet. He realized quite suddenly, with that premonition of
coming events, always his special gift, that some crisis was
approaching. Everything in the room seemed to share his
knowledge.

On his lap, as he was always afterwards to remember, was a
copy of Burke's *Reflections on the Revolution in France*. His
mother spoke. She had a fashion, when they were alone together,
of speaking, as it were, to herself, so that when he answered her
it was as though he were addressing the wall behind her or a
picture or a chair. But now she looked at him directly.

'Francis,' she said, and her eyes wandered over his face as
though she were seeing him for the first time. 'Why do you
stay here ? It is not, I know, to give yourself pleasure.'

'Yes, ma'am,' he answered. 'I am happy here.'

'No, you are not. I know exactly why you stay. It is from a
sense of duty. You think that you did me a wrong and repay
it by this attention to us. That is your duty.'

He made no answer. His heart beat thickly.

'Well, it is no duty. You have your own life to be lived. Will
is working in London, but there is money sufficient for you to

travel. Herman is honest enough and will see that everything goes smoothly here.'

Herman was the bailiff. The reference to Will was no new one. The inference was that Will was working hard at making money in London while Francis idled ... No new inference.

But Francis, tried by much practice, only nodded his head.

'If you wish me to go, ma'am.'

'I wish! I wish! Who cares what I wish? ... I am a dead woman.' Then a surprising thing happened. She turned to him almost eagerly, as though they were, for an instant, friends. 'You didn't know, did you, that one person can die and quite another take her place within the same skin? That other woman would have long forgiven you had she lived. Besides, she was your mother. She was gay and happy, foolish possibly in her trust of events, but she was only a child, although she bore children ... But this other woman here is not your mother, was not even when she was alive. You have often felt her unjust, I know ...'

'No, ma'am,' he answered her.

'Oh, but you have, you have! And rightly ... Only I am not sorry at any injustice. That belonged to your mother.'

As always a strange mingling of irritation and pity rose in him. He hated a sort of melodrama and extravagance in her speech, and yet he knew that at the heart of the extravagance there was a real cankerous sickness.

He felt deeply sorry for them both, so gently he answered: 'I do not want to go, Mother, unless you wish it.'

She got up, felt for her cane, walked towards the door, then turned and said roughly:

'I do wish it. We can have no life together, you and I.'

Then she went out.

He stayed there alone in a kind of impotent fury. So that was all he got for his years of faithful service! He had always had a sharp, keen sense of reality and also a kind of hunger for it. He felt now that ever since his father's death this house had been completely unreal, and it was his mother who had made it so.

Tonight, his mother's last words in his ear, he was moved to a passionate sense of rebellion. He paced up and down the little parlour, the spaniel following his movement with soft anxious eyes. Yes, if she wished him to go he would do so! No word of thanks for all the drudgery of these years! Here he had lamed his life at its most active and promising period to serve her, and all he received was a contemptuous reference to Will. Will, who had never, in all his days, thought of anyone but himself or of anything but his own advantage!

Poor Francis was one of those who are confident about ideas but doubtful about the human race. That Liberty, Equality, Fraternity must ultimately flourish, he was convinced, but he was hurt, with pitiful ease, by any act of human injustice. He found it difficult to believe that human beings were egoistic, jealous, cruel, niggardly, and yet on every day of his life he was injured by proofs that they were.

He *could* not credit that all his years of service went for nothing. They did not go for nothing. Did he but know it, it was his mother's acute knowledge of her own injustice that aggravated her bitterness. But ... 'Herman will do as well.' Herman, the stout, red-faced bailiff, who was honest only because he was stupid and faithful, only because he was without imagination.

Tomorrow, then, he would go. He would show them— He stopped abruptly. Wiser councils were prevailing. First he would ride out to Watendlath and see little Judith. She would help him. She was now, he sighed, his only friend. The spaniel came to him as he sat down by the fire, put her paws on his knee and gazed into his face.

Next morning he rode out. He took a magnificent white mare, Juno, his especial favourite, who knew the country so well that she could find her way over almost trackless paths and climb precipitous hills like a young pony. He was a fine figure in his purple riding coat with the high collar, his head up, like a king. But he didn't feel like a king. There was something surreptitious in his departure as he turned down over the fell towards Bassenthwaite.

He told no one where he was going. Mention of Judith to the Uldale household was a great deal worse than useless. He had seen her three times in the fifteen months since her marriage, once in Keswick, twice at Watendlath. Watendlath was an exceedingly remote little valley lying among the higher hills above Borrowdale. It could indeed be scarcely named a valley: rather it was a narrow strip of meadow and stream lying between the wooded hills, Armboth on the Grasmere side and King's How and Brund Fell on the other.

It was utterly remote, with some twenty dwellings, a dark tarn and Watendlath Beck that ran down the strath until it tumbled over the hill at Lodore.

Georges Paris had found here exactly the place that he wanted, an old house once a Statesman's but now belonging to a farmer, Ritson, who, owing to a ne'er-do-well son, now dead, was at money odds, but owned two farms. Paris bought one farm from him, but kept him there to maintain both. And here he deposited Judith, while himself, for much of the year, was engaged on all kinds of doubtful adventures on the coast, even in Holland and Scandinavia.

Francis had not seen Judith for some months, but at his last sight of her had been amazed by the happiness that radiated from her. He had regarded the marriage with that ragamuffin Frenchman as most certainly disastrous, had not had spirit even to contradict the self-congratulatory 'I-told-you-so's' of his mother and sister. When he heard that Judith had been banished to Watendlath, disaster seemed even more certain. But when he saw her he found her confident, assured, triumphant. It was true that it was then still the first year of her marriage and for most of that Georges had been away. But she had had six months in Watendlath alone – and had flourished on it. When he rode out there on the last occasion it had been veiled in rain and storm. It had seemed to him simply the end of the world. With the rain lashing his face and the gale tugging at his hair he had looked back to see that small indomitable creature laughing goodbye to him in the narrow doorway. Indomitable, yes! But the happiness was real. It was not assumed to reassure him. His heart was touched, and he loved her more than ever.

He thought, as he rode on this March morning of flushing sun and hovering cloud through Keswick and then beside the Lake water that now tumbled with a shiver of grey and then swam into straths of gold, that she was the only human being now in all the world whom he did love.

In old days, when she had been a child and told him insistently that she adored him, his own shyness and sensitiveness of taste had held him back, but, after his father's death and her flight to Gauntry's, he had realized to the full the courage, fidelity, warmth of feeling in her, yes, and her egotism and passion for power as well. How could that passion for power be satisfied in this lonely place where there were scarcely a hundred souls? He himself, who had no passion for power, but only for justice, could not be quiet there. No, he thought, sighing, as he turned Juno away from the Lake up the Fell path, nor anywhere else.

Where in the world now was Equality, where was Freedom?

He, who had killed his father with his joy over the fall of the
Bastille, must now in this March of 1792 begin to tremble at the
things that his Frenchmen were contemplating. After the Flight
to Varennes his sympathies, always so easily swayed by human
misfortune, had begun to turn towards that unhappy King
and Queen. Then the news in December of the ultimatum to the
Elector of Treves had moved him again towards this brave
country beset by so many external, as well as internal enemies,
but the latest news of the quarrels between Delessart and Brissot
in the Assembly caused him the bitterest disappointment.

He was afterwards to recollect that it was on that March
day of cold sunshine, riding out to Watendlath, that he foresaw
something of the cruel confusion that led to the September
Massacres.

As he rode into the higher air and crossed the little bridge
above the running stream he shook his shoulders with a sort
of indignant despair. He had never before felt his life to be so
lonely, so aimless, such a failure. He looked about him, and as
always the beauty of this beloved country fell on him like a
balm. Only a few days before there had been a March snowstorm
in the upper dales. He could not yet, riding among the trees, see
the rising Fell, but he could scent the snow in the air. He knew
that if the snowfall had been deep the shepherds would be
anxious for the sheep. He felt suddenly a touch of their anxiety
and with that kind of shame for bothering about unreal things
like politics when there were such real things as sheep close at
hand. Soon he would be clear of the trees for a while and see
how the sheep were faring.

He had reached now the spot where Watendlath Beck tumbled
into Lodore, and as always when he was here he must stop and
breathe in deeply that perfect beauty. This was surely one of the
loveliest places in all England – English, too, in its qualities of
old imperturbable age, a kind of wistful tranquillity, a cosiness
of beauty mingled with an almost fierce suggestion of force. Here
Vikings had stood, here two hundred years later his descendants
would stand, and at every time the cataract (when the rains had
fallen) would fling clouds of mist above the turning flower-like
whiteness of the water that leapt and fell and leapt again between
the thin brown stones. The dark bare stems of the larch and
oak stood sentinel on either side, and exactly framed by the
delicate pattern Derwentwater lay, in colour now snow upon
steel, a thin shadow of stainless white hovering over the silver
grey. Skiddaw and Blencathra seemed to sway under the chang-

ing passing cloud. Every colour – white and grey and brown – although so delicate, seemed to hint at the coming Spring; there was a promise of saffron and primrose in the stems of the trees, in the leaping water of the Fall.

Francis felt for a moment that here was the answer to all his unrest. With his hand on Juno's back, his eyes leaping with the water, he swore to himself that he would be true to this fragment of English soil, and that so long as he was so no other disappointment, whether in God or man, could deeply touch him. Here was his proof that there was something lovely in the world that made his life worthwhile.

He rode then higher on to the Fell, Juno picking her way on an almost trackless path, and could see now the sheep gathered into dark groups feeding on the loads of hay that the farmers had sent to relieve them. The whole sweep of the Fell was flooded with thin sunshine, and little rocks stood out in it like islets of ebony. The snow, on the farther Fell, was more scattered and lay in streaks like marking on a tiger's back. The sheep moved in black sequence against the running stone walls. There was silence everywhere, except for the rhythm like a humming voice of the distant falls.

He rode on, through forest again. As he approached Watendlath in his purple coat on his great white horse, the distant white fells, like pummelled pillows, shining down on him, he might have been some knight-at-arms riding into the Forbidden Land. He seemed to be more and more withdrawn from the world. He was high up among the hills, and yet this meadow and stream had the quality of a mysterious valley that would later on be rich with flowers and enchanted with the voices of birds. But today ice and snow and rock ringed him inexorably round.

Soon, looking down, he saw the odd dumpy shape of John Green House, Judith's home. A queer little place indeed, crouched into the soil as though it feared a blow, its narrow windows peering blindly on to Armboth Fell that here was split to allow a beck to tumble down the hollow. There was the chattering of the beck, the bark of dogs, the lowing of a calf, but before he had reached the door Judith had seen him, had run out, had almost pulled him off his horse in her eagerness, flung her arms round his neck and dragged him into the house.

John Green House was L-shaped with a double porch. From the 'hallan' or passage there were three doors, one that led into the 'down-house', now used for farm purposes, baking, brewings and the rest, the second that led to the garden, and the third to the 'house-place' or 'house', a beautiful room with lovely views, surrendered now entirely to Judith; beyond this room was a smaller panelled one, Judith's bedroom. A small staircase led upstairs to rooms that had been formerly open to the rafters but that were now ceilinged.

Judith took Francis into the 'house-place', shining now in the pale March sunlight. The walls were plastered. There was a stone mantelpiece over an open hearth; there was a settle, some carved chairs and a large oak table.

There were signs of Judith's passionate cleanliness everywhere. Everything gleamed and shone; china, candlesticks of beaten brass, an old spit with many hooks and a dripping-pan. Some early daffodils were in a china bowl on the oak table.

She stood back and stared at him.

'Now, let me look at you! Oh, how handsome you are, Francis! I had forgotten. You are more beautiful every day!' She stood on tiptoe, pushing back the high hard collar of his riding coat that she might see the white fall of his neck cloth and the beech-coloured waistcoat with the stamped silver buttons.

'I always put on my best when I come out to see you,' he said, laughing, and taking off his riding coat.

'That's more than I can do for you,' she answered.

She was wearing the country clothes, an upper-dress of undyed duffel like a man's and a skirt of native wool woven into a sort of serge – wool of the black sheep mixed with red and blue. Her stockings were of blue homespun, and she had clogs of uncurried leather. They were lined with straw to keep her feet warm.

Francis thought she looked extremely well, with her pale excited face and the pile of red-gold hair on top of it. She was, as always, immaculate from head to toe. She had an air of virginal purity as though the wind, the rain, the unchecked sun had cleansed her with an austerity of their own. In fact she was neither austere nor remote. She was wild with excitement at seeing him, could not keep still, went dancing about the room, touching first one thing and then another, talking all the time. Of course, she was yet a child, only seventeen, while he was thirty-two. But it was true what she said, suddenly turning to him and crying: 'You know, Francis, I've always loved you – from the moment that I was born!'

She had to have someone to love, and she had to have someone to dominate too. It amused him to see how at once she took

charge of him, telling him where he must go and what he must
do. It would soon be the dinner-hour, but first he must see
everything, and she danced in front of him, taking him along
the 'hallan' into the farmhouse of the Ritsons. He was aware
of a great fire roaring in the open fireplace, of a spit turning, of
sacks of corn, hams and sides of bacon hanging, the oak settle
screened by the 'heck', the 'rannel-balk' or great wooden beam
across the chimney, and a chain with hooks for cooking utensils
hanging. The big room seemed filled with men and women,
all busied with affairs, but he noticed in especial one magnificent
old man with a snow-white beard like a patriarch. Judith introduced him. This was Robert Ritson, the head of the Ritson
family, a man of seventy-four, who, in spite of his many troubles,
financial and others, was yet above the world, above it and
removed a little from it, with that touch of remoteness and
austere reserve that is in all true Cumbrians.

Then they went out. She led him over the boulders and the
foaming beck down the hill above the meadow to the Churn.
The Churn was filled just now with water from the snow off the
fells and toiled and tossed and seethed, an odd spot of turmoil
above the quiet silence of the long meadow. Judith said a strange
thing as they were looking into it.

'If Georges were to leave me I'd throw myself into it,' she
said. Then laughing: 'No, I would not. I would stick a knife in
his back.'

'Do you love him then so much ?' asked Francis.

'I do.'

'And does he love you ?'

'He loves no one at all but himself,' she answered.

Then they went and stood by the Tarn in front of the stone
wall of the house. All was very grey and silent. The hills streaked
with white, thick with naked trees, looked down on them while
quilts of wadded cloud rolled heavily across the sky. Francis
shivered.

'It's a black piece of water,' he said.

She told him that it could be every colour, that it had so
many moods that she could almost believe that it was alive,
as Mother West, the witch, said it was.

'Have you a witch then in this small place ?' he asked her.

They had, but a good and kindly one who gave the girls
love potions and the men cures for the rheumatism. 'She is an
immense woman, like a whale.' Then, as they walked back into
the house again, Judith told him about all the families in the

place, the Ritsons, the Wilsons, the Tysons, the Morrows, the Blythwaites, the Gibsons, the Robsons.

Judith knew everyone and, as Francis soon perceived, governed everyone. She was Mistress of Watendlath, knew it and triumphed in it.

But it was not until after their dinner that they truly talked. For dinner they had oat-bread baked on the girdle, a broth of onions and savoury herbs, and a goose pie that had been made at Christmas. To drink there was ale brewed in the 'down-house'.

When dinner was over they sat over the fire, while the logs hissed and crackled and spat and threw out tongues of flame against the blackened stone. He asked her first whether she were happy. As she replied, telling him everything in her mind with her accustomed honesty, he watched her. She had changed but little, and he thought to himself that her real struggle with Georges was yet to come.

She had all the audacity and self-confidence that she had always had. Nothing in life had frightened her as yet then. She had a woman's knowledge and common sense.

'This Georges of yours,' he said. 'You'd stick a knife in his back if he left you. But he's always leaving you. How long has he been away this time?'

'He has to be away on his business.'

'What is his business?'

'Oh, smuggling, stealing, anything bad. But when he has made money he will settle down here.'

'Such a man settle down?'

'Oh yes. You cannot know him, of course. I often think no one knows him but myself.'

'How much has he been here in the fifteen months of your marriage?'

'Three months. Three months and a half. There was the first month – oh, that was grand! We did nothing but make love to one another. I was new to him. It couldn't stay ... One morning he knocked me down, and before I was myself again he was gone. But he wrote me a beautiful letter from White-haven. He was away then six months. He came back one fore-noon without any warning and then we loved one another again – two weeks or more. Then he was away five months, and the last time he was here we were good company, not lovers. He had a woman in Whitehaven.'

'You knew all this,' he asked her, 'and didn't care?'

She looked at him with bright eyes. 'Most certainly I cared.

Night after night I cried myself sick; then if I made a noise he would go and sleep with the farming men. He has no heart. He is quite cold. When I saw that, I stopped crying.'

'And you love such a man?' he asked, disgusted.

'Certainly. He wants me to love him. And I find him charming. He is the most elegant company in the world. When he is here at home we laugh and laugh for hours together. If I am in love with him and troublesome, he is either in love, too, or he is drunk and doesn't care, or he goes away. He certainly cares for me more than anyone in the world, but not for me very much. He says it is the fault of his mother, who was a bad woman and beat him. Did I ever tell you, Francis,' Judith dropped her voice a little, 'how when I was little and ran away to Uncle Tom's I looked through a door and saw Georges' mother naked and a young man in his shirt kissing her knees?'

'No,' said Francis, 'you never told me.'

'Well, that was the beginning of it.'

'The beginning of what?'

'Of my love for Georges. I love him because he is beautiful and witty and cares for nobody. But one day I will make him think of me so that he can never get me out of his mind. It is almost so now. He is always writing to me ... and when he has stolen enough money from other people, we shall go to London and steal some more.'

Francis was aghast.

'But, good heavens, child, do you approve of stealing?'

'I would not steal myself. I wouldn't steal a halfpenny. But no one will ever stop Georges from stealing. It is in his blood. He steals my things all the while – and from the Ritsons too. But one thing about Georges – he never tells a lie. If I ask him whether he has had women in Whitehaven he always says Yes. He tells me all about the smuggling. He tells me everything. You cannot change people's natures. Isn't that what your Mr Rousseau said? I have read the *Nouvelle Héloïse* and find it too full of sentiment. Well, I love Georges and I cannot change him. He had a bad mother – so what would you?'

'And he beats you?'

'No longer. After the last time I said next time I would kill him. Perhaps I would. He knows my father was mad and my mother a gipsy. That is one thing he cannot understand – that I am so *practical*.' She said the word twice with immense satisfaction. 'And on the other side so wild. I tell him that is the Herries blood; what makes them so interesting a family.'

But,' cried Francis, still greatly distressed, 'there will be
some terrible scandal. He will kill someone or be killed or be
put in gaol or be hanged for a thief . . .'

She nodded her head. 'Georges says he will never die in his
bed. I would be for ever anxious while he is away if I were not –
what is it ? – a fatalist. That's what I am, Francis, a fatalist.
What will be will be, and nothing shall beat me.'

Then she went on eagerly. 'I want to go to London. London
must be fine. I want to see all the Herries, my relations. Will
lives there now, and they say his wife is as proud as a peacock
and has a cast in her eye. Georges heard about them. And there
is Pomfret, old Raiseley's son . . . Oh yes, and there are the
Rockages in Wiltshire. It was the greatest fun, Emma Furze
saw them.'

'Who is Emma Furze ?'

'She is my greatest friend. She was Uncle Tom's mistress,
and after he died she went back to the theatre again. She had a
season in Salisbury, and Lady Rockage had a meeting about the
wickedness of the theatre. Emma went, and she says Lady
Rockage is like an old pincushion and has two children at her
heels, and they have a house always in the rain—'

'It can't always be raining,' Francis interrupted, laughing.
Then he asked: 'But how can you endure it so long here alone ?'

'I am never alone,' she answered indignantly. 'Never for a
moment. I shall prove it to you. I keep a Journal.'

She ran, pulled out the drawer of a cabinet and brought back
to him a book bound in dark-green leather with heavy clasps.

He opened it at random and read, in her sprawling childish
hand, entries such as these:*

Nov. 3rd, 1791. Mrs Ritson had a Haunch of Venison this
morning from Mr Crosthwaite of Keswick. Obliging of him
but I think he has an eye on Mary Ritson. While I was in at
Tom Blythwaite's this morning their cousin Nancy B. from
Mardale was taken in Labour being only a quarter gone and
had a Miscarriage. No doctor nearer than Grange and he
not arriving till late afternoon.

Nov. 7th, 1791. The Carrier, Ned Wilkinson from Keswick,
round this forenoon. 2 Sauce Ladles pd twenty shillings.
Poor Rate from Lady Day to Michlms pd 1.5.2½. Oh I forgot
bought also of Ned Wilkinson a pair of Garters 0.1.0. To

* Judith Paris' *Journal* is still Herries property. See *An Old Border
Family*, published by Houghley & Watson, 1894.

Poor Travelling Woman walking over from Grasmere 0.6.0.
Mrs Mary Robson's little Boy by me for an hour while his
Mother baked.

Nov. 23rd, 1791. Mrs Watson of High Head Grange sent
us 2 Tubbs of Geneva. Very kind. The Robsons and Braith-
waites – John, Hob, Anne, Henry, came in last evening and
we had a Grand Feast. I gave them Pease Broth, boiled Leg
of Mutton and Caper Sauce, Mince Pye. After supper we
had Quadrille at which I lost 1d per fish – 1.0.0.

Dec. 4th, 1791. Mr Bletson rode up from Rosthwaite –
said he wished he could have driven up his new Curricle to
show me. Very smart painted Green with Red lines. Walked
down to Rosthwaite with him, he leading his horse. Walked
back through Snowstorm. Very heavy over the Langdales.
Fine Show of Sun betweenwhiles above Armboth. Pd 1.0.
per yd for 6 yds of white Cotton for Lining.

'Yes,' said Francis, looking up from the book to her eager
face. 'You're not dull – and you *are* practical.'

'It is to show Georges,' she answered, 'if he were ever to ask
where the money goes. But he never does. I have enough from
the farm, even though,' her voice lowered, her face grew dark,
'Georges were never to return again.'

'Then you don't know ... whether he comes, when he
comes— ?'

'No; even though he writes he never says. A while ago I had
a letter, and from it you might fancy he would be here any
moment. My eye is always on the road by the Tarn. One day
without a word he will be coming along.'

She came closer to him, sitting curled up at his feet, her hand
on his knee. 'I think so much of my father. I fancy that I am
the only person left alive who gives him a thought. Already
he has gone so far back for everyone else, but not for me. His
house, you know, was just below here at Rosthwaite. It is
tumbling down. Poor Father! Everyone thought him too mad to
be real, but I understand how he felt. He is alive in me still,
Francis. Perhaps none of us ever die.'

'Better the dead than the living!' Francis broke in so fiercely
that Judith turned to stare at him. 'Put no trust in anyone alive,
Judith – not in your Georges nor in me nor in your friends here.
The dead are faithful, but the living change with every breath.
What was my mother ten years back, Judith? You knew
her. No one kinder or more generous ever breathed; but now,

although I may break my heart serving her, she can only say that Will is making money in London or that the bailiff manages better than I . . . I am going away from Uldale. I can endure it no longer.'

She could feel his whole body heaving with his distress. She thought that in a moment he would break into tears.

'Nay, nay, it is not so bad. I mustn't speak of Sarah because, God forgive me, I never loved her, but it will be good for you, Francis, to go to London for a while. Perhaps I shall follow you with Georges.'

'Everything has left me,' he murmured. 'I am quite alone. I am not a man to make friends readily. Even Moore, with whom I had an intimacy, has gone too far for me in this French business. And now – my mother, my sister—'

She kissed him passionately. 'I will never, never leave you, Francis. After Georges I love you most in the world. Do you remember years ago when I crept in to look at Mrs Monnasett after she was dead and your father beat me, how you came and comforted me? I ever *adored* you!'

'And do *you* remember,' he said, holding her close to him, 'one evening when there were fireworks on Keswick Lake, how we sat together – you and I, Will and Reuben – and talked of our future, how Will said that all he cared for was to make money, and I talked like a ninny, and Reuben—'

He broke off.

'And where is Reuben now? I have not seen him these two years. Someone told me he was an itinerant preacher.'

Judith nodded. 'Yes . . . He preaches in the hills to anyone who will listen. They throw stones and mud at him and set dogs on him from the villages, but he says that he is happy now, and so I hope he may be. Poor Reuben! Francis, will it not be terrible for him if there is no God, and when he is dead he has had all the stones and mud for nothing?'

'There can be no God,' Francis answered. 'This world is too unjust and bitter. No God could suffer Himself to witness it, and it is His own doing . . . And yet I dream sometimes of a fine Heaven, all mercy and charity, where all men are free and there are no tyrants . . .' He sighed, rubbing his eyes with his hands. 'Certainly a dream – further from this world every day . . . But you, Judith, Will, Reuben and I – we are a mixed lot of Herries. All Herries is in us together. From a study of all of us you would get the Herries quality. All obstinate, all proud, all English, but in nothing else alike. But you are right. You have told me what I came to ask. I will go to London. And yet I doubt that I will be happy there. I love this piece of country like none other in the world.'

She would have answered him, telling him, too, how she loved it; but he saw that she suddenly stiffened. She rose slowly from his feet, straightening her small body as though under a spell. Her eyes were fixed on the window.

He followed her gaze and saw coming on the rough path above the Tarn a group of people.

'It cannot be! It cannot be!' he heard Judith mutter, and then, a moment after, she had broken from him with a cry, had rushed from the room, and, her red hair tumbling, had started down the path.

Standing at the window, he saw then a figure detach itself from the group and run ahead of the rest. The figure met Judith, raised her in the air, hugging her.

'This must be Georges,' thought Francis with a quick sensation of sadness and loneliness. It was right that Judith should run to him. It must be marvellous for her after so long an absence, but why must the fellow come just now and spoil the only happy hour that Francis had known for many months?

Judith cared for him, Francis, but at the sight of her husband she could forget him as though he had never been. So it was with him always. Everyone had someone else. He was first with no one. Well, what of it? Had he not courage enough for that rôle? He shrugged his shoulders and went out.

Standing in the little wind-swept garden, he could see that others had been attracted by the noise and had come to the doors. In front of a cottage not far from him stood an enormous woman, yes, like a whale. That must be the witch of whom Judith had spoken.

A wind blew up the little stream that tumbled from the tarn. Some fat Herdwick sheep wandered like sleep-walkers towards the Fell. The group was near enough now for him to distinguish them. The leader was a slim, handsome, dark fellow, Georges Paris. He had an arm round Judith, who was looking up, talking eagerly. In the other he swung carelessly a gilt bird cage that contained a bright crimson bird.

Behind were two pack horses laden with boxes; there were sheepdogs, some young men, a stout laughing girl with a red ribbon in her hair. Georges Paris was wearing a handsomely cut riding coat and a broad hat with a silver cord round it. The colours of the gilt cage, the crimson bird, the red ribbon, stood out sharply against the dark Tarn ridged now with the wind like a gridiron, the snow-streaked hills, the heavy grey sky.

The air quivered with excitement; there were the voices, dogs barking; everyone was laughing. A group of the Ritsons came out eagerly from the farm.

He felt that he could not bear to meet them. He slipped away, found Juno and rode off. No one noticed him. Within a week he had departed for London.

THE CRIMSON BIRD

GEORGES PARIS, running forward to meet Judith, did not know and would not have cared had he known that with those very steps he was influencing the future form and shape of branches of the Herries tree.

He was gay, he was honourably fatigued, he was hungry and thirsty, triumphant with physical health and money in his pocket. He hadn't seen his dear little Judith for many months. He was going to remain with her now and make her happy and make himself happy; but even as he greeted her he was able to notice that one of the Ritson girls, advancing now towards the little bridge, had grown uncommonly pretty while he was away and had exactly the figure that he preferred.

Judith, too, running forward to meet him, was unaware that she was running forward into the first chapter of her mature life, and that when he caught her up, putting the bird cage for a moment on the stones, and hugged her and rubbed his cheek against hers, this was the opening of a battle that would form her nature and mould it, affecting through her the whole future stock and texture of the Herries family.

That moment when Judith was caught up and felt Georges' arms about her and his mouth on hers was her last of peace. She did not at the time realize that. She was to have weeks now of happiness. But looking back long afterwards she saw clearly that that was so. The steps from that were so gradual, so silent, but the movement was sure. So, to the end of her life, she remembered that heavy grey sky, the snow-flecked hills, the ruffled water of the Tarn, the crimson bird beating against the bars of the cage on the wet shining stones, and that warm amused murmur of Georges' voice.

'My little darling . . . And is your hair still so lovely ?'

Afterwards she thought perhaps that she got what she deserved, because in all her excitement she forgot entirely Francis, never all that afternoon remembered him, sank into her husband's arms that night without a thought of him.

It is of no use, however, to be too solemn about it, for that day and many days after it were exceedingly happy for both Judith and Georges. Georges wanted only for himself to be happy, and if he was happy, why, then, he was charming to everyone. It was only when he began to be less happy that others began to suffer.

And Judith wanted only that Georges should be happy. She could not have believed that the world could be so lovely as it was in the weeks after Georges' return. They were still children, both of them, in their capacity for happiness. They could be happy at a moment's notice and over nothing at all, a bird's cry, a gooseberry pudding, a dance in the road, the sun on the Tarn.

The sun shone during those weeks. All the valley was illuminated. Nor was it ever a constant sun, whose glow can be wearisome. Not in this country. It was a sun attended by flights of happy clouds, and it shone upon all the running streams with the endearing tenderness of a passing hand, glittered in the heart of the bogs of peat and struck fire from the streaming rocks.

For the first weeks Judith had no conception but that she was going to be happy for ever. She knew that Georges was selfish, grabbing, thoughtless of others, a liar and a thief. On the other hand he was delightful to look at, a charming companion when he was pleased, and, although a liar about his deeds, quite honest about himself. But beyond these things she loved him. She loved him with all her being, and when one says that of Judith one means it.

She loved him maternally, because she knew that he was an evil small boy, who had not reached any age of discretion. She loved him physically. She loved him as a comrade. She loved him quite selflessly, never thinking at all of her own advantage in anything, but in her heart she was determined one day to dominate him. She could not help that in herself. It was so in her with everyone whom she met. She must *want* to dominate them.

But she loved him behind and beyond these ways, as only women can love – that is as though she had made him herself. She did not like altogether some of the things in him that she

had made, but it was her work. So she loved him with deep
tenderness and care, but also with the proprietary pride that a
craftsman has for his beautiful creation.

She knew that he did not love her in any sense of the word
as she understood it, but she did not want him to love her in
her way. She wanted him simply as he was. Well, she got him
as he was, and the first trouble came when he showed her a
little of what he was. This was in March 1793.

The suddenness of that first trouble took her breath away.
They had had a merry evening. They had had a 'rocking-night'
in the Ritsons' great kitchen, the women spindling while everyone told tales. Wonderful stories were told, stories of the 'Wise
Man' and 'Hobthross', sovereign remedies against witchcraft,
stories of the hunting of the 'hiding' men after the '45.

Suddenly Judith was aware that no one there liked her
husband. The Cumbrian can hide his true feeling better than
any other of God's people; there is no sober reticence anywhere
in the world so dignified, so impenetrable as his if he wishes.
Judith knew these people; they were her friends; they had taken
her in and made her one of them, and when the Cumbrian does
that you are safe. They had not, however, taken Georges.

How did she know it? She could not tell, unless perhaps it
were something that she saw in the bright unswerving eye of old
Ritson, seated in the settle, his body high and taut, his white
beard a prophet's. His eye rested on Georges, and Judith was
suddenly frightened. They did not like Georges. They none of
them liked him.

Later that night she was lying beside Georges in bed. They
could hear the tumbling water beyond the house. No other sound.
Driven by her queer uneasiness, she began to ask him questions,
questions about his life in Whitehaven; he kept always a dark
cloud over all his life away from her. It had always been understood between them that she left that alone. But if she asked
him anything he must answer her truthfully. As his answers
always hurt her she had learnt not to ask.

But tonight she was uneasy. Why did her friends here not like
him? He felt strange to her, as though she had never touched
him before nor heard his voice. She was very young and knew
nothing yet about marriage.

So she said a very foolish thing.

'Next time that you go to Whitehaven, I shall come with you.'

He laughed gently. He put up his hand and buried it in her
hair. 'Then I would kill you and throw you into the sea,' he said.

'But when you go to London you say you will take me with you.'

'Yes, I shall need you there.' He tugged at her hair.

'Don't, Georges. You hurt me . . . But perhaps you need me in Whitehaven.'

'I neither need you nor think of you in Whitehaven.'

'You don't think of me?'

'But why should I? I have quite another life there.'

'But you write letters to me.'

'Yes. Suddenly you come into my mind . . . Your smallness, your hair, how you laugh when you are amused. Then I write.'

She sighed with satisfaction.

'Then you do belong to me. I can make you do what I say.'

This was the instant of transformation. He sat up in bed and shook her until her head was, it seemed, separated from her neck. Then he pushed her out on to the floor.

She got up slowly, rubbing her hands in her eyes and staring at him in amazement. Then he jumped out of bed and chased her out of that room into the next. He caught her, dragged her by the hair and threw her on to the floor again. He was trembling with anger. She could see him only dimly in a pale-green moonlight that shadowed the sky and the room. But two stars quivered with laughter above the dark stern trees.

'Never you say that again!' he shouted at her. 'I'll beat you! That you own me! Never you say that again! You miserable! I'll whip you. By God, I shall show you!'

He was dancing with rage. She got up and stood against the wall, staring. She was too angry to speak. She sat all night in a chair under the green moonlight. She was bitterly cold. She couldn't think at all; she was so utterly surprised.

Early in the morning he came to her, kissed her feet and her hair, said that he was so sorry, so very, very sorry. Then he carried her to bed and warmed her cold body. She said not a word. She had never in all her life been so completely surprised.

All that day she was silent, going about her duties with a grave set face, and all day in her eyes there was that look of surprise. But she was not a fool, and she had the great gift that was to serve her again and again of seeing straight in difficult crises. When the situation was sentimental she was unsentimental, as indeed most women are. She was not in the least sentimental now, and when, in the evening of that day, Georges, made very uncomfortable by her silence, explained himself, she listened gravely, not thinking at all as to how she could snatch compensation from him for her wounded pride, but simply as to whether what he said really explained what had happened.

But in the middle of the explanation, Judith, looking up, saw the crimson bird, a cockatoo, in the gilt cage hanging from a nail. The bird had its head on one side and, with its beady eyes shining, listened attentively to everything that Georges said.

'I am bad,' he began. 'I always told you that I was. I have never had – what do you say? – any fine sense of morality. I am not at all like your Sir Charles Grandison. I despise the sentiments; they are for women. I have the devil of a temper and I have never tried to check it. My mother had it also. For myself I think that if you understand my temper it is very agreeable. It makes a change.'

'Do you love me?' asked Judith suddenly. She asked not at all from sentiment, but because whether he did or not was a practical question of importance.

'No,' he said. 'No, Judith, I do not. I love nobody. I don't know what it is to love anybody if by love you mean to be in a fever, to give up what you want, to run hurrying to the feet of the beloved. I have never been in a fever about any person except to sleep with a woman, and then it is quickly over. No, I do not love you.'

'I see,' said Judith.

'No, but you must understand. I do not love you, but I care about you more than anyone except myself. I am bad and worthless. Not that I am ashamed. Why should I be? It is the colour I was born, that is all. But I am nearer having virtuous feelings when I am with you than at any other time. I have always thought that I had no heart as my mother had none. The French people are not famous for their heart. But at times I suspect that you are giving me a little. For example, I have been unhappy today because I hurt you, and I have never before been unhappy about hurting anybody. I always want to come back to you when I have gone away, and I feel now that if ever I bring everything down about my head – as I shall one day – it is only you in the whole world that I want to come to. You are a wonderful woman, Judith. You have more strength and courage and sense than I have ever seen in a woman. I don't really care for women except for a moment. I prefer greatly men, and that is what I like, to be in danger, to be against the law. More than anything in life I like to be against the law. I cannot bear that anyone should say to me "Do this!" or "Go there!" I am like a bird in a cage. That was why last night, when you said that you could make me do what you wished, I hated you and wanted to kill you. I am no good, Judith, but I do not care. If I want to be in a rage I am in a rage, if I wish to steal I steal. Life is not important, not in the least. You and I are not important. No one is important.

'Only to break the law, to beat someone who plays against you, to take what isn't yours and make it yours, that for a short time is amusing. But I hope my life will not be long.'

After all this Judith nodded her head. 'I think I understand you,' she said. 'You are very honest with me, Georges, and it would be an easier matter if I did not love you. There is no reason for loving you that I can see, but I do. Only I must protect myself. You must not beat me nor drag me by the hair. That is stupid and sentimental. It is like Emma Furze acting in a play.'

He agreed that it was. They were reconciled and were good friends again.

But when two people live together, every struggle between them, however handsomely it is ended, alters the relationship. Judith was now on her guard. She watched Georges, even as the crimson bird watched her. Yes, the crimson bird was very like Georges. It was charming when it wished, and twisted its neck to be scratched and rubbed its beak against your finger. But it surrendered, for no very obvious reason, to the most frantic tempers, screaming its rage and rasping its claws against the cage; it was very proud of itself and its feathers, and its spirit was undaunted, which was also one of the fine qualities in Georges. Judith had no intention of surrendering to Georges; he should not dominate her, but he was now a little distance removed from her. She must be close to him without his knowing it. She thought that she was clever enough for that. But it is difficult for any woman who has a very tender heart and no sentimentality. She is for ever tempted into situations that seem to her foolish. And therefore she keeps back so much that she feels.

As the summer came nearer Georges began to grow very restless.

He was not restless with the place. In his fashion he cared for it almost as deeply as Judith did, and it did not worry him at all that the people did not like him. Ever since he had first come to Cumberland as a little boy, the Cumbrians had disliked and suspected him, and it had never disturbed him at all. That it did not was one of the things that in the old days amused Tom Gauntry about him.

Watendlath was the wildest piece of land that he had yet known. The fells towards the Langdales appeared endless, and their mingling of peat and heather, ancient rock, strange tumuli in human shape, and sudden streams rushing through the soil as though on some secret mission enchanted his lawlessness. On the other side there was Keswick. All England just then was gambling crazy, and Keswick had its little share.

Georges was a born gambler; one day he was a genius at cards and on another he would be so wild and reckless that he would lose all his advantage. Like Mr Fox and the superior gentlemen in London he would bet on anything, the fall of a leaf, the approach of a woman round the corner, the wax of a guttering candle. There were plenty of men, from gentlemen like Mr Osbaldistone and Mr Kenrew down to ostlers at the 'George' or broken-down wasters like Tom Fawcett, who, in Keswick, would oblige him. At first, after his return from White- haven, he was well in funds. Then less and less so.

Judith sometimes rode with him into Keswick. She had a few friends there; a Mrs Pounder who had come from Bath; a rather blowzy red-cheeked lady, who knew Emma Furze, had a warm heart but an uncertain moral code; a Mrs Dunn and her husband Henry Dunn, kindly people, crazy about dogs and horses; one or two more. But on the whole Judith did not care for Keswick and would have given thirty of it for one of her beloved Watendlath. What really distressed her as the weeks passed was that Georges might in a gambling fit rid himself of her adored farm. That he was capable of it, in one of his excitements, she well knew.

For her own expenses she needed almost nothing at Watend- lath. She shared with the Ritsons food and shelter. She was scrupulous in her record of expenses, chronicling every penny; Georges never looked at her laborious accounts. At first he was ready to shower money on her. He bought her scarves and dresses and shoes and bonnets. She didn't need them in the least. Now he was less ready. She didn't care. There would always be food and shelter for him at the farm.

But if one night he should suddenly tell her that the farm was gone?

On the other hand, she shared with him his excitement about London. She would like to experience that adventure. They were not so cut off in the North as they had been. There was plenty of talk about the old King, the Regent, Mrs Fitzherbert and the rest.

Beyond this she had a strong Herries feeling. The Pomfrets in Kensington, Will and his ambitions, the Rockages in Wiltshire, she wanted to see them all and maybe, herself, play some part in the Herries fortunes. Half of her was sober Herries – she could understand Will's ambitions – the other half was wild English, born of her mother and father, belonging altogether to these hills and lakes and streams. One half of her looked at the other half of her, partly in mockery, partly in wonder.

By the month of July, which was hot and green with no wind, she knew that a crisis was approaching. Even the crimson bird seemed to know it, for it rapped its nails no longer on the bars of the cage, nor fell into violent rages. It perched, with its head on one side, and listened.

And the crisis came. But before it came, she had a moment with Georges that she would never forget, one of the happiest of her life.

He rode in from Keswick, up the little rough path above the beck that was now thin and placid like a child asleep. The evening sun was deep and fair over all the landscape, and gold-dust was in the air. He came and sat beside her in the window-seat, took her hand, put his arm around her and drew her to him. These gestures were so rare in him that she knew that something critical had happened.

She sat there, her heart trembling lest in his next words he should tell her that he had gambled the farm away. But he did not. He told her nothing, and she, wise through much experience, asked no questions.

They sat in the golden silence for a long time. The little stream that ran down the break in Armboth was only an amber line now after the dry weather.

'Judy, you funny little thing, how can you stay here month after month and be happy?'

'Because I love the place. My father lived below the hill in Rosthwaite, and he was there without moving for years and years.'

'Yes, but your father was crazed.'

'Maybe I'm crazed as well.'

'No, but you're not. You have more sense than anyone in Keswick. I'm proud of you, Judy.' Then after a pause he asked her: 'Do you not hate me for riding into Keswick and gambling, leaving the business in Whitehaven to tumble?'

'No,' she answered. 'I could never hate you.'

'Why not? Cannot you hate?'

'Oh yes, I can hate very well.'

'I could almost love you,' he said, 'if I were quieter. Sometimes I dream of making a handsome fortune, and we have a big house with dogs and horses, and you have all you want . . .'

'I have all I want.'

He drew her closer, held to her as though someone would tear her away. She did not dare to let him see how happy she was. Wild ideas ran through her head that perhaps always life would be like this now. He would give up his dangerous ventures, they would improve the farm, sometimes they would go to London for a holiday, perhaps there would be children. She would be a hostess, as Sarah used to be in Uldale; on occasion she and Georges would escape from everyone up into the hills, Eskdale or Patterdale, away from everyone . . .

'How old are you now, Judy ?'

She told him. Nineteen in November.

'I should not have married you so young. Indeed, I should never have married you at all.'

She drew his head close to her childish breasts. She sat on the window-seat clutching him to her. She saw her feet dangling. How she wished she were taller! Of course, he could not love her, so small and insignificant. Then as she looked at his dark head and felt the warmth of his cheek against her thin dress she thought that she was as good as another, better than many. But she would love him all her life long, even though she lived to be a hundred. He was worn out. 'He was playing cards all night,' she thought – and he slept there, his head on her breast.

It was her last quiet hour for many a day.

The crisis came a week later, and the cause of it was, of all people in the world, Reuben. She had seen Reuben but thrice since her marriage, once at his mother's house in Cockermouth (little Mr Sunwood had died a year and a half ago of a chill), once in Keswick, and had once listened to his preaching in Borrowdale beyond Rosthwaite. Poor Reuben! On that last occasion her heart had ached for him. He wandered, so she understood, from place to place, belonging to no especial ministry or sect, simply preaching Christ and His message. Yes, simple enough in intention, but involved in every possible sort of loneliness, hostility, ostracism. Reuben had not even, Judith thought, the gifts or personality of a preacher. He looked clumsy, ill-shapen, in his awkward, ill-fitting black coat, and he had what no public orator must have, lack of confidence in his own gifts, and so he bred lack of trust in his audience. He gazed anxiously around, and, save when he was caught up on the wings of his devotion and imagination, he hesitated for words and moved restlessly on his feet. On the day when she heard him there was a gathering of farmhands, women, boys, who listened, some with a mild, some with an angry, interest, and before the end he had been driven away with mud and stones. She had hurried after him, but had not found him.

Now, on a lovely summer's day, Mrs Ritson ran in to say that there was an itinerant preacher on the nearer side of Brund Fell and that they were going to hear him. It might, Judith thought, be Reuben. Georges was away at a farm bargaining for a horse.

Indeed, it was Reuben. She saw him at once, standing in his black coat bathed in sun, while all about him the rough tumbled fell wore that rather sinister look that this country has in brilliant sunlight – something too naked and bold, as though the real country were only present in cloud and mist and had given way to some flaunting and scheming intruder. Reuben looked the more helpless, the more dishevelled in the glare, and Judith, her heart always instantly touched by anything at odds, longed to go and stand beside him. He had by now, however, his supporters. Since she had last seen him he had collected apparently a little band of strange and incongruous figures – a large stout woman in a man's jacket and a bedraggled green skirt, two rheumy old men who were so nervous of their audience that they could scarcely stand on their rickety legs, two girls and a boy. Reuben was stouter of body, Judith thought, but younger than ever in face, his eyes wide and anxious like a baby's, his cheeks plump, his chin indeterminate.

A crowd had collected, it had followed him from Seathwaite, Rosthwaite, Grange. It was a rough-looking lot of men, women, children and dogs, some there in evident sympathy, but for the most they were, Judith thought, strangers to the district. She had noticed of late a certain class of foreigner in Keswick and surroundings. There was much distress abroad. Food prices were high, work in many parts scarce. Transportation, too, was so much easier than it had been. This little world was no longer isolated from the older one. The days of its extreme remoteness were over for ever.

Reuben was speaking when Judith, Mrs Ritson, and two other women drew near. He spoke with a shrill, rather piercing note that dropped suddenly to a low bass. There was something ludicrous about this that almost at once set some of his audience laughing. As he talked he waved his hands in the air and rolled his eyes. Every once and again the little group round him would break into singing with a wavering and unsteady tone. Judith became with every moment more uneasy. He began a passionate evocation of the character of Jesus Christ, speaking of His charity, His unselfishness, His courage. Behind his uncertain voice there was a piercing sincerity, but he had not the power to evoke for others what he himself saw. Judith had the strange notion that the hills, the rocks, the peat seemed to understand him better than the people around him. She fancied that the sun was a little veiled, the colours a little milder. But he could not catch his audience; they were not fish that day for his net. Some of the more scornful men began to laugh. One of the dogs began a fight with another dog. When the quavering voices were raised other voices joined in derisively. And as the opposition grew, Reuben's voice was ever more shrill, and his eyes wandered more beseechingly to the heavens.

Then someone threw a stone, pretending that it was aimed at one of the dogs. Other stones followed. Two men had been drinking gin from a bottle and began to quarrel; a moment later they were rolling on the ground atop of one another. The dogs were barking, the women screaming, figures were running down the hill. Clods of peat were thrown, more stones; something cut Reuben's cheek. His little band clustered close together, and then, as the scene was wilder, the two old men and the stout woman started away quickly over the brow of the hill.

Reuben stood there, his hand on his bleeding cheek, as though he did not quite know what to do. Judith went up to him and put her hand on his arm.

'Reuben dear—' she said.

He started, at first seeming not to recognize her. The crowd was streaming away down the hill.

'Come and rest at the farm,' she said.

He followed her quite passively, like a child. She felt his arm trembling under her hand. Then when they had gone a little way he began to speak.

'They think it finer not to listen ... to throw mud ... I cannot hold them. You may laugh, all of you may laugh, but the day is coming when the spirit of the Lord will descend upon me ... Stay a moment, Judith, while I fasten my boot.'

He was wearing faded and stained green breeches under his coat. He bent to tie the worn string of his boot. When he raised his head his forehead was bathed in perspiration and his cheek was bleeding again. But he was smiling.

'God has but just spoken to me and told me that I do well. He watcheth over me and will see that I come to no harm.'

'Where are you living?' she asked him; she had to take many quick little steps to keep pace with his almost running strides.

'Like the birds of the air—' Then he shook his head. 'I cannot remember, but I must always be talking in Bible phrases like the Methodists. But with you, Judith, that's folly. I live nowhere. I have no home unless I go to Mother. You know,' he began more excitedly, 'now that God is the only real thing in my life, roofs and walls are constricting. I am happier in the open.' She asked him to stay with them for a little while and be rested, but he shook his head. 'No, no . . . I must go on. There is so much to be done.'

While he was sitting beside the big open fire, she brought water, and he washed his face. He took off his coat and his shabby riding boots and his soiled neckcloth. He opened his shirt and bathed his breast that was smooth white like a woman's. His hands, too, were soft.

He became more collected and told her of his brother's death in France, how he had joined the first ragged French army and almost at once had been killed in some squabble on the way to the frontier. As he spoke Judith saw again the desperate hunted man in Cockermouth. It had been, it seemed, since that day that both for her and Reuben active consciousness of life had begun. After his brother's death, he told her, he had been always restless, and at last had begun to preach up and down the country, simply by himself, attached to no creed. He didn't know whether he did any good; it seemed to him that he did not. But he must go on. He was the Bear, ordered to play his part . . .

She realized that he had no great interest in her affairs. He put up his hand once and touched her hair, but he asked her no questions about herself, whether she were happy, how she lived here . . . Once he broke out about women. They were his great temptation, the temptation of the Devil. He tried to lead his life without them, but they were always breaking in. Often he could not sleep at nights, and in the towns, in the taverns and inns . . .

She kissed him. 'Reuben, stay here for a little. It is very pleasant here, and I will care for you—'

She broke off. Georges was standing in the doorway, looking at them. She realized at once the evil temper that he was in.

Things had gone badly with him over the horse. Reuben rose. His coat and vest were on a chair-back, his long muddy riding boots on the floor. He looked doubtfully at Reuben.

Judith said: 'Georges, this is Reuben.'

Georges began at once. 'Yes, and we want no canting preachers here. I have heard of your doings, sir. Whatever my wife may say, this is not the place for you.' He was in one of his black rages, trembling with anger.

Reuben at once hurried to pull on his boots, drag on his coat. He said nothing.

Judith burst out: 'Georges, you shall not. Reuben is my relation and my friend—'

'A fine relation. A canting humbugging preacher who steals the chickens and kisses the maids. A fox! A fox—'

But Reuben was clothed and stood for a moment with a very fine dignity. He kissed Judith's cheek. 'Goodbye, dear,' he said, then staying a moment before Georges, quite, as Judith was afterwards to remember, without any fear: 'Good day, sir; I do not steal chickens, and that I am a preacher is true and is God's will.'

She ran forward with a cry. 'No, no, Reuben—'

But he was gone. She could see him walking swiftly, but still with dignity, along the little path by the Tarn.

She stayed, watching, until he was out of sight, and then she was a proper termagant. Georges knew well that she had a temper, but he had never seen it like this, and had his own rage not been too fierce for him to be clear about anything he would have marvelled.

Although now they were close together, they shouted at one another as though they were at far ends of the valley.

'That is the last time! This is my place. He is my relation, like a brother. He came here weary, soiled—'

'A fine brother with his thieving.'

'You to talk of thieving—'

'Well, at least, I do it in the open. There's no hiding in women's cupboards.'

'You *shall* not! He is more noble than you can ever understand—'

'Well, go to him then! Tie a string to his tail and follow him round the countryside.'

She looked at him, then, moving back to the fireplace, drew her little body to its full height and in a small chill voice, speaking now very low, said:

'You are cruel. I have always known it, but how cruel, not until tonight.'

He came towards her, not for reconciliation. At that moment he hated her: to set up her will against his, and she had been bathing his cheek, that mean canting rat of a preacher – she – his wife—

'Aye,' he said slowly, 'when I have a ranting woman to discipline.'

'Now learn this,' she answered him, looking him in the face as though she had struck him between the eyes. In his rage he was not so angry but that he could see some dignity of anger in her that gave her a dominance he had never suspected in her. 'Learn this. I am not your woman to be disciplined. Here was one who came to me, my kinsman, weary, hungry, beset, and you drove him out with a curse. That I will never forget.'

'And I will never forget,' he answered as fiercely, 'what you have been to me this day. I am master in this place.'

'You shall never be master of me,' she answered.

'We shall see.'

He came towards her as though to strike her. She never moved. Then he remembered something. He was held. She was the elder at that instant as he stood there like an angry boy, his black hair ruffled and damp. He had on still his riding coat, and he carried a whip in his hand.

They exchanged a long defiant look. Then he turned on his heel.

'I have had enough of this,' he said, and he went up the winding stair.

She never moved. Later – she had no sense of time, but her anger bore her as though on a horse with bright wings, timelessly, through dry air – he came down, pulling after him a box. It bumped on every stair. He stood in the doorway, dark in an evening glow all saffron, with faint blue light in the upper sky.

'I shall never return,' he said.

Still she did not move. She heard him call to young Jacob Ritson. She heard them lead the horse out and its sharp stamp on the stones, very clear on that summer evening. Then she saw him ride off, the box behind him. She saw him climb the Fell beyond the Tarn. And still her anger was so hot that it held her high in fiery space.

Many hours later, at some early morning time, she woke, and her brain was quite clear and her anger all gone. She did not

at first realize that he was not there. Half awake, she turned
as she was accustomed to do, to settle her small body inside the
curve of his arm. She would lay her head on his breast, even in
her sleep seeing that her hair was not in his eyes, then her hand
would fold inside his palm.

She stretched out her hand and touched only the cold bed.
Then she was fully awake. She sat up to hear some bird calling
its cry like slipping water beyond the open window. There was a
pale light, like stealing smoke over the room, and in her ear
as though a voice had called it from over the hill: 'I shall never
return.'

She waited weeks for a letter. None came. He was gone; and he
meant, no doubt, what he had said. It would be like him. She
saw now that she had never had any real hold on him. He did not
love her; he had very often told her so. He liked to tell her. She
knew nothing about his life without her. She envisaged Whitehaven and the sea as a strange town, the houses running down to
the sea-edge, figures moving on the foreshore, bales loaded in darkness, the firing of a pistol, or some woman, very opposite to herself, tall and dark, coming softly in a candlelit room, drawing him
towards her ... and outside these scenes a sea always angry, grey
and roaring, and some foreign coast, darkness again, men moving
on tiptoe. That was what her imagination did for her, and it was
to this land that he had returned. He would never come back.

She had great courage. She would show no one that anything
had occurred. She went about all her daily business, her head
up, poking her nose into every village affair, nothing too trivial
for her, deciding always what was best to be done, hypnotizing
them into believing that she was a woman, although she knew
now that she was only a child.

Her business now was to cut out all the outside world. She
would not think of Georges nor of anything beyond Watendlath
Beck.

All the souls of the village she brought into her world and
made them giant-size to fill the space better – old man Ritson,
patriarchal, aloof, believing fiercely in God and His angels,
whom he expected to descend from the skies at any moment, but
practical, too, about money so that he knew where every penny
went to; young Tom Ritson, deformed, with a crooked back,
a marvel at any job with his hands; Mary Ritson, the beauty
who lóved some imaginary man of her dreams and would wear
a lost faraway look when earthy young men courted her; Giles

Braithwaite the wrestler, famous in all Borrowdale already, though he was only twenty, later to be famous through all Cumberland and the North, at present a stupid young man who thought the French lived over Ullswater way; James Wilson, broad, brown-faced, kindly-eyed, the finest Cumbrian of them all, whose wife Jane gave him a child every year so that he now had fourteen; Mother West, the whale, the witch, perhaps at the last, when all was said, Judith's warmest friend in the place; the children, the babies, scattering like ducks, like chickens, like puppies in and out of the becks, the peat, the stony passages – all Cumberland, if you liked, held in this small space, among these few rocks and boulders. Nor so changed from today when the Herdwick sheep still pass from descendant to descendant, and the children still go, day after day, rain or shine, down the rocky path to school in Rosthwaite. They did not care that only a mile or two away by the sea the new Industrial England was beginning to show its dusky evil-stained face, nor that there was an old mad King in London. Here, between Armboth and Brund Fell, was, and is, the whole heart of England.

Soon, though, it was not enough for Judith. With all her resolve and courage, unhappiness crept closer and closer to her. She began to dread the waking moment of every day. She began to watch, against her will, more and more anxiously the path by which the carrier would come on his old fat horse from Keswick.

She realized for the first time for many years how lonely she was. These friends of hers in Watendlath were not enough for her. Reuben, even if she could find him, was not enough. Francis was in London. Deborah, Reuben's mother, was a widow in Cockermouth. Judith thought sometimes of going to visit Deborah Sunwood, but she shrank from it because it was there that she had one of her liveliest memories of Georges. She began to see, with a vividness that appalled her, that she had staked her whole life on Georges. She had not cared so much when he was away, because she had always known that he would come back. Like many another she discovered that true love is irreplaceable. There may be other later experiences as fine, but never *that* one again. There was no one else like Georges. There never would be. His very selfishness, ill-temper, childish reckless independence gave him his colour. And the fact that she had lost him made him twice as precious. She was growing through all this knowledge. Life taught her more now in these few weeks than in years before, but we do not thank life for teaching us *while* we are being taught.

She became more and more miserable. Sleep forsook her. She lay for hours, watching for the light, and when it came she watched the road. One evening she went to Mother West's dark smoky room that smelt of herbs and bacon, and made her tell the cards.

But the cards told nothing. Then one autumn afternoon her unhappiness was so deep that all her courage left her. She went out on to the peak of the Fell that looks down over Borrowdale and sat there, while the clouds rolled over Scafell in red and smoky splendour and all the bracken was gold. But she saw nothing. She sat there, her head in her hands, and cried her heart out. Only a stone's fall below her her father had lived, crazily alone for years.

'Oh, I cannot endure it any longer,' she cried as though to him. 'I cannot live without Georges. What am I to do?'

She dried her eyes and tried to be sensible. This was what she always despised others for doing, to have the vapours as the women in Keswick did, or to want a man who did not want them. Georges did not want her. Now, here on this hill, with only the sky about her, she must understand that he was never going to return. Her life with him was over, and she must make a new life for herself. 'No one can beat you but yourself.' She was young, strong, full of curiosity and eagerness to see the world.

Georges had never cared very much for her (but had he not always returned to her?), he was not a fine man (but was he not endearing with his dark hair and his sense of fun?), he was for ever in a temper (but was he not enchanting when things went well?), he would be hanged one day (would she not be proud to stand at his side when all the world was against him?), he was French, and the French were a bad nation (did she truly care *what* he was so long as he was with her?), she was an independent woman (who would live her life in her own way whatever men did). Perhaps (for queerer things happen in this world than facts allow for) an old man with a scarred face stood beside her then, his arm about her, he looking down through rock and stone to a little house tumbling to ruin.

So she went back over the Fell with her head up, and the first thing that she heard was that there was a letter for her. On the one day that she had not watched!

It was scribbled on some rough tea-paper and ran:

DEAR LITTLE QUEEN JUDY – I have got a Fortune and

We shall go to London to spend it. I am coming Home to
fetch you – Your loving husband,

GEORGES

She allowed the letter to drop. She ran like a mad thing in
to all the Ritsons, and she caught the Patriarch round the neck,
crying, 'He's coming home! He's made a fortune! He's coming
home!'

She danced like the child that she yet was, into the hallan and
over the cobbles, and ran into the whale's parlour and danced
all about between the stuffed birds and the snakes in spirits and
the bottle with the baby's thumb.

The smoke blew out of the chimney, and old Mother West,
smoking her pipe, nodded her head with pleasure, for she loved
this child.

The crimson bird in the cage woke up and scraped with its
talons on the wires.

HAPPINESS IN LONDON

THE ONLY PART of Georges Paris that was visible was his
nightcap, white with a red tassel that lifted and fell above his
nose with the rhythm of his breathing.

Through the open door in the larger room Judith Paris lay,
also sunk in sleep, her hair loose about the pillow, and on her
lips a happy smile, because she dreamt that she and Georges
were alone in a chaise made of silver that drove swiftly through
the clouds above Scafell.

All the cocks around Cheapside were crowing. Above London
a heavy dark mantle was slowly lifted, and soon over all the mud
and running water that clung to the toes of the red-bricked City
the sun would ride with an especial triumph, because it had not
been seen for so many days. It had rained for nearly a week, and
Jackanapes Row and Blowbladder Street were running with water.

Had Georges looked out from his little window into the street
below at the first cock-crowing hour, he would have encountered
Cheapside at the single moment of either day or night when all
life there was still, for the roisterers had roistered to their beds,
the 'Charlies' had not yet started their policing day, the watch-
men had completed their happy and far-too-easy duties. The

cocks, calling from St Dunstan's in the West to the Strand, from Butchers' Row to the Poultry, were kings of the hour.

Then as the light grew stronger he might have seen one small figure, little Jack Robinson, youngest son of Mr Jack Robinson, shoemaker, whose premises were on the ground floor under Georges and Judith. Mr Robinson, senior, had four small boys, who worked on his behalf sixteen hours of the day, and twelve children, fruit of his own loins, so that he was accustomed to children. That Jack, his youngest, should at this moment be earning his wages as 'climbing boy' seemed to him but right and proper, so that there he was with shovel, scraper and brush, and in his cap a brass plate with his master's name and address. He had had some bad chimneys that night, and was so sleepy that he had found his way home as it were blindfold, with chimneys dancing by his side all the way. His lungs were half-choked with soot, his knuckles were in his eyes, but he was home. In another five minutes he would have rolled under the blanket with six other young Robinsons, pushing in among them like a little bird. He was awake enough, though, to see that it was a fine day and to rejoice thereat, for there was to be a cock-fight by Bath Street that afternoon, and there would be rich gentlemen to beg pennies of on a fine day.

You can almost see Cheapside sit up, rub its fists in its eyes, give a great yawn and, jumping out of bed, start shaking its rattle. A light air has sprung up with the sun. For days these piles of little red houses, lifted, like boats on a stormy sea, on heaving cobbles, open sewers, sudden little hills that run up and down in the middle of narrow thoroughfares simply for fun, have felt the mud rise higher and higher about their doors. But this is June, and even in Cheapside the country is not far away. You can smell hay and roses as well as sewage and stale cabbage and the offal of cows and dogs and horses. The river, too, is close at hand; you can hear the noise from the steam-engines in the factories of the soap- and oil-makers, the glass-makers and the boat-builders. Were you to stand on the roof above Georges' nightcap, you would see the Pool, a forest of masts, the ships at anchor, the lighters and the barges . . .

But Cheapside has its own noises, and soon, its face rosy with pleasure, is waving its rattle like the infant that it is, while the sun grows stronger and stronger and the churches are ringing their bells.

The noise is now rocketing about Georges' room. He hears nothing because he is well accustomed. But soon it is ten in the morning, and Cheapside is going to make the best of the splendid day.

First there are the milkwomen, then the baker ringing his bell and calling out 'Hot Loaves', then the watercress men (three bunches for twopence), then the old lady (at this time there were two old ladies, one with a beard, who made Cheapside their headquarters every day from ten to one) crying 'Baking or Boiling Apples', charcoal stove and barrow attending them. And now there is the man with bandboxes, carried on either end of a pole (at this time in Cheapside and the neighbourhood a giant Negro), then the brickdust man with his small sacks and his donkey (the brickdust men are, after the lamplighters, the great trainers of bulldogs). There are the rat-trap dealers and the bullock-livers man, the basket man, the bellows man, the chair-mender and the doormat man. All calling together they are answered by the opening of high windows, the emptying of pots and pans, the rumbling of the country wagons, the first stir in the shops whose glass windows run round-bellied above the cobbles, the barking of dogs, the lowing of cows, the ringing of bells – such a hubbub that, although it is not yet mid-day, a lady with her servant meeting another lady with *her* servant must step into Mr Jordan's the silversmith's to exchange a word or two and, once there, there are clocks to be seen and necklaces, and there is a bull, they say, loose by St Paul's and a crowd running really for the fun of the thing, because it is a June morning with the sun shining, and here is an Italian with a peep-show and a monkey, and a man caught robbing Mrs Morris' fruitstall and no 'Charley' anywhere to be seen so that Mr Benjamin Morris, fresh from a good night's sleep and fit for anything, has given the thief two between the eyes and he has tumbled into the gutter, and the little Robinsons, thoroughly up and about now, throw choice pieces of dirt at him, and the bull they say, is really mad, has trampled down two flower stalls and a Jew's clothes-basket, and in the distance coming in veiled harmonies through the summer air there are the strains of a band, strains that mingle with the scent of the roses and new-mown hay and make the young dandy in his blue and silver, reading his paper in one of the Turk's Head Coffee Houses, think of Apollo Gardens and St George's Spa.

All this before mid-day, and while Georges and Judith are yet happy dreaming. The room in which Judith was sleeping was a large one, Georges' little more than a closet. A shabby place, Judith's room. The bed in which she was had over it a very heavy mustard-coloured canopy, covered with faded red roses. The mantelpiece was tall and narrow, surmounting a wretched stove, semi-circular, with a flat front. There was a bowed fender of perforated sheet brass, a scarred table, and a large china jar filled with roses. There were two cupboards, a mean stand with a wash-hand basin. On one of the stiff high-backed chairs some of Judith's clothing. On another most of Georges'. The crimson bird hung in a gilt cage by the window, but there was now a green baize cloth over his head. The sun poured in through Georges' room into Judith's, lighting up patterns of dust and the bare boards of the floor and the bright green silk jacket over the chair and the silver sheen of Georges' white waistcoat with buttons of emerald. There were lying on the floor two masks, a child's drum painted brilliant red and yellow, and a bunch of artificial flowers.

So they slept, but not for long. A door burst open. A woman's voice (it was Mrs Robinson's, who was at the moment stumbling down rickety stairs, nursing a naked baby, devouring a slice of bread and ham) screamed: 'You can have it your own way, ma'am ... You can have it your own way!'

In the doorway stood a lady of magnificent proportions, tall as a grenadier, as broad as tall, with a fine bosom, a grand im-passioned eye, an air of ruling the world. How magnificently, too, was she dressed! Over her hair, arranged 'hedgehog' style and powdered a very light yellow, she wore a high-brimmed hat of dark beaver fur, adorned with splendid trimmings of purple silk. The dress that covered her noble form was a long caraco jacket of brown striped silk, a light corselet of black taffeta with white trimming. She carried a cane with an ebony top. She stood, her head high, her large face rubicund and jolly, her arm out resting on her stick in a fine theatrical pose.

Her eyes took in the room. Then she saw the bed and moved nearer to it. She stood looking down on Judith, smiling, her eyes sentimentally soft, for she was a most sentimental woman and had not seen her dear Judith for two years.

Then after a while she tiptoed across the room and looked in upon Georges, who was snoring lustily now with his mouth wide open. She looked out of window and had the pleasure to see a grand coach, wobbling along like a fat woman, stick in a rut between cobbles, little boys run up to the windows, a lady in a beaver hat very like her own push her head out, and a man have his fruit barrow overturned in the general excitement.

After five minutes of this, back to the bedroom again and

back to the bed. With a magnificent gesture that it was a thousand pities there was no one there to see, she bent forward
and gave Judith a smacking kiss on the forehead.

Judith woke, sat up, pushed her hair from her eyes, then saw
her visitor. With a cry she was out of bed and had her arms
around the other's tremendous waist.

'Emma! my darling, darling Emma!'

'Emma it is, my love! Thy Emma, whom Fortune has constrained, but the Heart—'

She could say no more, for Judith kissed her again and again,
while Emma's great arms enfolded her in her thin nightdress
with the excited fervour of an amatory bear.

'Oh, Emma. Where *have* you been? I assure you I think it
most ungrateful in you—'

But Emma would let her finish no sentence. Words poured
from her. She had been in Ireland. She had been in Dublin.
She had had the greatest success in the Irish theatres since Venus
and Minerva took human form. Especially in *The Irish Widow*
or, maybe yet more, in Dryden's *Rival Queens*. Tragedy,
comedy or farce, as Judith knew, it all came the same to her.
And there had been a gentleman in Dublin . . . Oh, a gentleman
in Dublin! 'Everyone who knew us spoke of marriage as a
speedy and certain affair, and I could have cried myself ; to
the vapours had I not Resolution and Character . . .'

'Well, and what prevented him?'

'An impudent little Toad with the morality of a – but I shock
you, my darling Judith.'

'Never fear,' cried Judith, jumping up and down on the floor
in her bare feet and the greatest excitement. 'I have stood a
good many shocks.'

'But how are you, my dear little love? and how does Mr
Georges?'

'Very well. Very well . . . we are all very well. But why have
you been so long away from me? Two years . . .'

All this in jerks, in exclamations, in frenzied pauses while
Judith laughs and Emma laughs.

'And he pursued me, the monstrous wretch, through three
streets and an alley-way until I was forced to run into a toy
shop and hope to have the fortune to meet with a chair!'

'But you are handsome now, Emma, so handsome! And so
grand. You have money. You have wealth.'

'I have a little. Just for the moment. All to spend upon you,
my darling. I am hoping to have an engagement at Drury Lane.'

'Georges and I, we too have money, just for the moment . . .'

'Your Georges, he detests me. I am terrified of him. He finds me impossible.'

'But Georges is changed, as you will discover. He is older, more serious. He has still some bad friends, but I have now a little influence, a very, very little influence. When he is not gambling at the "Salutation" or at Offley's he does very well with the money that he made two years ago; he started a business in Whitehaven with Captain Wix. You know Captain Wix? I forget. He is huge as a barrel, and his heart is as big as his belly. He is all heart. Even his liver is heart. But he is also shrewd, and they have made money . . . Georges travels from London there and back again . . . Yes, when he is away from his wicked friends, Mr Charteris, Mr Mandable, and there is a White-haven young man, Mr Stane. I like him the least of them all. His father owns a ship that trades to Holland. Georges has a share in it. But Georges is good now. You will see that for a Frenchman he is very well . . .'

'Oh, God, yes!' cried Emma, throwing her arms abroad in ecstasy. 'I can see that you are the happiest of women.'

'I am indeed, indeed happy,' Judith cried, 'now that you are come.'

They settled down more quietly after that, and sat down to-gether on the bed under the yellow canopy, Emma's arm around Judith, Judith's red head on Emma's bosom.

There was no insincerity in their affection; there was even a certain relief in their pleasure at being together again, for with neither of them had the success of their fortunes been quite so great as they gallantly pretended.

Emma had great qualities, and one of them was constancy to those whom she loved – for so long, at least, as they loved her! For Judith she had an especial care: there was something brave and reckless and good-humoured that exactly appealed to her. She liked a woman to have both spirit and heart, and a friend-ship with Judith that extended now over a number of years had proved her both dauntless and passionate.

When Emma had last seen the pair they had but lately descended on London, and their position was hazardous. She suspected, looking about the room, that it was still hazardous. Judith, she thought to herself, had been through something in these two years. She was prettier, her features were maturely formed, her assurance greater, her recklessness also, perhaps.

There was something individual in the dark flame and shadows of amber light of her hair. Emma had never seen any like it – and beneath it the pale vivacity of her small face was so sharply featured. Her body was lit with energy and independence. Covered as it was now with only the lightest of nightdresses, the June sun warming it, there was something virginal, untouched, in its fire and purity. Emma had once again the sense, that she had known before, that there was something in Judith remote and separate. And yet there could be no one more human, more normal in her passion for all the adventure, all the fun, all the experience that life chose to bring to her.

They had talked then, two years before, upon the great things that were to come from the descent upon the Herries relations. Well, what had come of it. How were they all?

Judith jumped off the bed, caught Emma's beaver hat, seized her cane. 'Look, Emma! Look! Now I'll give you Will! He's very tall, you know, very tall. Oh yes, extremely! And he talks like a war-horse. "Oh yes! Ha, ha! Well, well! Dear me! How are you, my dear?"' (Here Judith bent forward, very grand, almost to the ground and shook hands solemnly with an invisible midget.) 'Just as though, you know, we hadn't been brought up as children together. He's the City Man, but he's also moving up. Oh yes, very much up indeed! He can tell you all the latest about the Prince and his bride, and what poor Mrs Fitzherbert is doing, and why Lady Jersey chose the Prince *such* a plain partner and what Mr Fox lost last night at cards. He moves doubly, you know, Emma, darling. There's the Will of the moment and the Will of ten years hence – the Will there's going to be if he has any luck. And Christabel. Oh, Christabel! She's like this!' (Judith rolled her eyes, stood on tip-toe and made her face as vacant as a saucepan.) 'She's so stupid you can't believe it! She's for ever running herself down that you shall run her *up*! "I am but an old wife," she'll say. "I have my principles but nobody cares to bother with *me*!" And nobody does, you know. But she's kind, poor Christabel. She has a heart. She's all extravagances. "That's a *sweet* fellow," she will say. "Oh, a *sweet* fellow."' (And Judith gave her voice such a pitch of stupid ecstasy that Emma roared with laughter.)

'And then there are the Herries from Kensington, Pomfret and Rose and dear James and sweet Rodney. Pomfret's kind, but he loves the women, and Rose is so busy catching him that she can think of naught else. Pomfret's stout and dresses grandly. He and Rose are socially finer than Will and Christabel, but they haven't the money. No Herries have as much money as

Will, and the house in Kensington costs a deal. I like Pomfret.
Georges and I found him the other evening at Ranelagh, with a
lady all simpers and jewellery. Oh, it was the loveliest thing!
They had a chicken and a dish of ham between them, and he was
feeding her with the merrythought . . . Mr James Herries puffs
himself like a bull when he walks. Like this.' (Here Judith gave
an admirable imitation.) 'His voice is all falsetto. He's at the
pimple stage.

'Then there are the Cards from Bournemouth. They come
every year to London for the Season. Prosper and Amelia and
the beautiful Jennifer, their daughter. Prosper is nearly fifty
years of age and is most distinguished. He wears a full-bottomed
wig, although it's the fashion no longer, and can tell you all
about the virtues of Bournemouth. He's so grandly dignified
that his knees won't bend, and he has buckles on his shoes as
large as saucers. Amelia's a little woman like a rabbit. But I like
Amelia. She'd be happier in a cottage with a sampler to work at.
But Jennifer, she's a beauty! She really is, Emma. Of the
dark kind! All cloudy splendour and proud as Helen of Troy.

'And then – oh, Emma darling, best of all there are the
Rockages. I've stayed there down in Wiltshire. Yes, twice.
Without Georges, you understand. Maria likes me – wherefore I
can *not* understand! But she does! She thinks I have a soul to be
saved, and so I don't doubt that I have. And what a place! They
haven't a penny between them, and the family coach has rats
in the straw, and they put buckets in the hall when it's raining
to catch the water through the ceiling. But Carey – that's Rockage – must have everything as grand as grand, although the footmen have holes in their stockings, and there isn't food to go
round. The last time I stayed there I half died of discomfort.
You know how it is in a country place where nothing is looked
after. Here it was the *extravagance* of neglect! All day long it
was nothing but pulling at bell-ropes that brought no answer or
always the wrong servant, or a pair of rusty tongs that let slip
a coal that is smaller than your head, or an asthmatic pair of
bellows, the coals always out, all the pencils with their heads
broken off, and *such* a mess of things in every room that was
lived in – phials, fiddles, books and knick-knacks, and the rooms
that weren't lived in as cold as tombs with all the family portraits
frowning from damp. And the gardens! Oh, Emma, the gardens!
All laid out in the ancient taste. You know – a mile's length of
clipped trees with spouting lions, fish ponds as round as a wheel,
with six or eight flights of neglected terraces and a summer-

house, all broken-down windows and decayed bluebottles.

'And the religion. Oh, Emma, the religion! Early morning, all the maids and the footmen with their patched heels in air, while Carey read a sermon, and trampling through the Wiltshire mud with Maria delivering tracts on the villagers, and Madeline, Carey's sister, mad with enforced virginity, talking to herself in the cupboard ... And yet, Emma, it's there that I feel all Herries and want to feel so. Half of me is so Herries that I understand Will's ambition and Carey's pride and am proud of Jennifer's beauty because she's Herries like myself. But the other half of me ... that's with Francis and Reuben and Georges and is lost in Cumberland peat. That's from my father, Emma, and I doubt it will ruin me in the end. But when I'm at Grosset or Kensington or Will's place I'm *all* Herries, and I would run all the establishment and see how the butter's used and where the beef bones go to and how every penny fares. Were it not for Georges I'd be mistress of Will's place by now, and Comptroller at Grosset, but they're afraid of Georges. They think he may be hanged any day, and they don't want a hanging relation.'

'Well,' said Emma reflectively, 'I'm glad that there's plenty of money. Money! Money! Judy, my darling, I'd sell my heart and lungs for money. I've never enough.'

'To tell you truth, neither have we,' said Judith, dropping her voice. 'I was speaking a trifle out of order, maybe, when I said that Georges' business was admirable. It might be if he'd attend to it, but we've been put to some odd straits, and it isn't twice or thrice only he's been in the lock-up.'

'But not today!' cried Georges, laughing. They looked up. He was standing in the doorway with his nightcap still on his head, a quilted blue bed-gown wrapped around him, rubbing his eyes and yawning.

This was an uneasy moment for Emma. In spite of her size she was a deeply shy woman, ready to burst into tears at any moment from sensitiveness. In the bad old days Georges had hated her; moreover, she was uneasy with anyone who had known her in the raggle-taggle times when she had been poor old Gauntry's mistress. Two years ago Georges had been polite to her and that was all.

Now, however, his regard was amiable. He was stouter than he had been, she reflected, but still very handsome. She was no trivial observer, and at once she realized that Judith's influence over him was now a very real one. Their relations had changed.

He was more good-natured, less self-willed, a little lazy, some of his earlier energy dissipated. All this she realized in the next half-hour, and with it her attitude to Judith insensibly altered. Judith had a new power. She was somebody now. Emma surrendered to her, but resisted her too, a mixed attitude that Judith would rouse out of many of her later companions.

They spent the happiest hour. Both Georges and Judith were of a ravenous hunger. In the cupboard there was a cold pie, a rice pudding, beer and cheese. They had everything out on the shabby table and ate as they were, Judith in a yellow jacket, her nightdress, and Emma's hat still on her head. Georges was kind to Emma. He had won money the night before over the contest between Battling Ginger and Monty Punt. He was right now for a day or two. He scattered his winnings on to the table among the pie and the rice pudding, and let Judith take what she wanted. Emma, encouraged, was able to come out with her project, which was that they should both accompany her to the 'Elephant and Castle' at Newington for supper. She had, she told them, a young friend, a Mr Audley, and the young friend had a coach, and he would drive the three of them, through the fields, to Newington. They should drive back under the moon with the hedges smelling of flowers; at the 'Elephant' there were sheep and cows and on a June night country dances on the Green.

So they all gave themselves up to being happy. They had a fine natural capacity for happiness, all three of them, and being in one degree or another all adventurers, happiness brought no kind of obligation with it. Georges dressed there in front of Emma, and there was no false modesty on either side. The bells of St Mary le Bow had struck three by the time that everyone was ready.

The usual dining hour was anything between three and four, but they would wait now until they could enjoy their supper under the trees of the 'Elephant'.

Georges, when dressed, was a dandy, and Emma sighed romantically, as she always did at thought or vision of a handsome man.

His stoutness, not yet pronounced, added to the impressiveness of his foreign good looks. He was a man now, not a boy, a man with a reckless air, a good-natured mouth, a roving and humorous eye. A man to be trusted? Emma thought not. A man for a woman to love? Of course. A man for Judy to love? Oh, Emma hoped so, but could not be sure. They made a fine pair. The colour of Georges' coat was dark cinnamon, no collar to it, single-breasted; the waistcoat fully seen, of light blue satin cut low under the pockets, under which, as well as down the front and at the bottom, was a border of rosebuds, jonquils and heart's-ease. He wore a lace frill, called a Chitterling, the ends of his white cravat trimmed with lace, and the ruffles at his wrists the same, his hair powdered, no curls, but brushed back from his face and hanging in a black bag with a rosette behind. Judith wore a jacquette of pale silver-coloured silk and the bodice and underdress were of dark wine colour. Her red hair was unpowdered and fell down behind with curled ends, and perched on it she wore a hat of light straw, also of pale silver. Her shoes had silver buckles.

Judith thought the clothes that she and Georges wore on this day important, for she describes them in her Journal minutely, and at the top of the page has written in a hand that is still very childish: 'The Happiest Day of My Life.'

Mr Audley's chariot-chaise was to be met in Holborn so they engaged a hackney-carriage and drove there, Judith with her head out of window for there was so much to see on this very fine day. They rattled along with a great deal of bumping, jerking in and out of holes, climbing little hills and running down the other sides again, along Blowbladder Street, past Butcher Hall Lane, Bath Street – sacred to the memory of Charles II – Ivy Lane, where Dr Johnson had his Club, under the ancient gateway beside Giltspur Street, up Snow Hill, past Cock Lane, Cow Lane, Fleet Market, then a steep climb up Holborn Hill, when they moved so slowly that little boys looked in at the windows, a gentleman with silver rings in his ears wanted Judith to buy a green parrot, the Bishop of Ely's Palace with his gardens, Thavie's Inn, Staple Inn and so to Holborn. Here, at a corner of Whetstone Park, was Mr Audley with his coach.

Judith had already asked Emma to tell her all she could about Mr Audley, but Emma could not tell her very much. It seemed that Mr Audley was a young man with a very rich City father (here it was Georges who pricked up his ears), that he was a great admirer of Emma's ('A passion for the Play, my dear. He was in Salisbury at the time, buying a horse, and he saw me in *Othello*. I am free to confess that Emilia is not so splendid a role, most especially in the version that we were playing, which was one with music, and Othello, Mr Barnstaple, had a fine tenor and played the flute in the third act, but I was wearing white satin, and poor little Miss Huxley, who was playing Desdemona, was a chit of a thing that you could fit into a nutshell. To be honest, my dear, he liked my size. He was heard to say loudly in the pit that the Furze was his style and – well, we were friends very shortly after. He is a nice young fellow with most agreeable manners.')

He flushed with pleasure when he saw them. His coach was very smart, of a bright bay colour with silver ornaments on the harness. He was attended by a stout driver in a blue and yellow striped waistcoat who, as they approached, was engaged from the box in a sharp and apparently rather bitter discussion with two gentlemen and a fruit barrow.

Everything and everyone was very lively, including the June sun, the shopmen standing in their doorways, the glittering glass of the shop windows, an old man with a fiddle to whose tunes several children were dancing, a stout lady with a bell who was selling pinks and roses, and a church near by ringing peals as though it were mad with joy.

Mr Audley was introduced, they all climbed in and started off. Judith gave herself up to complete enjoyment. Everything was as she would have it, except that she would have preferred a chaise to a coach, because in a chaise she could see more, but in a chaise there would not be room for them all.

Mr Audley was exceedingly attentive to her, so attentive that she was afraid lest Emma should be jealous. His method of attention was to ask innumerable questions, to which, however, he appeared to expect no kind of answer. He had a foolish expressionless face, but his questions were for the most part educational, concerning literature and the drama. Judith soon conceived a feeling of maternal care for him, as though he were an infant or a puppy. He seemed to her so very eager, inexperienced and untutored.

'Pray, ma'am, you have read *Evelina*, of course. Do you not find the Branghtons too amusing? Is it not laughable where the Captain throws Madame Duval into a ditch? Is not the close inexpressibly touching? Is London not dull in June – no Covent Garden, only the Little Theatre? Pray, ma'am, have you been to the Tower lately? Are not the tigers and lions fine? I saw recently Foote's play *The Minor*. It is all against the Methodists. I laughed myself into hysterics. I was at the Pantheon the other evening. It is never the same since it was burnt. I was at a Masquerade there, as mean as ever you saw. But the fireworks at Marylebone! Have you seen the fireworks at Marylebone? I hope you find this coach easy. I have a phaeton, bought only last week, but Mrs Furze told me that friends might accompany her. I trust you are comfortable.'

It was his way, she assured herself, of courtesy and politeness. She need not listen to his questions if she did not wish. She had once and again, an uneasy feeling that Georges was watching Mr Audley with a growing conviction that he would, a little later, be an easy friend to win money from. She pushed that from her. She did not care just now to consider that side of Georges' character. Yes, she surrendered herself completely to happiness. There had been many days in the last two years when she had been, it seemed to her, living on the very edge of irretrievable disaster. One touch and she and Georges would both tumble over into a bottomless pit, and no one in the world care that they had gone. She knew Georges so well now that the black side of the account of her life with him was fearfully familiar. But slowly, slowly she was influencing him. Month by month he was less drunken, attended more steadily to his Whitehaven business, submitted to her will.

By a constant good humour, a perpetual check on her fears and alarms, a refusal to be astonished at any sudden calamity, a trained restraint on her own nerves, temper, moods – by all these things she had gradually governed him, he not knowing that he was governed. The odd thing was that, although she knew now by heart all the iniquities of which he was capable, all his tempers, his violences, his infidelities, his shadiness, she loved him more than ever. He was still her created work, although she was wise enough now never to show him that it was so. And there was, when all was said, somewhere in his strange character, a strain of sweetness, of loyalty, of liberality, of boyish candour, that made him to her, with reason, endearing. But, when all was said, she loved him, had always loved him, would always love him. There could be no one else for her.

It was enchanting when, after crossing the river, they left the town behind them and passed into the open fields. The blue sky was cloudless. Everything was painted with a shining lustre, and the trees were dark at the heart of their green foliage. They were at the 'Elephant' almost before they knew it.

Here, indeed, there was liveliness! In the centre was the stout signpost with its four pointers, and round and about it all the world was on the move. There was a countryman on a donkey driving two other donkeys in front of him, two shouting peasants with whip and dog, urging their stupid but amiable cows, two coaches drawn up at the inn door, and another, loaded with people, nearly riding down a little collection of barrows piled with flowers, fruit and vegetables. There was a private coach crammed with six people, and led by four horses, chariots, hackney-coaches, groups of country-people stood about enjoying the lovely afternoon, a party of very fine ladies and gentlemen, moving as though they were creatures of another planet, brilliant in their colours of red and purple, children outside the gardens playing at ball, dogs everywhere, and a superb solitary gentleman riding his horse, his servant riding behind him on another. Judith's heart beat with ecstasy when she saw all this life. She put her hand through Georges' arm and walked as proud as a duchess with him into the inn.

Here everything was in a bustle with the arrival of the two coaches, so, very soon, they crossed the road to the Gardens on the other side. These were simple Gardens, not like Marylebone or Bagnigge Wells, but they were what Judith preferred. There were 'Chinese' benches, rough wooden tables, very childish amusements with a pillory for a gentleman to sit in until he was liberated by a kiss from a lady, a maze in which lovers might be lost and a peepshow rather the worse for wear and weather. But soon, Judith was attending to none of these things, for sitting on the bench, her mouth open with excitement at all the things and people to see, her legs swinging, her eyes shining with delight, she was aware that Georges, of his own volition, had come to sit beside her, had his arm around her, was pressing her to him. All the world was forgotten in the heart-beating discovery of that moment. He had come of his own will, there in the public view, he who was so shy of demonstration, of anything that could attract general attention.

Wise from experience she showed no great responsiveness, only moved a little closer to him. But her heart was beating, and within herself she was thinking: 'I must keep this in memory. Whatever comes in the future nothing can take this away!'

All she said aloud was: 'Oh, how hungry I am! It is almost six, and we have eaten nothing all day long.'

'There was the cold pie,' he reminded her; then he whispered in her ear: 'Judy, do you love me?'

'A little,' she answered.

'Are you happy?'

'Yes – but when I have eaten I shall be happier.'

'I think you are charming. I am seeing you today with fresh eyes.'

'Your old wife!' She turned round to him, her eyes dancing. 'After so many years you can find that she has charm?'

'You are better. You are vastly improved. You are a woman now and yet you are still a child. Life has taught you something.'

'Marriage with you has taught me something,' she answered, laughing. 'Striving to alter you—'

'I doubt your capacity to amend me,' he said. 'Nobody enjoys better spirits than I – at times. Today when the sun is shining and my French blood is warmed and you, my little wife, are beside me, and we are in fine clothes and have money . . . Then I think heigh-ho! how virtuous I could be! But soon it will be Mr Moss and cold mutton and flying down side-streets to avoid creditors and the fog and rain—'

'Meanwhile,' she cried, 'let us be happy now. We have a happy day. We must enjoy it.'

'We must enjoy it,' he repeated after her. His eyes lighted as he saw Mr Audley coming towards them.

'Sir,' he cried. 'I would have a wager with you. Guineas that the next person through that gate yonder is a female.'

Mr Audley looked rather nervous. Judith saw that he was no gambler by nature.

'Why, surely,' he agreed in his silly fluttering voice. 'Guineas it is, sir.'

They watched the gate. Judith saw, with an odd mixture of tenderness and chagrin, that Georges was watching with an eager excitement worthy of some great hazard. His body was tingling with his suspense. For a moment no one came. Then a stout man in a high beaver hat, very solemn in his claret-coloured coat, marched in through the gate.

'Damn!' cried Georges. 'It is against me! But double or quits, Mr Audley, that the next is a female.'

'No, no,' Judith broke in. 'For shame, Georges. I am famished. Food I must have . . .'

She saw his brow clouding. He would, in another moment, have forgotten all his recent affection for her had not, fortunately, Emma been seen arriving and with her a serving-man.

She was now in her proper and most happy element, arranging ceremonies that had to do with food and drink. They were to have their meal under a large spreading chestnut. They would have veal cutlets, a small green-goose and asparagus, a damson pie . . .

Judith was long afterwards to remember that scene, the soft warm air, the cool green benignity of the great tree, the children

playing on the sward near to them, the noise of the coaches and
the carriages, the voices, sheep bleating – all beyond the gate;
the laughter of lovers happily lost in the maze near to them, her
own happiness as she sat beside Georges, her hand once and
again resting on his knee.

They were all so happy, Mr Audley so proud of his entertaining, and Emma in her tall hat at almost bursting point with
pleasure at the food, the cheerfulness, the general sense of security. Poor dear! Her life did not provide her with so many
secure moments!

She complained, of course, of the cooking as in duty bound,
being herself so great a connoisseur, but hugely nevertheless she
enjoyed it. She shouted orders to the waiters, and herself, at one
moment, hurried forward to inspect the green-goose on its
way through the gate from the inn opposite.

Then, as the sun sank beyond the garden walls and everything
was suffused with a pale shadow of gold, the dark friendly
patterns growing lengthy on the grass, a silver star or two
winking through the trees, a fiddler drew near and with him a
woman, who had a strong sweet voice. She sang:

> 'Beauty clear and fair,
>   Where the air
> Rather like a perfume dwells:
> Where the violet and the rose
> Their blue veins and blush disclose
> And come to honour nothing else;
> Where to live near
> And planted there
> Is to live, and still live new;
> Where to gain a favour is
> More than light, perpetual bliss –
> Make me live by serving you!
>
> 'Dear, again back recall
>   To this light,
> A stranger to himself and all!
> But the wonder and the story
> Shall be yours, and else the glory;
> I am your servant and your thrall.
>
> 'Dear, again back recall
>   To this light!'

Oh, that this moment might last for ever, never to change. This voice, this shining light, enclosed in this garden . . .

Georges, too, must have felt something of it for he rose impetuously and pressed money on the fiddler, then turned back to them a little shame-faced. But he kissed Judith before he sat down. The dusk came; candles were lit. There was dancing on the green.

But, alas, when it was time to go it was found that the coachman was perilously drunk. He greeted them all with a warm and most appreciatory affection. He would have embraced Emma, quarrelled with a little gentleman near by, who had, he fancied, insulted her.

Mr Audley was greatly ashamed and not of much value in the situation. He twittered like a bird whose nest is in danger, looking at Emma as though to implore her not to like him the less for this accident. Georges was of excellent practical use. It was just the situation for his temperament. He helped to hoist the man on the box, frightened away the interested spectators, quietened the horses and threatened the coachman with such dire penalties were there an accident that for the moment he was sobered. So they started off down the road under the stars. There was a moon, and everywhere a radiant peace.

But not for long. After a while the coachman began to sing; the horses took fright; the coach rocked and rocked again. Georges attempted, with head out of the window, to bring the man to his senses. There he was with throat uplifted, singing to the moon. A moment later there was a fearful heave, and the coach was on its side in the ditch. Georges climbed through the broken door, ran to the horses' heads. The others, uninjured except for a shaking and a bruise or so, climbed painfully after him and sat in the hedge. The coachman, his singing silenced, was perched skywards, fallen almost on to the horses' backs, his thick legs dangling. Georges assisted him down, and he at once began to snivel, his fist in his eyes like a schoolboy's.

The shafts and one wheel were broken. The other wheel raised in mid-air made a fantastic gesture.

At length Mr Audley and the coachman, still snivelling, set off for the nearest village to find some other conveyance. Emma, Judith and Georges sat in the hedge over a ditch, and a network of fiery stars shone down upon them. There might be highwaymen, an added adventure, but it seemed not; for the whole world was still, holding its breath under the moon.

In the shadow of the fantastic coach with its clamant wheel Georges and Judith sat close together. He seemed to be, in the spirit of that beneficent night, a transformed creature. He declared his love as though this were the first night that he had met her. She held her breath, catching the divine moment that it might be with her for ever.

'Judith, I love you tonight. I have never told you that before.'

'No, never – and I have wanted it so.'

'It has grown in me. Through all my vagaries it has been ever drawing closer to me. *You* have been drawing closer to me.'

'And I love you, Georges. I always shall.'

'Perhaps this is the beginning of a new life for us.'

She shook her head humorously.

'No. Things will be up and down again as they have always been, but I am very happy for this moment.'

She was in a transcendent happiness. The two different strands of her life were suddenly united in one common glory – her practical daily Herries life, and the dream, that which separated her from the rest of her kind. Love had for a moment united them.

The fantastic wheel of the coach against the sky seemed to promise her something:

'Trust this moment.'

And to threaten her something:

'This moment is already almost gone.'

'Oh, let me keep Georges!' was her unuttered prayer. And if in the sequel her prayer was denied her, it was also granted. Her whole nature in that half-hour was fulfilled.

In the hedge, bathed in the warm flower-scented air, for a brief while they were completely united.

THE HERRIES BALL

MAY 17TH, 1796

JUDITH WENT TO the famous Masquerade at Will Herries' house, given there in the month of May of the year 1796, dressed as her mother.

She had never seen her mother, who had died in giving birth to her. She had seen no picture of her; nevertheless it was a link in the strange sequence of events that once there should have been a child sheltering in its mother's skirts at a Christmas games in a Borrowdale farm, that then there should have been a woman crying over her lost lover in Carlisle streets, that again there should have been a weary woman knocking at the door of Herries in Rosthwaite, that now Judith, dressed as a ragged gipsy, her red hair loose about her head, should be waiting in an almost breathless excitement for the coach to take her to another Herries house.

There were to be many consequences from the Masquerade on this night, consequences as important to the whole Herries family as the quarrel that rose out of this occasion, consequences that helped to make Judith's life afterwards what it was, and from that to affect generations and possibly the colour of England itself. For if, on that night, Judith had not been dressed as a gipsy, would the beautiful Jennifer have snapped the ivory stick of Mrs Will's fan – that famous fan!

It is still in dispute as to whether the mandarins painted on it were clothed in blue or silver. A letter still extant, written on the day after the Masquerade by Rose, Pomfret's wife, speaks of 'Christabel's *blue* Fan'. On the other hand, in Judith's own Journal, there are these words: '... And so, scarcely knowing what she did, so angry was she, she snapped one of the sticks of Christabel's Fan with the Silver Figures that had been lying on the Table at her side ...'

We may go back, too, and ask History whether if Francis Herries, senior, had not sold his mistress at a Keswick Fair, would Jennifer Cards have recollected the fable of old Maria and her spaniel, and, if she had not ... Of all the things of which we are uncertain in this world – and there are more every day – we can at least be sure that History has for one of its subjects the ultimate importance of trifles. A coin rolled on a table, a verse by Mr Pope, a cabbage grown in a stubborn garden, a foggy night in Carlisle, a players' booth in Penrith, scattered snow reflected like feathers in a lake – such things were the landmarks in the life of Francis Herries of Herries. Such things were to mark the life of his daughter also. And it is in the chronicle of such things that the history of the Herries family finds coherence.

Judith and Georges were ready dressed waiting for the hackney-coach, Judith as her mother and Georges as Mephistopheles. Four of the Robinson children, thumbs in their mouths, stood inside the doorway, wondering at the splendour, and a moment later there was Mrs Robinson herself, a baby in her arms, to announce that the coach had arrived.

Georges was superb and was well aware of it. He wore scarlet shoes, black silk hose and doublet, a crimson cloak, a red peaked hat with a black feather. His costume, tight-fitting, displayed his figure to splendid advantage. He knew that his ankles, his thighs, his chest, could suffer any display. He would, if he did not take care, soon be too stout, but that was not yet.

Judith's dress was orange colour, trimmed with silver; it was ragged a little, showing her neck and arms. She had a wreath of flowers in her hair. She looked a child of ten; her excitement gave her a colour of eager expectation. But although her excitement was great, she was yet able to be practical. She had her anxieties. Georges was in one of his wild moods. They had, during the last three months, been living very precariously. She was not sure – he would not tell her – but she fancied that he had been losing heavily at cards. Young Mr Stane (whom she hated) had arrived three days before from Whitehaven; in his sinister and complimentary politeness she had imagined threats and bad omens.

She was in the difficult position of attempting to protect Georges, but not knowing from what to protect him. He had been in his most cynical, mocking, restless temper, treating her as though she were a helpless child, assuming for himself an air of profound wisdom (which was, as she well knew, quite unjustified). She could only control or have any influence over him by asking him no questions. She would not ask Henry Stane anything. The lovely intimacy of that wonderful June day at Newington had never returned. She had been wise to tell herself that day that she must treasure it, for there would not be many like it. Her anxiety over him only made her love him the more, but she was working in the dark, fearing she knew not what, dreading some awful disaster. She never saw Henry Stane without knowing her fear increase. And she was not yet twenty-two years of age.

However, it was her nature to be concerned with the happiness of everyone who came near to her, and, before they started, she was busy with all the Robinson children. They were a dirty little group, as, indeed, necessity forced them to be. Judith, with her passion for cleanliness, had kept her place as decent as she might, but the rest of the house, although some of the rooms were let to gentlemen of means, was a pig-sty. Many of the window-frames were black with soot, windows were stuffed with paper and rag;

in one room eleven members of an Irish family slept in two beds; a drunken tailor on the floor above Judith kept a pig in his apartment.

Mrs Robinson had enough to do with her lodgers, her family and her husband's apprentices. She was not a bad-natured woman, and she had a deep admiration for Judith because she kept her room so clean, was always in a sensible mood and was connected with fine families. She had intended binding out her eldest girl Fanny, a child of eleven, to a tambour-maker, but very reluctantly, for she knew well enough the cruelty that these apprentice children must suffer. And Fanny was a bright, pretty child. But Judith had persuaded her to keep her at home, had even herself employed the child and paid her a wage. Then there was the little chimney-sweep (already out on his work this evening), who was falling into bad ways. Judith had been looking after him a little, letting him come into her room in the early afternoon when he had had his sleep out and was ready for any mischief. He was a funny old little boy and regarded Judith as just of his own age . . .

So now she pinched the cheek of one child, patted the verminous head of another, smiled at the harassed mother and then, followed by her splendid Mephistopheles, picked her way down the filthy staircase.

Chelsea was a great distance in the coach, and they had plenty of opportunity for conversation. Avoiding any display of sentiment as she always did when she wanted to get at the truth, she challenged him at once as to the position: things were bad? He shrugged his shoulders. He had been unlucky. He was always unlucky now. Henry Stane had come down from Whitehaven with his usual complaints. Henry Stane – she shivered. Why had he so much to do with everything now? Well, he wanted to be a partner with Wix and Georges. He was ambitious. Because his father had once been a simple fisherman, he thought it fine to have risen in the world as he had; now he wanted to rise still further. Judith, trying to think connectedly in the jolting coach, had an impulse to implore Georges to free himself from Stane, buy him out, do anything. She did not know why she dreaded him as she did. Her mind flew back to the night in Cockermouth when she had helped to save Humphrey. That dark cellar, the fugitive, they were connected in some way with Stane and his ambitions . . . But she said nothing. After the night of that quarrel in Watendlath she had determined not to question Georges about his Whitehaven affairs unless he wished.

'Don't sell the farm,' was all she murmured, as much to herself as to him.

'The farm?'

'Watendlath. You said once that if all else failed you could be happy there, in the life . . .'

'By God, I could! It's strange, Judy, but when you speak of it I could leave this London and the coin and the stinking candles – all shut up, closed – I'd give a fortune to see that water now tumbling over the stones and watch those smutty-nosed sheep pushing up under the stone wall . . .'

She, too, had for a moment a vision – the cut in Armboth Fell, the Tarn when the wind played on it, the ridge of the Fell looking over Borrowdale.

But with his French impatience and eagerness for practical things he drove all that from him. He had now an immense confidence in her common sense and a respect for her judgement. It had grown in him through the years. So he began to outline the schemes that he had for making use of all the Herries connexions. This was an old topic with him. He often blamed her for not making more of all her Herries family. They liked her. Those old Rockages would do anything for her. Will was like her own brother. Will Herries was becoming a very rich man. Everyone talked of him. Why could they not give up this hand-to-mouth existence? Why should she not get Georges some place in Will's City business? Tonight would be a fine time to work something. Will would be in great feather at having so grand a Ball in his house. Judith would be able to do anything with him.

Judith sighed to herself. This was an old, old topic. Georges always raised it when things were going badly. When things went well he loudly despised Will and his business, and that he wouldn't be tied in the dirty City for all India's wealth. It was only when he was in a corner that he thought of it. Yes, Judith sighed. The omens were bad. Georges must be desperate. And she could not tell him what was the truth – that all the Herries family regarded Georges as a wild adventurer, almost as a vagabond. That they would not have Georges, this little gambling Frenchman from nowhere, into any intimate connexion with them, not if you offered them all China! It was bad enough with the country crowded with French refugees as it was . . .

Georges went on. How clever Will had been about all this French War that was ruining so many men, and he had managed to make his profit out of it! There were rumours that he had been lending the Prince money. Everything that he touched seemed to turn to gold! And Georges was just the man for him! They were much of an age. Will could not be more than twenty-six or so. So young a man must need partners.

'He has partners,' Judith remarked. 'He is the youngest in his firm.'

Well, young or not, he was the lively one. What would he not be at forty? And he had been in the City for so short a time! Georges *must* make some association with him! Surely Judith could manage it. Judith had an impulse to turn to him: 'It's your own fault that I can't – you with your tempers and sudden idleness and bad company and gambling and the rest!' But she might as well have said: 'You, Georges Paris, because you were born Georges Paris.'

Their coach was going very slowly now, for they were approaching Ranelagh and there was much traffic. The road (that had been but a few years before all country, but now buildings were springing up) was crowded with chairs, private coaches, hackneys, boys running with lights, families walking – so much noise of wheels and shouting that Georges and Judith could not hear one another speak. Now, as always, she surrendered at once to all the excitement. She forgot all troubles, financial, domestic, thought only of the Ball and all the fun there would be.

Will's house stood in its own ground. The whining purr of the violins could be heard coming, as it were, from the heart of the trees. Above the wide staircase the long ballroom glittered under the wavering flutter of the candles that blew gently in their hanging silver lustres.

Will had taken a bigger house than his present needs when, at a moment, Sir Frederick Cottenham must sell at a ridiculously low price because of a night's loss at cards. Servants were so cheap as to cost almost nothing, except for mouths to be fed, and although, because of the French War, food was more costly every day, here there seemed to be always an abundance. It came from somewhere, Christabel herself scarcely knew whence.

But the events of that strange evening began for Judith not as she stood masked watching the fantastic medley of Turks, Nuns, Punchinellos, Italian Ladies of the Renaissance, Devils, Monks, Columbines and the rest, but rather at the sudden sight of Francis, disguised only by his mask, wearing otherwise a plain suit of black and silver. She would have moved at once to his side, but she must first speak to Will and Christabel. They were the only two unmasked in the room. There was something,

Judith felt at once, a little pathetic in Will's sense of triumph. She
had a divination (how utterly surprised he would be if he knew!)
of what this glorious moment would mean to him, and of the
jealousies, hatreds, contempts that his very success would rouse
up against him.

Yes, even now, this very room would be seething with them!
The Herries who were here would be resenting his power, but
resolving to make use of it, and those who were not Herries
would be scorning him for a City merchant who was pushing into
Society. And yet the Herries were as ancient and well-rooted a
family as any in England. But it was new, this pushing upwards
of the merchant by power of his wealth, this very Ball the symbol
of the reluctant yielding of the old world to the new.

Will would have no sense of any of this. She realized, looking
at his thin stiff body, marked with the sharp horse-bones of the
Herries, his eyes lit with a cold, nevertheless animated pride, that
he could feel nothing but his success. He might well be proud.
Little more than a boy, he yet had arrived at this power. But
Judith felt that in Christabel there was a real uneasiness. In an
ugly dress of a pale yellow, her hair done too high for the present
fashion, she seemed almost to be expecting sneers and insults.
Judith saw that this evening had been both her proud expectation and anxious dread for months before. She was in a
state of nervous tension that might lead to anything. And, in
fact, at this time moods, tempers, resentments, wild pleasures
were very near the surface. There was in the London of that
moment much social etiquette, but little social control. The world
was turning over, and everyone's foothold was a little insecure.

Neither Will nor Christabel had at that moment very much
time for Judith, and after a while she was free to find Francis.
A minuet was in progress. The coloured masked figures stirred
in the candle-shine like fragments of a pattern moving towards
a perfect arrangement. The moment when that arrangement was
achieved – would the world stop? But on every occasion something prevented perfection. Tall high windows were covered
with curtains of silver brocade. On the distant gallery the
musicians played. Judith could see, above the clouded colour
that was veiled with a kind of dim smoke, one fiddler, very thin,
his arm raised like a stick, a sharp-pointed nose that seemed almost
to be directing the whole room . . .

She found Francis and touched his arm.

'Sir,' she said, 'a word with you,' as though they were
strangers. Then she laughed. They stepped back into the curve

of the windowplace. They had not seen one another for six months.

Francis had, the year previous, made friends with a Mr Samuel Rogers. This gentleman was a poet, who had become famous with a piece entitled 'The Pleasures of Memory'. He lived at Stoke Newington, and Francis had stayed with him there. In January of this same year he had been involved in some of the troubles connected with what was known as the White Terror, the suspicious and terrified reaction in England of the Terror in France, and Francis had been able to show him some assistance during this anxiety. He was, from Francis' account, a sharp-tongued little man, bitter in speech about everyone, but of great active kindliness in deed. Francis, at least, seemed to understand him, and in his company lately had met many interesting people. Rogers had London rooms in Paper Buildings, and Francis had had wonderful evenings there with men like Horne Tooke, Parr, Sheridan, and even the great Mr Fox himself. Francis had taken to a sort of sporadic journalism, the political variety. He also had published essays in the *Gentleman's Magazine* under the pseudonym of Peter Mountain.

But he seemed tonight to have but little interest in his own career. He was making a new life for himself; but Judith soon saw that it was no more the life that he wanted than the earlier Cumberland one had been. He was as alone here in this sounding, moving gaiety as he had been beside the silence of the Watendlath Tarn.

He seized upon Judith with a kind of feverish thirst. His need tonight was for someone who could give him some sort of reassurance. Behind his mask his loneliness seemed for a moment to darken the candles, the coloured clothes, to put out all the splendour. She had her own excitements, her own anxieties, but as always when she was with anyone whom she loved she forgot her own life in her eagerness to benefit the other.

'Judith, let's escape together thousands of miles away – to some island where there are no people.'

'Only the savages,' she answered him, laughing.

'Well, we Herries are savages. I hate us in the mass. Behind the masks you can scent Herries a mile away. There, in that silly black costume, that's Maria Rockage, and near her in the red and gold that's Rockage. There to the right, the Punchinello, that's Montague Cards; there's Amelia, dressed as a Nun, dancing. We are a horrid family, so pleased with ourselves. For ever casting someone into outer darkness. "Oh, he's mad." "She's lunatic." "That's an atheist." And for what are we proud?

Because we are English, because we are Herries, as though you said: "Because I'm a cow." Judy, there was old Maria. Have you ever heard of Maria? She died in '45. She lived almost to be a hundred, within a month or two. When she failed her century Herries were angry all over the country. That is a record of the sort that they value. I have heard my father tell how your father visited them in Keswick after old Maria's funeral and found them all at odds. But her dog was there, the only thing that cared for her, and your father said that the scorn of them all in that dog's eyes . . .' He broke off. Looking at her half quizzically, he added: 'You know you have no right here, you and Georges. You are vagabonds. And I am one also.'

'I know,' Judith answered. 'And I had the whim to dress as my mother. I never saw her. But I fancied her at this Ball. What they would all say, if she came in from Borrowdale with the mud on her shoes! But I feel Herries as well, Francis. I would like to be the head of the family, very wealthy, telling them all what to do.' Then, catching his arm: 'Why, see, that must be Jennifer! Did you ever see anyone so lovely ?'

Francis turned, looking more closely into the room.

'Do you know,' he said, 'I have never seen Jennifer ? My lovely cousin . . .'

But he broke off. Quite close to them a beautiful girl was passing. Jennifer Cards was, in that year when Francis first saw her, twenty-six years of age. Francis Herries was thirty-six. That first sight of her was one of the more important moments of Herries history evolved on that eventful evening. She was dressed as Catherine de' Medici in a magnificent robe of slashed crimson, and behind her lovely head a stiff high collar of silver. Ropes of pearls were in her black hair. She was tall, carried herself superbly, her skin had the whiteness of a white rose. She walked lazily as though half asleep. Francis stared. He could not speak. It was as though, after all these years, his dream had been, by some favouring magician, created into fact for him.

'Her dress suits her nobly,' Judith said. But he did not hear her. He stood like a man lost.

Like a man lost! It was from that moment, perhaps, that Judith began to have the sense that this whole affair was a dream, and a dangerous dream too. Her excitement did not leave her, but the happy element in it. She began to feel that there was something evil in the air.

The dance had stopped, and the dancers broken up. A sort of wildness crept into the house. Not far away, in Ranelagh, down the dark alleys, couples were standing in the shadow, body strained against body in deep embrace. Although the music in the room had ceased it still seemed to linger in the trees, and little companies of wanderers gathered at the garden gates, watching the house so brilliantly lit, heard the lean fiddler. Was he seated among the chimney pots? Was it some strain from the Ranelagh musicians? Or an old beggar fiddling wildly down the road?

Judith saw that she had lost Francis. He cared no more what she said to him. And then she saw another thing. She saw that her own especial Mephistopheles was attracted just as Francis was. But he was more active. His eyes fixed on the lovely lady, Georges waited until he saw her a moment detached, alone. He went up to her and spoke. How exactly Judith knew what the tone of that voice would be, the softness, the charm! His mother's! She saw again, as she often did when she was with him, that moment of her childhood when in the bare room the young man had knelt to the naked woman! Mother and son. Ah, but he had charm when he spoke like that, when his body seemed to tremble behind his voice. She could fancy how his eyes would shine behind the mask! He spoke. Jennifer turned. She looked at him and laughed. He spoke again. She smiled, and they both moved away together, she leading, he following.

Judith shivered. She was cold there in the window. Francis and Georges, the two whom she loved best in the world, they would both leave her at any moment for a fine woman. She had done so much for Georges, but at any instant he forgot her. Indeed, it seemed that no one remembered her. She seemed to be as alone in that crowd as though she were by herself on Brund Fell. Her gipsy's dress, how shabby it was beside all these splendours! And her mother would have been shabby, too, had she been here. Once again she knew that sharp pang of alarm at her own insecurity in this harsh, indifferent world. She had no one but herself. Only her own pride to keep her. No one would care if this moment she vanished for ever. Not Georges? No, not Georges. Emma, perhaps, and at the thought of that large, comforting women the tears stung her eyes, were damp behind the mask. Then she pulled herself up. What did it matter if she *were* alone in the world? So her mother had been, so her father. Oneself was enough. She was aware then that a Mask, dressed as Punchinello, stood motionless at her side. He had been there perhaps for a long while. She turned, and as she did so he spoke:

'You would not expect to find me here,' he said.

She knew at once the voice. It was young Stane. How was young Stane here? She thought he did not know Will. Georges had not brought him. He was always to her uncanny, and his presence now only increased her sense of the strange wildness of the evening.

She said coldly: 'I did not know that you were acquainted with Mr Herries.'

'Yes. You would not know. I had said nothing to Georges. But I have known Mr Herries – for some time.'

She might have guessed that he would. It was like him to make use of every advantage, but to tell no one of what he was doing. He would go far. He was not now more than twenty-five. Ten years back on naked feet he had been selling fish in Whitehaven. Georges had told her of his father, a huge man with a white beard, always reciting the Scriptures, who worshipped this his only child. She turned and looked at young Henry Stane. He had large black eyes behind the mask. He was black-haired, sallow like Georges, but tuned, she knew at once, to a far greater determination. He would eat Georges up! She saw at once how Georges' laziness, good-nature, bad temper, self-indulgence, all these would be simply easy material for Stane's advancement. He was an adventurer too, but he was resolved not to remain one.

Meanwhile she had never hated anyone so much; instinct, fear for Georges, and her own innate repulsion. She was not at her best when she hated anyone. She showed her feeling too readily. She showed it now.

'I congratulate you, Mr Stane,' she said. She saw (and it was to explain very much to her afterwards) that his most maddening quality was his imperturbability. Nothing could touch him. That would infuriate Georges just as now it was angering her. Then his next words amazed her:

'Pardon me. I know how you regard me. All is love or hatred with you. I admire so much your sincerity. But although you dislike me so very much, would you not perhaps allow me to say a word about your husband?'

'No,' she answered.

'Very well. But you have much influence with him.'

'What is it, then?'

'Only that he is making a great mistake to neglect his business so constantly. It is a good business, but it needs attention. He has a good head, Georges, but no discipline.'

She hated the familiarity in his voice. From behind her mask she looked at him.

'I know quite well what you feel about my husband. You wait only to climb over him into his place.'

'No, I assure you, madam—'

'Oh yes, I know very well—'

'Then there is nothing more to say. I meant it civilly.'

As he went it was as though another little Punchinello leapt out of him and sat on his shoulder, its small, puckered, malicious face laughing back at her. How insulting of him! – but there was truth, too, in what he said. And Georges was whispering somewhere in Jennifer's ear.

She had not for many years felt so miserable, so lonely, lost, deserted. Again and again the hot tears gathered behind the mask, and she beat them back. She felt as though some influence separated her from everyone there. She had expected to be so happy, but now that sense of slipping on the very edge of some disaster frightened her so threateningly that all she could do was to start off in search of Georges, to be sure that he was safe. No, she did not care whether he were with Jennifer or no, so long as he were safe.

She was soon caught into the throng. She realized that everything was growing very wild. Couples whirled madly together, colliding with others. Both men and women were elated with their freedom. Many were unmasking. The fiddlers seemed to be playing mad, discordant tunes as though they were drunk.

She had an odd thought as some stout Cardinal tried to catch her by the arm. 'It's because in their hearts they despise Will that they do this. It would not be like this in a really grand house.' She suspected that any of the 'really grand people' who had come had left already.

She was confirmed in her suspicions by having thrown almost into her arms poor Maria Rockage. Maria and Carey had, she knew, come to the Ball with a great sense of condescension. For one thing, Will was young enough to be their son; for another, he was a City man; for another, nothing in London anywhere was so fine and superior as Grosset. So they had come with condescension, with Methodist suspicion, and with kindliness of heart. Judith, young though she was, knew every motive in Maria Rockage's brain, her poverty, so that often at Grosset there was not food enough, her passion for her offspring, her confused Methodism, her muddled benevolence and her real warmth of heart. It was on this last ground that the two of them met.

But now Maria was frightened. She could not find Carey. She *must* find him for they must leave at once. Even the servants downstairs were drinking. There was a little black boy on the staircase eating pie out of a dish. The whole affair was tumbling out of control. She must find Carey and take him home, back to their rooms in Berkeley Square. As a matter of fact, Judith knew that the rooms were not in Berkeley Square, but up a mews in Brick Street. Young Phyllis (safely asleep at Grosset) was for ever betraying her mother's tactics. Maria's terror rose. She especially resented that Jennifer Cards should be the belle of the evening. She disliked and condemned the Bournemouth branch of the family. Moreover, her own rather shabby black dress had been, in intention, a Catherine de' Medici. It had a stiff high black collar. 'She paints shockingly high. How Amelia permits her . . . But Amelia wishes to sell her to the finest bidder, and for all they were so grand when Carey stayed at Bournemouth last year, the rain came into the coach and the straw was soaked . . . and I'm sure that Robert (Jennifer's brother) is an effeminate young man as you'd find among the silks and gauzes at a dressmaker's. Judith, *where* is Carey? Oh, help me to find him! This is, indeed, pandemonium.'

Almost everyone now had unmasked, and the scene had a strange phantasmal beauty.

In the brilliant dusty light, figures moved now to country dances. One followed another, the 'top couple' always 'calling the dance'. There were Chain Figure, Allemand, Triumph, Swing Corners, Poussette and many more. The dancers kept their places, observed their decorum. It was beyond them, in the alcoves, up and down the stairs, in the hall, that the coloured figures, devils and monks, courtesans and milkmaids, Columbines and sea-captains tumbled and laughed, whispered and embraced. Silver and purple, cinnamon and orange, grey and crimson broke, melted, formed, as though from the gilt ceiling with the pink naked cherubs a figure solemn, sad-faced, remote, hiding a gigantic yawn, absent-mindedly pulled the strings.

In any case the Herries strings were pulled that night. By a kind of fate the little Herries figures were drawn together and with disastrous consequences.

For Christabel Herries the evening had become a torture. She was only a girl in years, although tall and gawky of figure. Will's wealth had come suddenly. Of the many persons invited she knew herself not half, and their masquerades made them only more mysterious to her.

At that time in London it was a very general complaint that many persons came to private Balls and Masquerades who were quite unknown to their hosts and hostesses. It was the increasing licence of these London seasons that led to the strict etiquette of Bath and other watering-places. With the divisions at Court, the uncertainty of the war with France, the consciousness of a lower class slowly but increasingly vocal, the new importance of the business man from the City, the advancing licence of Vauxhall, Marylebone and the many lesser resorts, no hostess during the last years of that century but knew alarms and terrors that would have horrified her grandmother. No smaller hostess, in any case – and Christabel was a very new hostess indeed. It is an old and very true axiom that nothing can harm a party save the anxieties and alarm of the host and hostess themselves. All would have been well on this especial evening had Christabel been able to command herself. Unfortunately, when the crisis arrived, Will was elsewhere. He in fact saw nothing the matter with his Ball. It would have taken a great deal more than a few riotous spirits to upset his complacent equanimity. He had also enjoyed no small quantity of his own wine, which he thought excellent; he congratulated himself on acquiring it cheaply from a Jewish gentleman in the City. He was dancing the Triumph with a lady quite unknown to him, but, in his eyes, of an especial fascination, when Christabel so desperately needed his support. There were to be many occasions afterwards when he would have given half his wealth had he only been there that he might have prevented what occurred.

Many times in the records of any family it must seem that the stage has been set with especial and malicious purpose. Had Will's house not been an old one of Queen Anne's date there would not have been the small ante-room leading from the ballroom itself, and had there not been the small ante-room . . .

It happened that Rose Herries, Pomfret's wife, from Kensington, began the trouble. Rose Herries was a woman thinned and raddled by incessant jealousy. By birth the daughter of a small Worcestershire clergyman, she had been amazed when the handsome young Pomfret Herries had proposed for her in marriage. Pomfret's father, Sir Raiseley Herries, had married the sister of David, the son of old 'Rogue' Herries, but there had been an old boyhood feud between Raiseley and David that David's sister had certainly done nothing to heal. It was because of the proximity to David's family at Uldale that the Raiseley

Herries had moved from Keswick to London. Raiseley, Pomfret's father, had always been delicate and ailing. When Pomfret had been around twenty-five years of age, Raiseley had moved for a summer into Worcester because of some doctor or other, taking his two children with him. It was here that one fine morning young Pomfret had seen the lovely Rose walking down a country lane. He had fallen in love with her on the spot. He had been often in love before, but never considered matrimony. Now he did consider it, and six months later was married.

Rose had never recovered from the shock of it. The most that she had ever expected was a local squire, but now to be a baronet's Lady, to have a grand house in Kensington and, above and beyond that, to be married to a man whose figure was everything that her most romantic imagination could have designed for her! Sir Pomfret was an amiable fellow, contented with all that came his way. He was as good a husband to her as was in his nature. But, after the first month, he was unfaithful, nor was he either then or later able to conceal his infidelities. And, so evilly does fortune arrange, Rose was designed to be jealous. She was made for it. The more jealous the more she loved, and the more she loved the more jealous. Pomfret learned, as all husbands learn, to conceal more skilfully his private life, but the less Rose knew the more she guessed. She was frankly a plague both to herself and to him. A Masquerade such as this was designed to torture her.

Sir Pomfret's stout figure (he had come to the Ball as Henry VIII) soon escaped her vision. She told herself, as, poor woman, she had told herself a thousand times before, that 'she must permit him his pleasure'. For five minutes she knew a sort of unhappy nobility. She was being fine, generous, the true wife; but the five minutes were as long as a lifetime, and soon, her long thin neck craning (she was dressed in a watery green and considered herself a Naiad), she looked for him everywhere. She had come to the Ball happy and expectant; Pomfret would stay by her side, he would dance with her and then, very handsomely, she would say: 'Now be off. You don't want your old wife at hand all the evening.' But he had left her so quickly; he had given her nobility no opportunity.

It is another of the signs that Providence had its long finger crooked in this affair that the men were all of them absent, Will dancing, Rockage talking of his place in Wiltshire to an elderly baroness, Pomfret making love to a very young but very worldly Nun, and Georges ... Well, Georges, his head singing with Jennifer's beauty, was betting with some young men on the staircase as to the number of young women's feet you could see moving across the ballroom floor.

So the men were away. This was a woman's affair. Rose Herries met Christabel by chance behind the bronze-coloured curtains that portioned off the ante-room from the ballroom. It was comparatively quiet here: the music, the voices came like water flowing up, ebbing away again. The room had been cleared of furniture; the walls had a blue and white paper recommended to Christabel within the last month as the very latest design. On it were depicted over and over again the sorrows of Werther, an elongated Werther watching a gigantic Lotte beside the spring.

It was unquestioned that Christabel did not, by this time, know what she was doing. It seemed to her that the whole thing was a devastating, world-shaking scandal. Tomorrow all London would be speaking of it. She and Will would be disgraced for ever. The scandalous Herries Ball . . . She had been always a delicate woman. Child-bearing had but shaken her nerves the further. Her stupid, wondering features, pale but strangely streaked as though with the marks of someone else's fingers, were puckered and childishly distressed above her ill-fitting yellow dress.

She had convinced herself that it was Jennifer Cards who had disgraced the Ball. She had always disliked Jennifer, always distrusted the Cards branch of the family, who, she was well aware, looked down upon Will and herself. She did not like Rose and Pomfret, the Kensington branch, very much better. Little Judith was the one she especially cared for. She would have liked to have her always with her. It was a thousand pities that she must live up in that rough Cumberland and be married to a scamp of a rascally Frenchman. Poor little Judith! Christabel knew that she would come to some catastrophe. But she liked her; Judith was kind and considerate, despised no one, understood one's troubles. How she wished that Judith were here now! Then she saw her with Maria Rockage and at the same moment Rose, in her ugly green dress, peering about among the crowd.

The four women drew together as though by instinct, standing just inside the ante-room as bathers, soaked with the sea, gather together on a rock for a moment's pause. They were all nervous and uneasy – Christabel because of her social anxiety, Rose because of her errant husband, Maria because she could not find Carey, Judith because the whole evening had been a failure for her.

The big room was thinning. The candles were burning low. The music had lost its vigour. In the distance a crimson Cardinal pursued a Dairymaid, who ran with little screams of pleasure across the shining floor.

'That Baddeley,' said Rose Herries scornfully. 'There is some resemblance to mankind in him. That is as much as you can say . . .' She was speaking of a Mr James Baddeley, an acquaintance of Pomfret's.

'It is scandalous,' said Maria Rockage, 'that Jennifer should be so monstrously without a chaperon all the evening. When I was a girl, to leave one's chaperon for an instant, except to dance with an acceptable young man—' She broke off. She thought of her daughter Phyllis at Grosset, and how she could not afford to buy her the dresses . . . that flaunting crimson with the silver collar . . . 'But, of course, the looseness of these Masquerades . . .'

Christabel felt at once that this was a criticism of her Ball. All over London tomorrow . . . Her long fingers closed and un-closed about her fan. (The famous fan. Were the figures painted on it of blue or of silver ? Who will ever know ?)

'I admit . . . 'Tis a failure, a monstrous failure . . . I am distracted . . . And Will has assisted me in nothing at all . . . I have had all the burden myself . . .' She did not mind now what she said. She was on the verge of tears.

The others were surprised. They had not been thinking of the Ball. They had not thought it out of the way. Everyone knew what these Masquerades were. Once you wore a mask . . .

'Why, Christabel,' Maria said amiably (for when she could rise above her own worries she was a kindly woman), 'the Ball is well enough. A very fine Ball. A Masquerade must always have a certain licence.' (But nevertheless she thought 'This is a pandemonium.')

Judith, who had been standing looking into the outer room, wondering where Georges was (she could not see with her small stature over the head of the dancers), thinking that at least he might once that evening have sought her out, felt an instant desire to take Christabel in hand, to reassure her, to persuade her that everything was well, to make her happy again (and behind that she was still wondering about Georges, thinking that her love for him was a sort of poison in her blood, a poison that she would never, never be rid of).

'Yes, Jennifer has no modesty,' Rose said, bending her long neck. (Was *that* Pomfret laughing with that girl in white, there near the window in the farther corner ?) 'Her father permits her to do as she pleases. Amelia has been playing cards instead of doing her duty. I never liked the girl: swollen with self-approval. They say that at Vauxhall the other week . . .' She broke off, for Maria Rockage's hand was on her arm. Jennifer was standing quite close to them, alone, looking into the ante-room.

It must be understood that the girl was elated with her triumph. She had not been so very much in London, and Bournemouth's triumphs were not very satisfactory. This was her first *real* Ball, and, more than that, it was in the very heart of the family. Although the Rockages had been there, yes, and the Herries from Kensington, it was she who had been the evening's sensation. She knew that socially the High World had not been represented here. But Jennifer was true Herries in that. Although she disliked all the other Herries except her own family, yet she thought them as good as anyone in the world – as good as the Pope or the Prince or Queen Charlotte or Lady Jersey. She wanted nothing more than to be the acknowledged Herries Beauty, and that not at all for the outside world but simply for the Herries world.

So here she was, panting with triumph, her mask in her hand, her marvellous dark blue eyes glittering with success and pleasure, her magnificent bosom half bare above the crimson, her carriage superb, her youth, vitality, self-confidence all alive and shining – and she glanced for a moment into the ante-room to see whether her mother were there. She looked and saw the four women, three of them, to her, untidy old frumps, and the fourth that strange girl Judith Paris, whose force of personality she felt. The girl had marvellous hair. She had character too. She didn't like her.

She might in fact have passed on had Judith's gipsy dress in some odd way not challenged her. Judith in her ragged dress with her unpowdered hair was unlike anyone else at the Ball. She had had, Jennifer knew, a vagabond for her mother and a vagabond for her father. Jennifer's grandfather had known 'Rogue' Herries.

So Jennifer stayed. She had not intended to look scornful. She was too happy. But there was an element of cruelty in her. She looked at Christabel's pale face and ugly yellow, at Rose's thin bones and ill-chosen green, at Maria Rockage's untidy hair, and before she moved away, she smiled.

Then she asked:

'Is my mother at cards ?'

The smile was, for Christabel, a statement of the whole evening's failure. Her voice trembling, she answered:

'No. But wherever she is, you should be with her.'

Jennifer came forward a little into the room. She wanted these old women to have a full sight of her youth and her beauty. Christabel was her own age, and yet how elderly, how worn, how awkward she seemed! And perhaps Christabel thought: 'This is what I should be! The Ball would have been a success tonight had I been!'

Jennifer stood there, swinging her mask between her fingers.

'Christabel,' she said, 'I must congratulate you on the evening.' She meant a compliment. She had no sense of irony there. But Christabel saw it as only ironical.

'I do not need your compliments,' she answered, 'and least of all when they are not intended. I know what you have felt this evening. I must tell you that you have failed entirely if you wished to conceal your feeling.'

With a shock of surprise Jennifer realized that Christabel was in a hysterical rage. The three girls were standing near to one another, the two older women farther apart. Maria, who wished that everything should be peaceable, but that at the same time she might satisfy a little her own sense that her daughter had not fine clothes and that the evening had lacked decorum, said: 'You should have been more with your mother, Jennifer, or your mother more with you. Chaperons are still in fashion, my child. Yes, your mother is at the card table. Pray give her my love.'

'Oh,' cried Jennifer, 'so that is what my sweet relatives have been settling with one another. That I need a chaperon!' She curtsied to them, and Judith thought that she had never in her life before seen anyone so beautiful. ('But,' she also thought, 'what a temper! My God, what a temper!')

'But for my own part,' Jennifer went on, addressing Christabel as though no one else were there, 'it appears ridiculous ostentation to me! At a Ball like this—' She paused, staring Christabel in the eyes. She had always hated Christabel, she thought, the mean pudding-faced thing, proud only because her husband had made money as a merchant, a vulgar City merchant.

'And what at a Ball like this?' Christabel whispered. They had come close together as though they were discussing some very intimate secret. Rose interrupted. She was aware that there was a very dangerous element here, something that threatened everyone's comfort. 'There!' she cried, laughing nervously. 'Why, I am certain that Jennifer meant nothing. The Ball is very

fine. We have all enjoyed a most handsome evening. Jennifer
had no intention—'

'But I had an intention,' Jennifer interrupted hotly, looking
only at Christabel. 'If you fancy that I am to have my manners
taught me – and my mother her manners also. There is a shabbiness here that one might have expected. Manners learnt from
Great-Aunt Maria, I don't doubt, who learnt them at the Battle
of Naseby . . .'

'Manners!' cried Christabel, beside herself with weariness,
hysterical exhaustion, jealousy, loneliness. 'Manners from you!'

She moved forward. Jennifer turned aside and, resting her
hand on a small table beside her, without knowing what she did,
picked up Christabel's fan that was lying there. She raised her
head contemptuously; her fingers tightened about the fan, and
one of the sticks broke with a little crack that sounded in
Christabel's ears like a pistol shot. It was her favourite fan, one
of her finest possessions.

She stepped forward and smacked Jennifer's face.

And this, exactly, was the true history of one of the most famous
and momentous quarrels in all the Herries history, so long as
events have been recorded.

THE HANGING

JUDITH SAT FACING old Montague Cards. He was not old in
years, being but twenty-nine. He was the only son of Morgan,
brother of Prosper and uncle of Jennifer, and was, therefore,
the lovely Jennifer's cousin. He was a bachelor and plainly
designed from the beginning for that character. He was thin
to emaciation, never varied in his dress, a bag-wig, a suit of
black silk. His nostrils constantly heaved in a sort of simpering
protest, as though he were offended by a bad smell. But he was
not. It was a sort of inner nasal irritation. His voice was affected
and often rose to a shrill note, but behind these absurdities he
was in reality a kindly, nervous, generous soul, who longed to be
liked but did not know how to set about it. He had a horror of
being made love to by women, although he liked their company,
for he adored gossip.

He was tyrannized by his manservant and his manservant's

wife. He had been, until Will's sudden rise, the wealthiest of all
the Herries. His grandfather had left him money, and he, by
careful investment, had increased it. He was very cautious and
reputed to be miserly. This he quite certainly was not, but he
found the reputation useful. Like all the other Herries he
thought there was no other family in England so fine and so
grand, but he quarrelled with individual members of it. He had
not, for instance, spoken to either Carey or Maria Rockage for
years until today. This cleavage was the result of the bursting
of a damaged water pipe upon him in the middle of a winter
night when he was staying at Grosset. He complained that the
Rockages thought it an honour to receive the contents of a burst
water pipe at any time, in any place, were it a Grosset water pipe.
He liked to stay with other Herries in the country. Visits saved
expense. At once, however, on hearing of the family crisis, he
had offered his rooms in Berkeley Square as an unprejudiced
meeting-place. The Ball had not, as Christabel had feared, been
the subject of any general scandal. It had in fact, in the outside
world, made absolutely no mark whatever, but among the Herries
themselves the effect had been terrific.

Judith, looking now at the various Herries seated in the fine
brocaded chairs round Montague's panelled room, saw, from the
barely concealed sentiments of pleasure in the various faces, that
here at last was the family battle for which they had all for long
been aching.

Carey Rockage, as someone outside the dispute and the titled
head of the family, was in charge of the conference, and delighted
he was. It had been no easy matter for the Rockages, economic-
ally, to be compelled to stay in London an additional week, but
their rooms in the Mews were cheap, and young Carey and
Phyllis would be living on short rations for many a week after
their return to Grosset.

Rockage had a round baby face with dimples. His suit was
rusty with age, his hair shabbily powdered, and one stocking
had a hole above the heel. But he was a real Herries. There was
dignity and discipline there. He could command men, and there
was a certain sweetness in his nature, as there was also in his
wife's, which had, in spite of their narrowness and Methodism,
long ago drawn Judith to them. Maria, his wife, was sitting near
to him, and in her excitement it was all that she could do not to
be speaking all the time. She hated so intensely the beautiful
Jennifer, jealous of her loveliness, the advantages she had over
her own dear Phyllis, but in the main thinking, quite honestly,

that the beautiful creature represented all the whoredoms of Babylon.

Jennifer herself was not present. It was thought more fitting that she should not be, but her father and mother, Prosper and Amelia Cards, were there in very truth; it would not be too much to say that their rage and sense of insult was as fine and pure an emotion as ever a Herries had known.

Prosper, in spite of his forty-eight years, was, by far, the finest figure in the room. His suit of crimson and silver, his elaborate wig of shining whiteness, the splendid ruffles at his throat and sleeves only served to emphasize his magnificent physique. He had the chest and neck of a bull, but his features were not common. They had, as Amelia was proud to emphasize, a classical correctness. He was not fleshy as Pomfret Herries was; his frame was gigantic. He carried on the Herries' physical tradition of David, Will's father. Curiously enough he was not proud of his beauty; he had been so, maybe, once, but now he had transferred it all to his lovely Jennifer and it was in her that the whole of his life – physical, material, mental – and his ambitions were centred. She was to marry a Duke. Nothing on this earth was too good for her. And that she should have been struck in the face . . .

He sat there outwardly calm, his splendid legs in their silk stockings stretched in front of him. Outwardly calm. But, if he lived to a hundred, as he and all the other Herries felt it their right to do, he would never forget this insult. Amelia, his wife, in a dress of canary silk, seated at his side, had the subdued and colourless appearance of a woman who has, her life long, played second to a splendid husband. She was not, however, as he knew, so colourless.

The round shining table between them, on the farther side of the room sat Pomfret, fleshy, unserious, gay in spite of himself; Rose, his wife, thankful that she had Pomfret secure at her side for an hour at least, eagerly excited at the human possibilities of the situation; Will, very stiff, trying to be grand, feeling desperately young, aware at one moment that he was richer than them all, at another that his wife had slapped the face of a guest in her own house, trying to calculate the social and family consequences of the incident, rather as a financier will balance his probabilities; Christabel, gauche, awkward, knowing that the whole family, save possibly Judith, was against her, a sort of rough obstinacy rising to support her, warmed too by an almost frantic hatred of Jennifer; a little farther from them again

Francis, elegant, aloof, looking out of window as though he were thinking of something else – and Judith.

She had not intended to come. It was only because Christabel herself, coming all the way to Judith's lodging in a coach, had persuaded her.

Christabel, bursting into tears, had protested that all the world was against her: even Will had scolded her, had told her that her temper had put back his affairs a dozen years at least. True, she had slapped Jennifer's face, but was she to endure impertinence from anyone who offered it her? Rose and Maria had been with her in that. But now – who knows? They were under the thumb of their husbands . . . Judith must come and support her.

Judith had her own private troubles – worse, she could not but think, than anything that Christabel had to suffer. In the week since the Ball, disaster had crept nearer, and now, for these last two nights and days, Georges had not been home.

He was attempting (how well she knew it!) to repair desperate fortunes with some desperate remedy. At every occasion when he left her she did not know but that she might never see him again. Maybe he was even now at the Thames bottom with his head battered or his throat cut. She thought, sitting in that room warm with the May heat, smelling the scent of the lilac bloom that came up from the Square below, hearing the cry of some vendor in melancholy tuneful cadence, 'Oh, if he would only come. Nothing else matters! It is strange how I love him!'

She had left word at the lodging if he should return there while she was away. Did any of those in this room love anyone as she loved Georges? She clasped her small hot hands together, smoothed her dress, and heard Prosper Cards' deep stern voice come to her as though from the heart of an abysmal pit:

'I am not indicting Mrs William Herries for anything,' she heard him say. 'That is too strong a word. There must be, however, an apology in writing.'

'Come, come, Prosper, my friend,' Pomfret's easy genial voice interrupted. 'Is there not altogether too much ado about a trivial matter? Nay, nay.' (He raised a fat white hand.) 'We are all one family here. It is among relatives. Jennifer and Christabel are young, life is beginning for them, they had both an intemperate moment. For my part I like a little hot blood . . .'

'Yes, Pomfret, we know you do,' Prosper answered dryly, crossing one splendid leg over the other. 'But I do not consider it a trivial matter, nor does my wife. We demand an apology in writing.'

Will's voice broke in. It trembled a little and was more human than Judith had ever heard it. 'If one apology is necessary, then so is another. My wife has already agreed that her action was hasty and undisciplined. The more reason that the affair was under her own roof. But what of the cause? Your daughter, sir, used words of gross discourtesy and in her temper destroyed one of my wife's most cherished possessions . . .'

'Cherished possessions!' broke in Amelia Cards. 'Fiddlesticks! A fan, and no extraordinary one either!'

'Fiddlesticks!' Will cried, now very hot and red in the face. 'Is that a word for a lady? . . .'

But Rockage interrupted, the dimples on his cheeks deepening so that he looked like a laughing cherub:

'Ladies! Ladies! Gentlemen! Gentlemen! You have invited me to preside over this conversation, simply, it was understood from the first, a friendly conversation that the little incident may be closed finally. It was with the wish of everyone that we met. Let us all part friends. The matter is surely clear enough. There was regrettable temper on both sides. The evidence has proved it. Mrs Will Herries has stated her own regret. It only remains for my friend Prosper on behalf of his daughter—'

'Not a whit! Not a whit!' answered Prosper, slapping his silken thigh. 'I must have an apology in writing. There is no evidence that my daughter showed temper.'

'She did! She did!' broke in Christabel, on the edge of tears. 'She spoke most insultingly, comparing me with old Great-Aunt Maria of Naseby Battle, and making a play of our entertainment, and all for no reason but her own vanity, because she thought that she was the beauty of the evening—'

'As indeed she was,' Prosper said with deep satisfaction. 'No one within a mile's race of her.'

The lilac, rich, warm, pungent, floated in through the open windows, bathing Judith's eyes with its lovely odour. Oh, why must they squabble about this silly business and her own life on the knife-edge of ruin? She was here, a grown woman, to help her cousin, to aid in the family councils, but she did not feel like a grown woman. She felt like a little girl, shut in a dark room expecting she knew not what terrible entry. What did they, these comfortable, well-fed Herries, know of the struggle that these last years had been for Judith and Georges, the scrapes for money, the taming of landladies, the corners of Coffee Houses, the night hours when Judith in her shift, her arm around Georges, had again and again persuaded him that all would yet be well? What did they know? . . .

Then Rose's introduction of her own name caught her attention.

'There can no no question about the impertinence offered. Ask Judith Paris.'

All eyes turned to her. Her head was confused. Her own personal anxiety pressed upon her heart like a hand closing down on it, and the hand seemed to crush lilac bloom in its fingers; lilac swinging through the sky, while the tops of the green trees in the Square flamed on the iridescent air.

She heard Prosper Cards' deep arrogant voice: 'Well, what has little Miss Judith to say?'

Years after, when she looked back and wondered at the sudden temper that she showed now (temper that had immense consequences), it seemed to her that everything rose together to influence her. Just as, had Christabel's fan not been on the table, there would have been no family crisis, so had there been no warm day, no lilac, no anxiety for Georges, nay, even no dimples in Carey Rockage's cheeks, and, most certainly, no 'little Miss Judith' from Prosper, why then there would have been no temper, no such public taking of sides, binding her, she often afterwards felt, to a whole lifetime of consequences. 'Little Miss Judith' indeed! There was certainly something insufferable about this Cards family!

She heard her own voice, rather shrill, not like her voice at all:

'I think that Christabel had aggravation. Contempt was shown for her Ball, not too civil in a guest who had been so kindly entertained. Christabel should not have slapped her face, maybe . . . but I would have slapped her. I would indeed. One's own guest . . . Oh, there was certainly cause!'

She realized with some satisfaction the surprise that everyone felt. For a moment she forgot even Georges, for she was doing what she loved to do, influencing a situation, a group of persons, above all, a group of Herries! She could feel how Rose Herries was thinking, 'Well I never; who'd have thought it!' and would wonder whether Judith's boldness might possibly titillate Pomfret's sensual side: how grateful Christabel would be, and even Will; how furious Amelia, Jennifer's mother; how scornful Prosper (but in his slow grandeur and handsome pride he would never forget it nor forgive it).

She stole a glance at Francis, who still was staring out of window, staring at the trees that shimmered like green glass in the sun. And what was *he* thinking of? She knew at once by a sort of inspired divination. He was thinking of the lovely, lovely Jennifer – had been thinking of her all day. Years later she was to know that her divination was true.

Meanwhile she had to fight to maintain her position. Prosper was regarding her through his large liquid brown eyes with a patronizing indulgence.

'Come, come, Miss Judith,' he said. 'Why so unkind to my daughter? How has she offended you?'

'She *has* not offended me!' (Judith thought – does he not know that I'm married, the great pompous ox? Oh, how once again she wished that she were larger, her legs longer, her brow more imposing!) 'I have nothing against your daughter, sir, I was present, and must say what I think. In my advice it would be more seemly for nothing more to be said of the matter on either side. There was temper shown both ways. It was a late hour, and everyone was weary.' She was surprised at the firmness of her voice. Her personality counted; she knew that they were all impressed with it.

Perhaps Prosper felt that also, for he said, his voice a little more angered than it had been:

'Why do we waste our time? I should be in the country by now. My wife and I are not here for some child's play. I demand from Mrs Will Herries an apology in writing.'

Will, his face pale with anger, the horse-bones of his cheeks emphasized with his passion, answered:

'It is clear enough from the evidence ... I also demand an apology in writing.'

Then everyone began to speak at once:

'No apology on either side.'

'Great rudeness.'

'For my part I'd have a public apology.'

'And what could you know of the matter? If you'd been beside your daughter as you should have been—'

'Most certainly she insulted me. She laughed at my entertainment and broke my fan—'

'I demand an apology in writing ...'

'After all, they are both young. Who should mind a slap in the face? ...'

'I would call you out, Cousin Prosper, for less.'

'Call me out then. I'll make mincemeat out of you!'

'Pomfret! Pomfret!' (This, shrilly, from Rose.) 'What are
you about? And at your age . . .'

And then a contribution from Cousin Montague, who had
said no word until now, had been completely forgotten by
everyone:

'The weather is so warm. There are refreshments in the parlour. The other room has a cooler outlook—'

Then from the hubbub, the decisive authority of Carey
Rockage. Strange, the dominance of that shabby baby-faced man!

'Friends, friends! This is a family affair. About nothing so
outrageous neither. Mrs Will has agreed that she will offer an
apology. As to writing, I am sure, Prosper, that your good-nature
will insist—'

'Good-nature be damned!' Prosper interrupted. 'My daughter
has had her face slapped and publicly. My wife is with me in
this. For the hundredth time – there must be an apology in
writing.'

'And I say there shall not!' cried Will suddenly jumping up
and tipping his chair over. 'This is our last and final word. My
wife has expressed her regret for her hastiness. We expect the
expression of similar regret from Miss Jennifer Cards. Otherwise
there is an end to any possible intercourse between this branch
of the family and the Bournemouth part of it. Greatly to be
regretted – but this is final.'

The boy, for he was little more, glared across the room at the
magnificent Prosper. It was a little, Judith thought, like David
defying Goliath. But she was proud of him. She saw now – perhaps for the first time – why it was that he was making himself a
solid figure in London.

Then came the real surprise of the occasion. For Francis, who
had hitherto been silent, spoke. 'I should wish to say,' he inter-
jected, 'that I am dissociated from my brother in this. I hold that
Miss Jennifer deserves an apology in writing.'

'Oh no, Francis – oh no,' Judith whispered under her breath.
She realized with an actual pang of apprehension that this silly
dispute about so trivial an affair was going much deeper than
she had ever supposed. Her memory spread before her in an
instant of vision, scene after scene – Uldale in the old years,
Sarah and David, Francis and Will; Francis hardly more than a
child, staring at Skiddaw, turning and picking Will up from the
long orchard grass, smoothing some fancied hurt; Francis and
Will bathing and running naked from the stream; Francis,
Will, Reuben, herself, watching the fireworks at the Lake's

edge. But Francis must be possessed by this Jennifer! That he should so defy his brother, so publicly . . .

And it was the last straw for Will. He caught Christabel by the arm, dragging her from her chair.

'No apology!' he shouted; 'neither now nor ever!' He shook his fist across the room. 'You can carry your Bournemouth manners back with you! I wish you good day.' At the door he turned. 'And your own betrayal of me, Francis, I am not likely to forget.'

He pulled Christabel through the door with him. Everyone broke into confusion. Judith could hear Montague urging: 'It is the warm weather . . . refreshments . . . a cool parlour.' And Prosper's measured tones: 'Young puppy! I'd call him out for a penny!' And Maria Rockage: 'Oh dear, oh dear! . . . That's a pity, and Carey so wonderfully discreet.'

Well, the thing was done. Judith sighed, turning away from Francis, who stood with his back to the company, looking out of the window down into the Square. It seemed, Judith thought, as though the beautiful shadow of Jennifer hung over all the room.

A moment later she had forgotten them all, for there, standing just within the door, looking at them all, a half-defiant, half-apologetic smile on his face, was Georges!

He was neat and tidy, in a brown suit, holding his hat in his hand, but – she saw at once – infinitely weary. His round face was ashen. He held himself as though at any moment he might fall.

Rockage knew him. Rose and Pomfret spoke to him. A moment later Judith was tugging at his arm.

'Georges, you had my note. I have waited two days . . . Where have you been? . . . What? . . .'

'I came to fetch you,' he said, looking at her with a great kindliness that caught at her heart. 'We shall talk better outside.'

She took his arm. He bowed to the assembled company. One last impression she had (that was to seem to her afterwards like the closing note on all her old life) of Francis, turning from the window and very gravely regarding them both. Then they were out of the room and down the stairs.

The Square was quite deserted and beautifully still in the dusty golden sunlight of the hastening summer afternoon. They walked along, she still holding his arm.

He spoke very rapidly, but still with a great and considering kindness.

'Listen, Judy . . . Everything is up. I have been a fool these two days, just as I have been a fool all my life. But worse now, much worse, Listen to what I say. I must be off this instant. There's a boat I know at Greenwich; away tonight for Copenhagen—'

'But what have you done ?'

'I've played two nights and a day. Once I was handsomely to the good, then lost it all again. But that's not the thing. There was a scuffle this morning at Jonathan's. I stuck a ninny – no, he's not dead – but they are out against me and several more. London's closed to me for a time at least.'

'And I ?' Her mind was active with a thousand possibilities.

'Go back to Watendlath and wait for me.'

They stood at the Square corner, and now she had actually just above her head a thick bush of purple lilac that leaned towards her as though it would brush her cheek. A Negro boy, with a silver turban and leading a spaniel by a thin chain, passed them whistling.

He spoke to her most urgently. 'Judy, I know you are brave, and most sensible. I'm sorry indeed that I have brought you to this pass, the more that these years in London have made us friends. I have no friend in the world like you. You've tamed me because you caught my admiration and kept it . . . Judy, I think I could love you for long now, were we quietly in Cumberland . . .'

At the word 'Cumberland' she broke out: 'Oh, why could we not go there ? Both of us. No one would look for you in Watendlath.'

'No,' he answered sharply. 'I must be out of England. I've come to think that they hate me here. They turn on me and hunt me like dogs a hare if they have the slenderest reason. I'm a man of no country. I'd rather be on the sea than on the land anywhere. Except for you I'd go to sea and never touch land again . . . But I always have to come back to you, and will come. Go to Watendlath. Be patient there. I shall write and send money if I have any. But you can manage in any case. You have a man's head on you. There's money enough in the lodging – the drawer by the fireplace. Here . . . the key. That will carry you North. I should pay the woman and leave tonight. Stay quietly there. Answer no questions if they ask you. One day, perhaps soon, you'll see me walk up the road. I *must* come back to you. There's no one and nothing else in the world draws me . . .'

She asked no questions. She hated people who asked tiresome questions at an urgent crisis.

He caught her by the shoulders, as he sometimes did when he was pleased, lifting her a little from her feet. He kissed her. 'Now – goodbye,' and he had turned the corner swiftly and was gone.

She stood there, looking up into the lilac, but not seeing it. Not from sentiment but because she knew that in the future it would often please her to remember, she repeated some of the things that he had said.

'I think I could love you for long now . . . Except for you I'd go . . . You have a man's head . . .'

And so she had. She wanted to commit some panicky folly like running down the street to find him and then insisting that wherever he went she would go with him, but she must be practical and do exactly what he had asked her.

She was glad that she must leave London. As though to be in tune with the urgency of her own affairs, the day was clouding. Thunder was behind the houses. She walked on, thinking how, with ease, she could catch the night coach to York. From there across country she might share a post-chaise if she were lucky. The very thought of Watendlath made her heart beat with pleasure. The cool breeze slipping down the mountain-side, the water, green-clear, tumbling into the Punchbowl, the Tarn, mirroring one white cloud, while the Fell looked down to Rosthwaite; the Ritsons, the children, the dogs, the smell of the peat, the dung, the Cumberland bracken (now there would be new fresh fronds springing up, curling above the stem) and, most lovely of all, the eternal running streams, so reassuring, so friendly . . . Why had she left it? Although she was only a step from Berkeley Square all the members of the Herries family, with whom she had so lately been, seemed unreal and unalive.

She hurried on, for her mind was set now on the practical business of doing what Georges had told her – leaving London and catching the night coach.

Soon she was in the poorer streets that hung like spiderwebs about Charing Cross. The heavy day was dark now above her head, and the noise of the traffic on the street, the stench of the gutter, the projecting windows and the roughness of the cobbled road held and confused her.

When she stood it seemed that almost at once people closed in upon her. She was in a narrow street that opened out until it became almost a small cobbled square hemmed in with uneven and overhanging houses. She was aware then that her own thoughts had hindered her from noticing that some event was going forward. Before she knew it or could resist it she found that a mixed and very evil-smelling crowd was pushing her on; then, looking about her, saw that beside a butcher's shop that had above it a large swaying sign a platform had been erected and on the platform a gibbet.

The sight of the gibbet sickened her; it had in its very rough newness and sharp angles a sense of torture and pain about it. She turned as though to go back, but found now to her dismay that the crowd behind her was too thick for her to pass through.

She had heard at one time that malefactors were sometimes hanged by the place of their crime, and she supposed that unwittingly she had tumbled upon some such scene. The odd mixture of emotions in her breast at that moment – her passionate feeling of love for Georges, the excitement of the recent family squabble, the sense of the exceeding importance that she should do at once what Georges asked her – threw her into a special state of nervous apprehension. Her first thought was that she must at once get away from where she was. She realized that in her abstraction she had moved into a crowd that must have been waiting there for a considerable period. All the windows of the neighbourhood were open and were crowded with figures. Boys were clinging to the lamp-posts, and along one side of the street a platform of boards had been arranged on barrows and tubs, and this was thronged. Above the roofs the sky was dark, and she fancied that she could hear distant rumbles of thunder. Whatever happened she must escape, so she turned to go back the way that she had come, but she was at once obstructed by a large man carrying an empty tray round his middle, and a group of women who, so soon as they saw that she wanted to pass them, with laughter prevented her.

'No passage this way,' one woman, who had a huge bosom and her skirt tucked up almost to her knees, cried.

'I beg you,' Judith began. 'It is an urgent matter – if you please.'

'If you please – if you please!' the whole street seemed to echo her. 'Only one thing urgent here, and that is a jerk with the rope and, lady or gentleman, it's all the same, we all go to heaven!'

She was so small that she had no hope of asserting herself. She looked about her to see whether some face were likely to help her, but she thought that she had never seen so many coarse mouths, bright hard eyes. There was in the look of every-one a flutter of the animal – the animal allowed for an hour a little freedom, to prowl into a larger cage and taste handsome food. The sense that she had had for a long time in London that times were changing, that the people themselves were now more actively conscious of possible power and were moving towards it, held her now. For the first time in her life she was afraid of people. She had never before been aware of what a crowd was. Her individuality was lost. If she were not careful she would be trampled down, not her body but something much more real and vivid than that.

She hated any public scene; her reserve and dignity came to her rescue. She turned back and found that she could move forward more easily. She might escape at the broader street-end. But when she had gone some way, jolted, pushed, with much unpleasant contact with clothes and hot breath, legs and arms, she came to a stop again. She saw to her great distress that she was almost under the platform where the gibbet was. Here was a thick ring of people, mostly women; she thought of France. It must have been often like this in France, the women knitting and singing, their ears straining for the rattle of the tumbrils.

She felt faint with the heat and the smells and the noise. Scarcely knowing what she did, she caught at an arm to steady herself and found that she was holding on to a little thin man in a large hat and a rusty black suit. He smiled at her kindly.

'Can you help me out of this, sir?' she asked gently.

He shook his head. 'I fear not, madam. It is best to stay where you are. The crowd grows thicker every moment.'

'Oh, but I don't wish to stay. I have a most urgent appoint-ment.'

He pointed with his finger. She looked and saw that escape was now impossible. The crowd had in the last five minutes flooded in. She could see the shining hats of the 'Charlies' at the crowd's edge.

'Is someone to be hanged?' she asked.

'A young man.'

'What had he done?'

'Stolen three shillings from his master's till – the butcher's there.'

She was a woman of her time, she did not feel the injustice of it as a woman of a later day would do, but it was as though, in that moment, looking anxiously into the little man's mild eye, pressed in on every side, stirred perhaps by the drama of her

own personal circumstances, she received some especial consciousness, ahead of her time, a sense of cruelty and persecution
that pierced her very heart.

'Oh, poor boy ... I don't want to see ... Please cannot you
assist me? What are all these people here for? If he must die it
should be by himself alone. Oh, help me, please! ...'

She saw herself the hopelessness of any escape. He was very
kind. He put his arm very courteously round her. 'There is
no way out. You can see for yourself. It will be over soon now.
It was to be at five o'clock. We shall have a storm if they are not
quick.'

Something compelled her to look around her. The people
near her were decent enough, quiet, grave-faced. They waited
indifferently, as though it were a peep-show they had come for.
Two women close to her were chatting about their own affairs.
A hush spread slowly over the crowd, as though a hand had been
laid upon them all. A man, burly and broad, carrying a cane,
mounted the steps to the scaffold. He went to the gibbet and
felt the rope. A flock of pigeons flew from one side of the street
to the other, and a sudden clap of thunder, as though someone
had fired a gun, startled them. They rustled their wings like a
shower of falling paper.

It seemed to Judith that this was her own personal tragedy,
that all her life she would be affected with her memory of it.
She was forced now to watch; indeed two opposite impulses
seemed to fight in her, one that she should hide her face, the
other that she should see every slightest thing.

The crowd was very still in the vicinity of the scaffold, but
beyond that, there were laughter and singing and beyond that,
in a great distance, all the noisy traffic of the day. The atmosphere
was strange, very dark above their heads, but pale beneath with
the flat colour of sunlight. The shops were like pale faces staring
from darkness, and the thunder muttered like an uncertain drum.

She saw all this with a sickness of anticipation. She really felt
sick, as though it were Georges or Francis or Reuben – someone
who was very close to her – who was going to suffer. The silence
grew and seemed to spread to the farther distance. She saw
individuals – a woman's face with a wart, an old gentleman in a
shabby brown wig, a girl with a sharp nose who lifted a child
that it might see better, a man, a foreigner surely, wearing a
bright green turban – and all these individuals seemed to belong
to her, to know all about her, and to have arranged to come with
her to see this sight.

Then, as though obeying some signal, a little procession mounted the steps. There was the stout fellow with the cane, a long thin man bare-headed, three officers in uniform, a clergyman with parson's bands carrying a book, and, last, between the officers, a boy with his hands tied. At once she could not remove her eyes from the boy. He was broad and short and ruddy-faced, like any strong country boy. His hair was cropped, he had large blue staring eyes that, Judith saw, were now mad with an ununderstanding terror. But his mouth, which was a child's mouth, uncertain and tremulous, was trying to be resolved and manly.

She was, against her will, so terribly close that she was forced to see these things; she fancied then (she knew afterwards it could have been only fancy) that as soon as he was on the platform the boy's eyes were seeking hers. What he was doing was searching the crowd, the houses, the sky; a wild animal at bay looking for escape, although he knew that there was none. But Judith fancied that she could help him. Raising herself on her toes she nodded and smiled and nodded again; even (although she did not know it) her lips were forming words: 'Be brave! I'll help you! I want to help you! Be brave!'

Indeed he tried to be, poor lad. Things moved very quickly. The parson, who looked shabby and had mud on his stockings, read from a book. The boy came forward. He was in his shirt and breeches; the shirt, open, had slipped from one shoulder and showed his breast. His face was ruddy in spite of his fear; he looked as though he should have been caught robbing an orchard.

He came forward and began to speak bravely enough. Now an absolute silence froze the scene. Carts could be heard rattling on the Strand cobbles very far away.

'Good people,' he began (his voice was fresh and very young), 'I am told to bid you all farewell and to beg you to stay in peace with God. Good people, it is very true that I took the shillings from the till – I never for an instant denied it. I was tempted by the Devil, good people, for I am very weary of the Town and was hungering for the country again. It was but an instant's temptation, and here I am, so that, good people, all learn by me to resist—' He had begun bravely, held up, perhaps, by the importance of the attention given him by the listening crowd, but suddenly it seemed to come upon him that he was really going to die, that, in a few moments, he would be fighting for breath . . .

He broke off, his voice rising to a shrill terror. 'No, no . . .

I must not die . . . I must not die . . .' He moved as though he would throw himself from the platform. The officers caught him, and then began a dreadful struggle. He was young and strong. The three officers wrestled with him all over the platform. His shirt was torn from him and he was bare to the waist. He cried again and again, 'No, no . . . I will not . . .' and other words that no one could distinguish, some private name that sounded like 'Nancy'. Then they had him. His arms were bound behind him; his naked chest, white and shining with sweat, pushed forward, his head, turning, twisting, turning like an animal's in the pen before execution. An agonized whisper came: 'Jesus! Oh, Jesus Christ!' Just before they had the rope round his neck his eyes seemed to find Judith's, blue, staring and asking some question.

Then he was swinging, his legs twisting as though with independent life. The body heaved, then his head hung and he was still.

'Now, madam,' said the little man from an infinite distance, 'I can assist you.'

Judith nodded her head. Reuben had been right. Until the Bear was safe from persecution nothing could be well in the world.

THE CLIPPING

SARAH HERRIES, widow of David Herries and mother of Francis, Deborah, and Will, died on the 3rd of July 1796, suddenly, at the age of fifty-eight.

She was walking in the garden with her daughter Deborah, wrapped in one of her strange and brooding silences, when she cried out suddenly in a proud and joyful voice: 'Davy! Davy!', ran forward, her arms outstretched, and fell down on the green sward.

Her heart had failed her, and she was mercifully relieved of a life that was only a torment and distress to her. Judith went from Watendlath to the funeral. Will and Francis naturally could not arrive from London. The distance was too great and the time too short. Deborah Sunwood, now an aged, white-haired, and very quiet little woman, long a widow and never the same since the death of her son Humphrey in France, came from Cockermouth, and she and Judith had a very loving meeting. Deborah

Herries, a stout, large, rosy-faced, cheerful woman, was now left
in sole charge of Uldale and its affairs. She begged Judith to
come to her whenever she wished. They had a friendly regard
for one another, but nothing whatever to say, and Judith knew
that Deborah, who loved social events and decent behaviour,
regarded Georges in her heart as a rogue and a vagabond, which
indeed he was.

The night of her return from the funeral Judith had wild
and fantastic dreams. It was a hot airless night, very still, and the
streams, thin though they were, seemed to leap in through the
open windows and chatter about the room. She had been sleeping
badly for a long time past. Wise though she was and determined
always to be sensible, a foreboding of distress and misfortune
grew on her day by day, as though a cloud with every hour
grew heavier and darker above her head. She had had one letter
from Georges since he left her in London. It was addressed
from Bergen in Norway, very short, sending his love, telling her
that he was busy and would return when he could. She thought
that she read between the lines a new sense of care and longing
for her, but that, with her usual good sense, might be a willing
imagination.

The nights were the bad times. During the day she was
surrounded with friends in whose affairs she took ever a more
active and dominating interest, but at night she was alone, and
that part of herself that she could least easily control – her wild
and restless part – seemed to have full power.

On this particular night she suffered especially from the
thought of Sarah. Her loving heart could not endure that she
had never been reconciled to Sarah. When she was a child
she had not thought that she cared for Sarah at all, but as she
grew, so she perceived that there was some deep loyalty and
submission in her feeling.

She had always been too proud to go to Sarah and ask her
forgiveness; besides, she did not think that Sarah had anything
to forgive, but she had supposed that some accidental meeting
would bring them together again. Now it would never be.

At least, if there was another conscious life, Sarah was now
with David, was happy again and understood everything. But
this supposition, a very doubtful one, as it seemed to Judith,
was poor comfort. She tortured herself, on the ride back from
Uldale, with the thought of all the lonely years that Sarah had
endured. She could never bear that people could suffer, and
especially that they should suffer through her fault, and now

there occurred to her a thousand ways in which, with a little courage, she might have approached Sarah and done something for her.

Her dreams that night were wild, entangled and desperate. She was again in the London street, where the boy was to be hanged. Pressed in, tossed about by a wild and revengeful crowd. But it was Georges who was to be hanged. She could do nothing to save him, but must stand there helplessly and watch. The sky was black, the houses ringed with flame, and from a high window Christabel, Will's wife, leaned out and cried that her fan was broken and Georges must suffer for it. Then Georges came sailing towards her in a little boat; waves, hot and angry, with cruel white tongues, filled the street and beat about the scaffolding. Young Stane was in the boat, and Georges suddenly caught him, held him in the air, then flung him into the waves while all the people cried.

She woke, trembling, damp with sweat. At first the deep quiet of the room with only the sound of the singing streams soothed her. She lay there and listened to her heart as it slowly diminished its terrible beating. How good that it had only been a dream! From her bed she could see, in the faint morning light, the shadows of the homely, familiar things, and beyond the open window the friendly breast of the rising hill.

She was in her own house with friends on every side of her. Since her return, although she had said very little to anyone, they had all understood, it seemed, that Georges was in some trouble. They did not like Georges, but with that wonderful silent sympathy that is perhaps the Cumbrian's finest gift, they had closed in around her, showing her their affection and loyalty. She had never been so near to them before as she was now.

Yes, but she wanted Georges. She wanted him with a fierce hunger that was an experience quite new to her. She was doing what he told her, staying here and filling her life with little daily interests, but, in the back of her mind, there was always the fear that after a while, if he did not return, waiting would be too hard for her, and she would run off to Whitehaven and search for news of him.

To conquer her desire for him she lay there, as the new light flowed about the room and a cluster of sharp steel-glittering stars faded out above the black hill line, saying over to herself, aloud, the names of places that she loved, and the names of people whom she loved. She said, as though she were addressing the shapes, with every moment less dim, in her room:

> *'Stonethwaite, Honister,*
> *Gavel, Watendlath,*
> *Rosthwaite, Uldale,*
> *Bleaberry, High Seat,*
> *Armboth, Grey Knotts,*
> *Glaramara—'*

They had sung her almost to sleep again, mingling with the streams that ran about the boards of her room when, with a sharp stab of awareness, she was conscious of an odd thing – that with every day she was becoming more frightened of leaving her own square of ground.

It was as though someone had told her that did she step over a certain line, something terrible would befall her. She had noticed at the funeral that she had to force herself to face people, even good friends like Deborah Sunwood. It was as though she expected that anyone at a moment's notice would cry: 'I have news for you. Georges—' The people here around her she could trust. They were her own people – the Ritsons, the Wilsons, all the children and the dogs. And her new great friend, Charlie Watson.

Watson had a farm, New Hope, towards Armboth. He had come there in the last year; he was from the village of Strands, near Wastwater.

He was a Cumbrian of the Cumbrians; that is, he was silent, often churlish, sharp, a marvellous shepherd and utterly loyal. She had met him one day coming up from Rosthwaite. He had two dogs with him. She had been startled by his looks, for he was broad and massive and his hair was of so jet a black, his cheeks of so warm a colour, that at first he seemed a foreigner. He had a short, sharply cut, black moustache that was not like the neighbours'. He was so broad of shoulder and thick of thigh that his height seemed moderate, but he was of good height nevertheless.

He would be thirty-five years of age. They began to talk. You would have said that all he thought of at that time was sheep, that or any time. He thought of other things later, though. He was proud, sensitive, suspicious, and hated foreigners till he knew them. He had worked in Liverpool five years in his youth. He was single; preferred sheep to women, he told Judith once. True enough then – not true later. On their first meeting he said

little more than 'Aye!' He looked at her as though he disliked
her. He stood, his legs wide apart, striding the fells.

He told her that his sister looked after his comfort, that it was
a dry month, that he didn't hold with politics – Regent or King,
it was all the same to him, but we'd better not take after the
Frenchies.

Judith said: 'My husband's French.'

He said: 'Aye,' looking at her meditatively and without a hint
of apology. Then abruptly, still looking at her, he remarked:
'You'll be Mrs Paris. I mind hearing of you.'

'Nothing bad, I hope,' said Judith.

'For t'matter o' that – nay,' he said, suddenly smiling a slow
deep smile. He strode away, not looking back, his dogs after
him.

After that first meeting they were always encountering one
another. He was a friend of old man Ritson's, but it seemed to
her soon that he came to the farm very much more often than
he had done.

Once or twice, without any conceit of self-flattery, she
wondered whether he were in love with her. He seemed to seek
her out so directly, with a simplicity that might elsewhere have
caused gossip. But, in a week or two, she realized that the
Ritsons and the rest knew just what his feeling for her was.
He was sorry for her, but without hurting her pride. They said
of him that he was mighty tender with all animals and rough
with women and off-hand with men. It seemed that he thought
that she needed protection as an animal might. He made himself
her protector. There was no sentiment between them. They
made a curious pair, he so large and she so small, and she could
have disappeared, she used to fancy, into the outer pocket of his
coat. He was an unusual man with his intense depths of feeling
unexpressed. One day they were standing together near the Tarn,
and three strangers, two ladies and a gentleman, rode up on
horses. They were sightseers, the first 'tourists', perhaps, that
Watendlath ever beheld. They called Watson 'my good fellow'
and, when he had given, very curtly, some information, the
gentleman threw him a shilling. The ladies, very grand and
speaking with affectation, looked at Judith, who was dressed
like Mrs Ritson or any of the people of the place. When they
were gone Watson threw the shilling into the Tarn. He was
trembling with anger.

'I'll tell them if 'tis t'right road. If they come again without
biddin' they maun stay a bit . . . I'll settle him.'

She laughed and said that she supposed that anyone had a right to the place.

'Nay, they havena ... the man's a lump of mutton off an auld tup.'

She didn't laugh any more, when she saw how deeply moved he was. It was as though these people had soiled the landscape for him.

Judith went one day and called on his sister. Then one evening, sitting in his kitchen, she told him everything: about her father and mother, her childhood in Uldale, her life at Stone Ends, her marriage with Georges, her time in London, her present distress and ever-growing anxiety, her love for Georges that seemed to grow ever deeper and deeper. He took her hand in his huge one.

'Aye, you want someone to look after you.'

From that evening it seemed to her that he was always at hand, although there were days when she didn't see him. Indeed he was a tremendous worker, had no time for idling with females. But he was behind her and beside her. The thought of him infinitely comforted her.

As, lying there, she considered him, his silence, his tenderness, her fears thinned away. It seemed that it was her fate to have these figures guarding her, protecting – Tom Gauntry, Emma, now Charlie Watson. The strange thing was that she did not want anyone to protect her. She was quite well able to protect herself. But she liked to have friends. She loved to be loved – that is, by the people whom she wanted to love her.

The sun flashed above the purple ridge of the hill. The sky was pale green like the wing of a young paroquet.

The Ritsons had their 'Clipping', and it was a grand day. The hot weather had lasted for over a fortnight, and this was the hottest day of them all. The sheep panted fit to burst their sides. Armboth Fell shone like a brazen shield and was so slippery dry beneath the bracken that it was flaming ice to the feet. The Tarn was shadowed with an ebony mist under a sky clouded with heat.

The clipping was perhaps the grandest day of the year for the Ritsons. They were farmers in a small way, but very popular. Neighbours came from miles, first to help in the clipping, then to eat of the feast and dance in the Ritson kitchen.

Charlie Watson came. He was the best clipper in Cumberland maybe; a Master. Then there was Tommy Blunden of Smoke, Robert Tyndale of Cardale, Will Bennett of Axholme, Roger

Perry of Thunder. They, their wives, their children, their dogs.

Judith was happy again. The night was far behind her. But the thundery weather distressed her; it had been ominous to her ever since that last day in London, and now, in the middle of helping with the great joint of beef, with the huge pease-puddings, with the arranging of the long table, she would go to the porch and look out over the Tarn to the hills and listen. Perhaps it was Georges, also, for whom she was listening.

In the kitchen there was tremendous noise and confusion. Old man Ritson was too aged now to move about, the rheumatism had him fast, and sometimes the pain was so bad that someone inside him yelled loud enough to bring the roof down, but the yell never passed his inside. He sat, his grand head high, his gnarled hands on his knees, watching and saying nothing. His daughters, his grand-daughters and a great-grand-daughter (in a cradle by the window) were all around him. A sea of femininity. But he said nothing. He sat there thinking of his youth, of fighting a man bare-skin in Whitehaven and throttling him, of tending sheep on the hills above Coniston Water, of the fugitives in '45 from Butcher Cumberland and his father hiding one up the kitchen chimney, of sheep and sheep, cows and cows, fine weather and bad, of women whom he had loved, his children and their ways, Armboth and Brund Fell and Glaramara that were live creatures to him, Gods maybe, carrying on their gigantic forms the rocks and tarns and streams that were their splendid properties. Yes, he had plenty to think of. And he sat there, looking straight in front of him, while the pains at his hip made him bellow inside.

When the table was laid, Judith, to escape the kitchen heat, went out to watch the clippers.

As the weather was so grand the clipping could be in the open air instead of in the barn. All the sheep had been brought in. There were eight hundred sheep and five hundred lambs.

Beyond the house in a grand half-circle were fifteen clippers striding the sheep stools, and each clipper held a sheep, shorn, half shorn, about to be shorn. There was a tremendous noise, for the gate of the farmyard was packed by five score of wooled sheep penned against it. They would be caught, one after another, by one of the boys, who, in a wild, excited pack, tumbled and fought and shouted, having the day of their lives. The sheep bleated and their lambs on the fell-side or in the fields bleated as well. The dogs barked and even horses neighed. It was strange to feel, beyond this excited whirlpool of sound, the glazen silence of the Tarn, the road, the hills, pulsating through the shimmering heat, but silent, as though holding their breath for the first peal of thunder that would release them from this spell.

Judith first looked for Charlie Watson, and a splendid sight he was. His shirt was open at the neck, and sweat beaded the thick black hair of his chest. His arms, red-brown to near the elbows then snow-white, bulged with muscle; his legs planted wide to hold the sheep between them seemed to be rooted in the ground; every once and again his head went up and his mouth parted, showing his teeth white under the short thick black moustache. (His perfect teeth were a phenomenon in the dale, for most men lacked one or two.) His short, thick hair had almost a metallic gleam in its blackness.

As always when at work, his dark eyes shone, his parted lips seemed to cry aloud his energy, his body worked in harmony with the fell, the running water. He worked with rhythm, as though the whole of English nature and the wheel of the brazen sky moved, back and forth, with the pulse of his blood; and he handled the sheep as though he loved them.

Tom Ritson was in charge of the clipping; an old man called Benny Held – with two fierce questioning white eyebrows and a face like a wrinkled turnip – kept the pitch pan heated and held the marking iron and the rudd stick. Young Roger Perry of Thunder, a lad nearly as thick and broad as Watson, held the animals while old Benny applied the marking.

Judith forgot her anxieties and trouble for the while. Now there came out in her all her passion for management. She could not be present at a scene like this without burning to 'arrange things'.

She looked fifteen years of age, with a high sunbonnet tied over her red hair and her legs bare as the other women's were, stamping about in her clogs. Her cheeks were flushed, her eyes shining. Her Cumberland blood exulted in the scene. This was the heart of England and so the heart of the world. Everything was right for her – the scent of the bracken, the still waiting expectancy of the hills, the sun shining on the little stone walls that ran up into the edge of the sky, the rough voices that had a sort of grumbling humorous note in them, the jokes and oaths and laughter, the bleating of lambs and sheep, the strange help-less whiteness of the sheep after they were shorn – knowing that they were so different, so changed that their own lambs did not recognize them – the life of this little community centred here in this circle of fells, so remote from the world but strong,

independent, asking nothing from any man (as for centuries they
had asked nothing, so for centuries more they would ask
nothing), and all of them looking at her, speaking to her as
though she were one of themselves (which, indeed, she was), the
sun slipping over the sky and, as the afternoon drew on, shadows
staining every hill with a different dye; Armboth saffron as
though sunlight had soaked into its very heart, Brund Fell
orange-red, then sinking, with almost an audible sigh, into a
gentle silver-grey, and beyond them the farther hills, violet
cloths spread before a sky white with evening haze, and, with the
evening, a breeze springing that had every scent of coolness in
it, young grass, water over shining stones, and the wet wavering
mosses that shadow the Tarn's edge. The sea also was not far
away.

Ale was brought out in pots, and there were hunks of fruit
pie. Then the sky was green, and the first star winked at a silver
moon half full. The fleeces were tied in small bundles, the loft
door was closed on them, and everyone moved indoors to the
feast.

There were rounds of beef and oat-bread, pease-puddings,
gooseberry pies, puddings 'touched' with rum. Soon everyone
was very merry. Benny Held had brought his fiddle. Robert
Tyndale, who had a fine tenor, sang Ewan Clark's 'Happy
Bachelor':

> *'A bachelor life of all lives is the best;*
> *No cares matrimonial disturb his calm rest;*
> *No lectures called* Curtain *shake sleep from his eyes,*
> *When tir'd he can rest, and when tir'd he can rise.'*

and 'Wey, Ned, Man!':

> *'Wey, Ned, Man ! Thou luiks sae down-hearted,*
> *Yen wad swear aw thy kindred were dead;*
> *For sixpence, thy Jean and thee's parted –*
> *What then, Man, ne'er bodder thy head.'*

Then, Charlie Watson, shy but determined, sang in a deep
bass: 'What charms has fair Chloe':

> *'What charms has fair Chloe !*
> *Her bosom's like snow !*
> *Each feature*
> *Is sweeter,*

Proud Venus, than thine !
Her mind like her face is
Adorned with all graces,
Not Pallas possesses
    A wit so divine.

'*What crowds are a-bleeding*
While Chloe's ne'er heeding:
    All lying
    A-dying
  Thro' cruel disdain:
Ye gods, deign to warm her
Or quickly disarm her;
While Chloe's a charmer,
    Your temples are vain.'

He sang without any expression whatever, and a disdainful look on his face as though he despised the song and himself for singing it, but, when it was over, and the applause had been terrific, he flushed with pleasure and looked down the long table to see whether Judith had approved.

Then the tables were cleared, Benny Held struck up his fiddle and everyone was dancing. Stamp-stamp-stamp, clamp-clamp-clamp along the kitchen floor, the dust rising, faces flushed, bodies a little unsteady with the ale, whispers and protesting laughter, kissing, and hugging, and old Ritson, sitting in his chair, looking straight before him, thinking of the time when he had taken the girl of his heart out of the hot room into the cold of the valley and wandering down to the Tarn's edge had kissed her for the first time. He fancied that now, although she had been dead so long, she was standing just behind the hallan, her eyes taunting him . . .

Charlie Watson asked Judith to dance. He clamped round the room with her, staring over her head, saying nothing. He trod on her toes, bundled her about, and his arm held her like an iron rod.

They stayed by the door, and he was about to speak to her. Alice Ritson, the only unmarried Ritson girl remaining, for Mary had died two years before, ran in from the garden path, waited an instant, looking at the crowded room, then went up to Judith, caught her arm and whispered: 'Judith, 'tis Mr Georges. He's coom back. He's there, in your own place.'

For a moment the room with its figures and haze of heat

swayed, in movement, almost it seemed, to the fiddler's tune. She remembered afterwards (looking back as she did so many, many times) that Charlie Watson put out his arm and for a moment held her. She felt (she knew afterwards, although at the time she did not notice it) the beating of his heart against her cheek. What an agony of joy, anticipation, and fear!

'It is my husband,' she said, looking up into his face: then she ran out.

Georges was standing in their living-room, near the staircase, down which he had once bundled his box. She ran to him, and at once knew by the way that he held her that something terrible had happened to him. He had never held her like that before, as though his only safety lay in his contact with her.

'I thought that I would never be here,' he said. He lifted her off her feet and looked into her eyes. Then he put her down and went to the door, which he closed, slowly, surely; then stood for a moment with his back to it. They could hear through the wall the scream of the fiddle and the tramp-tramp-tramp of the dancing figures.

'Will you come down to the Tarn?' he asked her.

'But you must eat.'

'I had food at Keswick.'

'Where's your horse?'

'I've tethered him. He had his corn. He can stay.'

'But here ... You must be so weary. I can make all comfortable.'

'No, no, no. I must be outside. Away from the music.'

Taking his hand, looking up at him, she said: 'What is it? Are you in trouble?'

'Yes,' he answered. 'I'm in trouble.'

She nodded her head, asking him no more.

They went out together, and the evening was sweet with all the summer scents. One lamb in a fold bleated incessantly; as soon as they came down the hill the music faded to a murmur like a voice in the Fell. The Tarn had a broad path of moonlight that quivered with little shudders of gold.

'Will you be cold?' he asked her. 'If you've been at the dance.'

'No. The air is warm.'

He put his arm around her; she was pressed close against his thigh, and they walked up and down.

'Judy, I've murdered Stane.'

She shivered, and he held her close. When she could steady herself she thought, at once: 'Now he will need me. He shall

want me always. He is mine to the end,' and directly afterwards:
'Are they searching for him ? I must get him away.' It was odd,
but she thought of Humphrey Sunwood and how sensible she
had been then.

She asked him at once: 'Are they after you for it ?' She had
always hated Stane. She didn't care that he was dead.

'No. It was two weeks back. Off Bergen. No one knows.'

'How was it ? Was it in a fight ?'

'No. Not a fight. I murdered him deliberately. I took him out
in the boat to do it.'

'And no one saw ?'

'It was evening. A storm got up. After I had drowned him I
turned the boat over and swam to land. But do you not shrink
from me ? First, before all else, I must know that—'

'No. I love you. How could I shrink from you ?'

'Because I shrink from myself. It was deliberate, Judy.
Planned. Intended. Not a drunken scuffle, not a hand-to-hand
struggle. I took him by the throat and squeezed it till I thought
my fingers would break. Then I toppled him over. The rain was
coming down in torrents, and there was a wild sea. I thought
I should myself drown, and I would have been glad of it, but
nothing can drown me nor hang me nor stab me . . . I shall live
for ever, Judy, with Stane around my neck – like a dead bird,
clammy, with talons scratching my skin.'

His hand was fiery hot in hers. She remembered afterwards
that in all her bewilderment, her determination to be sensible,
her tenderness for him, her hatred of Stane, which seemed now
to be double what it had been, was amazement at this new
Georges. He was like a man whom she had never seen before;
she loved him as deeply as the other Georges, nay more, because
he needed her, which the other Georges had never done. But
his French indifference, callous humour, self-sufficiency . . .
Where were they ? Was this man a coward ?

He seemed to know her thought. He drew a deep sigh of relief.

'Now it is better. If you are with me we will beat that damnable ghost. For he's been a ghost, Judy, keeping step with me
all the way. Afterwards it was like a spell. In Bergen they believed every word. His body was beaten on to the rocks the
day following, his face disfigured. It seemed natural that his
neck was broken. Three days after I set back to Whitehaven. In
Whitehaven I saw his father . . .'

He broke off.

'His father – a giant old man with a beard to his waist. He

had a mad worship for his son. You know it. I've told you. I thought that he must suspect, caring so much ... But no. He stood there without moving. He went blind, groping with his hands. Then he caught me round the neck and kissed me. He thought I was Stane's best friend. There was water lapping up against the room where we were and a man came in with a sword. I thought young Stane would slip from beside me, catch the sword and stab me with it. I would offer no resistance. But when later old Stane called his son, running up the staircase after him, shouting his name in the rooms, there was no one there.

'But he would not let me go. All night he sat there holding my hand.'

'But how did it come?' Judith asked. 'Stane's death, I mean. What made you do it?'

'You know how it was. You felt it as I did. Stane and I always hated one another. I've been bred in England, Judy. I speak like an Englishman, walk like one, in my behaviour am like one – is that not so?'

'Yes,' she said, but she knew in her heart that it was not so. He had never walked, talked or behaved like an Englishman.

'Yes, but there are times when I am French through and through, when I loathe England and the English. And some Englishmen I hate from the beginning. So I did Stane. So satisfied, arrogant *and* ignorant. That mixture of conceit and ignorance that is in all your relations, Judith – the most obvious thing in the English. And he was clever, too; he saw at once how I was, my laziness, excitement, that I was unable to stay with anything for long. He judged me well, truly – that was partly why I hated him. And he meant to supplant me. He saw that the others, Wix and the rest, were dissatisfied. He manoeuvred me to London and then worked on them ... My God, Judy, he was clever! And I a fool! Holy Heaven, the fool I was!'

The words broke from him in a despairing cry such as she had never heard from him before. It seemed to be echoed from the hills. She was afraid lest someone should hear.

'Hush, hush!' she said, leaning up and stroking his cheek as she might with a child. 'Not too loud. And then— ?'

'Well, he came to London to work his way into Will Herries' counsels. You saw him at the Ball that night. He gave a black account of me to Herries, worked promises out of him and then returned to Whitehaven to show them that he had power in the

City, while I diced and drank ... Oh, it was true enough! Every word was true ...

'Then when I had fled from London to Christiania he knew all of it. He must have been spying into every corner. I started some business in Bergen. Not much, but something. It was doing fairly, and I meant to return to Whitehaven, show them my steadiness, make all well again. For I knew Wix cared for me in his heart ... I hadn't heard that Stane had told him all the London affairs, my debts, the scuffle in the Coffee House, everything. He came over to Bergen, Stane, I mean. He pretended that it was an accident, but I knew well what it was.

'We met in an inn room above the sea. He was victorious. He had a letter from Wix to say that they were ended with me in Whitehaven, that I had best never return to England. Stane was triumphant. It was the moment for which he had been working so long. His face was lit up. He had a wart on his right eyelid. Behind his head on the green wall there was a map of China and the Indies. I can tell you, Judith, that I all but killed him there, drove his head into that yellow map, there, just where China was. But there were men about, a street with traffic, boats knocking with the tide against the wall.

'I waited. I waited two days. I was most friendly. I licked his hand, asked that I should be the clerk. Then he boasted, how his father had once been a common fisherman and he himself had sold cockles barefoot. And he went further. He paid for my drink and told me how easy I had been, what a simpleton, and then he said something about you, Judy—'

'I always hated him,' she said.

'Yes, but he wanted you. You were his size, he said. He liked small women – and he was haunted by the wish to plunge his hands in your hair—'

She said nothing, only came closer to him.

'So I made my plan. I said I would row him across an inlet to a house where there were paid women – drink, women, dancing. He could be lascivious. Contemptuously he permitted me. As I strangled him he called out for his father thrice. That was his only decency. Physically he had no strength; I could have broken him anywhere.'

He stopped and said hoarsely: 'I have a fearful thirst. My mouth is dry every hour.'

'We will go home,' Judith said, laying her hand for an instant on his brow, 'and sleep.'

THE OLD MAN OF THE SEA

JUDITH AWOKE, AS now she was accustomed to do, to find Georges standing on the floor wrestling in his sleep with his implacable enemy.

She could see only his shadow. The October night was dark; clouds hid the stars. The words came from him thick and fast: 'No, no. Leave me. I have done with you. That was to end it. Struggle then, and the water's cold ... Sharp, sharp. I'll not touch you again. Keep off me. No, no. I'll listen to no whisper. It is useless. Oh, God, keep me free!'

The last was a whisper of intense and gasping weariness. He sank to his bare knees. She knew that he was kneeling on the floor, his head in his hands, while his body trembled.

She got out of their bed, went to him and very gently put her arms round him. He stayed there trembling against her. Then slowly he woke.

'Where am I ?' he asked.

'Here with me.' She led him back to bed, he docile as a child. They lay down together, hand in hand. Almost at once he was asleep again. But she remained for a long time awake, wondering what it was best to do.

This was October. He had returned in July – July, August, September, October, and there seemed to be no end to it, no frightening away of the ghosts, no helping him to overcome them. For the first time in her life she wished that she were older – older and wiser. In the immediate weeks after his return her great fear had been lest in an instant of indiscretion he should confess to somebody what he had done. He never rode into Keswick but she waited in an agonized terror for his return. She never saw him talking to the Ritsons or walking with Watson (for whom he had conceived a great liking) but she expected the end of the talk or the walk to be some terrible revelation. But now, especially when she was weary or lying awake at that time of the early morning when fears are most pressing, she sometimes wondered whether it would not be better that he should confess to someone. The burden of sharing it alone seemed often more than she could bear.

She was not subtle about it. She was not made for subtlety. He had killed Stane, who had tried to bring him to ruin. That

seemed to her fair. She would herself kill, if need be, anyone
who threatened Georges. She would lie in bed, clenching and
unclenching her hot little hands, with such a hatred of Stane
in her heart that she would almost swoon of it. He had tried to
kill Georges, to kill in Georges' life everything that was of any
value in it: he would have taken from Georges his livelihood,
his friends, even his wife. Well, then – what crime had Georges
done?

No one had seen. No one guessed. It was over. What then
possessed Georges? It was perhaps the hardest part of her task
now that this Georges was another man from that careless,
wild, courageous, casual Georges, whom she had married and
loved. And yet they were the same! She saw dimly how the one
had become the other. She could trace back a thousand times
when, in the past, he had been afraid of his deeds and then,
because he was afraid, had recklessly covered the old fault with
the new one. He had never had any stability. He had refused to
dig deep into life. She had seen that in him again and again,
and now, when he had tumbled into reality, it had been *too* deep
for him.

His kindly casualness had always made him live for the
moment, but from his childhood – although he would never
confess to it because of his pride – he had had an anticipation of
fear like a child who is safe only while the lighted candle is in
the room.

She did not analyse this. Women of her day did not analyse
natures and motives, but she understood him at last.

The irony of it was that now at length she possessed him as
she had always longed to do, but as so often when in life we are
granted our desires, her gratification was tragic. For, although she
possessed him, she could not help him. He relied on her now
for everything. He did nothing without asking her. He hated that
she should be out of his sight.

There in the half-dark, he uneasily sleeping at her side, she
was teased by the odd mixture of her feelings. If she had killed
Stane she would see to it that she was not haunted by his ghost.
Once done well done! There was impatience in her love for
Georges. He must get some work to do: that would worry his
ghosts! The farm was theirs and the next farm the Ritsons',
both worked by the Ritsons. That just sufficed them for their
immediate needs, but she could not endure to see Georges
standing about, leaning against a stone wall watching the sheep
or the clouds or walking on the uneven stone path beyond the

farm outhouses, his hands behind his back, his head down, as though he were a prisoner. His only healthy days were those when he went off on the fells with Charlie Watson.

She was beginning to 'manage' him as she 'managed' old Ritson's rheumatism, Mrs Ritson's bad clumsy sewing, Tom Ritson's carelessness about money, young Alice Ritson's love-affairs; and like all managing people she always a little despised those who succumbed to her management. It was part of Watson's power over her that she couldn't manage him any-where.

But her real anxiety was that she did not herself know which way she would go. Part of her – her father's part – shared Georges' terrors to their depths. She knew how real that ghostly world was, how dark its valleys, how awful its inhabitants. But for the other part of her all ghosts were unreal, fantastic, just as her father had been altogether unreal and exaggerated for many people. As though, indeed, someone had said to her about her father: 'Fielding would not have drawn such a character.' No, but there were ghosts outside the books of Mr Fielding and Mr Richardson. But were there ? Was it not merely the colic ? How real were Georges' terrors ? 'Very real,' whispered a shadow by Rosthwaite. 'I spent my life in fighting them.' 'Balderdash,' said Will Herries and all the Herries.

But if only she herself could go one way or another! At one moment she wanted to shake Georges by the shoulders, to wake him thoroughly from a silly dream; at another she had only to close her eyes, and young Stane, the wart on his eyelid, his mouth curled contemptuously, his clothes wringing wet, crawled from the Tarn and slipped up the field towards her. Two events showed her very sharply the division between her two worlds. One was an unexpected letter from Francis. He wrote from Bournemouth saying that he had intended to send her a letter 'weeks back' but had been so closely occupied ... Closely occupied in Bournemouth ?

He was staying with Prosper and Amelia Cards. He had been there for some weeks. Judith, remembering the Ball, whispered to herself: 'Jennifer.'

... At first, dear Judith, I will be honest and confess that I found the country so desolate that I could have drowned myself. But there have been ameliorations, and now I find myself hanging on when the season is inclement and London calls. Moreover, my conscience tells me that I should come

North and assist poor Deborah and see my darling Judith. Not that yourself are my conscience, dear Judith, but rather my pleasure. However, I am kept here and by what I will one day tell you.

('By whom rather,' thought Judith.)

The Town is a nest of old women who drink nauseous water and talk gossip by the bushel. We have also had a Menagerie with two Lions and a Bear. I tasted the waters but once. Do you remember how once for a punishment my poor mother gave us a pint basin of thin gruel with a spoonful of salt in it for a week and how it tasted? Well, that's for these waters. I fear that the Dispute that had its commencement with that accursed Ball of Will's shows no abatement but only an increase. Brother Will will have nothing to do with me, and there is indeed now a Division in our family starting with Brother Will and Cousin Prosper and spreading into many directions.

I am myself deeply sorry for it. What a stupid affair to start with a Broken Fan! I console myself with the friendliness of my relations here and especially with my cousin Jennifer.

I fear that yourself, dear Judith, are held here to have taken sides most decisively, and that Amelia, at least, is not to be reconciled to you. Cousin Prosper in his cups is reconciled to all the world, but out of them – well, he has enough family pride for Sir Charles Grandison. I have been entertained by Godwin's *Enquiry concerning Political Justice*. You should read it, for if we are going the way of France, which is none too unlikely, there are wise words for us here. I am myself engaged on a paper answering some points in Paine's *Age of Reason*. We were never, I am convinced, in all our National History, more at the parting of the ways than we now are. All Europe is in an uproar. The People's Voice is making itself felt everywhere and splendid extravagances at Brighthelmstone are not sufficient satisfaction for such a heavy rise in prices.

You know, Judith, that I was always more Dreamer than anything. Now more than ever I dream my dreams. I am thirty-six years of age and have done nothing with my life. See Will, who is adding pound to pound with every breath he draws. Dare I venture into matrimony, little Judith?

Is there any woman would be fool enough to take me if I asked her? . . .

'Any woman?' thought Judith. 'Will Jennifer?'

The thought struck her with an added pang of loneliness and difficulty. If Francis married Jennifer, then he was lost to her, Judith, for ever. And with Francis gone it seemed to her that she would be, indeed, alone. But Jennifer would not have him. She was to make a far finer match than a poor North Country cousin ten years her elder.

Putting the letter down with a sigh, the world contained in its pages slipped into incredibility. How unreal, beside her present actual trouble, seemed that little pasteboard quarrel of the fan. Will's city life, Bournemouth's waters, Paine's *Age of Reason*, Jennifer's beauty, Prosper's pride and the rest. There *were* two worlds, and the secret of living was to know both to be real! But it was a problem. So she went out and rubbed old Ritson's back with ointment, looked at Tom Ritson's bull that he had bought in Keswick, advised Alice Ritson against young Humblethwath of Rosthwaite and stood, shading her eyes against the October sun, to see Georges ride up the path with Watson.

What she did see was incredible.

Georges was walking along the rocky path leading his horse and beside him was walking – Reuben! Reuben, as she could see, talking, gently, kindly, smiling, and Georges was smiling too.

At the first sight of them she had to recall that last time when she had seen Reuben, proud, master of himself, but driven from the house . . . and now, Georges was walking with him as though he loved him!

Reuben had been often in her mind. She was always thinking of him, but she had never seen him again since that day. Now, as she turned towards them, she loved him for being kind to Georges, and she loved Georges for being kind to Reuben. It was the first time she had had comfort since Georges' return. She met them and kissed them both. They stood there, the three of them, looking down at the Tarn, which was ruffled with little grey bird's feathers that ran in flocks under the pale sun, making the whole sheet of water quiver with life.

Reuben was different. He was far surer, more in command of himself and of everything. He was stouter but harder too. He was wearing black knee-breeches and stout black shoes and a broad black hat, but he was clean and neat; his white stock was

clean and the white bands at his wrists. His voice was quiet
and assured like his carriage. He moved and spoke like a man
who had discovered how to rule himself.

They all went into the house. Reuben said that he would stay
with them the night. He had come from Wasdale. Tomorrow
he had to preach in Mardale. He had walked from Waswater
over the Stye Head and up from Rosthwaite.

That evening they had a strange conversation that Judith
was never to forget. Oddly now Reuben dominated them both.
He had never dominated Judith before, he had always been subservient to her, but now, although he was as loving to her as
ever, being with her as though they had never been separated,
he had a new power that set him apart. Soon she knew where his
power lay. He was no longer afraid of anybody or anything.
She saw that Georges submitted to him like a child to an elder.
They sat, the three of them, close together by the wood fire
that blazed with a sharp exulting power in the hearth. Judith
sat at Georges' feet, her head against his thigh. She caught his
hand in hers and felt its pulse leap wildly against her palm.

She was always saying to him now with every movement,
'Don't be afraid, I'm here.'

Reuben had not very much to tell them about himself. He
went about, just as before, preaching everywhere, anywhere.

'What do you preach?' Georges asked suddenly.

'Jesus Christ,' Reuben said.

'I do not wish to be offensive,' Georges went on slowly. 'May
I say what is in my mind with honesty?'

Reuben smiled. 'Yes. If you will.'

'Well, then, Christ is a figure to me who died long since. A
Jewish rebel. The times needed a new religion. This was offered
them and they took it. I cannot believe in any God, or that Christ
was more than a brave man, mistaken ... This life is all that we
have, and, by God, it is a poor one!' His hand trembled in
Judith's.

'I do not think so,' said Reuben. 'I know Jesus Christ. I
have talked with Him.'

'But these are words,' said Georges. 'My mother was heathen
and her father before. My grandfather was an atheist, famous in
his day, in the town of Toulouse. It is true that I was always
taught that the Christian influence was a false one, but that has
not formed my mind. I have observed men and their actions,
and I find that there is no sign of a God in the world.'

'Then life is meaningless.'

'Yes, meaningless.'

'It is a question,' Reuben said quietly, 'that every man must decide by his own experience. Here we are, two men in the world. You are certain of your experience and I of mine. But if I had been to China and seen the Emperor and you had not, you would permit my right to my certainty, would you not?'

'Yes,' answered Georges impatiently. 'But the Emperor of China exists. Many people have seen him. The Christ is a fable.'

'You must permit me my experience. I know that God is in the world.'

'And I know that He is not.'

'Are you as certain,' asked Reuben, 'that He is not, as I that He is?'

Georges raised his eyes, haggard and restless, to Reuben's face.

'Then if He is, how can He permit this cruelty, this pain . . .' He broke off. His whole body was trembling.

'When I was a lad in Cockermouth,' Reuben said, 'I saw one day a bear baited in the street. I suffered torture from its helplessness. Now I know from my own life that all experience adds to one's riches. And pain possibly gives the most.'

'Was the bear the richer?' Georges broke out passionately.

'If the bear knew his gain. This is not the end,' Reuben said. 'Or so I believe. I have an immortal part, and Jesus is my friend to show to me that I have.'

'This world is enough,' Georges cried. 'A vile world in which we have no chance and are buffeted by a hidden enemy.'

Reuben was silent. He bent forward and gazed into the fire.

'Ah, but I have two worlds,' he said at last, 'and there I am richer than you. I must deny neither. I am citizen of both. In the one I am very young, an infant, but with the Grace of God I shall grow. In the other I eat my bread and pay my tax, but my body dies, my tax is paid and I go through the door, out of it, at any time.' Then he added, smiling to himself: 'The great lesson of life is patience.'

'Patience!' Georges broke out. He started to his feet. 'I swear to God, if there be one, that I have no patience. That I refuse to delay. I want my judgement. For my sin . . . for my crime . . .' He stood over Reuben, bent forward, shaking the other's shoulder.

'Reuben! Your sins, if you've committed any, do they stay with you? In your other world that you speak of, will you be punished for ever? Will there be no release?'

Reuben nodded his head. 'Yes, there is release for sin – after repentance.'

'But I do not repent. I have done no wrong. He merited his death. He . . .' Georges broke off, seeing what he had admitted. There was an intense silence between the three of them. Judith, whose guard over Georges was constant, turned to Reuben with some of her old ferocity, as though she would defend Georges with her claws. But there was no need. Reuben looked down at the floor; then, glancing up, he said:

'What I tell you must seem like empty folly to you. I can only warrant you that nothing is final; there is no end to experience – and there is no sin too large to keep Christ Jesus from your life.'

He rose and went over to Georges and put his hand on his shoulder. 'Pay for your sin – good worthy coin. Then travel on.'

He went up to his bed.

After he was gone they sat close, hand in hand. Georges said desperately: 'Judith, there must be ghosts. It is true, although I never thought it. He will not leave me. At every corner I think to see him, and now it is months since I broke his neck and he drowned.'

Then after a little he added: 'There must be some end coming to this. I can *feel* it coming. If I could fight someone with my hands, stand my trial, be hanged by the neck – yes, anything rather than this stealthy silence. I, all my life I have never cared what I did nor minded what I did, and I am young and have everything before me. And he's dead and no one knows. It is sentimental imagination, this fancy I have – but I can't be free of it. I can't! I can't! I can't!' He walked desperately about the room. Then he stopped sharp in front of Judith. 'Judith, do *you* think there's a God?'

'I don't know. No one knows.' (But she thought to herself: 'What he said about the two worlds is true. That is the way *my* life is going.')

But she rose and then, bending forward, said:

'I shall tell you what I think, Georges. That you are lazy. That you must go somewhere to work and forget Stane. Why should you think of him? If he were here and he had tried to hurt you as he did, and I were strong enough, I should strangle him with my two hands. He was our enemy, and you slew him fairly. Shake off your imagination! Go farming with Charlie Watson for a while. He'll teach you things. He has no business with ghosts—'

Georges looked above her head to the farther wall.

'Stane's father,' he said. 'His heart was broken.'

She herself felt a pang then. Yes, the consequences went, as always, beyond the act. But she faced them ... Stane, his father, all his relations – she'd face them all. Let them attack Georges and they attacked her too. But to fight for Georges, she now saw, needed more than physical combat.

A week later Judith lost her temper in the good old fashion of her childhood, and this loss of her temper led to an incident.

There was a man just then, Larry Tod, who was helping Tom Ritson with his cattle. He was a waster, this Larry, no good at all, and he wandered about the district doing odd jobs hither and thither and not much good anywhere. He was famous, though, as a wrestler. He was big, carroty-haired, broken-nosed. He liked to strip to his shirt and drawers and show a chest like a board, and, to quote the old description of the famous French wrestler, Le Bœuf, 'a stomach like a bale of wool'. He was very proud of himself, very sly, up to any mean trick, the right sort of figure for the villain in a wrestling bout. And that, on this occasion, because of Judith's temper he was.

On this day, an October afternoon of driving black cloud when the fells looked twice their natural size, Judith coming into the yard saw Tod bending down and twisting the tiny arm of young Walter Ritson, who was yelling his loudest.

Tod straightened himself when he saw Judith. He was always dirty with manure and mud and the rest. Now he wiped the back of his hand over the flat of his broken nose and said something about the child's laughing at him. Young Walter, the tears drying on his cheeks, stared up at them both in interested amazement.

Judith's temper was fine to see. She enjoyed it herself. She had been living in half-shadows with Georges for months back and she needed a change. Then she hated the huge oaf with the surly eyes, the tangled hair that seemed like a parody of her own. He was a sort of ogre personification of all that threatened Georges. She told him her notions about him. Slowly his brow darkened. What he would have said or done no one will ever tell, for Charlie Watson came by. Tod turned his rage in that direction. He hated Watson anyway.

A minute later Watson was stripping his coat. It was to be a wrestle. The news went round as though a bell had been rung. Everyone came flocking, and the match was moved to the green mound above the farm.

All the little village was there – men, women and children.

A ring was formed, Watson and Larry Tod stripped to shirt and drawers. Both men were open at the neck.

It was to be the best of three throws. The little crowd held their breath, while the sky tossed cloud after cloud as though there were some giant juggler over the hill, and the Tarn, black as ink, lay insolently below them.

In the front of the ring, squatting on the grass, was young Walter Ritson, the cause of the trouble, with his mouth open. He hated Larry, but he feared him too, and if Larry won he fancied that there would be trouble for him. Perhaps the others felt the same. Larry Tod had been prominent in the little place these last weeks, and with every day he was becoming more sure of himself and more insolent. And for Judith and Georges, also watching, although neither confessed it to the other, the result of this seemed like an omen. Let the red-haired ogre win, Georges thought, and he was pushed a step farther into his prison.

The men shook hands and got into holds. Larry tried at once the back heel, the simplest and oldest of all 'chips', for all the wrestler has to do is to lay his foot behind his antagonist's heel and bend him over it. But you must be strong to do it. Larry was strong, but so was Watson, who at once slackened his hold and moving his beautiful firm body with the most delicate grace, turned his side. Watson tried then for a buttock, but Larry's immense strength prevented him. Watson tried to get under him to lift him over his back. Then, when that failed, he stepped away and there they were again, their arms at one another's necks. They began slowly to step round. The little crowd drew their breath. This was to be an even match.

For Georges it was an agony. In his strange, over-nervous, harassed state everything was exaggerated. The dark furry clouds hung low, as though with an especial sinister message for himself. When the sun suddenly struck out from them with bright splinter-like rays, flinging the dry bracken into patches of amber light as though there were a secret flame beneath the soil, that, too, seemed to point the finger at him. Why was he thus persecuted? Could he not bring his mind to order? It was true what Judith had said, that Stane deserved his death. It was only his imagination that dragged with him everywhere the accompanying scene, the rain hissing on to the boards of the boat, the sudden consciousness in Stane's eyes of Georges' intention, the cry lost in the storm, the whip, whip of the wind.

The women were shouting. Watson had tried the right-leg trip, making Larry swing sharply towards his left. With a mighty straining of muscle, his thighs and buttocks forced to their uttermost strength, he lifted Larry up, hoisting Larry's left leg up with his right and – to a great shout of all and sundry – landing the ogre with a fine bump on his back.

First throw to Watson.

The two men stayed a moment, wiping their brows. The crowd were silent. Did they feel, perhaps, that there was something concerned here more deeply than the personal encounter? The women were all on Watson's side, and yet he was aloof from them. He had never tried to make love to any of them. There was a little feeling that he was 'a bit above himself'. Larry, when he was dressed up and had washed his face, was a great figure of a man and knew what love-making was. One and all, though, in their hearts, they loathed him and perhaps, like little Wallie, feared him too.

At any rate he looked now a man to be feared. As he stood there waiting, scowling between his sullen eyes, he looked as though he would kill Watson had he the chance.

When they came together again Larry tried the hitch-over, that is, he attempted to turn his left side to Watson, curl his left leg round Watson's right and, while Watson was standing on his left leg, cross-buttock him. But Watson was too quick for him, and soon they were moving round, slowly, cautiously, trying for some advantage.

You would not tell from looking at Georges, standing straight and grave, his rather round cheeks composed, his black eyes sombre and still, that his soul was in torment. If he had one! If he had one! That preacher, Reuben Sunwood, with his confidence in his Christ, his quiet happy assurance . . . Ah well, that was not for Georges! His life had gone for nothing, one silly mistake and foolishness after another! He had begun life with a sense of adventure, with a kind of bravado, as though he could dare the world and bring it tumbling to his feet. But the world had snapped its fingers at him. He had got nothing out of it. Nothing save Judy!

He half turned and looked at her, standing on tiptoe, her mouth a little open, her hair blowing, all excitement like a child. A child! But how courageous and independent! How she had held by him – from the first, through everything, her loyalty never for a moment wavering. If he could but get rid of this present burden and dread he would show her that at last he realized her worth. He had been a long time coming to it, through slow selfish stages, but he knew it now, that he had had the luck of the devil to get her – yes, luck far better than he deserved.

He heard the deep indrawing breath of the women beside him and saw, with a beat of excitement, Larry Tod turning his back suddenly, getting right under Watson and, with a great heave that had also in it a lightning quickness, sending Watson flying over his back. He had buttocked him. Buttocked him, fair and square.

Second throw to Tod.

Then, indeed, Georges' whole life and purpose seemed to be in the match. Watson must win; he must, he must! The very sight of Larry Tod strutting about there like a flaming peacock, pushing out his chest, stroking his arms, throwing glances from his narrow eyes to heaven as though he expected the clouds to acclaim him, that was indeed too much. If Watson lost now all was lost. It was as though Tod with his coarseness and his evil had been sent as a messenger to Georges threatening him with some low, vile dominion for ever.

Watson stood there quietly, no expression in his eyes, waiting. Above them the clouds were stripping the sky, which began to be flooded with a white pale glow. The Tarn, beneath them, was white like the peeled inside skin of an orange; all the houses of the village were black.

The men took hold again. First Tod, setting his teeth, tried the swinging hips, but this, if it is to succeed, must be a swing of great quickness, and Watson was too strong for him. Then Watson, in his turn, tried the chip, getting his knee behind his opponent's so that Larry might lose his balance. It seemed that Watson would succeed. Larry raised his head to the white sky, his teeth clenched, his eyes closed; you could feel that he thought that he was going. But his strength was too much for Watson. He escaped, and suddenly, a moment later, was clicking Watson's right leg with his own right and his left with Watson's left. The struggle now was fearful. Both men put out their uttermost. Watson resorted to the outside click to save himself from falling, placing his leg as near the ground as possible. The two men swung and strained; Watson's neck and upper chest were soaked with sweat. Then Larry's little eyes were triumphant; he crossed both Watson's legs quickly with his own, cross-buttocking, and with a shout, his huge frame seeming to double its natural size, he had Watson on the ground.

He stood there, smiling.

Georges turned. His fate was sealed then. He walked away down the hill. Coming to the little rough bridge he saw someone

standing there, someone with his back to him, a man of a great
height, in a long dark-blue coat. He knew, before the man turned,
who it would be. It was young Stane's father.

A few minutes later Judith noticed that Georges was not at her
side. She had been absorbed by the incidents of the last bout,
and when she saw Watson beaten she felt, as Georges had felt,
that there was some personal omen, intended for them both.
That was not like her. She realized it herself, but these last
weeks had tried her. Yes, she wished she were older and wiser
and, in general, more patient. She wished that she were not so
easily excited – excited by just anything, a piece of silk, a cloud
in the sky – and then by a man hanging! It was then that she
saw that Georges was not beside her and, at once, apprehension
seized her as it always did now. It seemed to hover over her like
a black bird – yes, and the sky white behind the bird, the Tarn
dead white and all the bracken dead.

Watson was walking slowly towards her, pulling on his coat.
She had to speak to him.

'Next time, Charlie,' she said, smiling.

'Aye.' She could see that he was bitterly disappointed. She
was not sure that there were not even tears in his eyes.

'I'll whack him – great oaf!' he said, half to himself, half to her.
She realized with a quick sharpness of perception that he had
done it all for her, all from the first to the last. She put out her
hand and it lay in his hot one, damp and sweating from the
tussle.

'I'll back you, Charlie Watson, against all the world.' And
yet, although she was so grateful to him and friendly, the truth
was that she was scarcely aware of him.

Over and over again she was saying: 'Where's Georges?
What's he about? Why did he go without telling me?'

She turned and ran down the hill. Pushing open their door,
she saw a strange sight. A giant old man stood looking at her.
He had long white hair that fell to the blue collar of his long
heavy coat, and he had a white beard, like the cleanest, most
shining wool. Above his beard a sharp pale nose and two pale-
blue eyes. All down his long blue coat were round brass buttons,
and he wore tall boots that gaitered him to the thigh. He was
so white and clean that he seemed to be wrapped in some mask-
like covering, and Judith had the odd sense that with a gesture he
could throw off all of this – the hair, beard, face, clothes – and
that he would be then a thin naked old man, sharp like a sword.

Another odd thing was that at once she knew him. She did not need to hear Georges' voice:

'Mr Stane, this is my wife. Judith, this is poor Mr Stane's father.'

She remembered always her sudden resentment that Georges said 'Poor Mr Stane.' There was weakness and cowardice there. She would never have said 'Poor Mr Stane' had a thousand of his fathers been there!

She went forward, holding out her hand.

'How are you, sir? Will you not sit down? You must be weary after your walk.' She saw at once that the old man liked her and that, very strangely, she liked him. It was always Judith's way, her life through, to know in the first instant whether she liked or disliked anyone.

The old man sat down. Georges had not moved from his place, standing against the wall, and Judith did not look at him. Rather she was compelled to notice everything about old Mr Stane, how, with solemn, dignified, cautious steps, he moved to a chair; how he slowly sat down, spreading on either side of him the long heavy skirts of his coat; how he put up his hand and smoothed his white locks, pinched his white nose, then, very carefully, as though he were dealing with something extremely precious, laid his hands on his immense knees. It was then that she was struck with his great strength. His hands looked as though they could wring the neck of an ox.

'Mr Stane,' Georges said, 'took a chaise to Keswick and walked from there to see us.'

'Aye,' said the old man. 'I was drawn like. My heart is aching for my son, madam, and your husband was the last to see him. It was a terrible accident and God's will. But he was all I had in the world.'

He spoke with very little accent in a soft mild tone. Then he went on: 'Whoso casteth a stone on high casteth it on his own head. He that worketh mischief, it shall fall on him, and he shall not know whence it cometh.'

Her heart beat wildly. He knew then? He had come here for some kind of vengeance? But he looked up and gave her a smile, so gentle, so friendly, so amiable that she could only smile back at him.

'The Scriptures, madam,' he said, 'have been a comfort to me all my days.'

'Yes,' she said, not knowing what to say. 'And now you must have some food.'

'Thank you kindly, madam. I could enjoy a bit of food. Although I like a walk, you understand.'

'Mr Stane, Judith,' Georges said, 'will stay here with us tonight.'

'Thank you kindly,' the old man answered, pinching his nose. 'I wouldn't mind.'

He smiled on them both, then sighed a deep heavy sigh.

TUMBLE DOWNSTAIRS

OLD STANE stood, as he liked to do, the blue skirts of his coat spread, before the fireplace.

Judith sat on the window-ledge, peeling potatoes from a large 'kist' on her lap, looking out of window at the gold smoke of the bracken that rolled in a low cloud up and up above the thin splintered blue of the Tarn. A late October afternoon, quite still, without a cloud in the sky, and the running everywhere of water, crystal clear.

Within the room, too, everything was sharp and clean; Judith, her lithe figure like a cut jewel, the flames of the fire like painted laths, old Stane's beard like the white of an egg, his blue coat without a spot, his long strong hands washed, you would say, with pumice-stone. Cleanest of all his long nose, always like the nose of a mask.

'Well, madam,' he said, 'I swore that my son should become a great man. I had myself sold fish with my feet bare on the Whitehaven cobbles, and the Lord thought it well for me to do so. My wife, ma'am, died in childbirth. She was a good woman, although with impulses not entirely Christian. When the Lord took her I accepted my rebuke that I could not have made her more godly, and I offered my son, even as Abraham offered Isaac a sacrifice to the Lord—'

('Young Stane,' thought Judith, 'a sacrifice to the Lord!' She could see his face, mean and ambitious, and his hands as they moved towards her . . . if she had allowed him—! She shuddered a little.)

'But as Abraham with Isaac, so with myself and my son. The Lord did not at that time demand the sacrifice. He knew His own good time . . .'

Oh, when would he stop! She thought that in these last weeks he had managed to creep into her very being. She would never be rid of him again. He had done nothing but hang about the house. He never went farther than the steps beyond the door. He was always there. At night they could hear him move his great body in his bed, yes, although there were a thousand doors between themselves and him! He ate but little, drank only water, spoke to no one save Georges and herself. He was quite silent if they were not there. Sometimes he would talk to them, sometimes only look at them. He would stare and stare over his long nose.

He had little movements that made her long to scream out. One was when he laid, slowly and almost sacramentally, his thick heavy hands on his thick heavy knees. Then he would stroke his beard with a purposeful meditation as though he were wondering whether, with a quick jerk, he would not tug it off and show it to be a disguise. He would raise a hand as though he would give a blessing. He was always gentle, kindly and patient. She liked him behind her terror of him. Had he not been young Stane's father she might have been his friend.

As it was he must go – and as soon as might be. But Georges would not let him go. He was fascinated by him as the rabbit by the snake.

Two days before this, almost hysterical with irritation (for it was absolutely against her character to be passive in this manner), in their room at night she had attacked Georges.

'Tell him to go!'

'I cannot.'

'Why not?'

'This is the least I owe him.'

'You owe him nothing! Georges, tell him to go!'

'You don't understand . . . So long as he wishes to remain he must.'

She could have shaken him until his head rolled on his shoulder.

'Georges, wake up! You are dreaming. You killed the man in self-defence. He would have finished you. He wished to. Well, then. The old man has no right over us.'

'I cannot tell him to go.'

'Then I will.'

'Tell him. You will see. Nothing will happen.'

'But what *is* it? What spell has he laid on you?'

'No spell. I cannot do otherwise.'

'But is he to be here with us always?'

'So long as he wishes.'

'But he makes you miserable. He reminds you always. If he went away you would forget.'

He came to her, put his arms round her.

'In this you *are* a child. You are too young to understand. It is not because I think I was wicked to kill Stane. I've done many worse things. But I'm not the same man since I did it. I feel that I must confess it to someone. Then it will be over.'

'But you have confessed it – to me.'

'You are part of myself or you have grown to be. We are both in this – as though you had been in the boat too.'

She stood up straight beside him, like man standing by man.

'Well, I shall tell him to go.'

And so, on this golden afternoon, she did.

She was not afraid to tell him; her earlier fear of him seemed to leave her as she spoke.

'Mr Stane,' she said, coming quite close to him, 'when will you be leaving us?'

He didn't answer: he was pulling at his beard.

'I ask,' she said, smiling up at him, 'because I may have a guest. Mr Francis Herries. He has written that he may be coming.'

The old man's nose seemed to probe into her, tickling her skin. As a fact he was bending down towards her.

'When you have no place for me,' he said, very gently stroking his beard and almost, it seemed to her, drawing her into the meshes of it, 'I may reside in the village. It is a pleasure for me to be near your husband, who was so good a friend to my son.'

She was on the verge of crying out: 'He was not good to him. They hated one another.' It was one of Mr Stane's peculiarities that he seemed to draw out of you your most secret thoughts.

He smiled on her very affectionately as he added:

'I am an old man, madam. The Lord has seen fit to take everything from me. These, your husband and yourself, are, it may be, the last affections of my life.'

After that what could she say?

That night they lay awake hearing him walk his room. It was a heavy soft tread like an animal's. They heard him get into his bed at last. Then there was only an owl's cry.

They clung together that night like children.

'Georges, let us run away.'

'Where?'

'Anywhere. London. Paris.'

'He would come after us.'

'Georges, I *must* help you. I must! I must! I'm not a fool. This is a ridiculous thing, to be hemmed in by an old man.'

He sighed, holding her very closely.

'It matters very little. I'm happy because now I love you. Judy, Judy, I love you so.'

'And I love you more and more.'

'But how can you when there is so little in me to love? I have never treated you well from the beginning.'

'Georges, I shall never love anyone again. That is true. I know it absolutely. This is for all my life long.'

He stroked her hair. That, at least, he had loved from the very beginning.

'Judy, if we could be rid of this I know now what we would do. I could settle here now, I wouldn't wish to move. I would farm with Watson. I have lived out all my restlessness. We would have enough. Perhaps you would have children. If only we could be rid of this!'

'But we can, Georges!'

They were whispering as though the old man in his room could hear them.

'He must go, and then you will forget it all.'

'What did he say when you spoke?'

She did not answer.

'Did he say he would go?'

'No.'

'You see.'

'Oh, but I shan't be beaten by an old man.' Her voice rose. She dropped it to a whisper again without knowing that she did so.

'Judy, I love you! I love you! I love you!'

'Oh, Georges, I love you so! It has come at last, both of us loving one another – both of us.'

'Yes – both of us . . .'

'It is very seldom that two people love with the same strength.'

'I did not know that I could love anyone for long. You have made me by being so good.'

They heard the old man in the other room rise from his bed. The boards creaked. They were silent, their hearts beating the one against the other.

But it was on that night that they both had terrible dreams. Georges dreamt that he was being hanged from a tree that was covered with white moss, and in that last moment before death the moss was alive with worms. Judith dreamt of a white horse that, plunging through dark water, leapt up the black hills beyond, and that, as it leapt, her father (she had never seen him, but she knew that it was her father) ran and jumped on to its back, calling to her to follow. But she could not, because Georges was struggling in the water and she trying to save him. The white horse vanished, a star fell from the sky into the water, and Georges was drowned.

In the dim musk-like shadow of dawn she waked and found Georges sleeping at her side. In her relief she laid her hand on his bare heart and felt its steady beat. Then she looked in his face and saw that he, too, was struggling in dreams.

She brushed his dark hair back from his forehead, kissed his eyes, stroked his breast, gently as a mother her child.

In the morning, however, all her sentiment was gone. They must be rid of this old man. The weather had changed. The sky was a fury of wind and rushing cloud. The clouds ran like messengers, and the sun struck like a whip on the hills, slashed and was gone. The bracken changed in an instant from dun to fire, from fire to sullen death. The clouds, after racing the sky, suddenly gathered into heavy bales of wool and then slipped down, enclosing Watendlath in mist. The rest of the world was shut away. Judith, in spite of her common sense, began to lose her wits, for now she, too, was conscious of a terrible impulse to catch the old man by the beard and tell him everything.

'Yes. It's true. I don't know whether you think it or not, but Georges killed your wretched son, and he deserved it. Now will you go?'

She had never felt any urge like this before. It was exactly as though someone were whispering in her ear. Their nights were broken. They were afraid to sleep because of their dreams. The old man stayed by the house, and they found that they, too, stayed there also. Charlie Watson was away in Carlisle. She did not seem to want to speak to anyone. She never went into the Ritsons' kitchen. The low wet clouds seemed to shut them off, the three of them, from all the rest of the world.

Judith sewed, cooked, sometimes walked to the Fell and looked down to Rosthwaite. That was the farthest she went. Georges sat, walked to the door and looked out, sat down again. It was as though they were both held by a spell. It could not, of course, continue like this. But what would happen? Old Mr Stane seemed to be perfectly content. He talked much and always about himself and his son. He gave no trouble, stayed for the most part beside the fire.

'You may be sure that I appreciate your kindness. The Lord will not suffer a sparrow to fall to the ground . . . My boy would have been wealthy had he lived. He had a fine head for business. Aye. Aye. All that I had, but it is the Lord's will, and His mercy must be great in our eyes . . . But it is a grief to me that he should have perished in foreign waters. Your husband, ma'am, did all that he could, but it was beyond human power to save him. I know that. For an old man it is a hard blow, but it will not be long before the Lord will take me to Himself . . .'

Nevertheless he did not give the impression of great sorrow, but rather of intent watchfulness. He watched with his nose, and when he stroked it with his thick slow finger it was as though finger and nose were communicating together.

One afternoon the rain came. It fell in hard relentless torrents. The country was blinded as though a hood had been drawn over its eyes. That night in the war of water and groaning trees Georges caught Judith's hands and told her that he could hold out no longer. He must tell the old man and be damned to him.

'When I have told him, I can take him by the neck and shove him from the door. He can take what revenge he pleases.'

For a moment she thought that perhaps this would be best. Then she saw what it would mean. Georges would be arrested and hanged. She told him that that would be the end of everything, of herself as well as of him.

'Well, maybe that would be best. Anything's better than this. He is strangling us as though he had a cord around our throats, and he knows it.'

She had a wild notion that they should start out then and there, run for their lives, on and on, reach some foreign country – China . . . Even as she said it she knew that it was hopeless. He had strangled all her energy.

On the next night the rain had ceased, and a cold pale stillness lay over everything. They sat around the fire, and Mr Stane told them about his home, his possessions, his clothes, his Bible, his intimacy with God as he had done a thousand times before. There never was such an egoist.

'The Lord giveth and the Lord taketh away . . .'

Georges sprang from his seat by the fire, stood up against him, front to front.

'I killed your son. I killed your son. I threw him into the water

and watched him drown. I hated him and hate him yet ...
Now be damned to you both ... You and your son ... both of
you.'

It was as though the words had been spat out and then
returned into him again. He put his hand to his throat. Judith
rose with a startled cry. She came close to him, as though to
protect him, so that they were all near together. In the silence
she heard the owl's cry that had been haunting her for weeks.

At last, after this great pause, old Stane slowly lifted himself
up from his chair, stood above them, then with his white hand
pushed them, breaking through between them.

He looked at them, nodded his head.

'I knew it ... a long time back. I wanted confirmation from
your own mouth. Bloody murderer of my son—'

'Well, he had been bent on my ruin for years. He wished to take
my place.' Georges panted the words. 'It was an old feud
between us. We hated one another from the beginning.'

Old Stane nodded his head. 'Aye – you hated him.'

'Now go!' Georges cried. 'Call in the Justice. I shan't run
away.'

He seemed like a man liberated. Judith went to him and put
her hand on his arm.

'We shan't run away,' she repeated.

But Stane did not move. Georges felt such a sickness of the
sight of him, a sickness that involved himself, his deed, the whole
world. He would never be free of all this until Stane was gone.

'Finish it,' he said, and went up the stairs.

Everything happened then with great swiftness. Georges had
reached the upper landing, when old Stane turned and was
after him. For so heavy a man he moved quickly, as though someone very young and vital were concealed in that bulk.

He was at the stairhead in a moment. Georges turned to face
him and they stood close together as though in amity.

Stane shouted:

'I came for this! ... I came for this! Down you go,
murderer—'

His arms shot up, he hugged Georges close to his heart as
though he loved him, lifted him like a baby, then hurled him
away from the stair, over to the floor below.

He waited, looking down, then rushed down the stair, bent
for a moment over the huddled figure, passed out through the
door.

* * *

It had happened in a flash, as lightning strikes a house. Judith had not stirred; now, liberated, she ran to Georges, frantically, crying she knew not what, knelt down beside him.

His head was bleeding and both his legs were bent beneath him. He was quite conscious and he looked at her and smiled.

'My back is broken . . . he has done for me.'

'No. No—' She lifted his head and placed it against her breast.

'There's nothing to do, Judy, my darling. I'll be gone in a moment. The old devil was strong . . .'

She tried to be clear-headed and wise. This was the crisis of her whole life, something for which she had been always preparing. Her hand was soaked in the blood from his wounded head, but she could think of nothing save his eyes, which stared into hers as though they would never let her go.

'I must fetch someone. They shall ride into Rosthwaite . . .' She did not know what she said.

'No. Don't go. Don't leave me. Soon I shan't see you.'

She began to cry.

'. . . It is just . . . Now we had come to love one another. Ugh, I can't speak. I am swimming in water . . . Sinking. Hold my eyes, Judy. Oh, Judy, darling, how I love you!'

'And I you, Georges. Always. Oh, Christ, for help. Someone to help . . .'

'Nothing to be done.' His head sank deep against her breast. His voice fell to a whisper.

'I love you – for ever—'

His hand touched hers and he was gone.

Part III

The Bird of Bright Plumage

FAMILY PAPERS

Letter from Judith Paris to Francis Herries, Esq

22, WESTBOURNE PLACE, LONDON,
16th of May, 1800

MY DEAREST FRANCIS – Dinner is over, Emma has gone out
to visit a friend, the candles are properly trimmed and now is the
time to do what I have for several days pledged myself to – write
a proper and informing letter. You know well by this time, dear
Francis, that I am never as informing as I would wish to be, but
on this especial occasion I have real news for you – for, what do
you think? I was actually present at Drury Lane Theatre last
night when the poor King was shot at by a ruffian and had a most
providential escape from death.

Mr Ross, with whom Emma has on several occasions acted
at Drury Lane, had given her two tickets and, as you may well
believe, we were all agog for we were promised that the King
and Queen and all the Princesses would be present.

Now fancy the event! Scarcely had the King entered the box,
before he had taken his seat and was yet bowing to the audience
(myself and Emma were on the floor and had a most excellent
view of it) when a wretch in the pit not far from us aimed at the
poor King with a horse-pistol and fired.

You can imagine the sensation! Everyone was screaming. It
was fortunate that there was not a panic. The King alone was
calm, for he turned, said some words to an attendant, took his
seat quite tranquilly and sat out the entertainment which was
She Would and She Would Not and James Cobb's *Humourist*.

It was terrible to see the people throw themselves upon the
wretched would-be assassin, who was pulled over the spikes
and hurried across the stage. Sir William Addington examined
him in an adjoining apartment.

After a while up went the Curtain and we all – on the stage
and off it – stood up and sang 'God Save the King'. Emma was
crying like a child and I must confess that my own eyes were wet.
Princess Mary fainted twice they say, but Princess Elizabeth
was most brave and we could see how the Queen nodded to the

Princesses that they should keep up their spirits.

They say today that the name of the man was James Hadfield and that the King was indeed lucky, for one of the slugs from the pistol was found only a foot to the left of the royal chair. The affair is the more mysterious it seems, in that only that same afternoon during his attendance at the field exercises of the Grenadier battalion at Hyde Park a Clerk in the Navy Office was shot while standing only a few feet from the King. It was thought at the time to be an accident but now it looks otherwise.

What times we live in! The whole world is disturbed and the wretched Revolution in France has been, I am convinced, the cause of it. Gold is scarce they say, and I know from my own experience how scarce food is. Everyone is complaining but nothing is done and many well-informed persons fear that we are on the verge of Revolution. Well, after all this public news you will wish to hear something more personal.

This is now my second year with Mrs Dudeney and her children. I go to her house in Mecklenburgh Square at nine every morning and am there until six, save for Saturdays and Sundays. I take my dinner with them and often drive out with Mrs Dudeney or her sister Miss Chalpaine.

I must confess that I have grown attached to the children. They are good little things, even a trifle too virtuous, for you know, dear Francis, I never care sufficiently for those I can completely rule.

Poor Mrs Dudeney misses her husband very sadly and this that we have in common should draw us closely together. But something holds me apart from everyone, even from Emma. It is as though my heart were indeed quite dead and, although time has now passed, I live in a dream. It seems to matter nothing where I am or what I do. My whole movement is external. I speak of this to no one else save yourself – even Emma has no notion of it but thinks that I am well recovered from Georges' death.

But oh Francis, I am not! Something has died in me for ever. That condition of living when one existed only for another is gone never to return.

That catastrophe was a dream. Hunt though they did high and low for old Stane, he was never seen again. Was he imagined by Georges and myself? I sometimes think so. But it is not that I cherish any illusion about Georges. He was neither strong nor faithful; I loved him as he was – not as a Perfect Being, whom, in fact, I should have detested. Forgive these sentiments. You are the only one with whom I ever share them.

Emma has now abandoned the Theatre or possibly it would be more truth to say that the Theatre has at length abandoned her. She is a strange Creature, quite devoted to me until some man crosses her path, when she is for a while like a schoolgirl. She has still her Charms and is less stout than formerly and as good a woman as ever was known.

Our apartment here is pleasant and looks out to a Square with Trees. There are sparrows, a man with a clarinet, a Poodle that walks every morning in the Square and an Artist up the stairs who quizzes me at every opportunity.

Write soon and tell me all about dear Uldale. Is the Museum still there at Keswick and have there been any Balls? Give Deborah my greetings and nod to every stream, hedgerow and little hill in the neighbourhood. Do the clouds still dance above Skiddaw? How I wish that I were there! – Your loving

JUDITH

Francis Herries, Esq, to Judith Paris

ULDALE, *14th of June, 1800*

DEAREST JUDITH – I was delighted indeed to have a letter from you, for it was several months since I had heard and I was beginning to feel some anxiety. When I saw you last year in London you had not been sufficiently with Mrs Dudeney to know how you would find her, and it is very gratifying indeed to discover that at least she is neither a bore nor a bully.

I cannot quite accommodate myself to the necessity of your earning a living in this manner, but quite honestly, dear Judith, I do not feel that it would be altogether wise for you to live with us while Deborah is here, nor would you yourself I think wish it.

Deborah is the best of women and the most kindly of sisters, but she must rule domestically any place where she is and will brook no rival. You also as you admit have a certain ruling capacity and when Greek meets Greek—!

Moreover, remembering Georges still as you do, work is I do not doubt the most helpful of Panaceas, and I know that you are of the greatest value to Mrs Dudeney and her family.

You do not say in your letter whether you have seen Brother Will. I hear that he is with every week a man of greater wealth and more important responsibility. I am told that they are to take a house in Mount Street (my information is from Bournemouth). I hear also that Christabel is no more in love with a grand life than she ever was, poor thing, and has in fact never recovered socially from the unhappy and now historic Ball.

Will will have no dealings with me and breathes fire and slaughter against his Bournemouth relations. Is this not foolish? But Will was always as filled with himself and his affairs as an egg with meat, and an insult to his wife is a snap of the finger in the face of the Almighty.

Nevertheless Will prospers and I do not. He is the other side of the Herries blanket from ourselves, dear Judith, and I think all the interest in our family's history must come from that, that men like Will are being for ever disgraced and made anxious by men like me. We break in upon their solid plans as a horse-thief breaks into their gold. So also on their side they break in upon our dreams. Where, I must ask myself, wandering among these fields and hills, do the two worlds join? Who may bring them together? Last week I rode up Borrowdale to Stonethwaite and wandered for an hour about the little overgrown court and garden of Herries where my grandfather and your father dug for so many years the hard and ungrateful soil. A shepherd, Wilson, now has it and lets it go as it will.

It was almost as though your father were at my elbow. I had forgot him but my father so frequently spoke of him that it is as though I had known him. I have only one memory of him, a tall gaunt black man with a scar on his face, riding up the white road to Uldale. I must confess to you that I was miserable enough that hour in that garden. All has gone wrong with me of late. Deborah's little sociabilities, the neighbours, their tea parties, cards and small festivities I can take no interest in. My writing such as it was has failed me; even my reading has little power over me. The country seems to me on the verge of ruin, the country people seething with discontent, the towns no better, a crazy King on the throne and a Prince – you do not need me to say anything there.

But you know what it is, dear Judith, that drives me. I am a man now of forty years and should be past such madness and should be master of such folly – but rather I am sunk in it deeper than before. Every breath I draw, waking or sleeping, seems to drag me to Bournemouth. They tell me that she is more beautiful than ever. She should be indeed now in the full flower of her loveliness. I hear also, and this has possibly given strength to my madness, that young Beaminster, the Duke of Wrexe's eldest son, is crazy for her. What a match for her that would be! But if anyone in our age is fitted to be a Duchess it is she! What a triumph for the Herries family if it should be so! I hear too that she is both proud and kind beyond ordinary measure – and truly in every grace and virtue she is over all others . . .

I will not burden you more with this. You ask whether Skiddaw stands where it did. Indeed it does. This is a perfect month for this country. There is a spot by Portinskill bordering the Keswick Lake where I love to be. The trees are now young flames and when the water is like glass they burn in their reflections. Then a breeze ruffles that glass and the fire is suddenly in the sky carried on the breast of a cloud. Were she with me here to see this beauty I know that I could win her to love me. I know it, Judith, I *know* it! But what is the value of such vain dreams? If you should hear anything of young Beaminster being at Bournemouth or of their meeting in Town, pray let me know – Your loving

FRANCIS

Miss Jennifer Cards to the Hon. Angela Painter

GROSSET PLACE, WILTSHIRE,
September 2nd, 1802

MY DARLING ANGELA – Forgive this odious hand for I cannot find my own pen and all the writing-tables here are filled with birds' nests and bones for the dogs. I speak with the utmost literalness for you cannot conceive the disorder in which Maria Rockage loves to confuse everything. But I have told you of this odd Place before and there is no need to make a repetition save that it is truth itself that there is a Basin on the floor of my bedroom at this instant to catch the drops from a crack in the ceiling, for it has rained for twenty-four hours without ceasing and every room in the Place runs with water. Not that we any of us are disturbed in the slightest degree. We are all True Britons in this respect and discomfort is part of our Birthright. There are but three of us here at the moment, Rockage, Maria and Phyllis, twenty last week and quite pretty in a milkmaid kind of style.

I fancy that she is the principal cause of my invitation here, for she had her Coming Out last Season and then must Go In again for they haven't a Penny amongst them and can make no sort of Show – while I, they suppose, have everyone in my Handkerchief from Mrs Fitzherbert downwards. They fancy too that I can give the Child some kind of a 'ton', but I am too amiable on the one side and too lazy on the other. And indeed she is not so bad in a simple kind of way.

But you know, dearest Angela, of what it is that I would write. Have you seen Beaminster since his return, have you spoken with him, if so did he mention me and what is his attitude now that he has seen China and all the Indies ? Perhaps he has brought back with him a young Chinese Woman and I will not care if he has. But will I not ? What is my mood ? Upon my word it is hard to tell. How perverse is the world! Here am I, thirty-two years of age and still Single. And yet I have had every Element in my favour, have no aversion to Matrimony. At least I have told Beaminster a thousand times that I do not love him and would marry him only to be a Duchess. I like him at least sufficiently to be honest with him and as you know have refused him a hundred times. But now, time passes. It will not be long before I am a Withered Hag. What is Love, Angela ? I swear I have never known it. My cousin, Francis Herries, swears that it is the Toothache of the Soul that no dentist can cure. I can only say then that my Teeth have no need of a Doctor. But why are the Virtues and Qualities of men so obstinately dissipated ? There is Francis himself, the best and happiest of company, but having nothing better than a small Place in Cumberland where it rains inordinately. There is young Stephen Hailes whose every breath showers gold pieces but he is so gross in his feeding and thinks of nothing but Horses. There is Beaminster (and I would adore to be a Duchess), but he whines through his Nose like a Parson and cracks at the knees.

And many another all of whom you know, dearest Angela. I'm not boasting that I tell you this, but only that I may remind myself of my Vast Age and how my Opportunities are slipping over me.

There is talk still everywhere of the Peace and it is the fashion only to hasten to Paris. Rockage has heard that Charles Fox is on a visit to Bonaparte and that Mrs Fox is for the first time publicly acknowledged.

I shall be soon returning to Bournemouth for Wiltshire rusticity is softening my Wits. Moreover there is shortly coming here little Judith Paris whom you have seen I fancy in London. Maria has an odd Affection for her. She is a quaint thing whose

French husband was killed some years back in a brawl in the North, since when she must be a Governess or Companion as he left her without a Penny. She is, as you will remember, an Oddity, being but a few feet in height and with hair of coarse flaming red.

Maria vows that she is a Noble Creature. I am not myself prepossessed too strongly in her favour as she supports the Will Herries part of the Family in that ridiculous squabble of which I have often told you and over which we have so frequently laughed together. In any case I prefer my Nobility over two foot and a quarter!

Write soon, dearest Angela, and relieve the Anxiety of Your loving Friend,

JENNIFER

Francis Herries, Esq, to Judith Paris

ULDALE, CUMBERLAND,
14th of September, 1802

DEAREST JUDITH – I am following my letter of yesterday with this brief note that I may enclose this silver chain and cross. Last night rummaging in some old drawers, I came upon some effects of my father's, a packet or two of letters, a book or two, a riding whip, this Chain and a small silver Box. The Box was the one of which he had often told me, decorated with the Picture of girls dancing round a Maypole and gentlemen hunting. It was given him when a Child by a Pedlar. The Chain also he had spoken of, and it seems that your Mother's Mother bequeathed it to your Father for some Service he had one time done her.

The Chain then is by right your own and it pleases me greatly that I have discovered it, as also the silver Box by which I know my Father held considerable store.

I have no further news than that of yesterday – Your loving
FRANCIS

Judith Paris to Mrs Will Herries, of 48 Mount Street, London

GROSSET PLACE, WILTS,
December 3rd, 1802

MY DEAR CHRISTABEL – It was most kind of you to write to me. I was most grateful. I have been here now for two months

and have as yet no regrets at having left Mrs Dudeney. Phyllis is
a charming girl, modest and intelligent, with a sense of fun that
enables her to see the Ludicrousness of much in her home and
her Parents, and yet in no way impairs her Love for them.

They are indeed Lovable and yet most truly there is also
something of the Ludicrous! Had you but now seen Carey
peeping over the banisters, his nightcap nodding above his eyebrow, his nightshirt flapping at his bare ankles, shouting for
Doggett, the man, because he heard that the sow had but just
now littered! Indeed this is no place for early rising, for even
now I was downstairs at ten o'clock to find such a confusion in
the breakfast room, fender huddled two yards high, into the
middle of the room, chairs, tables, shovel, poker, tongs anyhow,
carpet thrown back, dust everywhere, dogs everywhere, bees-
wax, rubber, brush, broom, mop, pail, and before a cheerless
grate Maggie the girl on her knees. All the doors on this house
have rusty refractory doorlocks of which the hasp invariably
flies backward, all chimneys smoke, going to bed the candle at
once goes out with a whiff and a stink in the passage and you
break your shins at every step, all the corks break and drop in
fragments *inside* the bottles, all keys are lost to all drawers, room
after room (there are dozens of unused ones) is piled with broken
bricks, scattered chisels and hammers, battered trunks mildewed
with neglect. No proper alliance is formed with any butcher,
carrier or baker, no salt-cellars have their spoons, no knife
its proper fork, every snuffer to every candlestick tilts off and
drops its contents on the carpet, every bell-rope breaks, or if it
rings, brings the wrong servant, every scissor pinches without
cutting . . . and so on, and so on! Dear Christabel, I could continue this for an hour!

Into this chaos it is hoped that I shall bring some kind of
order, and indeed I see a good ten years' work in front of me.
But after all these are my own people and not strangers, and as I
see Maria in an old silk Negligée padding around, her slippers
flapping on the carpet, dogs sniffing at her heel, and that kindly
amiable smile on her face, knowing that she loves me (as indeed
I believe that she does), I must love her in return.

All this must seem terrible to you in your smart Mount Street
Mansion, and you can understand what it must be to myself who
have, as you know, a Passion for cleanliness, but I have no longer
Energy to direct my own path and take what comes. Affection
seems to me everything just at present.

Your beautiful Enemy, Miss Jennifer, was staying here in

the summer. They report her proud, matter-of-fact, worldly, not over intelligent but kindly and not conceited. They were rather relieved though, I fancy, at her departure. They say that she has any number of times refused Lord Beaminster and that now he, after a visit to the East, is paying attention to Lord Garrison's girl, but I do not know what truth there is in these rumours.

Has Will still the same implacability about Francis? The Monynghams have been here. I dislike the name and am glad that Carey's father after being Lord Monyngham became Viscount Rockage – a far handsomer title!

What of Pomfret in Kensington? I hear that he has been ill and that James, the monster, is biting his thumb till he can be Baronet. Like his grandfather Raiseley, whom Will's father always so thoroughly hated, I never cared for James.

Love to all in Mount Street and if Mrs Dudeney pay a call, as I fancy that she may, pray be kind to her for my sake – Your loving

JUDITH

Francis Herries, Esq, to Judith Paris
(Portion of letter only)

ULDALE, *Jan. 6th, 1805*

... You know what it was that I read in the *Gazette*. And so she has surrendered! Well, it will become her to be a Duchess although I hear that he is sadly spindle-shanked and a dull dog. I will think no more of her. I feel stronger now that the blow has at length fallen. I must build my life on a sounder bottom.

One agreeable thing has occurred. A Mr and Mrs Coleridge have for some time past lived at a Keswick house, Greta Hall, and now he is joined by another poet, Mr Robert Southey, whose sister-in-law he had married. I have met Mr Southey and find him a most agreeable person of immense learning, but no haughtiness of manner. Mr Coleridge is an extraordinary man who lives for the most part in other worlds than ours. He is often absent from Keswick and, so gossip says, is on no very easy terms with his wife, but the Southey family is excellent and very friendly towards myself. I am even stirred once more to attempt something with my pen. But more of this later ...

William Herries, Esq, of 48 Mount Street, to Judith Paris

48 MOUNT STREET, LONDON,
Feb. 20th, 1805

DEAR JUDITH – You must forgive the brevity of this letter. I am but now returned from the City where I was consulted in certain important matters having no indirect connexion with His Royal Highness's affairs. Your enquiry on Carey's behalf concerning his City Investments I will prosecute further and send you information when I have it.

The Budget of two days back causes some concern especially the extra 6d per bushel of salt which will I imagine greatly hamper the curing of bacon and ham, but on the whole things might I consider be worse.

Have you heard how Jennifer's engagement to Lord Beaminster prospers? I can only say that I pity the foolish fellow from the bottom of my heart. He little knows the Tartar that he has taken to his bosom. After dancing round him for years she has condescended to be his future Duchess without I fancy intending him any return. He will discover his mistake in time. I must however admit that the Match is a fine one for our Family.

There is considerable anxiety in the City about the King's health. Stocks fluctuate accordingly. Christabel would I know send her love were she conscious that I was writing. She is lying in her room; she had a slight stomach affection today.

Pray give my regards to Maria and Carey. I am pleased to learn from Christabel that you find your stay with them agreeable. I must confess that I have little love for the Country save for our own Northern portion of it, which however for family reasons of which you are well aware I am little likely to see again.

With kindest regards, dear Judith, I remain – Yours most sincerely,

WILLIAM HERRIES

Judith Paris to Francis Herries, Esq

GROSSET PLACE, WILTS,
Feb. 25th, 1805

DEAREST FRANCIS – I hesitated whether to write after I had seen the news, but I feel that it would not be friendly on my part did I not tell you of my sympathy. She has made her choice and that she can prefer a marriage without love because of its Social Splendour is only proof to me of her unfitness for any marriage with a finer man.

Put her utterly out of your Heart, dear Francis. I do not doubt but that you have done so. I pity her for her unwise decision, for where there is no love there can be neither companionship nor respect. So at least I feel. I wish that I were with you. I myself have often a longing for the pressure of your hand. You remember how as a Child I loved you and how I would watch at the window for hours to see if you came. As it was then so is it still, save that I am a woman now and have learnt something of life and know what it is to be alone.

Do not fancy, however, that they are not all goodness to me here, for indeed they are. I have brought some discipline into affairs here, but the real trouble is lack of means. Poor Carey has no mind for business and he cannot keep more than one thing in his head at a time.

No sooner is he distressed by the loss of a silver spoon than he is told that a dog has the Eczema, and some woman is up from the village to beg something of him, or Squire Somebody or Another has ridden over from Somewhere and must have a Bed.

The Guest Room is always in disorder, there are rats in the wainscot and a window-pane is broken. Still time passes and I am tranquil, refusing to lament over milk that is spilt or a fire that has died. Only maybe the fire is not dead and burns the more fiercely because no one perceives it . . .

We have had a Visitor this last week and a pleasant one, Warren Forster of Alnwick. You recollect that he is the Grandson of Mrs Dorothy Forster who used to visit at Keswick. He is a man of some thirty-five years and has been visited by incessant misfortunes. When a child he was kicked by one of his father's horses and has been slightly lame ever after.

He has also, I fear, some affection of the Heart. In addition to these things his wife to whom, as I understand, he had been some four years married, last year abandoned him and ran away to America with a theatrical gentleman and has never since been heard of.

In spite of these visitations he is a man of great Character and much tenderness of Heart, never complaining and always cheerful. Maria dotes upon him and I must confess that I myself have a warm Friendliness towards him. I can see you smile at this point, and prophesy me a second husband, but that will never be – Georges remains with me as though he were yet living. I must go now as I hear Carey calling me – Your loving

JUDITH

Francis Herries, Esq, to Judith Paris

ULDALE, *November 9th, 1805*

DEAREST JUDITH – By now you must be aware that Jennifer has broken her engagement. Scarcely had the glorious news of Trafalgar reached us and we were in the midst of waving flags and hanging lanterns, when I received a letter written by herself informing me that she had broken off all relations with Lord Beaminster. She begged me to come to Bournemouth and you will not be surprised to learn that I am catching tonight's coach at Kendal.

I will write from there – Yours in haste,

FRANCIS

Judith Paris to Mrs Emma Furze

GROSSET PLACE, WILTS,
Dec. 8th, 1805

MY DEAREST DEAREST EMMA – Late though it is and mean and drunken my candle, I am scribbling a hurried word to you to tell you what I have only myself this evening learnt – that my dear Francis was married to his Jennifer secretly in London three days ago. I have only had the barest word from Francis acquainting me with the fact and that they have already set off for Cumberland. As I sit in this large bare room with the wind howling down the chimney and the mice scratching in the wainscot, it is hard not to be melancholy. How, how can this end? Only badly, I fear. She has but accepted him on the re-bound from her trouble with Beaminster. She does not love him and even though she did, could never endure the remoteness of our Cumberland country. I can see that they will move to London and poor Uldale fall into the tea-party chatter of Deborah's domination. And yet I have heard that Jennifer does not love London either and that that is one of the first causes of her quarrel with Beaminster. You know, dearest

Emma, that yourself and Francis are now the two human beings whom I love the most deeply and for Francis this affection has existed from my earliest childhood. He has been always a little remote from life and interested in notions more than persons – always, that is, until this passion seized him. He is one of the noblest of men, but reserved in the expression of his feeling. She must be proud and selfish, accustomed to adoration and her own way. What *can* come of this but disaster? I have heard, too, that she is lazy and idle and will sit for hours admiring herself in the glass but this, I confess, comes from Will Herries who detests her.

Where are you now – at Colchester or Nottingham? Is Mr Edwardes the Knight at Arms that you fancied and is the care of his two little girls as entertaining as you had anticipated? There are times when I am tempted once again towards London and Mrs Dudeney. She would welcome me with open arms back again any while.

Only my affections hold me here, for try as I may I cannot bring any order into the Place. This Country is at its worst in the Winter, all muck and mist, so unlike my own beloved Cumberland, where the Winter is the best, for the hedges sparkle with frost, the hills are powdered with snow and the air smells like wine.

Here, at Grosset, the Country is low and miry and one must walk in high, hard-bottomed fields not to be knee-deep at every step – one is like a frog kicking and sprawling through a welter of water.

My candle is at its last drunken nod and I must go to bed – Your most loving

JUDITH

Mrs Cards of Macklin House, Bournemouth, to her daughter, Mrs Francis Herries, of Uldale, Cumberland

(*Portion of a letter*)

MACKLIN HOUSE, BOURNEMOUTH,
June 8th, 1807

MY DEAR JENNIFER – Your father has requested me to say that we are both anxious at not having had news from you for so long a period. You must really, my dear daughter, try to oblige your loving father and mother more frequently in this respect. It is not kind to continue any sort of grudge against your father because he did not in the first place approve of your marriage. A year and a half have passed since that event and he has become as you know reconciled to it. He wishes only for your happiness and welfare and you know well that there is no human being on the face of the globe for whom he cares as he does for you. You know that it is our wish that you should lie-in in Bournemouth and I have written to Francis asking him his own feelings in this matter.

I have not much News for you. The talk is only of the Princess, whose behaviour since the return of her Champion, Mr Perceval, into power, has been, they say, outrageous. At a Ball at Mr Hope's she was truly a sight if eye-witnesses are to be trusted. Her figure is now as round as a drum and she paints monstrously. Her conversation is so wild that she seems often like a mad woman and she is not ashamed to be seen anywhere with her boy 'Billy Austin'. The Prince has broken entirely with the old Whigs and his hatred of Grenville and Grey is fanatical. Sheridan rules him in everything and in your father's opinion is nothing but mischievous.

The London dresses are now so tight that it is almost impossible to walk in them. In my old-fashioned eyes the *robes en Calecon* are quite shameless, all the outline of the figure being clearly seen beneath them. Very often there is nothing but a thin petticoat beneath and that is sometimes omitted. The skirt is now in two pieces, a third piece sewn in diagonally as a lateral gusset . . .

Francis Herries, Esq, to Judith Paris

ULDALE, *Dec. 7th, 1807*

MY DEAREST JUDITH – I wish you to be the first to know that last evening at seven-thirty of the clock Jennifer was delivered of a fine boy. They are both doing well and my happiness is beyond measure. I am convinced that now with a child in the house all will go well.

I will write later at greater length – Your loving,

FRANCIS, Father of John Herries

Judith Paris to Francis Herries, Esq

GROSSET PLACE,
March 29th, 1808

DEAREST FRANCIS – This is the first sign of Spring this year
and so I write to ask you whether you are yet living or have
changed into a Leprechaun or one of the Borrowdale Cuckoos?
What I would give to see Keswick Lake or Newlands Valley or
the Moor above Uldale on such a day as this – for at home the
skies are ever changing and streams are running and the bracken
is popping while here even on this Spring day all is Languid and
barely stirs.

But do you know, Sir, that of late you have very gravely
neglected your Half-Aunt or whatever is my true Relationship
to you? It is now some six weeks since I had any word from you
and I am feeling very gravely neglected. Two Nights back I had
a Dream about you and I awoke distressed, thinking that you
had called to me and I could not go to you. Do pray write and
tell me how you are and how Jennifer is and little John. I
am uneasy in my mind.

At this especial Moment it is necessary that I should write
to calm my Feelings, for this morning has witnessed one of my
most celebrated Tempers. I fear I give vent to them more
frequently than of old, whereas it should be the other way.
This morning I stamped and shouted like a Fishwife. I think
I had some reason though, and you shall judge. It was over young
Carey, who is at home just now and doing no good here. He
should have gone for the Navy, as was originally intended,
instead of this foolish notion that he should superintend his
Father's estate. For that he has no more gift than his poor Father
has, nor has he his Father's sweetness of nature. He is a thick
heavy Oaf as I had the pleasure this morning of telling him, for
I had but just, urged by the sweetness of the Spring sunshine,
directed the clumsy Maggie to the proper cleaning of the Drawing
and Breakfast Room when in Carey must come, knee-deep in
mud, cracking a whip and followed by four huge dogs so that he
breaks a China Ornament kissing Maggie (not knowing that I
was present) and sets the dogs after the cat, crying 'Halloo!
Halloo!' and riding the Chairs with all his lanes and bogs
clinging to them.

I treated him to a pretty Scene and then, when he laughed,
boxed his Ears. Although he is twice my height that flummoxed

him and while he stared I told him all I thought of him, that he was a selfish good-for-nothing nincompoop living on his Father's Bounty and doing nothing but chase Foxes and set the Dogs on the Cats. And I fear, although I did not tell him so, that he does worse than this with the Girls in the Village and thinks it all Fine Sport.

Well, in upon this comes Maria, who thinks him the Paragon of all Wonders. He went off in a Sulk calling me a fine collection of names, and Maria was altogether at a loss for she loves me and thinks I can do no wrong. But I am sometimes deeply weary of this life here, dear Francis. There is something in me that aches for Cumberland, even though there are scenes there that I could never have the Courage to revisit. This is not my place nor are these in truth my people. But where is my place and where are my people ? Like my father before me I have no Home and yet I am truly a domestic creature and could not live except for the affections of those of whom I am fond.

Warren Forster has been here visiting again and we are become the greatest of friends. I think his lonely situation touches me – not that we are melancholy together but rather laugh for most of the time.

Pray write to me soon and tell me how little John fares. In your last letter you mentioned that he was suffering with a Colic.

Francis Herries, Esq, to Judith Paris

ULDALE, *June 10th, 1808*

DEAREST JUDITH – I have not written frequently of late because I have not been in the merriest of spirits – nothing specific but only a Malaise that is, it seems, difficult for me to shake myself free of. But now I have two Items of News that I must give you. One is that Jennifer will be lying-in again this November. We hope that this time it may be a girl. She is well and seems to have no fears of the event. I am afraid that she sometimes finds me a Dull Dog.

My second Item is that Sister Deborah is engaged – to a Squire Withering of Summerhays by Carlisle. As Deborah is now forty-six years you can fancy that this event was most unexpected but Withering is of her own age and has already been twice married. He is a jolly red-faced Ox, whose interests are entirely bucolic, but he will I think suit Deborah well, for her desires are as you know of an exceeding Sociability, and now she may entertain the Neighbourhood to her heart's desire.

Her relations with Jennifer have been, as I have hinted to you before, of an armed friendliness and I doubt whether there will be many tears shed on either side at parting.

The Cotton Riots at Manchester have been I understand of a serious nature, houses have been broken into, managers burnt in effigy and many rioters lodged in jail. The People are making themselves more and more felt and I must admit that they and their Cause have increasingly my Sympathy. Jennifer is an Aristocrat of the Old School and would have every Rioter burnt at a public Stake – Your loving

FRANCIS

I am becoming good Friends with Mr and Mrs Southey and frequently visit them.

Mrs Francis Herries of Uldale, Cumberland, to
Mrs Judith Paris, at Grosset Place, Wilts

ULDALE, *Nov. 10th, 1809*

DEAR JUDITH – You will I fancy feel some surprise at receiving a letter from me, but indeed I would have written sooner had we not all been so occupied with the Jubilee which for my part I am most thankful that it is safely over. You would not, however, have recognized your little Keswick. We had grand Fireworks above the Lake, an ox roasted whole in the Market Place and many other Diversions.

It is not however of the Jubilee that I wish to write to you. I am Laziness personified and to write a Letter is always an agony to me so I will come sharp to the point.

It is this – that both Francis and myself wish that you should come and live with us. It is plain enough that Francis should wish it – he has always wished it – and therefore I write myself that you may believe in my own independent desire for it. In honesty I discover that, since the departure of Deborah, the two children and the management of the House are more than I can properly sustain. But beyond this I will admit that I consider that it will be of advantage both to Francis and myself that you should be with us. I have grown unaccountably sluggish of late and so I fancy has he. In addition to these things I have a real wish that you should love me – something that may at this present seem to you quite impossible, but juxtaposition and a Good Will may work wonders. – I am, Your sincere friend,

JENNIFER HERRIES

Judith Paris to Francis Herries, Esq

GROSSET PLACE,
Nov. 15th, 1809

DEAREST FRANCIS – I have but now received a Truly Extraordinary Letter from Jennifer which I have answered as honestly as I may. You doubtless know of it. But what am I to say?

Of course I wish to come to you and Uldale. I have wished it all these years when I have been in sober truth a real Exile from my own country. I have developed a fondness for Carey and Maria and Phyllis. I would leave them perhaps for no one else in the world, but you have always been – save for Georges – first in the world to me and I would go anywhere to serve you. Also it is a Happiness to think that I must have the Care in some part of your Children.

But does Jennifer truly wish me to come? Have you not pushed her into that Letter? I must know this before I give any Answer. I had fancied that she had in her Heart no affection for me. I am myself not easy, love to dominate where I am, am often in terrible Rages and am haunted by the past. But you know this, dear Francis, and you know your wife. It seems to me that if I come and things go ill I may imperil all our Happiness. Yet the House at Uldale calls me like a living person. I cannot refuse if you assure me that it is Jennifer's wish as well as your own. – Your loving

JUDITH

Francis Herries, Esq, to Judith Paris

ULDALE, *Nov. 19th, 1809*

DEAREST JUDITH – Come. It is Jennifer's wish most certainly. Things are not too Happy here. You can help us to understand one another. Come – Your loving

FRANCIS

Judith Paris to Mrs Emma Furze

(Portion of a letter)

GROSSET PLACE, WILTS
Nov. 29th, 1809

... If you can meet the Coach I shall be most happy. Farewells here are of a quite Tragic Description. Even young Carey weeps down the Barrel of his gun.

Oh Emma to what Adventure am I going? My Life is built on that piece of ground. I have tried to shake myself free of it, but how fruitless was that effort I now know as I feel the excited beatings of my Heart. It may be that I am committing the supreme Folly of my Life ...

ULDALE AGAIN

'LET US WALK up the hill,' Judith said to Francis.

They got down from the chaise and allowed it to draw slowly ahead of them. She put her arm through Francis'.

She was not going to tell him how frightened she was. This scene so amazingly familiar to her, the trees bright and bare so that the winter sun seemed to be shining in the heart of their branches, the thick soft carpet of leaves, the fresh sharp air with a breath of approaching snow in its stillness, all these were the friendly accompaniments of countless old winters. Soon, at the turn, the first houses of the village would appear, the black-smith's, the little house with the round bottle-green windows, and beyond them the first comfortable shoulder of the moor. All so familiar that they were part of her own blood, and yet her heart was beating with an almost agonizing apprehension.

She wished now that she had not come. Oh! how she wished it! She had been safe there in Wiltshire, safe even though she had not been alive. Now the pain was sharp as when the blood returns to a limb that has been numb.

At once, on her first sight of Francis in Keswick, she had been sure that he was not the same. She had seen him before he had seen her; he had stood in front of the inn, slim and dark, slapping his thigh with his whip, looking sternly out into a forbidding world.

She had instinctively drawn her shawl more closely about her and shrunk back as though she would prevent him from seeing her. He had kissed her, put his arm about her, given her a hot drink, seen to her baggage and, through the drive out of Keswick along the familiar Carlisle Road, had been infinitely kind. It had been her own fault that she had been so helplessly constrained. He did not know that with every step Georges was approaching more closely to her. Georges, Georges . . .

But that cowardice she had foreseen, and with every strength in her character she had beaten it back. Then, in place of it, as they turned away from the Lake into the heart of the woods, the thought of Jennifer increasingly possessed her. Why had she come ? Jennifer did not want her. She *could* not want her. She had yielded to Francis' entreaties, and now she thought that Francis did not want her either. It was true, in fact, that for Francis, too, there had been a little shock. When he had last seen Judith she had been a girl; now she was a woman, and, with that exceptional sensitiveness that was his curse as well as his blessing, he felt, at first sight of her, that she had become a woman whom he did not know.

This resolute, solid little person almost hidden under her shawl and pelisse, her small white face looking out at him from her rose-coloured bonnet with such seriousness, was very different from the fire and impetuosity of his own familiar Judith. He had good reasons – there had from the first been many – for doubting the wisdom of this experiment and now he suffered a sudden panic, foreseeing every kind of trouble and even disaster. He had, Heaven knew, enough already!

So, while they rode, a silence fell between them. Then, as they started on foot up the hill, she stopped, laid her hand on his arm, looked up into his face.

'I am frightened, Francis,' she said. 'I feel as though I cannot go on.'

'I am frightened also,' he confessed.

They looked at one another. Then she laughed, and it was as though a screen were rolled away, the old Judith of all his life was back again.

'Do you remember once when your father beat me and I climbed out of the window ?'

He nodded, smiling.

'I thought then that I could never be frightened at anything. I am wiser now . . . I am frightened of Jennifer.'

It was he now who put his arm through hers, drawing her close to him. They marched now steadily up the hill.

'There's no need to be,' he said. 'You can do so much for Jennifer, Judith. And for myself as well. We are in a tangle. You must clear it.'

'Do you think she will like me? Because if she does not – I can do nothing with anyone who dislikes me.'

'You must make her like you,' he answered. 'Everything hangs on that. She is proud, she has been spoilt by much admiration, for which she does not really care. She *could* be happy here. You can make her so.'

'Are you yourself happy?' She stopped again, looking up into his face.

'I, my dear?' He shrugged his shoulders. 'Have I ever been happy save for a moment or two? But I love her very dearly. I am not a wise man,' he added, lowering his voice as though he were speaking to himself. 'I have never been wise all my life. I killed my father. My mother hated me. It is not natural that I should be more fortunate with my wife.'

'I have come into a pretty business,' she thought. 'This will not be easy.'

But they had found one another again. Her resolution, obstinacy and common sense were all active now that she realized that there was something to be done. The dusk had fallen when they reached the house. She could see it only as a white ghost. The lights in the hall confused her, and it was a moment before she could realize that Jennifer was greeting her. Then she was almost shocked by Jennifer's beauty. It was a woman of forty who confronted her, but age here had nothing to say. Jennifer's loveliness came from her superb richness of colour and form. Her hair was dark with the darkness of clouded fire, when the flame is imprisoned by black shadow. Her skin had warmth in its ivory softness. She was very tall, a height that was emphasized by her high close dress with its waist just below the breasts, but her body was moulded by her maturity to a perfect fitness. She stood, her head up, her lovely neck and arms bare, save for a thin Cashmere purple shawl, as though she were receiving a deputation of loyal subjects. Only her eyes were a little sleepy, heavily lidded.

Judith had never in her life before felt so small, so insignificant. It was as though she were a servant coming for a place. She was weary, too, crowded about with old memories, homesick for she knew not what. But it was not her way to be beaten.

Only, as on so many other occasions, she wished passionately that she were taller.

The thought in Jennifer's mind as she bent down to kiss her was: 'Well, I need not be afraid of this little thing.'

Jennifer moved into the little parlour that was thick, for Judith, with pressing memories. She recognized at once gratefully that it was not changed. That was Francis' doing. But also, with a flash of intuition, she realized that Jennifer must be lazy. She would have altered things if she had had a mind for that. Here was the old spinet with the roses on its lid, the music-box with the King in his amber coat and the Queen in her green dress; there was the carpet with the pictures of the Battle, the leaping horses and the cannon firing. For how many years had it been there – and yet it looked even fresher than in earlier days. Best of all, here was the China wallpaper with the blue and white pagodas, the bridges, flowers and temples.

Jennifer helped her to take off her jacket and bonnet.

'You must be weary.'

'Oh no, thank you'; but she was. She sat down on the old brown sofa that was covered with a pattern of red leaves and little rosy apples. Francis had gone to see about the horses. She and Jennifer were alone.

'Did you have an agreeable journey?'

'Yes. The weather was fine. We had only one storm before Kendal.'

'You must rest now and take your ease. Life is very quiet here.'

Judith thought: 'She talks as though I had never been here before. I knew it before she did.' She was in that nervous state of weariness and loneliness that can rouse, very quickly, the Devil, but she had already faced the Devil so often in her life that it was easy to say to him now, as she did, 'Lie down!'

She smiled. She could not help it. Jennifer was so very beautiful.

'What lovely hair you have,' Jennifer said.

'It is sadly tumbled.'

'No, but you will want to go to your room. I will show you.'

They went up the staircase down whose banisters Judith had many times slid. That was something at least that Jennifer had never done. Jennifer moved upwards like a queen.

'I hope you will like this room,' she said, throwing open the door.

Oh heaven! it was Mrs Monnasett's room, the room where

once she had crept up to the bed and touched the cold body, searching for the little box . . .

'I trust that you will be comfortable here,' Jennifer said, staring with her sleepy eyes about her. 'If you need anything pray tell me.'

'I have known this room,' Judith said, also looking about her, 'all my life.'

The two women looked at one another – one swift appraising glance – and at once Judith knew it was going to be a battle.

'She is going to let me be happy here,' she thought, 'if I do what she tells me.' Then there was the further thought: 'You've never done what anyone told you – except Georges.'

But she was so weary that she could have cried if she had been a woman accustomed to crying. She was not.

'Thank you, dear Jennifer,' she said. 'You are very amiable.' She knew that Jennifer was thinking: 'I can manage *this* little thing.'

For several years after Georges' death the terrible time had been the night. If she slept, one horrible dream after another swept over her; if she were awake, loneliness and remorse weighed down her heart. Loneliness because Georges was not there, remorse because again and again she asked herself whether she might not have done something to prevent the calamity. Why had she not driven the old man from the house, driven him, with whips and scorpions? How was it that she had submitted to his presence so passively? It was as though he had cast a spell.

What could she have done? What? What? She tormented herself day after day, night after night. Then, as the years had passed, quiet sleep had come back to her. She was not one to bewail the past. She had her new life to make. But during the years in London and Wiltshire there had been no life. It had been as though she had walked in her sleep. Now with one step into the lighted hall tonight, life had swept back to her. Contact was made again.

She woke in old Mrs Monnasett's four-poster and looked about her trying to penetrate the darkness. It seemed that she could. Georges was alive again and at her side, and said with his old reckless impudence: 'Soon we'll have this house in our hand.'

So, leaning her head on his breast, she went happily to sleep. In the morning she met the two children, John aged two, Dorothy aged one, in the charge of a fat beetle-browed woman, Mrs Ponder. Judith knew at once that this was a bad, ill-disposed servant who was resolved to defy her. John was a square-made, sturdy child with the high Herries horse-bones and light blue eyes that reminded her of David. There seemed to be no nonsense about him at all. Dorothy was small and dark and nervous. She hid herself in Mrs Ponder's dress.

Judith loved children and had a swift power over them, perhaps because she was herself little and was amused by small things that seemed, however, to her important.

For John the only thing that mattered on that day when Judith first saw him was that Matt the stableman had made a ship for him and would take him later to the Tarn to sail it. As soon as he discovered that Judith also wished to see the sailing of the ship, she became part of his world and was never again outside it. He did not as yet talk a great deal, but expressed his emotions with wriggles of the body and small stern frowns.

'Pray, ma'am,' said Mrs Ponder, 'do not permit the child to be a worrit.'

'I care for children extremely,' answered Judith quickly, looking straight at Mrs Ponder's black eyebrows. 'To be quite honest, I do not think I can live without them.'

'That is very well, ma'am,' said Mrs Ponder, who was a woman of one idea at a time. 'But he must not be a worrit.'

Dorothy was another matter. Baby though she was, she was already nervous, suspicious and reserved. Mrs Ponder was her only haven. When Judith came near to her she screamed, which pleased Mrs Ponder very much indeed.

Indeed everything that occurred on this first day after Judith's arrival contained the signs and portents of the struggle – a struggle that involved the fates of all of them, and of many more besides them – that was to come. The prophecy of the walk up the hill had been a correct one.

Snow fell all day, snow most unusual for that time of the year, soft, feathery, gentle, at first not lying, then, as the day sharpened, lying with a silver radiance over all the world.

It always seemed to Judith afterwards that she gathered in her complete and final knowledge of Jennifer in that first winter afternoon. They sat after dinner in the parlour, drinking their tea, the two of them one on either side of the fire, where the logs crackled and hissed, the only sound save the gently whispering clock.

Jennifer sat very straight, working at a piece of silver embroidery. Erect, her splendid body, with its soft rounded arms, its swelling breasts, its crown of dark, slumbering hair, gave an odd impression of being on guard. Often Judith was in the future to notice that Jennifer's body seemed to have a life apart from the brain that directed it. Jennifer's brain, she was to discover, was not active. It moved very slowly from point to point and there stayed obstinately without stirring. It was not an animal brain at all – something quite other – but her body was entirely animal, wanted only to be cared for. That was why, perhaps, Jennifer was not conceited and minded nothing at all when her body was admired; why, too, men had deserted her at the moment of crisis.

But if she was not conceited she was intensely proud. She had all the pride of a woman who has no imagination, the most fundamental pride of all because the owner of it cannot look outside and make comparisons. Her pride had its origin in the fact that she was a Herries (though but a portion of one), and in fact that she had a father and mother who thought her perfect.

She did not admire herself because they thought her perfect, but admired *them* for that reason, and her pride was all the greater.

There were things that Judith, as she sat by the fire on that first day, wanted to know. First, how so gloriously beautiful a creature, who might (so Judith, rather simply and very modestly, thought) have had all London on its knees, could stay year after year in this little distant country place; secondly, whether or no Jennifer loved Francis; thirdly, why Jennifer had asked her, Judith, to come.

Before the hour by the fire was over, Judith had discovered the answer to the three questions. First – Jennifer liked the country better than the town because Herries were of more social value in the country, because she had always lived out of London and was a woman of habit, but in chief because she was lazy. The country demanded less energy than the town.

Second – she did not love Francis in any sense that Judith understood the word. But – she was lazy. That might explain it.

Third – she had asked Judith because, after Deborah was gone, there was too much to do. A housekeeper was impertinent. Judith, to whom, in Jennifer's judgement (she repeated this several times), Francis was quite devoted, would please Francis and keep him quiet. In short she had invited Judith because – she was lazy.

'Pray come nearer to the fire. It is monstrously cold.'

'Thank you. And is Deborah comfortable with her Squire?'

'I believe so indeed, as much as one may be comfortable in this world.'

She raised her slumbering eyes, lifted her white hand on which a great ring with a deep crimson stone glittered, to shield her face from the fire, and said: 'Are we to be friends, Judith?'

Judith bent forward, giving her glance for glance.

'I trust so. It is my own most earnest wish.'

'You will be on my side sometimes?'

'Your side?'

'Yes. You were not on my side in that most unseemly quarrel in London many years ago.'

'I was then quite unformed . . . And Christabel was then my friend. You were not.'

'Yes, we were young then. I wonder. Is it wise – do you think – that we have met again?'

Judith answered gravely. 'It is for yourself to decide.'

Jennifer's body became more active. You could see the life stirring through it, as still water is suddenly moved by a breeze.

'Are you passionate?'

'I beg your pardon?'

'Are you passionate? With that hair you should be. I hear that you have a temper that can be monstrously roused. I should like to see it.'

Judith laughed.

'There is time enough,' she said. Moved by a quick impulse and because she wished always to be friends if it were possible (she could be an enemy very easily if that was wanted), she went over to Jennifer, bent across her chair and kissed her. To her own surprise Jennifer put up her arm and with her soft warm hand drew Judith closer, kissing her again.

'It is by far more comfortable to be friends,' she said.

But was it Jennifer's body that had kissed her – or Jennifer?

That evening Jennifer, Judith and Francis sat in the parlour. The little clock with the china dairymaid struck. Jennifer rose stretched her arms, threw up her lovely head. Her eyes were almost closed. She seemed to be tasting some delicious food or smelling a marvellous scent.

'I am sleepy. I shall go to bed.' She moved, slowly, majestically to the door. She turned towards them, showing a sleepy smile. She yawned.

'Goodnight,' she said.

After a little silence Francis said: 'I am so happy that you are here, dear Judith. Jennifer likes you already.'

'Do you think so ? I am afraid that at first I shall be needlessly troublesome. In time things will settle themselves.'

'Is it strange to you to come back here?' He looked at her with eyes of deep affection. Now he had regained his old Judith. It was true that on the outside this was almost a middle-aged woman who sat near to him, a woman, too, who had known the most bitter unhappiness, who had suffered years of the harshest loneliness, but there was there also the child with the light of humour in her eyes, with her pugnacity, eagerness and acceptance of adventure.

'Strange ?' She looked into the fire. 'No. But, Francis, with what passion I love this house. I had not forgotten it – no, not a table nor a chair, not a print nor a carpet, and the garden, the high wall, every branch of every tree. But I had not known that I would be so touched by it, nor that it would lead me on into the country beyond it. *My* country . . .' She laughed. 'Perhaps it will be wisest in me to check my feelings while I can; I am determined against too much enthusiasm. In an old woman it is an absurdity.'

'An old woman!' he said fondly. 'Why, Judith, you are not changed.'

'No,' said Judith. 'When I was in my room this evening after dinner and pressed my nose against the pane, standing a little on my toes, just as I did when I was a child, I could see nothing but the snow falling through the darkness. Nevertheless, the country crowded about me – Scarness, Bowscale, Calva, Blackhazel, Mungrisdale.' She said the names like a spell. 'And so leading to Watendlath, which I must face if I am ever to have any peace here. On the first fair day I shall ride over to Watendlath.'

'Why, Judith,' he said, 'you are a poet.'

'Part of me is a poet, and the other part, I fear, most unpoetical.'

He sighed and stretched his long, thin legs to the fire, rubbing his hands in his hair. 'I also. Part poet, and the useless part, the only part for which I have any care. We are a strange family. It seems that the Dreamer must always destroy the Man of Deeds, and so either way you fail. Your father let the practical go and was called a madman. My own father was ultimately all practical and faded spiritually away. Will had always been for the practical – he has never known a conflict and is become a money-bag. There is Reuben who has rejected the practical and is saved, maybe, by his Maker. And you and I, Judith – our fates are yet undecided. But it would be a subject for an Epic, this

Herries struggle, with a changing England behind it. Which is real? Is there a soul? Are we for ever to be exiles from our true country? All my life I have been like a man wandering down a road that leads nowhere.'

'You should ask Mr Southey these things. He is a poet.'

'I have asked him. He is sure of his destiny. His answer is in his books and his family. I never knew a man more confident. But his brother-in-law, Mr Coleridge, has more genius, and so is more lost . . .' He drove his fist on to his knee. 'Judith, I must lose myself in something greater than myself. That is the only answer.'

'And your marriage?' She asked at length the question that had been hovering between them all day.

'My marriage is a failure, a damnable pernicious failure. How could it have been otherwise? Jennifer never loved me. She has never loved anyone. When she dismissed Beaminster she was frightened of her old age and she liked me better than the others. So she took me. And she has done her best with me. But there is a devil of selfishness in her. In a country life some sort of selfishness is, I conceive, a necessity. I also am selfish. But our selfishnesses – hers and mine – do not coincide.'

He stopped. Then went on eagerly, 'Judith, I say these things because all our lives we have been frank with one another, but also since you must live here you must understand what the situation is.'

'Yes,' she said. 'What is the situation?'

'I am as crazy for Jennifer as ever I was. She has a terrible physical spell over me. In a while you will feel it right through the house – the spell of her body. I care for her, too, in other ways; I have a great tenderness, sometimes an almost unspeakable longing to make her happy. And so long as she is comfortable she is happy, but let her comfort once be disturbed and the whole house is wretched.

'She is pure Herries, the unimaginative practical sort. Had she energy she would be the feminine Will of the family, turning everything to practical profit, but she has none and she wants none. She does not love me but she loves no one, not her parents nor her children. But she is proud of everything that is hers, myself as well. She will quickly be proud of you if you serve her. If you do not—'

'Yes – if I do not?'

'She will fight you until you do. And she has many strange weapons . . .' He went on after a pause. 'I had thought when I asked her to marry me that what she would not be able to endure would be the quiet and silence here. That she would be restless here, want people that would entertain her, admire her. But that has been the slightest of the trouble. She has settled here like a cat by the fire so long as she is comfortable.'

'Then why,' asked Judith slowly, 'did you ask me here? If she is comfortable . . .'

'I had to have you, Judith. I had to. It is turning me mad, this life here. It is not that I have not much to do. I have learnt much of the estate. I have grown a wise countryman. Things are prosperous here. I buy land, sell cattle. So far I have conquered my dreams. But I love her and despise her. I love her and despise myself. I know that she does not care for me, that my children do not care for me. I am in touch with no one here. And therefore I had to send for you. For the last three years I have had this longing, but beat it down. Now it has been too strong for me.'

Judith felt her heart leap. She had loved Francis all her life and at last her reward had come. He needed her and had told her so. This was perhaps the first moment of true happiness that she had had since Georges' death.

But she showed no emotion.

'Yes, but if we care for one another – brother and sister as we are, although, Francis, I am in reality your aunt, you know – what will Jennifer say?'

'There we must be on our guard. I do not know how it will affect Jennifer. If she is against it she will use every weapon to be rid of you.'

'She thinks,' said Judith, 'that I am a meek little thing. I saw it in her eyes tonight. But I am not. Francis, now that I have come, I cannot go again. Nothing can turn me out. I am resolved. This is my country, my home . . . even if Jennifer hates me.'

'You have no true realization,' he said slowly, 'of Jennifer's obstinacy.'

But she was astonished at herself. She felt rising in her breast a resolved determination on power. That other self – not the self that at her window behind the falling snow had in the gloaming traced every rise and fall of the fell, the peaked line of Skiddaw, the thin haze of the Scottish hills; but the self that had conquered Georges and these last terrible thirteen years, this obstinate self – was moving her forward to this new conquest.

She would make them all love her, Jennifer, children, servants, even the dogs. But – if they would not love her – then they should

obey her. But for Francis she felt an infinite tenderness. She
got up and knelt in front of the fire by his chair. She did not
touch him. She would never again kneel by a man to embrace
him. That had been for Georges alone. But she turned to him,
looking at him with so much sweetness that his heart was comforted as it had never been since the day of his marriage.

'Francis,' she said, 'in the way of love I shall never care for
any man again, but in the way of ourselves, of all our lives, I
love you most dearly. And I will win a victory here.'

He was about to put a hand to her. He stopped and listened.

'Hush,' he said. 'I thought I heard a door opening.'

But there was no sound. The door was fast closed.

PAYING A CALL ON MRS SOUTHEY

OPENING THE DOOR of her bedroom on a fine July afternoon,
intending to prepare for her visit to Mrs Southey, Judith stood
frozen to the wall.

In the far corner of the room could be seen the broad, ill-
shapen back of Mrs Ponder, its calico covering spread to its
utmost as she bent over the drawer of the little spindle-legged
escritoire near the window. In these drawers were Judith's
papers and personal odds and ends – old letters, legal documents,
programmes of dances and concerts, ribbons and faded flowers.

Most of these were now scattered about the floor while Mrs
Ponder, in furious haste and grunting like a pig, burrowed even
deeper.

'Yes,' said Judith. 'Good afternoon.' She had always hated
the woman; from the very first she had detested her, and now
there was such a rage beating in her throat that she had a most
childish impulse to rush across the room and seize the woman by
the neck and shake her head off.

Mrs Ponder's back jumped, then straightened itself; then
Mrs Ponder's pasty-faced, beetle-browed countenance turned
round, terror braced by defiance appeared in it.

'Yes, Mrs Ponder?' Judith said again, her voice small and
quivering in her anger.

'I was straightening things, ma'am,' the woman answered in
her sulky, deep-toned voice, 'helping to keep your drawers tidy.'

'You are not paid, I think, to keep my drawers tidy.'

Mrs Ponder was recovering her self-command. She had thought that she was safe enough, had just time enough. What ill luck that the little soft-footed, prying thing should come creeping up five minutes too soon! Oh well! she wasn't going to be put down by this red-haired leftover of a thief and a vagabond. She knew what she knew.

She put one hand on her hip.

'Excuse me, ma'am. I cannot say I am sure what I am paid for and what I am not paid for, only to do my duty, I should suppose.'

'And is it your duty to decipher my personal letters?'

'I do not know what you mean, ma'am, by deciphering. I was intending for the best.'

'You are very obliging, but it is a dangerous precedent, Mrs Ponder, as I think you will find. Leave this room! It will not, I trust, be long before you leave this house.'

The woman came forward. She was half of a mind to have her say. It was a year and a bit since this French Madame (for Mrs Ponder, like many another, confused facts when she wished to) had come to the house interfering and disturbing. She, Mrs Ponder, had hated her from the first. She would like to say now all the things that she knew and had picked up from gossip. What was she after all? The daughter of some road gipsy who had married a thief killed in a cheap scramble. If it were not for the Master, poor silly fool, she would not be here another day, with her red hair and standing on her toes to make herself taller! Mrs Jennifer didn't want her, that was plain enough. And then she was alienating the children. The little boy had never been the same since her coming . . . Mad she was, going off bareback with no hat on her head all the way to Caldbeck! Mad, as her rascal of a father had been, so she had heard, before her.

All these things Mrs Ponder would have liked to say, but there was something about Judith, something both in her rage and her dignity, that frightened the woman against her will.

She was about to go through the door when Judith stopped her: 'Why did you do this? For what were you looking?'

'I, ma'am? Looking? . . . Why, for nothing, I assure you.'

'Nonsense. Of course you had some purpose.'

Judith stepped forward, and Mrs Ponder, thinking she was going to strike her, retreated.

'No. I would not touch you. You are a bad servant. You have always been one. You will leave this house in the morning.'

'That is for my mistress to say.'

Yes. It was true. The woman was right. But Jennifer would not hesitate. After such a thing as this!

'I cannot understand what it was that you wanted. Pray inform me.' The disgust in Judith's eyes was more insulting than the anger. Mrs Ponder would not quickly forget it. But, for the moment, it would be better to withdraw. So she withdrew.

After she was gone Judith sat in her chair considering. They were to go to take tea with Mrs Southey at Greta Hall, she, Jennifer and Francis. She had come up to put on her bonnet. But she must speak to Jennifer before they went. She could not calmly join in the social amenities of the Southeys while this was raging in her breast. To break open her drawer and read her letters! There were packets of letters from Georges there . . . Oh, it was monstrous, it was impossible! The insolence of the woman. But she would go at once – that was one good thing. The affair would have a good issue, for the woman had been always impossible, and now there would be a fine reason for her dismissal. Jennifer would not hesitate. Of course she would not. Judith's heart seemed to stop a beat. Jennifer was so strange a woman. They had been friendly enough during these twenty months. She had been delighted for Judith to take the house in her hands; she had given her free rein. But Judith knew her no better than on that first evening.

She could not any more now than then say whether it were War or Peace. The time had gone so swiftly; there had been so much to do – the house to order, the servants to watch, the children to care for, Francis to make comfortable, new neighbours to know, and sometimes – twice or thrice – strange sudden expeditions into the mountains, to Watendlath, to Newlands, once so far as Ennerdale, when another life altogether had stirred and moved, a life that was not dead, although it was given so little freedom. The time had gone, Judith had even been happy because of Francis, because of the children, because the neighbours were kind, and chiefly because this house and the little village and the Moor were all hers. From Iredale to Caldbeck, from Threlkeld to Mungrisdale it was hers. And so, because of all these things, the central situation, the pivot upon which everything else turned, the relationship between herself and Jennifer, had never been examined.

But it had been growing; all the while it was growing. As she sat there, beside her bed, looking at the dove-grey bonnet that lay upon it, she suddenly shivered. *What* was Jennifer thinking? Had Jennifer? . . . And at the very suspicion of that thought, she, to whom honesty and cleanliness and fair dealing were the first rules of life, sprang indignantly from her chair. Oh no! that was monstrous ... Monstrous ... But she must go, at once, *at once*, and speak to Jennifer.

So down she went, and the first thing that she saw was the fat, handsome, sensuous face of Captain Fernyhirst in the hall. Captain Fernyhirst lived near Caldbeck. He had bought, only last year, old Uncle Tom's house, Stone Ends. He had a pale, ill wife there and two lanky children. And he was an admirer and friend of Jennifer's.

He was a fine upstanding man with a broad back and stout legs. His eyes were too small, his nose a trifle too large, but he looked elegant in his green coat, his hair curling above his ears, his spurred heels spread, yes, as though he owned the house and everything in it.

They were a handsome pair, a very handsome pair. He greeted Judith with the courteous patronage that he always used to her. He said something about the weather, and went. Jennifer was dressed in green and white, her lovely hair falling in thick ringlets on her bare neck. Very lovely, Judith thought, was her hair, parted in the middle of her fair smooth forehead, combed towards the sides, falling in curls that seemed to hold in their dark shadows a strange, steely lustre.

'Very lovely hair,' thought Judith, 'but I wonder whether Mrs Ponder ...' She was in fact too angry to wait, as she should have done, for a more favourable opportunity, and in that lost an important chance of commanding the situation.

Impetuously she led the way into the parlour.

'Jennifer, I must speak to you.'

'My dear ... but we are late, and Mrs Southey is most punctilious ...'

Slowly she followed Judith in.

'Jennifer, Mrs Ponder must be dismissed. At once. Tonight.'

'And why?'

'I caught her, now, five minutes back; I went to my room and she was searching my drawers. My papers were scattered about the floor.'

It was not Jennifer's way to speak quickly. It was as though slowly and with practised deliberation she sent a message through all her tall body that it must be prepared for a set of circumstances, that there was no haste required ... plenty of time.

She sat down, put her hand to her hair, looked out of window.

'Well, Judith, I must inquire. Mrs Ponder is an admirable servant. She was perhaps making tidy your effects.'

'Making tidy my effects? But who is she to make my things tidy? It is not her business. She had no place in my room. No, indeed. She was making nothing tidy. She was spying.'

'Spying? What is there for her to spy into?'

'Nothing, of course. I have nothing to hide.' Then amazement, increased by her anger, seized her. 'But, Jennifer – are you not yourself indignant? Do you understand what it is? She was *spying*! The woman was in my room, my letters were on the floor. Letters. Letters from my husband . . .' Her voice broke. She was very near to tears.

'Well, it shall be inquired into. I am convinced that you have judged too hastily. It *is* your weakness, Judith. You act too immediately on the impulse of the moment . . .'

'*My* fault! My fault!' Judith broke in. 'But Jennifer, I cannot understand! You appear to be blaming *me*! Do you hear what I said? That Mrs Ponder was discovered by me tossing my private papers about the floor, her hands among my effects. She did not deny it. She could not. She was most insolent. She must go . . . must leave . . . at once, tomorrow morning. You must tell her so. A fine thing to have in the house, a servant who opens drawers and carries her secrets, I have no doubt, to the kitchenmaids and the grooms. You cannot hesitate. Francis would insist . . .'

She pulled up. For her life she wished that she had not spoken those last words. Her rage had carried her away. The very thought of the woman's ugly thick back and the packets of Georges' letters . . . But she should not have mentioned Francis. Was she never to learn?

In the short silence that followed, the place seemed to fill with the summer scents, the radiant sun floated the room with shadows of gold. Some man called to his horse, wheels creaked on the road. Then Jennifer spoke:

'Yes . . . It was I who asked Ponder to search your drawer.'

She looked at Judith, and Judith looked back at her. Judith's pale face slowly flushed. This was an incredible thing. It was as though the spinet had leapt through the ceiling, or the little rosy apples on the sofa had rolled like little live bullets about the floor. An incredible thing. To Judith, in spite of the many events that had been her lot, the most astonishing, the most dumbfounding of them all.

'You . . . told her?'

'Yes. I wished to know what you were writing of me to London.'

'I . . . to London?'

'Indeed, yes. To dear Will and Christabel, who have so true an affection for me.'

'And so . . . you thought that such dishonest behaviour was in my character – that while I lived here and was your friend I would write . . .' She broke off. All words failed her. The sun had died from the room, which was grey in her eyes and chill.

'But why not? We must have common sense. When you first came here I hoped that we should form a friendship, but you had other ideas. You were determined to be mistress here. You alienated my husband, my children, my servants. I was well assured that your friends in London must have the benefit of your experience. Why not? If I had had your ambitions I should have doubtless done the same.'

'You thought that? I have been here for more than a year. All this while you have fancied me indulging in such treachery; you have known me so little that you suspected *such* things in my conduct? Why, then . . . why, then . . . if your mind has been of such a colour, you must have hated me! . . . And I thought that we were friends. For a year I have suspected nothing. And you have made your servant spy on me . . .'

She was shaking, quivering with rage, astonishment, but also with a dreadful miserable unhappiness that seemed to strike deep into her very soul. All her life long, through every difficulty and distress, she had been supported always by her sense of her own integrity and the conviction that everyone thought her honest. She had not had pride in that, but it had been her comfort; whatever else went, that remained. And now – to be charged with such treachery and to be hated when she had thought that she was cared for.

Her lip quivered. If she wept now it would be a humiliation for which she would never forgive herself.

Steadying her voice she said quietly: 'I have never suffered any disloyalty to you, Jennifer, in myself or another. I had thought we were friends and so acted. You have wronged me,' and left the room.

Once in her own place any tendency to tears was gone. Tears! No, indeed! She walked the floor like a raging little animal in a cage. The letters, papers, ribbons were still scattered about, where Mrs Ponder had left them. Mechanically, without knowing it, she bent down and put them back and closed the drawers. She remained, kneeling there, looking in front of her.

Her immediate impulse was, as it had always been in every crisis of her life, to take some dramatic action instantly – to find Francis, to tell him what had occurred, without either self-defence or accusation of anyone, and then to depart – to be, as swiftly as possible, as far from Jennifer as the world allowed her. But very quickly her temper cooled. Her intelligence reasserted itself. There was more in this than a vulgar quarrel. The whole of her own past life was in it, her father, her mother; the whole of the Herries family was in it, for what she was meeting now in Jennifer was the thing in the Herries blood that her father, her-self, Francis, Reuben, Georges had always been fighting – the unimaginative, calm, self-assured obstinacy and confidence.

At that she knew that she was herself now calmer. She rose from her knees and, as she looked about the room, realized something with an absolute certainty of its truth, as though some-one had whispered it in her ear. Jennifer had intended this quarrel. She did not hate Judith. Hatred was an emotion un-known to her sluggishness. She had decided – perhaps some while back – that Judith made her uncomfortable and that Judith must go. Francis would never allow her to go, unless there were some very obstinate reason or unless Judith herself was provoked to it. She must provoke Judith or she must find a reason. In all probability she was smiling now quietly to herself, thinking that she had succeeded.

At that Judith flung up her head and swore that whatever occurred she would not go. This was her place, and here she would stay. She could be as obstinate as Jennifer, yes, and more obstinate.

There was a knock on the door, and opening it she found Francis there. The carriage was ready. Jennifer was ready. He was smiling, had no consciousness that there had been any trouble. She looked at him and smiled too. She was there to make Francis happy, and make him happy she would, Jennifer or no Jennifer. She put on her bonnet and shawl and went down with him.

'I like the grey bonnet,' he said.

'I had it in Carlisle,' she said, 'a month ago.'

Jennifer, in her fine green and white bombasine dress and an ostrich feather in her bonnet, stood by the carriage, the moors undulating in hummocks and pools of green on every side of her. She smiled as they came towards her.

'Dear Judith,' she said, 'what a charming bonnet!'

So it was all bonnets, and a more agreeable trio, sitting behind the immense back of Fred the coachman, could surely not be found in Keswick. Francis might complain that Will made the money and that he was a failure, but nevertheless things were very comfortable at Uldale. That land that they had bought towards Caldbeck was turning out very well, and, in spite of the unsettled times, the shares in the Liverpool shipping business were for ever improving. And, in a year, Judith had brought the house to a fine discipline. Mrs Harper, the housekeeper, a widow from Carlisle, was an excellent woman. Jennifer herself was not at all extravagant. Whatever she wore seemed to be beautiful on her. She had no great taste for entertaining. An occasional little dinner with cards afterwards, a Ball at Christmas. No magnificence even then. Ten couples at the most. Yes, new bonnets could be afforded. They were very generous to Judith or, at least, Francis was. His allowance was most generous. She had never had so much in all her life before; never been so comfortable ... Comfortable? A glance across at Jennifer on the opposite seat, and it was as though everything sinister and destructive thickened the summer air.

To be charged with such malice and deceit, to be suspected of the basest treachery ...

'They say that Mr Coleridge dislikes his wife extremely and will never again return to Keswick. He goes often, I believe, to visit Mr Wordsworth in Grasmere ... How cool the woods are! ... The Southeys always seem to me very pleasant people. Judith my dear, if the sun is too hot you must change places with me. You know that I am never disturbed by the heat.'

She was not. She basked in it, or like a great bird of brilliant plumage bathed her feathers in it, letting the light strike gold and emerald and sapphire from her loveliness.

'Edith Southey,' said Francis, 'is a very pretty-behaved child, very pretty-behaved, indeed. And little Hartley, Coleridge's boy, is most unusual. But, of course, he is growing now. He must be fifteen, at least. He is at school at Ambleside. Yes, this is a most beautiful day; the air is exceptionally warm.'

Francis was happy today. He was always pleased when he was going to see Mr Southey. That she should set her servant on to spy and then, without a tremor, admit it ... How lovely that rather selfish droop of her mouth and the faint warm glow of her cheek, and the softness of her eyes as they looked out so calmly under their heavy lids! ... The falseness! That Judith had tried to alienate the children! John loved her. That was not Judith's fauit. And he was uneasy with his mother. He knew, as children always know, that she did not in her heart care for him. Or did she care ? Who could tell for whom she cared ?

'Look, Judith, how blue the Lake is! There is not a ripple.'

Yes, she had thought that she had got her way, and that in a week Judith would be gone. She was wrong. As they approached Keswick the air was rich with the scent of the summer flowers. July and August are the bad months for this country. There is rain, everything is heavily green without variety. But days come like this one when all the trees, larch and birch and fir and oak, are so deeply shadowed and so highly lit that fire runs from stem to stem, melting into cloud and climbing into swift eddies of green smoke. If only there are clouds in the sky the hills lie waiting to receive the shadows that slip like birds from shoulder to shoulder. The clouds have a great richness in this month, so proudly filled with white light that they quiver with their intensity, throwing paths of ghostly radiance on to the Lakes that are blue, here and there ruffled darkly like tarnished silver. On such a day the richness of the English scene, when the hay burns in the nostrils and every cottage garden has the dusky odour of snapdragon and sweet-william, is immortal. One summer's day is enough for memory to be enriched for ever.

Keswick was so small a country town that in the summer its gardens dominated all the rest. Greta Hall is at the entrance to it from the Carlisle side, and once they had crossed the little bridge they were almost there, but Judith could smell the flowers mingling with the soft friendliness of the cut hay that lay on the open fields.

She could see the peace of the town, the farmers' carts, Mr Probus the Apothecary standing at his door enjoying the sun, two young ladies laughing as they came out of Mrs Gray's, the bonnet shop, old Mr Fordyce the Antiquarian, who was said to sleep half the year on the Roman Wall, with his snuff-coloured wig and old-fashioned breeches. As the carriage turned up the drive she thought: 'It will take more than Jennifer's insults to drive me away from this.'

This was Judith's first visit to the Southeys. Mrs Coleridge and Mrs Southey had been to Uldale. They were quiet, comfortable women; certainly Mrs Southey was a comfortable woman. About Mrs Coleridge one could not be so sure; there were lines of discomfort about her mouth, restlessness in her eyes. You could see that they were sisters and had lived for most of their lives together.

Yes, the house was charming, a nursery garden on the right as they climbed the hill; then you could see an orchard with plum trees and apple trees behind the house. They were admitted by a cheerful motherly-looking woman, who conducted them into the parlour on the left of the passage. They waited in the parlour, gathered together in a kind of attitude of defence as people are when they are awaiting their hostess.

This was a charming room, with a large green shaped like a horse-shoe in front of the window. The room was comfortably furnished with old furniture, shabby but friendly. There were pictures on the wall – one really dreadful painting of a staring doll-like Mrs Coleridge.

Mrs Southey came in. There were greetings all round, words about the splendid weather, about the hay, the crops, being tired, not being tired, being hot, not being hot. But they must all come upstairs to Mr Southey's room. That was where tea would be. So upstairs they all went.

Oh! this was a wonderful room, so light, so well-proportioned, so airy! And the views were fine. Were the views not fine? They were indeed. The room had three windows. The large one that looked down upon the green and the flowerbeds and away to the Lake and the mountains, the two smaller ones whence you could see the lower part of the town.

The room was lined with books, and there were splendid volumes bound in vellum lying in heaps on the floor. And the family portraits on the wall; before long Judith knew who they all were – Mr and Mrs Southey by Downman, little Edith Southey and little Sara Coleridge by that fine artist Mr Nash; the other three Southey children, Kate, Isabel and Bertha, also by Mr Nash.

Much good furniture, Mr Southey's writing-table piled with books and papers, a screen, a desk. The room was decorated in quiet dignified tones, the curtains of French grey merino, the furniture covered with some buff colour. A noble room, the room of a poet, lit now with the summer sun, and all the summer sounds mingling beyond the open window.

It was, in fact, Mr Southey himself who showed Judith the portraits and then some of his books. At first she thought him a little alarming with his dark hair, his grave features, the dignified, rather remote way he had of moving, a little as though, she wickedly fancied, he were carrying the offertory plate in church. He was at first the official host, cold and ceremonial. He held up his head as though he knew it was a fine one; she thought that he certainly was aware that he was an important personage. She fancied, too, on their first arrival, that he had thrown an impatient glance or two at his writing-table, where his papers lay, as though he wished his visitors very far away. And he certainly had no idea as to who she was; he took care to give her no name lest he should be in error. She thought that he had difficulty sometimes in seeing her at all and would have spoken with the same grave courtesy if she vanished; he would not know that she had gone.

And then, when they moved to the large window, he became entirely another person. When he spoke of this country, this country that she loved as dearly as he, his voice thrilled, his face was lit, his black hair flung back.

'You know it is hard for me to speak of these things. When I first came to Keswick I assured myself that I should never settle down without a violet – no violet and no nightingale. But now I have long forgot those losses. My brother Tom was settled in the valley of Newlands, and I would not like to confess to you how we have been, the two of us, our childish behaviour. And now with my own children there is no stone or leaf of Walla Crag or Watendlath that we do not know.' (Watendlath – a quiver at the word touched her and fled.) 'And with my books – my books. Are you yourself a bookworm? If so you see in front of you the most impassioned of your clan. Let me show you—' He waved his hand and, eagerly walking to the bookcase, began to pull out volumes for her. 'Have you been ever in Portugal? Do you know Portugal? What! you have never seen Cintra! ... And is Verbeyst an unknown name to you? Verbeyst of Brussels. He has three hundred thousand volumes. Do you know what it is to open a chest of books? What are you going to find? ... No, let me show you this – *The Revelations of St Bridget*. See, not only are the initial letters illuminated, but every capital through the volume is coloured ... Fuller's *Church History* ... Is not Sir Thomas Browne a favourite with you? ...' A small tortoiseshell cat came and rubbed its back against his leg.

He was quivering now like a boy. His hands shook, his face was all smiles. Then ruefully laughing at himself: 'Ah, I am for ever making collections. It is foolish, is it not, for who will read them if I do not, and they arrive more swiftly than even I can peruse them. Time! Time! Why are the days not twice as long and the nights four times. Come, I must not weary you, but I can see that you have a fancy yourself this way. You have a fancy, have you not? you have a library? I hope that you have a library.' He smiled at her so friendlily and his eyes were so kind that she wished that they could be examining books for ever.

At tea, seated in a half-circle, Mr Southey, Mrs Coleridge, pretty Edith Southey, Mrs Southey behind the tea-table, they were all very gay. Judith had often noticed that when at parties Jennifer was present, everything went well. People were delighted with her beauty. Shadows and shapes of loveliness seemed to radiate from her passivity and composure. Then, being so beautiful, people assumed that she would be haughty and proud. But when she was anywhere, the first thing that she did was to secure her comfort and, as she was always the most beautiful person present, she was always the first to be offered a seat, food, drink, whatever it might be. So, assured that she had all that she needed, she was as amiable as anything, listened with apparent attention to everyone's stories (although Judith suspected that she never heard a word of them). There was, however, always a sense of thunder behind the calm. When suddenly out of her comfort she might, Judith thought, snap something in her fingers, even as on that old historic occasion she had snapped Christabel's fan.

But on an afternoon like today's she was entirely at her ease. She had had a fight and, as she thought, won it. She had been increasingly uncomfortable during the last six months; now that cause of that discomfort would be removed. Then the weather was hot, which she greatly preferred. Then the Southeys were reputable people; she had herself never read any of Mr Southey's long poems, but she knew that they were generally respected. What she liked was for the Herries to be gracious and condescending to families that were worthy of graciousness. The Southeys, she thought, were really worthy. Then Francis was happy here; he could here indulge his ridiculous passion for literature; and, although she only cared as to whether he were happy or no because when he was unhappy his sulkiness made her a little uncomfortable, yet, in warm weather like this, she preferred that everyone should pass a pleasant hour.

And lastly there was that little pushing nonentity Judith, who had been this very day told her place and at whom therefore it was agreeable, once and again, to look.

All in all, Jennifer that afternoon was very comfortable at the Southeys'. There would come a day when, looking back, she saw that warm, quiet afternoon as the beginning of all her trouble.

Mrs Southey was the conversational one; Mrs Coleridge had a

tendency to peevishness (which you could understand, Jennifer lazily pondered, if it were true that her husband was always away from her and was a slave to opium . . .).

'Are you partial to evening visiting?' Mrs Southey inquired. 'I must confess that we are not. Mr Southey has so much work in the evening and the roads are so often floated by the rain. Not that I think this is a rainy district in reality. It is only that it seems very hard when it does come down. Does it not rain hard sometimes, Mr Herries? I have never seen such hard rain anywhere.'

Mr Southey, who was offering cake and bread and butter with a graciousness that almost demanded the accompaniment of music, answered with gravity: 'It is the rainy hours that give us the opportunity for all our reading. Is it not so, Edith? Or rather, in my little girl's case, the writing out of charades and riddles into our book. Come now, Edith. Confess. How many charades have you copied in today?'

'None at all, Papa. I have been in the town with Mama.'

What Judith liked in him, she thought, was the warmth of his affections. As he spoke to his daughter his eyes looked on her as though he would surrender the world for her sake. And, as she knew, there was his boy Herbert whom he loved even more dearly.

'That is what my friend Wordsworth will never do. Copy a charade for a lady. No, he bows and regards her sternly and slips out of door and takes a walk. Are you acquainted with Wordsworth, Mrs Herries? The greatest man alive in England today. Yes, indeed, the greatest man in England, as the world will see one of these times. There has been a young man in Keswick this last winter, a Mr Shelley, with his wife. A most unusual young man. I have told him that when he is as old as I am he will grant the truth of my prophecy about Wordsworth. He, too, wishes to be a poet. We are all poets these days, Mrs Herries . . . Well, he is an unusual young man. Just what I was myself in '94. What it was hard for him to understand was that you may have Five Thousand Pounds a year and yet be a good man; I fancy that there are many young men like him today. The Revolution in France is responsible, you know. But I set him upon a course of Berkeley. That should do him good. He does not realize as yet that a man must put a bound upon his desires and work within them . . . Dear, dear, how sententious I am becoming! Pray, Mrs Herries, another of Mrs Southey's tea-cakes. They are quite famous in the neighbourhood, you know. John Wilson declares there are none like them even in Scotland, which is the land of tea-cakes.'

'Yes,' thought Judith. 'But will Francis be on my side? He must not know. He *shall* not know unless Jennifer herself tells him. And I believe that she will not.'

She had a horrible sense that the battle now would be underground, that no one henceforth would tell anyone anything, and that was so against her own character that it was as though she must twist her whole soul to conform to it.

'For my part,' Mrs Coleridge was saying, 'I would never encourage anyone to marry. There can be so many blunders in matrimony. Although, to be sure, young people must marry. 'Tis only natural for them.'

It was now that Judith saw enter the room a very extraordinary being. This was a boy of some fifteen or sixteen years of age; he had a small restless body dressed in clothes too young for it, the short blue cloth jacket, the white trousers and open frilled shirt of boys junior to him. Dark hair strayed untidily over his forehead, but his eyes were the strangest part of him, burning with intelligence and yet at the same time lost, as he gazed about the room, in a kind of abstract wonder. He saw them all seated about the tea-table and smiled, came towards them, stared at Jennifer as though he were mesmerized, then, pulling himself back with a jerk, nodded, still smiling, and stepped away to the farther part of the room.

'Nay, Hartley,' said Mrs Coleridge, 'you must wish Mr and Mrs Herries good day.'

He came back to them with an odd stepping dancing movement as though he scarcely touched the floor. Then he stood there, shook hands, seemed as though at any moment he would break into laughter. What was amusing him? It was to Judith exactly as though he had sprung through the wall, coming from another world. He was no resident in this one. All his real life was elsewhere, and as she watched him she became restless. She wanted to get up and run away from all of them – to Watendlath, maybe, find the old house, sit with the Ritsons by the great hearth and hear the lambs bleating beyond the window; then to pass into that other room and to stand watching that staircase, to see again that old man with the white beard as he turned to the stair. Georges would come in, wait beside her as he often did, take her and lift her, pressing her backwards against his breast. Oh, after all these years, after all these years . . . Was she never to be rid of it? If the battle were joined now between

Jennifer and herself, it was also joined between the one world
and the other. It was almost as though Georges were beside her
fighting Jennifer.

All this disturbance had come from that strange boy there,
moving away again, flitting now here, now there, regarding no
one and regarding everyone, humming (she fancied, although
she could not be sure) some tune to himself. They had all
moved away from the tea-table and so she found herself encountering Hartley. He was standing on one foot, one ankle
curled around another, and staring at Jennifer. He greeted
Judith as though he had known her all her life. Children often
did so because she was small and independent.

'That is the most beautiful lady, ma'am, I have ever seen,'
he said.

Jennifer was being shown books and manuscripts now by
Mr Southey.

'Yes,' said Judith. 'You are Mrs Coleridge's boy?'

'Yes, ma'am; there are Derwent and Sara and I. I go to a
school at Ambleside. Mr Dawes is the Master.'

'And what do you learn there?'

(It was the strangest thing, as though behind this outward
talk they were conducting a quite different conversation. As
though he said to her: 'I have just been with Georges and he told
me . . .' It was the boy's air of being not yet awake, of suffering
under some enchantment.)

His eyes were never still, nor his feet. He looked at her with the
most engaging friendliness.

'Oh, they try their best to teach me, but I cannot learn any
of the ordinary things. I shall dream of that lady for weeks and
write stories about her. She shall be the Queen of Ejuxria.'

'Where?'

'Ejuxria. It is a country that I discovered many years back.
She shall be the next Queen. Oh, ma'am, what a grand Queen
she will make.'

Oh yes, she will, and her servants will go spying in the drawers
of her Ladies-in-Waiting, reading their letters, undoing the
faded ribbons . . .

'Do you like to be here?' she asked him.

'I like to be everywhere. It is all the same, for if a place is
ugly one can make one's own picture of it, can one not, ma'am?'

How odd it was to see this small child, with his restless, unexpected gestures (so that he would crack his fingers or move
three steps on one foot as though he were playing hop-scotch,

or swing his little arms above his head), a child like none other that she had ever seen, and feel that she had so much in common with him. She felt no awkwardness. He understood her absolutely. His smile was the most bewitching part of him; it embraced and included her in his own delight.

'And what will you be when you grow up?' she asked him.

'I shall be nothing,' he answered, twirling round on one foot. 'I shall never grow up, I should think. I cannot learn the things that help one to grow up, and I know such a number of things that one must not mention. I have a secret name for everything. What is your name, ma'am?'

'Judith – Judith Paris.'

'Judith – I shall call you Florindascantinopolis. One day I will show you where Ejuxria is.' Then he added quietly: 'And now I must go and do my Greek lesson. And then we are going to play cricket – when the others come back from the Lake.'

Yes, they were going. Farewells were being said. Goodbye, Goodbye . . . How warm it is! Is it not warm!

'Yes, the laurels are in great profusion here – but the kitchen-garden is not really too extensive. So beautiful at Uldale! So fine a view of the Scotch Hills . . . But certainly we will come . . . very much obliged . . . too kind of you . . . Goodbye. Goodbye.'

So they rode home.

'Most agreeable people,' Jennifer said. 'When you are in London, Judith, you must read Mr Southey's poems. They are all the thing in London.'

'London!' Francis cried. 'London! But Judith is not going to London.'

'No. I am not,' said Judith.

The two women looked at one another. Upon Jennifer's fine smooth white brow a small, a very small frown appeared, the first, Judith thought, that she had ever seen there.

'Of course not,' said Jennifer. 'But we cannot expect Judith never to wish to leave Uldale.'

'I am very happy at Uldale,' Judith said, smiling at Francis. 'You are so very good to me.'

But afterwards when Jennifer had gone upstairs, slowly, majestically, like a green and white swan floating upwards, to take off her bonnet, Judith had a desperate, almost choking need of reassurance. She caught Francis by the broad lapels of his coat. He paused astonished. He was always shy of demonstrations, she knew. She looked up into his face and he saw that her eyes were filled with tears.

'Francis, you do want me here, do you not?'

'Want you!' He put his thin firm hand on her small one. 'Why, I will never let you go!'

She nodded and said in a low voice: 'I am glad. I wished you to tell me so.'

He added kindly, holding her hand more closely in his: 'You have altered everything here. The servants, the children all love you. And the best of it is Jennifer has grown so attached. I have never known her trust anyone so before. She relies on you completely. I cannot thank you sufficiently.'

'I am glad,' said Judith, moving towards the stairs, 'that you are pleased.'

GONE TO EARTH

ON A LOVELY October afternoon a post-chaise drew up outside Fell House and from it stepped a little short man in a brown hat.

He wore a dark brown 'carrick' with many capes, breeches of a light grey and very smart and shining top-boots. He was something of a dandy. He opened the gates, walked up the tiled path and pulled the bell-rope. He walked with a slight limp.

There was complete stillness round him. The thick, gold leaves of the trees in the garden, the little heads of amber chrysanthemums, never stirred in the blue air. Only the pigeons rustled in a flock above the pigeon-house at the sound of the bell, then settled again.

While he waited he sniffed the sharp beauty of the autumn weather and savoured the great spaces surrounding him on all sides. The edges of the hills were clear as though they had been cut out of paper. He could hear the sheep cropping on the moor beyond the garden wall.

A manservant opened the door and he inquired for Mrs Paris. He was shown into the hall bathed in sun, then after a pause into the parlour, where he stood holding his hat and looking anxiously at the door.

A moment later it opened and Judith stood astonished. Then she ran forward holding out both her hands.

'Warren!' she cried.

He laughed and was so glad to see her that his little grey eyes, bright and restless like a bird's, twinkled with pleasure. He had not seen her for four years.

'You are not changed in the least,' he said, holding both her hands in his.

'Why, of course not,' she said, leading him to the sofa. His limp made her seem protective towards him. 'And why should I be?'

'I have thought at times,' he said, looking at her very closely, 'from your letters, that you were.'

'In which way?'

'Oh, more serious, more grave.'

'I am a most serious person,' she said. 'You have never granted me that sufficiently.'

She was enchanted to see him. He was exactly what she was needing, an easy, good friend who cared for her, who was outside all the increasing perplexities and complications of this house and her position in it.

'But why are you here? And where have you come from?'

'I have been in Keswick a week.'

'In Keswick a week and only just come!'

'I had some business there and I would not come to see you until it was concluded.'

'But why not?'

'Because it concerns you.'

'Concerns me?'

'Yes. Wait an instant until I have seen you. I have been looking forward so impatiently to this moment.'

He was holding her hand a little harder than she wished. Very gently she withdrew it. He must be her friend, nothing more. But her *friend*! She had never in her life wanted a friend so badly as she did just now.

His face was very charming, ugly because the nose was too large and the mouth too small, but eyes and mouth both were wrinkled and lined with kindliness and humour. His looks had also that sense of strain common to everyone who has had a life of pain and ill-health. But he did not appear a weakling. His body was broad and sturdy, and he was alert and active save for his limp. He was now forty-three years of age.

'Well, what is your great news? I can tell that you are bursting with it.'

'Yes. You may not care for it when you hear it.'

She was quickly apprehensive; recent events had made her so.
'I had thought that you might have got wind of it.'

She suddenly knew. Of course! he was to be married. She
was disappointed.

'I know – you are to be married!'

He looked straight into her eyes, so that she dropped them.

'No . . . not yet,' he answered quietly. 'Nothing like that.
Will has bought Westaways and I am to be manager of the
estate.'

She drew back, erect with amazement.

'What!'

'Yes; Will has bought Westaways. The purchase was concluded last evening.'

Westaways was the house that old Pomfret, Raiseley's father
and David Herries' uncle, Francis' and Will's great-uncle, had
had built for him between Keswick and Crosthwaite Church.
It was called Westaways because it was one of the best examples
of the work of an old crazy genius of an architect who, a hundred
years ago, had lived in Keswick. It had been built for Pomfret
and his wife at great expense and it was a beautiful house. When
Raiseley had moved with his wife, Mary, to London, he had sold
the house to a Colonel Grant, who, however, had infrequently
resided there. Six months earlier Colonel Grant had died in
Spain and there had been much local speculation as to its next
owner.

Will had bought Westaways! Will was coming here to live,
eight miles from his brother with whom he was not on speaking
terms! Will was coming back to Keswick. Will with his money
and pride and scorn of everything outside London! Will! . . .

'Oh no, no!' she broke out. 'It is impossible! Westaways and
Will! Will and Keswick!'

'I know. But it is so. I have concluded the purchase myself.'

'And he is to live here?'

'He will come up occasionally. I fancy that Christabel and
Walter will be here more frequently. She has not been well of
late. Young Walter loves the country. He is mad on horses.'

'How old is Walter now?'

'Twenty-one. He was born in '92. He will make as good a
business man as his father. But different. He loves power even
more than Will. I never saw a young man so arrogant. He must
have his own way in everything.'

'But I cannot believe it. It is incredible. Does he mean to be
reconciled with Francis? He will not find it so easy.'

'No. I am afraid not. He is very bitter against Francis, and young Walter carries on the feud.'

'Then—' Judith waited. Suddenly she cried: 'Oh, he is coming here to show off! To triumph over Uldale! I see it all. Oh! it is shameful, shameful! With his money he thinks that he will humiliate Francis!'

'Remember,' Warren said, 'Francis married Jennifer.'

Judith could not grasp it. The change in everything that it would make, the unpleasantness, the rivalries, jealousies, personalities! The difficulties for herself, a friend of Will's and Christabel's as she was. She could not cut herself off from poor Christabel. That would be a disloyalty that no one would command in her . . . but how otherwise was her life with Francis and Jennifer to be possible, difficult as it was already?

In her perplexities she burst out: 'Warren, you should not have taken this. It is going to lead to nothing but hatred and ill-feeling—'

He nodded his head.

'Perhaps I should not. I hesitated, I will confess, but there was one thing that decided me.'

She said nothing. He went on.

'That you were here.'

'Oh no, Warren, please—'

He persisted.

'No, you have to hear me. I came to say this. From now we shall be living near to one another, and I do not care what you or any other may think. For four years I have tried to conquer my love for you, but it will not die. No, listen . . . listen . . . please do not send me away! No, Judith, please – please!'

She had risen and stood there looking at him: 'Warren, it is quite useless. You know that it is. We settled that four years ago. We were to be friends. You promised it.'

'I know, I know,' he answered. 'And so I intended it to be. But I cannot command it, try as I may. It is the last of my life. I shall have no more. My life has been always broken, everything has failed in it. This too will fail. I see that it must. But I am compelled to tell you.'

As she looked at him she longed to be kind to him, to give him anything that he wanted. What she had always desired, what she would always desire, was to give people what they wanted. And for seventeen years now no one had wanted anything very much. At Grosset it had been a carpet brushed, a window mended, a consoling word to Maria, a humorous word to Carey, and here it had been comfort for Francis, who after all was not comforted.

As she looked at Warren whom she liked so greatly, who was so courageous and bore pain without flinching, who never made complaint, she longed to give him anything. But how could she? She did not love him. He wanted passion, and she had no passion left for anyone in the world. And then it was absurd; she was thirty-nine.

'Dear Warren,' she said gently. 'I care for you very greatly. With Francis here you are the best friend I have. But love – love of the sort that you mean, I have none for anyone. It is true although it may sound fantastic, but I love Georges after all these years as dearly as I did when he was alive. Is that false, a sentimentality? I think not. Or, if so, I am myself deceived. And then I am so old. I am near forty.'

He got up and stood beside her, but did not touch her.

'Yes, I know everything. Nothing has altered since we talked at Grosset. You are not old to me. Besides, I am not myself young. There is nothing to do – I did not ask you to do anything. But I could not come here to live and not show you that there is no change in my feeling. I shall not do anything but what you would wish.'

He kissed her hand, gave a little bow, and limped away out of the room. She heard the carriage rattle off down the road.

The light was failing, and the little room was shadowed with yellow dusk. She stood there, her hand on the lid of the spinet, looking at the dim garden and the white road beyond it. Her head whirled. Will coming to Keswick! Will only eight miles away! Will and his family hanging over Uldale and flicking Francis' sensitiveness, Jennifer's pride, with every hour that passed! Oh, but it was impossible! The situation was impossible!

The door opened, and Jennifer came in.

'Who was that who was here?' she asked. She was wearing a dress of deep crimson that fitted very close to her body. She walked wearily. During the last months Judith had seen that something was distressing her, something that had nothing to do with her comfort. A curious perception of life was slowly, slowly waking in her. One could see it tremble in her like a faint flutter in a white sky before dawn. Her battle with Judith continued, but this was not the cause of her disturbance. It was from some other direction.

'That was Warren Forster.'

'Warren Forster? Why did he not stay?'

'He had a piece of news—' Judith hesitated. This same news was going to shake Jennifer's placid laziness as nothing else could do. Judith longed to see that shaken; in part Judith hated Jennifer as she had never hated anyone before. But, beyond that, there was something further. Jennifer's anger would include Francis' discomfort. They were all included in this.

'Well,' Jennifer said slowly. 'Cautious little Judith. You *are* cautious, are you not? With your own plans and purposes—'

She always, now, when the two of them were alone, tried any kind of irritation that seemed to her clever, but like all unimaginative women she could only think of the taunts and teasings that would goad herself if someone applied them. Quite different ones would be needed for Judith.

'No, I am not cautious!' Judith answered, smiling. 'But this is rather astonishing news that Warren brought. Prepare yourself for a shock.'

Jennifer, who was standing, drawn to her full height, looking out of window, had her mind only half on Judith's words. She was watching or waiting or listening . . .

'Well, my dear? What is your great news?'

'Will has bought Westaways at Crosthwaite and is coming to reside there with Christabel and the family.'

Judith had her reward. Jennifer turned; her eyes for once were wide and awake, her beautiful mouth open, her whole body stung to attention.

'What? What do you say?'

'It is true. Warren has just completed the purchase. He is to be Will's bailiff.'

At that same moment Francis came in. He had been riding and looked immensely handsome in his many-caped coat. His face was splendid now, very sharp and set, thinner than it had ever been; his whole body was drawn fine and alert.

'Francis? Do you hear? It is impossible, fantastic. Oh, no . . . he cannot . . . he would not dare. No, no. There must be a mistake.'

It was astonishing enough to see Jennifer pacing the room, her head up, waving her arms, in a flurry of agitation.

'Judith, what is it? What's amiss?'

'Only that Warren Forster has been here and has told me that Will has bought Westaways and is to come there with Christabel.'

'Will! Bought Westaways!'

'Yes.'

Jennifer turned sharply upon Judith.

'You knew of this. You had heard of this already. You knew this was coming.'

She was so frantically disturbed that for once she forgot the caution that she always kept before Francis.

He at once turned to her. 'Jennifer! Certainly Judith did not know—' He stared at her as though he were seeing something new.

'Well, then,' she cried, tossing up her head and moving towards the door, 'it is at least just what Judith would have. Her dear friends, Will and Christabel, next door. No one can wonder at her pleasure.'

Before she went, her voice shaking with rage, she said to Francis: 'You have brought me to this – to be humiliated before that City merchant and his chicken-faced wife, but I shall not sit under it patiently, you shall see.'

When she was gone he put his arm around Judith and drew her down in front of the fire.

'You are sure of this?'

'Quite sure.'

'Warren himself came to tell you?'

'Yes.'

'And of course you had not an idea of it?'

'Why, no – of course not.'

He sighed deeply, leaning his head on his hand, looking into the fire. He was still wearing his heavy coat. She slipped it off his shoulders.

At last he said: 'Will is doing it only to humiliate me. He could have no other purpose.'

She tried to reassure him. 'No. Why should you take it so? After all this is his home. He lived here all his childhood. He must care for it. He will come to make friends.'

Francis struck his knee with his hand, his favourite gesture when he was excited.

'Never, never. He hates me and Jennifer too. And besides – if he wished to be friends I would not agree. He has insulted Jennifer in every way, and now it only needs this—'

She said what she could, but what was there to say? It was quite true. She knew that there was only one reason why Will had bought Westaways.

Then quite suddenly Francis asked her a surprising question. Dropping his voice a little he said:

'Judith, has Fernyhirst been here this afternoon?'

'No. Why?'

'Oh, for no reason. I wondered. He seems to ride this way frequently.' After another pause he asked her: 'Why did Jennifer speak to you like that ?'

'Speak to me ?'

'Yes, in that manner – unfriendly, angry. Is she offended with you ?'

'Sometimes a little.'

'I have thought lately—'

After a while he said: 'Everything is turning wrongly. I feel as though some great misfortune were coming.'

She must get away. That, when she awoke the next morning, was her first and most dominating impulse. This was no new passion for escape. It had been constant with her all her life long. She was for ever wanting to escape – but never in the end escaping! That might be the just epitaph on her tomb were she ever to have one! Now she was going to escape almost exactly as she had escaped to Tom Gauntry's out of the window all those years ago after David Herries had beaten her. Only now she would not escape out of the window!

No one in the house seemed astir. It was as still as the lovely October morning around and above it. She left a note for Francis, laying it on his table in his study. She went round to the stables and brought out Peggy, who whinnied with delight at her approach.

Peggy was a small and very strong mare that Francis had given her, a brown mare with a most human expression, for she could look wicked and evil at the approach of Jennifer and most affectionate and engaging when Judith was near.

As she turned the corner at the bottom of the hill, leaving the house and the village behind her, her spirits rose with every clatter of Peggy's hoofs. She had told Francis that she would be a night away in Watendlath; but now she thought that it would be very pleasant were she to extend the one night into two. She wished to wipe Uldale and everyone in it out of her mind, yes, even Francis.

For two days she would not be the woman of Uldale, but someone quite different – the woman of Watendlath.

As her spirits rose she was like a girl of twenty instead of a woman of almost forty. Peggy, who was also, by mares' standard, a middle-aged female, became a very conscienceless child, pricking up her ears at sounds of birds and rustlings in the trees, although she knew that they meant nothing at all, and striking the stones of the road with an especially youthful gaiety because this piece of freedom was quite unexpected and the thing that most of all she enjoyed.

Judith was once more reminded with especial clearness of that evening when she had climbed out of window and ridden to Tom Gauntry's. It seemed only yesterday, and she remembered how lively she had been, swearing in good strong Cumberland at the men in the road. It was as though nothing of any importance had occurred in her life between that ride and this, except Georges. And yet she was middle-aged, riding off like a girl. Something very ridiculous about that, but then she often found herself ridiculous! Women rode on horseback very much less than they had done when she was a child. They went now sedately in chaises or barouches; it was quite a common thing now to go to Edinburgh or even to London, whereas in her girlhood it had been quite an adventure.

And how formal and careful in these days the women of her age were! Mrs Osmaston of Troutbeck (very far from sedate her old mother-in-law had been!), Mrs Worcester from Threlkeld, Alice Sandon of Keswick and Mary Robertson of St John's in the Vale, Mrs Southey, Mrs Coleridge – all stout, careful, sedate women who would never dream of riding on horseback from Uldale to Watendlath!

The matter with her, Judith, was that she was a trifle vulgar and common. It had always been so, always divided her from people. She had it, she supposed, from her mother. How enchanting it would be to see her mother appear suddenly now out from the hedge, with her hair about her face, her gay ragged clothes, her wild behaviour!

'I am your daughter,' Judith would say, jumping off Peggy, and then they would sit down in the hedge together and talk about everything. Judith would show her the silver chain that Francis had sent her; she always wore this under her clothes.

'Come away with me,' her mother would say. And away at once they would go for ever! No question of a real escape then!

She had never been a proper lady; even Francis, she suspected, found it so. That was why she had been so easily friends with people like Georges and old Tom Gauntry, Emma Furze, Charlie Watson, who were not ladies and gentlemen either. If only she had looked a little different! – here Judith, in spite of herself, sighed. To be so small, to have such unimportant features – and now she was a little stouter and her hair had lost some of its lustre.

She could not understand how Warren Forster could be in love with her! Nobody had ever been in love with her for her looks; Georges had only come to love her through propinquity. But that was her greatest triumph, the triumph of her life!

But to return to the vulgarity of her nature, that was the reason, no doubt, of her struggle with Jennifer. Jennifer detested anyone who was not a lady. She had hoped that Judith was a lady, and then, when she found that she was not ...

Well, Judith could not help it. She was not to worry her head on this beautiful morning about Jennifer. She bore Jennifer no kind of malice – only why was she, Judith, in that house at all? Some part of her was always dragging her back into Herries affairs. She did not want to go back. How splendid it would be if she could stay in Watendlath for ever – then her real life would begin!

She would not go through the town, but took the bridle-path at the back of it, along the lanes under Skiddaw until at last she joined the path that led up to the stream above Lodore.

Here at a clearing between the trees she was compelled to stop Peggy and watch, for a moment, the storm that struck the Lake. It had been, when she left Uldale, a perfect October morning, without one cloud to mar the pale delicate blue. But, with the dramatic splendour that makes these skies the most wonderful in the world, a rolling black cloud, like a great funnel of smoke, had rushed over from the sea, pouring over Cat Bells and Robinson like the issue of a conflagration. The Lake was yet blue, the hills still gold with their burnished bracken. But this cloud hurried with the gait of a drunken man. It had been a funnel of smoke, but now, even as Judith watched, it swung outwards as that same drunken man might wave his cloak in a gesture of defiance. Then it spread with ferocity, eating up the sky, frothing at its edge in spumes of grey vapour, its black heart catching a purple light, the stain of blackberries.

It ate the sun. The Lake shivered and fell into a trembling agitation of tones and circles; the hills, that had been so bright, raised their heads; they seemed before Judith's eyes to increase their stature, and shadowed gulfs of purple rent their sides. Around her still the bracken was gold, the sun beat upon her face. Then with a quick whirr of wind the raindrops fell. The woods sighed. Where, only a moment before, there had been gentle stillness, there was now a sibilation like the whisper of a thousand gossips.

Soon the rain was falling as though a huge bowl had been

opened over her head, but already, above Robinson, a thin line
of gold cut the black wedge; light, mysterious and lonely, fell
on one of the small islands and lit it with an unearthly glow. The
black cloud began to break.

This moment's storm seemed to mark her passage from one
world into another. As she moved on up to the road above
Lodore, she felt that all her other life was closed to her, and she
was so happy that it was absurd to think that she had ever been
otherwise.

It seemed a moment later that she was in the Ritsons' kitchen.
What a welcome she had! She had been to Watendlath three
times in the last two years, but only for very short visits. She had
not slept a night there, and, on one occasion, Francis had been
with her. Now she *was* to sleep a night there, maybe two, and
she was quite alone. With all Cumbrians, when, after long years,
much silent watchfulness and infinite caution, they decide that
you may be trusted, the fidelity and affection is all the more
fervent because of the earlier testing. But Judith was quite
unique in the lives of the people of Watendlath. Her appearance,
her history, her marriage with its extraordinary end, her long
years with the 'Grand Folk' down South, her character with its
odd mixture of fiery temper and great patience, of humour and
seriousness, of youth and old wisdom, half a lady, half anything
but a lady, her character honoured them by being both so
strange and yet so ordinary. In a way they took her quite for
granted now after all those years with them, but in another way
they never took her for granted. They were never sure what she
would do next. And, in addition to all these things, most of them
loved her (there are always grumblers everywhere who do not
love anybody) because she made them laugh, because she washed
dishes and scrubbed floors, because she was interested in everybody and everything, because she could talk the broadest
Cumberland and often did, because she knew as much about
sheep as anyone, because she could lose her temper with a man
like any good woman, because her rascal of a husband (they had
always hated Georges) neglected her, because she continued to be
fond of him long after he was dead, because she had no pride
and someone in one class was the sàme to her as someone in
another, because she was shocked at nothing that they did,
whether they were dirty, mean, lecherous, drunken, cruel,
spiteful (and at times as with all other of God's creatures they
were one or another of these things), because she was a plain-
looking little woman but also unusual, so that you always looked

at her twice – but chiefly they loved her because they trusted her, which, with a Cumbrian, is first and last the principal thing. She kept her word; her heart was warm; she was not 'stuck on herself'.

Old Man Ritson had died two years back, his daughter-in-law last year; now Tom Ritson and Alice shared the farm. Tom had married a girl from Cockermouth, a simple little woman who was a good cook, and Alice had married young Roger Perry of Thunder, who was so thick through, broad across and short of leg, that he resembled the small stone wall above the Tarn. He had a round red freckled face and was a very silent man. However, he liked Tom Ritson, loved Alice, had three small boys who rolled about the kitchen floor like little ninepins and was excellent with cattle and sheep. The Ritsons were now a very happy household.

They all rushed at Judith, even the three small Perry boys, who had not the least notion as to who she was, but, like puppies, felt that she was part of a good and friendly world. Alice was perhaps the best pleased of them all. She had an almost reverential love for Judith. Although now a quiet pale-faced woman who went about her work with little comment, she saw further into character than did the others. She understood a little of what Judith's feeling for Georges had been; he had not been for her merely the foreign rogue and rascal that the others had thought him.

As Judith sat down beside the huge open fireplace, realizing with deep pleasure that all the busy life of the kitchen was going on around her just as though she were not there, the men stumping in and out, the women in their clogs clattering about, baking, working at the butter, going after the chickens, shooing geese out of the doorway, looking into the sunny yard to see whether the men were coming for their dinner, Alice Perry quietly watched her. She was anxious for her, thinking of what none of the others would consider – for Judith had not slept the night here since the night of her husband's death; more than that, she had never since then entered that room. Alice knew that now, this time, she would enter it.

Then, just as the men came clattering across the yard, hungry and thirsty, Charlie Watson rode in on his horse.

'It's Charlie!' Alice cried. 'Charlie Watson!'

Judith ran to the door and then out to meet him. He jumped off his horse and stood there, his legs spread, his mouth twisted in that strange, shy, almost angry smile so peculiarly his. It was as though he said: 'Well, it's a foolish thing to feel this pleasure and one is an idiot to set one's affections on anything but a sheep – still, I can't help myself.'

It was a year and a half since she had last seen him. He had stoutened, but otherwise was little changed from the man she had met on the road from Rosthwaite seventeen years ago. His skin was as clear, his teeth as white, his colour as ruddy, his body as strong – and his tongue as silent.

'Aye. 'Tis good to see ye. Lookin' fine.'

Then they walked into the kitchen together.

While they were all eating. Charlie sitting among the farm-hands and with one small Perry on his broad knee, she watched him with exceeding pleasure. She knew from all that she had heard in the last year that he was growing to be a very important person, not only in that neighbourhood but beyond, as far as Ravenglass on one side and Mardale on the other. One thing for which he was becoming famous was his fighting the cause of the farmers against the cattle-dealers. In those days, when there were no railways and few newspapers, cattle-dealers did much as they pleased, naming their own prices and seeing that they got what they demanded.

He was already beginning to buy cattle himself at fair prices, and sending them to Liverpool. At present only in a small way; it was, later on, to become a famous thing. Then he was a great arbitrator in all local disputes. His scrupulous fairness, his even-ness of judgement, made him ideal for the settling of boundaries, squabbles about sheep and cattle, even domestic troubles. He was himself growing wealthy, but lived always in the simplest fashion on his farm. Although he was older now he was still a great wrestler and player at any and every game. She had heard also that he refused to marry, laughing at every suggestion. Many liked him but he had no intimates; he seemed to prefer to be alone. He liked her, she knew, but she could not flatter herself that she knew him. She was even at times afraid of him.

But now as she sat there watching the October afternoon fall behind the kitchen windows, hearing all the sounds that she loved, sheep slipping like a flock of anxious old women up the path, water being drawn from the well, the soft crooning song of little Mrs Perry as she rolled the dough on the long kitchen table, the screeching of the turkeys on the field above the farm, her own fear gathered about her. Because she knew that she was soon to do that of which she was most in the world afraid. The first time, after coming up from the South, that she had ridden over, she had intended to force her will, but Francis had been with her and that had been her excuse. The second time Alice Perry had been sick, and that, she told herself, had been her excuse. But today there was nothing to prevent her.

Her pale face grew weary and strained. Her hands were clenched on her lap. She answered Mrs Perry's chatter without an idea of what she was saying.

Then she nodded her head as though something spoke to her, commanding, and she submitted. She got up and went out into the yard. Watson stood there speaking to Perry. She nodded to him, and he came across to her.

'Charlie, will you come with me?'

He seemed to know at once what she meant and walked off with her without another word.

The distance was nothing, but at the door she hesitated.

'I have never been inside – since it happened.'

Gently he put his hand through her arm.

'Come in,' he said.

She felt as though she were leaving everything living behind her. The air was suffused with a purple dusk, and she turned back to see the Tarn one blaze of fierce white light. The hills seemed gigantic. She heard, exactly as though she were leaving them all for ever, all the sounds of life, the animals, the human voices, the running water; then they went in together.

The room that had once been her sitting-room was used now for lumber, and one end of it was piled with sacks. An old kitchen table, rickety on three legs, was in the middle of the room and on it stood a large swinging mirror whose glass was cracked. The glass reflected the staircase. Some hens were rooting about on the floor. The place was dusky, but everything was as clear to her as though flooded with sunlight. And everything had happened yesterday, that night, only a few hours ago.

'Old Mr Stane stood there in front of the fire. Suddenly Georges went up, as close as to touch him, and cried out: "I killed your son! I hated him! I killed him, I tell you, and you can do what you like." Then he went up the staircase and the old man ran after him and caught him and threw him down. Then he ran down the stairs again and went out. I saw that Georges was dying. There was nothing to be done – nothing at all. But before he died he caught my hand and he told me he loved me. He died at once. There was nothing I could do. No one could have helped. It was too late.'

'Aye,' said Charlie. 'It must have been terrible for you.'

She began to cry, hiding her head in his coat, holding to him, and he put his arm round her. He stood looking over her into the cracked mirror.

At last she whispered, so faintly that he could scarcely hear her: 'This is my home . . . I shall never have any other.'

She cried on, then went and sat upon the stairs, looking all round at everything, taking every piece of it into her so that she need never fear to come again. And he stood gazing at her and knowing that she had altogether forgotten him.

They stayed so long without moving that the hens grew bold and scratched in the dirt at their very feet.

GHOSTLY IDYLL

BUT, AS EVERYONE knows, just when Fate seems to have a fine bouncing climax in his hand he shakes his head, changes his mind (which is not nearly so settled a one as people seem to think) and puts the climax back into his pocket again.

It was so with Judith now. She came back from her two nights in Watendlath happier than she had been for many a year. She had slept in her old room again. Whether she had truly slept or no she could not say, but, without either sentiment or nonsense, it had seemed to her that Georges kept her company. Therefore, she returned to Uldale in a state of great happiness. She settled down into all the Uldale affairs again as though she were for a moment pitching her tent there. Very soon she would be back at Watendlath. Nothing should keep her. But everything kept her. It was to be months, and then even years, before she saw Watendlath once more. Members of the Herries family never escape so easily as that.

Her time now at Uldale was difficult, and it was the difficulties that kept her. Feeling that she must stay, she did not dare go even for an hour to Watendlath lest it should keep her for ever and her duty be broken. The first difficulty was Jennifer. Strange! Can one be so secret a woman without being secret at all ? For although Jennifer had now her mysterious preoccupation that caused her to twist her brows and bite her thumb, yet she was not really secret. She was wondering, Judith knew, whether to go further with Fernyhirst.

Judith suspected that Jennifer was moved, as a woman stirred by a man, for the first time in her life; that she was as uncomfortable, bewildered and disturbed as a child wakened up from a deep sleep by sunlight. She was finding one discomfort after another press in upon her. Always before she had been able to deal with discomfort. Now she could not. She had told Judith to depart, but she had not departed. She had tried to make Francis a convenient figure in her life and nothing more, but of late he had begun to frighten her. She had told Fernyhirst to cease to make love to her, and he had not ceased. She had told herself to be indifferent to him, but she was not indifferent. Even with Mrs Ponder she was beginning to be uncomfortable, for Mrs Ponder now was often insolent. Even with her children she was not comfortable, for they were growing and insisted on having lives and personalities of their own.

Because of all these unsettled discomforts Jennifer was at last beginning to live. Her eyes were no longer half closed. She was often alert, as though she were listening for some sound.

One thing for which she was listening was the arrival of Will and Christabel at Westaways; but the months passed, one year closed and another year opened. Still they did not come.

Warren Forster, who was often at Uldale, although Jennifer disliked him and showed it, said that This, That and the Other prevented them ... They would come ... Surely they would come ... A pity ... He had endeavoured to persuade Will to alter his mind. Westaways was not the house for him. But Will was obstinate. He did not know why he was so obstinate.

Francis, however, knew; Francis was an altered man. Biting, sarcastic, silent, even with men of his own mind, like Southey, he appeared to have lost all his sweetness.

'He's gone sour,' said Fernyhirst to Jennifer, and he stretched his broad chest and pinched his strong neck with a smile of satisfaction. It was a long business, this siege, but she was the handsomest woman in the country and it was a fine occupation for a dull country life. It could have but one end to it. He was an extremely patient man, as his training of horses and dogs (for which, in the North, he was famous) showed.

Worst of all, Francis had now shut himself away from Judith. If he spoke his mind to her he must speak of Fernyhirst, and that he was resolved not to do. He was now entirely alone, even as his grandfather and namesake had been before him. He was going the same road.

It was on a winter morning towards the close of '14 that family history took a stealthy step forward. Young John Herries, aged now seven, was the cause. He was a very typical Herries child, square and strong like his grandfather, rather sensitive, but with a more plentiful allowance of humour and less sentiment about his father than David had had about his.

In fact at this time he had no sentiment about either his father or his mother. His mother he quite honestly disliked. He knew that she did not care for him. He hated to be embraced by her. In his father he was more truly interested; but this was a bad period for anyone to be interested in Francis. John saw him as a thin, severe, august figure moving about the place giving orders. He admired his father, but was happier when his father was not present. For Dorothy, his sister, he had a feeling of mixed contempt and protection. She cried a great deal, and she clung to Mrs Ponder, whom he, John, without extenuation or limitation, detested. No, he thought very little of Dorothy.

His whole heart was given to Judith, and had been ever since she had gone to the Tarn with him to sail his boat. He was very tenacious of ideas and affections. He loved Judith because he trusted her, because she talked to him like a human being, because she did not mess him about with embraces, because she was always so clean and neat (he was already fastidious about these things), because she thought the things in which he was interested important, because she considered the things funny that he considered funny. He treated her as he would have treated another boy who was a friend of his (he had no boy friends). He never gave any sign that he was glad to see her. He would look at her, a little frown gathered between his eyebrows, and he would ask her opinion. When he was going to laugh, the laugh came first in his eyes, which would be twinkling with merriment while the rest of his face was quite grave. He liked to rub the flat of his hand up and down the side of his breeches. Another pleasure was to put on a sudden very deep bass voice which was supposed to be an imitation of Mrs Ponder's.

'Boney's coming to eat you!' he would say out of his boots. It was her favourite threat, but instead of fearing he would chuckle with laughter.

He would walk up to Judith with great gravity and say, with his chin sunk into his neck so as to bring out his deep voice better: 'Boney's coming to eat you!'

It was John on this winter morning who made history. Judith

had dressed and was ready for the day. She came out of her room on to the landing. On this landing the rooms of both Jennifer and Francis opened. Stairs led up to Mrs Ponder's sacred chamber and attics; stairs led down to the main hall. Standing there for a moment before she descended, Judith thought of all that she had to do. She looked what at that instant she was, a very competent housewife, with keys at her waist, a green apron, and a spotless lace cap on her head. She had much to do: there was Mrs Harper, there were the kitchen-maids, there was the dairy. Mrs Birket and some London friends of hers were coming to supper and cards ... She heard then, from a large ancient cupboard that had stood for many a day in a corner under the stairway, strange sniffs, and then – a most startling sneeze.

Opening the cupboard door she beheld an odd sight. Seated on the dusty floor was John, absorbed in the feeding of a large, and, it seemed, very greedy brown rabbit.

'Why, John—' she cried.

He jumped to his feet, catching the rabbit by its long ears. As always, in any situation, now or ever, he stood his ground, but he was very red in the face and his cheeks were marked with dust. The rabbit squirmed in terror.

'Oh, but, ma'am,' he said in his husky confidential voice, 'I was intending—'

She could see that he was really frightened. But why? She could not think that there was anything very terrible in feeding a rabbit ... But why a cupboard? Why this furtive secrecy? She asked him. He stepped out of the cupboard, holding the rabbit in his arms.

He dropped his voice so that it became even more husky.

'You see, ma'am, Mrs Ponder had forbidden me to keep it. Yesterday. You see,' he dropped his voice yet lower, 'she has an exceptional distaste for rabbits. She ordered Jim to have it killed, and so I have been hiding it in this cupboard—'

'But why did you not tell your father?'

'Why, ma'am, he says that I must do as Mrs Ponder orders. It is only,' he whispered, coming very near to her, 'for today. I have found a place in the field—' He broke off. She realized that he did not want her to know where the hiding-place was lest she should be inconvenienced by questions. She whispered back to him, smiling:

'My indulgence shall be given. I shall tell no one.'

Greatly relieved, he went back to the cupboard.

She remembered something in her room that she had forgotten, and, for a moment, was back there, opening and shutting a drawer. Before she had reached the door again she heard a clamour. A woman's voice, muffled as though she were endeavouring not to be overheard, but so passionate that it shook the air. Hastening out, she was horrified to see Mrs Ponder, her face all black eyebrow, hurry across the floor and, with a vindictive gesture, fling open the window and throw the rabbit out. John gave a cry, then stood there, his face twisted with anguish. Not seeing Judith, Mrs Ponder threw herself upon the boy and, in a convulsion of passion, dragged him by the hair towards the stairway. She moved so swiftly in her rage that she had knocked his knees against the lowest step before Judith could move. Then she was stopped by something else, for Francis had come out. Mrs Ponder heard him and stayed. She let John go, and he, as though driven by a sort of wild fury, uttering little sobs, his eyes staring, ran past them all down the stairs.

'What is this?' Francis asked.

Judith had once heard him described by one of the ladies of the neighbourhood as 'a pleasant gentlemanlike man'. He had, she thought, never deserved the description less than at this moment. To speak in the terms of the author of *The Italian*, he was 'cold fury nobly seething'. Mrs Ponder felt this, and for once in her courageous life was alarmed.

'Not at all, sir. Nothing, I mean. Master John has been disobedient.'

He moved towards her as though he would strike her. Judith remembered that she had once done the same. Mrs Ponder appeared to have that effect on her critics.

He drew up and, looking at her as though she should, were he magician enough, change into a rat at his feet, said:

'You will leave this house within the morning.'

And she, recovering some of her confidence, answered, as once before she had answered Judith:

'That is for my mistress to say, sir.'

It happened then (for this landing was as public a place as that generally chosen in the theatre for intimate confidences) that Jennifer came from her room, looking very lovely in some loose garment of a rosy shade and a white cap with rosy ribbons covering her dark hair.

'Well, Ponder—' she said, and, seeing Francis and Judith, stopped.

'This woman,' Francis said, 'will leave the house today.'

Judith then saw Mrs Ponder give Jennifer a very strange look. Jennifer said: 'Why, what has she been doing?'

'She has been in a bestial temper and has dragged John by the hair.'

Mrs Ponder folded her arms as much as to say: 'You have not the smallest chance of moving me.'

'And what has John been doing?' Jennifer asked.

'If you please, ma'am, he has been most disobedient. He had concealed a nasty filthy rabbit in the cupboard, and after my telling him that of all filthy animals and filled with diseases, and my doing all for the best, ma'am, as I always do—'

'She had thrown the rabbit,' Judith broke in, 'out of window and was beating John against the stair.'

It had been better, as usual, if she had not interfered.

Jennifer, looking only at Francis, said: 'Mrs Ponder was in the right if John disobeyed her.'

'I have said what is to be done,' Francis answered, his face cold with disgust. 'The woman goes today.'

'I shall do what I think right,' Jennifer answered.

They looked at one another, a strange long look. His unspoken words were: 'She has the command of you. You do not dare to let her go.'

But he would have no scramble before servants.

At the top of the stairs he said again: 'She goes today,' and went down.

Mrs Ponder began: 'I assure you, ma'am, I had no thought but for the best. I would always do my duty—'

But Jennifer returned without a word into her room.

This little scene, so swift and so impromptu, was to have a deep and lasting effect on all the persons concerned in it, but on the life of Judith most of all.

After it the house was as silent as a valley in the moon. The winter day was sharp and sunny. The hedge sparkled with crystal and the lawn was laced with silver frost. A very fat robin at the parlour window sang. He was the only live thing. Francis rode out. Jennifer stayed in her room.

Judith went about her work and felt very lonely. What would happen? Would Mrs Ponder go? Whatever happened she had for a long time to come lost Francis, who would now keep more within himself than ever, and John, whose look of terror and anguish as he ran down the stairs she would never forget. Meanwhile the rabbit lay, with its back broken, on the stones below . . .

While she was in the storeroom, marking in a book the jams, jellies and preserves while Mrs Harper, a small thin woman like an amiable radish, chattered along, she thought impatiently: 'I cannot endure this much longer. I can't stay in a house where nobody cares for me.' Although she was forty years of age she was as childish as that. But perhaps what she really meant was that she needed to be close to somebody, close in affection and sympathy. This house today was a prison.

So that when, an hour later, Warren Forster arrived on horseback, her reaction from that early morning scene was terrific. She had never before been so glad to see him. Had it not been for that early disturbance she would never have gone ·riding with him, and had she not gone riding with him everything in later Herries history would have been different.

As it was, she did not care. She was reckless that day, reckless through exasperation and a longing for someone who was not angry, was not hurt, was not deceitful.

Warren, his little figure so dapper on his large horse, was not angry nor hurt nor deceitful. He was enchanted to see Judith, who was kinder to him, more responsive to him, than she had ever been. The house was quite still. She looked around her and found nothing alive in it but the robin. The air was filled with distress and anger. So she gave the robin crumbs, took Peggy out of her stable and rode off with Warren.

Often, when afterwards she looked back upon this eventful day and tried to see how one step had so determinedly led to another, it seemed that it had all been planned. But it was not in reality so. Nothing was planned. They just rode into the cold and crystal air.

At first they talked lightly of general things: of how Napoleon had tumbled down at last; of the quarrels among the Allies at Vienna, and the clever man that Talleyrand was; that it looked as though France, Austria and England would soon be fighting Russia and Prussia; of Napoleon's exile on Elba, and whether he would be there for the remainder of his days. They talked of those things, but they did not really care any more than their descendants would care for similar figures and intrigues. Napoleon, Talleyrand, the Czar of Russia were as remote from them as they rode along the Cumberland lanes as figures on a Chinese screen. They talked about affairs in England: of the King and the Regent, and the high prices and the uncertainty of everything and everybody; of how the world was changing as it had never changed before; of how interesting it was to live in a time

of transition, but also how unsettling; of how there were no
great figures in the world any more, no great literature, although
Mr Wordsworth's poems were pleasant and *Childe Harold* had
some fine writing (and was it true that Lord Byron was both so
beautiful *and* so wicked ? Judith asked), just as their descendants
afterwards would talk. Warren said that Will Herries said that
trade was going soon to recover and that everyone would be
wealthy again, that there would be wonderful new industries,
and that everyone would soon be living in towns because the
country was too dull.

'That would be a pity,' said Judith, looking about her at the
grey hills, their tops scattered with snow like sifted sugar. 'There
is nothing so beautiful as the country.'

'I think so also,' said Warren, looking at her. He was madly
in love with her that day. He was never to know why his love
for Judith was so much fiercer and more sharp than any other
emotion of his life, his greatest happiness and his greatest distress.

It had been so from the first moment of his seeing her at
Grosset, although that had not been a good occasion, for it had
been a stormy wet afternoon and she had been standing in the
hall rating a servant when he came in. Her voice had had a
sharp and dominating note in it, as though she were telling all
the world to go to Hades. The fire in the hall had been smoking,
there were dogs all about the place and one of Maria Rockage's
garments hanging up to dry. Judith had turned on him like a
cross, exasperated child and had been anything but gracious.
So perverse are men, and so beyond all rules is love, that he had
liked her the better for her mood. He preferred, perhaps,
women who were of the ruling kind. Then as he came to know
her more truly he found that, although she wished to dominate,
she could be led by her affections almost anywhere. She could
not indeed be led to love him, but would do almost anything for
him out of kindness.

He was a man of great courage, humour, and spirit, and his
pains, physical and other, had taught him patience. So he waited
for a long time, and at last he had his reward.

They had no plan of direction, but they rode through Keswick
(where Judith did a little shopping), then out, above the Lake,
to the Grange Bridge and on into Borrowdale.

'My father lived her,' Judith said, 'all his life. They could not
persuade him to move away. His house tumbled about his ears,
but he died in it and I was born in it. Here,' she waved her whip
to a broad bend of the little river, 'they drowned a witch. My

father went before them all and took her out of the water and
carried her away.'

The trees, bare above the chattering river, had a rosy edge
to them in the cold air. The top of Castle Crag played with little
wreaths of mist that crowned its head with a thin light, behind
which the black rocks gleamed. His hopes began to rise, he
knew not why. She was so friendly today. There seemed to be a
new current of intimacy running behind her words. He did not
know that he was indebted to a rabbit for his happiness.

'Would you have an objection,' she asked, 'if we paid a visit
to that old house of my father's where I was born? I have not
for a long while visited it. There is only a shepherd there. It
must be bare and deserted.'

They turned off the road and across the little bridge.

In the little graveyard near here Georges had been buried, and
here her father and mother had died.

The house that stood behind a little courtyard, defended by a
rough stone wall, seemed quite dead against the pale blue sky.
It had been, Warren thought, two houses; on the right it was of
some height, with latticed windows and a gabled roof. From this
attempt at grandeur it fell away to a low rough place that had
what seemed to be farm buildings attached to it.

But all was now in utter desolation. As they led their horses
in through the gate, shabby and broken, their feet struck the
rime from the stiffened grass. Birds rose in a whirl of agitation
from the thin stems of the bushes; a large white cat with malevo-
lent eyes slunk across the fast disappearing stones. Yet it was a
scene of great beauty. Rosthwaite Fell and Glaramara in farther
distance rose above the fields in purple grandeur. Water ran
in silver skeins down the rocks, and its tumbling was the only
sound.

Warren had got down from his horse to lead it in, and now,
standing in front of the old door, he cried, 'Is anyone here?'

There was no answer. They heard some animal stamping in a
byre close by. They pushed the door back and entered.

A musty odour of decay, straw, animal dung, met them, but
they persevered and, climbing the stair, found themselves in a
large room.

This, it appeared, was the place where the shepherd was at
home. A sort of couch made from boxes, and a decayed chair
that had great arms from which the stuffing protruded like a
disease, had been arranged with cushions and a blanket before
the wide stone fireplace. There were remains of a meal – a loaf,

some cheese, a plate – on the table that was the only other piece of furniture there.

Judith stood looking about her. 'It is strange,' she said. 'It is as though I had lived here. I know where everything was. There are the marks on the wall yet where that picture hung. It was a picture of an old man of Elizabeth's time. It hangs in the house at Uldale now. When I was a small child he terrified me. Here they would sit, my father and mother, before the fire, and upstairs they died and I was born.'

'Ugh! It's cold,' said Warren, shivering. 'We will not stay.'

'We will make a fire,' Judith said. 'Why not? Perhaps we will bring their ghosts back with the warmth.'

He was eager to do anything that she asked. They climbed the rickety stairs, rotten now with holes, creaking at every step, into the upper storey. The rooms here were pitifully small, but had a more human air, for one of them was plainly used for sleeping by the shepherd and his wife.

'It was here I was born.' Judith stared about her. 'Uncle Tom has often told me. How he was riding through the snow and heard an infant crying. He came up here with all his dogs, and in the bed my mother lay dead, in a cradle myself, and on a chair the old woman asleep with drink. And in the next room my father dead. So he picked me up in his arms and rode off with me home.'

Warren would have wished to come close to her and put his arm around her. She looked so small and by herself. But he did not dare. In the next room they found a pile of logs. They carried some down and made a great fire in the open hearth.

They sat down near to it, close together, warming their hands. The house was filled with her father and mother. Georges seemed there too. Only dead people. And for that reason, because she could not get at the dead and her heart was so moved that she longed to be kind to the living, almost without knowing that she did it, she laid her hand on Warren's knee, and then, when she felt it throb in response, she did not care to take the hand away again.

It was the first demonstration that, unurged, she had ever made to him; after a little he, as though he were moving mountains or the heavens would fall, laid his hand on hers.

'The fire makes me sleepy – the fire and the cold air.' She took off her riding hat and shook her red curls about her face. 'Warren,' she said, 'you look most solemn. Well, I should also feel solemn. Perhaps I do, but I have often noticed that whenever I feel most solemn I want to laugh.' She went on talking

as though she would cover the emotion that she knew he
was feeling. 'This house, deserted as it is, is better than Uldale
just now. Everyone is at odds there, and I am weary of trying to
make them better. I want a life of my own, Warren.'

'Come away with me, then,' he said.

'But that would be no life of my own. Since Uncle Tom
carried me out of this place in his arms I have been for ever
mixed with the lives of other people.'

'You can go to a nunnery,' he said laughing. He came a little
closer to her. The fire was burning with splendid energy and
roaring up the chimney.

'No. I am mixed with other people because I want to be. I
am not such a coxcomb as to suppose that I am inhuman. I am
inquisitive; I must know just what their lives are, and then I
must tell them what they ought to be. And yet I wish to be by
myself. I am only happy in one place, and that is Watendlath.'

'Are you not happy now?'

'I shall soon be warm, and then, when I am, I will tell you
whether I am happy.'

He put his arm around her; she did not move away. Why
should she if it pleased him? And he was alive. His heart was
beating against her breast. She was tired of anger and disappointment. Her heart ached to be kind.

She went on talking. At last he said (his hand was trembling
under hers):

'Judith, I love you every day more ... What shall be done
about it?'

In ordinary times she would have checked him, but now –
what did it matter? Was she not too particular in guarding herself? After all, was she so important? She had only in all her
life been important to one person, and that was to Georges,
and even to him for only a little of a time. How much she was
making of her life, considering herself this way and that way,
when in reality she was nothing. The mother of no one, the
lover of no one, scarcely the friend of anyone ... She was not
pitying herself – rather laughing at herself – with a little interest
and tenderness, because she knew herself better than she knew
anyone else.

So she let him hold her hand, then tenderly kiss her cheek, then
with great gentleness stroke her hair. The trembling of his body
touched her infinitely. Warren, who had faced so many things
with such courage, needed her now to help and befriend him.

'Oh, Warren!' She liked him close to her, the fire was very

pleasant, and figures, friendly figures, seemed to be in the room.
'It is so long since Georges died. I wish I could let him go in
peace. I shall not be a free woman until I can be friends with
everyone and yet be independent. Does it make you happy to be
sitting here, the two of us beside the fire ?'

'Desperately happy.'

'I want you to be happy.'

Why not ? Oh, in God's name why not ? There was Reuben's
bear, and the boy hanged on the gibbet, and Georges thrown
down the stair, and John's rabbit . . . Why not be kind while one
may ? So soon it is all over and nothing done, no kindness
remembered, no indulgence or charity. She thought, looking into
the fire and feeling perhaps the figures in the room gather more
closely about her, that she had never been charitable enough.
If this life had a purpose (which she gravely doubted), it was for
us to learn charity. A dangerous lesson, because the more
charitable we became the less free we became, and this desire
for freedom was becoming with her a passion. But the bear
danced in the Square, the rope swung on the gibbet, Georges
lay with his back broken, little Hartley Coleridge was a prisoner,
the rabbit was flung out of window, Warren had a bad leg, and
his wife had left him, and he loved *her*, poor man – although
why he loved her she couldn't conceive.

'I have never been happy until now,' he said, resting his head
on her lap. It seemed as though Georges, and the child that she
had never had, and maybe her mother and father whom she had
never seen, were all represented in that little damaged body
holding her as though she were its only hope.

She smiled, looking out above his head. Why should she be
so proud of herself ? Why should she not be kind ? Why should
she not give anything she could that would make him happy ?
She sighed, touched his cheek and then surrendered, giving him
all he asked—

WILL HERRIES DINES AT EASTWAYS

SHE KNEW EARLY in February that she was to have a child
For some time she had been happy, and, when she was certain
of this new circumstance, it was as though life beat up in her like
a released fountain.

For years after Georges' death there had been no life, then
slowly, slowly it had returned, always finding its source in
Watendlath. Now she was going really to live again, and all she
had to do was to fight for her freedom. That she had not yet
secured, but she would secure it now that the child had come
to help her.

She was beginning at last to understand something about life.
A woman is made for the love and protection of someone or
something else; this is the mainspring of her nature. But in
order to employ this love and protection at its fullest she must
be free of any bond that is simply a tyranny without love. All
the women around Judith at this time were so bound – it would
be generations before they would begin to be free – and Judith
would have been held in the same way had it not been for the
lives and natures of her father and mother whom she had never
seen or known. The whole history of being a Herries is learning
to be free.

She took things as they came. What was coming was her child.
What was also coming was Will Herries to Westaways. What
was also coming was some decisive crisis between Francis and
Jennifer. And it seemed that all these things were arriving together.

Since the ride to Borrowdale, Forster had seen Judith less
frequently. He was shy now and uncomfortable, for he had never
realized so sharply that Judith did not and could not love him
as at the moment of her surrender to him. He did not know that
she was to have a child, but he did know that, on that day, she
did not surrender to him but to her memories. She had begun
by wishing to be kind to him, and then had recalled the voice
and movements of a man who was dead. That hour had been
filled with ghosts.

So, although he loved her with a fire that really ate into the
very nerves of his small and ailing body, he came to visit her less
often and, when he was with her, saw her as someone always
just beyond reach.

She was resolved that he should not know about the child.
It did not seem to her that it would be Forster's child at all, so
filled had the ruined house been with others on that winter
afternoon.

Passionately she wished that it should be born in Watendlath,
in that room where Georges had died, but her practical mind
saw beyond the sentiment of that desire. That her child should
be born in Watendlath would involve too many others besides

herself – the Ritsons, Charlie Watson, Jennifer, Francis ... She must go away, and the child must be born with only herself for its guardian. She did not know at present where she would go or what she would do.

There were more immediate necessities, for, in this same month, on a gusty evening of February 1815, Will Herries with his wife, his son and a vast deal of impedimenta arrived at Westaways.

On the morning after his arrival Judith and Francis had a talk.

Francis looked a man twenty years more than his real age. He was so thin that his facial bones, always prominent in the Herries fashion, gave shadows and lines to his cheeks and eyes. His dark, thick hair emphasized his pallor. He looked a man with his back to the wall. Judith knew that, besides his trouble with Jennifer, he was in great distress about the condition of the people around him. The long years of the French wars had brought hunger and unhappiness everywhere; in the agricultural parts of Cumberland and Westmorland, where life was largely self-supporting and where the narrow and remote valleys led to seclusion, the pinch was not so severe as in many parts of England, but in the last twenty years industrial life was beginning to make itself felt, a new phenomenon, and towns like Kendal, Whitehaven, Cockermouth knew something that was close to starvation.

He, who had been always on the side of the people against privilege, of the rebel, the under-dog, found himself now a rich man with a fine house and a body of servants. He would like to give away all that he had, but he was not free – he had a wife, children, dependants. More than that he saw that this new growing England did not want his charity. He was held to be an aristocrat, and to be responsible for taxes, bread prices and all the other evils. Of his class he found no one in sympathy with his ideas. The squires and landholders round him thought that a sign of encouragement to a poor man meant that the poor man would rule, as he had been doing in France. The French example was before every eye. So Francis was once more alone, as all his life he had been. But he was not only alone – he was inarticulate. He had the great misfortune of seeing the justice of both sides. He, who had once proclaimed exultantly the fall of the Bastille, now feared any kind of revolution for his own country that he loved so dearly.

Until now there had been no riots in Cumberland, as in the

Midlands and the South, but only a week or two ago rioters
had burnt some ricks and stable buildings of Osmaston's, and
he himself had received several threatening anonymous letters.

If only, Judith thought, he would speak to me, say frankly
all that was in his mind, as he used to do. But it was years now
since he had been honest with her. Silence had grown upon him.
He was shut up within himself.

But now today he began frankly enough.

'Judith,' he said at once, 'I want you not to avoid Will and
Christabel because you are living here.'

That, unfortunately, produced a feeling of irritation in her –
all in a moment when she had intended to be so kind and understanding. She was suddenly tired of the lot of them – Francis,
Jennifer, Will, Christabel, all of them.

'What do you wish me to do, Francis ?'

'Why ... to go to Westaways ... when you wish ... as often
as you prefer.'

'And Jennifer ?'

He shook his head impatiently.

'What has that to do—' He broke off. 'I often think you hate
Jennifer.'

She sat down, suddenly weary.

'Oh no – hate ? – oh no, dear Francis. Perhaps I am a little
tired. What would you say, Francis, if I went away altogether ?'

'Went away!' His thin pale face was aghast. He put his hand
up to his forehead in a movement of bewilderment.

'Oh no! You to desert us! It would be shameful!'

Then she was angry. There was the implied right here that
had always irritated her in him, as though, if he decided that she
was necessary for him, why, that was reason enough for anything. It was not selfishness but rather an obstinate preoccupation with his own ideas.

Her anger gave her the opportunity to say some things that
had long been in her mind. She looked up at him, and part of
her thought, 'Oh, poor Francis, how weary and despondent
he looks!' But the other part thought, 'How insensitive he is!
I have endured this long enough.'

'Listen, Francis. I am going to say one or two things. One is
that I have been here for over five years and have been a failure.
Yes – don't protest – it's true. I have been a failure with you.
Do you know that you have not spoken out your heart to me for
three years ? No, not once. I have loved you all my life. You are
the only friend I have beside Emma and Reuben, whom I never

see nor hear of, and one other. But of late you have shown me no friendship. You have never thought of me at all, never inquired how I did nor how things went with me. You have been filled with your own troubles. I have been the housekeeper here. Good enough.

'Then I have failed because Jennifer hates me. Oh yes, she does! When I first came she was too languid to hate anyone. But now she is not languid any more and is perfectly capable of hatred. Do you know that when I had been here a year or so I discovered Mrs Ponder searching my drawer for my private letters? No, you did not know. But I begged Jennifer that Mrs Ponder should depart. Mrs Ponder did not depart. Later, *you* ordered that Mrs Ponder should depart – but Mrs Ponder is still here. I have not failed with the children – John loves me, I know, but even that has been an added aggravation to Jennifer. Yes, although for five years Jennifer and Mrs Ponder have done all that could be done to make me miserable (and I am not happy, you know, when people near me dislike me), I have stayed because I love you and I love your children. Or no – maybe there is too much sentiment in that. If I am strictly truthful, I have stayed in part because I like to make people do as I wish. I have stayed even because Jennifer has wished me to go. I have stayed, perhaps, because I would not be defeated by a fat snake like Mrs Ponder.

'But you, dear Francis, have never given these things one thought. You have not asked yourself whether I were lonely or unhappy. In fact, I am almost frantic for my freedom. There is a place but a few miles from here where I could be happy for ever. But, although it is so nearby, I do not seem to be able to reach it. My father, by all that I hear, was the same. But he was not a complacent female as I am.'

She smiled up at him then, feeling quite friendly again now that she had said her mind.

But he, in a voice of horrified disgust, said:

'Mrs Ponder searched your private papers. You told Jennifer of it and yet Mrs Ponder stayed?'

'Well, but *you* told Jennifer about the rabbit, and yet Mrs Ponder stayed.'

She wanted then to rise and throw her arms around his neck, so terribly unhappy did he look.

'You are right,' he said at last. 'Dreadfully right. I have been most fearfully to blame.'

Then, of course, she repented of having said anything. She

did not want to add to his distresses. What she *did* want, how-ever, was to be free of them all and to have her life to herself!

She went on quietly: 'You see, Francis, I am the only one in this house who is friendly with Will and Christabel. What complications will come now from my being here! I cannot abandon Christabel, who was so good to me in London. And of course I cannot abandon you! I think it shameful of Will to have come here, and so I shall tell him, but I shall be a shuttle-cock between the two houses. I am nearly forty-one years of age, and that is too old for a shuttlecock!'

'You say you cannot abandon Christabel and you cannot abandon myself – but a moment ago you were implying that you wished to be free of all of us!'

'And so I do.' She shrugged her shoulders. 'And so I will. I am for ever promising myself. Tomorrow – the day following . . .'

She had risen and, instinctively, they came together. He drew her to him and they exchanged a long embrace, the first of real intimacy for years.

'Judith,' he whispered, stroking her cheek, 'do not leave me, I beg you. I beg you. I am unhappy. No one understands—'

She thought of the child alive within her, and then she was so happy that she thought humorously, 'Was ever a woman in so many complications? But this is living – every moment has excitement.' At that instant she was so much a child that she could have sat down at the spinet and strummed any discordant noise. For she loved Francis to love her. Never mind if she could not be free just yet. Time for that! She *loved* Francis to love her. He had not for so long!

'Oh, Francis, I love you!' she murmured. What would he say if he knew that she was to have a child, she who was, he thought, so faithful to Georges' memory? Well, so she was. But Georges would be glad for her to have a child. Then she could not have Francis back again without at once wanting to manage him. She drew him down on to the sofa beside her, holding his hand. She wanted at once, without delay, to make him happy! Somehow to make him happy! Her eyes were so glowing with life and eager-ness and vitality that she did not seem like a small, round, middle-aged female in a grey spencer, but rather she was the daughter of a gipsy, telling fortunes.

She held his hand lightly.

'Now listen, Francis. Here is what you must do—'

And at that moment Jennifer came in.

They were both silenced. They had nothing whatever to say. Jennifer, brilliantly attired, stood there and looked at them. She was dressed for going out.

Francis thought, 'She is going to meet Fernyhirst' and was at once miserable.

Judith thought, 'I really hate this woman at last.' But did she? There was something *ignorant* about Jennifer, as though with all her beauty, her husband, admirers, children and the rest, she had never learnt anything about life at all. Just as you pity a selfish, wilful child because of the trouble that is in store for it, so Judith pitied Jennifer. And where you pity you cannot hate.

She was dressed in a crimson spencer with long sleeves that she wore open. It was lined with white fur. Over it she had a delicate Cashmere shawl and under it a long, tight-fitting dress of grey. On her head was a tiny crimson bonnet, close-fitting to the head, decorated with an upright ostrich feather. Her low boots, ankle high, showed the beautiful elegance of her little feet.

Remarkably, at this critical moment – for it was the only one at which the three of them together discussed the Westaways situation – scarcely a word was said.

Jennifer, looking at Judith as a bird of Paradise might look at a sparrow, said:

'So I hear that Will has arrived at Westaways. You know, Judith, that your visits there will inconvenience us in no way whatever. Pray visit there when you feel inclined.'

Judith got up and, simply because she knew that it would annoy Jennifer, rested her hand on Francis' shoulder.

'Thank you, Jennifer,'

Mrs Ponder was in the doorway. 'Fred is there with the carriage, ma'am,' she said. She gave her two enemies, Francis and Judith, a dark look. Yes, she had stayed there although they had told her to go. And she would stay so long as she pleased.

Jennifer, her head high, her ostrich feather nodding, swung her way out.

When the door had closed, Francis said: 'Judith, do you think? . . .' Then he stopped.

'And now,' said Judith, pointing to the sofa, 'I will tell you what you must do, Francis—'

The first occasion on which Judith dined at Westaways was on a wild, stormy afternoon in March. She was generously allowed the closed barouche by Jennifer, who was for ever making attempts to suggest that Judith was a sort of poor relation. (And indeed was she not just that in reality ?)

'Dear Judith, I pray that you may have an entertaining evening. Do not encourage Christabel to call on us here.'

'I am sure that she will not wish to,' said Judith.

Jennifer looked at her closely. Was she beginning to suspect the child ? Then Jennifer was clouded by a glance of apprehension. She looked back to the stairs as though to be sure that no one was there.

'Judith,' she said. 'If they talk scandal of me at Westaways – as of course they will – even though you dislike me, well, I am Francis' wife.'

'Scandal ?' said Judith. 'What scandal ?'

'There is always scandal in a country neighbourhood.' She looked most beautiful in the candlelight. Her dark ringlets gleamed on the soft orange texture of her Cashmere shawl.

Judith smiled, compelled by that beauty to which she was always surrendering wherever she saw it.

'How little even now you know me,' she said.

But as she climbed into the dark carriage she stubbed her shoe against the step. In the dark she nodded to herself. 'I cannot *endure* these people!' It was as though her mother, puzzled and bewildered at Herries fifty years earlier, had spoken.

But it was a most interesting evening. Judith stepped, in a moment, back into her old place. There was James, son of Pomfret and Rose, great-grandson of old Pomfret, who had built the house; he was a short, stubborn-looking fellow of thirty-six, very silent, and, everybody said, waiting for his father to die that he might succeed to the baronetcy. There was Montague Cards, in whose London rooms the famous arbitration had once taken place. He was now forty-eight, looked as though his cheeks were painted and wore most affected clothing. He spent as much of his time as possible in staying with relations free of charge. He planned to remain at Westaways longer than Will had any idea of. Carey Rockage, now sixty, was a splendid old fellow, wearing loose garments that seemed to have been made for someone else, most absent-minded but always finding something interesting and amusing to entertain himself with. Maria was now an old woman of sixty-one and looked like a haystack on wheels. She moved with a kind of rolling motion. She had peculiar habits; she would whistle to herself or, at table, make little pellets of bread and flick them about. She was so untidy that no one of her garments seemed to belong to any other. Her hair was white and she wore a lace cap, none too clean and set rakishly at an angle. For Judith, who had such a passion for cleanliness, her untidiness was an agony. She found herself, before she had been at Westaways ten minutes, running after Maria, picking up her handkerchief, fastening a button, tying a ribbon.

Will Herries was not greatly changed, save that he was a wealthy man now of forty-five, and so had swollen in importance. Not physically swollen; he was as thin and stiff as a water-pipe, and he spoke like Moses delivering the Ten Commandments to the people of Israel. Christabel also was now a middle-aged woman, dressed better than of old, and was not so deeply terrified of functions and ceremonies.

She was, however, one of those people whose anticipation of catastrophe spoils every occasion. And expectation of disaster attracts it as surely as mountains attract rain.

Walter was now their only remaining child, his sister having died some years previously of smallpox.

Walter was terrific. He was, Judith thought, the largest young man she had ever seen. Horselike as all the Herries were one way or another, he resembled a charger for whom no general, however famous, could ever be grand enough. He had all the splendour of bone and muscle united to a supreme self-confidence and determination. He was the absolute symbol of Herries, blood, bone, and soul, all mingled together, engaged upon the same pursuit. He was neither dour nor aloof like his father. He laughed often, and his laughter, Judith thought, must make the inner confines of Borrowdale quake. His chest was the broadest, his legs the thickest, his neck the strongest, his arms the most muscular that she had ever seen. Set in all this splendour were very small eyes that had a strange meditative stare, even when he was most jolly. Later in the evening she was to perceive how instantly he could change from pleasure to business. She decided that he would become the most important of all the Herries family, and she was correct in her prophecy.

Already he dominated everyone there. He wore a huge stock, a vast purple coat and immense trousers, just then coming into fashion. His hair was a dark curly brown, and he had a snuffbox as big almost as a band-box.

He ordered the servants, arranged the details of the party as though he were master of the house. Two years previously he had married Agnes Bailey, daughter of a rich City merchant. She was not present this evening because she was expecting very shortly her first child. So Walter, roaring and laughing, informed Judith, adding that if the child were not a boy he would let his wife know of it! She was a little bit of a woman, he informed Judith, whom he could slip easily into his pocket. He spoke of her with all the pride that the Herries feel for any woman who had been wise enough to marry one of them. As always, when she was with anyone of great height, she was embarrassed by her own smallness. But she soon recovered. He at once chaffed her.

'Why, you are the pocket Venus!' he cried.

'Oh, Walter!' cried Christabel. 'Pray, pray—'

But Judith laughed.

'How much brain is there in all that muscle, Cousin Walter? I've seen bullocks at a fair—'

He thought that immensely good. She found that he laughed at almost everything. She rather liked him. After the restraints of Uldale this was rather refreshing. She discovered very shortly that it was he who had persuaded his father to come to West-aways. He was all for carrying on the family feud, partly from rancour and scorn of Francis, partly from pride and physical good health. And he had never been in Cumberland before, although it was his home. Of course it was his home. His grand-father had been the best fighter in the district, and his father had been born here. That was enough for him. She saw that he was determined to get Uldale into his hands before he had done.

She was happy at once when she saw how greatly pleased Christabel and Maria were to see her. Then speedily also the light of battle was in her eye. For she perceived that they were all there, that everything was done, to impress her. She was the spy from the enemy camp, and the intention was that she should return and tell them all at Uldale that they had no chance, that they had better surrender at once, pack up and go. Well, she was going to tell them nothing of the kind. She was fond of Christabel, but she loved Francis. Poor Francis, growing old now, with nothing to show for life at all save his children, who did not know him. Yes, she was on his side, and so she would let that great hulking elephant of a Walter know before the evening was over.

The house she had never been inside before. She knew well its charming exterior; she had often walked and ridden past it, its roof covered with rosy tiles, the beautiful wrought ironwork, the door with the fluted columns and the delicate fanlight.

Within it was by far grander than Uldale, with the pillared hall, and up the wide staircase to the grand saloon that had been decorated by old Westaway himself. The subject of the decorations was Paris awarding the apple, and there were three fine, plump, rosy goddesses. In this fine room, glittering and gleaming with the candlelight and the swinging splendours of the glass candelabra, they were all gathered. Soon they went down to dinner.

Judith was seated between Walter Herries and his father, who, his back erect, his thin neck raised like a hen's, should have commanded the assembly. He did not. Walter praised the food, guaranteed the liquor, chaffed old Maria, scolded and commanded the servants.

At the last moment Warren Forster slipped in and, with a nod and a smile to them all, took his place.

'You have nothing, I wager,' Walter said to her, 'like this at Uldale.'

Judith looked about her: a very grand room with a massive fireplace, the table piled with food, perfect organization.

'I prefer Uldale.'

'You prefer Uldale? But, come now, Cousin. I may call you Cousin? What can you prefer? There is no space at Uldale, no light—'

'No light! We have all the light in the world!'

'Well, well – so has a barn. I know what I know. You shall have your Uldale.'

She looked at him with great calmness.

'You have come here, Cousin Walter, to crow over Uldale. Well, you shall not do it for me. I am old enough to be your mother, Cousin Walter, and there are one or two things I shall teach you before we are done.'

He looked at her with admiration. He liked her. He had heard that this little woman had spirit. What was she? Born in a barnyard out of a gipsy? No matter. She had pluck.

'Is Jennifer as lovely as they say?'

'She is very lovely.'

'I would go a long way for a beautiful woman. But Francis, now – he is vexed, is he not, at our taking Westaways?'

'He has other things to think of.'

'Ha, ha! ... I warrant he has, and there will be more before long. Jennifer insulted my mother, you know ... in a public place too.'

'That is an old story – and there are two sides to it.'

'Not so old that I have forgot it. And you would smack my face if there were cause, Cousin Judith. By gad, I believe you would too.'

'Certainly,' said Judith gravely, 'if there were cause.'

'Well, I drink your health, Cousin. We are to be friends.'

'I am in the other camp,' she said, smiling at him.

'It will be all one camp one day,' he answered her.

She heard Will saying with great gravity:

'I have heard my father tell many a time how as a small boy he came to this house. It was your great-grandfather Pomfret, James, who had it then, you know. Yes, and he sat there with my poor grandmother – she died shortly, poor thing – and stared and stared. For it was a grand house to him. He had never seen the like of it. And there were all the things in the room that are here yet. I will show them to you afterwards, Maria. We had them in London and brought them up with us. Out of the parlour window the fountain with the bird that has been here from the beginning. The screen with the gold work on it, the clock with the sun and moon. We had them in our London house. You must have seen them often, Maria. But what frightened my father – he was only a small boy, you know – was his great aunt Maria, sitting there with a spaniel on her lap. He often told us children of it. She had a wig with flowers and a hoop as large as a tent, a black patch on her cheek, and her fingers covered with jewellery. She was born in the year of the battle of Naseby, you know. So here we are back to the battle of Naseby.'

Will, Judith thought, was quite human all of a sudden. He was so proud of being here, back in his rightful place. Yes, she understood him and sympathized with him. Then he looked at her, as though he would say: 'Here we are, you see, and we shall remain.' Then her cheeks flushed. So would Francis remain *and* his children. She would see to that while she had breath left in her body. (Odd that only an hour or two ago, in the carriage, she had wanted to be free of the lot of them! Now she was in the very middle of the battle, and glad to be!)

More and more food appeared. (They had not dinners like this at Uldale.) More and more wine was drunk. James began, in his stubborn determined way, to talk of the present discontents. He had nothing good to say of anyone – King, Regent, Parliament, Army – but the villains of every piece were the working classes. Oh! these working classes! What was it they wanted, the dirty dogs? Why were they *never* content? They complained of the price of food. Well, let them work harder and earn more. They said that their homes were not fit to live in! What did they expect? Palaces?

Nearly everyone joined in. At Manchester and at Liverpool there were disorders every day. Of course it would be right enough now that Napoleon was safe in Elba. But would it be? Someone said that we would be fighting Russia next ... Wars were endless. One led to another. And while there were so many wars, of course trade would be bad ... At the word 'trade' Will lifted up his sharp blue-tinted chin and told them all what he thought about Trade.

Money would be in the towns – Birmingham, Liverpool, Manchester ... This new machinery ... The country would be a dead place in another thirty years. Cotton? Had any of them thought about cotton? Well, he had. India and the East were all very well, but wise men were turning their attention to home products. Now that Napoleon was shut up and the Allies were in Vienna ... In another thirty years there would be no country in England, no *true* country.

Why, when his grandfather had come first to Keswick his father, as a little boy, had ridden into Borrowdale on horseback as though you were riding into China. His father had often told him. Why, nothing on wheels had ever been seen in Borrowdale a hundred years ago, and now he wouldn't be surprised but that one day they would be driving carriages with steam. He looked at them all grimly, just like an angry and emaciated Moses.

'They'd better look out,' he seemed to say, 'or they would have the surprise of their life!' For a brief moment he dominated all of them; even Walter disappeared.

Old Maria Rockage, on his other side, listened to him and thought what nonsense he was talking. She had drunk some wine – not her customary habit – and her head was a little fuddled. To tell the truth, she was homesick for Grosset. Oh yes, she knew that this was all fine, with the fountain in the garden, and the painting of the naked women upstairs and all the shining candles. Everything was very orderly, the servants moved most quietly. There was enough food to feed the village at Grosset for a week (and that when all the countryside was starving!), but she wasn't really comfortable here. She didn't care for that big shouting Walter, and Will wasn't kind to Christabel, and the large four-poster that enshrouded herself and Carey at night was not truly a *friendly* bed, and she missed her children; even though Carey the Younger *was* fond of doing nothing, she would rather have him than this hulk of a Walter, and Phyllis was a *sweet* child . . . She began to feel very melancholy indeed. A tear fell into the goose on her plate. Then she looked up and changed a smile with Judith.

She felt better. What a pity that Judith had ever left them! They had all been very happy together! And now she heard the strangest things about Jennifer. Judith surely was not happy there. But the child (for although Judith was over forty, Maria thought of her as a child) *looked* happy. She had grown stouter. What a sensible woman! Grosset had been in pieces ever since she had left them! And it was neither nice nor kind of Will to come here simply to triumph over Francis, all because years ago Christabel had slapped Jennifer's face. Not that she had ever liked Jennifer, beautiful though she was. And they said that Francis was most unhappy . . . It was not as though he were a boy any longer . . . He must be fifty-five or so, and had done nothing with his life, poor man . . . She piled up little pellets of bread beside her plate.

Behind the wall of talk and laughter they were moving on their secret ways. Will was stiff with triumph. This was a grand dinner. He would show brother Francis at Uldale . . . Christabel longed to have a real talk with Judith. She wanted that somehow, in one way or another, they should understand at Uldale that she was not their enemy . . . In her heart she would rejoice to have a reconciliation with Jennifer.

Walter was hot and thick and turbulent with the pride of life. He saw himself as a conqueror. Of what? Of whom? It did not matter. James had in his heart contempt for all these country bumpkins, the grand Walter included. The old-maidish bachelor with the painted cheeks was enjoying the food and the wine. Here was the place for him! He would stay . . . one month, two, three? Old Carey was thinking of a dog of his, Pluto, who was as game a dog . . .

Warren Forster, who had scarcely spoken, sat, his eyes secretly fixed on Judith. Judith, placed so demurely there, once in his arms while the logs crackled in the stone fireplace. Judith, the passion of his whole life . . .

And Judith herself began to wish to escape. She felt unwell, some great uneasiness at her heart. She *was* in the camp of the enemy! It was as though she could foretell in some secret way all the consequences that were to come out of this move into Westaways, a move made from vanity and vainglory. She had sympathized with Will, but now she felt that he was there only that he might snub Francis. And as for his son! He seemed to be more overbearing with every minute that passed, as the room grew more heated, the food more grossly devoured, the wine more carelessly drunk, the lights more brilliant. He seemed to grow and hang over her in a vast imposing shadow. He had drunk great quantities of wine, but it had not affected him. Will's speech was already clouded, poor old Carey was waving his glass with uncertain hands, Monty Cards was calling for a song in a shrill high tone, James scowled . . . It was time for the ladies to be gone.

They rose. Walter got up, bowed, then kissed her hand.

'Adieu, Cousin Judith!'

His purple coat with its high collar strained across his tremendous shoulders, his stock seemed scarcely to confine the muscles of his neck – but his eyes were very small. She looked up at him, glance to glance. What she would give for a few more inches! But his little eyes closed before hers. In a majestic procession the ladies left the room.

Upstairs, seated beneath the rosy goddesses, Christabel at once drew Judith aside. From where Judith sat, under the swinging glittering glass on the gilt sofa, she could look out through the curtains that were not yet drawn, to the Lake darkening now in the gathering dusk. Its bosom was shaken with trembling; its surface was crossed with paths of pale opalescent light, and one rosy shadow hung on to the green skirts of the hill. It moved Judith most strangely to see how the Lake was trembling; however, in another moment she was looking about the room and thinking how she would arrange it were it hers. That cabinet would be best in the corner and the large clock with the marble pillars . . .

'And so, Judith,' Christabel was saying in that hushed anxious voice of hers, while old Maria nodded her head, jumped awake and then fell off again, 'you must understand that I have no animosity. Bygones must be bygones.'

'No, *you* have no animosity,' said Judith, nodding her head and swinging her legs as well as she could in her long gown (for the sofa was a trifle high). 'Of course *you* have none, dear Christabel. But what of Will and Walter?'

'Oh! yes!' Christabel admitted, her brow wrinkling with anxiety. 'Should not the curtains be drawn? It is almost dark. Ah, here comes Wiggins with the tea – I am half afraid of Wiggins. We brought him from London. Monty found him for us!'

Judith looked at Wiggins, who was almost as mountainous as his master, Walter. Poor Christabel – to be crushed among all these huge men! But she would like to have the managing of Wiggins. He would be child's play beside Mrs Ponder.

'Yes, Wiggins. Here, if you please. You understand, Judith, that men look upon these things quite differently. Walter regards it as a sort of a game. He does indeed, and he is very chivalrous about any insult to myself . . . And Jennifer *was* rude to me, you know . . .'

'So long ago!' said Judith scornfully. (Yes, and the spinet would be better nearer the window. What a lovely pattern of flowers and leaves on its cover! And then you could have the sofa . . . Sofas were still rare and this was one of the finest Judith had ever seen.) What a lot of money Will must be making! Well, it was what he had always wanted . . .

'At least,' Christabel went on, 'you will not leave me, dear Judith. I must see you sometimes. I must indeed. It was my only comfort in coming here. You must not hate me because Jennifer does!'

'Hate you! Dear Christabel!' Touched as always by any appeal to her affection, she leaned forward and kissed Christabel's dry cheek. 'Alas, I hate nobody! Hatred is so difficult to sustain. Even Mrs Ponder—'

'Who is Mrs Ponder?'

'An odious female.'

'And Jennifer?' Christabel looked to see that Wiggins was gone and Maria fast asleep. 'They are saying very odd things about Jennifer, Judith.'

'What things?'

'Is there not a Captain Fernyhirst? And they say that Francis—'

'I suppose Walter brings you this gossip,' Judith broke in indignantly. 'Remember, Christabel, that I love Francis more than anyone in the world. I will not hear a word against him—'

'No, no,' Christabel cried, frightened of offending Judith. 'It is only that it is common talk—'

'There is always common talk,' said Judith. 'In every country place they talk.'

She was thinking: 'Well, there you are, now it has all begun. Christabel is different already, sniffing out things about Uldale. And soon Jennifer will be saying things about Christabel.' She saw Walter on a huge horse riding deliberately past Uldale and making rude gestures, mocking the smallness of the place and the bareness of the garden. Oh! it would be impossible! She had an impulse to rise there and then and run for her life.

Indeed, she did shortly run, but not before she had heard some astonishing news. The door burst open; all the men were there, Walter in front of them. They were shouting and crying out. Old Maria woke up, Christabel thought the house was on fire, Judith wondered whether Walter's wife upstairs was suddenly delivered of a child. But no! Walter was roaring out:

'What do you think? What do you think? Boney has escaped from Elba! Escaped from Elba, by God! He's in Paris, and the French are with him to a man! Esthwaite has looked in to tell us. There's news for you! Boney escaped from Elba! Whoop! Whoop! . . . What a fellow! By gad, I admire him! Escaped from Elba, by gad!'

They were all in a frantic excitement, even James, and Monty Cards was crying out like a woman:

'He'll be in London yet! We shall all be French before the year's out.'

Judith, standing by herself, beside the window, felt the news run inside her like wine. That marvellous fat little man, whose corpulent shadow had hung over them, almost all their lives as it now seemed, had done it again! Yes, it was wonderful. He was a wonder. She could see, looking through the haze of the candles, all Europe in a hurry and a scurry, hastening like ants, hither, thither, everywhere. Stiff and conceited Talleyrand, and the sentimental weak Russian, their own mountain of flesh, the Regent, the old mad King, all the bourses and the shops and the theatres, the country lanes, cottages, mountains, lakes – all suddenly quivering again under the shadow of that little indomitable monster!

The others in the room had for the moment forgotten her. They were all talking together; in the doorway Wiggins and another manservant stood listening.

Bonaparte free again! You could hear the cry from China to Peru! Well, if Napoleon could free himself so easily why should not she?

The news and a sudden glimpse of Warren Forster's anxious, pale face (even in the excitement he did not forget her) made her almost mad with eagerness to get away. Away! Anywhere . . . To have her child somewhere by herself. No Herries. No relations or duties or scandals. Napoleon had done it. She had as strong a will.

Moved by an irresistible impulse she was out of the room and had slipped down the stairs. They were not thinking of her. She felt as though she had the energy to escape down the road just as she was, and in a moment she would be in Paris! Well, why not ? Anything to escape. However, she found her bonnet and shawl, ran out into the garden, and then in the courtyard at the back discovered Fred. She told him that she wanted the carriage. At once! At once!

While she waited for him she smiled up at the stars that were beginning to break into the sky.

If Napoleon had done it she could! And it was as though the child in her womb laughed its approval.

JUDITH IN PARIS

THIS TIME JUDITH escaped some distance; she ran from Westaways to Paris.

In June the battle of Waterloo was fought and Napoleon's escape was concluded.

Judith told Francis and Jennifer that she would take a little holiday. She was going to stay with Emma Furze in London. Jennifer was kind to her and kissed her goodbye. Judith did not know whether she was aware of the increase in her figure or no. No one else seemed to notice anything. Francis was grave and reserved again. All he said was:

'It is not for long, Judith. Have you sufficient money ?'

'Yes, thank you . . . No, it is not for long,' she answered him. She did not know whether she were lying or no. It might be for ever.

But John made a scene. Quiet as he usually was, on this occasion he made a scene. He cried himself into being sick and scratched Mrs Ponder's cheek. Then, two hours after Judith's departure, he ran away. He was found on the road to Bassenthwaite in a hedge, fast asleep . . .

On a very hot summer afternoon, in the middle of the Café des Mille Colonnes, sat La Belle Limonadière, dressed in crimson velvet and covered with jewels, serenely looking down on her hundreds of clients, like an empress, but very accurate in the change that she gave to the waiters. Spread before her were dozens of portions of broken sugar, five or six pieces in each portion, arranged in little silver saucers like wine-funnel stands. This was the remnant of the respect for sugar induced by the period when Napoleon closed Europe against English commerce. There were at this moment no sugar basins in Paris.

La Belle Limonadière, although perhaps her best time was now over, was indeed a brilliant creature. A contemporary – a gentleman certainly to be trusted – describes her as having a complexion of Parian marble. He goes on (his letter is in the Herries' archives): 'Her black hair and eyes were in striking contrast with her complexion. The usual aids of colour to the cheeks were not forgotten, but quite what the French call *au naturel* – a word merely meaning something less artificial than the last stage of artifice. *La Belle* has an air and expression of great good nature; and, what most amused me, a most solemn attitude of correctest propriety. Nobody presumes to address her without previous formal presentation, and it is found impossible to give any coffee orders to her majesty except through the medium of a gentleman-in-waiting!'

To Judith and Emma, sitting almost under her nose, this brilliant, black-haired, crimson-clad creature was infinitely fascinating. They could not take their eyes off her! She reminded Judith a little of Jennifer, only that she was not so beautiful. She always afterwards seemed to Judith to be the symbol, the decorated figurehead of this strange Paris adventure – to have the colour, the audacity and also the sordidness and underground thunder of this fantastic Paris scene. During all that followed in these exciting weeks, La Belle Limonadière was marching just in front, the presiding deity of this affair.

On this especial afternoon she was very gracious to a noble-looking gentleman (plainly not a Frenchman) who sat with some friends near to her, eating an ice and smiling up at the queen's throne. This gentleman, someone confided to Emma, was no other than Mr Walter Scott, the famous poet. Judith looked at him with all her eyes, and loved him at once for his grand high forehead, his eyes beaming with kindness under their shaggy eyebrows, the courtesy of his mien. He was like a very noble sort of sheepdog. When he got up and, limping on his stick, passed down the hall, she felt as though all were indeed well with this strange world, which was neither so fantastic nor so threatening as she had thought it.

For although she was greatly enjoying it all she was also rather frightened. For one thing they had not very much money, she and Emma, for another she was not very well, she who had always been so strong and so healthy. And then she was taken with strange waves of homesickness, wondering whether Francis were in health, whether the meals at Uldale were served properly, whether John missed her and what the clouds were doing to Skiddaw.

However you cannot, as she was for ever discovering, both have your cake and eat it, and this was most truly a fascinating scene. Paris was now a hotch-potch of all the nations of the world. This splendid hall, mirrored all round, divided by fluted Corinthian pillars, made the company seem innumerably multiplied. Here were English officers, then Highlanders with their plumed bonnets, now Prussian hussars, and again Brunswickers in their sombre uniforms. The French ladies, in their walking dresses and in high-crowned, plume-covered bonnets and shawls, were attended by their beaux, who were as gay, lively and noisy as though there had been no revolutions, no devastating wars, and as though their country were not at the moment occupied by the triumphant foe.

But how dazzling this scene, thought Judith, and how unreal the figure of the strange crimson hostess, her figure, solemn, correct, almost austere, multiplied in all these mirrors, herself entrenched with peaches, sugar and nosegays of flowers!

Beneath all the gaiety and sparkle you felt that the ground trembled. The English were popular, but the Prussians were hated. She saw on every side of her the Prussian arrogance. She had heard that when Wellington had protested about some outrageous piece of conduct, Blücher had replied: 'Yes, but remember – the French were never in England.' The very fact that the French found it so difficult to submit to the domination of a people whom they had so long despised, caused those people to be more arrogant. In the cafés their behaviour made Judith, who, when the English were not in question, was, because of Georges, more French than the French, tremble with indignation. And the whole public life of the French, so that they seemed to be never at home but spent their whole time in the cafés, the theatres, or on the boulevards, made this trouble with the Prussians the more prominent.

But then, as she by this time thoroughly realized, the French themselves were scarcely, as yet, disciplined. They had not suffered a revolution in their country so long a while for nothing. The French boys in the street, for instance, were insolent beyond belief, and she and Emma were for ever encountering both men and women who seemed to them like dangerous animals just let loose from their cages.

She found evidence enough of it in the lodgings; they were in the rue Vivienne. They had two rooms in the apartment of Monsieur and Madame Dufresne. Little M. Dufresne, thin as a stick, with a funny black toupee and a tiny black moustache, had suffered some terror in his earlier years from which he seemed to find it impossible ever to escape. His chief pleasure was in animals, so that he had in his room a cockatoo, a monkey, three dogs, two cats and a tortoise. For animals he had, it would seem, a very special gift, but for human beings no gift at all. His wife, on the other hand, was a large brawny woman, whom Judith could well imagine knitting in front of the scaffold while the tumbrils rolled up. Her great muscular arms were always bared to the elbow and she had a deep bass voice like a man's. They were a pair who led their own lives – they interfered with neither Judith nor Emma in any way, but at night one could hear the thick, low rumble of Madame's voice through the wall; it seemed to threaten every sort of vengeance.

However, here they were in the Café des Mille Colonnes and enjoying every moment of it. For Emma, indeed, this stay in Paradise was simply heaven. She had her darling Judith to look after and care for, and there rolled all around her the very life that Fate should have designed for her. She was now a woman between fifty and sixty, handsomer than she had ever been, for her figure, tall and majestic, had thinned, and her grey hair, her sparkling eager eyes, her vitality attracted attention wherever she went.

She was more ready now to be spectator than actor, but the sight of almost any man stirred her blood and excited her curiosity. And had ever a city in the world's history been so grandly filled with splendid men as was Paris at this moment? Glorious men, and most especially the Highlanders, who, in their intriguing costume, simply had the French ladies at their feet!

She was always on the move, for ever seeing the sights. They went to the Opera, saw the King, a most benevolent-looking gentleman, the Emperor of Austria and the Duke of Wellington. They witnessed a ballet in which some of the performers were dressed as Highlanders, and heard the building ring with cries of '*Vivent les Ecossais!*' – a glorious moment. There were constant processions, and one morning they saw pass no less than thirty thousand Russian soldiers. They went to the Théâtre des

Variétés and saw 'Jean Bool' most amusingly caricatured. Best of all, perhaps, were their visits to the encampment of the English troops – the 95th Rifles, 52nd Light Infantry, and 71st Highlanders – in the Champs Elysées. This was one of the sights of Paris and immensely Emma enjoyed it. The world seemed only to exist to provide handsome military forms and fine ladies to gaze upon them.

She would, in fact, have known perfect happiness had it not been for a certain anxiety about Judith. Judith had been the one constant and unchanging devotion of her life. She would never have claimed for herself that she had a constant nature. She had not one herself, nor did she, any longer, expect constancy of others. She knew, she said, human nature too well.

But Judith was changed. You must expect it, of course. Judith was over forty and the child coming. It was no light matter to have your first child when you were over forty. But there was more in it than this. In the first place, Emma could not understand Judith's devotion to Georges. No, she certainly could not! It was true that Georges had never really liked her, but it was not that she was prejudiced. She could never have fallen in love with Georges herself; but one of the things that life taught one was that everyone must have, and be permitted to have, their own taste!

No, but Georges had not been good to Judith; he had been a thoroughly worthless, selfish fellow; and here she still was, after all these years, adoring him as though he had been a paragon!

But she was filled with contradictions. She adored Georges' memory, but some other man was father of her child. She had always seemed to Emma one of the most virtuous of women, possessing in fact a virtue that poor Emma herself could never hope to command. And yet she had apparently given herself to a man for whom she did not greatly care, simply from an impulse of kindness. Emma herself was kind, but she was also passionate, even now when she was nearing sixty. But Judith was passionate only in relation to Georges. And how ironical that she had offered all that love to Georges, who was never to give her a child, but that now, when she was almost past child-bearing, a chance moment with someone whom she did not love should accomplish everything! But life was like that. Emma herself could remember . . .

Beyond her nostalgia for Georges there was a deeper nostalgia, and this Emma could not understand at all. For it seemed from Judith's brief and broken confidences – Judith talked very little about herself even to Emma – that she thought that could she only get away to Watendlath, leave for ever all her Herries relations, and hide herself in the hills for the rest of her days, all would be well.

'Surely then,' cried Emma, 'in heaven's name, go! You are your own mistress!'

But that, it seemed, was exactly what Judith was not. She was for ever being dragged back into Herries affairs.

'But you are not so weak!' cried Emma.

'But don't you see,' Judith answered, 'it is a struggle inside myself. And one day it will be too late. I shall be compelled to choose, and shall make the wrong choice. And then I shall be inside the Herries for the rest of my days. And the worst of it will be that I shall like it – and I shall have lost all my real life for ever.'

Not that Judith often talked like this. But she was brooding, Emma knew, too much within herself. If Emma made a fool of herself, which she often did, she burst into a rage or a flood of tears and it was all over. But Judith took things to heart. And then of course you did brood when you were having your first child. Poor women! What a time they had! And then Emma would see a Highlander pass by, with a great swing of the haunches, and be glad indeed that she was a woman!

On this particular afternoon Judith was in the highest spirits. They came out into the Palais-Royal, chattering and laughing. Judith was full of Mr Walter Scott – what fine eyes, how kindly an expression, how interesting his limp made him! Emma had never read one of his poems – they looked so very long – but she was prepared to find anyone noble whom Judith thought to be so.

The Palais-Royal was a place of enchantment. Under the hot afternoon sun it glittered and glowed with its life and splendour. It was a little city in itself. In shape an oblong quadrangle with piazzas completely around it, a garden planted with rows of trees, laid with gravel, with flowers and grass plots enclosed. Under the piazzas were countless shops, far more brilliant, as it seemed to Judith and Emma, than the shops of London. On the ground floor, coffee-houses and restaurants; on the principal floor upstairs, coffee-houses, gaming-houses, exhibitions; higher up again, what a Herries traveller of the period calls in his Journal 'the abodes of vice and profligacy'. (This is from the Journal of Rodney Herries, the very pious younger brother of James, who in middle life took orders, and was ultimately Archdeacon of Polchester.) He goes on: 'The attics are inhabited by filth, misery, and crime, in endless variety and in a manner that renders it much safer to take that fact on hearsay than on actual reconnaissance. I should have mentioned,' he piously continues, 'that below the pavement are places much corresponding in character to the attics, though many of them are only cheap cafés, traiteurs, or pastry-cooks, of fair respectability.' He ends in a passage of particular eloquence by calling the Palais-Royal 'This immense gangrene'.

It was for Judith wonderful in all its mingled life, its wealth and poverty, fine ladies and scoundrels, triumphant soldiers and washerwomen, ordinary quiet Frenchmen and ruffians almost in rags, clerics and flower-sellers, tourists and solemn officials. They had been in it so often, Emma and she, that she wondered why it seemed today to have some special significance for her.

She stood for a moment under the burning sun, jostled on every side, trying to define her impression. She was being reminded of something. The broad space around her seemed to narrow. The dazzling sunlight on the white walls darkened. She was suddenly chilled. The movement was frozen. She heard a voice in her ear: 'No, madam, I fear the crowd is too great . . . Yes, he stole from his master's till . . . a butcher . . .'

She caught Emma's arm. 'Let us go home, Emma. We must rest before this evening.'

'Why, my dear, you are pale. You are unwell.'

'No, but I was reminded of something.'

Afterwards, in the dark little room in the Rue Vivienne, she said to Emma:

'Emma, I am sure that something will happen to us in the Palais-Royal. I shall not return there.'

And Emma thought to herself: 'It is beginning. These fancies that women get at such a time!'

She made her lie down, and sat beside her, telling her lively improper stories of her own past life. Through the wall they heard the odd plaintive chatter of M. Dufresne's monkey. It chattered like a child, then broke into an angry scream. Then the dogs barked. Then could be heard the deep menacing rumble of Madame Dufresne.

Their window was open because of the heat, and from far below them came the rattle of carriages, the crying of wares, the distant dreamy cadence of a band. In the air was the smell of Paris, the scent of carnations, the tang of baking bread, the hot touch of the iron trellises before the balconies, the sniff of crumpled paper, dry almost to burning-point. Judith was almost asleep. Once opening her eyes, looking at Emma, she said: 'I saw a boy hanged once in London. I thought of it today.'

'I know; you have told me of it often,' said Emma composedly. 'What is a hanging? You are too sensitive, my darling.'

'Perhaps I shall die when the child is born.'

'Nonsense. Nonsense. Die! I never heard such folly!'

'I know how cool it is now up Newlands, and how the breeze blows above the turf of Maiden Moor ... I rode once, but only once, with Francis to Hawkeshead, and then up the hill to where the two little tarns lie. Oh, Emma, you never saw a thing so quiet and so cool when a great white cloud floats overhead and Fairfield and Helvellyn watch over you ... Oh, how hot it is, and how sorry I am for Monsieur Dufresne's monkey ... Madame Dufresne will murder us one night in our beds. She hates us for Waterloo. And she will hide our bodies in that vast cupboard with the creaking door. I am sure there are rats in the wainscot ... Emma I *know* that something will happen to us in the Palais-Royal, and that great woman with the black hair and the crimson dress will sit above us and watch us torn to pieces while she arranges pieces of sugar ... I wonder how Francis is, and whether he has that blackberry preserve that he loves. They are always forgetting to have it on the table unless I am there ... I wonder if you can see the Scottish hills clearly today, and what they are doing at Westaways ... That crimson woman has Jennifer's air ... Jennifer would be fine in a café with mirrors multiplying her ... How I wish I knew Mr Scott! He has stayed, I know, with Mr Southey. Francis may have met him ...'

She dropped away to sleep while Emma, her eyes full of devotion, watched her and listened to M. Dufresne's monkey.

That evening they went to the Tivoli Gardens. Judith, after a long sleep, had recovered all her spirits and was ready for any amusement. Here there was plenty. They had quite agreed that the place could not compare with Vauxhall for size and splendour; but the summer evening was so lovely, the crowd so diverse and so intent upon enjoyment, that it was impossible not to be merry. There was a great crowd on this especial night, for it was said that the King and the Duchesse d'Angoulême were to be present to see the floating of an illuminated balloon. Emma had said that the Duchess would not be there, because she was so devout that she considered all amusement harmful. In fact no Crowned Heads were present, nor could they persuade the

balloon to rise, although a great many people paid five francs
to stand within the ropes to see it do so.

There were all the regular diversions. One of the principal
of them was to guess who were French officers; for in spite of
Blücher's order that any discovered should be at once appre-
hended and treated as prisoners of war, Paris was filled with them.
Then there was the gaiety of going around in a circle – the gentlemen on wooden horses, the ladies in chairs – in order to carry
off with a small sword a ring hung out upon a post for the purpose; or you might get into a boat and ride about on a small
artificial pond scarcely larger than the boat; or you might watch
Mlle Sachi, elevated sixty feet on a tightrope; or there were the
fireworks, *quite* as good as Vauxhall; or you might simply laugh
at the costume of the French ladies, which seemed to Judith
and Emma very ugly, with the high headdress, the hair drawn
tight from the temples and forehead over a coif, or hid with a
high-crowned bonnet covered with feathers, no perceptible
waist, but a loose robe hanging like a sack from the throat to the
ankles, carefully collected about the wrists, and a shawl worn
three-corner-wise. Emma and Judith thought these styles most
absurd and laughed together a great deal.

However, the grand feature of the Tivoli, as of every other
place of entertainment in Paris, was the dancing.

Everyone formed a circle round the dancers, who did everything possible to be as widely observed as might be. One
gentleman was pirouetting round on his wooden leg and vastly
enjoying it.

Soon a grave French gentleman with a square black beard
invited Emma to dance, and, old though she was, she eagerly
agreed, giving Judith a nod and a wink and setting off into the
middle of the ring as though she were not a day more than twenty.

Judith was tired and sat down on a little wooden bench. The
green of the trees was as brilliant as fresh paint under the
illuminations, and between the leaves the evening sky showed,
soft and delicate and tender. She loved to see people happy, to
hear their cries of pleasure, to see the children running, to watch
the sturdy simple faces of the English soldiers as they walked
about in pairs, gravely considering the French girls, to catch
the quick coloured flash of the fireworks, blue and green and
red, above the dark water of the little pond . . . She was tranquil.
She was waiting for the delivery of her child. She felt at peace
with all the world; she owed no one a grudge. When she
thought of how hazardous and desolate had been her entrance

into the world she was fortunate indeed to have had so full and adventurous a life. When her child came she would see that it had all that she could give it. Poor Warren! She thought of him with warm kindliness and affection. She was glad that he did not know what had happened to her.

She heard a familiar voice say 'Judith', looked up and saw Warren Forster standing in front of her.

At once she cried: 'Oh, Warren, how ill you look! Sit down. Sit down here beside me!'

That was at first all that she could think about. He did look very ill. His sharp face, always strained with the memory of past suffering, was grey and haggard. He was so frail that, although when she began to think of all that his being there in Paris would mean, she would be intensely aggravated, she wanted now to put her arm around him and protect him. He sat down beside her. She patted his knee. He thought as he looked at her: Had she any idea of what his finding her meant to him, of what burning dizzy happiness it was to him to look at her small childlike face with its honest eyes, its rather sharp ironical mouth, its clear smooth brow, the whole energy of her sturdy compact body, the independence, courage, humour that her poise always implied? No, she did not know. Had she known she would not have had the heart to leave him without a word.

'Well, Warren. What are you doing in Paris?'

'I have been searching for you for a whole fortnight, every day, all the time—'

'But how did you know that I was in Paris?'

'Francis told me.'

'Francis! – but he did not know my address.'

'No; that is why I have been searching for a fortnight. I have been looking everywhere. I had a feeling that today I should find you.'

'But what did you want to find me for?'

'Oh, Judith, you should not have left England without telling me! That was not kind of you. And the other also was not kind.'

'What other?'

'I know everything. Jennifer told me ... Yes. I went one day to Uldale. I had not seen you for three weeks. I must see you, so I went to Uldale. Jennifer was in a temper. She had been furious. When I stood in the hall, asking for you, she leaned over the stair and said, quite loud, anyone could have heard,

''Judith has run away because she is going to have a child!" '

'Oh!' cried Judith. 'Did she?'

'Yes. And so I then at once understood everything. How could I have been so blind, so selfish?'

'So now they all know,' said Judith slowly. 'Well – it does not matter.'

'I was crazy with anger at myself. All these months and I had never thought! I went to Francis and demanded to know where you were. All he could tell me was that you were in Paris.'

'Poor Warren,' said Judith, patting his knee with her gloved hand. 'You look so very unwell.'

'So then I went to Will Herries and said that I must be permitted a holiday. He made some demur, but Walter said that it would be right. It did not matter. Walter is staying at Westaways through the summer. So then I came to Paris.'

'But why do you look so ill, Warren?' she asked again. 'What have you been doing to yourself?'

'It is my heart – nothing at all. I have been so anxious about you. Oh, Judith, you should not have gone without saying anything to me!'

'Why not? It was no one's affair.'

'No one's affair! It is my child as well as yours. And I love you so. Ah, let me say that once again. For a whole fortnight I have been searching for you. I deserve to be allowed to tell you that I love you. And now you are going to be mother to my child. That is so wonderful that I cannot believe it is true.'

'It is true enough.' She sighed. Here she was – caught again! But he looked so unwell that she could think of nothing else. She would take any trouble now, when he looked so unwell, not to hurt him. She began to be very practical.

'Now listen, Warren. I am here with a friend – Emma Furze. You have heard me speak of her. We are in lodgings in the Rue Vivienne together.'

'I am in an hotel near the Palais-Royal.'

'Near the Palais-Royal. Very good. Then tomorrow morning—'

'Oh, not tomorrow morning!' he broke in. 'I have been two weeks looking for you. Allow me to stay with you for a little while this evening.'

'Our rooms are very small.'

'I do not mind what they are. I must see that you are comfortable. You must have better rooms. You must allow me—'

'Nonsense, Warren. Everything is very nice where we are.'

A moment later Emma arrived, very heated. She smiled at the square-bearded gentleman, who bowed significantly, as though they had agreed on a further meeting, and went away.

'Oh, such a charming man! And he speaks perfect English! He is a Professor of Languages, and his wife has been dead five years. He has a—'

'Emma, this is a friend of mine from England. Mr Warren Forster.'

So this is the father of Judith's child, thought Emma, this little pale insignificant man!

She was inclined to be resentful, because he had provided all this trouble for Judith, but when she saw how ill he looked her heart was melted and she was as eager as was Judith that he should be comfortable.

They hailed a carriage and drove to the Rue Vivienne. Oh, dear! thought Emma, how he does love her, poor man! For he continued to look at her as a dog looks at its mistress, a fashion that always irritated Judith, who thought that everyone should be equal.

Warren insisted that he should pay the carriage. That Judith permitted him. Then they went through the courtyard, climbed the dark and smelling stairs.

In the close little sitting-room Warren said: 'What is that?'

'It is the monkey and the cockatoo in the next room.'

Emma was very tactful and went away. She knew that they would want to talk to one another. There were only two chairs. He insisted that Judith should take the larger. So she sat there, her hands behind her head. She felt her child move beneath her heart, her child and his. He sat very erect in the stiff-backed chair, leaning forward, his thin fragile hands tightly clasped together.

'Oh, I am so glad that I have found you!' he said. 'If you knew how happy it makes me. And that you are to be the mother of my child – that is the proudest thing that has ever happened to me!' Then as he saw that she was going to speak: 'No, don't say anything yet – pray, pray do not. I know that you do not love me, that you have never loved me. But you have given me such great kindness, and now that we are to have a child, I do not know – I do not know—' He broke off, twisting his hands nervously together. He looked up at her, smiling like a child asking a favour. 'It is a bond.'

But that was exactly what she would not have it. How was she to be honest with him without hurting him?

'No – Warren. I must be free. I am bound to no one, and the

child will not be bound either.' She got off the chair and came to him and stood close to him. She put her arm round him, and he, like a child with its mother, bent his head against her.

'You know, Warren, I have told you before. I have only touched life deeply once. I have only once loved and I never shall again. At that time I was so young that I did not know that that would be the only time. But I could not have valued it more highly even if I had known. And at the end when he was dying and said that he loved me ... No, no,' she broke off, her hand trembling on his shoulder, 'that was my real life. Nothing, my dear friend, has been quite real to me since. And I came to France because I wished my child to be born in Georges' country, and if I have been unfair to you, forgive me. I did not mean it—'

'No, no,' he broke in, 'never unfair. You have been only good.'

He bent forward and kissed her. She went on eagerly:

'We will make you comfortable, Emma and I. We will all be together. I was wrong, Warren dear, not to see you more frequently in England. That was most reprehensible, but now we will make you well. We will all be so happy together—'

For he looked so ill, poor little man. He had sunk against the hard back of his chair. His fingers clutched her hand. His face was the colour of ash. His lips were purple.

'Yes ...' he murmured. 'I am ill ... my heart ... In my coat ... drops.'

She rushed to his carriage-coat that he had flung off when he came in. In a pocket she found a little bottle. He murmured directions. She thought that he was going to die. There seemed nothing so important in all her life as to save him. Little by little he came to himself. His lips were less blue. He even smiled a timid nervous smile.

'The pain,' he murmured. 'The pain is very terrible.'

'Oh, you must remain here!'

She knelt by him, stroking his hair, holding him close to her. 'Are you better? Are you better now?'

'Yes, I am better now.'

'Of course, you must remain.'

She thought what she could do. One of the beds must be moved out of the other room. She and Emma could sleep together. Reassuring him that she would return in a moment she went out to find Madame Dufresne, and behold that woman, who had been so fierce and so sinister, was now the very soul of kindness.

Emma also was there. All together they moved the bed. Then alone Judith helped Warren to undress, as a mother her son. She gave him one of her own nightdresses. Very small and wan he looked lying there, never taking his eyes from her face. The doctor had been sent for.

She sat down beside the bed, sewing at something for the child.

She could hear very faintly the street noises. The candle flickered and threw great shadows on the wall. He put his hand out, took hers and kissed it.

'Now, now . . . you are to sleep. That is what you are to do.'

But she bent forward, leaned over the bed and kissed his forehead. He closed his eyes as though in an ecstasy of happiness. She continued quietly to sew, to listen for the doctor. She felt the child move in her womb. How strange life was! That she should be sitting here in Paris, waiting for her child to be born, Warren in bed in her room!

How strange, incongruous, foolish and touching! She felt a strong pride as though she had her hand on life, a mettlesome steed, restive under her touch, restive but obedient!

PALAIS-ROYAL

'Son Altesse le Prince de Benevento!'

'That is Talleyrand,' whispered Emma, who was in so frantic a state of excitement that the feather in her head-dress wobbled like a live thing.

Oh! thought Judith, how I wish they were all here to see us – Will, Christabel, Walter, Pomfret, Rose, Maria, Carey, Francis, Jennifer and the children, John and Dorothy. How they would adore it – the brilliant colours of the uniforms, the flash of the decorations, the silks, satins, shawls, diamonds of the ladies!

It was not Judith's natural disposition to want to show off, even to the members of her family whom she disliked most; but this was one of the great Balls of History!

How was it that they were there at all? Well, Warren had encountered (on the first day that he was able to go out after his recovery from his heart attack) a business friend of Will's, a Monsieur Rakonitz of the famous Viennese jewellers, and he knew everyone: had supped with Blücher and shown rubies to the King of Prussia, and sold a bracelet to Fouché. He had suggested that he could find three tickets for Warren. In all probability he had some deal with Will in hand, or wanted Will's influence for something. In any case, he was a grand jolly fellow, with a big beard and his hat cocked on one side. Then, unlike so many men with their hats cocked on one side, he had remembered his promise, and Warren had had his tickets.

So here they were, as merry and excited as three children. Judith was very near her time, and, in consideration of her age and that this was her first child, it had been wiser of her perhaps not to have come, but she could not resist it. She could never refuse to have fun, nor could she refuse to be kind to anyone, and she knew that Warren's evening would be nothing were she not there with him.

Not so Emma. She was devoted to Judith; but whether Judith were there or no she would enjoy herself. Her purple gown, her splendid turban, gave her a fine dramatic air, as of a prophetess given to acting tragic roles at occasional moments. This was her pose while she remembered, but when she forgot she was simply a tall jolly libertine, ready to smile at anything and eager for every kind of attention, with a heart that Warren, who did not really like her, described as 'incredibly open'.

Judith stood beside her, insignificant in the white gown that hid her figure, a little, very ordinary, middle-aged woman, but to Warren more magnificent and splendid than any one there.

They stood against the wall under a huge galaxy of candelabra, and Warren told them who everyone was.

Talleyrand was an old, powdered, old-fashioned gentleman. He might have been any card-playing, gently-flirting, fussy-about-his-food-and-his-bottle, old gentleman – one of the milder, politer Herries, Judith thought. But when you looked at him more closely (and they had an excellent opportunity, for he stood near to them, smiling, bowing, his sharp eyes ceaselessly darting now into this face, now on to that stubborn back, now beyond the other ingratiating desire for recognition) you could see an elaborate calm, a dangerous mildness ...

'*Le Duc d'Otrante !*'

Fouché, the villain of the piece, the super-policeman, sly devil, malicious tyrant, admirable teller of indecent stories ...

'*Sa Majesté le Roi de Prusse – leurs Altesses Royales les Princes Royaux de Prusse – le Duc de Mecklembourg.*'

The Prince of Orange, pale from his recent wound, Lady Castlereagh, General Alava, the Prussian King, plain, kindly, stout, melancholy, the princes his boys, also melancholy ... Oh yes, it would be agreeable to have Francis here, *dear* Francis whom, now that one was away from him, one loved as deeply as ever ... he would enjoy this and would look so distinguished and for a moment would forget Jennifer ... and oh! if Jennifer suddenly entered how startled everyone would be! What a wonderful entrance she would make, moving lazily like a queen, ever so slightly smiling in her consciousness of the great beauty that she was, and Talleyrand would bend his little figure forward and inquire of Lady Castlereagh, and Fouché would turn his sharp eyes, and the Prussian King would stroke his melancholy cheek. Yes, Jennifer should have been a queen in some country where everyone admired her, where there would be little work ...

And then followed the great thrill of the evening. An important body of officers and aides-de-camp, a rather aged, not very interesting officer at their head, and the announcement:

'*Son Altesse Sérénissime – le Prince Blücher.*'

Everyone pushed forward to stare at him, and then what a moment! halfway down the salon, Wellington moved forward and, meeting with smiles, the two great heroes shook hands.

But for Judith even that was not the final climax, for, just behind her, she heard a voice say 'Look at that – a few weeks ago those two men delivered Europe' – and, half turning, saw standing quite close to her, whom but Mr Walter Scott?

His expression was one of rapt and intense fervour. His eyes, from under their heavy eyebrows, glittered with emotion. She thought there were tears in them. As he leaned forward, his high-domed forehead rising into an odd peak, his strong shoulders set, the nobility of his mouth speaking of all the kindness (and yet firmness and stiff obstinacy too) that a Scottish gentleman is capable of, she felt that she *must* speak to him, wisdom, folly, or no.

'It is not wonderful to be present at such a moment?'

He turned and saw a modest, stout little body in a white gown. As he greatly preferred modest and simple people to any other, he smiled like a brother and gave a little bow.

'It is indeed, madame.'

He turned his eyes back to Wellington and Blücher. She did not venture any more, but she pulled Warren away to a little distance and whispered in a voice husky with excitement:

'I have just spoken with Mr Walter Scott.'

She was so happy and Warren was so happy that they were united in this hour more than they had ever been. For some weeks she had been looking after him, and he had needed her so; she had grown as a sister, as a mother, fonder and fonder of him. And he *was* someone to be fond of. She had not known that he had so tender and gentle a nature, one so honest and sincere. And in knowing him better she perceived a new and a better side of the Herries character, something more generous, easy, and kind. Francis had had that strain, Maria and Carey had some of it, even Pomfret and Rose. If only their wretched ridiculous family quarrels did not obscure it!

She said to Warren one day:

'Although you are but *quarter* Herries you are the *right* quarter! You are what we all ought to be!'

He flushed with pleasure.

'You can say that when yourself—'

'Oh no, I am all wrong. I shall turn into the most awful old woman if I live. Always grab, grab at people, and they will all run -- and then I shall blame them and not myself.'

So tonight they both forgot Emma (who was quite capable of entertaining herself) and wandered about in blissful excitement together. Every once and again, laying her hand on his arm, she would say: 'Are you certain that you are quite well? You feel nothing? You are sure?'

And he would answer radiantly: 'I am too happy to feel ill.'

His features were very pale, she thought, but otherwise he had filled out again. His body was sturdy and firmly set once more.

They saw many interesting things. They saw a portrait of Napoleon resting against the wall, the stern fixed eyes gazing out upon this scene that emphasized his defeat. They saw in the ante-chamber of the great supper-room Wellington himself slip across to a small supper-table and join Lady Castlereagh and Mr Scott. They were all very gay and merry, Lady Castlereagh indeed screaming like a peahen.

They themselves went out into the gardens, where long supper tables were laid and hundreds of people were supping. They sat down at a table under the trees from which lights were shimmering. Everywhere there was a flood of noise like the sea, multitudinous voices, laughter, knives, forks, plates, the popping of corks, the rhythm and pattern of the distant band.

'Oh, Warren, I feel as though something wonderful were going to happen with the birth of our child. Will it, do you think? Am I cheating myself? I have not been so happy since I was with Georges. You know I came to Paris because of Georges, do you not? You are not angry, are you? Because now I am so glad that you came. I wasn't glad at first. I was so *sickened* of Herries. All quarrels and temper, and no one caring for anyone. I wanted to be rid of it all. But now you are yourself, dear Warren. We are splendid friends. I care for you so much. I am glad that it is your child. Is it not ridiculous that it cannot be always like this, you and I and the child? I don't *want* to go back to all the Herries character. It will catch me up, and I shall like it and become a managing, *nasty* old woman, and be too old to know that I am . . . You must save me from that, Warren.'

He put his hand on hers. 'You are so good, Judith . . .'

'No, I am *not* good. I have never done anyone good. Emma said that the other day, and that when I met her first she was drunken and lost. But Emma would never be lost. She has too great a vitality. And I did Georges no good either. But now perhaps, if I choose rightly and stay outside the Herries family—'

'You must eat some of this chicken,' said Warren. 'This chicken is excellent.' Then added inconsequently: 'I have not long to live. Another attack like that last one will finish me. But I want you to know, Judith, that you have given me the happiest days of my life. I did not know I could be so happy . . .'

'Yes, is not this chicken excellent? It would be nice to have Francis here, and Maria—'

'Ah, now you want others—'

'No. It is beautiful as it is. But I want everyone to be happy tonight. Imagine! All the Kings eating chicken only a yard away! And I spoke to Mr Scott and I heard the Duke say "Damnation". Would it not be funny, Warren, if I suddenly had my baby here on the grass, in a corner under the tree? And then we would ask Mr Scott to be its godfather. I do hope that it is a boy. What shall we name him? Some new name. Not a Herries name, like Francis or Pomfret.'

She sucked a chicken bone, holding it in her fingers.

There was a '*grimacier*' entertaining a crowd on the lawn away from the tables. At his side were the long windows flooded with light, phantasmal figures moving within, beyond him; behind him shadows pooled with dancing candleshine, and into the pools figures moved with white, excited, laughing faces. The King of Prussia's two boys were there, laughing at his antics. He was a long cadaverous man and wore a sheepskin cap. He made the most extraordinary faces, pulling his chin down, wrinkling his forehead, closing his eyes. He imitated the English,

did a Highlander making love to a French girl, 'Jean Bool' and
his wife eating at a restaurant, Napoleon running from Waterloo,
Mlle George singing a song.

Judith began to laugh.

'He is so clever. Is he not clever? Oh, Warren, see – look
what he does with his cap! Is not that marvellous?'

She laughed till she cried. They stood close together and then
hand in hand, while Emma, in another part of the garden, told
a stout Frenchman how comic he was; and Fouché took the
leg of a chicken in his fingers and cracked the bones with his
teeth as though they were so many condemned criminals.

Then came the fearful day, never to be forgotten by Judith as
long as she lived, September 4th, 1815.

On the early afternoon of that day they walked, the three of
them, to view the site of the famous Bastille. At first they had all
been in the highest spirits. Judith had, in the last few days, been
feeling almost incredibly weary, but heavy though her body was,
her heart was light. Since the day of the famous Ball she had
known a new relationship with Warren, a deeper intimacy. They
were now like brother and sister; she could care for him, watch
over him without any falseness on her side or irritation on his.
On these days he poured out everything from his heart, talked
and talked as though he could never tell her enough, and she
loved to listen. It was all thrilling and exciting to her as though
she had shared in it. Emma, occupied with many romances of
her own, left them much to themselves.

Then, early on this morning of the Fourth of September,
Judith awoke in a panic. She lay on her bed, feeling the child
kick in her womb, wondering whether it were a bad dream that
she had. Some figure seemed to be in the room with her, now
it was young Hartley Coleridge twisting one leg round the other,
now Reuben, now young Stane, and now, more definitely, La
Belle Limonadière from the Palais-Royal with her black hair
and crimson dress, arranging the lumps of sugar.

The figures faded as the light in the room grew clearer.
There was no one there. The panic remained.

They started to walk in the afternoon, but it was very hot,
and they called a carriage. Little light silver clouds flecked the
sky, the buildings were pigeon-colour, the air full of the scent of
flowers, there was the echo of bands, distant as though from
behind closed doors.

They crossed the bridge of Austerlitz, drove gently along the boulevards and then came to the site. Here they got out, dismissed the carriage and walked about, seeing, from every angle, where the famous attacks of 1789 had been made. For Judith this was an event of poignant memories. She could see now David advancing across the bright shining grass of the Uldale lawn to meet Francis, then the talk, the quarrel, the uplifted stick. If David had lived, had Sarah not 'gone crazy' ... Ah well, what was the use of that kind of memory? Every link in the chain must be there; she would not be here now had she not ridden over to Stone Ends and struck a small boy because he loved her hair; she would not be the woman she was had she not rescued Reuben's brother in Cockermouth, had she not ...

She dragged herself wearily after the other two (how tired she was, how hot the day, how heavy the child within her!), but she smiled when Emma, who was being very dramatic over the Revolution, turned to her; she put her hand through Warren's arm, and was interested in everything.

What they especially were interested in was an immense wooden shed, in the middle of the site, and a half-finished colonnaded tower of freestone. This was enclosed with a wooden paling and had a gate. Inside the gate on a stool was sitting a slim, pale-faced, elderly woman, one of whose cheeks had a painful twitch. Her eyes were sad and staring, as though she were looking for something that she could not find. She was clothed very decently with a shawl over her thin shoulders.

She begged them to enter and see the 'Elephant'.

'The elephant?' said Warren. 'Pray, what elephant? This is not the *Jardin des Plantes*.'

But it seemed that Napoleon had determined to erect a huge fountain on the Bastille site that its waters might wash away the memory of the awful events that had occurred there. This fountain was to spout its waters through the trunk of a great elephant. The melancholy woman, her eyes staring far beyond them while she spoke, pressed them to enter. Judith did not want to go; she did not know why, but she did not want to go.

However, Emma was all for seeing everything, so in they went.

The model was built of clay, indurated and whitened, exactly in figure and size what the bronze was intended to be, and it stood at the tremendous height of sixty feet. It had been intended that it should be placed on a stone pedestal and that then the water should pour out of its trunk into a succession of basins all round.

The woman, in a dreary unhappy voice, said that the English intended to finish this work, so she had heard.

'They have a number of other things to finish first,' said Warren laughing. But nothing at all seemed to amuse the woman.

She asked them gravely, as though she were accusing them personally:

'What have *you* done with the Emperor?'

'He is in charge of the Allies.'

'Will he ever return?'

'Never! . . . Never!'

'*Tant mieux! Mais l'Eléphant!*'

For some reason this huge white towering beast affected Judith with nausea. It looked so bare, so savage, so revengeful. With its great trunk it seemed to be ready to catch them, throw them up, and then, when they had fallen at its feet, riotously trample on them. In the hot quivering summer air it appeared to move, there was life in its vast body. The woman became more sinister, her cheek twitching, her hands moving; they would be prevented from escaping and the elephant would pursue them, trumpeting, within the palings. The air was so close that it was stifling.

She felt that in a moment she would be hysterical.

'Quickly. I cannot endure it. It is horrible. It is moving, cannot you see that it is moving?'

'Why, Judith—'

'No, no. I must get out. I cannot endure it.'

In a moment she would be laughing and screaming. She ran out into the street.

They followed her, wondering what the matter was.

'No. It is nothing. The heat was terrible. And the elephant . . . its trunk . . . And the woman hated us. Could you not see? Of course, she hated us.'

They sat down at a little table on the boulevard and ordered coffee. Judith was surprised to discover that she was trembling.

'But did you not feel it? I cannot understand why you did not. The elephant was alive. Oh yes, I know . . . But it *was* alive. In another moment . . .'

She drank her coffee, feeling that she had been too foolish for anything. She to give way to nerves! So that when they suggested that they should go to the Palais-Royal, although she hated to do so, she agreed.

Arrived there, they sat at a little table beneath a wide awning and watched the scene. The ladies with their high hats, their long sumptuous dresses, some of them with canes, all of them painted, vivacious and, it seemed, without a care in life, smiled at the men as anglers throw their baited hooks. The shops glittered, the sun shone down relentlessly; the moving crowds were like players in a game where something has to be found, now suddenly hurrying forwards as though the scent were 'hot', now hesitating, halting, the scent lost.

Judith's uneasiness increased. It was the heat, it was the noise, it was the smell of hot iron and dried dung and clothes. The long stretches of the square shone like glass. Some toy balloons, red and green and yellow, were floating like swollen puff-balls in the air. In one place a 'grimacier' held a little crowd, throwing on and off his headgear, changing his coat, dancing, bending backwards. Nearer her there was a Punch and Judy, and from within the little coloured box came the sharp rasping cry and the quick bark of the little frilled dog.

It seemed to her that everyone was hostile, and this was not all her imagination, for at this time in Paris, behind the gaiety and laughter, all nerves were taut, no one knew what was to happen next, no one could trust his neighbour. There was great hostility to the Prussians. French officers in disguise were everywhere waiting to pick a quarrel. One of the means was to sit in a public place with your feet stretched and trip up a Prussian. Duels were fought every day. Two Prussians had been murdered the night before in a dark street behind the Opéra.

Judith sat there wondering what was the matter. She was not exactly ill, but felt a deep apprehension. Was her time imminent? Perhaps she had best go home, but she did not wish to spoil Warren's pleasure. She knew that he would insist on going with her.

She looked at him while he talked to Emma; how fond she had become of him, what good companions they were! She liked to be fond of people, especially when they were not weak and yet did what she advised. The pleasantest people in the world were the selfish ones who were also kindly, so that in the middle of their selfishness they thought of you and did something for you. Unselfish people who were always eager to do something for you were so irritating . . .

A group of French people, eagerly laughing and talking, came out of the restaurant behind Judith and, not noticing her, bumped against her and almost knocked her chair over. She felt her heart leap, the shops and chairs and coloured clothes danced before her eyes. She could not drive that horrible white elephant out

of her mind. It would not surprise her to see it come trumpeting
and trampling, the crowd running before it. She would not be
able to move; she would be held in her place as one is in a
nightmare. Something had warned her not to come to the Palais-
Royal.

Then she noticed sitting near to her a young Prussian officer,
quite alone. He had large melancholy eyes and was little more
than a boy. He stared out into the pageant with unseeing gaze.
What was it? Was he sick for home? Was he thinking of someone he loved and wishing that she were with him, wondering
what he did there?

Warren turned to her smiling. He was watching the 'Punch',
laughing at the little dog. Always after she would remember
every detail of the next few minutes. A tall very handsome lady,
in a high green fur hat, was leaning across her little table, gazing
into the eyes of a stout frog-faced gentleman choked by a huge
stock. Some band was coming nearer, the music grew louder
and louder as though a door were opening. Two more crimson
balloons floated into the air; a small poodle, ridiculously naked,
ran forward into the crowd, lost, and a shrill feminine voice
cried 'Dédé . . . Dédé!' It heard the voice and eagerly ran back
again.

Emma was exclaiming: 'But the air was so ravishing that I
could not endure to return, so I waved my hand and he came,
running, such ecstasy painted on his features . . .'

Then everything happened in a moment. The band just
entered with a blare of sound, someone laughed, the lady in
green pinched the gentleman's chin . . .

A young Frenchman with a black moustache and sharp
beady eyes moved against the chair in which the young Prussian
was sitting; a glass fell with a clash, the Prussian was almost
tumbled from his seat. The Prussian started up, his hand on his
sword. The two faced one another. A pistol-shot cracked; the
young Prussian, his legs bent oddly beneath him, lay huddled
against the iron legs of the table.

At the sound of the shot the sky seemed to swing, the buildings
to bend forward.

Everyone came out running from the restaurant. There were
shouts and cries. Two officers in Uhlan uniform approached
the Frenchman.

Judith saw him struggling with them. She was quite near to
him, and could observe how, although his face was white, he
expressed a rage that was like a mad cat's. He repeated, in a

shrill treble voice, over and over again the word 'L'Empereur!'

He pushed back the men who were attacking him, turned with a swing of his body and looked straight into Judith's eyes – without of course seeing her, but, in the fiery meeting of sun, sky, roofs, and floor that seemed now to whirl in a wheel of flame before her, she saw the face of the hanging boy from London.

She felt herself now, just as she had done then, sick from a kind of claustrophobia, the crowd shutting her in. She had lost sight of both Emma and Warren. She was alone, as she always seemed to be in every crisis.

Then the young Frenchman, brushing his cheek with one hand, as though a fly had bothered him, flung out the other, and again a pistol-shot crashed like a stone flung through glass.

At that it was as though the Palais-Royal had been a plate in a second tilted forward, spilling its contents downwards into some abyss. The screams and shouts were detached. One shout was deep like a drum, another was shrill like the knock on a high gong.

Judith, struggling to escape from chairs and tables, saw Warren endeavouring to push through an absurd clump of bodies that clung together like plants in a storm. Behind them the whole Palais-Royal, still tilted, swarmed with figures as unreal as puppets worked by strings.

He called 'Judith! Judith!' He beat the bodies in front of him frantically aside with his arms. He reached her, fell against her. Horses were rising. A horse, mounted by a soldier, came charging through fallen furniture. Glass fell with a crash. A dog barked, and on that bark she caught Warren in her arms, for his face was purple. He could not speak. He dropped limp against her, so that she stumbled to the ground.

Kneeling there, her arms around him, she saw that he was dead, heard a bell ring just above her head, saw the horse (shaped like an elephant) go charging into the sun.

A wave of pain caught her, so frightful that some other person broken to pieces inside herself screamed. Everything was black.

She sank down on a descending shaft of pain. She slowly mounted again, to find that she was quite clear-sighted, was lying on a hard, dry sofa, her head on a pillow that smelt of cheese. She hated the smell, but also the row of lofty shining mirrors that reflected again and again the long room with empty tables, chairs piled high.

Somewhere in the distance shouting fell against the mirrors and died on the floor. She felt the sweat tumble into her eyes, wiped it away, and saw a vast Emma towering above her.

'Warren is dead,' Judith murmured.

A little stout man with two chins, who seemed also to smell of cheese, advanced to her. She saw that he was greatly agitated. A big silver ring trembled as his hand trembled. She heard him say:

'A screen! A screen! ... Where is a screen!'

Then she had one more absolute moment of clear vision.

Warren was dead. Her child was being born. She would die also, and history would repeat itself, for even as she had been born at the instant of her parents' death, so now would her child be born of their death.

The little man leaned over her. She saw the silver ring tremble. A cascade of pain hovered in the air – but before it broke over her she screamed out, 'I will not die! ... I will not die!'

'It is a boy,' said the doctor to Emma, quarter of an hour later.

They were bringing the bodies of the wounded into the restaurant and laying them in the shadow where the room was coolest.

Part IV

Mother and Son

THE HILLS

WALTER HERRIES rode up the hill from Hawkshead one fine summer's evening to get some air before spending the evening with his friend, Squire Thistleton, at High Grange. He had come over from Grasmere more swiftly than he had intended, having already eaten his dinner with the Bordens there, not wishing to invade High Grange before nightfall. Squire Thistleton's lady bored him most desperately: stay the night with Thistleton he must, for he had important business matters to discuss with him, but be bored by Mrs Thistleton he would not. Although he was so genial, for ever laughing at the jokes of others, yes, roaring and slapping his vast thigh at them, yet, like all very self-centred men, he had a watchful eye. If he must suffer at the jokes of others there must be excellent reason for it. He did nothing at all without an admirable reason. Immense in build though he was, he was not yet corpulent for his twenty-eight years. He looked exceedingly handsome in his green riding coat as the white horse picked its way carefully up the rough stone-strewn path. The summer is the worst time of the year in which to see this country: the naked blue sky does not suit its shape and size; the hills dwindle beneath the sun; the green carpet of field and brow has neither shade nor variety. But tonight fragments of orange cloud floated across a blue so faint as to be almost without colour, and the hills were so clearly outlined that they forced themselves, dark rocks of a mysterious country, out of a sea with no ripple.

Walter had no eyes for scenery; he left that to the romantic writers, now ever more numerous. But, pausing on the brow, and looking down to the left where the waters of Coniston lay bronzed and still, he felt all the pride of one who owns a fine property. For he had come now to feel that he, and he alone, possessed the whole of this charming and fruitful land. It was a natural and happy evolution of circumstance. He was at this moment well beyond his own actual territory, which was not as yet a very large one, but he felt himself to be so infinitely the most important person alive in the combined counties of Cumberland and Westmorland, and what he felt himself to be, that he was.

It was now over three years since Will Herries, his father, had departed back to London. He was to be seen very seldom at

Westaways. It had been made clear to him (Walter has assisted in the demonstration) that the City was the place for him. For one thing, there was nothing in life so pleasant for Will as the making of money, and although now much of his wealth had its richest foundations in Manchester and the Midlands, London was inevitably the heart of affairs. For another, Walter had helped him to perceive that, although Cumberland society did not object to wealth, it still objected to the City. The time was coming when a City man, granted that he had retired and had pocketed plenty of gold before retiring, would be admitted into good company, but that time was not quite yet. Moreover, Will had no intention whatever of retiring. He was now only fifty years of age and in excellent health. Business had never been so interesting as now when it was beginning to rouse itself, in the promise of so much fresh industrialism, out of the depression that followed the French Wars. The chimneys of the Midlands were gallantly smoking, and Will must be there to see that they were properly supplied.

Walter's ambitions were quite other. He disclaimed now all connexion with business. With his handsome person, his geniality, his ruthless selfishness, his happy disregard of the interests of any but his own, his fine place (but he already felt Westaways far too small for him) and, above all, his almost insane pride in the Herries name, he was excellently placed to dominate his country world. The men and women around him, he would say, had judged of Herries by the miserable specimens hitherto offered to them. *He* would show them what a Herries really was. Indeed, his earlier scorn of Francis and Jennifer had by now grown to an irritated and festering hatred. He would never dominate this country properly until Uldale and its occupants were wiped from the face of the land. They had not a chance against him; Francis weak and idle, Jennifer dull and scandalous. Only in their children could they rival him. At that thought, which constantly peered up at him out of the dark recesses of his mind like a malicious stinging animal, his whole body would tremble. For, in the spring of 1815, his wife had presented him with twins, a boy and a girl, and the boy was a weak and ailing cripple. Moreover, his wife would give him no more children, and, unless she died, Uhland must be his only son.

In his disgust at the puny and deformed baby he had not cared what they called him, and Mrs Herries, moved perhaps by the increasing wave of German Romanticism, or hoping, it may be, that the child thus named might make some escape from the

Herries nature, had had this outlandish fancy. The boy was Uhland, marked in this way, as in all others, from the common kind.

And Francis' children, John and Dorothy, were healthy and strong. Elizabeth and Uhland – John and Dorothy. He was beset by the contrast.

The horse moved forward. He turned down the hill to the two small pools that lay, in blue translucent stillness, under the dark guardianship of the wood. Behind the trees Helvellyn and Fair-field kept sleepy tolerant guard.

The day had been hot; their purple shadows slumbered.

There was perfect stillness all about Walter Herries as he sat on his horse and looked into the pool. There were other little things that had exasperated him today. He had been slowly riding by Grasmere Lake when he encountered that crazy old poet, William Wordsworth, and his mad sister as they walked along.

Walter, with his accustomed geniality, had stopped his horse to speak to them, as a king might to his subjects. Everyone knew that Wordsworth as a poet was a mock and a derision, and his sister, Dorothy, was as mad as a hatter. Wordsworth wrote poems about donkeys and daffodils. He was a joke to the neighbourhood, and that little sister of his, with her shabby clothes and fiery eye . . . And yet, speaking to them with all courtesy, he had been in some way rebuked. The comical pair! Wordsworth was going fishing; his sister said something about a bird on a tree. They did not seem at all gratified that he had spoken to them.

'Good day to you, Mr Herries . . . Good day to you,' Words-worth had said, as though he were impatient to be gone, and his sister had wandered about the road, following some bird with her glittering eye . . . Oh, mad, mad both of them! But mad or no they should have been impressed by his greeting.

Another vexation had been a queer one. As he left home that morning little Uhland, five years old, had limped to wish him farewell. He had felt a sudden pride in his heart at sight of him. Proud of that white-faced bony little cripple! But it was pride that he had felt; he had been moved; he had bent down to em-brace him. That was an absurd emotion – although, after all, when all was done, the child *was* a Herries . . . his only heir . . . In spite of himself he sighed, rested his hand on his great thigh and looked about him, breathing-in the sweet-scented summer air.

At that same moment there rushed past him, out of the wood,

the most astonishing figure, a small naked child. It was a boy, and, straight in front of Herries' horse, he splashed into the pool. Another moment and he was swimming vigorously, tossing his head and uttering cries of delight. The pool was deep – the two pools would be a fine small lake one later day – and this midge of a boy, screaming like a little shrill bird, dived, appeared a moment later at the pool's edge, and then sprang out, dancing about and waving his arms in front of Herries' horse.

The horse, alarmed by this unusual adventure, reared, and Herries, in anger, snapped his whip, catching the child's bare leg. The child laughed and plunged into the pool again; a moment later a peasant woman appeared at the wood's edge, then ran down to Herries.

'What are you doing, whipping a baby! Have you nothing better—'

She broke off. They had recognized one another. This woman was Judith. She was dressed like a peasant in some rough material of red and green. On her red hair she wore no covering. On her bare feet she had wooden shoes. She stood, her small body set, her little face grinning.

'Why, Cousin Walter, I did not know that it was you . . . It is a long time since we met.'

So it was. Years and years. He had not set eyes on her since that night in '15, when she had dinner with him, and they had heard of Napoleon's flight from Elba. None of them had seen her. She had been living in the hills with her bastard child. She had gone back to her origin.

'Well, well. Cousin Judith.' He took off his hat.

'Yes, and don't you whip my son or I shall have something to say.'

She was laughing, and he felt that in some way she was mocking him.

'Your son ?'

'Yes. Adam, Adam, come here!'

The child seemed to spring from nowhere and stood, naked and dripping, by the horse. Yes, this would be her child. It would not be a day more than five, born in the same year as his own. He saw, with satisfaction, that the boy was ugly. The small body was brown with sun, the hair – that lay thick and matted above his eyes – jet black. He had a short snub nose and a large grinning mouth, a strong sturdy body, but the legs and arms were too long. Yes, an ugly and common-looking child. He did not seem to feel cold, but Judith drew him to her, put her green shawl over him and her arm around him. He leant against her, wet as he was. She did not seem to care.

'This is Mr Walter Herries, a relation of ours,' she said to him.

How strong and sturdy the woman seemed! She must be between forty and fifty now. What a queer pair they made.

At that he recovered his self-command which, for a moment, he seemed to have lost. He leaned lazily towards her, resting one hand on his hip. The horse shifted a little and, bending down, began to pluck the grass. The stillness was exquisite. A cloud, like a bronze chrysanthemum, jagged at its edges, floated over the wood and darkened, like a hand, the little pool.

'Where have you been all these years ?' he asked her, friendly and patronizing.

'You know well enough.'

What clear bright eyes she has! he thought, and wondered whether there were specks of dust on his clothes. His hand moved down the lapel of his coat.

'And when will you return to civilization ?'

'It is quite civilized enough where I am.'

'Have you seen Francis and Jennifer lately ?'

'Francis has come to see me at Watendlath.'

'Well, I must be off to my supper.' He looked at the infant, and the infant looked back at him. 'So your name is Adam, young man ?'

The child grinned up at him, looking at him fearlessly.

'Adam Paris,' he said. Then he added most unexpectedly: 'I could make your horse jump more if I tried.'

'You try – that's all!' said Walter, suddenly angry again.

'Now you leave the child alone, Cousin Walter,' said Judith. 'He is not afraid of you nor of anything else in the world. But I will give you something to be afraid of if you touch him with your whip.'

He had a sharp consciousness (which he was to recall one day) of the force and vitality of her personality. Whenever he encountered her she compelled him to remember it, small though she was. While she was away he created, if he thought of her at all, his own picture of her as an insignificant sort of poor-relation-governess. But when he was with her it was another matter. And now he suddenly thought: 'I had forgotten *her*! Suppose that she should come back to Uldale!'

However, all that he did was to be gracious again. He took off his hat, bowed, invited her to bring her boy to see them at Westaways.

Judith was not ungracious. She always returned courtesy for
courtesy. 'Yes, I will come one day, Cousin Walter. I hope Mrs
Herries is well.'

'Oh yes. Well enough.'

Then Walter rode away, his figure for a moment gigantic at the
top of the bend against the soft glow of the milk-white sky.
Judith, her hand in her son's, started along the little path that
skirted the pool. Adam was wrapped up entirely in the shawl;
the end of it trailed on the ground behind him. He danced along.

'What a fat man!' he said.

'That is your Uncle Walter.'

'In truth my uncle?'

'Near enough.'

'I could have made his horse jump.' He skipped a few paces
and nearly tumbled. But she did not move to catch him nor did
she ask him whether he were cold, as any other child would
have been.

'Was the water agreeable?'

He wrinkled his nose like a little dog. 'I can smell the fire
burning.' He shouted and cried aloud with happiness. The shawl
fell off him, and bare as a young foal he ran towards the wood.
Judith walked soberly after him. She was thinking deeply about
Walter.

A small nondescript dog ran out to meet them. This was a
mongrel dog who, coming from nowhere, had attached himself
to them. He first ran eagerly towards Adam, moving awkwardly
on legs that were longer than they should have been, but with
eager excited joy. Then, just before he reached Adam, it occurred
to him that he might not perhaps be so popular as he had hoped,
so he crawled on all fours, dragging himself along with a bright
supplicating eye.

'Dog! Dog!' Adam cried, and picked him up and ran into the
wood, hugging the animal to his bare stomach; the dog's tail
wagged in an ecstasy of happiness.

Just inside the wood a bright fire was burning, and on the
other side of the fire sat a stout man in black, reading a book,
and with an absentminded hand once and again stirring with a
stick the pot that hung over the fire.

Adam, who was now almost dry, flung himself, dog and all,
into the stout man's lap.

'Uncle Reuben, a fat man on a horse tried to whip me, but he
could not. Can we eat now?'

'You must dress yourself,' Reuben said, putting his book down and reaching out to a pile of minute clothes near to him.

Adam stood up on Reuben's thighs, putting his hands round Reuben's neck. Reuben clasped him round his small naked body, holding him lest he should fall.

'And who was this fat man?' he asked, moving his face a little; the small dog, when he saw what Adam was doing, was trying the same with the addition that he would lick Reuben's cheeks. The fire threw a shining colour on Adam's body. He seemed to be surrounded with a nimbus of light.

'Mother said he was my Uncle Walter ... Can we not eat now?'

He jumped suddenly off Reuben's thigh and had scuffled into a shirt and a pair of diminutive blue trousers. His legs were bare.

'Mother, can we not eat now?' He ran towards Judith, who stopped to look into the pot.

'Whom do you think I have seen?' she asked Reuben.

'I know. Adam told me.'

He spread his black riding coat for her and she sat down, leaning her head against his knee. She looked up and could see the dark fans and wheels of the trees flecked with cool shell-white sky.

'Yes, Walter. After all these years. He looked huge and mightily satisfied. Do you know what he said to himself as he looked at me, Reuben?'

'No.'

'Here is slattern Judith and her bastard ... Adam laughed at him ...' She pushed Walter away for a moment and went on: 'You had a grand meeting this noon. The grandest I've seen.'

'Yes, praise the Lord!'

'But Reuben, you talked more of political things than religious. You were trying to make them discontented.'

'They are discontented already. They have been starving for years and now their masters will bring in machinery and they work in the dark like slaves.'

Judith shook her head.

'No. Not here. They are farmers and shepherds. There is no discontent in Kendal or Keswick.'

'No, but a little way out – at Whitehaven, Cockermouth ...'

She looked up at him and put up her hand. He took it in his.

'I like it better when you talk about God. Although I do not

believe in Him I like others to. At least . . . believe or not . . . I
haven't the wits to be so certain. But I like to hear you speak of
Him. You bring Him so close. You are so sure of yourself now,
Reuben, and yet as kind and good as ever you were. I had rather
people were kind than anything else. Yet I detest a fool, and so
many kind people are half-witted.' She let herself run on, looking
up and seeing that a little evening breeze moved, as a tiny boat
moves on a pond, through the trees. She looked down and saw
that Adam was playing with the dog.

'Reuben, are you still bothered with women?'

He laughed. 'No. I am too old.'

'Nonsense. You are not sixty. When did they cease to torment
you?'

'I will tell you. It was in Kendal some ten years ago. It was in
the wintertime and I had been preaching out on the hills. It was
perilously cold, and in the inn after supper a large red-faced girl
invited me to her room. Then, to be warm and to be comforted
by someone (for I was much alone at that time) I went into bed
with her. And she had but just blown out the candle when I saw
the Lord, a young man in silver armour standing on the floor.
The fire shone on him and he was glorious. He cried to me,
"Reuben, the pleasure is not worth the pain." And I answered
"Nay, Lord, I was so cold." And he came to the bed and touched
my forehead with his hand. I lay by the girl all night but neither
of us was harmed.'

'And do you truly think it was the Lord?' asked Judith.

'Who else could it have been?' said Reuben.

'No, no one else.'

'Well, then—'.

'But maybe you were already asleep—'

'Not before embracing the girl. No. It was the Lord. I have
seen him in such armour at other times too—'

'And women are nothing to you since then?'

'I like women,' he said. 'But the temptation is over.'

'What are your temptations still?'

He answered gravely, counting on his fingers. 'One, I am a
coward; two, I am greedy; three, I like a warm bed; four, I tell
tales; five, I hate the Methodist preacher at Cockermouth; six,
I am lazy – I can sleep all day—'

She interrupted him. 'Look up. There is a red cloud like a
crimson bird that Georges once had, hanging between two trees.'

But it was one of Reuben's defects that natural scenery meant
nothing to him. Any human thing, but a tree, a cloud, a moun-

tain – nothing. The pot was boiling. Judith commanded the whole situation. The three of them and the dog sat and had a splendid meal.

'We will go up the hill and see the sunrise as you promised?' Judith asked.

'Yes,' Reuben said, but in spite of himself he yawned behind his hand.

She had an impulse to be cross, as she always had when things were not to be as she wished them. Then she conquered her crossness. She had been expecting for months this evening with Reuben. About twice a year they spent a night together. Once before they had ridden up into the Langdales and seen the sunrise. And now he was sleepy. His head was nodding. It had been a grand meeting and must have wearied him, but she had been looking forward passionately to a long talk with him. It was so seldom now that she could talk with her own kind, and tonight, most especially, she wanted his advice, for she was about to pay a visit to Uldale again for the first time since her return from France. She was taking Adam with her. The sudden vision of Walter had been like an omen. She was not frightened, but she needed help and only Reuben could give it her. And now Reuben was sleepy. Only Adam was not. He was dancing about with the dog, eager for the next adventure now that his hunger was satisfied.

Reuben turned round, knelt on the grass and said his prayers. Then he leaned against a tree-trunk and in another moment was asleep.

'He's asleep,' said Adam, laughing.

The night was so warm and the scent of the trees so comforting, the uncertain flicker of the fading fire so bewitching that, standing there, she felt that she was under a spell.

She was in magnificent health because of the life that she had been leading since coming to Watendlath, the life of a peasant, harvesting, digging, helping with the sheep, riding off with Watson for a whole day on the fells, ploughing for hours through the quagmires at the top of the Fell after a lost or strayed lamb – and always in perfect content. That was the life to which part of her temperament entirely responded; but the other part would not have been content had she not had Adam. Adam now was her whole life, her soul, her body, her past, her future, her God and her destiny.

She had been waiting always for some such passion as this. Her love for Georges had possessed her, but it had not been returned until the last and, say what one may, a love that is not returned is only half a love.

Moreover, although she had not known it, she was a woman to whom motherhood was the only possible complete fulfilment. Her love for Georges, her affection for Reuben, Francis, Maria, Warren, Emma Furze, Watson, had been in its impulse maternal. But they had not been her own. Now she had something that was her own, and anyone watching her might have been frightened of the fiery, possessive, passionate element at the heart of her love for her son.

But she was not a fool. She kept her love in control as yet. And Adam was not at present difficult. His mother was his companion; he knew none other as good. He loved her quite naturally without thinking of it. He was independent but warm-hearted and, at present, he had no feeling that she threatened his liberty. There was as yet no cloud on his sky. The first five years of his life, two in France, three at Watendlath, had known no blemish. She had been able to give him all he wanted, because when Warren's will was read it was found that he had left her all his own small means – not much, but enough for her needs. The boy was of amazing health, and, so long as he was not shut up in a room for too long, asked for no attention. He trusted everyone as a puppy trusts everyone before his first betrayal. He was fearless, truthful and gay, the three best things a small boy can be. He would defend his mother against anyone or anything; he was obedient so long as she did not hamper his liberty. Once, for some small crime, she had locked him in a room; he had broken the window and disappeared until nightfall. She understood that because she had once climbed out of a window herself.

Their relationship was, at present, perfect.

Now as the light faded and the stars came out she tried to persuade him to sleep. She would not wake Reuben. She would walk up the hill and see the sunrise by herself. But she almost hesitated to speak because the silence was so glorious, broken only by the running water that is to be heard everywhere in this country, the gentle friendly crackle of the burning wood as it fell into crimson embers, the occasional movement of the horses behind her.

Adam, too, seemed to feel the silence, for he stood without moving, his legs spread, looking up.

'Now you must sleep, Adam.'

He shook his head, not saying anything.

'Oh no . . .' He looked at her, smiling. 'There's the moon.'

And there it was, sailing very calmly with a sort of smiling conceit between the trees.

She knew that he wouldn't sleep. 'Come. And we shall see the sunrise.'

So he took her hand and they started off, the small dog following. Adam was never very talkative. To be out at night was no very new thing to him. They left the little wood behind them and started to climb. They were now on the open moor. The Langdale Pikes, Fairfield, Helvellyn were beyond, and across Yewdale loomed the hump of the Old Man. The light about and around him was diffused as though shed by the multitude of stars. The pools of shadow, neither brown nor grey, lay below them like lakes of sleeping water. Fairfield and Helvellyn were marked with crags and precipices like the tearing made by some giant's fingers. How black, how black the hills against the luminous sky! A little higher on the moor and they were suddenly staring into the moon's face. They could see now the two little pools which seemed to blaze with moon-silver among the surrounding vapour. No wind stirred; somewhere some sheep were moving and the air was warm like the breath of a flower.

They sat down against a gigantic boulder; the stones around them rose in that moonshine like monolithic sacrificial monuments. As they sat in that stillness the hills seemed to approach them. Helvellyn, always a beneficent hill, leaned towards them, Fairfield embraced them, the pools below smiled at them. Somewhere in that wood Reuben was lying against a tree snoring with his mouth open. Adam curled in against Judith's side, the little dog curled in against Adam.

With her arm around her son Judith sat staring into the moon. She did not often think of the past, but tonight it came crowding towards her, figures issuing from the hills, events stealing up from the mist – the day that she had looked at Mrs Monnasett and David had beaten her, the moment when she had seen Georges' mother, the night of the fireworks when Will and Francis and Reuben had talked, the escape of Reuben's brother, David's stroke and death, Sarah's passion – and then all her life with Georges, from the first week (what a baby then she had been!) to the last awful scene with Stane's father! And then the dead quiescence of the years at Grosset, the semi-life with Jennifer and Francis, Will's coming to Westaways, the friendship with Warren leading to the drama in Paris – drama of death, drama, thank God, of life.

She did not believe in God, but she did feel tonight that every event, every character, had led her to this – this question that was now the dramatic crisis of her whole life – which world was she to choose, the world of Uldale or the world of Watendlath?

She had thought that it was settled. Only a month or two ago she had said to Charlie Watson that her Herries life was finished for ever; she would not leave Watendlath until Adam was grown. Then he should choose for himself, but she would remain.

She had thought that it was settled. Then came a letter from Francis. He implored her to come to Uldale. He gave no reasons. She was to come, if only for a night, and bring Adam with her. The most touching thing was that Jennifer had scrawled at the bottom of the page: 'The two of us need you.'

Well, she would go, but only for a few nights, only to show them that she was out of Herries affairs for ever. But was she? The invitation had stirred her. She wanted to see Uldale again – the dairy, the housekeeping, the servants. She was sure that it would be in a mess. And Jennifer, John, Dorothy . . . She was too proud to come to see them, after all the scandal about her, without an invitation . . . but if they asked her . . . For a brief moment Watendlath had seemed small, shut in, her domination there a poor thing, even her beloved Charlie a rough ignorant farmer . . . Then she had been ashamed, and in a day or two her true nature had recovered itself. For she knew that this was her true nature, the nature that she derived from her mother, the nature that outlawed her from the Herries blood.

Had she not written to Francis and said that she would come she would now have refused his appeal. But she had given her word.

Then the sight of Walter Herries this evening had revived all the struggle again. How proud and conceited he had been! It was thus, seated on his horse, gigantic against the skyline, that he remained for her, and, at the thought of him, her whole proud obstinate passion for dominating returned.

It was thus that he meant to wipe out Francis and Jennifer, John and Dorothy. She saw them helpless and cowering under his whip. She knew suddenly why Francis had sent that letter to her. How amusing to return to Uldale – she, the outlaw with her bastard boy – and fight Walter, make Adam – illegitimate though he was – head of all the Herries! Her heart beat triumphantly; she drew her arm more closely about him; he was sleeping.

She looked up at the stars as though to defy them. And the answer came back without question. 'Here is your country. Here is your place.'

But why? All the rebels were killed or disgraced. Georges had been murdered, Warren killed, Francis humiliated, her father an outcast, Reuben – well, Reuben talked more of social things now than of God. What of the bear, the boy hanged, young Hartley Coleridge? She was not sentimental about outlawry, but it seemed that if you fought against the laws of the House – if you broke the windows, rushed downstairs with no clothes on, rang the bells in the belfry, refused the common food or drink, brought the mongrel dog into the parlour – they all together, with one loud cry, threw you into the street; and then, how were you better?

For three years in Watendlath she and her boy had been outlawed; and how was she better?

'You *are* better,' the little dog, the cherry-faced moon, the scar like a sword on Helvellyn's flank answered her. 'You have never been at peace before. *This* is your world, not the other.'

But she was practical and not given to hearing voices. To beat Walter, to dominate all the Herries, to place Adam at the head of them. He would have, she was sure, all Will's genius for money, all Walter's physical strength, all Francis' brains ...

Which way was she going? Her whole life led to this crisis – or so she fancied, as we like to fancy that there is a line and a course and a climax, when it may not be so at all.

She remembered the way that the hens scratched in the room when she had first returned to it after Georges' death, the elephant in Paris, and that woman bending over, searching among her letters, and Adam trailing in the shawl, Reuben licking his fingers after the meal from the pot ...

Perhaps there is no line, only a gesture here, a leaf falling, the sheep huddling up the path outside the farm. But there was Adam ... She was responsible for the life that he would have. Would he be like Charlie Watson, blowing on his fingers for the cold, or Will sitting in his counting-house, or Walter at the head of his table, or Francis waiting for his wife's lover and pretending not to see? ... No, not that. Adam, even now, was as brave as a lion. Poor Francis ...

But before she fell asleep she was aware that the decision that she would make must affect many lives, much Herries history. She knew what she could do if she tried. She had never as yet tried with her whole heart. She had always been divided. Her son had united her. She saw him, as her eyes closed, reaching up with his hand, catching the stars and joining, with the light that streamed from them, her divided heart.

She woke to see one bright bar of gold above the ridge. The edge of the bar sparkled and quivered. Behind it a fleet of tiny pink clouds trembled, hovered, then merged into a fan-shaped shadow of rosy light.

She bent down and kissed Adam. 'Wake up,' she said, 'and see the sun.'

He looked up, rubbed his eyes with his knuckles, then jumped to his feet, caught her by the hand and pulled her to a higher ridge of the moor.

Little winds, little fingers passing over an instrument, blew against their faces. The sky was beyond depth, without end, but was flecked now with fire. Thick white mist lay like water beneath them, but this soon was touched and lightened, thinned; the rocks and the spear-tops of the trees rent and tore it. They, too, caught the gold, and Helvellyn was, as though it had rolled its shoulder towards the light, purple.

The mist broke everywhere, and the sky was showered with flecks of gold. The cloven mist streamed down the hills like rain. Light was everywhere. The valleys ran with sun.

'Now I'll race you!' Adam shouted, and started tearing down to the little wood.

JUDITH RETURNS TO ULDALE

WHEN JUDITH STOOD again in the so-familiar hall at Uldale she was deeply excited. It was her nature to be excited, and that nature had not changed although she was forty-six years of age.

A stranger would have seen only a little ordinary pale-faced, middle-aged woman, bewildered perhaps by the sudden light, dressed in bonnet and shawl, faded but scupulously clean, holding by the hand a very small, rather ugly boy. No romance there. Nevertheless the situation was romantic, for Judith was returning to the home of her childhood, after behaviour so scandalous that it should have ostracized her for ever, holding her illegitimate child by the hand – and she was there by invitation! She would not, she proudly assured herself, be there in any other way!

Her emotions were mixed and confused: she could never enter this house without a hundred memories crowding upon her, but it was characteristic of her that the first thing that interested her was that there were signs of neglect and untidiness every-

where. She saw that at once, and her fingers itched to put everything to rights.

For a moment the only person who greeted her was the very
decent woman who opened the door. She knew that her ancient
enemy, Mrs Ponder, had been dead now three years of a fever.
She gave the woman a quick friendly glance.

'Thank you,' she said, smiling.

Then her very next move, instinctive, almost unknown to herself, was to step forward, still holding Adam by the hand, and put
a picture that hung crooked on the wall straight again.

'That's better,' she said.

It was an old picture that she knew well, of a huntsman leaping
a little ditch. She gave it a friendly little pat.

Then Jennifer came out from the parlour. 'Judith! I didn't
know—' she cried; but even then she came forward a little
slowly, a little lazily, as though she were but half awake.

She was not as handsome as she had been; she was middle-
aged now, as Judith was, but she was still a very remarkable
woman, carrying herself with the same old dignity and grandeur,
and her hair, untouched with grey, was of the same superb
darkness. She was wearing a coloured bodice of orange over a
white skirt. The orange sleeves, puffed and slashed, were very
fine. But Judith saw at once that the dress was a little slatternly,
and that her cheeks were painted. Her eyes, too, were weary, not
with quite the old affectation of sleepiness. There was real fatigue,
disappointment, unhappiness there.

She towered over Judith and the little boy. She bent down and
kissed Judith.

'Is this Adam?'

'Yes. This is Adam.'

She kissed him, and he returned the kiss with fervour. She was
quite the most beautiful lady he had ever seen, as this was the
most beautiful house he had ever been in. He stared at the wallpaper with its Chinamen and castles, at the silver candlesticks, at
the broad staircase, at the tall grand lady with the wonderful
orange sleeves. From that first moment he and Jennifer were
friends.

'Here is Francis! Francis, Francis, Judith is come!'

Francis was coming down the stairs, and Judith, looking up at
him, felt a shock of dismay. He had been over to Watendlath to
see her a year ago, and she had thought then that he looked old
and ill, but now – how thin he was, how tired he seemed; he was
an old man, and yet he was not more than sixty!

in a way he was more handsome than he had ever been. His extreme thinness suited him; his high collar, frilled shirt, and dark blue trousers showed his figure to the greatest advantage.

Judith was proud of him and deeply sorry for him; she longed to put her arms around him and mother him. He took both her hands in his.

'Judith, this is famous! . . . After all this time! And is this Adam ? How do you do, Adam ?'

'Very well, I thank you, sir,' said Adam in his shrill piping voice that was apt to end in a squeak.

They all laughed to relieve the tension of the meeting. There was a bustle about the baggage.

Judith went out into the dark garden. Charlie Watson had driven them out from Keswick. He leaned over and held her hand. For a moment she clung to his touch. All Watendlath seemed to be personified by him.

'Goodbye, Charlie,' she said, raising herself on tiptoe. 'We shall soon be back.'

'I am not so sure about leaving you.'

'Nonsense.' His face was close to hers. She let her hand rest for a moment on his rough coat and thick strong arm.

'Watendlath is not far away.'

' 'Tis a world away,' he answered her gruffly, and at once drove off.

She went back into the house. Her thought was, before everything, of Adam. He must go to bed. They had left Watendlath early that morning and, wild with excitement, he had been awake at four. Then, too, putting him to bed would give her some excuse to be alone a little before coming down.

On the landing they met the two children. John was now thirteen and Dorothy twelve. John was oddly like his father in face, but would be broader and thicker in body. Judith knew that he had a most charming character, kindly, affectionate, loyal – a little weak perhaps, a little dreamy like father and great-grandfather before him. How strange! John's great-grandfather had been her father! She thought of it as she kissed him. Dorothy was good-natured, obedient and conventional, something like her Aunt Deborah, fair-haired, at present plump, at the moment conscious of her 'pantalettes', which were only fastened with tapes above her knee and gave her much anxiety. Such things were always to make her anxious.

Both children were delighted to see their Aunt Judith as they had always called her. Life at home had not been too pleasant of late; now that Aunt Judith had come it would be more gay.

They were exceedingly interested to see Adam. He was at once at his ease with them. He was always at his ease with everyone, because he trusted everyone.

He threw off his little riding coat, letting it be where it fell, and showed John how the horse that Charlie Watson was driving had thrown up its head and snorted, but in the middle of this exhibition he was excited by the sight of the room where he and his mother would sleep. He had been too young during those first years in France to notice or remember things, and since then the farm at Watendlath had been all that he had known.

Certainly the room at the Keswick Inn today had been grand, but that had been a public place with men drinking and a man playing a harp, and there had been a dog with a lame leg. This was *his* room and his mother's!

He ran round and round it, shouting cries of joy. For Judith it was strange enough. For, once again it was her old room, the room where Mrs Monnasett had died.

'I thought you would wish to be in the same room,' said Jennifer, standing in the doorway.

It was indeed the same room! In all these years the wallpaper had not been changed. Still there were those blue pagodas, there was the tallboy that had seemed to her as a baby so infinitely high, over the bed the blue tester hangings and overlay, the bed itself with the columns fluted and reeded and so charmingly carved with acanthus leaves. There Mrs Monnasett, with her yellow face, had lain, the candles flickering in the breeze, her lips fixed in a sardonic smile ... The room of all Judith's life. Nothing had occurred. Only yesterday she had bent forward to find the little box ...

'I will leave you,' said Jennifer. 'Come, children. Aunt Judith will soon come down.' There was a new note in Jennifer's voice, as though behind her words she was pleading for something.

But Judith now could think only of Adam. She undressed him and washed him. He would hardly keep still. She held him naked in her arms and kissed him. He lay back against her watching the leaping flames of the fire. His small dark head against her breast (he was quite suddenly sleepy), he asked her questions.

'Is that gentleman my uncle?'

'Yes, dear.' Impossible to explain now why and how he was not!

'Was my father like him?'

'No; your father was not so tall nor so old.'

'This gentleman is very, very old.'

'No. Not truly. He will not appear old when you know him.'

'Is that boy called John?'

'Yes.'

He yawned a huge yawn.

'I like him . . . ' Then he added, blinking his eyes at the fire: 'Is the beautiful lady his mother?'

'Yes.'

'But he called her ma'am.'

'Many boys and girls call their mother ma'am and their father sir.'

He thought about this. 'I cannot call my father sir because I haven't one, and I have never called you ma'am.'

'No, and you never will,' said Judith resolutely. She put on his shirt and carried him to the big four-poster.

He looked so small in it that she laughed. Then they both laughed. The touch of the cool sheets woke him up again and he rolled all over the bed. Then he lay still, watching her with wide-open eyes while she changed her dress, washed her face and hands, brushed her hair.

'This is a very grand house,' he said at last.

'Yes. I lived in it when I was a little girl, younger than you are.'

But the strangeness of it! In that bed, where her small son was lying, old Mrs Monnasett had once lain! She looked at him, her heart bursting with love, but her voice was quite severe when she said:

'Now go to sleep, Adam. Are you hungry?'

He could not be. He had eaten a tremendous dinner at Keswick.

'Yes, yes. I am! I am!' he cried, although until his mother had mentioned it he had not thought of it. But how wonderful he thought her in her evening dress! The colours of her gown were rose and lavender grey, and she had a turban with a plume of feathers.

When she bent down to kiss him he hugged her and pinched her nose, a favourite game of theirs.

'If I do not eat soon I shall be asleep,' he answered, grinning at her. Yes, he was ugly as proper standards went, but she would not alter him by a hair's breadth.

'Do I look fine?' she asked him.

He nodded and watched her with all his eyes until she was out of the door.

But she did not feel fine at supper. They had dined at three in the afternoon but she at five in the Keswick Inn, so they were hungry and she was not. It seemed very natural that Jennifer should enjoy her food. However severe the crisis her appetite was strong.

Judith was strongly conscious of her clothes. That was not like her, but for three years the rose-lavender dress and the turban had lain in a box under the stair at John Green House. Fashions had changed. Evening dresses were shorter and had a padded 'rouleau' at the bottom. Waistbands were directly above the hips. Nevertheless, although she was in fashion, Jennifer was not smart. She looked as though she had put on her clothes in her sleep. Jennifer was untidy, Judith was dowdy; that's what they were. Francis was the grand one, seated gravely at the end of the table, his head thin now, as though carved of a fine stone. The ruffles at his neck were of a peerless whiteness.

Their talk was stiff and awkward. They spoke of general affairs. People were still discussing the Cato Street business, although it was eight months since its occurrence. Judith noticed at once with what feverish excitement Francis spoke, as though ignorant desperadoes like Thistlewood and Edwards were in every town, hiding down every lane, concealed in every corner.

She noticed, too, that when he went on in this exaggerated sensational strain Jennifer's lips stiffened and her eyes were scornful. She looked at Judith once, as though to say: 'You see now what he has come to. Can you wonder if I despise this man?' and Judith thought again that there was an appeal for help there.

Matters became even more personal when they discussed the Coronation that was to be celebrated in the following year, the King's efforts for a divorce, and the Queen's eccentric behaviour.

Francis, who had been drinking, Judith saw, very much more than was his habit in the old days, broke into a demonstrative, emotional defence of the Queen. The King was a blackguard; he did not care who heard him say it. He was surely old enough now to say what he pleased. Besides, everyone knew what the King was. It was disgraceful that the country should have to suffer under such a man. And the poor Queen – well, she had been, perhaps, a little imprudent at times. She was eccentric, emotional. But who had driven her to her eccentricities? Brougham was a hero. He would drink to Brougham. They must all drink to Brougham. Judith noticed then Jennifer's irritation. She saw that such scenes as these were part of every evening's programme. Jennifer, looking across the table at Francis scornfully, praised

the King, said that he had been much calumniated. At least he
was no prig nor Methodist. For her part she liked a jolly fellow,
a man who knew what life was and lived it to the full . . . not a
half-alive pedant who skulked about the house . . . She stopped
abruptly. Then smiled at Francis.

'I am fortunate,' she said softly, 'to have a husband who strikes
the mean. Judith, do you not think that Francis is looking well ?'

'Very well,' said Judith, and she put out her hand and touched
his. He looked at her with a glance that had in it so much of
apology and unhappiness that her heart was wrung.

The food was badly cooked and warm when it should have
been hot. The meal dragged on interminably. No allusion was
made to anyone's private affairs. At last they sat there in silence
while the candles trembled and the old clock ticked like a miser
counting his money.

What was the matter with the house ? There was more in this
than the relations of Francis and Jennifer, more than Jennifer's
infidelity, more than Francis' self-disgust. An air of apprehension
was everywhere. She had detected it, even in the faces of the
two children.

When at last they got up to move into the parlour, Judith
thought of Watendlath with a longing that was almost irresistible.
She had an impulse to run out into the dark cool garden. She
would be closer to the hills there and would hear water running
somewhere. She felt the touch of her hand on Charlie Watson's
strong arm. Oh, there everything was so simple, so happy.

In the hall she stopped for an instant to hear whether there
was any sound from Adam. No, he would be sleeping quietly.
She was comforted again.

In the parlour the three of them sat like images. The outburst
was soon coming, but until it did they must be silent. Judith
herself was affected by the stillness that was so vocal. Seated with
her back to the window she had a sudden fancy that Walter
Herries was standing outside, watching them, peering in. It was
all that she could do not to get up and see.

Then Jennifer rose, said that she was going to bed, kissed
Judith and went out, her eyes half closed, yawning a little, just
as she had used to do.

'Well, Judith,' said Francis.

'Well, Francis.'

He got up with a quick impetuous movement and came to
where she was sitting. He knelt down by her chair, put his arms
around her, rested his head on her breast.

'Oh, I am so weary, so weary,' he murmured.

She thought of the time when she was a baby and had adored him, when David had whipped her, and she had not cared so long as Francis loved her. She smiled a little wryly above his head. Poor Francis!

Then to her distress he began to weep. He seemed to be completely broken down. He wept as though all his control must be abandoned or he would die. She had never seen Francis cry. She could not bear it.

'Oh no, Francis. No . . . No, no!'

Then at last he looked up at her, his cheeks stained with tears.

'Forgive me, my dear. It is many years since I wept last. I am not given to weeping. But seeing you come back tonight, after all this time, the same, so familiar, the only friend I have left – it has been too much for me. Truly, Judith, I am desperate. I don't know which way to turn.'

'Now sit here beside me.' She motioned to a place on the sofa. 'Let us talk over things quietly. They are never so urgent when one talks over them quietly. We will discuss everything just as we have always done.'

He came and sat beside her.

'But you are going to stay now that you are here, are you not ? . . . You are not going away ?'

'For a few days. Of course, we will stay for a few days.'

'For a few days ? Oh, but that is nothing. Judith, you must live here again – for a while at least – you and your boy . . .'

'Live here ?' She laughed. 'Francis, do you not realize that I am now a scandalous person ? I have had a child out of wedlock as everyone knows. With Jennifer and the children—'

'Scandalous!' he broke out. 'We are all scandalous now! Yes, I will say anything tonight. I have held myself in long enough. Jennifer has been that man's mistress for years now – quite an old family affair. As soon as I am away at Kendal or Carlisle he comes here, and everyone knows it. Everyone knows it, I tell you. It is the common joke! Walter sees to that . . . And all these years I have done nothing. I, the fine Francis who started the world with such grand ideas. I have done nothing, nothing at all.

'I have skulked in corners, taken his hand, offered him drink, while he makes my wife a common whore . . . Oh, my God, my God, I am the most despicable man on this earth, the most despicable and the most unhappy!'

She tried to calm him. He was trembling from head to foot.

'She hates me. She despises me. And, God forgive me, I love

her yet. It is because I love her that I have been able to do nothing, because with my cursed nature I have always seen two
of everything. She never loved me. I forced her into marriage.
Why should I have denied her all opportunity of love ?'

He caught her hand.

'Judith, do you remember that Ball all those years ago, the
Ball when Jennifer broke Christabel's fan ? Of course, you do.
It all started from that. It has all come from that. You remember
that I was talking to you when she first came by! How lovely she
was that night! Do you remember ? Catherine de' Medici with
the collar of pearls and her white neck and the crimson dress ?
Her excitement at the Ball – do you remember ? . . .

'And after – the meeting in Berkeley Square. Do you remember ? When I sat in the window and it was so hot and the scent of
the lilac came up from the street. I sat in the window thinking
of Jennifer, and then do you remember how I broke in upon
Will and how angry he was ? Our separation dated from that.'

Did she not remember ? And how, a moment after, Georges
stood there in the doorway, Georges in his brown suit, spent and
done ? . . .

'Before that,' Francis went on eagerly, 'everything had been
well – for all of us and for the country too, I think. What a good
old country it was when I was a child, so quiet and so cosy!
Everyone drank ale, and there was "oat clap bread", and no one
came to disturb us. The children would help in the spinning or
drive the sheep on the fells. Everyone was happy together. But
now there are visitors peering and fingering, and in the towns
children of six and seven years work in the dark, and the ma-
chines have come to take the bread out of men's mouths. The
sky is blackening with smoke, we have a King too drunk to sit
on the throne, and class is against class . . .'

He broke off. 'No, by God, what do I care for the country any
more ? There was a time when I cared. Did I not kill my own
father and cause my mother to hate me, because the Bastille
fell ?'

He laughed bitterly, striking his knee with his hand.

'But now what should a cuckold think of his country – a
cuckold plain to all his neighbours, and any who do not know of
it kind Cousin Walter will tell them of it.'

She tried to calm him. He was so dreadfully excited that she
thought that at any moment he might raise the house.

'Dear Francis, the country is well enough. This is a time of
transition, and such times always seem hard to those who are in

them. There is a grand new world coming . . .'

'And I don't care if there is!' he interrupted her. 'You can have your fine new world! If I could but get my fingers round dear Walter's large throat!' He stopped himself with a tremendous effort. 'You see how it is with me tonight, my dear. I am excited at seeing you again. For you are the only one I have left, the only one who understands me. I killed my father. My mother hated me. My brother and wife hate me yet. God knows but my children hate me too. But I ask for no pity. It is all my own doing. You and I, my dear, are misfits; and to be a misfit in the Herries family is to be slain.'

'We are neither of us slain,' she said, looking up at him quickly. 'It is perhaps true that we are misfits. But it is the misfits, I fancy, who give the value to the world. What would the Herries family be without us? A dull, poor lot. We are the ones who understand and because we suffer have charity. We can see into both worlds. We travel into strange countries where the others cannot go, and bring back the news.' She laughed. 'I am turning very poetical,' she said. 'It is not my ordinary fashion. But I must tell you, Francis, that if I am a misfit I am a very happy one. And so may you be too if you will. I am certain that Jennifer does not hate you. She must be long weary of that other affair. All will soon be forgotten . . .'

'Forgotten!' he broke in. 'Not with Walter Herries there! Ah, you do not yet know the villain of the piece!'

'Walter?' she asked. 'What can he do?'

'What can he do? What has he not done? He hates us, has always done, because, firstly, he says Jennifer insulted his mother, secondly, he must be king of the castle here and wants no other Herries round, and, thirdly, he has a deformed son, and my children make him mad . . .'

'But he can do nothing.'

'Do nothing? He can do everything. He is my perpetual enemy and has been these five years. He is so proud that he will burst his skin one of these days. He has all the neighbourhood in his pocket.'

He calmed himself that he might give the value to his words. 'Do you know what for five years he has been doing? There are spies all around me, and every small action of mine is repeated to him. It has been so for five years now. Fancy to yourself what it would be if a good friend of yours, who had known you well for a long while, drew a caricature of you in a book, using all your external habits, your tricks of speech, your eccentricities, and then, with a diabolic cleverness, twisted them all to mean and sordid motives ? You would be yourself bewildered. You would say yes, that it was true; you had done this and that, you wore your hair so, you laughed thus, and like all men you had your weaknesses, your follies. Was this perhaps a true picture ? And if you saw it as partly true how much more would others, who know you but externally, judge of your true self ? And you would begin to doubt yourself and to suspect every movement, every gesture. I tell you, Judith, that my neighbours here who have known me all my life long take rather Walter's picture of me now than their own. There is nothing goes on in this house that he does not know, nothing that he does not use . . .'

Yes, he would be like that. She knew instinctively that what Francis said was true. She felt, even here in the warm safe room, the force and danger of his overbearing vitality.

But she answered firmly:

'Listen, Francis. No one can traduce you but yourself. Even your bitterest enemy knows that a satire is a satire. Its very exaggeration must make him consider the opposite. One is alone in this world. No one knows one save oneself, and then it is only a glimpse of the truth that one has. Forget Walter, and if you cannot forget Walter fight him!'

She jumped to her feet.

'I could fight him! He should have enough of his spying and traducing if I got at him!'

'Yes, yes,' he cried eagerly. 'You must stay, Judith. Remain here. With you to help me I can be another man. Although I am old—' His voice faltered. 'Sixty is an age . . .'

She had had enough. She was infinitely weary. Francis' request that she should stay gave her a sudden flick of terror. She did not want to stay. She must get back to Watendlath. She and Adam safe in Watendlath, away from all these Herries . . .

She kissed him.

'Goodnight, Francis, dear. All will come right.'

But as she climbed slowly the stair she thought, in spite of herself, 'But how *could* he not have challenged Fernyhirst ? How *could* he let it go on as he has – all these years ?' But she was weary to consider it further. However, her evening was not yet done with. As she passed Jennifer's door a voice called her.

She went in.

Jennifer was sitting on her bed in her shift, her long white legs dangling to the floor. Her room was in a disorder. Clothes were flung about the floor, drawers were pulled open, the curtains were roughly drawn, a lamp by the bed was smoking to the ceiling.

Judith closed the door.

'What has he been saying?'

'Oh, it is so late!' Judith sighed. 'Dear Jennifer—'

'No, I must know.'

'He has been saying nothing, only that he is unhappy—'

Jennifer put out a long white arm and drew Judith to the bed.

'I am unhappy too! Oh, so dreadfully unhappy! It is all his fault. I hate him . . . I have hated him for years. Why was I such a fool as to marry him? He has been speaking to you of Edward.'

'Edward?'

'Fernyhirst. But that is all finished. Finished long ago. I hate him too.'

Judith looked at her, and again her tiresome maternal impulse that was for ever preventing her real action interfered. But what was she to do? This poor, tired, aged woman! And once there had been that brilliant happy girl, radiant with beauty and success, in the crimson dress, the collar with the pearls?

But she had still lovely legs and feet! How different might Judith's own story have been had she had such wonderful feet and ankles! She put her arm round her, but how she longed for her bed!

'Francis spoke for the most part of Walter!'

'That devil! He is determined to ruin us, Judith, all of us – my poor children—' and even then, when she should have wept, she yawned, kicking her feet a little, looking at her silver slippers. And in that yawn Judith saw once and for ever exactly what she was. She was true Herries. She had no imagination, none whatever. Had she had any she would never have married Francis, never have lived in Cumberland, never have suffered an intrigue with Fernyhirst, never have stayed here for years, doing nothing, understanding nothing, seeing nothing! And it was against the Herries in her that Francis had beaten in vain! Had she been of an age it was Walter that she should have married. They would have suited one another to perfection.

It was from that moment of comprehension that Judith's complete domination of Jennifer began.

'Dear Judith. You are such a consolation. There was a time when I was jealous of you. I know how shockingly I behaved. You need not tell me of my behaviour. But now I would do anything for you – and Francis too. It is the one point on which we are agreed. You must stay for a long, long while.'

Judith smiled and shook her head.

'I am an abandoned woman, Jennifer – myself and my little bastard. We do not belong to good society any more.'

'What foolishness! I am sure that an illegitimate child is nothing. Everyone is so free in these days. And I am as bad as you. Everyone knows about Edward. Certainly you must stay.'

'I have grown unused to society. I am a peasant, digging and ditching, watching the sheep. You cannot think how strange these clothes seemed to me tonight.'

Jennifer, looking at her naked legs with approval, answered:

'I am sure that is a very good costume. But we are two old women. What does it matter what we wear? My legs are still fine, although there is no one who cares any more. Nor do I wish there to be. Love is the most wearying thing I know.'

Judith said goodnight.

'Then you will stay?'

'For a day or two at least.'

'No, for always. The children worship you, and little Adam is a love.' She stood up in her shift that fell in folds to her silver slippers. For a moment there was something genuine and touching in her fine eyes that looked out above her painted cheeks in a true and human appeal.

She said what Francis had said:

'You are my only friend.'

Judith undressed and lay down beside Adam. She stared into the dark. She *would* not, no, she *would* not be caught by these two. She *would* not come back into these Herries affairs . . . But they were so alone. Francis had no one – Jennifer only her brother, who was a fat careless bachelor in Bournemouth. Both Prosper and Amelia were dead.

But she *would* not be caught . . . She seemed to hear beyond the window the water of Watendlath. She could see the Tarn lying in ebony silence under the stars. The sheep were pressing up the road, the cows were to be milked; here came Tyson, his arms loaded with hay for the cattle. Armboth touched the stars . . .

She was near to tears; she was so homesick.

She was too old, too settled in her quieter life to take up these quarrels again. Ah, but Walter, riding his white horse, striking at Adam with his whip . . .

With a gesture of protection she stretched out her arm and

drew Adam to her. He was deep in sleep but he grunted like a little pig and nestled into her side.

ROUND OF THE MOON

THE HOUSE WAS bathed in sunlight and ladders of dust quivered in the air. No room had been swept for months; the kitchen was a disgrace; the dairy – ah, how beautiful it had once been with its gleaming cleanliness, the stone floor like a mirror – and now! In the stables there were but three horses, two of them fit for little but to drag the carriage at a funeral pace along the rocky, uneven roads.

Judith swept through the place like a whirlwind. Mrs Quinney, the housekeeper, Martha Hodgson, the woman who had opened the door on Judith's arrival (she was cook and maid both), Doris, a stupid country girl, and Mr Winch, the thin cadaverous little tutor, were, in addition to Bennett the coachman and Jack the stable-boy, all the servants. Very different from David's day, different even from Jennifer's early day, but Judith must make the best of it. And make the best of it she did. In no time she had them all at her call, all save Mr Winch, of whom more in a moment.

She summed them up instantly. Mrs Quinney was lazy, greedy, gossipy, weak, amiable, gossipy, greedy and lazy. Martha was earnest, plain, silent, faithful, opinionated and earnest. Doris was little, if anything, removed from the beasts of the field and like them was hungry, obedient, and responsive to overtures of love from the opposite sex. Bennett had always reminded her a little of her dear Charlie. She liked him because of that. He was stouter, less intelligent, had far less personality, but was a man – that is, he was a Cumberland man and therefore silent, suspicious, obstinate, faithful and courageous.

Jack the stable-boy pleased her best of all. He was only a lad and had come from the depths beyond Mardale, but he had the makings of a grand gentleman. He, from the first, would do anything for her.

There they were, ready to her hand. For years they had been neglected. Francis had scarcely spoken to them, Jennifer had let them do as they would. Before the week was out the house looked a different place, the floors shone, the silver glittered, the food came hot to the table, the horses trotted, Caesar the dog barked at night when he heard a strange step, the spiders were broomed away, the carpets were dusted, the grass of the lawn was cut, a dead cat was removed from the Gothic temple, a mouse was found in the chaise, chrysanthemums, bronze and orange, lighted the parlour, the drawers in Jennifer's bedroom were tidied, Dorothy had fresh ribbons to her dress, and the holes in John's stockings were mended.

Judith was to stay only a day or two. It was nearly Christmas before she had the house entirely to her liking.

Then, one winter's day when the sun like a swollen red penny rolled between shifting orange clouds over Skiddaw, she looked out through the bottle-green glass of the parlour window and saw Mr Winch creeping round the corner of the house towards the stables.

Creeping he was. His thin lanky body was bent almost to all-fours. There was a moment when in actual fact he knelt on the path and looked ludicrous enough in that position.

Abruptly round the corner came Francis, his head bent, his arms behind his back, and almost stepped on Mr Winch, who was diligently brushing his trousers. Francis said a word to him and came on, lost in thought as he always was in these days.

Now what had Mr Winch been doing? With her accustomed impetuosity Judith had disliked him from the first moment of meeting him, and, it is to be feared, for no better reason than that his hands were damp. Afterwards there were other reasons. Whence had he come? He had been in the house for four years and yet both Francis and Jennifer were exceedingly vague about him. He had tutored Lord Somebody's son once somewhere; he said himself that he came from Warwickshire; Jennifer disliked him and behaved as though he were not there. Francis talked to him on a day, and then on another day disregarded him. It seemed that he taught the children something. John at least said that he did. Judith disliked him increasingly, and the more she disliked him the more obsequious he became. His appearance was most certainly not prepossessing, for his narrow grey eyes were so placed that you could not be sure whether he had a squint or no, his suit was always a shiny black and he was for ever blowing his nose.

This vision out of the window woke Judith to life. She had been alive indeed all these weeks, engaged on a business that she adored, but the house had swallowed her. She had not seen outside its affairs. Except in one matter, and that was the emotion that never left her, night or day, her love for her son, Adam. She was suffering for the first time in her life from jealousy.

For Adam, when he had been in the house two days, fell in love with John. He was in love so completely and absolutely that he forgot his mother altogether. For five years she had been everything to him, and now she was, in the flash of an instant, it seemed, nothing to him at all. Of course it was not so. It was simply that he was at the age when he could not think of two things at the same time. He had never, as yet, in his life had an older boy for companion, and he found it simply enchanting.

John was kind, amiable and easy. He had not had in these last years a happy life. The house had been smoky with unhappiness. The two children had been quite neglected. He had followed the hounds at a time, but then the horse had been sold. He went out shooting rabbits with Bennett. He witnessed an occasional wrestling or cock-fight. But he was 'soft' for his time. He hated cruelty of any kind. It made him sick. It was hard to say at present what he cared for. He was not a student like his father, he did not roam the country. He liked to stay at home, work in the garden, read stories. Although he was no student he could read tales and poetry to himself by the hour. He would sit curled up in a corner somewhere and pray that he would not be noticed. He had always detested Mangnall's *Questions* and Butler's *Guide to Useful Knowledge* – for such things he had no use whatever, but Goldsmith's *History of England* he devoured in all its four volumes because of the thrilling detail in it. Then there was Vicesimus Knox's *Elegant Extracts in Prose and Verse*, then *Marmion*, *The Lay*, the Waverleys, *The Parents' Assistant*, *The Fairchild Family* and, secretly, obtained from some of the Forresters who lived in Bassenthwaite, many volumes of the Minerva Press, *The Mysterious Hand*, *The Demon of Society* and the rest.

He read, he dreamed, his life was intensely solitary. It was an amazing thing for him when this ugly baby, so fearless, so interested and so happy, came into it. The two great characteristics of Adam Paris, then and always, were his interest and his happiness. In later years he was to exasperate many persons by these two qualities, for most human beings quite naturally call extensive interests selfishness, and happiness complacency.

John had not known much happiness yet in his life, and few persons had cared very actively whether he were happy or no. He was shy of his father as his father was shy of him, and afraid of his mother. Dorothy was a girl. Mr Winch was nothing. Only

Bennett was his friend, and Bennett had never much to say. Now this small boy came and worshipped, thought him a god, believed everything that John told him, trusted him utterly. Soon they were inseparable.

Adam did not forget his mother, but she was always there, while John was something new and showed him everything that he wanted to see.

When Judith realized that she was jealous she was amazed at herself. She liked John and trusted him; Adam could not be with anyone better. But her jealousy would not let her alone. She showed it to no one, but something told her that the first stage of her life with her son was over. She would never again have him so completely her own as she had had him during those first five years. She was alone again. It seemed to be the one lesson that life was for ever teaching her. Alone she was; alone she must ever be. She did not yet realize that it was the lesson that every other human being was also, with exasperated tears and helpless gestures, learning.

The fire of her love for Adam burnt her heart, it seemed to her. She stood listening for him. She called softly, then louder, then louder again. At last he would appear at the stairhead or at the stable door, John beside him. She would smile and wave to him and go away.

At night she had him. He would dance into bed, ask her one question after another on the wonders of the past day, and then instantly fall asleep. Then her time came. She would fold his small body in her arms and, with his head against her breast, would tell him how she loved him, how he was everything to her, how he was all that she had, how she loved him as no mother had ever loved her son, and the shadows of the fire would leap ironically on the wall and Adam would breathe softly in his sleep, lost to her even then.

But he was not really lost to her. In the depth of her being she knew it and was comforted. Meanwhile the discovery of Mr Winch on all-fours on the garden path woke her to important issues.

Having the house now tidied and disciplined, she was aware that, in spite of herself, Walter Herries' shadow was hanging over her as it was over the others. Not so grimly perhaps, nor so tragically, for she still maintained to herself with all her energy that her stay here was only temporary and that in another fort-night – after Christmas for certain – she would be free, in Watendlath, of the pack of them, never to return. She was not very sensitive as to her social position – she had never been sensitive – but she was aware that the visitors to Uldale in these last months had all regarded her with a very lively curiosity, and she thought that, behind their politeness, there was a kindly ostracism. They did not, she was aware, invite her to their houses, but that might have been as easily because of Jennifer's scandal as her own.

Only good, kind Mrs Southey invited her. She went with the secret hope that she would see again that strange boy Hartley. But Hartley was not there. None of the children were present. Mr Southey was very kind and a little distant.

Of Walter himself and his family she had seen nothing. The two households were cut off from one another as though they were as remote as China from Spain. But, rightly or wrongly, she heard the loud voice and saw the broad back of Walter behind everything and, in spite of her own good common sense, began to catch something of the superstition that Francis and Jennifer had of him – as a sort of malicious devil, horns on his head, hoofs instead of feet, and an eye in the middle of his back.

Seeing Mr Winch, one thing at least became plain to her: Mr Winch was Walter's spy. Assured of that, she was, in a moment, alive to a whole blazing bundle of circumstances, as suddenly bright and crackling as though she had seen it burst into flame before her eyes.

On looking back afterwards it appeared to her that everything and everyone sprang into action from that moment when she saw Mr Winch on all-fours. It was, in any case, very soon after that day that some of the worst and unhappiest moments of her life confronted her.

The awful day opened for her quietly enough. It was a fortnight before Christmas, and in the morning the sky was a bright shrill blue, the tops had a powdering of snow and the roads were hard with frost.

Adam was to go on some grand Christmas expedition into Keswick with John and Dorothy. She accompanied them, riding her own sturdy little mare, Phyllis, that she had brought with her from Watendlath. She thought that after she had seen them safely into the town she would ride on into Borrowdale and have a glimpse of Herries again. She had woken that morning with her head full of Warren. She could not tell why. She had not thought of him, she was ashamed to confess to herself, for months. But now, without warning, he had returned as the dead do unexpectedly return.

They had an agreeable ride into Keswick, passing many enchanting things on the way – a pedlar, a blind man with a trumpet, two drunken men fighting, a flock of sheep and a herd of cows. Adam had had his eyes and nose pressed to the windows of the chaise and was asking questions as fast as he could breathe, not waiting for any answers. The vast broad back of Bennett bobbed up and down on the box outside, the inside smelt of straw and mice, and Judith tried to feel no jealousy as she watched John holding Adam that he should not fall.

Then she rode on into Borrowdale. The road was still wild and uneven and unfit for a carriage, although carriages often used it, for it was the thing now to tour the Lakes and see 'the horrid precipices' and 'the thunderous waterfalls' that had so terribly frightened Mr Gray. Today, however, Judith had the scene to herself. Not a human being did she see, save an old man gathering sticks in a field. The Lake embraced the blue sky with a little tremor of excitement, and very lovely were the reflections of the snow-sprinkled hills in that blue water, hill-tops trembling like shadows in a swaying mirror.

The village of Grange was dead, and when at last she came to the Herries house, that was dead also. As before, when she had been with Warren, no one was there, but there were the remains of a meal on the table and a crumbling fire in the kitchen.

She sat on the old mildewed couch in the upper room for a while. Here she and Warren had sat . . . how long, long ago! Had they not sat there that day Adam would not be sucking lollipops (as she was sure that he was doing) in Keswick at this moment. Once again she asked herself why she had surrendered to Warren? For love of Georges' shadow? – and then with a sharp pang she realized for the first time how swiftly Georges was now fading from her mind. All the pain of losing him was gone. She did not miss him any more! Adam had taken his place.

She was not a sentimentalist. Facts were facts, and Georges, who had always wanted everyone else to be happy so long as he himself was not uncomfortable, would be glad. But Adam! She stood before the dead stone fireplace and pressed her hands before her eyes. Her passion of possession was terrific. She must govern it, guard it. Adam as he grew must be free. Looking into darkness, seeing into the future, she was afraid of herself.

The house dripped with damp and was of a fearful cold. She listened. Were there ghosts about? No; today Adam had slain them all. Father, mother, husband – one crick of her son's finger and they were fled.

She visited Georges' grave, then stopped at one of the cottages in Rosthwaite and ate and drank there. She knew every man, woman and child in Rosthwaite. It needed all her control not to push Phyllis up the well-known track. She was so near to Watendlath that, had Adam been with her, she must have gone – and then never have come down again! It was just over her head! If she listened she could hear Mrs Ritson calling and Molly the cow lowing for her calf!

She would not come this way again. It was dangerous. But she would not need to come, for in a fortnight Christmas would be here, and directly after Christmas she and Adam would leave Uldale for ever.

She started homewards and saw that the weather was changing. She looked back and beheld how over Scafell and the Gavel great black clouds were climbing. They were piling up as though out of a vast vat. The blue sky above her head seemed to tremble in anticipation of its destruction. The clouds had a sort of boiling rage and fury in their blackness. She turned on her horse to watch as though at some show or pageant. Then she saw a small white cloud, like a puff of smoke from a cannon, spring above the hill and start to fly from the enemy. The little white cloud spread across the blue, and the black clouds pursued it. She could almost hear them roaring in their fury. 'I hope it will escape! I hope it will escape,' she could fancy the bare trees around her, that were all beginning to tremble, saying. But of course the little cloud had no escape. The vanguard of the black army put out an ebony feeler, as an octopus might do, and the little white cloud was instantly swallowed. The landscape around her went dead as though a hand had struck it. The trees were shaking violently. A drop of rain smacked her cheek. She whipped Phyllis up and ran for it. By Grange she was caught. The rain slapped the earth like a woman beating a carpet. The drops danced on the ground with exultant joy. There was an empty outhouse off the road opposite the bridge. Pulling Phyllis after her, she ran in – and found Walter Herries filling the little place with his bulk!

They were at first very polite. His eyes twinkled with amusement. The noise of the rain on the roof was so loud that they had to shout. Then, quite suddenly, she sprang in.

'Walter Herries, you should know that shortly I intend to wring the neck of your shabby little spy and throw him into the stable.'

'My spy!'

'Nasty Mr Winch.'

He laughed, throwing his great head back and slapping his thigh.

'Cousin Judith, come and stay at Westaways for a little. Food and drink are better than at Uldale.'

She looked at him contemptuously.

'I would marry Mr Winch sooner than sleep under your roof.'

'I am not inviting you to share my bed, Cousin Judith.'

She flushed.

'That was worthy of you,' she said. 'But remember you cannot touch *me* anywhere. It may be in the end I can harm *you* the more.'

He seemed contrite. 'I said a dirty thing. For once you see me ashamed. Make the most of it.'

She looked at him with a quiet inspection that made him, she saw, uncomfortable.

'I believe I could be your match if I cared, but I have done with all the Herries affairs. I never was in truth part of them and I never will be. But you must understand that I have loved Francis all my life, and something will come of your persecution of him.'

They had to shout, and there was something very ludicrous in that. In spite of herself, and although she was feeling exceedingly angry and had never hated him more, she smiled. He smiled too.

'I think we could be very good friends,' he said.

'Never! Never!' she answered passionately. 'I hope very much I can do you some harm before I die.' Then, to her great vexation, she smiled again, for a little trickle of rain, coming in from the roof, fell down his cheek and made him look absurd.

'Why do you persecute Francis? It is a very small game and not at all worth all the energy you put into it.'

'Jennifer insulted my mother,' he said like a sulky schoolboy.

'What! You are going back all that way – because years ago at a stupid Ball Jennifer broke your mother's fan?'

'They can leave Uldale and go elsewhere. Francis is doing no good there. Jennifer is the countryside scandal. They do the Herries name harm.'

'The Herries name! And what good do *you* do the Herries name?'

That touched him. He started up.

'By God! I do the Herries name more good than your rascally father, or *his* miserable puling grandson.' He grew calm again, came near to her and would have taken her arm had she not moved away.

'Now listen, Judith. I have but begun. I am a young man, strong and healthy. I shall wipe your Uldale family out as though they had never been. I have wealth and power, but nothing at all in comparison with what I shall have. I am here for ever – I and my son after me.'

'I have not seen your children,' she said quietly.

It was cruel of her. She touched him there. His stout red face grew more crimson. For a moment she felt almost kindly towards him.

'Never mind,' he said, so low that she scarcely caught the words. 'My son has one leg that is shorter than the other, but he will have a head-piece that Francis' boy will one day fear.'

'So you carry the feud into a later generation,' she said scornfully.

'Not if they leave Uldale. Let them go South. I will not bother them.'

'I see!' She looked him in the eyes. They were now very close together and she could smell the stuff of his handsome brown riding coat.

'Had I not other plans for myself I should like to stay and fight you, Cousin Walter . . . I, too, have a son, you know. His father was Herries, even though distantly.'

'Yes. Poor Warren.' He laughed contemptuously. 'An illegitimate Herries, my dear.'

'But Herries blood,' she answered.

He caught her arm then, whether she liked it or no.

'We should be friends, Judith. We are of the same sort.'

'But we are enemies, Cousin Walter,' she answered. 'Good, sound, rock-bottom enemies. Good day to you.'

The rain had almost ceased. She mounted Phyllis and rode away. It was nearly dark when she reached Keswick, but the sky had cleared again. There were a few stars already and a fine frosty tang in the air. Soon there would be a grand full moon. The thought of the moon stayed her. There would be plenty of light to ride home by if she returned later. Francis had gone to Cockermouth for the night on a piece of business and she shrank from an evening quite alone with Jennifer. There was nothing more dreary, for Jennifer would either yawn and say nothing, or seek to abuse Francis, when Judith must stop her, or retrace the by now desperately familiar path of her affair with Fernyhirst, her weariness of him, the unfairness of everything and what would Judith advise her to do ?

When Francis was present things were better, but without

him – no, she could not endure it! Moreover, she was herself
tired. She was not so young as she had been. It had been a long
ride to Borrowdale; the visit to Herries, the encounter with
Walter had for the moment exhausted her.

So she stepped in to see the only two friends that she had now
in Keswick. They were a quaint pair, Miss West and Miss
Pennyfeather. They were one of the scandals of Keswick, and
about them Keswick was never weary of talking. They lived in a
very small house in Main Street, next to a smithy. They were
indeed an eccentric pair, devoted, original, entirely indifferent
to public opinion, clever and sarcastic.

Miss West dressed as near a man as to be no matter. She wore
a powdered wig and a coat with brass buttons. It was said that in
the evening in her parlour she wore trousers. She drank and, it
was rumoured, smoked a long clay pipe. She had a thin dried
face with a long nose and very bright keen eyes. Miss Pennyfeather was very feminine, round and plump, pink and white.
But she was even more sarcastic and cruel than Miss West in a
quiet soft way. In reality they were neither of them cruel, but
gave much in charity. They hated men and would not, it was
said, have one in the house. They liked Judith greatly and would
have seen much of her had she wished it. She liked them also,
but was not in Keswick sufficiently.

She knocked on the door, was admitted by their little maid
Betty, and found them by the fire in the parlour, Miss West
reading to Miss Pennyfeather from one of the novels of Mrs
Cuthbertson.

They were enchanted to see Judith.

Miss West threw Mrs Cuthbertson on to the floor, crying in a
deep bass voice: 'This is Stuff!'

Then they had supper off cold chicken, rhubarb pie and cheese
and, after that, played cards very frivolously. Miss West told
some scandalous stories about the curate of Crosthwaite, about
the wife of a coal-merchant who had recently come into money
and set up his carriage, and a French poodle owned by the
eccentric Mrs Mason, a widow. They all laughed very much and
Miss West imitated the Crosthwaite curate looking for his handkerchief in the middle of his sermon.

When Judith at last departed she wondered what had happened to her lately. It seemed so long since she had last laughed
with real abandon.

Phyllis was thinking of her stable and under a full moon
trotted with enthusiasm. It was late. The Crosthwaite Church

struck the hour of eleven as they turned into the Carlisle road.

As she went along she was happy and confident. 'Three old women! Never mind. We know how we can enjoy ourselves without the men – and I stood up to Walter. I enjoy standing up to Walter. I shall do it again.' She would tempt Miss West and Miss Pennyfeather up to Watendlath after Christmas. They were great riders. They should stay a day or two with her at the farm. They would enjoy the Ritsons . . .

When she reached the house it was five minutes to twelve by the round-faced clock above the stables. The moon shone with such brightness that the whole world of hill, fell and dead white road was recreated into unreality. The stars were fiery – all else was icy cold and like a dried bone in colour.

She put Phyllis into her box, patted her nose and then, almost startled by the sound of her own steps on the cobbles in the still world, crossed over to the house.

She let herself in and with soft tread went straight to her room. The stair was flooded with moonlight.

She lit the candles and, with one raised in her hand, went over to see that Adam was sleeping. With his cheek on his hand, his mouth a little open, he looked so entirely hers and hers alone that she gave a little gasp of happiness, put down the candle and sat on the bed-edge gazing at him.

She blew out the candle, drew back the curtain and let the moonlight spread a pool of liquid shadow about the carpet. She did not feel sleepy. She was immensely content. She sat at the window looking at the frosted slope of Skiddaw, the friend of her life.

She was thus idly watching and had listened to the clocks tell the half-hour when, muffled by the window but sharp on the frosted road, she heard the hoofs of a horse. She bent forward and saw, to her amazement, the horse stop at the gate and a heavily-cloaked rider, whom she quickly knew to be Francis, dismount. Francis! Here! Now! She stood up, her hand at her heart. Something told her at once that there was trouble. She saw him open the gate and lead the horse round to the stable.

Driven by some instinct, unreasoning but imperative, she softly went from her room on to the landing, and, as she did so, at the same moment Jennifer's door opened and she appeared, in her nightdress, her ringlets about her shoulders, a candle in her hand, and on her feet her silver slippers.

'What was that ?' she said, her finger to her lip.

'Francis is returned.'

'Oh, my God!'

Even as she breathed that they heard the outer door of the house open. Jennifer seized Judith's wrist. She never spoke, but pushed Judith into her room.

Six candles were blazing, a table with wine and the remains of a chicken was near the bed, which was tumbled and in disorder, and Fernyhirst in his shirt and trousers, his shirt open at the neck, his rather long grey hair untidily over his forehead, sat sprawling in a large crimson chair.

'What is it?' he asked, looking up; then saw Judith and his mouth stayed open. She thought that she had never seen a more unattractive creature, purple-veined, double-chinned, with a heavy stomach and thick unwieldy legs. Her disgust with both of them was so intense that for a moment it covered everything else. That they should thus – these two elderly lovers – have been philandering in the room next to her sleeping son seemed to her a foul thing. That Jennifer should thus have gone back on her word—

But beyond her personal sense of affront she knew at once there was something more important. Francis must not find them there. He must not. And once this hateful discovery of hers was passed she would see to it that Fernyhirst came to the house no more.

But they remained, frozen into silence. The room seemed chilled by an icy wind from the cold world outside although the fire blazed in the grate. They waited, the two women standing where they were, Fernyhirst sitting up in his chair.

Jennifer only whispered once: 'He always goes to his room.'

They heard nothing, for the door was closed: then, as though the house crashed about their ears, the door opened and he stood there.

Judith saw at once from his face that he had known what he would find. Instantly he flung himself across the room and fell upon Fernyhirst, pulling at his shirt, beating his face with his hand and crying:

'At last! At last! ... You bloody rat ... You whoring, filthy ...'

Jennifer ran to them, pulled feebly at Francis' coat and screamed. The table with the chicken and wine fell over, making a terrible crash.

Judith ran in among them.

'Francis! Francis! Listen! ... Be quiet! Be still! The house must not hear, it must not wake ... Francis! Francis!'

Francis seemed to hear her, for he stopped clawing at Ferny-hirst and walked away, trembling from head to foot, his breath coming with a strange shrill sob.

The scene indeed was very quickly over, for Fernyhirst, silent and, it seemed, unmoved, rose, felt the blood that trickled on his cheek, put on very calmly his waistcoat and coat, picked up from the chair his hat and riding coat and walked to the door.

There he turned and, looking at Francis, said heavily, 'You shall answer me for this.' He seemed not at all disturbed, and even looked at the decanter on the floor as though he had half a mind to pick it up. Then he went out.

Francis came forward, and, speaking very rapidly and, Judith thought, as though he had made up his speech in his head before-hand, addressed Jennifer, who was now sitting on the bed and crying very wildly.

'I go now,' he said, 'and I shall never return. Thank God I have seen the last of you ... I shall attend to your lover ...'

He stammered, as though he would say something to Judith, but suddenly hung his head and went swiftly out of the room.

He dragged his horse out of the stable and clattered up the road in pursuit of Fernyhirst, who was but a little ahead of him. He had but paused to take two rapiers from the corner of his room – the small room behind the parlour that was cluttered with guns, fishing-tackle, books, papers, swords and these rapiers. No one had touched them for many a year.

As he rode he did not feel the cold; he was rather bathed in a damp heat that was also dry, so that, although his forehead was wet with sweat, his hands had no moisture. That afternoon, walking along the street in Cockermouth to see some fellow on a land transaction, he had been touched on the elbow by a ragged man with a black patch over one eye, who had given him a dirty piece of paper. On this was scrawled in a rough unfamiliar hand: 'The Captain is with your wife tonight and don't leave till morning.'

Reading it, he walked on mechanically until he was almost out of the town without knowing it. He was no longer Francis Herries – that weak, lily-livered creature was gone for ever. He was a fiery man of action, but cautious withal, a crafty vengeful devil, murderous in intent, brilliant in device. This sly fiery devil waited until night at the Cockermouth inn, sitting in a room there, with a plate before him, but not eating. Once and again he held scornful converse with the pitiful Francis, who was imprisoned in a cage and could not get out.

'Let me out!' cried Francis.

But the fiery devil only grinned, while his hand trembled on the table and his eyes were blind.

Later he found them just as the dirty piece of paper had said, and now he was going to kill Fernyhirst.

He came upon him a quarter of the way to Stone Ends. He rode past him at a gallop and then turned and faced him. There was bare moor on either side and the moon cynically observant. Everything was as bright as day, and the smoke from the horses' nostrils clouded the air.

'Off your horse, Fernyhirst,' Francis said. 'We will finish this here.'

'Let me pass, you blackguard,' Fernyhirst cried. But he was a coward at a pinch, had always been. He did not know whether Francis had not a pistol. He climbed off his horse and began blustering.

Francis showed him the rapiers.

'We will fight here and now,' he said.

'This is monstrous,' Fernyhirst said. 'No seconds. No arrangements. I protest. I refuse—'

'We will fight here and now,' Francis repeated.

Perhaps it occurred to Fernyhirst that here would be a good opportunity to teach this puling husband a lesson, for although a coward he had been a skilled duellist in younger days, and the rapier was his favourite weapon. He knew, too, that this business would be scandalous if he let it go on. The quickest over the less said.

His hesitation swung to bluster.

'If you wish it,' he said scornfully. 'You are a poor husband, Herries, and poor husbands always make shabby fighters.'

Herries said not a word.

They drew the horses up the moor and over the ridge to a hollow where they could not be seen from the road. They fought in their shirts, although the cold was intense. Francis was a good swordsman, but it was years since he had had any practice. He fought in what was known as the Neapolitan style, with straight arm and straight back, his knees bent. Fernyhirst fought with a flourish, sweeping his rapier in the air. He knew instantly that Francis was a good swordsman, and cursed his own lack of condition, for he was fat and had been drinking heavily that same night. The scene was strange enough. Sheep came up the moor and stood bewildered. The two horses cropped the grass, and across a cloudless sky the full moon proudly sailed. The hills cut the sky sharply in the frosty air and seemed to bend their brows in attention.

They fought for a while without advantage to either side; then suddenly Francis, lowering his rapier a little, pressed upon his enemy. Fernyhirst retreated a step or two, then Francis made a short lunge in tierce. Fernyhirst backed again, but, after some clever feints, came forward and himself began to challenge Francis.

This extra exertion told on him. His breathing distressed him, and soon two moons circled in his vision, swinging about the shining length of Francis' weapon. Was he to be killed? In this bitter air with no witness? A sudden fear of Francis' intensity caught him. He lunged, his breath coming in pants, but he could not find Francis' body. Everywhere that stiff wall of steel met him. His legs were trembling, the ground rocking. The fear of death, of imminent and dreadful death, leapt at his throat like an animal from the moon.

He gave a yell that made the sheep scatter down the slope, turned and fled for his life. Panting, he flung himself on his horse, threw the rapier away from him and rode off as though all the Furies were beside him.

And Francis stood under the moon without moving. This had been the creature to whom for all these years he had surrendered his wife.

The agonized bitterness of a self-contempt that now would never find a cure stole slowly, quietly down upon him.

Gently his head bent; he went towards his horse.

FRANCIS IN LONDON

Spring 1821

FROM THE WINDOW of his little lodging off St James's Street Francis could see a pale green sky floating between the clouds of two smoking chimneys, a curricle waiting outside the bow-window of Ashton's, the hosier's, and a very elegant dandy picking his way through the puddles as though his life depended on the dryness of his boots. Both before and behind him spouts, charged with the rain that the flat roofs had collected, were pouring out their floods. He had navigated one. Now he paused before the other as though collecting all his resources. Soon the lamps on the little elevated posts that dotted the street would be lighted. The sun was almost set. One star, freshly washed, so bright it was, by the recent rain, hovered in the green sky. So agreeable was the spring air that Francis had his window open. He could hear the rattle of the carriage-wheels on the cobbles of St James's, could smell the damp and soot and sea-coal and the cooking that was going on in Mrs Morland's room downstairs.

In his melancholy depressed mood, to watch the dandy gave him some occupation. The man in his light pantaloons (surely his calves were padded!) his absurdly exaggerated hat, his ridiculous collar *à la guillotine*, his monstrous waist (he was wearing beyond question Cumberland corsets), seemed scarcely human.

As he paused, looking at the water-spout, raising first one foot and then another, Francis, in spite of his dejection, could scarcely forbear to laugh. Then there hurried past, his coat up to his ears, a little man with a pile of books under his arm, who, Francis fancied, might be Mr Lamb, to whose house his friend Daintry, the water-colour painter, had one evening taken him. Francis thought, for a wild moment, that Mr Lamb might be coming to pay him a call. Why not ? He had been most pleasant to him, talked to him of old plays and actors, asked him whether he had thought of playwriting, had appeared to be interested, had inquired his address . . . but no, it was not Mr Lamb. Of course not. No one ever came to visit him.

The green sky faded, the old lamp-lighter whom Francis knew so well by now, with his funny step that was a kind of dot-and-carry walk, passed down the street. Francis closed the window, drew the curtains, lit the candles, went to the table, drew out his papers; he was writing an article on Malthus which he hoped (very faintly) that the *Evening Chronicle* might look upon kindly. He wrote a few lines and threw down his pen. It was no good; the thing was a farce. He sat there, his head between his hands, muttering to himself that the end had come.

He had taken of late to talking to himself, for indeed he had for the most part no one else to talk to. Mrs Morland told Morland that the poor old gentleman was wrong in his head; she hoped he would do no one a mischief. Morland, who was a coal-merchant by trade and as kind-hearted as any man in London, shook his head and said that he thought that Mr Herries had lived too long in the country. He had lost touch with the Town. 'London's a big wild place these days, Maria, and not good for a gentleman who has no friends seemingly and is accustomed to country fields.' This was perhaps true. Francis *had* lost touch with the Town. He had been here now for nearly five months. After the wretched farcical fight with Fernyhirst he had ridden to Penrith, slept the night there and taken the London coach on the following day.

He had found rooms with the Morlands, and for a week or two had fancied that he might begin a new life. He had written a brief letter to Jennifer, saying that he would never return, but that proper provision would be made for her and the children. He had sought out some of his old friends, avoiding, however, any possible contact with any Herries relations. His principal success here had been with his old acquaintance, Samuel Rogers, who, only a year or two younger than Francis, welcomed him with the warm kindliness and good heart that that crabbed old poet hid under his sneers and oddities.

He welcomed Francis to his famous house in St James's Place, with its view of the Green Park, its collections of prints, its Etruscan vases. Here Francis could have found exactly the society suited to his taste, and many happy contacts might have come of it. He had real literary feeling, could talk excellently when he was in the mood. He had, however, developed an almost crazy spirit of suspicion and self-detraction. It seemed to him that everyone must know of the disgrace and misery that weighed so heavily upon him. No one knew and no one cared; but, after a few visits, some fancied slights, some momentary irritations on the part of old Rogers, he slipped away and hugged his loneliness. He had thought that writing would be his great recourse. He thought that now at last he had the freedom and independence. But always his own wretched thoughts broke into his imagination and shattered it.

He walked mile upon mile of London streets, but here, too, he was unhappy, for the old London that he had known was gone or going. The stucco of Mr Nash was rapidly covering with its pallid cloak the red and brown and grey of the earlier houses. A passion for building seemed to have sprung upon the town, and the suburbs were eating fields and lanes and trees as fast as they could be devoured. This was a busier, more serious London than he had known, and it seemed to have no place for him. Everywhere new shops were opening, no one appeared to have leisure any more, all were thinking of making a fortune or seeing some new invention. Housebuilding, experiments with machinery, expeditions to America, a visit to Paris and back, a tour on the Continent – all these were everyday adventures. It was a

world in which he was lost. He was altogether a lost man; he
had no foothold anywhere any more. On the little ink-stained
desk near the window lay a pile of letters from Judith unopened.
He had not read one of them; he did not dare to. She would
implore him to return, would tell him of John and Dorothy, of
himself and, worst of all, of Jennifer.

The awful thing, the poison that in his loneliness devoured
him, was that he still loved Jennifer. He loved her as ardently
and as hopelessly as at the beginning, yes, as madly as on that
first occasion when he had seen her at the Herries Ball. The thing
that had ruined him, apart from his own indecision of character,
was that his love had never been returned. That had not been
Jennifer's fault – she had been honest with him – but from that
misery of tantalization he had died. For now he was as good as
dead. Had he once captured her he would have found, likely
enough, that the thing captured was neither interesting nor
valuable, but he had been able neither to catch her nor leave her,
neither to admire her nor despise her, neither to fight for nor
against her; she had completed the ruin that his own miserable weakness had begun. As he sat there he did not pity himself
nor curse himself. He did not feel that he was altogether to
blame. He was a piece of pottery in whom the potter had carelessly set a flaw.

He might be, as Judith had said, one of the hopes of the
Herries; but they had been too strong for him and the hope was
lost. From the very beginning he had been frightened of Will's
efficiency, a rebel against his father, acquiescent in things as
they were, a slave to his mother's melodrama, subservient again
to his wife's lazy indifference. The Herries had beaten him every
time. He might have been a success in any other family. Judith
alone had understood him. Judith . . . dear, darling Judith . . . so
kind, so wise, so brave, so friendly and true . . .

He got up, made a step towards the desk. He had almost those
letters in his hand. But no, he must not. If he read them he
would return and there would begin that wretched half-life,
with Walter's spying and bullying . . .

Walter! He called the name aloud as though he were challenging it. He could see that swollen, red-faced, confident boaster . . .
There was a knock on the door. Mrs Morland looked in.

'A lady to see you, sir,' she said.

'A lady?' He turned back, smoothing his hair that had grown
too long and tumbled over his forehead. His heart beat nervously, as it did now when anyone approached him. There was

a pause, and then who should come in? Who but old Maria
Rockage?

He was so greatly surprised that he could not speak, but could
only stare at her with his mouth open. She was an odd enough
figure. She must be, he thought, nearly seventy. She was
wearing a black, rather faded costume of a fashion quite ten
years earlier, all in one piece, tied with a band of ribbon immediately under her ample breasts. Her shoes were muddy and
she had a black poke-bonnet. Her face wore its accustomed
expression of anxiety, nervousness, kindliness and assurance.

Her nervousness was for the actual moment, her assurance
for her general state. But, as always, kindliness was the pre-
dominating note. As a matter of fact, she was not so old as
Francis thought her – she was sixty-six – and she felt a great
deal younger than that.

'Cousin Maria! . . . But I never expected . . . Pray come in . . .
I am delighted . . . But how did you know my lodging?'

She smiled at him with great beneficence.

'Mr Rogers told me. Carey and I were at a party in St James's
Place the other evening, a very fine party . . .' (The odd thought
came to him that, in spite of her Methodist proclivities, she was
ever going to parties.) 'I had Phyllis and Carey with me. Literature and the Arts . . . And then Judith wrote to me. She begged
me to search you out. She is so greatly distressed—'

She was looking at him, and biting the fingers of her worn
gloves, and putting up her hand to pat the hair under her
bonnet, and screwing her mouth round in a strange way that
she had. What a funny old thing she was!

He cleared the papers away and sat her down at the table. Of
course, he said to himself, she was looking around her and seeing
how shabby everything was. She would tell Will and Christabel,
and everyone would know. How was he certain that she had
not come to spy out for Walter? She had but recently been staying at Westaways. Tiresome old thing! And then, to his amazement, he saw that tears were trickling down her cheeks! When
he saw that, it was all that he could do not to cry himself, so tired
and wan and miserable he was. She began to chatter with little
gulps and stammers.

'Francis, we have never known each other very well. We are
almost of an age. I fear it is an impertinence my coming like
this and intruding on your privacy. But I had to come. The Lord
told me to come; and although I know that you think me foolish
about my religion, still we are both old people now and can be

tolerant about one another. I have not come to interfere in any way, dear Francis. Indeed I have not. But I could not bear to think of your being all alone and away from Jennifer and your lovely children – although I have never quite agreed with Jennifer, yet she is no longer as young as she was neither, and the pomps and vanities of our life fade away, leaving us often much alone. I know, although I have the best husband in the world and dear Carey and dear Phyllis, I know what it is to be lonely and have only the Lord to depend upon—' She broke off and looked at him with mild kindly eyes, beseeching him not to be rude to her.

She smiled at him over her handkerchief, a watery but encouraging smile. He wished to be kind – but what was he to say?

'Dear Cousin Maria, this is very good of you. I fear I have no hospitality to offer you.'

'Oh,' she broke in, 'I want nothing. I want nothing at all, I assure you. Too good of you – and your room is very cosy, very cosy indeed. And right on the street, so that you have people passing. I always say that if you have people passing you cannot really be lonely. Always something going on – a carriage accident or a fire or a Punch and Judy. I would go anywhere myself to see a Punch and Judy. Carey is for ever laughing at me for it. "Why, Maria," he says, "I believe you'd run down the street if there were a Punch and Judy about" – and I believe I would, you know. So very amusing . . . One never tires . . .' She broke off and then said abruptly: 'And when was the last time you heard from dear Judith?'

'I haven't heard,' he said in a very low voice, 'for quite a while.'

She put out her gloved hand and laid it on his.

'Francis,' she said, 'go home. Think of your dear children. Forgive Jennifer and go home. We must all forgive one another. I am certain that Carey and I have forgiven one another a hundred times. Go home, Francis.'

He caught his hands one within another and looked straight in front of him.

'I cannot, Cousin Maria. I cannot. You do not know—'

She came closer to him, putting her hand on his arm.

'No, of course I do not know, but I cannot endure to see you looking so unhappy. We are not young any longer, Francis, you and I; and when we are old it is not at all easy to be alone. No, it is not easy. Carey and I miss one another if we are apart a day. What will you do here in this lodging alone? Come to us at

Grosset for a while if that will assist you. And then go home. Jennifer means very well. She means very well indeed. She had a selfish upbringing. Poor Rose never had a notion of how to bring up a family. She is the mother of your children, Francis.'

He was deeply touched. Her sincerity and true longing to be good to him were beyond any question. But he wished that she would go. No one could help him any more. He smiled at her and laid his hand on hers.

'Thank you, Cousin Maria. You are exceeding kind. But I must shoulder my own troubles. What you say is very true. We are growing old, and nothing is of very much importance any more. Thank you, Cousin Maria, but indeed I must stand on my own feet.'

There was something in his face that told her that it was so.

She hesitated, stammered, then broke out: 'Well, then – would it trouble you ... You would not laugh, I am sure ... but it might be a help to you. The Lord is always nigh. If I offered a prayer ...'

Her eyes gazed at him with the eager moisture in them of a puppy begging for a biscuit.

'Certainly, Cousin Maria. It is good of you—'

At once she knelt down on the floor beside him and, her bonnet falling back a little from her head, her gloved hands clasped, prayed.

'Oh Lord God, I pray Thee to look down on this Thy servant who has been sore troubled and in deep distress. Thou knowest what are our faults and failures, but there is in Thy heart an infinite patience and an all-preserving Wisdom. Take this Thy servant into Thy care and show him the way that he may find once again those whom he best loves and be restored into their company. Thou knowest what is best for him, and Thy will be done. In the name of Thy Son who was crucified for us on the Cross and whose Divine Example we would eternally follow. Amen.'

She waited a moment, her head between her hands, then she rose. There was thick dust on her black gown, but she did not notice. She stroked her nose with her hand.

'And now I must really be off,' she said briskly. 'Phyllis and I am to spend a little evening alone together. We are reading *The Task*. Remember, pray, Cousin Francis, that we are most eager to have you with us at Grosset, if you care to come. You have only to send us word. Yes, we shall all be delighted to see you.'

She bent and kissed him on the forehead; then murmuring

something to the effect that she did hope that it was not raining, she gave him a smile at the door and went out.

He sat on, lost in thought. In what was he lost? The candles flickered, the shadows leapt on the wall, carriages rumbled beyond the window, steps hurried by, voices rose and fell, but he was engulfed in his sense of utter disaster. Good old woman! She had wished to help him, but it would need more than Maria Rockage to help him now.

At last he rose, found his hat and coat and went out. He walked up St James's Street and into Piccadilly. He did not know why he was walking nor whither, but it seemed to him that a figure was at his side, keeping pace with him, murmuring in his ears: 'This is your farewell to the world. Soon, when the lights have dazzled your eyes sufficiently, you will return into your dark house.'

In the nervous state in which he was, it seemed to him that there was a babel of sound all about him. The lamps were lit, but there was still a great deal of traffic and business, and the fine spring evening after the rainy afternoon encouraged everyone to be out. London, although it was so rapidly growing in size and energy, had still something of the village about it. In this central part at least there was much recognizing of acquaintances, the cheerful intimacy of shopmen who knew their customers and, only a yard away, big houses, silent squares with lawns and gardens, the grandeur of the great mansions on the Park, footmen standing on doorsteps, coachmen from the boxes of their carriages looking down upon this world as though they commanded, shopmen filling their doorways, their legs spread, their noses sniffing the fresh evening.

To all this Francis was a stranger; he passed like a shadow, hurrying nowhere. At every moment something occurred to infuriate him. For some while a cart accompanied him. It contained it seemed, a thousand iron bars that rattled and rumbled and screamed above the cobbles. A drunken sailor, rolling by, ejected a shoot of tobacco and missed his shoes by an inch: an odour of meat seemed everywhere; the hackney coaches rattled his brains to pieces.

Infuriated by the noise, but still, as it seemed at him, driven on by this companion at his side, he turned up a side street hoping to find quiet, but first on a doorstep a footman was practising 'Paddy Whack' on a small fife, execrably out of tune, a headlong butcher's boy rushed by uttering a shrill cat-call; in a room just above his head there was a dancing lesson being

held. The window was open and he could hear the 'One – Two –
Three' and then 'Now then – Left – Right', and the shrill
discordant wail of a fiddle . . .

Despairing of freeing himself from all these miseries, he
turned back, found Piccadilly again and ventured into Mr
Hatchard's bookshop; there would be silence, the friendliness
of books, the courtesy of good Mr Sumner who, although he
looked like a prize-fighter, had all the delicacy and sensitiveness
of one who knew Byron and Scott and Coleridge, and had often,
under Mr Sheridan's direction, supplied the Prince, in earlier
days, with the best literature.

So Francis stepped in – and there was old Mr Rogers!

Yes, old Mr Rogers, the very last man in the world whom he
wished to see. Nor was he alone. He was attended by a stout
thick-set young man, badly dressed, with an untidy neckcloth
and a very supercilious air.

Mr Rogers gave him a finger and introduced him to his
friend.

'This is Mr Macaulay, who is at Cambridge and soon will be
having the world at his feet. Come, come, Macaulay. You know
you will. You know you will. You are as confident of it as I am.'

The thickset untidy youth raised a pair of very remarkable
piercing eyes and began to talk with great eloquence and
volubility. It was clear that he did not suffer from shyness.

Francis meanwhile hated the confident young man and hated
Rogers. He was sure that they were mocking him; indeed, that
everyone in the shop was mocking him. It was true enough,
perhaps, that Rogers was not over-pleasant, because he had
gone out of his way to be kind to this fellow who, of late, had
treated him casually.

'Well, Mr Herries,' he said in his sharp restless voice, 'it is
well met and farewell, for I am shortly taking a sister and niece
with me on to the Continent – Switzerland and Italy. I have
been trying to persuade Tom Macaulay here to accompany me,
but he has better things to concern himself with . . . Well, well,
Mr Herries – good day to ye. Good day to ye.'

The loquacious young man had already forgotten him and
was talking eagerly to Sumner about a book that he held in his
hand. Sumner also (who was, as a rule, so courteous) had not
noticed him. In a tumult of irritation Francis left the shop.
So Rogers had had enough of him? Even Sumner did not care
to speak with him, and so old and insignificant was he that an
untidy young man from Cambridge could turn his back on him.

It was true enough. He was old and shabby. He had no place in the world any longer.

At the corner of St James's Street he met a man whom he slightly knew, an effeminate bore, and this fellow would not let him go, but with one finger on his coat must, in a shrill piping voice, talk about the coming Coronation. It was all that anyone was thinking of, it was the finest and grandest the world had ever seen, no expense was to be spared, and they said that the Queen, poor thing— At last Francis broke away. As he hastened down the street he fancied that the man was looking after him, wondering what madness had taken possession of him. Well, he was mad if they liked. He had no place in this absurd world any longer – this absurd, monstrous crazy world.

When he entered his little room again and lit the candles once more, a sense of disgust took him. What a mean little place it was, with its smell of soot and cooking food! How grimy and foul the world had grown!

He went into his little bedroom, filled his basin with water, stripped, washed from head to foot, put on clean linen and another suit. Then he returned to his table, took out paper and pen and began to write:

DEAREST JUDITH – You have all your life forgiven me for my many faults and failings; once again – and this is the last time that I shall ask you – you must forgive me. For many weeks your letters arrived here and now they are lying in a pile on a table near me unopened. For it is only a part of my general weakness that I have not opened them. I did not dare, for I know that if I had done so you would have tempted me back. But I must not go back, dear Judith. Were you not so noble and generous to me you would be honest with me and tell me what I know well to be the truth – that I must never come back again. You have known me all my life long and once when you were a baby you loved me. Perhaps you love me still, for your heart is so generous that it can pass over all weaknesses and all mistakes. But I myself cannot pass them over. In these last weeks I have learnt to face myself and to see what is there. You will think that there is too much self-pity in what I have written, but it is not so. I have never pitied myself. I have had every chance to make something of life and I have thrown every chance away.

When I was a young man and you were a child I used to talk to you about all the things that I intended to do. I had great faith in myself, and because I have none any more is not a reason for pity, but rather for acceptance. I have failed everyone – my father, my mother, my wife, my children and my ideals.

I think that there are other men in like case. Men of our time have some of them been unfortunate because they have lived in an age of transition. The Great Time was behind them. The Great Time is coming again – but some of us have had our faith taken from us and have not been given, or have not found, a new one. I thought once that all men would be free now. I thought once that the poor man would have Justice. But the poor man is more a slave than before, and we are all of us in prison. I cannot write clearly; I see everything darkly, but I know that for myself I took the wrong path.

I am writing this only because you must not, *you must not*, dearest Judith, take the wrong path also. Return to your own life, take your boy, have nothing to do with the fortunes of our family. For such as you and I there can never be any happiness in Herries affairs. They are ruin and damnation to us. They deprive us of all that our souls need. I have been no good friend to you. I have not given you assistance when you sorely needed it. I have left you alone when you were most lonely. In this as in everything else I have betrayed myself. But now I am speaking truth from the heart. Your life is not with Will and Walter and Jennifer and the rest. They are strangers to you and you to them. Because I married a stranger and, God help me, love her now as dearly as I ever did, I have worked my own Destruction.

I know that you will be good to Jennifer and my children, but they are provided for, and *you must not stay with them*. Be true to yourself. You know well enough what you should do . . . Go back to Watendlath. I can see the light over the hill, hear the streams running . . . the streams running. My hand shakes. Tell Jennifer that I love her, I love her, just as I did . . . as I always . . . Embrace the children. John will be a fine boy . . . and your Adam. Go back to the light over the hill. There is so terrible a noise in this town. Dear Judith, think of me kindly, but better to forget me. I could not find a Balance. I was always fearful of Action. God be with you, but there is no God – none for me. Nothing . . .

He broke off; his pen rattled on to the table. He sat there for a long while, his head buried in his hands. Then he got up, folded

the letter and addressed it. He went to the window, pulled back
the blind and looked out. Two ladies were talking, laughing. A
little dog came sniffing up to the lamp-post. Another dog saw
him from the other side of the street and came slowly across.
A boy, carrying some parcels, stood idly and watched them.

Francis went to the drawer of his little ink-stained desk and
took from it a pistol.

He crossed to the mirror, cracked and seamed with age. He
saw with great clearness the faded green paper, the print of the
fight between Gully and the Chicken, the copy of Drayton's
Poems, that he had been reading, on the table. Then he put the
pistol to his mouth.

Mrs Morland, fancying that she heard someone tumble' or the
distant firing of a gun or the collision of two carriages, went to her
window and looked out. But no: in the street there was nothing
to be seen but two ladies laughing together and the cautious
intimacies of a Newfoundland and a King Charles.

MONEY

'WILL YOU NOT come in and pay us a visit, Cousin Judith?'
Walter Herries asked. He was standing at the high pillared
entrance to Westaways. The wind was blowing with a kind of
innocent child-like caprice and turning back the leaves of a
giant beech to a duller chillier gold. Judith, with Adam beside
her, felt the wind tugging at her big velvet-lined feathered hat.
Her hands were warm inside their muff. Her face for once
was rosy; the sharp air, the wild sky, the scudding fragments of
blue and the harp-like swing of the wind across the bare fields,
the ridges of snow on the brown range of fell, all exhilarated her.

Moreover, it was four days before Christmas and directly
Christmas was past she was returning with Adam to Watendlath
– yes, for ever and ever!

She had passed Watendlath as she had done a thousand times
before, walking from Crosthwaite to Keswick. The carriage
was in Keswick for the day; Jennifer was paying visits and after
their three o'clock dinner at the inn they would drive home.

It was now midday. The Crosthwaite Church clock had but
just told the hour. She had intended to take Adam to show to her

friends, Miss West and Miss Pennyfeather. The last thing that she had expected or wished was to be caught by Walter Herries.

Westaways looked gleaming and polished in the wet windy sunlight. On the eastern corner there were ladders and men working. Walter was for ever doing something to the place.

'Do come inside now, Cousin Judith, and taste a glass of sherry.'

She knew that he had a family party for Christmas – Will, Christabel, old Monty Cards, Rodney, the pious second son of Pomfret and Rose from Kensington, old Pomfret himself and his ancient old-maid sister Cynthia, and best of all, Maria's Phyllis with her husband, Mr Stephen Newmark, and two of their children; Phyllis had been married in 1818 and had already three babies!

It was Phyllis whom she would like to see; Christabel too, Will even. But she shrank from the crowd of them, all gathered in the parlour, talking scandal, most of it of the family order. In she would march with Adam, and Will's neck would tighten in its collar, and fat, over-decorated, 'Regency' old Pomfret would wink at her (she could bet on it!), and silly kind old Monty would stroke his powdered cheek while his corsets creaked, pious Rodney would look down his nose – only dear Phyllis, untidy like her mother, with some of the Grosset disorder clinging to her, only Phyllis would really welcome her, would be enchanted to see her. She had a curiosity, too, to behold Phyllis' husband, Mr Stephen Newmark. Maria, in letters, had informed her that he was a very fine man indeed, a wealthy religious landowner from Warwickshire. Wealthy *and* religious – not a very promising combination!

There was the other temptation, too, that this was her last opportunity for spying out Westaways. Was it not absurd, perhaps, to say that, when Watendlath was only a mile or two away? But Watendlath was more than a mile or two away, it was a world away. As poor Francis had said in that last despairing letter.

Strange to pass from the thought of that letter to that great brilliantly-coloured body straddling there in the gateway! But, looking at him, she suddenly wondered whether he were not already a trifle old-fashioned? The thought gave her a malicious pleasure. He was certainly over-dressed for the present times, with his billowing stock and its jewelled pin, his claret-coloured coat with the exaggerated waist (he was corsetted – and what immense corsets they must be!), the fawn-shaded pantaloons fitting so tightly over the calves. There were rings on his fingers. And yet he was a man! Do Walter all the injustice in the world, but you could never name him effeminate. He was the prize bull of the stock. Already, young as he was, there was a purple tinge to his cheek, but his eyes were hard and clear and his mouth firmly and confidently set.

'Come inside and drink a glass of sherry with us, Cousin Judith.'

She looked up at him from under her broad-brimmed hat with that air of humorous impertinent defiance that they seemed always to use to one another.

'I have Christmas shopping and calls to pay. Have we not, Adam?'

Adam, who was holding a little toy whip, had never taken his eyes from Walter since he had first seen him.

'Why, young man, you have some clothes on at last, I see.'

'Yes, sir.'

'And how old are you since I saw you last?'

'Six, sir.'

'Six, are you? Well, your mother shall bring you in out of the wind. Not too young for a glass of sherry, are you?'

'Of course he is, Walter. A glass of sherry indeed!'

'Why, I was drinking sherry before I was weaned, and look at me! Come along in! Come along in!'

So Judith went and Adam also, his eyes still following Walter's back as though he had never before seen anything like it.

She knew that he had been doing things to the house, and when she stood in the hall her astonishment was vivid at the changes that he had made. Everywhere were riches. On the wall facing the front door a great piece of purple tapestry showing Diana hunting, on either side of the door pieces of sculpture, one of a Pan playing his flute, another of a stout naked goddess drinking. (What, oh, what would Maria Rockage say to this paganism?)

At the stairhead, over the door of the saloon, was a sumptuous painting of a French king (Louis XIV perhaps) dining with his ladies, and, beside the door, a silver pedestal with a black bust of some Roman Emperor – and Walter, as he walked slowly up the stairs, gave the impression even in his backview that it was he and no one else who had wrought all these splendours.

They were gathered about a blazing fire in the saloon – Will, Christabel, Monty Cards, Rodney and his father, Phyllis, Carey her brother, and a thin upright man with a hooked nose who must be her husband, Mr Newmark.

As Judith crossed the long shining slippery floor, holding Adam by the hand, she felt that both herself and her son were midgets. She was not frightened but she could feel their intense interest as they all turned towards her. She was helped by Adam's absolute confidence. He nearly tripped and fell as he bent his head back to look at the gods and goddesses in their brilliant nakedness. He feared no one.

Christabel and Phyllis rose with cries of pleasure to greet her. Everyone made a display over Adam. Pomfret (still a very gay and brightly set-up dog in spite of his years) was the most pleased with him. He took him between his knees and looked into his ugly little face with a very lively interest. He asked him questions, and Adam, in his funny high voice, answered them all instantly.

Judith, sitting with her hand in Phyllis', thought: 'This grows grander every month. Up, up, up. And at Uldale we go down, down, down! Never mind. The battle is not ended yet . . . Yes, Adam is ugly. His mouth is too large by far – but he charms everyone . . .' That strange pang at her heart again! He charms everyone! He always will – and I shall be left . . . 'But I *wish* him to charm everyone, to be happy and honest and brave as he is now – always.' And then, following quickly on this, cutting across the self-sufficient tones of Rodney, who would be one day Archdeacon of Polchester and patronizer of the very Black Bishop, came this thought:

'In ten days we shall be in Watendlath, eating food with the Ritsons, and Adam will be mine, mine, mine!'

She could almost hear the sheep shuffling with the noise of the rustle of leaves across this shining floor. She could see the sun strike the flint in those rocks until they shone like spear-heads, dulling the painted goddesses. 'Oh, if anything should hinder my reaching there! But nothing can, now surely nothing can!' It was as though she were planning to get as far as China!

They were still discussing that now so wearily worn topic, the Coronation and the Queen's beating on the Westminster doors. Will, who was strangely aged now and thinner than ever, so that he looked like a stork standing on one leg and protecting his nest (only his eggs were money-bags), was all for upholding the Crown.

'What we want,' he said with his usual air of delivering judgement, 'is stable conditions. To counteract the lower classes.

Relax, and we shall have another Peterloo ... But the country is recovering its Balance. I am glad to be able to say that the country is recovering its Balance.'

Everyone looked greatly relieved. It was pleasant to hear from Will, who must know, that all was well.

Adam was passed round from hand to hand. They were all kind to him although he was a little bastard. But Judith knew that it was for the moment only, and that her presence made them uncomfortable, yes, even poor Christabel, who was restless under the eye of her lord and master. The thought came to her as she saw Rodney's eyes meditatively resting upon her: 'Oh, if Adam could grow into the master of them all, rule the pack of them! He could. He has even now twice their spirit ...' But she was going to Watendlath, and Adam with her, leaving the Herries behind them for ever, and Adam would be a farmer like Charlie Watson, and one day he would come down into Keswick, driving his sheep, and he would encounter Walter's children in their fine carriage, and the coachman would shout to him to clear his sheep from the road ... And after Adam would return, riding up the road to see the Tarn shining with the evening sun, and he would call to his dog, and the fields would smile up at him, the hills look kindly down ...

'Well, my little friend,' said Rodney Herries to Adam (he spoke as though to a little black child newly rescued from the heathen), 'and what is the game you enjoy the most?'

'To cut men out of wood,' said Adam with complete assurance, but his eyes wandering a little. 'I have cut Mr Noah and the Duke of Wellington and Mr Winch.'

'Very praiseworthy. Very praiseworthy indeed,' said Rodney, looking, however, bewildered.

'He is commencing,' said Judith, 'to carve figures. He has a true disposition towards carving.'

'Yes,' went on Adam eagerly, looking at everyone with an enthusiastic smile, 'and I colour them also. And Bennett gives me the wood. He says—'

'Hush, Adam, hush,' said Judith, drawing him towards her. He came to her, but with one last look round him and pointing at old Cynthia Herries, Pomfret's sister, who had a nose like a door-knocker:

'That old lady would be very fine for cutting.'

His manners, Judith could see them deciding, were not at all of the best, but what could you expect when his mother? ...

Then Walter came forward.

'Judith, you must see my improvements. Forgive me for taking you away an instant. I must show you the improvements.'

She knew that he wished to speak to her alone. She had known it all the time. The drama of the scene, the implication of it all, had been rising in her with increasing force. Poor Francis was dead, Jennifer bewildered, like a woman lost in a wood, the children helpless – and this power, this force, destructive and remorseless, hung over them. And something told her that she was the only one whom Walter feared; it had always been so. And it might be that she was the only one whom, of all that company, Walter respected.

She looked back and saw that Adam was safe with Phyllis' arm around him. Then she followed Walter out.

He preceded her into a little parlour off the saloon, a room so small that, when he had motioned her into a red morocco chair and himself stood, with his legs straddled, in front of the fire, the two of them filled it. There was nothing in the room save a Chippendale cabinet on which was a bowl of Christmas roses. They were full-blown and wore that look of patient expectancy that precedes death.

Walter began at once:

'Judith – how long will you remain at Uldale?'

'I cannot see that that is any business of yours, Cousin Walter,' she answered sharply. She had retained her white fur muff, and her fingers in it clasped one another with self-congratulation. What was it in her that made her love a battle? She was at the moment perfectly happy, all her faculties widely awake, her eyes on the rich panelling, the Christmas roses, and the brilliant person of Mr Walter Herries.

'No business of mine,' he went on. 'Well, perhaps not. And yet because I have a regard for you, Cousin Judith, I would wish you out of Uldale. That place and all in it are doomed.' He said this, a little swell of importance rising in his great chest.

'Really! That is exceedingly interesting. And by whom are they doomed, pray?'

'By myself.'

'Are you so powerful?' He was, she reflected, like a giant schoolboy fallen from some star where everyone was twice as big as nature.

'I am indeed,' he answered. 'And growing more powerful every day. It is my father's wish that our family should be the chief figures in this country. Natural enough, when you think of it. He was born here, and his father lived here till the end of his life. He has developed an affection for the place.'

'An affection so deep,' interrupted Judith, 'that he never comes near it save on Saints' Days and Festivals! No, no, Cousin Walter,' she went on, 'there are the two of us alone here, and we may be frank. I belong to this country far more than you ever can. My mother may not have been of the country, but at least for generation upon generation my ancestors have lived and thieved here, stolen cattle and ladies only too ready to be stolen. I love this country, and so will my son after me. I love it because it is dark and full of storms and rains every other day, and smells of bracken and sheep and cow-dung. But you have none of these reasons. You love it because you wish to impress it, and I can tell you, Cousin Walter, it is not so easily impressed. What have you got? You have one thing – money. Nothing else. You are not especial clever that I have heard; you are too stout to be beautiful; you are a bully of those weaker than yourself; you are as conceited as a peacock. I am almost old enough to be your mother, Walter. In fact, in Eastern countries I believe I might have been – so forgive me for my frankness.'

'Go on,' he said, smiling at her.

There were moments when she thought that she rather liked him. Hatred would make everything easier.

'Very well, then, I will. You have nothing but money. At Uldale they have much. Poor Francis, who took his life because he had so much more perception and understanding than you, loved this country with all his heart. He made an unhappy marriage. Oh! I am not blaming Jennifer. There was a time when I hated her, but it is hard to hate anybody long. It was not her fault that she could not love him. Now that is all over, and there are two very fine children who are *not* doomed, dear Walter, however much you may say it. They have more right to this country than you have. Money can't beat them, and don't you think it.'

Walter nodded.

'Very well, then. We know where we are. You have said nothing, though, of the scandals that we have all suffered for years past. It may be foolish' (again his immense chest swelled), 'but if I am proud of one thing in this world it is of being an Englishman and a Herries. I have as much right as yourself to any part of England, Cousin Judith, even though your ancestors *were* cattle-thieves. How agreeable has it been to us, do you think, that for years past, under our very noses, we should have a Herries who is too weak to challenge his wife's lover, who allows adultery any day or night under his roof; a woman so lost to shame that she receives her lover in the room next to her children; a man so lily-livered that he challenges that same lover, and then before the duel is fought runs to London?—'

'I do not believe that,' Judith broke in, her eyes flashing. 'We have only the word of that miserable oaf whom everyone knows for a coward—'

'Yes; and what about Uncle Francis for a coward, who let such things be year after year?'

'And who are you,' she broke in hotly, 'to be so virtuous? How have you treated *your* wife all these years? And what of milkmaids in Keswick and loose women in Kendal? Do you suppose that you are so sacred that no one talks of you?'

He threw his head back and laughed.

'I am no hypocrite, Cousin Judith. Nor are you. I am as other men. You had your little come-by-chance in Paris. But I have not allowed my wife a lover, nor have you blown off the top of your head with a pistol. But come . . . that is not the point. You may say that there is no power in money. But I say there is. And more. Money is going to be powerful in England as it has never been before. I am no such fool as I look, Judith. In spite of my size I have a trifle of my father's brains. But the long and short of it is just this. They must leave Uldale. It is my obsession that they should. I hate Jennifer, for she was rude to my mother; but beyond that they are a blot on the Herries name. I will pay them a good price for the house, but they must quit this part of the country!'

'Never!' cried Judith, springing up. 'Never! Never! Never!'

'Now come, Judith. Why should you care? What are they to you? You loved Uncle Francis. Good. I have nothing against it. But he is gone. Jennifer is a dull, heavy, stupid woman. You have never liked her. What is all this to you?'

'It is this to me! These are Francis' children. You would bully them out of existence. Well, you shall not.'

'What will you do to prevent it?'

'Never mind. You shall not.'

He shrugged his great shoulders.

'It may be true that I am a bully,' he said slowly. 'I hate the weak. They have no place here if they cannot stand up for themselves. You are the only one whom I admire, and you have put yourself out of court with your little bastard. Not that I have anything against bastards; but you are a little public with yours, are you not? It was worth seeing just now the way that prig Rodney's nose curved down his cheek. So leave them alone, Judith! Be quiet with your boy in some place and we will be good friends. But leave Uldale alone.'

It was on the edge of her tongue to tell him that he need not be disturbed, for in ten days she would be in Watendlath and free of him for ever. But she did not speak. As she faced him the dominating part of her longed to oppose him, to fight him, and beat him, to defend John and Dorothy, to show him that the little bastard was not so negligible as he pretended. She *could* fight him! And what a fight that would be!

Meanwhile there was Watendlath. She almost sighed as she turned away and saw a smooth white petal of the Christmas roses flutter to the ground.

'Good friends?' she repeated. 'Not if you touch Uldale.'

'Well I *shall* touch Uldale,' he said, moving towards the door. 'I have told you. And now, come up and see the children. Bring your boy with you.'

But at the door she paused.

'This is not a game, Cousin Walter.'

He stood over her.

'No. I have told you. It is a chapter in family history.'

'What have you ever done,' she asked scornfully, 'to be so proud of our family history?'

'*Non mi ricordo*,' he answered in the phrase that had been the popular catchword ever since Majocchi's evidence in the Queen's trial. He was determined to be amiable.

But, with her hand on the door, and with a passion that in these days she rarely showed, she burst out: 'I tell you, Walter, you must leave Jennifer and the children alone'; and he, smiling, murmured lightly that popular epigram:

> *Most gracious Queen, we thee implore*
> *To go away, and sin no more;*
> *But if that effort be too great,*
> *To go away, at any rate.*

They looked into the saloon and found Adam diving into old Pomfret's pockets and producing treasures – a gold snuff-box, some seals and a small watch set with diamonds. The old man was watching him with delighted pleasure, and Judith at once forgave him all his pomposities, sensualities, infidelities to Rose, every other crime or weakness.

Adam came at once running when she called him. He turned

when he was halfway to the door and waved his hand to the figures at the fire. Pomfret and Christabel waved back. Phyllis got up from her chair.

'Are you going up to see the children? You shall see my babies too.'

Judith knew how deeply intrigued they all were. What had Walter been saying to her? How much part did she play now in family affairs? She knew that Will was regarding her with secret alarm. She had always been a signal of danger to him, representing everything that was lawless and unsanctified. And she had been always Francis' ally. Perhaps he thought now of that old scene in Monty Cards' house when Francis had defied him . . . lured by Jennifer's beauty . . . Well, he had never been lured by anyone's beauty, and he was glad of it. But this pain in his leg was vexatious. This Northern air did not suit him. He was truly well only in the City. But she knew by this time that she was in the camp of the enemy and, as she went out of the room with her head up and trying not to slip ignominiously on the polished floor, her hand went quietly to the silver chain, her father's, that she always wore beneath her clothes.

So the four of them went upstairs, Walter leading. It was a fine high room where the children were. Almost a hundred years ago old Pomfret's children, Raiseley and Anabel and Judith, had sat there, the girls with boards down their backs to keep them straight, learning their Latin. But much had been done to the room since then. The windows were fine and high, with a great view over the Lake and Scafell, and the Gavel grouped handsomely at the end of it. The waves were running across it now as though in a race, and the woods by Manesty were black as jet.

Inside the room everything was warm and cosy – a great fire roaring, a decent-looking elderly woman sitting beside it sewing. On the carpet Elizabeth, one of Walter's twins, was playing with Phyllis' two babies; Uhland, the other, was sitting on a small chair by himself, his face absorbed as he pulled the hair out of the tail of a painted wooden horse.

Many, many times afterwards she was to look back to this moment when she first saw Uhland. (Poor child, that he should be burdened his life long with so outlandish a name!) How characteristic that he should be sitting gravely by himself pulling something to pieces! But, at the moment, she felt nothing but pity. He had already, although he was but six years old, the face of an old man, the high forehead lined and the corners of the mouth bitter, and those strange grey penetrating eyes. His legs were dangling over the chair, but she noticed immediately that, absorbed as he was, at once, when he heard someone enter, he drew them up so that no one should observe their inequality. His body was too small for his head; his hands, she saw, were very beautiful, and, later, when she had reason to know how proud he was of them, she was interested to remember how quickly she had perceived them.

What followed touched her deeply. Walter, in his magnificent claret coat and resplendent pantaloons, hurried forward to his son, caught him up in his arms and held him close to his breast. The child seemed unmoved. His face did not change. Only one hand rested on his father's big one. Walter kissed him many times, oblivious of everyone else there.

'You must say How do you do?' he commanded him, and brought him to Judith. The child's cold grey eyes rested on her and, she fancied, with an expression of instant dislike.

'How do you do, ma'am?' he said in a small, remote voice. She bent forward and kissed his cheek, which was chill and dry. It was odd to touch that pallid, small face and feel Walter's great red one just above it. Walter took him back to his chair and, kneeling on the floor beside him, talked to him about the horse.

Walter had shown no attention to his daughter Elizabeth. This was a charming child with fragile, delicate features and pale flaxen hair.

She glanced once at her father as though she would have liked his attention, but she did not seem at all unhappy; she talked eagerly, made friends with Adam, played games with the babies, who already, Judith thought, bore, both of them, resemblance to Mr Newmark.

After a little while they came away, but Judith saw that, as they left the room, Uhland stood up and gazed after them with an almost frightening intensity.

Judith, with Adam holding tightly to her hand, walked into Keswick. Even the road was alive with the stir of Christmas, but she moved for some while with unseeing eyes; she had a sense of danger – as though did she let Adam out of her sight for an instant Walter would get him.

The touch of his warm little hand in hers comforted her; but that was not enough. In one hand she held her muff, but with the other arm, had it not been so public a place, she would have encircled him that she might be the more secure.

He meanwhile had observed everything and had a hundred

questions to ask. Why did no one wear any clothes in the pictures? Why was the floor so slippery? Who was the old gentleman with the diamond watch? The little boy upstairs had one
leg longer than another. Why was the big man who had tried to
hit him with the whip so red in the face? Why ... Why ...
Why? ...

Then suddenly he was aware, with the perception that came
from their long-continued intimacy together, that she was
disturbed and wanted his help. He always knew when she needed
him, although he might not understand what it was that she
needed. Even at the time of his greatest intimacy with John (he
was as deeply devoted to John as ever, but the novelty was gone)
he would look up and run off to find her, although he could not
himself tell why.

She walked more slowly. She wanted him to understand
something.

'Adam, would you wish to live in a house like Uncle Walter's,
so grand and rich, with everything you could need?'

He put out his tongue at two small boys who were mocking
him from the hedge, then he applied his whole intelligence to the
question.

'I would like that rocking-horse,' he said at last.

'Yes. But besides—' Her step was slower. So soon she would
be in Keswick, and there would be Jennifer and gossip and the
outside world. At this moment she felt for him so overpowering
a love that it was as though she were saying goodbye to him
before he departed to America or the incredible South Sea
Islands.

'Besides – would you wish to live there – always?'

'Would you come and John and Dorothy and Bennett, and
might I cut things?'

'No. We would not come.'

He considered it.

'I should *like* the rocking-horse,' he said slowly. 'But *of course*,
you would be in the house.'

'No, I would not.'

'But you will be everywhere I am always.'

'No.' She shook her head. 'No.'

He laughed, for the two little boys were running along in the
hedge making faces at him, and one of them, not being able to
see in two places at once, fell down.

'The boy fell down,' he said, screwing his head round to see
better.

She stopped at the little stream that was now coffee and now a froth of foam.

'Listen, Adam. I wish you to hear this. No one will ever love you as your mother does now. No one can take you from me. No one. We will soon be in Watendlath with Charlie and Mrs Perry again. I could make you a fine man in a grand house, and everyone would do what you say, but I am going to make you a farmer like Watson, and when you are in the road with your sheep, the carriage that you should have ridden in will order you to clear the way. You will be walking and you might have been riding. You will be rough and poor and you could have been grand and rich.

'But we will be happy, you and I and Charlie and Alice; but the little sick boy will be rich and powerful, and you will be poor and nobody.'

He did not mind at all. He was looking to see a fish jump in the river.

But she put her hand under his chin and looked into his eyes.

'I want you to remember this, because all my life I have been making this choice. You cannot understand now, but one day you will look back and perhaps be angry with me.'

He knew that she was wanting him to understand something, so he screwed his forehead into a hundred wrinkles and did his best.

'Would you prefer that you were Charlie Watson or big Uncle Walter?' she said.

He laughed at the thought of being Uncle Walter and, then and there, puffed out his cheeks, swelled out his chest, and began to strut about. Then his face was grave. He turned, looking back down the road.

'If he hits me with his whip again,' he said, 'I'll *beat* him.'

The change was so swift that she was astonished.

'But you like Uncle Walter,' she said. 'He was very kind to you.'

'Why does the little boy have one leg bigger than the other?'

'He was born like that.'

His mind seemed to jump.

'It's Christmas! It's Christmas!' he cried, and began to run down the road in front of her. She walked after him. He turned back to meet her.

'Boneyparte was beat at Waterloo, Mr Winch says,' he remarked very gaily, dancing about. Then catching her hand again and dragging her along he shouted:

'And I will beat Uncle Walter when I am bigger!'

He ran, pulling her hand, calling like a song:

'And I love you better than everybody – better than John, better than Dorothy, better than Bennett, better than Jack, better than—'

But even as the litany continued, something caught his attention, a goat dragged along by a cord, and a very small girl in charge of it. He pulled his hand away and ran on to see this phenomenon, but as he ran he chanted in a high absent-minded refrain:

'Better than Bennett. Better than Jack. Better than—'

And she, feeling that it was an omen, followed after.

MOB

JUDITH IN A state half sleep, half wakening, heard a voice say: 'Dig deep here. The deeper you may dig the richer the loam.' She recognized that she had a choice either to stay in that square of country, hemmed in by hills, and dig down and down – for what? treasure perhaps – or to fasten to her shoulders a pair of very elegant gold wings and fly the country over, but, of course, be for ever on the surface. She had to make a choice, and she made it without hesitation. With a sense of great relief and satisfaction she shouldered a spade, and as she did so saw the pair of wings be drawn up on a gold wire through the dark sky.

With confused notions of Mrs Radcliffe, a novel that the night before she had been reading, *The Last Step; or The History of Mrs Brudenal*, Rousseau's *Confessions*, and *Isabella; or The Rewards of Good Nature*, she woke to see the thin January light covering the floor with a sort of pale mildew and to realize that Adam, having thrown off the clothes, was sleeping upside down with his feet on her breast. She turned him round, heard him sigh happily in his sleep, and staring up at the bed-hangings, thought: 'He— She— It was right. She must dig and remain faithful to the—' To what? That question woke her. She realized that the crisis of her life had come.

How often before it had seemed to be upon her – when David had beaten her, when Georges had married her, when old Stane had robbed her, when Jennifer had insulted her, when Warren had kissed her, when Adam had kicked his way out of her, when

Francis had called her back to Uldale, when Francis had written a last letter to her, when Walter had challenged her – but now at last the crisis had truly come, for today she must make Jennifer realize that within a week she was positively and for ever departing and that no prayers, no beseechings could alter her resolve.

She moved restlessly on the bed as she thought of it. No wonder that she had woken early with this in front of her! Again and again in the last year she had attempted the break; but first there had been poor Francis alive, and then there had been poor Francis dead, and then Jennifer had kept to her bed for weeks, and when at last she had been driven out of her bedroom had refused to attend to her affairs, refused to see Mr Bertram, the solicitor from Keswick, refused to do anything unless Judith were there to force her to do it.

During the last three months it had come to this. Again and again she had said:

'Well, Jennifer, I will do this for you' (speak to Mr Winch or Bennett, or talk business with Mr Bertram, or write to London about some shares or discuss with Mrs Quinney the fare for the coming week). 'But you had far better yourself, you know, for a week after Christmas I am off, and you will have to manage it all then.'

'Oh, a week after Christmas – besides, you will change your mind.'

'I shall not change my mind.'

After the discovery of Fernyhirst (who had never put in another appearance), Francis' refusal to return, and then his suicide, Jennifer's sluggishness had swallowed all the rest of her. Once she had been lazy because she was proud; now she was lazy because she was humiliated. She tumbled into a slattern over whom Judith had absolute command. Judith had seen her as lovely girl, proud and overbearing wife, self-satisfied mistress, betrayed beauty (her attitude after Francis' departure), and now she was humble, but yawning, slattern. Poor Jennifer! Parents who had adored her too deeply to educate her or to force her to anything that she avoided had begun her ruin. Her lazy and stupid indifference completed it. She cared now only for her food, an occasional fine gown, and sometimes to dress Dorothy up and take her into Keswick. (But when there always fancied that she was insulted, and returned in a state of indignation and confused panic.)

She went to bed of an evening ever earlier and earlier; the

time would surely come when she would never rise at all.

She had, however, one increasing terror, and that was of Walter Herries. He had assumed now quite gigantic proportions for her. He could do, she was convinced, any horrible thing that he chose. He was bent on her destruction. And in that last she was perfectly correct.

Poor Jennifer! She might have been, Judith thought, a brilliant, successful beauty at an earlier time. She was born too late for her period. Like many of her contemporaries, she was the victim of a transition world.

She would, however, now be forced to action. When Judith was gone, Mrs Quinney, horrid little Mr Winch, kindly but saturnine Bennett, would do as they pleased. And then John would grow and take his place. He was now fourteen years of age and as nice a boy as you could find – gentle and kind, thoughtful for others, but manly also; more resolute in character than his father. He was reticent; no one had ever known what were his real feelings about his father's suicide, or how much he knew about the scandal in the house. Judith suspected that he had suffered with intensity. She fancied, too, that he had a sort of irritated pity for his mother...

But John against Walter? That was the only thought that gave her obstinate departure a touch of treachery.

Today she must tell Jennifer that the matter was final, and, three days from now, she would be safe with Adam in Watendlath.

It was a kind of fate, as things developed, that before mid-day she should encounter Watson.

He stopped his horse by the Uldale gate. He would not come in. She came out to him.

Why did her heart beat so when she saw him? She was not in love with him. She had never been. He was a fine thick figure of a man, but it was not his figure that made her heart beat. Did a shadow pass? Behind him the hollows under Skiddaw filled like wine in a jade bowl – but it was not the hollow valleys. He did not love her, or at least had never given her reason to think that he did. They were two elderly people now, she nearing fifty, he over sixty. Was it their friendship and mutual trust that made her heart beat? But when she put her hand in his all the nonsense was over. He never had much to say. She had many things to do and could not waste precious time standing there in the cold.

Besides, after three days, she would be seeing him six times a week! There was a joy! It was so intense that she burst out:

'Now there's no need, Charlie, to keep me in the cold. I am busy this morning – and in three days I shall be in Watendlath, for good.'

'Truly, you're coming?'

'Truly, I'm coming.'

'Aye, but you've said it so many times . . .' Then he added, smiling, speaking his broadest, as he did when he was happy: 'I willn't believe tha, not without thou'll swear 't.'

'Oh, I'll swear it. In three days.'

'Aye, I'm glad!'

This was too much emotion for both of them, so she asked him what he was doing so early in their direction. He could give no connected account of himself, mumbled something about visiting for an account in Caldbeck, but she was aware instantly that he was troubled and had come to tell her something. He talked on about agricultural distresses – the old grievance of cash payments, the abundant harvest of '20 that had led to over-supply, the wet autumn of '21 that had destroyed the crops, the new contemplated Corn Law, Huskisson's speech in the House of Commons, all uninteresting enough to her with the wind driving down the road in icy gusts. Then at last he came out with:

'There's trouble about.'

'Trouble?'

'Aye. They burnt Squire Forrester's ricks last night over at Deddon.'

'Who did?'

'Oh, some of t'wild lads and men with no work, and others egging them on!'

'Poor Mr Forrester!'

'Aye. 'Hope they'll hev a long wait in gaol. Well, I must be moving. 'Tis true you're coming in three days?'

'Yes – true enough. And never going away again. Adam is to be a farmer like yourself, Charlie.'

'Reet.' He smiled a tremendous smile, his teeth as white and perfect as they had been twenty years before. 'I'll gang down and mak' all ready for him.' He gave her one of his long protecting looks as though he thought she was only safe when he had his eyes upon her; then he lifted his hat and rode away.

All day she remained troubled. Charlie was so cautious that

you had to guess from one spoken word the twenty that he had intended. But the remark about Forrester's could have no application to them. No one would want to burn *their* barns. Nevertheless she knew that this was a day of fate. She set back her shoulders as though a shadow had warned her that before nightfall she would need all her endurance.

In any case, without any shadowy whispers, she needed all her endurance for her talk with Jennifer. All her life she had detested scenes, but she was aware that Jennifer fell into them and out of them as easily as she washed her hands. A scene there would be – but it would be good to have it behind her, and, although there would be, in all probability, three days of silence and sulks, after that – liberty!

She chose her time well – six o'clock in the parlour, following an excellent dinner, the curtains drawn, Jennifer languidly – with a painted hand-screen to shade her face – before the fire, thinking of her food and the handsome flock-gauze gown that she was wearing.

'Jennifer,' said Judith. 'I think that you should realize that in three days Adam and I will be gone.'

'Oh dear,' Jennifer, stifling a yawn, answered. 'Not this evening, Judith, pray. You are for ever speaking of going. "Jennifer, tomorrow I am going – the day after tomorrow I shall be gone, Jennifer," but, thank Heaven, it is only a bagatelle like Mr Hume and his grey top-hat.'

Judith sighed. This would be indeed a tiresome affair.

'This time it is no bagatelle. It has been one often enough. I had intended to go a year and a half back, and I have remained on and on until I do not wonder that you hesitate to believe me. But this time it is true and certain.'

'But you cannot go in three days. Mr Bertram is coming from Keswick next Wednesday.'

'Well, it will be practice for you in something you will have to do very often – talk business with Mr Bertram.'

'Oh, but it is absurd! Of course I cannot talk business with Mr Bertram.'

'Really, Jennifer. A woman of your age and unable to talk business.'

Jennifer smiled and put her hand on to Judith's arm.

'Oh well, you do it so very much better than ever I can. You are made for business, Judith. Why, only last Tuesday—'

This would be interminable. She rose from her chair and stood between Jennifer and the fire.

'I am very serious. You *must* understand. I am going to Watendlath in three days' time to *live*. This was always temporary – my stay here. You have been very good. I have been happy here; but it is not, it has never been, my real life. I have been running away from this house since I was a baby, since I can remember, and I am for ever returning to it. Now I am running away for the last time.'

Something in Judith's grave serious gaze, something in the determined set of her small body, caused Jennifer to put down her screen and move her head uncomfortably.

'It grows wearisome, Judith, this everlasting talk about Watendlath. What you should want to go to the place for at all I cannot conceive; but if you *must* go – for a visit, to see your farmers and their wives – well, I cannot prevent you. Only, pray return as soon as may be.'

Judith stamped her foot with irritation.

'Jennifer, listen! I am going to Watendlath in three days and I am not returning. I am *not* returning. Now, do you understand?'

'You will leave me?'

'Yes, yes, yes. I have told you a hundred times.'

'Leave me?' The screen fell to the ground. Her big blue eyes widened, her hand began to beat on her dress. 'Leave us? Oh, but, Judith, you cannot! You cannot indeed!'

The note of terror was there. Jennifer was awake to reality; fright was the only thing that awoke her. Judith was suddenly compassionate. She put her arm around the large trembling woman:

'Listen, Jennifer. I have been trying to escape from this house ever since I was a baby, and I am now a woman of middle age and *still* I haven't succeeded! From the house, not from Francis or you or John. I have never been permitted to lead a life of my own. When I was with Georges I was devoured with love for him, so that I was not myself. Now I have Adam, and Adam shall not lead this false life, nor will I any longer.'

But Jennifer did not understand a word of it. She had no imagination, and she saw only things that concerned herself.

'False life? But this is not a false life here.'

'No,' said Judith, striving to be patient. 'The tables and curtains and chairs are real, but it is a false life to me, nevertheless; occupied with fears and ambitions that do not matter. You see, Jennifer, I am only half Herries. My mother was a gipsy. And even that Herries half is wild. You know what my father

was. So now I am going away where there are no Herries, and
I shall take my son with me.'

But Jennifer had not heard a word of it. Slowly, while Judith
was speaking, her brain had been taking in this fact – that Judith
was going away and that she would be alone and defenceless.

She gripped Judith's arm and cried out, her body trembling
again and her cheek white where it was not painted.

'No, no . . . you are going away, to leave me and my children
to Walter Herries! You cannot . . . You must not!'

Now the terror was real enough, and the strange thing was that
Judith felt it also. She looked for an instant at the darkened
window-pane. She had been troubled all day. She was, in her
final resources, alone in this house with this crying, hysterical
woman. Of course Walter could do nothing, nor did he wish to.
He was at this moment kneeling on the nursery floor embracing
his pale little boy. Nevertheless . . .

'Now, Jennifer. Come, this is absurd. Walter can do nothing.
You have Walter Herries on the brain. Everything is well here.
There is money enough, you have Mr Bertram in Keswick,
you have most devoted servants, John is growing a fine boy.
You cannot wish me to stay here and cosset you for ever. Besides,
I am blown on. Everyone knows that I have an illegitimate child
and that poor Warren was its father. What good can that do you ?
You will discover when I am really gone that it is much better so.'

But Jennifer, in full realization now that Judith meant what
she said, was past all control. She clung to Judith, holding her
with a frantic grasp.

'What can you mean ? You cannot be so cruel. You were never
cruel even when I was stiff with you in the old days. Walter is a
devil. You have seen it for yourself. All the scandal about me
everywhere is his doing. He will poison my children and—'

'Jennifer, don't be so absurd.'

'No, but it is not absurd. I am certain he will poison all the
water here before he is done. I see him at every turn. I dare not
walk out unless I should see him. I am quite alone here. I have not a
friend but you. Everyone hates me. Walter sees to it that they do.
He is everywhere whispering . . . If you go, Judith, I shall kill
myself and then you will have to come and see to my poor children, my poor deserted children. I know that Walter forced
Francis to kill himself. I am sure of it. He wrote him a letter or
something, and only because years ago I broke his mother's
cheap little fan. Oh! how I wish that I had never left my
dear father and mother. There has never been anything but

unhappiness since I left Bournemouth. But I will not be alone in this house . . . If you go I kill myself . . . '

'Come, come, Jennifer. You must not be so foolish. You are like a child.'

Jennifer was now in floods of tears. She waved her hands, beat with her feet on the ground and behaved like a madwoman. Part of this was stupid and lazy histrionics, but part of it was the true bewildered apprehension of a slow, but not evilly intentioned, woman who might, had she married a rich warm husband in a safe comfortable place, never have been exposed. It was because Judith knew this and by now understood her so well that she was touched.

'Come, Jennifer. Come upstairs and lie down.' (Always the recipe for Jennifer's distresses.) 'We will talk quietly. There is nothing for you to be so distressed over. Nothing at all. You have an obsession about Walter. He can do you no harm. Come and lie down.'

She surrendered as though hypnotized. Judith led her away. On the stairs she said:

'Well, but you were only laughing at me, Judith. You are not going away?'

Judith patted her shoulder.

'You will see in the morning it does not look so terrible. After all it is only a few miles. I shall be close at hand.'

But when at last Jennifer had been laid down and petted and quietened and she, Judith, stood in the still hall with the clock ticking the only sound:

'Phew!' she said to herself. '*That* was something.' But she was resolute. Nothing now could turn her. However, half an hour later she had to suffer another attack. There was a knock on the parlour door and John appeared.

He looked at her shyly. Of late she had noticed in herself a certain embarrassment which she was for ever trying not to show him. Was she not going to desert him? A look that he had of his father, although he was more firmly built, a look of delicate sensitiveness and courtesy, deeply touched her. Then there was his love for Adam.

He had fair hair, blue eyes, a very white skin and a proud mobile mouth. His worst fault was his modesty and his lack of self-assurance. Perhaps the unhappy history of his parents had encouraged that. She knew that his sense of honour was so scrupulous that decisions, their rights and wrongs, were often an agony to him.

'John,' she said. 'Come in.'

He came in and stood near her, twisting and untwisting his hands.

'Aunt Judith, Mother is crying. She says that you are going away.'

'John, dear, come here,' Judith said, drawing him to the sofa where so often she had sat with his father. He sat close to her, very erect, his thin white hands resting on his knees. She looked at him and loved him dearly. In that one look the foolish childish jealousy that she had had because Adam loved him too vanished altogether.

'I want you to understand. Adam and I are going away because it is best for you all that we should. I have managed everything for too long here. I am a managing old woman, you know. I cannot see a thing without wishing to arrange it. Now you are growing into a man, and this is your position, not mine. And then—' she hesitated for a moment, 'you know that I was not married to Adam's father, and people gossip. So – it is better for me to go.'

He gave a small gulp in his throat, staring into the fire.

'Yes, Aunt Judith.'

'You do understand, do you not?'

It was harder than she had expected.

'Yes, Aunt Judith ... But will you never come back any more?'

'You and Dorothy will come to visit us – only we shall be farmers, you know.'

'Yes.' He hesitated, then said: 'You and Adam are my best friends. I know Mr Winch says that I am not one that others can like very much—'

'What does Mr Winch say?' she burst out indignantly.

'Oh, he means it very well. And it is true. I like to be by myself unless it is someone I understand. And I do understand you and Adam. So – if you go—'

And then to her utter dismay he broke into tears, hid his head in his hands and sobbed most bitterly. She put her arms around him (a thing that she seemed to be doing to everyone today). He leaned against her for a little, then looked up, deeply ashamed and rubbing his eyes with his knuckles.

'I never cry,' he said. 'I don't know why now ... Mother was so unhappy ... and she is afraid of Uncle Walter. She says that if you go he will destroy us ... and I am not very old yet ...'

'John, John. Listen to me. Uncle Walter can do nothing to

you. You are here to care for your mother and sister. You are on guard over them. There is nothing to fear, and Adam and I will only be a few miles—'

She was interrupted by a loud banging at the door, a furious, impatient knocking.

They both started up, and she was never to forget that John put out his hand on to her arm as though he intended to begin, at once, to guard her from danger.

The knocking was repeated, more impatiently than before. She hurried out and opened the door. There was a figure against the dark, and then as he moved forward she saw who it was – it was Reuben.

'Reuben!' she cried, astonished. Then she saw that he was in the very greatest agitation. He closed the door behind him. Mrs Quinney was coming towards him.

'Quick, Judith,' he said, 'I must see you alone.'

She drew him into the dining-room, something in her saying: 'This is what you have been expecting all day long.'

When the door was closed she caught his arm. 'Reuben, what is it ? I thought you were at Whitehaven.'

There was perspiration on his forehead, and his breath came in gasps until he was calmer.

'Have you not heard anything ?'

'Heard anything ? No, of course not. What is it ?'

'I have ridden as swiftly as I could. I got away only in time ... My own men ... My own people ... They would not listen to me. They knocked me down, threw things at me. I tell you, Judith, they have thrown me over and it is because I have deserted God. I have been drawn more and more into earthly things, politics, money ... and now—'

He was incoherent, staring about him; scarcely, it seemed to her, recognizing her at all.

'No, but, Reuben, what *is* it ? Please, please ...'

'Yes, you are right. I scarcely know what I am saying. Listen, Judith; they are on their way now to burn this place down. I had dinner in Cockermouth and it was there that by chance I learnt of it. Holroyd, Atkinson, Bell, Wood – no, but of course their names mean nothing to you. There is a mob of them on their way now. Someone had put them up to it. They have been out of hand the last month. Last night some of them burnt Squire Forrester's ricks ...'

'Yes, yes, I know. But why here ? We have done nothing.'

'No. No. I don't understand.' He wiped the sweat from his

forehead. 'It was about Jennifer – some vastly improper things that they were saying.'

'Jennifer?'

'Yes – and Fernyhirst.' He seemed to waken then to the sense of the urgency. 'No, but no matter. They can be only a mile or so away. A good hundred of them. What are you going to do? What have you here in the way of servants?'

He stood staring about him. Then he went on quickly: 'Someone should ride for one of the Magistrates. Mr Fox at Holtby is the nearest. He is old but courageous. Only last year he wished to have me whipped off his grounds. Is there anyone can go? He should be there in an hour.'

'Yes. Jack. He's a brave boy. He'll go.'

She seemed to be transformed. This was a situation that she could understand. No tears and vapours and horror of some vague unknown danger. Something definite.

'We must have all the servants in' – and from that spoken word until the end of the affair she was in absolute command. She went out into the hall and found John and Mrs Quinney there, wondering.

'John – will you do a thing for me?'

'Anything,' and she knew that he too was glad that action had come at last.

'Go up to your mother. Sit beside her bed. Read to her. Anything. She must be kept quiet and tranquil in her room for the next hour.'

He gave her one look, asked no questions, and went.

'Now, Mrs Quinney, I want all the servants. Everyone. In here. I have something to say to them. Will you fetch them, please?'

Mrs Quinney went. Judith returned to Reuben.

'Reuben, you must have something to eat and drink.'

He nodded. He was sitting down and in his eyes was a look of utter dejection. Once again she was carried back to that day when she had given succour to his brother. The same incident – the same command. She brought him bread and meat and ale, and he ate and drank eagerly.

'But I cannot understand,' she repeated. 'Why here? Why Jennifer? Jennifer has done no one any harm but herself, poor thing.'

'Oh, they are mad. They have been so for months – indeed for years. This is only a little sequel to Peterloo, and there will be many another before all is done. But the wretchedness of this is that it is I who have been urging them to it . . . Oh no, not here, of course, nor to any violence. I have preached peace, but of late I have been filled with their material harshness and have forgot their souls. You yourself saw it when we were at Hawkshead. You spoke to me of it. And now today they would not listen to a single word from me. Bell and Holroyd are the worst. And only a year back Holroyd would have done anything for me.'

The door opened and they came in: Mr Winch, Mrs Quinney, Martha Hodgson, Doris, Jack Turner, Bennett.

At the sight of Bennett Judith's heart warmed. With his broad thick bulk, his utterly unperturbed air, his kindly protective eyes (just as Charlie Watson was protective), he would be the man for her now.

They stood in a group together, Mr Winch, with his pallor and nervous shifting eyes, a little apart from the others.

'Listen!' she said, smiling to reassure them. 'Mr Sunwood has ridden on to tell us that some rioters are on their way here from Cockermouth. It seems they mean mischief. Well, they shall find us ready for them. Jack, I want you to take Peggy and ride off at once to Squire Fox at Holtby. He is a Magistrate. Ask him to come as speedily as possible. You should be back with him in two hours. You know his place ?'

Jack nodded.

'Well, go then. Be as quick as you can.'

With another nod he was off.

'Fred' (this was Bennett), 'have we any firearms ?'

'There's two guns and an old pistol. I don't know if 'tis firing yet.'

'Good. Get anything you can. So soon as we hear them we will make the whole house dark. Do not disturb Mrs Herries or the children until we must. It should be an hour or more yet before they are here. They may not come at all. Now, Mrs Quinney, Martha, Doris, no fuss, now. At the worst it is only a few rough boys and men. Mr Fox will be here as soon as they – that is, if they come at all. You be quiet in the back of the house, will you ?'

They smiled and nodded proudly. They were Cumbrian women and not lightly disturbed. Nor were they garrulous. They showed no agitation at all. Bennett remained alone with Judith and Reuben.

'Dusta think,' he asked, 'there'll be many of them ?'

'A good few, I reckon,' said Reuben.

'Aye,' said Bennett slowly. 'T' height of wickedness. And

they'll suffer.' Then he added: 'Foreigners likely.' That was his
principal sentiment – that he was shocked. He did not know,
as he was often fond of declaring, what had come to the country.
However, he was really only unhappy when he was puzzled as
to which way he should act. It was the fear of his life that he
should act the wrong way and look a fool. Happily in this present
case his duty and his pleasure were clear.

He went off to the stables.

Reuben looked at her admiringly. This was how he liked to
see her.

'Judith, you should be the Captain of a pirate.'

She laughed. 'Perhaps they will not come after all, Reuben.'

'Oh yes,' he said. 'They will come.'

'Let us go out and listen.'

They went into the garden and then on to the road. Then up
on the moor. It was a fine night now, with a thin moon and
quivering sheets of dim smoky stars. On the ridge of the moor
the frosty air stung. Hills and valleys lay, under the deep shadows
of the moon, in up-and-down disorder like a quilt shaped by
the limbs of a recumbent giant. They listened, but there was only
the thin whistle of the wind, smell of earth and sheep and rabbits,
and the peaceful sleeping land.

'Maybe they will not come.'

'Oh, they will come. Not a doubt of it. Holroyd shouted filth
at me; I had lost all touch with him. Do you remember one night
when I came to Watendlath and Georges asked me about God?
I was in touch then. It was as though I had Him under my cloak;
but the world tempted me again, and I lost Him. First, when I
was a boy, it was my fear of being a fool; then it was women;
then I climbed over that and saw God as plainly as I see you;
then their politics tempted me, and I lost Him. So I lose them
as well.'

'You have done a good, kind thing coming to tell us, Reuben.
God will be pleased with that. For myself, if there is a God, I
will be grateful one moment and defy Him the next. It is no
use to be always on your knees.'

She was talking to cover her own fears. She was thinking
at that moment only of Adam. Her heart was wild with fear
for him. Had she not been ashamed she would have snatched
him out of bed, caught him up in her arms and run away with
him out of the back door. When she was in the house and there
was plenty to be done it was one thing, but out here in the cold
and silence quite another. An owl hooted. A little wind pulled

at their feet. The anaemic moon was enveloped by a thin cloud of gauze, and the world was veiled.

'Hark! Can you not hear something?'

She caught his arm. They both listened. The breeze rose and fell; a church bell from a great distance could be heard echoing the half-hour. On the wind for a moment there seemed to be the crack of horses. But it died.

'No. That was the church clock.'

They listened again. It seemed as though all the landscape were listening with them.

'Yes. I am certain I hear something.'

She stood close to him. He put his arm around her. The breeze came up the slope again and the moon rode out, her light stroking Skiddaw's shoulder.

'Yes. Listen. Listen.'

Then above the beating of their hearts they heard it beyond any question, the strike of horses' hoofs on the winter road.

'Quick! Quick! Back to the house!'

They ran down the fell, along the road and through the gate. As Judith turned in she saw a figure come out of one of the village houses; the black shadow stood looking down the hill. It was beyond doubt now, a clatter of horses, laughter and voices.

She ran into the house and up the stairs. First she went into Jennifer's room. It was in darkness. John came towards her.

'She is asleep.'

She went to the bed and shook Jennifer's shoulder.

'Jennifer! Jennifer! Wake up!'

When she was awake she told her as quickly as possible.

'Now, Jennifer, it is nothing. Only some drunken boys. But you must stay here. Don't move from here. It will be soon over.'

'Drunken boys? . . . But what do they want?'

'Reuben is here, and Bennett has a gun, and Mr Fox of Holtby is coming over.'

'Oh dear. Oh dear . . .'

But she had no time for Jennifer's 'Oh dears!'

'John, you remain with your mother. Adam and Dorothy had best be here as well. I will bring them.'

When she went into her own room her heart for a moment failed her. Adam was lying, his head on his arm, fast asleep. She woke him, wrapped him in a blanket so that he looked a young bewildered Indian, and told him quietly:

'Adam, there are some noisy men in the garden. If they shout

and throw stones, it is no matter. Mother is here and Bennett
and Mr Winch and Uncle Reuben. You stay with John, darling,
in Aunt Jennifer's room.'

He nodded his head, yawning and rubbing his eyes with his
knuckles. 'Where will you be ?' he asked.

'I shall return very soon. Now, go to John, darling.'

'Can't I see the men throwing stones ?'

'No. Not now. Be a good boy.'

He was always a good boy if his mother thought that it was
serious. He saw that she thought that this was serious, and
obeyed. She took him into the next room, saw that Dorothy
was also there, and Jennifer sitting up in bed and asking John
questions. She gave Adam to John and left them.

When she came downstairs another world had already burst
upon them. The house was in darkness, save for the candles in
Jennifer's room. The women were in the kitchen. Bennett and
Reuben, each with a gun, were in the hall. They all three moved
into the parlour.

She looked between the curtains and almost cried out at the
scene. At least a hundred men, women, and boys were gathered
in the road, dark and shadowy in the moonlight, but some of
them carried torches whose flames, leaping in the wind, jumped
from shadow to shadow. About a dozen men were on horseback.

She recognized at once a number of villagers among
them. Since Francis' death the men and women of the village
had held aloof from Jennifer, whom in fact they had always
disliked.

There was the strangest contrast between the black silence
of the house and the shouts, laughter, cries that came from the
crowd. She saw that one of them, a long thin bearded man on a
white horse, was their leader.

'That is Holroyd!' Reuben whispered to her. The crowd
moved backwards and forwards as though stirred by some impetus within themselves. Through the closed window she could
not hear what they were crying. White faces leapt into torchlight
and out again. Arms rose and fell. Suddenly the gates swung
back and they all tumbled pell-mell into the garden. Then there
was a pause and silence. They stood transfixed, as though a spell
had been cast on them, staring at the house.

That was queer – to stand behind the curtains with that
familiar room all about her, to look out and see that multitude,
faces like fish-scales in the moonlight, all still and waiting. All
for no reason! These were familiar things, the furniture, the

walls, the pictures, and yet these strangers had the impertinence to break through the gate, to trample on the garden, to insult the shadows of David, of Francis, of Sarah – perhaps to frighten the spirit of her own son, Adam! A furious indignation began to rise within her.

The silence cracked. A stone was flung and smashed through the parlour window, missing Judith by a breath.

'Take care!' Reuben whispered, pulling her back.

The throwing of that stone released them. They all began to shout at once. More stones were thrown. Figures were running down the lawn, others towards the stables. Meanwhile the thin man with a beard sat motionless on his horse.

'I must go out to them!' Reuben said.

'No. No. They will throw stones. Wait—'

'No. I cannot wait.'

He went out. She heard him open the door of the hall, and, before he shut it, a roar of voices reached her, like a sudden ripple of thunder. What had she better do? Her impulse was to go with him. The parlour door had closed, but now it opened to show the meagre black figure of Mr Winch, who entered with a lighted candle.

'Blow out that candle!' she ordered him sharply.

But he could not. He stood there, his mouth open, his eyes shifting from place to place, the candle shaking in his hand. He was in a sweat of terror. Indignantly she snatched the candle from him and blew it out, saying:

'No one will harm *you*, Mr Winch. Your place is with the children upstairs.' She heard him slip away.

From the intervals where the curtains were not drawn the glare of the torches, falling and rising, lit the room – the coloured top of the spinet, the crimson chair, the sofa with the red apples. She could also hear now through the break in the window that the stone had made. Reuben's voice came across to her, and it seemed that they were listening:

'. . . and if I had done so you might have charged me with a fault, but for many years now I have had only your interests at heart. What others could I ever have had? Have I not given my whole life to your friendship? . . .' She lost it again. Then it returned. '. . . and this house has never harmed you. It has not starved you as some have done, nor ill-treated your children as some have done, nor thrown you out of employment like some. But even though it had, this would not be your Court of Appeal. Violence of this sort has never won anyone any good,

and well you know it. Cruelty to women and children has never
been our Cumberland way . . .'

'A little too much of the orator,' she thought. '*I'd* speak to
them!'

But he was not to speak much longer. She caught the words:
'. . . and be for ever ashamed of as dastardly an action . . .'

Perhaps someone was stirring up trouble from the road. In
any case, there was a sudden rush from the rear of the crowd,
shouts and screams, and someone threw a lighted torch, whirling
through the dark until it fell with a hiss on the lawn and lay
there blazing. The man on the horse made as though he would
ride on to Reuben and so past him into the house; but, in spite
of his furious movement, his voice was sharp and controlled as
he cried:

'Enough words, Sunwood! Back to the stables, lad. And we'll
see them blaze!'

'Shall I fire? Shall I fire?'

Judith heard a voice in her ear, and putting out a hand felt
Bennett's breast and his heart beating like a clock.

'No . . . Wait, Fred. Oh, the devils! I cannot endure this.
And with the children upstairs. Oh, when will Mr Fox come?
I must go out to them! I cannot endure this here!'

'No, no, ma'am. Stay where you are!'

'No. I must go.' She tore herself from Bennett's hand and
ran from the room, he following her. She could never quite
clearly remember afterwards what occurred in that outside
pandemonium. The air was cold and yet the heat seemed intense.
There was smoke in her nostrils. Reuben was shouting. She saw
that his forehead was bleeding, and that seemed to loose a
fury inside her. She never knew what she cried, but she drove into
the middle of them; then, nearly stumbling over a mounting-
block by the door, she climbed on to it.

'Be ashamed of yourselves. Attacking women and children
who have done you no harm. Go back to your homes, you
bullies . . .'

The ineffectiveness of her words enraged her yet more.
They swept past her and around her, not even seeing her, shouting, some of them singing, the horses rising in the moonlight
like white seahorses. Then, as though it were a banner unfurled,
a shuddering, quivering flame leapt up into the sky from the
stables. The fire lit the whole scene; all faces were white, the
house like a black wall with the pale glass squares of the windows.
A woman's cry came from inside the house.

'The horses! The horses!' Judith cried, and began to push and fight through the mob, who, at sight of the fire, seemed dimmed and quieted as though they sank from the scene. Some man struck her in the breast. She turned, gasping for breath, and saw Bennett behind her, his gun raised.

'You shall have it then!' he cried, and fired.

Holroyd on his horse half turned, raised an arm, shivered and slowly fell. Reuben sprang forward, was for a moment illuminated by the fire; a shot rang from the road, and he too jumped as though, with arms lifted, he would touch the moon, and collapsed on the horse-steps.

The two shots, the crackle and gesture of the fire, the riderless horse plunging, seemed in a moment to change the scene. Men and women all turned. They fled through the gate.

A woman, her hair loose, turned and shouted in a shrill broken voice: 'Curse you ...' and something more about Jezebel and vengeance.

Then panic had caught them all, for they were flying down the road – horses, men, women – the white moonlit stretch was black with fleeing figures ... Then, save for Reuben's huddled body on the steps, there was nothing in the garden. Only the flames of the stable chattered, hissed, rose and fell as though they were busy with their own private important business.

Judith, with Reuben's head in her lap, looked desperately around her.

'Quick, quick, Fred. Someone fetch Doctor Borden from the village. He'll be hiding in his house. Tell him' (her voice was fierce and bitter) 'that it is safe now. He must come. The women must get buckets for the fire ...' She caught sight of some slinking figures in the gateway. Villagers who, now that the riot was over, had crept out. 'Force them. They must help. The house must not burn.'

Bennett answered. 'The house is safe. It is only the outside sheds. The fire is burning itself out. Oh, Mr Reuben, are you hurt, sir? Are you hurt?'

'He's dying, Fred.' She bent over him. His eyes were open, looking at her. He smiled.

'Goodbye, Judith. I did my best.'

She knew that he was dead. Her hands were soaked in blood. She stared out above him to the quiet sky and the stables lit by fire. She felt a hand on her shoulder and looked up. It was Mrs Quinney.

'He is dead,' she said quietly. 'Help me to carry him in.'

THE CHOICE

REUBEN WAS BURIED five days later in Ireby Churchyard. As Judith drove in the carriage, away back to the house again, she was so weary that the whole world was quite unreal.

A great crowd had been at the funeral. Men and women had come from all parts, for Reuben was in general much beloved, and the riot, the disorder, and his death had made the greatest possible stir. Nothing else was talked of. Holroyd (who had only a flesh-wound in the arm) and Bell were in Kendal gaol; other arrests were expected to be made.

All of this could do poor Reuben very little good; but Judith was aware as, a lonely little black figure, she moved through the courtyard gate into her carriage, that she was surrounded with sympathy. She had known already that Uldale village was properly ashamed and anxious to make amends. She did not care. Reuben was gone – and, very soon, oh, very, very soon, she would be away from them all, safe with Adam in Watendlath.

It was a most curious day, she thought, as she drove up the road. For three days and nights there had been unceasing rain, and as, night after night, she had lain awake the rain had seemed to shroud her in as though it were weaving for her a great suit of silver armour, and in this she could live, safe and protected, for ever after.

But this rain in the valleys had meant snow on the hills. They were more thickly covered than they had been for many years. Today the landscape was shrouded in mist. There seemed to be three veils, one upon another, and these were always shifting. The middle veil was faintly radiant and orange in colour, for it held the sun, sunlight enfolded and shrouded. The farthest veil was of a very dim blue, cold, with snow in it. The first veil was almost transparent, of the thinnest gauze.

All the land moved in mystery behind these veils, for it was the land that appeared to be moving as the veils shifted. Everything was on the edge of discovery, but nothing was clear, only the stones under your feet, trunks of birch and larch and oak at your hand. In the corner of a field leaves were burning, a blazing fire in smoke.

So, sitting in the carriage, only half awake, in this shrouded world, it did not seem strange to her that the forms of her four

friends, all dead from violence, should be sitting beside her –
Francis, Georges, Warren, Reuben – one of whom she had
loved and still loved, one the father of her son, two the friends of
her lifetime.

They none of them, she thought, looked at her with any
reproach. She had in a way been the cause of death in all of
them – at least she had been in the minds and hearts of all of
them when they died. But, unsentimental as ever, she did not
intend in any way to reproach herself. She had been honest with
them all, and she knew that they wished her well. They had all
died fighting – Georges fighting discipline, Francis his own soul,
Warren convention, Reuben fighting his way back to God.
They had all, in fact, been fighting Herries one way or another –
if you took Herries for fact against fancy, as she did.

However, she was too weary to do more than smile upon
them and assure them that they need not look at her with such
anxiety. She and her little son were on the very point of escaping.
The Herries would not get her, try as hard as they might.
Nevertheless, she knew that when she was alive again she would
discover that the unfair savage death of Reuben had placed something hard and bitter in her heart that had never been there
before.

When she had taken off her bonnet and cloak, washed her face
and brushed her hair, she thought that she would finish the
thing once and for all. Jennifer was down in the parlour looking
at the mist that trailed past the window. A small block of wood
had been placed where the stone had crashed; they would come
very shortly from Keswick and mend the window. Indeed, very
little damage had been done: two windows broken, a shed or two
destroyed – that was all there was to show for the flaring torches,
the flaming sky, the shouts and curses and Reuben's death.

Jennifer looked very fine in her black gown. There was no
paint on her face, and her magnificent black hair gave her today
some nobility. But the shock of that night had done something
to her. She was more properly controlled than she had been for
years.

'There is a letter come for you,' she said.

Judith took it and saw that it was from Emma Furze. Emma!
As she read it her heart glowed. And then, when she found that
Emma was in London, was well and happy and gay, and wished
to come up and spread some of her happiness around the Watendlath farm, it was as if the sun had broken into the room. She

should, indeed she should. In another week Judith and Adam
would be there. Then there would be Emma and Charlie and
Alice Perry . . .

'Were there many at the funeral, Judith dear ?' Jennifer asked.
Judith told her of the funeral.

Jennifer nodded to all the details.

'I am glad that I did not go. I am very unrestrained at funerals.
And I do not know that I shall ever have the courage to go out
again. Do you not know what they were calling . . . some of the
women ? . . . Doris heard them. "Jezebel." One woman wanted
to burn me in the stable.'

'Nonsense, Jennifer. You must not think of it. They are very
kindly disposed to us. They are ready to do anything.'

'To us ? To you, you mean. So long as you are here we are
safe. But I want to tell you. I have been thinking deeply and I
see how weak and wretched I have been. I am terribly ashamed.
And I mean to be a help to you, Judith, in the future as I have
never been. And to John and Dorothy too. Yes, I am most
wretchedly ashamed, and John, that evening, was so brave and so
good. I am sure no boy of his age anywhere is so brave. You will
find, Judith, that I shall be quite another woman—'

'Well, that is excellent,' said Judith cheerfully. 'It is what I
have always told you, Jennifer. You have been frightened by
shadows.' Then she went on more gently, but with great firmness. 'Next week Adam and I are going. My mind is quite
made up. You will find everyone here as kind as possible –
everyone in the village. Eager to make friends.'

'Oh no,' said Jennifer in a voice so low that Judith could
scarcely hear her. 'Oh, please Judith – it will kill me if you go
away.'

They had had it out already so many times. There was to be
no more discussion of it. But as she bent to kiss Jennifer's cheek
she had an appalling sense of weakness.

Oh, let her waste no time! Let her slip out now, this moment!
Jennifer was harder to resist now that she was so quiet, and there
was John who had been so brave and Dorothy who, on that awful
night, had been so good to Adam, telling him stories. As she
kissed Jennifer and felt the cold touch of her hands she cared
for her as she had never done before.

Another moment and she would surrender, moved and
softened as she had been by the funeral. She would surrender
and be lost, all hope of her happiness gone! She murmured
something and hastened out, almost expecting to find Walter

Herries barring the door of the house with his huge body, defying her to escape.

But in the hall, instead of Walter Herries, she found Mr Winch.

'May I speak to you a moment, madam?' he said.

'Yes, Mr Winch,' she said. She had a new gravity. She had noticed it herself. She did not dislike it so long as she was in Uldale. It would not do at all for Watendlath. She led the way into the small room that had been Francis'. Mr Winch, very pale, his hands clasped, his head up, looked at her.

'Well, Mr Winch?'

'I thought I should tell you ...' He hesitated. '... I wish to resign my duties here.'

She felt a relief. It would be easy to find some far better tutor, someone who did not go down on his knees on the gravel path. Indeed, had she had her way he would have gone long ago. Jennifer had some weakness for him. He read Minerva Press novels to her.

'But why?' she asked. In spite of herself she was scornful. 'Have the rioters been too much for you? You remained safely in the back of the house for the greater part.'

'I know,' he stammered. 'You must despise me – and rightly. But you do not know all. If ...'

Then to her amazement he burst into sobs, threw himself down to his knees, held up his hands.

'Mr Winch!' she exclaimed, stepping back, thinking he must be out of his senses, that the fear of the other night had unsettled his wits.

'No, no. Listen to me. I have been miserable for a very long time, and this terrible catastrophe, with the death of Mr Sunwood, has destroyed me. I was his murderer.'

'You!' She could have laughed at the little figure in the shiny black with the rather grubby hands. But his distress was real, his fear was real. She saw that this was a matter of importance.

'Please rise,' she said. 'Please get up. You cannot be Mr Reuben Sunwood's murderer, for I myself saw the shot fired that killed him.'

He was sobbing. He buried his head in his hands.

'I cannot speak to you unless you get up.'

He rose. He composed himself. His head bent a little, as though he were making a confession, he went on:

'No, not in positive fact his murderer. I did not fire the gun. But in everything else – Mrs Paris, ever since I came to you I

have been spying upon everyone in this house. Mr Walter
Herries of Westaways has paid me for that odious business.'

'I know it,' she said quietly.

'You knew it?'

'I saw you one day on your knees in the garden spying on Mr
Francis.'

'You knew it and you did nothing?'

'I did nothing because, once I knew it, you were safer than
someone I did not know.'

He went on a little more confidently.

'I have no excuse. None. I did not need the money. All my
life I have avoided shabby actions. But Mr Walter Herries had
a strange power over me. He could do anything with me that he
pleased. I do not urge that in my defence; there is no defence.
But so it was. He overtook me one day walking to Keswick
and from the first I was his slave. I brought him news of everything that happened at Uldale – everything. It was I who found
a man that should carry the note to Mr Francis when he was
in Cockermouth, telling him that Captain Fernyhirst was here
that night.'

'You did that?' He thought she would strike him and he
moved back, but she had not stirred.

'Yes, I. It was Mr Walter Herries' plot, entirely arranged by
him.'

Her face was so terrible that he could not look at it. He turned
away.

'Yes. And so with everything here. Every day he had news.
It was he, by my agency, who brought the rioters here.'

'Yes,' she said (but she was not addressing him). 'I understand.'

'He intended, I think, only to give you a fright. I was in
Cockermouth and saw Holroyd and Bell and the others. They
were given money. There was to be no real damage to life or
property. But they had drink on that afternoon. They went
further than they intended.'

'Yes,' she said. 'They went far.'

'I have been very miserable ever since I have been here.
Again and again I have gone to him to tell him that I would do
his work no longer but when I saw him . . . I cannot explain . . .
He had a power . . .'

He was trembling.

'Forgive me,' he said. 'I must sit.' He sat down, his head so
bent that she could scarcely catch his words. 'Again and again I

have tried to say to you that I must go. Something prevented me. And at the beginning of this week when I knew what was in hand I was in hell. I could not sleep nor eat. A hundred times I was on the edge of breaking it to you. But his presence seemed always behind me. I thought that he would kill me if I betrayed him. He has often said, in his jolly laughing way, that he would. But he did not mean it to be murder. I did not intend . . . But it is too late. You may give me up to the Justice, Mrs Paris. You may indeed. I would be happier . . .'

'You!' She turned to the window. Francis and Reuben both killed by Walter!

Her stomach was sick. Her knees trembled. She also sat down, but with her back to him. For a long while there was silence. Could she bring the thing home to Walter? She half turned, as though she would speak, but turned back again. No! there was no help there. He would have seen to it that nothing could be carried to him. Who would believe a creature like Winch? Walter's power! . . . And suddenly she saw him, as though he were there with them in the room, vast, blazing with colour and jewels, laughing, but so bent from conceit and arrogance on his purpose that nothing was too terrible for him, too mean, too cruel. And yet he was a jolly man and loved his son even as she loved hers. She got up.

'Pray go away, Mr Winch,' she said. 'Go away in the morning. What is due to you will be sent to you. I would be happier not to see you again.'

Without a word he got up, and, head still bent, went out.

Very slowly she went upstairs to her room. No one was there. She looked out. Behind the mist the moon of five nights ago was now full, but it was like a flat stone ridged with light and wrapped in wool.

She had been caught. Now she had no doubt. She could not go. She had been able to defeat everything but this. Now a hard determined anger such as she had never felt had come and would abide. Francis . . . Reuben . . . killed by that laughing man. How could she now leave Jennifer and John and Dorothy defenceless?

Oh, but the other life! Watson was expecting her. In the Ritson kitchen Alice at this moment perhaps would be speaking of her. And her home, the room where Georges had died. And Adam to be a farmer, to grow up knowing nothing of this world of money, deceit, jealousy, unkindness. The Tarn, wrapped in mist, would be waiting for the moon to break. Or, perhaps, there was no mist there tonight and the slopes of the fells, snow-clad, glittered.

'I cannot ... I cannot ...'

She turned, possessed by some strange madness, pulled drawers open, found a box beneath the bed, began, on her knees, to cram it.

Adam came running in. He was shouting and dancing.

'Jack says there will be a new barn. They will begin to-morrow, and the windows—'

He stopped, seeing what she was doing. She shook her head as though the battle were hopeless. Once as a little girl she had climbed out of window, but now – to leave them, Jennifer weak, John, Dorothy, so young, to that determined remorseless purpose ...

'They are doomed, you know,' Walter had said, and even as he said it, he was aware that he had killed Francis, was planning this.

She got up from her knees and went to the window again. As she looked the moon broke the mist. Skiddaw started up in dazzling white. Like a white rose, like a glorious white rose from heaven, she lifted her head, and the mist sank to lie in waves across the valley.

She looked and she wept. The tears blinded her. She said farewell.

She came and sat down by the bed and drew Adam to her. She had command of herself.

'Tell me something,' he said. 'Tell me about Uncle Tom.'

It was his favourite story. While her mind was fiercely working on her future, hers and his, mechanically she went on with the familiar words:

'Although it had snowed so bitterly Uncle Tom got off his horse because he heard the baby crying, and he rode over the little bridge—'

'Don't forget the dogs! Don't forget the dogs!' Adam cried.

'Yes. They were all there and they followed him solemnly over the courtyard and into the house. And they went up the stairs. And they went into a room, the dogs sat down by the door, the old woman was sleeping—'

Oh, who was moving in the hills ? What Rogue was wandering, calling for her, telling her that here was her home ? The dry bones of the dead were alive. They were calling for her, those two old ghosts, and she could not come ...

She had now complete command of herself. She drew him closer.

'Adam, I want you to listen. You may not understand, but do you remember that one day going to Keswick I talked to you about being a farmer?'

'Yes,' he said. He drew himself up very straight because she was reposing a confidence in him and he was proud. He stood up straight with all the pride of a very small boy, that pride that is perhaps the small boy's most lovely quality.

'Now everything is changed. I have had to make the most important decision of my life – a decision for you also. You and I are to fight, Adam. I had thought that it would all be quiet and at peace, but now we are going to fight.'

'Who will we fight?' Adam asked with great interest. 'Uncle Walter?'

'You are too young to understand, but later you will see that I could do nothing else than this. We have to be very strong, you and I, and very wise, Adam. We will beat them all, and you shall be the head of them. No, you cannot understand now. But you must trust me.'

He threw his arms round her neck. She was small, and it was easy for him to draw her head down; he could kiss her and lay his cheek against hers. Now, if she wished to fight someone, he would help her. He thought that perhaps she was sorry that she made him stay in Aunt Jennifer's room when they came to burn the stables. Now, this next time, he would go with her and help her.

While he hugged her, her pride was rising. Her pride, her deep and unchangeable hatred of Walter Herries. In that hour the second half of her life began.

She got up. Now she would take command. A fierce bright delight flowed in her veins. She would make Adam the master of them all. Walter's boy ... She saw him in his little chair, his deformity, his old, pale face, and the big man kneeling at his side. She caught Adam to her, kissing him passionately. Adam should be King.

With her head up, as though she already commanded a kingdom, she stepped downstairs.

She opened the parlour door. Jennifer was standing at the window. When she heard the door open she turned. She looked and saw a short pale woman in a plain black gown. But she saw also a woman on fire with determination, with pride and an almost fanatical purpose.

'Why, Judith!—' she began.

'All is well,' Judith said quietly, coming forward and stroking the red apples of the sofa. 'I shall not leave you, Jennifer. It is better I remain.'

Clare Francis
Red Crystal £3.99

The bestselling thriller by the author of Night Sky

The anger is there, the injustice, the repression. The situation just needs to be polarised – crystallised . . .

Out of the savagery of the Paris barricades there was born the most sinister of all the terrorist groups of the 1960s. Secretly funded by Moscow, trained in subversion and assassination in Italy, the Crystal Faction came to England. To wage war . . .

For Nick Ryder of Special Branch, finding and infiltrating the cell presented a daunting challenge. Hampered by the deviousness of his own superiors and lack of cooperation from MI5, he was drawn slowly but inexorably into a tangled web of sex, drugs, murder, intrigue and lost innocence.

And at the centre, the beautiful Gabriele Schroeder, leader of the Crystal Faction. A tough, daring, utterly ruthless woman for whom killing had become a pleasure . . .

'The climax is agonising, and made only too horribly likely by the author's careful groundwork and ability to maintain suspense.'
BOOKS AND BOOKMEN

'A sexy as well as a fast-paced thriller' DAILY EXPRESS

Lynda La Plante
The Legacy £3.99

At a Welsh pithead at the turn of the century, a gypsy girl, a romany princess driven out by her people, waited for the pitman father of the bastard son in her arms.

When he emerged from the black coal seam, he turned away and walked off with his pals to the pub, while her curse echoed after him down the hillside . . .

A vast and panoramic novel . . . possessed of a splendid narrative sweep . . . its pages teeming with compelling characters . . . its richness stemming from the age-old traditions of the romany people . . .

The Legacy is the first part of Lynda La Plante's splendid saga of four generations of a bloodline tainted by a romany curse . . .

After the death of Freedom, his sons are despatched by fate in very different directions. While Edward goes up to Cambridge . . . Alex goes into a remand home . . . and on to prison . . . serving his time for a killing he did not commit.

It was not until twelve years after the end of *The Legacy* that the brothers met again . . . standing at their mother's graveside.

Lynda La Plante continues her magnificent saga in *The Talisman* . . . following the curse down through the third and fourth generations.

All these books are available at your local bookshop or newsagent, or can be ordered direct from the publisher. Indicate the number of copies required and fill in the form below.

Send to: **CS Department, Pan Books Ltd., P.O. Box 40, Basingstoke, Hants.   RG21 2YT**.

or phone: 0256 469551 (Ansaphone), quoting title, author and Credit Card number.

Please enclose a remittance* to the value of the cover price plus: 60p for the first book plus 30p per copy for each additional book ordered to a maximum charge of £2.40 to cover postage and packing.

*Payment may be made in sterling by UK personal cheque, postal order, sterling draft or international money order, made payable to Pan Books Ltd.

Alternatively by Barclaycard/Access:

Card No. | | | | | | | | | | | | | | | | | |

Signature:

Applicable only in the UK and Republic of Ireland.

While every effort is made to keep prices low, it is sometimes necessary to increase prices at short notice. Pan Books reserve the right to show on covers and charge new retail prices which may differ from those advertised in the text or elsewhere.

NAME AND ADDRESS IN BLOCK LETTERS PLEASE:

....

Name————————————————————————————

Address———————————————————————————

——————————————————————————————

——————————————————————————————

——————————————————————————————

3/87